THE CHRONICLES OF
JEGRA

THE COMPLETE SAGA

VOL. 2

GLADIATRIX OF THE GALAXY

THE CHRONICLES OF

JEGRA

THE COMPLETE SAGA

VOL. 2

BOOKS 4-6

TRISTAN VICK

A REGOLITH PUBLICATIONS BOOK

The Chronicles of Jegra: Gladiatrix of the Galaxy
The Complete Saga Books 4-6 Vol. 2
DEXLUXE HARDCOVER EDITION
By Tristan Vick ©2018. All Rights Reserved

Published by Regolith Publications
First Edition, copyright © September 8, 2020

The Chronicles of Jegra: Origins of the Gladiatrix
A Cosmic Alliance Prequel Novella
By Tristan Vick ©2018. All Rights Reserved
First Edition, copyright © March 30, 2018.

Edited by Sheila Shedd
Box Set cover art by Tum Dechakamphu
Additional art by Jackson Tjota
Opening graphic by Ariel Diaz
Interior book design by Tristan Vick
www.tristanvick.com

ISBN-13: 978-1-950106-09-7
ISBN-10: 1-950106-09-7

CONTENTS

BOOK 4

THE CHRONICLES OF

JEGRA

GALAXY UNDER SIEGE

1

ISS lingered above the translucent shroud of Earth's thin, luminescent atmosphere. Although hidden behind the swirling, blue and white orb, the warm radiance of the sun's backlighting gradually collected along the circumference of the planet until it condensed into an incandescent halo of gold. A split second later, the halo flared brightly, exploding outward in a brilliant sunburst that crested over the mantle of the blue planet.

A new dawn washed over the continents and oceans of Earth, revealing a world rich in life and beauty. High above the waking planet, the *ISS* cut across the radiance of the morning star and shot into the dark gulf of the great expanse as it followed its embowed trajectory.

The sunlight gleamed off the solar panels and danced across the aluminum alloy hull of the station. Beheld from afar, the *ISS* sparkled like a diamond set against a dark sea sprinkled with a hundred thousand other sparkling gems; many of them billions of years older than Earth.

The station's crew was made up of two Americans—one man and one woman—along with a single Japanese gentleman, an Indian woman, and two Chinese, also one male and one female. The crew of six wafted about the various interconnected modules in zero-gravity and busied themselves in preparation for the Mars One resupply mission which would be arriving with new faces and supplies within approximately eleven minutes.

Captain Thomas Michael Drange floated over toward the view portal passing through the cabin effortlessly as his forward momentum brought him to the large glass window. Reaching out, he grabbed onto the padding around the window frame and caught himself, the change in force causing his legs to swing downward as he looked out the glass portal.

Drange steadied himself by hooking his toes under a yellow handle near the base of the inner hull. Then looking out the window he made visual confirmation of the inbound rocket. The rocket had passed the Karman line and was gradually making her way to them, right on schedule.

He smiled then reached up and pushed himself off the glass and spun weightlessly back toward the main cabin. Tom needed to get to the controls and man the station's docking arm to help secure the two vessels.

The *Ares III* spacecraft would arrive courtesy of a Super Heavy booster rocket. It would dock with the station and drop off additional equipment and supplies to the *ISS* crew before heading on to resupply the Mars Colony One installation.

Besides anticipating the resupply, Tom was looking forward to seeing the captain of the *Ares* again, one lovely Ms. Karina Nazimova. She was Russian-born but moved as a child to the United States with her father and mother.

Her father was the famed Anton Nazimova, expert rocket engineer. After being laid off by the Russian space agency, whose space program had been gradually shrinking over the decades, he'd secured a job with NASA and moved his family to the United States. Karina was only four years old when they arrived stateside. Viewed as a defector, however, Russia smeared Anton Nazimova's name up and down the World Wide Web making him out to be a villain rather than the brilliant scientist he truly was.

Tom knew all this because during flight academy he and Karina had dated for a stint. After their mutual separation, both putting their careers ahead of their personal lives, they remained on friendly terms with one another.

Karina getting command of the *Ares III* was a big deal. And he was glad it went to her. With as hard as she'd worked for it, she more than deserved it.

Not only was she perfectly suited for the job, she joined a long line of famous female astronauts like Peggy Whitson and Pamela Melroy, who both commanded highly critical space missions. Karina was an excellent officer and a brilliant astronaut. Tom couldn't think of a person better suited for command.

Even so, if he was being completely honest, he did feel a slight twinge of envy. After all, the *Ares III* was the most advanced spacecraft that humans had ever built. It was NASA's very first nuclear-powered space vessel and coming in three times longer and with twice as much cargo capacity as *Ares II*, it was the

Ferrari of all interplanetary ships ever built.

In fact, Tom practically salivated over the specs of that ship every time he looked at the schematics. To him, it was like ogling a pinup girl from an old Playboy magazine, but a hell of a lot sexier.

With a skilled crew complement of thirty, naturally, the *Ares III* was outfitted with everything from a full-sized gym to a botanical biosphere, which helped supply fresh food for extended missions. The biosphere also acted as a carbon monoxide filter, assisting the ship's scrubbers in recycling air. A natural air-freshener for the ship, if you will.

Additionally, plants were frequently transferred down to the greenhouses on the Martian surface, providing additional food for the astronauts living there.

Hovering above the space station's control room for the docking arm, Tom let his legs dangle in the air behind him as he flipped on the automated targeting and took a hold of the dual joysticks. "*Ares III*, I have you on the monitor. Please cut your momentum thrusters and switch to maneuvering only."

The ship continued coming in hot and Tom raised an eyebrow.

"They don't appear to be slowing down," Dr. Iwasaki said as he gazed out the same view portal that Tom had been looking out of moments prior.

"This is the *ISS* calling *Ares III*. Cut your thrusters and prepare for ship-to-ship docking. Do you copy?"

Still, no response.

Tom and Iwasaki shared a nervous glance then slowly turned their heads and looked out the view portal in time to see the white spray of compressed gas explode out of the nose of the *Ares* as she ignited her reverse thrusters.

Relieved, the two men let out a nervous sigh as the ship slowed to a near halt. A few more short spurts and the two ships came into nearly perfect alignment. It was definitely Karina's trademark flying: one part daredevil and two parts showoff.

"This is the *Ares III*," Karina Nazimova's voice came across the comm, "requesting permission to dock."

"Cutting it a little close there, don't you think?" Captain Drange asked with a chuckle. Then he added, "Permission granted."

Hands at the controls of the robotic arms, he reached out with the clawed arms and took ahold of the coupling unit of the *Ares III,* guiding it toward their airlock. There was a loud clunk as the ships came together, the mechanical sound of the docking clamps, and finally the magnetic seal locking into place.

Tom turned toward astronaut Melissa Thompson and motioned her to accompany him to the airlock to greet their guests. She was happy to do so, too, as she wanted to confront Captain Nazimova and remind her about the standard ship-to-ship docking procedures which she had clearly ignored.

As they floated up the access junction toward the airlock, Tom thought about the *Ares III's* mission. It was on its way to *Mars Colony One* with parts and supplies. Karina's mission was twofold. First, they were going to swing by the *ISS* and resupply the station, including providing additional food, lab equipment, and two fresh astronauts.

After their twelve-hour pit-stop aboard, they'd proceed on to their final destination where, after seven months of space flight, they'd arrive in orbit around Mars.

Once there, they'd take a shuttle down to the surface and join their fellow astronauts in studying the Red Planet for the next three years. The *Ares III* would become a space station, hovering above the planet, providing vital research assistance and acting as an orbital resupply vessel for the duration of the mission.

Arriving at the hatch, Tom caught the handle and lurched to a stop, his body swaying in the zero gravity. Thompson, who was close behind, grabbed onto some cargo netting and slowed herself down so she didn't collide with him.

When the orange light above the door changed to green, Tom used a foothold to keep himself in place then pulled down on the latch to the airlock.

The round door rolled opened smoothly and with very little effort, as both ships had matched each other's pressure. Once fully retracted, Thompson reached down and tugged the lever back up, securing the door into place.

She turned to Tom to give him a thumbs up when, without warning, Karina Nazimova shot past her. In fact, she almost collided with Captain Drange as she raced by, pulling herself into the space station and then hurtling up the corridor like a dart.

"Wait! Commander Nazimova, what are you doing?" Thompson called out, getting a bit red under the collar. "You have to follow protocol!"

"Commander?" Tom called out inquisitively, using his no-nonsense captain's voice. As much as he knew that Thompson wanted him to reprimand her, the fact remained that you didn't get hired as the lead astronaut for a critical mission by slacking on the rules. If Karina was breaking protocol, it was his bet that she likely had a damned good reason.

"Apologies, Captain," she called back. "I'll explain everything when I get the chance. But right now I need you and your crew to gather your essentials and get aboard the *Ares III* asap."

"Are you ordering us to evacuate the *ISS*, Commander?" asked Thompson in a skeptical voice.

"That's exactly what I'm ordering you to do." Karina floated up to the control station that Tom had been at moments earlier and, finding the keyboard, began typing in some code.

The keys clacked under her fingers and then an automated voice came onto the comm system. <<Automated self-destruct sequence in T-30 minutes.>>

"*What in the bloody hell do you think you're doing?* Commanding officer or not, I'm going to need you to stop what you're doing and give me your mission codes." Thompson kicked off the wall and flew across the cabin to try and stop the commander, but she bumped shoulders with Karina, who simply nudged her out of the way.

Slowly spiraling away from the commander, arms flailing, she tried to grasp onto Karina's sleeve. Thompson finally caught some electronic paneling and halted her freewheeling spin. She pushed off the wall and floated back to the control panel.

Back at the keyboard, she attempted to disarm the auto self-destruct and frowned when the computer didn't respond to her override codes. "Dammit! I'm locked out."

"You better have a damn good explanation for all this," Captain Drange growled. He eyed Karina sternly, but she casually unzipped her flight suit, reached into her overalls, and pulled out what looked like two, over-sized, red plastic dog tags. She tossed them to Thompson, who caught them and then, with a crack, snapped each red tab in half.

Thompson pulled out two slips of plastic, one red and one blue, and overlaid them. A series of green letters and symbols appeared on the previously innocuous seeming pieces of plastic. A code.

"What is it?" Tom asked.

Thompson looked up at him. "It's the evacuation codes, sir," she answered.

He floated over to her and checked the codes himself. Sure enough, it was an order to abandon ship.

As they were confirming the codes, Karina simply glided over to the view portal and peered out at Earth.

"No, no, no…" she whispered to herself. "I thought we'd have more time."

"More time for what?" Iwasaki asked, having overheard her. He sidled up beside her and peered out at the same glorious vista. Soon everyone was curious as to what they were looking at and crowded around the window.

Even doctor Asima and the two Chinese astronauts, Zhi Cheung and Quan Jing, who were watching the drama unfold with interest, decided to come over and join them. As they gathered around, one thing became abundantly clear, their order to abandon ship wasn't about leaving the space station. It was about leaving Earth.

"Oh, my god!" Asima gasped, scarcely able to believe her own eyes. Almost as soon as she'd taken another breath, her lip began to quiver and tears flooded into the corners of her deep brown eyes.

They all watched with dreadful astonishment as giant, orange glowing fissures opened up on the planet's surface.

Explosions of magma began shooting up into the air, and a daisy chain of events followed as every single active volcano on the planet's surface began to erupt simultaneously. It made the fatal eruption of Pompeii look like a child's baking soda experiment by comparison.

As dark ash and smoke rose into the atmosphere, forming dark, billowing, ominous clouds that threatened to blot out the sun entirely, the crew all had the same terrible sinking feeling in their guts. This wasn't just a disaster; this was an act of God. This was cataclysmic.

"What is going on down there?" Asima Krishnan asked in a low, steady voice. She spun around and fixed her exacting gaze on Karina. Following her lead, the rest of the crew turned to Karina too, hoping she'd have the answers.

"Look," Karina said, scanning all the stunned faces, "I don't have time to explain right now. We need to get aboard the *Ares III* and get our asses to Mars. That's our only hope."

"Only hope for what?" Tom raised an eyebrow as he stared at Karina with one inquisitive eye slightly larger, slightly more intense than the other.

"Our only hope of survival," she replied in a solemn tone that sent a shiver down his spine.

2

A sandy moon wrapped in a cerulean veil of oxygen rich atmosphere hung above the blue and green swirling mass that defined the Dagon homeworld.

With the recent sanctions placed on the homeworld by the Nyctan-Nephilim Fusion, however, very few ships came and went. The enemy had effectively laid siege to the entire planet. Those that tried to leave without authorization were shot down by the massive Nyctan and Nephilim battle cruisers that hung in the distance, monitoring vigilantly for signs of rebellion.

Authorized travel was only granted to small freighters shuttling supplies back and forth between Dagon Prime and Thessalonica, its moon. Being primarily a desert world, it didn't have the resources necessary to sustain itself. As such, cargo ships were allowed to resupply the moon, sparsely, but as needed. Random inspections by Nyctan security patrols ensured that nothing but the absolute most necessary supplies ever made it to the moon. And nothing ever made it back down to the surface of the planet except empty containers.

Raphine pulled back on the joystick of the Falcon, heavy drop ship and climbed toward the greenish-blue atmosphere of Thessalonica. As the ship peaked above the wispy clouds and stalled in the stratosphere, she glanced up at the encroaching darkness and glimpsed the outline of a massive Nyctan Vespa class destroyer lingering above the moon. Her ship's thrusters choked on the thin atmosphere and she rolled the sluggish craft over onto its back and guided the ship back toward the surface.

White vapor trails looped themselves into a figure eight as they trailed the Falcon dropship back down toward the rolling dunes and patchwork of oasis settlements scattered across the moon's surface. Water-evaporators, which syphoned the precious liquid from deep inside the moon and turned it into breathable air, exuded a constant stream of white spray that replenished the Thessalonica's atmosphere.

Out of the cockpit canopy, she watched as a series of small explosions flashed in sequence down on the surface. She knew it could be only one thing: Danica had finally tracked down her bounty.

Raphine smiled to herself and then flipped on the autopilot. She'd circle above the disturbance like a Torvian hawk circling high above an unsuspecting field mouse, and monitor the situation. If things went south, she'd swoop down, supply cover fire, and evacuate Danica out of there ASAP.

But it wasn't like she was worried. Ever since the loss of her and Jegra's child, Danica had been extremely cold and distant. And it wasn't only their son she'd lost. She had lost Jegra, too, in a manner of speaking.

The Empress had fallen into a deep coma after the incident and, like the hallmark sleeping princess of the fairy stories that Jegra had shared, lending Raphine her personal favorite books to read whenever she liked, she knew that it would take more than true love's kiss to awaken the sleeping empress.

In the meantime, she watched Danica cope the best she could. And she coped rather well, Raphine thought, by turning her anger into something productive and becoming a full-time bounty hunter. Not only did it give her an outlet to unleash her never-ending rage, but Danica had proved to be a rather talented manhunter, bringing in a constant stream of illegals and other criminals.

What Raphine hadn't anticipated in all this, though, was that Danica would start using again. And this time it seemed that she didn't care what the Nividium 3 would do to her. She just wanted that momentary high, that few seconds of mindless bliss.

And then there was one drunken night when they reminisced about the good old days, drank way too much wine and Dragonian brandy, and fell into bed together. It was a one-time thing. They both needed the other to act as a soothing balm for their pain. In that moment, in that desperate time of need, they were there for each other, and it had all just seemed right somehow.

Besides, the raw attraction between them made perfect sense. They trained together; fought together. And in the evenings, they consoled one another, a physical necessity now, seeing as ghosts haunted the empty corridors of the once thriving palace they lived in. They both knew it was bound to happen at some point on their road. So often did they feel compromised and in need of each other's comfort.

Raphine didn't regret that it had happened, but she did try her best to put it in the past. In spite of everything they shared, it wasn't a relationship that was realistic, let alone sustainable. It was what it was. Simple, brief, and bittersweet.

Raphine flipped on the comm. "Hey, you. How's it going down there? I see you're tearing up the terrain rather nicely."

"No time to chat," Danica's voice came back through the comm. She spoke loudly as the noise of what sounded like jet turbines droned in the background. "I have this son of a bitch in my crosshairs, and I'm not letting him get away. Not this time."

The electric powered turbines on the dune buggy roared over Danica's shouting. She raced at high speeds, somewhat recklessly, across a scorched desert terrain in pursuit of her bounty.

After a year of collecting bounties, she'd worked her way up the ladder of petty criminals to the kingpin himself, the drug lord and seemingly untouchable Gerard Van Zallek. What's more, Zallek had proven to be as slippery as a Brilaxian eel, so to speak. But her resolve was unfailing.

This was the man who'd gotten her addicted to an experimental drug from which she overdosed and nearly died, and she was out to make him pay. The fact that he'd taken advantage of her, using her to hurt those she cared most about, well, she'd punish him painfully. If he was very lucky, she wouldn't beat him to death with her bare hands but would toss him in the top max prison and let him rot away in a private cell for the rest of his miserable life.

"I have you now, you spineless, knuckle-dragging tosser," she roared above the screaming of her turbines. Kicking her head back in her seat, her purple-turquoise ombre hair falling across her shoulder, she floored it. The buggy's giant, paddle-tread tires kicked up a spray of sand nearly two stories high.

The jet engines she'd affixed to the dune buggy did their part, and she jammed the throttle up to full. Shooting over a medium-sized sand dune the vehicle soared momentarily in the air with an impressive hang time before crashing back down into the sand with a padded thump followed by another sky-high wake of sand jutting out behind it.

It had taken her eight months and sixteen days to track down Gerard Van Zallek's secret manufacturing facility and shut it down—by dropping a tungsten rod on it from orbit. Sadly, he wasn't there when she'd destroyed the place.

With the manhunt in full swing, it took her another four months before she finally got wind of his whereabouts. Each time she caught up, however, he'd always find a way to evade her. As it turned out, the man was like a snake, slithering out of every trap she set for him.

But not this time. This time she had him right where she wanted him. In her sights, on the run, with nowhere to go.

Zallek adjusted his sunglasses, then rose up from the passenger seat, blaster in one hand, the other firmly gripping the lip of the windshield, as his driver gunned it to try to lose the overzealous hag chasing them.

Of course, running wouldn't be enough. She'd caught scent of him, and Zallek knew that she would doggedly pursue him to the end of a thousand worlds. That was the type of crazy he was dealing with here.

He leaned over to his driver amid the roar of the engine and yelled something that was lost on the rush of wind and the sound of revving engines. The ATV pulled a hard right and plowed into a drift, and Zallek, swinging wide, took careful aim of his pursuer. He'd only get one shot at this.

Danica, of course, followed suit, and the two vehicles became locked in a tight donut, circling one another like two alpha sharks about to settle a territorial dispute.

A halo of sand plumed high from the speeding pirouette as Zallek trained his blaster, resting his forearm across the roll bar of his ATV to help steady his hand and get off a clean shot. Peering over the rims of his dark tinted shades he fired once sending a green plasma bolt zipping between the two vehicles.

Danica yelped when the blast hit her left arm—a lucky shot. Cringing she looked down at her singed and smoldering clothes doing her best to ignore the pain. She slammed her foot down on the brakes and throttled down the turbines bringing the buggy skidding to a halt in the sand.

In the distance between them, Zallek could be heard laughing above the rumble of his engine as they tore away from Danica's location. She looked up in time to see him shoot her a smug look, knowing he'd bested her again, and give her a two-finger salute as a taunting goodbye.

"Fuck!" Danica growled frustrated that he was getting away. She smashed her right fist down on the leather-wrapped steering wheel and screamed.

Still feeling the sting of the blast, she reached over and tore off the singed sleeve of her jacket and tossed it out the side of the buggy where the wind took it. It fluttered spastically away in the backdraft of the idling turbines.

She inspected the wound on her metal arm; the area that had been shot melted briefly into a metallic liquid; in the very next instant, the wound quickly filled itself in and a fresh layer of metallic skin congealed into place rendering her arm as good as new.

Wholly mended, Danica raised her clenched fist, opening and closing it repeatedly, flexing her metallic muscles out of sheer amazement that everything had been perfectly restored just as it had been before she'd been shot. "Amazing," she murmured to herself, admiring her high-tech arm.

Although it had cost her some major credits, Danica was happy with splurging on the self-healing memory metal upgrades. As far as prosthetic limbs went, it sure beat having to tinker with a clunky mechanical arm all the time trying to keep it in working order.

"Nice try, asshole," she said, gripping the steering wheel tightly with both hands—one lavender and one silver—and wrenching it in her fists so that the leather wrap whined and squeaked under duress. "But you'll have to do better than that if you're going to shake me this time."

With renewed determination, Danica spun the car back around, carving out a figure eight and kicking up another wall of sand in her wake.

Once she had gotten the nose of the buggy in-line with Zallek's tracks, she jammed the throttle up to full and the thrust of the turbines slammed her back into her seat.

Her purple-turquoise hair whipping along in the open space behind the headrest, she pulled down her goggles and aimed for the large dune off to the left of Zallek's tracks. He was circling around the dune in an attempt to lose her, but she had other plans.

The souped-up dune buggy hit the sandbank at two-hundred twenty-five kilometers per hour. Reaching for the dash she flipped up a red tab safety cover revealing a large red button. As she approached the cusp of the dune, she mashed the button and the throat of the jet nozzle opened wide as the afterburners ignited to full.

Triple shock diamonds formed in the tail of the afterburn as the custom buggy flew off the apex of the dune and out into the open air. Of all the jumps she'd ever attempted, this was the most insane, reckless—and thrilling!

Zallek looked up in time to see Danica's entire vehicle flying through the air like a flaming boulder launched from an ancient catapult—the kind barbarian warlords on primitive worlds often used to fend off Dagon landing parties. And in that moment he knew she was completely out of her mind.

Worse still, she was on a direct collision course for him.

At the last minute, he panicked and reached across the chest of his driver, grabbed the wheel, and jerked it as hard as he could to the right. Before his car could even respond to the abrupt direction change, however, Danica's front bumper plowed into his rear fender at a forty-five-degree angle and an impossible to escape downward momentum.

Metal grinding against metal, Zallek's ATV violently spun out of control, flipped up onto its side and tumbled three times before landing upside down where it scraped to a halt in the soft sand.

Simultaneously, the front bumper of Danica's car bit into sand at an extreme pitch, overturned, and was flung into the air from the excess momentum, spiraling violently as it became airborne. Her buggy went up and over Zallek's landing on the opposite side of his with a harsh thud, rolling twice, then settling onto the roll cage.

In the collision, one of the turbines tore off and launched itself into the sky. Untethered, it zipped away in a zig-zag fashion like a balloon darting aimlessly about until, finally, it crashed back down several meters away in a fiery explosion.

Wreckage lay strewn about, some of it still on fire, as a ghastly silence fell across the scene.

A gloved hand shot out of the sand, followed closely by Danica's violet face. Gasping for breath, she simultaneously coughed and spat up sand as she clawed her way out from underneath her overturned vehicle.

Luckily for her the roll bar had protected her from any serious injury, minus a minor case of whiplash. Seeing as the buggy had sunk fairly deep into the sand at a slightly skewed angle, she needed to squeeze out between the bottom part of the upturned ATV and the ground.

The loose sand didn't make pushing her way out any easier, either, as every time she made any headway she'd merely slide back down into the cavity of the buggy's cockpit.

Black smoke trailed into the sky over the various scorch marks left in the wake of the wreckage of both vehicles, along with a field of scrap metal that glinted in the mid-afternoon sun.

Somewhere a faint voice emitted from a buried radio smothered in sand. "Danica, are you all right? Dani, do you copy?"

"Gah!" Zallek emerged from the sand and gasped for air.

After catching his breath, he began pawing at the sand to get out from under his overturned ATV. His driver came up beside him and together they dug their way out from under the crushing weight of the vehicle.

At the same time, Danica was still digging herself out from under her own dune buggy. She looked over at them scrambling to try and beat her to the punch; she knew, just like the fights in the arena, the first person back on their feet usually prevailed.

It didn't help matters that Zallek's blaster lay in the sand an equal distance away from both their locations. Spotting the gun lying there, as if offering itself up to the victor, they turned to face one another, their eyes meeting with a familiar recognition.

Their dire expressions made it clear to them both that they shared the same thought. First one to get the gun wins. Not wasting another glance, both parties began to double-time their efforts, digging more frantically and kicking up sand everywhere.

Zallek was the first to free himself, but in his zeal to get to his feet he tripped over himself and bit the dirt. His sunglasses fell off and bounced to a stop an arm's reach in front of him. He swiftly retrieved his shades and placed them back on his face before scrambling back to his feet.

When he stood up, he saw that his hired man was closer to the gun than he was and thrust his chin desperately towards it, urging his man to hurry up and get it before Danica did.

Of course, Danica had two things they didn't—resolve, and a mother-fucking-bionic arm. Adrenaline surged throughout her entire body as she quickly sprang to her feet and marched toward Zallek and his henchman. Her fists tightened into compact wrecking balls which she planned to use to make him regret the day he'd ever crossed paths with the likes of her.

She knew the thrashing wouldn't fix all the wrongs he'd dealt her, but it sure as Helios would feel good.

Zallek's hired man made it to the blaster first and quickly drew it up. Aiming the weapon with unsteady hands, he sneered as he fired it at Danica.

The first shot went wild, pinging off the sand, making a scorching sound as it did. Realizing that the sights were off, his sneer melted into worry as the woman with a metal arm relentlessly closed in on him. Worse still, her eyes burned with a fury hotter than any flame and, in that raging fire, he could see an unconcealed desire to pummel him into meat jelly.

The gap between them closing, he hastily fired off another blast. This time his aim was on target, but Danica threw up her metal arm and deflected the shot. The plasma bolt bounced back toward him and, impacting directly in front of his feet, sent up a spray of sand—some of it getting into his eyes.

"Argh, I can't see!" he yelped. He staggered back and tried to open his eyes, but the sting of the sand blast forced him to close them again. Taking a wild guess as to where Danica was, he fired off a random shot. And then another.

Determined not to let her get to him, he drew backward and continued firing off a consecutive series of rapid shots.

Finally, he managed to crack open one eye just enough to find that she was nearly upon him, a stone's throw away. He screamed as he unloaded everything he had into her.

This time, however, she was ready for it. Throwing up a blue energy shield, her Dygra crystal glowing in her chest, the plasma bolts ricocheted off the forcefield and deflected back toward the idiot who kept firing at her.

Off to the sidelines Zallek scurried out of range of the blaster fire and dove to the ground to bury his head in the sand.

One of the bolts bounced back and hit him squarely. He stopped firing. A stunned look on his face, he looked down to see that the plasma bolt had burrowed inside his chest. Suddenly, a searing pain tore throughout every nerve fiber in his body and he let out a most wretched scream.

As the shock set in, his organs boiling from the inside out, he dropped his weapon and then, clutching his chest, sank to his knees.

Unable to comprehend that like a fool he'd inadvertently killed himself, he looked up at Danica, astonished. The look of astonishment faded into a blank expression as the life drained from his eyes and then, teetering ever so slightly to the left, he fell sideways and crumpled to the ground.

Not slowing her stride for a nanosecond, Danica stepped up to Zallek with the intent to mangle him. Alarmed, he threw up his arms defensively and began to back away from her, taking one additional step back for every step forward she took.

"Let's talk about this, Dani. You and I have history. We go way back, you and I. You owe me at least that much."

"I owe you squat, Zallek. You used me," she snarled. "And, now, it's my turn to use you. As my personal punching bag."

A metal fist came arching around in a vicious right hook and planted itself squarely across his left cheekbone. A resounding *thwack* and Zallek collapsed to one knee.

Stunned from the harsh blow he reached up to touch his jaw which felt rather numb. Something rattled around in his mouth and he spat up some blood-laced saliva and along with it a tooth. "You bitch," he mumbled.

"What did you call me?" she asked, her metal hand tightening into a fist, her arm flexing with the raw power of mechanical strength.

Zallek slowly turned his gaze toward Danica, staring up at her from behind half-shattered lenses. Before he could react, however, a second, even more unforgiving blow, met the side of his blue temple.

His mouth full of sand, Zallek pushed himself up to his hands and knees and spat out a muddy wad of dirt. The completely shattered sunglasses were left disregarded on the sand next to him.

When he saw Danica's foot take another step toward him, he scurried back, scuttling on all fours like a hermit crab in reverse. Falling onto his ass, he threw up a defensive hand and pleaded with her to have mercy.

"Wait! After everything we've been through. Somewhere...deep down inside...I know you still have feelings for me."

Although it was certainly news to her, she pretended to mull it over for a moment. Then, with a shrug, she replied, "Actually, I do have one overwhelming feeling for you. The urge to punch you in your stupid fucking mouth so hard that you'll have to shove a toothbrush up your ass just to brush your teeth."

"If you spare me," he said, changing tact, considering he wasn't getting anywhere with his previous line of impetration, "I'll make it worth your while. I'll make you an equal partner. Yeah, that's right! I'll split the revenue right down the middle." Thinking her brief pause was meant to hear him out, he quickly continued, "Just think about it, Danica. I can make you rich beyond your wildest dreams. Don't be a fool and throw it all away simply for something as childish as revenge."

Danica smiled. She raised her shiny metal fist high in the air and brought it down with a definitive blow to his head.

Zallek's lights went out like a bulb, and he hit the dirt with a harsh thud.

Casually bending over him, Danica threaded her metallic fingers through a tuft of his white hair. A subtle smile forming at one corner of her mouth, she trudged off into the desert, schlepping Zallek's limp body behind her like an oversized ragdoll, his feet leaving narrow traces in the sand.

3

A Pembroke Corgi paddled his stumpy white legs as he floated weightlessly across the passenger cabin of the *Ares III's* civilian section. Although the little animal was treading quite vigorously, he wasn't getting very far as he tried to make his way across to the other side, where his owner was strapping into their assigned seat.

The orange-tan corgi with white legs, who wore a doggy-diaper for zero-gravity strolls through the spacecraft, was tethered to his owner by a long, elastic leash. With a short tug on the leash, one moment the corgi was swimming in place and the next he accelerated across the expanse like a fuzzy tetherball and landed safely in the arms of his master; an older gentleman of Asian descent.

Captain Drange did a double take of the little flying furball and then glanced back over his shoulder at Karina with a look of equal parts surprise and curiosity. "Is that a dog?"

"Four legs, an elongated snout, and a cute fuzzy face," Iwasaki said in a droll voice. "Looks like a dog to me."

"You've really got to tell me how you convinced NASA to allow this."

"Simple," Karina said. "The world is ending. The *Ares III's* mission is no longer simply to resupply Mars Colony One but to save the entire Human race."

Drange nodded. He knew that getting off the planet couldn't have been easy. Not with the Avatars of Hastur, or whatever they were calling themselves, monitoring all human activity. But before he could inquire as to the specifics, Thompson beat him to the punch.

"How did you even manage to get off the surface of the planet with those…things…watching every little move?" she asked. Thompson titled her head toward the display on the wall that showed the news footage of the alien beings who referred to themselves as emissaries for some god-like being named Hastur. They'd arrived on Earth roughly a year ago and had proclaimed Earth as one of the spoils of this galactic conqueror. But what he wanted with the planet was anybody's guess, seeing as he'd never made his presence known except through his three avatars.

The reaction to the extraterrestrials ranged dramatically and you had a fair bit of crazy on both ends of the sociopolitical spectrum. Cults sprang up almost overnight and entire groups began worshipping these aliens as celestial supreme beings.

At the same time, governments wanted to learn more about where they'd come from. What their biology and physiology were. And how they manipulated natural law with such ease.

Scientists wanted to study them and often sent teams to try to collect any samples or data that they could, but the aliens proved resistant to any kind of social interaction that they themselves didn't instigate. Through it all, the one thing that became abundantly clear was that they weren't here to make friends with the Human race.

After the third month, the aliens held a summit at the United Nations, inviting all of the world leaders to attend—they promised to reveal what they called "The Great Plan."

As presumed, the world took keen interest in what the aliens had to say, and every leader and diplomat, as a sign of good faith, attended the summit.

Not even ten minutes into her speech, the golden alien female, who often referred to herself in the third person as The Voice of Hastur, switched tacks and, to the dismay of millions of television viewers tuning in live, ordered all the world's leaders, diplomats, and ambassadors in attendance to kill themselves.

Over half of the world's leadership was wiped out in the blink of an eye. This sparked panic and numerous countries immediately declared war on the aliens.

Protestors flooded the streets carrying signs which read "Go back to where you came from," and "Deport the illegal aliens."

Eventually protests turned into movements; movements gave rise to underground militias; and finally, the people rose up to take their planet back.

The war did not go well. One of the aliens could control time. To what extent, though, nobody knew. The larger, winged figure seemed impervious to nearly everything thrown at him, including a desperate nuclear attack that wiped out Phoenix, Arizona. But the woman, with her doll-like appearance and porcelain skin, was the most vicious of them all. Nobody could even get close to her without succumbing to her seductive persuasion.

Half a year after their arrival, the three of them had brought the Earth to its knees. All of the world powers pleaded for mercy. They tried to broker deals with the aliens. Radical militias fought in vain, hoping maybe to get lucky and find a weakness, but none was ever found.

Ten months into the occupation, a massive starship arrived in orbit around Earth. Soldiers in golden plated armor came down upon energy beams and began erecting all manner of machines. They sucked up the water. They took up plants, seeds, and soil. They plundered as much of the fertile world as they could. Then, within two weeks everything stopped. And all three omnipotent beings, along with their crews, returned to their ship.

That's how Karina had gotten off the world. The aliens had gotten what they'd come for and, now the planet, along with the life that once thrived there, was dying.

As a parting gift, the aliens had syphoned the energy from the Earth's core and had frozen it solid. The core turned into a solid ball of iron, stopped spinning and soon the entire planet would slow to a stop. Subsequently, the planet's magnetic field was already failing. At the same time, the magma that was shed by the iron core came under the capillary action of the fissures opened up by the alien's laser drilling, thereby setting off a chain of devastating volcanic eruptions.

The crew of the *ISS* had monitored the situation from above, but the damage had been done. The aliens' tampering of the planet had sent Mother Nature into frenzied chaos. Now it was only a matter of days, if not hours, before the planet simply came to a lifeless halt and burned on one side while the other succumbed to an eternal frozen wasteland.

Once everyone was safely aboard the *Ares III*, Karina turned, secured the hatch, and attempted to release the docking clamps that joined the *ISS* to the *Ares III*. The automated computer voice informed her that: <<Auto disengagement failure. Manual override is required.>>

Karina's head snapped toward Drange, and she shot him a worried look.

Without thinking, she catapulted herself up the corridor making her way to the main airlock. Drange was hot on her heels as she entered it.

"We're going to need to go outside to release the clamps manually," she said, stating the obvious.

"You mean...*I'm* going to need to go outside and release the clamps manually," Captain Drange clarified.

Karina reached up and grabbed the lip of the airlock's entrance and using her momentum swung herself inside. Inside the small room were two space suits waiting to greet the two astronauts like a couple of old friends with their mannequin-esque poses and welcoming, outstretched arms.

Drange appeared immediately behind her and clasped onto a side-bar halting his free-floating motion. He eyed her sternly and she glanced briefly at him. Then, resolute in her mission, began prepping the suit. He reached out a hand and gently tapped her arm.

"You already have your mission, Karina," Drange said, placing a hand on her shoulder. "I've got this."

She stopped what she was doing and bowed her head. She didn't look up but he could see a lonesome tear squeeze from the corner of her eye and wobble off into the center of the room.

He reached up and gently brushed her cheek with his warm hand. She reached forward and clasped his hand in hers.

"I didn't want to have to say goodbye like this." She slowly turned toward him, her body hovering in front of his as they clasped hands.

"I know," he said in a soothing manner that, for whatever reason, seemed to help all her other worries melt away.

She looked up at him with those blue eyes of hers that reminded him of the ocean. Her teary-eyed gaze only seemed to enhance the effect and, in that moment, as they stared into one another's eyes, they said a silent goodbye.

They didn't speak another word but worked in tandem getting his suit ready. She helped him into the space suit and did a double and triple check to make sure he was all set to go.

"Well, this is it," he said, shooting her his crooked smile.

She nodded but couldn't find it in herself to smile.

With nothing more to be said, Captain Drange had begun to turn toward the hatch when he felt her hand on his arm. She reeled him back to her and pressed her lips to his.

After a long kiss, he blinked twice and stared at her with a stunned expression. "What was that for?"

"Let's just call it a thank you."

"I haven't done anything yet," he replied.

"But you will," she said. She finally managed to smile, one last parting gift, and then kicked off the side of the wall and floated back out of the airlock.

Karina closed the hatch behind her then peered through the view portal of the airlock door and watched him. He put on his helmet, twisted it till the magnetic lock clicked into place creating an airtight seal. Then he reached up and depressurized the room.

Turning one last time to catch a glimpse of her beautiful face, he raised his thick glove to his visor and saluted her. She saluted him back. "Requesting permission to go for a walk," he said through the helmet comm.

She touched her earpiece and with tears in her eyes, replied, "Permission granted, Captain. And godspeed."

Climbing out of the airlock and onto the hull of the ship wasn't much of a challenge, but Captain Thomas Drange needed to get to the docking arms which were latched onto the *ISS* and pry them free.

As he floated down the length of the *Ares III's* hull, he looked up at the huge alien vessel hovering over the planet like a domineering citadel. It resembled the One World Trade Center back in New York City—in shape, if not appearance— and was just beginning to peek over the horizon of the planet. It hung vertically rather than horizontally as you'd imagine a ship of that configuration to hold in a fixed orbit. But even from this distance, he could tell the structure was huge. A feat of engineering that humans had yet to achieve.

"I'm closing in on the docking arms now," he said into his helmet's comm.

"Copy that, Captain, my captain," replied a voice.

Captain Drange paused, an expression coming over his face as though he'd just seen a ghost. Then, as his astonishment gave way to a larger, ear-to-ear grin, he asked, "Alice? Is that you?"

"In the flesh, big brother."

"What in the world are you doing up here?"

"Figured I'd have a better chance of not ending up on some cold slab with a dozen alien probes crammed up my tuchus by putting as much distance between me and them as possible."

"That's my lil' sis," Drange said, his smile widening. "Always able to put a smile on everyone's face with that quirky sense of humor and that winning personality of yours."

"The truth is, I knew you'd need all the help you could get."

"Is that so?" Drange asked. He chuckled to himself as he came into position over the malfunctioning docking clamps. Unlatching his tether, he hooked his safety line to the *ISS* portion of the arm, since it gave him a better foothold to address the malfunctioning areas.

"Well, big brother, it seems Karina needs to talk to you. But I'll see you when you get back."

"Yeah," Drange replied, "see you soon."

A brief pause followed and then Karina's voice came back onto the comm. "How's it going out there, Captain?" she asked.

"It would almost be a perfect evening sky if not for that phallic eyesore floating out there, reminding us that we all just got ass-raped by a bunch of world conquering aliens."

"Copy that," Karina replied, ignoring his colorful, yet undeniably apt, description of their current predicament. "So, what's the damage?"

Drange looked down at the arm and studied it. Then he reached around to the tool kit that was secured to the side of his suit with good old fashion Velcro. With a rip, he plucked off the tool kit from his utility belt and then set it beside him on a portion of the docking clamp. It snapped into place with a magnetic *clack* and latched onto the metal surface of the station.

"I'm in position now," Drange said, opening the tool box and pulling out the tools he needed.

Out of nowhere came a bright flash. He shielded his eyes then looked up. The alien vessel had jumped away. At the same time the entire planet began to swell like a beach ball being fed too much helium.

"Are you seeing this?" Drange asked.

"We're seeing it," Karina's voice came back over the comm. A long pause was followed by an order. "You'd better get to work on that arm," she said. "I don't know how much time we have."

"Already on it."

Captain Drange worked furiously on freeing the clamps, but they didn't want to budge. Another bright flash caught his attention and he looked up in time to see a quarter of the planet rupture into outer space. Large chunks of debris the size of entire continents spun out, freed from gravity.

"No, no, no," he said to himself as he forced his eyes back down. One problem at a time, he told himself.

"Captain, we have eleven minutes and thirty-eight seconds till we come around and that debris makes mincemeat out of us. You've got exactly eight minutes to get those clamps free and get back here before we bug out."

"Hey, Karina, have I ever let you down?"

"No," she said. However, the nervousness in her voice didn't abate. Because she knew that if he couldn't get the job done, she'd have to abandon him there and tear half her ship apart in the process. And that wasn't at all ideal.

"Hey, Thomas," Alice's voice came over the comm again.

"Yes, sis?" he replied, never pausing from his work.

"I just wanted to say…"

"I know," he replied, cutting her off. "I love you too."

Karina returned to the cockpit of the *Ares III* and took her seat and strapped in. She glanced out the port side and caught a glimpse of Drange's suit reflecting the sun's light. Reaching down she flicked on the comm. "Captain Drange, it's time. Get your ass back inside. We'll drag the *ISS* to Mars if we have to. But you're out of time out there."

"I've got two more minutes," he said in a low voice. Nearly every ounce of his concentration was on getting the clamp to release, which is why he didn't hear the other half of what Karina had said. But he knew she was just likely cursing his stubbornness and giving him a piece of her mind. It didn't matter. He knew what he had to do.

"Karina, you listen to me and you listen to me good. I need you to take care of Alice for me. You hear me?"

Another long pause and then Karina's voice came back to him. "I hear you. Good luck, Captain, and we'll see you over the rainbow."

That was their little code for meeting again someday. Even though they knew it was a complete fantasy, like Dorothy finding the wonderful land of Oz, if it ever happened it certainly would be a nice dream.

"Same to you…to you all."

Karina flicked off the comm and then sat back in her seat. After taking a deep breath, she announced to the rest of the ship. "Everyone strap in. We're going hot in T-3 minutes."

Outside the ship Drange unfastened his oxygen canister. His suit immediately began to warn him about his limited oxygen when he turned off the automated system. He had enough internal air to last two minutes; after that, it wouldn't matter.

Canister in hand he carefully wedged it into the portion of the clamp where the gears seemed to be frozen. Taking a large monkey wrench out of the toolbox, he raised it high and then said to himself, "Hi-tech, meet low-tech."

With a resounding clangor, he brought the wrench down on the nozzle of the canister with all his might, but it merely made a small *tink*. He then clamped the wrench onto the end of the canister and using as much leverage as he could muster, began to pull on it, straining against the resistance as hard as he could.

Beads of sweat appeared like dew on the surface of his face only slightly jostling whenever he moved his head. Eventually one of the plump droplets broke free and floated weightlessly inside his helmet. He did his best to ignore it and doubled his efforts on putting his back into wrenching the cannister free.

Without warning the metal buckled, a crack opened up, and the canister shot out a spray of gas.

Luckily, it was just the right amount to loosen the clamps and both ends finally released their grip of the *Ares III.* But the oxygen jet had also shifted the trajectory of the *Ares III* slightly off course.

"This is Captain Drange to *Ares III.* You're free, but mind your trajectory. Now go on and get out of here. That's an order."

Cheers erupted around the ship and filled his earpiece. He smiled to himself, glad that his mission was a success.

Just as the applause was dying down, the *Ares III's* thrusters ignited. The ship tore away from the *ISS* and pieces of shrapnel glinted and gleamed in the afterglow of the thrusters.

With a solemn expression, Drange watched them pull away from him. He raised his thick gloved hand as if to bid them a final farewell as they shrank into a white dot that gradually faded into the distance, only the bright blue glow of their engines alerting him to their position.

<<Warning: Sixty seconds of oxygen remaining,>> the suit cautioned him. He lowered his hand and then turned back to look at Earth one last time. As his final seconds counted down in the HUD display of his helmet's visor, he looked up and watched the blue and green sphere he called home swell to an impossible size. It seemed he could reach out and touch home with his own hands.

In the next instant the entire planet exploded outwardly in every direction. Giant chunks of rocky debris flew out into space and a hailstorm of rock and detritus rose toward him like a raging tsunami.

In the brief moment of solitude—he became the sailor looking out at the raging sea—he found peace of mind in the knowledge that he had helped saved the lives of all that remained of the Human race.

All good captains go down with their ship, he reminded himself. And Earth was his ship. Looking up one last time, a sad smile formed on the corners of his mouth and the edges of his eyes rippled with an excess of tears. It was always hardest, he felt, finding the words to say goodbye.

"Thou wast all to me...for which my soul did pine—A green isle in the sea...a fountain and a shrine."

4

A dark halo of sweat saturated the neckline of Danica's tan tank top as she hiked to the top of a large sand dune. Just as she reached the peak, a heavily armored drop ship flew overhead and circled back around. She looked up and waved to the woman peering out from the cockpit window. Raphine's smiling face met her gaze and she nodded, letting Danica know that she had eyes on her.

Smoking Zallek out like the cockroach he was had been a fun preoccupation, but now that she'd finally caught him, Danica knew it was time to start focusing on more important matters.

Dagon Prime lay in ruins. H'aaztre's avatars had decimated all their major cities in order to cripple the great empire and send a message to anyone thinking of resisting him. Nothing was out of their reach. Not even the mightiest empire the galaxy had ever known could stand up to them.

After the Avatar of War, called Nodengoth, had taken Danica and Jegra's child, the baby had disappeared off the face of the map. At the same time, the Nyctan and Nephilim allied armada, called the Fusion, continued to police the Commonwealth and everything in it.

With the occupation fully underway, Nyctan grew more prosperous than it had ever been. This was partly due to the fact that they were the descendants of the Nephilim, the chosen people of H'aaztre. The only difference in their porcelain skin and obsidian black eyes was that some of the Nephilim had wings like those of an Arkadian fisher hawk.

Favored by the new regime, Nyctan became an immense, yet inherently corrupt power—a new Mecca for evil in the galaxy.

Luckily for Danica, however, a place as barren and unimportant as the desert moon of Thessalonica was of little value to the Gilded God and his acolytes. So, for the most part, Thessalonica went ignored, left more or less to itself.

Other than the occasional port check, the Fusion patrols merely came down to collect offerings in the name of their God. Basically, every occupied territory was forced to tithe, to give as many assets as possible, as defined by the Fusion, naturally, in the name of pleasing H'aaztre. But seeing as Thessalonica hadn't much to offer in the way of natural resources, the Nephilim didn't terrorize them nearly as much as they did worlds which had bountiful resources.

The past was hard for Danica to think about, but not nearly as hard as it had been for Jegra. In fact, she and Jegra should have died that day on the *Shard*.

Fate, however, had other plans for them. And although Danica had been mortally wounded and Jegra rendered unconscious after a difficult birth and the emotionally shattering trauma of losing the child, it was Fate that had intervened.

With the entire ship ripping apart all around them, amid all the chaos, Lianica had appeared to them in a beam of light. She saved them moments before the ship went up. And, as usual, Raven showed up just when Jegra needed her the most; she and her crew had swooped in and whisked them away from the battle.

Raven brought them home, to Arena City on Thessalonica, and stayed for a stint. When it became painfully clear that Jegra wouldn't be waking from her coma any time soon, Raven wished Danica and Raphine the best of luck and returned to her mission of rebuilding the fleet and, with any luck, building up the resistance.

For Danica, though, the numbness and shock didn't seem to fade; it began to define her. After the loss of her son, she felt hollow. Empty inside. And her best friend, the only person she'd truly opened up to emotionally, had fallen comatose. As if to add insult to injury, she didn't lose one love that day; she had lost two.

Sand whipped about and caused Dani to shield her eyes as the drop ship landed in a clearing several meters in front of her. The ramp lowered and Raphine sauntered out.

The bounce in her step and her captivating swagger suggested she was almost as excited as Danica for having captured Zallek. At the same time,

Raphine's tight, khaki tank top slid up her taught abs from the motion of her swinging hips, teasing out her olivine midriff.

She tugged her shirt back down to her flight issue black pants which, in turn, ran all the way down into military issue desert tan boots. She paused at the end of the loading ramp, hands on her hips.

"You finally catch your great white whale?" Raphine asked, a pleased smile forming on one side of her mouth.

Danica shot Raphine a curious look. That particular cultural reference wasn't familiar to her. "Whale?" asked Danica.

"It's from one of Jegra's favorite books. It's about a maritime ship's captain, Ahab, who's hunting an elusive giant whale that bit off his leg after an encounter on the high seas."

"Did he ever catch the beast?"

"Actually, he spent his life hunting it, only ever coming close, again and again, but never managing to kill it. Then, in his old age he tracked it down wrecking his ship in the process. He fought it with a rope and harpoon, but got entangled with the creature in the frigid waters. It pulled him under the jagged waves and man and beast disappeared into the depths of the ocean never to be seen again."

"That's how the story ends?"

"Well, there's a bit after that. A boy gets rescued. But, that's the fate of Ahab. Battling a monster till the bitter end until, finally, they sink into the abyss together. It's the perfect metaphor for…well, you know." She nodded her head at the unconscious body being dragged behind Danica.

"Sounds like an intriguing story," Danica said, smiling at Raphine. "But I'm still here and this isn't any abyss," she informed, jutting a thumb over her shoulder at the baked wasteland behind her, "and this here isn't a white whale. Just an asshole."

Raphine laughed and then helped Danica drag Zallek up the ramp into the cargo hold of the drop ship. At Dani's prompting, they let go of his hair and his head smacked against the metal floor with a resounding *clunk*.

Raphine squinted her eyes at her reproachfully and Danica shrugged.

"It's the least he deserves," Danica said in her defense.

"It's not that," Raphine informed her. "It's just…" she paused and formulated her words carefully. "It's just that I was worried about you. That's all."

"Don't be," Danica replied, turning back to find Raphine's crystal blue eyes fixated on her.

Raphine placed a gentle hand on Danica's breast, the palm of her hand tenderly cupping the rounded fullness of her. "I couldn't bear losing you too," she said.

Danica placed both hands over Raphine's and smiled. "I'm right here," she said. "That has to count for something, right?"

Raphine flung her arms around Danica's neck and gave her a massive hug. After their embrace, Danica laughed.

"What was that for?"

"I was going to try and keep it as a surprise, but I can't contain myself any longer. I'm bursting at the seams to tell you…I have good news."

"What news, Raph?" Danica asked, more curious than ever.

"She's awake."

Danica froze, her eyes hanging on Raphine's face as she tried to process the news. Somehow it didn't feel real. It felt as though she was being pranked— as if it were all some kind of cruel joke.

After all these months, was it really happening? Were her prayers finally answered? "You mean…?"

"Yes," Raphine answered, her pearly white smile spreading ear to ear beneath her lush, forest green lips.

Danica cupped her mouth and, her legs growing weak, she sank to her knees. Warm tears streamed down both cheeks and quickly evaporated into the desert heat, disappearing again almost as quickly as they'd appeared. After catching her breath, she gathered herself, stood back up, and, clasping onto Raphine's arms, said, "Take me to her."

Raphine nodded and seeing how Danica was still beside herself with shock, helped her into a seat that lined the inside hull of the drop ship.

As Danica strapped in, Raphine turned and slapped the button next to the bulkhead to close the loading ramp. Without waiting for it to close all the way, she turned and marched back to the cockpit. It was time to go home.

Thirty-eight minutes later, the Falcon dropship landed at the far end of the palace lawn.

The grass compressed under the blast of the reverse thrusters, flattening in large circles beneath the powerful rotary turbines. As the landing skiffs of the ship touched down, palace security raced toward the rear loading ramp to assist in apprehending the fugitive, Gerrard Van Zallek.

Chief of Security, Raphine Agnar brought the criminal out in shackles while Danica, anxious to see her luv, leapt off the loading ramp and dashed across the garden toward the woman dressed in a white gown. She was standing by the fountain watching small bees buzz excitedly about the palace flower beds that encircled it.

"My god..." gasped Danica, stopping less than ten feet away from the angelic sight. "It really is you. You're awake!"

More tears trickled down her cheeks as her best friend and soul mate turned to her and smiled.

Jegra, wearing a form fitting white dress that hugged her body like a milky residue, studied the face of the blue woman standing before her. For a moment, Danica felt worried that Jegra might not recognize her. After all, she'd had cortical stimulators inserted into her temples to help stabilize her neurological framework and ensure she didn't slip back into a coma. Whatever else that did to one's mind, she wasn't entirely sure.

Danica, still crying, smiled in return. She raced over and took Jegra's hands in hers. Then, rising up on her toes, she gave Jegra a peck on the lips.

"Oh, how I've missed you," Danica said.

"Is that all I get?" asked Jegra, giving Danica a dejected look.

Danica laughed and then, reaching around her neck, drew Jegra into her Prussian blue lips. Pink and blue flesh mingled as the women shared a long, sultry kiss. Danica's forked tongue slipped inside Jegra's mouth and tasted that familiar flavor that drove her wild. That honey-kissed sweetness that only Jegra seemed to have.

After a brief reprieve, Jegra gave Danica another peck on the lips and then, clearing her throat, asked, "Our son?"

"He's gone," Danica said. Almost as soon as she said it a flood of emotions washed over her and her eyes instantly began to stream hot, wet tears.

"Oh, Dani," Jegra said, her heart breaking for Danica as she finally noticed the prosthetic. "I'm so sorry." Reaching out with her hand she gently touched the cool metallic surface of Dani's prosthetic arm and then ran her fingers delicately along its surface.

She wanted to tell Dani how sorry she was for having let her down. For not being there for her when she needed her love and support the most. But no amount of wishing could ever change the past. It was too late for all she should have done.

At the same time, she wanted to promise she'd get their son back. But that wasn't a promise she was even sure she could keep. All she could do was stand in silence, feeling as though a part of her had been ripped away—taken from her—and it quite literally had. And the woman standing across from her felt the exact same agonizing pain.

And it was in this shared sorrow, the very recognition of the pain itself, that they found the smallest quantum of solace. For in this recognition there stirred a sense of compassion. A desire to end one another's pain. And only by this recognition could they hope to end the other's grief and begin the healing process.

Until today, Danica couldn't begin to heal. But now that Jegra had come back to her—she knew things would gradually start to get better.

Danica placed her hands on Jegra's face. "Don't worry about any of that right now," she insisted. "We may be broken and defeated, but we aren't finished. Not by a long shot."

Jegra wiped a tear from the corner of her eye with the back of her hand and tried to smile. Her lips quivered, faltered, and she fell back into a state of melancholy. "I never knew you to be the optimistic type," she said.

"I'm not being optimistic," Danica said, her brow scrunching up into a scowl. "I'm being pragmatic. We lost. But we're going to do what any good gladiator does. We're going to get back up to our feet and pull ourselves together. Because, like it or not, the fate of the Dagon Empire, maybe even the entire Commonwealth, depends on you and me getting our shit together."

"Nice pep-talk," a third voice interjected.

Jegra and Danica turned to see Raphine standing several meters off to their side. Barely recognizing the girl because she had grown into a stunning and vivacious woman, Jegra raised an eyebrow.

"Raphine? Is that you?"

"In the flesh!" she said, strolling up to them. She fell into Jegra's arms and embraced her as though she were her own sister. She looked at Danica; they shared and awkward moment, her smile briefly fading; and then she looked back toward Jegra again. And again, all smiles.

"You've turned into a total babe, babe," Jegra said, scanning her from head to toe. She rubbed her head, like one would a child, and then pulled her in for another hug.

"Glad to have you back in one piece, Your Grace."

"Glad to be back," Jegra said, relinquishing her hold on the young woman.

Raphine stepped back and then bowed reverently. "If you'll excuse me, my empress, now that you're back up on your feet, I have numerous security matters to attend to."

Her eyes slowly lifted back up to meet Jegra's and she smiled one last time. Anxious to impress upon Jegra how serious she was about maintaining her safety, she wasted no time, and promptly returned to her duties. Pivoting smartly, her ponytail whipping around behind her, she sauntered off to resume her security checks.

"Our girl is all grown up," Jegra said proudly.

"Indeed," Danica agreed. "Of course, we'll have time for catching up with her later. Right now we need to get you up to speed with everything that's happened over the past year."

They shared another glance and then, happy to be reunited, turned to look out at the sunset together.

The Thessalonica sun was already beginning to sink into the distant dunes of the southern reach and it cast a brilliant orange hue over the rolling white sands, saturating everything with its warm glow.

Jegra's hand slid over toward Dani's and, fingers entwined, they stood watching the sunset intensify from orange to hot pink just before settling behind Arena City and the distant horizon.

As the cool of dusk swept over them, in that pristine moment where the warm winds give way to the cool desert night, they stood together in contemplative silence. Although Jegra couldn't imagine what thoughts flowed through Dani's head, she had a sneaking suspicion they weren't so dissimilar from her own. A deep desire for this sanguine, and positively happy moment to never end.

The evening breeze blew Jegra's chestnut brown hair about in soft undulations, as she watched the last sliver of light get swallowed up by the night. In that moment, she imagined she could hear the distant beating of war drums calling to her. Whether she was merely imagining it, or if the Arena games had implemented drums for entertainment's sake, she knew not. All she knew was that she felt the warrior's spirit inside of her stir and the gladiatrix of the galaxy had awakened once more.

5

"**Must you make** that infernal clicking noise with your jaw?" Dakroth griped.

"What?" Callestra said as she sat on the edge of a broken chariot that lay at the far end of the arena—the same arena that they'd been trapped in for over a year.

"I can't help it. When I get stressed or bored I pop my jaw. And right now I'm a whole lot of both."

Rhadamanthus Dakroth leaned against the stone wall of the arena and let out a disgruntled sigh. "This bloody endless mid-day heat. An entire year of non-stop swelter minus the beaches of Arkadia, brimming with the glistening skin of a hundred nude women from every imaginable species and world."

"Is that all your primitive mind can think about at a time like this?" Callestra asked. "Naked girls?"

"You're naked enough," Dakroth mumbled as he glanced at Callestra's flimsy, deerskin bikini. She looked like a pin-up jungle girl from the pulp books he'd read as a kid. Blue bosomed babes fighting for the glory of the Dagon Empire against foolish alien species too stupid to realize they'd fallen for the wiles of assassin women.

"Why are you staring at me like that?" Callestra asked, nervously. "Our dining date isn't for another two days."

Indeed, he thought, as his stomach grumbled from hunger pains. That was, perhaps, the worst part about being trapped in H'aaztre's terrible chthonic time-loop that continuously resurrected them. The mad entity had neglected to provide any food.

If they allowed themselves to starve to death, every seven days the nightmare would simply reset and begin all over again. What's worse was that they were just as hungry when they woke up as when they'd died. No amount of sleep ever seemed to help stymie the hunger pains. The only thing that did that was too terrible to think about. But they did think about it. How could they not? They were flesh and blood. And they were starving.

Over and over again the cycle of constant hunger, pain, and death recurred on an endless loop, never relinquishing their souls to the relief of eternal sleep. Driving them to the brink of madness. Driving them to cave into the depraved little voice in the back of their minds urging them to go through with the most unspeakable of crimes.

Finally, they came to a mutual agreement. Every six days one of them would sacrifice themselves by offering themselves up as food. The other would be forced, out of necessity of survival, to eat their partner in a cruel and gruesome act of cannibalism.

And like clockwork, once they'd died and the other had consumed their partner's flesh, a few hours would pass and the unlucky victim of the ritual would wake up in their cell, all the horrors of what had transpired fresh in their mind.

This gruesome ritual had gone on for 278 days. Although the number of times they'd cannibalized one another before the terrible reset slowly blurred in their minds, it went largely undiscussed, it was still a cruel fact of their existence in this place.

The rest of the time they tried to find things to preoccupy themselves with: throwing pebbles; sparring; telling each other jokes or riddles; and, of course, sex. Sex was, by far, the most readily available distraction. But today neither of them were in the mood for much of anything.

"Do you think…" Callestra began before cutting herself off.

When Dakroth realized that she wasn't going to finish the sentence, he let out another sigh and then asked, "Do I think what?"

"That we'll ever get out of this dismal nightmare?"

"Come now, we've discussed this a thousand times already. It doesn't serve any good to talk about the purely hypothetical. What we need to do is try and focus on finding a weakness in this place so we can exploit it and, with any luck, escape."

She shot him a frustrated look. "What are you talking about? We can escape. We've gone outside the walls; there's an infinite jungle out there to explore."

"Yes. A jungle with poisonous vines, acid rivers and lakes, and grass made out of crystalline needles that paralyze you. If anything this H'aaztre has a very morbid sense of humor."

"We've never made it to the end, though. If escaping is our goal then all we have to do is try to—"

"We have tried!" Dakroth grumbled. "We walked for days. I died, woke up back here. You made it slightly further, but if you didn't find the end to this trap, then maybe there isn't one."

"So, we just sit here for all eternity, fucking and eating each other, until all we know is this ritualistic madness?"

Dakroth pushed himself to his feet and dusted himself off. He didn't answer her question but took a few steps out into the arena and looked up at the domed ceiling.

They were in some kind of biosphere, a menagerie of sorts, that much was sure. It stretched on for dozens of miles in every direction, but as they had discovered, everything beyond the walls of the arena was viciously hostile: barbed plants that stung like wasps; vines that wrapped themselves around your legs with razor blade-like leaves; patches of quicksand everywhere.

The trees had sap that acted initially like morphine but always proved fatal, no matter how little you imbibed, and the rivers of pure acid were virtually impossible to cross without some kind of raft—which you couldn't fashion because it would require you to cut down trees that responded to attack by shooting paralyzing, multi-needled darts.

It was one giant death trap. The creation of a sadistic deity that found the torment of other beings amusing. In all his years exploring the galaxy, Dakroth had never encountered a world as lethal as this one which gave him the sneaking suspicion that it had been engineered this way.

The first time Dakroth had been immobilized by a needled dart in the forest, he had to endure agonizing pain, lying there in a crumpled heap of vegetative consciousness, waiting to starve to death so he could reset.

That was the one good thing about this place. As long as they were here, they had immortality. If only he could figure out how to adapt such a technology to the outside world.

Callestra stood up and broke a wooden spoke off from the battered wheel of a weathered and toppled chariot. The chariot had been there when they'd arrived and it always was there to greet them, and it always filled her with dread. Every time she saw it, she was reminded of where she was and the fact that there was no getting out of this place.

A week earlier they'd grown bored and decided to have a full-on gladiator match. Under the sun that never set, they took turns whipping one another as they yelled, "Faster, faster!"

They had exhausted themselves to delirium, running in circles, shuttling one another around in that chariot, and laughed in their madness as they set fire to it and danced in the euphoria of their sunbaked lunacy. But given enough time, even madness becomes a bore and they set it aside for another time.

Now everything was stuck in a lull. They had exhausted all meaningful conversation. They'd shared their most intimate secrets. Bared their souls to one another. And Callestra felt that Dakroth probably knew her better than anyone ever could and she felt she knew him better than anyone else ever would. But, in this place, she wondered if that meant anything.

That is what a year of being trapped with a person will do to you. Forge an inseparable bond. A kinship of sorts. And although, over the course of weeks and then months, she had learned that Dakroth was nothing like the man she used to idolize. But, at the same time, she knew she'd spend the rest of her life with him. Either as a servant or as a mistress, it didn't matter to her. She was a part of him now, whether he liked it or not. And he was a part of her, too.

She brought the spoke down on her leg and snapped it in half. Bringing up a jagged end, she held it out to him. "If you want, you can kill me."

Dakroth waved his hand and rescinded her offer. "I'm afraid we're beyond that now, my dear. All we have left is to find a way out of this place."

"You keep saying that," Callestra said.

"So?" Dakroth shrugged and turned to her.

"It's getting a bit old."

"Says the woman who clicks her jaw like it's a…a…"

"A what?"

"I don't know…the word escapes me at the moment."

"Apparently, so do your manners."

"Watch your tongue, girl. I'm still your emperor!"

"And you're still a giant ass too!"

"Now who's lacking in manners?"

"I don't know, ass-face, you tell me."

"Bitch!" he growled.

"Bastard!" she shot back.

A fiery rage compelled them to come together and, before either of them realized what they were doing, they'd torn the rags off of their haggard bodies and began to give into their baser instincts.

They tumbled to the ground, rolled around in a violent embrace, and soon, dust sticking to their sweaty blue bodies, he was on top of her, hands at her throat.

"Yes," she said, grabbing his wrist with her hands and forcing him to choke her even harder.

She gasped as he penetrated her, the granules of sand rubbing her tender flesh raw. But she didn't care. It couldn't be pleasant for him either, but at least it was something that caused them to feel. Caused them to remember that they were still alive.

"You like that?" he asked in a low tone, a crooked grin forming on one side of his mouth.

"Harder," she pleaded, "squeeze harder!"

The next thing Callestra knew was she was waking up in the dank, dark holding cell beneath the arena.

"FUUUCK!" she screamed, taking a massive gulp of air. As the world came back into focus, she realized that she'd died and reset once again. And once again she staggered to her feet and made the bothersome walk up the dreadfully long corridor.

When she arrived topside, she saw the emperor sitting in the shade of an archway that led to the lower holding deck for waiting gladiators. The only place in the arena that had any ounce of shade.

She went over to him and placed a gentle hand on his shoulder. He startled and reeled around, only to stare up at her with an awestruck expression on his face; a face that hadn't shaven in months. In fact, Dakroth's grizzled beard had fully grown in, and she couldn't help but wonder what was going on.

She could sense something was wrong. "What is it?" she asked him. He swiveled around and, wrapping his arms around her mid-section, clasped onto her waist and held her. His sobbing only grew more profound and she did her best to not let it get to her. She'd never seen him like this. "Please, tell me."

"You died," he said.

"I know. You strangled me to death."

"No," he said, looking up at her, his face serious. "You don't understand. Afterward…you didn't come back. At least, not right away. Not like before."

A puzzled looked came over her. From her point of view, everything had happened just as it always did. She died. She came back. When he died, he always came back too. *What's so different about this time?* she wondered.

"I'm back now, though," she said, stroking his hair.

"You say that as if a hundred days hadn't passed."

"*A hundred days?*" she echoed, drawing back. She looked down at his forlorn expression with a startled one. "Are you saying I've been dead for over three months?"

"I survived off your remains for as long as I could," he said. He nodded at the weapons rack which had what appeared to be strips of beef jerky strung up on it. When she realized the flesh was her own, she suddenly felt sick to her stomach.

"What's going on? Why can I see my dismembered, withered flesh? How can I have been gone for so long? What has changed?"

Dakroth started laughing manically. "Don't you get it?" he said. "Nothing has changed. This place's very design is to torment us. And that's precisely what it's doing!"

"No!" Callestra said, sinking to her knees and grabbing the sides of Dakroth's face, forcing him to look at her. "Don't let him get into your head. You're the Emperor of Dagon. Never forget that."

"Promise me you'll never leave me," he said. He began sobbing again and she brought his face down to her bosom. She coddled him, rocking on her heels and soothing him like a mother would a small child.

"I promise," she answered.

It pained her to see him this way…weak and sobbing like a baby…but, at the same time, her heart was warmed by the fact that he had revealed how deeply he cared about her.

Maybe now she could finally tell him that she had, in fact, found a way out of this place that fateful day they'd become separated in the noxious jungle.

She had been biding her time, unsure whether to reveal this secret, because the one thing she knew above all else was that Dakroth was ruthless. As ruthless as they came. And he needed to be broken down before she could rebuild him and make him into the emperor she had always known he could be.

That was the one good thing about this place. It had given her the ability to gradually shape and mold Dakroth into the man of her dreams. And to her pleasant surprise, it had only taken a year to get him to treasure her more than even his own life.

Not even the empress, Jegra Alakandra, could claim as much. Callestra smiled to herself as she stroked the emperor's silver hair. No, the emperor didn't belong to anyone but her. He was hers and hers alone.

"I promise," she consoled. Running her fingers through his hair, she added, "I'll never leave you again." And then she kissed the top of his head and smiled at her own cunning.

6

Shade of night settled across the white desert sands of Thessalonica as the last sliver of warmth faded behind the distant dunes. A purple veil settled across the landscape as far as the eye could see. And to the northwest, the city lights of Arena City lit up the valley while to the east the diffused glow of Mardok could be made out, to one with a keen eye.

Desert fireflies caught Jegra's and Danica's attention and they decided to watch the flickering dance of the luminous insects for a while longer before turning in for the evening. That's when they heard the barely perceptible sound of soft footsteps sneaking up behind them.

Alerted to the interloper's presence, Jegra spun around to face down whoever it was that was interrupting their romantic moment. When she saw that Raphine had returned, however, her aggravation quickly melted away, giving way to a welcoming smile. "Raphine? You startled us."

"Apologies, Your Grace," she said, giving the Dagon salute and bowing slightly. When she looked back up, her eyes were distant. "I'm afraid I bring bad news."

Danica noted the girl was standing frozen, as if in terror, unable to spit out whatever it was she was holding inside. She merely stood gazing at them both with deeply sorrowful eyes, which prompted Danica to ask, "What is it, Raph?"

"I-I don't know how to tell you this, but..." She choked on her emotions, which made the words almost impossible to get out, but she pushed through it the best she could. Looking the empress in her eyes, she said in a faltering voice, "Earth has been destroyed."

After grappling with the weight of the information for a moment, she cleared her throat and asked, "H-how?"

The news was so implausible that the shock hadn't even really begun set in yet. Then, all of a sudden, it hit her like a ton of bricks and she quickly felt weak in the knees. Reaching out, she grabbed Dani's arm and they slowly sank to the ground together.

"Let me guess," Danica said, looking up at Raphine, her face creased with a broiling rage even as hot tears streamed down her cheeks. "It was *him*, wasn't it?"

Raphine nodded solemnly. She waited a moment then cleared her throat again. When both women's attention returned to her, she informed them, "Long range sensors are picking up a distress signal emanating from the fourth planet in your solar system. It simply repeats the same message: S.O.S."

Jegra looked up with a hopeful expression. "Mars?"

Raphine looked to Danica for confirmation, who merely gave her a mystified look and a shrug, then back to Jegra. "The red one."

"That's the one," Jegra said, rising to her feet. She brushed the sand from her white dress and then, arching her back and craning her neck, peered up at the stars. "We'll need a ship."

"Even assuming we had the fastest ship in the fleet," Raphine informed them, "we'd still have to get past those blockades. And I'm afraid, first, we're fresh out of ships and second, that blockade isn't going anywhere."

"Umm…that's not entirely true," Danica said a bit sheepishly, as though she were keeping a vital secret.

Both Jegra and Raphine turned toward Dani with inquisitive looks.

"Well, spit it out," Jegra demanded. "What aren't you telling us?"

"After we lost the *Shard*, I had Raven dedicate all of the shipyard's resources to building you another ship. If her team is on schedule, the new and improved *Shard* should be in orbit as we speak. It was going to be a welcome home surprise for you when you woke up."

"I'm up now," Jegra said. She looked up at the sky, wondering if she could make it out if she gazed long and hard enough.

That's when she looked over at Danica, who had tapped something into her holovid bracelet. No sooner had her eyes settled onto Jegra's inquiring gaze, than the yellow beams of light came down and danced all around them.

Mouthing the words, "I love you," Jegra smiled at Dani.

Danica smiled back, mouthing the words, "I know."

In a flash of golden light, they found themselves standing on the bridge of *The Shard*, minus Raphine, who stayed behind to oversee the palace and act as power of authority in Jegra's absence.

Once fully materialized, Jegra looked down and noticed her white dress had been replaced with traditional, form-fitted black leather armor with silver ornaments detailing the breastplate which, in turn, depicted the Imperial seal of Dagon Prime.

If Jegra wasn't mistaken, it was the armor of Dagon Prime's liberating emperor, Cirius Ra'hallek, only tailored to fit her full-bodied, undeniably feminine figure.

"Armor of the King of Kings," Danica said, looking Jegra up and down with admiration. "I must say, it looks rather impressive on you."

"Thanks, Dani. But, just a quick question. Why am I wearing the armor of the emperor?"

"Because our emperor," she said in a blasé tone, "went missing over a year ago."

"Again?" asked Jegra, her hands poised disapprovingly on her hips.

Of course, it wasn't like him to give up power or, for that matter, abandon his people during their time of need. If Dakroth was missing now, she thought, then something was terribly wrong.

Danica nodded gravely, signaling that, although she had no love for Dakroth, she, too, was bothered by his disappearance.

"Which means," Danica added as she reached out and ran her fingers along the edge of the armor next to Jegra's shoulder, her fingers brushing Jegra's flesh unintentionally, "in a time of war, you're the Dagon Empire's officially sanctioned ruler. The Empress Regnant."

Not only was the armor symbolic of Dagon Prime's first emperor, Cirius Ra'hallek, but it also now symbolized Jegra's rise to ascendancy as the first fully female supreme ruler of the empire.

It was a little overwhelming to think that she was the first female ruler in five thousand years of Dagon history. Before her just a string of ambitious, power hungry men, from Dakroth Rhadamanthus to his father before him, Loki'Alloran, Rhadamanthus the Second, to his father before him, Loki'Alloran the First, all the way back to Emperor Ra'hallek.

Now the name Empress Jegra Alakandra would join them in the annals of history as one of Dagon's great rulers. And she was nervous to her core with butterflies fluttering about inside her stomach.

"Imperatrix on the bridge," a voice announced.

It took everybody a few moments to realize it was her, then her presence on the bridge caused a flurry of chatter to break out.

Captain Blackstar rose from the command chair situated at the center-aft portion of the bridge and raised her fist. This gesture was met with an abrupt silence. When she opened a flat palm, everyone drew up and came to attention. The officers turned one by one to face their empress, and crossed their right fists over their hearts in the Dagon salute.

Jegra returned their salutes and, unexpectedly, the entire bridge crew erupted in a round of cheers and applause.

"All right, all right," Blackstar said, smiling. "You missed your empress. Noted. Now, get back to work."

The crew did as they were ordered. Some officers periodically looked over their shoulders a few times just to be sure they weren't imagining it. The empress really had returned to them.

When she turned back to Danica, the smile on her face quickly faded. Dani's eyes looked sad, and she was giving Jegra a look she knew all too well. "What it is?"

"I'm afraid I won't be going with you on this mission. There are things I have to do down on Thessalonica. And, besides, Raphine's training isn't complete. Someone has to watch out for her."

Jegra took Danica by her waist and drew her in. "Then, I'm glad it's you." They leaned into one another, kissed, and, unable to fully relinquish hold of the other, stared into each other's eyes for what seemed like an eternity.

Neither one wanted to say goodbye. After all, they'd only been united less than a few hours ago. So they held their embrace as long as they could.

"I'll miss you," Jegra said, offering Danica a smile.

At last, Danica slowly drew back, holding Jegra's gaze. She shook her bracelet once and brought up the holovid display. Typing in her teleportation codes, she looked up and smiled at her beloved.

As the shaft of light came to fetch her, she smiled, but didn't reply. Instead, she simply glowed in angelic fashion in the beaming light.

Jegra raised her hand, desperately wanting to touch Dani's face before she vanished, but she was too slow and, in a flash, Dani was gone.

A stillness replaced Danica's presence, and Jegra stood for a moment and took a deep breath. She didn't know why, but it always felt strange seeing a person vanish like that. One moment they're standing in front of you and the next they're just gone.

Captain Lianica Blackstar's eyes met hers and she rose up from her chair and gestured for Jegra to take a seat, offering the command chair to her.

"It's good to have you back, Your Majesty," Lianica said, greeting Jegra. She then stood back at attention so Jegra could assume command position. Jegra nodded and slowly sank down into the plush leather seat.

The leather straps of her skirt slid to the side as she lounged back in the chair and crossed her long, bronzed legs. A couple of the pteruges jutted out at an awkward angle and she brushed them down, tucking them in with the others, allowing the top of her thigh to be fully exposed.

Every single muscle sinew in the empress's body was tighter than the cables of a space elevator. As she bounced her calf up and down on her knee, every ripple and crease in her powerful yet luxuriant legs flexed and twitched with raw energy.

"Let's drop the cloak. I want to send a message to those destroyers out there that I'm back."

Lianica waved her hand, signaling for the tactical officer to do as the empress ordered. The ship hummed and the warbling sound of the energy cloak dropping echoed throughout the ship's corridors and bulkheads. As soon as the cloak had dropped, the *Shard's* lighting returned to full brightness.

"The destroyers are changing to an intercept course," said Brei'Alas. She turned and looked at Jegra anxiously, waiting for further orders.

"Match their speed and course. But maintain our trajectory. Let's remind these assholes who they're dealing with here."

"You heard her excellence. Prepare for ramming speed!"

"Yes, ma'am," Brei'Alas answered, swiveling in her chair and inputting the coordinates as ordered.

"All firepower to aft plasma cannons," Lianica added. Jegra shot the captain an inquisitive look. She looked back at the empress and smiled. "There have been a few improvements made since you've been gone."

"I can see that."

Brei'Alas looked up from her nav-station and looked at the viewscreen and the giant enemy battlecruisers drawing near. "The lead Nephilim ship is hailing us, Captain. Shall I respond?"

"Negative, Lieutenant. Stay the course."

"Staying the course," Brei'Alas replied, confirming her orders as a puckish grin formed on her pursed lips.

Everyone watched with bated breath as the enemy destroyer slowed to a stop, giving in to the game of chicken. But the *Shard* didn't slow. It just kept barreling towards its target.

At last, the long silver tip of the elongated ship pierced the mammoth destroyer's hull and explosions lit up all around the impact point as gas hull fragments ignited in a fiery blaze.

None of it, however, slowed down the *Shard,* which flew into the enemy vessel as smoothly as a hot knife cutting through butter. It was designed, after all, to slice through enemy vessels in this exact fashion.

"Full ahead," Lianica shouted above the din of the crash.

The *Shard's* aft thrusters flared bright blue and propelled the vessel through the enemy ship like a bullet. The Nephilim battleship ripped into two segments, both halves sparking and hissing as they jettisoned gas and incrementally drifted apart from one another.

"Open fire on those other two remaining ships," Lianica said. Jegra rose to her feet and sidled up next to the captain as they watched the viewscreen.

The aft disruptor cannons of the *Shard* began spitting hot bolts of plasma at the remaining Nephilim and Nyctan battle cruisers. The ships tried to return shots, but the debris of their own sister ship cut into their line of fire and absorbed most of their defensive volley.

The few disruptor charges that did manage to make it through the debris field merely deflected off the *Shard's* sleek, metallic hull and ricocheted off into space. Eventually the plasma would cool then evaporate into a gas which would just disappear into the cold of space.

Captain Lianica Blackstar folded her arms across her chest and cleared her throat. "Let's introduce them to the drones."

"Yes, ma'am," Brei'Alas chirped gleefully.

"Drones?" Jegra asked.

Lianica looked over at her and smiled then turned back toward the screen as if to say, *you'll see.*

Jegra's eyes followed her gaze and she saw two smaller ships, the size of shuttle craft but shaped exactly like the *Shard*, rise up out of the front bow as if the *Shard* herself was giving birth to twins.

Both smaller vessels engaged the enemy and opened fire, pelting the Nephilim ships with two added sources of disruptor fire equal to that of their mother ship.

The barrage striking from all sides of the sluggish destroyers did massive damage, and the second enemy ship went up in a series of explosions.

The crew erupted with cheers of victory as the third ship went up mere moments after its compatriot. But Jegra merely sat back down in her chair and crossed her legs again.

"Well done, ladies and gentlemen. But my planet was just wiped off the face of the galactic map by these assholes, so you'll forgive me if I reserve celebration for another time."

Lianica raised a hand and the crew simmered down. She turned to Jegra and awaited her orders.

"This is now a rescue mission. I'm issuing a level Black alert. All communication will be severed with all vessels, friendly or otherwise. We will fly cloaked. We will not respond to any other distress signals. Rescuing the Human race from extinction is now our topmost priority."

"If anyone has a problem with that..." she reached up and, gripping her right fist in her left hand, popped her knuckles threateningly, "keep it to yourself if you don't want to eat your own teeth."

Lianica scanned the amused faces of the bridge crew then scowled. "Must I repeat her majesty's orders? Get us to the Sol system. Maximum speed."

"Aye, aye," the crew shouted in unison.

The stars in front of the *Shard* slowly stretched into spaghetti thin strands and the ship launched itself into hyperspace like the crack of a whip.

As the starry expanse washed over the ship, Jegra shifted in her seat, uncrossed her legs, repositioned herself, and then recrossed them again.

She stared at the kaleidoscope of colors outside the window. *Faster,* she thought. *Faster.* Then, cutting into her train of thought, the ship's computer chimed and a soothing voice with a posh, almost transatlantic sounding accent said <<Slipstream drive coming online in thirty seconds. All crew, please prepare for time dilation.>>

As per usual, everyone in the room slowed to an incremental tic. Even Jegra's own heartbeat sounded like the slow-motion thump of a distant drum.

It reminded her of the noble Native American tribes of the Western frontier and how they played the drums of war in preparation for battle. Right now her own heartbeat was her drum of war and it sounded her coming—the coming of the Imperatrix of the Galaxy.

7

Glinting silver against the backdrop of a dusty red planet, the *Shard* settled into a geosynchronous orbit of Mars. The massive, thirty-deck battlecruiser came up alongside a long and slender Earth ship called *Ares III* and matched its orbit.

Side by side, the smaller vessel looked like a sleek, silver harpoon against the whale-sized hull of the empress's gleaming battle cruiser. And, although the alien vessel was an undeniably impressive ship, its streamlined design had a disarming quality that suggested it was a vehicle of peace, not one of military conquest.

"Open all frequencies," Jegra said, rising to her feet.

Once Brei'Alas gestured with a nod that she was live, Jegra cleared her throat and opened her mouth, but had no words. She took in a deep breath, doing her best to calm her nerves, and pushed down the butterflies fluttering about inside her stomach.

"This is Empress Jegra Alakandra of the Dagon Empire. We monitored the destruction of your planet and received your distress call. If we can be of assistance, please, let us know."

When there was no reply, Jegra scanned all the puzzled faces of her crew. She understood why they might be hesitant, given the fact that aliens from another world had just destroyed their planet.

At any rate, their skepticism of her peace offering was well deserved, and there was no easy way around that, so she did the only thing she could. She shrugged, and, clearing her throat, tried again.

"I repeat, we are here to lend aid and assistance. We come..." She hesitated then sighed. "*In peace.*" She almost choked on the words; on Earth the phrase was so cliché, made somehow even more so once she'd heard herself say it aloud. Even so, she realized that, all things considered, it still needed to be said.

A long wait for a response ensued and time seemed to crawl by at an incremental tic. Jegra, full of anxiety, paced the floor. Why was she so nervous? It wasn't like she had sworn off her own kind. One day, she knew she'd have to deal with humans again, and, whether she liked it or not, today was that day.

Still getting only radio silence, she debated if she should send another signal. Ultimately, she decided against it; she didn't want to come off as a too pushy. They could, after all, just be convening, trying to figure out their next step and the best way to respond to her messages. For all she knew their coms could be down.

She glanced back over her shoulder at Brei'Alas and was about to ask her to resend the communication, when, to her relief, an incoming message came through.

"I'm receiving video," Brei'Alas informed her.

She nodded. "Put it on the viewscreen."

The image of an Earth woman in her early forties appeared on the monitor. She looked weathered and frail, yet, for everything she'd been through, her eyes remained youthful.

"Our planet was destroyed nearly fifteen months ago. I'm afraid you have arrived too late." The woman's eyes widened when her gaze settled on Jegra. "Y-you're human," she gasped. Then, looking over at the blue, elf-like woman in a white uniform standing next to the Earth woman in battle armor, she added, "You're not…one of them."

"Yes, I'm human," Jegra said, smiling. "And I'm the leader of these people." She gestured to the crew of Dagons standing around her. They bowed their heads as one in acknowledgement that what Jegra said was true.

"How do I know this isn't some kind of trick?"

"Why would it be a trick?" Jegra asked. "The only planet of value in this system was Earth. Mars is just a dead hunk of rock; let's face it, it's not a sustainable world. Not without some major terraforming. But, if you're still not convinced, why don't you join me aboard my ship for dinner. Or, if you prefer, I can come down there and meet with you on your own turf. I leave the choice entirely up to you."

Lianica leaned close and whispered something into Jegra's ear which caused the empress to shake her head and, with a wave of her hand, she brushed the secretive comment aside.

"The good captain here," Jegra shared openly, "doesn't feel it's safe for me to go down alone. But since I have nothing to hide, it's entirely up to you, miss…?"

"The name is Captain Karina Nazimova, Chief Astronaut of the *Ares III* spacecraft and NASA pilot," she informed. "I am now interim president of the *Human Martian Alliance,* here on Mars."

"How many survivors?" asked Jegra, her voice soft and her gaze demure. She dreaded the answer because any news was guaranteed to be bad news.

Billions of people had screamed out in agony and their voices were abruptly silenced as the planet was annihilated. And for what? So the Gilded Master and his legions could consume its resources and add it to the occupation of the galaxy.

Jegra was really beginning to dislike this H'aaztre person. Thing. Alien…entity…whatever he was. Not only had he ripped her newborn from her arms and left her and Danica for dead, now he had destroyed her homeworld. But he'd made one critical error: he'd left her alive.

"Three hundred and seventy-two men, women, and a handful of children are all that's left of the Human race, I'm afraid."

"My god," Jegra gasped. "That's all?"

"Not entirely. I mean, we also managed to save some livestock, along with a few dozen domesticated animals. We secured the Svalbard Global seed vault before we left the planet, and we have collected all biopository samples from all the leading gene banks, including zoological and agricultural, that we could get our hands on in short notice. So, if anything, we have a large enough DNA sample pool of Earth's animal and plant life to repopulate another world, should we find one that shares Earth's unique…" her voice faded out as she fought the emotions which bubbled just under the surface, took a breath to compose herself, and continued, "…the point is, we saved enough of home to rebuild ourselves a new home. Someday."

After wiping a tear from her cheek with her thumb, Karina leaned back in her chair and looked off to the side at someone off camera. Low voices exchanged whispers and seemed to be deciding what to do now that help had arrived. Karina seemed to agree with what they were saying, as she kept nodding in the affirmative in response.

Leaning back into view, Karina informed the empress of their decision. "Jegra, Your Excellency, the truth is things aren't going as well as we had hoped down here. Due to the added number of survivors, our rations have depleted faster than we'd have liked, and we are already running low on food, oxygen, and other resources. Our Co2 scrubbers were never designed to filter out this load and are already failing. In effect, we're stretched as thin as we can get. Our best estimates suggest we've got another three or four months left at best. So, I'm going to accept your dinner invite on one condition. You bring everyone down here up to your ship. Then we decide where to go from here."

"It would be my great honor to bring you all aboard the *Shard*," Jegra said, giving Karina a slight nod. Karina returned the gesture and Jegra smiled warmly.

"How long do you need for your preparations?" asked Captain Blackstar, taking a step forward and turning her golden eyes toward the Earth woman.

Karina seemed notably startled by the fact that the blue-skinned alien spoke to her in perfectly fluent English, but she shook the astonishment from her mind and replied, "Only about three hours." She checked her wristwatch and then added, "Just in time for supper—Sol time."

"You have your three hours to make the necessary preparations. Then we shall beam you, your crew, and the rest of your cargo and supplies up to the ship. I'll have the main cargo hold turned into a stable for the livestock, and once you're aboard, we'll assign each of you your own personal quarters which will be yours for the duration of your stay," Lianica informed.

Karina raised an eyebrow. "Beam us up?" she asked in an incredulous tone. "You mean like on *Star Trek?*"

"Actually," Jegra chuckled. "Their teleportation technology is a little more advanced than what you may have seen on *Star Trek*. I can assure you, there's absolutely no need to worry. It's perfectly safe. That is to say, the annihilation theory is bogus; if that's what you're worried about. Your data isn't destroyed and you're the same you as when you first teleport. Your information merely gets transferred by exploiting quantum entanglement."

"Intriguing," Karina said, mulling over what Jegra had said. The best humans had achieved in the 21st century was the nuclear engine aboard the *Ares III*, the most advanced ship ever built. But even their best technology looked like child's play next to this alien tech.

Jegra, growing excited about getting the chance to talk with another person—another human person—couldn't hold back her giddiness and continued to discuss the finer points of Dagon teleportation technology with Karina, even though she'd never asked for it.

"It's like this. Your particles are entangled with other particles spread evenly throughout the entire universe and these particles, if triggered in just the right way, will fold out of existence—sort of like dominoes toppling over. Each domino is a potential 'you' that could exist, but you're only concerned with the last domino. That's the potential 'you' in a different location. However, due to the uncertainty principle regarding quantum entanglement, most particles can only manifest in one place at any given time. So, how do you get the dominos to topple in your favor? You have to exploit them by triggering a daisy chain of wave function collapses where the first domino sends its information across the assembly of near infinite dominos until you find the precise domino you want to pop into existence."

Karina nodded her head along with Jegra's explication. So far it made perfect sense. And she was surprised by the fact that a muscle-bound Amazonian woman had such a keen intellect. But, then again, she knew better than to judge a book by its cover. And she was certain that whatever made this Jegra-woman tick meant she was likely to be one fascinating read.

Still on the subject of teleportation, Jegra summed up the whole experience as best she could.

"In effect," Jegra relayed, "the energy beam destabilizes your particles—not destroys them, mind you. Once you're turned into information, the teleporter system sends the information across the sea of dominoes…all the potential versions of 'you' that could possibly exist in the universe…in the form of a laser beam and then exploits the information so that it can be directed to a singular point at a different, separate location of space-time. The energy beam, in turn, tells the entangled particles, or dominoes, where to snap back into reality by triggering the collapse of the wave function. Subsequently, this allows your entangled self to manifest at the precisely calculated designation. And you re-appear at the exact spot where the final domino topples." Seeing as how Karina's eyes had begun to glaze over, Jegra took a breath and with a nonchalant wave of her hand, brought her little science lesson to a close. "It's just that simple."

"It seems I'll need to brush up on my quantum mechanics," Karina said, a cordial smile forming on her lips.

"I mean, I'm no expert, either," Jegra assured her, trying not to sound conceited. "That's just the summation I was given. At the end of the day, though, I suppose it's true what they say."

Karina raised a curious eyebrow and waited for the empress to complete her thought.

"Since you are your entangled self and your entangled self is you, wherever you go, there you are." She chuckled at her own joke but then stopped herself when she realized Karina wasn't sharing her same level of amusement. "Never mind," Jegra said, brushing the topic aside for another time.

"Yes, it's all very fascinating. I'm sure our scientists will be quite keen on delving into all the new alien sciences we shall encounter. In the meantime, however, I really should be helping my people with the preparations. Thanks for your time, and I look forward to meeting you in person." With that, she leaned backed, squinted long and hard at Jegra one last time and then flicked off the feed.

Jegra looked over at Lianica. She placed both hands on her hips, arched her back and then let out a long sigh. "Well then. That went about as well as could be expected."

Lianica threw her hands on her hips and stared out of the viewscreen at the red planet rotating below. After several seconds of contemplative silence, she took a deep breath and exhaled. "I don't trust that woman. She's hiding something. I can feel it."

"Don't be so paranoid," Jegra said, trying her best not to sound overly stern.

"It's my job to be paranoid," Lianica replied, her tone and demeanor brusque and to the point. "But this…isn't paranoia. It's something else."

"How do you mean?"

"Did you notice how she was acting…I don't know…reticent? She didn't divulge any information that our scanners wouldn't have already detected. But how would she know precisely what to withhold or divulge, not knowing anything about our scanner?"

"What are you suggesting?" Jegra asked, raising a curious eyebrow. She was genuinely curious, because even though she dismissed the awkwardness of the conversation, due to her blathering, she also knew that Lianica's instincts were rarely wrong. In fact, Jegra had felt something was off too.

"She's asking us, in effect, to rescue her entire crew, yet she didn't seem grateful in the least. In fact, just the opposite. In all honesty, your majesty, her manner of speaking seemed scripted to me. Which would only make sense if she knew we were coming or…"

"Or what?" Jegra asked curtly.

"Or if she's been brainwashed."

"Brainwashed? By who? For what purpose?"

"That's the part I'm having trouble wrapping my head around. Maybe you're right and I'm just being paranoid. But I'd rather be paranoid and safe than trusting and dead."

"In that case, you'd better get to the bottom of it." Jegra winked at her with the cool signal of a superior giving orders to her subordinate without the need for unnecessary words and then spun on her heels and marched toward the exit.

Lianica had Jegra's full trust. She knew exactly what needed to be done, and if Jegra had needed to tell her what to do, then she wouldn't be the best woman suited for the job.

Fortunately, Lianica was the best officer Jegra had ever seen. Which is why she had handpicked her from a long list of candidates that desperately wanted the position of commanding the flagship of the empire.

"Let's get to work, people. We have guests coming for dinner and I want everyone on their best behavior."

When there was no response, Jegra paused in the entrance and turned around. She shot the entire bridge crew a hardened look and glowered at them as if to say, *didn't you hear me?*

"Yes, Your Grace," came a cascade of replies.

Jegra smiled and thought, *that's more like it.*

With that, she continued on her way, disappearing through the automated sliding doors which swooshed shut behind her.

8

The molten glow of the door cast a warm, pale orange light across Callestra's skin as it heated to its melting point. It was the same door she'd stumbled upon just a few months ago. The very door she'd neglected to tell Rhadamanthus about. *Just a little more,* she thought to herself, her pointer finger firing off a concentrated laser. And soon they'd be free of this place.

"I can't believe you didn't notice this door before," Dakroth said as he focused his finger blast to a fine point. The Dygra crystal in his chest glowed hot pink as he pushed his energy level to its upper limits.

"As I said," Callestra groaned, as she, too, focused all her strength and energy on creating an exacting laser beam that converged on the same spot and effectively doubled their power output.

When the crystal in her chest flared bright pink and then began pulsing softly, she stopped and placed both hands on her thighs, panting heavily as she paused to catch her breath before continuing.

"It was covered with those barbed vines. I missed it the first time around. Luckily, you agreed to get off your lazy ass and venture out of the arena one more time, otherwise we would never have found our way out of here."

"Yes, well, all that lounging about doing a whole lot of nothing was getting rather tiresome."

Callestra laughed. "And here I thought it was because you realized how much you loved me and would do anything for me." She straightened up and, one hand on her titled hips, her other arm falling gently behind the curvature of her hourglass form, she shot him a sultry look that demanded he agree.

He turned to her and smiled. "Never doubt it for an instance, my luv," he

61

said in his most assertive voice. "You are, without a doubt, the best thing that's ever happened to me. Beautiful beyond compare, loyal to a fault, and someone whom I know I can always put my faith in. Callestra, when it comes to the matters of my heart, you have nothing to fear. I will always hold you in the highest regard."

That's more like it, she thought. *A confession of his feelings…and it sounded sincere.* After all she'd done for him, she deserved at least that much.

She smiled at him once more and brushed the hair out of her eyes as she studied the lines in his face. At a hundred and thirty-two, he was getting on in age. But somehow every crease and wrinkle made him look all the more distinguished.

After their shared moment, they turned and ramped up their energy output.

The door heated up even hotter and their chests began to glow so brightly it seemed as though the crystals would burn through their flesh. But if they didn't keep up the output, they'd never get through this confounded korridium door.

Dakroth figured it had to be an extremely pure form of korridium, too, in order to withstand the intense laser heat better than any armor plating on any battle cruiser he'd ever seen.

Determined to get through it, however, he dropped to one knee and gripped his left wrist with his right hand to better steady his laser. Callestra remained standing. Their two beams converged at the same point.

"We're almost through!" she said. "Just a little bit further."

"You said that three hours ago," Dakroth said.

"This time I can feel it."

"I sure hope so, because I don't know how much longer I can keep this up without a recharge."

Another few seconds later and the korridium metal dripped to the floor, and a hole opened up. Seeing this, they both let out relieved gasps; they had finally breached the impossibly heat-resistant metal.

"We need to make sure the hole is big enough for us to squeeze through," Dakroth said, taking a step closer and really giving it his all. Beads of sweat rolled down his temple and cheek but he merely doubled down with determination and continued welding away at the door.

Callestra finally let up and placed her hands on her knees again and panted heavily. Her chest heaved with each deep breath and once she'd caught her breath she said, "I'm spent."

Dakroth ceased his laser beam and took in a deep breath of the cool air. *At least*, he thought to himself, *the air is one thing that wasn't lethal in this place.*

"That ought to do it," he said victoriously, brushing his hands together as if to dust himself off after a long day's work. "Now all we have to do is wait for it to cool."

"How long will that take?" Callestra asked.

"I don't know," Dakroth replied. "But I'm sure we can find something else to do to help bide the time." His red eyes settled onto her and he grinned.

She could already detect the subtle tone of prurience on his voice. "Oh, yeah?" Callestra asked, matching his grin with one of her own.

She was enthralled by the idea of making love in their current condition—hot, sweaty, and well-seasoned with ash from the burned-up detritus of the vines and the grime of the dust from the arena.

"What did you have in mind?"

Before she knew it, his arms where around her waist and she was pressed into the side of the archway. Dakroth hoisted her up and she wrapped her legs around his waist. Soon enough they were doing what came most naturally to the both of them. Fucking like a Torvian weasel in heat.

For whatever reason, though, this time seemed better than the last hundred times combined. She didn't know if it was the excitement of the immediate moment coupled with the anticipation of gaining their freedom, or if it was something else, but whatever it was, she enjoyed every rugged thrust of his hips and every probing penetration of his tongue.

She kissed him with a perfect blend of hot passion and wet sultriness and laughed with hot breath as he finished inside her. "Feel better?" she asked him, kissing his lips once again before he could answer.

"The best I've felt in ages," he replied. When he didn't immediately pull out of her, she moaned with delight and sank down onto him, plastering his lips with another round of kisses.

After their quick, yet satisfying, round of fornication, she slowly climbed off him and lowered her legs back to the ground. Untangling herself from his neck, she brushed down her deerskin loincloth and then looked over at the door to check on how well it was cooling.

Although the edges were now a soft orange, it was clearly still hot enough to catch a stick on fire, definitely hot enough to do some serious damage to one's skin.

Anxious to get out of this place, she tapped her foot impatiently and folded her arms under her chest. "Well, what do you think?"

"I think we've waited long enough. But, just to be safe, let's assume that once we step beyond this barrier, the whole resurrection cycle thing ends. I have a feeling that whatever is keeping us immortal ends here." He nodded at the door and she nodded in response, agreeing with his assessment.

Although neither of them could explain it, she knew that he was right. There was this unspoken feeling...a sensation that one felt that, like a clairvoyant having a full-blown premonition, you just knew it was the place itself that was all wrong.

And as much fun as all the dying and coming back to life business had been, she knew it was time to move to the next chapter of whatever this nightmare world had in store for them.

Callestra was the first to squeeze through the opening. Her bare shoulder accidentally brushed the edge of the metal door and she cried out in pain as it seared her skin.

"Be careful," she warned the emperor, glancing over her still sizzling shoulder at him as he followed her lead, "it's still hot."

Once they were both safely through, they stepped out the other side of the opening and into a spacious valley surrounded by mountains and lush green forest land mottled by glistening lakes that stretched into the distance of the ring world as far as the eye could see.

"What is this place?" Callestra asked aloud.

Dakroth turned a full 360-degree circle, scanning their surroundings. It appeared to be some kind of ring world, more massive than anything he'd ever seen constructed before.

Not even the Seyfferian ring habitat, known as *Prytaneous,* perhaps the greatest structure in the Commonwealth, could match the sheer marvel that he beheld with his own two eyes.

While *Prytaneous* was about three hundred times the surface area of Dagon Prime, and was wrapped around an entire moon which served to help anchor it, this one was, given his roughest estimate, nearly three hundred million times bigger. What's more, it seemed to have its own white dwarf star at the center of it.

"It must be H'aaztre's lost planet," he mused aloud to himself.

"You mean, Aldebaran?" Callestra took a cautious step forward and scanned their surroundings.

Surprisingly enough, none of the poisonous or lethal flora they'd been plagued by seemed to exist on this side of the door. A huge relief, to be sure. Yet, at the same time, it still had an eeriness about it. They could see no evidence of animals anywhere, and no insects either. Everything was strangely…silent. Deathly so.

"I don't see any other possibilities," answered Dakroth.

"But the engineering it would take to build such a structure…" she said, admiring the fact that they stood on the surface of a ring world virtually impossible to build, given current technology they were familiar with. Somehow, though, an ancient race had managed to construct it using methods that were only theoretical to her—speculative at best.

"My dear, you almost seem taken by this place. Don't forget, it's still our prison."

"No, my dear Dakroth," she said, turning to him, a calculating smile spreading across her lips. "It's a beautiful new world for the Great Lord Emperor to conquer."

He smiled in return. But as much as he'd like to steal H'aaztre's own ring world right out from under him, he had other plans. Merely snatching another's property from them and gloating didn't send a powerful enough message. And Dakroth wanted nothing more than to put the gilded imp in his place.

"I think you may be right, my dear Callestra. It's time I stopped resting on my laurels and showed this imposter who the real Lord of the Galaxy is."

Out of the blue, a sudden blast of wind crashed into them and they had to brace themselves.

"What in bloody Helios?!" Callestra shouted over the loud turbines, shielding her eyes as her hair whipped frantically about her. She clung to Dakroth's elbows, her fingers digging into his blue flesh so she wouldn't blow away.

Once she could crack her eyes open, she looked up to see an egg white-colored shuttle craft hovering over them. A moment later, the shuttle set down less than a dozen meters away from them and the angel-wing door swung open.

Dakroth and Callestra turned to see a hoary bearded satyr standing in the opening, grinning at them.

The old goat hopped out and skipped up to them and, upon recognizing them both, abruptly stopped in his tracks. After a moment's reflection, his baby blue eyes sparkled and he began to bellow with laughter.

"Rhadamanthus, my good chap. Is that really you?!"

"It is I, you old fiend," Dakroth answered in a jovial tone, a diplomatic smile spreading across his Prussian blue lips.

"You know this foul creature?" Callestra asked Dakroth, a hint of disgust on her voice. She wrinkled her nose in revulsion at the sworn enemy of her people.

"Why of course I do, my dear. Everyone knows the infamous Grendok of Galliforn."

"You're Grendok?" Callestra asked, taken aback by the unassuming visage of the legendary satyr. "The war criminal?"

"I know, I know..." Grendok said in an aristocratic manner, stroking his chin hairs as a roguish grin spread across his caprine lips, "I'm taller than you imagined."

The joke going over her head, Callestra shrugged. She really hadn't given much thought regarding the notorious criminal's appearance. All she knew was that he was the galaxy's most wanted fugitive and was more slippery to get your hands on than a Brillaxian eel—which explains why he'd never been caught.

"How did you find us?" Dakroth asked, assuming the satyr was heading up a rescue mission.

"I didn't find you, per se," Grendok answered. "I was merely returning to basecamp when your biosignatures spontaneously appeared on my scanners as if out of nowhere. Just to make sure my eyes weren't deceiving me, I swung back around to see who it was. Needless to say, I am more than a little shocked to find that it was you two."

"How long?" Dakroth asked in a grim voice. "How long has it been?"

The satyr stroked his chin reflectively for a moment and then answered the question. "It's been over a year since you both disappeared. Vanished into thin air, just like that. We all assumed you'd been taken captive, though plenty had all but given up hope that either of you were still alive."

"And yet, here we are," Dakroth said with a wide grin.

"And here you are," Grendok answered, throwing his arms onto his hips and letting forth another raucous laugh.

"I don't know about either of you," Callestra informed them, "but I'm ready to get off this nightmare world." She turned sharply upon her heel, tossing her hair, and without saying another word began making her way to the ship.

Dakroth turned back toward the satyr and they looked at each other with blank expressions. Slowly, they turned to watch Callestra sashay back toward the shuttle craft, her deerskin loincloth and halter top barely concealing her voluptuous form.

Grendok cleared his throat and then gestured for Dakroth to follow suit and board his shuttle. Dakroth nodded his head with gratitude and the two of them walked together back toward the shuttle craft.

"I'm sure you're both exhausted. Most probably on the malnourished side. I did three years in a Dagon labor camp after the campaigns, so I recognize the signs."

"Apologies, for any hardship my people may have caused you," Dakroth said.

Grendok knew he was merely being diplomatic and playing his cards close to his chest. Right now they were allies, not enemies, and there was no reason for bad blood between them. The past was in the past.

"Water under the bridge," Grendok assured the emperor. "For now, however, we'd best get you back to camp and have you fed and cleaned up. It looks like you've been roughing it for quite a while."

"Roughing it may be the understatement of the century," Dakroth said, following the satyr aboard the shuttle. "It's one thing to take a trek through the wilderness. But when the environment is designed to kill you at every turn, 'roughing it' doesn't quite seem to catch the full extent of how awfully dreadful it all was."

"Of that I have no doubt," Grendok answered.

Callestra stood by the open doors of the craft, waiting for them and nodded as the satyr strode passed her and climbed into his shuttle.

Dakroth paused by the two stairs that led up into the shuttle and placed his hand on Callestra's shoulder. She reached up and touched it. After a moment, he withdrew his hand and boarded the ship behind her.

Still feeling a bit skeptical, Callestra glanced back over her shoulder and looked back out at the strange door that stood in an open field and led into a multi-dimensional prison one last time just to be sure she wasn't just imagining things.

In the time they'd been prisoners, they'd each experienced their fair share of hallucinations. If it wasn't poisonous mushrooms they'd found, it was poisonous flowers. And, the truth was, she wanted to be sure they weren't still trapped in the jungle somewhere, imagining their freedom…only to wake back up in the nightmare.

All she knew was, if this was a dream, it was a good one; she was simply glad to be done with it. She turned back and climbed onboard the satyr's quaint little vessel. The clamshell doors clamped shut behind her and, with a roar of the plasma-coil turbines, the shuttle slowly rose up into the air.

Once the ship was in motion, Dakroth cleared his throat as though he had a question and then leaned forward to speak into the ear of the satyr. "I'm afraid I'm not exactly up to speed on current affairs. How goes the war effort?" he asked.

Grendok laughed out loud. "What effort? H'aaztre's forces have obliterated the Dagon fleet. They've laid siege to every system in the Commonwealth. They've rounded up all persons of interest for questioning and have managed to cripple all means of transit between the allied worlds."

"That grim, is it?" Dakroth interjected.

"I'm afraid it's much worse than that," Grendok answered. "Interplanetary communication is banned and all ships leaving or entering the system are boarded and searched. Non-compliance equals instant arrest and seizure of all your property. I'm afraid the galaxy has fallen upon desperate times, Lord Emperor. Most desperate times, indeed."

"In lieu of the emperor's absence, it's the duty of the empress to protect the empire," Callestra stated, reciting Dagon Imperial protocol to the satyr. Scowling at the satyr, she snidely asked, "Has she not upheld her responsibilities as sovereign ruler and designated protector?"

"I'm afraid that Jegra's confrontation with H'aaztre left her in pretty bad shape. Not for lack of trying, either, mind you. She managed to destroy a quarter of his fleet before things went south. But, alas, the empress barely made it out alive and has been in a coma ever since. Like I said, desperate times."

"It would seem so," Dakroth said contemplatively as he stroked his chin.

A scowl settled over his brow, darkening his eyes, and he leaned back and folded his arms across his chest in displeasure. This unfortunate news wasn't filling him with optimism, and he felt somewhat responsible for the current state of affairs. If only he had been there to aid Jegra in her fight against H'aaztre, then, maybe, things would be different.

But the truth was H'aaztre was a cunning statistician and knew exactly what pieces to knock off the chess board. Not only that, he seemed to predict every possible move anyone could make well in advance, which gave him a definite advantage.

"It's a pity everyone just rolled over," Callestra said in a melancholy voice, lamenting the anti-climactic way in which the entire galaxy had succumbed to H'aaztre's forces.

"It's the smallest of our worries, Vice Admiral Van Morgan, I can assure you," informed the satyr. "Reports have been coming in from all over the Alliance that inhabitable moons and worlds beyond the Outer Rim are being drained of their resources and destroyed."

"Outer Rim worlds? Why?"

"If I had to venture a guess, I'd say because—"

"—The enemy is creating choke points for us," Dakroth said. "In every war, in every occupation, the occupied know their home turf better than the invaders. They will use this to their advantage to throw off the shackles of tyranny. But if you have the power to physically change the terrain, well, then it's an entirely different game altogether."

"So, he's preventing any insurgency by literally wiping out all the places a rebellion could hide or convene and thereby tightening the invisible noose around all of our necks," Callestra mused aloud.

"I couldn't have put it better myself, Vice Admiral Van Morgan," the satyr said, nodding along with her summation of current events as he understood them.

"*And the tiger, with its terrible gleaming eyes, shredded all of our hope,*" Dakroth said in a quiet aside.

"I beg your pardon?" Callestra asked, tilting her head with a vague expression.

"Oh, it's nothing. It's merely something Jegra once said to me about the nature of terrible beasts that only care about power. She said you could see it in their eyes. I asked her what she saw in my eyes. She answered…something more."

A subtle smile spread across his lips as he reflected fondly on his past with Jegra and Callestra's jealously flared red-hot.

"How romantic," she mumbled to herself in a tone dripping of sarcasm. She flicked her hair angrily and then looked out the opposite window as she sulked quietly by herself.

Dakroth shelved the memory for another time and returned to the conversation at hand.

"Without a united front, it's only a matter of time before different agendas arise and in-fighting begins to fracture a unified resistance."

"That's how it always goes," Grendok said, nodding along with the wisdom of experience.

"Then the resistance cannibalizes itself from the inside out," Callestra interjected, finishing his train of thought for him. Dakroth nodded somberly.

"If you can get the Alliance worlds to crumble without ever having to lift a finger against them, then there's very little you need to do in the way of defeating those you wish to conquer. Once they turn inward on themselves, all H'aaztre needs to do is sit back and wait till the dust settles and then march in, plant his sigil, and lay claim to the broken worlds."

Callestra reached over and placed her hand on the emperor's forearm. "If this gilded prick thinks he can simply lay claim to your empire without so much as getting the fight of his life, then he has another think coming."

"Of that you can be sure, my luv." Dakroth reached over and placed his hand on her thigh and then turned his face away from her and peered out the shuttle's window. "And we shall take the fight to him. Of that I can promise you."

Grendok produced a yellow toothed grin as he listened to the emperor vow to fight the cancer poisoning their sector of the galaxy. If anyone had the strength and sheer willpower to mount a resistance and surgically remove this blight from all existence, it would be Emperor Dakroth.

9

It took Jegra nearly the full three hours of waiting for the Earth-Mars delegation to arrive for her to read through the backlog of reports on her holovid tablet, a translucent glass plate that could manifest high resolution images but also project holograms for holographic vid-conferencing.

The first step of reacclimating to life after being in a comma for a year was to get herself brought up to speed on everything that had transpired in the past year, and she read through all the log entries by Lianica, checked the status reports of the Imperial armada, and reviewed more than a dozen of the important news feeds for the past ten months. She even checked on the status of the gladiatorial games.

While reading through the information, she came across two encrypted files that caught her attention and used her Imperial Access Code to unlock them. She was pleased to discover that, contained in the classified documents, was the summary of Brei'Alas's training and the discoveries and theories behind her unique time manipulation abilities.

She was pleased to learn that Brei'Alas had been practicing honing her time warping skills and that, according to the file, they were triggered anytime she experienced hyper-arousal. As such, she'd been conditioning herself to anticipate high-stress events and also how to trigger them herself.

Jegra had been so engrossed in her reading that she hadn't even heard the first door chime. It was only on the second one that she'd looked up from the holovid pad and said, "Enter."

Brei'Alas stood in the empress's doorway, hemming and hawing and looking as nervous as ever. "I'm here to accompany you to the banquet hall, Your

Grace."

It was only fitting, Jegra thought, that Brei'Alas should be the one to come and fetch her when the time had finally come to meet their guests. "Well, don't just darken my doorway! Please come in," Jegra said in a casual fashion, her eyes settling back onto the glowing text of her holovid pad.

Brei'Alas timidly stepped into the empress's room and patiently waited, startling only slightly as the doors closed behind her.

After a few more moments, brief enough not to constitute any kind of inconvenience, Jegra finished her article and tossed the pad beside her on the sofa. She swung herself out of her roost and stood up.

As she sauntered from the sofa and cozy reading nook in the corner over to her king-sized bed at the head of the room, she nodded at the dress hanging on the rack nearby and said, "I have my dress picked out—over here. But seeing as it's custom tailored to fit my figure precisely, I'll need your help getting into it."

Brei'Alas gave an affirming nod as Jegra peeled off her clothes right in front of her as she arrived at the edge of the bed. Her discarded clothes piled up on the floor at her feet and she stepped out of them and fetched the dress from the rack.

Stripped bare, she slid one shapely leg into the dress followed by the other. With a wobble of her hips, she wiggled into it. She nodded at Brei who took the fabric in both hands and pulled it up like a tube top until it became taut. She then bent before the empress, grabbed the hemline and gave it a tug, pulling it back down to its appropriate length, slightly above the knees.

Jegra adjusted her ample breasts until they were lifted and the fabric stretched smoothly across them. With a sideways glance, she turned and cleared her throat for Brei'Alas to help her zip it up from behind.

By the deep purple and hot pink of Brei's cheeks, Jegra could see that she was flushing bright with embarrassment at having seen the empress's nakedness with her bare eyes. It was the third or fourth time she'd managed to glimpse the empress in a compromising and quite revealing manner of dress or, rather, lack thereof.

Even so, Brei was one of the few people that Jegra trusted enough to consider part of her inner circle. There was something about the girl's primness; it didn't fit with the Dagon mold of always puffing up one's chest and walking around with one's nose stuck up in the air all of the time. She seemed almost...well...human, in a manner of speaking. And Jegra found that comforting.

"Are you excited to see your own kind again?" Brei'Alas asked, filling the awkward moment with some general small talk. She began zipping up Jegra's dress only to pause half way when the empress looked over her shoulder and shot her what felt like an exacting look.

Brei'Alas tensed and, her hand pausing midway up Jegra's back, she began apologizing profusely for overstepping her bounds. "Sorry, Your Grace. It's not my place to stick my nose in your personal affairs. Please forgive the intrusion."

"It's quite alright, Lieutenant," Jegra reassured her, flashing her a lighthearted grin before turning away again to look at herself in the standing mirror by her bed. "I feel more nervous than anything. I guess, I just don't know how to be or act around them anymore. I mean, I'm the Imperatrix of the Galaxy, for crying out loud. They're refugees from a dead world. I don't know...it just feels..." she paused and took a breath. "It's all so surreal."

"But they're your people, the few that survived the destruction of your planet," she said exuberantly. She finished zipping up the back of Jegra's dress and then turned toward the mirror. She peered over the empress's shoulder; her eyes met Jegra's, which stared back at her from the reflection. "That has to be a good thing, right?"

Jegra smiled to herself but did not respond. She honestly hadn't given it much thought beyond the present moment. The truth was, she'd grown quite comfortable having become the token Human Being in the far end of the galaxy. Apart from the random stray, like Homer, whom she'd run into at the Cove, she really hadn't given the fate of her species much consideration.

After everything she'd been through, she didn't feel fully human anymore. She had mixed feelings as to what her existence even meant in the grander scheme of things. Considering the multitude of species she'd encountered, what part of the galactic neighborhood she happened to be from didn't seem to matter all that much.

On top of this, she couldn't imagine rejoining the petty, self-centered squabbles of her race. The meaningless wars, the endless greed, the disregard for nature and one another. Not to mention all the terrible memes and selfies that dominated the fleeting, yet reflexively vain, existence of so many of her people.

Sure, she understood not all humans were crap specimens. Some were compassionate, had a surplus of empathy, and genuinely cared about making the world a better place. But they were far and few between.

But considering how hard the Human race seemed to struggle against its own better interests, she was always discouraged by the reality of it. For every four strides humanity made toward progress…be it technological, intellectual, moral, or otherwise…they always took three steps backward again. It was disappointing, to say the least.

She didn't feel that she could relate to any of that any more. The Human Condition, so to speak, was no longer her concern. And it hadn't been for quite a while. Her mind had been opened to a whole hidden universe just beyond the veil of cosmic understanding, and she wouldn't trade that for all the Earths in the cosmos.

Yet, even with her own personal reservations, it was as Brei said. These were, for better or for worse, her people.

Fate had given her a second lease on life, but now it seemed it had dealt her another challenge as well—the challenge to safeguard the entire Human race.

It wasn't the job she wanted. Not right now, at any rate. Not with everything else that was going on. But it was a job she'd been handed. Besides, not acting would only make her implicitly guilty in the genocide of an entire species. *Her species.* And regardless of her feelings about any of it, she couldn't sit by and let the uncaring indifference of inaction be the final arbiter on whether or not the Human race thrived or, ultimately, met their ruin.

"The truth is, Brei," Jegra informed the young Dagon woman, using her nickname to let her know she was speaking personally to her, as a friend, "I've always felt like the odd duck out. Like, I just didn't quite belong. I guess I was just happy to distance myself from my people and forget all about them because, for me, they didn't represent how I felt inside, or who I truly was or, for that matter, who I wanted to become."

"But they're a part of you," Brei said, watching Jegra's reflection in the mirror, which gazed back at her holding her hand over her heart in a subconscious gesture of solidarity.

Jegra turned around somewhat abruptly and the girl drew back so she could meet Jegra's towering gaze.

"How do I look?" Jegra asked, changing the subject.

Brei looked the empress up and down, biting her lower lip in contemplative admiration. "Metallic burnt orange looks good on you. It's very sexy."

"You don't think it's too much?" Jegra nodded down at the open front which trailed all the way to her belly button. It was a miracle the dress could hold her girls in at all, and it was sure to make a lasting first impression. Not that she was trying to go out of her way to impress; she just wanted to look good for her guests.

"It suits you…and isn't that what matters?"

"I'm just worried about something slipping out," Jegra said half-jokingly.

"Well, that's never seemed to bother you before," Brei teased. "It's funny, I've probably seen you naked more times this week than I have my own boyfriend." Brei'Alas chortled lightly as she mused over the comical series happenstances between her and the empress.

When she turned to see Jegra's inquisitive stare, she gulped hard and couldn't help but feel as though she was about to have a major panic attack.

"Oh, s…sorry, Your Excellency…what I meant was…you're just so beautiful…and you have the admiration of the entire crew. So, naturally, there are those attracted to you."

"Are you trying to tell me that you're attracted to me, Brei'Alas?"

Brei blushed and looked away, as though she were casing the room and making a mental log of all the nearest exits. Her face glowing steely pink with embarrassment, she fidgeted nervously, not knowing how to respond.

"Attracted to you, Your Grace?" Brei'Alas gulped down the painful lump in her throat and laughed nervously. "Oh, no. I mean, I'm not, you know…" she stammered, catching herself mid-sentence realizing she was about to insult the empress to her face when she abruptly back-tracked. "What I mean to say is, it's not out of the realm of possibility that I've imagined having a threesome with you and Barrion on more than one occasion. And he certainly didn't balk at the notion. Which is to say, it's not out of the realm of possibility that I may be open to being intimate with you…I mean…if Your Excellency doesn't mind slumming it with a commoner such as myself."

Speechless, Jegra just mumbled an uncertain "*Umm…*" and thought about how best to respond to such an oversharing of so much information without hurting Brei's feelings. Luckily, she didn't have to, seeing as Brei'Alas wasn't entirely finished yet.

Brei curtseyed for no discernible reason, and still chattering fretfully, added, "Not that I would ever presume to make your decisions for you." She curtseyed again for good measure.

"Brei, it's quite alright, you don't need to explain yourself to me. We're friends," Jegra said with a warm smile, halting the girl's apprehensive ramblings.

Brei let out a huge sigh of relief and took in a deep breath. She had nearly talked to the point of passing out. Then it occurred to her that the empress had just called her a personal friend. Her eyes lit up and a curious smile formed on her otherwise timorous lips. She looked up at Jegra as if awestruck and asked, in all sincerity, "We are? Friends? I mean?"

"Of course, we are!" Jegra laughed, placing a reassuring hand on Brei's shoulder and giving her a gentle yet encouraging squeeze. "It's not just anyone I ask to come visit me in my personal chambers and then let rave on about her personal sex fantasies about me."

"Oh," Brei, said, feeling terribly self-conscious for having let such personal confidences slip from her lips so recklessly. She hadn't meant to offend. "I didn't mean to imply you were overly promiscuous or anything. Because you're just so…fucking hot. And I'm, well…as you can clearly see. Not."

"Lieutenant," Jegra interrupted, craning her neck and cocking her eyes at the girl, a puckish grin forming on her tightly pressed lips. "Please, for the love of all things good, just stop talking."

"Oh, I don't think I can," she confessed, her whole entire body vibrating with the tension of her building anxiety. Spontaneously, Jegra reeled her in and their lips crashed together.

Brei's eyes widened to the size of saucers as the impromptu kiss had caught her completely off-guard.

It took her a moment, but she finally melted into it and the wet pecks on the empress's cherry lips gradually became sultry and delicious exchanges of passionate breath and swirls of sensual tongue. In that moment, Brei found herself wishing it would never end.

Eventually, however, it did end, and Brei'Alas drew back and gulped nervously as she stared at Jegra with a stunned expression which permeated her entire being. "You kissed me," she said, stating the obvious.

"Only to silence your rambling mouth before you said something you might have regretted," Jegra informed her, offering the young woman a frolicsome smile.

Their eyes locked and, in the aftermath of a really amazing and sultry kiss, they stood staring at one another, sensing feelings beginning to stir where feelings hadn't been before.

And for the first time since Jegra had known her, she realized that Brei, for all her eccentricities, also happened to be a true, natural born beauty.

"And, to set the record straight, you're totally hot."

"I am?" Brei asked, still insecure about her own looks.

"Totally fucking hot," Jegra reassured her.

This left a smile on Brei's astonished face.

"So," Jegra said, clearing her throat and returning to the task at hand, "we should probably get going."

She brushed her chestnut colored hair over her shoulder, trying her best to play it cool, even though that kiss had nearly rendered her into a puddle too.

If it wasn't for more pressing matters, that kiss might have led to something more. But Jegra couldn't explore those feelings now. She shelved them to return to them another time.

"Yes, of course," Brei said in a distant sounding voice. She too was taken aback by the unexpectedness of the encounter and was still in a state of utter disbelief.

It had been, after all, a knee quivering kiss and she simply didn't know what to do with herself. She'd never imagined in a million years that the empress would show any kind of physical affection towards her and, besides, it had happened so suddenly that it almost felt as though it had all been a daydream.

A moment later Jegra found herself waiting at the entrance of her own chambers calling out Brei's name as the girl stood swaying on her feet in a trance-like, besotted stupor. When she didn't respond, she cleared her voice and called again, a little more loudly this time.

"Lieutenant, are you coming or not?"

"Oh, right. So sorry. I don't know where my head is at."

"Well, you'd better find it fast," Jegra insisted, as they stepped out into the corridor together. "Because I'm going to need you right here beside me the entire evening. Lianica wasn't wrong earlier. There is something off about all of this. I can't put my finger on it, but I'm certain that President Karina of the Human Martian Alliance is hiding something."

"Ah," Brei gasped. She glanced around, as if they were being eavesdropped on and, cupping her hand around the side of her mouth whispered to Jegra, "Do you think this all might be some kind of an elaborate trap set by the...*you know who*...to get to you?"

"I don't know," Jegra answered, pausing in the corridor. She turned to Brei'Alas for a moment, her eyes speaking to the shared apprehension they both felt, before continuing up the corridor. "Regardless, I'm not willing to risk taking any unnecessary chances. Not at a time like this. Too much is at stake for me to grow careless now."

Brei lingered behind for a moment and admired the fact that Jegra was truly a fascinating woman. She was the smartest non-Dagon woman that Brei had ever met and she could see why Dakroth, despite whatever unscrupulous machinations inspired his madness and passions, had decided to make her his empress and co-ruler of the Dagon Empire.

Regardless of what anyone else thought, Brei, for one, was proud to call Jegra her empress. She knew not all Dagons felt that way, but that the empress still held the majority popular vote of confidence. And on Dagon Prime, really, that's all that mattered.

As long as the people trusted you to do your job, you were sitting easy. But the moment you lost the people's confidence, you'd be ousted by the next hungry up-and-comer. That said, Jegra was something of a Jack-of-all-trades and had managed to exceed the people's expectations on more than one occasion. Whether it be fighting in the arena or leading the Imperial armada against enemy forces, she had always met every challenge head on and without fear. And this had certainly worked in her favor.

"Lieutenant!" Jegra called out to her in a near holler, the strained continence in her voice hinting at the fact that she was growing impatient with Brei's aloofness.

Brei snapped back to attention. "Right! Coming!"

10

Darting across a cerulean sky like a radiant firefly, the shuttle cut across the radius of the ring world from one arch to another.

Grendok fired the thrusters and the ship accelerated rapidly, shooting across the empty expanse. Re-entering the atmosphere above the opposite section of the ring, down below in the cradle, lights illuminated what appeared to be a small settlement that ran along a river basin.

The eggshell white craft descended from the canopy of fluffy white clouds and then circled wide before coming back around to land just outside of a large base camp. The camp consisted of about two hundred prefab units; some of them linked together in quad units and stacked on top of one another to make cube-like apartments.

Half a dozen larger warehouse-sized units sat in the distance and scatted about the lush valley were another three hundred hard-cover tents. At first glance, one could tell by the number of people living here and the well "lived-in" look of the camp itself that it must have been here for months, if not longer.

Looking out the window of the shuttle Emperor Dakroth could see Dagon archeologists working alongside Galliforn geologists, scientists and engineers, mechanics and medics, and laborers of all kinds carrying out their assigned duties.

Impossible though it seemed, he couldn't help but feel amused by the fact that, here, of all places, there were Dagon and satyr folk working together, side by side. It wasn't a sight he thought he'd ever have the pleasure of seeing during his lifetime. But here they all were.

War had a strange way of uniting people behind a common cause, making old enemies into new allies. It was, after all, like the old adage said: The enemy of my enemy is my friend.

With a hiss of air, the hydraulic landing skiffs settled into place on the wild grassland and the shuttle doors swung open. Grendok stepped out, followed by Callestra Van Morgan and finally, the Lord Emperor himself.

Everyone stopped what they were doing and looked up when they saw the emperor. Dagon faces didn't know how to react getting caught colluding with the enemy. But none of that mattered any more.

Right now what Dakroth needed was the Galliforn people's help. Not only did he require their technical expertise to rebuild his armada, but he would also need their allegiance when he finally did go up against the Gilded imp.

Besides, he knew that if they remained divided, they'd fall. But if they combined their ingenuity and skill, they'd grow strong.

"Carry on," he said, with a regal wave of the hand, accepting the new alliance for what it was: necessary. "Today we join forces with all those opposed to the tyranny oppressing the once great worlds of the Commonwealth Alliance. Today we join the Resistance!"

The impromptu yet rousing speech drew cheers from the onlookers and Dakroth shook hands as he slowly made his way through the crowd. Once he'd made it to the lodge at the other end of the gathering, Grendok gestured for him and Callestra to go inside. They ducked under the low doorway and found a spartan suite set up for them.

"Shut the door," Grendok ordered, waving at Callestra. She rolled her eyes, not wanting to be relegated to the servant girl, but begrudgingly complied, none-the-less. When she turned back around Grendok pulled a bowl of fruit out of the refrigerator that sat in the corner of the small apartment suite. "Wait, is that...?"

Both Dakroth and Callestra rushed over to the table and greedily began to devour the fruits without so much as peeling them first. Juice and pulp ran down their chins as they bit deep into the flesh of the fruits. Moans seeping out as they inhaled the food, they appeared like rabid animals gorging themselves on a carrion feast.

"I was in a Dagon labor camp for three years during the campaigns. I know what the wear and tear of malnutrition and being over-worked looks like. When you're finished," Grendok added, gesturing toward the other end of the suite, "there's a shower in the back and a fresh set of clothes. Please help yourselves to anything here. We'll convene at the refectorium at 18:00 hours and sit down for a meal together." He flipped his wrist over and the holovid bracelet gave the time. "That's in two hours."

"Much appreciated," Dakroth said, wiping the sweetness from his chin with the back of his blue hand.

When Callestra didn't say anything Dakroth shot her an exacting look and she quickly turned to the satyr and bowed her head reverently in a show of genuinely-felt gratitude.

"Until we meet again." The satyr grinned, shot them both a wink, and then ducked back out the entrance.

Dakroth leaned back on the counter and stared out at the other side of the room, his eyes not fixating on anything in particular as he lost himself to thought. Callestra, having had her fill of fruit, also leaned back on the opposite wall and folded her arms under her chest. She, too, fell into a daydream-like trance.

After a long silence, both of them staring off into the distance, Callestra was the first to break the quiet. She asked, "Fancy a bath?"

He smiled as she took his hands and led him into the back room. It would be their first real bath in over a year, not counting the time they had unwittingly waded into the acid waters of their morbid menagerie.

In retrospect, that might have been one of her worst memories. The acid had melted the flesh off their bodies and, scrambling out of the water in a panic, they managed to stagger halfway back to the arena like a couple of undead corpses before succumbing to shock and unbearable pain. Dying in the middle of a clearing, they were holding one another in each other's arms as the life drained from them.

"I can't wait to get out of these rags for good and slip into something a little more...practical."

"And I can't wait to watch you do it," Dakroth said with a suave grin and a twinkle in his eye.

Upon entering the shower, they stripped, and he pressed her up against the glass. His bare chest pressed down on her back and her breasts squashed up against the glass wall.

Dakroth's lips dabbled the back of her blue neck with kisses as she turned the water on. Its coldness shocked them at first, but they were accustomed to a year's worth of shocks and pains that it actually felt good. Refreshing even.

They both laughed and then he went back to kissing her neck and running his hands along the curvature of her waist and thighs.

No sooner had she gotten into it than he bit her. He'd bit her harder than he had initially intended and, in fact, drew blood. But the love bite was so tantalizing that instead of causing her to pull away in pain the opposite happened. She moaned with pleasure and shifted her hips back making sure her ass rubbed up against him—all of him.

"Harder," she moaned sensually, reaching up with her hands and squeezing her own two breasts.

"I haven't entered you yet," he said, slightly puzzled.

"That's not what I meant," she said. Tossing her hair, she exposed the bite mark on her neck and batted her dark blue eyelids at him.

She desired him to bite harder, and to her pleasant surprise, he did. He bit so hard he tore a piece of her flesh off in his teeth, but this only caused her to scream out in sensuous passion. Simultaneously, she orgasmed. Her body reacting to the pain as though it were pleasure. Apparently, a year's worth of conditioning had primed her body to react in such an unexpected fashion to the extremes of rough sex—the taboo of pushing the limits of where pleasure passes the threshold into the territory of pain and vice versa made for a more gratifying experience.

Callestra instantly spun around and, throwing her hands onto Dakroth's firm chest, she dug her nails into his blue flesh and clawed long lines down his torso. She then started kissing his sternum, moving incrementally down to his left breast. She, too, bit into him, tearing off a piece of his flesh just above his Prussian blue nipple.

Dakroth moaned out in pleasure. Surprised that the pain had induced such a thrill, he realized that their year of captivity in the arena had changed them more than either of them realized. *But to what extent?* he wondered.

"I never properly thanked you," Dakroth said, water cascading down them both as they panted heavily, pausing to catch their breath.

"Thank me for what?" she asked, looking up at him with her magenta eyes.

"For sticking by me this past year. For your loyalty, your support, and your devotion. I have not known a more loyal woman than you."

Callestra laughed. He cocked his head at her and gave her a curious look as though to ask what was so funny.

"That's overly-sentimental, even for you," she said, her smile lingering on her face a little while longer. "Be careful, you king of melodrama and pandering to the crowd, because if I didn't know any better, I'd think you were in love with me."

"Maybe I am," he offered, wrapping his hands around her waist and drawing her close. "Deeply, madly, passionately…" his voice trailed off and he simply held her gaze, the words "eternally," slipping passed his Prussian blue lips.

"In that case," she replied. Her sunken eyes settled on his dark blue lips for a moment and then she rested her head on his shoulder. The cool water of the shower drizzled down their hot bodies, washing away a year's worth of accumulated dirt, sweat, and blood. "Let me silence your romantic blathering with a kiss." She wrapped her arms around his neck and, rising to her tiptoes, kissed him long and hard. In that moment, she knew that she never wanted this to end. After the kiss, she rested her cheek on his firm chest and whispered, "Just…hold me." And he did as she asked.

Dinner was a communal experience, just as the satyr had said. When Callestra and the emperor walked into the canteen, they were ushered to the front of the line. As he moved past the line of stunned onlookers, he shook hands and greeted both Dagon and Galliforn people alike.

He smiled pleasantly and chatted with them, making sure to show a keen interest in them and always remembering their names. It took him back to his campaign fund raising days before he figured out how to use the popularity of the games to fund his military ambitions. Luckily, it was a skill he still had in his back pocket for when he needed it. Even so, all that seemed like a distant memory to him now.

Dakroth and Callestra took their trays and received the food from the cooks. Callestra formally said, "On behalf of the emperor, I'd like to thank you for all your service."

She sounded more like his publicist than anyone genuinely caring about their service, but the cooks and food servers didn't seem to mind; they simply gazed with bewilderment at the face of the Emperor of the Galaxy.

After receiving his allotted food, Dakroth looked down at the tray. It didn't look like much. Some hash, a side of roasted Angorian turkey with gravy, some greens, a carton of sweetened koimen milk, and a slice of pickle on the side. Not exactly a feast, but he was dying to dig in.

Callestra sidled up to him and then pointed over at the left corner of the dining hall. "Over there," she said. Dakroth followed the angle of her finger and saw Grendok waving them over to him, entreating they come join him at his table. They obliged.

No sooner had they arrived than Grendok stood and clapped his hands, drawing the crowd's attention. He addressed the dozen or so members of his table saying humbly, "Excuse me, ladies and gentlemen, I hate to interrupt your meal time, but the emperor and I have some official business we need to discuss. If you'd be so kind as to give us some privacy, I'll see to it each and every one of you gets an extra dessert tonight."

The promise of an additional dessert caused them all to scurry away excitedly like a group of pigeons that had just been tossed some breadcrumbs.

"There, see? Sometimes using the proverbial carrot works far more effectively than hollow threats and brute strength."

Dakroth grinned tersely realizing it was meant as a criticism of his past leadership techniques. "That young man you once knew was full of ambition and had very little experience with the ways of the galaxy," he said, still smiling. He sat across from the satyr and, setting his tray down, continued on. "Were his methods a bit brutal and antiquated? Sure. Was he headstrong and full of himself? Some say I still am."

This uncharacteristic bit of self-deprecation drew a chuckle from the satyr and he smiled at Dakroth with sagely eyes and wisdom that far outstripped the emperor's own.

"It seems you're not entirely incapable of learning from your mistakes. The sign of a true leader," Grendok said, making sure to pay the emperor a compliment.

"Men with great power don't always have the greatest scope," Dakroth stated. "I learned that from watching my father. I feel that somewhere along the way to becoming a great emperor, he became obsessed with the quest to gain ultimate power. Of course, he could never achieve it because, although he wouldn't understand it, ultimate power doesn't exist. There is an equilibrium, I've found. The Universe, it seems, has a way of balancing things out. And no matter how strong or powerful you become something will always arise to match you."

"Do you think this H'aaztre is some kind of universal balancing mechanism?"

Dakroth shook his head. "No, but I think Jegra might be."

Callestra leaned back obviously disturbed by the mention of her rival's name. She didn't hate Jegra, but she didn't like her either. All she wanted was for Dakroth to speak of her like he talked about Jegra, whom he obviously held in high esteem.

"Power has never been my obsession," Grendok stated, clasping his hands together and resting his chin upon them. "But wealth certainly has been a preoccupation of mine. But, like you," he said pointing his hoary chin at Dakroth, "I, too, realized that the endless chase for the pot of gold at the end of the rainbow was unrealistic."

Glad to make the conversation about anything but Jegra, Callestra looked at Grendok with inquisitive eyes and asked, "Why? Why is it unrealistic? You've amassed more money than anyone else in living memory. You own your own space armada. You colonized a ring world that had only been rumored to have existed. And you found a way to make yourself immortal. Yes, I too know all about the legendary Grendok of Galliforn. But if an ultimate trophy was ever been within reach, it was within your reach."

He shrugged, as if to say none of that mattered. "You see, my dear," he continued, "it wasn't ever about being rich. It was the *acquisition* of riches that I found rewarding. It was the pursuit that thrilled and delighted me. Once I held the prize in my own two hands though, then the novelty faded. It just became another thing to me." Grendok looked down at their untouched plates. "Apologies, I've kept you from your dinner for far too long. Please, dig in."

Both Dakroth and Callestra leaped at the chance to enjoy their first real meal in over a year. They scarfed down their food like wild boars gorging themselves on truffles. Seeing as how they weren't slowing down, Grendok raised two fingers into the air and gestured for the service staff to bring over two more meals for them. They devoured those, too.

Her mouth full of food, a single tear trickling down the left side cheek,

Callestra let out a deep moan and said, "It's so bloody good." Another bite later, she moaned again, this time more sensually. And then again.

Both men paused mid-bite and looked over at her with stunned looks. She stopped chewing, gulped down her mouthful, and said, "What?"

"Nothing my dear," Grendok answered, waving his hand about as if to clear the air. "Eat until your belly is full and your appetite satiated."

Callestra let out another scandalous moan and both men briefly glanced at her before falling back into their conversation.

"I presume the plan is to destroy this world," Dakroth said.

"And you'd be right," Grendok answered.

"May I inquire as to how you hope to achieve such a feat?"

Grendok smiled. "We're going to flood the atmosphere with equal parts hydrogen and oxygen. Then we're going to detonate fifty-seven strategically placed neutron bombs. The explosions will ignite the gas rich atmosphere causing a pressure wave that will travel to the neutron star at the center. The additional mass will condense on the star, make it collapse into a black hole, and the ring should break apart."

"Should?" Callestra asked skeptically.

"Well, we've double checked the math regarding our considerable understanding of physics. But the construction of Aldebaran eludes even our best scientific minds. Quite literally speaking, a place like this shouldn't even exist."

"And, yet, here we are," Dakroth said, gesturing with a swipe of the hand at the imagined landscape beyond the walls of the dining hall.

"It's a gamble I'm willing to take," Grendok replied, his slatted eyes shifting to Callestra's face.

"If it can withstand fifty-seven neutron bombs and defy the very laws of physics, then maybe it's not meant to be destroyed," Callestra said, chewing her food softly as she talked.

"Perhaps," Grendok said nonchalantly. "But part of the fun is the challenge itself." He winked at her and she paused momentarily and then looked over at Dakroth, who was mainly focused on cleaning his plate.

"Why not just keep the planet?" Callestra asked. She turned to Grendok. "Your people lost their world because of H'aaztre. Why not keep his world as your own? It would only be fair."

"It's a nice thought," Grendok said, stroking his chin hairs. "But it wouldn't be satisfying. Right now, my people are hurting. They've suffered a great loss, and it seems the only way to ease their suffering is to pay back in kind what H'aaztre has taken from us. Besides, there are other worlds."

Callestra scoffed. "So, it's about revenge?"

"Don't underestimate the value of revenge, my dear," Dakroth said, raising a finger. "It can be a great motivating factor when going up against a seemingly undefeatable enemy."

"I'm sorry if I have given offense," Callestra said, bowing her head apologetically. "I only meant to suggest there may be better uses for this place than simply blowing it up to send a message."

"That may be true," Grendok replied, "but sometimes the message needs to be boldly written in the only thing that the enemy will understand. Violence."

"It sounds awfully close to terrorism, if you ask me," Callestra said. She put her silverware down on the table as she'd grown too upset to keep a healthy appetite.

"Oh, to be sure, my dear," the satyr responded with a wry grin and a gruff voice, "it is virtually indistinguishable. The only difference is, at the end of the day, it won't be the innocent who are unduly terrorized. It will be the villains."

Dakroth reached out and took his glass and then stood up. The entire canteen died down to a simmer of whispers as all eyes settled on the emperor. With his glass raised high, he shouted, "Long live the Empire!"

It wasn't the Dagon Empire or the Galliforn Empire. It was simply *The Empire.* Their empire. And one they were determined to take back at any cost.

A brief silence followed his toast, but then something amazing happened. Satyr and Dagon all stood up, unified by their oppression and their desire to end the reign of terror that had seized them. Together, they raised their glasses and roared, *"Long live The Empire!"*

KRA-THOOM!

"What in the bleeding Helios was that?" Callestra asked, startling at the deafening noise that clapped like thunder overhead.

Almost as soon as she had asked the question the scramble alarm came onto the speaker system.

The fighter pilots were the first to leap out of their seats and rush from the canteen. Grendok, Dakroth, and Callestra shared a quick three-way look and then leapt up and raced outside. They all filed out into the open field in front of the building and looked up at the sky. Hanging above them was the most massive Nephilim battle cruiser any of them had ever seen.

"It's him," Callestra said, her voice wavering with fear.

"We don't know that for sure," Grendok said.

"Unfortunately, my esteemed friend," Dakroth said, turning to Grendok, "*we* do."

Dakroth raised his forearm and pulled up his sleeve. The hairs on his arm stood straight up, as if static electricity were holding them erect. But it wasn't the static causing his goosebumps, it was the cold, unrelenting fear coursing through his veins.

Callestra raised her arm, holding it next to his, and showed that the same thing was happening to her.

Something about that prison they'd been held captive in changed them. Because, in this moment, they could both feel a terrible, dark presence. It almost felt like standing on the cusp of an event horizon, peering down into ultimate oblivion—only a million times more awful.

It was a fear Dakroth hadn't experienced since he was a small boy and had fallen into a viper pit; bitten repeatedly and left for dead—hundreds of poisonous snakes slithering over his small, frail body.

If his father's hunting hound hadn't sniffed him out, he would most assuredly have perished in that hideous dark nightmare. The sensation he felt now was just like that: pure, unabating dread.

There was another long silence between them and, then, they turned their gazes back up toward the ship.

"*Odengrat,*" Grendok grumbled under his breath. This was really going to put a kink in his plans.

11

A blonde woman, along with thirty delegates representing the Human Martian Alliance, sat at several large dining tables in the banquet hall. Although they looked rather haggard and were little more than skin and bone, they were cleanshaven and wore their formal dress uniforms for tonight's special occasion.

After a bit of waiting, the empress, Jegra Alakandra, along with her entourage of officers, imperial bodyguards, and servants entered the banquet hall. The bubbly and ever cheerful Lieutenant Brei'Alas stood to Jegra's right and Captain Lianica Blackstar to her left, while four Imperial guardsmen, two on either side, flanked them and provided protection.

Everyone in the room stood when they entered, yet it did not escape Jegra's attention that the slender blonde at the center of the table was the last to stand.

Naturally, the tall blonde woman was none other than President Karina Nazimova of the Human Martian Alliance, and one of the last remaining humans in the entire galaxy. When she made eye contact with the empress, Jegra smiled at her. Karina did her best to smile back, but she was still uncertain about this woman. More importantly, she was trying to figure out how an Earth woman became an intergalactic empress in the first place.

Jegra gave Karina a subtle nod of recognition to let her know she remembered her from the video chat they'd shared earlier. She answered Jegra's nod with one of her own in a show of affinity but did not smile.

Jegra couldn't blame her though, for being less than enthusiastic. She, along with her people, had just lost their entire planet. They were all probably still in shock—stuck in survival mode. Jegra doubted any of them had even had time to let the devastating loss sink in—she sure as hell hadn't.

Karina was taller than she'd appeared on the video, and rather slender, too. Jegra couldn't help but admire her piercing blue eyes and thought to herself that, out of the entire group of survivors, she seemed the most capable.

Lieutenant Commander Barrion stepped forward, raised a digital whistle to his Prussian blue lips, and gave the bosun's call. All crew came to attention and turned toward the entrance.

"Introducing her majesty, the esteemed gladiatrix turned empress, Jegra Alakandra, Imperatrix of the Dagon Empire, Jewel of the Commonwealth, and Mother to all of Dagon."

When the empress's entourage had passed by Barrion's position, giving a slight sideways glance, Jegra couldn't help but glean the fact that Brei'Alas did her best to avoid making eye contact with him. It was clear that Brei divulging her sexual fantasies about having a threesome with her had made her uneasy around him, given her present company.

Given Brei'Alas's propensity to be perpetually on edge, along with her penchant for blurting out whatever thought sprang to mind, however, Jegra felt it was probably for the best that she didn't start up a conversation with Barrion during tonight's proceedings.

Karina and Jegra met face to face behind the main dining table and greeted one another.

"It's nice to finally meet you in person, President Nazimova," Jegra said, extending her hand.

Karina Nazimova didn't smile. She seemed to have nerves of her own but, realizing her rudeness, quickly blurted out, "I'm sorry."

The apology seemed authentic enough, but something wasn't quite right with Karina's tone. Instead of sounding embarrassed she sounded frightened somehow.

Jegra raised an eyebrow when Karina drew out a korridium alloy blade from the back of her waist and, lunging forward, thrust it into the empress's gut.

Everyone in attendance gasped out in horrific shock at the sudden and unexpected attempt on the empress's life. Captain Blackstar was the first to step into the fray. She clasped onto the scrawny human's arms and, locking her arm behind her back, held her at bay.

Karina's eyes welled up with tears and, again, she apologized. "I'm so, so sorry."

"Silence, Terran," Lianica growled, her eyes flaring pink with energy from the Dygra crystal pulsing hot in her chest. "You will bite your tongue or I shall have it removed for you."

"It's alright, Lianica," Jegra said at last. Lianica and Karina turned toward the empress and watched as Jegra looked down at the blade lodged in her abdomen.

"Please. You have to believe me. I didn't want to do this. But *she* told me to do it. So, I had to…you understand, right?"

Jegra looked up at Karina and smiled casually, which caused Karina some confusion, as that wasn't the response she was expecting. With a grunt, Jegra ripped the dagger out of her stomach and tossed it onto the table along with a smattering of her blood. It rattled to a stop and she took a deep breath, doing her best to ignore the lacerating pain. Dismissing the transgression, she gently held her hand over the wound and then gestured for everyone in attendance to be seated.

"Everyone, please excuse the misunderstanding. Everything is fine now. I am fine now." To console any doubt about it, Jegra removed her hand from the gash in her dress to reveal her wound had completely sealed up on its own.

"But I don't…I don't understand," Karina said, stumbling over her words.

At first, she had been afraid that the empress would retaliate or that her security detail would pile onto her and drag her to the brig, but now she didn't know what to think.

Instead of arresting her, to her utter surprise, Jegra barely flinched and seemed to be rather calm about the whole ordeal.

"Don't you need to see a doctor or something?"

"I'll be fine," answered Jegra, rubbing her fingers along the slash in her dress and spreading it open for Karina to see that, indeed, her flesh wound was virtually gone.

What appeared to be white traces of scar tissue slowly dissolved into the coppery undertones of Jegra's sunbaked skin. A few moments later, her taught abs rippled with raw power beneath the tattered fabric; not a single trace of the knife wound left on her.

Astounded by Jegra's healing ability, which she knew to be more than human, Karina's mouth hung open in astonishment.

"But how…I mean…why would they have me to do such a thing knowing it would barely leave a scratch on you?"

"Like meeting an unfamiliar combatant in the gladiatorial arena…they're testing you. Looking for your weaknesses. At the same time, challenging your willpower and your resolve. They want to see if they can exploit those weaknesses and use them against you."

"For what end?" Karina asked.

"To see if they can make you and your people into subservient slaves, or, in your case, assassins. Either that, or whether they need to eradicate what remains of humanity because you show a resilience that threatens their rise to power."

"And I failed," Karina said aloud, looking down at her feet in shame. Not only was she ashamed for being weak to resist the influence of this alien force, but ashamed by the fact that, as the representative of her people, she was supposed to be the one who stayed strong. Who didn't cave in and who never gave up.

But here she was; her willpower truly tested for the first time and, contrary to what she thought she knew about her strength of will, she'd crumpled as easily as tinfoil.

A gentle finger brought her chin up and Karina raised her blue eyes and locked onto Jegra's gaze.

"Who said you needed to be strong?" Jegra asked, smiling at her with a puckish grin. "Leave that up to me. After all, I don't know if you've heard, but I am the Empress of the Galaxy." She winked at Karina and then gestured for her to be seated.

Lianica looked over at Jegra, who shot her a stern glance which told her to back off, and she bowed her head and stepped back, giving Karina room to breathe.

Although she didn't like it, since she couldn't be certain there weren't more sleeper agents hidden somewhere in the banquet hall, she reluctantly took her seat. Leaning over, she whispered orders into Lieutenant Brei'Alas's ear.

After a moment, when Karina was certain nothing ill-fated was going to happen to her, she let out a deep sigh. Finally, she looked over at the empress and said, "You're not what I expected."

"And what were you expecting?"

"I don't know. Less bodybuilder and more blue-collar American farm girl, perhaps?"

Jegra laughed. "I've never been to the gym in my adult life. Back on Earth, I was a librarian in Omaha, Nebraska. But, as you can clearly see," she said, fanning her hand across her hefty chest and drawing attention to her improved physique, "after my abduction my entire body was enhanced from head to foot and everything in between."

"Oh…" Karina said, taking it all in as her gaze settled firmly onto Jegra's cleavage and lingered there for a moment, "I see."

"Korridium blades are one of the few things that can cut through my enhanced flesh…proving I'm not invincible…just extremely…how shall I put it…resilient."

"I suppose you'd have to be in order to be able to adapt to another civilization's culture, let alone ascend to be its ruler."

She smiled at the compliment and then leaned back in her chair as a team of waiters brought the first entrée over to the table and, in a simultaneous motion, served the entire main table all at the same time.

As empress, Jegra liked the idea of a leader being served at the same time as her people. There was no reason a king should eat first when there are people starving throughout the kingdom. Such a king was either incompetent or cruel, if not both. As such, she always liked to be served along with her people, and feast together in a show of solidarity. It spoke to her sense of justice and equality.

She gestured for Karina to take a bite of what appeared to be a slice of pineapple atop a red sea bream, her favorite kind of fish. Although, noting it had six eyes, she knew it was some kind of off world alien variety.

Karina picked up her knife and fork and cutting into the fish took a large bite and began chewing her food with an almost euphoric delight. In fact, she'd gone for so long without a real, home-cooked meal that her eyes began tearing up from the sudden overwhelming joy of it. Still chewing a mouthful of fish, she wiped away a stray tear with the back of her hand.

Pleased that her guest was enjoying her meal, Jegra smiled and then, raising her cloth napkin to her mouth, she dabbed away any morsels of food and lightly cleared her throat.

"You're a scientist," Jegra asked, keeping her gaze fixed on Karina.

"Yes," answered Karina, her mouth full of food. "I have degrees in Engineering and Astrobiology."

"So, you of all people ought to know that we must evolve and adapt or risk extinction." Karina merely nodded along as Jegra talked. "That's my advice to you now, Madam President. You must evolve—not only as a species, but you must also evolve your way of thinking. You must adapt—not only to survive but also to persevere."

At this juncture, Karina put down her knife and fork to give Jegra her full attention. After all, here was a woman who had succeeded in surviving against all odds. Needless to say, it wasn't advice you simply brushed aside. It was advice you took to heart.

"Much of what I have experienced since my abduction has been about adapting to survive. Once you can will yourself to change, then a whole new world will be opened up to you. It's not easy. Not everyone can do it. But if you want the Human race to endure—you're going to have to become fluid. Be like water, Karina. Be malleable. Form yourself to the environment. But never lose sight of who or what you are—because like water—someday you will learn to move mountains."

When the Arkadian king prawn arrived, it sat on the central platter and was the size of a grown person's forearm. It came with a salad slathered in a savory vinaigrette wine dressing. Once everyone had been served, Jegra beckoned the delegation to dig in with a simple wave of the hand.

Some of the visitors moaned quietly as the savory juices of melted butter and sweet tasting prawn flooded into their mouths. Others, feeling overwhelmed by their first real meal in fifteen months, let tears of joy stream from their eyes. Jegra smiled warmly when Karina let a small moan of culinary satisfaction slip out of her own lips and then quickly covered them up with her napkin and blushed as though she'd been caught skinny dipping after stepping out of the local pond.

"That good, huh?"

Even Karina couldn't deny the humor of it and let out a small chortle, giving the empress a sideways glance as her cheeks flushed with further embarrassment. "Sorry," she apologized.

Jegra shook her head. "No need to apologize."

"My compliments to the chef," Karina said. "I haven't felt this good in…well, you get the picture." She paused and looked over at Jegra, studying the empress's face. To the contrary of what Karina had expected to find, Jegra was just as laid back as any girl from Nebraska could possibly be. There wasn't the slightest trace of arrogance or superiority about her, and she confirmed as much when she let out a loud belch.

Surprised, Karina's eyes widened and found Jegra's. When their wide-eyed gazes locked, both women burst out laughing.

A few moments later, as things settled down, Jegra stood up and clapped twice so loudly that the force behind it rattled the dishware and shook the lighting panels on the walls.

Naturally, this caught everyone's attention and as they looked up from their meals, harpsichord music began to play. Entering the dining hall from a side entrance, two Bre'lal women glided into the room wearing emerald green ballerina pointe shoes and see-through gowns that were part of the traditional Arkadian ceremonial culture.

Raised up onto their delicate toes, the green-skinned beauties leapt and twirled, their gossamer clothing showing off tantalizing glimpses of flesh as they performed a rather sensual dance as a type of greeting.

As Jegra settled back into her seat to admire the performance, she even caught a hint of some traditional Nyctan courtship movements thrown into the traditional Bre'lal dance. It was a fusion, representing the synthesis of cultures, peoples, and ways of thinking. The dance itself was a kind of language that reflected everything from the struggle for peace and harmony to the deep loss of violent wars.

As the last strings were plucked, the two bonnie dancers finished with the sensual embrace of lovers.

Once the performance came to an end, the attendees gave a standing ovation. The Bre'lal women, holding hands, turned to the crowd and curtseyed. Afterwards, they twirled and pranced away, exiting the same way they had come in.

"That was lovely," Karina said, slowly sinking back into her chair as dessert was brought out. The evening's dessert appeared to be a kind of gelato with a garnish of fresh berries and a warm sauce laced with edible glitter.

Anxiously awaiting the mouth-watering delights, Karina turned to her host and asked another question. She had so many that she was just dying to ask, but she didn't want to seem too fervid in her inquisitiveness. "How many species are there?"

Lieutenant Brei'Alas, who was situated on the other side of Karina, answered on the empress's behalf faster than she could so much as offer a reply.

"Oh, that's a great question. There are currently one hundred and fifty-seven cognitively advanced species listed in the official census of the Commonwealth systems. That's what we call the alliance of peaceful worlds and independent empires that have joined in commercial trade and have signed treaties declaring a truce of the thirty-year trade war between the Nyctans and Dagons. But all that, I'm afraid, has come to an end with these new invaders who have lain siege to our sector of the galaxy and destabilized the entire cosmic alliance."

"Yes, lieutenant, that's…highly informative, thank you," Jegra said, stopping the girl before she droned on at length about the peace accords and boring politics of it all.

It was no secret that Brei was a nervous talker, yet if you managed to get a glass of wine into her, and she'd had three already, she became even more of a chatter box. Often jumping from one topic to another at a brisk pace, with no rhyme or reason to her method of selecting said topics, but always finding connections among the most unfamiliar things.

She was a fascinating woman, to say the least.

Brei smiled and gulped down a hiccup. She picked up her glass of *pinot gris* and gulped it down hastily. Once she'd finished it off, she promptly extended the glass for the passing waiter to refill.

As fresh wine poured into her cup, a maudlin grin came over the girl's face as she watched the white liquid fill to the brim. The waiter continued on to replenish other glasses and Brei, sipped from the lip of the glass so as not to let a single drop spill over and go to waste.

"My people's world was destroyed too, I'm afraid," a gruff sounding voice informed their guest. Karina leaned over the table slightly and turned to see who had spoken when she noticed that sitting on the other side of the empress was a talking satyr. Her mouth fell open again as she beheld the mythical creature sitting so near her.

"Y-you're a…"

"Yes, my dear. A very dashing young-man of one hundred and eighty-seven of your Earth years old. But more to the point, I'm a noble satyr of Galliforn. Sadly enough, it would seem that both our peoples are in the same boat, so to speak, as the crazed entity calling itself H'aaztre also destroyed *my* homeworld."

"I'm sorry for your loss," Karina replied.

"As I am yours," the satyr responded with a solemn, yet somehow consoling nod. He raised his glass to her and then turned his attention back to his dessert, which sat in front of him, tempting him to put down his drink and partake of its luscious sweetness instead.

The evening wore on, and soon everyone had full stomachs and was pleasantly sozzled. Deciding it was as good a time as any to give a closing address and maybe let people retire for the evening, Jegra stood up and clinked her fork on her wine glass. This caused the delegation of dinner guests to stop whatever conversation they had drifted into in the amicable spirit of celebration and turn their attention to her.

"Ladies and gentlemen from all the esteemed worlds of the Commonwealth and beyond..."

After getting their attention, she brushed her dress down, feeling a little bit fidgety. Public speaking wasn't exactly her forte, even though she seemed to be doing an awful lot of it lately. She cleared her throat and continued on with her speech.

"I know we are facing trying times. But as long as we face these challenges together, there is no obstacle we cannot overcome. In the meantime, you are all free to stay as long as you desire, leave when you are content. My servants shall see you safely back to your personal quarters whenever you are ready to call it a night. Feel free to get to know one another. Mingle. Make new friends. And we'll convene sometime tomorrow...after all our hangovers have worn off."

There was a round of laughter and Jegra paused long enough for it to die down so she could finish her speech.

"Now, if you'll excuse me, I'm afraid I've had too much wine and must, humbly, retire for the evening."

Another round of applause accompanied her as she turned to leave. Only Brei'Alas and her Imperial bodyguards followed after her, while Lianica and the admiral remained behind as they continued getting to know their new guests.

Before Jegra could leave the dining hall, however, the entire congregation of Martian Alliance Earth delegates stood at attention and saluted as the empress strode by.

When she reached the door, she turned and gave the Dagon salute. Her crew and guests all returned the salute, even President Karina Nazimova paid her respects to the empress.

Overwhelmed by their gesture of gratitude, Jegra smiled one last time and then spun around and stepped forward, the sliding doors of the dining hall parting for her to leave.

Barrion stood in the entrance, blocking her exit. Nearly colliding with him, Jegra reflexively drew back. That's when she noticed that he was completely strapped with explosives in what seemed to be a fully activated suicide vest.

"Oh, my Goddess," Brei'Alas gasped.

"I'm sorry," Barrion whispered, tears streaming down his cheeks. "She told me to…"

The Imperial guards bull rushed him, but even so, they were too late. Barrion's thumb came down on the detonator.

The guards who'd rushed forward were picked up by the explosion and thrown back. In that split-second window, Jegra moved swiftly and shoved Brei'Alas behind her. "Watch out!"

Jegra threw up her hands as the fireball that had swallowed up her guards plumed toward her. But when it didn't vaporize her, she peered up over her extended hand to find the bubbling wall of fire frozen mere inches in front of her fingertips.

The look of stunned astonishment plastered on her face said it all.

"Hang on," a voice rang out.

The empress turned to find Brei's hand on her shoulder. Sweat trickled down her forehead and her nose bled. At the same time, her eyes seemed to be lacquered with the color of midnight. The trail of blood from her left nostril dripped from her nose down to her lip and then dribbled down her chin, and her eyes slowly filled with the swirling, star dappled, vista of a cosmic expanse.

Brei began to shake and the room began to wobble and distort. Everything blurred out of focus and reality began to fold in on itself.

"When we reset," she managed to say with some effort under the strain of her powers, "I'll be the only one who remembers what happened."

"Do your best to warn me, Lieutenant. That's an order."

Brei nodded and the room blinked out of existence.

12

Sticky, crimson blood dripped off of Danica's metallic fist like some repulsive mucus as she stood over a battered body tied to a chair, panting heavily as the dark shadows of the dimly lit room blotted out her eyes.

She'd worked up a sweat beating Gerard Van Zallek to a bloody, puss-faced, pulp. He slouched forward in the chair, his arms bound by rope, and spit a blood infused glob of saliva at her feet.

"Go ahead, you bitch," he mumbled through his swollen mouth. "Have your fun. But when I get out of here, I'm going to fucking kill y—"

Thwak!

Before he could finish his sentence, his head flew back with a *crack* as she struck him one more time for good measure. This time she had hit him hard enough to dislodge a tooth and he spat it up.

"If you have the energy to talk, then we're not even close to being finished here."

"Fuck you," he growled, his disdain for her clinging to every syllable.

This time his blood-laced saliva landed on her pants leg and she looked down at the disagreeable stain. When she looked up again, he was running his tongue along his swollen gums, doing a mental tally of how many teeth he had left.

"I can do this all day. So, do you want to move on to round two or do you want to tell me how Nividium 3 is finding itself traded off world during a siege? Who's helping you?"

"Helping me?" he scoffed. "My drug trade was already flourishing before you and I ever met, you stupid cow."

"Your drug trade didn't have Nephilim and Nyctan checkpoints to worry about back then. Now they do. But it's more than just expert smuggling tactics, because it seems like they're ignoring the fact that Nividium even exists. So, either you've figured out the loophole of the century or…you have help."

A dubious smile on his bruised mouth, he shrugged. "Even if I did have help, I wouldn't tell you a damn thing."

"Is that so?" she asked, cracking him again. *Thwak!*

"Ow," he said, rubbing his jaw. "That one actually hurt."

When she raised her fist to strike him again, he was finally prompted to beg for mercy. He'd been doing his best to put on a tough-guy act, but she was relentless. And he wasn't sure how much more of this pummeling he could take.

"Wait! Wait," Zallek pleaded. "I can't give you what you want, anyway, because she's protected. By the voice."

"She?" Danica asked.

Zallek turned his black and blue face away as if to say, *I've said too much already.*

With a merciless crunch, she stomped her boot down on his bare foot.

"Argh!" he cried.

Her hand reached out and clutched him vigorously by his hair. Jerking his head back, she leaned down to whisper into his ear. "Sorry, I may not have made myself clear earlier. We're not stopping until I get a name."

"Tell me, Dani, do you still have that cute little freckle on the inside of your left thigh? The one that greets you just before going down on—" *Crack!*

She elbowed him right across the bridge of his nose. His head was already back as far as it could go so the tension placed on his spine caused his head to rebound and whip forward. Leaning hunched over, blood gushed from his busted nose and mingled with the blood pouring from his mouth.

"You psycho bitch," he grumbled, blood and saliva drizzling from his mouth as he spoke. "You broke my goddamn nose!"

She stomped down on his other foot and he yelped like a wounded dog.

"I don't know if you're just dense or really *this* stupid. But you still haven't answered my question. Names. Or we go to round three."

Zallek just laughed to himself. When Danica drew out a knife he stopped laughing and gulped. "W-what's that for?"

"I'm going to cut off your balls now and feed them to you."

"You're joking, right?"

Danica smiled at him, leaned in, and said, "Sure." Then, not wasting another second, she grabbed his waistline and sliced through his belt. Then, gripping tightly to his waistband, using the blade to sheer the fabric, she tore off the pants in one swift jerk and looked down at his man thong.

"Seriously?" she asked, raising an eyebrow. "Budgie-smugglers?"

A crude smile formed on his battered mouth. A smatter of sticky red stained his teeth, giving him a hideous look—like a wild beast that had just gorged itself on a kill. "You better get to cuttin' sweetheart, because I have a huge set of balls and it's gonna take you all day long."

She ignored the lewd remark and clutched his underwear's waistband and started cutting through it. He watched nervously as she removed his underwear too. His half-flaccid dick unfurled and flopped onto the chair between his legs.

They both looked down at it together, admiring how truly long it really was. Then, Danica gently scooped it up in her hand and slowly squeezed down on it. This elicited a pleasurable groan from his lips and leaning over she looked into his eyes and smiled.

"So, do you have a name for me or not?" she asked. She continued to squeeze his cock, which was growing firm in her hands, and ran the edge of the knife along his inner thigh as she moved the blade incrementally closer to his scrotum.

Just as the blade touched the tender part of his perineum, he yelped, "Fine! Yep. Got it!" Realizing she might actually go through with it, he glanced down at the blade between his legs and quickly began to spill everything he knew.

"Onelle Te'Legra Agnar," he said in a distressed tone. "She and the Voice of H'aaztre have an agreement of sorts. She gets to have free rein on all trade during the occupation."

"And what does The Voice get out of all this?"

"All of the intel she gathers from shipping manifestos goes back to her. If anything on the manifestos should look suspicious, she sends in boarding patrols to take a look and neutralize any possible threats."

"Let's see if I have this down correctly. You get to send your narcotics to all corners of the galaxy and get bonuses for ratting out your competitors who lose their licenses on one-time offenses? And the Voice collects all of the information to keep tabs on every little thing being traded, sold, and smuggled."

"In a nutshell, yes."

"So, naturally, you climbed into bed with her."

"She's a woman, isn't she?"

"Ew, gross," Danica said, making a sour face. "I didn't mean literally, you Slurvian ass."

Zallek shrugged as though bedding any random woman was a common occurrence with him. One he obviously wore as a badge of honor evidenced by the smug half grin he wore on his swollen lips.

"I think this concludes our little chat," Danica said, dropping his cock back onto the chair.

She twirled the knife in her hand, raised it high, and then slammed it down with brutal force right between his legs. He jolted in fright and then sighed with relief when he realized it had only bit into the wooden chair. The blade barely missing his manhood, he sighed out in relief, happy to remain unscathed.

Danica fetched a nearby towel and wiped Zallek's blood off her hands. She had gotten what she needed out of him and was ready to retire for the evening.

"Wait," Zallek called out to her as she turned toward the exit. He looked down at the blade wedged between his legs, the sharp edge pointed toward him. "You're not just going to leave me here like this?"

Danica didn't reply. She left him there to contemplate his life choices, slowly turning away again and continuing on her way. She had better things to do than waste any more time on his sorry ass.

But she couldn't say that seeing him didn't stir up old feelings. With everything that had happened, the loss of her child, Jegra having fallen into a coma, every single damn day was a fight to just not use again.

Consequently, she turned all her pent-up frustration back onto the person who had been the bane of her existence. Sure, it wasn't Zallek who'd forced her to use in the first place—that was on her. But everything after that was a deliberate attempt to manipulate and abuse her. And for that, he deserved whatever was coming to him.

"What do you intend to do with him?" a familiar voice asked as she neared the end of the corridor. She looked over to find Raphine leaning against a large marble pillar looking over at her with inquisitive, teal eyes.

"I'm going to let him sweat it out for a few days. Then lock him up and throw away the key. The best thing for me to do is try and move on."

"We could use him, you know?"

Danica raised an eyebrow. She wasn't in the mood to talk shop, but Raphine never had a bad idea, so she was willing to hear her out. "Oh, yeah?"

"I was thinking we could put our own agents into his drug shipping operation and then gain intel on those gaining intel on us. Kind of a double sleeper agent, spy on spy situation."

"Sounds promising. But I'm washing my hands of Zallek's bullshit. This time for good. So you'll be overseeing this one on your own."

Raphine nodded and then sauntered over to Danica. She reached up and brushed Danica's hair out of her eyes and gently tucked it behind her right ear. Danica reached up and stopped her hand.

"Raph, sorry, I can't. I mean, what happened between us was…unexpected and…I do care about you. It's just…Jegra's back now and I can't…you know."

"I know," Raphine said, doing her best to mask her heart wrenching pain as Danica rejected her. "It wasn't meant to last. It was foolish of me to fall for my teacher anyway."

"Someday you'll find the person right for you," Danica said, bringing Raphine's hand to her lips. She kissed the top of Raphine's knuckles and smiled up at her. "I promise."

When Raphine smiled back, Danica turned up the stairwell and disappeared into the main palace.

Raphine waited for her to be out of earshot before she broke down sobbing. Wiping tears from her eyes, she turned down a side hallway and raced out a hidden back entrance and into the courtyard. When she stepped out into the crisp, evening desert air, she took a deep breath and looked up at the stars.

Somewhere up there, right now, Jegra was meeting with her people—the last survivors of planet Earth—now galactic refugees. They had a long, hard road ahead of them and Raphine knew she'd need to have the palace ready to receive them when they returned.

In the distance, new apartments were being built just at the edge of the city. The fifteen story-tall buildings were designed specifically for housing the human survivors.

"Raphine," a voice called out from over her shoulder.

She turned to find Danica standing there, eyes brimming with tears. "I may have been premature in how deep my feelings run for you."

Raphine laughed and then gulped, feeling equal parts anger for being jerked around and joy for Danica returning to her and admitting how cold and cruel she'd been.

Danica ran to her and threw her arms around her neck. Their lips met and they shared a satisfying kiss.

"Are you sure this is what you want?" Raphine asked.

"No," Danica replied. "But whatever it is we have," she pointed at her own heart, "it's worth holding onto. Don't you think?"

"What about your engagement? Don't you still want to marry Jegra?"

Danica looked away as though she were embarrassed. "Honestly, she seems different to me somehow. Maybe it's just me. So much has happened. And, not knowing if she'd ever wake from her endless sleep, I'd been mentally preparing myself for the fact that I'd need to move on. And the thing between us just sort of happened. And now…now, I just don't know."

"Maybe you both just need some time," Raphine said. "She only just came out of a coma to find the nightmare she had dreamed about for over a year was, in fact, a reality. That's not an easy thing to wake up to."

"No, but it's the reality we must all face," Danica replied.

"Like I said," Raphine reiterated, "just give her time before you make any lasting decisions. Who knows? She may bounce back to her old self and everything will be right again, you two will marry each other, and live happily ever after."

"And if not?"

"If not, then you'll still have me." Raphine cupped her hands around Dani's face then leaned in and touched her forehead to Dani's. They smiled, kissed briefly, and then returned to the glowing lights of the palace, hand in hand.

About fifteen hundred meters away from Arena Palace, a light breeze blew across the landscape, kicking up kernels of loose sand that rolled passed a medium sized rock perched on the crest of a sand dune.

Without warning, the rock sprouted legs and scuttled around like a crab. It moved into position and then focused its three, green-glowing night-vision eyes onto its target.

The telescopic eyes zoomed in on the two women entering the palace. After they disappeared inside, it zoomed back out again, widening its panoramic view. As a couple of palace guards rounded the corner, it automatically honed in on their positions and began tracking them. Each individual guard was flagged with a tracking number as the sand-crab gained intel.

Three dunes over, sitting cross-legged at the base of a rather large mound was a woman wearing full desert tactical gear, a VR headset, and the best equipment that a freelancer could buy. On her visor, she watched through the nigh-vision eyes of the robotic sand-crab perched on the crest of the dune.

In the silence of the desert night, the comm crackled in the woman's earpiece and a gruff voice came on the radio. "Sand Viper, report."

"The ex-vice admiral and the green-skin returned to the palace. Security seems to be minimal with the empress off world."

"Do you have a fix on the target?"

"Affirmative. The target is being held in a secondary basement. Likely a holding cell."

The robotic sand spider's eye flickered and changed to red then transmitted its infrared thermal imaging back to its viewer.

"What's the security detail like guarding the cell?" the voice in her ear asked.

"Nothing that appears on thermal imaging. But that doesn't mean there aren't bots guarding the prisoner."

There was a short pause before the voice came back over the comm. "Sand Viper, your mission objective has changed. Ghost recon is now an official rescue op. Your mission is to infiltrate the palace undetected, secure the asset, and get out again."

"And if there's unforeseen trouble?"

"You have permission to terminate any and all obstacles that get in your way. Sand Viper, I needn't remind you of the delicate nature of this op. I don't want any mistakes. Do I make myself clear?"

"Crystal," she replied in a calculating voice.

She cut her link and then slowly reached up and slipped off the VR headset. Pulling out her earpiece, she unwound it from her ear, letting it dangle from the cord. The insinuation that she'd ever make a mistake on a live op was insulting and she resented the accusation. Letting out a vexed sigh, she reminded herself that, although her current employer was a complete ass, she'd be sure to add a surcharge for putting up with his condescending bullshit.

Like most Bre'lal, she was extremely beautiful, even as she sported a shaved head. Slowly rising to her feet, she put on sunglasses with mirrored lenses that gave her an added mystique and then walked over to her ATV, parked a short distance away.

The Jeep-styled ATV was equipped with oversized sand tires that resembled giant tractor tires. The vehicle didn't have any doors, even as it appeared to be armored, and she tossed the VR headset into the open duffle bag on the backseat before leaning in and fetching the high-powered plasma rifle off the back windshield.

After breaking down the gun and folding it in half, she swung it across her back and it clamped down onto the magnetic harness with a resounding *clank*.

The desert camo and tactical gear she wore helped her blend into the surroundings well enough, but she opened up a carbon fiber suitcase in the rear cargo bed of the ATV and pulled out a hooded cloak. She slipped the cloak on over her head and body armor then pinched a touch sensitive patch on the collar.

All of a sudden, her visage wavered like a heat mirage glistening on the desert. Parts of her image faded then reappeared, while others reappeared only to disappear again. Finally, she disappeared from sight altogether as the invisibility cloak fully activated.

Invisible to the naked eye, she ascended to the top of the dune and looked out across the two klicks of sand which sat between her and the palace lights that glimmered in the distance like the lamps of a desert caravan.

Although the Bre'lal people didn't have a military to call their own, many Bre'lal were conscripted into the Dagon military as grunts. In fact, most of the Bre'lal men and a large majority of the women made up the backbone of the Dagon Imperial Guard. As it turned out, Dagon people were perfectly fine sending others into harm's way to do their dirty work for them.

The IPG were trained in space, desert, and amphibious combat, but once their tours were complete, job prospects were rather limited. Which is why retired Imperial Guard made excellent private contractors.

Of course, you could always opt to re-up your enlistment, but for Gaewen Feradorn, private gigs paid too well to pass up.

Besides, she'd served her mandatory time and then some, having done two additional tours on the front lines of Dakroth's endless war with the Nyctans.

That had been enough for her.

For Gaewen, as a Bre'lal woman, it was either take on private contract work or go for sex work on some island resort, playing the part of a bikini-clad goddess desperate to appease her guest's every fantasy. She'd be lying if she said killing wasn't more arousing than sex. Because…it most definitely was. In fact, getting her hands dirty was the fun part.

She didn't know if that made her a sociopath, or whatever, but she knew that it made her extremely good at her job.

Gaewen focused her mind on her new mission objective and began shuffling down the side of the dune. As her boots left lengthy skid marks behind her, she pulled her hood up and vanished into her surroundings like a ghost.

13

Hot white bolts of radiant plasma pelted the Nephilim ship. Hundreds of automated gun batteries honed in on the arrival of the enemy vessel and spat streaming hot javelins of energy at the mammoth cruiser that lingered in low orbit.

The flagship of the Nephilim armada was unlike anything Dakroth had ever seen. Its architecture was organic, its design didn't seem functional, but somehow it operated capably, and it shared more in common with the CSEs than any battleship he'd ever seen. He couldn't even make out where its cannons were, as the entire ship seemed to glow with a coating of the same skin as the space squids.

Perhaps more daunting, however, was that this glowing armor seemed to absorb the blasts from the plasma canons they'd set up around the basecamp. The skin of the enemy vessel briefly flared to hot white wherever a plasma bolt hit it, then it absorbed the energy and cooled back to its usual, soft yellow glow.

Unable to damage the massive cruiser that lurked over them like a domineering golden Kraken, Grendok turned to Dakroth, a grim look stamped upon his face. "We might as well be throwing pebbles and wooden spears at it," he groused in his usual gruff voice, "for all the good it would do."

"How do you want to play this?" Callestra asked, throwing her hands up on her hips. She shifted her posture, tilting her hips in the other direction and tossed her hair across her shoulder as she waited for his reply.

Dakroth rubbed his chin as he mulled over their options. Then he turned to Grendok and Callestra, who watched him with anticipation as he cleared his throat.

"Order a ceasefire. It's best if I meet with H'aaztre myself. While I'm keeping him distracted, you have your team get those explosives ready."

"Sounds like a plan," the satyr said. He turned to Callestra and taking her blue hand in his he kissed it. "It's been a pleasure my dear. You keep him safe."

"Always," she answered.

The satyr bowed and then turned and skipped off toward the rows of batteries calling out orders to cease fire. Groups of mystified faces stared back at him as he went. Even though the orders didn't make sense, they obeyed the satyr's commands and the thousands of plasma needles lighting up the evening sky fell silent.

Callestra turned back to face Dakroth and squinted at him long and hard. When he was deep in thought like this it was hard to read him. "What are you planning?"

"Just follow my lead," he replied. She nodded and then took his side. Tapping his wrist the emergency teleport signal was sent to the ship hovering high above them. He then grabbed Callestra by the waist and drew her into him. She chirped from the unexpected surprise and looked up into his red eyes with her magenta ones, a subtle smile hovering playfully about her lips.

As they held one another, the red teleportation beam came down to collect them. The lines of light seemed to divide their bodies up into thin strips and then, piece by piece, and in no discernible order, the strips whisked them away up to the ship.

When they manifested on the enemy cruiser, they found themselves standing on what appeared to be the command center, surrounded by a dozen guards all wearing glossy black and gold lined, laser resistant body armor.

Many of the Nephilim soldiers had what looked like rocket packs, which Callestra recognized as their wing sheaths. Metal wings could unfold from the backs of the soldiers, sending them gliding on the air. This allowed wave after wave of the soldiers to deploy from drop ships onto alien worlds without ever having to set the ships down. The Nephilim rained down from the skies like a plague of locusts. It's what made their military so terrifying—they were legion.

Dakroth and Callestra turned to find The Voice of H'aaztre herself, Azra'il Nun, standing opposite them with a thrilled smile on her face.

"You!" Callestra growled, coming face to face with her sworn enemy. Realizing that if the woman so much as opened her mouth it could seal their doom, she didn't take any chances and quickly lunged forward, both hands reaching out to choke Azra'il Nun's throat before she had the chance to speak.

Blue electricity crackled and before she could wrap her hands around the woman's neck, one of The Voice's personal guards intercepted her with his stun rod and she crashed to the ground, her body tensing up from the tendrils of blue electricity.

When the charge had stopped, Callestra slowly uncoiled, groaning from the intense pain of the jolt. Muttering some obscenity or another under her breath, she looked up at the guard with a fearsome glare.

He didn't seem much intimidated by it, however, seeing as he merely reached down and jabbed the sparking and crackling end of the rod into her tender side once more as a warning not to get any bright ideas.

"Azra'il Nun, as I live and breathe," Dakroth said with a diplomatic grin. "It's been a long time."

"Azra'il Nun is dead," the woman said in a vexed tone. "I am The Voice of the almighty H'aaztre."

"The Voice?" Dakroth echoed, rubbing his chin contemplatively.

"His Word is his Will and his Will is my calling."

"How quaint."

"Oh, yes, I nearly forgot," The Voice replied in a less than flattering tone. "You're the king who doesn't believe in anything but himself."

"And what's wrong with having a little bit of faith in oneself?" he asked.

She smiled but did not offer any reply as that would merely stroke his ego. Nodding at Callestra, who lay curled up at her feet, she insisted, "Why don't you help your girlfriend up and maybe we can have a civil conversation?"

"I'll show you civil," Callestra growled, staggering to her feet and taking a step toward Azra'il Nun.

The stun rod came at her again, but this time she was prepared for it. Reaching out, she clutched the guard's wrist, stopping the tip of the rod mere centimeters from electrocuting her whole face.

Little blue arcs of electricity crawled along the shaft and convened at its rounded tip. Drawing it near, Callestra opened her mouth and licked the tip. The sound of saliva sizzling could be heard and then she quickly pulled back, little tendrils of electricity stretching out from the rod and dancing across her teeth and lips.

Distracted by the lewd simulation of fellatio, the guard never even saw it coming. In the blink of an eye, Callestra twisted the guard's wrist inward, drew him into her body while at the same time wrenching his baton wielding hand, hard.

She dropped her shoulder, rolled him onto her back, and then, still holding his arm, used both the strength of her legs and the momentum of his fall to flip him over her body.

He went up and over and then crashed down onto the ground with a harsh thud. A bit rattled by the speed and strength of such a slender woman, he gazed up at her with bewildered eyes. Standing over her conquest, Callestra looked down at him with a disappointed smirk as she held the stun rod in her hand that she'd stripped from him. She clicked the switch and let it crackle menacingly, feigning to zap him with his own weapon.

Unimpressed by the guard, she tossed the stun rod to the ground and then looked back up at Azra'il Nun with a hard glare that dared her to come at her again.

Instead of playing her little game, however, Azra'il just grinned and said, "Stay put, my pet." She then turned to Dakroth and gestured for him to step out onto the main bridge with her. "Please," she insisted, her gaze settling upon Dakroth, "This way."

"Let's dispense with the formalities, Azra'il," Dakroth said, not budging. "You need something from me, otherwise we wouldn't be talking right now."

The Voice raised a fascinated eyebrow when he didn't heed her command. "Impressive," she said. "Not many can resist my powers of persuasion."

A debonair grin formed on Dakroth's lips. "My dear, silly woman. I'm not just anyone. I'm the Emperor of the Dagon Empire, Sovereign Lord of Seven Sectors, and the rightful heir to my father's legacy! And what are you but a glorified megaphone for an over-inflated ego that thinks itself a god?"

She struck him across his face with the palm of her hand. The forceful smack resounded throughout the whole bridge and caused him to drop to one knee. Her strength was impressive, but nothing he couldn't handle.

"How dare you speak to me like that!" she snarled. "I am no mere messenger. I am the Authority of the Gilded Master Himself. I am His Will, his Voice, and you will know your place, little man."

Callestra moaned through her clenched jaw as she tried to fight against the

Voice's influence, but her command to stay put was resolute. Still, seeing Dakroth bitch-slapped like that only pissed her off even more, so instead of giving up, she merely tried harder, the veins in her neck bulging as she attempted to will her muscles to respond and her limbs to move.

Slowly, Dakroth rose back up to his feet and stood his ground. He glared menacingly back at Azra'il, who stared at him with the same disdainful intensity. Then, without provocation and quite unexpectedly, Dakroth threw his head back and let out a loud, belly-clenching bellow of laughter.

"My how I've missed your beautiful, stubbornness, Azzie."

Azra'il drew back, confused by his unexpected change of character. "If you're trying to trick me into letting my guard down, I can assure you, it won't work."

"No. No, tricks," replied Dakroth with a casual sigh. He looked around at the guards, scanning each of their faces and doing a quick check to see if any of them posed any kind of threat to him. None did. Confident he wasn't in any immediate danger, he turned his attention back to Azra'il. "So, as much as I love to beat around a good bush, the real question is, what do you want, Azzie?"

She ignored his infantile pet name for her and cut to the chase. "Keeping you here for a full year was no accident. The only reason you escaped at all was because He willed it to be so."

"Is that right?" Dakroth asked in a skeptical tone.

"It is," she answered. "And what's more, the only reason you're standing here before me now is because I need you to do something for me."

"I'm listening," Dakroth replied.

"H'aaztre is worried that with Jegra out of her coma, she'll inspire a rebellion. Many of the worlds see her as a driving force of peace in the galaxy. Now, you of all people should realize that we cannot allow such disloyalty to be sown. As such, I need you to lure her here so she can be dealt with properly."

"Ah, so you want me to be the bait?"

A thin, narrow smile formed on her mouth in silent acknowledgement.

"And what, may I ask, is in it for me?"

"You get to have your precious empire back."

"Your master is willing to return to me the entire Dagon Empire simply to lure Jegra into a trap for you?"

"Is it so hard to believe? His Holiness is not without generosity. His

Magnificence is loyal to those who are loyal to him. The only question is, Lord Emperor of the Galaxy, are you with him or against him?"

"Even if your words could be trusted, why should I help a master who held me captive for a year, starved and tortured me, and messed with my mind to the point of losing myself to utter and complete madness?"

"That's just it, though. You didn't lose yourself to the madness. You persevered. And here you stand…stronger than ever. You see, even the strongest steel blades can snap without first being tempered. But you have been through H'aaztre's forge, you have been tempered to near imperviousness, and you have gained a strength you never knew you possessed."

Dakroth smiled. Regardless of whether or not Azra'il Nun was telling him the truth, he had only one thing on his mind. Revenge. But knowing that he couldn't take on her and half the Nephilim military all on his own, he acquiesced to her demands. It was about time he introduced The Voice to his lovely, royal pain-in-the-ass wife, Jegra.

"Fine," he said, pretending to be disappointed in himself for giving up the empress so easily, "I'll do it. But under one condition."

"Name it," Azra'il said.

"You let me be there to watch when you ruin her and her merry band of rebels."

Azra'il Nun smiled and, in an icy tone, said, "As you wish, Lord Emperor Dakroth."

14

Brei's purple cheeks flushed hot magenta when the empress stopped her short of her getting into the sex positions she liked. The empress was being extremely patient with her, even as she was rambling on about how much her own boyfriend wanted a threesome with her and Jegra.

"Brei, it's quite alright, you don't need to explain yourself to me. We're friends," Jegra said with a laugh, halting the girl's apprehensive ramblings.

Brei let out a huge sigh of relief and took in a deep breath. She had nearly talked to the point of passing out. Then it occurred to her that the empress had just called her a friend. "We're friends?" she asked, somewhat in shock by the revelation.

Never in her wildest dreams did Brei have any reason to think that Jegra would consider her more than a loyal servant. To be elevated to the status of someone in the empress's inner circle was both humbling and stupefying all at the same time.

"Of course, we are!" Jegra answered, placing a reassuring hand on Brei's shoulder and giving her a gentle yet encouraging squeeze. "It's not just anyone I let rave on at length about her lurid sex fantasies about me and her boyfriend."

"Oh," Brei, said, feeling awfully self-conscious for having let such private daydreams slip from her lips so recklessly. She hadn't meant to offend. "I didn't mean to imply..."

"Lieutenant," Jegra interrupted, craning her neck and cocking her eyes at the girl, a puckish grin forming on her tightly pressed lips. "If you say another word, I'll..."

Jegra stopped mid-sentence when she noticed Brei trembling with fear.

Tears were streaming down the poor girl's face and Jegra couldn't help but feel sorry for the dressing down she was about to dole out. But then it dawned on her that this wasn't about that. Something else was the matter.

"What is it?" asked Jegra, her voice growing serious.

Brei looked up at Jegra, wrapping her arms around herself and grabbing her other arm to try and hold herself still. "I just time jumped. Something terrible has happened."

Jegra put both arms on the girl's shoulders like a coach would an all-star player and looked her directly in her eyes. "All right. Start at the beginning and tell me everything."

Brei'Alas nodded, wiping the tears from her cheeks that had unexpectedly began dampening her face.

Lieutenant Commander Barrion stepped forward, raised a whistle to his Prussian blue lips, and gave the bosun's call. All crew came to attention and turned toward the entrance.

"Introducing her majesty, the esteemed gladiatrix turned empress, Jegra Alakandra, Imperatrix of the Dagon Empire, Jewel of the Commonwealth, and Mother of all Dagon."

This time, as the empress and her entourage passed by Barrion's position, Brei'Alas leaned in and whispered something into the empress's ear. She nodded and the girl broke from the ranks, grabbed Barrion by his arm and, to his surprise, dragged him out of the room.

Given Brei'Alas's recollection of what happened in the not so distant future with Barrion, Jegra thought, remembering everything that Brei had divulged to her in her chambers, it was probably for the best that she dealt with him personally during tonight's proceedings.

Karina and Jegra met face to face behind the table and greeted one another. This time, however, Jegra knew what to expect.

"It's nice to finally meet you in person, President Nazimova," Jegra said, extending her hand.

Karina Nazimova didn't smile. She seemed to have nerves of her own but, then, unexpectedly blurted out, "I'm sorry."

Jegra raised an eyebrow when Karina drew out a korridium alloy blade from behind her back and thrust it toward the empress's gut.

The entire banquet hall gasped in simultaneous shock. At the same time, Karina looked down in dismay at the blade only to find that Jegra had clutched her wrist and stopped it before she could do any real damage.

It almost seemed as though the empress had anticipated the move before she'd ever made it. Almost as if she knew the attack was coming.

"I'm so, so sorry. S-she told me to do it. So, I had to do it. You understand, right?"

Jegra smiled casually, then pried the dagger out of Karina's trembling hands and tossed it onto the table. Ignoring the transgression, she gestured for everyone who'd risen, waiting to leap to the empress's aid if necessary, to be seated.

"But I don't...I don't understand," Karina said, stumbling over her words. She was afraid that the empress would retaliate or that her security detail would pile onto her and drag her to the brig. Instead, to her surprise, Jegra had foreseen the attack and seemed to be rather cavalier about the whole ordeal. "Shouldn't you be angrier with me or something?"

"It'll be fine," answered Jegra, brushing down her dress and then gesturing for Karina to take her seat.

Astounded by Jegra's calm under pressure and her ability to maintain a diplomatic air even after an assassination attempt, Karina knew in her heart Jegra had to be more than human. "But how...I mean...why would they tell me to do such a thing, knowing it wouldn't likely succeed?"

"They're testing you. Testing your willpower. They want to see if they can make you all into obedient slaves. And if the strongest of you succumbs to them, then they win."

"And I failed," Karina said aloud, looking down in shame.

"Who said you were the strongest of us?" Jegra asked, her lips curling into a raffish grin.

"Remind me again what we're doing in the utility closet," Barrion asked.

Brei brushed the supplies off a countertop and then hopped onto it. Seated on the counter, she leaned back and pulled her dress up. Spreading her legs, she smiled and said, "What does it look like?"

A crooked grin spread across Barrion's lips. "You're serious? Right here? Now?" He looked around uncertain, before finding her sparkling golden eyes looking back at him.

She nodded and, spreading her legs even more to reveal she wasn't wearing any panties, he was already halfway done unfastening his pants when he got to her.

Before she could even finish unbuttoning her uniform, with a vigorous thrust of the hips he entered her. She squeaked with the light sensation of tender pain and pleasure at the dry entry. But she was young and nubile and her body was always willing, and soon enough, things were moving as smoothly as ever.

It was a quick, messy, and dirty fuck in the utility closet. Not exactly her style, but she knew she needed to distract him somehow and this was the best she could come up with on such short notice. Besides, all that talk about sleeping with Jegra had really gotten her in the mood. She was almost shocked by how much she desired that fantasy to be her reality. But Barrion was sweet, and she truly loved him. So, she closed her eyes and let out a moan, thinking of Jegra but feeling him inside her.

Pleased with how his evening was turning out, Barrion finished and then, pulling out, tucked himself in and zipped his pants back up. Surprisingly, before he'd even finished dressing, Brei's hand shot out and clasped onto his jacket lapel and confidently pulled him into her.

Their lips came together and after a deeply satisfying kiss, she slowly pushed his head down. He kissed her bare chest as he slid down her body and then paused between her thighs.

"Well, what are you waiting for? You got yours. It's my turn."

"It's a little messy down here," he said, reticently, looking back up at her in silent protest.

She slapped him lightly across the face. "And who made the mess?"

"I did," he said, diverting his eyes and looking away in shame.

She grabbed his head and forced his face into her vulva. "Then you'd better clean it up."

"Yes, ma'am," he mumbled in a muffled voice as her lips wrapped around his.

Fifteen minutes later, Barrion's head buried between her thighs, she screamed out as the orgasm rippled through her entire body. It began at her head, ran down her tight neck, taught abdomen, and down her quivering thighs until finally finishing its course in her curled up toes.

After the satisfying scream, she gasped for air, inhaling deeply. Immediately after taking her breath she began panting as Barrion went down on her a second time.

"I can't," she pleaded, pulling on his hair to try and pry him off her. But he resisted and buried his face even deeper into her.

"*Qui, qui, etvi-dagri zoffenqui'le!*" she screamed out.

Zoffenqui'le was the Dagoni word for *leaking*. She remembered looking up the English translation of it so that if something between her and Jegra ever did happen, she'd know what to say. But the English version didn't make any sense to her. It wasn't about "leaking," as that'd be too straight forward. It was about coming and going. But, she wondered, why would arriving at one's destination or leaving have anything to do with experiencing an orgasm?

Finally, managing to pry Barrion's lips off of her clitoris, she let out a deeply satisfied sigh. "That was..."

"Amazing?" Barrion asked, rubbing her residue off of his lip with his thumb and then sucking off his thumb. "I know."

She laughed and then drew him back into her. They kissed again and then paused mid-kiss. She pulled away only to find a vacant, trance-like look had found its way onto his face.

"What is it?" she asked in a worried tone.

"There's something I must do," he said, turning to leave.

She caught him by his arm and yanked him back. "Not so fast, loverboy. I'm not finished with you yet."

"But there's something I must do," he said in a monotone voice, glancing back at the utility closet door as if he had somewhere else he needed to be and was running late.

"And I'm saying you can't get me this wet without leaving me absolutely satisfied. *Capisce?*"

He didn't seem to hear her though, and whatever had mesmerized him, overrode his will and compelled him to turn toward the door again.

She swiftly hopped off the counter and pulled down her dress while reaching out for him. She caught him just as he was opening the door and, reeling him back in with one arm, she reached up with the other and slammed the door shut.

"What are you doing?" he asked.

She flung herself into him, mashing herself against his body and then began to dirty dance grinding and rubbing all up and down his body.

"I'm…uh…you know…dancing." Grabbing her own breasts and squeezing them as she dropped down and then slowly slid back up his thigh, asked, "Why? You don't like it?"

He placed his hands on her shoulders and gently moved her to the side. "Brei, please, it's been fun. But I must return to my duties now."

She gripped him and spun him back around, more forcefully this time. "No! You can't!" She practically shouted it at him. Realizing her reaction might have been too much, she added in an overtly sultry voice not entirely appropriate for the current situation, "You can't go out there." She licked her lips seductively, began biting her lower lip in an awkward fashion that seemed more like she was flicking it at him, and then laughed out loud as though he'd said something hilarious although he hadn't so much as mumbled a word.

"You're acting strange," he said. He gently nudged her out of the way, again, but again she forced herself into his path.

This time he gave her a good shove and sent her staggering back. She looked up, almost startled but more shocked and disappointed than anything. Rage instantly replaced her surprise and she leapt onto his back and clung to him like a Zondonian monkey.

"Don't you ever shove me like that again!" she screamed, pulling his hair.

"Ow! Get off of me," he yelped.

"I'm sorry," Brei said, "but I can't do that."

Fed up with her interference, Barrion reached up and flipped Brei over him and pinned her against the wall. She smashed into it, back first, upside down, and then toppled to the floor. By the time she managed to push herself back up, Barrion was walking through the utility closet door.

She chased him out into the hall and, running at a dead sprint to catch up to him, body-checked and pulled him down to the floor.

Once they'd untangled themselves and got back up to their feet, Barrion's fist clocked her across the jaw. She staggered back a couple of steps, touching her face and looking up in alarm. But she knew this wasn't him. The real Barrion would never strike her. This was The Voice controlling him, like her personal little puppet. She recognized as much by the fact that the same vacant gaze as before had settled over him.

"Oh, now you're asking for it," she said in a low voice.

"I have to go," he repeated, as though he were on autopilot. "I have something…"

"You've gotta go. Yeah, so I've heard," Brei quipped sarcastically.

Barrion turned and began heading up the corridor again.

"Wait, don't you need this?" Brei asked.

Barrion slowed up in the hallway and then patting himself down, realized he was missing something. Slowly, he turned around to face her. Grinning at him, she held up the detonator to the suicide vest and waved it around as though she were daring him to try to come and get it.

"Where'd you get that?" he asked, reaching out for it.

She drew it back, not letting him snatch it from her. "Oh, this little thing? I just found it laying around."

"Give it to me," he said, holding out his hand.

"Sorry, I can't do that," Brei shot back.

He pressed forward and she took another step backward.

"Give it to me," he insisted.

"No," she growled, standing her ground. As he came closer, she did the unexpected: thrust her knee forward and kneed him squarely in the junk.

Barrion collapsed to the floor, his face turning an extra dark shade of blue as he clutched his nut sack and groaned in terrible, immobilizing pain. "Why in Helios did you do that?" he asked after having caught his breath.

Brei looked down at him and tried to gauge whether it was actually him or not. "Barrion?" she asked in a sympathetic voice. "Is that you?"

"Who else would it be?" He rolled over and looked up at her. Then, realizing they were no longer in the utility closet but in the open hallway, he asked, "Wait, how'd we get out here?"

"It's a long story," Brei said, slipping the detonator back into her dress, tucking it under the left side of her breast just between her under-boob and armpit. The tightness of her dress held it in place and she went over to help her bewildered boyfriend up.

As she helped him up, he noticed the welt on her cheek. "Who did that?" he asked in an angry voice when he realized that someone had assaulted his girl.

"You did," she replied unenthusiastically.

"I did?" he asked in an astonished voice. "I'm so sorry, Brei," he said reaching up to touch it. When she grew tense, still not entirely certain he had regained full autonomy over himself, he stayed his hand. But then, seeing how hurt he looked, she took it in hers and pressed her face into its warmth.

"What could have compelled me to do such a thing?"

"Apparently The Voice has inserted sleeper agents all throughout the crew. I was able to snap you out of it before you did anything you'd regret, but there could still be others waiting to activate when you fail your task. I don't know how many more sleeper agents there are or how I'm going to find them, but the empress is counting on me to stop them. I can't fail her."

Barrion rubbed his chin contemplatively and then said, "Wait a moment. Before the *Shard* left orbit there was a cargo ship that brought supplies aboard. I was returning with the resupply crew from Dagon Prime and we were boarded for a routine inspection. That must have been when it happened."

"So," Brei said, a smile spreading across her beautiful mouth, "all we need to do is find the cargo ship's crew manifest and detain everyone who happened to be aboard that vessel."

"Precisely," Barrion said, snapping his fingers.

"Well, what are we waiting for? Let's get going." Brei turned and started up the hall but stopped when she heard Barrion let out a painful groan. She spun back around to find him limping toward her with a bow-legged waddle.

"Oh, you poor thing," she said. She glided back toward him and gave him an apologetic peck on the lips. Gently running her hand down to his crotch, she began to massage him. He groaned again from the pain but didn't try to stop her. "Do you need me to kiss it and make it all better."

Barrion raised an eyebrow.

"Maybe another time. I feel we should really get going," he said glancing down at her hand which rested on his crotch.

"Right," she said, drawing her hand away. She turned her back to him and then squatted down. Slapping her own ass, she said, "Saddle up, buddy."

He shrugged and hopped onto her back, graciously accepting the piggyback ride down the lengthy corridor.

15

A visual distortion, like the wavering of a heat mirage dancing along the horizon of the Thessalonica desert at sunset, slipped onto the palace grounds without so much as being detected.

The barely perceptible shimmer moved along the posterior edge of the palace wall until it came to a rear service entrance and stopped. From out of a narrow slit in the invisibility cloak, a hand with a lockpick manifested out of thin air. After a few clicks, the phantom shimmer picked the lock and slipped inside the palace.

Once inside, Gaewen Feradorn pulled down her hood so that only her head was visible. She looked up and down the long corridor, checking all choke points and watching for possible security patrols. When she was satisfied the coast was clear, she turned and went over to the security system wall panel. She placed an electrofoil key-card on the security box, and, after a few seconds, the silent alarm countdown shut off and the system reset as though nothing was out of the ordinary.

With a flick of her wrist, Gaewen double checked the palace blueprints on her holovid display and then determined that the East wing stairwell of the palace would be the most direct course to her destination.

While her body remained shrouded beneath the invisibility cloak, her head bobbed around the corridor like a decapitated ghost-head floating in mid-air. She darted from one column to another until coming to a large archway that led out into the great hall with its impossibly high ceilings.

A clatter of boots marching down the hall caused her to dart to one of the large columns and flatten against it. Keeping the column between herself and the guards at all times, she slowly edged around it to the dark side, the security patrol drawing near as they made their rounds.

As the security patrol passed by her location, Gaewen slowly pulled up her hood as she further receded into the shadow cast by the enormous column so that it appeared as though the darkness had absorbed her into itself.

After the two guards had gone on their way, Gaewen's face re-emerged from her cowl, her turquoise eyes watching them as they rounded the corner at the end of the banquet hall. She scanned the room for cameras or pressure sensors, but didn't detect any and so cautiously stepped back into the light. That's when she heard the clatter of dishes and a breaking of earthenware.

She froze, swiveled her head only to find a servant girl standing no more than a couple of meters away from her, slack-jawed and doe-eyed as she beheld the floating head. In that moment, Gaewen mentally berated herself for leaving her hood down. *Anything that can go wrong inevitably always goes wrong*, she mused unenthusiastically. Such entropic moments always had a way of sneaking up on you when you least expected them.

Gaewen's hand came up from the cloak, and the floating hand pressed itself upon floating lips and hushed the girl, warning her to keep quiet. When it appeared as though the servant girl may scream, Gaewen swiftly reached into her cloak and pulled out a paralyzing dart and flung it with lightening quick speed.

The mini-dart sank into the girl's shoulder and she looked down at it with a startled expression. Almost instantly she grew drowsy, her eyelids fluttering. When she began to totter on her feet, Gaewen rushed over and caught the girl under her arms, saving her from a rather precarious fall.

Averting such a close call, she gently set the unconscious girl down in one of the chairs at the banquet table. If anyone came upon her, they'd assume she'd had a spell and was resting herself. Upon reviving, if she mentioned anything about floating heads, they'd likely just think it was a stress induced dream. Either way, it bought Gaewen the time she needed to complete her mission.

Careful not to make a sound, she left the girl sleeping peacefully and scurried over to the flight of stairs that greeted her across the hall and slipped into the stairwell.

Once inside, she turned off her invisibility cloak to conserve battery power and the fabric, which was like a high definition televid screen projecting the surroundings back at you, flickered and then turned into a dark gray matte cloak.

Rendered fully visible, Gaewen had to be extra vigilant. After all, she didn't want another repeat of earlier. If people started finding multiple unconscious bodies strewn about the palace, she'd soon be found out.

Still, she had a job to do and she wasn't about to pass up such a rich bounty. Taking a deep breath, she cautiously edged up to the railing of the spiral staircase and glanced up and down the shaft. The coast was clear. She drew back, reached into her cloak, and pulled out two metallic silver balls the size of six-centimeter wooden dowel caps; or about the size of a large, menacing eyeball.

In one fluid motion, she tossed them into the air and as they reached the zenith of their arc, they sprouted four pairs of tiny wings like those of a dragonfly.

The balls hovered in place momentarily, their wings buzzing softly. Then, with the speed of a wasp, they darted away, following the spiral staircase downward to the secondary basement, where Zallek was being held captive.

In case the drones were spotted or detected any signs of trouble, they would release a smokescreen and then self-destruct. Since they were also flash grenades, their destruction would sow confusion to help her escape. *Such a fun little toy*, she mused, that made her job all the easier.

Her mark, Gerard Van Zallek was being held on the second level basement, two levels down from her present location. The blueprints had shown her that his floor consisted mainly of the palace prison and several storage rooms. The first level basement, just above that, was a garage that held ATVs, hover bikes, shuttle transports, a medium class drop ship, and a couple of class nine Imperial fighters. Luckily, the stairwell bypassed this level completely, since it had higher security and different external access points.

This, of course, was why she'd chosen the Eastern stairwell as her access point. Security would be that much less prevalent while simultaneously giving her a direct path to Zallek's current location.

The third level basement consisted of a fitness center with a full-sized indoor pool, a sauna, and a massage nook—and probably had even less security than the two levels above it. She didn't think it would be a problem, but had sent the drones all the way down just to scan the room for signs of hostiles.

She followed the spiral staircase downward, the drones scouting ahead for any possible signs of trouble, until she reached sub-basement two. Cracking the door into the hallway, she slowly crouched down and peered out at the two blue-skin guards sitting at a card table near the end of the long corridor, playing a round of Follow the Queen.

The bad news was that beyond those two, she didn't know how many more security personnel would be lurking around the bend and throughout the halls. The good news was that the guards sitting a short distance from her seemed to be engrossed in their game, which gave her a small opening.

As her buzzing balls returned from their short trip, she reached out with an open palm and their wings instantly folded up and they dropped into her hand. She tucked them back inside her cloak and then, pulling on her hood, re-activated the invisibility device and slipped out into the hallway.

"Did you hear that?" one of the guards asked, poking his head up and looking over at the stairwell doors.

"Hear what?"

"It sounded like a door shutting."

"You probably imagined it, cuz I didn't hear nothin'."

The first guard shrugged and went back to studying his hand. As he looked back at the door down at the end of the corridor again, just to be sure, his friend leaned over and stole a peek at his cards.

"See. I told you it was nothin'," the second guard relayed. When his friend turned around again, he was already casually leaning back in his chair, pretending to ruminate on how to play his hand even though he already knew he'd won this round.

As the two men bet with small polished pebbles of various colors and sizes, tossing them into a pile on the middle of the table, they missed the shimmer that swiftly moved passed them.

Gaewen rounded the bend to find a scorpion class battle Centurion standing in front of a heavily armored set of doors that were obviously the Sally port of the palace prison.

She stood frozen in her tracks; Centurions were particularly good at catching anomalous sounds and had the ability to scan the room in infrared to detect any heat signatures. If she so much as made a noise louder than a mouse squeak, the thing would activate and run security scans and she'd be entirely visible to it.

Instead of taking the machine head-on in a fight, however, she tiptoed right up to it and crouched down under its large pincer-arm canon. Reaching into a side-pocket on her cloak, she drew out what looked like a credit card with delicate circuitry printed on the surface. More accurately, it was a sticker of pre-printed techno-phage adhesive. The techno-phage adhesive, when applied to an electronic device, would meld with it and automatically upload a virus.

She slowly peeled off the adhesive and then slapped it onto a side-panel on the Centurion.

The Centurion's eyes lit up as it detected her presence then reared up to change its position and try to get a lock on her. As it scanned the room, unable to find her, it scuttled back on its stick-like legs and then switched into heat vision mode.

The techno-phage circuit began to glow bright white as it fed the machine a malicious code to take it out of commission. The Centurion's red eyes flickered briefly and then went dark as the whole machine slumped back down into its resting position.

"That's better," Gaewen whispered, squeezing past the slumbering metal beast. She flipped over the card and pulled off the back side then slapped the second piece of techno-phage adhesive onto the prison cell doors. The locking mechanism whined in protest, but the virus won out in the end and then, with a noisy clunk, the heavy doors unlocked.

Nervous that the rather loud door mechanism may have alerted the guards, Gaewen glanced back over her shoulder. When she was certain their attention hadn't been aroused, she quietly slipped inside the prison.

Quickly scanning the interior of the hexagonal waiting room, she found several smaller suites behind reinforced glass lining each opposing wall. Only one suite had any lights on signaling to her that it was most likely Zallek's cell.

Gaewen quietly went over to the access panel and typed in the security override code she'd stolen from the manufacturer of these prefab prison cells. If the code was valid, it would run a security bypass on a password reset. Then, even if the system required biometric data, she'd just input her own.

After a retina scan and a finger print scan, along with her personally selected security code, the glass wall finally opened and let her into the holding cell.

She turned off her invisibility cloak and, not seeing any signs of Zallek, casually walked toward the bathroom. Although there was no bathroom door, steam was billowing out of the entrance, alerting her to the fact that he was showering.

Gerrard Van Zallek stepped out of the shower, rubbing his hair with a white towel. Stark naked, he stopped what he was doing and looked up only to find a strange, green-skin woman wearing heavy tactical gear standing in his private room, staring at his naked body. He smiled. "And who might you be, my precious?"

"I'm Major Gaewen Feradorn. Senator Targon Van Morgan felt you needed to be extracted as discreetly as possible, so he hired me."

"So, you're a Spook?"

A "Spook" was a special operative who excelled at recon, extraction, rescue ops, and assassinations—if needed. The tech they used made them into veritable ghosts, allowing them to slip in and out of places undetected. And if Senator Targon had sent a Spook to collect him, Zallek took it as a bad sign.

Was he being rescued or was this woman an assassin? Although Zallek and Targon were allies, he still didn't trust the corrupt politician as far as he could throw him.

"This spook is going to save your sorry ass," she said, her eyes trailing down as she stole a glimpse of his male anatomy.

"You like what you see?" he asked, turning slightly, so she could get a better look at his tightly clenched butt.

Pretty enough, she thought, but she had no time for such distractions. "We don't have much time," she said with a crooked grin on her mouth. "Maybe a raincheck."

"I'll hold you to it," he fired back, his crooked grin growing into a full smile. Before he could finish wrapping the towel around his waist, however, Gaewen spun on her heels and hurried over to the ventilation duct. She swiftly drew out a small tool kit, fetched a power screwdriver from it, and revved the little thing in her hands as he watched.

"What in the world are you doing?" Zallek asked as he began to dress.

"The trick to getting in and out of a place undetected is to always leave a different way than you came in."

"I meant, won't that trigger the prisoner breach alarm?" he asked skeptically, nodding at the vent.

She pried off the panel and set it on the floor next to her, "I've already changed the security settings to your cell," she answered. She pulled her cloak off, revealing the charcoal gray, skin-tight smart suit she wore beneath. It hugged her womanly form with the delicacy of a fine satin glove.

"Impressive," he said, making a double entendre about both her skills and her body. He wasn't typically into the buff military type, but she was feminine enough that he couldn't peel his eyes off her perfectly sculpted ass.

After rolling the cloak up and fixing it to the elastic bands on her belt, she put back her tools and looked over her shoulder at Zallek. "Follow me," she said, and then squeezed into the small crawl space.

Zallek finished buttoning the collar of his copper colored shirt, leaving the top two unfastened so he could show off his chest. "By all means," he said, gesturing for Gaewen to go on ahead of him, "after you."

A degenerate smile formed on his mouth and he licked his lips, admiring Gaewen's tight ass as she disappeared into the ventilation duct.

16

After the giant Arkadian shrimp, the Bre'lal dancers, and dessert, Jegra felt it was finally time to give her closing speech.

When it seemed that everyone was satisfied with the evening's meal, she slid her chair back and rose to her feet. The delegation all stopped mid-sentence of whatever conversation they had drifted to in the atmosphere of celebration, and turned to hear what she had to say.

"Ladies and gentlemen from all the esteemed worlds of the Commonwealth and beyond...," pausing briefly, she brushed her dress down. She felt a little bit fidgety seeing as how public speaking wasn't exactly her forte, but gathering her nerves, she took a deep breath and then continued on with her address.

"I know we aren't meeting under the most ideal of circumstances. I know that you have each experienced loss and sacrifice that very few people have ever been burdened with. But I want you to know something. As long as we face tomorrow together, there is nothing that can stand in our way." She hiccuped in front of everyone, which drew a round of muffled snickers, and she blushed and excused herself. "Apologies, I may have been a little indulgent in my wine. Which means, I'm afraid, that it's time I humbly retire for the evening. Please enjoy the rest of your evening at your own leisure and feel free to get to know one another. Mingle. Make friends. And we'll convene sometime tomorrow after we're feeling better and our hangovers have worn off."

There was another round of laughter and Jegra turned to leave. Only her Imperial bodyguards followed. Lianica, being ship's captain, remained behind with the admiral to continue to get to know their new guests.

Jegra paused at the doors, turned around and gave the Dagon salute. She was surprised when the Earth Martian delegation replied in kind and she smiled and bowed her head ever so regally.

With that, she took her leave and stepped through the sliding doors. She paused in the empty opening, recollecting what Brei'Alas had warned her about, and was pleased to find that the lieutenant had successfully completed her mission.

It hadn't been forty-five minutes before Lieutenant Brei'Alas and the Imperial guard had rounded up all the names on the ship's manifest and had placed them in the brig for safe keeping.

Barrion was the last to step into his cell.

"I'm sorry," Brei said, raising her hand to the security glass. "If there was any other way…"

"It's all right," Barrion answered. "I understand."

"I promise I'll make it up to you," she said in a voice that hinted at another round of intimacy between the two of them.

"Oh yeah?" he asked.

"Promise," she answered. "Anything you want."

"Anything?" he asked, testing her sincerity.

"I can't make any guarantees, but I may have broached the subject with *you know who* and she wasn't totally opposed to the idea."

"You're kidding me," he said, skeptically.

Brei'Alas knew that the particular conversation she was referring to had been erased by the time reset and then sighed.

"Of course, I'm kidding!" she laughed. She made sure to overdo it, bringing it full circle to that awkward and cringey moment she was so well known for. "That's totally never going to happen." She snorted, for added effect and then batted her eyes at him.

"Way to get a guy's hopes up," Barrion said disappointedly, puffing out a blast of hot air.

"Just consider it payback for this," she said, pointing at the welt on her cheek.

"That's fair, I guess." Barrion crossed his arms and closed his eyes, recognizing he wasn't going to win this one.

"Chin up, lover boy," she said, placing her hand on the glass again. "We'll get through this."

He did the same. After a long pause, he said, "I love you."

"You'd damn well better," she replied, slowly drawing away from the glass. "Because if you didn't, I'd come in their and kick your ass all over again."

This brought a smile to his face and she turned toward the door. Once she arrived beside the guard, she glanced back one last time, offering a subtle wave goodbye before exiting the brig.

The guard nodded at her as she passed him and Brei strode into the hall determined to bring Jegra up to speed about everything she'd learned from the time jump.

Upon arriving at Jegra's quarters she rang the doorbell and then waited. When there wasn't any response, she reached out to ring it again, but before she'd even had a chance to push the chime a second time, the doors swiftly parted and a drunken Jegra swayed in the doorway.

The empress had a very large bottle of pinot grigio wine in her right hand and her mouth glistened light golden with the sweet residue bedewing her lips.

"Oh, it's you," Jegra said in a slurred voice, a half smile inadvertently forming on her face as if some amusing thought had occurred to her in that moment.

Brei smiled. "Yes, and I just wanted to check on you and see if..."

Jegra belched, interrupting whatever it was Brei had to say, the light scent of vitis vinifera grapes mingling with her sticky breath. Her sunken eyelids widened and slowly settled onto Brei. There was a moment of reflective thought on Jegra's face, then, unexpectedly, she reached out and clasped onto Brei's uniform. "You'll have to do," she said.

"Have to do what?"

"Quench my thirst," Jegra replied, drawing her into her chambers and dragging her along behind her.

As it dawned on her that the empress meant sex, she paused. "Are you sure, I mean, we could..."

Before Brei'Alas could even finish her sentence, Jegra leaned forward and kissed her on the lips.

Embarrassed, Brei drew back ever so slightly and was about to decline her offer as politely as possible when Jegra reeled her back in again. This time the empress's tongue slipped into her mouth and was swirling about, doing a playful series of pirouettes with her own forked tongue.

In her mind, she ran through every possible excuse to try and find the best way to rescind the offer without hurting the empress's feelings when Barrion's stupid lust-filled fantasy of the empress popped back into her head. Growing angry that her own boyfriend would rather sleep with Jegra than her, she said to herself, *screw it* and leaned into the kiss.

If either of them was to bed the empress, it was going to be her. And why not? At least then she could brag about it to Barrion. And maybe then, the very idea of her having been with Jegra would get him equally as excited to be with her and her alone.

She realized the rationale didn't make much sense, but she was a little bit distracted by Jegra's feeling her up and shoving her tongue further down her throat.

Unable to back out now, Brei decided to embrace the moment instead of shirking from it. When the empress's fingers slid down her arm, down her side, and then between her thighs, she leaned into the touch.

Brei reached up and wrapped her hands around Jegra's neck, and pulled herself onto her. Jegra moaned with a delicious kind of delight as Brei slipped effortlessly into her embrace, Jegra's hands cupping the fullness of her perfectly tight ass.

Both women stumbled through the room toward the bed, their clothes falling off one garment at a time as they hastened to the chase. Stumbling into Jegra's bed together, Brei landed on top of Jegra. As they lay entwined, they paused and looked into each other's eyes as if to take in the moment.

"Are you sure about this?" Brei asked hesitantly.

When Jegra's lips spread into a welcoming smile, Brei smiled in kind and, as though an unseen magnetic attraction was drawing them closer, their lips crashed together again and the kiss was quickly followed up with sensuous moans which resounded throughout the royal suite.

At the crack of dawn, Brei's eyes snapped open and she looked over at the elegant woman sleeping next to her in the king-sized bed. *"Oh, no, no no,"* she whispered to herself. "What have you done, Brei?"

Jegra slept peacefully beside her, one leg and one large breast peeking out of the silk sheets that only partially covered her nudity.

Cautiously, Brei slid to the foot of the bed until, unexpectedly, she fell out and disappeared over the edge. She hit the floor with a thump and then popped back up, eyes locked on Jegra, fear building in her chest.

"Don't wake up, don't wake up," she pleaded in a barely audible voice. When Jegra didn't rouse from her slumber, Brei let out a sigh of relief and slowly gathered her clothes.

She dressed hastily, forgoing her underwear, as she scurried toward the door, threading one leg into her dress at a time only to freeze halfway across the room when she realized that she was forgetting her shoes. She twisted her head back around only to find them laying by the end of the bed. Rolling her eyes, she tiptoed back the way she'd come.

Careful not to make any sound, she slowly squatted down and retrieved her pumps. As she was down there, however, she felt a strangely uncomfortable feeling between her butt cheeks. Reaching a slender hand down between her legs, she reached up the opening of her dress and felt around until she found it. Plucking it out, she held up a butt-plug and looked at it with a petrified sort of amusement.

For the life of her she couldn't remember getting into anything as kinky as this. But, in her defense, she had helped Jegra finish off five additional bottles of white wine.

Not knowing what to do with the rascally thing, she set it neatly on the small round table next to the entrance that contained an ornate vase and beautiful floral arrangement. Then, slinking up to the door, she glanced back one last time to catch a glimpse of the sleeping empress before slipping out of Jegra's chambers.

Relief washed over her once she was standing on the other side of Jegra's door. Through the thin fabric of her dress, the coolness of the wall felt good against her back as she leaned against it. It invigorated her and she looked up at the ceiling lights and took in a deep breath.

Her body ached in all the right places, and she couldn't help but smile. This wasn't a walk of shame. She liked the empress. Almost as much as she liked Barrion, if she was being honest. And, last night they'd shared a moment.

In her mind, even if Jegra turned out to be a little too drunk to remember much of anything, let alone who she'd done it with, Brei had no regrets. She'd fulfilled a long-standing fantasy. And she wouldn't take it personally if, after last night, the empress wanted to keep things strictly professional.

"*No regrets,*" she repeated to herself. Sauntering barefoot all the way back to her quarters, a light bounce in her step the entire way, she realized she was still beaming with the aftereffects of the prior evening's lustful affair. Pausing at her door, she quickly composed herself before entering her quarters.

The doors parted and she entered the chamber; a shaft of light cut across the room and lit up Barrion's sleeping face . Being roused awake, he looked up at Brei with weary, half-opened eyes that showed he was barely awake but, lucky for her, still mostly asleep.

"Where were you last night?" Barrion asked, stretching his arms over his head and letting out a yawn.

She tossed her high-heels on the floor. "Oh, you know," she sighed, "I just got back from the empress's personal chambers." A sly grin formed on her lips as she heard herself say it but she tried to keep it subdued.

"You two have a meeting or something?"

"No," she said, looking right at him. "We fucked."

"Ah-haha-ha," he laughed drearily. "Good one." Not believing her, he rolled over and went back to sleep, snoring as soon as his head hit the pillow.

She rolled her eyes and then went into the bathroom to take a shower and freshen up for her morning shift.

17

The escape plan was simple. First, they'd make their way to the boiler room where they'd escape through the large fans that cooled the boiler and regulated its temperature. Once they were out in the open, they'd use her invisibility cloak and tread through the long central pool which didn't have any pressure sensors. Upon reaching the rear exit, they'd then make a mad dash across the place lawn to the only segment where there was no wall—the part where the palace lawn met the desert.

It was rumored that the empress hadn't wanted any palace wall at all but was talked into it for security reasons. Even so, the Southern Reach that overlooked Arena City remained completely open. All it had for protection was a high-powered energy barrier which abdicated the need for any physical wall in that section.

As such, Gaewen had set up a field disruptor when she'd first broken into the palace grounds. If the energy barrier was activated, it would part the energy shield like an umbrella parting a waterfall, splitting the water like a curtain.

Once through the energy barrier, it was a clear shot across the dunes to her ship. They'd need to double-time it so as to avoid any teleport locks, but she had some scramblers to help mask their bio-signatures and avoid any teleport snares they might happen to run into during their escape.

If all went according to plan, they'd be out of there in fifteen minutes tops. What she hadn't counted on, however, was being teleported into a holding cell opposite Zallek's before they'd even reached the end of the ventilation duct.

When she finally finished materializing, she slammed her fists on the glass. "Evek'dam Gammut baqui'lock!" she cursed. There must have been a backup detector somewhere within the ventilation ducts she hadn't anticipated.

Obviously, she'd triggered it and was flagged as an intruder and teleported instantly into the holding cell directly opposite the one she'd just escaped from.

"And who might you be?" a voice called out from the shadows at the far edge of the room.

Danica Valencia stepped out from the darkness, both arms folded disparagingly across her chest. Her metallic shoulder glinted in the dim lighting of the brig as she glared at the Bre'lal mercenary who was trying to steal her prisoner out from under her nose.

"Major Gaewen Feradorn," the woman said in an icy tone that revealed her frustration of getting caught.

"Major, did you honestly think I'd idly sit by as you tried to make off with *my* prisoner? I implanted a genetic tracker in that asshole the first time I pretended to let him seduce me, over a year ago."

"What?" Zallek asked, realizing that Danica had been working against him from the very beginning. "You tainted me with your filthy mods?" He groaned in disgust. But she merely ignored him and continued on with her interrogation of the major.

"And who, might I ask, contracted you for this mission?"

As a prisoner of war, Gaewen had nothing more to say to Danica other than her name and rank. But as a woman who had watched Danica's humiliation bout last year, she couldn't help but be curious about the infamous traitor of the Dagon Empire.

"I recognize you from the games, you know. Did it feel good?" Gaewen asked. "Vindicating yourself and proving to the whole Commonwealth that you weren't the traitor that you were branded to be? Not many get to regain their honor like that. It must have filled you with an unspeakable satisfaction."

Danica squinted at the major, uncertain as to where she was going with this. But she allowed the line of questioning, if only out of her own morbid curiosity to follow this rabbit hole wherever it led.

"Let's make a deal. I'll tell you what you want to know if you tell me what I want to know about who contracted you."

"Fair enough," Gaewen replied. She folded her arms and waited for Danica's reply.

"Even though I won the fight, I can never undo the damage to my reputation. That's why I have devoted myself so fully to serving Jegra. She's the only one who has always stood by me, no matter what. When the lies were spread about me, she never believed them. Not for an instant. Instead, she expressed her faith in me. She's the only person in this whole bleedin' galaxy who stands up for the innocent. For the helpless. And she may be the last flame bearer of compassion and love in these ever-darkening times. And if I can help her in her fight for peace, love, and acceptance for all, then, well, everything will have been worth it. Does that answer your question?"

"Yes," replied Gaewen, smiling at Danica with a modicum of admiration. After a short pause, she cleared her throat and said, "As for who hired me, it was Senator Targon Van Morgan."

Such news was to be expected. Zallek, after all, had found a loophole in the siege and she was certain Senator Targon was going to ally himself with him so as to take full advantage of it. But in order to do so, he couldn't let his frisky pup off the leash, and was reeling him back in.

What Danica was more interested in, however, was why a woman like this Major Feradorn would agree to work for a man like Senator Targon. She wasn't Dagon. She had no vested interest in her world or her people's politics. And there were far better paying gigs than this, siege or no siege.

"So, Major," asked Danica, stepping closer to the glass of the holding cell, "tell me. What is it that you get out of all of this?"

Gaewen smiled. "A big fat paycheck," she proudly admitted. It wasn't any secret. She was in it for the money. Plain and simple. She threw her hands on her hips and then added, "Paying gigs are far and few between these days and every little bit helps."

"Helps?" Danica asked, her eyebrow rising to the top of her forehead. "With what exactly…are you in some kind of debt?"

"No," Gaewen laughed. "Helps with fending off the soul-crushing boredom of a galaxy under siege. Besides," she went on, waving one hand about nonchalantly, "a girl's gotta eat."

"And you'd sell out…just like that…for a man like Senator Targon?"

The major shrugged her shoulders, her palms facing upward as if to say it couldn't be helped. "A job's a job."

"In that case, what if I compensate you for your loss of earnings? That way, I get to keep my prisoner, you get your credits, and we all get to go our separate ways in peace."

Gaewen smiled. "How much were you thinking?"

"How much will it take?" Danica rejoined. If it was too much, she'd just leave the woman in the cell for illegal trespassing and be done with the whole ordeal. But if the sum was reasonable, she'd let her go. After all, Danica knew it was always better to have a freelancer like Gaewen in your pocket than to make an enemy of such a dangerous individual.

By paying her off, the major got to keep her integrity intact. By releasing her, she came into Danica's debt. Keeping her would only stir up the beehive of her indignation and make it impossible for them to play well together, or for that matter, ever do business with her again.

But, strangely enough, Danica had a good feeling about this woman. She didn't know why. There was just something about her. Something…endearing.

"Seven million credits ought to be enough to change my mind," the major said after giving it some thought.

Danica let out a sigh of relief. "Phew," she said with a laugh, "I honestly expected it was going to be a lot more."

"I meant to say eight million. So, do we have a deal?" Gaewen asked.

After a few moments, Danica smiled at the green-skin staring back at her from behind the glass partition. Reaching over, she smashed the unlock button and the glass parted, allowing Gaewen to go free. "Deal," she replied.

"I appreciate that," Gaewen said. She raised her wrist, her glowing holovid flickering to life. Danica did the same, brought up some funds, and then transferred the credits over to the major with a swipe of her hand.

"Eight million Commonwealth credits, in full."

"That should cover it," the major said, smiling pleasantly at having come out on top.

"Hey!" Zallek griped from his cell. "What about me?"

"What about you?" Gaewen asked coldly. She shot him a look that said he was no longer her problem and turned back to Danica. Extending her hand, she looked Danica squarely in the eyes and thanked her. "It's been a pleasure doing business with you, Danica Valencia."

Without so much as hesitating, Danica accepted her handshake. The moment Gaewen's hand slipped into hers, however, she felt the shock.

As a jolt of electricity surged into Danica's body, she had time to reflect on what a terrible mistake she'd just made. Letting her guard down like that was stupid. And now, she was paying the price for it.

Her eyes rolled back and she dropped to the floor like a sack of bricks. Unable to move, her every muscle seized with electricity, she looked up at the major with an expression of helplessness and betrayal—but most of all fury for being lied to and spurned.

"We…had…a…deal…" Danica managed to snarl through clenched teeth.

Gaewen stepped over Danica's immobilized body and said, "Once I accept a mission, I complete a mission. It's nothing personal," she explained, nodding at her wrist as she referred to their previous transaction, "it's just business."

The major went over to Zallek's cell and opened it for him.

Zallek sauntered out, relieved that things turned out in his favor. "For a moment there, Major Feradorn," he said, brushing his longish hair back, "you really had me going."

As he laughed like a nervous idiot, she glanced over her shoulder at him and rolled her eyes. Without so much as a reply, however, she went over to the weapons rack and fetched him a gun. Tossing it to him she said, "Move it, pretty-boy. We're wasting precious time."

With his blaster in hand, he raced out of the brig and out into the corridor. Zallek paused when he saw the sleeping Centurion but, fairly sure it was safe, slowly edged passed it. A few moments later he rounded the bend and his voice echoed down the hall, "Hey, fellas," followed by two plasma blasts.

Gaewen held back, pausing in the doorway as she looked back one last time to find Danica dragging her half-paralytic body behind her as she clawed her way toward them.

"Thanks for the bonus," Gaewen said in awe of Danica's unrelenting resolve. "Maybe we can do it again someday. Until then," she said in a sweet voice, "parting is such sweet sorrow."

She blew Danica a kiss and, their business concluded, reached out and slowly drew the heavy metal doors of the prison together. They creaked noisily and then slammed shut with a resounding clank, locking Danica inside. Free to make their escape, Gaewen smiled and passed the sleeping battle Centurion, stepped over the dead guards, and made her way up the spiral staircase.

18

Captain Lianica Blackstar was already lounging in her command chair, sipping a steaming hot cup of Angorian tea when Brei'Alas arrived on the bridge.

"Good morning, Captain," she greeted Lianica in her usual chipper fashion as she strode by.

"Morning Lieutenant," replied Lianica, looking at Brei from over the rim of her forest green mug, steam slowly wafting up from it. As Brei glided passed her, she caught a lovely scent of something. "Wait, Lieutenant…is that a new shampoo you're using?"

"Birtchkum shampoo and body wash," she replied with a smile. Nothing could ruin her day today. Even with the time travel drama of the past couple of days, she felt livelier than she had in ages.

"Ah, yes. The same kind the empress uses." When she saw Brei's face go white, she immediately felt bad. She hadn't meant to imply Brei was mimicking the empress. "What I mean to say is that it smells lovely. Excellent choice."

"Thank you, Lianica," Brei replied. She spun around and continued over to her station.

Lianica raised an eyebrow, a little surprised by Brei's bold use of informal language. In fact, there wasn't a moment in all of Brei'Alas's service that Lianica could remember a time when she hadn't strictly adhered to rank and protocol. Whatever had gotten into her had emboldened her to the point of having enough confidence to address the captain in the most informal of manners.

"And when we're on duty, it's Captain Blackstar, Lieutenant," Lianica said, blowing on her tea and eyeing Brei with a strict look.

"Right, Captain," Brei said, blushing. "Sorry, Captain. It won't happen again." She bowed respectfully and slunk away, glancing once or twice over her shoulder to make sure Lianica wasn't still eyeballing her with that evil-eye of hers.

A chime sounded and the comms officer, T'Zera, swiveled around in her seat and informed the captain, "We have an incoming hail. It seems to be originating from sector Alpha Tau. But the communique is too badly scrambled to play."

Lianica stood up, still cradling her tea in both hands. "Can you clear up the distortion?"

T'Zera swiveled back around, her fingers instantly dancing across the keyboard with agile strokes. "I'll try." After a few moments she shook her head in disappointment and then said, "I can't seem to get a lock on the frequency. Rather, frequencies. There are multiple frequencies, and they're all interfering with one another."

Brei'Alas leaned over her shoulder and studied the display. Then she looked at T'Zera and asked, "Do you mind?"

"By all means," T'Zera said, leaning back in her seat and gesturing for Brei'Alas to take over.

Brei typed in no more than three keys and, just like magic, the communication came in loud and clear.

"What did you do?" T'Zera asked, astonished at how quickly Brei had fixed the garbled message.

"It's not different frequencies, per se. It's the same frequency originating from multiple points in time."

"A spacetime dilation?" Lianica asked out loud, but the question was rhetorical. "What could be causing it?"

Brei looked over at Lianica with a big smile on her face. "I have no idea!" She then cheerfully slipped back into her seat. She may have sat down a little too vigorously, however. Pain shot up from her bottom and she groaned lightly and resituated herself to be more comfortable.

Lianica shot T'Zera a look which seemed to ask, "What has gotten into her?"

T'Zera merely replied with a shrug before returning to her duties. A few minutes later, when the captain wasn't watching, T'Zera leaned over and whispered in a sing-song voice, "Somebody got some last night. You don't get that sore unless you gobbled up an entire footlong—if you catch my meaning."

Brei looked around, cheeks flushing bright pink. "Is it that obvious?"

Both women giggled and T'Zera, keeping her eyes forward, whispered back, "You must have really worn Barrion out, seeing as he's late for his shift."

"It wasn't with Barrion," Brei let slip. She covered her mouth with both hands then looked over at T'Zera with startled eyes. "Oh, shit."

"You cheated on Barrion?" T'Zera asked, her eyes large with excitement and her ears perked up with interest. "Tell me everything."

"I can't," Brei replied. She looked away, embarrassed by the fact that she'd already said too much.

"Come on," T'Zera pleaded. "You have to tell me. You have to tell me before Barrion gets here."

Just then the doors to the bridge swooshed open and Barrion, late to his shift, stumbled onto the bridge. "Sorry, I'm late, Captain," he said.

Lianica eyed him with a harsh gaze that put him in his place and then said, "Don't let it happen again, Lieutenant Commander Barrion."

"I won't, ma'am," he answered with a Dagon salute.

In the middle of a sip of tea, she returned a quick, slightly perturbed salute, and dismissed him with a nod.

As he walked past Brei and T'Zera to man the science console, he leaned over, placing his head between the two women and said, "I had the wildest dream last night, Brei. You and Jegra hooked up in the most epic fling of the century."

"Ha-ha. Good one," she said, glancing nervously over at T'Zera whose jaw slowly fell open in revelatory shock.

Once Barrion had sauntered off to his post, Brei glanced at T'Zera only to find her staring at her even more intensely, her mouth agape. "No bleedin' way," she said at last.

"Please, don't tell him," Brei pleaded.

"No bleedin' way," T'Zera repeated, still in shock.

Brei did a double take of her friend's stunned expression but, seeing that it wasn't about to change, she turned back to her console and did her best to ignore T'Zera's incessant gawking.

Lianica raised an eyebrow as her officers seemed to be preoccupied by other matters and let out a long, exasperated sigh. "Will someone answer that bloody hail," she barked.

"Yes, ma'am," T'Zera said, snapping out of her daze. She tapped a series of buttons and a voice came onto the main comm.

"This is Emperor Rhadamanthus Dakroth. We're in the Alpha Tau sector. Please lock onto these coordinates and send help. The coordinates are…*skrrr*…I repeat, we request immediate evac…skrrr…Nephilim flagship has…skrrr…please, tell Jegra…skrrr…just like old times, and I need her to once again…skrrrr…my sorry ass."

Lieutenant T'Zera looked back at the captain. "I'm afraid that's all I could get before the message cut out, ma'am."

She glanced at all the faces of the bridge crew looking at her, waiting for her decision. Although she was loyal to Jegra, the emperor—who'd been missing for over a year—was her main priority.

"All right, ladies and gentlemen, attention, please. This mission has just become a rescue op. Lieutenant Brei'Alas, please take us to the Alpha Tau sector, maximum slipstream speed on my command."

"ETA, six hours and forty-seven minutes," she informed aloud after inputting the coordinates.

"Hit it," Lianica said with determination.

The *Shard* stretched into a long sliver the shape of a loom shuttle, and, in a flash of light, snapped away.

No sooner had they made the jump into the Stream than T'Zera abruptly sprang to her feet and practically shouted, "Bathroom break!" She reached down and grabbed Brei by her arm and hoisted her to her feet. "Lieutenant Brei'Alas has to go too."

"I do?" Brei asked, looking around the room with a perplexed look.

"Yes," T'Zera said, dragging her friend behind her, "you do."

After some girl talk, Brei and T'Zera returned to the bridge giggling. They both hurried back to their stations and T'Zera relieved Barrion, who was in her seat.

"Both of you, my ready room. Now!" Lianica barked, storming off ahead of Brei and T'Zera.

T'Zera gulped and Brei shot her a worried look. "Get ready for the dressing down of your lifetime."

"No regrets," T'Zera said.

They both rose to their feet and followed the captain into the adjoining ready room.

The moment the sliding doors had shut behind them, Lianica whipped around and glared at the two women who stood at attention.

"I don't know what is so important as to distract two of my finest bridge officers to the point of negligence, but it ends here and now. If you don't want me to write up a formal reprimand, I suggest you shelve whatever is going on here and get back to focusing on your jobs. Do I make myself clear?"

"Yes, ma'am," they said in unison.

"Dismissed," she snapped and pointed them toward the door, urging them to see themselves out.

Both women bowed, gave the Dagon Imperial salute and then, holding a half-bow for forty-seven seconds, as was customary after a dressing down, they slowly eased out of the room avoiding eye-contact with the captain.

When the doors shut, T'Zera looked at Brei and quipped, "What climbed up her butt?"

Brei held back a giggle. It wasn't appropriate. But it was funny. That's one of the things Brei liked about T'Zera. She was quippy.

"What was so important that you both had to cut out like that anyway?" Barrion asked, grilling them on the reason they snuck off to the bathroom for a bit of girl-talk.

"Like I said," T'Zera lied, "I had to pee."

"And you?" Barrion inquired, shifting his gaze to his girlfriend. Brei'Alas looked more nervous than ever and he couldn't help but wonder what was going on.

"Nothing. I, uh, peed with her."

"At the same time?" Barrion asked skeptically, one eyebrow raised in genuine curiosity.

"Ew, gross," T'Zera said, and shoved Barrion out of her chair. He backed away, raising his hands in surrender as he left them to it.

No sooner had Brei and T'Zera sat down at their posts than the empress herself, Jegra Alakandra, stepped onto the bridge, drawing the attention of everyone present. She glanced around at everyone's faces and then got down to brass tacks. "Report."

"We've received an SOS from Dakroth, Your Majesty," Barrion informed her. Since he was the highest-ranking officer currently on the bridge, it was his obligation to brief the empress.

He played her the message and as she listened, she looked over at Brei'Alas and stared at her for the entirety of the message.

T'Zera leaned over and whispered excitedly, "Your new girlfriend is staring at you."

"What?" Brei asked, looking over her shoulder. The moment she made eye contact with the empress, Jegra smiled.

"Lieutenant," the empress said in that special tone of voice that hinted at the fact that she had a favor to ask of her, "please notify me an hour before we get there. I'll be in the training arena if you need me."

"As Your Eminence wishes," she said, blushing slightly. With that, Jegra took her leave.

No sooner had the empress stepped out than T'Zera stood back up and turned to follow her out. As she went, Barrion cleared his throat.

"Where do you think you're going now?" he asked, folding his arms disapprovingly.

"I have to pee. But this time for *realsies*." She spun on her heels, whipping her ponytail in his face and sashayed her way right off the bridge.

After a moment, Brei rose up and stealthily snuck out. When Barrion glanced over at her position only to find her absent, turning just in time to see her slinking out the doors as she followed after T'Zera.

What has gotten into those two? he wondered.

As soon as one door closed another opened, and Captain Lianica stepped back onto the bridge only to find Brei and T'Zera's stations empty once more.

"Where in the bleeding galaxy are those two now?" she shouted, throwing her hands up in the air.

A rueful smile formed on Barrion's pursed lips as he tried to decide the best way on how to answer that. He opened his mouth to speak when, suddenly, she spoke for him.

"Never mind," Lianica said, taking her seat. As she leaned back, she slid herself to the edge and crossed her legs. Placing one arm on the armrest and resting her chin on her fist, she blew a stray tuft of hair out of her eyes and muttered, "I'm sure I don't want to know."

19

A **silver flash** glinted high above the ring world, Aldebaran. The *Shard* had arrived with the empress and the remaining survivors of the Human race.

The massive Nephilim battle cruiser hung in the distance as streams of dotted light pelted the massive ship from nearly every direction from the ring world's surface. This non-stop plasma fire resembled the spokes of a giant cosmic wheel and the central hub was the golden ship made of light.

Interestingly enough, the warship seemed unfazed by the excessive amount of firepower. It merely absorbed the plasma bolts in the same mysterious manner that the squiddies did.

Jegra stood upon the observation deck of the *Shard* wearing her trademark gladiatrix outfit. Hanging from her neck was metallic triangle pendant, a trophy from the first Scorpion Centurion she defeated bare-handed. She wove the feathers of the razor clawed Emriel Falcon—a bird the size of an Earth elephant—into various parts of her outfit. And she'd made a necklace from the teeth of the various monsters with whom she'd faced off in the Arena.

A discerning gaze settled on her face and she placed her hands behind her back as she took in the view of the firefight raging outside her window. It wouldn't be long now. Soon she'd show that bloated walking ego Et'vat H'aaztre precisely why she was the one called Jegra the Merciless.

She reached up and tapped a magnetic pin that was fastened to her metal bikini top. It chimed once she touched it, and she cleared her throat. "Lianica, this is the empress," Jegra said, opening a comm link to the bridge. "Prepare the *Shard* for ramming speed. Full ahead."

Lianica's voice came across the comm, "Copy that, Mother of Dagon."

Mother of Dagon was Jegra's call sign. It's also what the commoners called her. The refugees, mods, and destitute she'd taken in when she made Thessalonica a safe haven for all also referred to her as the Mother of Dagon. She liked it. And like any mother, she was extremely protective of her children.

And, speaking of children, it was her duty as empress to be the emperor's protector. He hadn't always made it easy on her, but he was still one of the pillars of the Empire. And if she was going to take down H'aaztre, she knew she was going to need Dakroth's help. Besides, something he'd relayed in the message caught her attention. Something only she'd pick out. "Just like old times," he'd said.

Old times. Those were the days when he continually manipulated her. Ensnared her. Double crossed her. And tried to ruin her at every turn. Indeed, those were the good old days. So, why would he tell her to come rescue him and then say it would be like the good old days unless he was trying to send her a message? Perhaps even some kind of warning.

The *Shard's* elongated teardrop shape began to stretch as its hull morphed into an even sleeker version of itself. The pointy tip extended menacingly outward like a harpoon seeking out its prey and the ship's plasma-coil thrusters ignited to full as it charged toward the Nephilim flagship.

When the two ships came within firing range of one another, the Nephilim cruiser unloaded hell, firing all forward-facing plasma cannons. Every battery spat out bolts of hot red energy which pinged off the *Shard's* reflective hull.

"You're not the only ones with an impervious ship," Captain Blackstar said under her breath as they flew into the hailstorm of plasma bolts.

Unable to do any damage, the enemy ship's cannons ceased their barrage, and, almost as soon as they'd stopped firing, swarms of fighters were deployed. Yet not a single one opened fire. Instead, one by one the enemy fighters sacrificed themselves, each one crashing into the silver teardrop-shaped vessel and exploding against its hull.

This too didn't faze the *Shard's* liquid metal hull which was designed to take just such a beating. The little ships, which were little more than gnats to it, merely rebounded off before exploding, or crashed into the hull and burned up. In the end, though, the *Shard* came out fine.

Out of nowhere, a deafening reverberation shook the crew of the *Shard* as the Nephilim cruiser ignited its thrusters to try and pull away from the fast approaching ship. But the *Shard* quickly corrected course and came spiraling down on the top of the Nephilim cruiser's hull.

Like a drill, the *Shard* cut into the massive battle cruiser. Four seconds later, it shot out the other side, followed by a massive fiery plume.

Aboard the Nephilim ship, Azra'il Nun braced herself. "Is she out of her fracking mind?"

"My dear Azzie," Dakroth said, waving his hand in the air in a sophisticated manner. "I'd like you to meet my better half. She may be a little bit unorthodox, but that's all part of her charm, I assure you."

"What in the galaxy are you prattling on about?" Azra'il snapped, turning toward Dakroth with an annoyed look on her face. Her eyes grew large with shock when she realized he wasn't just blathering on ad nauseam about nothing but, rather, was making a formal introduction.

"Hi'ya," Jegra said, her fist already cocked.

"Wait!" Azra'il said, throwing up her hand in distress.

Jegra paused, as if Azra'il Nun's words couldn't be disobeyed. She was, after all, The Voice of H'aaztre. Whatever she said, good or bad, you were compelled to do it. When Azra'il smiled out of relief, Jegra smiled in kind.

"Nah," Jegra said, her smile quickly fading. Pleasantries exchanged, Jegra launched her fist and struck Azra'il Nun across the right jaw and cheekbone with such force it sounded like the crack of lightning.

Azra'il crashed to the floor, knocked out cold with a single punch. Jegra turned to face the half dozen soldiers that were charging her and, with a powerful clap of her hands, she blew them all off their feet with a prevailing gust of wind.

When a large officer tazed her in the small of her back, she slowly turned and grabbed the stun rod. The volts of electricity crawled up her arm and through her body, but her rage was so strong that the ten-thousand volts merely seemed to tickle.

"Big mistake," she growled, and jerked it out of his hands. Startled by her raw strength, he staggered back. Jegra snapped the officer's stun rod across her knee, splitting it into two sparking halves which she casually tossed to the floor.

With a wave of her fingers, she gestured for him to come at her again.

He hesitated before lunging at her. As he came at her, she nimbly stepped out of the way and he overshot her, throwing a wild punch that went nowhere. When he turned around, she smiled and waved at him to try again.

Tired of her dancing about, he shifted his stance and prepared for another strike but, without warning, his vision blurred and he suddenly felt as though his entire body had been through a meat grinder.

That's about the same time his eyes rolled back in his head and he lost consciousness.

Jegra called it the praying mantis attack. The trick was to move so fast the enemy can't see the punches as they land, while, at the same time, the rest of you appears to move slow. Get them off balance, strike, and then as their equilibrium slowly spirals out of control, let them realize their mistake just before blacking out.

"Behind you!" Callestra shouted.

Jegra spun around in time to see a korridium hatchet spiraling through the air. She reached out with one hand and, pinching her fingers as tightly as she could, caught it before it could do any damage to her.

She flipped the hatchet up, took it by the handle, and then lobbed it back at the soldier who'd thrown it at her. Her throw was so powerful, that when the axe imbedded itself into his chest, his whole body lifted off the ground and he flew back into one of the large control monitors.

Glass shattered, metal fractured and sparks shot out as debris rained down onto the floor. The sound of tinkling of glass filled the air and more voices of soldiers rallying themselves rose above the din of the pandemonium that had broken out on the bridge.

"Get her!" they shouted as a group.

All of a sudden, red flashes ignited the room and the remaining two dozen soldiers all dropped to the floor, screaming in agony as their severed limbs smoldered. Others fared much worse, either decapitated or sporting new holes in the middle of their foreheads that smoldered with wispy strands of white smoke.

Jegra turned to Dakroth. "I had it under control."

"And I, my luv, was getting bored," he replied. He blew on his still hot, orange glowing finger to help cool it and, at the same time, the Dygra crystal in his chest was already dimming.

"What about her?" asked Jegra, nodding down at Azra'il Nun's unconscious body.

Callestra pulled out a knife and marched toward the unconscious woman. She crouched down and scooped the woman's head up into her lap, then reached into her mouth and grabbed ahold of her tongue. Prying it out of her mouth as far as it would go, she slowly pressed the blade into the wet, pink muscle, drawing blood.

Callestra rose back to her feet and tossed the slab of meat at Jegra's feet. Jegra looked down at the severed tongue, grimaced, then looked back up at Dakroth. "Remind me never to piss this one off," she said, jutting a thumb at Callestra.

"You're telling me?" he jested.

"You do both realize that I'm standing right here, right?" Callestra sounded less than amused as she eyed them with her fiery gaze. They both looked at her, then each other.

Jegra eyed her up and down, scrutinizing every aspect. After a few intense seconds of uncertainty, when the tension was so high that Dakroth took a step forward to maybe try to diffuse things, Jegra smiled at Callestra and said, "You're as pretty as you are vicious. I can see why he likes you."

Dakroth let out a sigh of relief and then smiled at Callestra, who was herself a little taken aback by Jegra's response. She half expected the empress to hate her guts, but instead, she just brushed by her and carried on with the mission.

As was custom, Callestra followed her emperor and empress the allotted ten steps behind. She gently slid her blade back into the sheath on her back.

It was smooth sailing all the way to the airlock. Once inside, they paused and looked at the three Dagon EV suits waiting for them among an entire room full of the Nyctan EV suits, which had a strange, almost organic quality to them.

"How'd you pull this off?" Callestra asked, picking up a helmet to the female Dagon spacesuit.

"I had them teleported up when I came onboard. I figured they'd be so preoccupied with the security breach on the command deck that a few EV suits wouldn't matter much. Besides, even if they did come down to check it out and found three empty suits, they'd probably still be looking for the mysterious Dagon infiltrators."

"A nice diversion," Dakroth said, getting his own suit prepped.

"Remind me why we're jumping out of a starship and onto a ring world again?" Callestra asked as she strapped her chest plate into place with Jegra's assistance.

"I want to fly off the radar," Jegra said.

Callestra gave her a confounded look. She wasn't familiar with that particular Earther idiom. "Off the radar?"

"Using the teleporter would give away our location. It's best we keep them off balance. We force them to predict our next move, not the other way around. That way we have the strategic advantage."

"That's all and well," Callestra replied, "but they could decide to launch an orbital strike and obliterate everyone from up here. Then what?"

"Do you have a better idea?" asked Jegra.

Callestra looked over at Dakroth, who gave her the go-ahead with a subtle nod. She turned back to Jegra and relayed her idea. "As Vice Admiral of the Imperial Fleet, it's my job to offer tactical options during an active space battle. I still think we should take the ship out and then worry about getting back to the surface."

"No offense, Vice Admiral, but I already thought of that. This ship is massive. There are at least seven thousand crewmen aboard, and even if we did get to the main engineering room undetected, then we'd have to get out again. At the moment, there are far fewer enemies on the surface."

Dakroth cleared his throat and then asked, "What about Callestra's concern about an orbital strike?"

Jegra smiled. It was cute that he was trying to support Callestra's opinion. It meant he really did care about her, that she wasn't just another fling for him.

"The *Shard's* scans detected about six hundred Nephilim and Nyctan forces setting down on the surface. My bet is they're first going to try and round up the resistance for executions. Make a public statement, squash any further rebellion. I intend to not let that happen. Nonetheless, as long as their forces are down there, they will likely try to avoid any orbital strikes."

"But we can't be certain," stressed Callestra.

"No, we can't," Jegra agreed. "But if we destroy the ship now, they'll just call in for more reinforcements. Right now, we have enough on our plate to worry about."

"I concur," Dakroth said, backing up Jegra's plan. "It is practically impossible to take on all of H'aaztre's forces. His army seems to be endless. Which is why we must switch to guerrilla warfare."

"Appear weak when you are strong, and strong when you are weak," Jegra said aloud, speaking only to herself.

When they both turned to her, mistakenly thinking she was addressing them, she realized she'd recited the words of Sun Tzu aloud.

"It's from the teachings of a famous military general on my homeworld."

"Wise words," Callestra said.

Once all three had fully suited up in the EV spacesuits, they depressurized the airlock and opened the hatch. Outside, fighters chased the *Shard* in the distance. A little bit beyond that they could see the arch of the ring world looping into the evening stars.

Jegra pointed her thick-gloved hand at their target. "It's just a freefall straight down to the landing zone."

"I don't see it," Callestra said. She zoomed in with full magnification on her visor and still had trouble finding it, until, finally a bright red flare down on the surface lit up the landing zone.

"There," Jegra stressed, nodding her head inside her helmet.

"Got it," Callestra said, and without another word, she leapt out of the hatch and into space.

"After you, my dear," Dakroth said, gesturing for Jegra to go on ahead of him. She jumped out, falling headfirst after Callestra.

As Dakroth edged up to the open hatch, he couldn't help but feel as though he was being watched. He turned toward the entrance to the ship to find Azra'il peering at him through the small rectangular window. She rubbed her jaw as blue blood seeped from her lips. Dakroth smiled and winked at her, and then spun and threw himself into the vacuum of outer space.

"Graah!" Grendok roared, ripping his battle axe out of the chest of a fallen Nephilim soldier.

Off to his right were several of his men and women, mostly scientists, doing their best to hold their ground. But the enemy forces kept advancing. That's when golden beams of light manifested all around them and a battalion of soldiers, courtesy of the *Shard,* appeared all around them. Several of the

Dagon forces drew up their plasma rifles and began laying down cover fire for the battered scientists to retreat to a safer distance and regroup.

A blue Dagon officer scanned the battlefield and spotted Grendok a short distance away. Since she recognized him, he assumed she must be familiar with one of his doppelgängers.

"My name's Lieutenant Brei'Alas Kusagara," she said in a rather chipper voice.

"You couldn't have come at a better time, Lieutenant," Grendok said smiling at the girl with his yellow teeth and strange slatted goat pupils. His face drained of any relief, however, when a Nephilim soldier reared up behind Brei with a Nyctan-forged flamberge blade.

"Watch out!" Grendok warned as the solder brought the wavy blade down onto the unsuspecting girl with all his strength.

Miraculously, the giant soldier and his sword froze mere centimeters above Brei'Alas's head. That's when she winked at the satyr, who raised a surprised eyebrow.

Brei drew out her sword and, holding it in both hands, swung around, her blade arching high and wide. She swiped at his neck and then came full around where she paused, holding her sword out to the side as cobalt blood dripped off it.

The deed done, she stepped to the side, time un-froze, and the big lug staggered forward, clasping at the slit upon his neck which spewed forth an azure mist. Then, gurgling some indiscernible gibberish, he toppled to the ground.

"By Pan's beard! I've never seen such an impressive trick, my dear. You have truly been blessed by the gods."

She smiled at him and then turned to face the oncoming wave of soldiers. As she beheld the intimidating numbers, her hand began to tremble. She took a breath and locked down her nerves.

You're a goddamn soldier, Brei, she reminded herself. *You've trained for this.* Holding her sword at the ready, she took a deep breath and prepared to meet the onslaught head on.

Grendok merely grinned, hoisted his battle axe up and, gripping it tightly in both hands, leaped and bounded across the terrain. He bounded over Brei and crashed down on three soldiers at once, knocking them over like bowling pins.

Then, spinning like a top, he sliced into another six soldiers.

No matter how many he cut down, though, more soldiers seemed to appear in their place. Upon the ridge, another dozen had surrounded him. He took wild swipes with the axe and bleated at them menacingly, but they held their distance. Instead of using their blades, they drew their plasma rifles and aimed them squarely on the satyr.

"Cowards!" he shouted.

Just as it seemed they were about to fire, everything around them slowed to a crawl. The explosions in the distance, the surrounding plasma fire, even the Dagon security troops all froze. Brei'Alas sidled up to him and he looked over at her. They were the only two on the whole battlefield still moving fluidly through time.

"Shall we?" Brei asked, finally catching up to Grendok's position. This time he winked at her.

They moved swiftly, each of them making sure every laceration was a lethal hit to the enemy. After they'd gone around like a couple of dancers doing dual pirouettes, Brei released her hold on time and a spray of blood erupted all around them as arteries tore open and spurted gallons of blood, drenching them in the blue blood of the Nephilim.

"I haven't seen a Time-Walker since the campaigns, girl. Out of curiosity, who were your parents?"

Brei turned to the satyr, her face hard as stone. "I never knew my parents. I was adopted," she said.

"I see," he replied. With yet another battalion of enemy troops marching toward them, he turned around, his back to the girl, and said in a low voice, "In that case, we shall make a name for ourselves here. Right here upon this battlefield."

Unexpectedly a horn blew, and the battalion that was marching toward them fanned out. It seemed as though every soldier had split into two. That's when Brei realized they weren't facing just a few hundred, but closer to several thousand enemy combatants.

She gulped hard and then drew up her plasma rifle in one hand and her sword in the other.

"Stay close, Lieutenant. As long as we keep a tight perimeter, we'll do fine."

She nodded but didn't speak. The truth was, she was so scared she thought she might piss herself. But she grunted a few times and then hopped up and down all the while taking in deep breathes as she got herself amped up for the fight.

"That's the spirit, lassie," Grendok said, appreciating her get up and go. Preparing himself for the fight, he crouched low, holding his trusty battle axe tightly in his hands.

The wall of soldiers seemed to keep widening with no end in sight. Then, about four hundred meters into the heart of the horde, something from the sky crashed down like a flaming comet and a massive explosion erupted.

Screams rang out as soldiers flew into the air in all directions. It looked like a small nuclear warhead had gone off, and a dust cloud rose up from the impact site.

When the dust had dissipated, rising up from the crater of bones and death was none other than the empress herself—Jegra Alakandra, Gladiatrix of the Galaxy.

"Yes!" Brei, shouted, raising her blaster into the air and firing off a few shots out of the overwhelming excitement of having the cavalry arrive.

Jegra's space suit was all but demolished from the massive impact and only small pieces of cloth and warped metal clung to her. She tore off the fragments and tossed them aside, her trademark metal bikini making its grand appearance.

She looked back and smiled at Brei and Grendok and then threw out both hands. A massive battle axe, twice as big as Grendok's, manifested as if out of thin air in Jegra's hands. She wheeled around and faced the soldiers, who were only just beginning to regroup.

Roughly two dozen soldiers turned, their black and golden armor shining even in the haze of the dust that lingered in the air around the crash site. They slowly tightened their perimeter and surrounded her. As they encroached, blasters trained on the empress, one of them got up enough gumption to shout, "Surrender yourself! You're completely surrounded!"

"All I'm surrounded by," she snarled, "is fear and dead men."

Jegra blurred out of focus. She moved so fast, and one by one she cut them down. Not a single warrior on the field seemed to have strength, speed, or agility that could match hers. Instead, Jegra made a mockery of the Nephilim forces by showing them what a real warrior was capable of.

Spartacus, an ancient Earth gladiator, led a rebellion that began with just a couple hundred well-trained gladiators and slaves, and these browbeaten men and women went up against the superior forces of the entire Roman army who were legend. And they won confrontation after confrontation, reminding all they faced off against that the title of Gladiator was earned, and meant something far more than an expendable, battling slave. The title of Gladiator was one of honor and dignity, and it was earned.

In his final battle against Crassus, Spartacus and two-thousand warrior slaves met forty-thousand Roman soldiers upon the battlefield. And while Crassus defeated Spartacus's rebels and crucified six-thousand of his men and women warriors, the man himself slipped away into the sands of time, only to grow into the legend that he's remembered as today.

As the bodies of Nephilim and Nyctan soldiers piled up all around them, Brei and Grendok shared a look that acknowledged it was now or never. Charging forward, they picked off the stragglers and the scraps that Jegra left behind in her destructive wake.

As Brei and Grendok engaged the enemy, they heard a familiar voice. "Mind if we join you?"

Brei turned in time to see the emperor and Callestra touch down beside them. Their EV suit thrusters fired blue as they set foot upon the battlefield.

"Your Excellency," Brei said, bowing reverently.

Dakroth smiled at her and then pulled out a side pistol and began firing off precisely aimed shots. Brei looked over at Callestra and offered her sword. "Vice Admiral Van Morgan, please, take this."

She smiled at Brei and then drew out a blade from the sheath attached to the small of her back. She then took the weapon in both hands and pulled it apart, revealing it to be two blades. "No, thanks, luv. I brought my own."

With that Callestra raced into the battle screaming like a banshee. Brei turned and stood still, watching the chaos unfold around her as if in slow motion. She hadn't realized she'd triggered a time wind-down. Looking up at the sky, the *Shard* was taking on a swarm of fighters, while the Nephilim cruiser had a gaping hole in its hull as it lingered motionless in the sky above them.

All around her, Dagons and satyrs fought side by side as they struggled against the Nyctan and Nephilim forces. But she knew that no matter how hard they fought, they were severely outnumbered and that before the day's end, there'd be more than enough death and bloodshed on both sides to make the rivers of Aldebaran run red.

20

Each gasping breath scraped along the walls of her throat with dryness as Jegra stood in the clearing she'd carved out. Smoke and dust created a uniform haze that surrounded her. In the thick of the murkiness, she could hear the cries of some injured soul whimpering with pain.

Jegra set down her massive, double-headed axe, blue blood smeared across the blade. She had but a few cuts and bruises, yet they were already shrinking away as her hyper healing abilities constantly mended the damage she endured.

Her chest heaved as she took in another breath. The trails of sweat that trickled down her chest and thighs left narrow, clear tracks through the grime of blue Nephilim blood that glazed her skin.

She looked up and saw Dakroth standing in the distance. Callestra, his loyal...whatever she was...by his side. Grendok and Brei'Alas stood a few meters beyond them and were looking about as exhausted as she felt. In her defense, though, she'd killed nearly seven times as many enemy combatants as anyone else on the battlefield.

The first forty-five minutes of the battle had been utterly brutal. Almost as soon as she'd crashed down and joined the fray, another one-hundred and twenty security officers from her ship teleported down along with three Centurion battle robots. Two of the machines survived the fight; one did not. The crippled machine lay thirty meters off to the side, its battered husk still sparking about every ten seconds or so.

Luckily, before they'd lost too many lives, Jegra had managed to get as many of the scientists and civilians into the main research facility—the only building made of proper concrete—and had posted Centurions, along with a dozen security guards, out front to protect those inside.

Dark motes of ash fluttered to the ground all around her after the firefight. Dakroth had vaporized his fair share of enemy soldiers and the Centurions did a hell of a lot of the lifting too. What really surprised her, however, was that Brei'Alas had killed nearly as many enemies as Callestra. She wasn't expecting that level of ferocity to be present in such a timorous woman.

"Brei'Alas," Jegra called out across the distance between them, panting. "Good work."

Brei opened her mouth to speak, but all she could do was take in more air. Her arms felt like lead weights at her sides and she could barely raise her plasma rifle, let alone a heavy metal sword. Instead of speaking, she merely smiled at Jegra and gave a thumbs up. Then, using her hip, hoisted her gun up and fired off a shot.

The blast hit near Jegra and she startled and pivoted to see what Brei was shooting at. It happened to be a Nyctan soldier who'd been crawling toward the empress, hiding behind the carnage and dead bodies, to try and sneak up on her. But Brei'Alas had seen and dealt with him, and now he lay dead among the heap of his fallen comrades.

Brei let the rifle fall back down and she stood hunched over, still trying to catch her breath.

The attacks came in waves, and Jegra had a feeling that this lull was nearly over. The next torrent would soon be upon them.

She turned to find that the Nephilim and Nyctan forces had pulled back to a safe distance. They still had a solid eight hundred warriors, and she was down to about eighty or ninety of her fighters, but her small band of soldiers had wiped out over six hundred enemies in the first engagement.

By the first hour and a half mark of the battle, the enemy soldiers had tried to flank Jegra's forces from the north and the west. Luckily, they had the emperor on their side and Dakroth had turned them into cinders, wiping out an entire battalion in the blink of an eye.

Dakroth's help had given them the edge they needed to actually win against seemingly impossible odds. And even Jegra had to admit that he was quite impressive on the battlefield.

The emperor moved so elegantly when he fought, like a dancer. It was amazing to her that he always managed to evade each and every little attack so effortlessly; nobody could lay a finger on him. Jegra knew that to fight like that, well, you had to be leagues above everyone else in both skill and strength.

And Callestra wasn't half bad either. She fought with a kind of rage Jegra had rarely seen on or off the battlefield. Although, the fact that it seemed as though she had been trying to keep with Jegra's kills for the first thirty minutes of the fight was, admittedly, a little bit strange. But Jegra chocked it up to a bit of friendly rivalry, and eventually Callestra began to tire, just as Jegra got her second wind.

Still standing in the clearing by herself, Jegra closed her eyes and breathed through her nose, inhaling deeply. She exhaled, expelling any remaining tension and then craned her neck upward and gazed with smoldering brown eyes at the Nephilim battlecruiser hanging over them. The *Shard* lingered further out and the crescent arc of the ring world loomed in the distance, far beyond either of them.

If Azra'il Nun had wanted to blast the ground forces into smithereens, all she had to do was aim those giant plasma cannons down at the surface. The fact that she hadn't done so suggested to Jegra that she was gathering intel on battle. In all likelihood, she was probably recording the fight, studying patterns and techniques, perchance to discover any potential weaknesses in her opponents that she could later exploit.

Honestly, Jegra couldn't blame her. She would have done the exact same thing. Watching your opponents' fights gave you a clear insight into their offensive and defensive strengths and weaknesses. At the same time, it helped you formulate counter attacks as well as give you an edge over the enemy, allowing you to predictably evade anything they might throw at you.

It was because of this that Jegra had ordered the *Shard* to keep the enemy fighters distracted. She'd studied the invasion footage. She had watched hours upon hours of holovid recordings of how the Nephilim consistently used their fighters to bomb cities and communities to rubble, sowing chaos and crippling infrastructure, only to teleport down with ground forces that swept through the streets, taking prisoners and killing insurgents.

She'd seen how they operated with blitzkrieg style attacks, always destroying their enemies' least protected areas at the same time they crippled their military and defensive positions. Because of the sheer number of Nephilim forces, it was impossible to match them head on, and so one was forced to engage in more guerrilla style warfare.

Even though Sun Tzu never had to worry about high-yield explosives raining down from the sky, his words of advice still rang true. Give the enemy no rest and when they are distracted, attack with deception. That's why she'd boarded Azra'il's ship. It was completely unexpected during a ship to ship collision.

Right now, though, Jegra knew that the last thing they needed were bombing raids. They simply weren't equipped to take on fighters from above. Which was why she was so thankful for the new, much-improved, and heavily armed *Shard*.

Fortunately, the *Shard* now had an entire battery of plasma cannons and high-velocity rail guns which could fire projectiles so incredibly fast that they'd shred an enemy vessel, leaving nothing but particle dust. And Lianica was keeping those fighters more than busy with her fierce and relentless volley of firepower. Although the *Shard* was only a fraction of the size of the Nephilim cruiser, it matched it in armaments, making it a fierce and formidable opponent.

After having caught her breath, Jegra plucked her axe out of the ground and turned and gazed across the clearing to the area where the enemy soldiers had pulled back. She could now make out the gray figures of the Nephilim and Nyctan soldiers working to re-form a front line as they readied themselves to push for another attack.

Then, to her surprise, the troops began to part in large numbers, making way for a tall central figure decked out in golden armor. He swayed through the throng of soldiers, his white skin glowing under the sunlight, his muscles bulging with raw power. His obsidian eyes with golden halos that encircled the iris turned their gaze to her and flashed hot with disdain.

Jegra remembered those eyes and the smug grin that came with them. Of the three avatars, it was this fucking asshole, Nodengoth, that Jegra would relish killing the most. He was the one who'd taken her son from her. He was the one who'd taken Dani's arm. And he was the one who'd left her for dead. Now, she was about to return the favor.

Nodengoth stepped out onto the field and his warriors began banging their armor with their fists and chanting "Et'vat Nodengoth! Et'vat Nodengoth! Et'vat Nodengoth!"

Et'vat, Jegra knew, was Nyctan for *Great One*. She'd heard it chanted incessantly for H'aaztre; now, they cheered on their great warrior.

Not much was known about Nodengoth except that he once was a skilled and noble warrior, since made into a puppet for a celestial entity of pure evil. Whatever greatness he may have once possessed had since been eclipsed by the tyrant king's ambition and bloodlust.

The red, vengeful eye of hate replaced any semblance of valor or compassion the noble knight may have once had. All that remained of the Nyctan warrior was his body, a mere bludgeoning tool—and a cold-blooded killing machine.

Each repletion of the warrior's name was followed by the rhythmic banging on armor. Et'vat Nodengoth! *Clank-ka-clank. Clackity-clank.* Et'vat Nodengoth! *Clank-ka-clank. Clackity-clank.*

The thrumming pattern repeated itself endlessly as the throng of warriors spurred on their champion. Et'vat Nodengoth! *Clank-ka-clank. Clackity-clank.* Et'vat Nodengoth! *Clank-ka-clank. Clackity-clank.*

Jegra raised the heavy, dual head of her battle axe and twirled it about with a bit of style and verve, and then flung it over her shoulder where she let it rest. She shifted her hips into a casual, yet dynamic pose, and watched with a smirk on her face as Nodengoth sauntered toward her position.

Unintimidated by the gladiatrix, he came to a stop about thirty feet away and raised a gauntleted fist into the air. Almost immediately, the chanting of his legionnaires died down and his black eyes with golden irises surged with golden light as he looked upon her with a nearly endless well of contempt.

"It's been a long time, pink-skin," he sneered. "The last time we met you were crawling through your own blood and fluids as I clutched your newborn in my hands. Tell me, Mother of Dagon, what does it feel like to lose a child?"

Jegra's eyes narrowed down to dark, smoldering coals of scorn. She tossed her axe to the ground and then, her fists balled tight, she lunged into the air and roared with all the fury her belly could muster.

Her first strike crashed down on his linked forearms, and even though he managed to block her downward punch, the force of the blow sent him flying backward. Digging in his heavy metal boots, he carved out gashes in the soil as he skidded across it.

Still in motion, his eyes widened with shock as she thrust herself forward and slid into him, landing several blows on his torso before he even managed to scrape to a halt.

Stopped, he blocked a flying knee to his chest, but she quickly ducked down and followed it up with a couple of hits below the belt. She caught him in the balls, and he lurched forward, shifting his stance to avoid another ball-tap. Even so, it seemed that's exactly what she was hoping he'd do, because Jegra leaped up and headbutted him, sending him staggering back once again.

Nodengoth grinned as he licked the trickle of blue blood trailing down the corner of his mouth and ran his tongue across his white teeth. As blue blood smeared and stained them, he smiled even more.

"Well done," he said, grinning like a maniac. Impressed that she'd managed to draw first blood, he circled her and shook his arms loose, preparing himself for what was turning out to be a real fight. "You may prove a challenge to me yet." He tossed his long dark hair behind him, adding, "I cannot tell you how long it's been since I faced a truly worthy opponent."

She smirked and raised her hand, motioning for him to come at her.

With an impossible speed, he blurred out of sight—and then was suddenly standing just over her right shoulder.

Jegra's eyes widened as she realized that he'd manifested directly behind her. Attacking her backside, where she had no defense, was the best way at taking her down. Even so, she'd fully predicted he'd make that exact move.

In her spare time over the past year, Jegra had studied every piece of available footage she could get her hands on regarding Nodengoth. And although he was fast and ruthless, he was also cocky and reckless.

It wasn't hard to predict his first attack. Even as he had manifested behind her in the blink of an eye, she was already shifting her body weight. She leaned to the left, bending one knee slightly and tilting just enough so that Nodengoth's arm and fist flew across her shoulder, narrowly missing her head.

Over extending, he looked down, an almost amused look coming over his face.

Reflexively, Jegra reached up, took his forearm in her hands, and pulled down on it. Hard. His arm joint snapped over her shoulder with a bone-chilling *crunch* and he let out a yelp as she dislocated his elbow, shoulder, and wrist all in single move.

She twisted her hips, pivoted, and, using his body weight against him, flipped him over her shoulder. With the force of a hammer, he smashed into the ground, ribs breaking, and coughing up blood.

Jegra rolled her head across her shoulders and cracked her neck. As she waited for her opponent to get back to his feet, she rotated her shoulders, hopped up and down, and shook out the tension in her arms.

Staying loose meant staying fast. As she bounced up and down, her meaty thighs bounced with her. Once she'd settled back into position, she widened her stance, raised her fists and nodded at Nodengoth to hurry it along.

"What's the matter, Nodengoth? Did you fall out of practice?"

"Silence, woman!" Nodengoth growled as he pushed himself to his feet with only one good arm.

Once up, he popped his elbow and shoulder back into joint with a grunt and then flexed his arm to make sure everything was back in order. As he flexed, his forearm tightened to the point that his wrist reset itself, almost as if he had self-healing properties and then he shook out the tension in his arm, flexed again, and then rotated his arm in its socket just to be certain everything was back in working order. It was.

"I thought you avatars were supposed to be tough. By the way, your pretty little girlfriend up there wanted me to give you this," Jegra informed. Reaching into a small leather satchel on her waist, she pulled something out and tossed it to Nodengoth.

He looked down at what he held in his own two hands. It took him a minute to process the information, then it dawned on him that it was Azra'il Nun's tongue. Sickened by the barbarity of it, he flung the grotesque appendage into the dirt and screamed out in rage. "You'll pay for that, you bitch!"

"Big words coming from such a little man," she taunted, making sure he was riled up. The angrier he was, the more clouded his judgement.

"Grah!" Nodengoth lunged forward. He blurred partially as a spray of dirt shot up behind him. Jegra merely kicked a powerful leg back and, to everyone's surprise, caught his punch with one hand.

"H-how is this even possible?" Nodengoth looked down at his fist clutched in her mighty grip. She smiled at him and then crushed his fist as though it were as brittle as eggshells.

"ARGH!" he shouted as he drew back, clutching his mangled hand.

"I have a message for your master. Tell him I want to meet face to face."

"He'll never meet with someone so unworthy."

"Unworthy?" Jegra balked. "Do you know who I am?"

A perplexed look came over Nodengoth's face.

"I'm Jegra Alakandra, commander of the Knights of Caelum, loyal wife to the true emperor, champion of the arena, and the Mother of Dagon. And I will have my vengeance, in this life or the next."

"Rousing speech," Nodengoth sneered, "but I can tell you're stalling."

Jegra shrugged.

"The question is why."

After a short pause, Nodengoth's eyes grew wide with shock as a red line slowly appeared on the top of his head, ran down his face, and continued the entire length of his body. By the time he was aware of what had happened, it was already too late.

His eyes flickered with rage as they refocused on Jegra. "You backstabbing, two-faced whore..." he wheezed with his last breath. He was unable to finish the insult, as cleaved in two, both halves fell apart at the seam and Nodengoth spilled to the ground in two separate piles of guts and gore.

Emperor Dakroth stood directly behind Nodengoth's corpse, radiant finger still glowing hot pink.

Jegra gave an appreciative nod for the assist. He nodded back and then casually brushed down his space suit.

Battles were won by not having to fight your opponent head on. By distracting Nodengoth with a well-timed flurry of attacks, he became too preoccupied with what she was doing to notice the emperor silently sneaking up behind him.

After all, Jegra wasn't looking to punish Nodengoth for his crimes. She wasn't going to give him a slap on the wrist and forgive him. She was looking to make an example of him.

A couple of Nephilim legionnaires rushed forward, roaring fierce battle cries as they entered the clearing. Hoping to avenge their fallen hero, they drew their weapons and charged Emperor Dakroth. That was their first and last mistake.

Without even looking at them, Dakroth threw out his arm and let off a prolonged laser blast that cut the two warriors down in their tracks. The blast was so powerful, however, that a dozen other soldiers still standing in formation a hundred meters in the distance teetered and then collapsed as well.

Bored, Dakroth reached up and cupped his mouth to stifle a yawn. Jegra couldn't help but smile.

In the brief repose, as the enemy tried to figure out their next move, she turned and looked up toward the Nephilim battlecruiser. "On second thought," Jegra said, addressing Dakroth. "Blow that fucking bitch out of the sky."

"I thought you'd never ask," Dakroth said appreciatively. Raising his glowing finger, he pointed it up toward the cruiser. Taking ahold of his own wrist, and locking it in place with his left hand, he steadied his aim.

The Dygra crystal in his chest began to pulse and his finger began to glow a hot pink. The crystal pulsed faster and faster until, finally, it flared in his chest like a miniature starburst; the intensity of it showing through the fabric of his suit.

A massive laser blast raced up toward the Nephilim cruiser and then, like a plasma welder cutting through steel, it sliced the enemy ship right down the middle. This was followed by a series of explosions but, even so, the ship managed to hold together.

"Hmmm…" he said, stroking his chin.

"What is it?" Callestra asked, sauntering up to them. She glanced over at the Nephilim soldiers, who seemed uncertain as how to proceed, now that their champion lay in a smoldering pile of entrails at their feet.

"Oh, nothing," Dakroth said, yawning again. "I suppose I'm just tired is all." On a full charge, he would have decimated that ship. But the battle had left him drained, and he was in need a bit of food and refreshment to get his powers back up.

Callestra placed her hand on his chest and said, "What you need, my luv, is a bit of distraction." She licked her lips as she stared longingly into his eyes and he bent down and kissed her.

Grendok and Brei'Alas arrived to lend their support to Jegra just as the first beams of red light came down to collect the remaining enemy soldiers. Jegra stood and watched until every last one of them had been called back up to the ship.

Good riddance, she thought. Then, looking up, they all watched as the Nephilim cruiser, ever so slowly, turned about and limped away, venting gas out of its open wounds as it went. A swarm of remaining fighters trailed after it like a string of ducklings following their mother.

The Dagon and Galliforn ground forces all let out a round of victorious cheers as the enemy tucked tail and retreated. Although outnumbered, they had proven themselves to be the superior fighters. Hopefully, this victory for them would be enough to catch H'aaztre's undivided attention. Unless he was looking forward to more setbacks, he'd have to take Jegra's rebellion seriously.

"Now what?" Brei'Alas asked.

"Now we get cleaned up and feast," Grendok answered in his usual gruff voice. When he turned to meet Jegra's gaze, the two of them stared at each other for a brief moment and then both smiled and threw their arms out as they drew together and embraced. "It's been a long time, old friend."

"How I've missed your hoary old mug," she said, squeezing and then letting him go.

As they embraced one another, Brei shrugged and, wrapped her arms around the both of them and squeezed until they all needed air.

Uncomfortable with all the sentimentality on display, Callestra turned away and merely twirled her knives, waiting for everyone to finish gushing emotions everywhere.

Dakroth placed his hands on his waist and stared up at the destroyer. Squinting hard, he aimed his finger again and let out another blast. Everyone turned to watch the red beam stretch into the heavens. A few seconds later there was a brilliant flash of light as the ship exploded, breaking apart into a million flaming pieces.

"That's more like it," he said, as if reassuring himself that he still had it. His work done, he turned and headed back to the basecamp.

Still gazing up at the glowing ring of light that used to be the Nephilim battlecruiser, Grendok said, "An impressive man, that Dakroth."

Callestra smiled, sliding her blades back into their sheaths on her back.

"For all his shortcomings, he sometimes manages to surprise you."

Callestra frowned. She didn't like the fact that Jegra would openly talk bad about the emperor, even in jest. Growing defensive, she responded, "Personally, I think he's perfect."

"Of course, you do," Jegra said, fixing her dark brown eyes onto the Dagon woman. "Because you're head over heels in love with him."

"I...you...that's not..." stuttered Callestra, not knowing how to respond to that. It wasn't a wrong assessment, but she thought she'd hidden her infatuation better. Yet looking around at all the grinning faces, it was clear to her that they all knew.

"It's perfectly all right," Jegra reassured her. "You have my blessing."

"I do?" she asked.

"I expect you to keep a close eye on him. He's a handful, that one." She gestured back over her shoulder with a stiff thumb in the direction Dakroth had headed. Callestra merely nodded.

Callestra took Jegra's hand in hers, knelt at her feet, and pressed her lips to her empress's hand. After offering her kiss of allegiance, she replied, "I shall do my utmost to serve both my emperor and the Mother of Dagon to the best of my abilities."

Jegra pulled the woman back up to her feet so that they were standing face to face. "I know you will."

"Seems it's turning into a beautiful night after all," Brei'Alas mused as she continued gazing up at the sparkling debris that filled the sky like ten thousand, thousand glittering fireflies.

"Quite right," Grendok affirmed. "A most glorious evening indeed."

21

Onelle Te'Legra Agnar stood on the observation deck of the Nephilim medical frigate. She watched as drones brought in badly damaged escape pods. Apparently, the Nephilim flagship had gone up in a blaze of glory and Azra'il Nun had been aboard it. Rumor had it, however, that she was alive and well. And Onelle, who had on a fancy, pearl white cocktail dress, waited in the observation lounge for her monthly scheduled meeting.

Azra'il Nun strode into the lounge wearing a golden gown that draped across her porcelain figure. Onelle noticed she had some recent suture lines where the laser welder had operated on her. But the most striking thing was the prosthetic jaw she had attached.

Onelle took the drink resting on the bar, sipped it, and set it back down. Seeing that Azra'il had spotted her, she rose to meet the woman. "I know it's none of my business, but what in the bleedin' galaxy happened to you?"

Azra'il tried to speak, but her prosthetic jaw locked up. She fetched a small screwdriver from a toolkit strapped to her thigh like a garter and tightened the servos inside her jaw. Opening and shutting her mouth a few times, testing to see if all the kinks were out, she replaced the screwdriver and then turned to those off duty patrons who convened in the lounge. "Leave us," she commanded.

Without hesitation, the crew set down their tools, stopped whatever it was they were doing, and quickly left the bridge as requested. Once the final crewman had shuffled out of the doors, Azra'il turned her attention back to the meeting at hand.

"Dakroth and his wild harem of savage women is what happened."

"I warned you they'd be trouble," Onelle answered.

"I barely made it off that ship alive. If I hadn't ordered the evacuation after the first blast, we'd all be dead right now."

"H'aaztre must be watching over you, hallowed be his name," Onelle said reverently, bowing her head.

"The Terran has awoken and she has banded together a small yet effective alliance of Dagon, Satyr, and even the emperor himself."

"Jegra," Onelle hissed, her brow settling into a scowl at the mere mention of her mortal enemy. "What can I do to help?" Onelle asked, offering her services.

The truth was, she'd do anything to see Jegra overthrown and brought to ruin. It was her sole mission in life to get revenge for Abethca's death, and she wouldn't rest until Jegra was frozen in crystalline as the centerpiece in her fountain room.

"Surely, as a business woman with eyes and ears in every sector of the Commonwealth, you are uniquely suited for sniffing out insurgency wherever it might rear its ugly head. Although I am the Voice of H'aaztre, you are his ears."

Onelle bowed her head, "It would be my pleasure."

Azra'il smiled rigidly, the prosthetic still rather stiff. All she could manage was an artificial sort of grin, which made her look almost manic. She quickly gave up on the smile, rubbing her jaw and trying to get the thing to loosen up.

"I want you to monitor any and all unusual shipments. Large quantities of medicine, weapons, and food must be accounted for. If there is a last-minute change in shipping coordinates and a shipment gets rerouted, I want to be the first to know about it. If a bulk order for coolant gels gets made, I want to be the first to know. Anything and everything that could be used to support a rebellion needs to be watched with a renewed vigilance."

"Yes, my mistress. Is there anything else you'd ask of me?"

"As a matter of fact, there is. Are you still in contact with your sister? The one who has allied herself with the empress?"

"Yes," Onelle said hesitantly. "May I ask what it is that you need her for?"

"I need you to tip her off that a shipment of medical supplies will be making its way to Dagon Prime. When the politicians hear about it, they will do everything in their power to see that the elite aristocrats get their hands on it before the general populace. If the empress gets wind of the shipment in advance, she may make a run for it to re-distribute it more equally among her people."

"You're going to play her compassion against her?"

Slowly, Azra'il rose to her feet and locked her hands behind her back. "We must dismantle her foundation. Erode her allies' trust. Take out her support network. Once that's taken care of, everything else will come crashing down around her."

A wicked grin formed on Onelle's dark green lips. "Your bidding will be my great pleasure."

She gave the Nephilim salute, which was two fingers pointed at a forty-five-degree angle in the air. The ranking officer responded by doing the same and tapping the fingers of the ranking officer. With civilians, the salute was unnecessary, but since Azra'il did employ the services of Onelle Te'Legra Agnar in an official capacity, she saluted back.

Onelle turned to leave when Azra'il Nun called out to her. "One more thing, Mistress Onelle. This isn't the time to question where your loyalties lie. If you're thinking about betraying me, I'd think again, if I were you."

"The thought has never crossed my mind," Onelle reassured her, glancing over her shoulder at the black eyes that stared back at her with a dreadfully bitter, almost hollow quality that always sent a shiver down her spine.

Although she didn't like being threatened in such a manner, there wasn't much she could do. As The Voice of H'aaztre, Azra'il Nun could literally command her to do something and she'd have no choice but to obey—including taking her own life. At least she was giving Onelle the choice in this instance, even if she was being a condescending bitch.

She pushed away the indignant feeling and managed a polite smile, flashing her pearly whites at the black-eyed woman. Once it was clear to her that Azra'il Nun knew where her loyalties lay, she spun around, and with a bounce in her step, she strolled out of the observation lounge.

After she'd returned to her signature edition luxury space yacht made by her own *Agnar Galactic Industries*, she flipped a switch and turned on the automated pilot. All systems purred as the ship came to life. The plasma coils of her Orion class-9 engines hummed as they heated up.

Instead of a quadcore, like a Hyperborean fusion drive, the Orion class-9 configuration only relied on a dual core engine. It made travel much more efficient, and since the yacht wasn't meant for extended space flights, there was less need for redundancy.

The pearl-white yacht rose off the landing bay platform of the medical frigate and slowly turned toward the opening bay doors. Once the doors were fully retracted, Onelle tapped the console and the ship handled the rest for her.

As it exited the open hangar doors, it passed through the blue negative-energy shield and a purple shimmer moved across its iridescent hull. Once the ship had completely cleared the bay doors, Onelle settled into her seat and typed in the hyperspace coordinates necessary to make the jump into FTL.

Initially, she'd made a wrong calculation, and the computer bleated an angry sounding tone in protest. "Infernal technology," she growled, not wanting to take blame for her own mistake. She quickly retyped the coordinates and this time the computer chimed gleefully in response, and the hyperdrive engines hummed to life.

"See? Was that so hard?" she asked the computer, rolling her eyes in exasperation.

Of course, she was accustomed to speaking to her ship as though it were a person. Even though it didn't have any fancy A.I. interface and couldn't actually respond to her, she still sometimes felt it could actually understand her. Even though most of the time it merely seemed to delight in aggravating her.

As the engines warmed up, she brought up a 3D holographic image of Jegra on the holovid and smacked her teeth in disgust. If she could rip Jegra's world apart, piece by piece, then maybe…just maybe…she'd be satisfied.

It was only because she'd had the foresight to hide a brain-slug in her ear that she was comfortable blaming the parasite for her unrelenting bloodthirst. But the truth was, it had been there long before the worm.

By creating a valuable diversion, however, she was able to pretend someone else had planted the slug inside of her, and this had sent the fools on a wild goose chase looking for a villain who didn't exist, never once suspecting that she'd done it to herself as a ruse to throw them off her scent.

The ruse had worked, however, and while they were pre-occupied with other things, she'd managed to make her grand escape. The rest, as they say, is history.

Now, all she wanted was to break Jegra, leaving her shattered and betrayed. In that crippling moment of sadness, Onelle wanted to freeze her with a crystalizer. Although crystalizers were banned, due to the fact that their damage was unrepairable, Onelle had pulled a few strings and managed to get her hands on one of the few remaining models that drifted around on the black market.

And the first step to destroying Jegra's world was to sow the seeds of distrust and get her closest friends to turn on her, abandon her…maybe even renounce her.

Perhaps the only one who could travel freely throughout the Commonwealth, Onelle set course for Thessalonica to meet with her other sister, Raphine, and ask for a parley. The time for a little family reunion, she felt, was long past due.

"No parley!" Raphine yelled, attempting restraint. She folded her arms across her chest as the Imperial Guards fanned out behind her. If there was anyone who could get under her skin, it was her eldest sister.

Onelle stood in front of her yacht, parked just beyond the perimeter of Arena Palace, Jegra's personal residence on the moon, Thessalonica. As she took in its grandeur, she couldn't help but feel slightly impressed. Dagon architecture was as sacred to them as their many religions. It never ceased to amaze her how beautiful, functional, and elegant they made everything. She supposed that's what one could afford, when one lorded over the rest of the galaxy with all one's wealth and power.

But who was she to criticize? Her palace on Arkadia was twice as big and twice as opulent. Still, she hadn't conquered entire civilizations to procure it, nor had she forced children to dig in the mines for blood-diamonds to acquire her great wealth. No, she'd built her financial empire brick by brick.

A bitter smile formed on her forest green lips and she looked into Raphine's Bisbee turquoise eyes. "I beg your pardon?" Onelle gasped. "You'd deny parley to your own sister? Your own flesh and blood?" She smacked her teeth in annoyance and turned her nose up, acting all superior.

"No sister of mine would climb into bed with the enemy," Raphine shot back coldly. "Tell me Onelle, what's it like, having your head so far up Azra'il Nun's ass that you can taste it? Bitter? A little salty, perhaps? Oh, let me guess. Sweet and sour…just the way you like your stank-ass whores."

Livid, Onelle slapped Raphine across her face with the palm of her hand.

When the guards stepped forward to subdue her, Raphine raised a hand and gestured for them to hold their positions.

"You're way out of line, you ungrateful brat. Who raised you after mom and dad died? Who paid for your education at the academy? Who fed and clothed you?"

"Abethca did," Raphine answered indignantly, staring at Onelle with a gaze that cut like a knife. "You were never around! Always busy with whatever important business call you needed to make or had some corporate meeting or another."

"I worked to take care of you and Abby," Onelle responded. "I always made sure you girls had everything you needed. It was only because of Abby's..." Onelle trailed off. She realized that if she besmirched her own sister's good name it would only anger Raphine all the more.

"What?" Raphine asked, fishing for the unadulterated truth she knew her sister was dying to share. "Because what?"

"Because of Abby's recklessness and her desire to seek fame in the Arena that she ever crossed paths with Jegra in the first place. If she had only listened to me, she'd still be alive."

Raphine raised an eyebrow and took a step forward. The Imperial Guards held their position. "What do you mean...she'd still be alive if she listened to you?"

Onelle turned her back to Raphine and in a dramatic display of emotional turmoil and buried her face in the palms of her hands. Weeping bittersweet tears as if on cue, she sniffled and wiped her nose with the back of her hand. "I thought you knew."

Raphine did her best not to roll her eyes at Onelle's drama queen antics, but she needed to know what she was on about. "I know everything I need to know. As chief security detail for the palace—"

"Did you know it was Jegra who killed Abby?" Onelle spun around, her eyes full of a fiery rage that caused Raphine to draw back. "Did you know she vaporized her without even checking for a pulse? She still had a heartbeat, Raph. It was faint. But the detectors Dakroth had installed to keep watch on the vitals of his prized fighters showed that Abby was still alive. Check the records for yourself if you don't believe me."

"That's not how it happened," Raphine said. "The assassin, Ishtar Bantu killed our sister. She snapped her neck. And even if she was still barely hanging on by a thread, she'd live out the rest of her life as a paraplegic? You know she'd never have wanted that. She would have rather died than have to endure such an existence."

Onelle threw her hands up and balked. "Fine, take her side." Onelle spun back around and raised a reproachful finger. "But I'm telling you, the meddling red-skin may have wounded our dearest Abby, but it was Jegra who murdered her. That's a fact."

Onelle flung her forest green hair over her shoulder, spun on her heels, and marched back to her ship. Raphine maintained her position and watched Onelle leave.

Just before boarding her shuttle, Onelle looked back at Raphine with sad eyes. "You don't have to believe me. I don't even expect you to forgive me. But I implore you, check the holovid files yourself. You owe Abby at least that much."

Onelle disappeared into her iridescent space yacht, the external doors sealing shut behind her. The medium-sized craft rose, its plasma coil thrusters beating Raphine's hair about in eddies of hot air. Then, rapidly ascending into the sky, it darted past wispy clouds and winked like a shooting star before finally vanishing into the depths of outer space.

Raphine watched her sister's shuttle go. Danica sidled up next to her. "Was that who I think it was?"

"My lovely sister," quipped Raphine in a sarcastic tone.

"And what did that traitor want?" She looked at Raphine, suddenly realizing she'd insulted her sister to her face, and quickly apologized. "No offense."

"No offense taken," Raphine replied. "She is a traitor."

Danica placed a blue hand on Raphine's shoulder. "Are you all right? I know her just showing up out of the blue like that couldn't have been easy for you."

Raphine laughed. "It was a bit of a shock, that's for sure. But she's always been a prima donna, that one. I'll be fine. It's just…"

"Just what?"

Raphine turned to Danica and stared hard into her yellow eyes. "She said that Jegra killed Abby, and that there's holovid evidence of it. She was adamant that Abby wasn't dead when Jegra vaporized her. I know it's probably all just lies, but if there's any amount of truth to it, I need to know. Please. I deserve the truth."

Danica immediately felt the lump in her throat grow thick and heavy as she gulped it down. But she couldn't formulate how best to say it and stood in silence until Raphine's face turned to one of dismay.

"What aren't you telling me, Dani? What do you know about this?"

Danica turned to the guards and waved her hand, "You're dismissed."

They looked at her and then to Raphine. Raphine nodded and the guards took formation and marched off.

"What I'm about to tell you not even Jegra knows about, so, if you're going to blame anyone you blame me. You got that?"

Raphine nodded. Tears starting to well up in her eyes, brimming on her eyelids and threatening to pour out like tiny waterfalls. It wasn't the sad news of her sister's death, or the fact that her friends had kept vital information from her, but she feared that she was about to lose her closest friend.

"It's true, what Onelle told you. Dakroth ordered Ishtar Bantu to assassinate Abby and pin it on Jegra. The way she did it was to make it look like she'd drowned her. She'd given Abby a syringe full of etorphine and then dumped her in the water."

"And then Jegra stumbled upon the assassin, catching her red-handed, and intervened."

"That's right. And Jegra assumed Ishtar had drowned Abby, killing her in cold blood. But she never gave up hope. She even tried to save your sister, administering CPR. But Abby never woke up."

"You still haven't answered me. Was she dead? Had Abby's heart completely stopped?"

After a long, hesitant pause, Danica answered the question. "No. But it was so faint that even Jegra, with all her enhanced powers, couldn't have been able to detect it. And until the drug wore off, there'd be no way of reviving her using traditional means. For all intents and purposes, she was dead."

"That can't be everything. Why does Onelle pin all the blame on Jegra and none of it on the assassin? What does she know that you're not sharing with me?" The tears were rolling down both their cheeks now as she stared at Danica, her eyes blazing and hands trembling.

"Because," Danica replied, her tone growing solemn, "Jegra disposed of Abby's body the only way she could have. Using the blaster Dakroth had given her. The blaster I told him to leave for her."

"I don't understand..."

Danica wiped a tear from her cheek, sniffled, and divulged her deepest, darkest secret. "It was all part of my plan."

"Your plan?" gasped Raphine. "What do you mean your plan?"

"Dakroth wanted me to frame Jegra for a crime so that she'd have a reason to want to escape the arena. Even with all his wealth, he couldn't purchase her from IGS until her contract was up. And that wasn't for another three years. As such, I did what I do best; I devised a plan to get Jegra into the emperor's possession sooner. I framed her for murder. But then the Nyctans attacked and made my scheme unnecessary, so I erased the data and covered my tracks."

When Raphine remained silent, merely stood there fuming, Danica didn't know how to respond. So, she continued confessing the sin that had been eating away at her on the inside for so terribly long.

"Listen, not even Jegra knew that Abby still had a pulse. She was manipulated by Dakroth and myself into killing your sister. And...I'm sorry, Raph...so, so very sorry."

Raphine glared at Danica, one eye squinting narrowly at her, the other one twitching with rage. "You?! Of all people, how could you? I gave myself to you! I slept with my sister's killer!!"

"Please," Dani said, reaching out her hand.

Raphine swatted it away. "You're sick!" she growled. "You are fucking sick, Danica."

"I feel terrible about what I did," Dani sobbed. "You have to believe me."

"I have to believe you?" Raphine asked, her face contorting and wrinkling with unheard of layers of disgust.

Raphine grabbed Danica's hand, and, forcing it down into her pants, she shoved Danica's fingers inside of herself. "You fucked me," she growled. "You fucking killed my sister and then fucked me." Pulling Danica's hand back out, she flung it to the side. "There, enjoy the taste of my cunt, you fucking bitch. Because that's the last time you're ever going to taste anything as sweet ever again."

"Raphine, I..." At a loss for words, Danica merely bit her tongue and lowered her eyes out of shame.

Raphine shot her one last menacing glance and then stormed off, making her way back to the palace.

Danica felt a crippling sense of remorse come over her. She turned and called out, "Wait, Raphine!" Raphine paused without looking back and, knowing the moment wouldn't last, Danica seized the opportunity. "I'm sorry."

"I've heard enough lies for the evening," Raphine answered, and continued on her way.

Danica, completely shattered, sank to her knees and sobbed. Raising her mascara-tarnished eyes to the sky, she scowled up at wherever it was Onelle had slithered off to.

She realized right then and there that Onelle's entire mission had been to turn Raphine against her and cause a rift so devastating it might even give her cause to doubt the empress.

It was, without a doubt, a master stroke by a master manipulator. And now, Danica had to figure out how to repair the damage and somehow prevent it from destroying everything she and Jegra had worked for.

22

The rim of Aldebaran's outer edge eclipsed the system's main star and cast a long shadow across the inner ring, one side in the shade of darkness, the other in a band of light. Like a giant wheel floating in space, it gradually rotated so that both sides had full day and night cycles. One side always spinning into the light of a new dawn while the other spun off into the dark.

Down on the surface, a small portion of the landscape lining the inner circumference was blemished with the charred remains of fallen soldiers and pitted with tiny craters from charged plasma grenades and high-powered plasma rifles. Coolant cartridges littered the desolate battlefield; scraps of Centurion battle robot lying alongside fragments of Nephilim armor could be found strewn across the blue stained soil.

As the shade of night settled over the landscape, Grendok barked orders at some officers who were hauling wounded off the battlefield and then turned his attention back to the empress.

"You go on and get yourself cleaned up for tonight. Your people are anxious to see you back on your feet and in good form, so a victory speech from the empress would give their morale a much-needed boost right now."

Jegra nodded in agreement and then took her leave. As she turned to go, she reached out and caught Brei'Alas by her wrist and towed her behind her. "Come on, Lieutenant, we need to make ourselves presentable for this evening's festivities."

"Uh, right," Brei said, looking back at Grendok as Jegra led her away by the arm. With her free hand she waved at him and he smiled and waved in return.

As their hands clasped together, Brei looked down at their interlocked fingers and wanted desperately to ask Jegra about the other night. She wanted to know why, of all the people Jegra could have chosen to be with that evening, she had chosen her.

But she quickly put such silly ponderings out of her mind. Who was she to question the empress or her choices?

A medical team teleported down from the *Shard* to assist with collecting the dead and wounded just about the same time Jegra and Brei walked into the nearest prefab unit. Once inside, Brei'Alas noted it was only a storage room.

"I think maybe we're in the wrong..." she trailed off when Jegra collapsed against a pile of boxes, prompting her to rush forward and catch Jegra around her waist. "Empress, are you all right?"

Jegra sank to her knees and began sobbing. Brei'Alas, her arms still clinging to Jegra's mid-section, sank down with her.

It dawned on Brei that seeing the entity that had stolen her baby from her had left Jegra emotionally drained and vulnerable. At a time like this, all she could do was try to comfort the empress. She leaned across Jegra's back, wrapped her blue arms around her and squeezed tight. Resting her face on the back of Jegra's neck, she placed her lips next to her ear, and whispered, "I have you."

Jegra continued to cry, nestled in Brei's arms. And Brei did her best to soothe her empress, stroking her hair and repeating that, "Everything will be alright."

She didn't know if it helped any, but she knew that Jegra, although strong on the outside, was clearly hurting on the inside. The worst thing Brei could imagine was having to suffer being alone in one's great anguish.

Although she'd never experienced the loss of a child, Brei understood that it must be the most harrowing event in a parent's lifetime. Even Dagon women, who prided themselves in their stoicism and emotional restraint were known to break down in tears over the loss of a child.

After a long cry, Jegra sniffled and wiped the tears from her cheeks with the back of her hand and then looked into Brei's amber eyes. Brei smiled at her and gently stroked her cheek.

"Come, let's get you cleaned up, Your Majesty," Brei said, using all of her strength to hoist Jegra back to her feet.

Jegra nodded and then followed after Brei who, this time, was the one who reached back and took the empress's hand. She led the way to a separate installation, an outdoor sign reading: "Unisex Showers" and they went inside.

Six shower stalls, all currently unoccupied, lined the walls in a spacious, communal bathing area. There weren't any dividers or curtains, but there were a series of wall hooks for hanging your towel and shampoo kit. Entering the stall, Brei reached out and turned on the tap and checked the water with her hand, making sure it would get nice and hot. Once steam started to fill the small shower stall, she turned the water off again and let out a sigh of relief.

"At least the water filtration is still working."

"Thank you," Jegra said, placing a hand on Brei's shoulder. Brei looked back at her and smiled. "Thank you for comforting me. And, also, thank you for being here for me now like you were for me the other night. I just needed someone to…you know…keep me company."

"Oh, you remember that?" Brei asked, acting surprised.

"Of course, I remember. And I know I have a reputation of sleeping with whomever my heart desires, but in that moment I desired you."

"You did?" Brei asked. She gave Jegra a puzzled look. "Why?"

"Why?" Jegra laughed, echoing the girls question. "Why wouldn't I?"

Brei blushed and looked away. "I guess I've always felt I wasn't good enough or important enough for you to take notice of me. I mean, not like that, anyway. We're not exactly close friends or anything."

"Who says?" Jegra asked, guiding Brei's face back toward her with a gentle nudge of her chin.

Brei smiled and then threw herself into Jegra's arms, embracing her with a big hug. "Thank you for thinking of me," she said.

Jegra smiled and hugged the lieutenant in return. She was an odd duck, but Jegra had grown quite fond of her.

Once they'd finished undressing, they climbed into piping hot streams of water in their individual stalls and finally began to relax. Almost as soon as they'd gotten their hair wet and began to lather up with soap, they heard a melodic whistling drawing near. The doors to the shower room abruptly slid open and appearing in the doorway was Grendok, a light blue towel wrapped around his waist and a shower cap with two holes cut in it to allow his horns to jut out.

He whistled a merry little ditty as he went over to his preferred stall and turned on the water. He disrobed right in front of them, allowing them time to take a gander at his satyric anatomy, almost seeming to pose for them, and then he turned on the shower and stepped in.

"*Ahhh,*" he sighed, letting the warm water run down his furry back. "That's much better."

The two women shared a glance of mutual astonishment and then had to choke down a fit of giggles.

"Care to help and old goat lather up, ladies?" Jegra and Brei'Alas leaned into one another and began laughing even harder. Grendok raised an eyebrow and asked, "Did I say something amusing?"

"No," Brei replied. She looked over at Jegra with large worried eyes that almost pleaded for Jegra to rescue her from this situation.

"Don't get any ideas, old man," Jegra said with a laugh and pointed a finger at him to let him know she was serious.

"I promise you, the thought has never crossed my mind. This one, on the other hand," he said turning around and pinching Brei's right butt cheek.

She yelped and then slapped his hand away as she sashayed back to her stall. As she scurried off, he looked over at Jegra with a lecherous grin which exposed his yellow teeth.

"As fun as this has been, my dears," he informed them, sensing he'd overstayed his welcome. "I must get back to my duties."

As he rinsed off, he began to whistle the same tune as when he'd first come in. Once he'd finished rinsing off, he hopped over to his towel, wrapped himself up, and glanced over his shoulder and winked at them both. Continuing his little ditty, he skipped out of the showers and ducked into the changing rooms.

Soon after that, the song faded until, finally, neither Brei nor Jegra could make it out anymore and it became abundantly clear that they were, once again, allotted a modicum of privacy.

"Finally," Jegra said, letting out a sigh of relief. "I thought we'd never get back our privacy." While she spoke, she filled her hand with a large glob of bodywash. Reaching up, she ran her hands across Brei's back. The coolness of gel and Jegra's unexpected touch caused Brei to startle and she reflexively pulled away.

"What are you doing?" Brei squeaked, surprised by Jegra's unexpected touch.

Jegra laughed at her overreaction to her touch. "What do you think? I'm going to wash you."

"I'm good, thank you," Brei answered.

Jegra squinted at her suspiciously. "Are you telling me you want to be a filthy girl?"

"I don't think I'm necessarily the filthy one here," she fired back, teasing the empress with a cockeyed look.

"Oh, is that so?" Jegra parried. "Well, if I'm so filthy, maybe you can do my back for me, then?" She turned her back to Brei and the young woman drew closer. Lathering up Jegra's skin with bodywash, she ran her hands in small circles all across Jegra's tight back, her fingers tracing out the creases in Jegra's musculature and her thumbs pressing hard into the empress's flesh. In no time, what had begun as a simple lathering became a full body massage.

Brei's hands worked like magic and prompted the empress to let out a long, drawn out sigh as the tension drained from her body. Jegra closed her eyes and focused on Brei's sensual touch. How her fingers effortlessly glided across her skin. How they caressed every crest and valley of her anatomy with a tender touch that sent a thousand shivers of pleasure down her spine.

Jegra raised her arms, crossing them over her head, and rested her forehead on them as she let a satisfied sigh pass from her lips. "Don't stop," she said, water pouring down her face.

Brei nodded in silence, and even though Jegra couldn't see her reply, her continued touch was answer enough. As water rained down both their bodies, Brei put her weight into her kneading touch, forcing a release of tension from Jegra's lips in the form of a moan.

"I think you missed a spot," teased Jegra, glancing back over her shoulder at Brei.

"Oh, you mean down here," Brei said, sliding her hands down the small of Jegra's back, down through the valley of her buttocks, and then reaching up from behind to find the holy grail.

"Yeah," Jegra whispered, her voice barely audible as her eyes fluttered in her head and sensual shivers shot up and down her spine. "That's the spot."

Brei smiled and continued to massage the empress.

That's when the doors slid open and Callestra walked in. Walking in on the scene of Jegra pressed up against the wall with Brei's fingers halfway inside her, she stopped in her tracks. "I can come back if you both need some privacy."

"No, it's fine," Jegra answered, straightening up. Brei pulled her hand away and then slid to the side as Jegra quickly rinsed off, grabbed her towel and headed for the changing room. "Stall is all yours."

Callestra shrugged and then looked over at Brei. "So, you're giving free massages?"

Brei'Alas, not wanting to be a poor sport, sighed and nodded reluctantly. "I…um…"

"Great," Callestra said, flinging her towel over the stall and climbing into the shower Jegra had just been standing in. Glancing back the way the empress had gone, she said, "I want what she had."

Angry for letting herself be used like a common servant girl, Brei squirted the body wash into her hands, squeezing the bottle so hard it nearly exploded, and gave a curt reply. "Fine."

Surprisingly, before she could get to work on Callestra, Jegra poked her head back into the showers. "Brei, you coming or what?"

Brei'Alas couldn't help but grin as she got a free pass this time. "Sorry," she apologized to Callestra. "Maybe next time."

Just as soon as she'd finished, the doors opened and five Dagon grunts walked in. The three men and two women all sported shaved heads and were covered in grime from the battle they'd just returned from.

They froze when they saw Callestra showering alone. Not knowing the protocol of such a situation, since ranking officers usually had their own personal bathrooms, they all threw their towels over their shoulders and saluted.

Callestra quickly wrapped her towel around her torso and saluted them back. "I was just finishing up here," she informed them.

"Yes, ma'am," one of the male grunts shouted out.

They all moved to the side, standing at attention, and allowed her to pass by freely. As she went, she paused and stole a glimpse of their anatomy. Even the women had righteously large cocks. All of them stiff with nervous boners. This brought a smile to her face. "At ease, men and women," she added with a smirk just before ducking out.

"Yes, ma'am," the same grunt said.

After she left, they all gave one another astonished glances, still barely able to believe they'd met the Vice Admiral of the fleet in the showers, and then burst out laughing.

23

Late into the evening, amidst the dining tent and the banquet tables set up outdoors, the survivors of the attack convened under the stars and the watchful protection of the *Shard.* The Empress of Dagon rose from her central seat at the head table and clanked her fork against her wine glass, drawing the attention of the crowd.

"I'd like to give a toast. I want to honor all those who lost their lives today. May we celebrate their memory this fine evening."

A round of applause and "hear, hears" made the rounds and then Jegra raised her hand, silencing the cheers.

"I also want to say that today's victory, as bittersweet as it is, was but a stroke of luck on our part. The enemy is as cruel as it is cunning, and, to be sure, they will not underestimate us again. As such, we need to be ready for next time. For the next attack. The next battle. But, now…is not that time. Now, we celebrate. So, my loyal friends and subjects, drink and be merry, for tomorrow we die!"

"Here, here!" Grendok shouted, rising to his feet. He raised his own glass and saluted the empress. He waited for her to drink first then, smiling, he downed the wine in one legendary swig. Grendok wiped his purple-stained lips and then let out a loud belch.

"Long live the Empress!" a robust voice shouted out from the crowd.

The voice was commanding and loud, and when everyone turned to see who it was, they were astonished to find Emperor Dakroth standing across the room, his glass raised to Jegra.

This elicited a flood of cheers and a full choir of voices that repeated the salutation. "Long live the Empress!"

Once Jegra had seated herself again, Brei placed her hand on Jegra's thigh and leaned over and whispered into Jegra's ear, "They honor you."

Jegra smiled and placed her hand over Brei's and an inebriated smile formed on the girl's wine stained lips.

"I'm sure they'd honor him, too," Brei said less enthusiastically, as she looked over at Dakroth who was mingling with the commoners and shaking hands.

"Lieutenant," Jegra asked in at pleasantly surprise voice, "how much have you had to drink?"

"Only four glasses, why? *hic*"

"Oh, nothing," Jegra said, her smile widening. "Here," Jegra added, taking an open wine bottle that was sitting on the table and pouring Brei another drink. "Allow me the honor, at least, of filling your glass."

"Thank you!" Brei gushed in her usually cheerful manner. She took a sip and then, when Jegra's hand gently pressed down on hers, which was still on Jegra's thigh, she blushed. "Oh," she said, embarrassed, withdrawing her hand from the empress's leg. "So sorry. I forgot it was even there."

Embarrassed by her brazenness with the empress, Brei buried her face into her glass of wine which fogged up as she let out a deep breath. Then, tipping her glass bottoms up, she guzzled it all down in one go.

"Don't be," Jegra whispered into Brei's bright purple ears which were flushing pink at the tips. She reached over and took Brei's hand and placed it back onto her thigh. "I like it there."

She gazed at Brei and took a moment to admire her cute button nose and the short-cropped hair she sported. She was an interesting woman and Jegra had grown quite fond of her and her many quirks over the last several weeks.

"Let the wine flow freely!" Grendok said, manifesting over her shoulder and pouring her another glass.

She raised her glass to him and then placed it to her lips and immediately started gulping it down. After finishing it in record time, Brei held it out and said, "More, please!"

"A woman after my own heart," Grendok announced and poured her another glass. He got her cup brimming and then skipped away to keep everyone's wine glasses full as well. Such was the satyr way.

Once Brei had downed her seventh glass just as quickly, she let out a muted burp and then announced, "It's sooo good."

"Indeed it is, my dear," Grendok said, returning from making the rounds. He refilled her wine glass once more, adding, "It's the finest vintage of wine from the vineyards of Galliforn's most lush and beautiful valleys, even if I do say so myself…" he trailed off as he studied the label with sad eyes, *Chateau Sybarios*. It was one of the very last bottles of Galliforn wine in all the galaxy.

Jegra thought maybe she should warn Brei to pace herself, but the girl was letting her hair down for once. A rare thing for any Dagon to do, let alone someone as mousy as Brei. Instead of coddling her like a child, she decided to let the woman have a little fun. Besides, even Jegra had to admit to herself it was kind of a kick to watch a side of Brei she'd never seen before.

"So," Jegra asked, leaning in close to Brei's wine scented breath, "what does drunken Brei like to do for fun?"

She looked over at Jegra with sunken, yet beautiful amber eyes glazed over with maudlin delight. "I collect vintage postcards," she said, quite unexpectedly.

Jegra, who was midway through her sip, unexpectedly spit wine out everywhere. "What?" she laughed. She fetched a tissue and began dabbing the purple juice that dribbled down her cleavage.

"I do," Brei said defensively. "I know it's not cool or whatever," she shared, waving her hands about. "But I love to see all the places I could one day visit. That's why I joined the military, you know?"

"To travel the galaxy?"

"I know I'm not what most people expect. But my aptitude scores were off the charts!"

"I'm sure," Jegra said, resting her chin on her palm and smiling at the girl.

"So, what do you do for fun?" Brei asked.

"I like to read books," Jegra answered. "Although I've been so busy as of late, I really haven't had the chance."

"I like books too," Brei said, gazing dreamily into Jegra's eyes. "Do you have a favorite?"

"Yeah," Jegra answered, smiling back at her. "Moby Dick."

Brei raised an eyebrow. "Why would you read a book about someone's dick?"

Jegra laughed. "No, the book is about a whale hunter who's tracking down a legendary great white whale."

"Oh," Brei said, sounding embarrassed. "Sounds…interesting."

"Brei…" Jegra said, leaning in.

"Yes?" she said, turning to face the empress's glowing face.

"Shut up and kiss me."

"Oh," Brei whispered. Before she knew it, their lips were pressed together and they were sharing a long, drunken, extremely public kiss.

Brei, feeling awkward, pulled back and scanned the crowd, searching for Dakroth. When she couldn't find him she let out a relieved sigh.

"Do I get one of those?" a voice asked.

Brei looked up to see the Lord Emperor himself standing over her shoulder. Panicking, she tried to stand, but the alcohol got the best of her and she toppled out of her chair and disappeared under the table.

Jegra smiled and reached up and took Dakroth's collar and drew him down to her lips. Leaning in, he kissed her long enough that the attendees would see them and then gently pulled away. "As sweet as ever, my luv," he said, delicately stroking her cheek with the back of his hand.

She smiled up at him and he moved down the table to talk to Grendok and Callestra, who were busy chatting.

"Brei," Jegra said, without looking down.

"Yes?" a faint voice came up from under the table.

"It's okay to come out now," she said.

"No thanks," Brei said. "I think I'll just stay down here for a while, if you don't mind."

Jegra shrugged and then took another sip of the delicious Galliforn wine, of which she couldn't seem to get enough.

After second moon had set behind first moon and the evening had worn on for several hours, everyone at the soirée had managed to find themselves in the Bacchanalian stupor of good wine, gratifying food, and tranquil song.

Thoroughly sozzled, Dagons and Satyrs alike fell asleep right under the stars. Some lay hunched over their tables or nearby them, while others had gathered around a communal campfire at the center of the festivities and sat in groups while they listened drearily as a bard played his fretted lute.

The bard's melodies wove themselves into the dreams of the slumbering guests and was accompanied by the steady and soothing crackle of fire. In the sky, there was no moon, but the glimmer of the *Shard* could be seen keeping a watch over the people on the ground.

Satisfied that the evening had worn on pleasantly, Jegra slowly pushed herself up, brushed down her dress as she scanned the bevvied faces of the crowd, and then staggered off in silence.

Brei, who'd solidly dozed off some time ago, was snoring lightly, her face resting on her crossed forearms which in turn rested on the white table cloth. Her lips were stained a dark shade of purple due to the amount of wine she'd imbibed. She was sleeping peacefully when Jegra, who was mildly tipsy from her own impressive consumption of the free flowing *vin de table*, accidentally knocked into the leg of Brei's chair with her foot as she passed by.

The small jolt roused Brei from her slumber and she mumbled something about a turquoise banana print not belonging in the fall fashion catalogue. She managed to crack her eyelids in time to glimpse the blurry image of the empress wobbling away from her.

Brei sat up and wiped the drool from the corner of her mouth. The empress blurred in and out of focus and she squinted harder and then widened her eyes to try and compensate for the distorted image, looking the part of a real-life cartoon as she contorted her face in animated ways.

Determined not to let the empress slip away during the evening hours without an escort, she forced herself to her feet and took a wobbly step forward. The dizziness rushed to her head and she swayed back and forth before catching her balance.

"Girl, you're sooo drunk right now," she said reflectively as she focused on keeping herself upright and just putting one foot in front of the other.

Interested in where Jegra was headed during the witching hour, Brei followed her, making sure to maintain a safe distance behind so as not to be detected. About fifty yards from the festivities, the drunken melodies of song gradually faded into the distance and, to Brei's astonishment, Jegra's posture stiffened and any trace of inebriation quickly disappeared.

Brei'Alas grew worried. Not only did she recognize Jegra's stride as that of a warrior marching into battle, but she also struggled to keep up since, unlike the empress, she was sloshed out of her mind.

If that wasn't bad enough, she kept falling behind little by little until, finally, it appeared as though Jegra had virtually disappeared. "Drats," she muttered to herself when she realized that she'd officially lost the empress.

Panic filled her chest as she looked in all directions, desperately searching for any trace of the empress. Doing her best to pull herself together, Brei entered the same grove of trees that Jegra had and roamed about aimlessly in the woods. She called out once or twice at random intervals to no avail, but felt compelled to keep looking.

What felt like an eternity later, but probably hadn't been more than ten minutes, she stumbled upon Jegra standing in a clearing. She was just standing there, staring out at something that Brei couldn't quite make out.

"Jegra?" she asked. But the empress didn't acknowledge her presence. Instead, she continued to stare intensely at a figure that stood at the other end of the clearing.

When Brei sidled up to the empress, she saw it too. It was a young boy of no more than seven or eight cycles. Brei found it strange that a child so young should be out playing in the middle of the woods on a night like this, especially so close to a war zone. What's more, he appeared to be half Dagon and half...that's when it dawned on her.

"Oh, my lord," Brei gasped, covering her mouth. Tears flooded into her eyes when she realized who they were staring at.

The young boy gazed back at them with eyes that were as black as obsidian—all but for a golden halo around the irises that glinted brightly in the darkness and seemed to glow with a radiant energy reminiscent of the celestial squid entities.

Mother and child peered across the clearing at one another in silence and, then, in silence, the boy turned and entered the shadows of the trees and vanished from sight.

"That was him..." Brei whispered, still in shock. "It was your—" Her voice trailed off as she couldn't bring herself to complete the sentence.

"It was H'aaztre," Jegra said, finishing Brei's sentence for her.

"It was your son," Brei said, touching Jegra's arm.

Jegra pulled away and shot Brei a glare so frigid Brei withdrew her hand and cautiously eased back.

"My son," Jegra assured, "is dead."

Brei lowered her gaze and bit her tongue. It was clear that Jegra needed some space right now and even as she had the best intentions, she realized that she was only inserting herself where she didn't belong.

The empress spun around and marched back toward the encampment. Brei, growing anxious as she stood there all alone, looked back at the far end of the glade and gulped hard. Feeling unnerved by the immense silence that seemed to permeate this place, she slowly turned away and then trailed after the empress.

"Wait for me," she called out, walking as fast as her wobbly legs could carry her.

24

Aldebaran's edges glowed like a golden halo as the alien sun passed behind it. The morning rays lit up the terrain of the planet and, stretching, Brei'Alas stepped out of the barracks and into the light.

As she stretched, her unfastened uniform parted slightly, revealing the navy blue of her chest underneath. She yawned and then looked around for any familiar faces. It was no secret, after what she'd seen last night, she was worried about Jegra.

She tracked down Grendok who was behind the counter in the mess hall serving Cambrios eggs and Te'lekkian bacon strips to the grunts, scientists, and whoever else wanted a nice early morning breakfast.

"Good morning, Lieutenant Brei'Alas!" Grendok said in his jovial tone. "Can I get you something to eat?"

She shook her head. Brei couldn't eat with a nervous knot in her stomach. "Maybe later, right now I'm looking for Jegra. Have you seen her?" she asked.

Grendok shook his head. "Sorry, but she hasn't shown herself today. Have you checked her prefab unit?"

"I just came from there," Brei replied. "The bed was made as though no one had slept in it."

Grendok shrugged. He had nothing more he could say that would help her. "Sorry, I don't know what to tell you."

Brei looked over her shoulder to find a line of angry stares and realized that she'd unintentionally held up the line for far too long. "Sorry," she murmured and then scurried off to continue her search for the empress.

As she was about to exit the mess hall, she spotted Callestra eating by herself. Brei took in a deep breath and went over to her. "Excuse my intrusion,

Vice Admiral, ma'am," she said nervously. Callestra looked up and raised one finely painted eyebrow.

"Are you here to offer me that massage?" asked Callestra, a sly grin forming on her lips.

Brei shook her head, no.

"Oh," Callestra said, sounding dejected. "In that case, what do you want, Lieutenant?"

"I am looking for the empress. Have you by any chance—"

"No," Callestra said, cutting Brei off. "I haven't seen her."

"Oh, I see. Thanks," she said, slowly backing away. "Sorry to have bothered you, ma'am."

Brei saluted and Callestra rolled her eyes and saluted back. Once Brei had scurried off, she went back to eating.

Another twenty minutes went by and Brei started to grow increasingly worried that she couldn't find Jegra anywhere. That's when she decided to retrace their steps from last night.

Although her memory was a little bit foggy from the wine, she eventually found the clearing they'd been standing in the previous evening. This time, however, she heard voices talking.

Careful not to make a sound, she snuck up behind a tree and peered around the edge.

"It was here where you saw him."

"Right over there," Jegra said.

"Alright then," Emperor Dakroth said. "I'll have my men plant charges over there just to be sure any multidimensional time pockets are collapsed when we blow this place."

Jegra raised her finger to her lips to silence him and then signaled with her hands that they weren't alone. Dakroth glanced around and Brei ducked behind the tree trunk before either of them spotted her.

Her heart raced in her chest and then she heard Jegra's voice. "Lieutenant Brei'Alas, I can hear your heart thrumming from all the way over here. Take a deep breath and come out. It's perfectly alright."

Brei did as ordered and stepped out from behind the tree. Dakroth looked over at her and smiled. She saluted.

"It seems your shadow has caught up to you," he said.

"You be nice," she laughed. "She's a loyal officer and a fierce warrior. And I know she doesn't look it, but she's a veritable sex goddess."

"I see," he said in the same blasé tone. "In that case, I'll leave you to it." He took his leave and passed by Brei, pausing briefly to look down at her from his shoulder. If Jegra was right, he thought, then this girl was full of surprises and he'd be keen to keep an interest in her.

Before Brei knew it, Dakroth continued on his way without so much as offering a morning greeting or, for that matter, returning her salute. But as the emperor, he needn't bother. So, she merely held herself at attention until he'd gone.

"I don't think he likes me very much," she said timidly, watching Dakroth walk off.

"Don't take it personally," Jegra said. "Unless you catch his fancy, he doesn't bother with small fish."

Brei turned back toward the empress, who just stared at her with curious eyes. "So, you think I'm a sex goddess?"

Jegra laughed. "When you need to be. The rest of the time, you're a little peculiar. Yes, it's true. But that's why I love you."

"You love me?" Brei gasped.

Jegra looked over at her and smiled. After a moment, she changed the subject and asked, "How may I help you, Lieutenant?" asked Jegra.

"I was going to ask the same of you, your Excellency. After last night, I just wanted to make sure you were…you know…doing okay."

"I'm fine," Jegra said curtly. She wasn't fine, but she had to at least pretend to be. It was her duty, as empress, to be a symbol of hope and strength in these difficult times. Anything less and she wouldn't consider herself fit to lead anyone, let alone be empress to a whole galaxy.

Brei opened her mouth to say something more but Jegra was pretty much finished talking about last night.

"I'll be returning to the ship shorty, Lieutenant. You can accompany me there or stay down her and help assist Grendok's team. They could use an officer to help lead them."

"Is that an order?" Brei asked harshly.

Jegra shot her an exacting look but didn't reprimand her. After rethinking it, Jegra answered, "Yes, it's an order. Stay here, Lieutenant, until the work is completed and then report to me back aboard the *Shard.*"

"Yes, Your Excellency," Brei replied. She crossed her fist over her heart and bowed.

Jegra touched the com-link on her wristband and said, "One to teleport up."

Almost immediately, golden rods of light surrounded her and, beneath the glowing shower of particles, her body began to break apart into hexagonal micro-packets of light. Holographic data packets that converted matter into energy and then reassembled that energy back into matter aboard the ship using Quantum Entanglement Buffers, or *Quebs* for short.

After the empress had teleported away, Brei'Alas wiped a single tear that had slipped down her cheek and let out a deep sigh.

"Ugh," she groaned as she turned to hike back to the camp. She wasn't looking forward to having to manage an entire team. She wasn't exactly the most social person in the galaxy and expressing herself in any manner was never easy.

But orders were orders, she told herself. And if the empress needed her space, then Brei would give it to her.

She puffed up her chest and, with a bounce of confidence in her step, followed the dirt path back toward basecamp and said to herself, "Maybe I'll take up that old goat's offer for some breakfast after all."

Sixteen hours later, Brei'Alas's team finished planting the neutron bomb charges. She knew that this many neutron bombs detonating all at once could theoretically cause a black hole. And that was the whole point. Destroy Aldebaran at any cost.

By adding a container of super-condensed antimatter at the core of the explosion, it would create the *Heigl-Brocknalius effect* whereby all the energy and pressure would reverse itself and implode, collapsing all that energy inward and creating a black hole.

If that didn't destroy the alien world, then she didn't know what could. The black hole would then feed on the nearby star and grow larger over time, eventually gobbling up the entire solar system. But she wasn't worried; they'd all be long gone before the explosion ever went off.

Brei'Alas tapped her bracelet and opened a com-link. "Mr. Grendok, sir," she called, "my team is ready to return to our ship now. Your transport will be arriving in ten minutes. I wish you all the best of luck."

A gruff yet jolly voice came back over the comm. "Thank you, my dear. And don't you let the empress out of your sight...not for one moment. She's grieving deeply and your well of optimism and warmth is exactly the soothing balm her wounded spirit needs right now."

"I'll do my best, sir," Brei replied.

"I know, child. And may Pan forever watch over you."

"You too," Brei replied.

She tapped the button on her bracelet and the com-link cut out. She then turned to see her team gathering their things and allocating them to a central location in an open field. She shifted her posture, making sure it was something more confident and less "Jr Officer," before strolling over to them.

When she arrived back at the group, she heard gasps and hushed voices talking in excited, short sentences and she turned to find Vice Admiral Callestra Van Morgan and the Lord Emperor cutting across the open meadow as they made their way toward them.

"Mind if we catch a ride with you, Lieutenant?" the emperor asked in a pleasant tone.

Brei could tell he was putting on his best show for his people. After the cold reception she'd received earlier, she wasn't too keen on being the ranking officer right about now. But it was her duty to answer him. Brei saluted, placing her right hand over her left breast, and bowed slightly, holding it for about eight seconds before rising back up.

A bubbly smile on her face, she replied, "It would be our great honor to have you join us, Your Majesty."

He saluted her back this time, as did the Vice Admiral, and Brei turned away from them in order to let out a nervous sigh. It was bad enough that she always closed up tighter than an Angorian clam around the captain, but to be in the presence of both the Vice Admiral of the fleet and the Lord Emperor himself was too much for her nerves to take.

As they stood in formation, waiting to be teleported up to the *Shard*, Brei fidgeted and kept glancing over at Emperor Dakroth. He finally noticed her about the third or fourth time she'd turned toward him, noting it seemed she had something that she desperately needed to get off her chest.

"Lieutenant," Callestra said, intervening on the emperor's behalf. "Are you just going to stand there gawking or come out with it?"

"Uh, yes, thank you, Vice Admiral." She looked at Dakroth, her eyebrows arched in a worried expression on her face.

"See, the thing is…I slept with your wife. What I mean is, technically speaking, she seduced me. But we fucked. Actually, we've fucked three times. And there's no denying that there's some sort of connection there. I just wanted to apologize and say it won't happen again…" she trailed off and looked up to find two astonished faces staring back at her.

Dakroth didn't reply at first but merely raised an eyebrow and looked over at the girl. An impressed grin spread across his thin lips and she felt a huge sense of relief that he wasn't angry with her. "I somehow doubt that, Lieutenant. Jegra fucks who she likes, and right now she seems to like fucking you. I won't stand in the way."

"Really?" Brei asked, half beside herself in astonishment. When Callestra shot her a harsh look, she corrected her mistake, "I mean, thank you, Lord Emperor. Your understanding and compassion is unrivaled."

Panic flooding her chest, Brei didn't know how to respond when, suddenly, Dakroth offered her his fist. She looked over at it, not quite understanding the gesture at first. But then she remembered something Jegra always did. She had called it a "fist-bump."

Timidly, Brei reached out her fist and gave him a light, awkward tap. He smiled at her and she smiled back. At the same time, she began to feel the fuzzy feeling of her molecules begin to transfer into energy.

Callestra Van Morgan merely watched with a raised eyebrow and an amused expression on her face. Then, in the next moment, all of them gradually dissolved into light and were whisked away to the ship.

When they re-materialized aboard the *Shard*, all of Brei's nervous jitters came back up in the form of a vomit explosion. She lurched off the teleportation pad and bent over the garbage canister in the corner and hurled right in front of Emperor Dakroth and the Vice Admiral.

Dakroth didn't pay any mind; he simply strolled off the pad and out of the teleport room. Callestra, however, held back and threw her hands up on her hips and watched Brei continue to puke out her guts.

"It all makes sense, now," Callestra said, throwing up her hands in a revelatory fashion. "She has taken pity on you. That's why she tolerates you." Callestra put her hand on Brei's back and started rubbing. "Do you need me to call a medic?"

"No, ma'am," Brei, said, wiping saliva from her chin with the back of her hand. "I just got extremely nervous in front of the emperor. More than usual."

"Oh," Callestra said, sounding confused. "I see." Of course, she didn't see. She didn't understand much of anything that was happening right now. "Well, I have things to do," she said. "Are you sure you're going to be all right, Lieutenant?"

"Yes, ma'am," Brei replied, straightening up. She saluted, and the vice admiral returned her gesture.

"Make sure you head to sick bay and get yourself checked out. That's an order. You may be coming down with something and we wouldn't want anybody else getting sick, now, would we?"

"No, ma'am. And thank you, ma'am," she said, as Callestra strolled over to teleportation room's exit. "I will."

After Callestra had left the room Brei placed both hands on her knees and retched all over again.

25

Shortly after returning to the ship, Brei found herself standing in front of Jegra's quarters, hemming and hawing, uncertain as to whether she should ring the chime or not. Determined to debrief the empress as ordered, however, she took a deep breath and pushed the button.

She drew back, almost as if in fright, when the door chime rang. Soon enough, the door slid open and Jegra stood in the entrance. She looked at Brei, then looked up and down both directions of the corridor and then reached out and grabbed Brei and pulled her into the room.

Before Brei had time to react, their lips were mashed together and Jegra's tongue was probing her tonsils. A half a second later Jegra pulled back, and smacking her lips and making a sour pucker face, she asked, "Did you vomit recently?"

"Yeah, sorry," Brei answered. "I just got back and have been so busy preparing this report I haven't had time to freshen up." Thumbing over her shoulder in the direction of Jegra's bathroom, she said, "Maybe I should go and brush my teeth first?"

"Please, do that," Jegra answered. As Brei headed into the bathroom, Jegra went over to her standing bar and rinsed her mouth out with a glass of whisky.

After Brei finished brushing her teeth, she fidgeted with her hair in the mirror. Her white uniform hung open and she gently tugged on the collar, separating it even more so that her cleavage showed. But her smallish breasts didn't do her any favors.

She let out a dissatisfied sigh, puffing at a tuft of hair in disappointment as she eyed her chest disapprovingly.

It's not your tits she's into, Brei told herself. *It's your kindness and your ability to listen and maybe the double flicker thing you can do with your tongue.*

She fiddled with her hair some more and then decided that none of it was working. Inhaling deeply, she quickly peeled off all her clothes except for her Salmon colored lingerie and kicked the pile of garments into the corner. Looking back in the mirror one last time, she clenched her butt and then, doing her best to keep them as tight as possible, walked with an uneven gait back into the bedroom.

When she appeared in the entrance, she paused to gather herself, took a breath, and then tried her best to sashay over to Jegra's bed with a seductive swagger. Almost as soon as she'd set off, however, she nearly tripped over her own feet.

She stumbled forward, throwing her hands out like a person balancing on a tightrope to stabilize herself, and then, having caught her balance, slowly stood upright again. She swiftly kicked off her work boots, but she'd given the second kick a little too much power and one of the boots flew across the room and knocked over Jegra's reading lamp.

Jegra startled at the lamp and when Brei'Alas scurried over to pick it up, she extended her hand and gestured for Brei to ignore it.

Disheartened by the fact that she was failing to pull off anything that resembled sex appeal, Brei gave up on the notion of trying to seduce the empress and just walked normally the rest of way across the room.

Brei felt herself growing excited as she drew closer to Jegra's bed. To her pleasant surprise, it appeared as though Jegra had changed into something more comfortable too. She had on a gossamer evening gown made of a tangerine fabric so transparent that it left little to the imagination.

With one knee on the bed, Brei began to crawl across the covers with catlike nimbleness when she noticed the mascara stains on Jegra's cheeks that looked like a watercolor painting melting away into the canvas. "Have you been crying?"

"I'm sorry, I didn't mean to ruin the mood, but you were there. You saw my baby," she sobbed, and then she clutched Brei so forcefully that Brei thought her arm might break. Burying her head into Brei's breast, Jegra let it all out in torrents of tears.

"It'll be okay. I don't know how. But we will get through this." Brei tried her best to console Jegra but, all things considered, her words seemed inadequate. She had no idea how to cope with such a heart-wrenching revelation. She wrapped her arms around the broken-down mother and just held her to her petite bosom.

She held Jegra until the empress fell asleep in her arms, and then, feeling awkward that she was in the empress's room half naked without any official purpose for being there, she slowly slipped her arm out from under Jegra's sleeping head and slid to the edge of the bed.

"Please, stay," a dreary voice called out and she looked over to see Jegra staring at her through half open eyes. She reached her hand out and took Brei's and gently drew her back into her embrace. Brei curled up beside Jegra, this time becoming the small spoon, and let the empress wrap her arms around her.

"That's nice," Brei said, as Jegra cupped her breast with one hand and the other resting on top of Brei's abs.

"It is, isn't it?" Jegra answered sleepily.

They lay there holding one another until Jegra's gentle snoring filled the room. Brei didn't go to sleep though. Too many things were running through her mind. In fact, she barely remembered falling asleep at all when, all of a sudden, her bracelet's ringing aroused her from her half-slumber, alerting her to the time.

"What is it?" Jegra murmured.

"I have to get ready for my shift."

"So soon," she said, sounding somewhat disappointed.

"Should I come back later?" Brei asked, looking into Jegra's smoldering brown eyes.

"I'd like that," Jegra said. She leaned forward and gave Brei a peck on the lips, enticing a grin.

Brei, not knowing what to do in such a situation, since she'd never really dated girls before—not that she didn't like girls; the opportunity simply hadn't ever presented itself—she leaned in and kissed Jegra awkwardly on the upper lip.

"I'm sorry," she apologized, missing her mark. "I can do better."

"Show me," Jegra said, a sleep laden smile forming on her full lips.

Brei kissed her again, this time hitting her mark. It was long and sensual and Jegra even licked her lips when she'd finished partaking in the most delicious kiss she'd ever shared with another woman.

"That was much better," Jegra said, touching her lips with her fingers as if in shock.

"I have to go," Brei informed the empress, still hesitant on what she should do. But for whatever reason, she felt drawn into Jegra's lips again, and before she knew it, they were making out like a couple of teenagers.

"I thought you had to go," Jegra stated between kisses.

"I do," Brei replied.

"Mmm…" Jegra moaned, leaning into the kiss.

Slowly pulling back, Brei laughed. "I'm normally not like this," she said, withdrawing from Jegra's embrace.

Jegra just leaned back and watched her.

"What?" Brei'Alas asked, brushing her hair back over her shoulder.

"You don't give yourself enough credit. Underneath that meek facade is a gorgeous woman."

"I've never felt all that beautiful," Brei replied.

"You are, though. Don't sell yourself short."

Another chime sounded from Brei's bracelet and she looked down. "Shit, I'm going to be late."

Before she could scurry off, though, Jegra shoved her onto the bed. "Wha—" Brei gasped out, uncertain as what exactly was happening. When Jegra's hands slipped off her panties, however, and she looked down as the empress buried her face between her thighs, she kicked her head back and gasped, "Oh, my…"

Eyes closed, Brei took in every sensation. Jegra worked her to climax and, legs clamping tight as she orgasmed, Jegra slid up and kissed Brei on her thin blue lips.

That's when the comm came on and Barrion alerted her to the fact she was late for her shift. "Brei, what's going on? You're late, and you're never late."

"Sorry, I was just…I um…"

Jegra winked at her and then spoke up, even as Brei was waving her hands and pleading her not to. "She was just enjoying some morning breakfast with her empress," Jegra informed.

"Apologies, Your Grace," Barrion replied, feeling bad for having interrupted the empress's breakfast. "I had no idea, I'll, um, inform the captain."

"Please, do that."

"And Brei, please, feel free to take your time. I'll cover for you as long as you need."

The comm cut off and Brei hit Jegra in the arm. "You're terrible." They both laughed and then Jegra slowly slid back down.

"What are you doing?" Brei asked.

"You heard your boyfriend. We have all the time in the world." She kissed Brei's thigh and then looked up into her amber eyes.

"I can't," Brei said, using her arms to sit up. She met Jegra's gaze and then said. "If this is turning into something serious, I can't let it interfere with my job."

"I understand," Jegra said, bending down and dappling kisses along Brei's other thigh. "You've gotta do what you've gotta do."

"I'm serious!" Brei laughed, taking Jegra's chin in her fingers and gently guiding her eyes back up to hers.

"I know," Jegra answered. Slowly spreading Brei's legs apart, Jegra put her lips right up to Brei's wet sapphic lips and French kissed her long and deep. Pulling her tongue out, she rose up and kissed Brei on her mouth.

"Satisfied?" Brei asked, smiling at her precocious girlfriend.

"Very," replied Jegra, licking her lips and smiling brightly.

"Good," Brei said, climbing out of bed. When she tried to saunter away with a seductive swivel of her hips, she tripped on the rug and crashed to the floor.

"Ooh!" Jegra gasped out in shock. "Are you all right?"

"I'm fine," Brei said, bouncing back up.

"Haven't really got that swagger thing down yet."

"Nope," she said, feeling embarrassed.

Jegra watched as Brei scrambled to get her clothes on and then race out the door.

Brei paused in the open entrance. She turned back and smiled at Jegra, who was still watching her with those smoldering brown eyes of hers. Brei blew a goodbye kiss and then slipped out into the corridor.

Her hair a mess, her body odor lingering on her from the lack of a shower, and a hickey on her neck that she had no clue how she was going to explain to Barrion, caused an abnormal amount of stress, but since she couldn't put it off any longer, she ignored her disheveled appearance and headed off to start her shift.

Brei'Alas popped up her collar to try and hide the hickey best she could, put her shoulders back, straightened her posture, and confidently strode onto the bridge. "G'morning, everyone!" she chirped in her usual manner.

Lianica looked over at her from over her cup of steaming tea, the tea-bag still hanging out over the lip of her mug, and watched the disheveled, yet strangely confident, Brei'Alas take her post.

The moment Brei had settled into her seat, a proximity alarm chirped. "Captain," Brei said, looking up at the main viewscreen. "The Galliforn flagship has just entered the system."

"If you'd be so kind, Lieutenant, please hail the *Chiron* and give them our greetings. And send them the coordinates for the ground teams. I'm sure they'll want to begin teleporting their people up ASAP."

"Yes, ma'am," Brei'Alas replied as she carried out her orders. Not even a few seconds had gone by when the expression on Brei's face turned to one of absolute horror.

"Sir, they're aiming their plasma canons at the surface," Lieutenant Commander Barrion shouted.

"Bring the *Shard* in between the *Chiron* and the surface. Now!"

The *Shard* moved into position, acting as a shield and began taking a heavy pounding from the heavily armed *Chiron*.

"Our shields won't be able to take much more of this," Brei shouted above the hiss of electrical sparks igniting in the background.

"Shields down to fifty-six percent," Barrion relayed.

"Start teleporting the remaining ground teams into the cargo holds. We'll worry about overcrowding later."

"Yes, ma'am!" Brei'Alas shouted and she jumped up from her station and sidled up to Barrion. As she leaned over, he glanced down at her neck and his eyes widened.

"Is that a hickey?" he asked, somewhat shocked.

"Now's not the time," Brei said as she frantically worked the controls to get a lock on the ground crew. The computer bleeped, letting her know the lock was good, and she ran her fingers up the teleport pad. "Activating teleporters now."

"Drop the shields," Lianica shouted above more electrical explosions and another flurry of sparks.

The ship's lights dimmed as all energy from the shields went to the teleporters. The plasma blasts from the other ship glanced off the hull of the *Shard*, barely scorching it, and the areas that did get singed moved like a gelatin blob and healed themselves before hardening again.

Even though the *Shard* was designed to take on direct plasma cannon fire, the high yield disruptors of the *Chiron* were powerful enough to do some real damage if they stayed in the line of fire too long.

It was like sitting under a tin roof during an acid-rain storm. The tin would protect you for a while, but eventually the acid rain would eat its way through. This was true with the hot plasma blasts and liquid korridium alloy as well.

"Structural integrity is down to thirty-three percent," Barrion said.

"I got them all," Brei'Alas shouted. "No, wait," she corrected. "All but for one."

"Who is it?" Lianica demanded to know.

Lieutenant Brei'Alas turned to her captain. "Grendok, ma'am. He's teleported himself to the *Chiron*."

"Then may Pan be with him," Lianica said. She turned to T'Zera and ordered, "Get us out of here, Lieutenant."

T'Zera slid out of her seat and into Brei's seat, situating herself at the navigation station, and dialed in the coordinates. She glanced at Captain Blackstar for confirmation and, with the captain's nod, she turned back to the controls and activated the slipstream drive.

26

The iridescent ship flew alongside the massive Nyctan battle cruiser as both ships made their way toward the Correll system and the Seyferrian Republic for peace accords.

Onelle stretched up and out of her chair and then went over to the teleportation pad at the back of the flight cabin. She stepped onto it, brushed down the pearl-white cocktail dress she wore, which emulated the lustrous quality of pearls exactly, and then took a deep breath. She tapped the small opal pendant she wore and it chimed, doubling as a communicator. "I'm ready," she said, wondering why teleportation pads made her so nervous.

Almost immediately, the red Nyctan light of the *queb beams* danced around her and her vision blurred, faded, then came back into focus again. When her eyes had finally re-adjusted to the new environment, she found herself standing aboard the Nyctan ship with a black-eyed Nyctan girl staring at her from across the room.

"My name is Aidora," the girl said, bowing slightly. Her raven black hair trailed down to the small of her back, the silkiest hair Onelle had ever seen. The girl rose up and cautiously inched closer, keeping a demure pose, so as not to startle her guest. "I'll be your personal equerry for the duration of your stay aboard the ship."

"It's a pleasure to make your acquaintance," Onelle said, stepping down off the teleportation platform.

The Nyctan girl clasped both hands timidly in front of her, and then bowed her head. "Welcome aboard the *Qui'tek'alon*, Mistress Te'Legra."

"Qui'tek'alon?" Onelle repeated inquisitively. "That's a Seyfferian word, is it not?"

The girl's eyes rose back up and she smiled with diminutive, thin lips that had a slight nervous quiver to them. "Yes, it means the Great Negotiator in their people's tongue." She could see by Onelle's confusion that more explanation needed to be done. "Our people often name diplomatic vessels in the tongue of the races we are dealing with. Minor things like this prove to be psychologically beneficial when engaging in diplomatic talks."

"Is that why the Voice called me here? Is this going to be the peace renegotiation summit that people have been whispering about?"

The Nyctan girl smiled more broadly, her smooth white skin giving her the appearance of a porcelain doll. "It may be more than just peace talks, but those are a part of it, yes."

"All right, then," Onelle said, stepping off the teleportation pad and walking up to the girl. "Please show me to my quarters."

Again, the girl bowed reverently, spun deftly on her heels, and led Onelle out of the teleportation room and into a massive corridor which was unlike anything she'd ever seen before. Ships this size made even her biggest space stations look like middling yachts; even her biggest space yacht would fit in the smallest hangar bay of this massive vessel.

But that was Nyctan design for you, always opulent, intricate; always over the top. The religious aspect of their towering cathedrals and religious monoliths back on their homeworld carried over into every aspect of their ship design. This ship even had arches and buttresses built onto the outside of the vessel, giving it an ornate, almost decadent quality, and it looked like nothing else she'd ever seen.

After a long, winding walk through the elaborately decorated interiors, they eventually arrived at Onelle's chambers.

"This is you," Aidora said, gesturing with a wave toward the entrance to Onelle's quarters. "Will there be anything else you require, my mistress?"

"I would prefer my dinner be prepared fresh. None of the synthesized stuff. And no animal flesh, either. Any of the Arkadian dishes should be fine."

"As you wish," Aidora replied, bowing slightly and then turning to leave.

Onelle watched her stroll up the corridor and then entered her quarters. The lighting was dim, and she said, "Computer, raise lighting by fifty percent."

"Belay that order," a voice called out from the darkness.

Reflexively, Onelle slipped her hand into the v-cut opening of her dress, reached under her left breast and drew out a compact blaster—no bigger than a digital stylus pen. "Who's there?"

"Somebody that has a proposition for you."

Her green skin bristled with goosebumps and her stomach clenched tight. Not believing the mysterious figure hiding in the shadows, she demanded, "Come out where I can see you."

An older, but well groomed, Dagon gentlemen with flowing white hair that rested past his shoulders stepped into view. Onelle recognized him from the galactic televid news.

"Senator Targon?" she gasped, wondering why he'd invited himself into her room like this. "What are you doing in my personal chambers?"

"I apologize for the cloak and dagger routine, but this vessel has eyes and ears everywhere." He drew out a small device from his tunic-styled senatorial gown and flipped it open like a compact mirror. It started flashing and sending out a strange, rhythmic chirp. "This," Targon said, nodding at the device laying in the palm of his hand, "will allow us to speak freely."

"What is there to talk about that requires a scrambler?" Onelle asked, tucking the pen-styled blaster back into her green cleavage.

"The Nyctans are going to open up limited trade with the colonies that acquiesce to the rule of the Gilded Protectorate. That's what they're calling themselves now. Predictably, Dagon Prime will not submit to any rule of law they themselves haven't erected. This means the siege will continue indefinitely for the greater systems, though you shall continue to oversee all the trade. You hold all the cards. Which is why you hold great leverage at these hearings."

"So, what is it you're asking of me, Senator?" She eyed him suspiciously.

"I want to establish a more robust black market."

"There's already a thriving black market," she countered.

"Let me put it another way. I want a limited share in controlling the black market. You, of course, would be the galactic kingpin of the operation. I would merely bring you access to the systems that do not comply with this so-called Gilded Protectorate."

He smiled, then took a step closer. "Consider it a partnership. I win by becoming the hero to my people. You win by having me at your mercy. And what is better than having a Dagon Senator who sits on the High Council at your beck and call?"

"At my mercy?" Onelle repeated, her curiosity piqued. She strode over to the standing bar, took a glass, added a couple of large ice cubes, and began to mix herself a drink. "It's a tempting offer, but it sounds like a lot of trouble. What if the Nyctans catch wind of our back-channel dealings? I doubt the Voice of H'aaztre would be happy we have allied ourselves against her interests."

"Ah" he replied, stroking his grizzled chin. "A very reasonable concern. But let me assure you, anything said here, in this room, stays here."

Onelle eyed the handsome gentleman up and down. He was older, but he looked nice enough. She imagined that if her mother had even been half as beautiful, well, she could see where Callestra got her stunning good looks.

Presumably to raise a leg comfortably on the nearby chair, Onelle slowly rolled up the hemline of her dress. She hiked the stretchy fabric up until her sky-blue lace panties peeked out.

"Prove you mean it. Seal the deal with a kiss," she said, a prurient smile forming on her lips, her drink dangling casually in her left hand.

Senator Targon slowly settled onto his knees before the woman and ran his blue hand along her bare thigh. Her green skin was the softest he'd ever felt.

Once he had his fingers curled around the waistband of her underwear, he looked up into her lime green eyes with purpose and slowly began to slide her panties down her slender green thighs.

Still holding her drink out, the ice cubes rattling in the glass, she looked down at him as he buried his face in-between her thighs. She kicked her head back and let out a loud moan as soon as she felt his warm tongue penetrate her flowery garden patch.

Onelle grabbed the back of Targon's head, threading her green fingers through his long white hair. She pulled him in so tight he could scarcely breathe. She held him there until panic set in.

When he squeezed her ass with such vigor, she thought she might scream, she pressed her crotch into him even more. After another minute and a half of him unable to breathe, she felt his body go limp and she dropped him to the floor.

Senator Targon fell to the floor with a thud, unconscious. Her blue panties around her ankles, Onelle looked down at him with a curious expression and then downed her drink in one smooth swig.

Crouching down next to him, she whispered into his ear, "I'll think about it." Rising back up, she pulled up her panties, rolled her dress down, and then looked around the room for the bathroom.

Once inside, she undressed, took a shower, and cleaned the Dagon stench off of her. After her shower, she put on the bathrobe and went back out into the main room, only to find Aidora with a silver dome sitting on a food cart.

"I took the honor of removing the gentleman caller from your chambers, Mistress Onelle," Aidora said.

"I appreciate that," Onelle replied.

"May I inquire as to what the senator was doing here?"

Onelle shot the girl a harsh look, but the girl did not flinch—which meant she was under obligation to ask such invasive questions. Onelle smiled at her own personal little spy. At least she hadn't committed to anything that would get her in trouble, so she decided the truth was the best option.

"He was…trying to negotiate a side-deal."

"And how did you answer?"

"I didn't," Onelle replied. "I don't do business with just anyone. Not unless there's something to gain from it. I'm afraid all the senator had to offer were empty promises."

"That's a relief," Aidora said, letting loose a pent-up sigh. "I'm glad you're as smart and cunning as they say you are."

"And who would *they* be, exactly?" Onelle asked. She was never one to let a good compliment go overlooked.

"Azra'il Nun, for one," Aidora answered.

"The Voice herself? Are you serious?" Onelle asked, half skeptical. "Did she actually say that?"

"Something to that effect, mistress," Aidora replied, her smile growing. "She was quite impressed with how you handled the 'Raphine' situation."

"Ah, I see." Onelle took another sip of her drink and then sighed deeply. "That's a relief to hear."

Aidora went over to the tray cover and removed it, showing a very lovely presentation of steaming vegetables garnishing a perfectly cooked Arkadian king prawn, her personal favorite. "Your dinner, Mistress Onelle."

"Oh, thank goodness it's not that Nyctan worm slag," she said in a relieved tone.

Aidora raised an eyebrow.

"I mean, no offense, or anything," Onelle said, back tracking a bit, "but Nyctan food doesn't sit well with me. A sensitive stomach, I'm afraid."

"Understandable," Aidora said. Her tone wasn't the least judgmental and she politely bowed again and left Onelle to enjoy her dinner in solitude.

After exiting Onelle's chambers, Aidora waited in the hall until the doors shut behind her. She locked her hand behind her back and a sinister smile formed on her thin lips. Her big, black eyes blinked twice, and then two golden halos appeared in them.

She turned up the hall and found Senator Targon being propped up by two massive Nyctan guards. He looked a tad roughed up, as though they'd done a bit of work on him after finding him in Onelle's room.

"You've been a very naughty boy, Senator," she said, looking up at him. "Now, what in the world am I going to do with you?"

"Why don't you just kill me and see how far that gets you?" he snarled.

"Tsk, tsk, Senator. Is that any way to be?"

"You and your kind can just burn in Helios for all I care."

"If I wanted you dead, Senator, you'd be dead. But I'm afraid I must tolerate your obstinance a while longer as, it seems, my master has plans for you."

"How about you tell your master for me that he can suck my—"

"Sleep," the girl commanded and, like a narcoleptic, Senator Targon immediately drifted off to sleep.

Aidora turned her back to the guards and, after a moment's thought, said, "Take him back to his quarters and tuck him into bed. Lay out some empty bottles of Dragonian ale and some Arkadian brandy and erase the last hour of his memory."

"Yes, ma'am," the soldiers said, and with that they hauled Senator Targon away.

Aidora took a deep breath, blinked her eyes twice, and the golden halo, the mark of H'aaztre, vanished. She looked around as though she were confused what she was doing out in the corridor, and then went back to Onelle's door. It chimed once and Onelle's voice beckoned her to come inside.

"I take it the meal is to your satisfaction?" Aidora asked, finding Onelle seated at the large dinner table off to the side of the main room.

With a mouth full of king prawn, Onelle replied, "It's so juicy...care to try some?"

Aidora shook her head and politely declined. After a few more bites, Onelle looked back up at the girl watching her eat.

"It's a little bit weird…you just standing there watching me eat like that. Just try some."

"Apologies," Aidora said, "I didn't realize I was being rude." She turned her back to Onelle and continued to wait for her to finish eating without watching.

"No, no, that's worse," Onelle informed the girl.

Aidora turned back around and resumed her staring.

"Just one bite," Onelle said, holing out a piece of the stringy white meat.

"Just one bite," Aidora said, leaning in. Opening her mouth, she accepted the morsel of king prawn and began chewing. With her mouth full, she mumbled, "Oh, my Gilded God, this tastes superb!"

"See? I told you," Onelle said, pointing the petite, three-pronged shellfish fork at the girl.

Wiping the corner of her mouth with the back of her hand, she lowered her gaze. "Apologies, I'm not supposed to…" she trailed off and looked back up at Onelle, who was smiling at her.

"Are you always this timid?"

"No, but I'm on duty. And there's a certain level of etiquette that my job requires. I've overstepped my bounds and must report my failings."

"And what will happen once you've done that?"

"I'll be punished for my insubordination."

"Punished how?" Onelle asked in a worried tone.

"By receiving ten lashes."

"Seems a bit extreme, if you ask me," Onelle replied.

Aidora looked her straight in the eyes. "Not if I deserve it."

"And do you feel that you deserve it?"

"Yes," Aidora replied without even the slightest hesitation.

Onelle shrugged. Aidora really was just a serf, after all.

"Will there be anything else?" Aidora asked as she gathered up Onelle's dishes and began setting them back onto the tray.

"Are there any Knights of Caelum aboard?" Onelle asked.

Aidora raised her black eyes and stared at Onelle for a moment and then replied, "Yes. Every Nyctan battled cruiser has at least one Knight aboard."

"Excellent," Onelle replied, leaning back in her seat and rubbing her stomach. "Be a good girl and call the knight to my chambers."

Aidora nodded, finished tidying up, and then rolled the cart out of Onelle's room. As she stood in the entrance, she looked back and said, "I'll see to it right away, Mistress Onelle."

Onelle Te'Legra Agnar smiled and watched the girl leave. Once she was gone, she sprang to her feet and hastened over to the small kitchen nook and prepared all the things she needed for the green tea ceremony.

She knew that Knights made a solemn oath to remain celibate, but she had always wanted to challenge herself and seduce one. As an expert courtesan, there wasn't a man or woman in the galaxy who could resist her. And she was determined to prove it by seducing a Knight of Caelum.

After a few minutes the door chimed. Onelle said, "Enter."

When the devilishly handsome Nyctan warrior stepped into her room, she finished setting the ceremonial table and gestured for him to come in. "Please, take a seat."

He did as she said, trying not to stare at her breasts as she leaned over to pour the tea. Of course, she'd deliberately loosened her robe so it would slip open easily.

She set the steaming pot down and gestured with a nod for him to drink.

She, too, took her cup, matching him movement for movement. When he sipped, she sipped. When he put his cup down again, so did she. "Tell me, knight," she said, taking the teapot and refilling his and her cup, "what is the punishment for bedding a woman?"

"Twenty lashes, my mistress. If it happens twice, there is a mandatory demotion."

"And what is the punishment for not obeying a ranking superior, sir knight?"

"Also, twenty lashes."

"Now answer me this…am I your superior?"

He looked over at her with uncertain eyes and then, after studying the feminine curvature of her body, cleared his throat.

"Azra'il Nun has appointed you Captain of Commerce, which means you outrank me, yes."

"So, if both punishments are equal, it doesn't matter which one of them you break, now, does it?" She set the teapot down and waited for his answer.

He shook his head, unable to come out with a clear answer. "I don't know, mistress. These rules of conduct and other protocols aren't laws, per se. But there are punishments for disobeying them."

"In that case…I won't tell if you don't." She raised her cup, beckoning him to do the same. He did, and they drank.

After finishing their tea, she rose up, letting her robe slip to the floor. Standing before him, naked, she said in a sultry voice, "Now, knight, join me in bed."

Onelle's pheromone production was off the charts, and she had nearly broken a sweat by secreting as many pheromones as she possibly could. After all, it was the only way she knew with certainty that she could seduce a Knight. In fact, the formal tea drinking ceremony was just a ruse. She was flooding her entire chambers with so many pheromones it would make any normal man lose himself to pure lust-induced madness.

"Yes, mistress," he answered, and slowly, almost reluctantly, began to unclasp the braided loops of his uniform.

Once he was standing before her in nothing but the nervous expression he wore on his face, she took his hand and led him over to the bed.

She lay down first, spreading out across the satin sheets. She swiveled her hips to the side, slowly raising one leg up and over, spreading her knees wide and displaying herself in all of her luxuriant splendor for him to behold.

The knight's cheeks flushed as he stood at the end of the bed, and he couldn't help but look away with embarrassment. He'd never seen a woman in all her glory before.

Yet, slowly, his eyes found their way back to her and a smile formed on her face. When she noticed him begin to stiffen, her smile spread wider and she reached up with her slender hand and gestured with a finger for him to lay down beside her.

His broad, rounded shoulders sank down as he climbed onto the bed with her. He crawled across the satin sheets toward her like an albino tiger, his black eyes locking with hers. She waited for his muscular form to hover over her and then, reaching up and taking his neck in her hand, she pulled him onto her.

She felt the tightness in his muscles as he resisted her touch, but as his white flesh came into contact with the green flesh of her breasts, she felt the tension drain out of him. She smiled up at him and wrapped her legs around his hips, guiding his pelvis into hers.

"There. That's better," she cooed, coupling with him.

Deliberate in her movements, she began to slide up and down on him. Although she could tell he was inexperienced, she didn't let that slow her down. She was more than used to handling all the work herself. And, if she was being honest, his inexperience excited her. The added fact that she had a certain amount of power over him excited her even more.

Onelle handled all the rest, and although he seemed as though he were only doing it out of obligation, she could easily tell he didn't regret it, either.

"How does that feel?" she whispered into his ear.

"It feels fine, mistress," he answered in a dry fashion, void of any emotion or hint of pleasure.

"Just fine?" she asked, feeling slightly offended. She bore down on him, hard, and took him all in, and then squeezed, tightening to a full-on Kegel contraction. Rubbing her fingers through his dark hair, she gripped tight and jerked his head back. At the same time, she kept herself tight and continued to ride him harder. Eventually, a subtle twinge of pleasure appeared on his face. Ashamed by his own weakness, he quickly tried to hide it by looking away.

Onelle smiled, knowing that she had him under her spell.

Roughly forty-five minutes into their session, Onelle fell back onto the sheets of her bed, completely drenched in sweat. Panting, she waved her hand and dismissed him. "I've had my fill, sir knight. You're free to go."

"Palamedes," he replied.

She looked over at him with a blank expression. "Excuse me?"

"My name, mistress. Is Palamedes."

"I see," she replied, trying to sound interested. "Nice to make your acquaintance, Sir Palamedes. Maybe we can do it again sometime."

As a Knight, Palamedes did not respond to her invitation but simply withdrew himself from her and slid off the side of the bed. After he finished dressing, he turned to her and asked, "Will you be needing any of my other services?"

"No, not at the moment," Onelle said in a sleepy voice. Satisfied, she yawned and waved him out. He bowed, acknowledging her unspoken command, turned and left her chambers.

Palamedes, stepped out of Onelle's chambers and into the corridor and the Mark of H'aaztre flashed on his eyes. As the golden halo faded, a cruel and soulless smile appeared on his lips.

What Onelle didn't know was that every Nyctan aboard the ship was under *his* control. They were the most subservient of the serfs, and so, the easiest for H'aaztre to control. The weakest knight, the most submissive servant girl, even the captain of this vessel was an indecisive lummox.

It was a ship of slaves, and once the peace summit was fully underway, the slaves would all be overridden with one single command: kill everyone. Including themselves, once the task was completed.

The official story would be that it was a coolant leak and a faulty warning system that, regrettably, led to a core breach and the unfortunate death of all the delegates. A scandal, to be sure, in these trying times.

But by murdering the world's peace ambassadors, H'aaztre would sow the seeds of distrust and fear on a galactic scale. Throw in some conspiracy theories for fun, and he'd have every world questioning one another's motives. The galactic governments would be at each other's throats demanding justice. And as they destabilized, he'd be ready for phase three of the occupation. Complete and utter subjugation.

27

Grendok watched from out of the nearby view portal as the *Shard* darted out of the system in a flash of light. He turned away from the viewing windows of the lower deck corridor and slapped the coolant cartridge into his plasma rifle and cocked it. Its high pitched whine signaled him that it was fully powered up and ready to go. "It's time to take back my bloody ship," he growled in a low voice.

The hoary bearded satyr stepped out into the main corridor. Red light washed over him as the ship's alarms rang silently in the background; only the light of the display panels pulsed in emergency hues. Grendok glanced up and down the corridor for any possible threats. Finding it empty, he let himself take a deep breath.

The only reason the *Chiron* would ever fire on the landing party was if The Voice had boarded the ship and brainwashed most of the crew. But since he didn't know who was and who wasn't affected by her hypnotic hold, he had to assume everyone was hostile. Cocking his plasma rifle, the gun warmed with a whine as it heated the plasma bolt inside.

Ironically enough, this wouldn't be the first time he'd had to fight his way to the bridge to regain a ship. There'd been a mutiny aboard the first ship he ever served aboard, some three hundred and seventy-nine years ago. A medical supply frigate called the *Nomios*.

The incident all began when the first officer, *May His Name be Ever Forgotten*, wanted to deny medical aid to a quarantined world stricken with a lethal virus that destroyed the immune system of the planet's inhabitants. The captain of the *Nomios*, the now famous Themis Pindar, ordered a landing mission to take down medical supplies and assist with creating a retrovirus that could save millions of lives. The only problem was, this would require at least two officers to voluntarily become infected while they remained on the surface.

Believing a suicide mission to try and save an entire planet's civilization was not worth sacrificing the lives of his fellow officers, the first officer led a mutiny against Captain Pindar, hoping to safeguard the lives of the crew. As it happened, several officers agreed with the commander's assessment that the mission was a death sentence, especially considering there was no guarantee a cure could be found in time to save the officers who volunteered for the mission.

Naturally, Grendok had sided with his captain. And with a small crew of loyal officers, they managed to take back the bridge, secure the ship, and arrest the mutineers.

Grendok himself volunteered for the mission, and, indeed, he became infected with the virus, but not before discovering that the aliens of the disease-stricken world of Qu'Mar had advanced cloning technology which he used to give himself a second life. And then another. And another.

Eventually the virus was cured, thanks to the efforts of Themis Pindar, Grendok of Galliforn, and Zendaya Briareos. Along with a team of Qu'Marrion scientists, Grendok and Zendaya were able to reverse engineer the virus and create a retrovirus that saved the satyrs of Qu'Mar. But the cost was great, and both Grendok and Zendaya, afflicted with the virus, died before they could receive the cure.

Luckily, however, Grendok had saved samples of their DNA, taken from the medlab aboard the *Nomios*, and had already cloned both Zendaya and himself. They lived on Qu'Mar, helping the people for a time, and then the war against the Dagon Empire brought the entire Galliforn alliance into the fray, forcing both of them to enlist in the military.

Always an eccentric, Grendok made numerous copies of himself and allowed his various clones to have lives of their own. But if they chose to continue on with their immortality, they had to stay loyal to one thing and one thing only—the Old Way. The way of the ancestors of Pan. The way of the nymph and the fawn-folk. The way of the noblest of satyrs of his clansmen and the forest-folk.

The Galliforn philosophy of life was simple: *Strength in the face of weakness. Honor over cowardice. Kindness in lieu of selfishness. Practice the old ways over the new. And always honor the Moon Goddess, Selene.*

It was Pan himself who'd first set down the law, and it was the satyrs who were the keepers of the Old Way. The way not to be forgotten; the way to be remembered and practiced.

After the war, which relied heavily on the labor of clones, cloning was banned altogether, made illegal all throughout the Commonwealth. This ensured that clones wouldn't be treated as second class citizens or made into slaves on worlds who might acquire the technology but not be morally advanced enough to take a cloned individual's natural and legal rights into consideration.

Grendok, however, rebelled against the system that wanted to take away the very thing that had granted him a second chance at life, and so he took his cloning operation underground.

Branded a criminal, a warrant for his arrest was issued. He then began selling designer clones on the black market to those who could afford it, and this led to him getting embroiled with some high-end gangster families who wanted more than just clones. They wanted the means to create their own clone armies so that one might be able to take over the other rival faction and vice versa.

Instead of sidling up with gangsters, however, he went behind their backs and sold the technology to the Seyfferian Republic, who then modified and improved the technology.

This didn't make him any friends with the factions of the criminal underworld, and they have had it out for him ever since.

See, he liked to think that, although not entirely corrupt, he has always been perfectly willing to break the laws when it suited him and aided in his agenda. As such, Grendok of Galliforn has lived out the past couple of centuries existing in the gray areas of galactic law.

Impressed by how much thinking he was able to do before reaching the first major junction, he quickly flattened himself up against the wall when he heard several voices approaching from up the corridor.

Not wasting a moment, he found a nearby door and ducked inside just in time for the two voices to pass by the other side of the closed door. *That was close*, he thought, letting out a sigh.

When he turned to inspect what room he'd hidden himself in, he was pleased to discover it was the ship's dry cleaners.

It only took him a nano-second to find a uniform his size hanging on one of the racks, and although it wouldn't have the medals or pins denoting his rank of Admiral, or, at least, the rank of one of his copies who was likely somewhere aboard the ship, he might be able to dupe a few low-ranking officers into thinking he was the admiral off duty.

Once he was dressed, making sure to leave his lapel hanging open, as many officers did when off duty, he picked up his plasma rifle and slung it across his back. Then, acting as if he owned the ship, he stepped out into the corridor and confidently made his way to the lift.

Just as he stepped up to the doors the lift opened. There were two stunned-looking officers standing before him.

"Admiral," they gasped in unison, both saluting him.

He returned their salutes and grumbled, "At ease, officers," and then stepped onto the lift.

They were halfway to the bridge when he couldn't help but notice one of them eyeing him suspiciously.

Out of his peripheral vision Grendok glimpsed the man cautiously reaching down for his blaster which was holstered at his waist.

"I wouldn't do that if I were you, son," Grendok growled in a low, threatening tone.

This prompted the second officer to step back while the first grabbed Grendok from behind.

Kicking his hind legs off the wall Grendok slammed the second officer into the opposite side of the lift with such force he was rendered unconscious. Breaking free Grendok circled behind the second officer and pulled his gun from his holster before the officer could and shot him in the back.

The officer collapsed into a heap next to his comrade and Grendok checked the weapon. "Pan must be watching over you, boy, because it was set to stun."

Both officers incapacitated, he tucked the additional blaster into his waist, feeling it might come in handy later.

"Sweet dreams, gentlemen," Grendok said, stepping over their unconscious bodies as the elevator's doors opened. Grendok stepped onto an empty bridge. As he eased out into the open, he drew both weapons and scanned for any potential ambushes. Only the glowing pulse of the red emergency lighting showed any signs of activity.

That's when the main viewscreen flickered, came to life, and Azra'il Nun stared back at him with her malicious smile. It looked especially eerie as the bottom half was completely mechanical and her grin seemed to exude a kind of agony that comes with injuries that haven't heeled fully.

"My dear Grendok, did you honestly think I'd just let you all off the hook after what you pulled?"

Grendok shrugged. "Hadn't given it much thought," he replied. Then, aiming his rifle at the monitor, he shot it. The plasma bolt pierced the monitor and it popped with a small internal explosion and went dark. Gray smoke started streaming out of the gaping hole.

Sure, it would have been easier to simply cut the feed, but this gesture was more dramatic. The last thing Azra'il Nun would see was the flash of his blaster's muzzle aimed straight at her head. Message sent and received.

Grendok turned to his ready room suspecting that his younger self was there waiting for him. That's when the automated countdown to the self-destruct began. It was set to detonate exactly one minute after Aldebaran blew, so that if he did manage to find a way to escape the neutron explosion and subsequent formation of a black hole, he'd still have only one minute to enjoy his short-lived victory.

The ready room doors slid open and he found his younger doppelgänger standing across from him holding a blaster to Almathea's head. Grendok stepped into the room and raised his hand. "Let her go," he said. "This is between you and me."

"The moment I let her go you're going to blast me and then place one of those infernal memory extractors into the base of my skull to get the kill codes to the auto-self-destruct."

"That's the plan, anyway," Grendok replied to his brainwashed other self, a wry grin forming on his goat mouth.

It was at this time that he noticed that Almathea wasn't struggling and he leaped out of the way just as she brought up a blaster of her own. The bolt missed him as he crashed to the ground behind the leather sofa off to the edge of the room.

Almathea and the admiral fanned out, moving around either side of the command desk, training their sights on the sofa.

"You're surrounded and out-gunned, old man. The best thing for you to do is surrender quietly."

"I somehow doubt that The Voice told you to take me peacefully."

Almathea's shrill laugh pierced the silence in the room. "Always one step ahead, as usual, eh, Admiral? But you're right. When we catch you we're to skin you alive in front of the entire crew," she said gleefully.

"Fine," Grendok said, raising his hands above the sofa in surrender. "I submit."

He tossed the weapons to the side so they knew he was serious, then added, "I'm coming out now. So, don't shoot. Or do. It's up to you how this plays out."

Slowly, Grendok rose to his feet and faced his attackers, hands raised at his sides in unconditional surrender.

"What are you doing?" the admiral demanded to know. He was unfamiliar with such a tactic. Surrendering now didn't advance Grendok's mission and only seemed to preemptively end things. Did the fool want to get skinned alive?

Almathea gave the admiral a confused glance as if to ask what they should do next as this turn of events was completely unorthodox.

The admiral retrained his blaster on the senior version of himself and glared down the barrel of the gun at him, narrowing one eye. "What's your game here, Grendok? I know you as well as I know myself. You always have an ace up your sleeve. So, what is it?"

"Ah, yes, and I was counting on you figuring it out, but, as you said, Almathea, I'm always ten steps ahead. Only this isn't a game of cards we're playing. It's a game of chess, and you've just been dealt a checkmate."

"What in Pan's beard is he talking about?" Almathea asked.

"*En passant,*" a mysterious voice answered.

They all startled except for the old goat himself and looked around for whoever had spoken. Before they could figure out what was happening, a resounding crack to the back of their skulls sent them to the floor with a thump; Almathea and the admiral collapsed in a heap. At the same time, a flicker of blue and purple light followed by some electrical discharge flashed and a shimmer of light, like a heat mirage on the Thessalonican dessert, slowly melted away to reveal a solid form.

Raven Nightguard, having manifested out of thin air, stood over them and casually holstered her blaster back at her hip.

"I'm glad you got my message," Grendok said. "I wasn't sure you had, with everything else going on."

"There's only one satyr I'm loyal to," Raven said, shooting Grendok a subtle grin. "Now, what do you say we get out of here before this entire place is swallowed up by that thing out there." She nodded at the ring world outside the view portal.

"I should have listened to you the first time," he said after a moment of reflection. Raven shot him a curious look. He turned to her with a sheepish grin. "When we first discovered this place, it frightened you. You warned me to stay away from Aldebaran, but I was too greedy. I wanted it as a consolation prize and now look where it's got us."

She sauntered over to him and, standing beside him, looked out the window at the ring world. "The ancients who built that place are long gone. Destroying it will bring death to the destroyer of worlds, and maybe then their souls will finally be able to rest in peace."

Grendok nodded then shuffled over to the admiral's desk. "In that case we best not keep them from a happy journey to the afterlife," he said, placing his palm down on the surface of the touch-display desktop. "Transfer all command authority to Grendok, Beta-Prime, voice authorization, Grendok Baphomet of Galliforn. Execute Broken-Sword protocols, on my command. *Execute.*"

The area on the display where his fingers touched the desk glowed bright red as it scanned his biometrics, after which the ship's computer chirped in a pleasant voice, <<Command override complete. All ship authority now rerouted to Grendok Baphomet of Galliforn, Horned King of the Satyrs and Heir to the Eighteenth Dynasty of Silenos.>>

"Baphomet is your last name?" Raven asked, shooting Grendok a surprised glance. In all her time knowing him, she knew that his true name was his most closely guarded secret. And, now, here he was sharing it freely with her.

"That's what you took from that?" he asked, somewhat perplexed that she ignored the whole part about him being the most notorious outlaw king the galaxy has ever known.

Able to guess exactly what he was thinking, she smiled at him. "If you wanted to be anything other than an outlaw you would have taken up that crown long ago. I somehow doubt it suits you, though. Lacking in moral fiber and what not," she teased, throwing in a wink just for good measure.

"Ah, yes," he replied with a chuckle. "I suppose you're right about that." He smiled once more, baring his yellow goat teeth and, then, together they dragged the bodies over to the sofa and propped them up.

The two satyrs slumped over and leaned against one another, but when Grendok went to correct their posture, Raven reached out a hand and stopped him. She shook her head, admiring the affectionate pose that the admiral and his favorite faun, Almathea, were stuck in.

Grendok smiled and then skipped out of the ready room and back onto the bridge. He immediately got into his command chair and began bringing all essential ship functions back online.

Raven slipped into the navigation seat and typed in the coordinates to get them as far away from Aldebaran as possible. Quite frankly, she was glad that Aldebaran, the accursed planet, was going up in flames. There couldn't be a more deserving fate for such a heinous place.

"Ready to go on your command, King Baphomet," Raven said. She used his actual name just to test it out. It sounded good on him. And, now more than ever, his people would need a strong leader to guide them out of the darkness. Whether he was ready or not, it was time for him to take up the mantle and accept his title of King.

Grendok chuckled. In all the time he'd known her, Raven had never let him down. Not once. For that type of loyalty, he was ever thankful and forever in her debt.

"Punch it," he said in his most authoritative tone.

Raven pushed the two bars to the top of the panel and then mashed the FTL button. The ship's FTL drive whined and then, in a flash, they leaped away from the system three full seconds before it went up.

The *Chiron* dropped out of FTL in the middle of a massive fleet of a dozen warships. Grendok stood up, the pit of his stomach beginning to tighten, when an incoming hail rang on the comm.

Raven answered the call and Lieutenant Brei'Alas's face greeted them on the secondary monitor. It was much smaller than the first, but Grendok had blasted the main viewscreen away, so it was all they were left with. "Welcome to the fleet of the Cosmic Alliance, you guys."

Brei'Alas leaned out of the way to reveal Jegra and Captain Blackstar standing just over her shoulder.

"I'm glad to see you both alive and well," Jegra said, smiling at two of her most trusted allies and friends.

Grendok rose out of his chair and knelt before the empress. "My allegiance is to you, and you alone, Empress Jegra Alakandra of the Dagon Empire."

"As is mine," Raven said, sliding out of her chair and kneeling beside him.

On the small viewscreen, Jegra stepped forward. "Please, rise and join me aboard the *Shard* this evening. I have a plan I need to run by the both of you."

Grendok and Raven stood back up and then gave Jegra the Dagon salute.

She saluted them back and then added, "See you both shortly. And, Raven…"

"Yes?" Raven asked, looking at the empress on the monitor. "Thank you for all your help. Once again, you've proven yourself to be our guardian angel."

"Just doing my part," Raven answered. There was a brief pause and then the monitor's feed cut out.

Raven turned to Grendok who looked up at her and, with a smile on his face, extended his elbow. "Care to accompany me to dine with the Imperatrix of the Galaxy?"

"Why Grendok!" Raven gasped in faux astonishment. "Are you asking me on a date?"

"If only I'd be so lucky as to find myself on a date with a woman as beautiful and supremely intelligent as you," he replied, flattering her all the more. "But alas, I'm well beyond my prime."

"Don't sell yourself short, old man," she answered, giving him a serious look. "The night is still young and there's plenty of drink to be had."

"Ah, yes," he said bashfully, blushing slightly. "If only plying you with copious amounts of alcohol was enough to turn you into an unreserved, salacious, coquette of a woman." He was only teasing, of course. He'd never dream of trying anything of that sort with Raven. Not unless he wanted to know what real pain felt like when she decided to put him straight again.

Even so, she completely surprised him when she leaned in and whispered in his ear, "You never know. I still haven't said no." This caused him to gulp hard, as he mulled over what to do with such information in a state of twitterpated confusion.

She stepped back and watched the tortured look on his face with a roguish grin. Then, threading her arm through his, she said, "It would be my great honor to accompany you this evening, Grendok Baphomet of Galliforn, Horned King of the Satyrs and Heir to the Eighteenth Dynasty of Silenos."

"Oh, hush, you," he chortled. She laughed too, and brushed her sapphire, purple and black ombre hair out of her eyes.

Arm-in-arm they strolled off the bridge together and made their way to the shuttle bay where they'd take Raven's personal shuttle to meet with the empress.

28

The *Shard* monitored the fledgling black hole from a distance. If there was enough gas and dust in the sector to feed it, it would grow. If not, it would collapse under its own weight and become a rogue blackhole. Either way, the good news was that their mission had been successful. Aldebaran was no more.

Jegra stared out the windows of the observation deck at the strange anomaly they'd created. Although at a public forum, she'd sealed herself off to be alone with her thoughts.

The two guards outside the door had been instructed not to let anybody in unless it was a code red emergency. Of course, when she heard the doors open, she knew there was only one person aboard the whole ship who could override her command as empress: the Lord Emperor himself.

Without looking back over her shoulder at him, she continued gazing out at the stars, acknowledging his presence with a simple sigh. "What brings you here, my darling?"

"Your warrior's ears are as keen as ever, my luv," he replied, sidling up to her. He locked his hands behind his back and gazed out at the vista along with her.

After a long pause, he took a deep breath and said, "A couple dozen ships aren't enough to go up against H'aaztre and his forces. We're going to need more allies."

"I know," Jegra said.

"It needs to be you who brings them together."

She shot him a sideways glance and then went back to looking at her stars.

"I've never admitted this to anyone, but I've done things…things I regret.

Things that have made me unpopular with many of the worlds out there. It's partially because of my actions that the Commonwealth is so fractured. I put too much stress on it and when a tyrant came, he was able to do what I could not: break the fragile ecosystem we had. I realize, now, that I may have gone about things in the wrong way."

Jegra gave him another sideways glance. "I'm glad you're strong enough to admit your failures, Rhadamanthus, but you can save your pitch for another time. I'll do it. Of course, I'll do it. Not for you. Not for the sake of the galaxy. But for myself…so I can have my peace of mind."

She turned back to the glass window and glimpsed her reflection looking back at her. It was her, but sadder looking than she remembered. It was as though the weight of a thousand worlds was bearing down on her shoulders, and like Atlas, she was forced to bear the burden forever—the only one able to support the weight through sheer strength of will.

"I have faith in you, wife," Dakroth said. "I've learned the hard way that you're not one to be trifled with. And those who cross you get what they deserve."

She suppressed a laugh, which drew Dakroth's attention to her. Without looking at him, even as she felt his eyes linger on her, she replied, "Don't think I'm done with you, dear husband. I have several scores to settle with you. Saving my life the other day on the battlefield was appreciated, but it doesn't even begin to make up for your wrongs."

Dakroth sniggered and then turned toward the windows. "I suppose not. Until then, however, I place my full confidence in your capable hands."

"I appreciate that," Jegra replied.

Her words were followed by another long silence and, eventually, Dakroth withdrew himself from the conversation and took his leave. As he left, he looked back over his shoulder at her. He felt as though he should say something, something to console her, maybe let her know that he was sorry about the loss of her child. Ultimately, though, he decided against it.

The Mother of Dagon, like any mother, was fiercest when she was fighting for the safety of her children. And with her natural born child ripped from her very arms, her friends and her crew became her surrogates. It would be these people she'd fight for and die for, if necessary.

Dakroth no longer wished to test Jegra's limits—for he couldn't do anything to her that she hadn't already endured. She was ready to become the warrior he always knew she had the potential to be.

His arms still linked behind his back, he turned and continued on his way. The observation deck doors slid open and the two guards outside stiffened at the sight of the emperor. His arms still locked behind his back, he disappeared out into the corridor and the doors drew shut behind him.

Jegra let out a long, drawn-out sigh and checked her wrist. The implant lit up, revealing a digital clock interface just beneath her skin in orange numerals which read 19 hundred hours 45 minutes. She shook her wrist which, consequently, turned off the display and slowly swiveled about as she began to make the long walk back to her quarters to change for dinner.

As she approached the door, it chimed and she froze in the center of the room, wondering who else might need her so desperately that they couldn't follow her strictest of orders to be left alone. "Enter," she said.

The doors parted and to her surprise standing in the doorway in her dress uniform was Callestra Van Morgan. She had on hot orange lipstick and neon blue eye shadow that made her look electric. The daughter of perhaps the most dangerous man in the galaxy—after Emperor Dakroth himself. She was stunning to behold, and Jegra could see exactly why Dakroth had taken such a liking to her.

"I brought you your dress for tonight. Of course, I had Lieutenant Brei'Alas help me pick it out for you, since I don't know you that well, and she seems to be rather close to you."

"I see," Jegra said. "Just leave it on the bar," she informed the woman, gesturing for her to set it on the countertop.

Callestra did as asked and then turned around to find Jegra standing directly behind her. In fact, when she'd spun around she'd almost collided with the empress.

Jegra took a step closer and Callestra leaned back into the edge of the bar. It filled the small of her back and as she leaned there she let out a nervous laugh. "What are you doing?"

Not explaining herself, Jegra grabbed Callestra, drew her in, and kissed her on the lips long and hard. Callestra resisted at first, but then, with an equal vigor, wrapped her arms around Jegra's waist and pulled her close.

"Mmm..." Callestra moaned as their kiss grew deep and wet with all the hallmarks of those kisses you only experience but a few times in your life.

Jegra abruptly stopped the act of seduction and withdrew herself, leaving Callestra light-headed.

"What was that for?" she asked, still dizzy from the kiss.

"I've implanted nano-bots into your bloodstream," Jegra informed her.

"*You did what?!*" Callestra's eyes widened with a sense of violation and glared at the empress.

"Calm your blue tits, sweetheart. It wasn't anything nefarious. They'll improve your healing factor, supply you with vital medicines, and boost immunity."

"You modded me without my consent," Callestra growled. She'd never felt so irate in her whole life. Without thinking, she reached up and slapped Jegra across her face. Then realizing what she'd done, she drew back.

"Apologies," she said, immediately feeling remorse for her sudden emotional outburst.

Jegra turned her half sunken gaze on the Vice Admiral. "Allow me to relieve your worries. As your empress, I command you to accept the nano-technology. You don't have to like it, but you will accept it. Do I make myself clear?"

"Crystal," Callestra said, her amber gaze flickering pink with the rage-sparked energy broiling inside her. "Will that be all, Your Majesty?"

She said it with so much malice that Jegra raised an eyebrow and turned to her with a look that said just try it and see what happens.

Callestra turned away when Jegra reached out and grabbed her arm. Callestra looked down at Jegra's hand and then up at her and waited for an explanation.

"I intend to win this war, Callestra. Losing is not an option for me. Everyone who serves under me will undergo enhancements. If they don't, they will have sided with the ambitions of the enemy and I will deal with them as I see fit. Does that answer your question of why I dare trample your people's purity laws into the soil beneath my feet? They are holding me back. They're holding you all back. And it's time to open your goddamn eyes and see the truth."

"Yes," Callestra said. She jerked her shoulder and pulled her arm away from Jegra's grasp and stared at the empress, who stared back at her. She couldn't gauge whether Jegra was simply staring her down or merely waiting for her to respond first, but the tension was overwhelming. Instead of coming to blows, however, she smacked her teeth in disappointment and then stormed off the observation deck.

"If you want my opinion," a weaselly sounding voice came from the other end of the bar, "she has a stick so far up her ass that she can barely function as a person."

Jegra turned to find a toad-looking creature sitting at the end of the bar, helping himself to a bottle of Tri'laxian brandy. He had on what appeared to be a golden tunic and robe and looked like an old hermit monk with white whiskers sprouting from his chin that were braided into a long rope-like beard.

"Ah, I was wondering when we'd meet. After all, I've had the pleasure of meeting your other two siblings. But they were, how shall I say this, a disappointment."

"Ha!" the toad man laughed. "Right you are. Muscles and good looks only get you so far in life if you don't have brains." He tapped his temple, bringing attention to the fact that he was the brains of the operation, and grinned a wide amphibian sort of grin.

"If any of you had any brains at all, then I wouldn't be winning this war at the moment."

"Is that what you think is happening? Ha! Ha-ha!" the small creature laughed, clutching his abdomen and rocking back on his stool. He glanced at her from over his shoulder and his eyes filled with black ink and then a golden ring flashed in them. The mark of H'aaztre.

"Let me show you something," Giddion said, extending his hand for Jegra to take. She hesitated but for a moment and then boldly took ahold of his hand.

The entire room spun out of control and continued spinning, only slowing briefly to stop. When everything returned to normal, they were standing next to Jegra's bathtub as she lay in it, both her wrists slit.

Jegra watched herself bleed out into the tub. And she looked over at Giddion and shrugged. "This was a week ago. So, what?"

Giddion smiled and reached up and touched her hand again. And, once again, the room spun out of focus for a minute before slowing down again. When the world around them refocused, they were standing in Jegra's personal chambers. In her bed was Danica and...

"Raphine?" Jegra asked, genuinely surprised.

"Apparently the affair has been going on since before you proposed."

Jegra shot the toad a harsh look. "That's a lie."

"Is it?" he asked, reaching up to touch her hand again. She pulled it away.

"It's inconsequential," she said.

"That's not why I brought you here," he explained. He pointed out her open balcony window out at Arena City. In the distance, the lights of the stadium flooded into the sky creating a warmth and glow that was inviting.

"Never forget, dear woman, that you were but a slave. And although you've been granted great powers, your mind is still that of something so infinitesimally small that you can't even begin to fathom the power of the Almighty H'aaztre."

"You're probably right," Jegra admitted.

This seemed to throw Giddion off his game. After all he was trying to intimidate her, but upon seeing she wasn't bothered by any of it, he stroked his chin and studied her for a moment.

"In that case, I only have one more thing to show you."

This time when he reached out for her hand she didn't slink away. At his touch the room blurred out of focus.

In a series of flashes she saw every single death that had been directly or indirectly tied to her. First, it was her boss, Donald Bloom, being vaporized by a ray gun aboard the slave ship the day she was abducted. Until that moment she hadn't even known ray guns existed, let alone entire alien worlds.

Next, Abethca's death replayed before her very eyes. She reached out to touch her face, but found she no longer maintained a physical form; she was ethereal, wraith-like.

After Abby's death it was the harem. Dakroth's seventeen wives. Jegra had slaughtered all those women. Blood soaked, she watched herself sit in shock, unable to believe what she'd done. Then it was time to relive Ellia's death. The poor girl was innocent and yet she had become collateral damage, just like all those before her.

She watched herself come to Danica's aid as she killed all twelve contestants of the humiliation bout which threatened to take Danica's life.

The subsequent fight with Ishtar Bantu proved rather difficult to relive. Not because of how gruesome or brutal it was, but for what it represented, her unyielding resolve in being the last woman standing. No matter what.

Finally, she watched herself give birth to her beautiful boy. She watched as the doctor wiped him clean with a towel and handed him back to her. And as she coddled him and looked upon that beautiful newborn with a love she'd never known, she watched as the doctor was sliced down all over again, right before her very eyes.

At the same time, Danica was cleaved in two by a powerful ray blast. And that mindless puppet, Nodengoth, carried out his master's bidding and ripped her child from her arms, only to be whisked away in a golden eddy of light particles.

"I've seen enough," she said, closing her eyes and turning her head away.

When Giddion didn't stop the horrific scene, she squeezed his hand crushing his bones.

"Egads, woman!" he yelped. The room stopped spinning and Jegra braced herself against the bar table as they came to an abrupt halt. They had never even left the observation lounge.

"Why did you show me all that?" she demanded to know.

Giddion massaged his sore hand, met her gaze, and smiled up at her. "Isn't it clear by now, Empress Alakandra? Everywhere you go, death and misery follow."

A scowl settled onto Jegra's face and she peered at the toad-like creature with smoldering brown eyes.

"I killed your brother," she snarled. "I could have killed your sister, too. Instead I merely took her tongue as a trophy. So, if I'm as bad as you say I am, what makes you think I won't kill you right now?"

"Other than the fact that I can control time and won't allow it?"

"Yeah, other than that..." she said, grinning at him with a sparkle in her wild eyes.

"Because, if you push H'aaztre too hard trying to get his attention, there's no telling what he'll do to you. Or your friends."

"Maybe I do," Jegra said. With lightning fast reflexes, her hand flew across the distance between them and clasped onto the toad's tunic. He looked down at her hand and scoffed. Then squinted his overly large eyes at her and concentrated.

When the room didn't spin out of focus, Giddion ran his tongue across his wide mouth and taught lips, adding a grunt just for good measure. Still nothing.

Beginning to get worried, he looked over at Jegra with a startled expression. "How are you doing this?"

Jegra smiled, then with her other hand flicked the top of the Tri'laxian brandy's bottle, shattering the neck so that it was jagged and sharp. "I'm not doing anything," she said, smiling manically at him.

Without even hesitating, she slammed Giddion's head down onto the counter. The sharp end of the bottle went straight into his right eye, killing him instantly. She then sat him back upright in his chair, wiped some of the blood splatter off on his robes, and slowly turned toward the shadows at the far end of the bar.

"Thanks, I needed that."

Brei'Alas stepped out from the shadows, her hands raised as though she was casting a spell. "My pleasure," she replied.

A small stream of blood began to trickle from out of Brei's right nostril; Jegra fetched a table napkin and handed it to her. "Here, your nose is bleeding."

"Oh," Brei said, accepting the napkin. "Sometimes that happens when I over-exert myself."

Jegra nodded. "Out of curiosity, did you know you could freeze time like that?"

"Nope," Brei stated in the most cheerful manner. "I just found out. In fact, there's a lot about my powers I don't fully understand yet."

"All in due time," Jegra said, offering her a smile. Her smile faded when she turned back to the dress laying on the bar and she remembered she had other responsibilities to return to. She let out a deep sigh and then breathed in the sweet scent of coppery air. Looking over at Giddion, she watched as his prune colored blood oozed out onto the countertop.

"You could always skip," Brei said, offering the empress a coy smile. Jegra laughed off the idea.

"I'm afraid that'll be Dakroth's play this evening."

"I see," Brei answered. She stood studying Jegra's face for a moment and then, holding her elbow, she looked timidly over at the door and then back to Jegra. "If you won't be needing me any longer, I should really get back to my post. My shift's not over for another couple of hours."

Jegra smiled and then stepped aside so Brei could lift up the flap in the bar top and let herself out.

"Shall I come to your quarters later?" Brei asked, pausing beside Jegra long enough to ask her question.

"It's up to you," she replied. Brei smiled at her one more time and then, trying to be sexy, sashayed her way out of the room. She looked back once from the hallway and practically tripped over her own feet as she still hadn't gotten it down.

After stumbling slightly, she popped back up in time to exclaim that she was all right when the doors shut on her, muffling her words, and her cheeks flushed bright pink with the afterglow of embarrassment.

Jegra held her fist to her mouth and stifled a chortle, praying that Brei didn't hear her laugh at her. She had to give the girl credit where credit was due, however, given the impressive number of failures she had racked up trying to be sexy, she hadn't given up.

Brei'Alas, if anything, was pleasurable. But, more than that, she'd proven to be a true friend over the past couple of weeks. And while Jegra was out in the cold depths of space, Danica was back home seeking refuge in the warmth of Raphine's arms.

Such is the way of things when two people who desperately need love in their lives get separated by too much distance. A little dalliance here or there is to be expected. It doesn't mean you've stopped loving your partner, just that you've opened your heart to new people to love.

Love, like food, came in all shapes and sizes, flavors, textures, and couldn't be locked down as one single thing. Everyone has their favorite food, Jegra mused, but that doesn't mean there aren't other foods you can't stop to enjoy and take delight in. Or that you'll never find a new food better suited to your unique tastes than one you preferred before. Loving others was very similar. And limiting yourself to just one person to love, in her estimation, was like limiting oneself to just one meal for the rest of your life.

True love was a myth. It was as real as rainbow colored unicorns. It simply didn't exist, and those who told themselves it did were only fooling themselves. That didn't mean that there weren't enduring forms of love with deep, lasting connections. If you found someone who completed you in some profound way, then great. But to assume that because you got lucky and found a match meant that this was the only form of love to aspire to was, quite frankly, delusional thinking.

Jegra knew that everyone had to face the music of their own mortality at some point. A life, like the brief, lovely cherry blossom, is a fleeting thing. All you can do is cherish the limited time you have. And, at the end of the day, everyone is in the same boat. You can either embrace nihilism and go mad from the indifference and cruelty of the universe, or you run from it straight into the closest warm embrace you can find.

It's not always the right thing to do, but it's better than having to face the inevitable existential crisis of staring into the well of that infinite and dreadful void all on your own.

It was this line of reasoning that helped Jegra realize that if she was going to win this war—if she had any hope of uniting the galaxy into one giant cosmic alliance—she needed to do so through love, not fear. Through integrity, not intimidation. And through hope, not desperation.

She'd win the galaxy back, just like she'd won the hearts of the fans of the Intergalactic Gladiatorial Games: one planet at a time.

She still had a long road ahead of her. Even so, she knew that H'aaztre wasn't done toying with her yet. Not when he taunted her in the forest of Aldebaran. And certainly not with The Voice still out there sowing havoc wherever she went. But all that had to wait. Right now, she had a dinner party to attend and she was already running late.

29

Danica, fresh from a shower, reclined in a wicker chair on the balcony patio and basked in the morning sunlight. She had on a salmon colored robe and crossed her lavender leg over her left thigh and bounced her calf on her knee.

Her bathrobe slipped open slightly, exposing her full leg all the way to her hip. She ignored it as she read a holovid of the day's news. She swiped the hologram hovering before her and flipped through the channels. Upon seeing an article of interest, she tapped the picture portion of the hologram and the still image flickered to life above the slowly scrolling text.

A tall, glistening glass of pink lemonade sat at the edge of the table, sweating profusely in the sun. Luckily, it was early, and the Thessalonica sun had not yet fully risen, giving her another hour of pleasant daytime before she'd need to retreat into the shade of the palace.

"Enjoying your day off?" a voice asked.

Danica looked up to see Raphine standing in the entrance, dressed in her tan and brown security uniform. It complimented her forest green hair and avocado colored skin quite nicely, Danica thought.

"You might say that," replied Danica, taking a sip of her lemonade before setting it back down on its coaster.

Raphine took a step forward and seemed to hem and haw. Danica just watched, waiting for her to spit it out. After all, if she pushed her to come out with it before she was ready, she knew that Raphine would just grow defensive. But after Onelle's outing everyone involved in Abethca's death, Danica knew she owed it to Raphine to be sympathetic and just offer her a listening ear and a shoulder to lean on, if need be.

"I don't hate you," Raphine finally said. "But I can't accept what you did, either. Jegra was a pawn in Dakroth's game and you...you hid the truth from us."

"To protect you," Danica said, but she stopped there when Raphine raised a finger as if to say, *let me finish what I need to say*. Danica obliged.

"I understand your justification. I just can't agree with it. And although I have enjoyed your company and friendship, I don't think we should see each other anymore."

"Is there anything else?" Danica asked, locking her fingers together underneath her chin. She uncrossed her legs, and then recrossed them the other way. She casually brushed the pleats out of the robe again and then stared at Raphine until she answered.

"I know Onelle has mental problems. I know she's a sociopath and is dangerous. But, she's still my sister. So, when the time comes, I will be the one to deal with her."

Danica nodded. Seemingly satisfied with that response, Raphine turned to leave.

"Wait," Danica said, rising to her feet. Raphine turned in the doorway and gazed over at the beautiful lavender face of Danica staring back at her with intense eyes that brimmed with tears.

Raphine could see that she wanted to apologize so badly, but knowing her, that would open up a Pandora's box of emotion she wasn't ready for. Instead, she merely nodded with a subtle thrust of the chin, as if to convey her understanding then wheeled around and strode off the balcony.

Although their affair had been brief, Danica knew she was going to miss Raphine's company terribly. At least they were able to part on good terms. Danica turned back to the balcony's edge and looked out over the railing. Out of the blue, a loud crack like lightening sounded followed by a low rumbling boom. She looked up to see the Intergalactic Gladiatorial Syndicate's collection ship—a massive corvette class battlecruiser with the sole purpose of collecting escaped warriors.

When it loomed closer to the palace, she grew tense. As its shadow blotted out the sun, she called out in a tense voice that betrayed her own nervousness, "Raphine, we have company."

Raphine didn't reply, so Danica tapped her wrist and tried the implanted comm link, but it was being jammed. That's when golden beams of light touched down all around her.

"No!" she shouted in protest, peering up at the ship as she began to teleport up.

Five massive guards dressed in glossy black armor and masked helmets surrounded her with stun rods when she manifested before them. A slender Dagon man dressed in a white pinstripe, hot pink suit with a monocle examined her and said, "Danica Valencia, you are hereby summoned back into the Gladiatorial Syndicate."

"What?" Danica gasped, unable to believe her ears. "What's the meaning of this? Explain yourself before I have you deported to the farthest moon to mine korridium for the rest of your miserable existence."

In typical Dagon fashion, he turned his nose up at her in a gesture of superiority and ignored her hollow threats. "Due to your final humiliation bout being terminated because of an account of interference, you must re-fight the match."

"You have to be kidding me."

"I assure you, Miss Valencia, I am not."

"We'll see about this," she said, and turned to storm away. "When the empress gets word of this, you're going to regret ever having crossed paths with—"

ZAP!

The stun rod barely kissed the back of her shoulder but she went down like a lead weight.

"Collect her and take her to her holding cell," the fancy Dagon collector said, cleaning his monocle with a fresh cloth he'd drawn from the inside pocket of his neon pink suit jacket.

As the IGS ship slowly turned about and rose into the sky above Arena City, Raphine emerged from the shadows of their chambers and stepped out onto the palace balcony. She watched the ship slowly gain altitude and then, with another thunderous boom, it jumped away, vanishing in the blink of an eye.

Several hundred thousand light years away, on the beach world of Arkadia, a short distance from the Colosseum that sat on Arkadia's largest island, a green-skinned woman wearing military fatigues lounged in a hammock. She fiddled with a large tactical blade as she trimmed her nails and, in the shade of the palm tree, glanced up at the IGS ship that jumped into view high above the sparkling oceans of the tropical planet.

"Just on time," Gaewen Feradorn said, smiling up at the ship. She brought up her holovid display and it read: *Contact Arena Palace.* She tapped the button and a comm channel opened. "She has arrived."

"Good. Keep me posted, cousin."

"Copy that," Gaewen replied, answering Raphine Agnar's request to keep a vigilant eye on Danica while she endured her stay on the island nation, Arkadia.

The holovid closed and Raphine, still loitering about on the palace balcony back on Thessalonica, strolled over to Danica's unfinished lemonade and picked it up. Examining the lipstick marks where Danica had drunk, Raphine held the glass up, as if to say cheers and good luck, and then placed her own lips over the very same marks and finished off the drink.

A sigh of satisfaction escaped her lips and she slammed the glass drink down onto the table. A pain laden grin formed across her mouth and a tear seeped out of the corner of her right eye and ran down her cheek.

What she'd done, handing Danica over to IGS like that, was unforgivable. But for the part Danica had played in her sister's death, it was fitting. Although Jegra believed Danica was redeemable, Raphine was beginning to think otherwise.

For the past three hundred years, Dagons had prided themselves in thinking they were the apex species in all of the galaxy and therefore also above the law. Danica had carried out kill orders on Dakroth's behalf. She'd wiped out entire colonies without a hint of remorse. And even when Raphine had grown to be her lover, she hid things from her. Like the fact that she was still secretly doping on Nividium 3 and the fact that she'd plotted Abethca's untimely demise.

Raphine felt bad about what she had to do. But, the fact remained, she had to do it. Danica was in need of an intervention, something that would shake her to her core. And with Jegra preoccupied with the war effort and everything else that was going on, Raphine needed to see to it that the palace was secured.

Danica was neither stable nor safe. She'd gone off the rails during her yearlong cat and mouse game with Zallek. Once she'd caught him, she didn't know what to do with herself and literally spiraled out of control into what seemed like a mid-life crisis coupled with a clinical psychological break. She was fucking her student, taking drugs again—albeit so secretively that nobody knew except for Raphine, whose job it was to know everything that went on at the palace.

As far as Raphine was concerned, another few months in the arena would do Danica some good. Maybe she'd snap to it and finally realize that her actions have consequences. Because, unless she learned that very vital lesson, Raphine was perfectly content to leave her in the hands of IGS permanently.

"Equim! Zammen'eth!" Danica reached up and touched the earpiece she'd been given and gave it a tap. The translator was on the fritz again. "Hey! Watch it!" she grumbled as the guards shoved her through the gate which led into the hypogeum.

Unfortunately, she still only had on her white bathrobe. She pulled it tight when she noticed some wandering eyes settle on the bare shoulder that peeked out from the luxuriant fabric.

"You can't wear that," a droll voice said. Recognizing it, Danica's eyes widened and she spun around to find an old but familiar face peering over at her from the shadows of the underground preparation chambers.

A slender Dagon woman with dark purple hair tied up into an elegant bun gazed back at her with a single good eye the color of cerise pink while the other hid behind a leather eyepatch. She had on fishnet stockings, knee-high brown leather boots, and a velvet coat with a green brocade collar and a plum satin lining.

The elegant jacket she wore had black lace accents which matched the stylish under-blouse, its deep cut V-neck surrounded by cascading ruffled folds. She adjusted her oversized cuffs with their brass-toned buttons, and smiled at Danica. "Ladgara Vassex? What in the bleedin' empire are you doing here?!"

"Nothing much," she said, waving her hand across her body nonchalantly. "You know, the usual, just trying to keep my hide all in one piece long enough to make my grand escape."

Danica walked up to her as though she were going to slap the living daylights out of Ladgara, causing the woman to tense, but instead threw her arms around her neck and embraced her.

"You can't begin to imagine how glad I am to see a familiar face."

"I think your standards of what constitutes a friend are slipping, my dear," Ladgara said, nodding down at Danica's chest. Leaning in, she whispered, "FYI, your robe slipped open as well."

Quickly closing her robe, Danica looked around, embarrassed by the thought of anyone having seen her breasts flop out.

"Nice to see the ole girls in tip-top shape, though," she added, smiling coyly. "Always a pleasure."

Danica blushed and then drew back. She shot Ladgara a curious look. "Seriously though, what are you doing here, Vass?"

Ladgara laughed. "Nobody has called me that in ages." She shook her head and, motioning for Danica to walk alongside her, they strolled through the underground corridor together. "I'm afraid Novac Tamoran had some not so brilliant plan to try and raid a Nyctan cruiser. It turned out to be a troop carrier. He was taken into Nyctan custody and tossed in the clink and I was sold to IGS." She fanned her hands and did a slight curtsey, just for show. "And here I am."

"That blows," Danica said. "The arena isn't for the faint of heart. But I've seen you in a bar fight, so I know you can do more than hold your own. If you want any pointers, don't hesitate to ask, b'cause I'd be more than happy to—"

Ladgara leaned in close to Danica, her chest pressing into Dani's shoulder, her grin spreading into a wide smile, she cut her off. "You don't think I actually intend to stay here, do you?"

Danica stopped mid-sentence and swiveled to face Ladgara. "Same old Vass. Let me guess, you already have an ingenious plan to get yourself out of here?"

Ladgara stopped and looked around, scanning to see if they had any eavesdroppers, and then turned back to Danica. "Be careful what you say in here, the walls have eyes and ears."

They resumed walking again and Ladgara directed Danica into a small alcove. It turned out to be a quaint living cell. Nothing fancy. Just the basics. A bed. A toilet. A shower in the ceiling which rained down onto a cement floor with a drain off to the corner.

Once inside the room, Ladgara Vassex fanned her hands across the small space and announced, "Home sweet home."

"This is what they gave you?" Danica asked, dumbfounded, unable to believe a woman of Ladgara's stature would be given something so small and unaccommodating.

"I'm afraid that Arkadia's Colosseum isn't like the one on Arena City. As you can clearly see, this place is…how shall I put it, oh yes…primitive."

"I see what you mean," Danica responded, stroking her chin as she looked around the confined quarters. Ladgara slapped the wall and a Murphy bed folded down, revealing a hidden bunk situated right above hers.

"Here's where you'll be staying…roomie," Ladgara said glibly, offering little in the way of explanation, other than a sly smile.

"Vass, you're kidding me, right?" Danica stood looking at her with her mouth agape, scarcely able to believe that the two of them had to stay in a room literally the size of a watershed.

"I kid you not, old friend. But, think of it this way; we have all the time in the world to catch up."

"I thought you said you weren't sticking around," Danica said, noting Ladgara's slip up.

"No need to be so litigious, Cass, it's just a figure of speech."

Danica looked over at the sliding closet and, with Ladgara's nod of approval, went over and opened it. Inside were thin strips of leather, a deer skin bikini, crab shell body armor, and leather wrapped sandals.

"For crying out loud," Danica groaned upon seeing the outfit they'd provided for her.

"It was here when I arrived," Ladgara informed her. "But there was no way I was going to be caught dead in something like that. Besides, it looks like you could use it more than I could." She glanced down at Danica's chest again and Danica looked down to find that the robe had slipped open again, exposing her breasts and perky, dark purple nipples.

She rolled her eyes and peeled off the robe right in front of Ladgara who simply watched with an ogling sort of amusement. Seating herself on the end of the small cot, she watched Danica wiggle and squirm her way into the leather bikini and fasten the crab armor to herself. Once she was suited up, she spun around, inspecting the strange get up for herself. She looked like a pinup girl for the Arkadian guard.

"Hopefully tomorrow's match lets you have a trident. That way you can be the Queen of Atlantis!" Ladgara covered her mouth and muffled a snigger as she watched Danica grow red in the face.

"Oh, shut up," Danica fired back, squinting at Ladgara.

"I do have to admit, though," said Ladgara, eyeing Danica up and down, "you look sexy as Helios in that get up."

"Don't get any ideas," Danica said, waving a finger. "I know how you like to sleep around."

"And you don't? Come on, sweetheart, we're both Dagon women. Promiscuity is in our nature."

"Is that so?" Danica asked.

Ladgara rose up and drew close to her. "You don't feel it?" she asked, taking another step closer. Their chests were practically touching as their gazes held with a building intensity. "You don't feel the electricity between your thighs and the overwhelming urge to tear all my clothes off and take me right here and now?"

"Stop," Danica whispered. She closed her eyes when Ladgara leaned in.

"Stop? That's not like you. Have you changed so much, Cass? Or is it something else?" Ladgara folded her arms. "Don't tell me you can't get hard anymore."

"No," Danica admitted. "That's not the problem."

Ladgara drew back and shot Danica a stunned look. "Are you trying to tell me you've fallen in love?"

"Yes. Although I don't see how that's any of your business." She held her own arms and swayed a bit as she tried to figure out how best to put it. "I mean, I don't know. All I know is that all I've done over the past three years is make one terrible decision after another. The sooner I can move forward, the sooner I can leave all this bullshit behind me."

"Good luck with that," Ladgara said with a laugh, and she went over and sat back down on the edge of her cot.

"What's that supposed to mean?" Danica asked.

"No offense, Cass, but you've always made terrible decisions. It's just part of who you are."

"The name's Danica, now," she said, her brow settling into a frown. The more Ladgara used her pet name, the more she realized how much she didn't like it. "Danica Valencia."

She folded her arms under her chest just to drive the point home. It used to be cute and all, Cass vs. Vass, but these days she just didn't feel like the same person anymore. Cassera Van Danica Amelorak was someone else entirely. A complete stranger to her now.

"Danica, then," Ladgara said with a shrug.

"What are you saying here, exactly?" Danica pushed, fishing for answers, knowing full well she might not like what she discovered. Ladgara looked at her with her vibrant pink eye, staring for the longest time.

"You're reckless, destructive, and dangerous to everyone who comes into your path. It's why Dakroth promoted you to Vice Admiral in the first place. You were his battering ram, with which he broke the back of the whole galaxy."

"You honestly don't believe that, do you?" Danica could feel her heart breaking inside her chest with every cruel truth that Ladgara shared. But she couldn't deny the accusations. She had done terrible things.

All this time, though, her perception of herself as this strong and independent woman that could do no wrong had been a misconception born of hubris and blind obedience to a complete enabler. And what he'd enabled her to do was act out her worst possible self.

Danica had pride, sure. What Dagon didn't? But this was more than a few mistakes she'd accumulated over the short span of a military career. She had sin after sin piled up that she needed to atone for, but instead all she could manage to do was become addicted to a silly drug and get herself beat up on a daily basis.

If she was being honest with herself, she genuinely thought this self-abuse would force her to come to terms with what she'd done. Not so much of an atonement as a serious pause to reflect on her past. But what she found was that, contrary to everything she thought about herself, she liked doing drugs, and she had such little self-worth that she actually liked getting the snot kicked out of herself on a daily basis.

Why? Because it reminded her that she was at least worth something to the fans who watched the gladiator fights. It was quite telling then, that Raphine had sold her off to IGS instead of locking her away in some rehabilitation clinic. She knew that the clinic would force Danica to wither away into nothing, while the gladiatorial matches might forge her into a new, stronger woman. But only if she put the past in the past where it belonged. Which is one reason she so detested her old name: it reminded her of a person she absolutely wanted nothing to do with.

"Let me ask you this, how do you come to find yourself back here, in the arena, a mere cycle from the previous time? What went so wrong in your life that you ended up back in the Games, of all the places you could have ended up? I'm no expert, but I'd say that's the very definition of self-destructive."

Heat flooded into her cheeks as she felt her temper flair. "Maybe it's not me. Maybe you're just a complete bitch and a royal pain in my ass!" Danica immediately regretted her words but was surprised when Ladgara merely laughed them off.

"Honey, that's you in a nutshell. Ask anyone who's ever brushed elbows with you and if they're half as honest as I am, they'll hit you with the cold hard truth."

"The truth being?" Danica asked snidely.

"You're unlikable."

"Screw you!" Danica shouted, and she spat at the dust covered floor, her spittle landing between Ladgara's feet. Ladgara merely leaned back on her cot and smiled at Danica as she stormed out of the room.

Shoving a large Dragonian out of her way, she growled, "Move it, leather neck," and marched down the corridor the way she'd come. When she arrived at the gate, she grabbed the bars and rattled it. "Let me out of here!" she shouted. "Do you hear me? Let me out of here!"

"That one!" a voice called out.

Without warning, Danica felt a hand reach out and jerk her back. She was manhandled and quickly shoved into a line of three other aliens. Then handed a three-pronged spear, she was shoved out into the arena.

As her eyes adjusted to the brilliant light, she looked out at her two fellow gladiators only to see them piss themselves.

"You've got to be kidding me." That's when she heard the terrible scraping, like the sound of a building coming down in a demolition. She looked up to see a two-story tall, spiny shelled crab. She sighed. "Perfect. Just bloody perfect."

The giant crab opened and closed its pincers; its massive claws making a terrible scraping sound. There was a purple skinned, black tattooed alien to Danica's right who appeared tough enough, but he dropped his spear and made a mad dash to the gate on the other side of the stadium. He ran directly under the crab's abdomen and made it safely to the other side. Leaping up he flung himself onto the gate.

"Not smart," Danica said, cringing. She knew what would happen because she'd seen it before.

With a loud *zzzt*, the man fell from the electrified fence like a bug falling from a bug-zapper. He hit the ground with a thud and before he could even regain motor function, the giant crab was standing over him.

The crab reached down and scooped the man up into its serrated claws. Unable to fend off the armored creature, he wailed with intense pain and then with a resounding crunch, his top half and bottom half fell away, landing in separate locations on either side of the crab's spiny leg.

In the gruesome rending of the purple alien, the spray of his lime green blood had splashed across Danica's mostly naked body. As the televid drone swooped down to get a close up of her wiping the green sludge off her blue chest, she ran her fingers across the humps of her breasts, collecting the green blood on her fingertips and then shaking her fingers, flicked it off.

Although she didn't have much to speak of in the way of proper clothing, she turned her gaze to the gladiator to her left who stood beside her trembling with fear. Seeing as he had a full cloth shirt, she merely wiped her hand off on his back using him as a makeshift towel.

After smearing green blood all over his back, she slapped him hard and said, "Avoid the fences. They're electrified."

He nodded taking in her advice. When she smelled the ammonia scent of piss burning her nostrils, she made a sour face and looked down to find the orange skinned man next to her pissing all up and down his leg. The piss puddled at his feet and touched her sandals.

A sour look settled over Danica's face as she took in the foul odor and the disgusting scene. Annoyed by the pants-pisser, she huffed and cleared her nostrils of the foul odor and then casually stepped away from him, leaving him to stand in his own puddle of urine all by his lonesome.

Men like him, she wagered, were probably best used as bait to distract the monsters so she could get a clean line of attack. Other than that, they offered little in the way of any value. At least as far as the rules of the arena were concerned.

After the replay of the purple alien's horrific demise up on the big screen monitor, the arena erupted with cheers. As soon as the cheers died down again, the announcer introduced the audience to the "Traitor of the Dagon Empire, the Treacherous and Two-Faced Hag of Helios, Danica Valencia!"

She stepped out into the arena amid an eruption of boos and hisses and glared up at the audience. This wasn't the worst day of her life, but it was pretty damn close.

She glanced to her right and found Ladgara leaning casually against the far wall watching through the slats of the barred viewing area.

"Nice trident," she shouted from the sidelines, smiling at the fact that they'd managed to find Danica an actual trident. After all, it did complete the whole ensemble.

Unamused by her witticism, Danica scowled at her and mouthed the word, "Cunt."

Ladgara smiled back and mouthed the word, "Flange biter."

Another round of aggressive clacking of giant reddish orange claws -- claws drenched in lime colored blood--brought Danica's attention back to the threat at hand and she raised her trident and widened her stance in preparation for the inevitable fight that was about to ensue.

The throng erupted with cheers as Danica raced forward thrusting the trident outward. Sparks shot up as the trident scraped along the armor plating of the giant crab's claw, which was nearly as hard as steel, and the crowd roared with excitement. It was shaping up to be a great day to be at the arena.

30

"**Mistress Agnar, you** must wake up," Aidora said, shaking the sleeping woman. The ship's emergency alarm blared noisily all around them and Onelle quickly sat up, threw up both arms and gripped her head due to a bout of vertigo that seized upon her.

"Aidora?" she mumbled, still groggy, her satin sheets slipping off her bare green skin. "What's going on?"

"I don't know, but whatever is happening it can't be good. I heard screams out in the corridor." Aidora looked fearfully over her shoulder toward the entrance which to Onelle's shock looked as though someone had tried to pry open the doors. They were bowed outward and gashes scarred the metal from something like claws.

She made a mental note to maybe ease up on the pills before bed. The question going through her mind right now was: what if whatever had wanted in so badly had gotten in? What would have become of her? She shuddered at the mere thought of waking up screaming as the jowls of some ferocious beast devoured her alive.

"Quickly, my clothes," Onelle said, snapping her fingers urgently and pointing over at her iridescent pearl dress still hanging on the back of the vanity's chair. Aidora promptly fetched it for her and Onelle, rising out of bed, quickly slipped it on, forgoing any underwear. There simply wasn't time.

Hand in hand they raced to the exit and when they got to the doors they found them jammed. Aidora tried to pry them open with all her strength, but it was no good. They wouldn't budge.

"They're stuck," she lamented, giving Onelle a rather helpless and pathetic look.

As annoying as the girl's weakness was, there was no time for a stern lecturing. Instead, Onelle grabbed ahold of the door on her side and said, "Here, I'll take this side you get that one over there."

Both women, applying their collective strength, pulled on the sliding doors together and managed to pry them another fifteen centimeters apart before they caught on their bent grooves in the floor and got stuck again.

"That should be enough for us to fit through," Aidora said, cautiously squeezing into the crack. She pushed her way through the narrow opening with no problem and then turned and extended her hand for Onelle to take. Onelle took it and followed Aidora's lead.

Halfway through, Onelle's dress snagged on the edge. She took a deep breath and sucked in her stomach and her chest as much as she could and then said, "Pull!"

Aidora, still holding Onelle's hand, gripped her tight and gave her a firm tug. A loud rip sounded as Onelle popped through the door, making it to the other side. She looked down at her dress; it had been gouged all the way down the right hip and thigh. She checked herself for any wounds and let out a sigh of relief when she found herself unscathed.

Just then, the ship's computer came over the comms.

<<All hands, abandon ship. This is not a drill. All hands, abandon ship.>>

"This way," Aidora said, turning up the corridor. "We need to get to the escape pods."

They raced together up the corridor as a crazed passenger flew around the junction point. All parties froze in their tracks and stared at one another.

"This is your fault!" the wild-eyed Seyfferian woman growled. She lunged forward, knocking Aidora out of the way and tackled Onelle. Aidora smacked her head against the wall plating and collapsed to the ground, unconscious.

With Aidora down for the count, the remaining two women rolled around on the floor for a minute before the crazed woman found herself on top, straddling Onelle's waist. With fierce screams, she clawed at Onelle's face. Luckily, however, Onelle managed to clasp onto the woman's wrists and held her at bay.

"Aidora!" Onelle cried out, turning her head to look at the unconscious girl. "Wake up! Aidora, I need you!"

Unable to break free of Onelle's grasp, the woman bent down and bit Onelle's hand. She screamed and let go of the woman's wrists.

Scared for her life, she kicked and flailed and scooted herself up against the wall.

The woman, who'd fallen off in the tussle, slowly stood up. Then turning to face Onelle, her hair dangling in front of her face and giving her an ominous look, she reached out and bashed her fist into the glass touch-panel of the corridor's computer interface, shattering the surface.

The black glass lay in a mess on the floor and the crazed woman shuffled through the discordant shards until she found a long, jagged piece. Picking it up, she held it out in front of her and begin to prowl toward Onelle.

Terrified of what the woman might to do to her, Onelle let out a fearful shriek and pressed her back flat against the wall. Reaching into her cleavage she fished for her mini-blaster, then realized she'd left it back in her room.

"This is all your fault!"

"It's all just a terrible misunderstanding," Onelle said, her voice wavering as she spoke. Her body trembled with fright and she tried to scoot away. But this only seemed to agitate the woman even more, so she grimaced and turned her face away.

"Look at me!" the woman screamed.

"Leave me alone!" Onelle shouted back, squeezing shut her eyes.

All of a sudden there was a loud thump, and Onelle, cracking one eye open, looked over to find the woman lying prostrate on the floor.

When she opened both eyes, she saw the knight she'd seduced earlier helping Aidora up.

"It's you," gasped Onelle, surprised to see any familiar face, let alone his. She didn't make much of it, other than the fact that it was his duty to secure high-ranking officials and see to their safety. One of the perks of being a VIP member.

"The name is Palamedes, if you recall, mistress," he reminded her. Turning his attention back to the young Nyctan girl, he asked, "Are you able to walk?"

"I think so," the girl replied, rubbing the knot forming on the top of her forehead.

"Good, because it's not safe here. We have to keep moving." Palamedes helped Aidora up and she thanked him with a subtle nod. Then he turned to

Onelle. "I can see you both to the escape pods, but then I must get to the bridge."

"You're not coming with us?" Onelle asked in a shocked tone.

"I'm afraid a Knight's duty is to the ship he serves upon."

Onelle eased up to him and gently placed her hand on his thick arm. "About earlier…I'm sorry I forced you to…"

"That's all in the past," he said to her. He smiled at her warmly, as if to reassure her that it wasn't all bad, and then turned and marched up the corridor leading the way to the escape pods.

In the crimson glow of the red emergency lights they followed after the Knight, Palamedes. The red wash gave everything an eerie post-apocalyptic vibe that didn't help to ease the tension of whatever was causing the crew to go mad.

Aidora and Onelle followed the knight to the end of another junction when voices rose up from the depths of the adjoining hallway. He threw up his arm and motioned for them to get as flat as possible against the wall.

They did so and almost as soon as they'd receded from view two men tumbled into the corridor. Each of them was soaked in sticky wet blood and, like the woman from earlier, were quite mad with what seemed to be a rage virus.

"It's all your fault!" the one man shouted, bashing his fists against the other man's face. With a crunch, the first man's nose broke and blood began gushing down his mouth and chin, but all he did was laugh.

Full of rage, the battered man returned the favor and swung his blue fist and it struck the copper man in the temple, drawing green blood. He immediately went down and the blue man scurried on top of him and began to bite his ear. Tearing off the copper-skinned man's ear in his mouth, he threw out his arms, kicked back his head, and howled like a common beast.

This short reprieve allowed the copper man to shove the blue man to the ground and he climbed on top, blood trailing from the hole where his ear used to be and drizzling down his neck.

Compelled by rage, the copper man began to pound the blue man's face in. Even after he'd rendered the man unconscious, he did not stop his brutal attack. Instead, he continued pounding away, a gleeful expression on his face. Blow after blow he continued to bash the copper man's scull in until his face was a bloody pulp.

Just then an orange skinned woman with blue markings and her top torn asunder, raced by cupping her breasts. She saw the two men beating one another to death and continued on her way, screaming frantically as she went.

Distracted by the woman's shrill scream, the copper man stopped his assault and looked up. He paused and stared in the direction the woman had fled, an almost contemplative look on his face, and then rising to his feet he took chase. "You bitch!" he shouted. "This is all your fault!"

She screamed again when she glanced back to see him chasing after her and then they disappeared around the bend of the other end of the junction. At the same time, the blue man gurgled something with his dying breath and then his head fell limply to the side.

"What in the bloody galaxy is going on here?" Onelle asked out loud. She looked over at her two partners and they each shrugged.

"We're almost there," Aidora finally said.

A few meters later they rounded a bend and found themselves standing in front of the escape hatch.

"It's here," Palamedes said. He slid a wall panel away to reveal a manual lever with a red handle. He grabbed it and pulled it down. This released the hatch and a concealed door that were built to blend in as part of the wall. This rose up to reveal the round entrance to a four-person escape pod.

"You two get in. I must return to the bridge and secure the ship."

Onelle reached out and grabbed his arm, delaying his noble exit, "But it's suicide."

"It's my duty," he answered. "Besides, I've already broken enough rules for the week." He smiled at her and then turned and jogged up the hall.

"Hey, knight," Onelle called out after him. He paused and looked back at her one last time. "Be careful."

He nodded, as if to say he had this all under control, and then continued on his way.

Once Palamedes was out of sight, Onelle turned back toward Aidora and they stared at one another, the shock of it all causing them to feel numb.

"Gruh!" a gruff voice grunted, startling both women. They turned to face the other end of the hall when a man stumbled around the corner of the junction and then crashed to the floor. He let out another agonizing groan and was holding onto his side which was bleeding profusely. The man staggered back to his feet and looked up to find two women standing at the other end of the passage.

Almost immediately he recognized them and called out, "Onelle!"

Onelle gazed back down the corridor at the Blue-skin and recognized his charming features and long flowing white hair. "Senator Targon?" she gasped.

A flurry of angry shouts came up from the depths of the corridor directly behind the senator. Alarmed, he looked back, eyes wide with fear. Not waiting around to see what the mob would do to him next, he limped quickly toward the two women. "Don't leave without me. They're mad here. They've all gone mad."

"Hurry!" Onelle shouted, ushering him into the escape pod. She shoved Aidora in after him and then grabbed the hatch and looked back down the corridor just in time to see an unruly mob of at least half a dozen demented crew members flood into the main junction.

Ratty and drenched in one another's blood, they made eye contact with Onelle. She tensed up then quickly closed the hatch behind her, climbing into the escape pod. She secured the door and then turned to see what her next step needed to be.

Aidora was already fishing out a first aid kit to attend to the senator who was sitting on the bench seat leaning against the wall. While the Nyctan girl dressed his wound, Onelle prepped the escape pod for launch.

"Everybody hang tight," Onelle said, going over to the controls anxious eyes searching the panel. She hit some buttons and prepared for emergency launch. "I'll get us out of here."

She flipped a series of switches then mashed a large green button on the side of the dashboard and the airlock hissed then spat out the escape pod.

The jettisoned pod wobbled away from the ship before the automated stabilization thrusters kicked on, igniting white hot. As the small ship settled into a steady flight plan, all three passengers looked out the window at the massive Nyctan cruiser hanging large in the distance. It contained all the delegates from all the worlds of all seven systems, and they were slaughtering each other like common livestock.

Suddenly, numerous orange explosions started erupting all along the hull of the cruiser.

"All those people," gasped Aidora, covering her mouth with both hands as she gazed fretfully at the flaming ship outside her window.

They'd barely made it off in time, Onelle realized. She took in a deep breath to help calm her jitters then quickly tapped a few buttons on the controls. Off to the side, Senator Targon grunted and sat up to get a better look at what she was up to.

"What are you doing?" he asked her.

"I've signaled my yacht for an emergency pick up."

Soon enough, her vessel came into view over them and docked with the escape pod.

Once the two ships had fully connected, Onelle opened the hatch and stepped into the airlock of her ship. She waited for the automatic pressurization to equalize then opened the inner airlock hatch. Turning back to her two guests, she said, "Welcome aboard my personal yacht, the *Miura*."

Aidora helped the senator climb out of the narrow confines of the escape pod and brought him aboard the ship. Onelle was there to greet him, extending her green hand for him to take. He looked at it almost hesitantly, but took it anyway.

"I appreciate your help," he said as she hoisted him up. Practically bumping into one another, he maintained a firm grasp of her hand and pulled her close. "I'm in your debt," he said, before finally relinquishing his grip.

Onelle helped him over to a seat and sat him down again. As she buckled his waist, he groaned in pain, his blood seeping through the fresh gauze they'd wrapped him with. "Does it hurt?" she asked him.

"Not too bad. More of a pinch, really. Don't worry," he said, looking over at her with a poised smile. "I'll manage."

She batted her eyes at him, her dark green lips tightening into a flirtatious grin. Nothing more to say, she headed to the front of the cabin, quickly found her seat, and prepped the thrusters.

Onelle swiveled in her chair while Aidora settled into the seat across from the senator. "All right, everyone," she announced, "you can all take a deep breath because we're officially in the clear."

The sleek yacht, escape pod still attached to the side of its hull like a bulbous tumor, turned away from the Nyctan diplomatic cruiser, the *Qui'tek'alon*, and fired all thrusters.

Even making escape velocity, the final annihilation of the ship behind them sent out a massive shockwave. The force expanded out in all directions, like a ring rippling away from a stone tossed into a pond, and quickly caught up to them.

"Hang on!" Onelle growled through her clenched jaw. "Things are about to get rough."

As soon as she'd warned them, the ship began to shudder so violently that it sounded as though it would tear itself apart. There was a strong jolt, then another as the turbulence picked up. It felt like they were in a giant barrel crashing over the rapids, their harnesses digging into their flesh with each gut churning lurch. Before she could correct it, the vessel was knocked off its trajectory and spiraling out into uncharted space.

Onelle fought the controls, trying to get the ship back under her control, but the shockwave had been too strong and had knocked out her main thrusters. Simply put, there was nothing she could do.

"Graddack!" she cursed, smashing both palms on the dash and then looking back at her passengers. Senator Targon had already blacked out from the inertia and Aidora was struggling to maintain consciousness with all the g-forces of the uncontrolled spiraling pushing her to the verge of darkness.

Onelle reached back to try and touch Aidora's hand but she, too, felt the darkness tightening around her vision. What began as tunnel vision incrementally grew into a full-on blackout, though only momentarily. Fighting as best she could to remain conscious, Onelle reached out for the glowing orange button at the center of her darkening vision that read: *autopilot.*

She fought with all her strength against the unrelenting g-forces and, finally, her fingertips brushed the button just as she felt the walls of her consciousness collapsing in on her.

The strain was too much, and with tears streaming from her eyes she gave into the darkness, never knowing whether or not she'd succeeded in pressing the button that would save them.

31

A chandelier aboard a spaceship still seemed odd to Jegra. But the new *Shard's* design had been overseen by Lianica, whose taste leaned more into the decadency of Dagon aesthetics.

Even if it wasn't to her specific tastes, she did find that the soft light it cast basked everything in a wholesome glow that reminded her of a warm cabin fire.

Jegra rose to her feet, held her glass high, and cleared her throat. "It seems I've been giving a lot of speeches as of late." An unexpected round of laughter caused her to smile and briefly reflect on why that was funny. She understood the irony though, a woman of action, a warrior, becoming a diplomat and a ruler wasn't common. But, somehow, it felt right. "We've won a small battle, it's true, but the larger fight lays ahead of us. Tomorrow we take back Dagon Prime! So, eat, drink, and be merry—"

"For tomorrow we die!" they all cheered in unison.

It was a grim acknowledgement that war never truly brought peace, only suffering. The only real peace was in death. And you could either shirk from that fact or face it head on, courageously. Not recklessly, but with the awareness that life is only a fleeting, bittersweet existence.

Jegra raised her glass and shouted across the room for all to hear. "To those who will lay down your lives, I salute you!"

It was the gladiator's salute. A way to honor those they faced in the arena, each knowing that they had no choice and that, ultimately, one would die. For that sacrifice, they paid tribute to one another.

Everyone mimicked her gesture and uttered the same and then began their feast, for which the ship's cooks had slaved over for the past fourteen hours.

Instead of the stereotypical five course dinner most commonly prepared for dignitaries and guests, she had the equivalent of a Thanksgiving feast prepared. At least, the close approximation to one she could get with alien cuisine. However, for all their effort, the cooks couldn't seem to crack the gravy recipe and ended up having to synthesize it.

When Jegra hadn't touched her food for several minutes, Lianica leaned in, the many medals and pins on her dress uniform glinting in the chandelier light as she did so. "You haven't touched your meal. Is everything all right? I can send it back, if it's not to your liking."

"It's not that," Jegra replied. "I just have a lot on my mind."

Unexpectedly, the ship's red alert blared and the lights in the room changed from their soft golden color to a bright red.

"Saved by the bell," Jegra muttered to herself.

"What was that?" Brei asked. Jegra turned to her and smiled.

"Nothing," she said, "but gather all the senior staff and let's find out what is going on."

"Captain Blackstar to the bridge," Lt. Commander Barrion's voice came over the comm.

Lianica looked over at Jegra, a sense of urgency on her face. They rose simultaneously to their feet and headed toward the exit of the dining hall together. The senior officers all rose too and followed them out, including Lieutenant Brei'Alas.

Before she left the dining hall, Brei'Alas turned around and said, "Everyone hold tight. The empress and senior staff have everything well under control."

She didn't know if that would help console them or even ease their concerns, but she didn't want them panicking. She turned again to leave when a hand came out of nowhere and placed itself on her shoulder. She looked over to see Karina staring at her.

"How can I help?" Karina asked.

Brei was short for a Dagon woman, so she assumed Karina must be large for an Earth female, because Jegra had told her that most Earth males were the larger of the sexes. But both Jegra and Karina were larger than any of the males in attendance. This made Brei curious as to whether or not the human species carried an Alpha female gene, like her own species did.

Jennica had been an Alpha female. Danica, back when she was Cassera, had also been an Alpha female type. But Brei'Alas was just your average looking Dagon woman—only, in her case, a woman with hidden talents.

She smiled at the offer. "Thank you, Madam President. But I'm sure we can handle it." When she saw the disheartened look on Karina's face, she reached out a blue hand and placed it on her shoulder. "On second thought, it's probably better if I keep you in the loop of what's going on. Come with me."

Karina smiled and followed Brei out of the dining hall.

"What do we have?" Lianica Blackstar asked as she stepped onto the bridge. Lieutenant Commander Barrion turned to the captain to find an entire entourage of senior officers shuffle in behind her.

He had nearly forgotten about the evening's dinner party. After the last one, he felt it best to keep a low profile. Even though most of the crew was completely unaware of what had transpired, thanks to Brei'Alas resetting time, there were still enough people who knew what had happened for him to feel a sense of shame over it.

He realized it wasn't his fault, seeing as The Voice was nearly impossible to resist. So far, only Dakroth and Jegra seemed to be immune to her influences. And it was Jegra and Brei'Alas who'd intervened on his behalf. Something he was eternally grateful for.

"It's Aldebaran, ma'am. It wasn't destroyed. In fact, our long-range scans are showing that it's behaving...oddly."

"Define oddly," Lianica said.

"It's better if I just show you."

Barrion activated the onboard telefield array. It was a direct link to a network of spy satellites littered throughout the Dagon Empire. Of course, the array was set up under the pretense of astronomical research. Using one of the telescopes closest to Aldebaran, he brought up the image on the screen and zoomed in.

"What's it doing?" Jegra asked as she peered at the screen. The ring world was rotating around the fledgling black hole in a strange, unpredictable manner. On close inspection, though, it did seem to have a pattern about its gyration and sudden pivots.

"The ring world has become stuck in a bistable state," Barrion answered.

Jegra looked at him as though that didn't help answer her question. She turned to Lianica.

"Basically, there's no gravity in space, so if there are equal and opposite forces, the object will continually flip between the two states of inertia."

"And that's why it's gyrating and flipping around like that?"

A bright flash forced the entire bridge crew to cover their eyes, and when they looked back out, there were two ring worlds, one slightly larger than Aldebaran, undulating in an inverse bistable rotation.

"Uh…what just happened?" Karina asked.

They all looked to find that Brei'Alas had brought the president aboard the bridge. Although not protocol, Lianica allowed it, gesturing with a wave for them to come join her.

Barrion checked his scans. "It's…also Aldebaran. Just a different version…from a different timeline.

Another bright flash forced them to wince once more, and when their vision readjusted, there were now three different sized ring worlds nested together in a massive spinning armillary.

"Impossible," Barrion said, checking his readings again, just to be sure.

"What is it?" Lianica asked.

"The ring worlds are using the blackhole as an energy source. And they seem to be charging up."

"Charging up?" Brei'Alas gulped nervously. "That doesn't sound good."

"No, it doesn't," Jegra said. She turned to Lianica and gave her a look that seemed to be asking what their next move was.

Lianica scanned the worried faces of her crew. She knew that every mission had its own set of challenges, especially when facing the great unknown. But she'd never faced anything like this before. Regardless, part of being a commander was making the best decision she could given the information available to her, even when that information was inadequate at best.

"I think we should—"

"You all look so serious," a voice came over the viewscreen. Everyone turned to find a young man, no older than fifteen, sitting upon a golden throne in a lavish throne room. He gazed back at them with eerie, obsidian eyes, although he did not look Nyctan. Rather, he had pale blue skin, like the clearest of blue lagoons, and Dagon features, including their species' trademark elfin-tipped ears.

Jegra stepped forward, making it known she was the one in charge of the situation. "It was my plan to blow your world up," she informed the young man. "If anyone is to blame, it falls squarely on my shoulders."

"That's very noble of you, mother."

Everyone looked at Jegra, shocked by the realization that this was her child. A child born a mere thirteen months ago.

"How is he that old?" Barrion asked.

"Time displacement," Brei stated, addressing his question. "All three Aldebarans exist in different timelines. That's the only logical explanation."

"Then how can we see them?" Karina asked. She looked clueless, but Earth technology was still far behind even the most rudimentary star-faring species. Still, she was smart enough to grasp the concepts.

"It seems," Lianica relayed, "they are using the immense gravity well of the black hole as a kind of wormhole."

Karina scanned everyone's faces, searching for the slightest clue as to what all this meant. "So, they're traveling from the past and the future to meet at the present? But why?"

"Indeed," Jegra said, looking up at the young man who was studying his gold painted nails, apparently out of a state of sheer boredom. "Why are you bringing all three worlds into the present?"

"Ah!" the boy said, leaping up. "I thought you'd never ask." The young godchild walked over to one of the massive windows of his empty ship and pointed out at the vista. "Do you see that?" he asked. All they could see was a darkness filled with black orbs. "This is the future that awaits us all."

"It's full of nothingness," Jegra answered.

"Exactly. And I designed this ring world, what you people call Aldebaran, as a prototype world that could harness the power of black holes and continue life—even beyond the death of the known universe."

"You want to repopulate the future with remnants of the past?"

"In a manner of speaking. I want to send ring worlds into the past, using the black holes of the future, as they touch every point in space and time."

"To do what, exactly?" Brei asked timidly. She wasn't entirely certain she wanted to know the answer, but since everyone was thinking it, she felt obligated to ask.

"Why, to rule the universe ad infinitum, of course," the young H'aaztre said with a sinister grin parting his lips. A halo of gold flashed upon his obsidian eyes and sent shivers down everyone's spines. "What's the matter, mother? I can tell by the look on your face that you're worried. Was it something I said?"

"Don't call me that," she said. "You have no right to call me that. You're not my son."

"But you are my biological mother, are you not?" The boy asked the question with so much credulity that it broke Jegra's heart to have to reply.

"I am. But any hope of raising a loving, compassionate human being is long gone. The child that would have been can never be, and so doesn't exist."

The young boy looked puzzled for a moment, then he smiled. "I see what you mean. I suppose it was a tad bit cruel to take this vessel so early. But you see, time waits for no one. Not even for a god like me." He shrugged as if there was nothing that could be done about it and went back to staring at them with his dark creepy eyes and wicked smile

"Is that what you are?" Brei asked. "A god?"

Jegra turned to her and was surprised to find that little, meager Brei was feeling all the indignation that Jegra also felt, but was having trouble suppressing it to the same degree Jegra had managed.

Her fists balled up tight, Brei'Alas took a step forward. Her eyes fixated on the young man. That's when Jegra noticed her nose begin to bleed.

"Not now," Jegra said, placing a hand on Brei's shoulder. All of a sudden Brei let out a huge breath of air as if she'd been holding it and began panting.

"But you see, time waits for no one. Not even for a god like me," H'aaztre repeated. He paused a moment, frowning slightly as he seemed to be running through different timelines in his mind. Looking back up, he raised a curious eyebrow. "That wasn't from the black hole's time distortion. Did you just..." he began asking. But by the look on her face he knew it to be true. "Impressive. The ability to control time is a rare and valuable gift. Even so, you're limited in scope and can only manipulate the time around you by hours. Possibly days...depending on your skill level. Certainly nothing for me to be concerned about."

"Maybe you should be..." Jegra added at the last minute. "After all, your generals are dropping like flies. You might want to up your game."

"Tsk, tsk," he chastised. "Getting cocky at the eleventh hour is not very prudent, mother dearest."

The boy squinted at Jegra menacingly and then smiled in the most pleasant of ways, his eyes going from a narrow gaze to a joyful squint. "Anyway, it's been fun catching up. Let's do it again sometime."

The viewscreen went black and another bright flash blinded those on the bridge. When they could finally look again, they found the space being broadcast on the monitor completely empty. Nothing was there. Not even the black hole.

Lianica turned to Barrion. "Where did it go?"

"Unknown, Captain," he said, studying the readouts of the various screens that made up the science station. "It's the correct coordinates but, it seems, Aldebaran has completely vanished."

"Sorry to interrupt, but how in the world do you people expect to fight someone with near omnipotent powers?" Karina asked. She looked to Jegra and then Lianica, hoping that one of them had an idea.

"That's a good question," Lianica said. She turned to Jegra, hoping Jegra might have a more suitable answer.

Jegra's eyes panned across the room before eventually returning to Karina. "There's no such thing as God with a capital G. But there may be a god," she replied.

"I don't follow," Karina said.

"As a scientist, you of all people understand that 'God' is simply a construct of human imagination and superstition. H'aaztre is nothing more than an ancient, highly advanced alien. It's Clarke's Law."

"Whose what?" Brei asked.

"Arthur C. Clarke. He said something like: *Any sufficiently advanced technology is indistinguishable from magic.* I'd assume that the alien beings who created such technology would appear to us as gods."

"That doesn't seem to make things any easier for us," Brei said, folding her arms.

"No. But it takes his power over us down a notch; he's not omnipotent. In fact, I highly doubt he was the first advanced being in existence or, for that matter, the last. There must be others out there. Beings so ancient that they'd seem like gods even to someone as technologically advanced as H'aaztre."

"So, let me see if I'm understanding you correctly. You want us to enlist help?" Brei'Alas asked in all seriousness, her amber eyes fixing onto Jegra's brown ones. "From a god?"

"Something like that," Jegra said with a wry smile.

"Why do I get the feeling she's not telling us everything?" Barrion asked, leaning over to whisper into Brei's ear. She turned and smiled at him then looked back at the empress.

"And where do you expect to find such a being?" Lianica asked. "Our *allobiological* database doesn't contain any alien species with the incredible lifespan or abilities that H'aaztre seems to exhibit."

"Maybe not," Jegra answered. "But the Enchiridion predicted him, along with a host of other Progenitors."

"Let me get this straight," Brei interjected, "you're saying that because an ancient sacred text correctly predicted H'aaztre, that other entities it makes mention of might also exist?"

"Right now," Jegra said, her gaze roving from one face to another, "it's the best lead we have."

"And if it just turns out to be more primitive superstition?" Karina asked.

"Sometimes, Madam President," Jegra said with a reassuring smile and a warm hand on the shoulder, "it's about having a little bit of faith. If not in some higher power, then at the very least in ourselves."

3 2

Back in Arkadian space, Onelle finally let it all out in the form of a long, drawn-out sigh meant to draw everyone's attention to her flustered state. She did a quick glance to see if she'd garnered any sympathy, and although Senator Targon Van Morgan had almost certainly heard her, he pretended as though he hadn't. Only Aidora, with her large black eyes, gazed back at her sympathetically.

"Are you all right, Mistress Onelle?" Aidora went over to Onelle and tenderly placed her hand on top of Onelle's.

"It's just all this stress," she said, letting out another overly dramatic sigh. "I never expected Azra'il Nun to double cross me. Me! Of all people. Can you believe that? During this whole thing I've been her greatest ally. And how does she repay me? By using my connections to broker a peace accord meant to try to erase me off the face of the galactic map."

Senator Targon cleared his throat and then looked over at both women. "If she tried to kill you once, there's no guarantee she won't try it again. I recommend we all lay low for the time being, including you, my dear."

Onelle was nodding in agreement when, all of a sudden, the ship's proximity alarm went off.

"What in the blazes is the infernal racket?" Targon grumbled, covering his blue, pointy ears with both hands.

Onelle leaped up and rushed into the cockpit, her forest green hair flowing behind her. She peered out the view portal, scanning their surroundings. "It's the proximity alarm, a Nephilim scout has just spotted us."

"The Fusion?" Aidora asked. "They shouldn't be patrolling Arkadian space. Arkadia and Nyctan are the two allied worlds of H'aaztre. Why would they..."

her voice trailed off as she looked over at Onelle with a dreadful expression. As one, both women turned their frightened gazes onto Senator Targon.

"Of course," he mumbled to himself, even though his bellyaching could be overheard by all. "No loose ends."

"Quickly now," Onelle said, brushing past him, "follow me."

They went to her personal quarters where she kicked away the elaborate Nyctan rug on her floor to reveal a secret panel. She crouched down, opened the panel, and gestured for the senator to get into the recess.

"It's shielded to mask your bio-signature, and it locks from the inside. There's also a false top, so if they do try to pry it open, all they'll find are rows of circuit boards and a bunch of random wiring."

"I don't exactly like enclosed spaces," he said with a nervous gulp. As he swallowed, his Adam's apple seemed to get stuck in the back of his throat.

"Do you like living, exactly?" Onelle asked.

Targon nodded and said, "Ah, yes. Excellent point."

With a gentle nudge to his arm, she guided him down into the small recess, no bigger than a coffin and padded just the same. Obviously, Onelle had outfitted it for comfort during raids where she had to keep out of sight.

Before she could set the panel back into its rightful place, Targon's arm flew up. He caught her green hand with his blue one and his golden eyes looked up into her turquoise ones. "Don't forget me in here."

She nodded and gave his hand a firm squeeze, letting him know everything would be fine. With his concerns assuaged, she promptly placed the panel back into position above him and thumped on it twice with the heel of her hand, letting him know that he was secured.

A second later the sound of the locking mechanism could be heard as the panel bolted into place.

Not wasting another second, Onelle quickly covered the secret alcove back up with the rug and brushed out its creases so that it would look natural if anyone came into the room. Once she'd finished with that, she looked over at Aidora's quivering lip and nervous black eyes staring back at her.

"Can I trust you?"

"I serve only you, mistress," Aidora said with a reverential bow. The girl's long black hair flowed over her shoulder like an obsidian waterfall, and when she rose back up, the strands slid off her white porcelain skin and settled back into place along the curvature of her petite spine.

"I hope so, because I'm getting sick and tired of being double crossed. First, that bitch Jegra handing me over to that infernal bounty hunter. Then, Azra'il Nun trying to expunge me..." She raised her hand to the top of her head as if measuring her height. "I've had it up to here with insincere, back-stabbing, cunt-faced bitches."

Aidora nodded silently and stepped aside so as to let Onelle storm out. After Onelle had exited the room, Aidora's black eyes flashed with a halo of gold and she smiled menacingly.

"Are you coming?" Onelle's voice called impatiently out from the corridor.

Aidora regained her composure and timidly answered, "Yes, mistress. Right away."

Both women arrived at the airlock just as the clunking sound of the scout ship could be heard docking with Onelle's yacht, the *Miura*.

"Anxious" didn't even begin to explain how she felt or how tight her stomach was wound, so she took a deep breath and then said in a low voice, "Just follow my lead, Aidora."

Aidora nodded again but jumped when the hiss of the airlock pressurizing startled her.

The clunk of soldiers' footsteps could be heard on the other side of the door. Onelle peered through the small window on the airlock to see two Nephilim patrol guards, wearing their typical scab-like black armor with yellow traces of light pulsing at the seams.

"Open up," the guard said, looking back at her through the small viewing portal. He pounded his fist against the door twice, knocking to be let in.

Not knowing the exact reason they were boarding her ship, Onelle motioned with a thrust of her chin for Aidora to get behind her. The girl obliged and Onelle mashed the green button that unsealed the door.

Another pressurized hiss could be heard as the two ships matched each other's atmosphere, and two bulky guards crouched under the door frame and boarded the ship.

The brutish men, obviously of low rank, shoved the two women aside and marched directly into the corridor and split up. Each one headed in a different direction so as to scour the ship from both ends, searching for anything out of the ordinary.

"What's the meaning of this search? As Supreme Commander of the Trade Federation, I demand you tell me who ordered this illegal search."

"Your title is merely honorary," the guard informed her, ignoring Onelle's posturing.

Angered by his dismissal of her rank, if not her status as the wealthiest woman in the galaxy, she marched in front of him and planted her heels, blocking his path.

"This is my ship and I demand you go no further!"

He paused momentarily and looked down at her with an annoyed expression on his face, then reached out and shoved her aside as though she were nothing more than an inconvenient nuisance.

Her back slammed up against the wall and she gasped out in dismay at how he had so rudely brushed her aside. "Why, I never..." she balked, her temper flaring as she pushed off and continued after the guard with a reinvigorated determination to give him a piece of her mind.

"You do realize I answer to The Voice, right? And when she hears about how you've illegally boarded and searched one of her closest ally's ships, she'll be furious!"

The guard merely laughed. "Where do you think our orders came from?" he fired back, not in the least bit concerned over her hollow threats.

Slender white fingers reached out and took Onelle by her arm and stopped in her tracks. "No, Mistress Onelle," Aidora whispered, "it isn't safe."

"Fine!" Onelle growled, pulling defiantly away from Aidora's grip. Once she'd freed her arm, she pointed a condemnatory finger at the Nyctan soldier who was busy opening and closing overhead storage bins as he inspected the ship. "But I'll be complaining to Azra'il Nun personally. You have my word."

"And you have my word," he replied, shooting her an exasperated look, "I still don't care."

After a thorough search of the ship, both guards met back at the airlock. The first guard, who Onelle had chastised, looked at his comrade and said, "Report."

"It's all clear," he answered. "No sign of the senator."

The first solider nodded and then both turned toward the airlock to return to their ship when, unexpectedly, a clangor rang out from the back recesses of the ship.

"What was that?" the second guard asked, spinning around in the direction of the noise.

"What was what?" Onelle asked, feigning ignorance.

"I heard it too," the first guard said, stepping forward as he began to make his way down the corridor to the back of the ship.

"No!" Onelle, screamed. Without thinking, she flung herself into the soldier, knocking him back. In his shock at being assaulted, he reached up and clasped her neck to try and choke her out, but she reached down and snatched his blaster from his waist and fired two shots into his abdomen, point blank.

His gloved hands slipped from her throat, and her eyes wide with fear, she fired another five shots into his gut. The soldier fell into the wall and then sliding down the wall paneling he slowly settled onto the floor, the life draining from his eyes as he slumped over in a sitting position.

"Drop it!" a voice demanded from behind. Onelle dropped the gun to the floor, her hands trembling with a cocktail of fear and adrenaline. "Now, put your hands behind your head and step back toward me. Nice and easy."

"No!" Aidora cried, and she grabbed the second soldier's wrists and threw her entire weight into shoving his arms away from Onelle. He managed to fire off three shots, but Aidora was strong enough to redirect his aim, and the blasts simply scorched the inside of the ship's hull.

Without hesitating, Onelle bent down and quickly picked up her discarded blaster. She reeled around and pointed it squarely at the guard, but Aidora was still struggling with all her might and was in her direct line of sight.

"Aidora!" Onelle shouted. "Get down!"

Before Aidora could react, however, the guard backhanded her across the face and she crumpled to the ground. This gave Onelle the opening she needed and, without hesitating, she quickly pulled the trigger.

The first blast hit the guard in the shoulder and he looked up in shock. Then growing furious, he lunged for her, hands reaching out to grab her. But she pulled the trigger again. This time the shot tore through his chest armor and stopped him in his tracks. Seeing the rage in his eyes, she feared for her life and fired again. And then again. And, finally, one last time, just to be safe.

The Nyctan guard, smoldering in white smoke that billowed from gaping holes in his armor and his body, collapsed to the floor. The shot that did him in, however, was marked by a red glowing ring in his forehead.

As the soldier lay face up, staring at the ceiling with eyes frozen in alarm, a short distance away from him sat his comrade, who stared vacantly at the wall across from him.

"You got him!" Aidora cried out excitedly. She walked over to the guard lying on his back and nudged him with her foot, just to be sure he wasn't going to reanimate and try to attack them all over again. Satisfied, she turned and smiled at Onelle, but seeing that Onelle seemed a little jarred by the whole ordeal, she rushed over to her and began rubbing her back.

Off to the side of the corridor, tarnished by the black stain of plasma fire, Onelle stood hyperventilating. Although she tried desperately to catch her breath, it seemed a rather impossible thing to do at that moment.

Her hands shaking, she looked down at the weapon she held and then, startled by the revelation of what she'd done, she dropped it to the floor. She drew back from it as it rattled about as though it were a copperhead snake and stared down at the weapon in a state of complete disbelief.

"What have I done?" she asked, her voice wavering with the combined stress of shock and excitement of the kill. Oddly enough in all the turmoil she hadn't even given it any thought. She just acted, as if by instinct, doing whatever she needed to in order to stay alive.

And with a thousand different emotions running through her mind, she honestly didn't know whether to laugh or to cry.

Aidora rushed to her side and got under her arm, as it looked as though her knees would buckle at any moment. Guiding her back to the bridge, Aidora said, "What's done is done. When these men don't report back as scheduled, they'll send more soldiers to check on them. That's how they operate. They even run patrols in groups, so there's bound to be two or three more scouts nearby."

Onelle nodded thoughtfully. She looked at Aidora with her big green eyes and said, "I must thank you."

"For what?" Aidora asked.

"For staying true to your word and standing by my side even when things got scary. I appreciate that. And I don't forget who my friends are in the same way I don't forget who my enemies are. Just know that you'll be well taken care of if you decide to stay on as my personal servant."

Aidora nodded finding the offer quite agreeable.

Finally, back in the flight cabin, Onelle sank down in her seat, the white leather squeaking and whining as she slid into it, and made herself comfortable. "Aidora," she said in a soft voice as she stared vacantly down at the flight controls.

"Yes, mistress?"

"Please board their ship and erase any record of this search from their database. Our names, the name of the ship, even the name of the sector they were canvasing. I want it all erased. Then place the bodies aboard and decouple that scout ship with the auto destruct set to blow as soon as we're out of here."

"Yes, mistress."

Aidora scurried away, anxious to carry out her duties. Onelle looked out at the stars and the distant green and orange nebulae that filled the background like a grand oil painting and let out a heavy sigh. Another bout of rattling came from the back of the ship causing Onelle to frown.

"You almost cost us our lives, you stupid blue bastard," she murmured under her breath. Ignoring the fact that she had locked Senator Targon in the confines of the holding nook to ensure he didn't panic and prematurely release himself before the search was over.

Of course, for all their troubles, she'd decided to leave him in there for the duration of their flight, at least until their return to Arkadia. It'd only be another six and a half hours.

Another twelve minutes had lapsed when Aidora returned and quickly took her seat opposite Onelle. "It's done," she replied, "just like you asked."

"Excellent," Onelle said. She smiled at the girl and then, turning her attention back toward the control panel, she typed in the coordinates for Arkadia, a veritable pleasure paradise and homeworld to the Bre'lal people.

Her hand on the throttle, she powered up the FTL and, in a flash of light, her ship blinked into hyperspace, leaving the scout ship behind.

It hung lifeless in space, floating adrift like a castoff bottle floating across an endless sea.

A few moments after Onelle's gleaming white space yacht, the *Miura*, had blinked out of the system, the scout ship exploded in a glorious flash of hot plasma. Blue and white fire bubbled out of the ship's plating and the hull ruptured along the seams of every bulkhead. The flames quickly collapsed back in on themselves as they ate up all the gases until nothing was left except for the all-encompassing vacuum of space and the cold, charred, skeletal husk of what used to be a shuttlecraft.

33

Danica had always wanted to create energy discs that were akin to throwing stars. She pressed her palms together and generated a small energy shield and flattened it down until its edges were razor sharp then spun around on her heel like a discus thrower. She launched the glowing blue energy disc at the giant crab beast, angrily clacking its claws and watching her from its extended eye sockets.

Arkadia's gladiatorial arena was slightly smaller than the one on Thessalonica, but not by much. It was, however, quite different looking. It was designed with a pleasing, tropical beach aesthetic that allowed it to blend right into the surrounding islands without being an eyesore. The spreading tent roof was shaped like sails of a seagoing vessel, creating quite a striking look from a distance.

In fact, it was the largest structure on the surface and took up the most area of any structure on Arkadia. It was imposing in comparison to the relatively topographically flat resort islands, with their ocean villas that stretched out in every direction as far as the eye could see.

A small tourist-trap of shops and food places surrounded the arena, making the large island by far the busiest of all the resort islands. In fact, the arena took up so much space that the landing port for inbound vessels was set up on the adjacent island. This meant visitors had to boat over to the main island after making their way through customs. Even so, all of this added to the quaint, islander way of life that so defined Arkadia. The arena, however, was only the second biggest draw to the island world; the first was the pleasure resorts and the beautiful Bre'lal men and women who catered to their guests' every need.

Attendance at Arkadia Arena was up this season, as everyone who tuned in to the games eagerly anticipated a new reigning champion. There were a lot of fan favorites, a lot of predictions of who might step into the number one spot, but none of the contenders seemed to be able to clinch the title.

Danica was hoping to change all that.

Her energy blade arched high on its trajectory, wobbling unsteadily as it went, and finally swooped down and imbedded itself like a throwing star into the side of the giant crab's spiny shell.

After being wedged in the shell for about twenty seconds, the energy disc dissipated, leaving only a small gash where it had penetrated the thick armor. Before the crab even realized what had hit it, Danica began forming another energy-star. This time she made it twice as large and was determined not to miss the creature's vital areas.

The crab seemed to be more interested in the orange-skinned man who was scurrying to the other end of the arena, which was fine by Danica. The slight distraction allowed her to add some extra energy to her disc, and she gave it serrated, saw blade-like teeth, just for good measure.

Spinning on her heels, she launched the massive energy blade up into the air. It arched high, soaring over the people's heads as they *oohed* and *awed* from the stands, before spiraling back down where it sliced off the crab's right-side pincer.

The massive claw, along with the reedy arm that somehow held it up, dropped to the sand and the crab let out a terrible bray that sounded like a gigantic horse's whinny from deep under water. Danica didn't know if crabs even had voice boxes; maybe it was just a trick of the air passing over its oversized gill slats, similar in shape to a hover bike's air intake for powering the turbines.

She made half a dozen smaller discs, about the size of old laser-discs, and launched them all in a consecutive volley of energy attacks. Most of them missed, embedding themselves in random points of contact all across the crab's thick shell. But one lucky energy blade managed to slice off one of the eye stalks atop the crab's head. The entire eye, along with its stem, fell to the ground with a thud.

She looked down at the giant eyeball protruding from the end of the stalk and smiled to herself. It resembled a magic crystal ball on the end of a long scepter.

The eye twitched, startling her, and just as she refocused her attention on the beast, the crab spun around and, raising its smaller yet still formidable pincer high, lumbered toward her.

Immediately throwing up an energy shield, Danica absorbed the brunt of its attack. The size and weight of the crab were too much, however, and even though she blocked it in time, its momentum impacted against her with such force, it was like trying to stop a runaway hover-train.

Danica rebounded off the creature and was tossed into the air like a child's plaything. She flew halfway across the arena before tumbling into the soft beach sand of the Arkadian arena. She rolled a few times and then slowly pushed herself back to her feet.

Sand clung to her sweaty skin. As she slowly rose back up, the audience hollered with a round of confidence boosting cheers. She recognized a roar of cat-calls and lewd whistles and looked up to the large monitor. The televid drone had swooped down to zoom in on her sand plastered ass as she got up.

She ignored it and brushed the sand off her shoulders and then adjusted her bikini and shell armor, the seashell necklace adorning her neck rattling as she did so. Satisfied she was in performance condition again, she turned to see the crab knock the orange man down and skewered him with one of its spiny appendages.

The man screamed out as the crab's leg penetrated his mid-section, but try as he may, he couldn't free himself. When the crab took notice of Danica again, it began to scuttle toward her, the man sticking to its foot like a piece of gum. His lifeless body flopped about as he remained stuck to the crab's foot all the way across the arena.

"You just don't give up, do you?" she asked out loud. She let out a sigh and then started generating more energy discs. "Good, because neither do I."

She launched them one after another until she'd sent off a dozen or so, each one making small nicks in the crab's armor plating but doing very minor damage.

A thousand scrapes weren't going to bring this thing down, so she fashioned a massive energy sheet, raised it high above herself, and spun it in the air above her head. Just as the crab started charging her, she brought it down like a giant circular saw blade and placed it squarely between them.

Still spinning, it bit into the ground and kicked up dirt and sand. This time she firmly planted one leg behind, bracing herself for the inevitable collision, as more energy shielding slowly wrapped around her to provide additional protection.

The crab hit with a resounding crash that echoed throughout the stands, but the shield held. Unfortunately, so did the crab's thick shell. Although the energy blade wasn't enough to penetrate the thick shell, it did manage to cut off a segment of the crab's left middle leg, leaving the pointed tip lodged in the sand.

Dizzy from the crash, it staggered about on wobbly legs. In all the confusion, the orange man finally fell free of the creature's leg, but not before his entrails were ripped out of his gut when his intestines got snagged on the spiny appendage of the crab's back leg.

"Ew," Danica said, making a sour face, squinting as the wet slop fell to the ground. That wasn't a nice way to go out.

Of course, the dizzy spell wouldn't last, and Danica knew she needed to act fast if she wanted to take advantage of the situation. If she missed her window of opportunity, she'd risk ending up a shish kabob herself.

Danica traipsed across the soft sand, her muscular thighs flexing and rippling with raw power as she made her way over the difficult terrain. That was one difference she'd come to notice between Arena City's stadium and this one on Arkadia. Arena City had dry, packed sand with a red clay base to it. Here on Arkadia, however, the arena had beach sand.

Naturally, this made it extremely difficult to fight in. Every step shifted in an unpredictable direction, jumping required more energy as you sank in whenever you kicked off. And, although it was softer on the body for those nastier tumbles, getting back up was that much more of a struggle.

Running on the sand wasn't easy either. In fact, it took double the effort, and she wasn't used to it. She was a little worried when she became winded just traversing from one side of the arena to the other. But, eventually, she arrived at her destination and reaching out with both hands she began to pry at the bottom half of the severed pincer.

She tore off half of the claw and then, holding it in both arms like a lance, she turned back toward the crab, who watched her with its one remaining eye.

Danica hollered as she tore through the sand, her bikini and shell armor scarcely providing any security as she went. Using her powers she generated a ramp out of energy and ran up it. When she was high enough, she threw herself over the edge, spiny-lance-crab-leg in both hands.

She sailed through the air and came down onto the back of the startled creature with a thud. Using its own jagged claw against it, she swiped at its remaining eye. The first hit didn't do much but the second hit cracked the eye stem. A third broke it open more fully, and a fourth chop finally took it down like a pesky weed.

Unable to see, the crab grew panicked and began to scuttle in a tight circle. Danica lost her footing and toppled off the shell, landing in the soft sand with a padded *thump*. She rolled out of the way as the crab's needle-like toes came dangerously near and then pushed herself up and dusted off her hands.

She didn't like seeing the creature in agony and knew exactly what she needed to do—put the poor thing out of its misery. Bringing down another energy barrier, between herself and the spinning crab, the crustacean collided so hard against the energy wall that it knocked itself out. Then Danica spun the biggest energy disk she could muster and launched it high into the air. It sailed all the way to the top of the stadium's sail-shaped canvas roof, sliced clean through it, and then came right back down again, slicing through a second time in a different spot.

A silence fell across the crowd as they watched with bated breath. The spiraling energy blade came back down and landed directly on top of the crab's back with a squealing sound of energy and armor grating against one another.

Sparks shot up as the disc cut the crab right down the center. As the orange serration line began to cool, both halves broke apart and fell to the sand.

Smoke rose from the smoldering insides of the two halves, which were well cooked by Danica's energy blade, and the audience erupted into cheers. Danica, still on a high from her victory, climbed halfway up onto one of the larger legs and raised her fists over her head triumphantly.

As the cheers and applause began to die down, she shouted, "Dinner's on me!" and sparked another flurry of celebratory ovation.

As the crowd went wild, as if on cue, some Bre'lal men dressed in white chef's hats and aprons, came out and dragged the various fragments of the crab to the fringes of the stadium. They began tossing large chunks of crabmeat up to the spectators, who greedily feasted upon the spoils of Danica's victory. A larger portion of crab was carted off and taken down to the kitchens under the arena where it would be prepared for the other gladiators' evening meal.

When Danica returned to her shared cell, Ladgara, stood leaning against a wall pretending to ignore Danica's presence.

"Well?" Danica asked, throwing a hand onto her hip. "Pretty good for someone who always messes up, right?"

Ladgara's languid glance with her one good eye sparkled pink. She smiled pithily and said, "It wasn't half bad. And, if I'm being completely honest, you looked quite fetching in that get up."

"You're only saying that because you're horny as hell and want to mash this." Danica gestured at her rockin' hot body and grinned. Then licking her white teeth, she smiled even brighter and said, "But you ain't getting any of this, sweetheart."

"I'll take that as a challenge," Ladgara said with a light hearted laugh.

Danica shrugged. Then looked around and asked, "So, where are the showers?"

Ladgara pointed at the ceiling. Danica looked up and, sure enough, in the center of the room where a light fixture would typically be, there was a rain-styled shower head instead.

She looked back at Ladgara. "You can't be serious?"

Ladgara shrugged.

Danica rolled her eyes and then quickly undid her armor and slipped out of her bikini. She peeled off the bottoms and tossed them in the pile with all the rest. Then placing her hands on her hips again, she struck a pose and, facing Ladgara, said, "There. Satisfied?"

Ladgara's grin grew into a full smile and reaching up she mashed a blue button on the wall. Icy cold water instantly shot out of the shower head. The freezing water prompted Danica to squirm and wiggle and otherwise do a strange and unnatural dance.

"Cold…" she gasped, hopping around under the frigid shower, "too…bloody…cold!"

Once the sand and sweat had been cleaned off, Ladgara hit the button again and the water drizzled to a standstill, only a few stray plips squeezed their way out of the small holes in the shower head after the fact.

"Maybe in the next fight you can use those spears you call nipples to flay your enemies with," Ladgara quipped, nodding at Danica's chest.

Danica looked down and embarrassed by how far she was nipping out, quickly covered herself. Scowling at Ladgara, she said in an agitated tone, "Oh, shut up," and then flipped her off.

Ladgara laughed it off and, then, just to mess with Danica, hit the button again.

"You bitch!" Danica screamed as the cold water drenched her once more, raising massive goosebumps all over her body.

Ladgara laughed, finding it absolutely hilarious. Her laugh, which began as a throaty chuckle, slowly grew into a bawdy, head back, full on torrent of laughter. It was so infectious that Danica cracked a smile across her pursed, icy-cold, doubly blue lips. Eventually, they were both laughing, just like they used to back in their academy days when they were dorm roommates and were fresh and still had an air of innocence about them.

"Admit it," Ladgara finally said. "You missed me."

Danica, her entire body drenched in nothing but goosebumps and freezing droplets of water, smirked and reaching out, she clutched Ladgara's elaborate pirate shirt and reeled her in. At the same time, Danica hit the button and turned the showers back on.

Ladgara screamed playfully as she was drawn into the cold water with Danica.

"There, let's see how you like it," Danica said, not relinquishing her grip for an instant—not even when Ladgara tried to pull away and retreat.

Both of them stood frozen, gazing at one another, remembering the passion and heat of their mutual arousal. Then, Ladgara quickly began peeling off her layers of clothes.

Screw it, Danica thought, giving in to the temptation, and quickly assisted her, anxious to help her get out of her clothes.

A heap of wet clothing piled up around her ankles, Ladgara pushed Danica up against the cold rock wall and began kissing her neck. Her Prussian blue lips dappled Danica's lavender neck with warm kisses that made her feel amazing as the cold water ran down their bodies.

After a few pecks on the lips, their chests bunched up together, Ladgara looked at Danica with her one good eye and asked, "Do you remember our first time?"

"How could I ever forget?" Danica asked. "I'd never been with a woman until you."

"And, as I recall, I was so good that I turned you off of men for that whole year." She licked her lips in a salacious manner, her gaze never shifting off of Danica for an instant.

Instead of answering as expected, Danica shot her a curious look. "I don't remember that." A slow, devious grin formed on her mouth and she added, "Maybe you should remind me."

Ladgara hadn't been wrong. What she could do with her tongue had made Danica forget all about men. And just like back in their academy days, she was busy refreshing Danica's memory on precisely why she was called the silver-tongued she-devil of the empire.

34

Aboard the *Shard,* the holo-gymnasium walls were lined with matte gray paneling and stippled with silver holo-vid orbs lining every surface. Off to the side, there was some commotion; Jegra shouted at Callestra to duck down.

Callestra dipped low and Jegra leaped over her, shooting into the air with such speed she blurred out of sight then reappeared again once she'd reached the zenith of her jump. Here she seemed to hang in air for an impossible amount of time before abruptly plummeting down onto the back of the Centurion battle scorpion.

It wobbled with the weight of her coming down on it and then took several clumsy steps before finding its footing. Rising back up on all six legs, it tried to shake her off, but it was no use. She merely dug her fingers into its armored back and began prying off its metal plating with her bare hands.

Callestra heard the metal scream as if in agony as she wrenched it open, exposing the red and blue fibrous wiring of the inside, which looked exactly like sinews of densely packed muscle.

As this was happening, a tall and athletic Dagon woman, wearing only a sports bra and spandex athletic shorts, dashed onto the scene. She held a massive battle axe in her hands and struggled to carry it due to its ridiculous size. With a grunt, she called out, "Here!" and swung her whole body in a full circle, like a shot putter, gaining enough momentum to toss it up to Jegra.

Jegra reached out with one arm and caught the handle of the axe in her hand, holding it straight out as though it were a wooden staff.

"Thanks," she said. Then taking it in both hands and raising it high above her, with a grunt, she brought down the pommel of the axe directly onto the exposed circuitry of the robot.

Sparks hissed as the loud crunch of the axe's head bit into the strands of wire. A grouping of frayed copper wires curled up as she struck another blow to the soft, exposed area, sending up another spray of sparks which danced along her sweaty bronzed skin.

The robot's servos whined in protest as it tried to continue fighting the two women, but already handicapped, its mainframe fried, all it could do was kick spastically.

Eventually, the Scorpion toppled over and Jegra rode it all the way to the ground like a surfboard. It plowed face-first into the dirt and she leapt off its back and landed light on her feet, hopping and skipping to counter the momentum, until she skidded to a stop. She made it look so effortless; it was as though she'd done it a thousand times before.

"Impressive," Callestra said, smiling at Jegra as the empress swung her axe across her shoulders and casually sauntered over to her.

A demur smile formed on Jegra's chapped, sunbaked lips. "When you invited me to join you in the gymnasium for some vigorous training, I wasn't exactly looking forward to it. You know, on account of you being an insanely competitive, raging bitch and all."

This caused Callestra to laugh. "I assure you, you're a royal pain in my ass, too. And I wouldn't even be here right now if Lord Emperor Dakroth hadn't ordered me to do so."

This caught Jegra by surprise. "Really? What did he say, exactly?" she asked, her stern gaze softening into one of genuine interest as she gazed inquisitively at Callestra.

"That's it. Just…get to know Jegra better," she answered with a shrug. "And since we're both warriors, I felt this would be an adequate bonding experience."

Jegra let the axe head drop to the ground and using it like a walking stick to lean on, she rested both hands on the pommel and laughed. "And how's that going?" she asked.

Callestra eyed Jegra up and down. "It's not completely…awful…" she admitted with a bit of reluctance. A wry grin formed on her lips as she assessed the empress.

In that moment, as they giggled like a couple of old friends, she felt that maybe she'd misjudged Jegra. She wasn't so much her rival as she was the sort of warrior that Callestra aspired to be. That admission was hard enough to realize, let alone make. But maybe that had been Dakroth's intent all along?

There moment was interrupted by the chirp of an incoming call and Jegra answered it.

Lycia appeared as a blue glowing hologram before the two women. She looked at them both and then taking an over dramatic bow, said, "My Grace."

"You needn't do that," Jegra said. "You're like my own daughter."

Lycia straightened herself and then looked over at Callestra and made a lewd purring noise.

"Who's this snot-nosed *gahki?*" Callestra asked, scowling at Lycia and folding her arms across her chest in disapproval at the unwelcome intrusion.

When Callestra looked back, the girl was making two sets of scissors with her fingers and mashing the wedges together in an explicit manner. Wriggling her eyebrows, she made sensual moaning noises which prompted Jegra to speak up.

"Callestra Van Morgan," Jegra said, gesturing to the hologram of Lycia, "meet my daughter, Lycia Alakandra."

Callestra shot Jegra a stunned look. *"Your what?!"*

It didn't make any sense. First of all, the girl was half Jegra's age, and she knew for a fact that humans didn't have extensive lifespans. Not like Dagons or Nyctans, whose species each lived in the range of two and three hundred cycles, respectively.

What's more, she was positive Jegra hadn't been impregnated at thirteen cycles young by any Dagon person. So, how in the bloody Helios could she have an eighteen-year-old daughter of Dagoni lineage?

"It's a long story," she replied, waving her hand as if to brush aside the details and shelve them for now. "What's up, Lycia?"

"I don't know how to put this," she began, throwing her hands on her hips, "but your girl, Dani, is…well…" She paused and took a breath for dramatic effect before continuing on. "It's probably better if I just show you."

"Then show me," Jegra said somewhat impatiently, tired of all this dancing around the subject. Whatever it was, she was sure she could handle it.

The hologrid flickered all around them and suddenly they were standing in the middle of an arena on some distant world.

Lycia waved her hands and the hologrid of the gymnasium flickered and then the battleground simulation faded and reformed as the arena back on the planet Arkadia.

There was a loud, throaty scream, and all three women turned to see Danica, dressed in traditional Arkadian shell armor and a scarcely supportive, sand colored bikini that did little to dissuade the ebb and flow of her bulging bits.

"What's all this?" Jegra asked, puzzled by what she was watching.

"This is from yesterday," Lycia explained, waving her hand and skipping through the holovid to the point she wanted to show her.

Danica clutched another female gladiator, an orange skinned Polletesian from Gamidon's fourth moon, Pollex, in her arms. The opponent struggled in vain to break free of Danica's standing chokehold.

With a crunch, the Polletesian's neck snapped and her arms fell limply by her sides. She sank to her knees; her lifeless eyes stared out in shock as the unbearable weight of the realization of her demise remained permanently frozen onto her face.

Danica relinquished her chokehold and the woman tottered briefly then toppled onto her side. Dead.

Thick orange blood dribbled down Danica's lavender skin as she stood over the dead woman. Panting heavily, she turned to face the crowd, ignoring the large dagger that was lodged in her back, just over her left shoulder blade.

A large Dragonian man, his body emblazoned with a cross-hatching of scars, roared out and thumped his chest domineeringly as he postured for the crowd.

Danica huffed angrily and sent a tuft of loose hair fluttering away from her eyes. She looked over at the towering meathead who stood a dozen or so meters off looking unimpressed. He suddenly decided to take her lack of intimidation personally and charged her, roaring out his most daunting battle cry as he lumbered toward her.

Without even hesitating, she reached behind her back, ripped the dagger out and, with the snap of her wrist, flung it across the arena at him.

It spun through the air and impaled the lizard man squarely between his eyes before he had made it halfway to her. His combined momentum and muscle-memory carried his lifeless body forward another couple of steps before he crashed to the dirt and his corpse, finally, skidded to a stop.

His jaw dislocated, his tongue flopped out onto the ground and there was a short silence that settled across the stadium while the audience took a moment to process what had just happened.

Right at the moment it became clear that Danica had won her match, the crowd erupted with roars and applause. As was her style, she fought fast, dirty, and lethal. And she never resorted to using any of her powers—a fact she was personally proud of.

Exhausted from the match, Danica stood hunched over, barely able to stand, her lungs burning as she gasped for each breath, which seemed not to want to come. Amid the ongoing laudation, she finally took a large, achingly deep breath and then, mustering up her last ounce of remaining strength, raised her left arm victoriously.

The arena erupted with another burst of roaring ovation and the telecaster announced her new ranking, coming in at twenty-fourth on the competition bracket and still climbing.

"Ladies and gentle creatures, with this string of victories, the Traitor of Dagon is a traitor to us no more," the announcer informed the crowd. "Redeemed in the arena, Danica Valencia has regained our confidence as a warrior elite…as…" he paused as he contemplated the best suitable name for this new, meaner, version of Danica then finally revealed, "The Queen of Menace and Mayhem!"

The crowd cheered again. This time it was for the rebirth of Danica as a champion.

Jegra turned to Lycia with a half angry and half astonished look. "What's this?" she asked, still trying to figure out what the Helios it all meant.

"Exactly what it looks like," Lycia replied dryly. "Your girl's back in the thick of it."

Callestra folded her arms across her chest and stood patiently by, watching the drama unfold in real time. Although she had no dog in this fight, she still was curious as to what it meant. Danica was always fairly calculated. Everything she did had a reason behind it. Most Dagons were logical like that. But this…this wasn't logical. This was impulsive.

Jegra opened her mouth as though she were going to speak, but then closed her mouth again, opting to say nothing instead. Upset, she wheeled around, and stormed out of the room without saying another word.

Once the empress had left the gymnasium, the blue hologram flickered and

Lycia appeared beside Callestra.

"End of discussion, I guess," said Lycia with a shrug of her shoulders. Her blue flickering visage looked over at Callestra who was standing off to her side looking down at the ground, deep in thought.

"I appreciate you bringing this to my attention." After another few seconds of mulling things over, she added, "If you hear of anything interesting on the outskirts of the Outer Rim, don't hesitate to inform me."

"So does that mean you're giving me your personal number?" Lycia asked, a prurient smile forming on her pursed lips.

Callestra extended her arm and Lycia did the same. The blue holochip under Callestra's skin glowed as Lycia's holographic wrist brushed hers. The information exchanged hands and the two women stood looking at each other with intense gazes as they studied each other.

"I don't just give my number out to anybody."

"I'll try not to let it go to my head," Lycia quipped.

"I'd appreciate your digression in this matter," Callestra said. She shifted her posture, placing both hands on her hips in a stern fashion.

"I got it," Lycia said, leaning in close and smiling. "Oh, and speaking of favors, maybe next time I'm in your sector of space, maybe you let me take you out for some drinks."

"Don't push your luck. I don't just sleep with anyone either."

Lycia ignored Callestra's dismissive quip and simply took a step back. Her eyes fixed themselves on the gorgeous Dagon woman and she smiled. A flicker interrupted her blue glowing image and, a nanosecond later, the hologram dissolved into thin air.

Callestra locked her arms behind her back and stood thinking for a moment, her eyes fixed on the drab gray floor in front of her. The fact was, it appeared as though Dakroth had spliced his DNA with Jegra's and, indeed, created a designer clone.

Illegal in the highest degree, but, even so, it wasn't her place to question the Emperor's motives. And she was sure that he'd divulge his reasons for creating Lycia all in good time. Until then, however, she was more curious as to what Danica was up to.

With the entire galaxy edging toward all-out war, why in the seven systems would she re-enter the arena at a time like this? It simply didn't make any sense.

As far as Callestra could tell, there was no reason for Danica to rejoin the gladiatorial fights at all. Jegra had given her a royal pardon, something which even the Lord Emperor couldn't dissolve let alone IGS. As such, according to galactic law, Danica was a free woman. Why risk her life in a series of death matches for no good reason?

No matter how Callestra looked at it, Danica's motives remained a complete mystery to her. And this vexed her. After all, Danica wasn't a simple-minded savage. She was from a noble and prestigious line of pure Dagon pedigree.

She turned back to the center of the room and said, "Computer, resume live televid broadcast of Arkadia arena."

A scene of two unfamiliar gladiators came onto the holovid display. One held a spear and the other a morning star. They parried and attacked with such clumsiness that it was a wonder they didn't impale themselves.

Unimpressed and not knowing who these warriors were, Callestra frowned and grunted in disapproval. "No. Find Danica Valencia's feed."

The hologrid display wavered briefly as everything transformed to a different broadcast channel and Callestra watched Danica materialize into high def glory. She panted and groaned as she got reamed from behind by a strong, powerful Dagon woman with a full sleeve of tattoos on either arm, jewel studded eye-patch, pierced eyebrows, pierced nipples, and an impressive piece of male anatomy with a Jacob's ladder, replete with a dozen D-rings all up and down the frenum.

Some Dagon women were better endowed than others when it came to their male organs. Vestigial organs which, obviously, worked well enough to cause Danica enough pleasure to make her scream out loud with each penetrating thrust of Ladgara's hips.

Between Danica's metal arm and the woman's numerous body modifications, Callestra couldn't help but feel disgusted by the lewd conduct on display here. The lack of purity was unwholesome and, quite frankly, a huge turn off. But, for whatever reason, she couldn't take her eyes off of them.

"Computer, identify the tattooed woman."

<<Female Dagon is identified as Ladgara Vassex, first officer aboard the *Avarice* and second in command to the outlaw pirate Novac Tamoran.>>

"Threat assessment."

<<Considered highly dangerous and is wanted for murder in five systems. Currently being held by IGS on a code-blue warrant. Code-red warrant suspended in exchange for a thirty-year contract to fight in the gladiatorial games.>>

"Code red?" Callestra asked, raising a surprised eyebrow. That was more than a simple bag and tag warrant. It was a kill order. And only the extremely wealthy and powerful could issue such warrants. "Who issued the code red on her?"

There was a brief pause before the computer answered. <<Vice Admiral Cassera Van Danica Amelorak,>> the computer replied in a prosodic, almost soothing tone.

"The plot thickens," Callestra said in a hushed voice. The woman currently taking it from behind like a ten-dollar hooker was the very same person who'd issued the death warrant on the woman vigorously pounding her with every inch of her Dagon male anatomy as though her life absolutely depended on it.

It escaped Callestra's comprehension, how two women willing to kill one another on principle were currently engaged in such carnal delights. Regardless, she was bound and determined to get to the bottom of it.

She looked down at the glowing numbers that hovered just near the floor which gave the active Needle stream viewing numbers. She nearly balked. Eight million active viewers were watching Danica get off with some pirate chick in real time.

"Computer," Callestra called out again, making her way to the exit, "transfer all files you have on Ladgara Vassex and Cassera Van Danica Amelorak, aka Danica Valencia, to my personal data console. Highlight any and all files that show a connection between the two of them and mark it as priority reading."

The computer chimed with affirmative tones from over her shoulder just as she stepped out into the corridor. The holovid gymnasium doors slid shut behind her, and she turned up the corridor, a smug smile curling on her lips.

Whatever Danica was plotting, she was going to get to the bottom of it. You didn't just get engaged to the empress of the whole bleedin' galaxy and then enter yourself into the gladiatorial fights simply to hook up with an old flame. No. Something else was going on here and she was bound and determined to explore every avenue until she discovered exactly what it was.

35

Six heavy Nyctan battlecruisers hung in geosynchronous orbit around Dagon Prime. Three more held a fixed position just beyond Thessalonica and tracked any and all ships entering or exiting the hyperspace lanes. If any ship came through without the proper access codes, they'd be immediately shot down.

Azra'il Nun was done with polite warnings and mundane boarding searches. Jegra had somehow managed to kill both Nodengoth and Giddion. Which meant, if she was careless, she'd be next on the chopping block.

Of course, she couldn't have that. She planned to live a long and healthy life. So, in addition to the Nyctan ships, she had thirty Nephilim destroyers cloaked and waiting for whatever bold move Jegra had in mind.

The empress's propensity to come in guns blazing and fists swinging meant Azra'il had to beef up Dagon security. And her spies had informed her that Jegra and the emperor would be returning to Dagon Prime in order to reclaim their beloved planet within the next forty-eight hours.

Perhaps more exciting than lying in wait was that, with her siblings dead, she was able to syphon more raw power from H'aaztre, making her three times as powerful. All she had to do was think a solitary thought and someone would carry out her orders.

But right now, everyone was preparing for the looming battle, and she was doing her best to try and clear her head as she stared out at the vast expanse of stars. But even this lingering bit of solitude was beginning to grow tedious.

Luckily, an alarm sounded, sparing her from any further stretches of boredom. She looked up as a giant vessel flashed into view outside her view portal. It was the *Chiron*.

She ignored the comm hails as the bridge tried to contact her, and she watched, waiting, hoping the *Shard* would soon follow. After a minute, it was clear that the *Chiron* had come alone. Probably to negotiate their terms of surrender.

Still ignoring her incoming calls, she marched all the way to the bridge. Her black leather corset and tight leather pants squeaked softly as she strode up the hall. Her black, flowing cape wafted behind her elegantly as she strode onto the bridge and settled into pleated folds when she came to a standstill. All the white faces and black eyes fixated on her as she fanned her cape to the side and took her seat at the large command chair on the upper central region of the three-tiered bridge.

"Report," she said, stretching a slender leg out and then crossing it over her right knee.

"It's Admiral Grendok, mistress," an officer with a headset informed her. "He's requesting a parley."

"A parley?" She laughed at the mere thought of allowing any further negotiations.

No. She'd given Jegra and her rebel forces more than enough chances to throw down their arms and surrender to the almighty H'aaztre. But they continued to defy her will, H'aaztre's will, at every turn. For their insolence, it was clear to her now that she couldn't accept anything less than their total and utter surrender.

"Request denied," she barked without giving it a second thought. "Arm missile tubes and prepare to fire."

Before the vessel *Qui'tek'alon* could arm itself, the *Chiron* began spewing out little metallic balls. Thousands of the small probes all rushed off in every direction, where they formed a hexagonal grid pattern all around Thessalonica.

The automated drones established a perimeter around the entire moon which looked like a gridwork of metallic orbs, or something along the lines of a miniature Dyson's sphere. Once they'd locked into place, essentially creating an orbital defense grid, the *Chiron* maneuvered itself between the enemy fleet and Dagon Prime, where it began releasing more of the probes.

"Fire a single warning shot across the bow of that ship," Azra'il Nun ordered. A red plasma blast streaked across the divide and struck the *Chiron*.

"Direct hit, mistress."

Although the Galliforn warship took the brunt of the blast with its shields down, it ignored the attack and continued releasing a flood of metallic balls which began to spread out in the same hexagonal pattern as those that surrounded Thessalonica.

"All ships converge firepower on that battleship," she snarled, rising to her feet and making a fist.

The darkness of space lit up with flashes of disruptor canon fire. All nine ships converged all their firepower on the *Chiron,* which finally responded to their volley by raising its shields.

"As the Voice of H'aaztre, I must warn you that my ships are prepared to continue firing on your vessel unless you meet my demands and do exactly as I command. Power down your shields and surrender yourself to *The Children of H'aaztre* and the Nyctan-Nephilim Fusion. If you do as I say, you will be spared wasting away in the giant sundew pits of Nyctan's moon, Endiva"

"Ho there! Who, may I ask, do I have the great pleasure of speaking with this fine morning?" a hoary goat with wonky sky-blue eyes called back. His slatted pupils stared off in different directions, making it difficult for Azra'il Nun to tell if he was looking at her or at something else.

"I just said," Azra'il said in a vexed tone, "you are addressing the Voice of H'aaztre and the Nyctan-Nephilim Fusion."

"What's been fused?" he asked in an agitated manner. Bleating in typical goat fashion, he shook his head in protest. "No, no, no. I told them to keep the plasma conduits shut. Shut!"

Azra'il looked around the room only to receive numerous shrugs and people staring back at her with the same look of confusion that she wore on her own face.

She turned back to the satyr and asked, "Who are you again?"

"I'm Phipps. Grog Phipps. Pronounce P-i-p-s, not Fips. Fips is my cousin. Cousin!" Again, he shouted the last word for no apparent reason then bowed reverently. Once the formalities were out of the way, he went over to a console and began typing something out on the keyboard.

"Mr. Phipps, is it?" Azra'il said, a polite smile struggling to maintain itself on her taught lips. "Would you be so kind as to enlighten us as to what your purpose is?"

"Oh-ho! I'm so glad you asked. My duty is to lay these mines," he answered, a big yellow-toothed grin forming on his maw.

"Mines?" Azra'il gasped.

"Mines!" he shouted as though he had a strange form of Tourette's syndrome.

"What mines?" she asked him, ignoring his outburst.

"Of the magnetic variety, Your Worshipfulness," he said, shooting her a wink.

"Would you mind not doing that?" she asked.

"Oh, ho!" he laughed. "But it's my duty! I must oblige lest I make the captain upset with me. And you know how that old goat gets." He laughed again.

Azra'il huffed in annoyance.

She wheeled around, her cape sprawling out behind her, and turned to the officer with the headset. "Order the closest ship to move in on the *Chiron* and fire all missile batteries. I want that ninny and his ship blown out of the sky. Right. This. Bloody. Instant!"

The tactical officer followed her orders, and the bridge crew all turned to watch as the Nyctan armada changed course, converging on the *Chiron*. As they came within weapon's range, the magnetic mines began tracking the ships, moving closer to them the closer they got to the *Chiron*.

By the time Azra'il Nun's ships were within firing range, approximately three hundred metallic balls had attached themselves to each ship's hull.

The missile launch bays of the closest destroyer opened and then, launching its missiles as ordered, it went up in an instantaneous explosion.

"What just happened?" Azra'il demanded to know.

"The mines detonated and took the ship with it, mistress. What are your orders?"

"Cancel my order to fire on that ship and call in a squid. They aren't made of metal; they won't attract any of those mines."

A female Nyctan officer confirmed the order and, with a nod, hit a call button. A low whine, almost like whale song, filled the bridge. It changed tones a few times, as if making music, and almost immediately there was a flash off the port bow.

"As prompt as ever," Azra'il said with a smirk. "Now order it to carve us a patch through those silver orbs."

"Yes, ma'am," the female Nyctan officer replied. She looked down at the keyboard, her black eyes blinking rapidly as she typed in the orders and sent them in song to the squid entity.

They watched the CSE swim through space and into the minefield. But the mines just moved around it like water across grease. Nothing stuck. They just slipped around the entity only to settle back into their original position once the beast had passed on through.

"It's no use, mistress. Those are smart-mines. They can't be jostled out of the way."

"I can see that," she growled, growing even more vexed than before. "Fire a Helios python missile at one of the mines and see what it does."

The missile launched from the front firing tube and Azra'il peered out the viewscreen as its thrusters flared white-hot and tore away from the *Qui'tek'alon*.

A single mine matched the missile's velocity, trailing it as if caught in its wake. But then it promptly accelerated, latched on, and detonated itself before the missile could even cut half the distance between itself and its intended target.

Azra'il rolled her eyes and turned back to the ship's viewscreen. "Excuse me, Mr. Phipps. Are you still there?"

"I'm here, ye bonnie lass. How may I help you?"

Her black eyes lit up with a halo of gold and H'aaztre's energy surged through her. With her power of persuasion turned to full, she grinned menacingly. "Mr. Phipps, please be my hero and give me the deactivation codes for these mines of yours."

"Aye, miss," he replied. "But first, who may I ask is wanting the codes?"

"I want the codes," she replied.

"And who might you be again?" Mr. Phipps pulled out some spectacles and placed them on his wonky eyes, which didn't seem to help in the slightest.

"I've already told you," she said in a controlled fashion, speaking through her teeth. "I'm Azra'il Nun."

"I thought you said you were the Voice of Pasture, or some such?"

"H'aaztre," she corrected.

"So," he said, growing annoyed with her, "of the four of you, which might you be? Azra'il, H'aaztre, the Voice, or the Nun?"

She looked at more blank faces and then back to the monitor. "I'm...what I mean to say is...all of us are the same person."

"You're telling me that your full name is Azra'il Pasture Voice, the Nun?"

"Yes," she growled through clenched teeth. It was better to agree with his butchering of her name than to try and argue with an obvious dolt.

"Oh, ho! I see," he laughed in his jovial fashion. He went back to typing, almost as if he'd forgotten she was there.

After a minute, Azra'il Nun raised her fist to her mouth and cleared her voice, reminding him that she was still there.

"Ello, dear. What can I do you for?" he asked.

"What?" she asked, confused. "I have asked you for the codes."

"What codes, dearie?"

"The drone kill codes," she replied, her voice strained as she fought the urge to bite his head off.

"Oh, ho! I don't have those," he announced.

"What do you mean you don't have the codes?"

"Above my pay grade, I'm afraid."

"I'm dealing with a halfwit!" she cried out, throwing her hands into the air in defeat. Clearly this conversation was going nowhere.

Azra'il's persuasion affected everyone but the utmost simple minded. For some reason, the stunted and brain damaged didn't respond to her powers. And whatever was wrong with Mr. Phipp's head was jamming her mojo in a major way. She was so aggravated by him that all she wanted to do was to bash her head into a nearest bulkhead. Repeatedly.

Tired of getting nowhere with the nitwit, Azra'il ran a thumb across her throat, signaling for the comms officer to cut the link. The screen went black and the stars reappeared on the viewscreen.

"All ships, this is Azra'il Nun, High Commander of the Nyctan-Nephilim fleet. Fire everything we have at that idiot and his ship. Mines or no...that's an order."

The thirty ships decloaked and all vessels began launching their missiles and firing their plasma cannons. Even so, every missile was prematurely detonated by a smart-mine and every plasma blast was absorbed by the *Chiron's* impossibly powerful shields. Short of a ship-to-ship collision, there wasn't any way to take down the *Chiron*.

A giant laser blast flashed and then three frigates went up in a ball of fiery gas and debris, igniting in a glorious series of explosions.

"Where the Helios did that blast come from?" Azra'il demanded to know.

"It seems as though it came from the moon, mistress."

"Thessalonica?" she asked, her jaw half agape with astonishment. Had they developed a super-weapon? And if so, how had they built it right under their noses?

Another blast took the ship out that sat directly across from hers. She watched it go up in flames.

"Move us away from that moon," she shouted.

The armada slowly pulled back away from Thessalonica and Dagon Prime. As they did, a second armada of two dozen ships jumped into the system. It consisted of a wide variety of vessels, some more heavily armed than others. But the only ship that concerned Azra'il Nun was the shiny silver one that sat in the middle of the fleet.

"Mistress," a voice shouted out above the alarms. "It's the Dagon Imperial Armada."

Azra'il was down to twenty-five ships, so by her reckoning, it was as close to a fair fight as there ever was going to be. But knowing that Jegra had a talent for the unpredictable, she was worried this would give her the leverage she desperately wanted.

"Everyone, stay vigilant. The Mother of Dagon has returned to protect her children. And she's angry."

36

Glistening beads of sweat dappled Onelle's luxuriant chest as she fanned herself with an Arkadian folding fan made of a fine lavender silk. As a few of the beads dribbled down her sternum and into the valley of her cleavage, she tossed her verdant locks of hair over her shoulder and gave her form-fitting iridescent pearl cocktail dress a tug, allowing a rush of air inside that briefly cooled her lustrous skin.

Senator Targon, along with the servant girl, Aida, sat across from her on the roof of her sinking yacht in the middle of the Varuna Ocean, looking forlorn as the hot mid-day sun beat down upon them. They'd crash-landed but, luckily enough, set down in the ocean and had come out of it all in one piece.

Everything had gone awry immediately after they'd entered orbit above Arkadia. The airlock seal to the escape pod ruptured, tearing the pod away from the Miura and causing an explosion that took out the aft starboard thrusters and half the rear bulkhead with it. Not only that, but the mishap had rendered her landing skiffs non-functional. Unable to set down lightly anywhere, the ship rerouted to crash land in the Varuna sea.

Serendipitously, nobody had sustained any serious injuries. But the ship was wrecked and was taking on water. So, now, they sat on the belly of the upturned vessel and waited to be rescued.

"I thought you were supposed to be the prefect of this bloody miserable paradise," grumbled Senator Targon, taking a handkerchief out of his back pocket and dabbing his face dry. "How long does it take a rescue boat to arrive around these parts? On Dagon Prime we'd already be teleported back to the mainland by now."

The sun beat down on his deep blue skin and reminded him of the harshness of a world with a tropical climate, as this one. It wasn't to his liking. *It beats landing on some barren ice world or a desert moon*, he supposed.

"That's no way to show your thanks," Aida hissed as she scowled at the senator's clearly miserable state. "Mistress Agnar saved both of us, got us out of a deathtrap, and brought us safely to her planet. The least you could do is have a little class and show Mistress Agnar the proper amount of gratitude."

The senator took a deep breath then let it out in one long drawn out huff. Turning back to Onelle, his eyes softer now, he apologized. "I beg your pardon, Mistress Onelle. The sun is hot and I'm prone to heat stroke. But that's no excuse for my excessive griping. I do appreciate all your help."

Onelle nodded in acceptance of the apology. She knew that a man as proud as Targon would never think to apologize for something so trivial, as it would make him appear weak, unless he absolutely meant it. After a few more minutes of the three of them basking in the impossibly bright sun, they heard the distant roar of turbines approaching from the southwest.

"It's about time," Onelle said, rising to her feet and placing her flattened palm to her brow to blot out the sun as she peered across the sparkling surface of the ocean.

In the distance, two slender hydrofoil rescue boats skimmed the water, kicking up jet sprays behind them as they made their way to the crash site and the distress beacon that Onelle had activated.

When the boats finally pulled up alongside the sinking vessel, the copula's hatch to the first one opened and a man in a white uniform with gold cuffs and a black rimmed captain's hat stepped out onto the deck of the vessel. He tossed a rope to Senator Targon who reeled it in and held it taught so that Onelle could climb aboard. As she did so, three sailors climbed out of the second craft and hopped aboard the sinking vessel. One of them took the rope from the senator while a second helped him leap over to the first ship.

When Aidora tried to follow, the third man raised his hand, stopping her, and apologized. "Sorry, miss. You'll have to join us on the second ship," he informed her.

Aidora was a little surprised at first. She'd heard that other species were prejudiced against Nyctans, but she'd never experienced it herself. But, then again, she'd never been off world for anything more than an ambassadorial mission aboard a diplomatic cruiser.

"It's alright," Onelle said, waving Aidora aboard the first boat. "She's my new girl."

"Apologies, ma'am, I had no idea," the sailor said and he turned and hoisted Aidora up onto the deck of Onelle's boat.

"What was that about?" Aidora whispered, leaning in to address Onelle.

"Unregistered servants are not permitted to ride with their official guardians. However, since I am the owner of eighty percent of the resorts on this world, my word is law."

"Thanks for vouching for me."

"When we get back to Varuna resort, I'll see to it you're properly registered as my personal girl. My last one was a dear friend and trusted advisor; even after I gave her her freedom, she stayed with me."

"I'll try my best to honor her legacy," Aidora said.

"I wouldn't expect anything less," Onelle said and then she climbed down the copula hatch and into the sleek boat.

Aidora found her seat and then looked out the view portal at the white spacecraft half-submerged. As the second boat pulled away, it launched something into the water. It took a couple seconds before Aidora realized that it was a torpedo.

The torpedo struck the spacecraft and detonated. Pieces of the ship shot into the sky while others broke apart under water. Aidora was just thinking it was terrible to pollute such pristine blue ocean like that when a fleet of maintenance drones flew overhead. The drones, which were painted a drab gray with yellow stripes, had orange and green flashing lights that alerted everyone to the fact that they were busy working. Roughly half a dozen of them dropped nets into the ocean and began combing the surface for debris while another dozen dove into the water and activated their amphibious mode to dive down and collect pieces of the craft that had already sunk to the bottom.

"Impressive, isn't it?" a voice asked.

Aidora looked across the aisle to see Senator Targon smiling at her. She shrank under his heavy gaze and shifted nervously in her seat.

"The Nyctans are a proud race. Almost as proud as we Dagons. I'm sure you'll be missing your culture and people soon enough. Just let me know when you grow homesick, my dear, and I'll personally book your transport back home."

She blinked at him with her large black eyes. "Yes," she answered in a demure voice. "I'd appreciate that."

His smile, which he wore as a mask, quickly faded and his old eyes hardened and filled with disdain. Always the consummate politician, however, he brought the smile back out and used his diplomatic voice. "It's true, our people don't like one another, but as long as Onelle Te'Legra Agnar vouches for you, I'll ignore our little differences for the time being. But should you so much as step outside your lane, I'll have you arrested and shipped off to the gladiatorial fights. Am I being clear, my luv?"

The way he said it was anything but loving. Be that as it may, she didn't want to stir up any trouble and kept her feelings of indignation to herself. She nodded quietly and then turned to look back out the window and gazed out at the beautiful teal ocean streaking by her, the white wake of the boats spreading outward behind them.

Over the side of the boat, down in the water, some colorful fish were leaping into the air alongside the hydrofoils. She watched them for a short while with keen amusement, but even as she tried to focus on the fish, she could still feel senator Targon's eyes lingering on her.

It took everything she had just to suppress the skin-crawling shudder that threatened to ripple down her spine when, at last, he got up and left. Once he was out of earshot, she exhaled heavily.

"Forget that asshole," a young man's voice said. When she looked up there was a sailor making himself a cup of tea in the galley just behind the half-parted, gray curtains.

"You heard all that?" Aidora asked, blushing from the embarrassment of it.

The Bre'lal man turned to her and smiled. "I heard enough to know that the senator is just a big old windbag."

Aidora smothered a snigger and then smiled at the young man. He offered her the piping hot cup of tea that he had just made.

"Hot tea, on a day like this?" she asked him, giving him a peculiar, cockeyed glance.

He shrugged. "You looked like you could use a hot drink."

She took it from him and gave him an appreciative nod. "Thank you," she whispered. After taking a sip and discovering it was still too hot for her, she cradled it in her hands while she looked up at him, a subdued smile forming on her dainty lips. "Why are you being so nice to me?"

"This is Arkadia. We're nice to everyone here, as long as they pay their tab and keep our one law."

"You have only one law on this world?" she laughed. Her large eyes blinked curiously.

He smiled at her. "Just don't harm anybody and you'll be fine. Everything else," he added, leaning in to whisper into her ear, "is fair game." After slowly pulling away, he nodded down at her cup of tea and said, "Enjoy the tea."

"Aidora?" Onelle's voice rang again like an annoying call that just wouldn't stop ringing and Aidora's smile faded from her face.

"Yes, Mistress Onelle," she said, rising out of her seat and passing under the curtain to go and see what was needed of her.

"Why didn't you answer me when I called you the first time? When I call you, I expect a prompt reply," Onelle informed her rather harshly.

"Yes, mistress," Aidora said apologetically. "Forgive me."

"Never mind that," Onelle said, shaking her head and quickly correcting her mood before she let it derail her train of thought. "It's not important."

"Yes, mistress," she replied, continuing on to Onelle's seat.

Onelle tilted her head, gesturing for the girl to sit down across form her. "We're almost to Varuna City. Once we're there, I'm going to leave you for a few hours while I get things in order. Will you be able to manage on your own?"

"I shall try, Mistress Onelle," she answered.

"Good." Onelle reached into the v-cut opening of her dress, jostled her cleavage for a bit, and then plucked out a white plastic card. "This is a versatile card for servants. Since slaves aren't allowed to be chipped, in case they secure enough funds to run off, all servants are given one of these limited debit cards. There are some credits charged on here for you to buy clothes, food, and other amenities. Also, it will serve as your room key for a suite at the Varuna Luxury Beach Resort. That will be your living arrangement until I can find you some proper accommodations."

"Thank you, mistress," she said, taking the versatile key from Onelle and examining it with wide-eyed curiosity. "It's more than I require."

Onelle nodded and then waved the girl off. "Dismissed," she said, glancing back only once to see if Aidora had made it back to her seat all right. She had.

The young sailor, who had returned to his post, raised his eyebrows at Aidora as she smiled at him.

"You may want to be seated now," he said to her. "We'll be docking shortly."

"I'd like to dock with you," she whispered aloud.

"What was that?" he asked, genuinely feeling he'd missed something important.

She blushed. "Um…nothing. It was…nothing."

He nodded and smiled back at her and she did as asked and took her seat. Looking out the window, she could see a large island looming on the horizon. It had about two dozen seaside resorts, lovely white beaches that wrapped around the entire island, and jutting above the treetops of the tropical foliage was a giant amphitheater which was made to look like the billowing sails of ancient marine vessels.

It is glorious, she thought. That's when she realized it was the gladiatorial arena and a thrill of excitement ran up her spine. She'd never been to a live event before, and, if Mistress Onelle wouldn't be needing her for a few hours, she wanted nothing more than to steal away and watch her first ever gladiatorial match.

37

Heavily seasoned biltong wafted on the breeze as vendors went up and down the stadium aisles selling their spiced meats.

Nyctans didn't eat meat, so the pungent smell of well-cooked spicy flesh took some getting used to, but after the vendor had passed by and the scent dissipated on the air, Aidora thought it smelled rather nice. Almost sweet, but with the distinct smell of charred edges and burned fat.

Being new to the arena, she wasn't accustomed to finding her seat and looked in all the wrong places. She was still looking when, finally, the match began. Eventually, she discovered her seat, a front row aisle seat that overlooked the arena from about two stories up. Apparently Onelle's card bought excellent seats; got you right up close to the action.

When she went over to sit, however, a young Dagon teenager and a group of his friends quickly sat down in her assigned seat and the surrounding seats without any regard to her.

She doubled checked her ticket, just to be sure she wasn't mistaken, and then cleared her throat. "Excuse me, sirs, but I think one of you may be sitting in my seat."

They ignored her and laughed loudly at seemingly nothing when she cleared her throat and began again. "I beg your pardon, but I think that maybe you've taken my seat by mistake. It's E-34," she informed the teenager in her seat, reading the number off the ticket and holding it up for him to see.

He looked up and shot her an annoyed glance and then said in a condescending fashion, "So? What are you going to do about it, snow-sow?"

His group of friends began laughing; they all turned away and began chatting amongst themselves.

Aidora reached out her finger and tapped the young Dagon man on his shoulder. "Please, sir, it's my first time. I just want to enjoy the show."

"You want to enjoy the show, do you?" The young man stood up and got right up in her face.

His friends all stood up with him and tightened in around her, not giving her any room to breathe or to escape, if she needed. Suddenly, she felt trapped and the fear welled up inside her.

"Maybe I'll just go find a new seat," she said, diverting her gaze. "Sorry to have troubled you."

As she turned to leave, the young man's voice called out to her. "Wait. It's your first time at an arena show, yeah?"

She nodded shyly.

He looked around at his friends, a malicious grin spreading across his lips. Offering her the original seat, he apologized. "I'm so sorry. If only I had known it was your first time. Please, by all means, enjoy the show."

She looked up at him to see if he was being sincere; she couldn't tell by the look on his face. But scanning his friend's faces, which were all smiles, she was convinced of their sincerity.

"Thank you," she replied excitedly, and quickly scurried over to take her seat. Before she could pass the young man, however, he reached out and shoved her over the railing.

Aidora screamed as she fell.

The wind rushed out of her as she crashed onto the arena floor from the second story balcony and she looked up to see the group of Dagon teenagers peering down at her and laughing.

The mean boy who'd pushed her spat at her. She raised her hand to block it, but luckily the slight breeze diverted its trajectory.

"Serves you right, you Nyctan bitch!" the Dagon kid shouted down at her. Without warning, a massive wave of blood, guts, and gore splashed across the young man and his friends. The force of it was so strong it knocked them off their feet and drenched them in the thick, sticky goo of a slain razorback lion of the planet Scalios.

With three giant porcupine-like needles sticking out of her metal arm, which hung limp at her right side due to the venom darts shorting her servos, Danica was glad it hadn't been her flesh and blood arm. If the razorback lion's needles had hit her anywhere else on her body, the venom would have paralyzed her and she'd be little more than the evening's entrée.

Electric blue venom seeping out of the holes of her silver metallic arm, she edged up to Aidora and said, "Get behind me. This one's pissed. I killed its mate."

Aidora scrambled to her feet and got behind Danica as ordered. As soon as she was behind her, Danica erected a forcefield. Several more poison tipped needles pinged off the energy shield with such force they deflected back up into the stadium and pierced the underside of the balcony seating. The crowd erupted with startled cries which quickly changed into cheers.

"I don't know if I have enough energy left to deflect the brunt of another attack," she said through a clenched jaw, her blue hand raised as she maintained her forcefield.

Aidora put her hand on Danica's back. It had red claw marks which trailed down her blue skin in the form of three bloody gouges. "You're hurt," she said, sounding genuinely worried for Danica even though they had never met before this moment.

"I'll live," Danica replied stoically. Wanting to keep it that way, she promptly reached over and tore one of the quills out. Her metal arm sparked and then settled down again after a moment.

No wonder razorback lions are so formidable in the arena, she mused, *they can kill you with their claws, teeth, and needles, if need be.* There were extremely lethal.

"Stay close," Danica said, and she began to jog. As they headed for the lion, Aidora grew nervous.

"Are you sure this is a good idea?"

"No," Danica said, leaning into an oncoming volley of needles, using her metal forearm as a makeshift shield to deflect several of the quills. One of the quills pinged off her arm and lodged itself in the dirt a couple of meters to her right. The others were wide of the mark and the reddish-purple spines peppered the ground all around Danica and the young Nyctan girl.

Aidora pulled back at the last minute and watched Danica charge the lion. The lion roared at her, warning her it was the apex predator on this field, not her, and then pounced.

Together, woman and beast toppled to the ground, the lion's massive jaws biting down on Danica's metal arm.

The weight of the lion was crushing, but she held it at bay, reinforcing herself with an energy bubble. The lion gnawed at her arm, trying its best to tear the non-functioning appendage off of her body. While it was preoccupied with its new chew-toy, she drove its own quill through its right eye and into its brainpan.

It was an instant kill, and the lion collapsed on top of her and, with a grunt, she shoved it off. Rolling away, she clambered to her feet and, resting her palms on her knees, panted until she finally managed to catch her breath.

Looking back over her bruised shoulder at the Nyctan girl, she asked, "Are you all right?"

The girl nodded and tried her best to smile.

Danica straightened up and said, "Good," and walked over to the girl.

Aidora looked up into Danica's golden eyes. She was a little intimidated by the woman's size. Although she was only six foot three, by Nyctan standards, that was extremely tall, and only the males ever got that big. To see a woman so large was both awe inspiring and, quite frankly, rather impressive.

"Thanks for saving me," Aidora said as Danica hoisted her up onto her shoulder and allowed to her climb up onto the entry level railing.

"Next time someone pushes you around, don't just sit there and take it. Push back," Danica offered in the way of some friendly advice. Aidora nodded in the affirmative and watched the gladiatrix turn and limp off. Without looking back, Danica shouted, "Because next time I won't be there to save your sorry ass."

Aidora couldn't believe her luck was holding. Not only had she survived the mass slaughter at the trade summit days earlier, but she'd survived a ship crash from high orbit, and now she'd survived falling into a live battle in the arena.

Adrenaline coursed through her veins and caused her to have the shakes. Succumbing to a mild state of shock, she did her best to answer, even though it came out in a barely audible voice. "I will," she said, clutching her ticket close to her chest.

It was funny. In all the turmoil, she'd never once let go of her ticket. Now, it was a keepsake she'd cherish forever.

Still on her cocktail of adrenaline and excitement from her experience in the arena, Aidora checked in to the Varuna Luxury Beach Resort and made her way to her room.

Upon entering, she was left speechless. It was more than a master suite. It was a royal suite. She'd never had a room to herself, let alone one as fancy as this. As a servant, she'd always shared her accommodations with two or three others, and this seemed so grand that she could scarcely believe it.

The floors were made of white marble and the counter tops of the island kitchen were set with black marble. A set of stairs descended into a den replete with a gas fireplace, and rugs that were of the finest and most elaborate weaving she'd ever seen.

It even had a crystal chandelier that hung from a high ceiling.

After roaming through the mansion-sized suite, she found the bathroom. The bath was basically a small pool, a hot and cold portion partitioned off from one another. The hot side filled a long rectangle and the cold filled a small square at the end. But the two pools spilled over a low partition separating the two sides and bled into one another, their waters mingling to form a lukewarm area.

Excited to take her first ever bath like a true *sachem*, she stripped off her soiled clothes, stained with the blood and sands of the arena, and rinsed before turning to the pool.

Slowly, she dipped her snow-white toes in and, finding it wonderfully pleasing, sank into the warmth of the inviting waters. Swimming about, she took a deep breath and submerged herself.

Overextending herself, she came up for air and gasped out loud. As soon as she'd taken in a fresh breath of air, however, she felt gloved hands wrap themselves around her throat and hoist her out of the water.

Startled, she tried to scream but couldn't. The hands crushed her throat with such force that she thought her neck would snap like a twig. Her eyes shot open and she clutched the wrists that held her in their vice-like grip. She kicked and squirmed, trying to break free of the wrists she clutched in her hands. But it was no use, her attacker was too strong.

The next thing Aidora knew, her head was smacked hard against the sandstone floor. Raising herself slightly, she touched the gash on her temple and inspected the smatter of blue blood on her fingers.

In a state of shock, she sat there not knowing what to do. As she caught her breath, her vision began to come back into focus and she cautiously looked up to see her attacker's face.

"Senator Targon?" she gasped.

He was already undressing himself as he stood over her. "What happens here tonight stays between us. Do you understand, snow-sow?"

She nodded yes, but then the words of Danica came back to her. *"Next time someone pushes you around, don't just sit there and take it. Push back."*

Wet, scared, and desperate to scream, she leaped to her feet and shoved Targon back with all her strength. He tripped on the lip of the pool and fell in. As he splashed around furiously, trying his best to get out of the water, Aidora sprinted into the main room.

She raced across the floor, panic filling her chest, but she was dripping wet and slipped on the marble floor and crashed down hard, her entire back and head slapping against the surface with a *thwack*.

Aidora knew she must have hit her head hard, because the next thing she knew, the light dimmed as redness encroached upon her vision. She wanted to scream for help, but her voice was so coarse only a raspy half whisper escaped her lips and by then, it was already too late. The darkness had taken her.

As she came to, all the horror of her worst nightmares became a reality. She could feel him inside of her. She wanted to throw up, but she couldn't.

With a sinister grin, Targon pressed his leathery blue skin into her pristine white skin and groaned with a sickening pleasure that only one as debauched as he would feel for violating a young woman in such a manner.

She squirmed to try get out from under him, but it was no use. He outweighed her by several stones and all her struggling was in vain. She gave it one last effort, but abruptly felt his hand pressing down on her throat to try and force her to stop. When she looked up at him, he was grinning down at her taking great delight in violating her. *Sick bastard.*

Silent tears streamed from the corners of her eyes as Targon Van Morgan had his way with her, then, with a depraved grunt, he finished inside of her.

"Let that be a lesson to you, snow-sow," he whispered into her ear. "Next time you try to embarrass me like that in front of anyone of stature, I won't be so forgiving."

Senator Targon pulled out, dressed in front of her, and then left her lying naked in a puddle of cold water, blood, and his semen. Curling into a tight ball, her shivering and tears melded into a trauma-wrought sobbing.

Aidora clasped her knees to her chest and cried so hard that she had to gasp for air. All she wanted to do was be a good servant for Onelle. She hadn't asked for any of this. But everyone seemed to despise her race. At every turn, people lashed out at her in terrible and vicious ways. Were her people really so loathsome?

Even with the lingering resentment of the occupation and the fact that her kind had taken the side of the invaders, she didn't deserve this kind of treatment. She didn't deserve to be bullied, beat, raped, and then left bloodied and broken as though she were little more than refuse.

She forced herself up, even as the pain of his violation lingered, and she covered her body—not because anybody could see her, but because of the overwhelming sense of shame she felt for allowing herself to be violated—and went back into the bath. She sank down and let the blood of her wounds seep into the bath, dying it a pink color.

As the pool thickened to a uniform rosy hue, she stared at the open entrance and whispered, "I tried. I did."

Even though she had pushed back, like Danica had told her to, she hadn't been strong enough to protect herself. Ultimately, he was stronger and far angrier than she. And this anger fed his violence.

If only she'd been stronger, like Danica, like Jegra, like Anaïs Nin and all the women she looked up to and admired, then maybe none of this would have ever happened to her.

Her faint words were quickly overtaken by another torrent of sobs and she buried her face in her hands and cried bitter and salty tears which bled into the pool and mixed with the rest of her sorrow.

38

Six heavy Nyctan battlecruisers hung in geosynchronous orbit around Dagon Prime. Three more held a fixed position just beyond Thessalonica and tracked any and all ships.

"Knights, you're with me," said Jegra, marching into the shuttle bay in full power armor. She wore a purple sash across her armor with the Vorteshian symbol of the tree of life embroidered on it in gold. Even though she knew the Nyctan people called it a Vorteshian knot, it resembled the woven roots of Celtic images from old Earth.

A troupe of twenty Knights of Caelum, fully suited up, marched behind her in single line formation as they made their way to the drop ship sitting on the hangar bay deck.

Deck crew stepped aside to let the heavily armored soldiers pass. It was a little unnerving to the ship's crew to see elite Nyctan warriors aboard the flagship of the Dagon Empire, especially seeing how they were currently at war with the Nyctans. But the Knights were loyal only to the head of their order, who, unfortunately, had been murdered by a megalomaniacal space entity with a god complex.

Of course, this meant command of the Knights fell to the next highest-ranking officer in the holy order, which just so happened to be Jegra, who held the rank and title of Vorteshian Emissary to the Knights of Caelum.

This made her the High Voroxian Priestess of the order of all female knights, long since disbanded. And subsequently, the seneschal—when there was no grandmaster or administratrix to lead the order of Knights of Caelum.

Vortesh, an ancient Nyctan theologian, had interpreted the Enchiridion in such a way that allowed for females to join the holy order of celestial knights, or the Knights of Caelum, as Vortesh had named them. This gave rise to the order of female-only warriors who took the name Vortosh, which later was simplified linguistically to Vorox, the root of both being the same in the Nyctan etymology.

Since only a high priestess could join the Knights on missions, all female knights were so christened Voroxian High Priestesses. A special order of warrior priestesses who could fight alongside the Knights in battle and of whom Jegra was, as far as she was aware, the only living member.

Despite all of the religious rules and theological subtleties, nobody could find a religious or cultural rule that objected to Jegra's position. Even the current High Priestess of Nyctan, Yolkai Estan, assured Sir Lance Bishop and the Knights that Jegra's rank and title were official.

As such, with the High Priestess of all of Nyctan vouching for her, the knights all swore their undying allegiance to Jegra Alakandra, Voroxian High Priestess, Empress to the Dagon Empire, Mother of Dagon, and the Gladiatrix of the Galaxy.

And the Knights of Caelum gladly welcomed her leadership, for they were lost sheep without a shepherd until she had arrived on Nyctan, six months ago.

Lance Bishop, her first in command, had reassured her that his men's loyalty was to her and her alone and not to the imposter god that had killed their queen. And although the queen had considered Jegra a traitor, her time in prison had abolished her sins, as far as any of the knights were concerned.

And despite all the twists and turns, the lost flock had found their shepherd in the form of a warrior cut from the same spiritual cloth as them.

Jegra stopped in front of the loading ramp to the Falcon heavy drop ship and turned to address the knights.

"Honor. Death. Glory," she said. She scanned their faces. As was typical of the Knights, they all stared straight forward with emotionless gazes. Pacing in front of them, she repeated herself, this time much louder. "Honor. Death. Glory!"

There was a pause, and she stopped and faced the knights. "Honor! Death! Glory! Honor! Death! Glory!" the knights all roared in boisterous reply. "Honor! Death! Glory!

She smiled and then stepped aside. "Board the ship and prepare for zero-grav space-drop."

Their armor clanked in unison as they gave the Dagon salute. This unnecessary but respectful gesture brought a smile to her face. She returned the salute and then ushered them inside. Remaining behind for a moment, she turned just as Captain Blackstar and Lieutenant Commander Brei'Alas stepped onto the hangar deck.

Brei'Alas had on her white with burgundy striped EV spacesuit, helmet tucked under her arm. "I'm going with you," Brei'Alas said in her usual chipper way.

"Like Helios you are," Jegra replied.

"I'm afraid you're overruled, Your Majesty, seeing as it's under my orders," Lianica informed Jegra, pulling rank.

It wasn't often that Lianica overruled Jegra like this, but it was her ship, and she had final say on all mission objectives and assignments. If she was doing it now, then she must have her reasons, and Jegra backed down.

Jegra nodded silently and then nudged her chin in the direction of the ship. "What are you waiting for then, Lt. Commander? Get your ass onboard that ship, ASAP."

"Yes, ma'am!" Brei'Alas saluted, a smile curling onto her lips, and then scurried up the loading ramp.

Jegra watched her disappear into the opening of the ship and then slowly turned back toward Lianica, her gaze weighted with concern.

"You have command of the fleet while I'm gone. Just make sure to give those enemy ships Helios and the Knights and I will handle the rest."

"Yes, Your Majesty," Lianica answered, crossing her fist over her left breast and bowing slightly. With that she spun on her heels and marched back out of the hangar bay.

Jegra slapped the side of the bird and, looking up at the canopy motioned for the pilot to spool up the thrusters and get going.

As the ship began to rise off the hangar deck, the rear loading ramp began to retract. Jegra, still standing on the open landing pad, tapped a small button on the neck of her armor. A knight's helmet unfolded from seemingly out of nowhere and wrapped around her head and locked into place. Her visor flashed a menacing red.

Fully suited up, Jegra started jogging alongside the drop ship as it made its way to the blue shimmering energy field that looked out onto space.

She arrived quickly at the end of the hangar then leapt through the forcefield at the same time the ship shot out of the *Shard's* hangar bay doors. Both Jegra and the ship entered zero-gravity with a smooth transition. She reflected back to her first zero gravity space walk and how nervous she'd been. Now, she'd gotten accustomed to falling through the empty vacuum of space.

Her armor's thrusters fired and propelled her to cruising velocity. She straightened her body, flattened her arms to her sides, and entered a zero-gravity freefall.

She turned her head to the side and glanced at the drop ship. She made eye contact with the pilot, and he tapped his fingers to his helmet and saluted her, letting her know he had eyes on her, and she nodded and turned her attention back toward the web of glistening silver balls that formed a protective barrier around her fleet.

Jegra brought her arm display up and tapped a passcode into her holographic HUD. The smart-mines parted, allowing Jegra and the drop ship to pass through unaccosted. Once they were safely through, the gaping hole sealed itself up behind them.

"We're through," Jegra said into her headset.

"Copy that," Lance Bishop's voice came back over the comm. "The knights will run their final drop status check and join you shortly."

"I'm looking forward to it," Jegra said, smiling behind the glowing orange and green lights of her visor's heads up display.

Lance turned toward his brotherhood of knights and said, "Helmets on." Everyone, including Brei'Alas secured their helmets and then prepared for zero-gravity space drop.

Once his helmet was secured, his visor flashed and he checked his own HUD, making sure they were all a go. Everything checked out, so he turned and gave the thumbs up.

"Alright brothers and sister, we are go for a ship-to-ship space jump. Prepare for depressurization in three, two, one..." Reaching up to the red button on the wall next to the rear bulkhead, he smashed it and the loading ramp opened right into the blackness of interstellar space.

The air of the cargo bay seeped out with a swoosh that ruffled Brei'Alas's EV suit and caused her to brace herself so she didn't get blown out the back.

All 1,800 meters of the *Qui'tek'alon* came into view and Jegra used her maneuvering thrusters to bring the ship into dead center of her freefall. The drop ship opened up above her and one by one the knights leaped out from the ship, fired their thrusters, and joined her in the freefall.

Lance Bishop and Brei'Alas were the last to make the jump.

All twenty-two of them fell into formation and Jegra gave the signal for them to fan out. They did as commanded, and then, the *Qui'tek'alon* coming up fast, the knights fired their reverse thrusters and set down all along the ship's hull with barely a sound.

Lance Bishop set down next to Jegra and gently placed Brei on her feet. She nodded, thanking him for the assist, and he nodded back. Then, drawing out his plasma sword, he thrust it into the hull of the ship.

All twenty knights did the same, all along various strategic access points on the ship, cutting their way inside.

"Knock, knock," Jegra said into her helmet as she dropped down through the glowing ring of molten korridium and onto one of the upper decks of the ship.

Almost as soon as they'd breached the ship's hull, the structural integrity shields came on with a flicker and then solidified into a static field of blue energy.

As soon as the deck had pressurized, Jegra tapped the side of her helmet and it unfurled itself and automatically retreated back into her suit. She motioned with two fingers for Sir Bishop to go left and she gestured toward Brei to accompany her right.

"Where are we going?" asked Brei.

"Hunting," Jegra replied without looking back.

39

Several heavily armed Dragonian lizard men escorted Danica, bound and shackled, out of the arena and down a winding trail which led to a white sandy beach along the shoreline. It was ironic, she thought, that the Dragonians were now the slave race. They were once a race of galactic conquerors, but now, they merely comprised the hired help.

Roughly five thousand years ago, if her memory served correctly, the warrior lizard race of Dragonians had led an invasion force to Dagon Prime and, using their brute strength and sheer force of numbers, sacked the ocean city of Korsa.

What the Dragonians hadn't counted on, though, was Ra'hallek, the warrior emperor's, love of battle. A genius level strategist, he gathered his finest warriors and marched into battle right alongside them.

That marked the Blood Campaigns, as he had used EMPs to knock out the Dragonian's unshielded technology and then laid them to waste in hand to hand combat. Although the lizard men and women were fierce warriors, the Dagon soldiers matched them in size and strength. It was like letting two Titans go at it.

But the Dragonians had made a grave miscalculation. They didn't know about the Dagons' fusion with Dygra crystals and were not aware of the energy abilities of the blue-skins. As such, even without working technology, the Dagons had the clear advantage.

With the war won, Ra'hallek erected the first official gladiatorial games in honor of the fallen men and women who had valiantly defended their homeland and their world.

At first, the victorious Dagon race forced the Dragonians to fight one another to the death, as punishment for their war crimes. When the novelty of watching leather-necks die finally wore off, Ra'hallek issued a decree that opened up the games to other war criminals.

After a few hundred years of sending the worst criminals to die in the arena, however, the games were dissolved, being considered degrading and unnecessarily cruel under the new Commonwealth Alliance peacetime accords.

It wasn't until Loki'Alloran Rhadamanthus, a rebel in his own right, and Dakroth's father, reinstated the games as a means of prisoner control and as a way to regulate violent offenders and maintain a peaceful republic. But there was one caveat. The Intergalactic Gladiatorial Syndicate had to oversee them. This third-party oversight served to avoid any potential corruption from within the Imperial government.

IGS now acted as the largest warrant collecting agency in the galaxy and were known as the "Peace Keepers." They were, essentially, space marshals, and had near unlimited jurisdiction. They were also the ones that outsourced to bounty hunters like Raven Nightguard. Space was a big place; it was easier to pay a freelancer a meager sum than have to run an entire team, ship, crew, and supplies to catch one lowly bail jumper.

And, speaking of IGS, that's how Danica came to find herself stuck on Arkadia, wearing nothing but a flimsy floral patterned bikini two sizes too small for her.

As they wound down the path toward a grove of palms, the scorching hot beach sand burning her feet, Danica felt like she'd melt beneath sweltering heat of the sun.

"My how the mighty have fallen," a voice quipped as Danica approached a small outdoor encampment set up in the shade of the leafy palms.

Stretched out on a sunbathing bed, a Bre'lal woman basked in the hot, mid-day sun. She had on a white bikini with an exotic purple print, and beneath the spaghetti straps of her back she could make out the light olive colored lines where her dark olivine skin had kept its original pigment.

Although her face was turned away, making it impossible to tell who she was, she had three servant girls who diligently attended her every need. Coincidentally, Danica recognized one of the girls as the same one who'd fallen into the arena yesterday. The girl she'd rescued.

One of the girls fanned their mistress with a giant palm leaf while two others kept her margarita topped off and applied a healthy lather of tanning oil to her skin, keeping her glistening and beautiful.

The woman tossed her forest green hair to the side and slowly raised her face, her eyes opening slightly as she turned her maudlin gaze toward Danica before lackadaisically taking another sip from the straw of her margarita, which sat on a small table next to her.

When Danica saw that it was Onelle Te'Legra Agnar, she rolled her eyes and grumbled, "Onelle? I should have known it'd be you. Only you require this much pampering just to take a stroll along the beach."

"It's true," she admitted. "I have a taste for the finer things in life. But there's nothing wrong with that." Waving Danica over, she gestured for her to stand in the shade. "Care for a drink?" Onelle motioned for her servant girl to pour Danica a margarita.

"No, thanks," Danica replied. When Onelle went back to sipping on her straw as though she had nothing more to say, Danica sarcastically quipped, "If that'll be all."

She turned to leave, but stopping her were the crackling tips of six charged stun-rods and a group of angry looking Dragonian guards. Deciding it was probably against her best interests to take on six Dragonian security officers while in shackles, she raised her hands in surrender, blew a tuft of hair away from her eyes in a fit of annoyance, and pivoted back to face Onelle's smirking expression.

"We're finished when I say we're finished," Onelle informed the gladiatrix. Sitting up, Onelle swung her legs over the edge of her long beach chair and rose to her feet. The girl from yesterday handed her a towel so she could dab herself dry, and once she'd finished, she handed back the towel and turned her attention to Danica.

Beads of sweat already reforming on her green skin, glistening trails began to run down the humps of her breasts, which were being held in place by the white and purple bikini top. Onelle cleared her throat, as if to say *my eyes are up here*, and waited for Danica to look up.

Onelle placed her hands on her hips, met Danica's gaze, and held it, showing she wasn't in the least intimidated by her.

"You have my undivided attention," Danica answered, her voice betraying her as it sounded awfully impatient, as if she had better things to be doing.

"Imagine my surprise when I heard that the infamous Cassera Van Danica Amelorak was fighting in *my* arena," Onelle said, trying her best to sound imperious. "Now, imagine how much more surprised I was when I was told that you'd denied my pardon." She paused and, then, in dramatic fashion, threw her hands up and added, "I just don't get it."

"What's not to get?" Danica replied. "I didn't ask to be pardoned."

"You also didn't ask to be tossed back into the lion's den, quite literally speaking," she said, glancing up at the bandage wrapped around Danica's arm, which concealed the puncture wounds she'd received in her bout from the quills of the Scalios razorback lions.

"It's my burden to bear," she answered stoically, "and mine alone."

"If I didn't know any better, it almost sounds as though you're punishing yourself for something, my dear Cassera. But for what? Tell me, what is it you're running from?"

"If you must know, it seems my whole life has been a series of failures. I failed my emperor. I failed my empress. I even failed myself. You probably wouldn't understand this, but getting sent here was Fate. This, right here, right now," she said thumping her chest, "is my chance at redemption. I'll either die in the arena, or I'll be victorious and gain my freedom."

"You're absolutely insane," Onelle said, shooting Danica an unamused look. Danica merely responded with a shrug.

After a moment's reflection, Onelle let out a long, dramatically overly vexed sigh and replied, "Fine. Have it your way."

Danica bowed and then uttered a diminutive, "Thank you."

"Won't you have at least one drink with me?" Onelle grinned and offered Danica another margarita of which she politely rescinded.

"I'd better not," Danica answered, maintaining her posture and standing off to the side like a statue. "I have a match later this evening."

Onelle waved her hand in a dismissive manner and let out a disappointed sigh. "In that case, our conversation here is done. You're free to return to your dank cell and play with your little pirate girlfriend."

"She's not my girlfriend," Danica growled angrily.

Onelle, startled by the unexpected vitriol in Danica's voice, looked over at her and smiled. Seeing her rage seep out like this was delightful.

"Really? In that case, you truly don't have anything better to do." She offered Danica the drink a third time and this time Danica gave in and accepted it.

"Excellent," Onelle chirped cheerfully.

Danica looked over at the slave girl, who was familiar to her, then back to Onelle. "Do you think, maybe, that I might get an oil massage, too? It helps with the circulation and rejuvenates the muscles."

Onelle thought about it for a moment then smiled and snapped her fingers. "What's mine is yours, Cassera," she said, using Danica's old name. Turning toward her three servant girls, dutifully waiting for her commands, she cleared the frog from her throat and said, "Bring another long chair for our guest and a decanter of my finest birtchkum seed oil."

The three girls raced off, their feet leaving dainty footsteps in the sand as they scurried off to do her bidding.

"And what about these?" inquired Danica, holding out her arms and showing Onelle her shackles.

Without hesitating, Onelle snapped her fingers at one of the Dragonian guards and pointed at Danica's shackles. "See to those, will you?"

The guard hesitated, looking warily at Danica then back at Onelle. As a trained gladiator, he knew that she could kill all of them in the blink of an eye and then take a leisurely sunset stroll along the beach afterward.

"Did I stutter?" Onelle barked. "Unshackle her, now!"

The guard quickly undid Danica's shackles and then drew back. Danica rubbed her wrists and, looking up at Onelle, said, "I appreciate that."

Onelle smiled briefly then waved off her guards. "Your services will no longer be needed here gentlemen, return to your posts."

The guards bowed and then, in unison, spun on their heels and marched back toward the arena in formation.

Once they were on their merry way, Onelle swiveled back around and sprawled out on the towel laid out for her on her tanning bed. A couple of servant girls, waiting in the shade of the palm, poured birtchkum into the palms of their hands and began lathering Onelle's back up with the glistening oil.

Onelle looked up at Danica and motioned for her to lay down on the long chair that had been set out beside her. Once Danica had settled in beside Onelle, the servant girl from yesterday came over to her.

"This is Aidora, my personal girl. She'll see to it you get the best treatment while you're here on Arkadia."

Aidora bowed reverently and then poured some oil into her palms. "If it stings your wounds, please don't hesitate to let me know."

Danica looked at the girl from the corner of her eyes and recognized that the spark she'd seen in her eyes yesterday was completely missing. Something, or someone, had snuffed out that joyous innocence less than twelve hours ago.

Although Danica couldn't help but feel sorry for her, she also had tried to warn her. If you want to do well in this life, you have to do more than just try to survive. You have to fight for everything you need.

"I'll let you know if it gets to be too much," Danica said. She waited till Aidora had lathered her up before adding, "Sometimes, you have to embrace the pain. Because the pain is what reminds you what you need to grow stronger so that you won't ever experience that kind of pain again."

Aidora nodded. It made perfect sense to her. She needed to learn how to fight. How to defend herself so that she never had to endure what she'd gone through yesterday ever again.

"Maybe after this evening's match, you can send Aidora around to my chambers for another massage. I have a feeling I might need it after tonight's fight," Danica said.

Onelle, her face buried between the ribbons of the chair, waved her hand as if to say go right ahead. "My servant girl is yours for as long as you want her."

It was of Aidora's opinion that Onelle didn't actually need her. But for some reason she was keeping her around. Maybe it was that philosophy thing again. That saying she'd heard once before. Something about keeping your friends close but your enemies closer. If Onelle felt for one second that Aidora might be an enemy, then keeping her close made sense.

But Aidora didn't want to be anyone's enemy. What her people were doing was out of necessity of survival. If they had disobeyed H'aaztre's wishes, then their world would have ended up like Galliforn and Earth. Obliterated.

Of course, her people's hyper religiosity did seem to make a large portion of her society more prone to blindly following H'aaztre, no matter how evil he proved himself to be. But ever since he'd destroyed Earth simply out of spite, she had begun questioning whether his motives were pure. And she knew that other Nyctans were starting to have their doubts, too.

She shook the thought out of her head and got back to running her fingers through the folds of Danica's soft skin. Even though she was toned, and had ample muscle definition, a year of the easy life had given her an extra layer of shapeliness that only seemed to enhance her beauty.

The muscle was still there underneath, but now she looked more feminine and more voluptuous than ever. Gently, Aidora traced the scars of the lion's claw marks. Danica had obviously had a medic close her wounds with a binding wand, but the scars would remain there, without further treatments.

"Will you be keeping these," Aidora asked.

Tickled by the question, Danica smiled. "As a matter of fact, yes. Why? Don't you think I should keep them?"

"It's not up to me, Mistress Valencia."

"Imagine you were me," Danica continued. "What would you choose to do?"

"I'd most definitely keep them." Aidora grew so excited over the prospect of having actual battle scars that she began to dig into Danica's deep tissue harder than planned, and solicited a light moan from Danica's lips. "Oh, I'm sorry," she apologized for her mishap.

"No, it feels great. Keep doing whatever it is you're doing."

"Alright," she replied, glad that her little mistake had actually proved to be a win.

"That settles it," Danica finally said. "Alright, you've convinced me. I'm going to keep every battle scar I receive."

"Really?" Aidora asked, taken aback by Danica's courageousness.

"Really?" Onelle echoed, her voice filled with disgust at the very idea of having to live in an ugly, scarred and tattered skin suit. "You're going to let your flesh become disfigured simply to prove a point?"

"And why shouldn't I?"

Onelle groaned and then said, "Suit yourself. But don't come crying to me when you gain the title of ugliest gladiator ever."

"I shall do my best not to let it come to that," Danica reassured her.

"You do that," Onelle said in a dreary voice. She yawned, took another sip of her margarita, and then promptly fell into an alcohol induced sleep. Both Aidora and Danica were alerted to the fact by her gentle snoring.

As soon as it was clear that Onelle was out for the count, Danica sat up and turned to Aidora. The sudden change in demeanor and mood caused Aidora to cautiously draw back.

"Who did that to you?"

"Did what?" Aidora asked, unconsciously touching her neck. She'd tried her best to cover up the bruises with makeup, but maybe she hadn't gotten it all. Maybe Danica had seen right through her disguise.

Danica pointed down at her teal, wrap-around skirt. When she looked down, she saw the blue stain; her blood was seeping out and trickling down the insides of both her legs.

"Only an act of violence can tear a woman up that badly."

Embarrassed, Aidora dropped her things, clutched her skirt and scurried off, hot tears streaming from her eyes as she fled. She wiped the tears out of her eyes and then disappeared into the crowd gathering at the entrance gate for this evening's games.

Danica stood up and looked over at the other servant girls, who looked to each other, trying to figure out what to do in such a situation. When it was clear that Onelle couldn't be revived, they all bowed their heads and allowed Danica to gather her things and follow after Aidora.

She'd shadowed Aidora all the way to the main square in front of the arena when she was all but certain the girl had spotted her. She made a beeline for the buildings, weaving through the crowd. When Danica stepped out into the square, however, she was surrounded by a mob of ecstatic fans begging for autographs and selfies with the famed gladiatrix.

"Please sign my poster," a young fan cried out.

"Sign my breast," a Bre'lal woman shouted over the din. She lifted up her shirt and flashed Danica.

The commotion drew more attention and, subsequently, more bodies until Danica was cornered. She let out a frustrated sigh and then began signing autographs and taking selfies with all the plebeians.

An hour later, Danica slowly inched her way back to the main gates of the arena. Coming to the side entrance of the gladiatorial chambers, she rattled the gate and caught a nearby guard's attention.

"Hey, you. No tours beyond this point," he grumbled.

"It's me," Danica said.

"Me who?"

"Me, Danica Valencia."

The guard, an elderly Dragonian on the gaunt side, drew closer and studied her face. Realizing she was who she said she was, he frowned and then smacked his teeth in disapproval. "What in the bleeding Helios are you doing out there?"

"It's a long story. Just let me in."

He unlocked the gate and then quickly pulled her inside. Locking the gate behind her, he turned to her and grumbled, "I've heard of gladiators trying to break out, but this is the first I've ever heard of one trying to break in."

She looked out through the bars, across the crowd gathered in the square, and into the narrow city streets. "I owe you one," she said, addressing the guard who merely grunted approvingly. She peered out across the courtyard and gave up any hope that Aidora would return.

When Danica returned to her shared cell, she found Ladgara being completely double stuffed by two Dragonian guards.

"Oh, for crying out loud!" Danica shouted, throwing up her arms in disbelief.

Both guards startled and withdrew themselves from Ladgara's orifices. Fetching their things, they ducked out of the room as fast as they could.

"Are you quite finished?" Danica said, folding her arms and giving Ladgara her best reproachful stare.

"Not even close," Ladgara lamented, sitting up on her cot. "I was planning on a triple orgasm tonight and you came in and ruined everything." She pulled out a pack of smokes and lit up.

"Hey, I'm not the nymphomaniac here," Danica said.

Ladgara held out the pack of cigarettes and offered one to Danica who hesitated at first but then reached in and took one.

She helped Danica light up and then, just as Danica brought the fag to her lips, Ladgara slapped it out of her hand.

"Wha—?"

"Now you know how it feels," Ladgara said, lighting up her own cigarette and puffing a cloud of smoke in Danica's general direction.

"Oh, very mature," Danica said, waving her hand in front of her face to disperse the cloud of smoke.

"If you whip that Dagon cock of yours out and pound me into oblivion, I might just reconsider killing you in your sleep," she said.

"In your dreams," Danica replied. She bent down and picked up her cigarette from the floor, dusted it off, and then put it to her lips. She snapped her fingers impatiently and made Ladgara hand over her lighter.

Danica got her cigarette lit and then puffed out a near perfect smoke ring. After a long silence, Danica said, "You're a bloody hot mess, Vass."

"You too, sister," she said, smiling at Danica.

Pissed, Danica flicked her half-spent cigarette onto the floor and then stormed off.

Perhaps the part that stung the most was the fact that Ladgara wasn't wrong. Danica had been a hot mess ever since her academy days.

Walking through the tunnels beneath the hypogeum, Danica found her way to the armory and grabbed a shield and a sword from off the rack.

Ladgara, it seemed, had a way of getting under her skin. And if she couldn't stand being in the same room with that nympho, she figured she'd might as well blow off some steam fighting in the arena.

A Dragonian soldier motioned her to come over to him and she obliged. He glared at her sternly and folded his arms across his meaty chest. "What do you think you're doing?"

"I'm going to fight."

"You just fought," he grumbled.

"I'm going to fight again," she assured him.

"It's your funeral," he muttered, turning away to let her through.

She stepped through the gates with half a dozen other gladiators, all of them fresh meat, except for a couple, and then she heard the terrifying sound of a creature's roar.

The announcer came onto the speaker and said, "Ladies and gentlemen and species from all worlds! It has been brought to my attention that a new beast has, with great difficulty, recently been procured from a hostile alien world from beyond The Rift."

The floor parted, and the sands pulled away from the underground storage area. Up from the *hegmata* came a beast like nothing she'd ever seen before, but she recognized it by Jegra's description. *What was it she called it again? Oh, that's right.* It was a Tyrannosaurus Rex.

"Nobody's ever volunteered for a venation before," a bulging eyed, sniveling creature of short stature and unknown species said, looking up at Danica.

"I'm not nobody, now, am I?" she shot back, glaring at him harshly.

He looked her up and down and then shrugged. "I guess not."

The horn blared, signaling the start of the match, and its noise startled the beast. The roar of the crowd only seemed to make things worse and the animal pulled on its chains.

The chains were as thick as Danica's arms, and still they torqued and whined against the raw power of the monster.

"What in the bloody Helios have you gotten yourself into now?" Danica asked of herself, regretting her hasty decision—and the margarita.

"Hey," a voice came from behind her.

She turned to see Ladgara smiling at her from behind the bars of the viewing area. She was about to say something snooty when, unexpectedly, Ladgara said something she wasn't expecting.

"Good luck out there." There was a short pause before she added, "Because you're going to need it."

Ladgara casually balanced her fag back on her bottom lip and smiled as she watched, through one good eye, Danica being ushered out to meet her imminent demise.

Danica mustered up a fake smile and flipped Ladgara the bird. Ladgara replied by winking and blowing Danica a kiss, which caused her to roll her eyes and turn away in irritation.

When the horn sounded a second time, the beast's shackles automatically unlatched and it reared back its head and let out the fiercest roar she'd ever heard.

40

Dead bodies littered the bridge of the *Qui'tek'alon* and Jegra stood panting. Blue and purple blood dripped from Jegra's metallic gray battle armor and Brei'Alas stood close behind her, wielding dual plasma pistols, both of their muzzles glowing hot orange from overheating.

"I'm out of coolant cartridges," Brei'Alas said, checking the readout on both guns to find each of them down to their last notch. She might get a couple more shots out of each before the safety auto-shutdown rendered her plasma coil offline.

Jegra bent down and pulled at the ammunition belt of one of the dead Nyctan soldiers lying at her feet. Wrestling with it, she finally managed to pry it free and tossed it to Brei'Alas.

"Here," Jegra said, "use these."

Brei'Alas fumbled a bit as she caught the belt, but she quickly saved herself any embarrassment by throwing it over her shoulder so that it sat across her chest like a sash.

Brei'Alas ejected both coolant cartridges and then, with an extremely impressive level of expertise, brushed her guns against the fresh cartridges in the belt and, in one fluid motion, slid the new coolant cartridges into their rightful place.

The coolant indicator crawled back from the last red tick on the indicator and filled all the way back up to a cool blue. Once the coolant readout was back to full, the guns chimed, letting her know they were ready for action.

She twirled her guns around on her fingers with a bit of gunslinger style then looked up to find Jegra staring at her with an unusual expression. "What?"

she asked in a tone that had an edge to it.

Jegra raised an eyebrow and felt genuinely impressed. She hadn't seen this more aggressive side of Brei before. "Where'd you learn to do that?" she asked, eyeing Brei with a newfound sense of admiration.

Although Brei'Alas had her share of shortcomings, was aggravatingly timid, talked incessantly when she got nervous—usually at the most inopportune times—and occasionally was on the clumsy side when it came to wielding a firearm, she was an outright maverick.

Poised, level headed, and a crack shot, Jegra scarcely recognized this new woman standing before her. At the same time, she found herself becoming aroused by the hidden strength of this woman she'd come to think of as more than a friend in the past few weeks.

"I was top of my graduating class in marksmanship," she informed the empress. She twirled her blasters in her hands and then shot Jegra a badass look. A look which instantly made Jegra weak in the knees.

What had begun as a booze-laden fling had blossomed into a genuine friendship. And while Danica was far away, she saw no reason why Brei and she couldn't enjoy one another's company. But now, well, she realized she might have feelings that went a bit deeper than just friendship. And this confused her.

She was supposed to marry Danica. But Danica seemed so distant to her now. In fact, in the past two weeks, Dani hadn't even called her once. And it wasn't until Lycia, of all people, alerted Jegra to the fact that Danica was fighting in the arena on Arkadia that she even knew how she was doing.

Why wouldn't she share something like that with her? What was going through her mind? Jegra almost felt as though she didn't know her anymore.

"Consider me impressed," Jegra said, a pleasant smile forming on her lips. "And a little bit turned on," she added.

"You know you want me," Brei said confidently, winking at Jegra.

"I beg your pardon?" Jegra laughed and shot the girl a surprised look. Her newfound confidence was a bit outré, especially coming from her.

"Was it…too much?" Brei asked, her timid voice returning as though it had never gone. "I was trying to exude confidence…like you always do."

"Brei, you're perfect the way you are. Don't ever feel that you have to change for me or anyone else."

"You mean that?" she asked, her eyes widening with joy. They shared a look and Brei felt it too. There was definitely something there that hadn't been before.

Brei was about to say something about this unspoken attraction between them when a blast ricocheted off the wall next to her and a spray of hot sparks burned her left shoulder.

Brei'Alas screamed out in pain as she jerked her shoulder away from the scorched wall and raised her right-hand blaster, returning fire at the asshole standing in the doorway.

A sharp yelp escaped his lips when she hit him squarely in the chest. The Nephilim officer looked down at the smoldering hole in his chest that had vaporized his lungs and heart. His eyes wide with shock, he crumpled to a heap upon the floor and let go of his last breath.

"Are you alright?" Jegra asked, running up to Brei'Alas and gently touching her shoulder, removing some of the singed fabric of her uniform.

"I'm fine," Brei insisted. "It's just a slight burn."

Jegra leaned down and kissed her blue shoulder. Brei'Alas raised an eyebrow, and when Jegra looked up at her again, she knew it was the thing she'd been wishing for since the first day she'd met the empress.

"I'm in love with you," Brei blurted out as though she couldn't constrain her feelings a moment longer.

"I sort of pieced that together" Jegra replied, her eyes locking with Brei's.

Their lips crashed together and they kissed like two lovers who'd been reunited after a long separation. Brei moaned into Jegra's mouth and Jegra swallowed it up thirstily.

After a short make out session amid a throng of dead bodies, Jegra pulled back and said, "I don't want to overstep my bounds here. I know you're with Barrion and all this is confusing, so...maybe..."

"Shut up and kiss me," Brei said, trying on her confident look once more. She pulled Jegra in and locked lips once again.

Jegra smiled as she melted into the kiss. Reaching up, she grabbed Brei's EV suit by its collar and pulled her in close.

"When this is over, I'm going to treat you to a real dinner date. Maybe someplace nice, like Padua of Themecca."

"An actual date? With me? In public? In the love capital of all Dagon?" Brei asked, scarcely able to believe her ears. "Won't people talk?"

"You better believe it," Jegra said, nudging Brei's nose with her finger. "And we'll give them a whole lot to talk about."

Brei smiled and the two began to lean in for another kiss when the squeal of blaster fire echoed up the corridor.

Both women pulled back and Brei raised her blasters while Jegra ignited her plasma sword. The edges of the blade lit up hot orange and crackled on the cool air as the feared weapon of the Knights of Caelum came to life.

"How many of these assholes are there?" Brei asked aloud.

"Always one more than there needs to be," Jegra answered, her voice shifting to a hard and unforgiving tone. "After me," she said, looking at Brei, who nodded in the affirmative.

Jegra charged out in the corridor, shouting her battle cry at the top of her lungs. Brei trailed after her, both pistols raised, ready for action. But when they stepped out into the hall, they halted in their tracks.

Lance Bishop was on his knees and Azra'il Nun held his own plasma blade dangerously close to his throat. The blade hummed with energy and the white-hot edge was close enough to cause his flesh to blister and sizzle.

"My dear Jegra, can you believe he just gave it to me?"

"Don't harm him!" Jegra pleaded, throwing up her hand and lowering her blade. Brei sidled up to her, both guns trained on The Voice, but Jegra shook her head warning her not to engage.

Azra'il looked over at Brei and then smiled. "I recognize you. I saw a photo of you in your boyfriend's holovid files. Tell me, how is my little pet, Barrion?"

"He's well, no thanks to you," Brei growled.

Azra'il Nun shrugged. "It wasn't anything personal, mind you. Creating sleeper agents is my specialty."

"What do you want, Azra'il?" Jegra asked, redirecting the conversation back to her.

"I want you to surrender yourself freely into the custody of the Fusion and give yourself willingly to our Gilded Lord."

"If he wanted me, he could have had me twelve months ago. Instead, he took my child from me." Jegra stared menacingly at the Nyctan woman, who merely blinked at her with those oversized black eyes as a golden halo flashed.

Azra'il blinked a couple of times, looked around the room and then back at Jegra. "Mother, is that you?"

Jegra's eyes instantly flooded with tears. "My baby?" she whispered.

A hand reached out and touched her arm and she looked down to find Brei's blue hand resting on her forearm. "Don't trust her, or him, or whoever. It's some kind of trick."

"Mother, please, join us. If you join us, I promise you…no harm will come to you."

"What about my friends?" Jegra asked.

"Submit to my will, the will of H'aaztre, here and now and your friends' lives will be spared. But resist and I'll have no choice but to end the lives of everyone you've ever cared about."

"Don't do it," Brei pleaded. This time her words seemed to catch H'aaztre's attention and The Voice turned her scornful scowl toward Brei.

"Starting with this one," the Voice snapped, glaring at Brei'Alas for her continual interruptions. "Place that plasma pistol to your temple and keep it there."

As if possessed by a spirit taking control of her body, Brei's arm slowly rose up, and she pressed her own gun to the temple of her head. Brei looked over at Jegra, clearly terrified. "I don't want to die," she whispered.

"Oh, and do be quiet. The adults are trying to have a conversation here."

She tried to speak again, but could only mumble through her closed lips, which would not open, no matter how hard she tried. Screaming into her mouth with frustration, she turned her worried eyes to Jegra.

"Leave her alone," Jegra pleaded. "I'm the one you want, not her."

"You know, Empress Alakandra, you've proven to be a much bigger thorn in my side than I initially assumed you'd be. I'm not often surprised, but I have to give credit where credit is due. You've upended my designs time and time again."

"I'll take that as a compliment," Jegra replied.

The Voice merely nodded in an amused manner, acknowledging Jegra's little quip. "At first, I couldn't figure out how you were doing it. You know, your influence over these simple-minded people," she said, her eyes flitting to Brei'Alas and then gently settling onto Lance's head. Looking back up, she continued. "Your influence seems to be every bit as strong as mine. But then it dawned on me. They…love you." She balked as if the very notion of it was absurd.

"Do I detect a hint of jealousy?" Jegra smiled brusquely. "Is that why you feel you must either kill all of us or force me to surrender to you? So that they will follow suit?"

"I could no more be jealous of you than one could be jealous of an ant. But, when it comes to your ability to influence all the ants, well then, it seems I do have a problem. See, one ant is meaningless to me. But, as you know, when there is an infestation…well…an entire colony can prove quite the nuisance. So, consider this my one and only offering of the olive branch. You can have the peace you seek. The freedom you so desire. But you must swear your allegiance to me and me alone. Resist me, and you seal your doom and the doom of all of those you care about."

Jegra looked over at Brei, who saw the reticent look in Jegra's eyes. "I'm sorry," Jegra said, and, with a lightning quick chop to Brei's neck, she knocked the girl out. It was for her own safety.

She caught Brei in her arms and gently set her to the ground, then, setting down her plasma sword, she picked up Brei's twin blasters.

"And what do you intend to do with those pea-shooters?" The Voice asked, watching Jegra with an amused half-smile.

Without wasting her words, Jegra responded with action. She began blasting away at Azra'il Nun, who had no choice but to raise the glowing sword to deflect the plasma blasts.

Steadily, Jegra marched forward, both guns blazing. As Azra'il Nun was fully preoccupied defending against Jegra's onslaught, Lance Bishop slipped to the ground and rolled away.

"Get her out of here," she shouted, nodding at Brei's unconscious body lying on the floor.

Lance nodded and rushed over and scooped the girl up into his arms, flinging her over his shoulder. He looked back at Jegra one last time, but she was focused on her battle.

When the coolant cartridges ran dry, the indicator flashed red and the gun bleated at her in an agitated tone that relayed it was spent. She tossed the guns to the floor and then charged Azra'il Nun like an enraged bull.

Azra'il was panting heavily, and sluggishly raised the heavy sword. Not wearing any power armor, however, she was barely able to hold it up. She backed away from Jegra, the sword crackling menacingly on the cool air.

"Stay back," she warned, "or I will be forced to kill you."

Jegra laughed. "Let's drop all the unnecessary pretenses. You were already going to kill me anyway. My bet is you'd have ordered Brei to do it so that I wouldn't fight back or harm the person attacking me. Make it so I sacrificed myself to save her. Then you'd just off her too. See, I know what being a heartless monster looks like. It's the ugly shadow I see looming over my shoulder every damn day. The part of me that wants to be unleashed. The part of me that would just be so relieved if I just set it free to run wild."

Azra'il smiled. "And why don't you let it loose?"

"Because," she replied, "then I'd be just like you."

The Voice flicked off the plasma sword, set the blade town, resting the tip on the floor, and looked deep into Jegra's eyes. The golden halos flashed brightly in her own eyes and her lips parted in a seemingly affronted grin. She huffed. "And what, in your infinitesimally limited understanding, do you think I am?"

"A being completely incapable of love."

Azra'il Nun threw her head back and cackled. The cackle turned into a deep, throaty and demonic sounding laugh, and when she looked back at Jegra, the two halos were spiraling around her black eyes like a couple of rings of fire.

"Why, Jegra? Why do you do it? Why do you continue to resist me, continue to fight? Is it because you believe you're fighting for something? Is it for peace? For freedom? Or for something as mundane as survival? Could it be for love? You say I am incapable of love. But let me fill you in on a little secret, my pet. Love is an illusion. It's fleeting. Impermanent."

Standing nose to nose, Azra'il reached up and gently ran her finger down the bridge of Jegra's oily nose. Then, rubbing Jegra's oils between her white fingers with a slight look of repugnance settling across her face, she continued on with her speech in a manner that did little to allay the disgust in her voice.

"It's but a thousand unseen chemical reactions of a flawed physiology playing out in predictable ways. It may *feel* real, because you're a slave to your biology. But it's not real. The universe is indifferent to your pathetic concepts of love. Like your fleeting existence, in the grander scheme of things, it's all meaningless. Only oblivion is certain. And you, the only one to stand up to me in over seven millennia, put your faith in something as fleeting and insipid as love?"

She balked, disgusted by the mere thought of entertaining a notion as absurd as love. Waving her hand, she brushed it aside for the moment.

"When your existence ends, so too will your precious concept of love. But I am the End of Days! I am the one who will be there at the end of time to watch the universe blink out of existence. Oblivion is the only real truth, not love. Love has no place in this universe. You must be able to see it by now, Jegra. This universe was an accident. Like your existence, like love…all accidents, random convergences of nothingness. All of them ultimately meaningless. So, why? Why do you persist?"

Jegra smiled and, taking a deep breath, replied, "Because I have felt love and I know it's more powerful than even the darkest abyss. And regardless of what some seven-thousand-year-old alien thinks, perhaps it's something worth fighting for. Maybe, as farfetched as it sounds, the universe came into existence so that love, however fleeting, might be possible."

"Unlikely," the Voice interjected, a nauseated look settling upon her pale face.

"More importantly, though, since you asked," Jegra reminded her, hoping to fend off any more interruptions, "I resist you because I may be the only one in this entire stinking universe who can. Nevertheless, it's a charge I gladly accept, because even if it's all meaningless to you…it's not all meaningless to me. So, let me ask you something, H'aaztre, *Embracer of Oblivion*. Knowing that I've been able to resist you at every turn, what makes you think that I care one iota about your idle threats? You want to come after me? Fine. You want to come after my friends? I dare you to try it. But every single time I defeat you, and I *will* defeat you, remember my words. It's because of love that I will win. And it's because of love that you will lose."

Jegra reached up and gently caressed the side of Azra'il Nun's face, returning the delicateness of her enemy's previous touch with one of her own.

"And it's because of my resolve that I will look into your eyes as I am doing now, and I'll deny your evil to continue."

"Then we are of like minds," the Voice said, smiling as though she'd won some kind of wager.

"Yes. It appears that we are," Jegra replied somberly. "And that's what scares me."

She knew what she had to do but did not like it. She knew that a mother bear would kill to protect her cubs. She knew that people would help a loved one to die, if their pain and agony was so great that death was the only reprieve. And now, she found a new reason: to prevent genocide on a galactic scale.

In a split-second, Jegra's hand was wrapped around Azra'il Nun's face, her fingers bearing down onto her flesh as though she were palming a basketball. A quick flick of the wrist later, Azra'il Nun's neck snapped with a hideous bone shattering crack that reverberated off the walls and the bulkheads of the corridor.

The golden halo of light faded from Azra'il Nun's eyes and, just like that, The Voice of H'aaztre had been silenced.

She relinquished her grip upon Azra'il Nun's body and let it collapse at her feet. Yet Jegra, feeling terrible for having been left no other choice but to kill the being Azra'il had once been, could not simply discard her enemy as though she were unwanted refuse.

Instead, she gently scooped the lifeless form up in her arms and carried it back toward the rendezvous point.

After all, the fact remained, Azra'il Nun was also a victim of H'aaztre's minacious influence.

Before he'd sunk his manipulative and direful hooks into her, Azra'il Nun was a hero. It was Azra'il Nun's actions at the battle of Sector B-13 that had saved everyone. She'd sacrificed her life to save Jegra's and all the others. That wasn't something which Jegra could ever forget.

And it was of Jegra's mind that that's how this great woman, this noble warrioress, ought to be remembered.

Jegra cradled Azra'il Nun like a sleeping child in her arms and carried her back toward the rendezvous point. As she strode gracefully forward, several Knights of Caelum, returning from their mission of planting bombs throughout the ship, met her in the corridor.

They paused, exchanging glances, and then opened their helmets. As they gazed with sad eyes upon Azra'il Nun's dead body, the knights slowly stepped to the side and let the empress pass. They all saluted, one by one, as she passed them and continued on her way. Once she was at the head of the pack, she sniffled and let a single tear trickle down her cheek.

The battle was won, but the war was far from over.

Compassion and turning the other cheek weren't enough to fight an evil of this magnitude. Monstrous, devouring beasts didn't care if you ran or hid.

They simply wrought destruction and misery wherever they went, littering the centuries with the blood of innocent victims.

It was clear to Jegra that true evil needed to be combated.

And, feeling the portentous dread steadily growing in the pit of her stomach, she knew that they needed to regroup. H'aaztre, the baleful and self-proclaimed *Enemy of Love* and *Embracer of Oblivion*, would be coming for her. And she was fairly certain that the next time he wasn't going to be pulling any punches.

Next time would be all-out war.

41

In honor of Jegra's great victory over Azra'il Nun, The Voice of H'aaztre, Dakroth ordered a celebration to be held on Dagon Prime. Not only had the Empress of Dagon returned sovereign rulership to their world, but she'd broken the enemy blockade, destroyed a large portion of their fleet, and sent them scurrying back home with their tails tucked between their legs.

The message was clear: the Pearl of the Empire would not give in without a fight. And, after the past three years, one with a foreign ruler, one with the emperor missing, and one with Jegra in a coma, the people of Dagon Prime came out en masse to celebrate a return to greatness—a return to purity. If not in blood, then certainly in spirit.

"Noble women and men, it is my great pleasure to introduce to you my wife, the woman who brought us back from the brink of darkness and showed the galaxy why Dagon Prime is the sparkling Jewel of the Empire! Our enemies are vast, but our resolve is unwavering. We will not go into the night to embrace oblivion, no! We will stand steadfast next to our protector, our hero, the Mother of Dagon, Jegra Alakandra Rhadamanthus!"

The Lord Emperor stepped away from the podium, which was being broadcast live on all the televid screens in the Imperial Square, in the arena, on all the digital billboards throughout the metropolis. At the same time, the Needle stream was being cast across the entire Commonwealth and beamed into every home from here to the Outer Rim colonies.

His *coup de grâce,* however, was that he'd had deep space relays set up to boost the signal so it would find its way all the way to Nyctan, just to rub their victory in, and maybe deal a critical blow to their religious-born certitude that their Gilded God was impervious.

The roar of applause was deafening. It rose up from the city center and spread out in waves across the quaint townships and farming villages, from every hamlet to every mountain top, the cheers rippled all the way to the seaport and back down the populated beaches until arriving back at the palace again.

From sea to shining sea the people cheered with one voice—the voice of triumphant. At last, when the roar of the crowd seemed to lull, Jegra stepped out and took her side next to the Lord Emperor, and the rush of four billion voices swelled to a deafening ovation.

Dakroth smiled and placed his hand on the small of Jegra's back, his blue fingers delicately settling onto her bronzed skin of which the open back dress left on display. As she moved, the burnt umber dress hugged her every curve like wet, glistening mud, and shone with a reddish metallic gleam that made it truly something to behold.

Jegra wore her hair up in traditional ceremonial fashion for this momentous occasion, and her blue eyeshadow matched the hue of Dakroth's skin; her purple eyeliner made her brown eyes pop. Her lipstick was a rich burnt umber that nearly matched the dress she wore, and her earrings consisted of two, elongated sapphire crystals the shape and length of an Arkadian goose feather. She was glorious to behold.

Something new in Jegra's glittering attire was the sapphire and diamond studded pendant she wore around her neck. The deep blue of the sapphires complimented her dress and her dark, sun kissed skin. If this wasn't eye-catching enough, Jegra's newly pierced nipples drew lots of eyes as well, especially since the studs were prominent through the tight-fitting dress.

The gathered masses began chanting, "Speech! Speech! Speech!" in unison, and Jegra nodded graciously at Dakroth then stepped up to the microphone at the podium.

She cleared her throat and the chanting simmered down as the audience waited with bated breath for her words.

"I am but a foreigner in a foreign land. Many of you are aware of my backstory, but let me share it with those new faces I see out there in the crowd. Let me tell you in my own words the trials and tribulations I went through to get here."

She paused and smiled, waiting for the cheers to die down before continuing on.

"I was abducted by poachers, sold into slavery, and eventually wound up in the gladiatorial matches. That was a dark time in my life and, if I'm being honest, I was not strong or courageous back then. I had all but given up any hope of living and told myself to get comfortable with the fact that I was most certainly going to die. Then fate intervened." She turned and smiled at Dakroth, taking his hand for show. "And I was given a second chance at life."

Cheers rose up again and Dakroth, holding her hand in his left hand, reached up with his right and waved at the audience.

"Not wasting this rarest of gifts bestowed upon me by the powers that be, I fought with everything I had. I became a champion. It wasn't easy. But it sure as Helios beat the alternative."

She paused once more and drew Dakroth's hand to her lips and kissed it. She smiled at him, he smiled at her, and for a fraction of a moment, it really did feel as though they were in love again and not just pretending.

He squeezed her hand, then waved again to the crowd. After his show of gratitude, he returned her affection and brought her jewel encrusted hand to his lips and kissed it. The crowd went wild with roars and applause.

Jegra turned back to the podium, took a deep breath, and continued with her speech. "I'm not one for making speeches, but ever since accepting the dutiful role of being the Lord Emperor's queen, I seemingly have been put on the spot at every opportunity."

A wave of laughter reverberated through the crowd on the lawn of the palace where she was giving her speech and she was sure it got a chuckle elsewhere as well.

"The truth is, I was ill suited for such a position. There were far better, more capable women than I. Women of pure, noble blood and breeding. Beautiful Dagon women who could please the Emperor in every possible way I could only dream to aspire to. But, love is a fickle thing. And, like the bold spirit of your emperor, it knows no bounds and has no limitations. So, I accepted the responsibility, as daunting as it seemed. I may have struggled at first. But like my first time surviving a bout in the arena, I knew what a precious gift I'd been given and that I'd be crazy to waste it.

"My victory over the Nyctan-Nephilim Fusion and their false god, whose name shall not be mentioned, is the proof that I am worthy to call myself your

Empress. I've earned it. And if you still don't agree—then feel free to join me upon the battlefield in the coming war. Bleed with me, so you know what it means to sacrifice for something you believe in. Die with me, if necessary, to prove that what you're fighting for is worth any price. But spare me your petty criticisms and your negative gossip, because unless you've fought and bled alongside me, then your spirits are not pure. Though to some, my lineage may appear disgraceful, my spirit is the purest of the pure—of that I promise you. And love me or hate me, that fact will never change, I am your empress! I am the Mother of Dagon."

If the thunderous applause could shake the palace, rattling the glass window panes, she knew that the sound in the city square must be deafening, down amongst the throngs of spectators. In fact, when she looked over her right shoulder at the valley, the cityscape rising in the distance, she saw a flock of birds take to the sky, startled into flight by the uproarious cheers and applause.

Jegra smiled, waved to the televid drones that buzzed about, filming her speech in virtual high def, and took in a deep breath. She smiled to the camera, blew a kiss, and then turned and sauntered toward Dakroth, who kindly extended his arm for her to take.

She took it, linking with him at the elbow, and arm-in-arm they headed back into the palace, waving to the crowd and shaking the hands of the noble men and women lining the garden path back to the palace.

Once they'd arrived at the tall glass doors of the main entrance, they turned and waved one last time and then disappeared inside as the applause continued to roar unabated behind them.

The tall doors came to a shut, reducing the sound to white noise, and Dakroth and Jegra unlatched their arms. Callestra pranced up to Dakroth and chirped, "You were magnificent, my luv." She leapt up into his arms and kissed him with a sultry and unnecessarily deep, penetrating kiss. The entire time she kissed him she kept her eyes fixed on Jegra who, in turn, rolled hers out of exasperation of the ridiculously competitive display.

Callestra ran her fingers through Dakroth's flowing white hair, and whispered into his ear, "Seeing you out there in your element got me so wet."

Dakroth laughed and then put his arm around her waist and looked over at Jegra. "Care to join us?" he offered.

"Maybe another time, my luv," she said in a sarcastic tone. But her mockery went unnoticed. One of the downsides to Dagon culture was that they were so literal. The two merely shrugged and sauntered off to enjoy a good afternoon fuck.

If she was being honest, though, she had to admit that she was secretly happy for them. Besides, Dakroth had quit being such a pain in her backside ever since Callestra had arrived on the scene. She kept his idle hands busy, and genuinely seemed to be into him. Much more than Jegra ever had been.

In the meantime, she finally felt as though this entire wild carrousel ride that was her life was finally slowing down and, for the first time since she'd left the arena, felt as though she finally had a handle on things.

Jegra had returned to her personal chambers and was taking out her earrings when she heard a familiar sound. The yellow flash in her mirror alerted her to the fact that an unlawful teleport had just transpired.

Cautiously, she reached under her vanity and drew out the blade that was hidden there, strapped to its underside, for just such an occasion. Spinning around, dagger in hand, she saw the face of a petite Nyctan girl she didn't recognize. She looked the worse for wear, as though she'd been tortured to within an inch of her life.

She had numerous scrapes and bruises as well as a pretty severe burn mark on her left shoulder from where a plasma blast had scorched her delicate flesh.

"You have to help," the girl said, her voice trembling. "She's completely mad with power and is going to kill us. Kill us all."

"Who is?" Jegra asked, lowering her blade.

"The Voice of H'aaztre," the girl answered.

"Impossible," Jegra replied. "I killed her."

"No!" the girl practically screamed. She coughed; her voice was raw and her lips were chapped and bleeding. "You're not listening to me. She's back. She..."

A coughing spate interrupted her words and the frail girl sank to her knees. Jegra stowed the knife in her waistband and rushed over to help the girl up. She walked her over to the reading nook, set her down on the leather sofa, and poured her a cold glass of lemon water.

After handing her the glass, Jegra asked, "Who?"

Just then, a security team burst into the room. Jegra raised her hand and halted them, letting them know she had things well under control.

After a short pause, the Nyctan girl gazed up at the empress with her black eyes and, in a weak voice, replied, "It's true. The Voice of H'aaztre was never silenced. It merely found a new host."

The girl tried to whisper the name, but she choked on her own words. She looked over at the security team reticently, and Jegra motioned for them to lower their weapons.

It was clear to Jegra that the new Voice had ordered this frail girl not to divulge their true identity. And yet she'd come all this way to warn her. The question was, why?

Regardless, Jegra knew that it was simply a matter of time before this new, terrible identity would be revealed to them.

Jegra snapped her fingers and said, "Get a medical team in here, now. The rest of you, leave us."

Two guards rushed off to fetch the medic while four others took up positions at the door and out in the hall.

The empress waited for her doors to close before turning back to the girl. "What's your name?" she asked.

"Aidora," the girl replied.

"It's nice to meet you Aidora." Jegra smiled and Aidora took another sip of the water as she sat trembling.

"There's no need to be afraid," Jegra said. "You're safe here."

Aidora adamantly shook her head in the negative. "No," she said, her face as hard and unmoving as stone. "You've provoked him. Angered him. Now, none of us are safe."

42

All the televid screens on Dagon Prime and throughout the Commonwealth flickered with a wave of interference, cut out briefly, then resumed again. Instead of the continued celebration, however, there was something terrible, something stomach-churningly gruesome plastered upon the screens.

A man, completely eviscerated, bound and strung up by his feet with sturdy rope, writhed as a pair of bloody hands carved away his flesh, skinning him and removing entire slabs of tissue like thick bacon.

Worse than the brutality and the gruesomeness of it, though, was the anguish heard in the man's screams. For this poor soul wasn't yet fully dead, and he cried out in abhorrent, gut-wrenching agony.

It was an agony so hideously penetrating that it sent chills down the most hardened warriors' spines and put the very hairs of one's arms on end with his every miserable shriek and grievous wail.

The audience, stunned by what they beheld, shuddered with terror-stricken revulsion at those ghastly screams. The sounds rising up from his throat and lungs were almost other-worldly—sounds that no man should ever make.

Onlookers shared distressed looks with one another and wondered among themselves, who this poor wretched soul was, being skinned alive before their very eyes. What had he done to deserve such a lamentable fate?

"No, please, I beg of you!" the victim's wet, sticky voice called out. "Have mercy!"

"Mercy?" a woman's voice asked. "Like your empress showed mercy to my emissaries?"

"I beg of you…I cannot take this torture any longer. Please, let me die."

The bloody hands continued sawing at the man's flesh and he bellowed out in torment. His body jerked and twitched as he tried to escape the lacerating kiss of her blade, but it was in vain, for the ropes were far too tight to escape.

The audiences gasped and drew back in horror as the camera panned down to show his ghastly face—or rather the lack of one. Two bulbous eyeballs sat atop the white bone and sinewy muscle tissue of a smiling skull, the horrifying grin of Death.

It was to this dark realm of the unliving that its desperate gaze shifted, and the bloody face looked right at the camera, drawing shrill screams and startled gasps from the distraught onlookers.

One minute they had all been watching the empress give a rousing speech, followed by the talking heads of popular news personas discussing the nuances of every word and every gesture made. Then, in the middle of their review of the highlights of Jegra's speech, their commentary was interrupted by this revolting live-feed of a psychopath's snuff film.

Who, they wondered, was bold enough to cut into the feed of the Imperial house of Rhadamanthus with this torture porn? Who dared interrupt the Dagon people's celebration?

The camera gradually pulled back to reveal the one and only Onelle Te'Legra Agnar grinning viciously, blood splattered upon her face. Although, it did not seem to bother her.

She wore a black leather jacket with spikes that ran from the pointy shoulders all the way down the sleeves and encircled the cuffs.

She didn't bother fastening the metal clasps of her jacket, though, and it hung open, revealing her gore dappled green chest and abdomen.

Instead of pants, she had on what seemed to be a leather bikini, which met fishnet stockings that trailed down to thigh-high leather stiletto-boots. The heels of the stilettos were just more spikes and matched her dominatrix styled jacket.

She brandished a bloody carving knife and played with it in an almost careless fashion as chunks of raw meat and burgundy muck dribbled down to her naval.

Onelle tried wiping away the gore with her hand, but there was too much of it, and wiping it only smeared it around and made it that much worse, coating her like a sticky balm and leaving a glistening streak of claret upon her viridian flesh.

She sighed out lackadaisically, as though she was getting bored with this game, and then bent down next to her victim's mutilated face. "Tell them, Senator Targon Van Morgan. Tell them what they're dying so desperately to know."

The onlookers gasped out when they heard the name of her wretched victim. Senator Targon...he was one of their own.

He merely whimpered, and she thrust her hand into the meaty sinews of his thigh muscles, causing him to wail out in ear-splitting agony. This only seemed to cause the smile on her face to tighten with a twisted sort of pleasure.

"I said *tell them*," she growled, digging her fingers in deeper and moving her hand around inside his tissue without remorse.

"The Voice," he answered in a feeble, pathetic manner, sticky strings of blood oozing from his mouth as he spoke. With no lips to catch his blood-saturated drool, all he could do was make a mess of himself and look the part of the, wretched, broken creature. "H'aaztre's Voice cannot be silenced."

"Good boy," she said in a voice that dripped with unadulterated disdain. Then, to everyone's astonishment, she drew her blade up and sliced open his lower gut.

As the thin, red line split open like a gaping mouth, she thrust her bloody hand inside the gash and, ignoring his ear-piercing screams, tore out his bowels.

The senator's insides spilled from his torso and slithered down his upside-down body like mucus covered bloodworms. The ends of his entrails coiling on the floor like a brood of snakes, he gurgled an inaudible last sound and then went silent as his body fell limp.

His lidless eyes and skeletal smile grinned back at the viewers with a perpetually manic look that forced people of weak constitutions to look away. The only redeeming quality of Targon's grisly death was that with his slaying, his miserable screams had finally ceased.

The televid feed refocused on Onelle, who daintily sucked the glistening red goo off her fingertips and then turned to the camera with a blood stained grin.

"My dear servants, I'm so sorry to have interrupted your joyous celebration. But, you see, I just wanted to let you all know that I haven't forgotten about you. In fact, truth be told, I'm just getting started."

She slurped on her thumb, lapping up the senator's blood thirstily. Then, she let out an overly dramatic sigh, took a deep breath, and turned toward the camera with drooping lids and the detached gaze of an insomniac.

"It seems there are those among you who insist on defying me at every turn. Well, I'm putting an end to that. Side with them if you will, but know this. Everyone who joins Jegra Alakandra's cause or helps her ragtag band of rebels in any way will meet the same fate as our friend Senator Targon here."

She slapped the slab of dead meat hanging beside her and laughed. Then she turned back to the camera, her eyes pitch black except for the halos of gold encircling her obsidian tinted irises.

"I am the new The Voice of H'aaztre. And I am placing a one trillion credit bounty on my lovely, dear sister, Raphine Agnar. Oh, and listen up boys and girls…I want her *alive*. The condition you bring her to me in, however, is up to you. Thanks for listening. You may all go back to your celebration now."

Onelle waved her fingers as if giving a slow-motion single-handed clap and bid her viewers goodbye with a breezy: "Ta ta for now," just before the televid feed cut out.

When the regular news broadcast resumed, the crowd, who had been cheering on the empress's great victory, were now deathly silent. So much so that somewhere in the distance, a *Quilox* cricket could be heard chirping.

The newscasters touched their earpieces, taking in the frantic chatter of their producers and then, composing themselves, made their announcements.

"This just in. Emperor Dakroth will be giving a formal response within the hour. Stay tuned for any further breaking news. It appears that the war with The Fusion is here, folks. Again, I'm being told that we'll be bringing you a live televid broadcast of the Lord Emperor's official response to this startling revelation. Please, stay tuned and we'll keep you apprised of every detail as our team of reporters get information to us."

Cameras flashed and televid drones swarmed the Imperial palace lawn as the glass doors parted and Jegra, along with Dakroth, marched back out to the podium situated at the foot of the stairs. They'd come this way merely a little less than a half hour ago, and here they were, returning to give more speeches. This time, however, the news was grim.

An entire contingent of Imperial Guards lined the palace stairs as Dakroth and Jegra descended the red carpeted steps one foot at a time. Behind them trailed Raphine, along with the empress's private security.

Jegra felt worried for Raph. She now had a target painted on her back in the form of a trillion credits. Even if it was H'aaztre pulling Onelle's strings, it still had to sting, and Jegra couldn't imagine the heartache Raphine was feeling right about now, realizing that her own sister had given herself over to H'aaztre and was now calling for her head; it was almost too much to fathom.

Jegra tried her best to give Raphine a comforting look, but with what they just learned, things seemed the direst they'd been since Jegra had slipped into that coma.

When the Lord Emperor stepped up to the podium, Jegra clasped her hands in front of her and stepped to the side, dutifully supporting her husband. Those in attendance watched with great suspense as they waited for the emperor's speech.

Lord Emperor Dakroth put a fist to his mouth, cleared his throat, and then, leaning into the microphone, opened his mouth to address the startling revelation that had just shaken the entire galaxy.

"People of Dagon Prime, I don't know about you, but I'm fed up with being pushed around. Enough is enough. That is why, instead of giving in to The Voice's threats and demands, I ask you to heed my words. I will match the traitor Onelle Te'Legra Agnar's one trillion credit bounty with one of my own—bring me her smug, grinning head on a pike, and I won't only pay the trillion credits in full, but I'll give you a complete royal pardon for any previous transgressions that might be dogging your good names."

Staring long and hard at the camera, as if he were peering out at her, he added, "You picked the wrong empire to invade. You picked the wrong emperor to challenge. And you picked the wrong people to piss off!"

Cheers erupted all across Dagon Prime and all the worlds of the Dagon Empire. Their emperor was championing them. For the first time in their collective memories, the Lord Emperor himself was standing in their corner—rallying them to a unified cause.

Emperor Dakroth brushed down his royal dress uniform and paused, letting the cheers die down naturally before resuming his speech.

"I've listened to your words, Voice of H'aaztre, now hear mine. You don't intimidate me. I don't care if you think yourself a god. I don't even care if you're just a puppet on a string, doing your master's bidding. You wanted my attention? Well, now you have it. And I am coming for you. First you, then your army, and then H'aaztre himself. And so is the whole bleeding galaxy! Do you hear me?" Dakroth pointed at the camera and wagged his finger angrily. "You wanted a war? Well, now you have one!"

Dakroth spun dramatically on his heels and stormed back to toward the palace. Jegra gestured for Raphine to accompany her and, sidling up to one another, they quickly fell in line and trailed after Dakroth, the Imperial Guards closing rank behind them.

The people's cheers soared to the skies and a sound never heard before in the entire existence of the planet echoed all the way to the heavens: the sound of four billion voices joining one another in support of their ruler, of Jegra, and of the inevitable war that was at hand.

As they made their way back into the palace, Jegra and Raphine paused beneath the archway and looked back at the cheering throng of people.

"Are you ready for this war?" Raphine asked, turning her inquisitive gaze to the empress.

Jegra didn't return her look but, rather, kept her gaze fixed on the blue faces of the Dagon people.

"War, I'm afraid, is inevitable while we wish to defend our lives against a destroyer who threatens to tear us asunder and bring ruin to everything that we hold dear. And here we are, ready to let slip the dogs of war once more. Am I ready? Nobody is ever truly ready for war. Not even the conquerors. I suppose that is the inevitable truth of our existence. But there can be no greater glory in this life than fighting for something worth dying for."

Finally, Jegra turned to Raphine, her gaze settling on the young, green-skinned woman, a sagacious and somewhat uplifting smile forming on her burnt umber painted lips.

"Is all this worth fighting for, though?" Raphine asked, glancing back out at the city that filled the valley at the foot of the great palace. "Are they?"

Jegra's warm touch upon her left bosom brought her gaze back around. The empress smiled at her as she pressed her hand upon Raphine's heart.

"This is worth fighting for. And, maybe I'm foolish for believing in such fine things as peace, freedom, and equality, but these are what matter to me, because in everything I've seen they're the only weapons we have against evil. And above all else...I believe in love. These, I think you'll find, are worth fighting a thousand wars."

BOOK 4
EPILOGUE

Space and time distorted, the stars warped and then cascaded toward a central mass, as though they were all being sucked down into a funnel. The gravity well grew deeper and denser until a blinding flash followed by an aftershock that kicked out an energy ring like a supernova going off. The energy ring raced away from the radiant golden squid entity that had manifested in the middle of an uncharted sector.

La'Garren hovered for a bit in orbit of the purple and green world. Bright blue flashes sparked on the surface as though a storm was raging in multiple hemispheres all at once. But they quickly dissipated again.

His tentacles probing the space around him, he finally sank into the atmosphere and descended toward the planet. As he broke through the cloud cover, the lightning storm appeared to be giant electrical arcs leaping from mammoth crystals the size of thirty story buildings. La'Garren flew between the crystals, some emerald, some topaz, others a deep ruby red. Another electrical arc danced over La'Garren who flew casually beneath the raging electrical discharges.

Several kilometers later, a valley dipped down and the crystals multiplied by several hundred. Then by the thousands until the very terrain bellow looked like the inside of an amethyst. Only, with the array of colors, it was like looking at a multi-colored rainbow amethyst.

The crystals all thrummed and vibrated to certain melodic tones as La'Garren flew passed them. It almost seemed as though they were singing to him.

At the center of the outcropping was a massive crystal in both girth and height. Its very tip was so massive that it looked like the ancient pyramids of Vallorian City on Nyctan. La'Garren flew closer and closer, noting that as he did, the electrical discharges began firing more rapidly. Before he could even reach the central obelisk, a thunderous sound wave crashed into him and sent him freewheeling backward.

La'Garren righted himself as another loud wave rushed over him. This time it was less shocking and the decibels had dropped considerably. Finally, a third wave came and with it a voice. A voice which seemed to speak directly into his mind in his own language.

Little one, you are far from home. What brings you to Kruos?

La'Garren sunk down, one of his wavering tentacles floating toward one of the smaller crystals. When he touched it, the crystal warmed with an infusion of energy and a small electrical spark leaped from it to a larger crystal, and then from that crystal all the way along the rows of crystals until the energy ran up the body of the massive crystal at the center of the crystalline garden.

We see, boomed the voice. It seemed to emanate directly from the crystal's inner energy. Each sound wave arose from the harmonic vibrations of various crystals, all of them working in tandem to produce tones that carried their message, like a song carried on the breeze. The crystals themselves were talking to La'Garren.

You've journeyed all this way to ask for our help. So that you may help your friends? This altruistic predisposition impresses us, and we find no objection to your request. Our answer is, yes. We will help you and your friends, little one.

A tremor shook the crystals and then, the very ground split open. A new protrusion rose up and it was a bright red Dygra crystal.

This crystal, which is a part of Kruos and the Great Dygra, contains indescribable power. Use it wisely, for not only can it spark life into existence, it can also extinguish it.

La'Garren's numerous tentacles wrapped themselves around the slender crystal and with a glass like clink, the crystal fractured and broke off in La'Garren's arms.

Weighted down by the hefty size of it, he began dropping in altitude. His body, exerting more energy to compensate, began to glow bright yellow with a radiant energy and he flew up. Another tentacle brushed one of the nearby emerald crystals and La'Garren turned and flew away. As he departed Kruos, the voice followed him up into the sky.

You're welcome.

Once he found himself back in orbit, La'Garren did one more pass of the sparkling planet. As he approached the atmosphere, it all became clear to him. The electrical arcs weren't storms. They were the discharges of a planet sized neural network that was linked together by the crystals.

The entire planet of Kruos was sentient.

La'Garren picked up speed, using Kruos's gravitational well to slingshot himself back toward home. As he rounded the planet, his body lit up with golden light that poured out of him and into the darkness of space. Then, in another blinding flash of light, he jumped out of the system, the red Dygra crystal he'd procured clutched safely to his underbelly.

The glowing light of La'Garren faded into the heavens and the crystals all died down to a dimly lit glow. They stayed this way for a while and then they all began to pulse.

Each pulse had a slow, rhythmic, and almost soothing quality to it. Then, incrementally, their collective pulsating grew quicker and more frenetic.

A ripple wavered over the dark glittering sand and then a humanoid figure decloaked, the shimmer melting away to reveal a navy blue and charcoal gray EV suit fitted to a feminine form which, in turn, stood in the middle of the large clearing surveying the alien terrain.

The astronaut's visor was reflective gold and reflected the rainbow colors of the various crystals and their pulsing lights. The form-fitted suit was compact and the armor plating and materials seemed to be made with a technology light years beyond anything currently available.

Each step left boot prints in the soft soil and the astronaut bent down and took a soil sample. After that she took a reading of the air and of the radiation levels of this world.

Somehow, although she didn't know how, this crystalline planet had a breathable atmosphere. Maybe underground vents, perhaps hot springs with oxygen producing algae that shot up steam from one of the thousands of fissures she detected on her scanners. Whatever the cause, however, the oxygen rich atmosphere was optimal for breathing.

She turned and took a step toward the giant crystal protruding from the outcrop in the central region of the crystalline growth. The closer the female astronaut came to the large crystal, the faster and more frenetic the other crystals pulsed.

At the same time, they vibrated too with increasing pitch and frequency. In fact, it seemed for each step she took nearer to the primary crystal, the more the crystals seemed to grow agitated.

Soon they were humming loudly enough that she could pick up their sounds inside her helmet. She ignored their vibrating warnings and continued to cautiously walk toward the central crystal, the humming growing steadily with every step until it turned into a high pitch whine. When she was about fifty meters from the central column, the shrill noise increased in both decibel and frequency until all that filled her ears was a crippling tinnitus that would not relent.

The high-pitch screaming of the crystals all vibrating in such a way that they literally erected a sound barrier that forced her to take a step back. As she did so, the crystals vigorous vibrating died down substantially. Curious, she took another step back and the debilitating sound became a soft rhythmic hum again. It had an almost song-like quality to it.

The astronaut with golden visor tilted her head back and looked up at the giant glowing crystal at the center. If crystals of Kruos had a leader, she assumed this must be it. She stared for a while and then, very slowly, reached up to her helmet and tapped a button on the side.

Automatically, the helmet seemed to fragment with a series of fracture lines. Each fragment, however, seemed to fold up into the previous, and one by one the pieces folded away from the woman's face and retracted themselves back into the back of the suit just at the base of her neck.

Gray hair tied in a bun adorned her head and she peered up with old, wise eyes replete with crow's feet. Smiling up at the massive crystal, her face was beautiful and youthful looking, even though she was clearly approaching her late sixties. Luckily though, her eyes hadn't lost any of their color and remained a dark and smoldering walnut brown.

The crystal pulsed in an unusual manner and the woman laughed out loud. "I understood that," she said, tapping her temple with her gloved hand.

In response, the crystal pulsed and vibrated again, resonating with different harmonics. It sounded as though it were playing melodies on crystal wine glasses. But even though such a form of communication was expressly alien to her, with every melodic intonation, she seemed to understand as though it were speaking her very own native tongue.

The woman smiled and tilted her hips as she rested her hands on them. "So, you're the great Dygra," she said aloud. "I have heard stories about you. The most ancient of beings in the entire universe."

Again, the crystal played its prosodic melodies and the woman smiled wider as though it had said something funny.

"No, I'm not here to destroy you," she reassured the crystalline entity. Almost immediately after receiving her answer, the melodies became chipper and more optimistic sounding.

"Apologies," she said, her eyes narrowing as she smiled. "I didn't mean for my harmony to interfere with yours." She pulled a small shard of an old, cracked burgundy crystal out of a pouch on her pocket and held it out. "I need you to revitalize this."

All the crystals started pulsing frantically and the shrill noise between her ears grew to migraine inducing levels. When the woman shouted "Stop! You're hurting me," the crystals quickly died down again.

She took a step toward the massive crystal at the center, easing forward on one foot and watching to make sure she didn't startle it. She knew it could sense her vibrations and so any sudden movements would alert it to an imminent threat.

This time the crystals didn't react. They merely remained steady in their song. She drew close and, then, bending down, removed some of the glittering dark soil which seemed to be made of crystal dust from eons and eons of shattered crystals and whatever other strange geology thrived on this world. She dug a small hole and planted her crystal fragment inside.

After packing some soil on top of the crystal she slowly rose to her feet and took a few steps back and watched as the crystals all around her pulsed in strange rhythms. About thirty seconds passed when, unexpectedly, a new crystal sprouted from the ground. It was no bigger than a beanstalk, but it flashed a brilliant hot pink.

All the crystals began to vibrate in strange ways. The harmony they once had changed to a discordant cacophony. Eventually, however, they reharmonized in a manner that almost sounded like speech.

She listened carefully and in due course their words became clear. The vibrations floated through the air and mimicked, to the best of their ability, human speech.

"Old lady..." was the first part. The second word that the crystals had managed to utter in their mimicry of language was a name. A name the woman hadn't heard in a very long time. "Jegra."

"Yes," she said, brushing a lose strand of gray hair out of her eyes and tucking it back behind her right ear. "I am an old lady. That tends to happen when you're three hundred years old."

The crystals flashed random colors and tones and Jegra had to steady herself because the sounds and vibrations were so foreign that they messed with her inner ear and caused her to lose her balance.

"No," she said. "I've come back in time through a wormhole to warn my younger self not to trust H'aaztre's words. His promise of lenience is a lie. I have to warn her that if she surrenders herself, like I did, he still will kill everyone that...I...she...ever held dear."

There was a brief pause as she grappled with her grief, then, taking in a deep breath, she continued.

"I may have lost everything, but it doesn't need to be that way for her. I can still change the future. I can save them all. But I need your help, Great Dygra. I need you to bond your power to me one last time so that I may have the strength to finish this bloody war once and for all."

BOOK FOUR
FINIS

THE CHRONICLES OF

JEGRA

GALAXY AT WAR

1

Three hundred years ago the Commonwealth crumbled. An alliance of eight great empires shattered like a precious gem fractured by the pressures of a million eons of tension all coming to a head. And, then, in the cosmic blink of an eye, everything was lost forever.

The greatest of them, the Dagon Empire, weakened by endless wars and imperial expansion, faltered and left a power vacuum. This allowed for an evil force from another universe to take root and infest the galaxy. An ancient entity known as H'aaztre of Aldebaran, re-emerged with a single-minded mission to destroy the universe and recreate it in His image.

The hope of freedom rested with the prophecy of a woman destined to come from a distant world to lead a rebellion that would rise up to defy this ancient evil. Called the Daughter of Sol, one such woman fitting the hallowed description did arise. It was she who was able to finally bring H'aaztre to a standstill; her strength of will proved to be an immovable object which he could not overcome.

But the cost of victory was great. And, after the Great War of Light, as it had come to be known, the galaxy lay in ruin. Struggling to piece itself back together, new factions emerged to replace the once great cosmic alliance. Not all of them were just, however, and numerous worlds became co-opted into spheres of power and corruption.

Chaos and lawlessness reigned supreme. Justice was only a fading memory from a bygone era of peace and prosperity that the galaxy would likely never see again.

For Jegra Alakandra, however, everything else was pretty much as it had always been. There was always another galactic tyrant to replace the previous one, always another corrupted empire to topple. As ever, another oppressed people cried out for liberation.

But at three hundred forty-seven years old, she was finding it rather difficult to give a damn about any of that anymore.

"Who writes this rubbish?" Jegra mumbled to herself and tossed the holopad of the latest galactic hit, *The Savage Jegra: Vol. IX*, onto the console beside her.

After the Great War, she'd become something of a legend, and a popular novelization of her adventures manifested shortly after her retirement. She didn't know who wrote these far-fetched tales, but they were highly exaggerated and focused way too much on her sexual exploits for her taste.

She let out a sigh and leaned back in her seat, stretching her arms over her head. One thing the novels had gotten correct, however, was how harrowing it had all been and how deeply scarred the trauma of her past had left her. It wasn't something one simply "got over."

In fact, she was finding that the only way to combat the miserable voices that haunted her conscience was to drown all ghosts' cries in endless bottles of the crimson liquor called Nova Centauri Red.

Although rather pricey and hard to come by, it was worth getting one's hands on. It always went down smoothly, so easy to imbibe that, like a fine brandy, you never realized exactly how much you'd had.

She closed her eyes and took in a deep breath. She'd accomplished much in her three-hundred plus years, but now she seemed to be cruising through life on autopilot. How long she'd go on living, she didn't know; it wasn't something she dwelt upon. It wasn't fun, like life in the old days. She'd lost her taste for adventure.

While her exploits lived on in the stories of *The Savage Jegra* and in the archived televid footage of her gladiatorial matches, the silver-haired vixen with a few more lines around her eyes, a few more wrinkles across her forehead, preferred not to draw attention to herself.

As for the fame of being the champion of the arena, she'd put all that behind her. Besides, it was Gamagor Dar'Vek's great, great, great, great granddaughter, Evelangor, who was reigning champion now. And she pandered to the crowds just as much as Jegra ever had.

These days, Jegra preferred to hang out in unassuming, backwater dives, drinking away the memories of her past. Out on the fringes of the galaxy, very few people knew who she was anymore, with the exception of die-hard gladiator-heads who loved the entire history of the tournaments and held high esteem for what they deemed the golden age of the *Intergalactic Gladiatorial Syndicate*. But IGS had become a pale imitation of what it once was and acted more as a booking agency for gladiators these days.

Instead of being slaves to the arena, all modern gladiators were volunteers. Mostly bloodthirsty ex-cons and psychopaths all chasing their fifteen minutes of fame. Very few pure athletes ever appeared these days because nobody ever had to fight to survive—not like Jegra had once had to do. No, these days a gladiator could throw in the towel at any time. Which made for far too many anti-climactic matches, in Jegra's opinion.

Times change, though. Things change. And she preferred the anonymity which, ironically, came with a past that was larger than life. People who recognized her doubted their eyes; what they saw never stacked up to the legends about the great savior of the galaxy.

In the end, it was all just bittersweet memories. She'd given everything she had to bring peace to the galaxy, and it had blown up in her face. Everywhere she went, she met nothing but assholes. It was as if the universe simply liked to breed them, like a neglected garden sprouts weeds with abandon.

This seemed a universal fact, which is why she'd all but given up caring. And, in her impoverished state of depression, she looked forward to the next bottle of Nova Centauri Red over everything else.

Jegra sighed at the emptiness around her, knowing she'd soon be in space traffic and back amongst the living. She wore a black suede jacket over a brown leather corset; her denim hotpants were ripped across the thighs and buttocks, revealing tantalizing peaks of her sun-kissed skin.

She swung her legs off her console and sat up. Leaning over the blinking lights and buttons, she plugged in her landing coordinates and then let the autopilot handle the rest.

Still stiff, she stretched again, pressing her hands against the small of her back and leaning backward as far as she could manage without toppling over. The stiffness receded, and she reached up and touched the headrest of her leather seat and smiled to herself.

About the only thing she valued anymore was her ship. She'd christened it the *Valencia*, in memory of Danica. Jegra shook the thought from her mind and rubbed her thumb under her eye to brush away the rogue tear. Like she said, *bittersweet memories.*

Then she grabbed her nearly empty bottle of Nova Centauri Red from where it sat on the console, kicked her head back, and lapped up the last few drops of the glorious liquor.

The fire of the brandy warmed her belly and she belched out loudly as she scratched an itch on her right butt cheek.

A little lightheaded, she swayed as she stepped out into the corridor, pausing to catch her balance before heading down the circular passage that wrapped itself around the ship's core. Her quarters were in the aft portion of the ship and, as she passed the engineering bay windows, she took a peek at the hyperborean drive running her ship. It looked old, but it was a workhorse of an engine. *Don't make them like that anymore,* she reflected.

Finally, she came to her quarters and tossed her long white hair over her shoulders. The platinum color had replaced her original chestnut; it had happened on her one-hundred and twenty-first birthday. The color just evaporated, and all that was left was silver.

A glimpse of herself in the mirror reminded her that, although her aging had slowed to a *vorpian snail's* crawl, she could definitely see an older self behind her eyes. Luckily, she still retained her physical prowess and outward beauty; she didn't look a day over...*fifty-two-ish*, she thought. But, deep down in her bones, she definitely felt like Old Lady Jegra.

As she gathered up her things, she felt the ship set down on the dusty, korridium mining planet of *Pentanox*. Slinging a rucksack over her shoulder, she half-drunkenly headed back down the corridor to the cargo bay.

She waited for the loading ramp of the gondola section of the ship's underbelly to slowly open before exiting. Proceeding down the ramp before it even managed to clank down onto the rocky surface outside, she hopped out, her loosely tied boots crunching as they landed on coarse gravel.

She draped a laurel colored tunic over her bare, angular shoulders to help shield her from the biting dust storms of Pentanox and pulled up the hood. The air was thick with silicate that sparkled like glitter in the haze of the yellowish-orange dust. She wrapped her face with a scarf she wore around her neck to help protect her from inhaling the jagged fiberglass like fibers of the sand.

"I hope they have some nice brandy," she mumbled to herself through her scarf as she began her long walk toward the dusty village that sat in the distance. She was growing tired of all the micro-ales and turpentine liquors that tasted like piss. Which is why she always shelled out her hard-earned credits for the good stuff whenever she could find it.

The whole town was constructed from corrugated tin and welded steel and looked like a second-rate hovel. But most mining towns beyond the Outer Rim did. And this one was no exception. It was just further out than anywhere she'd previously visited, meaning it was all new frontier.

It never ceased to amaze her, though, how so many of the places she encountered far from home always seemed so familiar. Regardless of what aliens she encountered, or what intelligent beings she came across, people were still people. And most were still assholes. Everything else, whatever differences that may exist between all the lifeforms she'd ever encountered, given enough time, just blended into the background.

Still, refilling her supply of alcohol wasn't the only reason she'd come here to Pentanox. The other, and, perhaps, more important reason, was that it was the only planet in the system with an Obsidian Gate.

Obsidian Gates were a recent archeological find, a galactic game-changer, really. They consisted of a series of ancient, wormhole-based jump gates, and popular speculation was that only a fraction had yet been uncovered. The technology, left by an alien race long since extinct, allowed one to instantly transport oneself from one portal to another.

What's more, the Obsidian Gates were infinitely more efficient and quite a bit faster and more reliable than traditional teleporters. The downside was, the code hadn't quite been cracked yet; they seemed to pop up on random worlds with no rhyme or reason to their location or purpose there.

Jegra didn't know if the Obsidian Gate on Pentanox was operational, but she needed it to be. It was the only one she knew of in this system, and she didn't want to make the eight-month journey to the neighboring system to use theirs.

In any case, first things were first. She needed to be sloshed before she took on any serious work.

She swayed down the sparse main street of what resembled a futuristic frontier town right out of a Western. Upon finding the pub, a place called *Zordak's*, she stumbled through the entrance and scanned the unsmiling faces that stared back at her.

The regulars, long time patrons by the looks of it, eyed her up and down with uneasy gazes. When she undid her cloak, her massive cleavage swelling in the v-cut of her bodice, people looked away.

She sauntered over to the bar and flung her tunic casually across the barstool, taking up extra space to ensure she wasn't bothered by some half-drunken nitwit wanting to get into her pants, and then settled down onto the one beside it. "A pint of Brilaxian ale, if you have it."

A mug of green liquid, which practically glowed, slid down the bar and she caught it in her hand. She downed the entire pint in one go and then let out a wet sounding belch.

Jegra wiped her mouth with the back of her hand and, in a loud voice, demanded another. "Barkeep, keep them coming!"

A tall, strikingly handsome man dressed in fine threads appeared beside her and leaned on the bar, his eyes slithering up and down her figure.

"And what, may I be so bold as to pry, is such a fine and elegant woman such as yourself doing in these galactic boondocks?" the young man inquired.

When her second drink came, she took a sip, and then, without looking at him, Jegra answered, "I appreciate the compliment, but I won't be sleeping with you."

Surprised by her blunt, unorthodox response, the young man merely chuckled to himself. "The thought hadn't crossed my mind, I assure you…miss?"

Jegra knew he was fishing for her name, but continued playing coy and smiled without answering.

"Suit yourself," he said, turning away to regard the other patrons in the bar.

She sighed and looked over, planning to tell him to get lost. But as soon as she set eyes on him, she forgot about any lingering irritation.

Here was this demigod, approximately six-foot-three, eyes that were as cool as brushed steel, and shoulder length flowing black hair—but, she assumed, he was *human.*

She had never seen another human this far out from the galactic core. Her curiosity piqued, she asked, "And who, pray tell, might you be? I haven't seen you around before."

"The name is Alendar. I'm what you might call a wanderer."

"Aren't we all?" Jegra turned back to her drink and took a long swig of her ale then stifled another loud burp.

"Let me tell you what. If I can guess your name, you let me buy you the next one." He nodded down at her drink and she shrugged, as if to say *what could it hurt?* After all, it was a win-win for her.

"Alright then," she said, swiveling around on the barstool to get a better look at him. She crossed her legs in a lady-like fashion, resting her elbow on the counter and her chin on her open palm. "You have yourself a deal."

"You're Jegra Alakandra," he said, a sly grin trying to conceal the fact that, judging by the look on her face, he'd gotten it in one.

She shot Alendar a sideways glance and asked, "Read minds, do you?"

"No, nothing like that," he chuckled. Alendar leaned back, placing his elbows behind him, on the counter, and scanned the hung-over faces of the patrons. "I am just a knowledgeable man, Ms. Alakandra."

Jegra swiveled in her chair and stared at him long and hard.

"Don't be so surprised," he laughed. "Half the galaxy knows who you are."

"Tell me, Alendar, are you a descendant of one of the Mars survivors?"

"No, no," he said, waving a hand as if to dismiss the notion. "I was one of the early asteroid miners back in the late twenty-first century. Worked for Archer Industries Interstellar Mining Group, AIMG, for short."

"Never heard of it," she said, turning her attention back to her drink. She ran a slender finger along the lip of her mug and made the synthetic crystal glass sing for a moment.

He shrugged before continuing on with his story. "At any rate, there was a...mishap on one of the asteroids; about a dozen of us got blown clean off the rock and out into space. About ten hours later, my oxygen warning went off and I resigned myself to a quiet, uneventful death. A Dragonian cruiser using an illegal cloak picked me up, just in time."

"Poachers," Jegra mumbled under her breath.

Alendar smiled. "Are you sure you're not the one who can read minds, Ms. Alakandra?"

She made a tart face and shook her head. "You make it sound like I'm some old schoolmarm."

"Sorry," he apologized. His tone genuine, he slid a hand across the counter and placed it over hers. "Jegra, then?"

She looked down at his hand, deliberated whether to break free of it or just break it. Ultimately, her curiosity got the better of her and she decided to see where this was going; she would allow the touch—for now. She took another drink.

"Unlike you, however," he continued, leaning back on the counter again, "I wasn't sold into the Arena. Rather, I was sold to a collector of rare alien species."

"Let me guess...Vorgalen?"

"You know of him?"

"I've run across him a few times. Let's just say the meetings never ended well…for him."

"I see. I'm afraid," Alendar said, taking a moment to compose himself, "I wasn't so lucky. I was put in crystalline stasis for over three-hundred years, as a, well, a trophy piece."

"How'd you escape?" Jegra asked, her curiosity in the man's tale beginning to grow. At least he wasn't boring; she'd give him that much.

"A cargo ship was transferring some of Vorgalen's prized possessions to his new Imperium Cruiser when they came under attack by marauders. Space Pirates, active on the fringe worlds, ransacked everything they could get their hands on and took my stasis pod along with the rest of their spoils. The next thing I know, I'm coming out of a deep-sleep, staring up into the face of the Pirate Queen Li'lek Zira Baroco the VII. She brought me onto her crew as a hired hand, and there I learned the finer side of intergalactic piracy."

"So, you're a thief?"

"No more so than you're a drunk," he rejoined.

"Touché," Jegra replied, raising her glass to him. She downed the last of the ale and held the mug up to the bartender and pointed at it, signaling she needed a refill.

Alendar continued on with his story. "When I couldn't find any other humans, I began researching what happened to my people. That's when I learned about you. The Great Exodus, as the history books call it. The greatest rescue mission ever. You single handedly saved the human race. Gave us a fighting chance as a species on the verge of extinction."

Jegra balked at his version of events and was about to educate Alendar on what really happened when her drink arrived. She quickly forgot what she was about to say, and washed away any interest in reliving her past.

"I suppose," the young man said, rubbing his fingers through his thick main of black hair, "I've taken up too much of your time. It was nice meeting you, Jegra." Alendar touched his fingers to his brow and gave her an informal salute.

He was about to head off when Jegra reached out and grabbed him by the arm. "Wait."

Alendar raised an eyebrow and turned to her with a suave look and a warm glimmer in his eye. "Yes?" he asked, his eyes roving up and down her amazing figure.

"Maybe we could…?" Jegra let him fill in the blanks. She let go of his arm and went back to drowning her sorrows in her ale as she waited for his reply.

"Barkeep," Alendar called out, his eyes never once diverting from Jegra's ample cleavage, "a room for the night, if you'd be so kind. Make it your finest suite."

The bartender returned with a keycard and slid it across the counter. Looking at Jegra, Alendar held out his hand to her and asked, "Shall we?"

"I thought you'd never ask." Jegra slammed her mug down on the table and then showed her wrist. Her holovid turned on, glitched a bit, the image wavering, cutting out, then solidifying again. "This is for whatever I owe plus the room."

The barkeep scanned her wrist with the small glowing gem that was imbedded in his, and then nodded at her once the transaction was complete.

Jegra stood up a little too fast and realized all too late that her legs had turned to rubber. A dizzy spell snuck up on her, compounding matters, and before she knew it, her knees buckled and she nearly toppled over. To her surprise, Alendar swooped in and caught her from behind. She looked up at him and smiled.

"My hero," she said, drunkenly.

"Let me help you to your room," he said, setting her back on her feet. His hands slid down to her waist as he helped steady her.

"I should tell you now, pirate, I have nothing to steal but the clothes on my back."

He laughed and fetched her cloak from the nearby stool before placing his hand on her side again and helping her to the back stairs. "I may be a thief, it's true. But I'm no scoundrel," he assured her.

"A gentleman, are you?" she asked.

"Let's hope not," he replied with a laugh. This bad-boy edge compelled her to smile and she batted her eyes at him.

They swayed down the hallway and found their room. Once inside, Alendar helped her lay down on the bed.

Slowly, he ran his hands down her shoulders, to her thighs, and down the length of her legs. He helped her slip off her boots, removing them one boot at a time, like a regular Prince Charming. His eyes never once broke from her gaze as he helped to undress her.

Having removed her boots, he began to massage her feet. "Just relax," he said, his voice deep and soothing.

She could tell by the smoothness in his voice he'd done this a thousand times before, but she didn't care. She was lonely, tired, and hadn't been with anyone in ages.

His hands were firm, yet strong and rough enough to alert her to the fact that he was no mere pretty boy. Hands like that don't come without a bit of rigorous labor.

"You don't need to do that," said Jegra, smiling at him from over the rise and fall of her chest.

"Are you not an empress?" he asked. "Shall I not serve you and acquiesce to your every beck and call?"

"Oh, shut up and fuck me already," she said, reaching down and grabbing him by the collar. She drew him up and onto her, their lips crashing together. She quickly pulled off his shirt, taking in his taught physique as they kissed, and growing even more excited at the prospect of bedding this gorgeous man. Their hands undressed one another hungrily. They settled back onto the bed, and a thrust of his hips drew from her a sensuous moan like a terrible thirst had been quenched.

Fifteen minutes later they lay in bed panting as they gazed up at the ceiling. Their chests were glazed with the residue of their lusty encounter and, Jegra's leg resting across his, they took a moment to catch their breath.

Jegra was the first to break the silence. "That was…"

"Sorry," Alendar replied, cutting her off. "I usually have better stamina than that."

"You did just fine," Jegra said. "I'm a little rusty myself."

"Nonsense. You felt smoother than a well-greased Cambera shaft," he said.

"Thanks…I guess," she replied, looking over at him.

He smiled at her.

"Are you thinking what I'm thinking?" she asked.

"Depends," he said, climbing onto her and kissing her neck. Gradually, he worked his way down to her bellybutton, dappling her body with kisses as he went. Then, gently sliding between her thighs, he looked up at her probing gaze.

She smiled and watched as went down on her.

She threw her head back, the veins in her neck throbbing as pleasure coursed through her. "Don't stop," she said in a hot, wet voice.

As he buried his face even deeper into her, Jegra closed her eyes and imagined Dani's face. She missed her terribly, as she had for over two hundred years. But there wasn't much she could do about that. People aged and died. She, on the other hand, didn't—not really, anyway. It was complicated.

She aged so slowly that it was barely discernible. The passage of a hundred Earth years was only five years to her enhanced metabolism. Three-hundred plus years, then, was merely fifteen by her estimation. Which meant she had, possibly, a millennia still to live before she was properly old.

But the very thought of living that long filled her with dread. She'd already outlived almost everyone she ever cared about, and she was miserable for it. She would not wish this isolated, lonely existence on anyone.

The only one from her past still kicking about was the wily satyr, Grendok. He'd continued cloning himself over the years, and he was well into his tenth generation of enhanced clones, intact with all the memories and personality of the original, to boot. But seeing him always dredged up painful memories of those mortals not so inclined to live forever, so, she limited her contact with the satyr as much as possible.

Jegra must have fallen asleep mid-cunniligus, because the next thing she remembered was waking up in bed the next morning, face down on the sheets, buck naked and with a puddle of drool slowing soaking into her pillow.

After staring at the wall for a while, she sat up, wiped the excess saliva from her chin with the back of her hand, and basked in the warm morning rays beaming into her room. Alendar was nowhere to be found, but she figured it was probably for the better. She really wasn't a morning-after kind of girl.

That's when she heard the sound of all-too-familiar plasma-ion thrusters roaring to life. Jumping up, she ran over to the window and promptly drew the curtains, only to find her ship, the *Valencia*, slowly rising up into the air. Its plasma-ion drive thruster burning hot blue, the ship kicked up a veritable dust storm in its downdraft.

"*No, no, no, dammit!*" Jegra cursed. Without wasting another nanosecond in this dump, she spun around and quickly gathered her clothes in her arms, though, time being of the essence, she didn't bother to dress. Instead, she dashed out of her room wearing nothing but a frown.

Her long legs stretched out in front of her as she darted down the hall and scrambled down the stairs, nearly crashing into a housekeeping android at the bottom. The robotic maid bleeped and chirped a mechanical warning at her, which she conveniently ignored. Narrowly dodging the chamberbot, she glanced around the saloon only to discover it was empty.

Outside was a different story, however. She burst through the front doors of the saloon and shot into the main street. She found it bustling with locals going about their daily business, and almost too bright, after the morning spent inside the dim interior.

Startled onlookers watched with astonished faces as the naked human raced through street. Her clothes wadded up in her arms, she was a stranger here, and quite unusual to them.

"Gradack!" Jegra stomped, looking up at her ship pulling away from the city and climbing high into the drab gray sky.

In a rage, she threw all her clothes at the ground, kicked dirt at them and growled, "Just fucking perfect."

Fists balled up tightly at her sides, she looked around at all the blinkered faces. "What? Haven't you ever seen a naked Terran before?" she shouted at them.

Not wanting any trouble, they all wisely looked away and continued about their business. Spinning around, she merely kicked dirt at her own clothes again and let loose under her breath a string of uncouth obscenities.

A throat cleared just over her shoulder, and she gradually turned around to find a four-armed Bulovian standing over her.

Bulovians were wiry, seven-feet tall, and were the spitting image of what science-fiction writers back on Earth used to imagine Martians would look like.

They had green skin with darker green sunspots and large eyes atop sweeping, oval heads. Four fingers per hand instead of five...and no real nose to speak of.

This one had on what appeared to be a cowboy hat and wore a kind of duster trench coat over a fine black vest with a gold watch chain leading from the pocket to the button it was clasped to.

The Bulovian tapped the star on his chest, signifying that he was the law around here, and Jegra let out a disgruntled sigh and puffed at a tuft of loose, silver hair.

"I can explain," Jegra stressed, hoping he'd hear her out.

Instead, the Bulovian sheriff raised a pair of magnetic shackles and gestured for her to turn around.

As the lawman clasped the shackles onto her wrists, Jegra groused in a sarcastic tone, "*Wonderful.* Just fucking wonderful."

2

The Commonwealth Alliance, three hundred years prior.

Blast marks scorched the sides of the walls of the docking arm and sparks rained down onto the korridium alloy deck plates then quickly fizzled out of existence. Grendok's hooves clapped against the metal floor as he leaped over his dead copy and landed in a crouch on the other side of the deceased satyr.

"Sorry, ole chap," he said, reaching into the left breast pocket of his clone's blue suede waistcoat and pulling out a communicator device, "but it would seem you've reached the end of the line. Enjoy the long sleep."

The only discernible difference between him and his dead doppelgänger was that his vest was burgundy. Other than that, they were virtually indistinguishable: white fleece beard, four-foot-eight stature, bovine face with black markings, cloven-hooves, an upright posture, anthropoid hands, and a couple of swept-back curving horns adorning the top of his head.

As heavy boot steps clamored up the corridor behind him, Grendok wasted no time. He promptly reached into his own vest and pulled out a weapon. Inspecting his communicator without looking up, he held out the blaster and let loose a slew of aimless shots.

The charged plasma bolts splashed the corridor's surfaces, leaving blackened carbon on the walls and floor. Not that it mattered much anyway–the entire station was a veritable junkyard of cannibalized starships held together by twice-recycled parts. It was a wonder anything worked at all. *A few more blemishes will only add character,* Grendok mused.

Another spray of sparks lit up the corridor as return fire came streaking down the tube of the docking arm. Ducking out of the way, Grendok grew fatigued by the doggedness of the three bounty hunters who pursued him.

Not wanting to kill the bounty hunters, as irritating as they were, Grendok crouched down off to the side of the corridor, took aim at the pipes that ran alongside air ducts above his pursuers, and fired.

The blast broke open a hot water vein and steam began to pour out into the hallway, providing a white-shroud of cover. The air ventilation system helped disperse it quickly, so it quickly filled the entire corridor.

Grendok fired off another round of shots into the billowing haze, forcing the trio of nimrods to duck into the inlet of an adjoining airlock for fear of getting vaporized. This momentary distraction allowed Grendok to skip away with hastened strides.

As he reached the end of the enclosed docking arm, Grendok paused briefly to admire the sleek new Seyferrian shuttlecraft poised there. Its elongated teardrop design and chrome anti-blaster coating glistened beneath the docking bay's running lights. *Nobody builds ships like the Seyfferians.*

Holding up the wireless communicator, he dialed in the access codes to the shuttle. The door bleated at him impatiently, and he retyped the code. But it still fussed and denied him access.

"Blasted Seyfferian encryption! You and your perfect three-tier protocols. You couldn't have picked a worse time to lock me out of my own ship."

"You there! Ssstop!" a booming voice welled up from the far end of the corridor.

Grendok ignored it. Hoping to rattle it into working order, he smacked the communicator device across the top with the palm of his hand and then tapped it against the side of airlock door for added measure.

"I said *ssstop!*" the disgruntled voice from down the hall reiterated.

Nettled by the constant string of interruptions, Grendok let out a long, fatigued sigh. Slowly, he turned his slatted eyes toward the trio of bounty hunters emerging from the misty corridor at the opposite end of the passage.

A musclebound, scaly, green Dragonian with well-worn body armor and an oversized blaster gripped in his four-digit hand shoved his two comrades aside and postured threateningly. He glowered at the satyr with lime-green reptilian eyes and an intimidating python-like brow.

Dragonians, Grendok lamented. *It had to be Dragonians.* Although not a fan of the warlike and gratuitously violent species, he did admire their warrior spirit and the drive that compelled them to never give up the hunt.

"Did you hear me, space-goat?! If so much as a single hair on that curlicue tail of yours twitchesss, I'm going to put a few more breathing holes in you. Capisce?"

"My good sir," Grendok said in his erudite fashion, "Although I have been known to traverse these galactic backwaters on occasion, you should know that I am not overly fond of the pejorative label 'space goat.' It sounds…how shall I put this…uncivilized. I, sir, am a noble *satyr* of Galliforn."

The Dragonian glanced at his two partners with an incredulous look. "Isss he lecturing me?" Nictitating eyes turned back toward Grendok. "Are you *lecturing* me, ssspace-goat?"

"Indeed, I am. And I'm glad to report your mental acuity is not as slow as we all first thought."

"You insolent little…" the brawny Dragonian growled. "If you weren't so valuable to me alive, I would have blasssted you to ashes already."

"Is that so?" Grendok asked amusedly.

As he kept the Dragonian preoccupied with idle chatter, his hands worked furiously trying to correct the malfunctioning communicator.

"Believe it, ssspace-goat," the Dragonian hissed. "Lucky for you, though, I ain't gonna blassst you just yet."

"That's wonderful news," Grendok chirped as the light on the airlock door to the ship turned green. "But, alas, I must be getting along now. Good luck to you, chaps; here is where we must part ways." Taking a deep bow, he added, "I bid you adieu."

With a pneumatic hiss, the airlock door behind him rolled open and, stowing his blaster inside his dapper vest, Grendok backed up, smoothly crossing the threshold. Once he was safely inside the confines of the ship's airlock, he winked at the Dragonian bounty hunters and slammed the hatch shut again.

The larger Dragonian raced up to the porthole window on the door and pointed a thick, clawed finger at the satyr. His nostrils fogging up the glass window with angry huffs, the lizard-man hissed, "You! Open thisss door, now!"

"No can do, friend," replied Grendok receding further into the safety of the ship. He tapped his brow and gave a casual two-finger salute to his would-be captors, bidding them farewell. Then, without so much as another word, he turned and sauntered into the main cabin and planted himself in the pilot's seat.

"Gradack!" the Dragonian cursed and slammed his fist on the glass window. That infuriating weasel of a goat had slipped right through his fingers…again.

Delighted by the success of his grand escape, Grendok chuckled to himself and sank down in his chair. Seated at the controls, he let his fingers dance across the console with finesse as he released the docking clamps.

Outside the hull, there was a resounding clunk and the clamps relinquished their hold on the small craft. The sleek shuttle tilted slightly starboard as it fired its maneuvering thrusters and pulled away from the docking port.

Gradually, the shuttle moved farther from the asteroid space station. The giant hunk of space-rock spiraled away from him at a measured counterclockwise rotation. As darkness surrounded his vessel, the flashy lights of the station receded into the depths of the star-spackled void, stretching out infinitely behind him. He suddenly got the feeling he wasn't alone. He reached for his blaster, but a cool, calm voice urged him to reconsider.

"I wouldn't do that if I were you…*space-goat.*"

Grendok slowly turned in his seat to find Raven Nightguard lounging in the co-pilot's chair opposite him. In his haste, he had completely neglected to see her sitting there when he'd come in.

She sat in a relaxed manner, her feet up on the dash, her blaster resting casually in her lap. It was trained on him with inexorable precision, though, and he knew if he made even just one wrong move the notorious bounty hunter wouldn't hesitate to vaporize him.

"Yes, well, if you ask me, that little *nom de plume* is growing a bit old," he said, glancing down at her weapon with trepidation.

Raven's enhanced body pulsed with circuitry just beneath her indigo skin. She tossed her purple and blue ombre hair over her left shoulder and looked at Grendok with amethyst eyes as crystal clear as the purple oceans of Dagon Prime. As always, her gaze was penetrating.

"Slowly and carefully, open your vest," she told him.

He complied. After all, this wasn't the kind of woman with whom you pushed your luck.

Raven Nightguard was famous throughout several systems as the bounty hunter with the most impressive capture rate; a near perfect track record, last he checked. If she came after you, it was a sure bet that your luck had plumb run out.

Cautiously, he looked back up into her eyes and held his vest open for her. She reached over and slid out his piece. While she leaned forward, he couldn't help but examine her womanly features, and noticed signs of further augmentation. "I see you've had some work done."

"Minor enhancements is all. Nothing major," she answered.

"By the way," he said, turning back to the controls and checking the monitors. "Where's that sleek little Corvette of yours?"

She grinned at him roguishly but didn't reply.

Grendok scratched his chin contemplatively for a moment and then, snapped his fingers as it came to him. "Oh-ho! You enhanced your ship as well. Let me guess. A type-9 cloaking device?"

A demure smile formed on her lips, but she still kept silent.

"Well! I see someone has been doing quite well for herself."

"Stall all you like, Grendok. There's still a two million credit bounty on your head, which I intend to collect."

He whistled in an impressed tone. "That much already?"

"I could get myself an X5 series battle droid for that kind of cred," she replied.

"I'm sure you could."

The smile lingered on her face a while longer, then, as it slowly faded, she stared at him seriously for a moment. "It's nothing personal, just business."

"Naturally," he replied. He turned to the viewscreen and fanned his hand across the swath of Percheron black sky painted with luminescent pin-pricks of distant stellar light. "It's a vast galaxy, my dear. There are unimaginable riches to be had."

"No hard feelings, then?"

He waved his hands to show that it wasn't a concern.

"Speaking of business, what have you got stowed that's so important it set off a code blue alert and a systemwide warrant for your arrest?" Raven said, nudging her chin toward the rear cargo hold.

"Oh that?!" Grendok hemmed and hawed as he tried to figure out a way to change the subject. "It's nothing. I can assure you. Just a misunderstanding. That's all."

Swiveling in his chair to face Raven, he steepled his fingers, leaned forward, and propped his chin up on his hands. He grinned sheepishly at her.

Raven slid her legs off the console and sat up. Her relaxed posture dissolved and her entire body language stiffened, as though it were speaking a much more formal dialect. Her blaster, too, awakened from its perch on her lap and met Grendok's more aggressive posture with one of its own.

"That happens a lot, does it?" Her smart-contact lenses zoomed in and tracked his facial movements, scanning him for any signs of duplicitous intent.

Grendok casually sat back in his seat and chortled lightly, stroking his beard. "It seems we've gotten off on the wrong foot here. Let's start over, shall we?"

"I'm listening," Raven said, urging him to proceed.

"If I am to divulge these rather sensitive matters, I ask only that you hear me out. What I have back there, Miss Nightguard, might benefit the both of us."

"Wheel and deal all you like, Grendok. But what's to prevent me from just bringing you in, collecting the bounty, and taking your precious cargo for myself?"

"You wouldn't dare," he gasped in astonishment.

"Look, if you have a better offer for me, I'm all ears. Otherwise we're done here." She refocused her aim onto his head to drive the message home. Her patience, after all, had its limits.

"Hold on—just a moment," he pleaded, fanning his hands in front of him as he beckoned for her to hold up. "How about I pay you ten million credits upon my safe arrival at Rivelon–cargo intact–and, as a show of good faith, I'll throw in half a dozen clones of your own to sweeten the pot."

"Ten million credits for being your escort?" Raven practically balked at the offer, thinking it too good to be true, but she kept her voice to a professional cool. "Why so generous all of a sudden? What's the catch?"

"No catch," Grendok replied. "Just a matter of professional courtesy. You scratch my back, I scratch yours."

Raven lowered her blaster as she mulled over the offer. The truth was, she wasn't likely to find a better deal than this all year. Besides, it was an easy take, and the syndicate never paid all that well anyway.

It didn't take her long to make up her mind. Ten million credits was ten million credits. Why, each clone cost at least as much, and here she was being offered six of her own.

Raven holstered her weapon and, sticking out her hand, answered, "You have yourself a deal."

Grendok let out a pent-up sigh of relief as the tension drained from him. "You won't regret this. Of that, I can assure you." He took her hand in his and shook with a renewed vigor.

After their handshake, she reached up with indigo fingers, nails varnished patent black, and slipped her hand beneath the layered tresses of her purple hair, brushing it to the side and revealing hot-pink underneath. She gently squeezed her earlobe once. A golden pulse of light running through the circuitry in her neck flared briefly then dissipated. "Did you get all that?"

"Indeed we did, Captain," a voice came back over the shuttle's comm.

"Drop the cloak and open the landing bay. We're coming aboard."

Grendok's eyes widened as the cosmic expanse outside the viewscreen began to waver and ripple unnaturally. Out of thin air, a sleek starship appeared. Not just any starship. Raven's ship. The *Skywend*.

"Remind me, again, how you got your hands on a top of the line Dagon Corvette fresh out of space dock?"

A wry smile formed on Raven's Prussian blue lips. "A girl doesn't kiss and tell."

"Very well, keep your little secret."

"I will," Raven said, a demure grin spreading across her face. She leaned back in her seat, crossed her legs, and regarded the satyr, who smiled back at her with his yellow toothed grin.

3

The Pentanox townsfolk watched their sheriff guide the naked female primate down the street and toward the local jail. A robotic horse whinnied and pulled over to the side of the road to let them pass. The sheriff merely tipped his hat at the horse's driver as an unspoken *thanks* for the small courtesy.

Although this wasn't the first walk of shame Jegra had ever taken, she did begin to feel her cheeks flush as she gradually grew more and more self-conscious.

Modesty was never her strong suit, but she realized the passersby gawking at her as though she were some common zoo animal had a degrading quality to it that made her regret how undignified she had been.

It also forced her to realize that she needed to sober up and get her shit together.

Ushered past the reinforced doorway of the local jail, the Bulovian lawman brought the naked Earth woman into a holding cell, shoved some blue workman's overalls into her arms, and then tapped the wall panel and put up the blue, shimmering security forcefield.

"You have a right to legal counsel," he informed her, "but I doubt any highfalutin' lawyer types would be willin' to come all the way out here to the ass-end of the galaxy for it. Pentanox ain't exactly a destination resort. Nothin' but miners, felons wanting to hide from the Imperium, and fools come out this far."

"I guess that makes me the latter," Jegra replied, slipping into the overalls. She zipped up the onesie, but the zipper got stuck upon the hump of her enormous chest, snagging midway over her J-cup sized tits.

Determined to try and make it work, she gave the zipper another few tugs, but it was no use. The geometry just didn't work in her favor. And, to make matters worse, the metal tab broke off in her fingers.

She let out a vexed sigh, seeing as half of her massive chest bulged out over the top of the overalls. At least her nipples were securely hidden by an elastic panel. Unable to do anything about it, she headed over to the cot that was built into the wall, and slouched down onto it.

"So, what's your name?" Jegra asked the Bulovian.

"I'm the honorable Constable Nikkota, at your service," he said, tipping his cowboy hat and turning to her. His gesture had been in vain, however, as she'd already tipped over onto the bed and was noisily snoring.

Nikkota shrugged and then left his prisoner to sleep off her drunkenness in her cell until tomorrow. After twenty-four hours, he'd have no choice but to release her back into the wild. Hopefully, she wouldn't be any more trouble…the last thing he needed was more trouble.

"Rise and shine, Your Grace," a gruff voice said.

Jegra's eyes cracked open and she mumbled something about a Black Friday sale on apricots and rolled over, turning her back to the glimmering forcefield.

She dozed off again, but the steady hum of the forcefield generators cutting out, followed by a warm hand on her shoulder roused her awake.

Without looking back at whomever was interrupting her beauty sleep, she snarled, "If you wanna keep that hand, you best remove it before I remove it for you."

"Oh, my dear Jegra—you're as feisty as ever, I see."

Recognizing the voice, she rolled over, wide-eyed and, upon seeing a familiar face, squealed with excitement. Sitting up, she reached out and embraced her age-old friend.

"Grendok!" she chirped, and, drawing him in, she squashed his face into her voluptuous chest, his eyes bulging ever so slightly as his muzzle was enveloped by her fleshy bosom.

The satyr wheezed, "I've missed you too, Your Grace."

She finally let go of him and, gathering himself, he brushed down his forest green suit. He checked the pocket watch that was clasped to his suede moss vest, and then promptly tucked it back into its rightful place again.

"What in all the blasted worlds are you doing here?" she asked excitedly, resting her hands on his shoulders and giving him an affectionate squeeze.

"I was about to ask you the same thing, Your Excellency."

"Please. It's just Jegra," she said, shooting him a stern look. "Has been for years. But, tell me old friend, what brings you out this far?"

He nodded. "I'm here on business," he relayed, and then let out a sigh, "but korridium sales aren't what they used to be. Not with the recent find of the Yagothon asteroid belt. It seems to be nothing but."

"Knowing you though, you surely must have your hands in numerous other business ventures."

"Multiple income streams, my dear. It's what's kept me in business all these centuries. But I turn the question back over to you, Jegra. What brings you to the farthest extremes of the outer spiral and to a forlorn, dusty ole rock like Pentanox, for that matter? There's nothing of value out here."

Jegra leaned forward and put her elbows on her knees and rested her chin on her clasped fingers.

"An Obsidian Gate," she informed him.

Grendok raised an eyebrow. "I see," he replied in a rather unenthused tone.

She narrowed her eyes at him as a look she knew all too well came over his face. "What's the wrong, old man?"

Grendok sighed. "Over the past fifty years it seems to me that you've been gradually becoming more and more obsessed with the idea that you can somehow use an Obsidian Gate to travel back in time."

"I must go back in time," Jegra said. "I have to convince my younger self not to make the same mistakes I did. Not to agree to H'aaztre's terms. It only ends in ruin and heartache."

Grendok looked down at the floor, his own memories weighing heavy on him. "Yes, well, it simply can't be done."

Jegra clutched the satyr by the collar and hoisted him off the floor with one hand. The security shield automatically raised itself when it sensed a violent threat, but Jegra merely charged through it, leaning in with her shoulder.

The shield stretched and then melted away as though it were flimsy as rice paper as she tore through. Slamming Grendok into the wall on the opposite side of the holding cell, she growled, "Don't tell me what can and cannot be done!"

Grendok coughed up blood, and Jegra, realizing she'd lost control, instantly felt remorse and promptly let go of him. He crumpled to the floor and she drew back, dismayed at what she'd done. "I'm…I'm so sorry," she said, cupping her mouth.

Constable Nikkota arrived on the scene with dual plasma blasters drawn. "Is everything all right in here Mr. Grendok, sir?"

Grendok slowly pushed himself up onto his feet and, in his usual gruff manner, raised a cautionary hand and said, "Everything is fine, constable. You may stand down."

"If you wish to press charges," the constable said, eyeing Jegra disapprovingly, "I'd be more than happy to throw this one back into lockup for you."

"I assure you, constable, that won't be necessary. In fact, I think I'll pay her bail and we'll be getting out of your hair."

"Suit yourself," he said, shooting Grendok a surprised look. "But I have to warn you, this one is a handful."

"You have no idea, Mr. Nikkota, at what an understatement that truly is."

Jegra almost laughed, but she held back, noting how Grendok seemed to be struggling after her loss of control. She'd actually hurt him, and, although it was an accident, she felt bad.

"Grendok, I'm…sorry."

He raised his hand again as if to say her words were unnecessary and then nodded at her to follow him. "Come along, my dear. Let's get you processed and off this dustball of a world."

As they strolled out of the prison and out onto the street, Mr. Nikkota folded his top two arms and leaned against the edge of the doorway. A toothpick dangled from his lips as he watched them leave, while his bottom two arms fiddled about with his Bowie knife, shaving off bits of his oversized fingernails, trimming them one finger at a time.

"I should have been clearer in my meaning," Grendok told Jegra, as they walked along the dusty street. "The Obsidian Gates aren't wormholes. At least, not in the traditional sense. They work more like quantum entanglement portals. They simply aren't capable of taking you back through time."

Relieved to be back in her own clothes again, she nodded as Grendok filled her in. "I see," she replied, clearly saddened.

"Don't give up hope, my dear. Perhaps, there's another way."

"You've found a stable wormhole?" Jegra asked, her eyes lighting up with excitement. She stopped and turned to face him, her face beaming with optimism.

He paused in the middle of the street and looked back at her. "I'll do you one better. I've found a wormhole generator."

"I had no idea such a thing existed," Jegra said, half beside herself in awe. This was, quite literally, the best news she'd received in more years than she cared to count.

"Well, technically, It does and it doesn't. I mean, it most certainly is *real*. But it simply can't drill into the fabric of spacetime. Not without a very specific power source."

"And what, pray tell, is this generator's power source?"

"Dark energy, naturally."

"That's a good thing, then. Right? I mean, we already know how to tap into the dark energy layer of spacetime to power our ships. So, we should be able to make this machine of yours work, right?"

"I'm afraid it's not quite that easy," he said, continuing up the street again. She quickly followed behind him. "We'd need to siphon a whole lot more dark energy than what's required to power a starship. By Pan's beard, we'd need to siphon more dark energy than there are stars in the entirety of the universe."

"So, you're basically saying it's impossible."

"No, not impossible," he informed her. "We know of at least one device in existence that can do this with ease."

Jegra paused in the middle of the street and watched as Grendok continued on ahead without her.

"Don't tell me..."

He looked back at her with a troubled look which only confirmed her worst fears.

"Aldebaran," she spoke in a hushed tone.

That despicable planet was the one place she didn't dare venture back to. She couldn't. Not after everything that had happened.

"It's the only way, I'm afraid," Grendok assured her. He waited a moment and then added, "But if you've changed your mind about going back, perhaps you can accompany me aboard my new ring world, Galliforn II, and join me for dinner?"

"I've been running for so long," she said. "Running from my past. Running from my future. I've been running for so long that sometimes I don't even know why I'm still running. All I know is, I'm tired. I'm tired and I just want to go home."

Grendok extended his hand to his oldest of friends and, in a soothing voice that sent chills of excitement through her entire body, he said, "Then, my dear, let's go home."

The nano-second her fingers touched his, golden light engulfed them. The very next moment they were standing aboard an Imperium Cruiser.

"Really? You stole an Imperium Cruiser?" she said, shooting him a curt glance.

Grendok shrugged. "I have found that people tend to steer clear of me when they think I'm with the Imperium. Otherwise, what can I say? Old habits die hard."

She laughed softly and then turned to look at the giant monitor sitting before them. On the screen, a massive ring world encircled a small golden ball of light. When she realized that the sphere of light was no ordinary star but, rather, Aldebaran itself, she gasped.

"You built a ring world around a ring world?"

"Aldebaran acts rather like a perpetual motion machine. I suppose it has something to do with keeping H'aaztre's network open across the multiverse. My scientists have studied it keenly for hundreds of years, but we could never crack the algorithms that allow it to establish stable wormholes." He paused for added effect and then added, "That is…until three weeks ago."

"What are you saying?" asked Jegra, turning back toward him. Her eyes widened as she focused intently on the satyr's face.

"I can send you back," he said, a sheepish grin spreading across his bovine lips.

Jegra folded her arms under her chest. "I'm sensing a big but."

"*But* it's a one-way trip, I'm afraid. We can tell it to go to *one* point. It will. But without another several hundred years to decipher the other half of the algorithm, we have no way to recall it back to the present."

"Couldn't you just reopen it again?"

"Yes, but if you try to jump through on your side, it will simply loop you back; you walk out of the very same spot you entered from."

"So, if I go back, then, I can never return?"

"That's correct," he said.

She smiled. Her smile was so bright and infectious he couldn't help but smile too. Almost as soon as he'd joined her in an ear-to-ear grin, however, she began crying.

"What's the matter, my dear?" He reached out and took her hand in his, patting it lightly to help try and console her.

She dropped to her knees and threw her arms around him. Embracing him, she whispered, "I've searched for so long...I'd almost given up hope."

"Hope is what sustains us," Grendok replied.

She sniffled and wiped the tears from her eyes. "Thank you, old friend. From the bottom of my heart. *Thank you.*"

"And it's a big heart at that," Grendok said, patting her left breast in such a way that it jiggled. She laughed and then playfully punched him in the arm. He staggered back about six steps before planting his hooves and skidding to a stop in the middle of the floor.

"One last adventure, old man?" Jegra replied affectionately, the crow's feet bunching up in the corners of her smiling eyes.

"One last adventure," he replied, still rubbing his shoulder.

Jegra rose back to her feet and turned to peer once more at the main display. Her wish had finally come true. She could finally go home. Even so, there was one last thing she needed to do first.

The guardian of the gate of Aldebaran was a being who'd been given great power, including immortality, by H'aaztre. Nobody who had ever been permitted to pass through the gate ever returned. It was, for all intents and purposes, a one-way trip. And those who tried to enter without permission were quickly cut down by this impenetrable guardian.

Jegra neither had permission or the desire to face the guardian. And, yet, despite her own apprehensions, she had to try. Even if it meant that only one of them would be leaving that room alive.

4

Raven Nightguard returned to her quarters, exhausted, and stripped down to her coral colored underwear. Letting out a long sigh, she fell forward and toppled onto her bed. Burying her face into her pillow, she reached up behind her back with one hand, and, contorting her arm, she unhinged the clasp of her brassiere.

It snapped open and she took in a deep breath of fresh air as a feeling of relief settled over her. Her entire body seemed to grow impossibly heavy as she sank into the comfort of her duvet. All she wanted to do was lay there until she descended to the realm of blissful sleep.

It was only a short time after Raven had drifted off when the proximity alarm of the ship unexpectedly sounded.

"What now?" she mumbled groggily as she wiped a strand of drool from the corner of her mouth with the back of her hand. Looking up at her clock, eyes half open, she saw that she'd only been asleep for about forty-seven minutes. Not exactly the satisfying rest she'd been hoping for.

She let out a groan and forced her somnolent limbs to move. She swung her legs over her bed and sat up, the straps of the brazier sliding off her shoulders. She didn't care; she let it fall off and then nudged it aside.

Still moving sluggishly as she did her best to wake up, she stretched out of the bed, went over to the wall, and gently touched her fingers to it. A hidden panel popped open, revealing a drawer full of clothes.

She rummaged around, trying her best not to mess up the neatly folded garments. She grabbed a charcoal-gray tank top and slipped it on over her head, stretching it tightly across her body. It clung to her voluptuous form like a second skin, her indigo cleavage swelling in such a manner that it easily filled the opening of the v-cut top.

She gave her shirt another tug and was brushing away the few remaining creases when, without warning, a harsh jolt nearly knocked her off her feet.

The shuddering echo that rang up and down the corridors of the ship snapped her awake—along with everyone else on the vessel—and she quickly slipped her feet into her boots and rushed out of her chambers.

Raven was halfway to the bridge when she met Gyllek in the corridor. An orange tuft of hair covered one of her bright green, feline eyes; the other one shone brightly in the dim lighting of the passageway.

"What in the thirteen dimensions of hyperspace was that?" Gyllek asked.

"I have no idea, but it sounded solid, as though something struck us."

"But the computer sets the ship on a precalculated flight plan that avoids any asteroid fields," Gyllek said. "And the long-range sensors would pick up space debris…the computer would have merely autocorrected our course for us or dropped us out of FTL."

"Exactly," Raven replied. "Which means the computer didn't have time to react. Something must have entered hyperspace at the same point and time we happened to be."

Both women arrived on the bridge to find Grendok standing alone at the center of the view portal, peering out at something. A strange golden light, similar to candlelight, filled the room. When Gyllek and Raven drew closer to the windows to see what the satyr was staring at, their mouths fell open with astonishment.

"What in the seven moons of Primea is that? It looks like…" Gyllek's voice trailed off as she staggered up alongside the satyr. Her cat-like ear twitched nervously as she peered out the ship's window, her face bathed in the same mysterious golden light.

Raven sank into her seat and began working the controls.

"Vessel of some kind," Grendok said, finishing Gyllek's sentence for her. "By the looks of it, it's quite ancient, too."

"But the size of it…it's simply not possible. I mean, physics-wise, it's an engineering impossibility. Nothing that big can withstand breaching the hyperspace barrier without losing all structural integrity."

"And yet…" Grendok said, nodding his head at the object looming outside the ship's window. "There it is."

Raven tapped the display readout and, then, slowly turned toward everyone with a staggered look. "It's three kilometers wide and…" she looked back down to double confirm, "and the length isn't even registering. Which means…"

"It's an orbital ring," Grendok said.

"But orbital rings cannot enter hyperspace," Gyllek interjected. "It's physically impossible. Each time it entered or exited hyperspace, it would create tsunamis and other natural disasters so cataclysmic that it would destroy all life on the world, making the entire concept of the ringworld a pointless exercise."

"Apparently not," he observed. "What we are looking at, my dear, is, well, *alien*. There's no other word for it."

"We're all aliens here, Grendok," Raven stated, pointing out the obvious. Her violet eyes flashed a hot pink then cooled back to their regular purple hue.

Waving a hand in frustration he grunted and said, "Oh, you know what I mean."

Raven tapped the panel on her console and checked some additional readouts of the super-structure. As she read the monitor, she folded her arms and bit her lower lip in contemplation.

"There. See that?" She pointed her finger up at a rectangular inlet along the rows of box-shaped formations jutting out like buildings running along the hull of the alien vessel. "That looks like a docking port."

Raven tapped a sequence onto the control panel and then said, "I'm taking us in to get a closer look."

The intercom chimed and Skuld's voice came up from the lower decks of the ship. "Captain, are you seeing what I'm seeing?"

"You mean that enormous orbital ring hanging in the middle of hyperspace? Yeah, we see it."

"Good. Just wanted to make sure I wasn't catching a case of cabin fever and losing my mind out here," he jested.

The comm cut off and everyone looked at one another with dumbstruck faces. Orbital rings weren't a new concept. The Seyfferians had built one. But this…this was something else.

Raven knew that the technology they were looking at was so far advanced that it made her state-of-the-art Corvette class battlecruiser look like the seafaring ships of old.

"So. Who wants to head on over and see if anyone's home?" Raven asked.

She turned and smiled at everyone, her arms still linked as she studied the reactions on their faces.

Grendok silently raised his hand and grinned. Gyllek stood adamantly shaking her head, *no*.

"Not me," she said emphatically. She crossed her arms to drive the point home. "There's no way in Helios will I ever go aboard an abandoned ghost ship."

"Come, now, my girl. Where's your sense of adventure?!"

"You ever hear the saying 'curiosity killed the satyr?' No? Well, now you have."

Grendok waved his hand in front of his face, shooing away her negativity. "Suit yourself. But I, for one, am more than keen to learn about what awaits us on the other side of those miraculous walls."

"When you find whatever it is that's over there and it wants to eat your face, or worse, mate with it," Gyllek quipped, arms still folded in disapproval, "don't say I didn't warn you."

"All right, all right," Raven said, bringing the *Skywend* into position to dock. Rising to her feet, she turned to Gyllek and said, "I want you to monitor us from here."

Gyllek let out a sigh of relief and then slid into the co-pilot's seat. Grendok turned toward Raven and politely waited for directions.

There was a loud clunk as the ship latched onto the orbital ring. They all looked over and then turned back toward Raven.

"The rest of us will get suited up."

"Excellent!" Grendok said excitedly, rubbing his hands together in anticipation of the mission.

Gyllek nodded at Raven, letting her know she had things under control, and watched as she and Grendok exited the bridge. Once they were gone, she slunk down into the captain's chair and began chewing her nails nervously as she stared up at the giant alien megastructure.

On the way to the airlock, Raven reached up and tapped a nearby touch display on the wall panel that ran along the corridor walls and got on the comm again. "Skuld, meet us at airlock 2A. We're going on a little excursion."

"Righteo, Captain, my captain," Skuld replied, his words warbling up from the back of his throat.

The respirator he wore, which allowed him to breathe with surface dwellers, gave his voice a partially mechanical tone. He sounded a bit like a friendly A.I. whenever he spoke.

Several minutes later, Raven was fully geared up and was wearing a top of the line EV suit. She went over to the wall, opened a storage locker, and pulled out an additional helmet and a reusable air tank. She handed it to Grendok, who only managed to get the top half of his suit on.

He accepted it, sliding the oxygen canister into the slot on the back side of his suit, then placed the helmet over his head, but his horns clanked the top of the inner helmet, and he had to forgo the spacesuit for a standard plastic breathing mask.

Skuld, meanwhile, was always ready to go, since he had to wear his EV suit at all times. He stood next to the airlock, checking the holopad display on his suit's forearm.

Raven slipped on her helmet and locked it into place. Looking at Skuld and Grendok, she took a deep breath to help calm her nerves. "Let's do this."

Skuld hit the unlock button, and the primary hatch to the airlock rolled away. "Mind stepping into my parlor, ladies and faun-folk?"

Raven and Grendok did as asked, and Skuld shut the door behind them. Once the room was sealed, Raven walked over to the outer airlock door and tapped a button. The ship's computer chimed and a soft-spoken woman's voice stated <<Docking clamps engaged. Extending docking seal.>>

There was a loud hiss of air expelling and then a shudder as the two ships matched pressurization.

"That was painless enough," Grendok said, his voice muffled by the oxygen mask.

Raven glanced over her shoulder at him then turned to the airlock door and muttered to herself, "Keep your eyes and ears open and stay safe."

With a pneumatic hiss, the airlock door rolled away. Raven slowly stepped out onto the docking ramp and cautiously walked over to the alien vessel. Skuld followed after her. When he got to the door, he looked over at Raven, who was merely standing there, staring at it.

"There's no keypad," she informed him.

Sure enough, he couldn't find one either. There wasn't any access panel to get inside the ship.

"How do they expect anyone to get in?" Grendok asked from the safety of his side of the docking platform.

Raven searched the edges of the alien vessel's docking port for any signs of glyphs or anything that might indicate a switch or a button but found nothing resembling a control mechanism. It was all smooth surfaces.

Skuld drew out a handheld scanner from his EV suit's utility belt and began scanning the surface of the strange metal. "Here," he said, pointing at a nondescript section of the door. There's a heat signature."

Raven looked at him and shrugged. Turning back to the ship, she reached out and placed her hand over the warm-spot. Suddenly, the door before them dissolved as though it had been eaten away by acid and revealed a long corridor to them.

"Whoa," she said, taken aback by the vanishing door. "Didn't expect that."

Raven stepped inside the darkened corridor of the alien vessel. Only her helmet-mounted spotlights illuminated the section of the vessel's strangely uniform interior. As she took another step forward, though, the ship's lighting came on automatically.

She paused and took a moment to study what appeared to be just an ordinary passageway. She drew out her own handheld scanner and checked the atmosphere.

"That's odd," she said.

"What is?" Grendok called out from the other end of the docking ramp. He was still waiting for the okay before boarding.

"The temperature and atmosphere reads exactly like that aboard the *Skywend*."

Skuld came in behind her, held up his scanner, and fanned it across the archway of the ceiling. "It seems to have automatically adjusted itself to match our own atmospheric preferences."

Raven looked at Skuld. "But we were never scanned."

"Possibly someone else was here before us. Or the alien's scanning technology doesn't register."

"Is it safe to come aboard?" Grendok called out to Raven. She looked back and waved him over and, finally, gave him the A-OK sign.

Raven reached up and tapped the side of her helmet. "Gyllek, are you there?"

"Here, boss lady."

"Try running a narrow spectrum scan on the ship now that the entrance is open. See if you can peer into the vessel for us."

There was a momentary pause and then Gyllek's voice came back with a light static crackle. "Apologies, Cap'n, but I'm not getting anything. It simply reads as negative space."

Skuld raised an eyebrow, which Raven caught out of the corner of her peripheral. "What's that mean exactly?"

Skuld reached out and touched the wall of the corridor. "Negative space, Captain, in an object this size, would suggest Tesseract technology."

Gyllek's voice came back over the comm. "Right. That was my guess too. But such technology is only theoretical. Even the finest minds in the Commonwealth agree that it can't be done."

"And, yet, here it is," Grendok said, running his hand along the surface of the wall.

"Alright," Raven said, reaching down and tapping a panel on her EV suit's thigh plating.

A small, disk-shaped wafer popped out and, taking it in her hand, she flicked her wrist and flung it like a Frisbee. The ring spun like a tiny flying saucer, hovering for a moment, fluorescent green LEDs pulsing in the dim corridor. "I'm sending in the drone now."

Raven threw her hand outward, fingers spread wide, and then gripped tight and made a fist. Responding to her hand signals, the drone flew down the corridor, scanning with a series of probing directed beams that lit up the passageway like a laser light show.

"Well, what are we all standing around for?" Grendok said, a hint of impatience in his voice. Overcome by a sense of anticipation, he quickly took the lead, only briefly turning back toward Raven and Skuld with a smile. "Adventure awaits."

With that, he turned, and, hooves clapping along the metal floor, headed deeper into the ship.

After following the passage for about half a kilometer, they emerged from the seemingly never-ending corridor and came out onto a tiered balcony. It was like stepping out of a tunnel into a massive stadium. Only this stadium wasn't a mere football field, it was an entire world.

Raven gasped at the sudden, sprawling vista that extended before them as far as the eye could see. In every direction were trees, mountains, and lakes. An entire planetary ecosystem lined the inner surface of the ring.

"Impressive, no?" Skuld said, nudging her elbow with his.

She raised her scanner, making sure it was still safe to breathe the air. Satisfied that the atmosphere was still acceptable, she holstered her blaster and unlatched her helmet.

With her helmet tucked under her arm, she tossed her feathery purple hair and took in a deep breath. Her violet eyes flashed hot pink momentarily as she scanned the terrain using her enhancements. There were no signs of trouble. In fact, everything seemed quite still and lifeless. Not even the sound of birds chirping or bees buzzing.

"It smells like a nice summer day at the beach on Dagon Prime," she said, a faint smile forming on her lips as she recalled a fond childhood memory from her homeworld—one of the few she had before her family was exiled for being political dissidents.

Grendok followed the captain's lead, pulling down his oxygen mask and breathing in deeply. "It smells like spring on Galliforn," he added.

"Since I have gills, I'll just have to take your word for it," Skuld lamented, tapping on his aquarium-esque helmet, his shoulders slumping in disappointment.

"Let's split up and run some additional scans," she said, latching her helmet to her belt with a magnetic clasp. "We'll meet back here in fifteen kekals, so don't wander off too far. We're not staking a claim," she said, eyeballing the satyr, "*just looking.*"

Grendok shrugged and stepped out of the archway and onto the lush terrain. They seemed to be in a clearing within the middle of a pine forest, judging by the towering conifers and the low, mossy undergrowth.

Beyond the forest, a verdant valley stretched out as far as the eye could see. It was dappled with glistening lakes, but by the size of the world, he guessed those distant lakes were likely the size of entire oceans.

After taking a few steps, he paused momentarily. "The gravity here feels like…" his voice trailed off as he tried to think of what planet felt similar to this.

"You're right," Raven responded. "Feels like the gravity on Nyctan."

"You've been to Nyctan?" Grendok said, raising an eyebrow.

Raven grinned. "Does that surprise you?"

"What with the ongoing war between the Dagons and the Nyctans, I just assumed that you wouldn't have risked it."

"I actually carry Seyfferian membership," she said.

"Is that so? Fascinating."

Her violet eyes flashed pink again and a subtle smile crept onto her plum colored lips. "I think you'll find I'm full of surprises," Raven informed him. He nodded respectfully in reply.

She turned and walked several meters into the clearing until she came to an outcrop of rocks. She climbed up the boulders another couple of meters to get a better look around. From her perch, she continued taking scans, hoping to find something more interesting than trees and boulders.

"Guys!" Skuld shouted out, waving at them. His abrupt excitement startled them and they both spun in his direction to see what he needed. "Come have a look at this!"

Grendok and Raven shared a quick glance and then rushed over to where Skuld was kneeling down beside a shrub.

"What's up?" asked Raven as she approached his position.

He pushed the shrub out of the way and showed them a symbol that was etched into the base of the inner wall of the superstructure.

Raven held up her scanner, inputting the symbol. "I'm searching all known linguistic data logs, both ideogrammatic and glyph-based texts, to see if there's a match."

"Over here," the satyr said. "I found another one."

Skuld hurried over to Grendok. "It's similar to the first glyph, yet it appears to have a more angular characteristic."

Grendok skipped away and located another symbol. And then another. While he was hunting down glyphs, Skuld began taking detailed scans and processing them through the computer's translation matrix.

About twelve minutes later, they'd amassed enough symbols to run them through the sequencer. As the computer crunched the structural and logographic properties of the symbols to decipher their meaning, the first icon locked in.

"We've got one," Raven said.

As they waited for the next symbol to lock into place, Grendok sniffed the air. "Peculiar."

"What is it?" asked Skuld.

"There's no trace of animal life. Only plant life."

"By Helios!" Skuld said, snapping his webbed fingers. "That is peculiar. Something has to be pollinating all these plants and flowers. Insects alone could do perhaps half the work, but you'd still need small mammals and birds to do the rest." He smiled. "Yet another mystery to this wondrous place which needs unraveling," Skuld said cheerfully.

The scanner chimed and another symbol locked into place. And then another, until, finally, it came to the last box.

"Why does this look so familiar?" Raven asked, speaking aloud as she stared down at the glowing glyphs on the monitor.

"Wait," Skuld said, taking the scanning tablet out of Raven's grasp, rotating it 180 degrees, and then placing it back into her hands in its proper, upright position. "There you go."

Raven's eyes widened with realization of the forbidden word before her and she immediately drew out her blaster and dialed it up to full. "We've gotta go. *Now.*"

Before either of her companions could inquire as to what she was on about, she had already turned around and was marching back toward the ship. Her eyes glowing hot pink, she was on hyper-alert for any threats.

"What is it?" Grendok said, scratching his head in bewilderment. "What does it say?"

Skuld patted him on the shoulder and answered his burning question. "It's ancient Nyctan. It says… *Aldebaran.*"

"Aldebaran?" Grendok repeated, still as confused as ever. "Wait…isn't that the legend of the exploding star that destroyed a god? What of it?"

"As the story goes, in the final days of the gods, a supreme being by the name of H'aaztre hid away on a planet far from anything in the known universe. This planet orbited a single star. A star called…Aldebaran."

Grendok cut in. "I know the tale well. It supposedly went supernova, killing the last of the ancient gods. But don't tell me your captain is superstitious. H'aaztre, Aldebaran, all of that religious mumbo-jumbo…it's all just myth and legend."

"Or so we were led to think," Skuld said. He turned and placed his hands on his hips, his lanky arms jutting out behind him as he stood and took one last look at the beautiful scenery.

Raven slowed up and shouted over her shoulder. "You two cut the chatter and get your asses moving. I'm not sticking around to see if H'aaztre is still tending to his garden."

"Come, now, Captain. Let's be reasonable," Grendok pleaded. For him, this was the discovery of the century. A find that one couldn't simply walk away from.

"Reasonable?!" Raven snapped. She spun around with a wild look in her eyes. "I was indoctrinated with these stories as a child. They talk about how H'aaztre enslaved the whole galaxy and forced countless alien worlds to worship him. Those who refused perished in the 'great culling,' where H'aaztre would kill off half their populations. In these stories there was nothing but terrible suffering and the loss of innocent life, all to please a cruel and maniacal deity. If there's even one micron of truth to these stories, you bet your fuzzy ass I'm not going to stand around waiting to find out. Besides, you said it yourself. There's not a single trace of life anywhere in this place. So, you do the math."

"What about the myth? If Aldebaran exploded and took out this evil god along with it, then why are you so scared, Captain?"

"Because we were wrong. We were all wrong. The archeologists, the historians, the linguists. Aldebaran wasn't the name of a star."

"Then what was it?" Grendok asked.

"You're standing on it," Raven said, gesturing to the whole world enclosed around them.

Without saying so much as another word on the subject, Raven turned and marched back into the corridor, making a hasty departure.

"You heard the captain," Skuld said, slapping Grendok across his back. "If there's one thing I've come to learn about Raven Nightguard," he added as he turned to follow after her, "it's that her gut is rarely ever wrong."

"Indeed," Grendok muttered, disenchanted with his partner in crime. He was hoping to land the biggest score of his life, but, instead, they were running away from ghost-stories.

Even as Skuld left him standing there by himself, he decided to take one last look, peering out at the panoramic vista one last time. He let out a long, disappointed sigh.

A pity, he thought. There was so much more waiting to be discovered here.

Perhaps, another time.

Just as he was about to turn and head back, something caught his attention out of the corner of his eye. Slowly, he turned back around to see what it was.

Standing in the open meadow was a woman he didn't recognize. She had pale skin and long, flowing platinum hair. She wasn't Dagon, even though she was wearing the ceremonial armor of a Dagoni empress. Perhaps stranger still, she had appeared as if out of thin air.

They stared in stunned silence at one another from across the distance, gauging whether or not the other was a threat.

When it was finally clear that neither of them posed any danger, they both relaxed. And, in that moment, he waved to her, and she returned the gesture and smiled at him in such a way that he was all but certain he knew her from somewhere, and knew her well.

5

The massive battlecruiser settled into the orbit of Aldebaran with the lethargy of an ancient airship. It dropped down low enough into the atmosphere that they could use the teleporters. Jegra, dressed in a special ceremonial battle armor designed for her future funeral, stepped onto the teleportation pad alongside Grendok and took a deep breath as she tried to calm her nerves.

"Are you ready for this?" he asked her.

Without looking over at him, she replied, "Ready as I'll ever be."

Grendok nodded at the chief of operations, a female satyr who was rather easy on the old goat eyes. She smiled at him then tapped the controls. In a sparkling wash of golden light like a cloud of champagne, they were whisked off Grendok's ship and planted securely on the surface of the ancient ring world.

Jegra took in a deep breath. The fresh air smelled like a summer afternoon on her family's farm back in Nebraska. The light scent of her mother making lemonade and sandwiches for her father, the faint sweetness of soybeans growing, and the smell of a recent harvest wafted on the air.

If she didn't know any better, this place would almost remind her of Heaven. It always seemed to automatically cater to your preferences, even the ones you weren't aware of. It also weirded her out because no matter how many times she set foot on Aldebaran, it felt alien to her. Unnatural.

Grendok pulled out a GPS scanner and began taking readings, triangulating their position on the ringworld. "That way," he said, raising a finger. "The temple is that way."

"Then what are we waiting for? Let's get moving."

Jegra and Grendok walked side-by-side in silence all the way to the temple gates, which ran the outer perimeter of the ancient monolith. Passing through the towering gates, she looked toward the large central spire rising up at the center of the garden, which was surrounded by seven additional smaller spires—all ornately carved with ancient runes of a dead language. It looked eerily similar to the ancient Wat Arun temple in Bangkok, back on Earth.

She'd never believed in those old alien conspiracies before, but the similarities of certain alien architecture, which always seemed to crop up on ancient Earth, was too much of a coincidence to simply brush aside as trivial. The more she saw, the more she realized that there must have been alien influence stretching back through most of Earth's history.

But none of that mattered anymore, because H'aaztre had sent his avatars to destroy Earth. Something she'd never forgotten—or forgiven. In fact, it was that very chain of events which led to the Great War and to her losing everything. Ultimately, it's why she found herself standing here, on Aldebaran again, staring at the one place she dreaded as much as she despised. The home of her sworn enemy—H'aaztre, the embracer of oblivion.

Once they arrived at the massive entrance pylons that towered over them, Grendok paused. The entrance sat at the top of a long series of stairs and, turning toward her, he gave her an apologetic look.

"I'm afraid this is as far as I'm allowed to go," he said.

"I understand," Jegra replied. She reached out and touched his shoulder. "It was good seeing you again, old friend."

"The pleasure was all mine," he answered with a wink.

Drawing back, Grendok stepped aside and watched Jegra ascend the stair and then, pausing to look back just once, step through the dark entrance. Before she disappeared completely, he called out to her, "Your Grace!"

She turned back toward him just as he tossed her something. Reflexively, she reached out and caught the item in her hands and looked down to see what it was. It was an old Dygra crystal. Probably something he'd discovered in one of his numerous archeological finds. However, now it was nothing more than a lifeless gem with a few too many cracks.

"You may need it."

She smiled and looked up at him. "I'm afraid its energy has been completely exhausted, but I appreciate the thought."

Grendok nodded and then waved goodbye one last time.

She raised a single hand and watched as he dissipated in a swirling eddy of sparkling light.

After taking a deep breath, Jegra tucked the Dygra crystal down under her cleavage, where it rested securely in the crevice between her underboob and the quilted lining of her gambeson.

She stepped through the pylons and into the mouth of the temple, then made her away across a wide main hall to a series of stairs. She climbed the steps and paused at the top to study what appeared to be a throne sitting in front of an archway, which formed a half-circle just behind the throne. Almost immediately, she recognized it as a gateway of alien design.

The gate's portal wasn't activated, but the metal architecture itself still seemed to hum with a strange energy. Almost as though it were somehow alive.

The eerie sound reminded her of the deep rumbling of an active volcano, and how one, should they be so inclined, could put their ear to the ground and listen perchance to hear the sounds of an entire planet's insides slowly churning about, folding in on themselves, coiling like a giant serpent made of lava and brimstone curling up inside the bowels of the great planet.

"After all these centuries, you've finally come to face your destiny," a gentle voice said.

Startled, Jegra spun to her right to find a stunning, blue Dagon woman with pointy ears and eyes white as snow stepping out from behind an ornate support column.

The woman didn't look a day older than when Jegra had last seen her, and she realized that she'd been frozen in time. *All part of the curse of being indentured to H'aaztre for all eternity*, she supposed.

"I used to believe that destiny was whatever we made it. But now, I'm not so sure. It seems I can never fully escape my fate," Jegra replied. She shifted her footing as the woman circled around her, keeping her body in a defensive position the entire time they eyed one another.

The woman smiled and drew closer. The thin gossamer dress, replete with golden liana embroidered along the edges of the translucent white fabric, did little to conceal her Prussian blue nipples and dark areolas. She was, for the lack of a better term, a porcelain doll, immortalized in a glass case.

And although Jegra's heart ached, she turned and faced the other half of her soul. "Dani," she said in her gentlest tone, "you know why I've come."

Danica's eyes may have grown white, but she wasn't blind. She saw the world in the way H'aaztre saw the world. She glimpsed the past, present, and future all at once. And although the far future might blur into uncertainty, it didn't impede her ability to surmise what would happen in the next few minutes or hours. For, the closer the coming event was to the present, the more certain she could be of its probable outcome.

As such, and as the keeper of the gate, Danica knew the outcome of everything that would transpire here in the next few minutes. And even if Danica foresaw her own death, she wouldn't simply allow Jegra to pass through the gate—not without a fight.

"Dani, please, I beg of you to search your heart."

"You cannot kill Him; you must see that by now. He is eternal. He existed before the spark of creation and He will be here when the last ember of that glorious creation fades into nothingness. He is the Alpha and the Omega—time has no meaning to Him—He is a fixed pillar in an eternal multiverse. He is a God!"

"I don't need to kill your god," Jegra said, reaching up to touch Danica's face. Tears streaming down her own cheeks, she smiled bittersweetly. "I only need to go back and convince myself of another way."

Danica's white eyes widened. "Another way?"

Jegra, her hand still resting on Danica's cheek, leaned in and kissed her cold lips. The woman she knew and loved had been dead for centuries. All that was left was this hollow vessel. A soulless automaton who served her master, the Yellow King.

"I don't need to destroy H'aaztre to defeat him. I only need to convince my past self that the path she will choose is the wrong one—that it ends in the death of her friends. In a lonely existence, a life not worth living."

"I do not understand," Danica replied in a monotone, her white eyes blinking curiously.

"I need to tell my past self to reject H'aaztre's offer."

"But you would doom the galaxy to an endless war. Is not the peace you have acquired in your reconciliation better than the alternative you strive to create?"

Jegra withdrew her hand from Dani's face and wiped the tears from her own cheeks. "For years, I thought so. But I've come to understand that it's better to stand up to evil and cruelty, at whatever cost, than sit idly by, tolerating it."

"You would doom all those who enjoy peace today to the nightmare of your past, simply to feel at ease with your own conscience?"

"He destroyed the universe, Dani. He spared only our galaxy, as I agreed to. I thought I was making the right decision. I have come to see it was the wrong one. Look around you," Jegra said, fanning her hand at their surroundings, "we live in a snow globe. Isolated in space and time with nothing outside our borders but an infinite blackness.

"Beyond the fringes of our galactic borders," she continued, "exists a most hideous nothingness. An all-consuming darkness that we cannot ever escape. You ask me if I am comfortable consigning everyone in this galaxy to a life of misery? If it means getting back what we lost, then I'm more than fine with it. I must do this to save all the countless worlds and peoples I doomed the first time around to an infinite oblivion." Jegra raised her finger and pointed at the gate. "That blackness out there…H'aaztre didn't create it. I did."

"Is this your final answer to me, Jegra Alakandra, the Insolent Scourge of H'aaztre?"

Jegra slapped Danica across the face, but the woman merely took it without so much as flinching. Lacking the slightest expression of pain on her face, she turned her gaze back toward Jegra.

"It is," Jegra replied. She was ready to fight, if that's what it came to. But to her astonishment, Danica merely stepped aside.

"Then, so be it, Daughter of Sol." She stretched out her arm and summoned a staff. A golden glowing light took the vague form of a staff in the air as she raised her hand high above her. The golden light solidified into a solid rod, and Danica twirled it about like a martial arts master.

The staff came to rest behind her back and, with a wide stance, she raised her palm as if to say *thou shall not pass.*

As soon as Jegra stepped toward the gate, Danica lunged at her. She easily evaded, but Danica's speed and agility had been heightened by whatever power she drew from this place—with whatever terrible power surged through her body. The blue veins beneath her turquoise skin thickened and bulged as she moved with lightening quick speed. Even the veins on her face and around her eyes began to form a pulsing blue webbing.

The rod flew over Jegra's head as she ducked low, narrowly evading it. The end of the staff collided with one of the pillars and the stone marble exploded as though a wrecking ball had hit it. Debris and chunks of rock sprayed out across the floor and Danica twirled around, staff spinning, and took another swing at Jegra.

This time Jegra leapt backward, the end of the staff barely missing her nose. It was so close that it kicked her hair up in its wake. The two women paused for a moment to look at one another, and Jegra shook her head as if to say *don't make me do this. Don't make me fight.*

Danica ignored the subtle warning and attacked with a series of lunges and jabs. Jegra easily evaded these, but Dani was able to get in close. Using the opportunity which presented itself to her, she got Jegra into a choke-hold, using the staff to crush Jegra's larynx.

Jegra grabbed the staff in both hands and flung her upper body forward, flipping Danica up and over her. Danica, although more powerful, still weighed about half of what Jegra did. She somersaulted through the air as though she'd been launched from a catapult. She tumbled to the ground with a thud, her staff slipping from her grasp and rattling across the floor.

Before Danica could push herself up, Jegra manifested behind her in a flash, her white hair streaming behind her as if in slow motion. Placing Danica in a choke-hold, Jegra whispered, "You know the future, Dani. You know you can't win this fight."

No matter how much Danica kicked and squirmed, she couldn't break free of Jegra's hold. Jegra sank to her knees as Danica's struggling grew weaker and weaker, until she was barely hanging onto consciousness.

"You…will…not…pass…" Danica hissed, her throat getting pinched off so she couldn't breathe.

"I love you, Dani. If you're in there, please know, I love you with all my heart." With a deep breath, Jegra squeezed until a bone chilling crack alerted her to the fact that she'd successfully broken Dani's neck. The blue woman went limp in her arms, and Jegra whispered, "Rest in peace, my love. He can't control you now or hurt you ever again."

Jegra scooped Danica up and walked over to the large throne chair. Gently setting her down on it, she posed Danica's lifeless body as though she were the queen of all space and time. Then, with tears in her eyes, Jegra gently placed Dani's hair over her shoulders then reached up and brushed down her open eyelids. "May we meet again, in the next life."

It took everything she had to hold herself together. She'd just killed the woman she loved more than anything in the galaxy. But it was a mercy killing, one she should have mustered up the courage to do three hundred years ago but couldn't. Instead, she had let Danica languish in an eternal maudlin stupor of H'aaztre's influence.

At least, now, her soul could finally rest in peace.

Jegra composed herself best she could and then turned back toward the gate. Its humming seemed louder now—angrier, somehow. She tapped on her collar and opened up a comm-link to Grendok. "I'm ready," she said.

There was a crackle of distortion and then Grendok's voice came back over the comm. "We're initiating the startup sequence remotely. Godspeed, milady. And may Pan be with you. Always."

Jegra let a morose smile form on her lips—a sad reflective expression one might see in a classical portraits painted by the great painters of antiquity—and then cut the comm-link. A few seconds later, the gate lit up with a swirl of purple and black energy.

The sudden rush of energy washed over her as the gate came to life and she felt Aldebaran shift beneath her feet. The portal began to spin and swirl as it tapped into the infinite dark energy of the universe and, in a short time, it stabilized.

Before her stood a glossy purple portal filled with liquid the consistency of oil. It shimmered; a strange, dim light emanating from the mysterious fluid. Jegra paused at the mouth of the portal and looked back at Danica's body one last time. But it wasn't the woman she once knew—simply the discarded husk of something else. Something she scarcely recognized.

Jegra gathered her nerve and turned back toward the swirling energy. Taking a deep breath, she passed through it as if she were Alice stepping through the looking glass.

As she came out the other side, Jegra looked around; she was inside the very same room. And, to her surprise, a fetching blue Dagon woman rose from her throne chair and turned to face her. Finding Jegra dressed to the nines in ceremonial armor and standing in front of the portal, which was slowly dying down again, the woman spoke.

"I sensed your coming."

"I know," Jegra replied. She had to fight her urge to run up and embrace the woman before her. But if Danica could see the future as well as the past, then she already knew the outcome of her fate—she already knew that Jegra had killed her and would do it again if she had to.

"You wear the ceremonial armor of the Dagon death ritual and the passage into the underworld," she said, observing Jegra's elaborate costume.

"I do."

"Fitting," she replied.

Jegra almost sensed a smile, but she turned away from her at the last second. With a seductive swivel of her hips, Danica sashayed on ahead, pausing briefly to beckon Jegra with the wave of a hand. "Follow me."

Jegra did as asked, following Danica to the entrance of the temple. They stood at the great mouth of that ancient place, looking out across a sprawling landscape of purple mountains, glistening lakes, and lush green forests that wrapped all the way around them, inside the massive ring.

"In six hours, a ship will arrive just over that bluff. Explorers will disembark and venture into the inner sanctum, just beyond the grove of trees to the southeast." She raised her hand and pointed at a small patch of land down by some ruins. "It will be your only ride out of here for five years, so I suggest you board that ship."

Jegra built up the courage to ask her one last question. "Is she in there, somewhere? Does the Dani I know still exist?"

"She does," the woman replied, facing Jegra. Her vacant, white eyes fixed themselves onto Jegra's brown ones.

"May I talk to her one last time?"

The gatekeeper who wore Dani's face paused a moment, then blinked. "No. H'aaztre forbids it."

"I see," Jegra said, looking away. She wiped another stray tear escaping from the corner of her eye and blinked a few times. She knew that H'aaztre was punishing her for her defiant attitude toward him. But to be so spiteful as to deny her the pleasure of one final word to her beloved was beyond the pale.

Jegra placed a warm hand to Dani's cold cheek, leaned in, and kissed those cold, marble lips one last time. "Until we meet again," she said.

Then, without another word, Jegra turned away, her armor rattling softly as she descended the stairs and saw herself out.

She glanced back only once to glimpse Danica watching her from the top of the temple stairs. But no matter how much she wanted to break H'aaztre's spell over her love, she knew she couldn't do it here. Turning back, Jegra began her long hike in the direction of the distant outcropping that had been pointed out to her.

6

The Skywend dropped out of hyperspace. A thunderous boom erupted as it crossed the terminal shock barrier of the stellar medium.

Even though empty space was mostly a vacuum, it wasn't a hundred percent vacant; it was capable of echo. There were still dust, ice, and gaseous rich nebulas to contend with. If you jumped through the atmosphere of a world or into a gas rich environment, there would always be a terminal shock wave, followed by a deafening boom.

And even if you couldn't hear the sound waves from where you were, you could still feel them as they made contact with the hull of your ship, inevitably causing the bulkheads to rattle something fierce.

"Do you think we'll ever see that vessel again?" Gyllek asked the captain, her voice timorous.

"I don't know," Raven replied. "But, personally, I'd be more than happy if it never showed itself again."

"It really freaked you out, didn't it?" Gyllek asked.

Raven gave her a sideways glance. "More than you'll ever know," she answered, an edginess permeating her typically liquid smooth voice.

"Well, if you need to talk about it, you know where to find me." With that, Gyllek hopped to her feet, stuffed her hands in her pockets, and strolled off the bridge.

Raven slumped back in her chair and crossed her long legs. She looked out at Thessalonica, the dusty moon that orbited her homeworld of Dagon Prime.

It was beautiful and hung like a pearl in the star speckled sky. Thessalonica was home to Arena City and the famed gladiator matches that were broadcast on televid systems all across the empire.

As she sat, lost in thought, a voice called out to her, drawing her out of her daydream, bringing her back to the present. "Pardon?" she asked, not catching what had been said.

"There's something we need to discuss, Captain Nightguard."

She swiveled in her chair, and sprang to her feet. In the same instant, she drew her blaster and pointed it at the stranger standing on *her* bridge.

"Computer! Intruder alert!" she barked, annoyed that a stowaway had somehow not only gotten aboard the *Skywend* but had, somehow, bypassed all the security protocols.

The computer chimed with an alarm and, soon enough, the entire ship was at red-alert, blaring with the infernal racket of a digital klaxon.

Jegra reached out and smashed the controls on the side of the hatch and the bridge doors slid shut behind her, sealing Raven and herself inside the room together.

"You have precisely ten seconds to tell me who you are and explain what you're doing standing on my bridge."

"My name's Jegra Alakandra, and you have nothing to fear from me." Raven didn't seem to take her at her word, so she responded in another way, one which might be more convincing.

With a single verbal code uttered in Dagoni, she shut off the ship's alarm. "*Octenorrex, ebbesek vorgek, kek' amalorek.*"

The ship's bleating alarm stopped, and, with a chipper voice, said, "All ship commands rerouted to Jegra Alakandra, reigning Empress of the Dagon Empire."

Raven gave the console a shocked look, as though the ship were a friend that had just betrayed her, and then turned back to glower at Jegra.

"Give me back control of my ship or, so help me goddess, I blast a new breathing hole in you, pink-skin."

Although this mysterious woman standing before Raven had the long, silver hair of a Dagon royal, she didn't have blue skin or even pointy ears. In fact, Raven wasn't even sure what species she belonged to.

"I'm a Human Being from a planet called Earth," Jegra informed her in a soft voice, so soothing it served to disarm any lingering tension.

"Then why are you wearing the armor of a Dagon empress?"

"Because, in your near future, the Lord Emperor Rhadamanthus Dakroth falls for me hard, and, at your urging, I join him as his wife and become the first non-native Dagon empress in the history of the Dagon Empire. It sets off a political coup, and, to try and save face, the emperor double-crosses me and hands me over to the Nyctans as a peace offering. When that backfires, he sends an assassin named Ishtar Bantu after me."

"That does sound like the emperor," Raven said.

Nodding, Jegra continued with her story. "Ishtar kills a friend dear to me then sets a trap to try and subdue me. I eventually best her in hand-to-hand combat before teaming up with you to put the emperor in his place. All that will become apparent in time. Right now, though, I need to ask you a favor."

Raven shot her a curious look. A woman she barely knew, who, like an insane person, claimed she was the queen of the whole bleedin' empire, was now asking her for a favor.

Normally, she'd write her off as a complete loon. But since everything she'd told her thus far seemed to make sense, she decided to hear her out. "I'm listening," she said.

Although doubtful as to the veracity of this woman's claims, she still couldn't help but feel there was genuine congeniality about her. She spoke with calm and measured words, and it was clear that she knew how to comport herself like a true ruler.

More interestingly, perhaps, was the fact that she seemed to be a product of the arena. Raven recognized it in the way Jegra moved and the way she carried herself.

Her words never revealed more of herself than necessary, and while Raven had scanned her, she'd noticed the woman scrutinizing her in return. She'd been sized up with a subtle precision that only veteran warriors had any awareness of.

Raven was *mostly* certain that, if this woman's story at all checked out, it would be virtually impossible to best her in hand-to-hand combat. Still, for all her doubts, she was willing to listen to the woman's incredible story. She knew, no matter how far-fetched it seemed to her, there was an element of truth in everything the woman told her. This only made her all the more curious, and she had to follow this rabbit hole wherever it took her.

"By having set foot on Aldebaran, you set into motion a chain of events that will alter the course of history forever."

"If you truly know me, then you know I'm a woman who likes to have all the facts before I act. So, tell me, Jegra of Earth, how do I know you're not just taking me for a ride?"

"Listen to me, Khatri'LaGharia. I know you."

Raven's arm stiffened and the blaster steadied in her hand as she fixed its sights onto Jegra's head. "How do you know that name?" she barked defensively.

"Because, Raven Khatri'LaGharia, you taught it to me."

"Nobody knows my real family name but for…"

"You and your sister, Lianica. I know everything about you, Raven. And, in the near future, you shall know everything about me, too. And, right now, I'm asking you to trust me."

Raven squinted at the mysterious woman standing before her. It was all so odd, and, all things considered, she wasn't certain of anything anymore. No alien had ever before become an empress of her people. And she'd never heard of any Jegra Alakandra. It all sounded like the ramblings of a delusional fanatic.

Even so, she couldn't deny the fact that this woman was wearing ceremonial Dagoni armor tailored to her. Moreover, this woman knew things she couldn't possibly know, like Raven's true name, not to mention the command codes to her ship, which she had never uttered to another living soul.

Then there was the matter of the *Skywend* itself. The ship's own quantum computer believed Jegra was the empress. That compelled Raven to take this woman seriously, even though everything she'd claimed sounded to her like an elaborate lie told by a con artist.

Jegra looked at Raven and cleared her throat. "Computer, return command of the *Skywend* back to Raven Nightguard."

<<Command has been restored to Captain Raven Nightguard, by authority of the reigning Empress of the Dagon Empire,>> chirped the female voice of the *Skywend.*

"What's this favor?" Raven finally asked, lowing her blaster.

Relieved to see Raven come around, Jegra let out a deep sigh. "Help me out of this armor. It itches like a bitch."

"It is the ceremonial armor of death, you know."

"I know," Jegra said. "And I was prepared to wear it for my own end…" There was a long pause as both women looked to one another. "I've come back here to die."

Raven raised an eyebrow. Before she could respond to that cryptic comment, however, there was banging coming from the other side of the door.

"Captain?!" Skuld hollered. "Are you all right in there?"

"Captain," Gyllek's voice called out immediately after, "we'll get you out of there in a jiffy—just hold tight."

"And if that woman—who I totally did not let onboard—has harmed you in any way," Grendok informed, "we shall avenge you!"

"It's all right," Raven hollered back. "An old friend decided to drop in unexpectedly and surprise me." She then turned to Jegra and, in a hushed voice, asked, "Grendok let you onboard, didn't he?"

"Yup," Jegra replied with a puckish smile.

Raven rolled her eyes and then smiled warmly. She cautiously walked up to Jegra and extended a friendly hand. "In that case, welcome aboard."

Jegra took her hand in hers, but before she could shake on it, a powerful surge of electricity zapped her.

She clutched Raven's arm to try and pry herself free, but the voltage merely increased. Dropping to one knee, blue tendrils of electricity crawling across her entire body, she looked up at Raven with a stunned expression. "Why?"

"If you know me as well as you say you do," Raven replied, "then you already know the answer to that."

Jegra collapsed onto her side, rendered unconscious by one last high-voltage electrical discharge. Raven stepped over her unconscious body and mashed the control panel on the wall and opened the hatch.

Skuld, Gyllek, and Grendok were standing on the other side of the door; they peered through the opening with curious faces, looking past Raven to try and catch a glimpse of the mysterious sleeping woman on the floor.

"You two, help me get the intruder down to the brig," Raven ordered, pointing her chin at Skuld and Grendok. She then turned to Gyllek and, in a soft voice, she said, "Please chart a course for Mardok. I have a new recruit I want to proposition."

"A new crew member?" Gyllek chirped excitedly. "Oh, please tell me it's a girl. Please, oh, please!"

Raven laughed. "I'm afraid it's a Dragonian," Raven replied, letting the girl down as gently as she could. "We could use the extra muscle around here."

"I've got muscles," Gyllek said, flexing her fourteen-year-old cat-girl arm and showing off her little bulge.

"Indeed you do," Raven answered with a smile. "Just get us set down somewhere discrete and make sure the cloaking device is on. Then we'll see about maybe arranging a girl's night for just us."

"You mean it?" Gyllek chirped.

Raven nodded in the affirmative and Gyllek, moved by the wonderful news, spun on her toes like a ballerina and pirouetted her way to the console where she promptly plopped down into the seat and began to type in the jump coordinates.

Raven ducked under the archway of the entrance and followed after Grendok and Skuld who were struggling to carry—or rather, drag—the massive woman down the corridor toward the brig.

A stiffness ran the entire length of her body and, letting out a groan, Jegra finally came to. Opening her eyes, she looked around to discover that she was inside a holding cell aboard the *Skywend*.

The cool recycled air caused her skin to prick with goosebumps, and she looked down to find she wasn't wearing anything but a pair of gray cotton panties and a matching sports bra. At least Raven had listened to her request and had gotten her out of that cumbersome armor.

She sat up in her cot and sluggishly turned to find the captain sitting on a chair just outside her cell, watching her intently. She stretched her arms and rotated her neck across her shoulders to try and chase out the lingering tension in them after being electrocuted.

Raven leaned back in the chair and crossed her legs as she kept her gaze firmly fixed on Jegra. Her eyes flashed hot pink as her smart-lenses activated the lie-detection mode, which would monitor Jegra's breathing, heart rate, sweat, and record the discussion for review later.

"Start at the very beginning," Raven said, "and don't spare a single detail. Once you've finished telling me everything—and I mean absolutely everything— then I'll decide what to do with you."

"All right," Jegra said, brushing a tress of silver hair behind her ear. "But, I'm warning you, it's a long story."

Raven simply gestured with the wave of her hand for her to proceed.

Jegra put a fist to her mouth, cleared her throat, and then proceeded to tell Raven everything from the moment she'd been abducted by aliens from Earth, all the way to how she came to find herself the empress of an alien empire far away from home.

One hour turned into two, two turned into four, and four into eight. Soon, it was the next day, and Jegra was just finishing the part about how Raven and Grendok had helped her take back Dagon Prime and brought an end to a terribly long siege.

"And after that?" Raven asked, now sitting on the edge of her seat as she took it all in.

"War," Jegra replied. She looked away and stared off at the corner of the room with a solemn look. "A war that ends with me caving in to H'aaztre's ultimatum. I made a deal with the devil and it bit me in the ass."

She turned her gaze back toward Raven and rested both hands on her hips as they read one another's faces.

"I can't live with that decision any longer, so, when a chance presented itself, I decided to return to fix that mistake and set this timeline back on its proper course."

"And what if you can't alter the events of the past? What if things unfold exactly as they did before, which, according to my understanding of the time continuum, is more likely?"

"I can't accept that. If the universe is truly more deterministic than we initially thought, well, then nothing has any meaning and we might as well let H'aaztre have his way. But that's not the universe I care to live in. Something deep inside me believes we can still make our own destiny."

"And your destiny has put you on a path that has crossed with mine," Raven said, rising to her feet. She approached the cell and turned off the energy shield.

Jegra stepped up to Raven and, although she was slightly taller, causing Raven to look up, there was a genuinely mutual respect for one another.

"Thank you," Jegra said. "Thank you for believing me."

"It sounds as if the future me believed *in* you wholeheartedly. Who am I to argue with myself?"

Jegra laughed. Then an unfamiliar silence settled over them, and slowly they moved closer together until their lips were practically brushing up against one another.

"I'll help you on one condition," Raven said, her breath hot and sweet.

"Anything," Jegra replied. "Just say the words."

"We keep you a secret. If word gets out that you've come back in time to alter the past in order to save the future, we'll lose the only ace we have up our sleeve."

"I completely agree."

"Good," Raven said, her lips smiling playfully as she drew away. "We're in agreement."

Raven pulled back and looked Jegra in the eyes one last time. She blinked twice and then her pink eyes flickered and went back to her natural, purple amethyst.

"One last thing," Raven said, reaching in and drawing out the faded, cracked ruby the size of her fist she taken off Jegra's person. She held it up, and inspecting it, asked, "What in the living galaxy is this? The ship's scanners couldn't find anything in the database like it."

"You don't recognize it? It's a Dygra crystal," Jegra replied. Reaching over, she gently poked Raven's left breast with a slender finger. "You have one right here. But it's cracked, so you never use it."

"But Dygra crystals don't get this big. And why wouldn't it be registered in the ship's database? I mean it's a common evolutionary trait in my species. It grants us great powers. But…this isn't any ordinary Dygra crystal, is it?"

"It's the crystal I used to open a breach into the eleventh dimension. In your time, you call it *The Rift*—a cross-dimensional, multiphase, space-time anomaly. But I failed to seal H'aaztre inside it the first time around. Instead, he called upon his army of celestial squid entities to come through it onto our side. They entered our own galaxy only to lay waste to our fleet. Once our fleet was crippled, H'aaztre's army was able to take over the galaxy one system at a time until, at last, everything fell under his dominion."

"In that case," Raven said, handing Jegra back her crystal. "This belongs to you."

"Are you sure?"

Raven nodded.

Jegra accepted it and held it up, allowing the light to seep into it, causing it to glow a soft red. "When the future me gets her crystal, I'll recharge this one.

With two crystals, I'm certain we can send H'aaztre spinning into the eleventh dimension before he destroys the universe."

"Let's hope you are right," Raven said. Jegra merely nodded in reply; she had nothing more to add on the subject.

Just as they were about to head out into the corridor, Jegra felt her intestines gurgle and she quickly handed off the crystal to Raven who fumbled to keep ahold of it.

"Sorry," Jegra said as she hurried back into her cell. She went straight over to the toilet, slipped off her underwear and sat down. The stream of pee sounded as if it had blasted out of a firehose before her cheeks ever settled onto the seat. "Sorry," she said, looking up with flushed cheeks. "I've been holding it since we started chatting." She glanced up at Raven, who merely stared at her, amused.

"Do you often pee in front of others?" Raven asked.

Jegra shrugged as she broke off some tabs of tissue paper to clean herself with.

"I suppose it happens more than I'd care to admit. But you know the saying, when you gotta' go, you gotta' go."

"Actually, I'm not aware of any such saying," Raven replied, a half smile forming on her face.

"Oh," Jegra said, waving her hand over the motion-censor to flush the toilet. "Well, now you are."

As she approached Raven, the Dygra crystal flew into the air and Jegra had no choice but to catch it. Jegra held the crystal in both hands and looked back at Raven, who shot her a subtle smile and then turned and ducked under the archway.

"And so," Jegra said in a hushed voice, "the adventure begins, again."

7

Electrical sparks rained down from the wiring directly above the ship's cockpit. Deunan Atiyah yelped as some hot embers kissed her skin; she promptly brushed them off her copper toned shoulders. "Blasted ship," she growled, gripping tightly to the flight joystick. "Don't fall apart on me now!"

"Should I be worried?" Lycia asked, tossing her fuchsia died hair over her blue shoulder, which peeked out from the tight-fitting charcoal gray tank top she wore.

As her hair shuffled from one side to the other, the shaved undercut she sported helped to show off the multiple ear and eyebrow piercings she'd gotten at a private salon during their last cargo pickup on Veridion, roughly three days ago.

She currently donned a combination of multiple rings and studs per brow and per ear, including two electric purple sapphire earrings that matched her current hair color. She'd even let the cute Bre'lal girl at the tattoo parlor pierce her tongue, naval, and nipples, among a few other things she wasn't at liberty to share with anyone.

Deunan squinted disapprovingly at Lycia's bold new fashion choice. Although Seyfferians were all about mods, this was a bit excessive, even for her tastes. Lycia caught Deunan giving her a sideways glance and shrugged. "What?"

"Nothing," she grumbled, putting her hypercritical opinion back on the shelf where it belonged. After all, she wasn't the girl's mother. It wasn't her place to tell her how to act or dress. Even so, she still couldn't help but feel a nagging responsibility for the young woman.

A loud clunk of something impacting the ship's fuselage brought Deunan's focus back to the task at hand and, gripping the joystick with both hands, she pulled back on the controls and brought the nose of the ship up.

Then, veering hard to the right—as hard as she could—she maneuvered the ship in a spiral pattern as she cut back down through the gaseous nebula.

The ole girl didn't fly gracefully, like a fighter, or even some of the newer mid-sized freighters, but it flew well enough. Well enough, that is, to keep the skin on their backs from getting sheared off by the Suk'Naath'Degas they'd managed to royally piss off.

"Nothing? Tell that to the Suk'Naath'Degas out there that's literally breathing down our necks," Lycia quipped, gesturing reticently over her shoulder.

"He doesn't exactly seem to be in the mood for a chat at the moment," Deunan answered through a clenched jaw. She gritted her teeth and pulled back hard on the joystick, her arm muscles rippling as she fought the soupy consistency of this strange nebula.

Deunan looked up out of the cockpit window and saw the giant octopus-bat-creature that lived in dense gas nebulas and which breathed nitrogen and oxygen through massive alien gills like those of a prehistoric Dagoni megalodon shark.

Although Suk'Naath'Degas were typically weary of interstellar travelers and tried to avoid them whenever possible, Deunan had accidentally charted a course directly through the galactic leviathan's mating grounds and disturbed one of the more aggressive males. Now considering the ship a rival suitor and feeling challenged by their presence, it was attacking them. Quite aggressively at that.

Although not much bigger than Deunan's freighter, the beast was still big enough to do some serious damage with its winged talons and spiked tail, which whipped about behind it like a medieval battle mace.

One crushing blow from that spiky ball-like appendage could cause a breach to the outer hull. And, given the wear and tear of the ship already, not to mention her age, Deunan wasn't about to start pushing her luck.

Lycia snapped her fingers. "I've got an idea!" She swung herself out of her seat and daintily leaped over Allie, the indigo Lafor'allenthal panther grooming herself in the middle of the walkway without a care in the world for what was going on around her.

She hurried over to her battle android, which stood at the back of the cabin charging. "Wakey, wakey…eggs and bakey," she sang melodically as she unplugged X-5 from the charging station.

There was a three-second pause and then the hum of his internal servos whirred to life and his eyes lit up bright white. He sat up rather abruptly, posture stiffening as he repositioned himself.

"How may I be of service to the Lycia?" the automaton asked in a strangely realistic tenor voice; it had only the slightest reverb to it, the only reminder that it wasn't fully biotic.

"The Lycia was wondering…" the young Dagon woman said, speaking about herself in the third person, "if your feet are equipped for zero-G space walks?"

"Affirmative. The X-5 series can operate in the vacuum of space using a combination of its magnetic appendages and fully functional thrusters."

Lycia giggled to herself at the mention of magnetic appendages because she kept imagining something else. Shaking the arbitrary thought from her mind, she answered with a nod and quickly headed over to the weapons hold.

"Great," she said, reaching up and taking down a plasma rifle from the rack on the back wall.

She turned back toward the robot and tossed it to him. He reached out reflexively and caught it then looked down at the weapon with his bright, almost inquisitive eyes. His head jerked back up mechanically, and he looked at her, his eyes glowing softly as he awaited his orders.

Wasting no time, Lycia had moved onto the next step of their mission. She was climbing into a space suit, preparing for a jaunt outside the ship.

"Does the Lycia have a mission directive? Will we be going into zero-G battle?" X-5 asked her, waiting to receive his commands.

"Not so much battle," she informed the robot. "It's more of a rescue mission."

"Will the Lycia be joining X-5?"

"Yes," she informed him, slamming a palm on the rear airlock entrance. "I will need your help out there."

"Who will we be rescuing?"

"This ship," she said as she slipped her feet into the magnetic boots and latched them shut. "More importantly, though, our own asses," she added, standing up and fetching her helmet.

The door hissed and rolled away, which was enough to catch the attention of Allie. Her cat ears perked up and her head rose to see what the hissing was all about.

Once she was satisfied it wasn't anything in the way of competition or food, she lost interest, closing her eyes to take a short nap.

After ducking into the airlock, Lycia fixed her helmet, locking it into place with a metallic clack. She waited for X-5 to amble inside after her then pulled the hatch shut behind them.

Static gurgled up from the speaker and Deunan's voice came over the comm. "Be careful out there, kid. That Suk'Naath'Degas looks rather roiled at the moment."

"Copy that," Lycia answered. She turned her gaze from behind the glass of her visor to the android standing beside her and signaled with a nod that it was time to head outside. Reaching up to the airlock depressurization lever, she followed protocol. "Magnetizing boots now."

Both hers and the robot's feet clanked onto the metal floor and hummed with a soft rhythmic sound as the magnetic coils inside their footgear warmed up. She then pulled down on the lever and, in a rush of air, the connecting chamber depressurized as the inside matched the vacuum of space. Turning slowly, she tapped on her helmet to signal X-5 that it was go-time then slammed her gloved fist down upon the button and opened the outer hatch.

The hatch rolled away, revealing a beautiful pink and purple nebula outside. It looked like a watercolor painting, bright colors splashed upon a black canvas, and she stood breathless for moment, admiring the sheer beauty and grandeur of it.

"Remember," she said to X-5, her finger pointing down at the yellow line at the edge of the entrance. "Once we're past this line, the artificial gravity cuts off."

X-5 paused, as though he were processing the information, then raised his blaster and stepped out onto the hull of the ship. Lycia shrugged and followed after him. She desperately wanted to get him an A.I. upgrade so that he could have a greater selection of personality settings. Anything other than Stoic Gunman, which seemed to be his only setting, would be nice.

The comm in her helmet came on, and Deunan did a comms check then broke down the situation for her. "Remember, kid, the adult Suk'Naath'Degas is heavily armored, so you'll have to aim for the sensitive areas. The wing flaps, the soft area on the neck where its gills are, should sting it enough to send it scurrying back home."

"Don't worry, *D*," she grumbled, irritated, "I'm on top of it." She tapped off her headset and turned to X-5 and rolled her eyes. She didn't need to be pampered every damned nanosecond of every kekal. She was perfectly capable of taking care of herself.

Both Lycia and X-5 moved several meters out onto the top portion of the ship's outer hull and took up a defensive position. Scanning their surroundings, they made sure to keep an eye on the ominous gas clouds that grew thick around them.

Through the vaporous haze, a shadow loomed large above them. The dark silhouette of the creature, the color of ash hidden beneath the layers of its gaseous shroud, circled back around and made a sharp beeline straight toward them.

The vapors parted in a gust of swirls which wrapped around the hideous beast. A bat-like face with eight eyes, half a dozen horns protruding from the back of its head, and wings like those of a dragon stared back at them.

If that wasn't terrifying enough, the pair of barbed tails that whipped around behind it like a double-headed flail and its brutal talons, like those of an Arkadian Fisher-hawk, were perfect for catching prey and shredding up unwelcome intruders.

Its reddish orange skin was streaked with electric blue glowing veins and was chromatophoric. In an instant, the creature's skin could change colors to blend in with the violet and pink clouds in which it thrived, disappearing into its background in the same way a deep ocean dwelling octopus would.

When the creature opened its mouth, massive ropes of sticky, mucus enriched saliva dripped from its numerous rows of shark-like teeth. Whatever properties its saliva had, it didn't freeze solid in the cold of space, but large strands did break off and collect into globules that floated aimlessly through the nebula.

"Ew, gross," Lycia said to herself, leaning back to avoid one of the globules that wafted past her shoulder. After she was in the clear, she straightened up and faced the creature, which was coming around for a second pass. Shouldering her plasma rifle, she breathed in deeply through her nose and took aim.

As the creature drew nearer, she let off a warning shot to try to startle it away. Its hair-raising shriek traveled on the gaseous atmosphere of the nebula and filled her helmet. It was a scraping of nails across a chalkboard, teeth-grinding, demonic yowl; without a doubt, one of the most bone-chilling sounds she'd ever heard.

Unable to cover her ears, she turned her face to the side and cringed. Orange glowing light from the HUD of her helmet's visor cascaded down her blue face and cast violet shadows across the contours of her skin. As the shrieking died down, she opened one eye, targeted the beast, and let off another blast.

The shot pinged off the creature's underbelly as it flew over them but did little in the way of any real damage. Deunan wasn't mistaken; the beast was heavily armored. And all she'd managed to do was leave a few scorch marks on its tummy.

X-5 followed the creature with precision aim, his waist swiveling atop his legs which, subsequently, remained firmly planted on the ship's hull like a camera tripod. He let off three shots in consecutive bursts.

The first knocked the beast's forked tails out of the way, the second hit the Suk'Naath'Degas's right wing, causing it to veer left. And the battle android's third shot hit the creature directly in the left-side gills as it circled back around.

It shrieked again; this time its screams were filled with the agony of a plasma fire choking its lungs. Amid the excruciating cries, Lycia took aim and steadied herself. This time the monster was coming in hot, a wild look in its numerous blinking eyes.

Its gills are singed rather good, she noted, and she imagined the brute wasn't too happy about it, either. Plasma burns hurt bad enough on the outside; she couldn't imagine how unbearable they must feel on the inside.

Once the beast came within range, the Suk'Naath'Degas reached out with its curved talons and dragged them along the hull of the ship, sending up a spray of sparks and letting forth a shrill scream of metal shearing open.

The blaze of dancing sparks momentarily blinded her, and she had to raise her forearm to shield her visor from the firestorm that whipped about her. Just then, something crashed into her with such immense force that it knocked her off her perch and, subsequently, sent her hurtling into deep space.

"Graddak vendel la'terren'graft!' she screamed out loud as she spiraled away from the ship. In the Dagoni tongue, it roughly translated to: "Mother fucking shit-balls!" And, in that moment of dreadful frustration, there wasn't a better phrase to describe it in all the languages of the Commonwealth.

All things considered, though, it could have been a lot worse. At least this time the zero-gravity worked in her favor, as the EV suit had managed to absorb the brunt of the blow like the protective shell of a tortoise.

Nevertheless, now she was spiraling out of control, pinwheeling deeper and deeper into the nebula.

Before Lycia could even catch her bearings, Deunan's shouting voice came over the comm as she frantically barked emergency protocols in her ear. But with everything else going on, she tried her best to tune out Deunan's voice and just focus on getting her free-spinning cartwheel under control as she steadily drifted away from the ship.

It took a few moments, but she finally calmed herself, taking in several slow, deliberate breaths followed by long exhales. Opening her eyes, she looked out her visor; the stars had stopped spinning in a dizzying fashion and solidified as distant pinpricks of light.

Her EV suit's emergency thrusters had gradually slowed her to a near weightless halt. Coming to a stop, she got a hold of her thoughts before looking around for the ship. It was nowhere to be found. She let out a deep sigh and looked out at the vista wrapping all around her like a 3D panoramic photo.

In the distance, she watched as hot flashes of static discharge popped in random patterns across the deep violet nebula with no particular rhyme or reason. Each flash lit up the nebula like lightning illuminating dark storm clouds, allowing a myriad of hot pinks and electric blues to manifest momentarily in mottled patterns that bled into the deeper purple surroundings like a watercolor painting. It was breathtaking.

A loud screech drew her attention back to the present danger, and she snapped her head in the direction of the creature's loathsome cry. It was making its way back around to her.

"Deunan, if you're out there, I could really use a little help right about now," she said.

The Suk'Naath'Degas looked pissed as it came for her, its slimy jowls opening once more as it closed in on the attacker.

Lycia gulped hard as it drew closer and then, without warning, the ship came up out of a gas cloud and bumped into the massive creature's underbelly. The Suk'Naath'Degas pulled up to evade the ship, and Lycia looked over to find X-5 laying down suppressive fire, attempting to scare it away from her.

Half the shots missed their mark, and the beast ignored the robot's blasts and came about. Instead of being intimidated by the ship, it merely focused all of its ire on Lycia.

"That's right, you ugly, beady-eyed, scrotum-speckled space-leech. Come and get me!"

It shrieked again, its awful cries rippling through the gaseous clouds and crashing into Lycia with a terrible, spine-tingling force. She shook it off and aimed her blaster.

Nearly upon her, the beast opened its slimy maw, giant fangs ready to devour her whole. Squeezing down on the trigger, she began firing into the beast's open mouth, making sure to aim at the soft spot at the back of the throat.

The volley of blasts rocketed her backward, spinning her out of the way just in time to avoid getting eaten alive. The Suk'Naath'Degas flew over her, nearly clipping her in the process. She narrowly escaped getting snagged on its razor-sharp claws as it soared past her, and, once in the clear, she maneuvered herself back around and took careful aim.

She held the riffle one-handed which, in zero-G, was a total cinch. All she had to do was make the shot count. One deep breath. She steadied her aim. Then, squinting with one eye half closed, she pulled the trigger.

The blast spun her around, but her thrusters automatically kicked on and slowed her back down. She turned her face to the edge of her glass visor and saw that her shot had hit its mark.

"Bullseye," she shouted triumphantly, an instant wave of relief washing over her.

The Suk'Naath'Degas let out one last tortured shriek and then, turning tail, it flapped vigorously to get away from these pesky intruders. Eddies of nebulous gas swirled about as it flipped around without so much as a backward glance. Clearly, it had finally had enough of this irritation and had decided to retreat into the thick of the gas cloud and tend to its wounds.

Deunan's voice came back onto the comm. "What in the bloody Helios did you do to get it to take off like that?"

"I shot it in the nut sack," Lycia responded proudly.

"You would do something like that, wouldn't you."

"Look, I simply used his animal instinct against him."

"Oh, and how's that, exactly?" Deunan chuckled.

"Easy. He had one of two choices. Go back and bone one of those ugly ass females of his species or continue to dick around with the little spaceship and its insect—me, that is. I merely reminded him of where his priorities were."

X-5's robotic voice cut into the conversation. "Does the Lycia require rescue?"

Lycia smiled. "I wouldn't mind a pick up."

Moments later, X-5 rocketed toward her. Built-in thrusters fired in small spurts to bring him in-line with his mistress. He, of course, was tethered to the ship with a cable. When he got to her, he pulled out a lead and slapped a carabiner onto her belt. Using a pulley system built into his forearm, he then towed them back toward the ship.

"Thanks, big guy," she said, shooting X-5 a smile. He seemed to appreciate her thanks; his eyes glowed pleasantly as he studied her face.

"It is my job to keep the Lycia safe," he answered.

"I appreciate that," she said, smiling once more. She patted him on the shoulder and then turned her gaze one last time to the clouds and watched as another static discharge lit up the pallet of deep blues, rich purples, and soft pinks that blossomed here and there.

8

Hot sand pressed into her back as Danica lay sprawled out in the middle of the Arkadia arena, panting for breath. Beads of sweat rolled down the side of her face and neck as she looked up at the ominous strands of drool hanging over her like jagged stalactites.

The saliva, as thick as rope, dangled from the prehistoric lizard's four-inch razor-sharp teeth as it eyed her hungrily. Using her energy-based powers, she fended it off with an energy shield, but she didn't know how much longer the barrier would hold, given that she was already pressed to her limit.

Her violet-blue skin glistened with a uniform sheen of perspiration; she grunted from the strain of holding back the mammoth beast with her forcefield powers. The tyrannosaur weighted at least two tons and was relentless in its attempt to make her its next meal.

Due to the fact that her left leg was completely mangled from when it had nipped her and tossed her clear across the stadium, she wasn't able to get out from under the hefty beast. At least not without some serious strain on her body. It took everything she had to ignore the searing pain and focus her mind on her energy barrier.

She wriggled back in the sand, her shoulder blades helping her along as she tried to put as much distance between herself and her opponent as she could. But this only seemed to excite the beast, and it moved with her, snapping its jowls and deflecting off the energy barrier, to its great frustration.

With her arms fully extended, flat palms facing outward, she projected her energy barrier outward in the shape of a dome and gradually began to expand it. She had to be careful not to overexert herself, however, because if she pushed her powers too hard, she would experience a burn-out and be completely at the beast's mercy. The last thing she needed right now was to pass out as her body shut down.

Luckily, she managed to erect the energy barrier without losing consciousness. And, as long as she could keep it up, she'd stay safe.

Having bought herself a little extra time, her eyes darted around for a weapon—anything she might use as a defensive tool.

Unfortunately, there was nothing within reach. However, off to the side of the arena, she spotted Ladgara, smiling at her from beyond the gated entrance.

Ladgara nodded at the monstrous lizard as if to say, *see what you got yourself into?* Danica merely scoffed and turned her gaze away. If she wasn't going to help, then *screw her.*

Danica had been in worse situations before. None came to mind at the moment, but she'd be damned to Helios if she was going to let things go down like this. Especially in front of Ladgara. There was no way she'd ever give her the satisfaction.

With a grunt, Danica caused the energy bubble to flip up and wrap around the Tyrannosaurus Rex's head like a wet blanket. Capturing its massive head in the bubble, she clenched her fist tight and the energy blanket tightened itself around the creature's face like shrink-wrap. She hoped to suffocate it to death, killing it before it killed her.

Startled by the sticky barrier plastering its face, it began shaking its head wildly about like a cat stuck in a paper bag. When this didn't work, it reared up in a panicked fright and smashed its head into the side of the stadium wall, fracturing the reinforced cement.

It rebounded off the wall, lurching back before making a mad dash across the arena like a blind bull. A thunderous impact shook the stadium as the monster crashed against the opposite wall. A careless spectator, standing too close to the railing, lost his footing and toppled over the safety rail. He let out a scream as he fell into the arena.

The scrawny alien, a Dipthok, had long, lanky arms and legs and tiger-like stripes on his slender figure. Dazed by the fall, he gradually stood up in the worst possible location—directly in the path of the lumbering T-Rex.

Unable to move out of the way fast enough, he was solidly trampled by the beast. The loud crunch of his bones breaking prompted a roar of excitement from the audience, along with a round of cheers and shrill whistles.

Eventually, the tyrannosaur made its way back to where Danica lay in the sand. She'd barely had enough time to catch her breath, and she was a little surprised that the monster could hold its own breath for so long.

She watched as it stretched its jaws open with formidable strength until, at last, the energy barrier ripped like tissue paper being pulled apart.

"Oh, fucking Helios!" Danica yelped just as its menacing snout came down again to try and snatch her up.

Slightly rattled from its previous encounter with her, the beast was more cautious this time. So much so that its aim was off and the snapping jowls fell a bit short of nipping off her head. Subsequently, it somehow managed to get its front teeth snagged on her crab-shell armored bikini.

As it reared back on its hindquarters, she rose up with it, reaching around its snout and hanging on for dear life so as to avoid sliding into its gaping maw. The last thing she needed right now was to fall prey to those bone-crunching teeth.

Not finding it particularly appealing to have a blue creature sticking to its face, the T-Rex gave a couple of violent shakes of its head and flung Danica off. She flew through the air and crashed down onto the ground several meters away with a padded *oomph*. She rolled a few times before skidding to a stop in the sand.

Rough granules of sand made their way inside the flesh wound on her leg, and she gritted her teeth against the pain as she slowly pushed herself up onto her hands and knees. Her heart pounded in her chest but she continued to force herself up; there was no time to rest.

She staggered to her feet and, balancing on one good leg, swayed about like a reed in the wind. She finally managed to steady herself and looked up to find the T-Rex was still shaking its head in an agitated manner.

It took her a moment before she spotted her bikini top still stuck between its teeth like a strand of dental floss that had somehow gotten snagged there. That's when it dawned on her what else that meant and, sighing loudly, she looked down at her bare chest, her breasts half-caked with yellow sand which clung in patches to her sweaty body.

As embarrassing as it was to find herself topless, her dark blue nipples on display for everyone to see, she pushed the embarrassment down and focused on how she could survive this. Things weren't going well, and she was injured and exhausted. If she couldn't figure out a way to beat this creature in the next sixty seconds, then she wasn't going to defeat it at all.

The televid drones swooped down and took the liberty of broadcasting her nudity onto the large stadium monitors to rile up the crowd. Ignoring them, she turned her attention back to her opponent; it had managed to yank the garment out and was already prowling the arena for her.

Spotting her quickly, the monster let out a roar to remind her who was boss. Then, with a renewed vigor, it galloped over, its tail whipping to and fro excitedly as it barreled toward her. She braced herself as it opened its mouth wide and chomped down, engulfing her with one bite. With that, she was gone.

The audience let out a round of stunned gasps as the tyrannosaur ate Danica whole. But after a brief silence, so quiet you could hear a pin drop, a wave of murmurs rippled through the crowd.

The audience's low grumblings quickly erupted into cheers as Danica, her leg muscles rippling against the strain, slowly stood up inside the beast's mouth, prying it open like a jack ratcheting open a bulky freighter door.

This she thought, *was why you never ever skip leg day.* That, and the fact that squats kept her ass so perfectly sculpted it would have made *Alle'drexia*, the Dagon goddess of love, jealous.

Defiant till the end, Danica braced herself inside the beast's mouth, her metallic arm arched over her head protectively. She grunted so hard that her own saliva flew from her mouth as she agonizingly pried open the monster's jaws from the inside, her shoulder pressed firmly into the roof of its mouth.

Danica finally managed to get the maw halfway open when her metallic arm's internal servos sparked and hissed in protest of the strain they were forced to endure before sending up a spray of sparks.

"Don't give out on me yet," she groaned as her artificial arm began to falter. Without her arm, she wouldn't have the strength to fend off this beast.

Its slimy tongue came up between her quivering thighs and slithered across her body like a Brilaxian eel. Its tongue slid back down her front, between her breast, and down through her legs again, molesting her for all to see.

She groaned in disgust as it slid back up her backside, starting between her legs before slipping between her butt cheeks and swirling around her taught back, coating her in sticky, saliva-infused mucus.

She turned her face to the side as its tongue continued devouring her with an insatiable hunger; its foul breath wrapped around her like a cloak of death. "Ugh," she muttered, her nose wrinkling up with the stench of the beast's hideous breath.

Just when it looked like she was going to be eaten alive, a stealth battleship decloaked over the stadium. Danica looked up in time to see a hatch open beneath the ship and an absolute specimen of a Dragonian warrior, each arm bigger than her entire torso, leapt out of the ship via a tactical rope and rescue harness.

Rappelling downward, he wielded two triple barrel plasma blasters and began firing them as soon as he'd jumped out of the bay of the ship.

The scorching hot plasma bolts bit into the thick hide of the T-Rex, causing it to relinquish its hold of Danica and angrily snap at the Dragonian whose hot sting was sorely felt.

Danica flopped to the ground with a thud, landing on her back. Rolling over, she quickly raised her gaze to see what in the bloody Helios was going on. Sand caked her entire body as it mixed with the thick blood laced saliva that coated her blue skin, but she didn't care. Right now, she was more concerned with figuring out her next move.

As the Dragonian warrior held the giant lizard at bay, the IGS televid drones buzzing about her head sensed the interference of the hovering ship and changed from their default setting of entertainment drones into seeker-destroyers.

Their typically green bug-like eyes flickered to red as their camera equipment retracted and was replaced by the gleaming muzzles of laser cannons. Converging on the Corvette class battleship hovering over the arena, the fleet of drones opened fire, but the low-yield laser blasts did little damage to the heavily armored warship.

As the pesky televid drones continued their assault, a heavy-ordinance, dual-barrel plasma-canon dropped down from a gun-bay beneath the nose of the ship and made quick work of them.

The drones erupted in a daisy-chain of fiery bursts, the concussion of blasts sounding like noisy popcorn exploding overhead. The firefight rattled the stands and forced the spectators to cover their ears as flaming debris crashed down around them.

When the televid screens went blank, the audience began to hiss and boo. This was not a part of the show, and, as might be expected, they weren't all too happy about it. Many even began to shout and throw things up into the air at the ship; most of the items fell short, though a few pinged off the armored hull with no noticeable effect.

Danica sat up in a puddle of dinosaur drool and looked at her rescuer with probing eyes. "Kregor?" she asked, dazed and confused.

Kregor Zekkidion was quite literally the last person in the galaxy that she expected to ever come to her rescue...and here he was with the crew of the *Skywend?* It didn't make any sense.

Kregor landed on his feet a short distance from her, his heavy boots clanking down noisily even amid all of his blasting.

Danica sat up on her knees, her robotic arm still sparking near the shoulder socket, as she tried to make sense of the whirlwind of activity going on all around her.

"What in the seven moons are you doing here?"

"I'm rescuing you, hot-tits, that's what," he replied, glancing down at her bare chest as he continued providing cover fire.

She looked down again and, having forgotten that she was mostly nude, rolled her eyes when she grasped his innuendo.

Kregor sidled up next to Danica, and, crouching, threw one of his guns across his back where it snapped down onto the magnetic holster. With his freed-up arm, he bent low and effortlessly scooped her up and drew her into him, sending the crowd into a frenzy of cheers and catcalls.

The coolant cartridge of his plasma blaster glowed bright orange, signaling his weapon was close to overheating, but he continued to lay down suppressing fire long enough to give them time to escape.

Pressed up against his massive chest, Danica looked into his lime-green eyes as he radioed the ship. "I've got her, *Skywend*. Reel us in."

With that, they rose into the air as the *Skywend* drew them up. Just then, several green plasma bolts flashed past them, and they looked down to see two IGS guards rush out onto the arena field to try and stop their escape.

"Oh, no you don't!" a voice shouted.

There was a loud *thump* and the two guards mysteriously dropped to the ground, both of them incapacitated. Standing over their unconscious bodies was Ladgara, holding a spiked club.

"If anyone's going to kill that wench, it's gonna be me."

Ignoring the T-Rex off to the side licking its wounds, she bounded over the guards, and, before Kregor and Danica rose out of reach, she leapt into the air. Extending her hand as far as she could, she managed to barely clasp onto the leather straps of one of Danica's sandals.

"You're not leaving without me!" she shouted up at them.

Kregor and Danica merely looked down at the woman dangling from Danica's leg and then back at one another. "A friend of yours?" he asked.

"I wouldn't exactly say that."

He accepted her vague answer then helped them both up into the belly of the ship. As soon as he'd secured both women inside the hangar bay, he looked down one last time to see the T-Rex turning its aggression onto the guards.

Aroused from their blackout by slashing teeth, they shrieked in blood-curdling agony as the dinosaur dismembered them.

Entertainment resuming as usual, the crowd grew uproarious at the grisly sight, letting out raucous cheers as the *Skywend* pulled away, rapidly disappearing behind a cluster of clouds.

9

Deunan's ship emerged from the nebula a little worse for wear. Its confrontation with the Suk'Naath'Degas ensured that she'd need to get the ship overhauled the next time she was at a spaceport. Unfortunately, she didn't currently have enough credits for a complete tune-up, so it was a good bet they'd be looking rather raggedy for the next five months or so.

Lycia finished her decontamination process and then stripped off her EV suit, piece by piece and layer by layer. Once she'd gotten out of the spacesuit, she dabbed her chest, arms, and legs dry with a towel. The events outside had been rather intense, and that stress had soaked through her clothes.

She tossed the towel onto a nearby bench, walked over to the hatch that led into the main ship, hit the button, and stood aside as she waited for it to slowly roll open.

The hatch slid away. Deunan stood outside the airlock with folded arms and a scowl on her face. She tapped her foot anxiously and let out a loud, exasperated sigh when Lycia appeared in the opening.

"Don't you *ever* go and do anything like that again. Do you hear me? You could have been killed!"

"Don't get your panties in a bunch, D. X-5 had my back. And…besides," she said, stepping up to Deunan's side and leaning in close, "I saved your ship."

She started off, but Deunan caught her by the elbow and spun her back around, forcing Lycia to face her. "You're not getting off that easily. Latrine duty for a week!"

"What?" Lycia gasped. "Why? That's totally unfair. I saved the ship!"

"Unfair? You don't even know what unfair is. Unfair is me letting you stay on with me free of charge. Unfair is looking out for you as though you were my own child and never *once* getting a thank you. Unfair is worrying my head off that I've put you in harm's way. *Again*."

"I'm sorry for being such a burden," Lycia snapped. "You can drop me at the next mining colony and be rid of me."

Royally miffed, Lycia turned and stormed off, her fists balled up at her sides.

"Wait," Deunan called out, reaching for the girl. But she drew back her hand at the last minute.

She instantly felt a surge of regret for being so hard on her, and of course it wasn't that she wanted the girl out of her hair. Contrary to it. She was actually quite fond of Lycia. And, perhaps just as importantly, she genuinely enjoyed her company.

The last year had been one amazing adventure after another. But if anything had become clear during their time together, it was that the girl was full of rage. A rage that was always just skin deep. And, to be honest, Deunan didn't know how to help alleviate that broiling anger that constantly threatened to bubble to the surface at the slightest provocation.

Deunan lowered her hand and then looked over at the X-5 droid standing in the airlock, watching her with glowing eyes. If she didn't know any better, she might even say it was silently judging her.

She sighed, letting her shoulders sag in defeat then made her way back to the bridge in a melancholy stupor.

She found Lycia already seated in the co-pilot's chair, feet up on the console, legs crossed. She sported black jeans with rips in them exposing streaks of blue flesh and black, tactical boots which she hadn't bothered to tie.

"What'd I say about boots on the console," Deunan said, slapping Lycia's feet away. The girl swung her legs off and folded her arms, determined to pout some more.

Deunan sank back in her chair and stared out at the nebula for a moment. "Look," she said, keeping her eyes fixed on the horizon, "I care about you. I truly do. But what you do with your life is up to you. I won't interfere. So, if you want to leave, that's fine. If you decide to stay, that's fine too. I'll stay out of your hair from now on."

Lycia looked over at Deunan and saw that she was being sincere. Her guard softened and she slowly unfolded her arms. "If I'm being honest," Lycia began, "I've heard better apologies."

Deunan shot her a sharp glance only to find that she was desperately trying not to laugh. "Oh, you little snot-nosed brat. You're just trying to get me riled up."

"I won't leave you," Lycia said, swinging her legs back onto the console and placing her boots on the dash. "You're too much fun."

Deunan smiled pleasantly at her, as though they'd made up. Then, with the same forceful swat as before, she knocked Lycia's feet away, sending them to the floor again.

"Good, because someone needs to clean those toilets and it's not going to be me."

"How about this...I'll give you a full hour foot massage every night for the rest of the week if you handle the toilets."

Deunan squinted at her, a coy smile forming on her lips.

"Make it a full body massage and you have yourself a deal."

Lycia raised an eyebrow, thought about it for half a second, and then threw out her hand. "You have yourself a deal, D."

Deunan accepted the girl's hand and they shook on it. "Deal," she said.

"Good," Lycia replied.

Deunan turned back to the controls and dialed in their destination. "Next stop," she said after clearing her throat, "Brexis mining facility."

"The Outer Rim?" asked Lycia.

Deunan nodded cordially. "The last bastion of free trade unbeholden to any Commonwealth laws in this part of the galaxy. If there's something you want, they'll have it. If there's something you need that they don't have, someone will surely be able to acquire it for you."

A wide grin formed on Lycia's face. "I want to get a tattoo," she said, fiddling with one of her ear piercings as she spoke. "A full-body tattoo."

Deunan smiled over at her, eyes wide with surprise. She wanted to chastise her for what she considered a huge mistake, but she was done policing Lycia for now. Instead, she simply asked, "Of what?"

Lycia shrugged and then looked over at Deunan and laughed when she saw the look of astonishment lingering on her face. "Don't worry, D," she informed her, "It's just a tattoo. It'll be good. Trust me."

"I'm trying," Deunan answered skeptically.

"It's not like I'm planning to host an orgy and accidentally infect all my guests with a lethal nano-virus," Lycia continued.

Completely taken aback, Deunan gasped. She tried to speak, but only a dumbfounded squawk came out as she balked noisily. She composed herself, and, face red with embarrassment, asked, "How did you…I mean…those documents were sealed by a court order. How in the bloody Helios did you hear about that?"

Lycia swirled her tongue stud in her mouth and smiled at Deunan. "You were a real wild one once, weren't you? Tell me about this girl gone wild, D. She sounds like someone I'd like."

"A couple of things. First off, I wasn't the one hosting the party. I was merely attending it. And secondly, I had no idea that NIDs disease was contagious across species lines."

"Still…it sounds pretty bad. All those people could have died, D. NIDs is a serious nanobot inflicted immune disorder."

"Nobody died. And now, thanks to my mistake, there's a cure for NIDs."

"Just one question, D. How many people did you have to bang to get the nanobots in your body to go haywire and mistake other hosts as a viral threat?"

"Look. I'm not proud of it. I just wasn't thinking about the consequences of mingling with non-technologically enhanced species. I never imagined that my own nanobot enhanced immune system would invade theirs and slowly take them over—let alone nearly kill all those people."

"No, seriously," Lycia said, shooting Deunan a serious look. "I'm going to need a number."

"Oh, hush, you."

"Like a dozen? Two dozen?"

Deunan ignored Lycia's prodding and explained what NIDs was in a little more detail. "It wasn't a well-known disease back then. Cases of it were extremely rare, and it always presented itself masked as other diseases, so it was truly hard to identify."

"Until you came along, that is," Lycia teased.

Deunan rolled her eyes. "At any rate, NIDs disease arises when a person with nanotech enhanced regenerative nanobots engages in unprotected sex with a non-modded person. Usually, a small number of nanobots makes it into the other partner via bodily fluids, such as saliva and semen. That sort of thing."

"Yeah they do…" Lycia said with a wink.

Deunan ignored her and continued on with her explication. "Ultimately, the nano-probes would leave their host and infiltrate the new host. To prevent serious infection, ideally, they'd been programmed to recognize that their environment had changed—by taking DNA samples and analyzing them—and then self-terminate. The other person would be completely fine."

"But…?" asked Lycia. "Something went wrong, didn't it?"

"Extremely wrong. As we discovered, the early nanobots had slow processing speeds, and whenever they were introduced into more than two or three hosts successively, they couldn't process the new DNA readings and defaulted into an immune system defense mode to protect the original host from invasive diseases."

"Go on…"

"However, not realizing they weren't actually in their original host, they would begin to attack the red blood cells in their new environment, thinking they were foreign bodies, thereby damaging the person's immune system."

"And these pissed-off nanobots then got swapped into new partners?"

"Exactly. And this created the perfect storm which led to an epidemic illness and, if not treated, could eventually have ended in needless deaths."

Deunan sighed, again. It wasn't her best moment, that was for sure. And the memory of it still haunted her.

"Hey, but you solved the problem. You saved all those people. The way I see it, you're a hero."

Deunan shook her head, dismissing any such notion of heroism. She'd merely gotten lucky.

Nevertheless, if Lycia knew about this, then she most certainly knew that Deunan hadn't always been a freighter captain either, but once had an illustrious career as one of the leading biotechnicians in all of the Seyfferian Republic.

In fact, she probably knew it was because of the NIDs incident that Deunan had lost her medical license in the first place. She would certainly have come to the conclusion that, as a disgraced physician, she really had no other choice but to eek out a living on the Outer Rim as a freighter pilot.

"Let's just…focus on the job, shall we?" Deunan urged, changing the subject so she wouldn't have to deal with the embarrassing trauma of her past any longer than necessary.

"You bet, D," Lycia replied, throwing her boots back up onto the console without regard to Deunan's feelings or reproachful glare.

Unable to tame the girl, Deunan rolled her eyes and blew a huff of disgruntled air out of the side of her mouth.

"I'm still getting a full body tattoo," Lycia said, just to mess with Deunan. Deunan slapped her boots off the console again, and shot her a dirty look—as if to say I dare you to try it.

Another moment passed and, unprompted, they both burst into a fit of laughter. The camaraderie and banter made these long hauls a little less dull. And they'd be lying if they said they didn't enjoy one another as much as two friends could.

Allie yawned and they both looked down at the indigo panther, who looked back at them with sleepy eyes, stretched, then re-curled itself and went to sleep.

"You can sleep through anything, can't you, girl?" Lycia said, reaching back and ruffling the tuft of hair on the panther's head. Allie just purred softly, the light rumble catching X-5's attention.

"The Lycia's animal seems to be experiencing technical difficulties."

Deunan and Lycia looked up at him with curious expressions on their faces.

"How so?"

"The motor that drives it is vibrating arrhythmically. Your cat may be in need of calibration."

Lycia laughed. "It's called purring," she informed the robot. "All cats do it."

"Oh, I see." With that he turned around and, with his rigid mechanical gait, walked back over to his docking station. He stiffly climbed onto the charging pad and sat down, the dock on his back locking into the charging port.

Deunan shot Lycia a wry smile and Lycia looked over at her.

"What?"

"Nothing," Deunan said with a light chuckle. "I'm just glad to have things back to normal. It feels like a family again."

Lycia reached over and put her hand on Deunan's thigh. Deunan looked over at her and smiled.

"I'm sorry I bit your head off back at the airlock," she said.

Deunan nodded. "You don't need to apologize. I'm the one that overreacted. I just worry about you."

Lycia reached out and brushed a tuft of Deunan's hair away from her dark, copper toned face. But, as she leaned in to kiss her, Deunan drew back.

"What are you doing?"

Lycia looked at her, suddenly tense and uncomfortable, and then, after lingering over her lips, let out a breathy laugh.

"You little snot!" Deunan said, shoving Lycia back into her seat. "Don't mess with me like that."

"Who knows?" Lycia said with a shrug. "You might have liked it."

"It would be like kissing my own daughter."

"Your loss," Lycia said.

Deunan merely rolled her eyes and went back to checking the readouts on her console.

"That's strange," she said, leaning forward and tapping the console.

"What's strange?" Lycia asked, leaning in and examining the digital readouts with her.

"For a second there it looked as though a ship was trailing us, but it's not there anymore."

"A cloaking device, maybe?"

Deunan looked at Lycia, a stern expression coming over her face. Turning to the controls, she said, "I don't want to take any chances," and spooled up the hyper-drive to full.

In another instant, her clunky old freighter made the jump into FTL, leaving the nebula and the Suk'Naath'Degas behind for good.

After the freighter blipped out of sight in a brilliant flash of light, the space where the vessel had previously been rippled with a strange distortion, and, for a brief second, another ship appeared, but quickly faded again.

10

Aboard the _Skywend_, Danica soon found herself standing in the smoky glass cylinder that was the infirmary shower. A warm spray of anti-bacterial wash expelled through several hundred micronozzles, blasting her skin. Although it stung slightly at first, after the initial shock eased, it began to feel really good, like a deep-cleanse of every pore on her skin.

The sprays died down and hot air flowed over her as the nozzles became blow-dryers, evaporating every drop from her body. Once the cycle of wash-and-dry was completed, she took in a deep breath to brace for the pain of her injured leg and stepped out of the shower. Careful not to put any unnecessary strain on her wounded leg, she hopped lightly over to fetch the white medical gown from the hanger on the nearby wall and quickly slipped it on.

The medical gown did its best to cover her for modesty, though as the backside hung open, her ass was put on display no matter which way she tied it. Ignoring the inconvenient draft, she hobbled over to the hospital bed and, gathering the gown behind her, took a seat as directed by the ship's physician and chief science officer, Skuld Lor'ellem.

As a Vreelax fishman from the ocean-world Kree'alek, Skuld typically wore over his head an aquatic EV suit which acted like an upside-down fishbowl. But for medical procedures, the inflexible helmet only got in the way. Instead, he opted for an apparatus that hung over his shoulders with pads that wrapped around his neck-gills, allowing him to work unhindered by the bulkiness of the full EV suit. It didn't take up any more room than a scarf, and the tubes which ran to the water tank on his back were discretely bundled together under his surgical scrubs.

Danica gathered her damp hair and tossed it over her shoulder as she patiently waited while Skuld attended to her wounds. She watched as he bent over her and gently pulled up her gown, exposing her entire leg and wound.

Skuld leaned over and ran a healing-wand over the lacerations on her thigh. Almost instantaneously, the shredded skin crystallized and wove itself back together with each pass of the wand. It was almost as if it were mending itself.

In a rare display of affection, she placed a hand on his shoulder and smiled at him. "It's been a long time, Skuld."

"Indeed, it has, Vice Admiral."

"It's just Danica now. But…my friends call me Dani."

"In that case, Mistress Dani, I'll have you in tip-top condition in no time." His giant, fish-like eyes blinked twice and he smiled at her with such warmth and sincerity that she couldn't help but smile back.

Kregor stood off to the side in the sickbay, leaning against the white wall as he picked at his sharp, lizard teeth with a toothpick the size of a pencil. Before Danica had time to thank him again for rescuing her, the sickbay doors slid open and Raven Nightguard briskly strode into the room.

"Danica Valencia, by order of her Excellency, Jegra Alakandra, wife to the Lord Emperor Rhadamanthus Dakroth, Imperatrix of the Dagon Empire and the Mother of Dagon, you are hereby recalled to Dagon Prime."

Danica nodded understandingly and then waited for Raven to reprimand her or lecture her on her lack of moral fiber for getting in over her head, for self-destructing her life, and for turning tail like a coward. Instead, Raven merely smiled and then said, "It's good to have you back."

"It is?" Danica asked, half perplexed. The last time they'd seen one another, Danica had been a total bitch to her. There was no reason for Raven to be kind, but here she was, welcoming her with a warmth and affection she honestly didn't deserve.

"You're a friend of Jegra's, and so, a friend of ours. Never let it be said that Raven Nightguard, Captain of the *Skywend*, was unreasonable." She winked at Danica and then strode back out of the room with as much urgency as she had arrived.

"I don't think I'll ever get a bead on that woman," Danica said in a hushed tone.

Skuld tore the sheath off a sterile pad with an organic gel healing compound plastered to one side and gently stuck it onto Danica's bum leg. Its coolness caused her to suck in a deep breath, her breasts heaving as she gazed down at the newly applied bandage.

She expected the excruciating pain to return, but whatever was in the gel worked wonders; it began to soothe her leg almost immediately. A wave of relief settled over her as the throbbing pain that had badgered her since the arena quickly faded away.

"Let's just say she's a sophisticated woman," Skuld replied to Danica's earlier comment about trying to figure out Raven Nightguard.

"And you, Kregor? What do you think of the captain?"

"She brought me onto her crew when I was at my lowest. Gave me a job when nobody else would. She gave me purpose. I would probably be in the mines of Brexis working off a prison term if it hadn't been for the captain taking me under her wing. I owe her a debt of gratitude I can never repay."

"Loyal to the end," she said, smiling at him. "That's rare in a man."

"You better believe it, hot-stuff." He moved the toothpick around in his mouth, swinging it to the other side, and grinned at her.

This was the second time he'd complimented her beauty. *Is he trying to flirt with me?* she wondered. Danica simply wasn't used to such affection. Or, maybe, she'd just forgotten that there were actually still decent people in the universe. And it seemed that Raven and her crew were among this rare breed.

"You two are on rather friendly terms these days," observed Skuld. "Anything I should know about?"

As he spoke, he gently reached down and grabbed her metal arm by the elbow, and, with his other hand, reached up under her armpit then rotated it backward and upward, until it clicked. Having unlocked the hinge, he removed the prosthetic from her shoulder socket, and pulled the metallic appendage off.

Kregor looked over at her and she met his gaze, both of them recalling her sweaty chest, back in the arena. She smiled at him with a look of amusement and waited for him to react to her gaze, but he didn't so much as flinch. He just grinned and continued to look into her eyes.

"Let's just say Kregor is a gentleman and leave it at that."

"Ah," Skuld said, glancing between the two of them as they held one another's gazes. "A sensitive subject, I surmise."

Kregor just huffed proudly and went back to picking at his teeth with his toothpick.

Danica turned her attention back to Skuld, who now had her arm sprawled out on a table and was using a laser welder to make alterations.

"Can you get it working again?" she asked.

"The damage seems to be extensive, but probably nothing I can't fix. However, it may take a day or two before I can get it properly functioning again."

"I see," she said. She brushed the sleeve of the gown down over her nub out of habit of concealing her injury. She felt that it often made others squeamish. She looked back up at Skuld. "So, am I free to go?"

Skuld nodded. "I give you a clean bill of health. Just try to stay off that leg for a few hours. Give yourself time to finish healing."

"I will do my best," she said, sliding off the medical table. When she turned to leave, she found Kregor waiting for her by the door. She cocked her eyes at him curiously and then asked, "Why do I get the sneaking suspicion that you've been ordered to be my personal chaperone for the duration of my time aboard?"

"The empress gave explicit instructions to ensure you return," he said. "Even if it means I have to toss you over my shoulder kicking and screaming."

She gave a sympathetic nod and answered, "That certainly sounds like Jegra."

Still, part of her felt wounded. She wanted to ask Jegra why she was always coddling her. She wasn't a child. And if it was out of compassion, or pity, or simple affection—it wasn't cute. It only made her feel useless. As though she couldn't take care of herself.

Danica would rather Jegra just give her the benefit of the doubt and trust her. But these days, they didn't seem to have much of that anymore.

"All right then, but I'm going to need you to help me get dressed, seeing as I only have one arm."

His eyes widened and then he nodded, as if to say it was no problem. She smiled again, reassuring him, "It's quite all right. Besides, you've seen everything anyway."

"Not everything," he grunted in his usual, gruff manner.

With a puckish grin, she turned and sashayed out of the medical bay with the large Dragonian following after her like a lovestruck pup.

"Ah, to be young again," Skuld sighed as he held up the metal arm and went back to studying Danica's prosthetic.

Once Kregor had seen Danica to her assigned quarters, she invited him in, again, under the pretext that she needed his help dressing. He stood nervously beside her bed as she reached back and undid the ties on her gown.

Then, letting the white medical gown slip from her violet-blue shoulders, she glanced back at the Dragonian, who quickly diverted his gaze when she caught him staring. She laughed and said, "It's all right. No need to be shy."

She turned to face him, and his eyes slowly settled on her womanly figure.

"Do you like what you see?" she asked, sounding almost timid.

Kregor gulped and then nodded. "You are a fine woman," he said. "But you are also engaged to the empress, are you not?"

She sauntered over to him and pressed her chest into his body, reached up with her one hand, and clutched him by the back of the neck.

"I'm feeling vulnerable, Dragonian, and the window for you to seize this opportunity is closing fast. So, what will it be?"

"Oh, what the Helios..." he said, taking her by the waist and kissing her lips.

Her eyes narrowed with delight as he took her in his meaty arms, and together they slowly settled down onto her bed.

Just then, Kregor's comm crackled and Angellyk's voice came over the speaker. "Hey, babe. I'm down in engineering trying to replace a coupler in the main power conduit to try and give the ship a power boost and was wondering if I could borrow your strength for a minute."

He reached to tap the pendant on his uniform to reply, when Danica swiftly removed it and held it out of reach.

"A girlfriend?"

Kregor nodded as he fished for the pendant, but she smiled deviously and dropped it onto the floor so he couldn't reach it.

"Will she get jealous if she finds out?"

"I don't know," he said, drawing back to think about it. "We only started dating a couple weeks ago. I'm still not sure she's the one for me. I mean...I enjoy her company, but we bicker constantly. And...she's athletic and has a body like no oth—"

"Look," Danica interrupted, "I just want to fuck. You can save the life story for another time."

"Ah," he said, rubbing the back of his head. Then, leaning in, he kissed her neck. She closed her eyes and waited for more kisses, but when none came, she opened her eyes to find him climbing off of her.

"What's wrong?"

"As much as I want to," he said, "it wouldn't be right."

"Ugh!" she sighed out in frustration. "You and your people's codes of honor. It's so…infuriating."

He smiled down at her naked body sprawled out on the bed before him and said, "Another time, perhaps."

With that, he fetched his communications pendant and left her room.

Unsatisfied and still horny as Helios, Danica let out another deeply frustrated sigh then rolled over onto her side and slipped her hand between her thighs.

As she played with herself, she also began to drift off to sleep. It was a race to see which would come first, the ecstasy of her imminent orgasm or the peaceful bliss of deep, undisturbed slumber.

In the very next moment, she let out a lust-filled groan and took in a deep breath, panting lightly.

At that same instant, the door to her quarters chimed again and, startled, she sat up in bed. She covered herself with the sheet and wondered who would come calling at this time of night.

"Who is it?" she asked, calling out to the unexpected visitor.

"It's me," Kregor's voice replied in a hushed whisper.

"It's open," she said, a smile forming on her lips.

With a *whoosh* of air, the doors to her quarters urgently parted and Kregor reappeared inside the small room. She looked up at him with wide, curious eyes, wondering what he was thinking.

"I changed my mind," he said.

Danica's grin spread ear to ear, and she quickly began unfastening his pants belt. At the same time, he stripped off his shirt then fell into bed with her.

"And here I thought you were one of the loyal ones," she teased, a touch of that Dagon cynicism lingering on her voice.

In Dagon culture, monogamy was viewed as grotesque. It was akin to a form of slavery to hold another person hostage to your love. But she knew that

Dragonians were fiercely loyal to their companions, which is why it was such a surprise that he'd returned to her.

She reached down and helped guide him into her. As she brushed his head against her delicate petals, he asked, "Don't you need to get ready first?"

"I've been ready for the past thirty minutes," she said with a sly grin. Just then they gasped out together as he entered her.

With a forceful thrust of his hips, she yelped. He was much larger than she had anticipated and the pain of his girth mingled with the pleasure of how he hit all the right spots.

Kregor grinned down at her smiling, violet-blue face as she reached up and ran her good hand across his beefy chest.

"I never said I was loyal to a fault…" he informed her, addressing her earlier statement. "That was your assumption."

"Are you saying I mistook you for being a nice guy?" she asked as the rhythm of her body settled into his ebb and flow.

She was about to speak again when he silenced her mouth with a kiss. His long, lizard tongue filled her mouth as it spiraled around like a corkscrew, but she accepted it happily and sucked on it—even playfully nibbling a bit.

Under the weight of his muscular body, she felt confined, crushed almost. Even so, his crushing weight excited her. In fact, she grew so excited that she drew his hand up from her breast and placed it on her throat. He squeezed down—not too hard—just enough to cause her to gasp with excitement, and to make that gasp raspy as it wheezed from her parted lips.

Never in a million years did she think she'd fall so low as to be slumming it with a Dragonian, let alone allow him to have his way with her, but she wasn't the same woman she once was.

On that point, Ladgara had been mistaken.

But, even she had to admit that Ladgara had been right about one thing— she did make mistakes. A lot of them.

This…right now…was just one more mistake from which she wouldn't learn a single damn thing. Still, right now she couldn't care less about her past indiscretions. Right now, all she wanted was to feel *wanted*.

She knew it was selfish of her. If half the things Ladgara had said about her were true, she was the most unlovable bitch this side of the galaxy. Damaged goods, to be sure.

Nevertheless, to be cared for by someone with a tender heart, to be scooped up in his strong arms and, in the throes of passion, forget for a nanosecond how much of a crap person she had become was, well, a welcome change.

And here, in this rough exterior of a brawny man, there was a sensitive and loving person on the inside. And she reveled in the fact that, for this brief moment in time, he'd chosen her above everybody else.

11

Rock and ice were all that made up the outer system asteroid belts. And, as every deep-space traveler knew, Brexis, a dwarf planet situated amongst an endless sea of korridium rich asteroids, was the final waystation for those venturing past the Outer Rim territories into uncharted space.

Beyond Brexis lay the Badlands, an extended area of unprotected space that ran along the outskirts of the asteroid belt. It was a well-known place for space pirates to lie in wait for passing ships, using large asteroids for cover. They'd harpoon, board, and raid freighter vessels and any ships that were attempting to fly outside the detection of the Imperial patrols and the IGS's jurisdiction.

One had to be either desperate or borderline insane to risk traveling way out here, beyond the safety of Commonwealth protection. Out here, along the asteroid belt, space was ripe with smugglers, black market dealers, pirates, petty criminals, and the occasional fearless bounty hunter who was just as much a criminal as he was a lawman.

Several of the asteroids along the stretch of the Badlands contained spaceports where ruthless pirates and illicit entrepreneurs could convene and do business without the meddling intrusions of the law. These dives acted as refueling stations for the smaller transports and the mining ships that hopped from belt to belt.

Mining vessels were about the only ships off limits to pirate raids, since the miners always put up one hell of a fight and the pirates usually came away battered, bruised, and empty handed.

Additionally, the administrator of the Brexis colony, a fierce Dragonian woman and legendary ex-gladiatrix named Gamagor Dar'Vek, was known to hunt down and destroy entire pirate armadas for steeling her property. As such, the pirates steered clear of her wrath and stuck to easier prey—mainly cargo vessels and merchant ships trying to bypass security checks along the main trading routes.

Brexis was part of the Commonwealth, yet was so far away from any of the major systems that the laws were lax enough to allow for a certain underground economy to thrive there. A blackmarket of galactic proportions.

With a population of about two-hundred and seventy thousand inhabitants and another three-hundred and fifty thousand miners, Brexis was the main strategic trading hub in all of the allied worlds.

Gamagor Dar'Vek governed the Brexis colony with strict discipline and her own system of law. At the same time, however, she allowed the blackmarket to thrive, making a fortune regulating it. As long as you followed her three rules of law, you'd be fine.

First, you showed mutual respect for all those living on Brexis. Secondly, you didn't put your nose where it didn't belong. And last but not least, you always paid your dues.

Keep to Gamagor's simple rules, and everything was peachy keen.

Deunan Atiyah brought the freighter down onto the yellow striped landing platform that sat a klick outside the main dome. Once the freighter had touched down, a transparent wall, built of hexagonal plates of aluminum oxynitride, rose up like an intricate latticework and engulfed the entire platform in less than a minute.

Fully extended, the hexagonal plates locked into place with a resounding series of *clacks* and instantly sealed themselves shut within an energy shield that rippled over their surface. The forcefield turned the otherwise clear dome into a giant, blue glowing bubble.

Deunan heard the air outside pressurize, and she powered down the ship. Looking over at Lycia, who was fiddling with her tongue stud, she said, "Well, we're here."

Lycia squinted out the front windows and peered at the domed city in the distance. A much larger dome capped the Brexis mining colony, which sat at the end of a long series of pneumatic tubes that shuttled transport pods back and forth from the central base and the landing pads.

"I was expecting something more archaic…but this place is state of the art," she said, more impressed with Brexis than she'd expected to be.

"That's one of the benefits of being privately funded by a quintillionaire."

"You're shitting me? Gamagor has a quintillion credits?"

"More like forty quintillion," Deunan informed the awestruck girl. "Korridium mining pays well."

"Pays better when you're the Queen of the Underworld," Lycia observed, taking another gander at the cosmopolitan mining facility.

Deunan shot Lycia a disturbed glance and said, "Just don't call her that to her face, if you don't want her to rearrange all of your teeth."

"Got it," Lycia said, acknowledging Deunan's warning about Gamagor's testiness. Touching her fingertips to her brow, she gave Deunan a quick two-finger salute to assuage any further worries.

<<Prepare for ship-wide security scan>> the automated voice of the ship chimed.

Deunan raised her hand and motioned for Lycia to keep still while the red energy beam, a wall of light that seemingly sliced through the whole ship, incrementally made its way through the entire vessel, deck by deck.

It was simply a precautionary measure. Any dangerous or toxic cargo could be quarantined away from the main colony before ever risking a facility breach.

The CT scan could map every item in a ship in perfect 3D, including any hiding nooks that stowaways might be utilizing to sneak into the colony. Additionally, using interlaced infrared laser technology, it was capable of sniffing out explosives, biological contaminants, and even unregistered livestock.

This transparency was one of the prices you paid for setting down on Brexis. Nothing came or went without Gamagor's explicit knowledge and approval.

If flagged as a problem, the passengers and their cargo would be instantly rerouted and sent back to their landing pad, along with a ten-minute disembarkation warning.

After ten minutes was up, the landing pad shields dropped and anything still there would be sucked into the vacuum of space.

It was a well-known rule that anyone setting down on Brexis had to be certain they had their shit in order lest they risk being jettisoned off Brexis and slapped with a strike on their permanent record.

A second-time offense and you'd have your docking permits banned for a full three years. A third time and you'd be banned from docking at the spaceport ever again. At least, that's what it said in the Trade Federation manual of rules and regulations.

Lycia swung her legs out of her chair and sprang up to her feet. She tossed the holopad she'd been reading onto the console and then, giving her charcoal gray tank top a tug to flatten out the wrinkles, started for the cargo hold to help Deunan with prepping and transporting the cargo.

Allie, not wanting to be left behind, rose up, stretched long, her front paws spreading as her massive claws popped out, yawned, and then followed after her girl. As they exited the cabin, X-5 turned his head to track them.

Lycia noticed his bright eyes following her, and she paused and looked over at him. "Stay here, X-5. I need you to guard the ship and the cargo while we're gone. Apparently, marauders are a thing out here."

"Marauding is illegal," X-5 stated, preparing to quote Trade Federation rules and regulations to her.

She nodded and laughed softly, holding up her hand to halt him. "Yes, that's right." She cleared her throat, finding a more serious tone. "Yes. And that's why I need you here. To keep the peace."

"Won't the Lycia need protecting?" asked the android.

"Allie and Deunan will be with me, so I'll be well protected," she assured her concerned robot. Although she didn't think his A.I. was advanced enough to actually be capable of worrying, he was, however, programmed to protect her at all costs, and needed to be ordered to stand down.

"Just stay here and protect the ship," she insisted, "that's an order." She slapped him on the shoulder in a reassuring manner and then smiled at him.

"Copy that," X-5 replied. His eyes changed from soft white to an orange glow. He stood and moved to the center of the flight cabin, positioning himself facing the large windows of the ship. Eyes glowing as he scanned for marauders, Lycia wagered he'd make a fine sentry.

Soon enough, Lycia arrived at the aft cargo hold with Allie in tow. Deunan looked up as she ratcheted the rigging tightly to the hover skiff and secured the metal crates that they were bringing to Brexis. "Almost done here," she said pointedly, intending to draw Lycia's attention to the fact that she hadn't helped.

Lycia shrugged as though there was nothing she could do about it. She wasn't the one that wanted to hurry up and get off this boat. "If I didn't know any better, D, I'd say you had a hot date you were rushing out to meet."

Deunan raised an eyebrow at the girl. "I honestly have no bleedin' clue what you're on about."

Deunan finished securing the supplies, which were mostly medical, and a few "special-order" items that they'd managed to smuggle past all the checkpoints. Special-order items like the vintage Dragonian ale that Gamagor was fond of, and an entire case of Alpha Centauri Red. Last but not least, they had a container of the recreational drug, Nividium 3. The latest shipment to come out of Dagon Prime…it was all the rage right now.

"There," Deunan said, dusting off her hands then standing up straight, hands moving to her hips so she could stretch out her back.

These long-range hyper-hauls were several months in and several months out. And she swore that half of that time she spent lounging in her chair which, as it happened, was murder on her lower back.

"Cargo is secured and ready for delivery," she said through a strained larynx as she stretched the tension right out of her taught neck muscles.

Lycia, standing at the top of the loading ramp, went over to the wall and smashed a large yellow button positioned next to one of the aft bulkheads. The red warning light started flashing on the back wall and the loading ramp began to gradually lower.

With a clank, the ramp clamped down onto the landing pad, followed by the hiss of the hydraulics decompressing. The two women looked at each other, and Deunan nodded at Lycia to follow after her then sauntered down the ramp.

Before debarking the ship, Deunan fetched her brown leather flight jacket off the wall hook and threw it on. It complemented her black leather pants and favorite pair of tactical boots that, rain or shine, she always wore.

Already following after her, Lycia paused midway on the ramp to look down at Allie, who, sensing she'd stopped, gazed up at her with those emerald cat eyes of hers and forced Lycia to fall in love with the fuzzy-wuzzy purple face all over again.

"Don't worry, girl," she promised, "I'll do my best to keep a low profile."

When Lycia and Allie finally stepped off the landing ramp and sidled up next to Deunan, she stepped to the edge of the ramp and raised a transmitter in one hand. With her thumb she tapped the large green button which read "Autonomous Mode." A flurry of blinking lights signaled something going on in the computer-brain of the skiff's limited A.I. and, with the resonant hum of anti-grav coils, the hover skiff rose up and slowly began to follow after them.

A short jaunt to the loading platform of the transit tube, and a pod whisked up to them moments after they'd arrived. Its sliding doors spread open, Deunan tapped the button on the transmitter, and the hover skiff boarded the capsule. Deunan squeezed in behind it and turned to Lycia. "It's a bit cramped in here. You guys take the next one. I'll wait for you on the other side."

Lycia nodded and watched Deunan through the glass as the doors slid shut, first the shuttle pod's doors and then the tube's outer ones.

A loud gush of air sounded and the pod whisked off with the speed of a Maglev train shooting out of a tunnel.

Allie growled lightly for attention, and Lycia looked down and scratched behind her ears. When the second pod arrived, the double set of doors promptly slid open all at once, and Lycia boarded. She looked back to find Allie pacing in front of the entrance, eyeing the gap between the platform and the pod timorously.

"Well, aren't you just a big ole fraidy-cat?" she laughed. "Come on you fluff-butt, there's absolutely nothing to worry about. These things," she assured her nervous travel companion as she gestured to the interior of the capsule, "are perfectly safe."

Reluctantly, Allie leapt onboard and then hopped up onto the bench-style seat. Lycia looked back across the landing platform to see X-5's orange glowing eyes lighting up the inside of the ship's canopy. *At least the ship will be safe*, she mused.

Lycia plopped down into her seat, settling in next to Allie, who licked the girl's blue hand with her bright pink tongue. Having seemingly conquered her fear, Allie stretched out onto the bench and let one of her hind legs dangle lazily off the edge.

Sensing the passengers were aboard, the automated voice informed them to <<Stand clear of the doors>> and the pod doors closed. A green light above the doors turned on, alerting the passengers that the pod was secured. Then, in a surprisingly fluid momentum that felt like a horizontal elevator, the pod whisked off toward its pre-programmed destination of Customs and

Immigration.

A minute and thirty seconds later, the doors opened and Lycia and Allie stepped out. A guard greeted them with a security wand and said, "I.D. checkpoint. Show me your wrist."

She held out her wrist and he waved the baton over it. An area just below the surface of her skin lit up green and a holoprofile rose from her arm to show her face and personal data.

Of course, her information was all forged, including her name, since she had no real identity.

"Mrs. Bobertson?" the man asked.

Lycia smothered a giggled. "Yes, I'm Mrs. Bobertson." The snicker stifling drew the guard's attention. When his eyes locked onto her, she promptly put on her best poker face. Finally he was satisfied nothing fishy was going on.

He then turned his attention to the large, indigo cat. As a companion animal, Allie needed animal tags, proving her shots were up to date and that her exotic animal permit was in order which, of course, she neither had nor was capable of obtaining. Those, too, had been forged.

All the same, Lycia thought, *this security guy doesn't need to know any of that.*

"Anything to declare, Mrs. Bobertson?"

"Just my pet cat," she answered, jutting her chin toward Allie, who sat obediently at her feet. "She's my companion animal," she added at the last minute, to ensure there was no confusion about Allie's purpose here.

He eyed the indigo panther suspiciously, his gaze getting momentarily lost in those wide, emerald-colored eyes. As Allie watched, the man fell into a sort of trance, and Allie made a low growling in the back of her throat which caused him to snap out of it.

The guard shook his head, as though he were coming out of a deep sleep. Not quite understanding what had happened, he grew rather anxious and gulped hard. As the cat eyed him with a frightening kind of gaze that sent shivers up and down his spine, he decided it best not to test the limits of the animal's patience and waved them through the checkpoint with his baton.

"Move along," he said, urgently stepping aside so they could pass without any further delay. "Move along."

Lycia and Allie shared an amused look as they filed out of the checkpoint.

"That's a neat trick," Lycia said, patting Allie on the head. Allie merely pranced along beside her, happy to be taking a stroll.

Once they'd stepped out into the open concourse, however, they immediately drew to a stop again. To Lycia's dismay, a full security detail had surrounded Deunan and was, at that moment, shoving her to the ground, forcing her to her knees as they detained her.

A crowd was already gathering to see what the commotion was, when Deunan looked up and caught Lycia's shocked gaze and subtly shook her head *no*, warning her to keep back and not to get involved.

"*Mev'lek*, tell us where it is," one of the security officers demanded.

Lycia recognized the belter term for *foreigner*. But the truth was, a more accurate translation of *mev'lek* meant something more along the lines of *invader*.

Deunan leaned back on her heels and looked up at the security guard. "I don't know what you're talking about, *ba'vek*."

Lycia had to hold back her smile. *Ba'vek* was belter speech for *moron*. In Dagoni, moron was *ba'vekleth*. As such, she saw the linguistic DNA shared between two languages and how belter speech had merely altered and simplified Dagoni, filing it down to a more practical, easier to understand form.

The officer grabbed Deunan by her jacket collar and jerked her toward him then shoved her back, manhandling her a bit, trying to frighten her and show her that he was the one in charge. "Don't lie to us, Ms. Atiyah. We know you have it. Space Marshal Xarthon Dovek tipped us off that you were in possession of it."

"I don't know who this so-called Xarthon is," Deunan lied. "And I certainly don't know whatever it is you keep referring to."

"Don't play dumb with me, *mev'lek*. The precious cargo. I want to know where it is."

"Over there?" she said, nodding at the hover skiff that was still tracking her signal.

The security officer raised his hand and signaled for his men to check out the crates on the skiff. They undid the metal clasps and opened the lids, tossing most of the contents into the street. Not finding what they were looking for, they turned back toward their superior and shrugged.

"Satisfied?" Deunan grumbled, annoyed by their mistreatment of her.

Of course, the look on the guard's face said it all. He had been expecting to find a great treasure but, instead, had found nothing of importance to him.

Deunan realized this meant that Xarthon had probably lied to Brexis security just so that she'd get detained by the authorities and maybe held up long enough for him to catch up to them. Typical marshal strategy.

The officer held up a holopad and scanned her face, getting her personal information from her biometrics.

"Deunan Atiyah of the Seyfferian Republic. Commercial freighter license tag Delta 5-00-75-75. Clearance, green." He glanced back down at her and scowled. It was clear he was trying to think of some trumped-up charges to stick her with, but was having trouble thinking of any he could pin on her. She truly was squeaky clean.

"Are we done here?" Deunan shook off the guards to either side of her that tried to help her up and rose to her feet using her own power and volition. She shot them all a menacing glare and waited for her answer.

The chief security officer turned his head and saw Lycia standing there, watching him with a keen interest, and he eyed her shiftily.

"Can I help you with something, *ba'vek vargathal?*"

Ah, yes, Lycia thought. *More insults. Ba'vek vargathal* meant: insolent child.

"Unless you want me to write up a formal complaint to your supervisor for unnecessary harassment," she said, using her aristocratic entitlement to put him in his place, "you could kindly step out of my way."

She turned her nose up at him and scoffed for added effect. When he reluctantly complied and did as she said, she added insult to injury by saying in an audible voice which his compatriots were sure to hear, "That's what I thought, bootlicker."

That, apparently, had crossed a line; his eyes immediately grew wide with rage and his whole countenance became incensed. Reaching out to grab her, he growled, "Now, listen here you stuck-up Dagoni slut. You might think you're the queen of the anthill where you come from. But out here, we belters make the rules."

The security officer grabbed her wrist as though he intended to continue scolding her like a petulant child when Deunan sprang forward and hollered, "Don't touch her!"

Deunan's fist collided with the officer's jaw, sucker-punching him and sending him staggering back. She'd successfully drawn all attention back to her, just as she'd planned. And, now, he had his excuse to detain her.

Stunned, he rubbed his jaw, trying to massage away the pain then growled, "Arrest her!"

The two additional security officers gripped her by either arm and held her tight. "On what charges?" Deunan demanded to know, making sure he gave her a valid reason for stopping her this time. "Of shutting up a loud-mouth, asshat?"

"Assaulting an officer," he replied, unamused, still rubbing his jaw and opening and closing his mouth as he tried to massage away the soreness.

"*Graddak!*" she cursed, squirming obstinately as they forced her arms behind her back and slapped the magnetic restraints onto her wrists.

As the guards hauled her away, Deunan looked back over her shoulder at Lycia with a roguish grin and winked.

A few moments later, they shoved her into a side-by-side patrol UTV parked at the edge of the street. The two guards hanging off either side held onto the roll cage while they kept Deunan pinned between their uniformed bodies.

The lead security officer shifted the SxS patrol UTV into drive then slammed down onto the accelerator. The tires skidded a few times before making purchase with the road and the high-pitched electric whine of the motors signaled bystanders to get out of the way as they raced up the street.

Lycia, still a little shocked by everything that had just transpired, looked down at Allie and sighed. "Maybe I was wrong about it being just another quick pit stop."

Allie cocked her ears back and made a curious sounding whine that almost seemed as though she were asking what their next move was.

"I don't know about you, girl," she informed the indigo panther, "but I don't intend to leave D behind for a single nanosecond on this blasted rock. Unfortunately, breaking her out of jail might be easier said than done."

Allie paused momentarily and cocked her head as Lycia pushed through the crowd, almost as if the large cat were ruminating over her mistress's every word. Seemingly satisfied with the plan, she continued on after the blue-skinned girl.

Making their way together down the promenade, Lycia glanced around at all the flashy signs for casinos, eateries, and other forms of more lewd entertainment that adorned both sides of the street. Everywhere bustled with the sounds of customers and merchants haggling over overpriced goods, prostitutes soliciting clients, and blackmarket dealers trying to push Nividium 3.

Entering down a side street, she shuffled through the dense crowd and headed toward the central location of the bustling merchant district. Opening up before her, as if she'd stumbled upon a magical garden, was a tattoo parlor. She paused in her tracks and, desperately wanting to get her full body tattoo, stepped toward the glowing neon entrance.

No, she told herself. *First things first.* Rescuing Deunan was her top priority now. Getting a tattoo would have to wait.

If the shit were ever to hit the fan while visiting this rock, Deunan had told her to seek out a locksmith named Melehkor.

"Come along, girl. Stay close and follow me."

12

Ladgara paced back and forth in front of the hangar bay exit, mumbling obscenities to herself. She'd tried to follow Kregor and Danica into the ship after their rescue, but that good for nothing Dragonian leather-neck had locked her inside the hangar with no way out. She'd been down here for three hours now and was losing her sanity.

It was a good bet that they were all deliberating on what to do with her. Danica wasn't her biggest fan, and Raven and she had unfinished business. So, in all probability, it was a fifty-fifty chance whether they would decide to let her stay onboard or jettison her out of the nearest airlock.

Bored out of her mind, she sauntered up to the large hangar doors, which led into the ship's interior and waved her hands about, thinking it might be a faulty sensor. Still, nothing. The doors merely bleated at her in polite dismissal of her frantic gesturing.

Angered by their stubborn defiance of her desire to enter the ship, she pounded on the doors with her fists. The banging did little to convince them to open, however, and, feeling like a Qui'loxian rat trapped in a maze, she growled, "Let me out of here!"

The doors merely bleated at her again, as if to say "no dice," and she kicked them with her boot then threw up her arms in defeat. Spinning around dramatically, she leaned back against the doors, looked up at the ceiling, and let out a vexed sigh.

As soon as she'd exhaled, the doors parted and, with a startled scream, she fell backward into the corridor behind her.

Sprawled out on the floor in the middle of the passageway, she blew at a lock of pink and purple hair and let it fall down the side of her face.

Once she'd gotten back on her feet, she looked up and down both ends of the long corridor. Not knowing which way to go, she decided to make a blind guess and turned left.

After strolling about the meandering corridors for a while, she stumbled upon the chatter of hushed voices. *Finally*, she thought. *Other people.*

She cautiously entered what appeared to be the rec room of the ship only to discover that someone had left the televid on. It was playing a gladiator match on some distant world she didn't recognize.

Having been through it herself, she wasn't in any mood to watch the fights. Snatching up the remote and aiming it at the monitor, she said, "Enough of that nonsense."

The screen went dark and she tossed the remote control onto the nearby white-leather sofa.

She looked around the room. There was a 3D digital air-hockey table that doubled as billiards, a standing bar, and kitchen nook where she found a decent sized refrigerator.

Thirsty, she went over to the fridge and cracked it open. Leaning forward to peer inside, she let the soft glow of the inner light and the cool air wash over her. There were plenty of MREs stacked neatly in the back, but she was much more relieved to find a couple of bright orange Dragonian ales just waiting to be downed.

She pulled out a bottle, pried the cap off, and returned to the sofa, just letting herself sink into it. Slouching down, she kicked off her sandals and put her blue feet up onto the coffee table.

She wriggled her toes, her patent black nails shimmering in the fluorescent light, and took another sip of the orange ale. She belched loudly, assuming nobody was watching her, then realized she wasn't alone. "I know you're there. You might as well stop hiding."

"*Ah, shucks,*" a dejected sounding voice lamented, "how could you tell?"

A nanosecond later, the air wavered and the petite form of a young girl dressed in a military-grade optics suit appeared before her. She was perched on the coffee table like a feline, hands between her knees and thighs as she gazed curiously at Ladgara from behind a massive visor that resembled a VR headset.

Gyllek reached up with one hand and raised the visor to the top of her head and looked at the pirate with large, lime-green cat-eyes.

"And what, may I ask, are you?" Ladgara had never seen an alien species like this girl before, and she knew that she must be one of the rare finds hailing from a distant fringe world, so far out from the galactic core that most never pay it any mind.

"I'm Gyllek," the girl said. "I'm supposed to watch you and make sure you don't get into any trouble. Captain's orders."

"As you can see," Ladgara said, raising her beer in an amicable fashion and dispelling any notion that she was there for trouble, "I'm staying well behaved."

"But you stole *that* beer," Gyllek said, tilting her head toward the half-empty glass bottle in Ladgara's hand.

Ladgara smiled and then, leaning forward, cupped a hand to her mouth and whispered, "I won't tell if you don't."

Gyllek gasped. "Now I know why the captain wanted me to keep an eye on you," she said. "Space pirates are always up to no good."

"That's me, a regular ole rotten apple." Ladgara winked at her and took another drink.

"You seem nice enough, though," Gyllek added, still not entirely certain what to make of this space-pirate lady.

"Nice?" Ladgara laughed. "I'd hardly consider myself nice."

"You haven't tried to kill me," Gyllek chirped.

"Yet," Ladgara deadpanned. She pointed at her eyes with two fingers and then motioned toward Gyllek's, letting her know that she'd be watching her every move.

Gyllek gulped nervously.

"Just ignore her, Gyllek," a voice came from behind. "She's all bark and no bite, this one."

Both Ladgara and Gyllek turned to find Raven standing behind them, arms folded across her chest.

"Captain!" Gyllek said, springing up to her feet and hopping off the table.

"Gyllek, I'm sure Skuld would like some help tinkering with Danica's robotic arm. Would you mind assisting him?"

"I'm on it, boss lady!" Gyllek stiffened up and saluted Raven then bounded off on all fours.

Raven watched her leave, a quaint smile on her face. When Gyllek had disappeared from sight, though, the smile quickly faded. Raven turned back toward Ladgara with a stern glower, her dark green eyelids adding subtle contrast to the intensity of her amethyst gaze. Her eyes lit up brightly with hot pink Dygra energy as her biometric lie-detection mods turned on. Across the HUD of her optical lens flashed the words: *Interrogation mode* activated.

"What are you doing aboard my ship?"

Ladgara turned her back to Raven and sunk back onto the sofa. "Look, I have no beef with you, Raven. I just need a lift. Drop me off at the nearest starport, as long as it's out of IGS jurisdiction, and I'll be on my merry way."

"I'm not running some galactic taxi-service, sweetheart."

"Could have fooled me," Ladgara retorted, thumbing over her shoulder in the direction Gyllek had left.

"Look, I'm a reasonable woman, so I'll give you a chance to change my mind and explain exactly why I should keep you around. Otherwise, you might be taking a space-walk, and the next unlucky sap who finds you floating about can pick you up. Maybe your charms will work on them."

"You wouldn't?" Ladgara asked, shooting Raven a hurt look.

"Try me and see," Raven fired back, leaning over Ladgara, one arm on the back of the sofa. Both women stared at one another as if they were going to go at it, and then Ladgara broke her gaze.

Uninterested in all this posturing, Ladgara glanced over her shoulder, one corner of her mouth curling into a mischievous grin.

Although she'd never admit it, the truth was she didn't have any other option but to rely on Raven and her crew. So she decided to come out with the truth of it.

"Alright. I can make it worth your while."

"Go on..." Raven said, drawing back and folding her arms again as she listened to what Ladgara had to say.

"I've managed to get my hands on the access codes to the Nephilim communications array. If that's something that would interest you, then I'm willing to make a trade."

"You don't expect me to seriously believe that you're in possession of the access codes to the enemy's entire communications network, do you?"

"I didn't say network. I said, *array*. A single array in the Zargora system. But once you hack into it, you should have no trouble hacking into the rest of the network. And that, I should think, is worth a measly ride to the nearest space-port."

"All right, then," Raven said, squinting at Ladgara, "I'll bite. Give me the access codes and you'll have yourself a deal."

Ladgara let out a loud and lengthy sigh and then looked away. "I would…it's just that…"

"I knew it," Raven said. "You don't even have the codes."

"Fine, you caught me," Ladgara said, rising to her feet. Raising her hands defensively, a bottle of Dragonian ale dangling between her thumb and the edge of her right hand, she gestured with a half-curtsey in polite submission, as if to say she wouldn't dare challenge Raven's cunning and intellect. "I don't have the codes at the moment. But I know who does."

Raven shot Ladgara an uneasy look. "No. No way." She shook her head vigorously and added another, "Just nope."

"What do you mean, 'no way?'"

"There's not a chance in Helios that I'm helping you break out Novac Tamoran from Nyctan galactic penitentiary."

"Did I say anything about you breaking anyone out of anything? No. I'll be doing the breaking out myself. There's no risk to you or your precious little crew."

"Somehow I doubt that very much. Besides, even if he did have the access codes stored in that pea-sized brain of his, and even if I did go *completely* insane and decide to do this, it's simply not worth it. That place is in the heart of enemy territory, and there's no way we can infiltrate a maximum-security facility without months of planning first."

"In that case," Ladgara said, stepping forward, a subdued grin forming on one side of her mouth, "you're in luck."

Raven raised a curious eyebrow. "How so?"

"I've had months to plan. All those gladiator matches were mostly so the audience could see my top fall off. They only ever gave me exhibition matches— low level fighters with barely an ounce of skill to speak of. The rest of the time I spent bored out of my mind. So, I decided to create a plan to break Tamoran out as a way to fend off the boredom."

"So, you had a lot of free time on your hands. So what?"

"You're not listening to me, Raven. I did it. I figured out a way to free him."

She tapped the side of her forehead and smiled. "Everything is all right up here, safe and secure."

"What? All in your head?" Raven raised her hands and said, "That doesn't exactly fill me with confidence. So, thanks, but no thanks."

"No, not in my mind. In here…" Ladgara reached up and removed her eyepatch. She then plucked a holochip from the inside of her robotic eye socket and held it up for Raven to see, and she did all this with the bottle of ale still in hand.

She let the flap of her eyepatch fall back into place automatically and then informed the skeptical captain, "This chip has all the schematics of the prison, the blueprints, every single security update, as well as the plans to break him out, including at least fifty backup contingencies for if anything should go wrong."

Raven mulled it over for a moment and then, shaking her head slightly, sighed. "I still don't like it. The risk is just too great."

"Look, Raven, the risk may be high, but so is the reward. Tell me that cracking the encryption of the Nephilim's communications network wouldn't be a huge win for the Alliance. Tell me that, and I'll drop the whole thing."

"You're not wrong. Cracking the enemy's encryption protocols could be the thing that gives us a leg up in the war. We could listen in on ship deployments. We could analyze their strategy. We could decipher their strategic weaknesses. It would be a huge boon to the war effort."

"That's what I've been saying! So, Raven, are you in or are you out?"

Ladgara raised a hand, gesturing to seal the deal. Raven's eyes slowly settled onto her blue digits and stared at them for what seemed the longest time. Realizing that they all needed a win right now, as dangerous as it would be; it was too good of an offer to refuse.

"All right. You have yourself a deal. But I lead the mission. Not you. Not Tamoran. I don't need any backseat driving and that's final. If you can agree to that, then we're good to go."

"It's a deal, then," Ladgara said, clasping Raven's hand in hers.

Before Raven knew it, Ladgara had pulled her in close and, wrapping her slender fingers around her neck, leaned in and kissed her long and hard on her mouth.

Raven drew back in surprise and Ladgara let out a hearty laugh. A space-pirate laugh. "I seal all my deals with a kiss," she informed Raven. "It adds a more personal touch than your boring ole handshake."

A wry smile spread across Raven's face and she reached up and took Ladgara by her collar. Drawing her close, she kissed her back. "There," she said, finally letting go of her collar. "The deal is sealed."

Ladgara laughed as Raven turned and, with a seductive swagger of her hips, glided out of the room.

She watched Raven take her leave and let out a playful cat-call whistle as her eyes honed in on Raven's perfectly delectable ass. The sapphic stirrings in her caused her to bite her bottom lip as sinful and deliciously prurient thoughts danced through her head.

Once Raven was gone, she took another swig of the orange Dragonian ale and let out a hot and bothered sigh before twisting around and sinking back into the comfort of the sofa.

Ladgara threw her feet up on the coffee table and, with her free hand, reached down into her pants and let her fingers work their magic. A few moments later, she let out another sensual sigh that was part moan and part release of sexual frustration.

Once she managed to free Novac Tamoran, she'd finally have her ship back. Because although Novac was the self-proclaimed "Pirate King," she was the *de facto* "Pirate Queen." It wasn't just a title; it was a fact. She was the real brains behind the operation, not Tamoran. He could barely tell his left shoe from his right, and relied on her to ensure his piracy operation ran smoothly and without a hitch.

But the truth was, she'd outgrown him, and he was proving to be more trouble than he was worth. So, once she got the communications codes from him, she was going to have to find a way to dispose of him, permanently.

And, with the full firepower of the *Avarice* at her command, she'd leave her stamp on this war-torn galaxy—if it was the last thing she did.

13

Deunan Atiyah stumbled forward and slammed into the opposite wall of the holding cell. If there's one thing she didn't appreciate, it was being shoved by rude assholes. Pushing off the wall, she spun around and glowered at the two guards standing in the entrance with her fiery eyes.

The implants in her eyes lit up bright orange and light emanated from her gaze in the darkened corner of the cell, giving her an enchanted sort of look. "Watch it, ass-wipe! I'm a Seyfferian citizen, and I know my rights."

"Seyfferian?" the guard scoffed as he turned his back to her and exited the cell. "That don't mean *shaznik* around here. Not now that the Fusion runs everything."

"I'd bet credits to creylons," she snarled, "that you'd happily bend over backwards for your new overlords."

On the other side of the door, the head guard turned to face her and sneered as he smashed the button on the control panel. The holding cell's door slammed shut right in Deunan's face, and she flinched. The guard merely continued to gaze at her with a look of disgust.

Upset, she roared out in frustration and hammered both fists against the glass door with a resounding *thump*, but the security guard merely laughed and turned away.

She took a breath and tried her best to calm herself. Losing her cool now wouldn't do her any good. Shaking the tension out of her hands, she mumbled to herself, "Boring conversation anyway."

At least Lycia didn't get picked up too, Deunan thought, thanking her luck as she paced the room back and forth. After a few more minutes of nervous striding, a throat cleared.

"Deunan Atiyah, is that really you?" a voice asked in a rather breezy tone.

She paused her anxious pacing and looked up to see who it was that had come to pay her a visit. After all, it was too soon for anybody to know she'd been arrested. So, who could possibly know she was here?

Deunan turned toward the glass viewing pane of her cell and found a familiar face staring back at her. Standing on the other side was none other than Gamagor Dar'Vek herself. Her white fauxhawk looking rather fetching centered on her shaved green head.

Surprised to see her old friend, Deunan threw her hands on her hips and eyed the woman up and down. Gamagor sported a tight-fitting leather corset, which pushed up her already ample bosom. Additionally, the black fishnet stockings she wore ran down her muscular green legs and disappeared into black patent leather tactical boots, giving her the look of a Dom that liked to kick ass.

"And to what do I owe the pleasure of a personal visit by the Praefectus herself?"

Gamagor crossed her powerful green arms under her robust chest, the humps of her green breasts swelling to the top of her leather corset. "What? I can't just drop by to see an old friend?"

Deunan laughed. "We're old friends, are we?" She scanned her surroundings with a less than amused look and then locked eyes with Gamagor. "And, is this how you treat all of your friends?"

"Apologies, Deunan," Gam said, heading over to the control panel and waving her wrist over the scanner. The door unlocked and slid open. When Deunan hesitated, Gamagor gestured for her that it was safe to come out.

Deunan eased out of the cell, scanning the room for any signs of trouble as she still wasn't entirely convinced this wasn't some kind of elaborate trap.

"It's not a trick," Gam laughed, "but you know how I like to dot my I's and cross my T's. I needed to make it look like I was detaining you from some official offense or another, which is why I ordered my men to hassle you at immigration."

"Gee, thanks," Deunan replied sarcastically.

"Word is on the street that a bounty hunter named Xarthon has put an Orange Alert out on you. Any idea why?"

"None springs to mind," Deunan answered. Again, she was playing her cards close to her chest. Even if Gamagor was on her side, she still needed to protect Lycia at all costs. And the less Gam knew, the better off they'd all be.

"Are you certain?"

Deunan gave Gamagor a stern look that said she was sure. "Why? What would I have to hide?"

"Alright then," Gam said, uncrossing her arms so as not to appear too discriminating. "I trust you well enough to know you wouldn't bring any trouble onto my doorstep. But it seems trouble has followed you here nonetheless."

"What do you suggest we do about it?"

Gamagor edged up to Deunan so they were practically standing nose to nose. "It's we now, is it?"

"If what you say is true, then I could use the help."

Gam rubbed her chin as she mulled it over and then nodded her head as if Deunan's terms were acceptable. "Alright then. You shall have it. Besides, I still owe you."

One corner of Deunan's mouth curled into a crooked grin. "You don't owe me a thing, Gam. You never did."

"I'm merely stating the facts. If it weren't for you smuggling me out of the empire when I ran from IGS, I never would have wound up a free woman. Who knows, I might still be fighting in the arena taking C-grade games on some inhospitable moon as a washed-up has-been. But I'm here, on Brexis, a free woman. A filthy rich woman. And that's all because of you."

"I appreciate the sentiment," Deunan said, smiling at Gamagor. "But I was only doing what's right."

"Like I said, it's my turn to pay back the favor." Gam swiveled around on her boot heels and marched toward the door. "You can stay in my personal suite until this whole mess blows over. It's completely shielded from orbital scans, so when this Xarthon gets here you can remain completely off his radar for as long as you need."

"There's just one more thing you should know…" Deunan said, the tenor of her voice causing Gam to pause and turn back to find those familiar orange-glowing eyes peering at her.

"I'm here with a Dagon girl and her pet cat. Although she can take care of herself, I'd like to get to her before Xarthon does. If he finds her, I can guarantee you'll have a much bigger problem on your hands than you need right now."

"I'll send my personal assistant out to fetch her immediately. Do you know where she might be?"

After thinking about it for a nanosecond, Deunan answered, "I think so."

"Well, then, you can brief me along the way."

Their business settled, both women marched over to the exit, finding two Dragonian guards standing like sentinels at the entrances. When Gam stepped up to them, they came to attention.

She clicked and clacked a series of Dragonian sounds that were barely comprehensible. The fact that the universal translator hadn't been able to pick it out meant it was either slang or some kind of unregistered dialect.

Both guards nodded in compliance and then turned their backs to the women as a gesture of "out of sight, out of mind." The prison doors parted and Gamagor gestured for Deunan to go on ahead of her.

They slipped out into the corridor, and walked another fifty meters, came out a tunnel, and entered the busy concourse of the promenade. Deunan, nervous she might be recognized, popped up her leather jacket's collar to better hide her face and trailed after Gam as she weaved expertly through the crowd.

As they moved through the street, Gam's reputation preceded her, and she began to draw a lot of interest. She looked back at Deunan with a smirk and then tapped the upper left breast area on her corset. A holovid mask flickered briefly, and Gamagor's green Dragonian face unexpectedly disappeared beneath the shroud of a dark, copper toned Seyfferian man.

Smart, Deunan thought. Seyfferian women were not as large as Dragonian women, so having herself become a man not only added another layer of subterfuge, but it allowed her to blend in more naturally. And nobody would think twice of Deunan, walking beside a handsome Seyfferian, since they'd simply assume that they were a couple.

"This way," the undeniably gorgeous man beckoned to her, waving for her to follow him.

"You look hot," Deunan teased, practically treading on Gamagor's heels as they wound through the bustling streets.

"You like it?" she laughed in a burly voice. "I picked it out just for you."

"Did you, now?" Deunan asked, her curiosity piqued.

She couldn't tell if Gam was coming onto her or if she was just being playful, but either way, the connection was real. And whenever they came together, it always felt natural. It always felt like being partners in crime.

It took about twenty minutes to escape the throngs of the marketplace, but they finally came to the end of the promenade and found the housing district.

The streets were too narrow for vendors to set up shop between the series of cube-like apartments stacked five, sometimes seven, cubicles high. As such, only foot traffic passed through the narrow, encroaching walls of the residential area.

Each unit was large enough to contain a studio-sized apartment, but had the added benefit of being designed to link other units together. As such, a person who rented out multiple cubes could form full-sized quarters.

Family units often consisted of three or four cubicles linked together to create L-shaped homes. And those who could afford it often had two family units stacked on top of one another to form two-story apartments.

The wealthiest denizens, such as the sex parlor owners and some of the wealthier pub managers, would buy out an entire five or seven stack of units, usually leaving the bottom one or two levels to be rented by their respective employees.

Gamagor turned up a narrow staircase and began climbing. Deunan looked over her shoulder, an old habit that was hard to kick, and then followed after her.

Once they'd reached the top, Gamagor took out a keycard and ran it through the slot on the card reader of the door to the apartment on their left. The light flickered to green and she opened the door and slipped inside.

Deunan raised her eyebrows, curious as to where this adventure was taking them. She followed her in, letting the door slam shut behind her.

The unit was completely empty, apart from the kitchen counter and refrigerator. Gam turned off her holovid mask and the handsome Seyfferian man dissolved, revealing her bright green eyes and a pretty smile spreading across purple painted lips.

Gam flicked her tongue, smelling the air around them and then nodded. "It's all clear."

"I see that, but where are you taking me? Whose apartment is this?"

"It's mine, of course," she replied, a quaint smile forming on her lips. With that said, she went over to the smart-fridge and typed in what seemed to be random keystrokes on its interface. With a loud clunk, the fridge unexpectedly retracted into the wall.

"A secret passage," Deunan gasped excitedly.

"It's my secret entrance into my mansion—for when I want to be discrete," Gam informed her before stepping into the dark tunnel. "By building it into the backside of the rockface, I was able to disguise my back entrance with a row of apartments."

Deunan followed her in and the fridge slid back into place behind them, cutting off the light.

As darkness engulfed them, Deunan blinked twice and her eyes flickered from orange to night-vision green. A rocky tunnel extended before her and came into high-definition focus; she followed Gamagor deeper into the cavern.

Fifty meters later they came out into a small opening with dim lighting. Deunan's night-vision automatically reverted to standard, and her eyes glowed orange again.

That's when Deunan realized they were standing beneath a waterfall.

Gam tapped a button on the wall and the curtain of water parted as naturally as any automated drapery, giving them an exit. Gam stepped out into a luxurious bedroom, and Deunan followed her.

Unexpectedly, Gam immediately began stripping off her clothes. "Quick, take off your clothes."

"What?" Deunan asked, growing self-conscious at the mere thought of having to strip naked in front of someone else, let alone Gamagor.

Her clothes bundled in her arms, Gam turned back to her. "It's not like that. Nano-trackers are probably embedded in your clothing fibers. Bounty hunters use them to stick to potential targets. And because they're as innocuous as common gnats, our minds don't necessarily detect them when they latch on to us. We need to shed and burn everything."

Reluctantly, Deunan complied and stripped before Gam, who couldn't help but take a sneak peek at the bronze-skinned beauty. After stripping bare, she shoved all her belonging into Gam's arms. Everything except her boots.

"Those too," Gam insisted, eyeballing Deunan's boots.

"Over my dead body," Deunan said, pulling her boots close to her chest and refusing to hand them over.

Gam sighed and then said, "Fine. Most nano-tackers are airborne anyway; they float around like pollen. There's less chance that your boots got contaminated, but if they are, then that's on you."

"I'm willing to risk it," Deunan said. "You're not getting these boots."

Although intrigued as to the reason why Deunan felt such an attachment to her boots, Gamagor shrugged it off for now. "Suit yourself."

She turned and walked over to a receptacle and placed their clothes inside. Slamming the lid shut, she hit a button and, with a flash, the clothes were incinerated.

In the clear, Gam placed her hands on her hips and turned to Deunan, a sheepish grin on her face. As they stood gawkily around, trying not to stare at one another's nudity, Deunan was the first to break the awkward silence.

"What now?"

"I suggest a quick sonic shower and a change of clothes. Then we can go find your girl. Or we could…" she paused momentarily as she let her eyes slide down Deunan's body, "you know." She let the innuendo speak for itself.

"I appreciate the offer, Gam. But I'm not looking for anything serious at the moment."

She lied, of course. She was desperate for companionship. But she wasn't entirely confident that Gam was on her side or, for that matter, whether she might even be attracted to her in that way.

In her estimation, it was best to let things play out a little more before deciding if whatever this feeling was between them was real or not.

Gam shrugged. "It was worth a shot. With a rockin' hot bod like that," she said, leaning over to get a better look at Deunan's ass, "you can't blame a girl for trying."

Deunan laughed nervously. "Maybe ply me with a few drinks first, and we shall see what we shall see."

"Is that so?" Gam asked, taken aback by Deunan's offer. In all the years she'd known her, Deunan always shied away from the more adventurous aspects of sex—at least, ever since her incident with the whole nano-virus thing. This was a side of her Gam had never seen before, and she was dying to see how deep the rabbit hole went.

Excited as she was, she knew that appeasing her more baser desires would have to wait. Right now, they were in a race against bounty hunters to rescue Deunan's friend.

"The shower is in here," Gam said, sliding a standing mirror, which doubled as a door, out of the way.

Still clutching her boots to her chest, Deunan hurried into the bathroom and turned to close the door, only to find Gam standing in the entrance, her green eyes peering at her. Enticing her. Imploring her to reconsider Gam's offer.

Unable to deny that there was a certain chemistry between them, Deunan tossed her boots to the floor and then leaned in and whispered, "Like I said, drinks first." Then she slid the door shut in Gam's beaming face.

Once she'd secured the bathroom door, Deunan leaned up against the wall and placed a hand over her palpitating heart. "Oh, lordy," she said to herself.

Small beads of sweat began to glisten on her forehead and she fanned herself.

14

The matte-gray space station's large, saucer-like dome incrementally rotated high above the Nyctan home world's only inhabitable moon, Endiva. Although it was primarily a swamp, with mud and vines and too many bogs to count, it did contain a rich underground wellspring of natural gases, ripe for fracking.

As such, numerous factories littered the surface of the swamp world and puffed out a green haze. The haze, of course, was due to the pollution and smog being run through algae based air-scrubbers. The engineered algae let out a gaseous green vapor that was dispersed by large turbine fans, adding to the moon's overall verdant hue.

From space, the entire moon was just one big green swirling marble hanging in the balance. And orbiting this moon, was Nyctan's prison station—simply known as Endiva Penal Station.

The station looked like an inverted saucer shaped tower or a giant UFO with a long tail-like spire that hung all the way down to the upper atmosphere of the moon. Many lights illuminated the saucer section, giving it the look of a city floating in space. Everything but for the officer's portion of the station, the small bulge on the top of the saucer section, however, was a prison cell looking out into the depths of space.

Among its residents was none other than the notorious space-pirate, Novac Tamoran. His crime, as far as was officially logged in the books, was his attempt to commandeer a Nephilim battlecruiser for his own nefarious purposes.

Little did the Nyctan and Nephilim Fusion realize, however, that this grand theft starship was all part of an elaborate ruse. The real goal of the hijacking was to upload the communications codes of the enemy fleet. And this he had succeeded in doing—but before he could take his new toy for a joyride, he'd ended up getting himself caught when he boarded a luxury yacht to pillage only to find it was a trap.

That's precisely why he missed having Ladgara around. She would have seen through the ruse and warned him against it. He probably still wouldn't have listened, but he sure missed having her to get him out of a scrape.

Now, he waited. And like the rest of his ilk, he sat in his quarters, staring out at the indifferent blackness that hung outside his window.

There was nothing more humbling to the over inflated egos of killers and arrogant cads than being forced to stare into space, grappling with their own fragile mortality. On the other side of that cold pane of glass was an infinite void of lifeless, frigid, nothingness. A constant reminder of what awaited them, should they not change their ways.

More than anything, being forced to face this crippling expanse scared career criminals into walking the straight and narrow, though many went mad with the modern-day equivalent of cabin fever. Either way, it was the price you paid for doing something heinous enough to get you sent to a maximum-security prison in the Commonwealth.

Novac Tamoran rose to his feet and squinted as he peered out the window of his cell. For a brief moment, he thought he saw a barely perceptible shimmer, denoting the faint outline of a cloaked ship.

Under the veil of its optical cloak, the *Skywend's* outline rippled ever so slightly as it pulled up to the long, protruding, tail-like spire of the space station.

Ladgara's plan, as Raven understood it, was that once they'd cut their way into the main access tunnels, they'd use the zero gravity of the spire's utility passage to float all the way up to the rotating saucer section. There, they'd cut the security feed, break into the main facility, subdue a couple of guards, play a bit of dress-up, and break out Novac Tamoran before anyone was the wiser.

In the dressing room just outside the airlock, Raven and Ladgara stripped down to their underwear and slipped on a couple of optics suits. Getting in undetected was key, so going invisible was about the only way this plan was going to work.

Kregor, Gyllek, and Danica entered the paddock just as Raven and Ladgara had finished suiting up. Raven looked up to find that Danica had received her improved cybernetic arm, and smiled.

"How's the arm treating you?" she asked, glancing down at Danica's shiny new prosthetic.

"It's a bit stiff still," she replied, opening and closing her left hand. The artificial musculature flexed and whined as the pumps and servos made her sinews bulge like real muscles.

The fluid metal wrap on the outside acted like organic skin, and Skuld's enhancements gave her an extra twenty-six percent power hike.

Gyllek grabbed Danica's arm without asking and held it up, tapping an area under her wrist. The arm made a strange whirring sound and then the smart metal alloy opened up on the top of her forearm, parting like a wound being separated by medical pincers. To everyone's surprise, including Danica's, a built-in blaster sprouted and armed itself.

"It also has some upgrades," Gyllek said excitedly.

Danica shook the girl off her arm and shot her a stern look which seemed to go unregistered.

Then, with a mere thought, she retracted the canon back into her arm and the liquid metal skin melted back to its original configuration.

She flexed her hand again to make sure everything was as it should be then looked back toward Raven.

"I appreciate all the help," Danica said. "But I know you need Gyllek and me to keep the engines spooled up for when we ditch this place, so I'd best be getting to the bridge. Come on, kid. Let's get out of their hair."

Gyllek smiled at everyone and saluted Raven in her usual sprightly manner. Then, with a bounce in her step, she scampered off. Trailing closely behind Danica as they stepped out into the corridor, she chirped, "I want a metal arm someday."

"No, you don't," Danica assured her, and with that, they ducked under the archway and continued on their way.

Angellyk entered the room just as they were parting and exchanged nods in the passing. Pausing at the entrance, she scanned the faces in the room until she found her man. Smiling, she went over to Kregor and placed a gentle hand on his shoulder then, rising onto her tiptoes, gave him a peck on the cheek.

"Angellyk," Ladgara said, narrowing her rose colored eyes at her. "Long time no see."

"Vassex," Angellyk said coldly, her gaze falling on the woman with a scornful look.

Raven raised a curious eyebrow. "Do you two know each another?"

"Vassex killed my cousin," Angellyk said, bitterly.

"Yep. I killed a drug-dealer who stole a hyper-drive from us," she said.

"I know that Zee'dak wasn't perfect," Angellyk said, "but he was still family."

Raven stepped between the two of them to prevent tempers from flaring.

Ladgara place a hand on Raven's shoulder and calmly shook her head to let her know everything was cool. "It's all right." Then, drawing out a knife, she twirled it about fancifully, flipped it over, and extended it, handle end first, for Angellyk to take.

"You want revenge? Take this and stab me. Avenge your cousin's death, if it will make you feel better. I won't stand in your way."

Angellyk took the knife and looked at it. Kregor and Raven merely gave the two women space and watched with keen interest to see where this would lead.

"Nah," Angellyk said, handing the knife back to Ladgara. "You're totally right about Zee. On his best of days, he was still just an asshole."

Ladgara laughed and retrieved her knife.

Annoyed that she'd wasted everyone's time, Raven shot Angellyk a sharp glance. "Are we done here?"

She didn't like unnecessary drama. Especially right before a critical mission. And this classified as both unnecessary *and* drama.

Of course, that's probably one of the main reasons Angellyk and she had never worked out together. Angellyk, like most Bre'lal people, was overly temperamental and wore her every emotion on her sleeve. Raven, meanwhile, tried to bottle hers inside.

Even so, having to constantly deal with Angellyk's mood swings caused her to grow exceedingly vexed. The need to spark controversy simply for controversy's sake was the thing that had led to all their shouting matches and, eventually, their divorce. They'd lasted seventeen months before calling it quits.

After that, Raven promised herself the next person she married had to be one-hundred percent compatible, otherwise she wouldn't bother with the whole marriage nonsense.

"Yeah, no problem," Angellyk answered. "I'm good."

She turned to Kregor and whispered something into his ear that made him smile, and Ladgara rolled her eyes.

Ladgara leaned over and asked Raven, "What did you ever see in that woman?"

Raven shrugged. "At the time, I was completely smitten."

"Well, at least you did the smart thing in calling it off. Bre'lal are simply too emotional to make good long-term companions."

Raven didn't appreciate the Dagon smugness of Ladgara's remark. About the only thing that bothered her more than the temperamental nature of Angellyk's people was the imperious snobbishness of her own.

She glanced over at Ladgara with a stern look. "Let's just focus on the mission, all right?"

"Fine by me," Ladgara replied, and she finished zipping up her optics suit.

Their optics suits had an iridescent sheen to them, and resembled the colorful luster of pearls. Depending on where the light bounced off them, they reflected a rainbow of colors. Placing their helmets on, Raven turned to Angellyk and Kregor and briefed them.

"We'll breach the outer hull and disable the security grid. Once we're safely on the inside, I'll give you the signal, and you two secure the access tunnel. We're going to need a fast escape route once we have Tamoran in our possession, and we can't afford getting jammed up. I repeat, I need you two to keep the corridor clear."

Kregor nodded. "You've got it, boss."

Raven tapped the holodisplay on her wrist and opened a channel to Gyllek. "Gyllek, how's the hacking coming along?"

"I've bypassed their security protocols and have overridden the cameras, giving you a straight path through all the plotted access points."

"Danica, keep those engines warm. I want to split the moment we have Tamoran in our custody."

The comm crackled and Danica's voice replied, "Spooled up and ready to go, Raven."

"Good work, ladies." Raven turned back to Ladgara then slapped the button on the wall and opened the outer hatch.

They both stood back as the pressurized docking arm connected to the side of the spire, revealing a square-shaped access hatch. It hissed with a minor depressurization and then slid open. "Right. Let's do this."

Ladgara tapped her own holodisplay pad and activated her optics cloak. A shimmer wavered over her as she became invisible. Raven looked once more to the others, gave them a nod, and then she, too, activated her cloak.

"How long do you think it will take them to reach the main section of the space station?" Angellyk asked Kregor.

He puzzled over it for a moment, stroking his chin thoughtfully. "I don't know. About ten minutes, I'd reckon." Curious as to why she wanted to know how long they had until then, he turned to her. "Why do you...*oh, my.*"

Angellyk had already peeled off her top and was unfastening her bra as fast as her fingers would allow. She let it flutter to the floor and began unfastening her belt in haste. "We have just enough time for a quickie."

"Right here and now?" Kregor asked, a dopy grin spreading across his lips.

She finished stripping and began to help him out of his clothes. She got his pants down around his ankles and was about to reach up and help him remove his underpants when all of a sudden, they heard a muffled giggling.

"Gyllek!" Angellyk growled angrily, turning abruptly to the corner of the room. "I swear by the seven moons, I'll tan your little hide with both sides of my hand!"

Before she could finish her rant, however, Kregor's hand touched her shoulder, letting her know there was no harm, and so, no foul. She stopped her rant mid-sentence and took a deep breath.

Gyllek's optics suit decloaked on the back bench as she scrambled to gather up her holopad and make a hasty retreat.

Still upset, Angellyk picked up her boot and threw it at the seventeen-year-old girl, who quickly ducked out of the way, all the while still giggling as she scurried out of the room.

Once Gyllek was gone, Angellyk turned back to Kregor, who had finished undressing. She smiled at him. "Now, hot stuff, where were we?"

Novac Tamoran leaned back in his cell and relaxed. Being a prisoner in a Nyctan facility wasn't so bad. They were clean and luxurious. And he had every televid channel there was...but all of the television in the universe wouldn't help his sentence go by any faster.

According to the computer that had sentenced him, he had eighty some odd years to spend here, working off his penalty. But worse than this was, he was quite positive that if he didn't get to have the comfort of a woman during this time, he'd literally go out of his mind.

Just then, two guards appeared in front of his entrance and the forcefield dropped. Startled by their impromptu visit, he assumed the worst and scurried to the back of his room.

Their masks concealed their identities and their heavy armor made it impossible to know what gender they were. But Novac knew well enough not to test them. The last time he'd pushed things too far with the guards, he'd received a severe beating—one he still had bruises from after five weeks.

With a loud *thud*, one of the guards slammed a stun-staff on the ground. It spat out blue sparks and hissed menacingly, prompting the prisoner to shudder in fear.

"W-what do you want?" he asked.

The second guard ignored Tamoran's question and merely snarled, "Prisoner NT-31, assume the position."

Novac Tamoran obediently made his way over to the blue circles printed on the white walls and placed his hands on them. Spreading his legs, he assumed the position, and the guard came over and began frisking him for contraband.

"May I ask what this is about?"

"The prisoner will only speak when spoken to," the gruff voice said, and with a forearm to the back of his head they slammed his face into the wall so hard it forced him to groan.

The guard continued with the pat-down and, to his surprise, Novac noticed they were getting a little too friendly with their hands. Before he knew it, one of the guards was groping his package. Knowing that if he opened his mouth to protest, he'd only get another wallop, he cleared his throat.

"What is it, prisoner?" the guard's voice asked in an agitated manner.

"It's just that...you're squeezing my...you know...a little too...um...vigorously," he said, his voice rising a few octaves as he winced from the pain.

"You mean like this?" the guard asked, taking his junk fully in his hand. The guard clamped down on his family jewels so tightly that Novac yelped.

"Stop playing around," the first guard said. "We don't have time for this. The real guards will be here in three minutes."

"Wait, what?" Novac said, turning around. "What real guards? Who are you?"

The guard who had been molesting him pulled off her helmet, revealing a roguish smile and one rose colored, sparkling eye. The other eye was obscured by a black leather eyepatch.

"Ladgara?" he gasped in relief.

"Miss me?" she asked, taking his face in her hands and kissing him.

Raven slipped off her helmet and watched as Ladgara shoved her tongue down Novac's throat. Their kisses quickly grew wet and heated—and overly sexual for a time like this—and Raven had no choice but to clear her throat. Loudly.

They stopped their make-out session and looked over at Raven Nightguard, who stood glowering at them. "You two finished here?" she asked in an unamused tone. "Or do I have to wait around till one of you knocks up the other one?"

"Ah," he said turning toward Ladgara. "Very funny. But I think you'll find I'm all man and then some."

She folded her arms and cocked her eyes at him skeptically. He did a double take, but realizing he was outgunned, he gave up the fight with a shrug.

"Really?" he asked, sounding wounded. "You're going to take her side?"

Ladgara shrugged.

Not wasting any further time bantering, Raven nodded at them to stay close and turned to race out into the corridor, only to bump into two additional guards making their rounds.

Without hesitating, Raven stunned them both with her staff and they dropped to the floor, their bodies spasming with the lingering effects of the electrical shock.

In all the commotion, however, she neglected to notice the third guard down the hall. Before she could react, he'd sounded the alarm and the entire facility went into lockdown.

"Bloody Helios," Raven cursed.

"I think they're onto us," Novac said.

Raven shot him a harsh glare as if to say *'really dumbass?'* which put him back in his place.

"This way," Ladgara said, looking down at the map glowing on the underside of her forearm-mounted holovid-display.

They followed after her, heading up the corridor to the Y-junction at the end, pausing in the archway to check which way the escape route veered from there.

Before they could figure out which of the adjoining corridors to take, however, a troupe of Nyctan guards appeared in the mouth of every entrance.

Pinned in, Ladgara shoved Novac Tamoran back against the wall and they slipped between the bulkheads. "Quick," Ladgara shouted, "in here."

"This rescue op is going just fabulously," Novac Tamoran quipped, his every word dripping with sarcasm.

Raven got on the comm. "Gyllek, we're pinned down. I need a new exit strategy."

"Got it, boss lady," Gyllek's squeaky voice replied over the comm.

"Any day now," Raven urged, leaning out of the way of the sudden onslaught of plasma fire that scorched the walls and bulkheads. Each splash of hot plasma narrowly missed them as it squealed against the metal paneling.

"The garbage shoot," Gyllek replied. "It leads to the incinerator room. From there you will have to remove a wall panel, but you will have direct access to the shaft, and that leads back to the ship."

Raven handed the stun rod to Novac and then drew out her blaster. She cocked it without loading a plasma round and fired off a shot. The coolant cartridge released an icy blast that froze the grate. She cocked the gun again, loading in a fresh bolt. The plasma heated up, and she shot the frozen grate.

The temperature change caused the grate to explode off its hinges and, looking back up, she nodded her head and motioned for Ladgara and Novac to go through the smoldering hole.

"I'm not going in there," Novac said.

"Oh, for the love of all things sacred, stop your yellow-livered whining already and just go!" barked Raven.

She reached across the divide and grabbed him by his collar then shoved him down into the opening.

"Seriously?" Raven asked mockingly, shooting Ladgara a baffled look. "You're attracted to *that* spineless cock-biter?"

Ladgara shrugged. "What can I say? I just really like pussy." She winked at Raven and then, without saying another word, dashed across the passage and leaped into the mouth of the hole.

Raven let out a sigh and, with no time to waste, darted into the corridor. She let loose a flurry of blasts in both directions then yelped out in pain when a plasma blast grazed her left arm.

Luckily, it was just a flesh wound, and her arm didn't get vaporized. But it still burned like a son-of-a-bitch. Gritting her teeth, she turned and, diving head-first, leapt through the opening.

A wild twisting and turning ride down the chute eventually spat them all out in a pile of refuse. Sitting up, Raven plucked a banana peel out of her hair and looked around the huge garbage collection and incineration room.

Luckily, there weren't any Nyctan guards stationed way down in the bowels of the space station. Automated worker drones scooped up the garbage and loaded it onto hover skiffs which then floated over to a giant stove-like incinerator and dumped their contents into a slide that fed the ovens.

"Over here!" Ladgara shouted from across the room. She waved at Raven, signaling that she'd found the access panel they needed to remove in order to get back to the ship.

Raven slid off the mound of waste and then quickly made her way over to their position.

"This access panel should lead into the shaft, but it's bolted shut, and we don't have anything to pry it open with."

Just then they heard a loud clank, followed by another loud clank, followed by the sound of a high-powered electric drill revving.

As the whirr of the drill died down, to their relief, Kregor's voice came from the other side of the wall. "Y'all might want to stand back," he said.

Raven motioned with her hand to Novac and Ladgara to get clear of the wall. Almost as soon as they'd stepped aside, an explosion sounded and the panel fell to the floor with a clangor.

Poking his head out of the opening, Kregor scanned the room then smiled at them all. "Good. You're all here."

"Not for much longer, I should hope," Novac said.

Kregor had begun helping him and Ladgara through the opening when, without warning, all the worker drones in the room stopped what they were doing and froze in place. Raven turned back toward the entrance and braced herself. An automated shut-down only meant one thing. They were about to have company.

The double doors slid open and two Centurion battle scorpions scuttled into the room. Their claws spread open, and a hefty plasma canon extended from each claw. At the same time, their tails curled over their hooded heads as they produced a third tail-canon.

"Shit," Raven mumbled out loud, "Centurions."

"I've got this," Kregor said, squeezing through the small opening then reaching back inside. "Gun," he said.

"You got it, big guy," Angellyk answered, and she shoved a large Gatling gun through the access hatch. The gun had a six-barrel cluster and two oversized coolant stacks that jutted out at forty-five-degree angles, thereby leaving the line-of-sight open to the gunner.

Kregor hoisted the Gatling plasma gun up then turned on the barrel cluster, which spooled up to a noisy whir. With a broad smile stretching across his face, he squeezed down on the trigger and opened fire on the Centurions.

The bubble-like shields of the large war-bots flickered as an onslaught of three-thousand plasma bolts per minute rained down on them. The robots staggered backward, not accustomed to being chewed up by such heavy firepower. One by one, their energy shields faltered and they fell.

The war-bots were torn to shreds by repeated strikes by hot bolts of plasma. Their metal plating glowed with so many orange holes, that their mechanical bodies looked like neon Swiss cheese.

Finally, both robots collapsed under their own weight and died a slow death. Behind them, half the wall had been melted away by the plasma fire and the opening was much larger than before.

Raven slapped Kregor on the shoulder. "Thanks for the assist, now get your butt back on the ship. That's an order."

He nodded then went back through the narrow opening. He pulled the massive gun in after him and was gone.

Before she could do the same, however, half a dozen guards sprinted into the room through the still molten orange opening and drew their blasters on her.

"Freeze," said the lead security officer. "You're under arrest for aiding and abetting the escape of a fugitive."

She raised a finger, asking for a cool-headed moment, and then slowly proceeded to unzip her iridescent optics suit, gradually revealing her blue cleavage to them.

A little further, her Prussian blue areolas began to peek out from the obscenely tight plastic material, and just when it seemed like her breasts would burst out of the suit, she began to swing her hips and dance in a provocative manner.

Having their full attention, she ran her fingers up and down the center area of her chest, letting her fingers delicately brush the swelling curve of her breasts in a sensual manner.

At the same time, she gyrated her hips and slid down and back up in a seductive manner, her other hand running through her hair as she performed an erotic dance.

The guard's eyes watched her with wanton desire as she did a little strip-tease for them. A couple of them, growing stiff, adjusted their crotches to more comfortably continue enjoying the erotic show.

While they were fully distracted, Raven cautiously reached behind her back and drew out a slender cylinder, no bigger than a tube of lip balm, from her back pocket. She ran it up and down her chest, and then to her lips, where she rubbed it all around, fondling herself with the device. She even licked it before sliding the moist tip back down her chest.

Its small size, and the fact that it looked like lipstick, ensured that it was no perceptible threat to the guards, so they merely ignored it while glancing at one another with dumbstruck grins.

Raven smiled and pressed the top of the device with her thumb. A red band lit up in the center of the cylinder and she quickly lobbed the device into the air.

The guards followed the cylinder with their eyes, hoping it wasn't a smart-grenade she'd thrown at them.

Instead of being devoured in a fiery blossom of raging plasma, however, a clear bubble expanded outward from the device, engulfing them as gently as a rolling wave.

It was no ordinary grenade. It was a time-dilation grenade. The bubble, which warped time, slowly wrapped itself around them.

From her viewpoint, they'd all but stopped moving. In reality, they were merely moving extremely slowly. As the bubble grew incrementally outward, it swelled until it filled the entirety of the opening in the wall, ensuring that nobody else could squeeze into the room without walking into a slow-motion reel. Time on her side, Raven quickly ducked down and disappeared through the access hatch.

She arrived in the airlock of the *Skywend* with the others and shut the airlock hatch behind her. Panting to catch her breath, she paused to take a deep inhale so she could talk. "Danica," she called up to the bridge, "get us out of here, ASAP!"

Danica's voice came back over the comm, "I'm on it." They felt the ship break away from the station and slowly bank to make a stealthy getaway.

"Kregor," Raven said, turning toward Novac Tamoran. "Please escort our guest here to the brig."

"Wait…what?!" he asked, hurt by her distrust.

Kregor grabbed him by the bicep when Ladgara raised her blaster. "I'm afraid I can't let you do that, big guy."

Raven bristled at her insubordination and shot Ladgara an ice-cold glare. "You'd better holster that blaster before I put a hole in your *other* eye-socket," she growled through clenched teeth. Her hand slowly slid down to her holster and, gently unsnapping the safety strap, she rested her palm on the butt of her gun.

Ladgara looked over at her and, without so much as a worry, smiled and holstered her weapon. "Fine," she said, securing the gun back inside its holster. "Have it your way. But let me make one thing clear, he won't be going into another holding cell."

"Confined to quarters, then," Raven said angrily.

Kregor nodded as she looked to him to handle it and he turned and roughly escorted Novac Tamoran out of the room.

"Hey, gentle," Novac yelped as they went. Kregor merely chuckled in a low, baritone as he shoved him forward and forced him to pick up his pace.

Raven's head snapped back around, her eyes biting into Ladgara with a knife-like intensity.

"What?" A touch annoyed, Ladgara exhaled and spun to confront Raven face to face.

"You," Raven growled, brushing past Ladgara and deliberately bumping into her with her shoulder. "A word."

Ladgara rolled her eyes and followed after Raven. She knew that she was going to get a royal dressing down, but she had no choice in the matter. She still needed Raven's help to get back to the *Avarice* and regain control of the pirate fleet. So, she went along with it. For now.

15

A black stealth gunship of unknown design dropped out of hyperspace a short distance from Brexis. It came to a stop a safe distance from the mining station and launched a single fighter. The fighter, a split-wing design, shared the gunship's angular, black stealth aesthetic.

The small, two-man fighter craft raced toward the blue dome of the shield that protected the colony without slowing down for security scans. The main gate on top of the dome started to retract just in time for the fighter to enter the narrow opening without any collision.

Once inside the protective dome of the colony, the ship set itself down in the main courtyard, the same one where Deunan had been arrested earlier. Its massive plasma thrusters kicked up a whirlwind of dust and hot air.

No markings or insignia of any kind; the fighter could equally be friend or foe. This prompted nearby security teams, uncertain as to the nature of this unexpected visitor, to come rushing out, dressed in gray and black body armor.

With their blasters drawn, they took aim of the stealth ship. One of the security guards got on the helmet-mounted megaphone and said, "Cut your engines and step out of the vehicle, slowly."

Moments later, the canopy of the fighter popped open with a pneumatic hiss and out climbed a darkly clad Seyfferian man with dark, shoulder length hair and angular body armor that matched his stealth fighter.

His boots clomped to the ground and he flashed his wrist for the security detail to see. A red holovid display popped up showing his authorization. It read: *Xarthon Tyana of Correl, Special Operations. Clearance level: Alpha Blue.*

Not only was Alpha Blue the top security clearance, equal to that of a fleet captain, he also had top level clearance for every sector in the Commonwealth, indicated by the colors assigned to each system.

Blue meant all allied star-systems, whereas purple clearance meant the Dagon Empire only, yellow was reserved for the Nyctan Dynasty, and green for the Seyfferian Republic.

Conveniently enough, this blue clearance level allowed Xarthon to traverse any and all jurisdiction in the Commonwealth and bypass any treaty-restrictive laws, including those of non-extradition treaty safe-havens like Brexis. Border restrictions didn't mean anything to Space Marshals like Xarthon.

"You're cleared to proceed," the security officer said from behind the dark visor of his helmet after examining the readout. He dismissed the other guards with a wave of his hand and watched as they returned to their posts.

As the security detail left him, Xarthon tapped a button on his forearm-mounted holovid touch-display and the canopy of his fighter automatically began to close behind him.

Bringing his forearm up level, he held the holovid in front of himself like a heads-up display. Swiping the image of his cockpit control panel left, an orange glowing map appeared. He tapped it, and a green glowing line with a large flashing dot at the end demarcated his destination: the office of the Praefectus Urbanus, Gamagor Dar'Vek of Dragonia, the lizard people's kingdom and capital of the planet Skallek.

Xarthon flicked his wrist, effectively shaking the screen off, and the holovid collapsed back into the arm-mounted computer.

Resolute in his mission, he marched into the crowd, shoving civilians aside, like the brute he was, and stormed toward the mining colony's administrative building.

Arriving at the steps of the building, which was constructed directly into the rockface, he paused at the bottom to look up at the long flight of stairs lined with towering columns and various statues of Gamagor, in her loincloth and nothing else, poised dynamically—capturing epic scenes from her most well-known gladiatorial bouts.

Unimpressed by the naked statues glorifying the lizard woman, he let out a perturbed grunt. It wasn't only the nudity that rubbed him wrong, but Gamagor had a fondness for the old ways and refused to put elevators in her building.

The stone aesthetic lent itself to a classical air of a bygone age, but the climb was a pain in the ass. He'd rather just teleport to her office, but she had scramblers in place, making it a bad idea to try and drop in on her unannounced.

Several minutes later, he came to the top landing and passed two beefy Dragonian security guards who merely nodded at him, acknowledging he was expected. He strode past them and walked up to the ceiling-high wooden doors that led into Gamagor's office.

When he came to the office doors, he reached up to knock, but before he could even tap the doors just one time, they automatically parted for him, and he entered.

Inside the stately office, Gamagor was lounging at her mahogany desk, legs up on the edge. She leaned back in her chair and filed her Komodo dragon-like claws as he approached. When she heard, she glanced to the side without turning her head and went back to her filing, making sure to let him know he wasn't much of a threat to her.

She had a chic, sky blue, pleated dress with no under slip to conceal any of her anatomy. Every centimeter of her figure rippled with the taut strength of a bodybuilder's physique and showed through her gossamer dress. Even her perky, olive-green nipples rose under the semi-translucent fabric, her slightly darker areolas orbiting them like the rings of Gamidon.

Without looking up from her manicure, she re-crossed her legs and sighed. The shift in position caused her dress, sliding down her raised thigh, to reveal a glimpse of the natural curve of her buttocks. She looked up at him, greeting her guest with smiling lips painted a glossy royal purple.

"Xarthon, welcome. Please, help yourself to the bar and have a seat." Pausing from her manicure, she gestured to the standing bar off to the side of her main desk.

He declined the offer, choosing to stand instead. Arms folded behind his back, he stood in front of her desk, his posture rigid and militant. "As per our agreement," he stated impatiently, "I've come for the girl."

When he didn't accept the offer to have a drink with her, she'd stopped filing her talons and looked up at him with her lime green, serpentine eyes. Her reptilian, diamond-shaped pupils gave her an exotic, almost hypnotic appeal, and she smiled at him, baring rows of sharp lizard teeth.

"As per our deal," she replied, uncrossing and then re-crossing her legs as she went back to filing her nails, "you can have the girl, but I'll be keeping Deunan for myself."

Xarthon's posture stiffened and his fists clenched into tight balls at his sides. Through a rigid jaw, he growled, "Deunan isn't my concern anyway. Do with her what you please. But the girl belongs to me."

"Then we're in agreement," she said, uncrossing her legs and swinging them off to the side. Sitting up in her chair, she stopped what she was doing and stared hard at Xarthon. "Will there be anything else I can help you with?"

Xarthon looked away and, folding his arms, he answered, "It's my job to return the girl to the Seyferrian Republic to be placed back into cold storage. In the spirit of diplomacy, any further assistance you might be able to provide in securing them, or *her*, would be greatly appreciated."

Gamagor nodded her head and then smiled tersely and, leaning back in her seat, started filing her finger-claws again. "Don't get your panties in a bunch, Xarthon. As long as they're on Brexis, they're not going anywhere."

He didn't respond, just continued to stare at her. Leather-necks repulsed him. But he knew that she was a powerful ally, one he couldn't afford to piss off or make an enemy of.

Finished with her manicure, Gam blew the dust off her nails and then, in one swift move, rose to her feet. Walking around her desk, she settled down, perching halfway as she leaned on it.

"Patience, Xarthon," she insisted. "When I know the girl's location, so shall you."

Xarthon frowned. It wasn't his preferred way of doing things, but he supposed it could have gone a whole lot worse. Realizing there was nothing left to discuss, he turned to leave. Gam watched him without saying another word.

Pausing at the door, he peered back over his shoulder and narrowed his eyes at her. "Don't get any ideas, Gamagor. The last person who double-crossed me is still rotting away in a max penal colony on Typhon Eight."

Her eyes widening as the gladiatrix stirred within her, she smiled tersely. She wanted nothing more than to leap across the room and snap his scrawny Seyfferian neck. But she knew better than to cross an agent of the Seyfferian Republic. If she killed their asset, the next Space Marshal she'd be seeing would be coming to collect her.

"Have I given you any reason to doubt me?"

"No," he replied, his scowl matching hers with the same loathsome intensity. "I suppose not."

"Then we are good here," she said, rising up and returning to her seat behind the desk. Sitting comfortably, she clasped her hands together and, feigning a smile for his benefit, added, "And I look forward to working with you again in the future."

Without replying, he turned and pushed the doors open, exiting her office with haste.

When he was finally gone, Gam let out a disgruntled sigh and leaned back in her chair. She swiveled around to face the ceiling-high office windows, which overlooked the entire concourse of the Brexis colony, and crossed her legs again.

She watched the colonists scurrying about their business down in the narrow strip of the promenade. An endless line of shops lit up by neon lights advertising everything from noodle vendors to sex parlors for the overworked and underpaid miners ran along both sides of street. The night traffic was just starting to get busy as workers came off the late shift and headed into the entertainment district for food, drinks and girls.

Somewhere in the depths of all of that flashing neon-saturated asteroid life was a girl with a secret worth more than all the money in the Commonwealth. A secret so damning it could topple an entire empire. For that, Gam would happily betray Xarthon and a thousand others like him just to claim the honor for herself.

As enticing as such a fancy was, however, she knew that right now, she had to make a choice of whose side she was on. Was she on Xarthon's side or Deunan and the girl's side?

It wasn't an easy decision. Betraying Xarthon would pose a potential problem for her down the road. Betraying Deunan did nothing…except cost her a friend. A friend she was starting to rediscover she had long lost feelings for.

She knew which the better payout was, but she also liked to think her moral compass wasn't entirely eroded, either. Which meant, she needed to decide what to do: keep a promise and ruin a friendship, or keep a friendship and ruin a promise. It was complicated. And she really hated complicated.

The neon hues washed over her green skin as she sank into her chair and contemplated what course of action to take. Before she could finalize a decision, however, the side door leading to her personal chambers slid open and Deunan stood in the opening.

She was dressed in a fresh set of black denim jeans, a form-hugging burgundy t-shirt, and her trademark black leather boots, a matching jacket draped over her shoulder.

"You look hot," Gam said, returning the compliment from earlier.

"You think so?" Deunan asked, blushing slightly.

"Without a doubt," Gam replied, not giving it a second thought.

The two women laughed and Deunan went over to the mini bar and poured herself a drink. Downing it in one swig, she turned to Gam and said, "All right, I've had my drink. Now, what do I have to do to get you to help me?"

Stunned by the realization that Deunan was offering her anything she desired in exchange for her help, she slowly rose to her feet, a smile creeping across her purple-painted lips. "You don't have to do that," she said, reneging what she'd said earlier.

Even though she was a business woman through and through, she considered Deunan an old friend. That much was the truth. And it felt wrong forcing her into something she didn't want to do just to acquire one measly favor.

Deunan, realizing what she was getting herself into, popped open a bottle of ale and headed over to where Gam was seated. Standing before her, drink in hand, she cleared her throat. "Nonsense. A deal is a deal."

Seated in her plush leather chair, Gam's face was level with Deunan's sternum. She looked up into her orange glowing eyes and debated her next course of action. If she went through with it, it could put an unnecessary strain on their relationship. Then again, it might blossom into something amazing.

All things considered, there was only one way to know for sure.

Enticed by Deunan's offer, Gam took the girl's shirt in her hand and pulled it up, exposing her taught stomach. Flicking her lizard tongue, she ran it along Deunan's dark copper flesh, taking in her scent and flavor. Fresh from her shower, the taste of berry-blast bodywash lingered on Deunan's skin, a nice sweetness that delighted Gam and made her senses dance.

As she dappled Deunan's stomach with a flurry of feathery kisses, leaving purple butterfly-shaped lip prints wherever her mouth touched, her hands slowly began to undo Deunan's pants.

Unaccustomed to having someone else undress her, Deunan tried to help, but Gam gently brushed her hands aside and finished the job herself. Peeling down Deunan's pants, she slowly hooked her freshly filed claws into the thin elastic straps of her thong and pulled it down off her hips.

Gam didn't waste a nanosecond to take advantage of this moment. She slid off her chair and settled onto her knees, wrapped her green hands firmly around Deunan's dark copper buttocks, and buried her face between Deunan's thighs.

The moment Deunan felt the flicker of Gam's reptilian tongue find its way past the feminine folds of her flesh, her face contorted with all manner of intense pleasure and uncertainty. When the probing, flickering, tongue found her trigger button, she gasped out loud, "Oh, lordy!"

Deunan fell back onto the desk, Gam's face pressing deeper and deeper into the apex of the holy land where her thighs came together. Her face flushed beet-red and, leaning back and thrusting her hips forward to get better situated, she kicked back her head and let the waves of pleasure wash over her.

When she was about to explode, Deunan clenched her thighs tightly and orgasmed, slamming her bottle down on the desk, ale sloshing out and spilling everywhere as she screamed out in ecstasy.

The sad thing was, she couldn't recall the last time that something like this had happened to her. And since she'd never done anything like this with a woman before, something about the newness of it all continued to titillate her, sending chills up and down her entire body.

When Gam came up for air, she licked Deunan's nectar from her lips and grinned up at her. "Do you want me to stop?"

"Helios, no! Don't...ever...stop," pleaded Deunan between gasps of air. Feeling an overwhelming lust surge through her, she grabbed Gam by the back of her head and drew her back in.

Gam wasn't one to disappoint. She gladly went back to doing what she did best. This time, when she wrapped her claws around Deunan's ass, she left little red trails in her flesh. Even so, her lover was so caught up in the throes of ecstasy that she didn't even care.

Another fifteen minutes passed before they both had had their fill. Sucking on her lower lip, Gam stood up and opened a desk drawer while Deunan dressed.

A deal was a deal, Gam told herself, deciding that since Deunan had stayed true to her word, she had no choice but to help her. Drawing out a blaster from the desk drawer, Gam looked over at Deunan, who'd finally finished dressing.

"Here, you'll need this," Gam said, and tossed the blaster to Deunan.

Instinctively, Deunan caught the gun and looked down to find a class nine series, oversized barrel plasma blaster in her hands. She quickly flipped the gun around in her palm, popped out the coolant cartridge from the grip, checked it, then slapped it back in. Looking back up, she noticed Gam hadn't armed herself.

"What about you? Don't you need a weapon? A blaster or a battle axe, perhaps?"

Gam smiled. She pounded her fist into her open palm; the crack of her punch sent a gust of air across the room from the sheer strength of it. Deunan's hair jostled about in the breeze and she shared an impressed smile.

"No need," she replied, winking at Deunan, who merely smiled back in tickled amusement. "I've got these." She flexed her massive, gladiatrix arms, showing her that she was fully capable of pummeling even the largest of opponents.

"All right," Deunan said, tucking her gun inside her waistband. "Let's go and get our girl."

Gam fixated on the beautiful woman standing before her with an oversized blaster filling up her pants, and couldn't help but blurt out, "God, I love you."

Deunan froze in her tracks and slowly spun back to face Gam, a stunned expression on her face. "What did you just say?"

"Uh…nothing," Gam replied awkwardly, doing her best to walk back her statement. "It was just a figure of speech. I mean, you're a hot babe with a gun. What's not to love?"

Deunan stared at her long and hard, her digital eyes reading Gam's quickened pulse and increased body temperature. In that moment, she realized that Gamagor was truly, sincerely, deeply in love with her.

"You *do* love me," Deunan said, still taken aback by it all.

Gamagor blushed and tried to divert the topic. "Never mind. It just slipped out. Please, forget I ever said anything."

Seeing no other way out of it than just to drop it, she stormed past Deunan, hoping she hadn't messed up their friendship by blurting out her stupid feelings like a common *mugwah*.

A dark copper hand reached out and halted her retreat. Spinning Gam around, Deunan flung her arms around the tall, Dragonian woman's neck and rose up to her tiptoes. Their lips locked in a passionate kiss and, to both their surprise, they melted into one another.

After a long sultry kiss, Gam drew back, surprised, and asked, "What was that for?"

"Consider it a thanks for showing a girlfriend a good time."

"Girlfriend?" Gam asked, an undeniably pleasant smile forming on her lush purple lips.

"I'm not saying I want to be exclusive or anything, but I'm tired of denying myself happiness because I'm too damn scared to take a leap of faith. So, screw it. You only live once, right? Might as well be happy, regardless of who it's with."

When Gam looked down again, she found that Deunan was holding her hands in hers. With that, Deunan turned and, making haste, towed Gam out of the room behind her.

D's words replayed in her head. *Might as well be happy, regardless of who it's with.* It was, in her estimation, a little hard to believe Deunan had so perfectly encapsulated her own feelings. Because no matter how hard she had tried, she'd never felt entirely pretty. She'd always wondered, *how could anyone be happy with a hulking, she-monster like me?*

Sure, she'd had cosmetic surgery and augmentation to look less lizard-like and more Dagon. She'd even had her tail removed. After all, that was the standard of beauty. Dagon perfection.

But no matter how feminine she tried to look, no matter how big her breast implants, or how high an artificial bridge she had put in for her nose, or whether or not she raised her cheek bones, or burned permanent makeup into her flesh, no amount of augmentation ever made her feel desirable.

Yet, here was this dark, smooth, metallic-skinned beauty admitting that Gam made her happy. And that meant the galaxy to her.

If it had been anyone else telling her that, she wouldn't have believed it, would take it as flattery with an ulterior purpose, and would have merely laughed in their face. But because it was Deunan Atiyah, the most honest and upright person she'd ever had the pleasure of knowing, she believed her completely.

Whether or not their relationship would pass the test of time was a different matter. But, for now, she decided to enjoy it for what it was. A fun fling among old friends who needed each other more than either of them cared to admit.

16

Ladgara reluctantly followed Raven all the way back to her quarters. A couple of times she thought about ditching out and dealing with her later, but she owed Raven for helping free Tamoran, so she decided to tough it out and take her dressing down like a true soldier.

Once they stepped through the door and into Raven's quarters, to her utmost astonishment, Raven pulled her inside, slammed her up against the wall, and began attacking her with hot, wet kisses. Albeit somewhat confused by getting a different type of dressing down than she expected, she decided to see where it went and relaxed into Raven's embrace.

As Raven's purple lips dappled Ladgara's blue neck with moist kisses, Ladgara reached up and laid both hands on Raven's gently curving hips. At the same time, she felt Raven's own hands began to unfasten her pants buttons. Ladgara gasped when Raven unexpectedly slipped her fingers down into her underwear.

"W-wha..." she murmured, but Raven's lips found hers and silenced her with a kiss.

Ladgara moaned out with pleasure as Raven's blue fingers found their way to their destination and she couldn't help but draw back as she shot the captain a stunned look.

Caught completely off guard, she asked, "Seriously, Raven. What is happening right now?"

Raven's lips came back up to meet hers once more, and between their soft mouths she sighed with hot breath and whispered the words, "What does it look like?"

Ladgara was about to reply when she felt Raven slip her fingers further insider her and she chirped and bit her bottom lip as intense pleasure surged up through her loins and into her body.

This electric feeling was followed by a lascivious and quite sensual moan as she peered into Raven's alluring amethyst eyes to see if this was all real—or some kind of weird dream—or, perhaps even a trick. Realizing this was actually happening, however, she quickly seized the moment and began undressing the woman standing before her as hastily as her fingers would allow.

Although she didn't have the foggiest notion what had brought on this sudden seduction, the nympho in Ladgara didn't really care. She decided to just go along with it and kissed Raven back.

As an orgasm built inside of her, her curiosity got the better of her, and Ladgara grabbed Raven by her wrists and held her at bay, glancing down briefly to see her own nectar glistening on Raven's fingertips. "I'm, sorry," Ladgara said, "But I have to know. What's going on here, sexy?"

"I helped you with your thing," Raven said, moving back in and dampening Ladgara's neck with more epicurean kisses, "now you need to help me with my thing."

Before she could answer, Raven's fingers found their way back into that hallowed garden and Ladgara moaned again, this time leaning into it and resting her face on Raven's shoulder "And what is it you want, exactly?"

"It's complicated," Raven answered. She slowly peeled Ladgara's optics suit down over her shoulder, exposing her cobalt skin. Ladgara had slightly darker blue freckles speckling her bare shoulders and Raven leaned in and proceeded to try and kiss every single one.

"Hit me with it, hot-stuff," she said, craning her neck to bare as much flesh as she could so that Raven could continue stippling her neck with more luscious kisses.

"I need you to get me pregnant."

Ladgara gulped and then pulled away from Raven's embrace. "You want me to do what now?"

"Like I said, it's complicated. I have a rare nanotech related autoimmune disorder. The nanites in my blood are disrupting my entire immune system. Essentially, they've turned on the white blood cells they're supposed to assist, and my body is eating itself alive from the inside out."

"I'm sorry. That sucks," Ladgara said, her one eye growing sympathetic as she listened to Raven's harrowing story.

"They'll continue to attack one another until my immune system is so utterly compromised that I'll likely die of something as trivial as a common cold. But if I get pregnant, the hormones produced by my body will reset the nanites into their default setting as they upload the new firmware for safeguarding the fetus. As such, the update will reset everything, and my disease will be as though it never existed."

"Can't you just inject yourself with the necessary hormones to reset them manually? Isn't that how NIDs was fixed the first time around? Or, I dunno, just do a hard shut down, cleanse out the bosh, and then get new ones?"

"It's not that easy. This isn't NIDs disorder. It's something new. A glitch in the programming, I think. But I've already tried the hard shutdown. It didn't work."

"But you actually think that getting pregnant will do the trick?" Ladgara gestured for Raven to continue on with her explanation.

As she spoke, she nervously rubbed her fingers through her purple hair. "Look, I know it sounds counterintuitive. But I've done the research and know that I can be cured. The nanobots are programmed to update their firmware when they detect a pregnancy. Theoretically, this firmware update should rewrite the nanites, effectively patching the glitch."

"All you need is for me to put a baby inside of you?" Ladgara reiterated. She pointed at Raven's uterus and Raven looked down and then back up. She watched as Raven's cheeks flushed hot pink with embarrassment for needing to have to make such a request in the first place.

The very thought of a woman needing to get pregnant to save her own life seemed unfair. But those were the cards she was dealt, and Raven wasn't going to lose the entire game on the account of just one bad hand. No, she was going to figure this thing out.

"Basically, yes."

"Kind of a big favor, there, Raven. And, even if I do decide to go through with this, let me be absolutely clear about this, I'm not taking care of any snot-nose kid. Got it?"

"I doubt I'll take the child to term," Raven said in a soft, almost ashamed voice.

Still, it was her body. Her right. And when it came to matters of life or death, more specifically, her own life or death, then it was nobody's business but her own. Furthermore, anyone who tried offer any unsolicited advice would soon find their teeth rearranged on the back-side of their head.

"A child sacrifice, then?" Ladgara said sardonically, raising an intrigued eyebrow. "Now, I really am getting turned on."

"So, you'll do it?"

"One last thing, if you don't mind my asking. Why me?"

"Because of all the people I could possibly ask, I knew that you wouldn't get hung up on the moral implications of it."

"Right, because I'm a cold-hearted, self-serving bitch with a cock that actually works."

"You said it, not me," Raven said, smiling coyly.

Ladgara stroked her chin and thought about it for a while. Although the Dagon species was intersexual, the male's vestigial ovaries didn't show, unlike the female's male organs which had a way of sticking out like a sore thumb.

And although the male and female gender distinction was blurred to the point of it being a moot topic, the basic chromosomes still dictated assigned biological sex, even though that was merely a clinical definition to help categorize physiological type as a means to make better medical diagnosis.

Dagon society had done away with gender normative roles long ago. If you wanted to express yourself as male, you were seen as male. If you wanted to express yourself as female, then you were accepted as female. If you wanted to be androgynous, then you could express that identity however you best saw fit.

Nobody judged you for your appearance in the Dagon culture. They were much more concerned with your status, your family lineage, and pedigree. Which was a different genetic matter altogether.

That said, those with any particular XY chromosomal variation, as there were about half a dozen biological karyotype sexes in the Dagon species with male defining characteristics, passed in appearance as fully male, even as they still had non-functioning ovaries hidden on the inside.

The Dagon female's vestigial genitalia, on the other hand, did show. And on rare occasions, for a slim few, these typically ornamental genitals sometimes even worked.

Ladgara was one of the rare Dagon intersexual women with two working sets of genitals—one set of each. How Raven knew about it, however, was beyond her; unless…yes, she had a sneaking suspicion she might be able to guess how Raven might have found out.

While most Dagon women opted to keep their vestigial male reproductive organs as ornaments—mainly used to enhance sexual relations—Ladgara had thought it would be fun to actually put hers to good use and get some slutty space pirate groupie-whores knocked-up just for the Helios of it. And she did. And frequently, at that.

By her last count, she had approximately a dozen bastard children floating around the galaxy. Possibly more. She wasn't entirely sure; she didn't keep count of all her conquests. And there were far too many of those to even count.

If Raven had caught wind of her whoremongering, then that's how she'd likely learned about her unique condition.

Regardless of how she found out about it, though, this was a win-win for her. She'd get out from under her debt to Raven and she also got to fuck one of the hottest bitches this side of the galaxy. There really was no downside to this.

"And then we're completely even?" she clarified. "No strings attached?"

"Then we're even."

Ladgara smiled at Raven and, licking her lips, she unzipped her optics suit the rest of the way and let it fall to the floor.

Vulnerable, she stood before Raven stark naked but for the numerous tattoos and raging erection she wore, as her male anatomy reared to life. Catching Raven staring at it with curious eyes, she threw her hands up on her hips and said, "You like what you see?"

Raven glanced back up and smiled.

Ladgara smiled back. "Let's go then."

Raven drew close to her and reached around Ladgara's neck, threading her fingers through her thick purple mane. "You're sure about this?"

Before Raven could go any further, though, Ladgara briefly broke away from the kiss to whisper upon heated breath, "Sweetheart, you had me at child sacrifice." Then, drawing her in, Ladgara kissed Raven with the most sensual kiss she'd ever given anyone in her life.

As their tongues danced a tantalizing pirouette between their parted lips, Ladgara's trademark roguish smile returned and she clutched Raven tightly in her arms. The two of them crashed together again and fell back onto Raven's bed, sensual sighs and moans escaping their parted lips as they made love.

Ladgara woke up two hours after making love and sat up in bed. She desperately craved a cigarette or some Nividium 3, but there wasn't any lying around.

Leaning against the headrest, she stretched her arms over her head, yawned, and then tucked her male organ back inside as she returned herself to her more feminine look.

She didn't feel like a male, despite her masculine anatomy. She felt like a woman. But she enjoyed both forms of sex, so really it just depended on how the mood struck her, or what her partner preferred.

She looked down and studied the gentle slope and curve of Raven's elegant backside then slowly climbed up and over her. Gathering her things on the side of the bed, she quietly dressed herself and then snuck out of Raven's quarters.

Beneath the optics suit she wore black biker shorts and a black sports bra. She slung the plastic suit over her shoulder and headed for Novac Tamoran's quarters, but not before making a quick pit-stop at the rec room first.

When she arrived at his quarters, she could swear she heard more than one voice. Putting her ear to the door, she tried to listen to who it was he might be talking to.

Unable to make out the other voice clearly enough, she typed in the security override on the magnetic lock-pad that Kregor had placed over the door then walked in.

Novac Tamoran promptly cut a holovid feed and turned to see who'd entered his room. When he found Ladgara leaning in the doorway smiling at him, a couple of bottles of orange ale dangling from one hand, he felt much relieved it was her, rather than anyone else, and he let out a lengthy sigh.

"Thank goodness it's just you. I thought it might be that uptight captain or that overly righteous lizard brain."

"Who were you talking to just now?" Ladgara asked, pointing one of the bottles at him nonchalantly. When he didn't reply right away, she folded her arms and gave him a harsh look.

"Oh, nobody important," he said, waving his hand to brush her curiosity aside. "I did, however, speak with the League of Pirates. They want to convene at the Cove to discuss this war that our beloved empress seems to be itching for."

"We supported Dakroth during his campaigns; I don't see why this would be any different."

"The League feels…otherwise."

Ladgara raised an eyebrow. "What are you saying, exactly?"

"I'm not saying anything. Just that there are those who feel, maybe, Jegra's bitten off more than she can chew. It's true; we supported Dakroth's war efforts, but we always managed to play both sides and, I might add, we became filthy rich in the process. But Dakroth didn't go around picking fights with veritable gods."

"Are you saying they don't believe Jegra can win this war?"

"If you want to put it in simple terms, yes. The odds are against her. In fact, the odds are against all of us."

Ladgara stepped into the room and let the door shut behind her. "You didn't answer my question from earlier. Who were you talking with on the holovid?"

Novac Tamoran rose from his stool by the corner desk and walked toward Ladgara. "Like I said, it's nobody of concern."

"As your first…" she began, but he quickly wrapped her up in his arms and pulled her tight to his chest.

"As my first, I need you to know that I've suffered months of loneliness and isolation aboard that prison. As your king, I am letting you know that I would love the company of a woman."

Ladgara forced a smile even though she wasn't in the mood. Raven had satisfied her more deeply than she'd felt in years, but she knew Tamoran would persist until he got his way, so she decided to treat it like a cool down.

Instead of resisting his advances and causing him to be disappointed in her, she merely handed him a bottle of Dragonian ale.

They both took a step back from one another, twisted off the caps, and *clinked* their bottles together before each taking a long swig of the orange liquid.

"And what would you do with that woman?"

Novac Tamoran finished the rest of the bottle and then slammed it down onto the desk beside him. Reaching out, he placed his hands on her hips, leaned in, and kissed her. The kiss wasn't good or sultry. In fact, it was a little dry and wooden, but she accepted it nonetheless.

When he tried to kiss her again, she shoved him back so that he tripped on the edge of the bed and sat down.

"You don't need to wine and dine me, Novac. I'm as easy as they come." With that, she guzzled the last of her beer, tossed the bottle over her shoulder without a care as to where it landed, and promptly peeled off her top.

A large smile spread across his stubble speckled face as she leapt onto him, both of them tumbling back onto the bed together.

"I've been a *bad* boy," he said, looking up at her with a dopy grin. "I recently broke out of a super max penal colony, you know."

Without warning, Ladgara backhanded Novac across his jaw so hard that the crack echoed off the cold metal walls. Rubbing his jaw he slowly turned his wide eyes back to her.

"Shut it," she demanded. "Only good little boys can address me in such a casual fashion. You, my little hellion, must refer to me as Mistress Vassex."

"Yes, mistress," he said, gnawing on his finger in giddy excitement of the rough sex he was about to have.

She bent down and tore open his shirt, buttons pinging everywhere. Then, she reached down and pinched his nipples so tightly he gasped out in distress. Not relinquishing them, however, she made him whine and squirm.

"Now, tell me…what you're going to do to make up for your sins?"

When he didn't respond as she wanted, she twisted both nipples in her unrelenting grasp. Hard.

He yelped and then quickly, with short breaths, said, "I'll do anything. Anything you ask."

"That's better," she said, finally letting go of him.

Kregor opened the refrigerator and peered inside for a long time. "Who keeps drinking my beers?" he grumbled.

"I'm not old enough to drink," Gyllek said as she flipped through the various televid channels.

Angellyk sat on the white sofa with her feet up on the fixed aluminum and glass coffee table, painting her nails a fetching azure called *Neon Rain.*

Without looking up from what she was doing, she stated as a matter of fact, "I don't touch that orange stuff. I'm more of a Nova Centauri Red kind of girl."

"All that's left is this Johnnie Walker Blue stuff that Jegra requested we track down for her."

"Is it any good?" Angellyk asked.

Kregor shrugged and then twisted off the top. Taking a large swill, he immediately spit it all back out in a misty spray.

"That good, eh?"

"It tastes like fire!" Kregor said, hacking and coughing.

"Liquid fire? How fascinating," Gyllek said, rising to her feet. "Let me try some."

"Nice try," Angellyk said, reaching up and grabbing the girl by the back of her shirt and drawing her back down to the sofa.

"What'cha all doin'?" a voice asked.

They all turned to see Danica standing in the middle of the room, clutching her metal arm with her blue hand, and shifting about nervously. By the shocked looks staring back at her, she couldn't help but feel like a kid on the playground who wasn't sure she'd get picked by anyone to play on their team.

Angellyk was the first to break the silence. "I'm painting my nails. Gyllek here has been channel surfing for about thirty minutes straight. And Kregor is drinking fire water."

"Sounds interesting," Danica said, plopping herself down at the bar next to Kregor. "Mind if I join you?"

He shrugged and drew out a couple of shot glasses. "Be my guest." He poured her one and then himself one. They raised the glasses, *clinked* them together, and then kicked back their shots.

Kregor stifled a choke as Danica burst into a coughing fit.

Not only was her throat burning, but her lungs seemed to catch on fire too. "What in the seven moons is this stuff?" she asked, fetching the bottle out of Kregor's hands and examining it.

"It's Johnnie's Blue Walk, or some such," Kregor replied.

She smiled awkwardly as she handed the bottle back to him, and said, "It hurts."

"I know, right? Wanna another?"

"Sure! Why not?" she said, holding out her glass.

He poured them both another round and they downed those as well. This time they managed to sufficiently suppress their coughing fits as they grew accustomed to this mysterious fire water.

"Let me guess," Danica said, "this is one of Jegra's crazy requests."

"You got it in one," Kregor answered.

"It's not the weirdest thing she's ever ordered," Danica stated. This seemed to catch everyone's attention and she smiled at their inquisitive faces.

"What's the weirdest thing she's asked for?" Gyllek inquired, her probing eyes drilling into Danica for answers.

"There's this fizzy sugar drink called a Co-co-colas, or something…it gets in your nose, makes you cough, sneeze, and your eyes water all at once, and then you burp. You should hear her."

"It sounds awful," Angellyk said, squinting up her face in disgust. Her expression quickly settled back down, however, as she continued to concentrate on painting her toenails.

"It sounds like torture," Kregor added, but not before letting out a subdued burp himself.

"It sounds glorious!" Gyllek sang out. She flicked her wrist and used the televid's motion sensors to turn off the monitor. Then she slid along the couch and placed her head onto Angellyk's lap. Angellyk just looked down at her beaming face and smiled at her.

"Want me to do your nails next?"

"Oh, yes, please." Gyllek slid out and, sitting beside Angellyk, put her feet up on the table and copied her posture. Angellyk dipped the nail polish brush in the Neon Rain and began doing Gyllek's toes for her.

"I believe it's on file in the replicator data base. If you want I can order one…" Danica said, walking over to the dark panel on the wall that was supposed to be the food synthesizer.

Gyllek shook her head. "Actually, the ship's food synthesizers aren't functioning, at the moment," Gyllek informed her. "They kept causing a power feedback and were constantly shorting out critical systems, so Raven had them taken offline."

"I see," Danica said, stopping in her tracks and then returning to her perch on the stool at the bar. "Maybe another time."

Upon her return, Kregor poured her yet another drink, this time without asking if she wanted any, and raised his glass. "Long live the empress."

"Long live the empress," she replied. And with that, they downed another fire water.

As the warm buzz of alcohol surged through her, Danica leaned against the counter, her chin resting comfortably on her palm as she watched the smiling faces of Angellyk, Gyllek, and Kregor.

Soon Skuld joined them, bringing some playing cards, and they all gathered around the coffee table and began to play *Joh-Jong*. Joh-Jong was a hexagonal card game that relied on cunning just as much as skill. Each card had a number and a color.

There was red, blue, green, and yellow. Each player's number could add or subtract by connecting to another player's cards with a black series of cards with pluses, minuses, and neutral linking cards. Another player could dissolve the allegiance by placing a card of higher value than the total sum of the allied cards next to it, opposite the black cards.

The goal was to make and maintain allegiances for the most points while diminishing another player's points by using special blue attack cards. If you used a blue attack card, your combined points in an allegiance would subtract that many points from the enemy's cards. If the number went into the negative, as when a team with a plus ten attacked a five card, then that card would turn into a minus five, and you could divide the points among surrounding cards in your cluster.

The thing was, though, if you were already in an alliance, whosever turn it was could opt to subtract the points from their own cards or their allied partner's cards. This allowed more unscrupulous players to get ahead in points, at the expense of sacrificing their ally's points.

Granted, if you stabbed your ally in the back like this, they might opt to dissolve their alliance with you and join a rival player to wipe you off the board.

"I love Joh-Jong," chirped Gyllek as she blew on her freshly painted nails and watched as Skuld divvied out the cards.

In this moment, looking out of blurry eyes, Danica couldn't help but feel part of a larger family. And although they were rogues and misfits, she felt right at home among them.

17

Thirty-one days of celebration were held on Dagon Prime in honor of the great victory over the Nyctan and Nephilim force and the retaking of the Dagon capital, *Primea*. Dakroth rose from his bed and threw on his claret colored silk kimono. Not bothering to tie it shut, he made his way over to the palace balcony.

Callestra Van Morgan sat up in bed, bite marks adorning her neck, shoulders, and all up and down the insides of her thighs, and smiled at him. Likewise, the bite marks she'd left on him would keep him sore for days and ensure the next time he lay with her that every ounce of pain he felt making love to her would remind him exactly why he was with her and nobody else.

"What is it?" she asked him, sensing something was wrong. "Did I play a little too rough with you, last night?"

He looked down at himself and then shook his head. "No, I'll be fine."

She slipped out of bed and wrapped herself up in a gold silk kimono. Sidling up to him she slipped into his arms and, guiding his hands around her waist, secured herself in his embrace.

Callestra tossed her silver hair to the side and, baring her long, elegant neck, looked up at him with magenta eyes that sparkled with a warmth he didn't deserve.

"Talk to me, Rhadamanthus," she said in a disarming voice. "Share with me what weighs on your mind."

"I fear the end is near, my luv."

"The end?" she asked.

"The end of everything. Of this war. Of my reign. Perhaps, even the end of us."

Her eyes widened briefly as though she'd taken offense to the very notion, that he could even have the thought, but then she smiled bittersweetly and reached up with her delicate hand. Gently touching his face, she redirected his gaze down to hers.

"Don't talk like that. You are the Emperor of all Dagon. You are strong. You are capable. I have faith in you."

He smiled in return. "That's because I have impeccable taste," he teased.

"Taste?" she asked, drawing his lips near. She craned her neck, rising to meet him, and whispered, "Refresh my memory of the taste, my lord?"

Their lips came together and after a long, sultry kiss, he pulled away and answered her. "The sweetest taste my lips ever have encountered."

"A good taste indeed, my lord," she said, eyes gazing into his, her smile beaming with affection for the man she loved.

She turned to him and, still nestled in his arms, placed her cobalt hands onto his masculine chest. "Come, my lord, we have a war to prepare for."

He nodded solemnly. He looked back out over the balcony railing and peered out at his beloved city one last time. Primea was the most beautiful city in the empire; he hated that he had to leave it all behind.

Who would watch over it after he was gone? Jegra might rule for a while in his absence, but he needed an heir. With no blood heir to the throne, his empire would soon dissolve, regardless of the outcome of the war. He realized that Callestra was his last hope at making a child.

Grabbing her by her shoulders, he spun her around and slammed her up into the door frame and pressed himself firmly into her. "There's just one thing I must do first."

She threw her arms around his neck and bit her lip in heated anticipation as he had his way with her right there on the open balcony.

"Yes," she whimpered with every thrust of his hips; "Yes," she cried softly, and each soft cry was saturated with that sweet seasoning of bliss, for every centimeter of her flesh thirsted for his touch.

They continued to make love in that fashion until they were thoroughly exhausted and then, after a short reprieve, they made love a second time. And then a third.

At sundown, Dakroth and Callestra dressed to the nines in their ceremonial all-white military uniforms. They traveled through the streets of Primea via military entourage. As they rode along in the open top hover-car, they waved to the tens of thousands of denizens lining the streets that had gathered to see them off as they headed to their ship and, then, to the front line.

Their white military uniforms gleamed with the embellishment of full honors and decorations; they smiled regally and put on a noble air for the crowds.

In a few minutes, they would board the space-elevator at Primea's central spaceport and head up to the low-orbit docking platform where the newest Dagon battlecruiser, *The Imperatrix*, fresh from space dock, awaited them.

Although smaller than his last ship, *The Imperatrix* boasted superior technology and greater fire power than anything in the system. What's more, ignoring Callestra's dissatisfaction, he had christened it the *Imperatrix*, in honor of Jegra. Because, the truth was, without her there would be nothing left to defend. No Dagon Prime. No Empire. And certainly no rebellion.

Jegra had defied the odds and come back from the brink of oblivion—that eternal void of a broken mind—and had somehow fought her way out of a listless purgatory, to victory, or at least to hope of one.

Sunken beneath the rubble of a shattered heart, the loss of a child—the inability to save the most precious thing she'd ever held in her own two hands—to be beaten and broken—nobody would have blamed her for retreating into that black void forever, to hide from the crippling agony of facing the harsh, blistering sting of the real world.

But, against the odds, she'd clawed her way out of an eternal damnation of trauma-wrought misery and found her way back to the living.

In honor of such a strong, relentless, fighter, both mentally and physically, Dakroth only felt it fitting that his fiercest battleship be named for her.

Emperor Dakroth and the Vice Admiral didn't speak a single world on the elevator ride up, but it was a comfortable silence. They both wore their gamefaces and were ready to take the combined might of the Dagoni, Galliforn, and Dragonian fleets to the front lines.

In an exciting turn of events, the Seyfferian Republic had offered a hundred battlecruisers to help defend Dagon Prime and Arkadia during the main fleet's absence. Meanwhile, the Vreelax fleet would hold back and safeguard Kree'alek and Skallek from any potential ambushes by the enemy fleet.

Additionally, space pirates looking to take advantage of the weakened borders around the Alliance worlds would find themselves sorely disappointed when they ran into Dragonian and Seyfferian warships.

Really quite impressive, he mused. The remaining species and planets had all come together in a Cosmic Alliance, all under the steady-handed guidance of his empress, Jegra Alakandra. And although they'd had their fair share of rough patches, he still held her in the highest esteem.

She may not be the perfect blue empress that Dagon had always wanted, but she turned out to be the empress that Dagon had always needed.

Jegra had done the impossible. She'd united the warring and disenfranchised worlds by becoming the voice of hope and inspiration.

It was her rousing speech and call to arms that had convinced the diverse worlds it was time to stop resting on their laurels, squabbling over petty desires, and join the fight to take back the galaxy from the ancient evil that had infested it.

Although Dakroth knew he wasn't the best at governing or ruling his people, he did have mastery over one subject. The art of war. And with Callestra by his side, he was looking to make H'aaztre rue the day he ever heard the name Rhadamanthus Dakroth.

The lift arrived at the top floor of the orbital platform in a matter of minutes, and with a chime, the doors opened. Admiral Grendok and the Seyferrian ambassador, Hayden Greene, greeted them.

"Gentlemen," Dakroth said, a suave smile curling onto his lips. "Care to join me in picking a fight?"

Grendok let out a boisterous laugh and slapped the Seyfferian ambassador's back so hard he almost toppled over.

Jegra looked up from her work and peered out over the development project. On the outskirts of Arena City, the blue sky hung over the bustle of construction workers and heavy machinery as they added an entire new sub-district for the human refugees.

She set down the steel I-beam she was carrying over her shoulder and watched for a while as the other humans, along with the help of a host of volunteers from all three Thessalonican cities, built up a new home for the survivors of Earth.

She wiped her glistening brow with the back of her hand and watched as Karina Nazimova organized the others with a skill and strong leadership that seemed to come naturally to her.

The small suburb consisted of three, fifteen-story cylindrical apartment complexes joined by a lush garden square in the form of a Reuleaux triangle with curved sides that connected them.

Surrounding the base of the buildings, which were only halfway complete at the moment, were solar panel fields that stretched out for a kilometer in every direction. Thessalonica saw very few overcast skies, and this solar farm provided all the necessary sustainable power and energy to the whole of the complex.

The solar panels gleamed like the surface of the ocean in the hot afternoon sun, and were raised two meters above the ground, allowing ample room for vertical, vine styled gardens to grow. Right now, a group of human herbalists and gardeners were being led by NASA botanist Zhi Cheung, while irrigation design was headed by lead engineer, and NASA specialist, Dr. Iwasaki.

In their time on Thessalonica, the NASA scientists and survivors of the International Space Station imparted their wisdom and knowledge to the other survivors so that everybody would be equipped to handle the harsh conditions of intergalactic survival. During the day, all learning was hands-on, while more academic styled classes were offered in the evenings by leading scientists, as well as the scholarly Grendok.

This Professor Grendok was, naturally, one of the great satyr's many clones. He headed the Intergalactic Studies and foreign relations courses as well as the Commonwealth History 101 course. He also wore spectacles and fancy silk and tapestry waistcoats, without a suit jacket or top coat. And because he was a real-life satyr, a creature right out of their ancient mythology, the humans all greeted him with a fascination and a reverence he'd never expected to find (nor felt he deserved), but he accepted it as graciously as one could under such unique circumstances.

Beyond the silver gleaming solar farms, mottling the outskirts of the colony, were a series of water evaporators sprinkled across the barren landscape. They sucked the clean water from deep reservoirs beneath the ground and ionized the air, supplying enough moisture to the Thessalonica atmosphere that it could support life, even with a less than diverse ecology and limited biosphere.

Raphine, along with a crew of evaporator technicians from the palace, taught the humans the fundamentals of farming water for both drinking and for aiding the terraforming of desert worlds like Thessalonica.

Grendok Baphomet of Galliforn had also supplied the humans with a cloning facility, which had been built beneath the central park, allowing them to repopulate their species at a rate ten-fold what they would likely have been capable of doing, even if every woman had agreed to bearing fifty children in their lifetime—a near physical impossibility.

Although they had initially resisted the idea, Jegra had convinced Karina that cloning was in their best interest. And because it would only take three years to gestate a fully-grown adult clone, complete with memory implants, they'd have plenty of time to teach the clones as well.

Infantile clones could also be prepared, and because the turnaround time of creating a baby clone was the same as a regular pregnancy, people were already signing up for having children. And, of course, many of the women survivors did opt into bearing three or more kids in their lifetime.

In the end, there was no doubt that humanity would have a fighting chance to come back from the brink of extinction. And it was all thanks to the empress, Jegra Alakandra.

Karina fanned herself as sweat stains soaked through her light blue t-shirt. She sidled up to Jegra and stretched her arms high above her then pressed down on her hips and leaned back to crack her lower back. Jegra produced a bottle of water from the back of her tool belt and handed it to her. She smiled and accepted the refreshing drink.

After taking a mouthful, Karina screwed the top back on, swallowed, and then let out a thirst-quenched sigh. She threw her hands onto her hips, and, squinting against the scorching hot sun overhead, said, "I can't ever thank you enough, Jegra. Over the past few months, this project has allowed us to refocus our energy and let us be productive again. Feel alive again. For many, it has been just the catharsis we needed. For others, it has provided an outlet to vent their frustrations, some in very productive ways. To everyone else, at the least it's been a much welcomed distraction from the culture shock of being, well, thrust into an alien world."

Jegra nodded. She looked over at Karina's bright blue eyes and smiled.

"We're all strangers in a strange land here, Madam President. I'm glad to have helped."

"You didn't just help," Karina shook her head, "you saved the entire human race from extinction. In the first history book we write, your name will appear as the most important figure in human history. You'll be right up there with our most famous and beloved names: from Jesus Christ to Alexander the Great to Joan of Arc."

Jegra's smile faded and she looked back out over the progress being made. After a long pause and a deep breath, she composed herself and shook her head as if to deny the accusation that she was some great person worthy of being immortalized in the annals of human history.

"It was my fault he ever found out about Earth in the first place. If it wasn't for me, Earth would still be there. A pristine blue dot, hanging in the deep expanse in some distant corner of a vast galaxy."

"But it wasn't your fault he found us, and it certainly wasn't your fault that he destroyed Earth. That unforgivable sin rests entirely on his shoulders. You could have idly sat by and done nothing, like so many others. But you stood up to him. You challenged him. You are on the side of what is right, of what is just and noble. And I, for one, don't at all think that's a trivial thing."

"Even so," Jegra lamented with a heavy sigh, "I still can't help but feel somewhat responsible."

Karina held up Jegra's bottle to give it back to the empress but she merely shook her head and held up her hand to dismiss the offer.

"You keep it," she said, and then turned and sauntered off.

Karina shrugged and took another sip of water.

Raphine was returning to the palace at the same time Jegra was and jogged to catch up to her. Even from a distance, she noticed that something seemed wrong as Jegra stormed into the palace.

"What's the matter?" Raphine asked, meeting her at the entrance to the palace.

Unzipping her work overalls, her cleavage swelling to fill the opening, Jegra let out another burdened sigh.

"I just can't shake this terrible feeling lingering over me like some kind of perpetual dark cloud. I don't know what it is, but I know that whatever it turns out to be it's not going to be good."

"You worry too much," Raphine said. "Your mind used to be clear of all these burdens. Day to day life was about surviving the next battle in the arena. Now you have a thousand and one daily things to think about. I'm sure it can be overwhelming. But, listen to me; have yourself a nice massage and a good rest and then, I guarantee, you'll wake up feeling refreshed. What do you say?"

"I wish I could, Raph," Jegra replied, turning away. "But I've just been called to the frontlines." She raised her wrist and the holovid display on the underside of her forearm lit up with an incoming call from Primea, the capital. It was time.

The *Shard* dropped down into view just beneath the waning cusp of Thessalonica's golden southern hemisphere. The mighty new war vessel, *The Imperatrix*, took its place alongside her, and both ships took point, jointly leading the allied fleet.

Jegra strode onto the *Shard's* bridge and looked around at all the familiar faces. She smiled at Brei'Alas and then turned to Lianica, who merely clapped her heels together and, giving the Dagon salute, shouted, "Empress on the bridge!"

Everyone paused what they were doing and turned to face her, and with a fist over the heart, they extended their hands toward her.

"I'm glad to see all of you again," Jegra said, scanning the smiling faces of her crew. "Just know that whatever we face, we face it together. For the Empire!"

"For the Empire!" they shouted in unison.

"Stations," Lianica called out and she turned to face Jegra. "You ready for this?"

Jegra shot her a hard look that was neither entirely confident nor entirely insecure. It was, simply, uncertain. "I wish I had a good answer for that, Captain Blackstar. But the truth is, I simply don't know."

Brei'Alas approached them hesitantly and Lianica gestured with a wave of her hand to join them. "What is it, Lieutenant?"

"Permission to be informal," she asked.

"Granted," Lianica said.

Leaping up into Jegra's arms, she kicked up one heal and squealed out loud, "I've missed you so much!"

Jegra, caught off-guard by the sudden display of affection, simply laughed as she peeled the young woman off her.

The sound of Lianica's throat clearing forced Brei'Alas to calm herself and fall back into line. Brushing her uniform down, Brei curtseyed and then swiveled in place and began to make her way back to her station.

As she went, she glanced over her shoulder and chomped her teeth, biting the air seductively, and winked at Jegra. At that very same instant, she tripped over her own chair and toppled to the ground. Springing back to her feet, she blurted, "I'm fine. Everything is fine, now. Thank you."

Now that the show was over, everyone else turned and went back to what it is they were doing.

Lianica let out a sigh and rolled her eyes. "I simply don't know what to do with that one."

Jegra smiled. "Don't let her know I said this, but I think she may be my favorite."

Lianica smirked and raised an eyebrow. "Favorite what?"

Jegra smiled at her and then, keeping the answer to herself, turned and strode off the bridge. Lianica merely chortled lightly to herself and, linking her arms behind her back, turned back to her duties of overseeing the mission.

Outside the bridge, Jegra stood in the corridor and took a deep breath. But for whatever reason, it didn't seem to help calm her. There was just too much pressure to deal with right now. She glanced down at her hands, and they were shaking.

"Ugh," she groaned. She was so stressed that her entire body was going haywire. Maybe Raphine had been right all along. Maybe she had needed that massage more than she'd realized.

Just then the captain's voice came over the ship's speakers. "All hands, prepare for jump to FTL."

Jegra threw a hand up on the wall of the corridor and let the wave of vertigo pass before continuing to the observation lounge. She took a stool and held up two fingers. The Bre'lal bar tender nodded and drew out two bottles of Nova Centauri Red and slammed them down in front of her. He uncorked the first bottle and Jegra grabbed it by the neck and took a lengthy swill.

"Mind if I join you?"

Startled by the voice, Jegra spun to find Vice Admiral Callestra Van

Morgan standing beside her. Their eyes met and she felt like a stray alley cat which had inadvertently run into another stray cat. She didn't know whether to hiss or accept the friendly company.

"Callestra?" Jegra asked, slightly confused. "Shouldn't you be commanding the *Imperatrix*?"

"I teleported over here to ask you something."

Her curiosity piqued, Jegra offered her a seat and gestured for the bartender to open her extra bottle of Nova Centauri Red.

Callestra sat on the barstool next to Jegra and took a long swig of the best brandy in the galaxy. Then she took a deep breath.

"In Dagon tradition, if the emperor is to take a new wife to add to his harem, the woman must seek the permission of the current empress."

"Are you asking me for permission to marry Rhadamanthus?" she asked in an amused tone. She peered into Callestra's magenta eyes and sensed something she'd never sensed in her before. Vulnerability.

"Yes."

"Then you shall have it."

"Really?" Callestra asked, somewhat dismayed by Jegra's quick answer. She had expected an argument or some kind of lecturing intended to put her in her place. Instead, she got the simplest and, luckily for her, best possible answer she could have hoped for.

"Why are you surprised by that?"

"Because...you and me," Callestra said, gesturing between the two of them, "well, we don't exactly get along."

"Look," Jegra said, turning toward her. "It's not you I've ever had a problem with. It's him. But you genuinely seem to love him, and he loves you back. I'm not going to stand in the way of that. Besides, I'd be proud to call you my sister-wife."

Callestra slammed the bottle onto the counter, threw her arms around the empress's neck, and embraced her. "Thank you," she whispered into Jegra's ear. "Thank you, thank you, so much."

"You're welcome," Jegra said.

"I'm so happy right now, I could kiss you!"

Jegra smiled and was about to brush off the remark as another bit of flattery when Callestra put her hands over Jegra's face and kissed her long and hard.

When she finally pulled away, they gazed into each others' eyes, both sets wide with surprise.

Barely able to get out the words, Jegra gasped, "That was…"

"I know," Callestra replied, finishing her sentence for her. "Good."

With a sly grin, Jegra teased, "Just be careful, or I might invoke my right of *jus primae noctis.*"

Callestra touched her chest with her fingers, taken aback by Jegra's words, and laughed. "You want to sleep with me?"

Jegra nodded and the bartender set another bottle in front of them, opening it smoothly. "Why don't we finish that bottle and then we'll discuss it further."

Callestra, raising an intrigued eyebrow, picked the fresh bottle up and, kicking back her head, guzzled the entire thing.

Once she'd finished, she slammed it down on the table, belched loudly, wiped her lips with the back of her hand then reached down and took Jegra's hand in hers.

"If we must, we must," she said with a playful wink. As she towed Jegra behind her, Jegra leaned back and grabbed her first bottle, still half full, and then, together they left the observation deck to complete the outdated custom of sleeping with the bride to be before her wedding night.

Dakroth stood with his arms locked behind his back gazing up at the main viewscreen and watching the stars streak by in all their colors. Behind him, Callestra stepped onto the bridge.

Not having seen her for several hours, he'd begun to wonder what she'd gotten up to. Beckoning her to come over to him, he greeted her with a kiss and asked, "Where have you been, my luv?"

She laughed and, linking her arm around his, answered, "You wouldn't believe me even if I told you."

She leaned on his shoulder and joined him in his stargazing. As she peered out at the stars, she felt him glance over at her. It was rare for her to keep a secret from him, so he could only surmise it was either too embarrassing to talk about or too sinful for her to divulge, even to him. Not that it mattered, because he trusted her implicitly. And, besides, it was a well-known Dagon maxim that one needed to keep a few secrets to maintain a sane marriage.

"You asked her for her permission, didn't you?"

Callestra reached over and took his hand in hers. Then, her voice growing giddy with excitement, she answered, "Yes."

He looked at her and smiled in return. For the first time in what seemed a lifetime, Dakroth felt truly happy.

"I'm glad."

"When the time comes," Callestra said, turning to look back out at the kaleidoscope of stars, "all you have to say is…I do."

"I shall," he replied.

She turned her gaze to him one more time, lingering on his chiseled features long enough to take him all in. She had found her prince charming and he had agreed to marry her. It was happiness she'd never expected to find in this life. And, yet, here she was—holding her happiness in her arms.

It was such a shame then, that she would have no choice but to kill him on their wedding night. Just as the Voice had instructed her in the garden of Aldebaran that day. She sighed; all was well. *H'aaztre's will must be done.*

18

Neon lights cast colorful hues across Lycia's cobalt skin and her deep blue pet panther, Allie, almost seemed to glow in the radiant light. As they came to their destination, they both slowed to a stop in the middle of the street and glanced around at their surroundings. "Well," Lycia said hesitantly, double checking the address on her holovid display, "this is the place."

They stood in a dank alleyway, looking down a flight of stairs leading to an entrance of a rather dodgy strip club.

"*Merow?*" Allie seemed to ask the very question Lycia was asking herself. *Was this place the home of the Locksmith or some kind of skin parlor?*

Lycia knelt on one knee and took the cat's indigo face in her hands and said, "You stay out here, girl. If I need you, I'll whistle."

"Murrrr-rrr," the cat answered in a half purr, half growl.

It was as if she understood every word. But Lycia knew it was more than that. Allie seemed to have low-level psychic abilities and was in tune with her thoughts and emotions.

"Good girl," Lycia said, rubbing Allie's ears and forehead. After petting her oversized kitten, she took a deep breath and walked down the staircase. She glanced back up at Allie just once to check on her, and, seeing she was fine, took a deep breath, pushed passed the red, diamond-quilted plush doors, and entered the establishment.

Upon finding her way inside, Lycia was greeted by the sounds of lewd jeers and a couple of naked women, a Bre'lal, a Salamandarian, and a Kur Vagnorakian five horned, red-skinned demon-looking-woman, all gyrating and thrusting their hips into one another as they touched and squeezed themselves for the pleasure of half a dozen patrons.

The Bre'lal woman went as far as to lick the demon-woman's breasts and the Salamandarian girl moved her plump tail across both women's bodies like a phallic serpent meant to tease and tantalize. The Kur Vagnorakian woman even did a mock fellatio on the tip of the Salamandarian's tail, getting a rush of hot and bothered sighs from the captivated audience.

Lycia ignored the erotic dancers and wandered over to the bar where a Jacquardian bartender, wearing a white apron over his purple t-shirt that was a size too small, greeted her from behind the counter. He had dreadlocks, coppery, metallic skin, and black tattoos of traditional Jacquardian tribal designs running up either arm till they vanished beneath the sleeves of his tightly stretched t-shirt.

"What'll it be?" he asked, without looking up as he dried a beer glass with a towel. When he did look up and found an attractive Dagon woman standing before him, he raised a curious eyebrow and tossed the towel over his shoulder, giving her his full attention.

"I would ask you if you're Candy, but you seem to be a little too young to be a stripper," he said, eyeing her up and down.

"Obviously, I'm not a stripper," she replied, jutting a thumb over her shoulder without so much as glancing back at the naked dancing girls. "But I am old enough to take it all off, if the price is right."

"Is that so?" the bartender asked in his thick, Jacquardian accent. They didn't get many blue skins here, especially young ones. His obsequious gaze gradually slid down her figure once more, as he slowly undressed her with his eyes to ensure she'd be worth the credits to have dance up on the stage. Eventually, his eyes settled on her ample chest and he licked his lips with mouth-water approval.

Luckily, Lycia had been endowed with her biological mother's genetically enhanced assets, and he was distracted by her feminine wiles. As he gawked at her breasts, she leaned into his gaze, letting him fall deeper into her pheromone trap.

"I'll give you a hundred credits plus tips, if you take it all off on stage," he offered. It was a good deal. Perhaps not the best for a woman of her lineage, but given the nature of the establishment, it would be a hard offer to match.

Flattered, she batted her eyes at him and replied, "I would if I could, but I'm afraid I don't have the time."

He shrugged as if to say it was no big loss, though his eyes said otherwise. She didn't need to degrade herself, and he still had money in his pocket. The offer was left on the table, just in case she changed her mind.

Once he had breathed in enough of her hyper-exuberant pheromones and was fully enamored with her, she said in a helpless, pleasingly innocent voice, "I need a little itty-bitty favor, if you'd be so kind."

"What kind of favor?" he asked, going back to drying his glass and trying not to stare at her, even though he'd already been fully ensnared and probably couldn't break out of her trap, even if he tried.

"I'm looking for the locksmith, Melehkor," she said, leaning over the counter and fiddling with a strand of her fuchsia hair. She made sure to lean forward far enough so that he could see fully down her shirt.

She wasn't wearing any bra, so while he was preoccupied with her breasts, she reached over and nicked the card-key he had resting next to the register and stealthily slipped it into her back pocket.

"Spouting out a name like that in the wrong company could get you into a heap of trouble, little lady," the bartender warned her. Being enamored with her now, however, his voice had softened to that of a protective, father-figure.

"If you couldn't tell," she said in a flirtatious tone, "I'm the kind of girl that likes to get in a bit of trouble now and again." She seductively nibbled on her lower lip for added effect and smiled at him wantonly.

The bartender nodded, agreeing with her. He took another leisurely glance at her chest before raising his eyes to meet hers. She smiled when he finally caught up to her gaze.

The Jacquardian leaned in, looked around the room as though there might be spies, and then whispered, "Go into the back kitchen, head down the stairs toward the rear, and go all the way down the hall till you find the bright green door at the end. You can't miss it."

"You've been a total doll," she said, blowing him a kiss. He smiled and nodded.

"Anytime," he replied bashfully. He watched her ass a little too intently as she sashayed her way to the kitchen and let out a catcall whistle once she went inside.

Lycia glanced back out the swinging doors to find him still staring at her like a complete pedo. She bit her lower lip again and winked at him coquettishly then let the doors swing shut behind her.

"Perv," she mumbled to herself, the frisky expression melting from her face the moment the doors clamped shut.

Lycia turned around to find a cook, a dishwasher, and a waitress staring at her with blank expressions on their faces. When it was clear she wasn't there for them, they ignored her and went back to work.

Following the bartender's directions, Lycia headed down the stairs that ran along the back wall and came out of the stairwell to find a long passageway. She followed it to the end where she found a large steel door painted bright green, just as he had said. Why green, she had no idea, but it was bright enough that even in the dim lighting it almost hurt her eyes.

Strangely enough, there was no touch panel entry, no old-fashioned knocker, and no door handle, either. She stared curiously at the smooth surface of the door and then figured it might be voice activated.

"Hello?" she called out. "Anyone home?"

When there was no answer, she reached up and banged forcefully on the door. "Hey," she hollered, "you might want to return this door to the manufacturer because they forgot to put a handle on it."

She waited for an answer, but there wasn't one. "*Hellooo?*" she called out again, looking around for maybe a secret keyhole or something. Unable to figure it out, she reached up to give it another knock when the door inexplicably swung open.

Spooky as that was, she ignored her own trepidation and poked her head inside to take a look around. It was dark, and she didn't see much—other than an old, purple velvet sofa, a large, antique laser disc collection gathering dust on a shelf which ran the length of the back wall, and a fairly modern stereo system.

She cautiously stepped into the dusty room; it smelled of old books and moth-eaten rugs. She closed the heavy metal door behind her; it shut with a resounding clank, and she called out again, "Hello? Is there anybody home?"

Again, no answer.

Lycia shrugged and roamed deeper into the rustic looking domicile, studying the books on the shelves as she walked past a small library wedged into the far corner.

After a couple of meters, she turned down a secondary hallway and walked past a pair of sealed doors. She rattled the handles of each as she came to them, checking to see if any of the rooms were open, but everything was locked up tight.

After a bit of exploring, she finally came to a double door entrance at the end of the hall. She assumed it was the master bedroom and checked the handle. With a click, the doors swung open on their own.

Lycia stood in the wide-open doorway, a surprised look on her face, as she peered into a large bedroom suite. To her relief, nobody was in the main room, but she did manage to pick out a couple of voices talking in hushed tones somewhere within the confines of the adjoining room.

Slinking inside the master bedroom, she sidled up to a tall armoire that stood against the far wall and poked her head out. She could just see a back room off to the side of the bedroom, door half open, as it cast a shaft of light into the darker, larger room she stood in.

Needing to get a better view of whomever it was that was talking, she crept up to the entrance and found a small office filling the narrow opening before her. Inside, she could make out a square table situated in the back corner, and, there, leaning on the edge of the table, was none other than Deunan Atiyah.

In the seat directly across from her sat an older Jacquardian gentleman in what appeared to be the dark gray and black robes of a monk. He had on dark-tinted, circular sunglasses and was in the middle of pouring his guest a cup of tea from a handmade ceramic teapot.

Lycia gasped out loud, surprised by Deunan's presence. It was something of a shock finding her here, especially considering the last time she'd seen D was when she was being hauled away by Brexis security.

"*Deunan?!*"

Deunan stopped talking and casually turned toward the girl standing in the entrance and smiled at her. "Hey there, kid. What took you so long?"

"But...I saw them haul you away! How in the bloody Helios did you get out of jail before I even got to the locksmith?"

"Let's just say I called in a favor from an old friend, but we'd best pin that for now. Lycia, I want you to meet another old friend of mine," she said, gesturing with her hand at the elderly Jacquardian gentleman seated at the table beside her. "This is Melehkor. The Locksmith."

"Nice to meet you," Lycia said, holding out her hand.

Deunan put her fist to her mouth and cleared her throat. "He's blind, dear."

"Oh," Lycia said, retracting her hand. Her cheeks flushed pink with embarrassment. "Sorry. I didn't know."

The man laughed. "It's quite all right, my child. Happens all the time."

"It does?" she asked.

"No. Not really. I was just trying to be polite."

Lycia opened her mouth to say something, but finding there wasn't really anything she could add to the topic, she closed her mouth again.

The old man laughed. "Don't look so worried," he said, sensing her uneasiness. "The shades merely help conceal my disability. I find it helps others feel more at home around me."

"Pardon my intrusiveness," Lycia asked him, "but why haven't you gotten implants?"

"True vision, my dear, is less about the outside view around you and more about what you can see with your inner sight."

"Inner sight?" she asked, slightly confused.

"You have five senses, correct? What if I told you there was a sixth? A sense that allows you to probe the fabric of reality itself. A means to gain vision beyond sight, so to speak. This ability to see deeper into the very essence of the 'real' is one's inner sight."

"So, why are you telling me all this?" Lycia inquired, looking over at Deunan with a perplexed expression on her face. "Is this some kind of philosophy lesson?"

When she turned her gaze back toward the old man, he was gone. It was as though he'd evaporated into thin air.

"Because..." a voice said from her immediate left. Startled, she spun around to find Melehkor standing directly beside her. "You will need to learn how to hone your sixth sense, if we are to defeat the darkness that is gathering at our doorstep."

"Wait a minute. How did you do that?" gasped Lycia, shocked by his sudden appearance. She glanced back at where he had been seated, and then back to where he now stood, amazed that he could just appear like that without actually teleporting.

He chuckled lightly then turned and made his way into a small passage she hadn't noticed before. "All in good time, my dear. We have lots of work ahead of us."

"You mean, like training?"

"Something like that," he chuckled. "Now, follow me." With a wave of his hand, he beckoned the both of them to follow him. "There are hunters knocking at the door. They are looking for you. Both of you. We'll slip out the back."

A loud crash in the den could be heard echoing from up the hall behind them as soldiers breached the apartment. It was followed by another loud bang; this time the explosion of a flash grenade going off.

Lycia looked over at Deunan with a worried expression.

"What is it?" she asked.

"Allie's back there."

"Allie is a panther. I'm sure she can take care of herself."

Reluctantly, she put her worries aside and followed after Deunan and the old man.

Melehkor swiftly and quietly led them to a back wall with a large tapestry draped across it. He pulled the tapestry aside, revealing a hidden door. "Through here," he motioned to them, pressing a stone and letting the door pull away to reveal a secret passage.

Deunan stepped through first, but before Lycia could go through after her, Melehkor grabbed her by her arm.

"Please, take this," he said, slapping an electronic bio-patch onto her skin. She looked down and watched the circuitry melt into her forearm and bond with her flesh.

"What was that?" she asked. She knew it was Seyferrian technology since only they had bio-organic circuitry, but she wasn't sure what it was for, or, for that matter, what it did.

"It's a skeleton key," the old man replied, staring off to the side as he addressed her. "It can unlock any digital doorway in the Commonwealth and hack into any mainframe you might come across."

She looked back down at her arm where the patch had melted into her and brushed her blue skin with her thumb.

"Is that even possible?" When she looked up again, Melehkor had vanished without a trace.

What a weird little old man, she thought to herself.

The sound of boots clomping up the darkened hallway compelled her to hurry her ass up, and she quickly slipped into the secret entrance, letting the tapestry fall back into place behind her.

Once inside the passage, she quietly shut the door behind her, secured the bolts, then turned and raced up the winding staircase.

Her enhanced eyes adjusted to the darkness after about thirty seconds and she raced up the stairs until, at last, she came out a side entrance in a random alleyway somewhere in the market district. She found Deunan waiting for her there, and when she appeared, Deunan nodded at her to follow.

The alley joined a side street that bustled with noodle vendors and miners coming home from the late shift, stopping to get a bite to eat and maybe have a few belter brewskis before calling it a night.

"Don't tell me we came all this way just for this," Lycia said, showing Deunan the pinkish irritation on her forearm from where the organic-microcircuit slash digital skeleton key had bonded with her flesh.

Deunan popped the collar to her leather jacket, stuffed her hands into the pockets, and answered, "I learned a long time ago not to question the old man. Besides, even when he makes sense he still doesn't make sense."

"By the way," Lycia began, eyeing Deunan's new clothes, "did you go shopping without me?"

"What? Oh, this," Deunan said, looking at her new threads. "These were a gift."

"How many people do you know on this rock?"

"Enough to get by," Deunan said with a wry grin.

As they merged with the busy crowds moving through the food district, the scent of street-meat and spicy noodles filled their nostrils.

Lycia paused in the middle of the street, turned to look back the way she'd come, and put her fingers to her mouth. Letting out a shrill whistle, she watched and waited.

A few moments later there were cries of shock and a bit of commotion down the street. Lycia smiled when she saw Allie bounding up the narrow promenade, knocking people out of the way as she went.

"Hey, girl," Lycia said as Allie skidded to a halt right in front of her. She bent down and rubbed the cat's head and Allie nudged her to get more attention. Lycia laughed then said, "Come on. We're getting off this rock."

The three of them managed to find their way back to the security checkpoint and the pod ride back to the ship. The only problem was, there was an imposing stealth fighter parked directly in their path.

About half a dozen of Xarthon's men had teleported down to the colony and were busy patrolling the foot traffic of those coming and going, diligently scanning the faces of the crowd for Lycia and Deunan.

"Bloody Helios," Deunan mumbled under her breath and then turned to Lycia. "We're cut off from the ship."

"Maybe we could cause a distraction," she suggested.

Deunan shook her head. "It might buy us a little time, but not enough to get all the way back to the shuttle. And, besides, if I were Xarthon, I'd have a contingent of men waiting for us at the other end of the line too. Either way you cut it, we're screwed."

"Not if we took that," Lycia said, pointing at the stealth fighter. Her eyes sparkled with equal parts mischief and determination. She was certain that if they could only get their hands on it, it would be their ticket out of here.

"That? You're kidding me, right?" Deunan asked. She looked over at Lycia to find the girl was being dead serious.

"At least that way they wouldn't be able to follow us."

"Even if we could get onboard, we don't have the security key to activate the ship's flight system."

"You're forgetting Melehkor's skeleton key." Lycia held up her wrist and showed the organic circuitry to Deunan. "He said it would help me get through doorways I couldn't access on my own. I think the security system of a Seyfferian stealth fighter counts as an impossible to break security door." She flashed her arm at Deunan again.

Deunan raised both eyebrows as if to say, *I get it*, and then grabbed Lycia's wrist and gently lowered her arm. It wasn't the most prudent course of action but, right now, it was their best option.

"Alright then. Tell me what you have in mind for this grand distraction of yours."

Lycia smiled as if to say, *glad you asked!* Then, she leapt up and ran out into the open square screaming for help. Allie waited thirty seconds before pouncing into the square and letting out a ferocious roar.

The moment the large panther roared, bystanders startled and ran for safety. While pandemonium broke out all around them, Lycia screamed out, "Help me! It's after me!"

The guards all turned to see a beautiful Dagon woman running frantically toward their position, a giant indigo panther loping along after her.

Lycia pretended to stumble and fell into the first guard's open arms. She tugged on his sleeves, and in a frantic panic, pleaded, "You have to save me. That thing is trying to eat me."

"We've got this, ma'am," he reassured her and the five guards charged forward to meet the cat head on, plasma blasters drawn.

Allie dug in her paws and skidded to a halt when the guards drew their guns on her. The cat flinched when the whine of the blasters discharging all at the same time sounded. But to her surprise, not a single discharged shot had hit her, and her glorious indigo fur went unsinged.

Cautiously, Allie opened her eyes to find all five guards face down in the dirt, a blue energy bubble glowing around her. As the energy bubble slowly dissolved, Lycia blew on her hot pink glowing finger. Not only had she managed to throw up an energy forcefield to protect Allie, she also managed to blast all five guards in the back, demonstrating that her Dygra power levels were off the charts.

Lycia stepped over the guards' bodies, their armor smoldering with white smoke rising from orange glowing holes left by her laser blasts. She went over to Allie and wrapped her arms around her, nestling her head into the furry creature's soft neck.

Allie began to purr and Lycia, still embracing her big furry pussycat, whispered, "Good job, girl."

"Nice work, you two," Deunan said, arriving at the scene and stepping over the dead bodies. Then, turning to toward the stealth fighter, she rubbed her chin and asked, "Now, all we need to do is figure out how to get onboard this thing."

"That won't be a problem," a masculine voice growled.

Out of the blue came two dozen black-op soldiers, plasma rifles trained on Allie, Deunan, and Lycia. As the soldiers surrounded them, Allie's fur stood on end and she growled menacingly.

"You're making a big mistake," insisted Deunan, turning to face Xarthon, who stood before them smirking as if he'd already won.

"The girl is Seyfferian property, and she's coming back with me, whether you like it or not. If you want to file a complaint, take it up with the Council."

Lycia turned to face Xarthon Tyana, famed galactic bondsman, space marshal, and major pain in her blue ass. She stared at him with pink glowing eyes as she grew incensed.

When he saw her charging her powers, he pulled a blaster from the hip and aimed it at her. Its high-pitched whine signaled that it was loaded and ready to vaporize her with a single point-blank blast. "I wouldn't, if I were you," he cautioned. "So, just cool your jets there, hot stuff, and everything will go smoothly."

Lycia's eyes lost their charge and the mystical energy dissipated. Deciding on a different tactic, she took a deep breath and released a flood of pheromones into the air.

Instantly, some of the guards' eyes swiveled toward her, but they were well trained and didn't budge a muscle.

"Do you have a wife? A girlfriend, perhaps?" asked Lycia. She battered her eyes at Xarthon and played with her hair in a flirtatious manner. Slowly, she ran her hand down her side, gently caressing the curve of her own breasts and hips.

Xarthon merely extended his arm outwardly and brought the barrel of his gun to Lycia's forehead. "Enough games, you little coquette. Now, listen to me and listen good. I suggest you do what's right and surrender yourself peacefully since, as you can see, I'm immune to your wiles. And, if you persist in misbehaving, I'll have no choice but to blow your brains out all over my ship. Then I'll be stuck with a cleaning bill I don't need. So, you need to ask yourself, which will it be? Peace or brains?"

"I think I'll take a third option," Lycia said, grinning at Xarthon with tight lips that strained to fake politeness.

"There's no third option," he snarled, growing impatient with her constant obstinance.

"Are you sure about that?" she said, a sneer forming on her lips as she nodded to something just over his shoulder.

Xarthon spun around to find Gamagor Dar'Vek with an entire squad of security officers, their blasters trained on his men. They opened fire almost immediately, without any warning, and took out half a dozen soldiers in the first volley.

"Back stabbing, no good, scale-necked whore of a—" A scorching plasma blast flashed by, nearly melting his face and cutting him off mid-sentence as he was forced to duck out of the way.

Thanks to Gamagor's interference, Xarthon and his team had no choice but to retreat to the safety of the stealth ship. Taking cover, they exchanged fire with Gamagor's forces. Green and red plasma bolts crisscrossed in the open square and soldiers on both sides screamed out as they dropped to the ground, clutching the searing holes that had penetrated their body armor.

Igniting handheld energy shields, ten security officers formed a perimeter around Lycia, Deunan, and Allie and walked them back to safety.

Gamagor looked over at them and smiled. Lycia nodded appreciatively and Deunan smiled back, mouthing the words, "*Thank you.*"

Xarthon shouted across the divide from behind his ship, his voice cold and bitter. "It's clear now whose side you've chosen."

"It wasn't a hard decision," she assured him.

Deunan reached out and touched Gamagor's arm. She looked over at her and smiled again.

A wide smile spread across Gamagor's face and, then, reeling Deunan in, they shared a steamy kiss...tongue and everything.

"Ew. Get a room you two," Lycia teased, making a sour face for added effect.

"We already did," Gamagor replied, not breaking her gaze with Deunan.

"Ew, no, ew," she said, her reaction genuine this time. "I was just kidding before. But, seriously, that's TMI."

"Ignore her," Deunan said. "I like it when you're being romantic." This compliment excited Gamagor and she scooped Deunan up in her arms and gave her a big hug.

After Gam set Deunan back down on her feet, Lycia leaned in and sang in a melodic sing-song voice, "Somebody's got a girlfriend."

"Oh, hush, you," Deunan retorted.

A rogue plasma blast hit the top of the building above them and sent sparks raining down. They shielded their eyes and batted away any lingering embers that might have landed on their clothing.

"Alright, best not hang around here," Lycia said. Allie put her ears back and whined, as if to say she agreed with Lycia on that one.

"Access to our ship is still blocked. Unless we can get past that stealth ship."

"Don't worry," Gamagor informed them, "I'll get you off on mine."

Deunan shot her a hard glare and folder her arms in protest. "I'm not leaving here without my ship."

"What is it with your boots and your ship?" Gam chuckled.

"Oh, the boots!" Lycia interjected. "Don't even get me started on her obsession with those raggedy ole things."

"Lycia," Deunan snapped, "now is not the time."

Lycia raised her hands defensively and eased back as if to say: *no trouble here.*

"In that case, you go get your ship. I'll take the girl and the cat. Meet us at these rendezvous coordinates." Gam touched her wrist to Deunan's and their holochips flashed, signaling the exchange of information.

Deunan nodded and then took off toward the pneumatic transit. Gamagor gestured for a team of soldiers to accompany her and eight guards with energy shields jogged along with her, providing cover fire the whole way.

Once Deunan was in the clear, Gamagor slapped Lycia on the shoulder and tilted her head in the direction they needed to go. "Best be getting along, now," she said.

Lycia and Allie followed after her. "What about him?" Lycia asked, jutting a thumb over her shoulder in the general direction of Xarthon, explosions ringing out behind them.

"My security patrols will keep him busy," she said, pausing in the street and looking up. She searched the skies with her naked eyes for the stealth battlecruiser that was lying in wait for them. And the gladiatrix inside her thirsted for one last great adventure.

The pneumatic tube opened and Deunan stepped out, her blaster raised. Two of Xarthon's guards rushed toward her but she quickly took them out.

Not slowing her pace, she marched toward her ship. Suddenly three guards on either side of her ambushed her from behind strategically placed cargo crates.

"Throw down the blaster and kick it over here," one of the guards demanded.

Deunan dropped the gun to the ground as demanded and then kicked it. But instead of kicking it toward him, she kicked it in the opposite direction, toward the crates.

It crashed into the bottom of the crate and the soldiers looked over at it to see where it stopped.

"Now why did you go and do a thing like that?" he asked, placing his blaster to her forehead.

"To distract you," she said.

He turned his head just in time to see his men drop like fruit flies. Bright green plasma flashes lit up his and Deunan's face, and his jaw fell slack as an X-5 battle android, all four arms with four hands holding series nine blasters, made short work of his men.

Deunan quickly disarmed the man, snatching his gun from him and quickly turned the tables.

The guard raised his hands and, with a whimper, said, "Please, don't shoot. I surrender."

Deunan looked at X-5 and said, "Deal with this one X-5, will you?" and marched past the war android and onto her ship.

As she walked up the loading ramp behind them, X-5 turned his menacing, red glowing eyes toward the cowering man who stood trembling before him.

"Wait," the man said, drawing several fearful steps back.

X-5 raised one of his arms and swiftly brought it down on the man's helmet with a *thunk*.

The guard crumpled to the ground, unconscious.

Once the threat was neutralized, X-5's four arm-split battle configuration reset to his normal two-arm configuration. As the double set of arms merged back into place with their partners, X-5 turned back and made his way onboard the ship.

As soon as he'd climbed onto the loading ramp, it began to close and Ole Birtha's plasma thrusters lit up hot blue. With a bit of effort, the husky freighter rose off the platform and gradually pulled away from the pile of bodies littering the landing zone.

19

Blazing green bolts crisscrossed between the two armadas, nothing for a backdrop but a vast, star spackled expanse stretching out infinitely behind the battle. Onelle Te'Legra Agnar looked out of the wide viewscreen as more ships popped into view, manifesting as if out of thin air. Jegra and her allied forces had arrived above the Nyctan homeworld in force and more were arriving every second.

"Ma'am," one of her officers called out. He shot her a nervous glance and waited for her response.

She didn't know anything about rank, not being a military woman, so she just wagged her finger at him and said, "Speak."

"The enemy forces have currently matched our numbers and are steadily growing."

"Where did they get three thousand ships?" she asked. Not having an answer for her, he shrugged. His uselessness prompted her to let out a vexed sigh and pout. Slouching down in her command chair, she twiddled her hair and tried to guess at how they'd managed to sneak so many ships past the Fusion patrols. It was, quite literally, impossible.

Even with the so-called Cosmic Alliance, there was no way they could have doubled their ships in a single year—unless they had a secret shipyard. So, how come she didn't know about it?

The evidence of it, however, stretched out before her as far as the eye could see. It appeared that Jegra had a few tricks up her sleeve yet.

Rising to her feet, Onelle Agnar stepped down upon the back of the man that knelt on his hands and knees, forming a step for her petite figure to descend with grace and elegance.

She tossed her hair as she daintily walked across his back with her bare feet and then, stretching her long legs, she elegantly stepped down onto the cool plating of the command room floor.

A chill ran through her body as her feet settled onto the cool floor. She wore a gossamer dress of sky blue that matched her eyes. Her verdant skin was as lush as a forest canopy and her forest green tresses fell all around her bare shoulders.

"I guess," she said, watching the vivid fire exchange, "I have no choice but to execute plan B."

"Plan B?" the officer asked in a credulous tone.

She smiled at him and then ordered the crew to maintain their posts and the Fusion ships to hold their current positions. If they couldn't hold the front line, then Nyctan would be lost.

She knew, deep in her soul, that such a defeat would be unforgivable and that H'aaztre would torture her for a thousand years. She knew this because it's exactly what she would do.

"Hold the line and never surrender. Death before surrender!" She shouted the last bit and roused the moral of the crew.

"Death before surrender!" the crew shouted in unison, raising their fists into the air in solidarity. It was almost spooky how they all answered as one in near perfect sync, but that was often a side effect of dominating people's minds for too long.

As so often seemed to be the case, their egos simply faded into the background in lieu of the domineering presence they felt. Their desires muting as their personalities became subservient to her will—because her will was *His* will.

It was only the strongest willed individuals that could resist H'aaztre's power—a power that she was the vessel of—and it vexed her to no end that Jegra was one of the most impermeable minds she'd ever encountered.

"Maintain your posts," she said turning to leave. They all continued working as ordered as she strode off the bridge.

A few minutes later, Onelle arrived on the hangar deck and walked over to her personal shuttle craft and climbed aboard. She closed the ramp behind her and slipped into the navigation seat.

A pair of boots sat by her chair just in case her bare feet got cold or should she need to walk around rough terrain. Otherwise, she preferred to go barefoot.

After typing in the coordinates, she sat back and waited as the shuttle's autopilot took control. With a whine of the turbines, it rose off the hangar deck and, plasma thrusters igniting with the fulmination of a gas stove being lit, the ship headed toward the large glowing energy barrier of the open hangar doors.

The sleek shuttle, almost Gothic in its angular design, shot out of the Nyctan battlecruiser and darted into space. Phosphorescent stars sparkled in the distance as she cut across the space between the Fusion armada and the Alliance ships. Behind her, the flashing plasma storm raging outside her ship continued without any hint of abating. She ignored the battle and turned her gaze toward the pirate ship armada looming in the distance.

<<Preparing for short-range hyper-jump>> the computer announced.

The shuttle's FTL spooled up and then, in a flash, a massive Dagon cruiser with pirate graffiti and giant skull and crossbones painted on its hull in white with thick, yellow borders filled her entire window.

On the side of the hull, written in large bright orange and yellow paint, was the word: *Avarice.* Agnar recognized the name immediately. It was Novac Tamoran's ship.

Perfect, she thought. A simple-minded man like Tamoran would be completely powerless to resist her wiles. She wouldn't even need her supernatural abilities to control him, either.

Alarms rang out, alerting her that the *Avarice's* sensors had detected her. No sooner had she turned off the infernal blaring than the massive gun turrets of the war ship hanging outside her windshield swiveled about and locked onto her ship.

Before they could blast out of the sky, however, she quickly sent out an SOS, calling for their help.

"You have three seconds to identify yourself," Novac Tamoran's voice growled over the comm, "before I send you to the afterlife."

Onelle smiled and then flicked the comm switch. "This is Onelle Te'Legra Agnar," she said in a frantic voice. "I've escaped my captors and am seeking asylum."

A female voice came back over the comm. It was cold and simply wasn't buying her little story. "Nice try, bitch. But you'll have to do better than that."

A sinister smile spread across Onelle's green lips and her eyes flooded with an inky-wash which grew thicker and thicker until every part of her eyes had turned an oily black as dark as the Percheron night.

"Invite me aboard," she said, her voice sounding several octaves deeper and quite demonic with a slight reverberation to her words. It was almost as though she was speaking over someone else's voice, or vise versa.

"Please, join me aboard the *Avarice*," Novac Tamoran replied, unaware of why he had even said it. He shook his head, trying to snap out of the strange trance that had overcome him.

Ladgara shot him a scornful glower with one hot-pink eye. "What are you saying?" she growled.

"It's the Voice," he answered. "Her desire is my desire. Her will is *my* will."

"Listen to yourself," Ladgara chastised. "I didn't break you out of prison just to have you roll over and take it lying down like some mangy bitch!"

He blinked vacantly, his expression remaining just as blank as his gaze. It was as though he was doped up, high on drugs. All he could do was sway where he stood and wait for Onelle to come to him.

"Listen to me, and listen to me good, Captain. Raven Nightguard let us rejoin our fleet without so much as a request. But look out there," she said, pointing at the firefight that was lighting up the sky like a firework show. "They need our help. And I for one intend to give it to her."

"Her desire is *my* desire," he intoned, stuck in an infinite loop like a broken record. "Her will is *my* will."

"Fire on that shuttlecraft," Ladgara barked angrily. She spun around and glared impatiently at the gunner.

"Belay that order," Tamoran shouted. He turned toward her, his eyes completely black—as if he'd been possessed by a great evil force. "Open hangar bay three and give her permission to land. I'll see to her personally."

"Like Helios you will," Ladgara said, reaching up and seizing him as he tried to shove her out of the way and move past her, but she wouldn't relinquish her grasp of his leather trench coat.

"Unhand me!" he growled. "As your captain I demand that you…"

"I don't have time for this," Ladgara said, drawing out her blaster. "If you don't stand down, I'll have not choice but to put a bolt right between eyes."

"This is mutiny!" he snarled, shaking his fist at her.

Ladgara shrugged. "Stand down and hand control of the ship over to me."

"Never!" Novac Tamoran growled, spittle flying out of his mouth as he shook with rage. "The *Avarice* is mine! Do you hear me you traitorous wench? She's mine!"

With a flash, Ladgara put a bolt right between the eyes of the Pirate King. Then, turning to the stunned faces of the crew, she barked, "I'm the new captain now. If anyone has a problem with that, now's the time to speak up."

Not a single crewman challenged her. Instead, they slowly turned back around and quietly returned to doing whatever it was they were doing before her mutinous overthrow of the captain.

"Long live the Pirate Queen," Ladgara mumbled to herself as she holstered her weapon.

She took a deep breath and calmed herself best she could. She had loved Novac Tamoran about as much as one could love a womanizing, perpetually drunk, completely self-absorbed scoundrel. They'd shared some good times.

But, in the end, she knew that his weakness would be the death of them all. And she couldn't let him bring her down—let alone the entire Alliance.

She rubbed the single tear from her only eye away with her thumb and then coolly and calmly holstered her blaster.

"Should I give her permission to come aboard, ma'am?" an officer asked in a nervous voice.

Ladgara breathed deeply and then said, "Yes, give her permission to board. I'll handle this personally."

Although she'd merely echoed what Tamoran had said, she knew that Onelle would grow suspicious she'd fare better, since she was the only one who had remained unaffected when the Voice's influence took control of everyone else's minds. That gave her hope that she was strong enough to resist her a second time, too.

With that, Ladgara stormed off the bridge, leaving Novac Tamoran's corpse lying on his back in the middle of the floor, wisps of white smoke still rising from the glowing hole in his forehead.

Sparks rained down all around Callestra Van Morgan as the *Imperatrix* drew heavy fire.

"Shields down to thirty-eight percent!" an officer shouted over the series of electrical explosions. Without warning, his console blew up and sent him flying backward with an electrical jolt and a spray of glass. The officer slammed into the wall with a back-breaking *thud* and slid to the floor, unconscious.

Callestra gestured for someone to attend the injured man and then turned toward the monitor. "Reroute auxiliary power to the shields. Chanel the whole bleedin' life support into them if you have to."

"Yes, ma'am!" a female officer shouted as she slipped into the nearest console that hadn't been completely fried.

Dakroth stood at the foot of the view portal, hands linked behind his back, and watched the raging battle. Neon green and hot red bolts of plasma hatch-marked the sky. An occasional purple or golden blast of high-powered laser canon could be seen cutting across the sky.

Both sides were evenly matched in terms of firepower. Which, of course, meant that it would ultimately come down to stamina. And cunning. Which is why he'd ordered the pirate armada to hold back.

First, he'd wear out the enemy forces until they were rattling apart at the seams right along with them. When both sides were barely smoldering embers, he'd order the pirate forces to feign a retreat, only to circle around the enemy forces and make their advance.

"Vice Admiral, do you have any word on where the empress is?"

"Still no word, Your Grace," Callestra replied. She could tell by the subtle waver in his voice he was worried about Jegra, although he'd never let anyone know it by the look on his face and by the way he carried himself. Only she could tell.

But she'd given up being jealous. Jegra had given them her blessing. Now she could marry Dakroth, as she'd always dreamed. And she could slit his throat and bathe in his blood, just as The Voice had commanded her to do on their wedding night.

She had neglected to tell Dakroth about that day in the garden—the garden back on Aldebaran. The day she'd ventured out alone and found the exit. After she'd discovered it, she had turned back, anxious to tell him the good news. But that's when she ran smack dab into *The Voice*.

It was then that *The Voice* had instructed her to wait a full year. A full year was needed to break the Commonwealth while Dakroth suffered needlessly. The way out always being within his grasp.

That year, however, also had the happy side effect of bonding him inseparably to Callestra's side. That way, he'd never see it coming.

And even though her heart was breaking inside, she couldn't resist the dark influence compelling her to kill the one she loved the most.

Worse still, she was forbidden to tell anyone about it. And she was forbidden from taking her own life to save his. It seemed that Onelle Te'Legra Agnar had thought of every conceivable angle. And Callestra despised her for it.

All she could do was obey and carry out the orders she was being fed. It was as if she'd been taken over by a hideous parasite, turned into a zombie, while that black voice in the back of her mind was constantly whispering—always whispering—nightmarish things to her.

The most terrible aspect of it all was, no matter how hard she tried to ignore it, it became stronger. The whisper that had begun as an obnoxious earworm had grown into a roaring waterfall and was so loud, she couldn't ignore it. The whisper screamed in her mind, and it only seemed to grow more and more powerful each day.

It was building inside her—and although she resisted it with every ounce of strength she had—the growing blackness was inescapable. Eventually it would consume her from the inside out and take her over entirely. And, then, she'd be *His*.

High up in the Nyctan atmosphere, a blinding flash followed by a boom louder than a clap of thunder rang out. The *Shard* had FTL jumped directly into low orbit and the entire destroyer was now plummeting in a freefall down toward the bay just outside the capital city of Vallorium.

"T-minus fifty-two seconds until reverse thrusters," Brei'Alas shouted as she gripped her console with white-knuckled tension.

Reverse thrusters ignited, shooting out massive candle flame shaped jets that created shock diamonds, due to the power and speed that they fired at.

The massive ship drastically slowed, but it wasn't enough to stop its downward plummet. In fact, such a maneuver would be a death sentence for any lesser captain, but Lianica Blackstar had it well under control. She'd deliberately dropped it over the port for the very reason that, according to her precise calculations, the water would break their fall.

With a massive splash, like that of a Vorgathian whale-shark breaching, the *Shard* crashed down into the bay. It bounced back up, kicking out another massive spray—the white foam waves that rippled away were at least four-stories high.

The small tsunami it kicked off crashed onto the shore and sprayed the first and second rows of buildings before receding back out to sea.

The cruiser rocked gently, bobbing up and down in the bay, like a massive commercial cruise liner, when hundreds of yellow beams of sparkling energy lit up the beach just a kilometer away.

Jegra, dressed in her trademark gladiatrix bikini armor, held her battle axe in both hands as she materialized on the beach.

All around, a whole host of Dagon, Dragonian, and Vreelax soldiers joined her.

Brei'Alas and Lianica materialized by her side. Jegra looked around, expecting the Nyctan army to greet her, but instead found a desolate seaport. She motioned for her soldiers to advance, and they marched into the city streets of Vallorium.

After walking through several blocks, it was clear that the city had been completely deserted. She wondered if they'd abandoned it for the war or if something much more sinister had transpired here. Either way, she didn't like it, and she motioned with a flat palm for everyone to move slowly and cautiously.

"I don't like this," Jegra whispered.

"Where do you think everyone is?" Brei'Alas asked as she scanned the tall buildings, looking for signs of life. But there were none. "Do you think they all evacuated?"

"Not likely," Lianica said, holding her blaster at the ready. "Vallorium has a population of eighteen million. They didn't just vanish into thin air."

Brei'Alas shot her a startled look. "Do you think he killed an entire city of his own people?"

Both Jegra and Lianica turned to Brei. Neither of them had any answers.

"Over here!" a voice shouted, drawing their attention to a side street. A soldier waved them over to his location and they jogged over to him.

Another soldier was down on his knees offering part of a chocolate bar to something, or rather, somebody. "It's all right," he said in a soft, unthreatening voice. "I won't hurt you."

Jegra appeared and the soldiers drew back and saluted. She nodded at them and then looked down at a child cowering behind a dumpster. Her large black eyes blinked up at Jegra curiously, but when Jegra reached out her hand the girl timorously drew back.

"It's all right," Jegra reassured the child, dropping to one knee. "I'm here to help."

"You are the one my father talked about. You are the woman from the prophesy, yes?" the girl asked in a meager voice.

"The Daughter of Sol? I am," Jegra replied, kneeling down to be less imposing. It was just a legend, but the Nyctans were extremely religious, and in their zealotry, believed Jegra to be some kind of savior destined to save them from a great evil one day.

The girl came out of her hiding place and rushed into Jegra's arms. Throwing her own small arms around Jegra's neck, she clamped on tight like a koala and clung to her for dear life.

Jegra took the child in her arms and stood up. She shot both Lianica and Brei'Alas an astonished look.

Then, stroking the child's hair, she looked the young girl in her eyes and said, "I know it will be hard, but I need you to tell me what happened here. Where is everybody?"

"The golden monster killed them all with a blanket of light. Only, I hid," the girl said. "I hid in that bin from the terrible light monster." She pointed behind her at the dumpster and Jegra nodded.

"Light monster?" Lianica asked.

The girl buried her face into Jegra's neck and began to sob. Jegra rubbed her back and tried to calm her the best she knew how.

"What now?" Brei'Alas asked. "If he's killed everyone..."

"Then he made his first real mistake," Jegra said, finishing her sentence for her.

Handing the child off to Brei'Alas, she said, "Take her back to the ship and make sure she's given a full medical evaluation."

"Yes, Your Grace," she said. She held the girl's hand and smiled at her. "I bet you're hungry. Do you want to go get some food?"

The girl nodded but felt too timid to speak. Brei merely continued to smile at her and gave her small hand a reassuring squeeze.

A beam of golden light came down and fetched them, and Brei'Alas and the girl were quickly whisked away.

Lianica turned to Jegra as if to ask *what now?* Jegra nodded in the direction of the capitol building. A monolith at the center of the city that towered over everything else. It reminded her of the Burj Khalifa. A building that soared above all others.

"Why do I get the sneaking suspicion that all of this is a trap?" Lianica asked.

Jegra just shot her an apprehensive look which seemed to articulate that she was feeling the exact same thing. On the same page about what to expect, she turned back up the street and continued making her way toward the monolith.

Onelle Te'Legra Agnar met Ladgara on the hangar deck and they engaged in a stare down.

"Aren't you going to arrest me?" Onelle asked, holding out her dainty green wrists.

Ladgara drew her blaster and trained it on Onelle. "This is a pirate ship. We don't arrest people here; we jettison them out of the airlock."

Onelle laughed. "You Dagons always think you're so superior, don't you? Well, I'm here to set the record straight, you're all insignificant to *Him*."

"Don't insult my intelligence, green-skin," Ladgara growled, her pink eye flaring bright. "He's nothing but a parasite that latches onto the weak and defenseless and leaches their souls out of their bodies like a common bloodsucker."

"Sublime, isn't it?" Onelle retorted, her eyes bright and her smile beaming. "How He so effortlessly breaks you before brushing you aside like the worthless dust you are."

She took a step closer to Ladgara, but Ladgara straightened her aim and let off a warning shot. It pinged off the back wall, hissing as hot plasma scorched the metal surface of a bulkhead. "I wouldn't come another step further. Not unless you want to learn first-hand how I lost my eye."

Onelle raised her hands and took a step back. "Ah, yes. I heard about that. You survived a shot to the face. Quite miraculous when you think about it." Her smile turned grim and she added, "Too bad whoever shot you didn't finish the job."

Ladgara's eye narrowed and her finger slowly tightened around the trigger. She was done talking and was about to blast a hole in this bitch's head, but when she tried to pull down on the trigger, she found that her finger wouldn't respond.

"Listen to me," Onelle said, her eyes changing from crystal-clear blue to obsidian black. "I want you to jettison yourself out of the nearest airlock."

Ladgara hesitated but then slowly lowered her blaster and began walking to the large energy field of the hangar bay. It was a negative-energy forcefield which kept the pressure in but allowed ships to pass through.

The science was quite simple; any ship with a deflector array or forcefield emitter could match the negative barrier frequency and pass through. It wasn't dissimilar to how a soap bubble can pass through and enter another soap bubble without popping.

But, if a living thing walked into the negative barrier field, it would fry them like a microwave oven. If Ladgara walked through it without a suit on, her skin would sizzle and blister and burn right off her body.

The moment she passed through it, she'd be a meat-popsicle floating out into the icy-cold vacuum of space. And if the shock of having her skin melted away her didn't finish her off, the freezing cold of the frigid vacuum of space would.

She slowly walked all the way across the hangar deck and paused before the shimmering wall of blue energy.

"What are you waiting for?" Onelle asked, malice dripping from her every word. "Go on through."

"I…I can't…I can't do it," Ladgara said, resisting the Voice's influence with all her might.

The veins and tendons in her neck bulged as she checked herself against the involuntary movements. Barely able to hold her muscles tight enough to prevent any further movement, it took everything she had not to walk through the forcefield and shear off her flesh. "I won't."

Ladgara slowly turned back toward Onelle, her body moving sluggishly, like one crippled by a terrible pain, but she pushed through the agonizing torment and slowly raised her gun.

Onelle laughed out loud. "My, you are a stubborn one, aren't you? Defiant till the last breath. Oh, well. A pity no one is around to see your heroic moment."

"You can't win," Ladgara said, her hand shaking as she fought against her own body to regain control. This struggle to regain basic motor function, however, prevented her from getting a clear shot.

"Oh, honey, I already have won. But I like your feisty spirit. So, I'll rescind my first order."

Ladgara's entire body relaxed and she let out a massive sigh of relief.

"Wait for me in my personal shuttle until I get back."

Before Ladgara could protest, Onelle turned and strode off the hangar deck.

Unable to stop herself, she did as commanded and boarded the shuttle. Sitting down in the co-pilot's seat, she tried to reach up and touch the controls, but her hands merely dropped back down to her sides as though they'd miraculously turned into lead weights.

"That lady is strange," a small voice chirped.

Startled, Ladgara snapped her head to the side. Just then, in Onelle's seat, a petite cat girl appeared.

"Gyllek? What in the seven moons are you doing here?" Ladgara whispered. "You can't be here…it's too dangerous."

"I'm keeping my eye on you, like Ms. Raven asked." Gyllek smiled at her and then, reached into her pocket, pulled out a device, and slapped a transponder to her shoulder. "Don't worry, pirate lady, I got this."

Two golden beams of light came down and fetched them off of the *Avarice*. When they rematerialized, Ladgara found herself back o board the *Skywend*.

Raven stood across from her, a concerned look on her face. "Are you all right?"

"I think so," she said, pinching the bridge of her nose as though she was dealing with the onset of a bad migraine headache. Although, this was just the after effects of having been in the presence of the Voice.

It was this throbbing pain in her head which made her envy those who were immune to psychic powers. People like Dakroth and Jegra merely felt a fuzzy tingle. But for Ladgara, it felt like her entire brain was being squeezed by a vice grip.

"I found her just like you asked, Captain," Gyllek said in her cheerful manner.

"Good work, Gyllek. You can go help yourself to a pizza, if you want."

"Wow! A pizza? Really?"

Raven nodded and the girl raced out of the room.

Ladgara staggered forward, but still unable to regain full control over her own motor functions, she toppled into Raven's arms. "I've got you," Raven said.

Ladgara looked up at her and smiled. "You do, don't you?"

Before either of them knew what was happening, their lips came together and they were kissing like old lovers reunited after years of separation.

"I thought I was stronger," Ladgara said, her eyes welling up with tears. "I thought I could..."

Ladgara buried her face in Raven's shoulder and began to weep. Raven held her tight in her embrace, hushed her gently like a mother would a child, and simply repeated, "I've got you."

A few minutes later, Onelle Te'Legra Agnar returned to the hangar deck of the *Avarice* to find her shuttle completely empty and her bounty missing.

She snickered and then in a nonchalant voice said, "It seems that one may have had a stronger will than I initially gave her credit for. A mistake I won't be repeating anytime soon."

Onelle boarded her shuttle, closed the hatch behind her. She kicked off her boots and threw herself into her chair. Crossing her legs in her chair, she plotted the course back to her ship and the shuttle began to rise off the hangar deck. Its thrusters pulsing blue, explosions started to erupt all throughout the pirate ship, including the hangar bay.

Flames leapt out of the airducts and the doors. As Onelle's shuttle slowly turned toward the shields, a fiery explosion erupted from within the ship, blowing off the panels of a side-conduit. A plasma conduit leak had met an oxygen leak and a large ball of flame engulfed her small shuttle.

Still intact, Onelle's shuttle shot out of the hangar and into space just as the hangar bay went up in flames, loud explosions belching flames chasing her out like a ferocious dragon chasing a trespasser from its cave.

She glanced back as the entire ship continued to go up in flames and smiled cruelly. They had obeyed her every word—and now the entire pirate fleet would pay the price for choosing the wrong side.

"Order the pirate fleet to begin their run," Dakroth barked.

Callestra pointed at the comms officer, signaling him to send the encrypted message. He tapped a few buttons on his control panel and then swiveled around in his chair and nodded to her once it had been sent.

They all turned and waited for the pirate ships to move out of the system, feigning a retreat, only to jump back behind the enemy fleet in a strategic ambush. But, after another moment of waiting, it was clear that something was wrong.

Instead of the pirate fleet following the plan, the ships all started to self-destruct, one by one. Including the pirate flagship of the self-proclaimed Pirate King himself, Novac Tamoran.

The *Avarice* slowly lost its engines and, being tugged on by the gravity of the planet below, started to do a nose dive right into a fellow vessel.

The two-ship collision sent up plumes of fire which quickly evaporated into space. But fire continued to ignite in the atmosphere, being vented into space by the two damaged vessels, causing a daisy chain of explosions that tore through the hulls of both ships.

"What the bloody Helios is going on?!" Dakroth shouted out in a broiling rage, his pink eyes flaring with energy.

Callestra didn't have any answers for him, but before they could look into the matter, the nav-com officer suddenly interrupted Dakroth's tirade and, turning to give them an urgent look, said, "Ma'am, we have incoming bogies."

Jumping into the system were hundreds of squidies. Giant celestial space squids that fed on energy. The squids instantly went over to the exploding pirate armada and began feasting on their energy discharges.

"That weak-minded fool!" Dakroth snarled. His eyes flared hot magenta as a discharge of pink Dygra energy seeped out of the corners of his eyes like pink-tinged smoke.

"Shields are down to twelve percent, ma'am. What are your orders?"

Callestra turned toward Dakroth, cleared her throat, and gave it to him straight. "Once those squids finish off their meal, they'll be wanting dessert. And it's only a matter of time before they latch onto our fleet and cripple what remains of it."

"Then move us into the enemy fleet," Dakroth said.

Surprised, Callestra raised an eyebrow. It was a bold move. But at close range, the squids would have a harder time distinguishing between the Alliance vessels and the Fusion ones.

"You heard him," shouted Callestra. "Move us into that fleet."

The *Imperatrix, Verlag, Chiron,* and the *Galliforn,* along with the rest of the remaining Allied forces, slowly moved their ships into close quarters with the enemy fleet.

As Dakroth's fleet inserted themselves into the spaces between the enemy vessels, the squids were already turning about and heading their way.

20

Asteroids pinged off the hull of Deunan's freighter as she took a detour through the outer belt, cutting through the *Badlands*. No sooner had she dropped *Ole Birtha* out of hyperspace to navigate the asteroid belt than Xarthon's stealth gunship appeared directly behind her in the blink of an eye.

The military vessel fired off some warning shots. Red plasma bolts tore through rock and spat up a spray of detritus that rattled along Deunan's hull like a hailstorm.

"Dammit," Deunan growled. "That's gonna peel off my thermal paint."

Outside her window she saw Gamagor's jade yacht flash into view and pull up alongside her. She looked out her window and peered through the large glass view portal of the yacht's command deck to see Gam standing on the bridge with Lycia and Allie by her side.

Lycia waved at her from across the short distance between the two ships and, at the same time, Deunan's comm crackled as a call came in. She flipped the *on* switch, making the broadcast handsfree.

"You sure about this?" Gamagor asked from the other ship. "It's a little bit..."

"Risky? I know. But it's the best way, I'm sure. We can lose him in the asteroid belt."

"I sure hope you're right," Lycia's voice came back over the com. "Because, I for one, don't want to die in a fiery death."

"Just trust your instincts and you'll do fine," Deunan reassured her.

"You stay safe out there," Gamagor said, worried about Deunan. It was nice to care for someone other than herself for once.

"You too," replied Deunan. She smiled, feeling warm and fuzzy that Gam was thinking about her, and then cut the comm link.

It was no secret that *Ole Birtha* could take a hard hit, but Deunan knew she wouldn't last very long against those bigger asteroids. Taking the controls in her hands, she took a deep breath and prepared for one hell of a flight.

"X-5," she said, glancing over her shoulder at the robot sitting in the charging nook at the rear of the cabin. "You might want to strap in. Things are about to get bumpy."

The robot nodded his head and then looked over for the seatbelt. Finding the buckle, he pulled it across his torso and, with a satisfying *click*, secured it.

Xarthon may be driven, but he'd have to be mad to follow us into this, thought Deunan, leaning forward in her seat and looking up at the asteroids spiraling about upon irregular rotations just outside her window.

As she watched, a couple of large ones crashed into one another and fractured, breaking apart into smaller ones, which flew every which way. Anything getting caught in that asteroid storm would be pulverized almost instantly.

Making sure to keep her distance from the dense regions of colliding rock, Deunan carried on her plotted course, Gamagor's yacht sailing just off her starboard bow.

Back aboard Gam's ship, Lycia turned to look out the cockpit windows at the much larger stealth gunship looming just over their shoulders. All of a sudden, two additional stealth fighters launched from the open bay on the gunship's underbelly.

"Um…I hate to be the bearer of bad news, but we've got company," Lycia informed everyone.

The comm crackled and Deunan's voice chimed in. "I've got a few tricks up my sleeve yet. Deploying magnetic mines now."

Deunan reached over and hit a button and a small cargo hatch opened on her freighter and an entire swarm of metallic mines the size of Seyfferian golf balls poured out.

Once both ships were a safe distance away, she activated the swarm of mines and they snapped into a hexagonal grid formation, creating what appeared to be an explosive minefield in the shape of a net.

"That ought to slow them down."

As soon as she'd said it, though, the two fighters launched a couple of Python missiles and detonated the mine trap. A daisy chain of explosions ignited behind them and a large, empty pocket of space manifested in the wake of the explosion.

"Looks like we're going to have to do this the hard way," Gamagor said, shoving aside the helmsman and taking hold of the e-controls herself.

Jamming the throttle forward, the yacht's blue thrusters flared hot white as she raced forward into the empty pocket of space before it refilled with debris.

Small fighters tore away from Deunan's location and took chase. As they pursued their new target.

The pocket of asteroid field closing up ahead of them, Gamagor gunned it, giving everything the luxury yacht had to offer, and taking it into the rapidly closing tunnel.

The ship disappeared behind the veil of rock. One of the fighters pursued them, but the other turned and went after Deunan instead.

"If it's a fight you want," Gamagor growled, "then it's a fight you'll get." She looked over at Lycia and pointed at a tilting, gyrating chair that had a three-way split screen monitor attached to it. It looked like a fancy video game rig.

"What's that?"

"The ship's weapons console. You'll have direct access to the plasma cannon. Do you mind manning the guns for me?"

"Would I mind?" Lycia laughed, sarcastically amused. "I'd absolutely love to." She raced over to the chair and quickly slid into it. After strapping herself into the harness, she flicked on the system and the whole thing came alive, gyroscope mount rising up on hydraulics.

Cracking her knuckles, she rocked her neck from shoulder to should and then said, "I've got this."

Deunan's cargo ship wasn't nimble or graceful, but it could take a beating. Still, the drone of the collision alarm was driving her mad and she reached up and flicked a switch, killing it.

As more meteoroids pelted her hull, giving it a few hundred extra dents, she looked in the rearview monitor. The enemy fighter was still trailing her, and since it was a stealth ship, keeping a visual on it was about the only way to track him.

"That's right, you dumbass *krag*, get closer so I can see you."

A large asteroid came into view and she guided the ship toward it. If she could only park it in one of the craters and shut down her systems for a while, she'd turn invisible and the enemy fighter would just shoot past her. The only problem was on how to go about doing it without being seen.

If she set down in plain sight, the fighter would make short work of her. She needed a distraction.

She'd already deployed all of her mines. And her freighter didn't have any heavy ordinance like missiles. There was only the sad state of its plasma cannon which was barely holding together as it was.

In fact, they weren't so much canons, per se, as they were pea-shooters. They weren't even powerful enough to melt armored plating, let alone fry a *krag*. Just good enough, she reckoned, to blast a few rocks out of the away and scare off some emboldened marauders.

That's when it dawned on her what she was carrying in the cargo hold. She had stasis containers of superionic ice.

The unusual black ice burned hot and could be detonated by supercharging it with lasers. Conveniently, it also could be made into drinkable water in much the same way.

Because of its unique crystalline properties, a small cube of it could produce enough water to fill a bathtub. A few tons of it could create enough water to terraform a planet—which is primarily what it was used for—drinking and terraforming.

Making superionic ice into a bomb was a tricky procedure, though. Too little energy and it stayed as it was. Too much energy too quickly and it evaporated into a steam cloud. You needed to charge it slowly enough to allow the crystalline structure to become highly unstable, but not so unstable it collapsed like a house of cards.

This finicky and taxing process was the very reason the black stuff really wasn't used for explosives in the first place. But Deunan knew it could be done, *because science.*

The way she liked to visualize it was to picture a house made of cards where all the cards were heated up until every single card was about to burst into flame, then, by triggering a cascade effect, every card would fall into one another at the same point, at the same time, at the same speed. This additional friction of already super-charged particles would, subsequently, ignite and expel huge amounts of energy.

It was essentially creating a massive hydrogen bomb, since all the active components simply consisted of water. The perfect clean bomb, so to speak.

And Deunan had enough technical skill to modify the stasis containers into bombs. She'd just need to buy herself enough time to make the necessary modifications.

Luckily, she had just the plan for such an occasion.

"Computer," she barked. "Execute *needle in the haystack* protocol."

The computer chimed, bleeped and gargled some strange tones and then sent a series of holographic projections of the ship into space, disguising itself within about thirty exact holographic copies of itself.

If she couldn't go stealth, she'd do the opposite and multiply her vessel with holographic emulations. This way, the fighter would waste time chasing fake copies which continuously shifted position with one another, buying her the time she needed to build a few bombs.

With the clock ticking, she swung her legs out of her chair, the momentum carrying her up to her feet, and then double-timed it to the cargo hold to begin the alterations to the superionic ice containment canisters.

Lycia's chair automatically swiveled around as it tracked the fighter's whereabouts, always keeping it dead in her sights.

The stealth fighter moved nimbly through the labyrinthine spaces between the asteroids, which made tracking it that much more difficult, but she managed to do well enough. When it came into the crosshairs of her monitor, she squeezed down on the trigger of the joystick and fired off a couple of powerful plasma bolts. They were intercepted by rogue meteoroids and, having missed the ship, she cursed under her breath.

A large meteoroid collided with the ship and caused the yacht to lurch as the engines groaned to make the required course corrections. Almost immediately after that close call, another equally big, if not more jolting asteroid pinged off the hull.

"Could you hurry it up, princess?" Gam growled, frustrated that her luxury yacht was taking such a beating. "We're getting pretty chewed up out here."

"Hey, it wasn't my idea to take us into the thick of it," Lycia reminded her. "It was Deunan's...and which you agreed to."

"Just...stick to your job of killing the bad guys and I'll stick to my job of keeping us in the sky."

Lycia looked down at the red flashing light on her controls and found that it was suggesting a missile strike. Of course, she knew luxury yachts didn't come from the shipyard with fully functional missile batteries, which meant Gamagor had gone out of her way to make her sleek little vessel a mean, green, fighting machine—just like her.

"Here goes nothing," she said, and she flicked off the safety on the joystick and then mashed the button with the picture of a python snake on it.

A hollow *thwomp*, like the sound of a torpedo launching, sounded and a Python missile shot out of the jade yacht and raced toward a giant asteroid in the distance.

"The *krag* is over there," Gam shouted above the rattling sound of a light meteoroid shower peppering the hull. She nodded her head in the opposite direction from where the missile launched.

"Cool your tits, hot mama," Lycia shouted back, shooting her a polished grin. "Everything is copacetic."

Gam rolled her eyes as she turned hard to port and the ship veered left, narrowly missing a large spiraling meteoroid, its jagged edges resembling the teeth of a circular saw.

The missile finally impacted with the large asteroid, fracturing it but doing little else in the way of damage. Even so, Lycia fired off another Python missile, then another.

The second missile was aimed at the first, and when they collided, a massive shockwave pushed all the surrounding debris outward. The pressure bubble of the two explosions feeding off one another carved out another, this time, much larger hollow.

"See," Lycia said, looking over the monitors at Gam, who merely shrugged, "I told you everything would be fine."

"Good work, kid," she said, and steered the ship into the new hollow that Lycia had made.

As they entered the empty space, Gam throttled her thrusters up to full.

The engines roared to life and the thruster nozzles blazed orange hot as blue shock diamonds trailed out of the back of the five main plasma coil thrusters.

"I'm picking up low level atmosphere," Lycia said as she glanced down at the monitors.

"Good," Gam said. "Maybe we'll ignite something and smoke the *krag* out."

"We might ignite ourselves," she replied, shooting Gam a nervous glance.

Gam merely grinned wider and Lycia puffed at a tuft of dislodged hair. It was no use talking to the woman, she seemingly had a death wish. *Death before defeat, victory before death* and all that gladiator nonsense.

Lycia just would prefer it if Gam's heroics didn't take them both down with the ship.

The space yacht reached the far end of the vacuum pocket and Gam cranked the wheel hard. The ship flipped back over and she got the enemy fighter in her sights.

Lycia took the gunner's joystick in her hands and flipped around in the chair as she locked onto her target. "Gotcha'!" she said excitedly and pulled down on the trigger.

The yacht's plasma cannons fired a volley of hot red needles across the void. She held the trigger down and blasted away at it with everything she had. If the canons overheated, they overheated. All she wanted was to take that fighter out.

The enemy fighter returned her fire as the both of them streaked past one another.

Lycia shouted, "Graddak vela'qui!" as the enemy ship broke away from her attack.

"Hang on!" Gam shouted as she pulled back hard on the wheel, which tilted forty-five degrees backward. Using all her strength, her green muscles bulging and flexing against the g-forces that threatened to tear her from the wheel, she got the ship to do a barrel roll.

Barely able to believe her eyes, Lycia stared at Gam with mouth agape, completely awestruck. "Magnificent," she whispered to herself.

Snapping herself out of it, she quickly swung back around in her chair and locked onto the fighter again. When the auto-lock engaged, the fighter countered the yacht's reverse barrel roll with a displacement slide.

The two ships charged one another once more, playing a second game of chicken. Plasma blasts crisscrossed between the two vessels and Lycia let forth a relentless volley. "Hold still you little piece of—"

One of the *krag's* plasma blasts grazed the yacht's emerald colored hull, leaving scorch marks along the pristine metallic paint. The jolt roused Allie, who, for the first time during all the chaos, got up and began to pace the floor in a nervous circle before settling down again.

"Hang on, Allie. This is going to be a close one," Lycia shouted, as the two ships seemed to be on a collision course with one another.

Lycia armed her missiles again and fired off all remaining ordinance. This time she was going to race the shockwave. "Get us out of here, Gam—and step on it!"

Again, Gamagor spun the ship around and ignited her thrusters to full. As they pulled away from the detonation, the blue sheath of the shockwave chased them toward a storm of rock raging in the distance.

Lycia glanced down at her aft monitor to see the enemy fighter trying to maneuver out of the way of the shockwave, but to no avail. The shockwave tore through it as though it were a piñata.

"Yes!" Lycia screamed victoriously, pumping her fist.

"Don't get cocky, kid," Gam said. "We're not out of this yet."

"I'll try to clear a path in that debris field so we don't flatten against that rock wall," Lycia said.

When she squeezed down on the trigger, nothing happened. Looking down at her monitor, the holovid readout showed that the guns were overheated. And she was out of missiles.

"Dammit," she growled, smashing her fists down on the dash.

"What is it?" Gam asked.

"The cannons are overheated."

"Use the missiles," Gam said as she stared down an angry looking blizzard of rock.

"I used them all," Lycia informed her. She, too, looked out at the meteoroid storm and gulped.

"In that case," Gam said looking over at her and Allie, who now seemed to be showing the first signs of edginess, "hold on to your butts."

Deunan finally finished hotwiring three of the stasis containers and attached the laser charging device to each of the canisters.

The ice was about as hot as the core of a planet, so the stasis containers were necessary to maintain the pressure and also act as shielding from the intense heat.

With the bombs prepped, she dragged the first container over to the airlock and set it inside then went back for the other two. Halfway across the cargo hold, the ship jolted as though it had been hit by an energy blast rather than a rock. Which meant that she'd been found out.

"Dammit," she grumbled. The little bastard had found her.

But she didn't have time to bother with the *krag*, not if she wanted to get those containers off her ship before they blew.

She hurried along with the second stasis container and worked up a good sweat getting it all the way to the airlock in record time. The third one, however, fell over halfway there and with plasma blasts tearing her ship up, she scrambled to get it upright so she could fit it through the doorway.

It took a bit of struggle, but she finally got it inside with the other two. Once she'd set them all alongside each other, she stepped back, exiting the airlock, and shut the hatch. With a tug of the handle, she sealed the room up tight and then slapped the red emergency purge button on the wall.

A loud hiss sounded and all three containers jettisoned out into space. She watched them spiral away from her when another plasma bolt up the tailpipe reminded her she wasn't done yet.

She raced up the corridor, back to the bridge. Darting past X-5, she ran to her seat, hopped over the arm of the chair and slid into her seat, all in one fluid motion. She unzipped her flight jacket, letting the cool air lap at her glistening chest and took ahold of the controls.

Before she could maneuver the ship to a safer location, another blast rocked the ship and sent sparks raining down from the overhead paneling. "Oh, that does it," she growled, and pulling back on the controls she brought the battered ship around.

Yet another blast scorched the bow of her ship and she flinched. *Ole Birtha* took one hell of a beating, but luckily no vital systems had been hit. But she knew it was only a matter of time before that *lactating meat stick* got a clean line of sight on her thruster nozzles and unleashed Helios on her.

She flicked off the holograms outside, as they were no longer helping any, and the duplicates of the ship vanished in the blink of an eye. Deunan steered the freighter back in line with the path leading out of the asteroid field and, hand on the throttle, she turned her engines up to maximum.

Although the old tub was slow to get its start, it could keep up with the best of them. She had, after all, retrofitted her engines with a phase-three Hyperborean fusion drive for those extra-long hauls.

Although it wasn't a fancy quad core like the newer cruisers had, it was an extremely powerful three core system that could run continuously and maintain a steady increase in thrust the whole journey.

The bright flash of the explosion alerted her to the fact that the first container of superionic black ice had gone critical. Soon after, it was followed by the second flash which lit up the asteroids all around her. And then a third.

She even glimpsed the outline of Xarthon's stealth gunship directly ahead of her in the light of the flashes, hiding behind the wall of scattered rock and debris like the coward he was.

Deunan checked her monitor for the enemy fighter, but just as planned, it was gone. Destroyed in the explosion.

Science, one, Space Marshal Dickless, zero, she thought to herself, a wry smile forming on her lips.

With the pesky fighter out of the way, all she needed to worry about was the big gunship. And now that she had eyes on it, she decided to continue on a collision course with Xarthon's top of the line stealth gunship.

Compared to most vessels, a freighter like hers was a veritable sledgehammer. She was betting that when it came to a game of chicken, Xarthon would buckle. After all, she had a fairly strong hunch that his ship was delicate and full of expensive equipment he wouldn't risk letting get damaged just to prove he was the manliest of space dunces.

Whereas he had everything to lose, she had relatively little to lose. At the moment, she carried little more than superionic ice and old memories. So, even if her hunch turned out to be wrong and his ship was, in fact, built like a tank, at least she could be content in the fact that she'd helped Lycia escape. Because, right now, that's all that mattered.

When it came down to it, between her and him, she was fairly certain she had the bigger set of balls.

Deunan reached down and twisted a small dial next to the throttle. This killed the redundancy setting to the trifold fusion core and opened all three fusion engines simultaneously. With three times the power pouring into the thrusters, the eight, blue arrowhead-shaped tips of her thrusters grew to be several times longer than the ship itself.

"Let's see you flinch," she said, getting pinned to the back of her seat as she accelerated toward the enemy vessel.

21

Celestial squids of glowing energy wrapped their tentacles around the starships and began suckling the energy from the ships' fusion engines. With roughly a third of the armada crippled, Dakroth frowned as he watched the space battle take a turn for the worse.

It wasn't only the Allied fleet that was being attacked, though. Bringing his armada into theirs was smart, because, as he'd predicted, the squids followed them in and then began latching onto the first power sources they could find. Which meant the Fusion forces were taking on CSEs too.

Callestra edged up to the emperor and looked out at the massive ships which hung outside their window. They were so close it seemed as though you could reach out and touch them.

"We won't be able to take much more of this close quarter bombardment," she informed him.

"Until Jegra can engage H'aaztre's forces on the ground, we need to hold this position, no matter what it takes."

"Understood," Callestra said, and she turned to return to her duties. Before she could take her leave, Dakroth's hand reached out and grabbed her by the arm.

They shared a moment and she brushed her hair back behind her ear and smiled at him. Having taken too much of her valuable time, he let go of her and turned back to his fireworks show.

In the distance, through the tartan of red and green plasma fire streaking across the sky in every direction, he saw a familiar ship cutting through the storm of disruptor fire. It was the *Skywend,* and it was headed for the planet's atmosphere.

A smirk formed on Dakroth's mouth. He had no love for Raven Nightguard or her obnoxiously eclectic crew, but if she was going down to the surface then his confidence in Jegra's mission was that much greater.

There were very few people who had ever outsmarted the Lord Emperor, and Raven had done so on more than one occasion. She was a formidable adversary for anyone, and he half expected that with Raven's brains and Jegra's brawn, they might actually have a fighting chance.

Down on the surface of Nyctan, Jegra's forces were met with resistance when they tried to enter the citadel. The Nights of Caelum had taken up position outside and they were being led by a knight she was unfamiliar with.

"Who is he again?" Jegra asked. She leaned over to speak confidentially with Lianica in front of the knight she wasn't familiar with.

"He said his name was Palamedes."

Jegra nodded and then straightened up. Staring him in the eyes, she asked, "Where's Sir Lance Bishop?"

"Sir Bishop is attending to other duties," Palamedes said. "I have taken command in his stead."

Palamedes stood before the empress dressed in his black captain's armor. Behind him was a full battalion of armored knights. And behind them were about three hundred regular enlisted Nyctan soldiers.

Palamedes strode out to meet Jegra. He had an over confident swagger that suggested he wasn't in the least worried about her or her army.

"You will have your men stand down and surrender to my forces," Jegra said in all seriousness.

Palamedes laughed. "I was going to say the same thing to you."

There was a long pause as they gauged one another before Jegra finally broke the silence. "You do know that I'm the highest ranking commander in the order of the Knights of Caelum, do you not?" She stared at his big black eyes but he merely smiled at her with a malicious sort of grin.

"Not everyone recognizes the articles of Vortesh or the Voroxian warrior priestesses," he blithely intoned. "You may be a High Priestess in the warrior order, but we of the noble blood of Caelum do not recognize your authority as anything other than symbolic."

Jegra glowered at this Palamedes. Such semantic word games did not go over well with her. In her mind, it wasn't a matter of interpreting ancient texts.

The articles of the Knights declared that the warrior priestess would take command in lieu of the administratrix during her absence. And minus their regnant queen, the responsibility fell to Jegra to lead the knights in battle.

"In that case, I won't order you to stand aside as the High Priestess. I'll order you to stand aside as the Imperatrix of the Galaxy."

Palamedes laughed off her remarks.

"Such arrogance in a woman. If I didn't know any better, I'd think you had Dagon blood in you."

"I'll take that as a compliment," Jegra snarled. She was growing fed up with this pompous ass who insisted on ignoring her royal titles as if they were meaningless monikers.

They stared at one another for an intense ten seconds and then he drew back, smiling at her with a strained grin that betrayed the ventriloquist behind the dummy. It quickly became apparent that she was never really truly dealing with Palamedes in the first place, but rather just one more Avatar of H'aaztre.

Before Jegra had time to react, a high-powered laser beam came out of nowhere and pierced the side of Palamedes' temple.

It was so fast that, initially, Jegra didn't quite know what had happened. In the ensuing confusion, it seemed neither did anybody else. As she turned to scan the horizon, Palamedes' body tottered briefly just over her shoulder and then toppled to the ground.

"Sniper!" Lianica shouted. She grabbed the empress by her arm and yanked her behind a Battle Centurion war robot which turned and began scanning the city rooftops in the direction the shot had originated.

Jegra slowly stepped back out into the open, raising a hand to halt Lianica from stopping her. She stood beside the Battle Centurion and glanced around for where the shot had been fired from.

The beam, as far as she could gauge, came from over five kilometers away. She knew this because the angle of the shot lined up with the street which ran all the way to the port. The lighthouse at the port was the only place high enough for such a shot to be taken from.

"Centurion," Jegra said, "Keep your sites on that lighthouse roughly five clicks off. If you see any movement, obliterate it."

<<Affirmative>> the war machine replied.

There wasn't time to figure out who'd fired that shot, however, because the moment after Palamedes' body hit the ground, the knights ignited their plasma swords and began to advance.

Jegra turned back in time to draw her battle axe and block a plasma sword that came striking down above her. With a combined hiss and whine, her korridium axe blocked the scorching hot plasma blade.

Whereas a plasma sword could cut through tempered steel in a handful of seconds, korridium was a different matter. It would take at least a full half an hour to cut through her korridium axe, but that's assuming the plasma sword had time to cut in the same spot for the entire duration. A lot of time that Jegra wasn't about to give this rival knight.

"Death before defeat," the knight growled, his helmet masking his voice.

"Victory over death," Jegra replied through gritted teeth.

These were the words of the Knights. Words she had drilled into her during her training aboard the *Light Bringer*.

As empress, the moment she engaged in combat, her army rushed in to engage the knights, roaring out their fiercest battled cries as they clashed with the enemy forces.

Although the Knights were elite warriors and were notoriously difficult to take down, Jegra currently boasted the bigger numbers. Hopefully it would be enough to push the knights back and secure the citadel.

Five kilometers away, Gywen stood up and began breaking down her high-powered sniper rifle. As she dismantled it and put it back into its case, a call came over the comm for her.

"Is it done?" She recognized the Lord Emperor's voice instantly.

She tapped the Voroxian pendant on her armor and answered. "It's done," she said with a smile.

"Good," Dakroth answered. He'd kept his word and picked a fight just as he'd intended all along. But the battle was just far from over. "Now, take up the high ground and provide cover fire. Protect your empress at all costs."

"You've got it, Lord Emperor," she said, and she tapped the pendant to turn off the comm.

Gywen worked as a gun for hire, but just like any modern Voroxian priestess, they were loyal to one and only one person, the High Priestess of the order—and that was Jegra.

Packing up her gear, she headed into the desolate city to find a rooftop to set up on. From there she'd pick off knights until there was nobody left but the smoldering corpses of nameless, forgotten heroes.

Jegra backflipped out of the way, spinning in mid-air, her body twisting as one blade passed over her while another passed under her. As the blades passed her, one of them managed to nick a lock of her hair.

She landed in a kneeling crouch, strands of her hair fluttering to the ground soon after her, and then glanced over her shoulder at the knight behind her and slowly panned her gaze back toward the one standing in front of her.

She narrowed her eyes, angry that they'd messed up her hair, and growled in a low, imposing voice, "My turn."

With lightning quick reflexes, she flung her battle axe in the air, spinning it so that it twirled up into the sky with the speed of a circular saw blade. She then sprung backward, ran up the chest of the knight behind her, and sprang off his chest. When she kicked off, he tumbled backward and rolled across more than half of the battlefield as if he'd been hit by a hover-train.

Jegra flew into the air, caught her axe with one hand, and then grabbed the handle with both hands as she hung in the air for a split-second. Coming down, she brought her battle axe firmly down on the other knight, lodging it in the trapezius of his armor.

The force of her powerful downward blow dropped him to his knees and, gripping her axe's handle, she raised a foot and booted him in his chest.

He flew back and bowled over two other knights in the process, clearing a path for some of Jegra's men to advance on the capital.

The first knight had managed to get back on his feet and was charging toward her, blade humming. Slashing his plasma blade downward, Jegra drew back, as the very tip nicked Jegra's right shoulder and she let out a yelp as the blade seared through her flesh, leaving a burn mark.

By the time she shifted her stance to face him, however, her wound was already rapidly healing itself thanks to her hyper-active healing factor.

The scar would last about ten hours, but even that would begin to fade over time. In twenty-four hours, no cuts or abrasions would be seen anywhere on her body—assuming she didn't sustain any more serious injuries.

"That was a mistake," she said, the bridge of her nose winkling as she scowled menacingly at the knight.

"My only mistake," the knight answered, "was not striking you down dead the first time."

Jegra nodded. "As I said…" She then gestured with her fingers for him to come at her.

The moment he moved a micron, she leaped thirty feet into the air. While soaring above the knight, who craned his neck to track her, she threw her axe downward. It spiraled through the air like a tomahawk and, with ease, passed through the knight's arm severing it at the shoulder.

The axe lodged itself in the ground and a brief moment late the knight's arm *thumped* down next to it—sword still in hand. The knight reared back and roared out in pain.

His cries were quickly silenced when Jegra's knee guard crashed down on his head. She landed on top of him with such force that she shattered his helmet and knocked him to the ground.

As he struggled back up, she grabbed the remaining half of his helmet with her bare hands and pried it off. Then, with a powerful punch that echoed like a clap of thunder, she pulverized his skull.

The indent in his deformed head showed the power of her strike and the other knights, looking at her with trepidation, reconvened at the entrance gate of the citadel.

Jegra was about to order her forces to advance on them when, all of a sudden, the citadel doors opened and wave after wave of Nephilim and Nyctan soldiers poured out.

Three hundred more enemy combatants joined the fray and Jegra raised a fist, signaling her soldiers to hold their position and brace themselves for a second wave.

"Looks like you could use a bit of help," a gruff voice said to her right.

Jegra's eyes widened as she looked over to find Kregor holding her axe. His green beefy arms rippled with strength and his scales gleamed in the light in such a way that she couldn't help but have carnal stirrings for him. He raised the axe and, extending it toward her, handed it back to her.

"Hopefully we didn't miss much," Raven's voice chimed.

Jegra turned to her left to find Raven and Gyllek.

She looked back over her shoulder and found the rest of Raven's crew including Skuld, Angellyk, Ladgara, and Danica all having arrived to support her.

"Dani?" Jegra gasped. She almost didn't recognize her seeing as how Dani was wearing one of Raven's brown leather outfits, but it suited her well enough. Dropping her axe to the ground, it stuck in with a deep sinking *thunk*, and she ran to Danica.

They crashed together and Jegra, placing her palms on Dani's face, leaned forward and touched her forehead to Dani's. "I've missed you so much."

Danica took Jegra's face in her turquoise and silver prosthetic hand and smiled, but she didn't say anything. Jegra was going to ask if something was the matter, but before she could inquire as to Danica's strange mood, warning cries pierced the air.

"We've got company!" Angellyk hollered, drawing her dual plasma blasters and twirling them fancifully about like an expert gunslinger.

Kregor pulled his giant Gatling gun off his back and flicked on the motor, spooling up the plasma bolts.

Gyllek stepped forward, pulling out plasma blades and twirling them about with a practiced finesse. She may be small, but Raven had taught her to hold her own in a fight.

Raven drew out a plasma rifle and slid out her oversized coolant cartridge, checked it, then slapped it back in.

Jegra turned around and picked her axe. Then scanning the faces of her closest friends one last time, she turned back to the advancing throng of enemy combatants and shouted, "Let's show these golden-boot-licking sons of bitches exactly who they're dealing with!"

Red-hot laser beams and green and orange plasma bolts crisscrossed through the hazy air, making a tartan of intense energy that singed the air. Plasma blades clashed with the squeal and whine of metal against metal, every molecule protesting the scorching heat.

The blades heated up the air around them which hummed as it reverberated through the cool air. Dirt and steam mingled creating an unclean smog, and warrior met warrior—but only the best and most skilled walked away from the confrontation.

Like the sands of the arena, this was just another tired ole blood sport. Combatant against combatant, fighting for one goal and one goal only: *victory or death.*

22

Holding its position, the stealth gunship aimed its plasma cannons at the oncoming freighter, which was barreling toward it like a flaming kamikaze.

The korridium hull of Deunan's ship creaked and groaned as it collided with fragments of rock that made up the wall of the asteroid belt. Beads of sweat began to drip from her forehead as she wasn't entirely sure she would make it out in one piece.

"Hold it together," she murmured to the ship as if it were listening. "You can do it. Just a little further."

Debris exploded out and trailed after the freighter as it shot through the barrier of rock and ice like a bat out of hell then continued on its accelerated afterburn toward the stealth ship.

Collision being imminent, the stealth ship opened fire as the freighter broke through the asteroid field. Several direct hits scorched the thick hull of the small cargo ship but did little to slow it down.

Ole Birtha was the closest thing to a space sledgehammer there was. And there was no stopping her now.

At this range, firing off a Python missile would be unwise. It would only cause serious damage to both ships. And Xarthon would have to be a bigger fool than Deunan thought for him to detonate a massive warhead capable of destroying both of them.

Betting that he wasn't a complete idiot, however, she maintained her collision course.

"Break off now," a frantic voice came over the comm. "Or I'll be forced to blow you out of the sky."

"You would have already done it by now if you could have," Deunan responded.

Another barrage of plasma fire erupted from the glowing cannon muzzles of the stealth gunship. One lucky shot drilled into *Ole Birtha's* plating and ruptured the starboard side coolant tank.

Almost immediately, the afterburn cut out and the engines died down. Without coolant to cool the thruster engines, they simply burned themselves out. The ship was adrift.

Stalled out, Deunan's freighter drifted weightlessly, its momentum carrying it incrementally toward the gunship. Deunan had to work the maneuvering thrusters like a bloody magician to keep *Ole Birtha's* nose pointed at her target.

But without the afterburners, the maneuvering thrusters slowed the freighter down too much and, eventually, it lost all of its moment and came to a standstill off the bow of the gunship, its menacing maw looming over her.

"Var jong hylek!" Deunan slammed her fists down on the console and then looked up at the menacing black gunship sitting outside her front windshield like a bloodthirsty beast silently stalking her.

Ole Birtha was the worse for wear and there wasn't a time Deunan could remember her being this singed and marked up before. She'd been through hell and back, and was currently leaking coolant into space.

Purplish globs of coolant congealed and wobbled by her port window as she tried to figure out her next move.

"Ready to surrender yourself and the girl?" Xarthon's voice asked, the comm crackling with background static as his voice paused and waited for her response.

"Screw you, *slag!*" she barked angrily. Not only was she mad as Helios about being helpless, but she was pissed that he assumed she would just give up. She wasn't the giving up type. However, she was out of *joh-jong* moves—and he knew it.

Out of the blackness, bright red streaks of plasma rained down on the stealth ship like a maelstrom of angry fire.

When Deunan looked up to see where the attack was coming from, she saw Gamagor's glinting emerald yacht come out of the left quadrant and drop in between the two vessels, providing cover fire for her.

Deunan smiled. "Your timing couldn't be better, Gam."

"I couldn't just leave you in a lurch," Gam said.

The ship-wide comm crackled and hissed angrily. "You're making a *big* mistake," Xarthon snarled, his voice suppressing his broiling rage best he could. "All of you!"

"Wrong. It's you who has made the grave mistake," Gam shot back with her usual matter of fact boldness. "Allow me to introduce you to the *Epsilon*, personal ship to the Scourge of the Arena, Gamagor Dar'vek of Dragonia, offering assistance to the freighter under attack by an unknown alien ship."

Deunan smiled and then gripped her joystick and brought the weapons online. Although her plasma blasters were basic, she turned them onto the gunship and joined Gamagor and Lycia's relentless volley.

Although the stealth ship's armor plating could take a beating, it wasn't exactly built for close quarter engagements. They'd made it stealth for a reason. "Grah!" Xarthon growled, throwing up his hands with the indignation of defeat.

"Sir, our shielding won't be able to take much more of this beating. What are your orders?"

"Break off the pursuit," he said, clearly displeased. "We'll let them think we've retreated and then track them via long-range sensors."

"Yes, sir. Terminating pursuit now."

The stealth ship slowly turned away amid the barrage of sweltering plasma fire. A few moments later, in a flash of light, the stealth warship jumped out of the system.

Deunan let out a deep sigh of relief and sank into her seat.

"You okay, kid?" she asked, her finger on the comm button.

"Couldn't be better! How about you?" asked Lycia.

"Tired, kid. Damn tired. I could use that massage you owe me right about now."

Lycia laughed. "Message received. But since the freighter looks a little banged up right now, I suggest you come aboard Gamagor's yacht."

"Copy that," Deunan said.

A half hour later, all three women were lying face down on massage tables, moaning as though they were three Verusian fire-tail lionesses in heat.

"Don't stop," Deunan cried out. Her plea for more was followed by a salacious moan that escaped her lips without her meaning to, but she went with it.

This caused a fit of giggles from Lycia, who looked over at her and asked, "Did you just have an orgasm?"

"Oh, shut up," Deunan fired back. Lycia laughed again.

"If you want," Gam said, "you can order any of my man-servants to please you in any way you desire."

"Is that so?" Lycia asked. She craned her neck and looked up at the young Bre'lal man wearing nothing but a loincloth who diligently applied another layer of scented oil to her back.

Like the other two well chiseled male servants, he wore headphones designed to block out anything said in the room as per orders of his mistress.

Naturally, he was a fine specimen. Most Bre'lal were. The women were luxuriant and sensual and the men were fit and docile. The perfect combination for making them desirable and compatible lovers for most races.

Worlds like Dagon, with strong women and men, preferred keeping at least half a dozen Bre'lal workers on staff for comfort reasons. It seems Gam had the same taste in subservient men.

Lycia reached out and grabbed his wrist, stopping him from continuing on with her massage, and, then, sliding down off the massage table, she led him behind her glistening blue body.

"We'll see you in a few," she chirped as she ducked out of the room with her prize in tow.

"She's all hormones, that one," Deunan said as her masseur dug his thumbs into her lower back.

"I was meaning to ask you about her," Gam said, resting her head on her crossed forearms and gazing over at Deunan. "She's the one Xarthon is after, yes?"

Deunan didn't reply; she merely grunted as the masseur hit the right spot while working out a knot.

"What is it that makes her so special?" Gam asked, taking Deunan's silence as a yes. Only a mother like Deunan, who had raised her own brood, would be overly protective of this girl she barely even knew.

After carefully deliberating on how much she could safely share about

Lycia's unique situation, Deunan finally answered. "I suppose you'll find out one way or another. But what I tell you stays confidential."

Gam nodded and then pretended to lock her lips and throw away the key. "My lips are sealed."

"You saw how powerful she is. Killing those guards in the square was child's play for her. Lycia has the strength of Jegra, the powers of Dakroth, and the intelligence to match. She's a genetically enhanced hybrid clone. And she's supposed to be the future of Dakroth's military."

"Dakroth is breeding super soldiers? Isn't that illegal?"

"Very illegal. Which is why he contracted the Seyfferian Republic to do it for him. A gray area of Dagon law, for sure. But it's well known that my people embrace genetic engineering and body modification. So, it was only natural he came to our government with an offer they couldn't refuse."

Gam raised an eyebrow. "What kind of offer?"

"Not only would he cover all costs, but he'd share Lycia's genetic code with the Seyferrians so that we could construct a protectorate for the whole of the Republic."

"It's probably lucky he did," Gam said.

Deunan shot her a look. "How so?"

"Seyferria has stayed out of the Nyctan and Dagon politics for far too long. But given the nature of this war, they're bound to be drug into the conflict sooner or later. It's better to have protectors on hand than to be vulnerable to attack."

Although Gam's reasoning was very Dragonian in nature, she wasn't wrong. "I guess you're right," Deunan agreed. "But I hate to see her become yet another pawn in other people's never-ending conflicts. More war has never brought peace to anyone."

"And then there's Xarthon," Gam said with a vexed sigh. "A tenacious imbecile with a badge who doesn't know when to quit."

"Obviously, the Seyfferian Republic doesn't want it to get out that they are creating a secret army and so they dispatched a Space Marshal to track her down and take her in."

"Just an over glorified bounty hunter, if you ask me," Gam said, dismissing Xarthon's title as nothing more than a man for hire. Space Marshal was just a fancy word for a bail bondsman, in her estimation.

"Perhaps. But he's proved persistent enough that he's become a constant thorn in my side."

"I'm going to be honest with you," Gam said, her cheek still resting on her forearms as she turned her lime green eyes toward Deunan. "At first, I was sure whose side to take. But I've decided to help you get rid of this pest and make sure your girl stays safe."

Deunan shot Gam an astonished look. She knew Gam was the quintessential business woman. Seeing as there was nothing in it for her, she had to ask. "Why?"

"Why help you? Because I can. And I want to."

"Ah," Deunan said in a revelatory manner. "There it is."

"What?" Gam asked, feigning surprise.

"You're happy to let the girl go as long as she leads you to the other clones."

Gam smiled pretentiously. "Am I so transparent?"

"Just a little bit," Deunan said, pinching her fingers close and then a little bit closer.

"Fine. You've figured me out. But, the fact remains, Deunan, you still need my help. So, you can either keep running from Xarthon the rest of your days or let me work with you on this."

"Did I miss any juicy gossip?" Lycia asked, stepping back into the room. She returned to her table settled down, making herself comfortable.

When Gamagor saw that the servant she had been with hadn't returned, she wagged a finger at a standby masseur and he came over and began working on Lycia's back, running his strong, green fingers across her soft blue flesh. She looked up and shot him a prurient smile.

"As it turns out, Gam wants to help us," Deunan informed the girl. "She's willing to help us track down your cloning facility and find out who made you."

"Cool," Lycia said in a non-cavalier manner that surprised both Gamagor and Deunan. They both looked over at her with blank expressions on their faces.

"You're fine with that?" Deunan asked.

"Sure," Lycia said, giving a one shoulder shrug. "We need all the help we can get, right?"

"In that case, I shall seek out my contact on Correl and maybe poke around some of the Seyfferian Republic's archives and look for any flagged or encrypted files related to the cloning industry there."

Another lull in the conversation took over as their minds grappled with what the next step would be. As they were thinking, Lycia cleared her throat and looked over at Gam and Deunan.

"Have you two known each other for very long?"

"We're old acquaintances," Gam answered. "As you may be aware, like your genetic progenitor, I, too, was a gladiatrix once."

"A fine one at that, too," Deunan added. Gam smiled at her.

"I had over two hundred undefeated matches. A record that stood until Jegra bested it. Things changed though when Dakroth implemented the death bouts. Then it became about Victory or Death. The honor of a fair fight evaporated and then it became every person for himself."

"Why did he implement the death bouts?" she asked.

"The same reason Dakroth does anything. For prestige. Indeed, the fame and glory of his combatants was his fame and glory too," relayed Gamagor.

"Not to forget his need to revitalize the ratings which pulled in the credits which, in turn, he poured right back into the war effort," Deunan added. Gam nodded.

"When he changed the rules of the game back to the old ways, everyone in the system started coming for me. Every gladiator, big and small, wanted a pound of flesh. A shot at knocking the crown off my head and claiming the title of grand champion of the arena for themselves."

Enthralled by her harrowing tale, Lycia asked, "And then what happened?"

"It was rough going for a while. The matches grew brutal rather quickly. Every day became a fight for my life. A fight just to exist. And I was well past my prime. It was only a matter of time before some hotshot up and comer got lucky and got the best of me. It was Deunan who helped me escape that terrible situation. She smuggled me out of the system, hid me from IGS, and I ended up as a refugee on Brexis."

"It was only when Dakroth pardoned her on live televid to spike ratings again that she was able to come out of hiding."

"I don't get it. Why would he try to have you erased only to pardon you?"

Lycia didn't understand the logic behind it. But she wanted to understand her father's thinking. If she could grasp that, then she might better understand her own origins.

"It goes further back than just Gam," Deunan informed her. "It was because of the first Dragonian war with the Dagons that so depleted Loki'Alloran Rhadamanthus's reserves that the Dagon Empire was able to subjugate the Dragonian Empire and force Gam's people into indentured servitude."

"It's true. It was strictly a political move on his part. When the Trade Wars with the Nyctan Dynasty broke out, Dakroth pardoned me in a show of good faith so as to bring the Dragonians over onto his side. If he could create a temporary allegiance with his old enemy to combat the new, then he'd have the strategic advantage."

"The enemy of my enemy is my friend," Lycia muttered. She shook her head. She didn't know where the knowledge of that saying had come from, but it was stored in her memory—perhaps a residual epigenetic memory from one of her parents.

"A ploy that worked, too. And my people, being the proud warrior race they are, jumped at the chance to fight alongside the Dagon Empire perchance to get out from under the emperor's thumb and decades of oppression. Even if we still weren't viewed as equals in society, at least we could be equals on the battlefield."

"And you marched onward to victory or death," Lycia said somewhat ironically.

Gam reached up and snapped her fingers and a servant brought her a fresh towel. "I think I'll retire to my quarters for supper," she said, wrapping up. "Either of you care to join me for an evening meal?"

"I could use a bite," Lycia said, hopping to her feet.

"Not me," Deunan said, "I'm fine right here." She moaned again as the masseur continued working out the knot on her back.

Lycia wrapped herself in a towel and then edged up to Deunan and whispered in her ear. "Don't do anything I wouldn't do," she said with a wink.

"Hush you!" Deunan said, and she swatted Lycia's butt. Lycia laughed out loud, taken aback by the random swat. She stuck her tongue out at Deunan, who merely ignored her and then skipped over to Gam and linked elbows with her.

"Shall we?"

Gam smiled and walked with her into the changing room. The moment they passed through the beaded curtains, Lycia slammed Gam up against the wall and pressed her lips to hers.

"*Mmm-mmm,*" Gam mumbled through the girl's kiss. Drawing back, she asked, "What are you doing?"

"What does it look like I'm doing?"

Gam gave her a curious look. "I'm flattered, but I think you may be a little young for me."

"Nonsense," Lycia said. "I'm a fully mature woman." She pulled Gam into her and forced another kiss. Gam tried to resist again, but the girl's strength was phenomenal. That's when she felt the slender blue fingers slip up inside her towel.

"What are you do—" Gam gulped as Lycia's fingers found their destination and, before she could mount any further protest, she bit her lower lip and let slip a deep moan.

"I can go deeper if you want." Lycia dropped her shoulder and began to slide her hand further up into Gam when she clutched her wrist, stopping her.

"If you insist on doing this, then we best move things to my personal chambers." Gam looked back out into the main room through the crack in the curtain. She could still see Deunan's legs and knew she'd feel terribly guilty if she let this act of seduction continue any further.

Lycia ignored her and continued on with her sexual advances. As a surge of pleasure coursed through her, Gam reached up, grabbed the back of the Lycia's hair, and gave her head a strong tug. Lycia's eyes lit up when she felt the Dragonian's strength handling her in such a rough fashion.

"Yes," Lycia said, her hot breath passing from her lips and brushing against Gamagor's. "Rougher."

Gam's lizard tongue came all the way out and slipped down into Lycia's mouth. She almost choked on it, but then began treating it like a mock fellatio. After sucking on Gam's tongue for a while, she grabbed her and spun her around, pressing her against the wall.

Lycia tore off her towel, letting it fall to the floor, and then sliding down Gam's back, dappling her flesh with a thousand wet kisses, she settled onto her knees. Squeezing Gam's ass, Lycia buried her face inside Gams meaty cheeks and began to lick and nibble at her nifkin.

Once Gam was thoroughly aroused, Lycia rose back up and let her male anatomy unfurl. With a light grunt, she penetrated Gam from behind, who groaned from the pleasure of it. It filled her nicely and she was a little taken aback by the size of it.

"I don't know why, but always forget that you Dagons are both male and female."

Instead of replying with words, Lycia replied with a thrust of her hips. Gam spread her legs wider, allowing for deeper penetration and reached back around to stroke Lycia as she pounded her from behind.

Just as Lycia began to work up a nice sheen to her body, unexpectedly, Gam stopped their session and shoved Lycia off of her. "No, I'm sorry," she said, grabbing a robe off the hook and throwing it on. Shaking her head as if she'd changed her mind, she added, "I can't do this."

Then, her face flushing with embarrassment, Gam dashed out into the corridor.

Lycia shrugged and then stepped into the shower to clean off. Once she'd finished bathing and drying off, she tucked herself back in, dressed and headed to Gam's quarters.

Lycia rang the chime and a voice called out in a less than enthused tone, "Enter."

When Lycia stepped through the entrance, bottle of Centauri Red in her hands as a peace offering, Gam rolled her eyes.

"What is it now?"

"I wanted to apologize," Lycia said. "I took advantage and it was wrong."

Gam looked over at her with her lime green eyes and blinked a couple times. "If you agree to no more acts of seduction, I'll agree to sharing this meal with you." She gestured at the four-course supper set out on the table and Lycia's eyes lit up.

There were sweet yams, wild Torvian turkey, steamed green beans, and three kinds of gravy. There was even a honey-glazed, six-legged ham from the planet Quillox.

Licking her lips, she said, "I promise. No more acts of seduction. Because the only thing I intend to eat out here is that turkey."

"Good," Gam chuckled, "because there's more than enough food here to feed an entire Dragonian brood."

Sitting down at the table across from each other, they smiled and then began to help themselves to the small feast laid out before them.

23

A flock of Meridian crimson beaked birds fluttered away just as Gywen stepped out onto the rooftop of one of the taller buildings, which stood three blocks from the action.

She set down the large hard case she had slung over her shoulder and opened it. Unpacking her gear, she assembled her rifle and was busy attaching the scope when she heard a voice call out to her.

"It's beautiful isn't it?"

She looked up to find a young, beautiful man with powder blue skin and flowing platinum tresses of shoulder length hair. He looked roughly seventeen or eighteen years old, yet had an air of imperial authority about him.

The young man wore a purple tunic with gold print arabesques, the lengthy obi styled belt ends flapped on the breeze as he stood precariously on the edge of the high-rise and peered down at the battle raging in the streets of Vallorium.

He turned his face slightly, glancing over his shoulder at her, a subtle smile forming on his thin, pale blue lips. A halo of golden light flashed upon the Percheron abyss that were his eyes, and she knew instantly from the fear that seized her, who this was.

"The violence and the destruction," he continued. "It's beautiful, no?"

Gywen dropped what she was doing and swiftly drew both her blasters. She fired two shots but the young man just raised a powder blue hand and deflected them as though he were some kind of ancient sorcerer.

He shot her a disappointed look—one which seemed to suggest she should have known better. Letting it go, however, he turned back to gaze out at the battle raging in the square below. Locking his arms behind his back, he inhaled a deep breath of fresh air and then slowly let it out again.

"What do you want?" she asked him, her eyes narrowing on him as she tried to gauge his next move.

Like most cunning enemies, the trick in not allowing oneself to be deceived was to learn to see past the subterfuge of an amiable pretense. A true enemy only wanted one and only one thing—to drink the wine of their victory from the hollow of your bleached skull.

"Isn't it clear?" he asked her. "I only want the absolute, complete and utter destruction of all life. A simple enough plan, but in the light of recent events it has proved much more difficult to execute than I had initially anticipated."

Gywen frowned as she holstered her blasters. "That much is clear. I meant," she clarified, "what do you want with me?"

"Ah, yes," he said, his mind coming back to what he wanted to say. He turned his eerie gaze to her and looked at her from over his shoulder. "I want you to be one of my Avatars. The Avatar of War. I want you to lead my army to victory against that infernal thorn in my side, Jegra Alakandra."

Gywen laughed. "If you're so powerful, why do you need a host of middlemen to do your bidding?"

"Because, I have yet to transcend this physical form. And the prison of my flesh doesn't permit me to be everywhere at once. So, I make good use of my vessels. And as one of my Avatars, you'll be well rewarded."

"As a Voroxian priestess, we seek neither praise nor reward. Doing what is right, what is just, is reward enough. But you still haven't answered my question. Why me?"

"As a Voroxian priestess," he relayed, "you have a unique understanding of Jegra Alakandra. You know her strengths and her weaknesses. You've studied her, emulated her, and there's no one better suited in predicting what moves she'll make and how she'll make them. As the leader of my legions, you'd become the most powerful woman in the galaxy. Even more powerful than your beloved empress."

He smiled at her, but it brought her no joy.

"If I refuse?" she asked.

He reached out his hand from afar, as though he were reaching out to clutch her throat, and even though his fingers never made contact nor brushed her flesh, she could feel his grip bearing down all around her neck.

Choking, she clasped her throat to try and pry his grip off, only to find nothing there. She continued to choke and slowly sank down to one knee.

Finally, just when her eyes began to roll back and flutter in her head, he relinquished his psychic-telekinetic hold on her. She gulped in a huge gasp of air and breathed heavily for a moment.

Her chest heaved as she panted to catch her breath, but even so, she managed to speak. "Truth be told, I'd rather die, my oath to the Voroxian order still intact, than help bring about your sick and twisted vision of a lifeless universe."

"I'm sorry to hear that," he replied, his tone steady and calm.

Her head snapped up and she peered at him from defiant blue eyes. "Never!" she growled. "I'll never join you."

H'aaztre raised an eyebrow and then sighed in disappointment. "Suit yourself, warrior priestess."

Then, with a delicate wave of his fingers, she flew into the air—as if compelled by some unseen force—and shot over the ledge of the thirty-seven-story building.

Gywen screamed as she fell through the air without a parachute, her arms and legs flailing.

H'aaztre smirked as he watched her plummet to a violent death. "Don't worry, my dear, you're not the only candidate. There are others."

Danica deflected the flurry of plasma blasts with her metal arm and raced past a fallen knight, snatching up his plasma sword as she went. Wielding the sword, she came up alongside Jegra and they shared a brief glance before moving deeper into the fray.

Covering each other's backs, Jegra sliced anything down that came her way. Danica expertly carved out an opening as they both made their way toward the main tower.

"What's in the tower?" Kregor called out over the din of blaster fire as Raven's team formed up the rear.

"Credits to creylons, H'aaztre is," Jegra shouted back.

Kregor raised an eyebrow and gulped. Taking on the big bad himself was a bold move, but he trusted Jegra's judgement.

"In that case, let's knock and see if anybody is home," he replied and continued mowing down enemy soldiers with his Gatling canon. Once it was spent, he tossed it to the ground and pulled out two massive shotgun style plasma blasters.

As he fired the plasma shotgun, giant, donut shaped plasma rings spun out of the gun like smoke-rings.

The plasma donuts wobbled through the air and took out numerous soldiers. If a piece of a donut broke off on an enemy combatant or obstruction, the rest spiraled away in globules which plastered everything in a fiery goo and melted or set fire to it.

Messier than a standard blaster, plasma shotguns did the most amount of damage. The only downside was that they used up so much coolant they could only get off four shots before needing to be reloaded.

Once Kregor had spent all four rounds, he flipped the gun up into the air, caught the barrel in both hands, and started using it as a bat to bludgeon enemy soldiers.

Raven cut through enemies with the speed and dexterity of a cat. Using the HUD display of her enhanced eyes, she could get a read on them and anticipate their moves before they even acted on them. She seemed untouchable, and of all the people on the battlefield, she was the only one who hadn't even been scratched.

Angellyk lowered her smoking barrels and looked across the growing pile of dead bodies. She raised a finger and pointed at something just beyond the wall of haze. "Guys, over there. What's that?"

Everyone paused long enough to look at what she was pointing at; they saw their own soldiers floating in the air as if caught up in some invisible spider's web.

The bodies swirled about as if circling a sinkhole and then, to their horror, the bodies crumpled up, bones breaking, and screams piercing the air.

Their limbs were wrenched from their sockets, folded in on themselves, and, after the bone cracking, came the hideous snap of muscle and sinews stretched beyond their breaking points.

More screams echoed out before suddenly being silenced as all the bodies were brutally compressed into a giant ball of bloodied and mangled figures. A mist of blood spread out from the horrific ball as the pressure continued to squeeze the two dozen or so soldiers into oblivion.

"What in the tri-horned beast of Quillox is that?!" Kregor asked, dropping his useless shotgun and sliding a korridium battle axe from the magnetic catch on his back.

Torn limb from limb, Jegra's army was slowly and meticulously being pulled apart and then compressed into a throbbing meatball of pain by some invisible force.

"This has to be him," Raven said.

"Now!" Jegra shouted, touching a finger to the earpiece that had remained tucked into her ear.

Just then dark specs filled the sky. At first it looked like a swarm of birds, but as they drew nearer, it was clear that they were Dagon fighters.

"Converge all firepower on that spot!" she said, pointing her finger at the citadel.

The fighters, hooked into her comm link, obeyed and began launching a dazzling assault on the exact location she'd targeted.

Strangely enough, their blasts seemed to fall short. In a matter of seconds, it was clear there was an invisible energy barrier preventing any of the heavy ordinance from breaking through.

Some of the fighter jets dove too sharply and, though they tried to pull up and veer away, it was too late. They crashed into the invisible forcefield.

Fiery explosions rang out, warning the other fighters to hang back. Luckily, the majority of the fleet managed to break away and circle around for one more pass.

Wreckage of downed fighters created sparks and more explosions erupted all around.

Jegra shielded her eyes as she peered through the smoky haze. Unexpectedly, there was a gust of wind and the smoke and haze parted, creating a clearing where they all stood.

Jegra blinked twice just to be sure her eyes weren't deceiving her and when she was certain they weren't, she grew deathly quiet.

Standing in the clearing was a gorgeous young man. He tossed his flowing, shoulder-length hair and then smiled at her.

"It's been a long time, Mother."

H'aaztre sauntered across the blood-soaked ground, delicately stepping over the debris and dead bodies as he calmly walked up to greet Jegra and her team. As he approached, she glimpsed Raven cloaking and disappearing into a wall of smoke.

Jegra raised her hands and cautioned the others to keep their distance, and they did as requested. All but Danica, who stayed steadfast by Jegra's side.

"You can end this war right here. Right now. Just tell your people to cease this foolish attempt at resistance and allow them to peacefully and willingly hand themselves over to me."

"You still don't get it, do you. Nobody is giving up until one side yields. And it won't be me."

"And you assume I will yield?"

"Perhaps not to me. But to the whole galaxy? Perhaps the entire universe? You must. You may be powerful, H'aaztre. But you're not all-powerful. After all, you need this vessel to even stand before me now. A limitation that places you well within the realm of us mere mortals."

He threw back his head and laughed. "Oh, how little you truly know, my dear mother." After having a good chuckle, he wiped his eyes and then examined the residue glistening on his thumb.

It sent a chill up her spine every time he called her that. She was no more his mother than he was her son. The babe she'd given birth to no longer existed. What stood before her now was a soulless, insidious monster.

"Right," Jegra said sarcastically, "my mistake."

"Don't worry, Mother, I'm only just beginning to demonstrate my true power to you. But right now, I'm here to talk to her." His eyes shifted to Danica, who gulped and touched her chest as though her heart were breaking all over again.

"Me?' she asked, her voice wavering slightly.

"You are also my biological mother, are you not?"

She nodded, her eyes welling up with tears.

"Then you are family. And, as family, we should be together." He held out his hand toward her. "Come, Danica Valencia, join me by my side and together we can rule this universe as mother and son." He continued to hold out his hand, waiting for her response.

Tears streamed down both her cheeks and Jegra looked over at her only to see her take a hesitant step forward. "No, Danica! He can't be trusted. You have to see that."

"Join me as one of my noble Avatars. Be my Time Lord. And together, we shall reign over the entire galaxy for all eternity."

Danica took another step closer to him and he smiled. His eyes widened with the acknowledgement that she was truly considering his offer.

"No, Dani," Jegra said, reaching out and grabbing her shoulder. "I forbid it."

Danica swatted Jegra's hand away and then turned to confront her. "Don't baby me. I'm not a child. And I'm certainly not yours to command. I can make my own choices. And I choose to be with my son."

Jegra frowned and reached out to touch Danica, but she merely pulled further away.

"Admit it, Jegra. Things haven't been good between us for quite a while. And as much as it pains me to say this, I don't think we're going to work out. Besides, he's my child too." Danica turned back toward H'aaztre and he smiled at her. "I want this."

"Please, Jegra pleaded. "Don't do this."

Danica shook her head, as if to say there wasn't anything more that needed to be said on the subject. With that, she marched over to H'aaztre and took his hand.

They slowly turned together and began making their way back up the street toward the citadel. H'aaztre glanced back only once, to sneer at Jegra mockingly, as if to rub in the fact that he'd taken the thing she loved most in this world, a second time.

Jegra scanned the wreckage all around her and then dashed over to a large plasma canon that had shorn off from one of the downed fighters.

The cannon was the size of the stovepipe from her old farm house back on Earth, but Jegra hoisted it up to her shoulder as though it were a bazooka and took aim.

She reached into a hole in the metal plating, and operated it manually, firing the plasma cannon.

Ten orders of magnitude more powerful than a standard blaster, it spat a needle of red hot plasma which promptly deflected off of the energy barrier.

The shot rebounded and impacted a nearby building. Chunks of concrete and glass blew back and a large piece clipped Jegra and knocked her to the ground.

Shoving the car-sized slab of concrete off of her, she rose to her knees, wiped the blood from her chin with the back of her hand, and watched helplessly as Danica disappeared with H'aaztre into the monolith.

Unable to hold back her emotions, Jegra broke down sobbing on the battlefield. Her hands, palms facing upward, rested on her powerful thighs as she sobbed.

Although the fighting lulled around her, she was a sitting duck in the open like that, and Raven's crew quickly took up position around the heartbroken empress.

In all the tumult, none of them noticed the Nephilim female warrior sneak up behind them. She raised her blaster, pointed it squarely at the empress's head, and began to squeeze down on the trigger.

Raven appeared as if out of thin air and blasted the Nephilim soldier right in the side of her helmet. She dropped to the ground with a thud, smoke wafting out of the glowing hole in her temple.

"Protect the empress at all costs!" shouted Raven.

Jegra's sobs caused her entire body to convulse with the weight of her sorrow. She could barely catch a breath when a cold and cool voice spoke to her.

"Stop your whimpering. You'll see her again."

Outraged, Jegra's fiery gaze snapped up so she could stare down the rude asshole who'd made such an insensitive remark. She was about to tear the person a new one when all of a sudden, her jaw went slack.

Standing over her was a silver haired version of herself. Slightly older, but no less as impressive or powerful. She even wore the same metal armor bikini, albeit slightly more tarnished and worn and she had added trinkets and additional shoulder pads for extra protection.

"Your Grace," Raven said, nodding at the other Jegra, "allow me to introduce to you the Imperatrix of the Galaxy. Jegra Alakandra."

"W-who are you?" Jegra asked, still mystified by this strange turn of events.

"I'm you," the silver-haired Jegra said, extending her hand.

Young Jegra took it and old Jegra hoisted her up.

Coming face to face with her younger self, the old Jegra said, "There's a lot to explain, but before I do…" she slowly turned to face the intense battle raging all around them. "We've got work to do."

She cracked her knuckles and then her neck. And with a gleeful smile, picked up her battle axe and rushed into the fray.

Jegra looked to Raven, who smiled at her and shrugged before turning and providing Old Lady Jegra some cover fire.

Kregor sidled up to Jegra and let loose an impressed yet undeniably salacious hoot as he eyed Old Lady Jegra's ass. "That's one fine woman right there."

Jegra turned to him with a cold glare. "That's me."

He smiled at her sheepishly, and replied, "I know." He followed it with a wink and then turned to join the other Jegra on the battlefield.

She rolled her eyes and planted her hands firmly on her thick, curvaceous hips. Not knowing what any of this meant, Jegra decided the only thing she could do was regroup and then, maybe, once the dust had settled, get around to grilling this other Jegra on where she came from and what the Helios she was doing here.

24

Another violent jolt threatened to sweep Callestra off her feet, but she steadied herself even as the lights flickered and the bulkheads of the ship groaned out as if the entire ship was in agony.

She stepped over her navigation officer, who lay dead on the floor from an electrical discharge, and took over the navigation controls herself. The circuit breaker cut it off in time to salvage the console, but not before frying her officer till he was nothing but an extra-crispy corpse.

Sparks rained down like flickering fireflies all around her as she manned the station and guided the ship further into the enemy fleet. Another volley of heavy cannon fire made the *Imperatrix* shudder, rattling Callestra's nerves along with the bulkheads.

"Come on you fat-ass-bitch, get yourself in gear!" she growled, as the ship was sluggish to respond to her newly inputted coordinates.

Once the *Imperatrix* began to move forward again, she leaped over the bodies strewn about the command deck and returned to her seat. She quickly opened a comm to the entire ship and, tugging at her uniform to straighten out any wrinkles, she took a deep breath and then gave the announcement.

"This is the Vice Admiral. All hands, abandon ship. I repeat, all hands abandon ship. We will regroup aboard the *Verlag*, as she's the only vessel left in the fleet with shields. Again, we are abandoning ship. Evacuate to the *Verlag*. Emergency teleport and shuttle evac has been authorized."

She cut the comm link and then looked up at the three remaining bridge officers. Another spray of sparks flew as more electronic circuits overheated with surges of energy. Electrical wires shorting, there was a hiss and a pop, and another panel exploded.

Callestra pointed at the doors and shouted, "What are you waiting for, you have your orders. Go!"

They scurried off, leaving the charred remains of their fallen comrades where they lay. She turned to the view portal to find Dakroth still watching the battle with a cool and collected gaze.

Even though they were on the verge of losing the ship, so was the enemy fleet. Both fleets had crippled one another, and there was nothing else either side could do but continue firing until their reactor cores melted down and exploded.

Callestra opened her mouth to speak, calling Dakroth's name, when the console on her command chair exploded. Electrical tendrils reached out and licked her arm and she screamed out in agony and dropped to the floor.

Dakroth spun around, startled, and then, seeing her lying unconscious on the floor, rushed over to her side.

Kneeling down, he checked her for a pulse. Luckily, her heart was still beating, but there were signs of cardiac arrhythmia.

Dakroth grabbed her uniform and, giving it a firm tug, he ripped open her jacket and shirt, exposing her chest. Placing a hand over her left bosom, he created a small energy field and discharged it into a jolt of electricity.

Callestra's torso heaved, her chest rising and sinking again. He zapped her again, using his Dygra crystal energy, and again her back arched and chest heaved before settling back down.

Placing his ear to her heart, he checked to see if he'd gotten her heartbeat back in sync. Satisfied she was back to normal, he scooped her up in his arms.

"Computer," he said, as he cradled Callestra in his arms, "initiate self-destruct sequence."

<<By order of the Lord Emperor, Rhadamanthus Dakroth, self-destruct sequence initiated>> intoned the posh sounding computer voice.

Dakroth reached around her body and, fingers stretched out, tapped a pendant on his uniform and opened a comm to the *Verlag*. "Dakroth to the *Verlag*, two for emergency teleport."

A golden beam of light swirled about them as explosions began to ring out all across the ship and, in the sparkling eddy, their bodies were whisked away on hexagonal packets of light.

The *Imperatrix*, although her commission was short lived, lit up like a firework in one last hurrah. The explosion took out five enemy vessels in close proximity, leaving nothing in its wake but for debris and sparkling space dust infused with the tiny remnants of the ship and its deceased crew.

Covered in blood and sweat, Jegra collapsed to one knee, panting as though she'd just finished a triathlon.

Exhausted, she propped herself up on the pommel of her axe and looked around the battlefield. Dead bodies of both friend and foe littered the streets, glistening with the swirl of blue and red blood that mingled in areas to create purple flourishes.

The streets' gutters ran thick with deep purple and crimson as though it had rained blood. The sounds of blaster fire and blades clashing had all but ceased and a deathly calm settled across everything. Smoke coiled up from the crashed fighters and battle droids lay strewn about the main square in front of the citadel. Both sides had fought till nobody was left standing.

Jegra did her best to catch her breath, but when she tried to rise up, she promptly crashed back down onto her knee, her axe pommel tucked under her arm like a crutch. It was no use, since her legs had turned to rubber, and her adrenaline was already dying down.

Raven's team sat scattered about the empress, all of them taking a brief rest before regrouping.

A loud boom drew their attention to the citadel and the doors to the capitol building were flung open as another wave of knights marched out.

A dozen more Knights of Caelum stepped onto the battlefield and another hundred or so foot soldiers followed them out. It was the reserves.

Jegra struggled to stand but collapsed back onto her knee yet again. That's when a thick arm reached down and hoisted her up. She came nose to nose with her older self and the two, gripping one another's forearms in a powerful embrace, stared deeply into one another's eyes as they tried to assess what the other was thinking.

"Thanks," Jegra finally said.

"Any time," her doppelgänger replied.

"Ladies," Raven said, touching her earpiece. "The Lord Emperor has just given the order to regroup."

Jegra raised her arm and shouted, "Everyone…pull back!"

Her army quickly retreated back the way they'd come and raced through the streets back toward the *Shard* which was still parked in the bay.

When they arrived on the beach, Lianica was already there waiting for them with a small contingent of security officers. Jegra paused and looked back. Her mind was on Danica; she hated that she had to leave her behind.

"Your Grace," Lianica said. "We have to be going now."

"You go on without me. I'll catch a ride out with Raven." She looked to Raven, "If that's all right with you."

Raven nodded.

Lianica looked at the older version of Jegra skeptically. When they locked eyes, Lianica held their gaze until it grew uncomfortable and then she turned away, tossing her ponytail, and strode back toward the ship.

As she marched toward the ocean waves lapping at the shore, her body broke into golden light and teleported back to the ship floating in the distance.

Jegra and Raven's crew waited until every last remaining soldier was off the battlefield. That's when they heard the clank of metal incrementally marching toward them. Looking back toward the city streets, the Knights of Caelum stopped just at the edge of the boardwalk.

They didn't advance any further, but they ignited their plasma blades and allowed the menacing hum to ward off any who dared oppose them. Jegra could see by the style of their armor that these were the elite knights. The ones that served under Lance Bishop.

She wondered if any of those men behind the dark masks was her friend. Was he being manipulated like all the rest? Or was his mind strong? Did he resist H'aaztre's evil? If so, she knew he must be enduring a most terrible form of torture.

"We'd best be going," Kregor said.

Raven nodded and motioned for everyone to circle up. The Skywend decloaked overhead and its massive gun turrets dropped down and swiveled into place. Locking onto the knights, the ship's massive thrusters drowned out the hum of their blades. Then, as if on cue, the *Skywend* fired off several warning shots that pelted the sand and shot dirt into the air.

By the time the sandstorm had abated and the dust had settled, Raven's crew was but a flickering ember of light energy fading into the thin blue air.

The *Skywend* rose into the sky alongside the *Shard* and the two ships, in a flash of light, jumped into FTL to rejoin the rest of the fleet.

Several blocks inland, situated on an abandoned city street, a broken window pane slipped out of its shattered frame and *clinked* onto the ground. The glass pane shattered into smaller fragments, adding to the already plentiful mess of the caved in storefront.

Inside, what had once been a clothing store showcasing the latest in Nyctan fashion, a woman with forest green hair lay unconscious in a pile of clothes, the blue glowing shield of her stealth suit flickering as it finally started to give out.

<<Power reserve depleted. Safety shield failure imminent.>>

The suit's shield sputtered one last time then cut out. Almost immediately the woman sat up, taking a huge breath of air. Her lungs rattled in her chest as she gulped down the revitalizing breath of life.

Gywen slowly tried to push herself up to her feet, but abruptly collapsed back to the ground again. She grunted and spat up blood, some of which dribbled from her mouth, staining her chin red. Shaking her head as if to say *this isn't good*, she rolled over then brought up her forearm and checked her holovid display.

With a grunt, she forced down the pain and typed something into the holopad. Just then, a 3D hologram of her ship appeared and she mumbled, "Get me out of here," her voice thick with pain as she dealt with three broken ribs and a fractured collar bone.

Red light energy came down and fetched her. As her body was broken apart on small needles of red light, she closed her eyes and sighed out.

Once she rematerialized on the other end of the transport, she found herself seated in the cockpit of a Nyctan fighter she'd commandeered. Typing in some coordinates, her ship rose out of the empty swimming pool it was parked in out in the suburbs, several clicks from downtown, and flew up into the sky.

Gywen charted a different path than the Allied forces had taken, veering to the right. Then, FTL spooled up, the small ship darted into the sky and vanished in a flash.

Aboard the *Skywend*, Raven turned to both Jegras and said, "I'm sure you both have a lot to talk about. So, I'll leave you to it."

Raven walked off in her normal brisk manner before pausing briefly in front of the entrance. She cleared her throat and said in a stern tone of voice, "Gyllek!"

"Ah, man," Gyllek said, decloaking next to the two Jegras. "I never get to have any fun."

Raven waited for the girl to catch up to her and then they exited the teleportation room together.

"Care to get a drink with me?" the elder Jegra asked.

Jegra nodded and followed her to the small rec-room aboard the ship where they cracked open a couple of Dragonian ales and sat down across from each other at the kitchen table off to the side of the standing bar.

"So," Jegra said, "let me guess. You're from the future."

"I am. Approximately three hundred and seventy years from now," she answered.

Jegra smothered a gasp. "You're three hundred years old?" She looked the ancient woman up and down and couldn't get over the fact of how good she still looked. "You look...absolutely amazing."

"Thanks," the older Jegra replied, brushing a lock of platinum hair from her eyes and tucking it behind her ear.

Although Old Lady Jegra was literally hundreds of years older than her younger counterpart, aside from her silver hair and her slightly lighter shade of brown eyes, she didn't seem more than ten years her senior.

"Why come back to this moment in time?"

"Actually, I arrived three years ago. Raven has been keeping me under wraps all this time."

"She has? Why?"

"Because I asked her to."

Jegra raised an eyebrow when her other self wasn't more forthcoming. "I'm sorry for the twenty questions, but is there some reason you chose now? Is this point in time significant for some reason?"

"You might say that. You see, I was given an offer by H'aaztre. An offer he'll present to you shortly."

"What kind of offer?"

"He assured me that he'd spare everyone I loved and let me reign over the galaxy as its sovereign ruler if I agreed to give in to him and surrender to his supreme will."

"And…did you?"

The silver haired Jegra looked down in shame. "I did." When she looked back up there were tears brimming in the corners of her eyes. "But it's all a lie, Jegra. He never intended to keep his word. He killed everyone I ever cared about and then let me live with the grief. It was the greatest mistake I ever made."

In the lingering silence that followed, they both took a drink of Dragonian ale and then looked into one another's eyes; both searching for traces of meaning in the depths of those brown eyes.

"How do you know I'll make the same mistake? I'm not you," Jegra said.

"You *are* me," the silver haired vixen fired back, her eyes narrowing intimidatingly. "Which is why I searched for more than three hundred years to find a way back in time. I took a one-way ticket to come back and warn you not to repeat my past mistakes."

Jegra thought about it long and hard. Then she smiled warmly and raised her bottle to the old woman. "To learning from others' mistakes."

Old Lady Jegra smiled and then, raising her own bottle, clinked them together and they both kicked back their head and took another drink.

"There's just one more thing," the silver haired Jegra said, drawing up a large, dark ruby the size of an apple and setting it onto the table with a resounding *clunk*. "I need to get this recharged."

"Is that a…?"

"Yes," she answered, "it's a Dygra crystal."

Jegra picked it up in her hands and examined it.

"Whose is it?"

"Mine. Yours." She shrugged. "I don't really know."

Jegra looked up, slightly puzzled. She was human, not Dagoni. How could they possibly be in possession of a Dygra crystal? "But I don't have…"

"You will," the older Jegra interrupted, answering Jegra's concerns for her. "And you'll need it to defeat H'aaztre."

Young Jegra slid the gem back across the table to her and nodded. "I see.

In that case, we best find out where this came from and get it recharged."

"I'd appreciate that."

There was another brief silence as they finished off their drinks. Rising to her feet, Jegra went over to the fridge. "Want another?"

"Yes, please."

She tossed her older self another bottle and they both pried off their bottle caps in the same manner and same fashion at the exact same time. They both downed the bottles in one go and both belched within a hair's breadth of the other. With satisfied looks, they each wiped their mouths at the same time and looked at one another and laughed.

The idea of meeting your other self was absurd. And yet, here they were.

A pleasantly inebriated buzz warmed their bosoms and meeting one another's gaze, the younger of the two laughed.

"What?" her older counterpart asked.

"It's nothing. Never mind," Jegra said, changing the subject.

Old Lady Jegra shrugged. Then, looking down at her filthy, blood encrusted body, she sighed out long laboriously. "I supposed I could use a shower. Maybe even two or three."

"You and me both," Jegra said.

"Come along then," Old Lady Jegra said, waving for her younger self to follow after her. "You can use my shower."

Desperate for a shower, she agreed and, rising from her seat, followed the older Jegra to her quarters. When they arrived, the older Jegra began peeling off her clothes and shedding them where she stood.

Jegra felt embarrassed watching herself strip at first but then realized they were technically the same person and, shrugging off any further hesitancy, quickly followed suit.

Cramming into the shower together, they scrubbed each other's backs and then let the hot water wash every trace of grime from their battle worn bodies.

Jegra ran her finger along a curious scar that was on her counterpart's back. "Where'd you get this?" Jegra asked. After all, she didn't have any such scar. At least, not yet.

"A plasma sword cut through my back. And for some reason the wound never fully healed. I guess my healing factor is slowing down in my old age." She sighed, leaning against the glass wall of the shower stall and let her younger self trace the contours of her scar with delicate fingers.

Old Lady Jegra finally turned off the nozzle of the shower and the shower head drizzled to a stop. She looked over her shoulder at her younger self and then a devious smile formed on her lips. "You want to…maybe…I dunno…?"

"Mess around?" Jegra asked with an intrigued laugh.

"What?" Jegra balked. "Don't tell me the thought hadn't crossed your mind."

"Won't it be…I dunno…weird?"

"There's only one way to find out," the older Jegra said, pressing herself into her younger self.

Their lips drew dangerously close and their breath passed through parted lips with the same carnal curiosity that caused their loins to quiver with anticipation of experiencing the other in a way she'd never experienced before.

They gazed into one another's eyes for a brief moment longer and then, unexpectedly, their mouths crashed together. Their tongues swirled about playfully, breaching one another's mouths with deep and penetrating kisses.

Stumbling out of the shower, they didn't bother to dry off, seeing as they'd be drenched in sweat soon enough anyway.

Falling back onto the bed, they rolled around, crashing into the bedside lamp and knocking over some books that were balanced on a shelf.

Roughly forty-seven minutes later, they lay entwined, their arms and legs tangled up as they panted to try and catch their breath.

Chest glistening, the older Jegra sighed out and said in a rather pleased sounding voice, "That was…"

"Yeah…" Jegra replied to herself, finishing her sentence for her. "Pretty fucking amazing."

"We should do it again sometime," her older self said, a puckish grin on her face.

"Alright then," Jegra said, rolling back onto herself and getting ready for round two.

Her older self-laughed and they sunk back down into the sheets for another round of love making. Her hands reached around the younger Jegra and squeezed her buttocks firmly and said between the feathery kisses of their lips, "That's my girl."

Seventeen minutes later, they lay soaked in their own sweat, breathing heavily. "I think I need another shower," Jegra laughed.

"Do you think this makes us vain?"

"What? Because we love ourselves so much?"

They both laughed again.

"I have no idea. It's uncharted territory."

"Unless…"

Old Lady Jegra raised an eyebrow. "Unless what?"

"Well, Grendok might use his clones to…"

"Ew! Now I can't unsee that disturbing mental image."

Jegra laughed. Then, rising from the bed, she turned toward the bathroom.

Old Lady Jegra caught her by the hand, and asked, "Where do you think you're going?"

"I have to pee."

"Oh, yeah?" she said, her eyebrow raised. Instead of letting her go though, she reeled her back in.

"Seriously," Jegra pleaded as she watched the older Jegra slip her hand between her sweaty thighs. "I really have to…"

"Yeah?"

Jegra bit her bottom lip and moaned as her older self knew exactly how to touch her. Every touch sent a wave of pleasure though her body. Moaning, she leaned into Old Lady Jegra's touch, letting her use her magical fingers in ways that made her feel as though she'd go insane with ecstasy.

"I don't think I can…" she warned, her voice wavering. She bit her bottom lip again, her face and neck growing bright red, the veins taught like guitar strings as she did her best to resist exploding in one massive orgasm.

"Sometimes, it's not about being in control," the older Jegra relayed to her younger self. "Sometimes it's about letting others take control for you."

Jegra groaned as she fought her body's urge to simply let go. And the more she fought it, the more the pain turned to pleasure. Soon, she gave in and simply didn't try to fight it anymore…and released everything she'd been holding back in one massive splash of orgasmic nectar.

"See?" Old Lady Jegra consoled. "That's much better."

Jegra looked down between her legs and then, with wide eyes filled with panic, back up at her other self. "I'm so sorry…I didn't mean to…"

"It's fine," Old Lady Jegra said. Then she leaned in and kissed her younger self's abdomen, slowly making her way down to her mons pubis. Once she nestled her face between Jegra's glistening thighs, Old Lady Jegra said, "Relax."

Jegra closed her eyes and took in a deep breath as her wiser, more experienced self dappled the insides of her dripping wet thighs with hungry love-bites and more hot kisses.

Before Jegra knew it, the silver haired woman had her face buried deep between her thighs and was doing things she'd never felt before. Things that drove her so wild she wanted to scream out. She covered her mouth with both hands and smothered a scream.

"Oh, god," she gasped, releasing her hands from her mouth. "Keep doing that."

Old Lady Jegra looked up from between Jegra's glistening thighs and with a delicious sounding moan, smiled up at her. Then, she got to work.

The *Verlag's* medical bay bustled with nurses and doctors in white medical coats as they raced to and fro to attend the wounded. Off to one corner, the emperor stood cradling Callestra's hand in his.

"Will she be all right?" Dakroth asked. He stood by Callestra's bedside looking upon her beautiful sleeping face with large, worried eyes. He resented the fact that she made him vulnerable, but he couldn't help it. He was in love with this woman.

Doctor Darius Ebbedon, personal physician to the emperor, came over and pulled down his medical mask.

"She has suffered minor burns and abrasions. The shock to her system overpowered her, but with a bit of rest I'm certain she'll be fine. I gave her some painkillers to help her sleep."

Dakroth nodded and the doctor placed his arm on Dakroth's arm. "And the baby is fine too, so you don't need to worry, your Grace." With that, the doctor strode off to attend other patients.

"Baby?" he stammered, unable to believe his ears. A stunned expression gave way to a smile and soon he was filled with a newfound sense of excitement and accomplishment all at once. "Did you hear that, babe? We're having a baby!"

Dakroth, tears in his eyes, leaned over and kissed Callestra on her forehead. "Just...stay with me, luv."

He watched her sleep and thought to himself he couldn't live without her. He'd truly only loved two women in his life, and they were both with him here and now.

It's true, Jegra may not love him anymore, but he'd brought that on himself. At least he still had Callestra. At least he could still make a life with her. And now, serendipitously, he finally had an heir to the throne.

Onelle Te'Legra Agnar helped Danica out of her clothes. Aidora, a familiar face to them both, entered their chambers with a cleansing balm. The balm had gold flakes in it and Aidora applied it liberally to Danica's turquoise flesh.

"It's cold," Danica gasped as the cool gel was lathered onto her.

"It's the essence of H'aaztre," Onelle said. "If you close your eyes and focus, you will be able to feel him working within you. Eventually, you will be able to hear his thoughts. Don't try to resist it. Just let him consume you."

"And what happens when I do?"

Aidora smiled, golden rings flashing in her dark eyes. "Then you will become one with him. One with our ever-living God."

"I'll leave you two alone while I prepare for the ceremony."

Onelle strode out of the room and Danica turned to Aidora. "What ceremony?"

"In order to become one with him, you must let him enter you so that he may impregnate you with his essence."

"Enter me? How do you mean?"

"You'll see."

After covering her body in the balm with golden flakes, she drew a ceremonial blade and shaved the gel off Danica's flesh. All traces of hair below her neck came off. Aidora even shaved her delicate areas with a gentle touch that was light and feathery.

Danica's bare flesh bristled in the cool air, only golden flakes sparkling like glitter on her skin remained.

Aidora gently slipped on golden breast petals that covered her dark areolas and then helped her into a merkin made of gold.

The merkin was a golden mold of a shaved vulva replete with lip petals which she wore over her own nudity. Once she was dressed in the strange golden coverings, Aidora slipped a white cloak over Danica's shoulders and motioned for her to accompany her to an adjoining chamber.

When Aidora opened the door, a brilliant golden light washed over them. Aidora instantly fell into a trance and Onelle stood a few feet away, also stuck in a trance.

Ever so slowly, Danica incrementally turned toward the golden light and peered into it. As her eyes adjusted to its brilliance, a sense of dread filled her. Without even realizing it, she had screamed out in terror and was still screaming when it came for her.

"No!" she cried out, slowly backing away. "Stay back!"

She tried to retreat, backing into the room she'd just come from, but, before she had time to react, a large golden tentacle seemingly made of light stretched out and wrapped itself around her squirming blue body and drew her back into the room.

She clasped onto the door frame, resisting best she could, and let out a rattling scream. But no sooner had she screamed out than the feelers constricted tighter, forcing her hands down to her waist to try and pry them off, but in relinquishing her grip she was quickly drawn into the room.

The door slammed shut behind her, cutting out the light and muffling any further shrieks she might have cried out in her desperation. H'aaztre had her now.

25

Lycia woke up with her arm hanging out of the bed and something the consistency of damp sandpaper licking her hand. She opened her eyes to find Allie situated on the floor, grooming her.

Yawning, Lycia slowly sat up and stretched her arms over her head and then crossed her legs and sat in bed zoning out for a moment as she tried to force her mind awake.

Allie licked Lycia's hand again, drawing her attention back to her, as if to say they weren't finished with the bath yet. "Do I smell that bad?" Lycia asked with a laugh.

She raised her right arm and sniffed her armpit, instantly making a sour face. She smelled of sweat and black cherry flavored sex jelly—sweet but still a little bit salty. "Yeah, I guess I do," she sighed, letting her arm fall back onto her lap.

Lycia slid out of bed and staggered half-drunkenly over to the shower. When she climbed into the stall it asked her if she wanted a sonic shower or a hydro shower. She opted for water.

As a uniform spray poured out of the rain-style shower head directly above her, she rested her forehead against the cool metallic plating of the back wall and let the water glide down her neck and shoulder blades. It felt glorious.

After a long hot shower, she got dressed and headed to Deunan's quarters. When she arrived, she hit the chime and waited. When there wasn't any reply, she rang again. Yet again…only silence. Growing worried, she tried to enter, but the door bleated at her. It was locked.

She looked down at her wrist and debated whether to use the skeleton key.

It was a short deliberation, though. She promptly ran the bottom of her wrist over the control panel; it flicked to green and the door slid open.

Worried for Deunan's safety, Lycia burst into the room only to find her concerns weren't any better off than before she'd entered. The room was completely empty.

Even more peculiar was the fact that D's bed didn't appear to have been slept in at all. This worried her even more, and she rushed out of the room and ran all the way back to the massage parlor.

When she arrived, she found Deunan fast asleep, face-down in the hole of the massage table. She was completely naked except for the white towel covering her butt and Lycia rolled her eyes and then cleared her throat.

When Deunan didn't rouse, she cleared her throat more loudly a second time. "Rise and shine, sleepy head."

"Whuh? Who's it?" Deunan said, raising her head. She wiped some drool from her mouth with the back of her hand and looked over at Lycia. "Oh, it's you."

"Good morning to you too, sunshine," Lycia laughed. She tossed Deunan an extra towel to cover up with and then folded her arms. "Did you sleep here all night long?"

Groggy, Deunan sat up, stretched with a follow-up yawn, and then slid off the massage bed. "I've gotta piss like a *Njord* race horse," she said, sharing too much information with Lycia, who rolled her eyes.

"There's no restrooms on this level," Lycia revealed, "you'll have to go up a deck or use the shower over there." She pointed at the showers.

"I can't piss in the shower," Deunan said, squirming.

She eyed the showers again, the pressure unbearable, and realized she wasn't likely going to make it to one of the other levels of the ship. This caused her to laugh nervously.

But she really had to go and was already using every ounce of strength she had to hold it back, her thighs pinching together as she desperately tried to hold it back for as long as possible.

"The waste water all goes to the same place..." Lycia said, glancing over her shoulder at the showers. "The recycle plant handles the rest. It doesn't matter where you pee as long as it goes down a drain," she informed her.

Deunan's forehead wrinkled with worry lines and her eyes grew as large as saucers as she looked at Lycia. "All right, you convinced me!" hurried over to the shower stall and climbed in.

Without moments to spare, she unfastened her towel, squatted down over the drain, and then waved at Lycia to turn around. "Don't watch me! It's too embarrassing."

Lycia shrugged and leaned against the wall, folding her arms casually as she continued to stare directly at Deunan, intent on watching her pee.

"Oh, you brat," Deunan said, scowling at her. Lycia merely grinned back at her mischievous.

"I never took you for a nervous pee-er," she teased.

"Oh, hush you!" Unable to hold back any more, Deunan opened the floodgates and the rush of piss came out of her like the waterfalls of *Cresia* back on Dagon Prime.

"Could you piss any louder? I don't think they heard you all the way up on the command deck."

Deunan, still mid-piss, merely glowered at her.

Lycia laughed and then, grinning ear to ear as she deliberately eyeballed her cooch, shot her a playful wink then fetched a change of clothes for her.

A crooked smile on her face, Lycia handed Deunan the kimono styled robes and, not relinquishing them as expected, Deunan looked up at her.

"I don't see why you're single, D," Lycia said, "You have a rockin' hot bod and you have the nicest looking honey pot I've ever seen. And I should know; my fish taco is top notch," she shared, nodding down at her own set of lady bits.

"Uh huh," Deunan answered, jerking the clothes out of Lycia's arms and using them to cover herself up, hopefully salvaging whatever modesty she had left.

"But I'm serious, Mamma Bear, you need to get some."

"You're still young, Lycia. Your hormones are raging, and being of Dagon pedigree, your promiscuity levels are off the charts. Feel free to bang everyone and anyone you want, but please, leave me out of it. Are we clear?"

"Like a Dygra crystal," Lycia replied with a two-finger salute.

Deunan cocked her eyes at her curiously and then let out an exasperated sigh. It was the same sigh that every parent knew well. That sigh that expressed, in not so many words, one's frustration when one's child does or says something so unbelievably stupid you have no choice but to either go insane or let it all out.

As she turned around to get dressed, Lycia slapped her bare ass and then skipped out of the room giggling. Deunan rolled her eyes then let out a soft chortle.

For all of Lycia's mischief and coarseness, she was still fun company. Having her around for the past year had kept Deunan on her toes. Kept her feeling alert and aware and in the moment. And, for the first time in a long while, she didn't feel so lonely.

It only took Lycia a few minutes to locate Gamagor in the ship's dining hall. She grabbed a breakfast tray with a yogurt, half of a banana, a protein bar with dried fruits mixed in, and what smelled like mango juice but was green for some reason, and went over and sat down across from Gam.

"Morning," Lycia said, plucking a grape off of Gam's plate and popping it into her mouth. "Did you sleep well? I mean, you must have felt extra rested because you were in my bed when we fell asleep but weren't in my bed when I woke up this morning."

Not having swallowed the grape yet, she held it in her teeth and then bit down, letting it pop and flood her mouth with its sweet juices.

Gam shot her a tepid look. "Look, yesterday was a mistake," Gam said. "I should have never let myself…what I mean to say is, it's all in the past now, so let's just forget this ever happened."

"I see," Lycia said, looking down at her tray as she processed Gam's distancing of her. Although she wasn't happy about Gam's reaction, she wasn't entirely surprised either. Before she could apologize for her behavior though, Gam slid her tray away and looked up at Lycia's amber eyes.

"Sorry," Gam said, seeing as Lycia wasn't taking rejection well. "I didn't mean to mislead you."

"Nah, it's fine," Lycia replied. "I get it. Fun is fun until it's not."

Gam frowned and pushed her seat back and stood up. Standing over Lycia, she leaned over the table, both palms pressed firmly on the tabletop. "Look, you're a nice girl. But I need my space, that's all. Thanks for the fun, and I'll see you around."

Lycia settled into the chair opposite the empty space and sighed. She hadn't touched her yogurt when a voice called out to her from over her shoulder.

"Aren't you Lycia Alakandra?" it asked. She turned around in her seat and found a handsome young Dagon man sitting at the table directly behind her.

Since nobody was supposed to know who she was, she found it a little intimidating that he not only recognized her but knew her full name, too.

"Why don't you mind your own business," Lycia said in a disgruntled tone.

The young Dagon looked over his shoulder at her and then, picking up his tray, helped himself over to her table. "I meant no offense. I logged in your boarding pass yesterday and recognized you from your permit photo."

"Uh-huh…" she said in a less than enthused voice. She looked at him sitting across from her, self-invited, and then said. "Fine, I give up. Why don't you make yourself comfortable?" She gestured at the seat he was already sitting in and then let out a perturbed sigh.

"If you don't mind my asking," the young man inquired, staring intently at Lycia's beauty. "Is Alakandra your real name? I don't know of any other Alakandras in the galaxy, except for the empress. And as far as I know, she hasn't had any children."

Although it was a common question among Dagon people who were endlessly curious about one's lineage and pedigree, Lycia didn't have a ready answer for him. In fact, she really hadn't thought about how to respond to such a question. It wasn't like she was socializing with Dagon people or, for that matter, advertising she was a hybrid clone.

"Maybe we can finish this conversation another time," she said, rising to her feet. She shot him a forced smile and then left the dining area.

"What conversation?" the young Dagon man said in an ironic tone. After watching her leave, he went back to his meal.

The doors to the dining hall slid shut behind her and Lycia let out a big sigh of relief. *That was a close one,* she thought to herself.

Although the guy wasn't half bad looking, she didn't know what a Dagon was doing serving aboard a private entrepreneur's yacht. Gamagor had to be paying him a virtual fortune to entice his services. Either that or he was a complete dunce.

She shrugged and then continued up the corridor. She wanted to see what other services this luxury yacht offered. After a while, she decided nothing was for her and wandered about until she found herself standing on the observation deck.

It was empty except for a Seyfferian bar-tender that manned the back bar. But he kept disappearing into a back room to do who knows what.

Lycia stood in front of the towering glass windows that overlooked the kaleidoscope of stars passing by at faster than light speeds outside.

Stars moving toward them stretched into blue lines, stars moving away stretched into red lines, while stars that were aligned with their trajectory stretched into white lines. Occasional green or orange lines would streak by, signifying a passing comet or nebulae. It was mesmerizing.

The ship was headed to Correl, Capital World of the Seyfferian Republic. There they'd follow up a lead on whoever it was who was employing Xarthon and root out the secret to her origins.

Their ETA was still sixteen hours away, which meant she had more time to kill.

"Enjoying the view?" a voice asked from behind her. She turned around to find a flickering hologram of the most unexpected face.

"Jegra?"

The empress smiled. Her blue holographic visage cutting out briefly before resolidifying. "You look surprised to see me."

"Just unexpected is all," Lycia said, throwing a hand up on her hip and cocking her head a bit as she studied Jegra's cocktail dress.

"Looking as slutty as ever, *Mom*."

"Thanks," Jegra said, turning and showing herself off to the girl.

"The 'mom' bit was meant to be sarcastic," Lycia said.

"Sure, it was," Jegra replied, not buying the dodge.

Lycia shrugged. "Whatever. Was there something you needed?" she asked, acting smugger than she intended.

"I just wanted to check up on you. See how you were doing. I know tracking you down like this might seem like an invasion of your privacy, but I was genuinely worried."

"I'm fine," Lycia answered. "Really. Besides, you don't need to worry about me. I can take care of myself."

Jegra smiled and nodded. "If there's anything you need, please, don't ever hesitate to ask. I'll always be there for you." Tearing up slightly, Jegra raised a holographic hand and ran it across Lycia's blue cheek.

As a genetically modified clone, calling herself Jegra's daughter made more sense in the colloquial than calling herself a copy, because she wasn't an exact copy. She was as equal part Dakroth as she was Jegra. So, in effect, she was as close to a natural born daughter as she could be. At least, from a genetic standpoint, that is.

"Anyway," Lycia said, slowly drawing away from the uncomfortable holographic embrace. "I should probably go track down Deunan and see if she needs me."

"Right," Jegra said, wiping a single rogue tear from her cheek. "It was nice seeing you again," she said, her voice full of an overwhelming earnestness that made Lycia want to cry too. "I'm glad you're safe."

"You too," Lycia replied, smiling back at Jegra.

When the hologram transmission finally ended, Lycia took a huge breath and tried to get a hold on her emotions. Seeing Jegra with so much love in her eyes for her—a girl she barely knew—moved her to tears.

In her mind, she didn't feel like she deserved that level of compassion. But, at the same time, her human side of her knew that Jegra was probably just trying to fill the galaxy-sized void in her heart for the loss of her own child.

It wasn't her place to tell the Imperatrix of the Galaxy whom she could and could not love with all her heart. If she wanted to dote on Lycia, well, she was fine with that. Not having any real family to call her own, Jegra was the closest to a mother she'd likely ever get. Likewise, Deunan was like the big sister she never had. And Lycia was fine with that.

A bright flash drew Lycia's attention back to the view portal. The yacht had dropped out of hyperspace and was now being flanked by two Nephilim battle cruisers.

"This is the Nyctan and Nephilim Fusion, in service of the Almighty H'aaztre. Prepare to be boarded for inspection," a litigious and self-assured voice said over the comm system.

"Well, fuck me sideways and call it a goddamned Wednesday," Lycia grumbled at the unlucky turn of events.

She had the sneaking suspicion that things aboard Gam's ship were about to get dicey.

26

The chime sounded, rousing Jegra from her slumber. But being too exhausted to answer, she mumbled "Go away," waving her hand dully before letting it drop back onto the covers and promptly falling back asleep.

The chime to her quarters rang again but when she didn't answer there was the sound of Raven's voice followed by the override command. Entering the room, Raven looked at both women lying in a heap on the bed together—naked limbs braided together, leg over leg, arm over arm, both Jegra's snoring peacefully.

Young Jegra's face rested on older Jegra's chest, drool seeping out and running down the curve of her breast—a very Jegra sort of thing to do to herself, Raven mused.

A wry smile formed on Raven's lips before she shook the thought from her head and forced herself to get serious again. This wasn't some purple-heeled courtesan; this was the empress of the entire galaxy she was gawking at.

When the older Jegra yawned and stretched, slowly opening her eyes to find Raven standing over her, she smiled.

"Apologies," Raven said, looking the other away but finding her eyes drawn back to the curious entanglement, "when you didn't answer my call, I just assumed…"

Old Lady Jegra sat up and stretched her arms over her head, arching her back and pushing out her chest. Noticing the drool on her chest, she wiped it off with her fingers and rubbed it on the bed spread without thinking twice about it.

Jegra smiled at Raven and tossed her flowing silver hair over her shoulder and then looked down at her younger, still gently snoring, mouth slightly ajar.

"I used to be a real looker," she said, admiring her youthful visage sprawled out before her. It was a little bit surreal gazing upon a body she hadn't seen for over three hundred years.

Instead of a taught six-pack of abs, she now sported a small padded gut and enough insulation to round out her features a little more. Gone were the harsh edges of a sleek ten percent body fat and rippling muscles. Now, she was a curvaceous vixen.

Even her chest and ass swelled in size with the extra body fat—but she wasn't complaining. She rather liked her mature body. It was softer and sexier, in her estimation.

The added weight was negligible by most people's standards. In fact, she was fitter than half of the gladiators who still fought in the arena. Her hyperactive metabolism made sure of that. Of course, after three centuries, even her metabolism had grown slower than it used to be.

"You still are a looker," Raven stated, throwing her hands on her hips as she studied the older Jegra with a warm, affectionate gaze.

Jegra's eyes locked onto Raven's and she smiled at the unexpected compliment. Sitting up on her knees, she scooted to the edge of her bed, and reached out and placed both hands on Raven's gently curving waist.

A few of her fingers slipped beneath the folds of Raven's shirt and brushed against the soft lavender skin of her tender midriff, sending small tingles of excited energy racing into her surprisingly soft skin.

Raven blinked twice and her eyes changed from pink to purple, then to blue and finally turquoise-green.

"You never came to bed last night."

Raven gave a subtle nod toward the gently snoring Jegra. "She doesn't know about us... and I just thought it might be... you know... a little bit weird, all things considered."

"What's weird about a threesome?"

"What's *not* weird about a threesome with the woman I love and her younger self. A woman who I admire more than anything and who doesn't know I'm in love with her, you mean?"

"Just think of it as bedding two hot sisters," she teased.

"What?" Raven laughed. "That's worse!"

Jegra stood up and brushed her long platinum hair over her bare shoulder. "I'm going to take a shower and get dressed. We have a long journey ahead of us if we're going to get the Dygra crystal recharged.

Raven nodded and, stealing one more glance at the sleeping beauty just to make sure she slept soundly, confidently turned back to *her* Jegra and, drawing her close, leaned in for a kiss.

Jegra's strong arms wrapped around her purple waist as their mouths drew together. Their tongues wasted no time penetrating one another's parted lips and their hot breath filling the other with the most delectable form of passion.

Jegra began undoing Raven's tactical vest and almost got her breasts out when she broke off the kiss and drew away. "I can't," she whispered, nodding down at the slumbering empress. "It just makes me feel too vulnerable."

"All right," Old Lady Jegra laughed. "Be that way. Leave me wet and unmet. But tonight, it's just going to be you and me…no distractions. I promise."

"Don't make promises you can't keep," Raven said, pointing an accusatory finger at Jegra as she slowly backed out of the room. Jegra just folded her arms across her chest and pouted.

Raven had met this version of Jegra a little over three years ago, and for the past three years she'd been having an on again off again styled affair with her. And she was madly in love, but if the Jegra in this timeline found out about how crazy in love she was with her other self, it could lead to an awkward situation, to say the least.

She liked to keep her personal affairs personal, but at the same time it was growing more and more difficult to hide the older Jegra from everyone. And now that this timeline's Jegra had found out about her, it was becoming increasingly difficult to keep her three-year-long love affair hidden too.

More importantly, she didn't want to lose someone she considered a dear friend. She didn't have many she considered reliable and true friends. But Jegra was the closest she'd had to a best-friend her entire life. Which is why falling in love with her had been so easy.

Still, when she thought about it, things got really confusing really fast. She didn't know if she loved them both equally, or if she simply loved one so much it seemed like she loved the other one the same. Or, maybe she simply loved this timeline's Jegra and was settling on the Jegra from the future because there wasn't any romantic history between them to get in the way of them being together.

Whatever proved to be the case, she didn't want to lose Jegra—either of them—not ever.

Playing with her platinum hair, Jegra bit her bottom lip as she watched Raven gradually back out of her quarters. Raven deliberately zipped her vest back up and then blew a kiss as if to rub it in that Jegra wasn't getting any from her today.

Jegra laughed through her nose, keeping it light and airy so as not to wake younger herself sleeping peacefully on the bed.

Once Raven had taken her leave, Jegra let out a deep sigh and looked once more at the sleeping version of herself before climbing into the shower.

The sound of running water aroused younger Jegra from her deep slumber. She wiped the drool from her mouth then slowly sat up in bed, strands of light brown hair along with the plum colored sheets slid off her sun-kissed body.

"How long was I asleep for?" she asked in a groggy voice. She stretched and yawned as a voice answered her question.

"About five hours," a voice said over the sound of rushing water. "We've entered the slipstream and it will be about six days before we reach our destination."

"Six days?" Jegra echoed, her voice still a little bit raspy. "What will we do for six days?"

The water turned off and the shower stall slid open, steam billowing out and then quickly fading. A nude glistening Jegra stood in the opening wearing only a smile. "I can think of a few things."

"Anything in particular?" Jegra laughed.

Old Lady Jegra waited till the automated dry-cycle finished blow drying her body and hair and then strode over to her younger self and kissed her on the lips.

"Whatever comes naturally to us," she whispered in a sensual tone that dripped with the lingering aftertaste of their all-night love making.

When Jegra moved in for another kiss, her older self pulled away—a puckish grin forming on her mouth. "Right now," she said with an airy sigh, "I have to go help Raven with some things. Please, get some rest. You've more than earned it."

The younger Jegra flexed and massaged her jaw, still sore from last night's marathon enraptures, and nodded.

Old Lady Jegra turned toward the glossy gray wall opposite the bed and ran her hand across a panel which lit up blue. A hidden drawer popped open revealing a variety of outfits for her to wear.

Pulling out some autumn colored clothes, she slipped a charcoal gray knit sweater over her fulsome chest and then slipped into some black sweatpants without bothering to put on any panties.

Dressed for comfort, Jegra tied her platinum hair into a bun, using chopsticks she had in a small accessories tray set within the drawer, and then turned one last time to the sleepy-eyed Jegra and said, "I mean it. Get some rest. I'll be back in a while and we can talk some more."

"And by talk you mean…?"

Jegra laughed as she sat on the end of the bed and bent down, fetching her black tactical boots from the cubby under the bed. As she slipped her feet into them, she answered, "I mean, we can continue getting to know one another better, sure."

Jegra smiled, and still feeling the high from her lust-filled evening of ravishment, she grabbed a pillow, curled herself around it, and promptly drifted off to sleep.

"Sweet dreams, gorgeous," Old Lady Jegra said and with that she darted out into the cool corridor.

As she rounded the junction at the end of a corridor, a hand reached out from behind and, wrapping itself around her mouth so as to muffle any cries for help, pulled her back out of view.

Grendok Baphomet of Galliforn, heir to the throne of the tenth satyr dynasty as well as sworn defender of the Republic, beamed aboard the *Verlag* with urgent news.

The recent coalition under Jegra Alakandra had made the once sworn enemies of Dagon Prime and Galliforn close allies, their bond growing closer with each passing day of the war.

It was the cold hard fact of the matter that the spilled blood of their warriors bled together on the battlefield, uniting them as brothers and sisters—

and as people who fought for the same thing—freedom from a tyrannical cosmic being from another universe.

Light sparkled about in a controlled eddy above the teleportation pad while the teleporter buffers hummed loudly. A few seconds later, Grendok materialized on the teleportation pad wearing his admiral's uniform. With a blink and a nod at the crewman manning the teleporter console, he skipped off the pad and urgently entered the adjoining passage.

In his hand he carried a holofoil, a kind of translucent aluminum paper that could show videos and be written on like real paper. It also had the benefit of being flexible enough to roll up into a scroll for easy storage.

He made his way with haste to the infirmary where he'd been informed Dakroth was waiting for him. There, he found the emperor lounging in a chair next to a sleeping Callestra, his boots up on the edge of her bed as he gazed out one of the side view portals and watched the glittering stars hanging in the sky outside.

The satyr entered the infirmary with haste and promptly locked eyes with Dakroth who waved him over to the bed. Swinging his legs off the side, Dakroth sat up.

Stubble had appeared on his chin and it was the first time Grendok could recall not seeing the emperor in pristine condition.

"What is so important that it couldn't be spoken over the holovid display?" Dakroth wasn't angry, he just wasn't in the mood to discuss strategy at this time. But he had an admiration for the old goat, and decided he'd hear him out.

"This," Grendok said, handing him the holofoil.

He took it, unrolled it with both hands, and then examined its content.

A puzzled looked came across his face and he raised an eyebrow. "Is this what I think it is?"

"It's an official truce to be signed by you and the empress, myself, along with the generals of the allied forces. If we agree to H'aaztre's terms, then the war will come to an end."

Dakroth rolled the holofoil back up and rose to his feet and began pacing the floor. He did his best thinking on his feet.

"What do you think?" he asked, turning to Grendok.

Grendok shrugged. "My people are a single-minded folk. And until they have their revenge for the destruction of our homeworld, nothing that monster says will ever be trusted."

"And yet, I fear if we persist in continuing on with this war, we will be marching ourselves into our own graves."

"What of the empress? What would Jegra say to this?"

Dakroth laughed and locked his hands behind his back, still clasping onto the holofoil scroll. "She's unpredictable, to say the least. One day she's all about forgiveness, the next she's crushing in skulls to teach a lesson in respect."

"Sounds about right," Grendok chuckled, stroking his hoary beard contemplatively.

"But I know this much," Dakroth continued, "she has no love for this cosmic nuisance calling himself the Gilded Master. Of that much we can be certain." After a moment's rumination, Dakroth turned his head and, looking at the satyr's slatted eyes, asked, "By the way, where is my wayfaring wife at this moment?"

"On a top-secret mission with Raven Nightguard, Your Excellency. Not even I know their actual whereabouts."

"Probably for the best," Dakroth said, turning his gaze back toward the window. "If we're to win this war, we will need her at her finest."

Grendok bowed and then, taking his leave, skipped off.

Dakroth acknowledged his departure with a slight sideways glance but had his attention redirected to the bedside when a diminutive voice called out to him.

"Rhadamanthus?"

He turned to find Callestra looking at him with her magenta gaze. He smiled and moved over to her bedside.

"My luv," he said, bending down and kissing her forehead. "At last, you've come back to me."

"I'll always come back to you," she said, smiling weakly.

She tried to sit up in bed but he gently nudged her back down onto the soft pillows.

"Relax," he said. "We have all the time in the world."

"And the war?"

"I ordered a strategic retreat. Both sides had decimated one another to the point of a stalemate and we must regroup before coming up with a final strategy to end this conflict once and for all."

"It's unlike you to play things so cautiously," she said.

"Maybe your good sense is wearing off on me," he replied with a wry smile.

"Maybe it is," she answered. Her own smile spread ear to ear and then she took a deep breath. Then, with every ounce of strength she had, she slid out of bed.

Dakroth rushed over to her and wrapped his arms around her, helping her steady herself. "I told you to rest," he said, his voice worried for the woman he loved.

"I've rested enough," she said, steadying herself. She then looked into his eyes and smiled. "The time for rest is over. Now, we get to work."

"As you wish," he said, leaning in. She threw herself into his arms and, standing on her tiptoes, kissed him on the mouth.

As they kissed, unseen by them, a small glowing squid shot by their window on his way to deliver a very important crystal. With a flash, the tiny squid jumped to a different sector of space.

27

Eddies of golden light danced along the walls and chased Lycia up the corridor. She ran at a dead sprint, desperate to get back to Deunan. But a team of Nephilim soldiers came marching up the opposite corridor and she skidded to a halt.

The ship had been boarded for a routine inspection courtesy of the Fusion, and finding her path cut off, she mumbled some obscenities under her breath and then turned to head back the way she'd come.

Lycia hadn't even made it ten steps when the young Dagon officer she'd met at breakfast came racing around the corner and almost crashed into her.

"Hey, watch where you're going," she snapped, throwing up her hands in case she needed to deflect him away from her with a forceful shove.

He ignored her rudeness, grabbed her by her wrist, and continued up the corridor, towing her behind him as he went. As they ran, their hands slipped into a natural embrace. "Come on, a boarding party is back that way."

She dug her heels in and brought them both to a stop. "Slow down, hotshot," she said before sharing the bad news, "they're up ahead too."

He stopped in the middle of the passage and glanced up and then down, mulling over what to do. "They have us boxed in," he said, scanning their immediate surroundings for a place to hide.

As he searched for a way out, she glanced down at his hand, which was still holding on to hers. A subtle smile had begun to form on her lips when he announced, "Over here!" Pulling her into a side entrance with him, they shut the door behind them and panted softly, trying to catch their breath.

Locked in an auxiliary breaker room, their heaving bodies pressed up against one another. Inside the tight space there wasn't much but electrical cords, reserve cable used for repairs, and a lot of blinking lights signifying which wires were routed to where. As the changing colors danced across their skin, they looked at one another, their gazes meeting.

"What now, genius?"

"I don't know," he said. "It was the only place to go."

The clomp of heavy footsteps bearing down on them from outside in the hallway grew incrementally louder and Lycia made a split-second decision.

Bending down, best she could, given the cramped quarters, she slipped off her pants and began to peel off her panties. "You're going to have to fuck me," she said.

"What?" the young man asked, shocked by her brazenness.

"Look, these bastards are the biggest prudes in the galaxy. One look at my glorious wet pussy and they'll probably just die of shock. If they walk in on us having sex, they're going to feel all kinds of religious guilt and the undying need to lash themselves until they forget everything they saw here today."

"So, your plan is to scare them away with sex?"

"Got any better ideas?" she asked him.

"No. But what if your plan doesn't work?" he asked her, still nervous. "What if they just drag us out and start beating us right in the middle of the hallway?"

She stared at him intently for a moment and not having an adequate response for that scenario, she said, "Shut up." After another brief pause, she added, "It'll work. Trust me."

He hemmed and hawed for a moment longer than shrugged. "Alright," he agreed, and began to unbuckle his belt. "But I'm only doing this to save both of our asses."

"My hero," she quipped sarcastically as she helped him undo his pants zipper and drew down his trousers.

A few minutes later, just as predicted, the doors slid open, and a boarding team of three Fusion soldiers stood outside, mouths agape at what they'd stumbled into.

Lycia was pressed up against the wall, her arms high above her head, fingers threaded through wires that protruded from the walls. The young Dagon officer's sweaty body pressed up against hers as he thrust his hips into her and she let out a licentious moan.

The Nephilim soldiers, alarmed by this lewd sex act, immediately drew back from the entrance. Startled looks adorned their faces forcing a smirk onto Lycia's face as she peered at them from the corners of her eyes.

"Yes!" she screamed. "I'm cumming! I'm cumming!"

She clenched her fingers around the cords and pulled herself up just as she exploded with a spray of female ejaculation. Her juices shot everywhere and one of the guards standing outside turned away from the disgust of what he'd witnessed.

The lewd sex act was too much for them to bear and all three guards groaned in disgust. Not wanting to see what happened next, they immediately slammed the door shut.

From the other side of the door, Lycia could hear a heated debate break out amongst the Fusion soldiers. The leader wanted to drag them out, but the other two were reluctant to deal with them in their current state and opted to wait until they were finished.

After a moment, a stern voice came from the other side of the door and informed them, "When you're finished with this act of debauchery, report to—"

"*Ohhh,* my Gilded fucking God!" Lycia cried out, interrupting him. She gasped with the richest sex-laden moan she could muster which shut the officer up quite nicely. "Oh, my god, oh, my god!" she cried out in an exaggerated fashion. "Some of it squirted in your mouth!"

"I don't mind!" said the Dagon officer in a louder than usual voice. "It's both salty and sweet," he added for good measure.

Lycia shook her head and whispered, "Don't over do it."

"Sorry," he replied.

"Let's go," the lead guard said, turning to his comrades. "These two are obviously not the ones we're looking for. Otherwise, they would have hidden better."

The other two soldiers nodded, and with that they marched away, heading back down the corridor the way they'd come.

"It worked," the young man said. When he turned to fetch his clothes, Lycia stopped him and drew his gaze back to hers.

She clutched the back of his head tightly and pulled herself up onto him again. "We're not done," she said.

"We're not?" He looked at her and then realizing she wanted more, he smiled and then happily obliged her.

Between gasps of breath, Lycia said, "I think it worked. I think they've gone." They slowed down and paused to listen. When there was no longer any sound on the other side of the door, she looked at him and smiled.

"You're amazing," the young officer said, his face beaming as he peered into her amethyst eyes. "I think I might love you."

His candor denoted a deep infatuation which made her uncomfortable considering they'd only just met and hooked up. She drew back, startled by his sudden admission of love for her, and brushing her hair behind her ear as she stared at him stunned. "Don't be ridiculous. You can't love me," she laughed. "We just met."

"I'm sorry. I don't mean to freak you out. It's just that... you're the first woman I've ever..." he stopped stammering and looked her in the eyes. "I know I can make you happy. Just give me another chance."

Oh, great, she thought. *I deflowered a virgin.*

She knew what that entailed: Infatuation. Obsession. Constant desire to please her. To be with her. Which wouldn't be so bad if it wasn't for the awestruck puppy-love and clinginess which was a total turn off for her.

"If there is a next time," she said, sliding off of him and setting her feet back down onto the cold floor.

"My name is Arnott Jovarius, by the way."

"I didn't ask," she said more bitterly than she had intended. Even so, he didn't seem to take any offense to her candor.

Arnott rubbed his fingers through his hair and smiled at her sheepishly as she dressed. "So...do you have a boyfriend?"

"Not at the moment," she said, as she pulled her panties back up. Cocking her eyes at him, she asked, "Why?"

"No reason," he said, looking away bashfully, cheeks flushing red. They'd just had sex and he knew right there and then that he was in love with her.

Annoyed, she hurried to get her ripped jeans back on and grunted impatiently as she repeatedly slapped the door release button. It was like waiting for a damn lift that was taking far too long.

"What if they're still out there?" Arnott cried out, grabbing her hand and pulling it toward him.

Just then the doors parted and she looked out at the empty corridor and then back at him. "There. Empty. You happy?"

She nodded her chin at their clasped hands and, respecting her wishes, he promptly let go of her hand.

Lycia stepped out into the cool recycled air of the corridor and slipped on her yellow top.

Once they'd finished dressing, Arnott scanned both ends of the corridor and then went over to the wall panel to check on the progress of the search.

"What are you doing?" she asked.

"They've logged into the computer that the ship was searched and everything was in order." He looked over at her with a big grin on his face. "It worked."

"Of course, it worked, you big idiot," she replied. She was deliberately being mean to him so he'd catch the hint. But he merely grinned at her like a dope.

Arnott continued to stare at her until she felt her blood begin to boil, and fed up of his wasting her time she huffed in annoyance and turned up the hall.

"Where are we going?" he asked, following after her.

"I'm going to get myself some breakfast," she stated. "I'm starving."

Arnott nodded his head in agreement and bobbed along behind her. "Do you want some company?" he asked.

"Not particularly," she said.

"Oh," he said, drawing to a stop in the middle of the corridor. "I see."

She paused, thinking about a nice, quiet peaceful meal to herself before sighing out. Then, glancing over her shoulder at him, she saw the dejected and absolutely pitiful look on his face. This caused her to feel bad for him and, letting out another huff of annoyed breath, she rolled her eyes so hard she thought they'd tear out of her eye sockets.

"Oh, for crying out loud. If you're going to act like a love-struck pup I might as well make use of you."

Arnott immediately perked up again, his forlorn posture melting away only to reveal the optimistic idiot who had fallen helplessly in love with her.

"You mean it?"

She let out another vexed sigh and simply ignored him as she continued making her way back to the ship's dining hall.

Roughly an hour later, Lycia finished off her glass of pink lychee juice, dabbed the corners of her mouth with the cloth napkin, and then tossed it onto the table. Leaning back in her seat, she sighed contentedly.

Arnott brushed aside the table cloth and crawled out from under the table. As he rose to his feet, he wiped away the glistening residue on his lips and turned to her and smiled, his big dopey grin spreading across his face as he stared at her far too intently.

"How was your breakfast?" he asked her.

"It could have been better," she said nonchalantly. "How was yours? Not too salty, I hope?"

"It was more than satisfying," he said cheerfully. "Everything I could have ever hope for and then some."

"I'm glad," she laughed.

She rose up from the table, pulling up her panties in one smooth motion and then, walking side by side, they left the eatery together and headed for the bridge.

Unintentionally, their hands brushed up against one another and she glanced at him. Embarrassed to be caught ogling her as though she were food, he looked away. When she turned away again, he glanced back at her to study her beautiful features perchance to etch her heavenly visage into his mind forever.

She knew he wanted to hold her hand, but that seemed too intimate to her. They'd literally just met a little over an hour ago.

And although Dagon culture wasn't about romance, per se, it did have certain expectations.

Upon first meeting someone you were outwardly physically attracted to, you quickly hooked up and had sex. If you pleased someone sexually, then you could get to the romance part—because then, that way, at least you knew you were physically compatible. And, if it was meant to be, the rest would come naturally.

It never made sense to her why other species went through all the endless courtship rituals before picking a mate. It seemed like a complete waste of time and energy.

In truth, using all that mental energy, resources, and galactic credits for courtship, wooing, and eating fancy dinners just to find out whether or not you *might* be compatible enough to *maybe* get lucky was backward, in her mind. Why would you suffer months of agonizing uncertainty just to slowly condition one another into being comfortable for a once off intimate encounter? It didn't make any sense.

It was far better, she felt, to get the uncomfortable bit out of the way and then, if you still liked the person afterward, explore your feelings.

Even so, if he took her hand she wouldn't shy away, because so far, he was slowly but surely winning her over.

"Where are we going?" asked Arnott.

"The bridge," replied Lycia. "I need to make sure Gamagor and Deunan are doing alright after that little shakedown by the Nephilim soldiers."

"Seems like something you could have done before eating all those hotcakes and DorVidian strawberries."

She stopped abruptly, let go of his hand, and then placed a stiff finger against his chest.

"Look, here. A girl has needs," she said in a reproachful manner. His eyes wide with shock, he merely nodded along to whatever she said. "I needed to fill my stomach after working up a sweat with you. So, if you ever want to be lucky enough to experience that again, then you don't question my life's choices, *capisce?*"

He nodded along with her and then she reached up, cupped her hands around his face, and pulled him into her lips. After a long, sultry, wet kiss she let him go and continued marching up the hall.

All Arnott could do was stand in a daze, watching as she walked away from him, a dumbfounded expression on his face. His heart raced in his chest and he felt light-headed. She was the woman of his dreams. Feisty. Strong-willed. Sexually voracious.

When Lycia realized Arnott was no longer following her, she wheeled around and shot him an irritated look. Snapping her fingers to try and snap him out of his trance, she asked impatiently, "Are you coming or what?"

"Gamagor won't be on the bridge," Arnott informed her.

Lycia's hands dropped to her sides and she shot him a prying look. When he didn't divulge where it was she'd be, she cleared her throat and with a bit of snark, asked, "Where exactly, might I ask, will she be, then?"

Reluctant to reply, Arnott Jovarius hemmed and hawed for a moment and then gave in to her probing gaze. "In case of a boarding party, a faux captain assumes the role of Gamagor and she retreats to a safe-room where she can monitor ship's activities."

"So, she's laying low?"

"She's a wanted fugitive with a death sentence in five of the seven systems. So, yeah."

Still staring at him with the same intensity, Lycia folded her arms. "Right. And where exactly is this secret safe-room?"

Arnott gulped. "It's...it's, well, it's a secret."

It was no use. He wasn't going to tell her. Not unless she enticed him with something he'd be willing to trade for that juicy morsel of information.

"You drive a hard bargain," she said at last.

Confused, he cocked his head and squinted suspiciously at her. "I do?" he asked, his voice cracking with uncertainty.

She took his hand again and dragged him into a side corridor. The moment they stepped off the main concourse, she reached down and began to pull off her shirt.

Before she could pull it over the hump of her breasts, however, he grabbed her arms and stopped her. Her blue midriff showing, she just stared at him with an inquiring expression on her face.

"Right here and now?" he asked nervously, looking around to ensure they weren't being watched.

They were exposed. Out in the open. If the guards came back, or more embarrassing still, someone he knew, a member of the crew perhaps, it would be utterly mortifying.

"What's the matter," she asked, glancing at him with a perplexed look. "You don't want to?"

"I do," he answered, not wanting to give her the wrong impression. "It's just that..."

Disappointed in his hesitancy, she lowered her shirt and glared at him. "I thought you were a Dagon male. Are you trying to tell me you're not willing to fuck a woman of high pedigree because you might get caught by some lowly staff member? Where's your Dagon pride, man?"

"I'm only half Dagon," Arnott confessed. He immediately tensed up and looked at her, his face seizing up with fear. "Please, don't think I tricked you. It just happened all so fast."

"It's fine," Lycia said, waving her hand nonchalantly and dismissing the whole purity nonsense as trivial. "I'm actually only half Dagon myself," she admitted to him.

"You don't look it," he said.

She turned and stared at him long and hard, arms folded. She didn't know why, but she felt she could trust him. He wasn't like other Dagon men. He wasn't domineering, predatory, or full of himself. And that was refreshing.

Arnott was just an inexperienced young man. And she couldn't fault him for that. He'd learn.

"It's because I'm a genetically enhanced clone of the Empress, Jegra Alakandra," she finally revealed to him. She waited for the look of disgust to come across his face, but when it never did, she looked him directly in the eyes. "What is it? Why are you looking at me like that?"

"Purity is overrated anyway," he said, blushing.

They stood smiling at one another and then, brushing the turquoise bangs out of her eyes, she felt her heart skip a beat.

No, no, no she told herself. *Don't let yourself get caught up in this.* She immediately recognized that his pheromones were mingling with hers and creating a pheromone storm. About the only way to resist one was to either be dead to the world or give in to it.

"So," she said, twiddling a tuft of hair between her thumb and fingers. "Do you still want me?"

When Arnott leaned in, she leaned forward to meet his lips when, all of a sudden, a sharp sound startled him and he looked away. By then it was too late—her lips landed on the most awkward part of his jaw, just below his right ear.

"Sorry," she said, wiping the wet imprint of her lips off the side of his face with her palm.

He clutched her hands and then said, "Someone's coming."

She pulled him closer to her and then, nudging him behind her, she raised a glowing finger and prepared a complimentary laser blast for whoever was about to barge in on them and ruin their romantic moment.

When Deunan rounded the corner with Allie, the purple Lafor'allenthal panther, Lycia let out a huge sigh of relief and lowered her finger. "Bloody

Helios, D!" she gasped, the tension draining out of her. "I almost vaporized you!"

"I'm glad you didn't," Deunan said. She turned her attention to the young man standing behind Lycia, timidly peeking out from over her shoulder. "Who's this?"

Lycia glanced over her shoulder and said, "Oh, yeah. This is Arnott Jovarius. He's…uh…helping me evade the Nephilim patrols."

Arnott stepped out from behind Lycia, his posture stiffening into that of a regiment officer, and extended his hand for Deunan to shake. She looked down at it contemplatively but chose to ignore it.

"I'm Ensign Arnott Jovarius, at your service. A pleasure to meet you, ma'am," he stated in a manner that sounded as though he was introducing himself to her parents.

When Deunan merely stared at him with a critical gaze, he gulped and then gestured to Lycia and then himself. "We had sex," he said, oversharing in the most awkward fashion and at the most inopportune moment possible.

Lycia rolled her eyes and, then, firmly smacked him in the arm to express her dissatisfaction with him.

"Ow!" he yelped, rubbing his arm. "That really hurt."

"Why would you even tell her that, you idiot?"

"It's true, isn't it?" he asked in a credulous fashion, still rubbing his arm where she walloped him.

She glared at him. "Too much information, you dummy," she growled under her breath, jabbing him again with her elbow just for good measure.

"It's fine," Deunan finally said, attempting to defuse the situation before it got any worse. She turned and glanced up and down the hallway as she scouted for any unwanted company. "Apparently, so has half the ship."

"*Heeey…!*" Lycia said in a long, drawn-out manner, turning toward Deunan with a shocked expression and a blossoming smile as D's little jab came completely out of left field.

"I beg your pardon?" Arnott asked, turning to Lycia for clarification of this distressing news.

"What *aunty* Deunan means to say," Lycia said snidely, glaring at Deunan for the uncouth remark about her personal sexual habits, "is that she's jealous that I'm keeping my bed warm every night while her dusty ole glove box only manages to gather dirt and cobwebs."

"Sounds like…uh, a hygiene issue," Arnott answered.

Deunan rolled her eyes and began to make her way up the hallway. When Arnott turned to follow after her, he was stopped by the growl of a large indigo panther that sat directly in his way.

"Um…Lycia?" he asked, hesitantly. He made sure to keep both eyes on the big cat.

"It's alright, girl," Lycia said, glancing down at Allie. "He's with us."

That seemed to satisfy the cat's skepticism and she turned and followed after Lycia and Deunan.

Arnott shrugged as though it were no big deal then trailed after the women. As he walked up the corridor, he couldn't help but picture a long and happy life together with Lycia. In all his years, he'd never once imagined he'd meet the woman of his dreams way out here beyond the Outer Rim.

And, now that he'd found her, all he could do was think about what their wedding day would be like.

"Hey, ground control to Major Tom!" Lycia barked, drawing his attention back to her. She nodded as if to say, *hurry it up*, and he grinned and quickly scurried after her.

Once they'd all convened on the bridge, Gamagor waved them over, where she lounged in her command chair, sipping glowing orange Dragonian ale of the finest vintage.

Displayed on the viewscreen was the glowing Nephilim patrol ship as it gradually pulled away.

"Ladies," Gam said, turning to them. When she saw Arnott with them she raised an eyebrow and then included him as well. "Arnott." Raising her glass to them, she toasted, "Here's to living another day of freedom and finding yet another adventure."

It seemed that for the first time in a long while their string of rotten luck had finally come to an end.

Arnott, not wanting the moment to slip by, cleared his throat. "And I would like to propose another kind of toast." Slowly getting down on one knee, he reached out to take Lycia's hand. Smiling up at her, completely lovestruck, he opened his mouth to speak when, unexpectedly, Deunan's hand intercepted his.

With a hard jerk, she brought him back to his feet and then whispered in his hear, "Cool your jets, lover-boy."

They all laughed at his expense and he merely batted his eyes and gave an embarrassed grin. When Lycia leaned in and gave him a peck on the cheek, all his troubles seemed to melt away.

Another round of laughter followed when one of Gamagor's manservants brought over a tray of ales for everyone. They took their bottles and raised them high. Clinking them together, they made an unspoken oath to always remain loyal to one another. To always have one another's backs. And to stay friends forever.

Arnott looked down at Allie and grinned. He was just happy to be a part of the group.

Unimpressed by this new stranger, Allie turned away from him, walked in a tight circle, then plopped down at the feet of Gamagor. Surprised by the cat's sudden affection toward her, she looked down at the cat and then over at Lycia, who merely shrugged.

They all shared another round of laughter and continued chatting as they finished off their drinks one sip at a time.

28

Jegra broke free of her attacker, slipping out of his hold. Fists raised, she spun around to find Skuld Lor'ellem pressing a long, gangly finger to his fishbowl like visor, beckoning her to remain silent.

Instantly relaxing, Jegra whispered, "What is it?"

"I can't be entirely sure, but I think there's an intruder on the ship." He drew out a holopad and showed her the screen. On it was an image of the ship's schematics, including a cutout of the ship broken down deck by deck.

"What am I looking at, exactly?" she asked.

"Right here," he said, as he swiped away some pages, cutting through the layers of the ship. On the screen were green dots that represented the crew's life signs. "The green dots are us and the other crew members." But there was also a yellow dot just around the corner from them at the end of the junction.

"What's this yellow one?" Jegra asked, pointing at the new blinking dot.

"My question exactly," he replied. "It reads as a life sign, but the ship's scanners cannot identify it."

"And what room is that?"

"It's the armory," he replied, growing nervous. "Whoever they are, they may be planning to arm themselves and take over the ship."

Jegra laughed. "I think I know who it may be."

"You do?" he asked, somewhat perplexed. But, then again, she was the empress. Of course, she'd be privy to information he wasn't.

She stepped back out in to the corridor and Skuld reluctantly followed after her. Checking both ends of the corridor as though he were a child looking both ways before crossing a busy street, he cautiously stepped out into the hall and scurried after her.

"I'd better come with you," he said in his bravest voice. "It might be dangerous."

"If it is who I think it is…they're simply gorging themselves on some battery packs."

"Battery packs?" he asked. *It would be a curious creature indeed that eats battery packs*, he thought.

When they arrived at the armory, a golden light was seeping out from between the cracks in the door.

"What in the seven moons is that?" he gasped, his curiosity compelling him to move incrementally closer to the door.

Jegra slapped the touch-sensor and the doors parted. Inside the armory was a glowing squid entity, roughly the size of a blue bottle-nosed dolphin from the ocean moon Demaxian, its radiant tentacles full of battery cells.

"Skuld, I'd like you to meet an old friend of mine. This precarious little fella is La'Garren."

"You have a pet celestial space squid?" he asked, entering the room and inspecting the creature.

Inside his helmet, a monocle styled apparatus slid into place and he zoomed in on the squid entity, his magnified over-sized eye blinking curiously as he familiarized himself with the creature.

Jegra laughed. "Yeah, we sort of just found each other. Two strangers in a faraway land, you might say."

"A very apt description," Skuld said.

One of La'Garren's tentacles unfolded and extended itself toward Jegra. She reached out to touch it but was surprised when a glowing red rock tumbled out of his coils and into her open palm. Looking down, she recognized it instantly.

"A Dygra crystal?" Skuld asked, his curiosity piqued.

"It appears so," Jegra said. She looked back up at La'Garren and placed her hand on the side of his floating body.

"I'm curious about how they levitate," Skuld said, waving his hand beneath the squid's radiant body.

He reached into his pocket and pulled out a scanner to further study the squid, but the batteries instantly drained from his device.

Skuld tapped the scanner to try to jostle it back to life, but it merely beeped at him then shut itself off.

"Drats," he lamented and looked over at the power cell rack. They, too, had all been drained.

"How's my hungry boy?" Jegra said in a cutesy voice as she rubbed her hands over La'Garren's tummy. The squid rolled onto its back and let her rub his body just as a loyal dog would.

Satisfied that they were no longer under threat, she turned to Skuld and smiled. "Keep an eye on him, will you? I need to go talk to Raven."

"Of course, I'll endeavor to learn as much as I can about this unique species," Skuld informed her. She nodded and placed a hand on his shoulder, smiled at him again, and then exited the armory.

"Well, my friend, it seems we have plenty of time to acquaint ourselves with one another." Reaching over, he snatched up a still fully charged power cell and offered it to the squid. "Care for some dessert?"

La'Garren stretched out his feelers, touched the power cell with the tip of his tentacle, and drained its power.

As the notches of the power cell faded away to nothing, Skuld blinked his aquatic eyes and murmured, "Fascinating."

Old Lady Jegra arrived on the bridge to find Ladgara leaning in awfully close to Raven as she checked the readout on the star chart.

"The planet Kruos isn't on any maps. But if my memory serves, the last time I saw it, it was floating somewhere in this sector."

"Why wouldn't it be on any star charts?" asked Jegra.

Ladgara stiffened up and pulled away from Raven who just shot her a smile for getting all fidgety next to her girlfriend.

Smiling, Ladgara replied, "Because Kruos is a sentient planet, and it can jump to other locations. About the only way you can track it is via gravitational lensing. It has a very unique light signature."

"A planet that wanders about really lives up to its namesake," Jegra said, smiling at them. When they both gave her blanks stares, she chuckled and said, "Never mind."

"How did you find Kruos the first time?" Ladgara asked suspiciously, glancing down at the hefty, ruby like rock in Jegra's hand.

"I tracked one of the CSEs that I knew would go there."

"So, you still think you're from the future and not a clone?"

Raven shot Ladgara a harsh glower, but Jegra just raised her hand, letting her know that Ladgara's skepticism was perfectly all right. In fact, it was well justified.

"Why would a clone be older than the original she was copied from?" asked Jegra.

"I dunno," Ladgara said, smacking her teeth and folding her arms. "Maybe accelerated aging?"

"For what purpose?"

"Beats me. Maybe somebody's grandmother died and they needed a new one."

This made Raven laugh and Jegra widened her eyes at her.

"Alright, alright," Raven said, rising out of her seat. "You two can argue the finer points of cloning grandmas later. Right now, I think all three of us need to suit up."

"And why's that?" Ladgara asked, not breaking away from Jegra's gaze as they stared one another down.

"Because of that," Raven said, jutting her chin.

Both women swiveled their heads to look at what Raven was pointing to out the window. Just off the bow of the ship, coming into view, was a massive planet with pink and blue lightning-laced electrical storms.

"Kruos," Ladgara murmured under her breath.

"Still don't believe me?" Jegra asked, leaning in to whisper into Ladgara's ear.

Ladgara narrowed her one good eye at Jegra and forced a smile. "So, you were telling the truth. So what? All I know is that Raven trusts you, so I have no reason to distrust you. Best not give me one."

With that, Ladgara nudged Jegra out of the way with her shoulder as she walked off the bridge.

Jegra turned back to Raven. "She's in love with you, you know?"

Raven balked at the notion. "I highly doubt that. We only had sex the one time."

"Then you must have rocked her world. Because she's clearly got it bad."

Raven grew serious. "That was just sex. When it comes to my feelings...there's only one woman who knows the real me." She reached up and touched Jegra's face. "And she's standing right here."

The two drew close as they stared longingly into each other's eyes. "So…you love me?" Jegra asked.

"Is it so hard to believe?"

"You've just never said the words until now."

"I felt now was the appropriate time to…" Raven's words trailed off as Jegra's lips drew closer.

"Yes?"

"To let myself get emotional."

"And what do you feel right now?" Jegra asked in a sultry voice. She embraced Raven and held her in her arms as she waited for her reply.

Raven smiled, her lips practically brushing the older Jegra's. "If I'm being honest, I feel like kissing you."

"Then what's stopping y—"

Raven silenced her with a kiss. Before they'd even had time to come up for air, their hands were hastily grasping at each other's clothes.

Determined to make love right there on the bridge, Jegra hoisted Raven up onto the console and began unfastening her leather pants. The console beeped in protest to this gross form of abuse. Her ass sat down on top of the touch controls, making it cry out even more, but she ignored it.

Their kisses grew wetter and hotter and, without pausing to even take a breath, Raven slid a hand up Jegra's shirt and began groping her breasts. She squeezed so hard that Jegra's flesh rose between her fingers like yeasted dough. Jegra moaned into Raven's mouth as their tongues swirled about.

At the same time, Jegra slipped her hand into the crevice of Raven's partially open pants and, gradually, slid her fingers beneath the delicate fabric of Raven's black lace panties.

Raven leaned back, her body stretching out across the console as though it were a bed, and peered up into Jegra's brown eyes.

In the heated make out session, Jegra's bun had come unwoven and her silvery hair fell down across her shoulders like a cascading waterfall.

Jegra leaned over her indigo-skinned elfin lover, their chests pressing together as they kissed, and nibbled on her lip with soft bites in a way that sent a surge of pleasure-laced pain into Raven.

She pulled back, her bottom lip stretching as Jegra held it firmly in her teeth. Finally, when she let go, Raven threw back her head and gasped loudly.

The silver-haired paramour's fingers still inside Raven's pants, she continued massaging with delicate strokes, sending shivers of ecstasy up and down Raven's spine, forcing her to let out a prurient moan.

At that moment, Raven clenched as she orgasmed, the veins in her neck growing taught as her face turned a bright shade of pink.

"*Guphaaah...*" she gasped, trying to take in a deep breath as she buried her face into Jegra's neck, panting heavily.

Just then, the unexpected cry of a squeaky voice cut through the room, rudely interrupting their bout of passion play.

"*Ew, gross!*"

Startled, Raven and Jegra pulled apart from one another and scanned the seemingly empty room. Raven, looking up at the ceiling with closed eyes and a scowl, and screamed, "Gyllek!"

Gyllek quickly decloaked and scurried out of the room.

Raven huffed in annoyance and blew a purple tuft of hair out of her eyes and then sighed out loudly.

She and Jegra shared a look of utter bewilderment, topped by the embarrassment of getting caught wet-handed and then, at the exact same time, they burst into laughter.

"I think I'll need to have a talk with her," Raven said, looking at the door.

"She's just curious," Jegra said. "I remember when I was fourteen. Hormones raging. I fell for every boy who'd talk to me, let alone kiss me."

"There aren't any boys 'round here," Raven said, leaning back on her elbows. Notch by notch, she began to unzip her tactical vest, her purple cleavage bulging out as she slowly, deliberately, undid the restrictive garment. This prompted Jegra to raise an eyebrow.

"No. No, there are certainly not. Just a whole lot of sex-starved women, apparently."

It was true, though. Months on end in the cold reaches of outer space with nothing to do often led to unexpected hookups. Most of the time they were just mistakes, or folly. But, sometimes, you'd find a genuine spark of attraction. And it was this spark of attraction which Raven and Jegra had unexpectedly walked right into.

"And this woman wants you to finish what you started," Raven said, drawing Jegra back down onto her. Guiding Jegra's hand to the holy grail between her tender thighs, she smiled at her with a salacious grin and thirsty eyes full of longing.

"Now, where were we?" Jegra replied, kissing her on the lips. She paused just long enough to add, "Oh, yes. Now I remember."

"Less talking," Raven said, clutching Jegra by the back of her neck.

"Yes, Captain," Jegra teased, and fell into her lover's arms.

Callestra finished dressing as Emperor Dakroth sat up in bed. "Are you sure you don't want to go for round three?"

"No thanks, luv. I'm satisfied."

He patted the empty sheets next to him and gave her the sad, puppy-dog eyes. "Please? I've missed you."

She turned and, waving her hand across her uniform, let out a sigh. "I just finished dressing. You'd have me take this all off again?"

He smiled, but said nothing.

She rolled her eyes and then, with a shrug, replied, "Very well then." Reaching up, she began unbuttoning her uniform as she made her way back to the foot of the bed.

Dakroth rose to his knees and ripped open her white jacket with lust fueled haste and clawed at her mauve colored bra.

She tossed her purple-turquoise ombre hair over her shoulder and arched her back to push up her perky blue breasts with their budding maroon nipples.

Wasting no time, Dakroth quickly wrapped his dark blue lips around her left tit and began sucking. She let slip a salacious moan and ran her fingers through his flowing white hair.

Before he could help her out of the rest of her clothes, there was a thunderous *boom!* accompanied by an abrupt jolt that was so violent, she fell forward onto the bed, landing beside him.

Rolling back off the bed, she sprang up and began tucking her girls back into their rightful places. Racing out of the room, she tapped the royal pendant on her uniform and called to the bridge, "This is Vice Admiral Van Morgan. What the Helios is going on up there?"

"We're under attack, ma'am," a harried voice came back over the comm.

Callestra burst onto the command deck and looked out at the view portal. A massive space squid, nearly the size of a small moon, wafted outside the ship.

"Where the hell did that thing come from?" she asked.

"It just jumped into the system, ma'am. The shockwave rattled the bulkheads some, but there was no structural damage."

"It seems H'aaztre has sent his cleanup crew to deal with the remaining Allied ships."

"What do we do, ma'am?" the officer asked, sending her a frightened look. Although fear was unbecoming in a soldier, there were things in this galaxy too terrible to set eyes upon without quaking in one's boots. This was one of those things.

"Unless a miracle occurs, Ensign, there's not much we can do." Callestra tugged down her jacket, straightening out any lingering wrinkles and then turned to the crew. "Alert the fleet that we're executing an emergency jump. Jump coordinates, Zeta one-six dash seven-three Echo Prime."

"But ma'am," the ensign said, looking up from his console to meet her hardened gaze. "That takes us dangerously close to the Rift."

"I know," she said, locking her hands behind her back and turning back to the view portal. "You have your orders."

"Yes, ma'am." The ensign swiveled back around in his seat and typed in the asked for coordinates.

The computer chimed with acquiescence; the stars began to stretch all around them ever so gradually, and, then, with a snap and a flash of light, the *Verlag* entered faster than light travel.

29

Old Lady Jegra fetched her Dygra crystal from under her bed while the younger Jegra finished dressing. She strapped on her trademark metal bikini and armor and then, placing a hand on her hip, tilted her head and asked, "Are you certain that this will work?"

When the silver haired version of herself stood back up, she held two red crystals in her hands—one new and lustrous, the other old with numerous cracks running through it like withered veins. "If it doesn't, then we might as well throw in the towel, because this is our last chance to set things right," she replied in a grim tone.

"Well, that's depressing."

Raven poked her head into the room. "I've found a clearing where we can land the ship. Angellyk, Ladgara, and Kregor are getting the antenna prepped to try to channel some of that electrical storm. And Skuld is waiting for the both of you in the infirmary."

"Nothing like open-heart surgery during a lightning storm," Jegra said, smiling at her older self.

"I survived it the first time. So will you."

Jegra placed a hand on her doppelgänger's shoulder and smiled warmly. "Thanks," she said.

"For what?"

"For being kind. For continuing to be kind after all these years."

The platinum-haired Jegra smiled and placed her hand over that of her younger self.

Raven accompanied them down to the infirmary and the Jegras stood on either side of her. "Skuld, I want you to take the best care of these two you can. You hear me?"

"I hear you, Captain. And don't worry, it's a procedure I did many times when I was yet a practicing physician back on my homeworld. Luckily, my medical license doesn't lapse for another six revolutions, so we're all good to go here."

Raven let out a sigh and said, "I'll be right here by your side the whole time." Before Jegra could answer, Raven turned to her and placed both hands over the sides of her face and drawing her in, kissed her on the mouth.

Jegra, wide-eyed with surprise, graciously accepted it and even leaned into it, kissing Raven back.

After a moment of it going on for a little too long, the sound of a throat clearing brought Raven's attention to the fact that she was kissing the wrong Jegra.

"I'm over here, sweetheart," the older Jegra said, an amused smile causing the corners of her mouth to subtly curl upward, a hint of artfulness in her grin.

Breaking the lip-lock with the Jegra of her time period, Raven stared in horror at her, uncertain as to how she'd react to her abrupt and wholly intimate kiss.

"I'm so, so sorry," Raven mumbled, shaking her hands as they began to tremble with nervousness.

"No," Jegra replied, taking her hands in hers and steadying her. "It was good. Better than good. I actually didn't mind it." She then drew Raven in and gave her a quick peck on her lips to show there was no hard feelings and that she'd gladly kiss her anytime.

Raven chuckled nervously and then turned to the older Jegra, who couldn't stop giggling. Losing her cool, Raven hit her in the arm. Hard.

"Ow!" Jegra yelped.

"It's all your fault!"

"It is?"

"Yes! You're the one that got me into this mess in the first place by making me fall in love with you."

Old Lady Jegra laughed again. "I can't help it if you've been so blinded by love that you just go around kissing any woman you stumble across who resembles me!"

"Oh, shut up you," she said and hit her in the shoulder again. Jegra laughed, shot her younger self a wink, and then drew Raven in and French kissed her deep and sultry.

Young Jegra raised an eyebrow but didn't say anything of it. It was news to her that Raven was in love with her—at least the older version of her. But she didn't mind the idea of it. In fact, she'd consider herself lucky to win the heart of a woman as smart, beautiful, and noble as Raven.

"So, you two are…?"

"Yes," Raven replied guiltily.

"And you both…?"

"Yes," her older self replied, not letting her finish that sentence, knowing that the thought behind it was just as lewd as the one she was having.

"I see," Jegra said in an understanding tone.

"Ladies," Skuld interjected, "I hate to interrupt, but we're ready to begin now."

Both Jegras lay down upon a medical table on either side of Skuld. Along with the assistant surgeon, a robotic arm capable of performing advanced surgeries and other medical operations, he explained to them the details of the procedure.

"I'll be creating a small incision on your sternums so I can open up your chests. Once the Dygra crystals are charged, I will surgically implant them inside of you. If they take, we'll know so immediately, due to the nature of your sped-up healing factors. I will then close you both back up and stitch you back together using the laser suture. The combined surgeries should take roughly ten hours to complete."

"Sounds like a walk in the park," Jegra said.

Her older self nodded along, as she was the only one who understood the idiom.

"I don't know about that," Skuld replied, "but as your physician, I do have to inform you that I will have to put you both under for the duration of the procedure."

Jegra nodded as she lay down on the table.

Older Jegra reached up and took Raven's hand. "Whatever happens, just know that these past three years have been the happiest years of my life."

Raven, gulping back her emotions, said, "Stop it. You're going to make me cry."

Young Jegra smiled as she watched them kiss one more time and then, lying across from one another, they shared a pleasant smile.

"Good luck," Jegra told herself.

"You too."

Skuld came over to them and placed a neural inhibitor on either side of their temples. Once the electronic patch was secured, he turned it on and both Jegras fell into a deep, anesthetized sleep.

Raven nodded at him to begin, and he acknowledged her subtle order with a slight nod in return.

The allied fleet flashed into view just ahead of The Rift. Its purple and black swirls spiraled down to a central region that was dense, like a black hole, yet not a black hole.

The strange anomaly wasn't fully understood, but everyone knew that ships which entered it never returned again. As such, warning buoys were set up all around it for two hundred million kilometers in every direction to alert passing ships to alter their flight plans and avoid the anomaly at all costs.

Where wayward ships vanished to after passing through, however, was anyone's guess. By using gravitational lensing, it was the general working theory that the rift contained some sort of fulcrum planet that helped stabilize a wormhole which led through to a different pocket universe.

It was believed by many that was where the CSEs were coming from and, in all likelihood, where H'aaztre had originated from. It would also explain why no ships had ever successfully returned.

The moment they made it onto the other side, it was all but given that the CSEs would attack them and drain their power. This meant that what lay on the other side of The Rift was, effectively, a ship graveyard filled with the unlucky corpses of those who had passed through to the other side.

Of the Allied fleet, the total remaining ships only tallied one hundred and forty. It was still a sizable fleet, but a far cry from the three-thousand they'd started with.

Vice Admiral Callestra Van Morgan marched onto the command deck and barked, "Open a fleet-wide comm link."

The comm's officer nodded and soon she was being broadcast to every remaining ship in the fleet.

"This is Vice Admiral Callestra Van Morgan of the *Verlag* and head of what's left of the Allied fleet. I'm ordering every ship to fire five of your highest yield Python missiles into the breach. We need to take out that planet and collapse the wormhole."

"All ships responding in the affirmative," the comms officer replied.

"Good," Callestra said, turning to the view portal as she peered out at the golden tear in space. "On my mark…fire."

Seven-hundred Python missiles screamed toward the fissure in space. Soon, the planet would be pulverized by the force of a myriad of simultaneous neutron blasts and, if all went to plan, the planet would be destroyed and the tear in space would collapse in on itself.

She waited with bated breath as the missiles disappeared into the glowing fissure. When nothing happened, she turned to ask for a status update. But as she turned her back to the fissure, a bright flash lit up the bridge, forcing the crew to divert their gazes and cover their eyes. She spun back around to see the fissure slowly shrinking away.

"Ma'am, we have a problem. The collapse has sent out a gravitational shockwave strong enough to destroy the entire fleet."

"Issue an emergency fleet-wide jump on my command," she said. But before she could give the order, a dozen space squids, along with a behemoth sized one jumped into the system directly behind the fleet, preventing their rapid escape.

"Ma'am…the shockwave will hit us in T-minus 3 minutes and 39 seconds."

"Take the *Verlag* into the path of that shockwave. Maybe we can absorb the brunt of it and spare the rest of the fleet."

The officer hesitated and she shot him a stern look.

"What is it, Lieutenant? Were my orders not clear?"

"It's just that…isn't the emperor aboard?"

Callestra turned to the view portal and locked her hands behind her back. "He is," she answered coldly. "But this is my ship and you have your orders."

"Yes, ma'am," the officer said reluctantly. And he typed in the coordinates.

The *Verlag* slowly broke away from the fleet and placed itself between them and the incoming shockwave. It would most likely be destroyed, but it was the only remaining ship besides the *Chiron* that had enough shield output to deflect a portion of the shockwave.

A holovid call came through and Callestra looked up to find the 3D image of Grendok staring back at her, stroking his hoary beard and gazing at her inquisitively with his blue slatted eyes.

"Vice Admiral," he said in a worried tone, "that shockwave will tear your ship apart. You need to get out of there!"

"Better to sacrifice the one and save the many," she said.

"Spoken like a true Gallifornian."

She smiled. "Maybe. But the *Chiron* is now the flagship of the fleet. Lead them well," she said. "Lead them to victory."

"You have my word," Grendok said. And, in an unexpected gesture, he gave her the Dagon salute.

She smiled and saluted him back. Once bitter enemies were now brother and sister in arms.

Static interference caused the holographic image of Grendok to waver and distort and, he took a step back just as the holovid call cut out.

Callestra clasped her hands behind her back and turned once more to look out at the hot green and purple energy wave rippling through space that marked her inevitable fate.

"*No, no, no!*" Gyllek grumbled. "The yellow cable goes there. The blue one goes over there. Don't touch the red one! Red is bad."

Humid winds whipped her short purple hair about as they all stood on top of the *Skywend's* hull, preparing the lightning rod. They were going to try and catch some lightning in a bottle, or, in this case, Dygra energy to charge the crystals.

"Calm down," Angellyk said. "I've got it under control, she added casually.

She brushed a fluttering strand of forest green hair out of her eyes to help her see, and when she plugged in the cable, it sparked and hissed and spat smoke.

She pulled it instantly back out; an embarrassed look came over her as she looked up, holding the fried cord in her singed hands. "Oopsies! Wrong socket."

Gyllek rolled her eyes and then turned to Kregor, who was propping up the antenna array like a pair of old-fashioned televid rabbit ears.

At the same time, Ladgara bolted down the clamps using the electric drill. The drill torqued against the nuts and bolts and ground to a stop.

"That should do it," Ladgara said, raising the drill into the air like a blaster and throwing her other hand up on her waist.

"Good," Kregor said, stepping away from the lightning conducting rod. "Because I don't want to get fried up here."

"All finished here, too," Angellyk added, finally managing to find the proper socket to plug into.

They all looked up at the raging pink-and-neon-blue electrical storm flashing above them and then, one by one, slipped back down inside the hatch of the ship.

Kregor, the last to head down, looked up at the raging storm one last time. The giant crystals in the distance hummed, and for a brief moment, he could almost hear their song.

While Jegra was under, she dreamed of being back on Earth. It was like one of those dreams within a dream. She was just a little girl, probably no more than ten, and found herself back on her family's farm in Nebraska.

It was near the end of summer, the weather was warm, and she could hear crickets chirping in the distance. As things came into focus, like an old memory crystalizing in her mind's eye, she found herself standing in the hallway of her childhood home, by the stairwell.

Pictures adorned the walls. Most of them were of her and her parents doing things about the farm. A flower vase sat on the antique credenza at the foot of the stairs near the entrance.

Voices talking in soft tones, the laugh of her mother, her dad's dry humor, slowly became audible. They were talking in the kitchen—and that's when it came to her—she remembered this day. It was the day she chased after her dog, Ishmael, who'd run out into the soybean crops. When he'd disappeared, she'd thought she'd lost him for good and sat down and cried.

She cried for about half an hour before Ishmael found her, licked her face, and led her back to the house. By the time she'd reached home, it was supper time and her mom had baked a rhubarb and strawberry pie.

Before entering the screen door of her porch, she turned to look out at the crops one last time. The setting sun cast a golden light across the dried yellow plantation. She thought it strange that the plants looked as though they'd withered and were halfway toward being dead.

That's when she noticed something peculiar. In the distance, she saw a figure standing in the field. A strange young man she'd never seen before.

Curious as to who he was, she called out to her parents, "I'm going outside to play."

"Alright honey," her mother called back from the kitchen. "Stay safe!"

"Jesse," her father's voice called out to her. She spun around and saw him leaning in the archway of the kitchen.

"Yeah, dad?"

"Why don't you take Ishmael with you, just to be safe."

"I will, dad." He smiled at her and she smiled at him. She'd forgotten how much she'd missed her father. She loved him with all her heart and always would.

Once outside, she paused on the porch and let the old green screen door slam shut behind her. She called out for Ishmael, but the Australian shepherd was nowhere to be found.

Jessica shrugged her ten-year-old shoulders and headed out into the field to talk to the strange boy. *Maybe he's seen Ishmael,* she thought.

The closer she got, the stranger he seemed to her. His skin was a beautiful shade of blue, he had long pointy ears, like those of an elf from the fantasy stories she loved to read, and he wore what seemed to be a tunic, something like the one ancient Japanese samurai wore.

"Hello there," she called out. "Are you lost?"

The boy glanced over his shoulder at her and stopped her with his gaze. He had bright golden eyes that almost seemed to glow. "Lost?" he asked. "No, I've been looking all over for you."

"Looking for me?" Jessica repeated with a laugh.

"I've come from…let's say I've just come an impossibly long distance to meet with you, young Jegra."

She puzzled over his words, as they held no particular meaning to her. She turned to see what he was staring at. In the distance, Ishmael chased some magpies that were trying to steal some grain.

"Are you a space alien?" Jessica asked.

"What if I am?" the young man asked. "Would you be afraid?"

"No," she said with a smile.

"And why not?"

"You're blue, like a Smurf," she explained.

"I'm sorry," he said, looking down at her, "but I don't know what that is."

"Never mind," Jessica said, waving her hand. "It's not important."

"May I ask you something, Jegra?"

"Jegra?" she asked. "You keep calling me that. But my name is Jessica. All my friends call me Jesse."

"Ah, yes. My apologies, young Jessica."

She smiled at him. "Sure. You can ask me anything."

"What is it that you fear?"

"Fear?" she echoed, still uncertain as to what he was getting at. "Do you mean, what am I afraid of?"

"Yes. What are you afraid of?"

She considered it for a moment, holding her chin as she thought. After another moment, she shrugged. "I don't know. I guess I'm afraid of people not being kind to one another."

"That's a very mature thought for one so young," the strange man said. She smiled at him, accepting the compliment.

"What are you scared of, Mr.?" she asked.

He raised an eyebrow and thought about it for a moment. "I fear that I won't be able to accomplish my dream."

"And what's your dream?"

He turned to her, his eyes filling with black ink, and his voice grew cruel and cold. "I want to watch this world and everyone and everything on it burn."

Fear seized her as he began laughing callously—as if this morbid dream of his delighted him. Realizing this blue man was some kind of monster, she screamed and turned back to her house.

Almost as soon as she'd begun to run, however, she heard Ishmael's whimper. This drew her attention back to the strange elfin man who clutched her dog in his blue hands.

There was a terrible crunch, the sound of bones snapping, and the man let Ishmael slip from his hands. Her puppy collapsed at his feet, her broken body unmoving.

A wave of anger like she'd never known surged through her veins, and picking up a rock from the field, she threw it at the young man, striking his forehead.

The young man staggered back, and, stunned by her attack, reached up and touched his bloodied forehead.

He turned to her and smiled. "Even at such a young age, your defiance knows no bounds. I see now why you make such a formidable adversary to me."

"Go away!" Jessica screamed. She bent down and picked up another rock and threw it at him. She missed her mark, but the boy looked at her as though he were utterly appalled.

A trickle of blood ran down his temple. Reaching up, he touched it then examined his glossy fingers. "You struck me."

"You killed my dog!" she fired back.

They stared at one another, both eyes raging with unbridled hate. But although H'aaztre's hate was eons old, hers was only blossoming.

Still, Jessica knew that this boy—whoever he was—was pure evil. She could feel it in her bones.

"The *Verlag's* shields are down to seven percent!" the chief engineer shouted over the rattle of the ship's bulkheads.

The energy wave had collided with them and the *Verlag* was getting jostled about like a leaf being carried down rapids. The stress on the ship was simply too much, and its structural integrity wouldn't hold for much longer.

"I don't care where you get the power, Chief, but I want those shields to hold."

He nodded and turned back to his station. "I'll do my best, ma'am."

Just then Emperor Dakroth stumbled onto the bridge. The entire ship bobbed and swayed beneath his feet and he felt disoriented.

"What's going on?" he asked.

"We're getting slapped by the shockwave we set off when she collapsed the the Rift. I don't know if the ship will survive this." She turned to him and was surprised to find him smiling at her.

"It seems Jegra's compassion has rubbed off on you," he teased her.

She raised her middle finger and flipped him off.

Dakroth just laughed and then turned to the view portal. Raising both hands, he extended a massive energy shield that protected not only the ship, but the entire fleet.

The shockwave split against his energy barrier, breaking as an ocean wave breaks against the rocky shore.

A light sweat broke out on his brow, but he managed to hold the shockwave at bay. Once the wave had deflected onto another course, he dropped to one knee, panting.

"Will wonders never cease," Callestra said, extending her hand for him to take. She helped him back onto his feet and he smiled at her.

She was about to speak again when her navigations officer interrupted their moment. "Ma'am, the large squid is moving along an intercept course right toward us. Your orders?"

She looked at Dakroth, who raised his eyebrows, deferring to her judgment.

"If we go critical, we can detonate the engine core and take that thing down with us." Turning back to Dakroth, she held his gaze as she opened up a ship-wide communication. "All hands, this is the vice admiral. Prepare to abandon ship. This is not a drill, we are abandoning ship."

30

Deunan's bulky freighter and Gamagor's sleek and stylish space yacht simultaneously jumped into orbit around the Seyfferian planet, Correl, only to be immediately swarmed by planetary security attack drones. The drones had angular, ablative armor and highly aggressive, sharply cut edges that demonstrated their capabilities were just as intimidating as their looks.

<<You have entered restricted space>> an automated recording informed them. The drones scanned the ship, getting the freighter's serial numbers, then came back with another preprogrammed response. <<What is your cargo and destination?>>

Along with rapid-fire, high-yield plasma canons, they were also equipped with three-prong pincers, which gave them their trademark stag beetle look. They would latch onto a hull and bore their way inside a vessel using their plasma cutters—very much like a robotic tick.

Nicknamed "Penetrators," once inside, the swarm would burrow deep and work closely together to dismantle the ship's weapons, engines and hull, piece by piece. Taking out all the critical systems first, they'd cripple the vessel, then several of the drones, worming their way through the insides of the enemy vessel, would self-destruct in a collective daisy-chain of explosions powerful enough to obliterate virtually anything they came across.

Penetrator drones could render even the biggest destroyers and battlecruisers into nothing more than a gleaming cloud of scrap metal drifting in the black expanse.

This meant you needed to be quick with the orbital defense grid access codes, otherwise a swarm of very angry drones would descend upon you like a plague of demon possessed locusts and devour you from the inside out.

Luckily, Deunan had called in some favors and managed to acquire the up-to-date codes for a two-ship pick-up of several crates of holovid data-cubes, which she was delivering to Correl.

She quickly typed in the security code and waited to be granted shipping access. Even though she trusted her data, there was still a fraction of a chance they'd already cycled through to new codes. Waiting on the edge of her seat, Deunan let out a big sigh of relief when the drones pulled away, giving them the go-ahead to proceed.

<<Access granted. Please follow the designated shipping lane coordinates. Enjoy your stay in the Seyfferian Republic.>>

"Home sweet home," Deunan said, speaking mainly to herself, seeing as Lycia had her face buried in a VHD headset and was watching something on the Needle stream.

The Needle stream condensed high amounts of data into quantum bits using spacetime crystal relays populated throughout all of the Commonwealth by Von Neumann nanite probes. The unique quantum entanglement of the crystals conveyed data by the rate and angle of their spins, and allowed for instant data transfer from one end of the galaxy to another in a matter of seconds.

It was the greatest communications achievement of all time, as far as Deunan was concerned. It was the first truly unifying event that had linked all species and worlds together.

Lycia took off the VHD headset she was wearing and let out a disgusted groan. Deunan looked over at her as the drones outside the view portal formed an opening for the two ships.

"It was so realistic. I literally saw the droplets of blood flying past me in real-time."

"And who is it that's so worthy of holding your interest?"

"Danica Valencia," Lycia replied with a wry smile. Deunan raised an eyebrow. Lycia could see by the look on her face that she'd been unaware of the recent development. "Apparently she's back in the gladiatorial fights. And she was doing quite well, too, until Raven Nightguard swooped in and snatched her back into space."

"Does Jegra know about any of this?"

Lycia shrugged. "Beats me."

Deunan frowned at the girl. Then, thrusting her chin at the headset, added, "Why don't you be a good girl and give your mother a call? See if she's savvy, okay?"

Lycia rolled her eyes and sighed in annoyance. "I don't ever know what I'd talk with her about. She's just so...*alien.*"

"And you're half alien. What's the problem?"

Lycia folded her arms over her chest in frustration. "Don't remind me." After a long pause, she looked over at Deunan and decided to change the subject to something a little more meaningful. "So, how are things going with you and Gam?"

"You mean, since you slept with her?"

Lycia's eyes widened as Deunan shot her an exacting look. The kind of look that said, "I caught you red-handed."

Rubbing the side of her arm nervously, she replied, "You know about that?"

"I've known Gam far longer than you have. We talk."

"Are you mad?"

Deunan shook her head. "Not really. Gam's a big girl. She can sleep with whomever she wants. And, besides, it wasn't like we had committed to anything. What happened between us just sort of happened."

"Look, D," Lycia said, swiveling in her chair and turning toward her, "I overstepped."

"You think?" Deunan couldn't help but laugh. She liked Lycia, lots, actually. But she was audacious as they came.

And although Lycia might be having sex left and right, when it came to intimate relationships, it was clear that she was still just a virgin, in that respect.

"I'm sorry. I guess...I'm just new to all this relationship stuff. It's not always...you know..."

"Easy?"

"Yeah." Lycia leaned forward in her seat and steepled her hands in front of her face as she looked at Deunan. "Look, D, all I know is, as long as you two care about each other, that's what counts. I mean, wouldn't it at least be worth giving it another shot with Gam? She really likes you. I can tell."

"I suppose you're right," Deunan answered. "She has it bad for me. It's just…I'm the one with the issues, not her."

"So, do you know what you're going to do?"

Deunan shook her head, as if to say, *not really.* "I guess I'll try it for a while. I mean, we do get along. And there's a definite connection there. Besides, maybe it's time I dated someone who likes me for me, instead of settling for all the wrong types of guys."

"All the assholes, you mean?"

Deunan laughed. "Yeah. All the assholes."

The elevation alarm alerted them that they were now entering traffic-controlled airspace and Deunan checked her monitors. "Once we set down," she informed Lycia, filling her in on the details, "I'll file the necessary permits. You take Allie and X-5 and try to locate the cloning facility that created you."

"And how will I do that exactly?"

"You can trace your barcode."

"My what?"

"It's more of a kind of holographic watermark in the bottom right of your eye. Just scan it and it should trace back to the very facility which produced you."

Lycia turned on the holovid mirror and was pulling her eyelid down, exposing the white of her eyeball, and looking for the watermark. She zoomed in sixty-percent and then saw it. The computer scanned the mark and a number came onto the holographic display hovering before her.

"0009-1X-003," she read aloud to herself.

Deunan input the number into the Seyfferian databank and ran a search. Almost immediately, a red bar came up on the screen and flashed "Restricted Access."

"I thought as much," Deunan said, gently shaking her head with disappointment. "It seems that Dakroth didn't want to risk anyone finding out about you and covered his tracks."

"Maybe we can hack into the mainframe," Lycia said, stretching her fingers and cracking her knuckles before attacking the keyboard with a flurry of keystrokes.

Deunan's hand flew up and stopped her before she'd even cleared the first firewall. She shook her head in the negative, warning her against it, and gently lowered Lycia's hand again.

"Even a wizard level hacker wouldn't make it through the third-tier encryption of that firewall. And Seyfferian data encryption is literally impossible to break into anyway. And even if by some miracle you do, there are a million different booby-traps set at every conceivable back door which will trace back to you before you can even pull the plug."

"So, how does anyone get into the system?" Lycia asked.

"You need a key," Deunan said, nodding at Lycia's wrist.

"That's right!" Lycia said, remembering the digital skeleton key that the locksmith had implanted under her skin.

She raised her wrist to the hologram and it scanned her. The red bar flickered and, just like that, changed to green. Instead of saying: "Restricted Access" it now read: "Welcome Administrator."

"Administrator?" Lycia said, raising an eyebrow. "That's swanky."

"Swanky?" Deunan repeated, shooting the girl a confused look. She wasn't familiar with that term.

"It's an Earth word. Means super impressive."

"Ah," Deunan replied in a revelatory exhale of breath.

The port city of Chi'don in the southwestern hemisphere of Correl came into view, and Deunan brought the ship down on a landing pad. Dialing in Gamagor's number, she said, "Gam, this is Deunan. Have your people set down in the bay and begin delivering the cargo. While they're busy with that, meet us at these coordinates."

She keyed in the coordinates to the cloning facility, which Lycia was studying on the holovid screen. She logged off and swiveled in her seat and looked at her.

"Worried?"

"A little," replied the girl.

"Don't be. You've come this far."

"I know. I guess I'm just freaking out."

A loud explosion off their bow shook the entire ship. The fiery plume that billowed up and kissed their glass caught their attention. When the smoke finally cleared, they spotted Xarthon standing across the docking platform, loading a second rocket into his anti-aircraft rocket launcher.

"That bloody idiot better not damage my baby," Deunan said, springing to her feet. "Or there'll be Helios to pay."

"I don't think he cares about the ship, D," Lycia said. "I think he may have actually lost it."

They both stood over the console and peered out the windshield at the wild-eyed man. He laughed hysterically as he locked the new rocket into place and swung the launcher up onto his shoulder.

"You think you can run from me?" he shouted up at them. "I'll track you to the ends of the galaxy! Do you think you can hide from me? Think again! Wherever you go, I'll be waiting for you."

Sirens blared and red and blue light washed across Xarthon's face. A spotlight lit him up and a voice over a megaphone said, <<Lower the weapon. You are in violation of Seyfferian safety and trade laws. Surrender yourself and prepare for processing.>>

"I am a Space Marshall and this ship belongs to a couple of fugitives I've been tracking," he shouted back up at the drone, which was scanning him.

<<Negative. Your clearance has been revoked.>>

"What? That's impossible."

<<Negative. You have exceeded the time limit to recall the fugitives.>>

When it became obvious to Xarthon that he wasn't getting anywhere with the drone, he turned the rocket launcher onto it instead and fired.

A bullseye. The drone exploded in midair, spinning out of control, until, finally, it crashed to the ground in a small flaming heap.

"Mind your own damn business," he growled. "This bounty is mine!" Then, turning back to his prize catch, he snarled, "As for you two—"

CRACK!

Xarthon dropped like a sack of bricks, landing face-first in the pavement between two metal feet. Deunan and Lycia leaned forward, shocked by what they saw.

"My duty is to protect the Lycia at all costs," X-5 stated as he stood over the unconscious bail bondsman.

Lycia and Deunan turned toward one another, stunned looks on their faces. All Deunan could think to reply to such a twist of events was, "Swanky."

Lycia smiled broadly, and covered her mouth to prevent herself from breaking into a fit of laughter.

A few minutes later, Lycia lounged against one of the two giant hydraulic cylinders of the loading ramp, a smirk plastered across her face as she watched Deunan handcuff Xarthon.

When another couple of police drones showed up, she straightened up and slipped back into the steam and shadows of the ship, keeping just out of sight.

<<Citizen,>> the drone beckoned, shining its spotlight on Deunan, <<please wait here until security arrives to assist you with processing your Citizen's Arrest. The people of Correl thank you for your assistance.>>

"My pleasure," Deunan said, a wry smile forming on her face. She dusted off her hands and then looked over her shoulder at the girl lurking in the shadow of the ship. Shooting her a pleased grin, she shrugged, as if to say, *well, that happened.*

Confident the drones weren't for her, Lycia reemerged from behind the hydraulics and gave Deunan a big thumbs up.

31

Luminous golden tentacles wrapped in a thick, translucent skin slowly constricted around the *Verlag*. Initially only three then more tentacles slowly slithered up the side of the vessel and gradually coiled themselves around it. Soon, the Verlag was completely entwined, unable to break free.

With a *phssst* of maneuvering thrusters, multiple escape pods launched from the ship. After the first volley, more followed. It only took twelve kekals to fully abandon ship.

"I'm ordering you to go!" Callestra growled. Dakroth merely folded his arms across his chest and defied her orders.

"My place is by your side," he said. "Forever and always. Remember?"

"Now is not the time to be chivalrous," she said. Pointing a finger at the viewscreen, she added, "That thing has us in its clutches and I don't know how much longer the *Verlag's* structural integrity will hold."

"It will hold long enough for one last kiss," he said, drawing her into him.

She pounded her fists against his chest in protest, but unable to resist his strength, she melted into his arms and let his revitalizing warmth seep into her with a kiss that made all their previous kisses mundane by comparison.

She literally had to gasp for air the moment he relinquished her, and, taking a step back, she held his hands in hers and gazed dreamily into his ruby red eyes.

"I guess the wedding is postponed," she said.

"We don't need to be married to be in love," Dakroth relayed.

She nodded. "I know, I just meant—"

Metal cried out in agony as the bulkheads bent from the crushing pressure of the tentacles that had ensnared them. The lights flickered sporadically as the ship's energy slowly drained. Shortly, they'd lose life support, and the ship would grow cold. Once the power went out, the structural energy buttressing would fail and the ship would crumple in like a tin can.

Then, in an ironic twist, as they sat on the verge of freezing to death, in a blink of the eye, they'd be enveloped in flame as the ship's core went critical and detonated.

"Your Excellency," she said, her face growing stern. "This is not a noble death for a man like you. An emperor deserves a more glorious end than to be snuffed out like a common candle."

"Don't talk nonsense," he said reproachfully. "There is nothing in this galaxy nobler than standing by your lover's side in the face of overwhelming odds. If we die this day, then I am proud that I can share my last breath by your side."

Callestra began to tear up and immediately brushed a rogue tear away. "You fool."

"I think you meant to say, I love you."

She smiled and leapt into his arms. Once again, they found their lips come crashing together like the ocean tide and the shore—always coming back for more.

The ship's hull whined in protest, refusing to buckle, when, unexpectedly, a loud explosion erupted on the command deck. Dakroth and Callestra dove to the side, evading the brunt of the blast.

Dakroth hit the ground first and caught Callestra in his arms. Their eyes locked briefly, but their moment was ruined by a spray of sparks and several consoles exploding all around them.

Dakroth had pushed himself onto his feet and began to help Callestra up, when a harsh and completely unexpected jolt knocked them back off their feet and onto the floor again.

On the second try, however, they both managed to steady themselves. Not a kekal had passed when the bulkheads buckled, bending inward like giant fingers made of metal, slowly clutching them tightly, and the ship's paneling began to rend and sheer itself apart.

They looked at each other for what they knew would be the last time when, to their astonishment, golden light came down and began to swirl all about them.

When they rematerialized again, they looked around to find Raven, Angellyk, and Ladgara staring back at them. That's when it dawned on them;

they'd been snatched from death's grip at the last possible second and brought aboard the *Skywend*.

"Your timing couldn't have been better," Dakroth said in a surprisingly grateful tone.

Callestra strode up to Raven, who merely looked at her with an uncertain expression. "Of course, it would be *you*," she said, her voice icy with disdain.

"You're welcome," Raven laughed. Then, spinning on her heels, she whipped her hair around so that the ends brushed Callestra's face, forcing her to flinch and wrinkle her nose.

"Now, if you'll both accompany me, there's something I need to show you."

"Ishmael!" Jessica cried, falling to her knees before the bloody remains of what was left of her dog. Hot tears streamed down her cheeks as she cried for the loss of her beloved pet.

"It was just a lowly beast. Its life, in the grander scheme of things, meant very little."

"No," she cried, stroking the dead animal's fur. "You're wrong! He was my friend. He was family."

"There's that word again," H'aaztre said, a tinge of disgust on his voice. "*Family.*"

Jessica looked up at him, her eyes red from crying. "Don't you have a family? A mother, a father, a place you call home?"

He stared at her with those ominous black eyes. It dawned on him that nobody had ever asked him that before. And after a long pause, he finally replied to her unconventional question. "Honestly, I can't remember."

"You don't remember if you have a family?" she asked, a touch of sarcasm in her voice.

"I can't remember where I come from," the young man answered. "That's the truth of it." They stared at one another for a few more seconds and then he turned to leave.

"Where are you going?" Jessica asked.

He paused and looked back at her. "I came here to see what drove that indomitable spirit of yours. Now I see; you were born with it. You are, for the lack of a better phrase, a force of nature, young Jegra."

"Jessica," she corrected him, again.

He smiled at her one last time and turned to walk away.

"What's your name?" she called out to him before he was out of earshot. It had taken her that long just to get up enough nerve to ask him.

He paused again as though he were debating whether to tell her, and, then, without turning around, he decided it best to keep it to himself and continued on his way.

She watched as he disappeared into a bright flash of golden light. The light was so bright it forced her to cover her eyes. When she looked again, he had vanished.

After he was gone, she took off her jacket and wrapped it around Ishmael's body. Then, scooping him up in her little arms, she turned back toward the farmhouse, which stood a kilometer in the distance.

Jessica let out a long, yet determined sigh and, taking a deep breath, began to carry her dog, who was nearly the same size as she, all the way back home.

"I'm sorry this happened to you," she whispered. "I'm sorry I couldn't save you."

Several neon pink and blue bolts struck the pinnacle of the lightning rod sticking out of the *Skywend*. The energy surged down the pole and into the collector units on the ship.

"Is it working?" Angellyk asked, biting her nails nervously.

Ladgara, who stood next to her, replied, "I don't know," and then slapped Angellyk's hands down, forcing her to stop her incessant nail biting.

No sooner had Angellyk shot her a nasty look than Emperor Dakroth and Vice Admiral Callestra Van Morgan strode up to the observation window.

"Oh, great," Callestra said in a sarcastic tone. She threw her hands onto her hips as she gazed at the two women lying on the operating table on the other side of the glass. "Now there's two of them."

"Indeed, there is," Dakroth said, a lecherous grin spreading across his face.

He glanced over to find Callestra staring at him with a scornful look that warned him to not even think about it. He merely shrugged and went back to peering lasciviously at the two Jegras on the operating table.

At the same time, Gyllek clung to Kregor, hugging him fiercely as they watched through the glass wall as Skuld operated on both women, implanting Dygra crystals into their chests.

The only other one allowed in the room was the captain, and she wore a light blue medical mask and assisted Skuld as best she was able.

"Laser suture," he said, extending his hand.

She fetched it from the tray and delicately placed it into the open palm of his hand.

Very carefully, he reached up and threaded his arm through the open loops on the robotic arm, slipping into it as though it were a glove. The robotic arm would assist his movements, allowing him to be much more precise.

Skuld, with his robotic appendage, bent over young Jegra and sealed up her chest. Once her sternum was welded shut, he continued on with the same technique, sewing up Old Lady Jegra as well.

Once he'd finished closing them up, he took his hand out of the surgical appendage, and the robotic arm, now running on its own programming, came down and used a healing-wand to help mend the Jegras' flesh.

A job well done, he looked up to meet the captain's gaze. "All things considered, I think that went rather well."

"Excellent news," Raven replied. "How long till they're back on their feet?"

"Normally, I'd say about six days at the earliest. But given her healing factor, it could be as soon as three hours. We really won't know until either patient wakes up."

Raven nodded, then, pulling down her mask, she said, "Keep me posted on their recovery."

Looking down at the Jegra she adored, she reached out and touched Old Lady Jegra's arm. A sudden flood of emotion welled up inside of her and began to rise to the surface. She quickly turned and exited the room so as not to let anyone see her grow overly emotional.

Skuld turned to the window full of familiar faces and gave everyone a thumbs up. They all let out a collective sigh of relief and then took turns hugging one another.

Ladgara even threw her arms around Dakroth's neck and slipped her tongue down his throat. As he wrapped his arms around her, squeezing her ass, Callestra was already prying his hands off her. Once she'd untethered them, she shoved Ladgara off to the side and stepped in between her and Dakroth.

"What about all the old times we shared?" she said.

Callestra folded her arms. "That was before we were engaged. And, no offense, but I'm not going to allow Dakroth to slum it with a disease ridden space-whore like yourself."

Ladgara poked a lavender finger into Callestra's blue breast and growled, "You weren't complaining when I was eating out your—"

"Heh-hem…" A throat cleared drew their attention; the two of them looked over to find Kregor. He stood gazing at them sternly, arms folded across his chest.

As first officer of the *Skywend*, he had some clout, so both women took notice when he nodded down at the fourteen-year-old girl standing by his side. "Ladies, there are children aboard."

Ladgara just rolled her eyes and stalked off to the side of the room to sulk. Callestra turned back to her man and slipped her arm around his waist, as though she were claiming him all for herself.

"*Riiight,*" Angellyk said, scanning everyone's faces. "And with that out of the way, what I think is, we should all celebrate."

"Celebrate?" Gyllek's ears perked up and her eyes grew large with excitement. "What kind of celebration?"

"A dinner party," Angellyk replied.

"Can we have pizza?"

"As much as you can eat, child!" Angellyk rubbed the girl's head between her feline ears and then turned towards the kitchen to begin preparing their pizza feast.

"What's peet-zah?" Callestra asked, turning toward Dakroth for any clues as to what this strange sounding cuisine might be. He merely shrugged as if to say, *beats me.*

"It's a native Earth food that Jegra loves," Gyllek informed her. "It's basically a bread-crust covered in tomatoes and six kinds of cheese."

Callestra made a sour face. As most Dagon's were entirely lactose intolerant, the idea of a dough disc slathered in oily cheese was less than enticing to her. "That sounds absolutely repulsive."

"It actually tastes quite glorious," Ladgara shared.

Callestra shot her a cold glance that said: *nobody asked you.* "Not all of us have tainted and corrupted ourselves with impure technology just to give us immunity to the effects of animal juice, you fat cow-suckling cheese-lover."

Ladgara smacked her teeth in annoyance. "Then eat a salad, bitch!" With that she stormed out of the room to help prepare the evening's festivities. Because, although she could be rough around the edges, Ladgara could never say no to a good old-fashioned party.

Dakroth put his hand on Callestra's shoulder and said, "Relax, my luv. These people are not our enemy."

Callestra bowed her head and tried to calm herself. "I'm sorry, my lord, it's just that...having lost the fleet for a second time in my career, I'm feeling as though I cannot win at anything. That I'm not good enough. I'm not worthy to hold the rank of Vice Admiral, let alone be betrothed to you."

He gently pinched her chin and guided her face toward his and waited for her eyes to fix themselves on his own. "Nonsense. If you weren't good enough for me, how could I ever have fallen so madly in love with you?"

She stared into his ruby red eyes and then sighed. "Apologies, my lord. I won't let it happen again."

Back on the bridge, Raven leaned back in her seat and scanned the monitors. The cloak was working and no CSEs had followed them. As she gazed out, a million things raced through her head. Her priority right now, though, was to get both Jegra and the emperor safely home. Her hands expertly danced across the controls as she set course back to Dagon Prime.

She knew that H'aaztre would be pooling every last soldier and remaining ship he had to mount one last attack on her homeworld, for, without a doubt, he'd pick her homeworld. Being a vengeful and petty entity practically made sure of it. Fortunately, in Raven's estimation, it made him easy to predict.

Almost certainly, once the Gilded Dickhead's demands for Jegra to surrender were rejected, he'd want both Jegra and the emperor to suffer a fate worse than death. And, what's more, he'd want all of the galaxy to witness it.

As such, she had one more call to make before they left Kruos. Flipping on the sub-space communications, she opened a Needle-cast channel to the homeworld of the Seyfferian Republic.

As Raven waited for her call to go through, Skuld, sitting on the back of La'Garren, floated past the open entrance. The squid, along with his rider, casually wafted through the air at the speed of a lazy dirigible, moseying on his merry way, tentacles streaming behind him.

"Truly, fascinating," Skuld said as they passed the doorway.

Thinking she'd heard something, Raven glanced over her shoulder only to find an empty corridor. She shrugged and returned to her call.

A sea of blue, purple, and green flesh writhed together in one mass orgy. Every inch of the grand throne room was filled with the bodies of Dagon men and women, Bre'lal, Dragonian, Jacquardian, and a few of the more unique species from around the system.

Even the red-skinned, five horned, demon women of Kur Vagnorak, a volcanic world on the Outer Rim with a sulfur rich atmosphere, joined the sex party. Their barbed tails whipped about in sensuous gyrations as Dragonian men made love to them.

Moving through the sea of participants was a single green-skinned Bre'lal woman with black eyes.

Onelle Te'Legra Agnar, wearing a white, gossamer dress that left little to the imagination, strolled through the tangle of bodies. They parted before her as if she were the empress herself, as she moved to the dais that led up to the throne.

As she looked up at the skylight in the fifty-foot-high ceiling, she saw flashes as the Allied fleet arrived in orbit above Dagon Prime.

She sat down on the throne and, crossing her legs, her forest green lips twisted into a sinister smile. "Sir Bishop, prepare the Knights for battle. Empress Alakandra and her entourage of fools have arrived."

Sir Lance Bishop, who stood off to the side of the throne chair like a guardian sentinel, bowed his head. His face was stoic, devoid of emotion, and his white skin was marked with a webbing of nasty scars, resembling acid burns, from the "reprogramming" he'd undergone.

Slowly, he looked back up and, without uttering a single word, turned to carry out The Voice's bidding.

Onelle leaned on the arm of the throne chair and waited till the knight exited the orgy. Once he was out of earshot, she sat up in the throne and looked across the undulating bodies. Growing bored of her lecherous experiment, however, she rose to her feet and cleared her throat. "Everyone, may I have your attention, please."

The entire throng of mouths, breasts, genitalia, hands and feet ceased their licentious movement, and all eyes turned toward her.

"I want you all to do something for me, my precious children. On my word, I want you all to tear each other's limbs off, gouge out your eyes, and smash your heads in. I'll leave it up to you to decide the best order to go about it; leave none alive. Oh, and one more thing, have fun doing it, and don't forget to smile."

She settled back down into the throne and, leaning on the lion-paw sculpted arm, pushed out her chest and took in a deep breath. "Begin."

Chaos erupted around her as her guests began struggling to untangle themselves from the intimate positions, so to better murder one other.

Men and women clawed and tore apart one another's flesh, scratched at faces and eyes, wrenched arms and legs from sockets.

Shrieks of agony filled the grand hall as bones cracked and teeth and nails rendered flesh into bloody ribbons. And they all did it with maniacal smiles on their faces.

Blood slickened the floors and splattered against the walls; those with only bloody sockets where eyes once were began bashing their own heads into the marble floor and columns.

A Dagon woman gouged out her own eyeballs and, shrieking wildly, flung herself through the glass window of the palace and fell four stories to her death.

An ocean of multi-colored blood poured from the wounds covering numerous aliens, melding together, forming colorful, almost artful swirls upon the palace floor.

Onelle kicked back her head and laughed. Her evil cackle cut though the din of violence and chaos. Soon, all of Dagon would succumb to her desires. Soon, she'd tear it all down in the name of H'aaztre!

32

Xarthon's eyelids shot open and he tugged against the restraints that held him down to what appeared to be an operating table. Straining his neck, he turned his head only to find himself looking back from the reflection of a two-way mirror.

Another feisty jerk against the leather straps reaffirmed the fact that he wasn't going anywhere anytime soon. He looked around the darkened chamber, soon realizing he wasn't alone. His head snapped to the corner of the room where a slender woman in a lab coat sat jotting something down on a digital holovid tablet.

She had on black, triangular rimmed eyeglasses, a white medical jacket, and was definitely a blue-skin.

"Where am I? What is this place?" Xarthon demanded to know.

It concerned him that this wasn't the prison cell he'd expected to wake up in. Rather, it appeared to be a standard hospital room, minus the two-way glass, that is.

When he looked down at his arms, there was an IV drip feeding into his veins, but to his consternation it wasn't saline. Instead, he was being pumped full of some kind of mysterious, yellow liquid. That's when he noticed the subtle, yet distinctly real, burning sensation of whatever it was coursing through him.

"You failed us," the female physician said in a droll monotone. She looked up from what she was writing and peered at him from over the rims of her glasses.

"Who are you? What do you want?" Xarthon asked, surprised by the youthful sounding voice.

Regrettably, his vision, still having trouble focusing, was blurry. All he could make out were her basic features, her color, the fact that she had a nice figure, and by the way she spoke, that she was rather young—and entitled. Most definitely a Dagon.

The doctor rolled back on her chair and swiveled around to reveal a slender Dagon woman with sparkling amethyst eyes and raven black hair.

As she studied him from over the rims of her spectacles, he couldn't help but feel she looked familiar somehow. Feeling as though he was under the microscope, he opened his mouth to protest, but before he could speak, she swiveled away from him and went back to writing things on her tablet.

Xarthon squinted hard, forcing the face before him to come into focus. When she did, he laughed. "You?! What do you want with me?"

"It's not what you think," the young woman said.

"Don't lie to me. Whatever drugs you've got me on have no effect on my faculties and, now that I've seen your face, I know who you are."

"I am a doctor," she answered nonchalantly as if his assumptions weren't even worth bothering about. She pushed her glasses up on the bridge of her nose then added, "I'm not her."

Xarthon stared hard and peered into the girl's eyes. If she was lying, he'd be able to tell. The only problem was, she wasn't lying.

In fact, her eyes were cold and unfeeling, and she had a sociopathic vibe to her. He'd dealt enough with killers and criminals to know how to spot one a feylon away.

The Lycia he knew had a spark of something warm. She was spirited, vibrant, and most of all kind. He almost felt bad for having to bring her in.

This Lycia, or whoever she was, whatever she was, was not the same. That much was clear. And although she was the spitting image of the Lycia he knew, apart from the hair color, this girl seemed her complete opposite.

"You're one of…them," Xarthon said in disgust.

The girl simply looked upon him with her emotionless stare. "A clone? Yes. And I resent your tone."

Xarthon got a chuckle out of that. She was far too young to be telling a Seyfferian of his age how he ought to address her. But, at the same time, he recognized that she was all kinds of twisted inside; he didn't push the matter.

He glanced down again at the yellow drip feeding into his veins and cleared his throat in a nervous fashion. "You never answered my question, what kind of juice do you have me on? Some kind of military grade cocktail? A vitamin enhanced IV drip? Perhaps something new?"

He paused, waiting for the girl to answer, but when she didn't, he continued guessing other possibilities.

"Let me guess. It's top secret, and you're not allowed to talk about it?"

After an even lengthier pause leading to a permeating silence and the keen sense he was being ignored, she finally set the tablet down in her lap and asked him one simple question. "What do you know about Dygra crystals?"

That was random, he thought. "You mean that gem your people have inside their chests which give them all kinds of unnatural powers?"

She raised an eyebrow and answered in her stereotypical droll fashion, "Yes. What can you tell me about them?"

"I know that they originated as a disease. A bio-organic crystalline virus from someone who came into contact with the Dygra entity tens of thousands of years ago. I know that your scientists subsequently found a way to stabilize the infection which ultimately led to condensing the crystalline particulates all in one place, solidifying them into a single crystal. Then, the crystals absorb electrical energy and store it, like a battery, which the host can later use in the form of energy-based powers. Yeah, I took Dagon biology at the academy. I know your species inside and out."

"And what of the power source? Do you know anything about where the crystal syphons its energy from?"

"Apologies, doc, but what's this got to do with anything? Or with me, for that matter?"

"I was just making small talk," she said, answering him in such a clinical way, sufficiently dry and boring to effectively shut down any further inquiries and cutting short the "small talk."

Uninterested in discussing the topic any further, she turned toward the two-way mirror and said, "Bring the subject in."

The doors slid open and two large Seyferrian doctors, more resembling bodyguards than medical staff, dragged a young, naked Dagon woman into the room and propped her up.

It was yet another clone of Lycia, but he could tell by the gleam of her perfect skin that this particular copy was quite fresh. Still covered in stasis gel and a bit wobbly, she looked over at him with sunken, lethargic eyes, as though she were caught in a deep stupor and was unable to rouse herself awake.

"Is she all right?"

"Not for very much longer," the good doctor said. She reached over and began unfastening Xarthon's restraints.

Once she'd unbound his wrists, he sat up in bed and rubbed the tender areas of his flesh from where he'd struggled against the restraints. As he massaged his wrists, he looked down and watched as she undid his ankle braces too.

"What are you doing?" he asked, growing concerned.

"Just what it looks like. I'm unbinding you." After she finished unfastening all of his restraints, she turned to him, peering over her rims, and asked, "Can you stand?"

"I think so," Xarthon replied.

The doctor got up to help him. It wasn't that she was concerned for her patient, it was just habit. Most couldn't manage on their own once they'd received "treatment." Not desiring her help, Xarthon raised a hand to halt her and stood up on his own.

"How do you feel?" she asked.

"I'm not quite certain." He walked in a circle and rotated his arms and flexed them. When he flexed his muscles, his veins bulged and began to glow with yellow light. "Um...Doc?"

"You have been infused with Proteus E6."

Alarmed, his head snapped to her and his face ran pale. "You did what, now?"

"Relax," she said, touching his forearm. "In small enough dosages, it will take months to kill you."

"Proteus E6 is a banned biological weapon, doctor...? Even being near the stuff is a death sentence. And you're pumping it straight into my body?"

"It counteracts the effects of Dygra crystal energy. It should make you immune to any attacks from the girl. And," she added, drawing out a blaster and aiming it at his chest, "this gun has been modified to emit Dygra energy blasts."

Before he could raise his hands in protest, he shouted, "*No!*" just as she hit him with a full-on laser blast.

But the energy dissipated entirely the moment it touched his skin. It was as though he'd simply absorbed it like rays of sunshine beaming down onto his copper skin.

Xarthon clenched his fist tight, making his veins glow golden, then released his grip and the yellow energy faded. He did it a few more times before he was convinced. "What's the catch, doc?"

She gave him a blank look. "I don't follow."

"You've enhanced me to be the perfect weapon against the perfect weapon, infusing me with the deadliest substance in the whole galaxy, right? So, there has to be a catch. There always is."

"You might be smarter than you look," she jested. He didn't think she meant it as a compliment. "The catch is this. You must capture and bring the original Lycia in for testing and re-storage. After that, I give you the cure for the Proteus E6, and we part ways amicably."

"An incentive to get the job done, then?"

"The council is giving you a second chance. I suggest you take it."

"And if I fail?"

"Let's hope, for your sake, you don't fail," she said.

The young woman's lips curled ever so slightly. The smile wasn't sweet or innocent but, rather, that of a mad scientist deliberating over the ghastly details of their diabolical plan.

Xarthon thumbed over his shoulder at the naked girl standing off to the corner of the room. "And what is she for?"

"She's a test subject."

"A test?" he repeated, confused as to what she meant.

"Alpha Charlie Tango India Victor Alpha Tango Echo," the doctor said and then, placing her hand on Xarthon's arm, she smiled at him and wished him, "Good luck."

The doctor turned to leave the room, her white lab coat fanning out behind her. As she walked out, the naked blue girl's unstable posture stiffened and her eyes blinked several times as though she were an android booting up.

The doctor latched the door behind her, and when Xarthon went over to check it, he found that he was locked inside the room.

Without warning, the blue girl screamed, startling Xarthon. He spun around just in time to see her leap into the air and hurl herself at him.

"W-wait!" he said, throwing up his hands.

It was too late. She tackled Xarthon and they toppled to the ground together. She scurried to get on top of him, her powerful blue thighs straddling him as she clawed at his face.

He clutched her wrists and held her at bay, surprised by her sheer strength. It took everything he had just to shove her off himself.

Using one leg, he hooked her foot and tripped her to the ground. Their gazes locked as they slowly pushed themselves back up to their feet, never breaking eye contact, not even for a second.

Xarthon took up a boxing stance and motioned for the girl to come at him again. "If you want to dance, let's dance!"

She charged him and he swung a right hook. But she was so fast, she ducked the wide swing and tackled him. They flew up into the air and crashed down onto the medical bed, their momentum flinging them off the other end.

As they tussled about on the floor, the girl got a few good licks in before Xarthon scrambled to his feet.

On the way up he managed to hook her heel and quickly latched onto her ankle. With his hands clamped down around her lower leg, he caught her punch, gripped onto her right wrist, and picked her up off the ground. Holding both her leg and arm, he spun on his heels, swung the girl around a full 360 degrees, then flung her like a discus.

She flew into the two-way mirror and crashed through the glass. There was a small viewing room on the other side; luckily, it had been vacated. The girl sprang up, hopped over the windowsill and landed back in the room with Xarthon. Her feet crunched down on broken glass, but she didn't seem to care.

She charged him, trying another tackle move, but he caught her and flung her to the side. She hit the wall, hard, and rebounded off, crashing onto a medical cart full of surgical utensils.

The surgical tools rattled and skittered about on the floor, and when she rose back up, she held a wicked looking surgical knife in one hand.

"Now, hold on there..." he cautioned, throwing up a hand to urge her to stay back. "Let's think about this for a moment."

She swiped the blade at him and he lurched backward, narrowly escaping her lacerating blade. She stepped closer, taking another swipe, and again he drew back.

"Look, it doesn't have to be this way. I can help you."

The naked blue woman standing before him didn't even seem to register his words, and in the next instant, she came at him, screaming like a wild banshee.

Xarthon ducked low, prepared himself, and, letting her crash into his shoulder, he raised her up and catapulted her into the door. The door buckled but didn't go all the way. "To Helios with it!" he grumbled and, lurching forward, he rushed toward her at full speed.

He crashed into the girl's body like a battering ram just as she was standing back up and, with a loud *thump,* they slammed into the door together.

This time, their combined weight and momentum forced the door to give way, and they tumbled out into the hallway.

By the time Xarthon got back onto his feet, he felt a twinge of abrupt pain in the back of his left shoulder. Reaching behind himself, he plucked out the surgical knife that had been lodged there.

A grunt escaped his lips and he dropped the knife then turned his attention back to the girl.

She lay motionless on the floor, her back to him. She appeared to be unconscious, but Xarthon wasn't going to take any chances. Raising his bare foot, he nudged the back of her right leg. He gave her a stronger kick but, again, she merely rocked slightly without responding to his touch.

Since it didn't seem like she was conscious, he released a deep sigh and finally let his guard down.

Just as soon as he'd exhaled, however, the girl rolled over, clasped onto his right leg with her arms and, using her legs to lock onto his torso, took him down with a single guard-style sweep.

Before Xarthon knew it, he was flat on his back and the girl was straddling him, pounding his face in with her two tiny, but vicious, fists. Again, the power behind her punches was not that of a slender girl, but of a true brawler.

And although he was twice her body weight, he also tired twice as fast and barely had the energy to throw her off his torso for a third time. That's when he looked over and saw the discarded medical knife laying just out of reach.

As he took the pummeling, he extended his fingers and tried to get to the knife. But it was no use; the blade was just beyond his reach. And if he tried to shift his weight any further, she'd know something was up and get to the knife before he could.

Her knuckles dripped with blood, whether hers or his was anyone's guess. All he could do was wait for her to tire as well.

At the precise moment she faltered, he quickly reached up, grabbed her hair, and jerked hard. Pulling her down toward him, he used her hair to reel her in and head butted her as hard as he possibly could. The *crack* was so loud that he swore at least one of their skulls had fractured.

Her head flew back, her back arching away from him. Her breasts jutted out, erect, dark blue nipples pointing at the ceiling. This small change in leverage gave him the wiggle room he needed, and he reached out and snatched up the knife.

Just as she came at him again, he swiped out with the blade, cutting her left bicep and the upper part of her breast. The girl leaped off him with a yelp and tears welling up in her purple eyes, she drew away from him like a wounded animal, gently touching the cut to see how bad it was.

Xarthon staggered to his feet. Now, completely exhausted, he was fighting for his very life. "I'm warning you, girl. I don't want to have to kill you. But I will if you come at me again. It's your choice as to how this plays out."

Obviously, his words didn't have much sway over her because in the very next instant, she lunged at him, clearly enraged, her fingers curled like bloody talons.

Xarthon frantically back-peddled away from her, swinging the blade wildly. But even as he cut into her flesh, she seemed unphased by his lacerating blows. She merely sacrificed her body so that she could get to him.

It seemed he might have an opening to duck out, but she leapt up and thrust her knee directly into his sternum. Hitting him with a flying tiger knee-kick, he flew backward and slammed into the wall.

Disoriented, he rebounded off and fell back into her chest. She caught him under his arms and, using his momentum, she twisted her hips and flipped him up and over her body.

Xarthon crashed to the polished concrete floor with a harsh smack and spat a clot of blood out onto the floor.

A loud groan escaped his lips, and Xarthon rolled over to see that he still had the surgical blade clutched tightly in his hand. *Thank goodness for that*, he thought. But before he could catch his bearings, a blue foot slowly and deliberately stepped down onto his wrist.

He looked up to see the blue face and pink glowing eyes gazing down at him without a trace of emotion. She ground her blue heel into the tender area of his wrist, just beneath the palm, and he winced from the pain. What's more, he had no choice but to relinquish his hold on the knife.

"You psychotic bitch," he said, cursing her. But to no effect; nothing seemed to get any rise out of her. For all intents and purposes, she was an automated assassin: nothing more. Her only purpose was to carry out an order.

That's when he realized what the lesson was about. He had to stop thinking about this woman as a flesh and blood person and start thinking about her for what she was—a ruthless, programmed, killing machine.

And Lycia was, all things being equal, just another version of her. Catching his second wind, Xarthon pulled his arm away and rolled to safety.

Somehow, he found the energy to spring up to his feet and he charged the clone, roaring as he tackled her to the ground.

Back on the cold cement floor, he got on top of her and gripped her neck tightly in both hands. Slowly raising her head up, he brought her down hard, slamming the back of her skull onto the concrete.

Her head hit with a loud *thunk* and she faltered, trying to resist him. Falling back to the floor, she raised her glowing finger and shot Xarthon in the chest— point blank—with a full-on energy beam.

Shocked, he reflexively clutched his chest and then slowly looked down. All he found, however, was a smoldering hole in the front of his medical gown. Amazingly enough, his flesh was unscathed. His body had absorbed the energy blast entirely.

Still in awe that he'd survived such a devastating shot, he rubbed the area where the wound should be and then smiled to himself. When he looked back up, for the first time since they'd started fighting, he sensed a hint of fear in her eyes.

On the verge of exhaustion, Xarthon slid to the floor to catch his breath. As he rested, Lycia crawled back into the medical room. A trail of blood trickled behind her as her head continued bleeding.

Once inside, she used the bed to help herself up. Sensing someone over her shoulder, she turned to find Xarthon darkening the doorway. He was panting just as heavily as she was, and all he wanted was for this brutal, no-holds-barred contest to finally end.

"We don't have to keep fighting," he said.

The girl smiled. It wasn't a joyous or even particularly pleasant smile. It was a malicious smirk that took pleasure in causing pain. The grin of a psychopath.

Was that all these clones were? Designer psychopaths?

Xarthon took in a deep breath, preparing to go one final round with the girl when, all of a sudden, a bright pink flash of light caused him to flinch. When he opened his eyes, he saw the girl teeter then collapse abruptly under her own weight.

A smoldering hole in her temple alerted him to the fact that she'd just been shot. He looked over to the other end of the room to find the doctor standing there, a plasma pistol in her hands.

When Xarthon took a step toward her, she trained the gun on him and urged him to stay back. "I wouldn't come any closer, if I were you. High yield plasma is not the same as Dagon energy. And if you want to keep breathing, I suggest you keep your distance."

"I wasn't going to harm you," he said.

She shrugged. "Let's just say I'm extra cautious."

Xarthon nodded at the dead girl lying on the floor. "Why'd you go and do that?"

"She was underperforming;" the doctor gave a wry grin and then added, "and I was growing bored watching you two beat each other into submission without even realizing the reason behind it."

"You wanted to be sure that I would have what it takes to kill her when the time came."

The doctor raised an eyebrow. "I could see how you might think that, but no. I was hoping she'd kill you."

"*What?*"

The doctor turned her gaze to the dead girl. "It's my job to hone the clone's killer instincts. This test was about facing an enemy that was immune to her powers. In such a situation, I was hoping that she'd let her savage-self take over and use her bare hands to tear her opponent limb from limb; you in this case."

Xarthon gulped. "So, I was just your Guinea pig then?"

The doctor ignored his concerns, as they were neither here nor there.

"It appears there still seems to be something blocking her rage mode. I've traced it to the human part of her genetic makeup. No matter how emotionless and apathetic I make them, there's still something resisting my programming."

Xarthon laughed out loud, which startled the doctor. She gave him a peculiar glance and then asked, "What?"

"You're going about it all wrong. They won't kill with reckless abandon because Jegra would never kill with reckless abandon. But they'll kill just fine if you give them a reason."

"What are you suggesting?"

With the back of his hand, Xarthon wiped the blood from his upper lip and then looked over at the doctor with swollen eyes, a fat lip, and a knotted and dented head. "Who is it you want dead?" he asked.

The doctor shot him a chilling glance and then said, "My mother."

"The empress?" he asked.

"The Lord Emperor wanted this army so that he could conquer the stars. But I want it so that I can be with him."

Xarthon made a sour face. "But, he's, like, your father, isn't he?"

"No, you idiot. I'm his clone, just as I am her clone. I am made up of a combination of their DNA. Not like a child, whose genetic makeup is half from each parent. I share an entire genome from each of my so-called 'parents.' I *am* them. No. I am *better* than them."

"I see," Xarthon said, stroking his chin and doing his best to try and ignore her weird incestuous desire. "But you need me to stop Lycia."

"She's an unforeseen random variable. I could have never predicted her hybrid consciousness would have fully awakened and she'd set out to find her progenitors. But she has. And her little journey has brought her all the way back to me."

"And, if you don't mind my asking, who are *you*, exactly?"

The doctor laughed and tossed her hair back giving him a harsh smile. "I'm clone number eighty-seven, batch sixteen. But you may call me, Hela Alakandra."

"In that case," Xarthon said, extending his hand in a gesture of greeting. "It's my great pleasure to meet you."

Hela lowered her blaster and smiled. "I'm sure it is," she replied and then, ignoring the body of her sister on the floor, she breezed past him and exited the medical lab.

Puzzled, he looked down at the dead clone of Lycia lying on the floor when, from out in the corridor, Hela glanced over her shoulder at him and asked, vexed, "Well, are you coming or not?"

Not knowing what else to do, he shrugged and followed after her.

33

Screams pierced the thick haze of the smoke which gradually rose from the charred remains that littered the floor of the grand throne room. Onelle had ordered the knights to burn the bodies.

Half a dozen Knights of Caelum guarded the steps up to the throne and were ordered to cut down anyone who tried to pass them without authorization from Onelle Te'Legra Agnar herself.

Perched on the arm of the throne, Onelle dangled one leg over the edge, casually bouncing her foot up and down. She slid her leg down and sat up, her eyes widening, as a golden beam of light came down from the sky.

A smile spread in anticipation of her showdown with Jegra. But when the Lord Emperor himself materialized in the middle of the great hall before her, a disappointed frown replaced her grin and she huffed in displeasure.

Dakroth stood before her dressed in regal purple and gold-trimmed robes that resembled a *Shogun* lord or ancient Japan from Earth. He remembered Jegra comparing his wardrobe to such and she'd even drawn him some sketches to show him part of her planet's ancient warrior culture. A noble warrior class called *Samurai* had fought with a similar fierceness and discipline, or so she'd told him.

He glanced around at the blood spackled walls, the gore stained hall, and the litany of still smoldering corpses then smirked. "I wish I could say I love what you've done with the place, but I'd be lying."

Onelle brushed aside his attempt at levity. Instead, she slid back in the throne as if it were her own and crossed her slender green legs.

"My dear emperor," she said in somber tone, "as The Voice of the Gilded

Master, Lord of Nyctan, General of the Fusion Legions, and Supreme Ruler of a Thousand Galaxies, I am hereby offering you one and only one chance to see reason and surrender."

Dakroth looked up at her and smiled briefly. "Amusing that your so-called master believes that he has the authority to invoke his will where it is not wanted."

Onelle's eyes widened and her nostrils flared with indignation.

Slowly rising to her feet, the golden halos flashing brightly in her eyes, she snarled, "I am the expression of His will. And you will submit or be crushed by His merciless resolve."

Dismissing her little tirade, he nonchalantly brushed his braided hair back across his shoulder and said, "Yes, yes, but I believe you're sitting in my chair."

He took a step forward, but the moment he moved toward her, the knights, all in unison, clanked their boots and marched two steps forward, creating an armored blockade that protected Onelle from any imminent threat and forced him to stay at the bottom of the stairs, like a commoner in his own throne room.

Onelle smiled vindictively then settled back down into her throne, her glittering gaze staring back at Dakroth's ruby eyes with sinister intent.

"If you insist on defying His will, you will only bring ruin upon you and your people. Don't be a fool, Lord Dakroth. Accept His generous offer and surrender peacefully."

"I don't think you understand," Dakroth sneered, "I'm not afraid of this Yellow King of yours. He might as well be called the Yellow-Bellied King, since he insists on cowering behind the weak-minded puppets he manipulates. I've slit the throats of kings braver than him, and I'll slit your throat just the same if you don't step aside."

He scanned the faceplates of the Nyctan knights to see if they dared test his resolve, but they didn't move. Instead, they remained statuesque sentinels guarding their precious emissary.

Leaning back in the chair, Onelle shifted in her seat, uncrossed her legs, and re-crossed them again. She stared back at Dakroth, adjudicating how this would play out when she heard a voice from just over her shoulder.

"Just let me kill this bitch already."

Out of thin air, Callestra, wearing a military grade optics-suit, decloaked right beside the throne where Onelle sat. She had a blaster pointed at Onelle's temple and her finger was itching to pull the trigger. Its plasma coils hummed with excitement, and Callestra, having caught Onelle completely off-guard, grinned at her.

"I think you may be mistaken who you're meant to kill, my dear Callestra Van Morgan."

"Oh, yeah? And how's that exactly?"

Onelle's eyes flashed, the golden halos in each eye broke apart into two golden orbs that swirled about like grease on water. After congealing into a steady rotation around the iris, the golden circles spiraled down into one another, forming the appearance of a *taijitsu*—the *yin and yang* symbol of universal balance.

"Remember what we discussed in the garden," Onelle said in a tone void of any emotion, the taijitsu filling the central region of her eyes like hypnotic medallions.

Callestra slowly removed the gun from Onelle's temple and, turning, trained it on Dakroth instead.

A look of genuine surprise came over his face and he took a step back. "What is this?"

"She came to me," Callestra said, her eyes welling up with tears as she had no power to stop herself, "in the garden of Aldebaran. It was there that she showed me the way out."

"You knew the way out of that Hell yet never told me?"

"I... I..." Callestra stammered as she fought to resist The Voice's influence. "I had no choice. She swore me to secrecy."

Her hand shaking as though she were straining against an invisible force, she turned the gun back onto Onelle.

"Really?" Onelle sighed impatiently. "You're still fighting us?"

Blood began to trickle from Callestra's ears and nose, her brain hemorrhaging as she used every ounce of strength to resist the evil incantation. "I c-can't k-kill him. I love him."

"In that case," Onelle said, raising her hand. She flicked her wrist and motioned for her knights.

One of the bulky knights charged forward and slammed into Callestra. She crashed to the ground with a *thump,* and that same knight kicked her in the gut to ensure she'd stay down.

With a rib-shattering crack, she rolled twice before coming to a stop. Lying motionless, she clutched her chest in pain and tried to regain her breath.

Dakroth looked back at his unconscious lover and smiled upon her affectionately.

"Is something amusing?" Onelle asked.

"Love conquers all."

"What? Am I supposed to know what that means?"

"Nothing," he said turning back to her. "Just something Jegra always says."

"Oh, yes," Onelle hissed, "and how is our darling Jegra?"

Dakroth merely grinned and then, clasping his fingers together, he stretched his hands and popped his knuckles.

Once he'd limbered himself up, he did an ancient kata and let out a powerful energy wave. It was a kind of modified shield that rippled through the air like a magic carpet and picked Onelle, along with all the Knights of Caelum, up off the ground and tossed them clear across the room.

Onelle, being closest to the back wall, slammed into the stones with bone shattering force. She gasped for air as blood dribbled from the corners of her mouth.

The energy wave momentarily pinned her there, making sure she was unable to move. Finally, the force dissipated and she collapsed to the ground. Her chest heaved and her lungs wheezed as she gulped down air.

Raising her arm, she pointed a finger at Dakroth and growled, "Kill him!"

The knights slowly got to their feet and turned back toward Dakroth. One by one, all six warriors drew their plasma swords, shuffled their feet into fighting stances, and marched toward Dakroth.

Dakroth's eyes narrowed and he sneered, scanning the approaching warriors. Widening his stance, he focused and sought his center by doing his martial arts katas.

The Dagoni martial art of *BaiJamin* was known throughout the galaxy as one of the best forms of defensive and offensive hand-to-hand combat techniques there was. Even the Knights of Caelum trained in the form so they could better predict their enemy's attacks.

Armored fists flew through the air and Dakroth deflected them with expert skill. He back-flipped over scorching hot blades of plasma and landed on his hands and feet with the dexterity of a cat.

He let out a grunt and elbowed the knight behind him in the face plate—a small, saucer-like energy shield forming at his elbow like a protective body armor.

With a kick, he sent the knight in front of him staggering back. His knee glowing bright blue with the energy shield, he slowly lowered his leg and turned to face the others.

Then, with glowing eyes, he clasped his hands together, extended his pointer fingers like the barrel of a gun, and let out a magical blast of Dygra energy.

The laser beams slammed into the chest of the knight that he'd just sent sliding back. Naturally, the knight's armor was designed to deflect Dygra crystal energy and it split off, parting in different directions and blasting holes in the walls of the throne room.

Before he could react, two knights seized him from either side, clutching his arms and holding him tight so that he couldn't wriggle free.

"A little help would be appreciated," he growled through clenched teeth.

"Oh, but you were doing so well, Daggie-poo."

Jegra stepped out from behind one of the massive pillars of the grand hall and looked over at Dakroth and smiled. In the very next moment, golden beams of light came down all around the empress; like the calvary arriving at the eleventh hour, her backup had arrived.

Raven and Ladgara wore power armor, while Angellyk sported an optics suit and slowly faded into the air.

Kregor drew out two curved Dragonian Ram-Dao styled swords, and announced, "Perhaps today is a good day to die."

Dakroth glanced to his right and shot Jegra a debonair smile. "Shall we dance, my queen?"

Jegra smiled broadly at him, the warrioress inside of her attracted to his warrior spirit. "I thought you'd never ask."

With that, Jegra's team of expert mercenaries, pirates, and misfits entered the fray.

Outraged by the interference, Onelle drew her kukri blades and, with golden medallions for eyes, snarled, "The empress is mine!"

A clash of steel sent up sparks as Jegra blocked Onelle's assault with one of her two trusty battle-axes. Eyes glowing white-hot, the medallions spinning in Onelle's eyes like ominous orbs, she mounted another attack.

Every swing and every strike bit down on Jegra's metal, but the empress refused to fight—she only parried, and inched further back. Dodging and ducking, she receded deeper into the heart of the great hall.

"I know what you're doing," Onelle said. "You're trying to wear me down."

"And it's working so far," Jegra retorted.

As the others fought with the knights, another golden beam of light came down. To everyone's surprise it was the boy-king himself, H'aaztre.

"Stop!" he shouted above the clash of metal and din of fighting. "I demand you stop this folly at once!"

The knights backed off and Jegra and her team regrouped.

"My dear Jessica..." he began, only to cut himself short and change his tact. "I mean...Mother. Please, can't we discuss your surrender like a couple of level headed adults?"

"I don't know," Jegra said. "Why don't you ask her?" With a nod she gestured to the figure standing directly over his shoulder. He turned around; his eyes widened as he saw a ghost from his past.

Old Lady Jegra smiled and then, pointing a glowing finger at his forehead, said, "Hi, sweetheart. I'm home."

With a Dygra crystal blast, she shot H'aaztre point blank through his temple.

The blast pierced his skull, cutting clean through, and shot out the other side. It blasted into the wall, resulting in massive blowback that picked everyone in the room up off their feet and scattered them everywhere, including Onelle and her knights.

Once the dust had settled and the steam from the heat of the blast dissipated, H'aaztre stood grinning at the silver-haired Jegra.

"I see you've upgraded yourself, mother." While he spoke, the hole in his head slowly shrank away as his healing factor mended the wound. Looking over his shoulder at the other Jegra, he added, "But it makes no difference. Even with your combined strength, you're still not powerful enough to challenge me."

"Maybe," Jegra said, a subtle smile forming on her lips as she held up a hot-pink glowing hand. "But, then again, we shall see what we shall see."

Dakroth sidled up to her, his eyes leaking Dygra energy which wafted through the air like fluorescent pink smoke. Together they raised both glowing hands and trained them on the young man.

H'aaztre braced himself, but not before his ear caught the sound of more Dygra energy crackling on the air behind him. Looking back over his shoulder, he saw Old Lady Jegra and Callestra aiming their glowing hands at him too.

"Nooo!" he screamed just as the room filled with the neon pink light of Dygra crystal energy.

The air outside was peaceful and calm like that on a summer afternoon. Bird's flew over the castle and the clouds sluggishly wafted across a vast pale blue sky. The green foliage of the trees which surrounded the palace swayed gently in the slight breeze, and somewhere in the distance the faint chirp of some kind of cricket could be heard.

This tranquil existence was abruptly interrupted when the palace exploded as if a bomb had detonated. With a deafening boom, the cathedral-like spires imploded as the debris of the walls exploded outward. Large chunks of rock soared through the air as if launched from a catapult, and the opulent furnishings and decorations that populated the vast halls were rendered into little more than burning embers and ash.

Raven and Kregor, having been furthest from the blast, were flung fifty meters away from the main palace. Their body armor had done its job and protected them; they slowly stood up and checked themselves for any serious injuries.

Ladgara, having used her body armor to shield Angellyk, found they were in the same situation, having landed forty meters away from the palace in the opposite direction of everyone else.

Both Jegras had used their own bodies to cover Callestra and the emperor, and their bodies were glowing hot orange like heated steel, their skin steaming as they cooled.

After the heat had dissipated, they stood up and looked around at the rubble and debris strewn about them. The palace had been all but obliterated in the blast.

Onelle, who'd ducked behind two of the knights, climbed out from under their dead corpses. For, although the knights were strong, even their armor had limits. Luckily, it had been enough to keep her alive.

Picking up her korridium daggers, she bull rushed Old Lady Jegra. "I don't care which one of you I kill, just so long as one of you dies!"

The dagger pierced Old Lady Jegra's back on the right side, and she let out a pain filled shriek.

Just then a plasma blast to Onelle's temple blew out her brains. Callestra immediately tossed the blaster to the ground, stepped over Onelle's dead body, and rushed over to help the wounded Jegra up.

"You have to get up," she pleaded. "We still need you."

With a groan, Old Lady Jegra rose to her feet. And although she still had a blade sticking out of her back, the adrenaline surging through her veins helped mask the pain.

Raven came trotting up to them and immediately hoisted Jegra's arm across her shoulders. "I've got you," she said. Noticing the dagger, she added, "You're wounded."

"Ignore it," Jegra said, not thinking twice about the blade wedged in her back. Besides, if she tore it out it might do more damage than she cared for and opted to leave it in.

Angellyk and Ladgara moved over to where Kregor stood, regrouping so that they'd have a better chance when the fighting resumed.

Nearby, one of the knights was trying to get up, but his suit was so badly damaged in the explosion that it was faltering, and he collapsed to the ground on his hands and knees.

With a grin on his face, Kregor repeated the words, "Indeed, today is a good day to die. But it shall not be me."

With that, he sliced off the knight's head. It tumbled to the ground and rolled away.

A slow, methodical golf-clap drifted through the hazy air and they all turned to find H'aaztre smiling at them, perched on the smoldering remains of the throne—which was little more than a singed stone slab. "Bravo," he commended, "well done indeed. But, you'll have to do a whole lot better if you hope to defeat a God."

With a snap of his fingers, one brilliant flash of white light instantaneously teleported the full force of the Fusion army. Just a small demonstration of his true power.

Completely surrounded, he looked over at Jegra, her skin still steaming with radiant energy, and said, "Checkmate, Mother."

"We can't win this," Ladgara said in a hushed tone as she scanned the hundreds of additional soldiers, including another dozen knights, led by Lance Bishop himself.

Over six hundred Nyctan and Nephilim soldiers raised their plasma rifles and trained them on Jegra and her band of noble warriors.

Ladgara leaned over and whispered to Kregor, "You were saying, big guy?"

He merely grunted in displeasure as they scanned the hundreds of enemy soldiers ready to gun them down at H'aaztre's command.

High up in the stratosphere, the Fusion armada engaged the Allied forces. The *Chiron* took a heavy beating as it engaged five enemy ships at once.

The rest of the fleet, now down to forty-one ships, was taking on heavy damage as well.

The Fusion forces had been wise to hide their numbers until the final battle; now they jumped into the system, seventy-eight ships strong. Almost twice that of the already wounded Allied fleet.

Almathea turned toward Admiral Grendok. "Sir, the fleet is taking a heavy pounding."

"Well, let's pound them right back," he said.

"Yes, sir."

Just then, a flash off the port bow drew their attention to the fact that the Nyctan flagship, the *The Golden Rod of H'aaztre*, had just jumped into the system.

As soon as it appeared, its massive cannon turrets swiveled into position and began firing at the Allied fleet.

Almost as soon as it unleashed the barrage of relentless plasma fire, two of the weakened Allied ships went up in balls of flame.

She turned to Grendok, a worried look on her face. "We lost the *Raideck* and the *Scorpios*. What do we do now?"

"Prepare for ramming speed!" Grendok shouted.

"Aye, aye, sir," Almathea answered. Then, turning toward the view portal, her arms clasped behind her back, she bleated, "Full speed ahead!"

The *Chiron* and the *Rod of H'aaztre* crashed together high above the Dagon atmosphere. Both the vessels went up in a massive explosion that shook the entire fleet.

"Everything that has transpired has done so according to my design. Your friends up there, dear mother, have walked right into my trap. Soon your pitiful insurrection will be squashed and my forces will sweep through this blasted galaxy of yours, wreaking destruction and bringing its people to their knees in humble subservience."

"We haven't lost yet," Jegra said, as if to remind him there was still some fight left in her.

"If you wish your friends to remain unharmed, mother, you will surrender to me now. Because, if you do, I will spare your loved ones. I may even spare this feeble empire of yours."

Jegra looked up at Old Lady Jegra, whose eyes, wide with worry, seemed to plead for her not to do it.

She looked to Dakroth, who stared at H'aaztre with all the hate he could muster.

Behind her, she turned her head to find that her friends were battered but not broken. Raven gave her a nod, just one look that said, *you've got this.*

She knew they'd fight till the bitter end. They'd fight to the death for her. But could she bring herself to ask them to commit such a sacrifice?

Could she live with herself if they fought and died for her and still ended up losing the war? Would that be fair?

Perhaps, for the first time, she understood Old Lady Jegra's struggle. The offer was simply too good to pass up. To save everyone she loved simply by giving him what he wanted—by kneeling before him and kissing the ring. Then again, if the old woman was right about it all being just an elaborate lie, it would be the greatest mistake she'd ever make, again.

At the end of the day, there was only one thing she knew to be true; she'd never lie to herself. Not when it came to the lives of her family and friends.

"Face it, my dear mother. You've already lost."

She turned to H'aaztre and cleared her throat to speak.

34

Slinking down a dank alleyway, Lycia's boots splashed through a puddle that sent the reflection of overhead neon lights scattering in a ripple of expanding rings. She'd never before seen a city as bright or colorful as Correl. But to be fair, she hadn't seen very many cities at all.

Regardless, Correl was a proper city, replete with towering skyscrapers and cluttered, neon-lighted slums. Everything here seemed so highly advanced; every surface exuded highly advanced technology.

Three dimensional displays selling the ideal vacation getaway lit up a giant, holographic billboard. Next to that, virtual hookers, four stories tall, broadcast their solicitations in high-def. Their neon-purple nipples stood erect on their beautiful, modified, bronzed bodies.

There was something alluring about Seyfferian women. Lycia had noticed it with Deunan. And although she was like a big sister to her, if she ever wanted to mess around, Lycia would be more than happy to oblige her. *But that would likely never happen, knowing how tight-lipped Deunan could be*—and she didn't mean her mouth, either.

The streets were filled with dimly lit noodle shops that would scan the glowing holochip in your wrist as you sat down so you never had to reach for your billfold.

The steaming and musky odors of hot bone broths and street meats permeated the air. It was a shock to the senses at first, but then she found herself growing extremely hungry. But food would have to wait.

As exhilarating an experience as it all was, she wasn't there for sightseeing. Rather, she was here for business. And she was bound and determined to find answers for herself.

Lycia turned to look over her shoulder, checking up on Allie, who tagged along behind her, albeit at a frequently distracted pace. There were so many piles of garbage to sniff and strange greasy puddles to taste.

"Come on, girl. We're almost there."

Allie, pulled her nose out of a box of old takeout food and sauntered up beside Lycia, still licking her chops. Lycia laughed and together, they turned down the dark recesses of an alleyway.

After searching the various possible side entrances, Lycia eventually found the door with the correct apartment address, the one that Deunan had scrounged up using one of her numerous contacts on Correl.

Easing up to the entrance, Lycia waved her wrist over the sensor panel on the side of the door.

To her surprise, the door unlocked and slowly creaked open. She looked over her shoulder out of paranoia, just to be sure she wasn't being followed, then made a clicking noise with her tongue asking Allie to follow her inside.

They entered the building, letting the door swing shut behind them, and proceeded to walk down a long, creaky corridor.

An orange and green wash of neon lighting seeped in through the cracks of the boarded-up windows, casting everything in muted hues.

As she studied her surroundings, looking for anything that might be familiar to her, she found lots of empty offices and cubicles, but otherwise there wasn't much to see. She couldn't even tell what the place had been used for, other than some kind of generic office work.

Allie sniffed a pile of old rags and sneezed, shook her head in astonishment at the sting of the foul odor that filled her feline nostrils, then sneezed again.

"You all right, girl?" Lycia asked, looking down at her with an amused expression.

Allie simply gave her a look that relayed she probably shouldn't stick her nose in strange places and the two of them, seemingly on the same page, turned together and roamed further up the hallway.

When they reached the end, Lycia stood in front of a flat wall with nothing on it, not even a clock or a company slogan. Just a flat, empty wall.

It was precisely where an elevator should be, but strangely enough, no elevator doors. Also, the wall happened to be a brighter shade of white than the surrounding walls, meaning it either had a fresh coat of paint applied to it, or it was a new wall entirely.

"That's odd," she said, running her hand along the wall to check for seams, thinking that it might have been covered up in a renovation or something.

She flicked her wrist, the bottom facing upward, and a holographic projection of the building's blueprints rose up from her arm and filled the space in front of her face. Using her fingers, she pinched and rotated the model of the building, then, finding the right angle, she zoomed in on her precise location.

Lycia carefully studied the blueprints only to discover that something was not quite right. Unmistakably, right there in front of her on the original blueprints, was the missing elevator shaft.

She zoomed back out, double checking the address to see if she'd come to the right place. She had. *So, what gives?* she wondered. *Why is there a wall here?*

With another flick of the wrist, she turned off the holovid projection and took a step back. She looked down at Allie and informed her, "You may want to scoot back, too."

Allie's ears folded back as she gave a worried expression, and then walked to the rear corner of the room. She did a nervous circle and, then, sat down on her haunches and watched Lycia with her big green cat eyes.

Lycia turned her attention back to the wall, and, raising a glowing finger, she carved out the area where the elevator doors ought to be.

Once she'd carved through the slab of sheetrock and plaster, she pushed her fingers into one of the incisions she'd made and began breaking the pieces out little by little.

Piece by piece, she tore out the wall with her bare hands. It felt invigorating to rip it all down, and after a few minutes of demolition work, she gasped, coughing on the chalky dust of the sheetrock, and turned to Allie with a big smile on her face.

"See? I told you it was the right place."

Allie whined curiously. Lycia shrugged off the cat's obvious skepticism. She went over to the elevator doors. Since the power was out, mashing the button did no good, so, she began to pry the sliding doors open with her bare hands.

"You shouldn't be here," a voice called out from behind her.

Allie jumped and growled and Lycia spun around to find a Dagon woman dressed in a lab coat standing in the center of the hallway where they had just been moments earlier. Her face was shrouded by shadows and stood just out of the light which beamed through the windows from the neon city outside.

"Who are you?" Lycia asked.

The woman carefully stepped forward, inching into the light, revealing that she was exactly like Lycia in every way.

"My name's Hela, and, like you, I'm a clone."

Lycia gasped. "I knew it!" she exclaimed. "I just knew there were others."

Allie merely looked at one Lycia and then the other in confusion. Her whiskers twitched with consternation. Soon, though, she seemingly gave up trying to figure it out and started to bathe herself instead.

The only distinguishing physical difference was that the woman had dark purple, neatly cropped shoulder-length hair and wore eyeglasses, while Lycia had perfect vision and long hair, like Jegra's.

Her clone brushed past her, nudging her out of the way with her shoulder as she stepped up to the elevator.

"Come, we'd best get going. You triggered a silent alarm when you decided to blast through this wall to get to this door. They'll be coming for us any minute. So, if you want answers, now is the time to get them."

"Who'll be coming for us?" asked Lycia.

The anxiety in the woman's voice was unmistakable and Lycia looked back over her shoulder all the way down the hall to the entrance. She half expected a crack team of commandos to burst through the door any minute.

"Biosphere Genetics, or more accurately, their security detail," the woman said, drawing out a magnetic card key.

"Are they the company that was hired to make us?"

Hela nodded in the affirmative. She took out an electronic card key and waved it in front of the wall, and with a clunk, the elevator doors parted. A hiss of stale air shot out and jostled their hair, but sure enough, there was a lift waiting for them.

Hela stepped inside the lift then turned to find Lycia hesitantly peering inside. "Well? Are you coming or not?"

"I just don't know if it's safe," Lycia replied.

"It's probably not. But the question you have to ask yourself is, is the risk worth it? Is the risk worth finding out the answers you've come here searching for?"

That settled it. Lycia took a deep breath and climbed into the ancient lift with this perfect stranger who wore her face.

Allie jumped up and hustled inside just in time, sneaking through the opening and narrowly beating the closing doors. Lycia scratched her behind the ears and said in a cutesy baby voice, "Good, girl. Yessh, you are. You're such a good, good girl."

"Who woke you from stasis?" Hela asked, after waiting a few moments for Lycia to finish coddling her pet.

Lycia turned and stared long and hard at Hela. It felt weird, looking at someone with her exact features, mannerisms, and tics.

But even though they were unmistakably woven from the same whole cloth of genetic material, for whatever reason, she knew she couldn't trust this woman. Something was off about her at such a fundamental level that it made Lycia's stomach knot up.

"I don't know. I woke up in freefall inside an escape pod over Thessalonica. The emergency landing set off the reactivation protocols and I was pumped so full of endorphins and adrenaline that I must have pried my way out of the wreckage with my bare hands. The rest is all just a blur."

"Being sent to Thessalonica gives us some clues to who might have broken you out."

"If you mean Jegra, it wasn't her. The empress didn't even know I existed until we accidentally stumbled across one another's paths."

"I was thinking more along the lines of one little nefarious satyr," Hela responded.

"You mean Grendok?" asked Lycia.

Hela nodded. "He's been trying to steel top secret Seyfferian cloning tech for ages. I'd bet credits to creylons he was behind it."

There was a brief pause and Lycia turned to Hela. "Why are you helping me?"

Hela smiled at her just as the elevator slowed and, with a jolt, arrived at its designated floor.

The doors parted and Lycia turned to see a massive underground chamber with rows and rows of blue glowing cryostasis pods, all stacked on top of one another.

The series of stasis pods rose up three levels high as well as three levels below a maintenance walkway made of galvanized steel. And behind the frosty glass view portal of every single cryostasis pod there was a sleeping Lycia.

"Oh," Hela said, in a cheery fashion which seemed out of character for her dull monotone. "I can assure you, I'm not helping you. I'm putting you back into storage, where you belong."

Lycia's eyes snapped back to Hela's; she saw the cruel grin form on her copy's lips. Looking down, she found that Hela had drawn her plasma blaster and it was trained on her.

Allie had noticed it too, and growled at the woman, but Hela merely turned it on the large cat and pulled the trigger, firing off a low yield blast. The blast hit Allie in her side and, with a whimper, she collapsed onto the elevator floor, stunned by the unexpected shot.

"No!" Lycia screamed and fell to her knees beside the wounded cat. Placing her hand on Allie's side, she examined the plasma burn to make sure it wasn't fatal.

"It's all right, girl. It isn't that bad."

Allie's whimpers begged to differ, but there wasn't anything Lycia could do for her at the moment.

"Why not just use your energy blast?" Lycia asked, curious as to why Hela was relying on such primitive technology instead of her Dagon powers. Finding the blaster trained on her again, she slowly raised her hands and cautiously rose to her feet.

"I'm afraid I am just another failed prototype. My Dygra crystal never matured. So, unlike you, I'm without powers."

"I bet that pisses you off."

Hela shrugged and then waved the barrel of her blaster, gesturing for Lycia to step out of the lift. "I've adjusted."

Lycia, doing her best to stay calm, raised her hands and slowly stood up and did as Hela asked. She cautiously exited the lift, glancing down at Allie with a worried look. Allie whimpered softly in pain as if calling out to Lycia for help, but Lycia's hands were tied.

Hands still raised, she turned to face her captor. "So, are you just a stooge for the people who made us? Or do you have a mind of your own?"

Hela balked. "You simply don't have the first clue, do you? It doesn't matter, because soon you'll be back on ice and I'll be back in my lab running every imaginable test on you."

"What tests? Why?" Lycia asked, taken aback by the revelation that she'd become an unwitting lab rat.

"You've exceeded your specs. And, naturally, we want to ensure that the rest of the clones are just as capable as you are. But first, I have to figure out how and why you outperformed your design parameters."

"So, you're just going to put me under the scalpel, dissect me and experiment on me, just to find out what makes me so special?"

"If it comes to that," Hela answered with a shrug of her shoulders. A cruel grin spread across her lips as though she took pleasure in the thought of cutting and probing Lycia like a common science lab dissection, placing her under a microscope to nitpick every cell of hers down to its genetic base components— down to her very strands of DNA.

"You can't do that!" muttered Lycia under her breath. "I've come too far to be put back on ice without any answers."

"What do you think, Xarthon? Should we give her the answers she so desperately seeks?"

Lycia spun around again, this time finding Xarthon standing about fifty meters behind her on the large platform. He grinned menacingly and then raised a blaster of his own.

"I can take it from here, Hela."

Hela smiled and slowly drew back into the elevator. Allie dragged herself out, and Hela, annoyed at the slow pace of the wounded animal, gave her an unforgiving shove with her boot.

Allie flopped out of the lift and onto the metal floor plating.

Hela looked up at Lycia one last time and smirked just as the elevator doors slammed shut, cutting off their intense glares.

Lycia glanced down at Allie again who was now licking her wound and, had, luckily, only suffered minor plasma burns.

Pissed off, Lycia whirled back around and stared down Xarthon. She had questions. Lots of them. And if he wasn't going to divulge any answers, well, then she'd have to compel him to do so. She tightened her fists and then took one step forward when he gestured for her to stay where she was with a warning shot that pinged off the galvanized steel at her feet.

"How gullible can you be?" he scoffed. "What, were you born yesterday?"

"Basically, yes," Lycia replied, scowling at Xarthon.

Xarthon thought about it for a second and then nodded his head, grinning, as he realized that his figure of speech really did seem to capture the irony of the situation.

"Never mind," he said, changing the subject. "All that matters now is that I get you back inside your stasis pod."

"And if I refuse?"

"Then I'll have no choice but to do this the hard way." He raised the blaster and fixed its sights on her chest. She looked down at the green laser dot on her left breast and then up at Xarthon, her eyes narrowing to let him know she didn't appreciate his insinuation.

After a short pause, she raised her hands and, pointing two glowing fingers at him, said, "Hard way it is, cock-face." She fired off two high energy blasts, but she wasn't convinced she'd hit him, despite the close proximity. So, she fired off another two shots. Again, the blasts seemingly had no effect on him.

She didn't know how, but Xarthon was impervious to her Dygra energy.

He laughed at the futility of her attempt on his life. "You're not the only one with enhanced powers anymore, little girl. Your sister, Hela, has seen to that. Now, if you'll stop this schoolgirl charade and come with me peacefully, I might see to it that your kitten gets a good home."

Lycia looked down at Allie, who was panting heavily but, luckily, still hanging in there. She didn't want to leave her all alone, but Xarthon cleared his throat irritably, letting her know that she didn't really have any choice in the matter.

"Fine," she grumbled, raising her hands in surrender. "You caught me."

As they walked along the metal catwalk between the hanging cryonic stasis pods, she studied each and every face. And each and every face was her own. All their naked blue bodies lay in a deep hibernation, soundly catatonic in cryosleep containers, oblivious to the injustice happening a few centimeters beyond the glass of their casket-like pods.

She could scarcely believe that a few months ago one of these sleeping faces had been her own. It almost felt as though she were having an out of body experience and was looking down at herself.

But then, shaking her head, she reminded herself that these were her sisters. They were her genetic copies and, like identical twins, they had rights, too; they deserved to be free.

Right there and then she vowed to wake them all and save them from this life of frozen purgatory, not quite alive but not quite dead, either.

Caught in Morpheus's dream, they'd go on sleeping, dreamlessly, for an eternity if nobody ever woke them. And she knew she had to wake them. She had to set them free. It was the only way she'd ever feel at peace with herself.

"You won't get away with this," Lycia informed Xarthon in a bitter tone of voice that caused him to raise an eyebrow. "I have friends that will come looking for me."

Xarthon didn't reply. He merely gestured with his gun for her to hook a left at the junction ahead. Instead of doing that, however, she spun around and, breaking into a run, she tackled Xarthon, taking him to the ground.

They tumbled to the walkway and she wrestled the gun away from his hands. The weapon fell onto the catwalk and, in the struggle, he reached for it but knocked it further away from himself instead.

The gun skidded dangerously close to the edge of the catwalk where it got hooked on the lip of the metal gridwork.

Xarthon staggered to his feet and began to move toward it. Lashing out, Lycia scissor kicked his shin, tripping him. He collapsed back down, landing on the gangplank.

Lycia scrambled up and over him, trying to beat him to the gun, but as she stepped over him, he threw an upward punch and clocked her right in her v-hole.

Lycia hit the ground, hard, and clutched her crotch. "You fuckwad!" she spat.

"Serves you right, you little slut," he fired back. He rushed to crawl past her; but she wasn't having it and grabbed onto his leg. As she held him, she started bashing him in the nut sack with the strength of the gladiatrix herself.

"I'm going to pop your nuts like grapes, you fucking piece of shit!"

Xarthon yelped out in pain and rolled away, clutching his junk. As soon as he'd moved aside, Lycia struggled to her feet and lunged for the blaster.

Almost in reach, her fingers came up short and she looked back to find Xarthon, purple-faced with rage and scrambling after her.

She kicked at him as he caught her boot in his hands and dragged her backward across the metal grating. Her shirt came up and her back began to scrape across the hatched metal and she shrieked out in pain.

Safely having put distance between them and the weapon, Xarthon flung Lycia to the side; she tumbled into the railing with a hollow sounding clank. The wind rushed out of her, and Xarthon managed to scurry over and pick up his gun.

Lycia slowly sat up, the back of her shirt shredded and stained with blood. She rested her head against one of the support bars of the railing and stared up at Xarthon who, having regained his weapon, spun around and aimed it at her.

He bellowed with a triumphant laugh. "Ha-ha!"

"Go to hell," she growled, and spat at his feet.

Xarthon ignored her insult and trained the barrel of the gun on her. "Now, let's try this again. But this time, if you try any funny stuff, I'll splatter your pretty little brains out all over this catwalk."

Lycia struggled to her feet and gave him a frigid glare. Then, out of nowhere, a panther's roar descended on them and, before Xarthon could even turn to see the danger barreling toward him, a big blue panther pounced on him, taking him down. Hard.

Xarthon yelped as the giant cat got a hold of his forearm and dragged him to the ground. His screams continued to fill the cavernous underground chamber as she mauled him with her massive claws.

He tried to fire off a shot, but it flew wide. Allie, remembering the sting of the blaster, bit his wrist, crushing his bones. Xarthon screamed out, and relinquished his gun. It fell out of his grasp and skidded to floor again. This time it toppled over the side of the catwalk and fell out of sight.

Lycia put her fingers to her lips and let out a high-pitched whistle. "Allie, we have to go. Now!"

The cat halted her vicious attack and turned to follow after Lycia, who was already running full speed down the walkway, heading deeper into the facility.

Bloodied, battered, and cut up something fierce, Xarthon struggled to right himself, sliding up to the railing and propping himself against it.

Cuts all over his body, his clothes tattered and torn, he clutched his broken arm with his good one and spit off the side of the railing. "You'll pay for this, you blue Dagon cunt!"

A fiery rage filled his eyes as he watched her and her indigo panther disappear into the mist of the vapors stirred up by the coolant system.

Lycia raced along the gangplank with Allie treading closely on her heels. She didn't stop to look back, but just kept running. She ran until her lungs burned and then, finally coming to a large set of doors, paused to catch her breath.

She couldn't find any access panel, but the moment she stepped close, a red laser spread out and settled over her like a translucent blanket as it scanned her features.

<<Lycia 0009-1X-003, welcome home.>>

A resounding *clunk*, followed by a mechanical rattle of wheels and gears turning, could be heard. Then, with a heavy shuddering, the doors began to part, slowly revealing a warm, golden light.

The doors opened up to a balcony that overlooked an open air, stadium-sized pavilion. Down in the center was a garden being attended to by a whole host of Lycia clones.

Lycia and Allie edged up to the balcony railing and stared in awe as they beheld an entire underground colony.

Beyond the garden were loft-styled treehouses, hundreds of them, all filled with more clones going about their daily chores of hanging wet laundry, bringing supplies up from the garden, and cooking.

About half the clones were just hanging out, chatting with one another, while others trained on a dojo styled mat set out for sparring and martial arts practice at the far end of the garden.

A waterfall shot out of the rockface to the left and filled a pond with fresh, natural spring water. Several Lycias peeled off their clothes, and leaped into the pond naked, giggling, and splashing about. When a third Lycia who was gathering water in a pitcher rebuked them for tainting her drinking water, they turned on her and splashed her for all her troubles.

A stream winding away from the pond fed crops in a garden where more Lycias tended the vegetables and the fruits.

"Can you believe it, girl?" Lycia said, practically breathless by what she beheld with her own two eyes. "It's a self-sustained Lycia village!"

One of the Lycias down in the garden heard her speak and looked up at her. There was an awkward pause as they stared at one another. In that moment, the other Lycias all stopped what they were doing and turned toward her and

Allie, which made her nervous.

The Lycia in the garden smiled up at her, quelling her worries. And, then, to Lycia's surprise the clone strode over to the base of the wall and looked up at the balcony. Extending her hand, she said, "Welcome home, sister."

35

Six hundred plasma rifles trained their menacing muzzles on Jegra and her crew, coolant cartridges cocked and loaded. The dim glow of their muzzles and the whine of their plasma coils filled the air. Unphased by the show of firepower, she remained poised. She turned slowly to H'aaztre and shot him a brusque smile.

"It's time you admitted your defeat, Mother, and kneel before me, the galaxy's one true ruler," he said in a condescending tone.

"It's too bad I wasn't there to properly raise you, because if I had, I'd warn you not to be so cocky."

The boy-god raised an eyebrow and, amused, laughed out loud. "Oh, really, Mother? And what would you have done? Took me over your knee?"

"Couldn't have hurt," she said, holding his gaze.

Linking his arms behind his back, his golden robes flapping on the breeze, he walked toward her. "Is that what I'm being? An incorrigible reprobate? An egotistical knave? An all-around bad egg?"

"You forgot bastard," she added.

He frowned. "You don't think I can back up my boasts of power and dominance? If that's the case, I can assure you, Mother, you're gravely mistaken."

"Let's just say, you might be able to intimidate these people with your fear tactics, but you don't scare me."

"Then you are as unwise as all the rest."

"Perhaps," she said in a cavalier, non-threatened way.

"Pray tell, Mother, what is this ace up your sleeve that gives you such blind confidence?"

"This," she said, her burgundy lips widening into a smile. With a tap on her wrists, numerous Corvette class Dagon warships decloaked above their position. Each ship spewed out Falcon heavy dropships until the swarm filled the sky above them.

Each of the dropships swooped down and, buzzing the battlefield, opened their bay doors. Hundreds of blue women, clad in special iridescent pearl armor, dove from the bellies of the ships.

The first of them landed beside Jegra. The strangely familiar-looking girl stood up beside the empress and looked over at the young H'aaztre.

"Is this him?" she asked, her lips turning into a sneer. "He doesn't look like much," she scoffed.

This seemed to offend him; he looked the girl up and down, trying to figure out who she was.

Jegra cleared her throat and introduced the two of them. "Son, I'd like you to meet your sister, Lycia Alakandra, future ruler of the Dagon Empire."

"Sister?" he balked. "I have no sister." His black eyes settled onto his so-called sibling, golden halos flashing brightly as he studied her. He smacked his teeth in disgust. "You're merely a mongrel. A half-breed. The genetic equivalent of the leftovers of two incompatible species. You are for, all intents and purposes, a bastardization of a tumor. And that's all you'll ever be, *dear sister.*"

Lycia laughed. "Wow, you weren't kidding, Mom. He really *is* a pompous ass."

Jegra raised her hands as if to suggest she had no skin in this heated exchange and was keen to stay out of it.

What's more, even in her deepest conscious mind, she took no responsibility for his upbringing. The babe she'd once held in her arms—what seemed like eons ago—had been lost to her the moment Nodengoth snatched him from her. His life, his behavior, and his destiny was, for lack of a better turn of phrase, completely out of her hands.

"I may be nothing more than a tumor in your eyes," Lycia said to him, "but you're still just the *wittle* baby brother of a tumor."

In that moment, something caught her eye and she glanced over at Dakroth standing across the battlefield from her. When he caught her gaze, he nodded at her. It was the first time they'd ever set eyes on each other, and, although it was just a look, his acknowledgment of her filled her with joy she didn't know she could ever have possessed.

To her uncouth remark, H'aaztre merely glared at the young Dagon half-breed. "I should cut out your tongue for such insolent remarks!" he snarled.

She turned her gaze back toward him and pretended to shiver. "*What's the matter, wittle brother, did I touch a nerve?*" Then, tilting her head at Jegra, she asked, "Permission to teach this little snot-lick a lesson in respect?"

"By all means," Jegra said, gesturing for Lycia to proceed.

As more and more Lycias rained down all around them, the original one and only daughter, standing beside her mother, waved her back. "You should stand back, Mom. This may get...heated."

Deunan and Gamagor appeared beside Jegra and she nodded at them. "Thanks for coming."

They nodded in return and Deunan replied, "We came as soon as we got your call. And we brought backup."

"I see that," Jegra said, smiling. "And your timing couldn't be better."

"If only we could have awakened the rest of the clones," Gamagor said.

Jegra shook her head as if to say it was alright. They'd only learned about the clones five days ago. It was a miracle they'd managed to get them here, ready for battle, as fast as they had.

Then, all three eased back, giving the two overpowered combatants room to go at it. Lycia cracked her neck and her fingers and then hopped up and down in a happy-go-lucky way, her ponytail bouncing behind her as she smiled at H'aaztre like she knew something he didn't.

H'aaztre's black eyes targeted Lycia like a couple of heat-seeking missiles, and he roared out like a rabid beast. "You won't win."

"We'll see," Lycia replied.

"I'll remind you that you said that when I'm crushing your skull with my bare hands, *dear sister.*"

Lycia put her fingers to her lips, but before she whistled, she got the last word in. "Suck my meaty Dagon cock, you punk-ass dickwad."

A shrill whistle pierced the air and nearly half of the six-hundred Lycias swiftly began unleashing their powerful Dygra energy, each of them blasting away at H'aaztre from every angle.

He deflected the incoming blasts, promptly throwing up an energy shield, while the other half of Team Lycia turned their firepower onto the Fusion forces.

The combined energy beams came to a head, forcing H'aaztre to stagger back, all of his power going to sustain the shield. Eventually, one of them would have to tire, and he was quite confident he had the stamina to outlast this mongrel.

Nyctan and Nephilim soldiers turned into charcoal visages of their former selves as they were vaporized in mid-air. Their ashes fluttered to the ground only to be tread upon by the marching boots of more Lycias.

Not only were the Lycias capable of rapid healing and energy blasts, they could wield forcefield powers and were also programmed with every form of martial arts known throughout the Commonwealth, including the Dagoni form of *Bai'Jamin* as well as the Dragonian style lizard wrestling knowing as *Hrsh Varlek.*

Entire squads of Nephilim and Nyctan soldiers dissipated on the wind as various Lycias made short work of them. And for every Lycia they managed to take down, each one of her managed to take down at least three or four of them.

Fed up with the devastating assault his side was taking, H'aaztre raised a hand and let out a white energy blast. It tore through the dense center of action and seventeen Lycias went up in smoke, vaporizing in the blink of an eye.

Their screams, along with their remains, dissipated on the breeze.

Lycia Alakandra frowned as her sisters died all around; she nodded at one of the nearby Lycias. That Lycia nodded back and turned to H'aaztre.

"Hey, wittle brother," the Lycia shouted. H'aaztre looked over at her and she pulled up her top, flashing her tits at him.

"*Whaaat?* Why?!" he shouted, clearly revolted, and turned his gaze away from her mammoth, jiggling breasts.

Seeing her opening, Lycia charged forward and tackled her brother in his moment of distraction. H'aaztre and Lycia tumbled to the ground and rolled around together. Coming to a stop, she got on top and slapped him across the jaw. Hard.

Stunned, he looked up at her with his eyes filled with shock. Apparently, his physical form was yet a virgin to pain, and the thousand natural shocks of an unforgiving reality.

His blue fingers rose to his lip, which trickled blood, and he looked down at his blood smeared fingertips in silence. Then, his forehead wrinkled with a heavy scowl and his veins bulged and throbbed with an unbridled fury.

"Get off me, you filthy creature," he roared out in rage and backhanded her.

Lycia flew through the air like a rag doll tossed out of a moving vehicle and crashed to the ground. The momentum, combined with the rebound, forced her back into the air and she cartwheeled out of control until someone caught her.

"I got you," a voice said. She looked up to see yellow grinning teeth and two blue, slatted bovine eyes staring at her. It was Grendok—at least, a Grendok.

This one was decked out in full military gear and was mid-air, paragliding toward the battle raging down below.

"My hero," she said, and gave him a peck on his fuzzy white cheek.

"Ah," he said affectionately, "you're far to kind, milady."

Hundreds of satyr paratroopers filled the sky, their slatted eyes flitting around as they picked off enemy troops from above with their scoped plasma rifles.

"The cavalry has arrived," Kregor shouted above the din of blaster fire and explosions. He looked up at the hundreds of Grendoks floating down toward the war zone.

"It's raining clones," Gyllek said, decloaking next to Kregor. He looked over at her as she stood holding two plasma blasters in her hands. She continued on, "Blue clones, furry clones, big tittied clones, and clones with hooves."

"I thought the captain told you to stay aboard the ship."

She shrugged, then tapped a tab on her optics suit and vanished into thin air again.

"Kids," Angellyk said, letting out a deep sigh.

Kregor turned back toward the chaos swirling around them and nodded in agreement. "Can't live with them. Can't eat them."

Angellyk merely shot him a stern look that seemed to say, *not funny.*

"What? What'd I say?"

"Someday I might want to have kids with you, you dumb oaf. And there's no way in Helios I'm letting you eat them!"

"Kids?" Kregor gulped. "Who said anything about wanting kids?"

She turned to argue, but realized this was neither the time nor place for this discussion. "I'm pinning this for now," she said, pointing a slender green finger at him. "Until then, don't eat any children."

"Not even the annoying bratty ones?" he teased, grinning at her stupidly. She merely punched him in the arm, which made him laugh.

"Incoming!" a voice shouted, and Kregor dove on top of Angellyk just as a massive blast hit too close and buried them beneath a pall of dirt and debris.

"My hero," she wheezed, coughing lightly as the dust settled. Kregor merely smiled and then, leaning into her, kissed her long and hard.

"What was that for?"

"Yes," he said. "I will have kids with you."

This forced a smile to her lips.

"Will you two stop smooching already," Gyllek's voice came from the thin air, "cuz more bad guys are coming."

They looked up to see several red beams of light manifest all over the battlefield as more Knights of Caelum appeared. It was H'aaztre's reserves.

After the satyr paratroopers landed, Grendok set Lycia down and they all took up positions around her.

Jegra threw a fist into the air and shouted, "Now!"

All the remaining Lycias stopped what they were doing, letting their assigned Grendoks step in to protect them from any ambushes as they focused their energy beams.

Jegra threw her korridium battle axe high into the air and, in succession, all the Lycias trained their Dygra energy onto the twirling axe.

Caught in the blast of a thousand energy beams, the axe began to glow orange-hot, then white-hot, and, finally, it melted down, turning into a super-heated plasma.

Dakroth looked over at Jegra and she flashed him a coy smile as she turned to meet Old Lady Jegra's gaze and nodded.

All three joined the Lycia army, adding their own energy blasts to the mysterious laser show.

"What are you doing?" H'aaztre asked, confused by this unconventional stratagem. But only his servant, Aidora, was within earshot, and she looked over at him with a blank stare and shrugged.

He grumbled in an agitated fashion and tried to take a step toward Jegra, but a giant hoofed foot came down from the sky and squashed him like a bug.

"Leave her alone," the massive Grendok's voice boomed over the hum of the Dygra energy discharging.

"I forgot he could do that," Old Lady Jegra said to herself, as she watched Grendok grow in size to giant proportions. Memories of her first time in the arena flashed before her eyes, when she, too, faced off a giant, and utterly terrifying satyr.

Soon the korridium plasma began to sparkle, and when it seemed so full of energy it would explode with the force of a supernova, a strange thing happened. A golden tear in the fabric of space-time slowly began to open.

Unexpectedly, the giant Grendok screamed out in agony as his leg vaporized. The giant goat fell to the ground with a ground quaking thud.

H'aaztre dusted off his robes, his eyes glowing hot-white with radiant energy.

It was a stark change to his typically Percheron black gaze, which meant he was finally feeling the pressure of the combined might of the Allied forces. It was the first crack in his seemingly indomitable power.

"Enough," he snarled, marching up to Jegra. She stopped her energy blast and turned to face him, but she was too late. He clutched her by the arm and, spinning around like a discus thrower, whipped her about in one fluid motion and flung her into the air.

She went up then came down, tumbling across the ground. She rolled to try to break her fall, finally scraping to a halt in the dirt, a large mound piling up behind her in the process.

She stood up in the small pit at the end of a gouge that stretched a hundred meters long, and stared back at her foe with smoldering brown eyes.

"Don't you dare touch my wife," Dakroth yelled, as he turned his full energy blast onto H'aaztre.

H'aaztre immediately countered with a blast of white energy of his own. The red and white energy crashed together like the icy waves that crash violently against the rocky cliff face of Primea's northern shores.

Their feet skidded across the ground as they both increased their power output, gradually pushing one another further back.

"I admit, you have a surprising amount of power for a mere mortal, but you're still no match for me," H'aaztre said, grinning with an air of superiority.

"Son," a voice called out.

H'aaztre, not ceasing his assault, looked towards where the voice had come from. His eyes softened when he saw his mother, Danica, standing near him.

She wore the gossamer gown of gold lace he'd given her. Her purple-turquoise ombre hair had been died black with red highlights and was coiffed into an elaborate, rose petal shaped up-do.

She was the Guardian of Aldebaran—her new role as servant to the Gilded Master was to protect Aldebaran and prevent anyone from interfering with H'aaztre's plans.

In addition to this, she had gained the power to manipulate time, and could see both into the past and the future simultaneously. To her was granted immortality, a gift he had bestowed upon her so that they could be together...forever.

"Please, end this," she begged.

"I cannot. You, of all people, know this, Mother. You have seen the future. You know what must come to pass."

"The future hasn't yet been written," she said. "The farther in time you look, the less certain it is. There are elements at play now that have already changed your probable future. This war, your plans, are now in jeopardy, my son. But you can still prove yourself merciful and end this."

"Never," he growled. "Now fall back in line, Mother."

With sad eyes, she drew out a very special blade. A blade, given to her by her father, and his father before him: the korridium blade of her great ancestor, Thorgon Van Danica Amelorak.

"You wench!" he spat, "This betrayal will doom you to an eternity of suffering!"

"It is not for me to kill you," she said in a sad voice. "You are in my heart, and my hand shall not move against you. But there are those you've wronged. Those whose vengeance is as inescapable as death itself."

She let the knife slip from her hand and the moment it hit the ground he lunged for her. Gripping her by the throat, he hoisted her off her feet and began to choke the life out of her.

The moment his attention was focused on Danica, he stopped his laser game of tug of war with Dakroth, who collapsed to his hands and knees, panting as he tried to catch his breath. That little standoff had nearly depleted him.

Choking, Danica gasped for air but could not find it. Soon, her eyes fluttered back in her head. But before she faded away entirely, she heard a scream pierce the air. She was released, falling backward and landing on her ass.

Astonished to find H'aaztre looking down at the blade of her knife protruding from his chest, she smiled. She smiled because she understood something no one else did. She understood that if they didn't defeat this evil entity this day, they'd all die in the most terrible ways imaginable.

Everyone but for her. She'd outlive them all. She'd continue living, for all eternity, with the shame of what she'd done driving her to a madness she could never return from.

H'aaztre looked down at the blade dripping blood. He staggered forward once, and then slowly turned to see who'd stabbed him in the back. Standing behind him was Aidora, eyes blazing with the fury of a woman scorned.

"That's for letting him rape me!" she shouted. "And for what? So you could lure him into a false sense of security before catching him and skinning him alive?"

She spat on his face in disgust and he wiped at it ineffectively and stared at the sticky saliva dripping from his fingertips.

Abruptly, H'aaztre's eyes turned pitch-black and, so too, hers. His darkness filled her and she was frozen with terror, unable to flee, only able to watch as he held her in his grasp.

His hands reached out and squeezed her throat, and she could feel him trembling with rage as he strangled her. "Why you…insolent…little…wretch."

Ruthlessly, the knife was ripped out of his back and he yelped from the pain. As he spun around, the knife came back down and entered his chest, just above his heart. A near miss.

He looked down at the handle protruding from his left breast and, in that moment, his face was grief stricken as he stared back at the face of his own mother, Danica.

"Why?"

"Because, my son…you are evil."

The blade hissed as it melted through his layers of clothes and super-hardened flesh. Like Jegra, he was virtually invulnerable, with but a few exceptions; this knife being one of them.

"All you have is your threats and your fear. But listen to me, child. Your hate is nowhere near as powerful as her love."

Danica slowly turned her face and nodded at Jegra, who stood in the distance. Then, leaning in, she whispered into his ear.

"Look around you. Look at those countless warriors laying down their lives for her. They do so willingly—out of love for her. Your soldiers only do so because they are compelled by fear of you."

"And your point is?" he grunted.

She twisted the knife to make him pay closer attention. "My point, son, is that no matter how powerful you believe yourself to be, you're not just fighting against Jegra. You're fighting against everything she stands for. You're fighting the ideology of love itself. And that is not a battle you can win."

"How can you be so sure, Mother? What have you seen in that distant fog you call the future?"

"At the end of the day, who do you think these people will be most loyal to—the despot who rules over them with threats of violence and fear, or the queen who rules over them with love and acceptance?"

"I see it now," he said with a chuckle and a nonchalant wave of his hand. "I was foolish not to see it before. You love her more deeply than anything in this whole, mad spiraling galaxy."

"Am I so transparent?" Danica asked, a subtle smile forming on her black painted lips.

"You have betrayed me, Mother," he said, the blackness fading from his eyes. She drew back as the oily dark of his demonic gaze washed away, leaving only his natural blue eyes. "And for that, I'll take the very thing you cherish from you. I shall isolate you in my temple to ensure that you two shall never meet again except for the day that Jegra shall come to you, and out of mercy for you and the eternal torment you endure, end your life. And as you look into one another's eyes, your dying thought shall be how your sacred love failed you— and that, my dear mother, will be your fate."

At that very moment, Dakroth's red energy blast engulfed the young H'aaztre, and he vaporized in front of them all.

Danica staggered back then sank to her knees. She began weeping for the loss of her only son, when a gentle touch pressed down on her shoulder. She looked up to find Jegra standing over her. "You did the right thing, Dani."

Danica placed both her hands over her heart, which ached terribly, and asked, "Then why does it hurt so badly?"

A deep and throaty demonic laugh cackled, interrupting their reunion;

they looked around for where it was emanating from.

It continued to cackle like a madman, and everyone stopped fighting, both sides frantically searching for the source of that booming, diabolical laughter.

"Over there!" Raven shouted.

All eyes followed her finger up into the sky where the young H'aaztre, his white skin fracturing with eggshell thin cracks of golden light, hovered roughly seventy feet above them.

"You pathetic fools," H'aaztre's voice boomed, "you are but ants to me. I am a God! I cannot be defeated."

Little by little, his skin flaked off and, swelling up from inside, a massive golden creature tore through his broken flesh and entered this reality through its vessel.

"*Nooo!*" Danica screamed out, as the flesh and bone of her son gave way to something nightmarish.

A gigantic squid entity made entirely of radiant golden energy, larger and more hideous than any to have come before it, manifested before the innumerable eyes that watched in horror.

It unfurled hundreds of tentacles which slowly stretched out across the sky as it continued to grow bigger and bigger until, finally, it was the size of the largest battlecruisers ever constructed.

Soon, the terrible being blanketed the battlefield for several kilometers in every direction and blotted out the sun.

Four sets of bat-like wings extended from the creature's back, and its face, vaguely anthropoidic, but at the same time unmistakably alien, peered down at them with a dozen blinking eyes that were as black as the darkest night.

"Watch out!" Raphine's voice cried out, breaking the silence.

Jegra's head snapped to the right as she spotted Raph. In all the commotion, she hadn't even realized Raphine had joined them on the battlefield.

Curious as to what she was pointing at, Jegra looked up, turning her gaze toward the sky. Debris from the *Chiron* and *Rod of H'aaztre* hung in the atmosphere, slowly, incrementally, falling toward them.

"Take cover!" Jegra shouted.

But it was too late. Flaming debris had already begun to crash down all around them like a hailstorm of flaming steel. The ground beneath their feet swelled and then erupted with the impact of a hundred craters. Soldiers on both sides flew through the air while others were impaled by razor sharp shrapnel.

The larger chunks of the ship's massive bulkheads crushed dozens of warriors unable to get out of the way fast enough. And even then, some of the large fragments that had pierced the ground tilted, melting the earth around them and slammed down, crushing countless more beneath their unbearable weight and girth.

Screams echoed through the chaos and were quickly silenced by the quake of the main fuselage, which crashed two klicks away. An atomic-level explosion plumed high into the sky forming a mushroom cloud in the distance.

Once the shrapnel and debris had finished coming down, people slowly rose to their feet and checked themselves to see if they were still intact or merely dead-men walking.

Stunned, enemy glanced at enemy, unable to bring themselves to continue the battle due to shock and exhaustion setting in. They merely stood looking around at the world shattering events, flaming debris peppering the entire landscape. Utterly drained, they were left trying to figure out what they should do next.

All of a sudden, Gamagor Dar'Vek let out a fierce battle cry—the cry of a gladiator. "Victory or death!"

Drawing her own battle axe, she charged forward, lodging the blade into a knight's chest, picking him up off the ground, and slamming him down onto his back.

Before she could pry the axe out of his chest, more shouts rang out and the Allied forces joined her and let slip the gladiator's cry: "Victory or death!"

"Victory or death!" the Lycias cried.

"Victory or death!" Grendok and his soldier clones bleated.

Jegra smiled, and whispered those words, perhaps for the very last time: "Victory or death.

Both sides began their merciless grudge match and the onslaught grew to its bloody zenith.

Amid the bloodshed, Jegra helped Danica to her feet and the two of them, still gripping one another's forearms, looked around. Their eyes finally met Dakroth's and they were astonished to find him standing amid the swirling chaos, eyes full of tears, weeping.

When they looked over to see what he was staring at, they saw that

Callestra had been pinned to the ground by a sharp piece of shrapnel from one of the downed starships.

739

36

Swords clashed and plasma fire was exchanged as both sides charged into the heat of battle.

With the help of the Lycia and Grendok clone armies, Jegra and her forces were finally able to push back the enemy just enough so that a small clearing opened up around the empress and her friends. In that hollow space, Dakroth let out a gut-wrenching scream and everyone nearby turned to watch as he raced over to Callestra where, upon reaching her, fell to his knees at her side and took her up in his arms.

She smiled up at him even as blood dribbled from the side of her mouth. The shrapnel had pierced her abdomen, and unbeknownst to all but her and Dakroth, had taken the newborn growing in her womb.

When she tried to speak, more blood gurgled up over her lower lip, her words choked by the thickness of her own blood.

She coughed violently, her body expelling as much as it could from her throat, some splashing across Dakroth's uniform, but he did not care.

"I need to...*cough*...I need to tell you something...*cough*"

"Don't speak, my luv," he whispered. But before either of them could utter another word, the life in her drained away and her gaze grew vacant.

As her face grew expressionless and her head tilted to the side, Dakroth was overtaken with violent sobs that rattled in his throat. Clutching his dead love in his arms, he buried his face in her hair and wept for the loss of both his greatest love and his unborn child. Both of them, taken too soon.

Dakroth choked down any further sobs, and sitting upright, he gently pressed his hand to her forehead and ran his fingers down her cobalt face and aquiline nose. With the gentlest touch, he closed her amber eyes so she could rest in peace.

An emotional whirlwind churning inside of him, he threw out his arms and kicked back his head. Rising from his lungs came a roar of pain and anguish so great that half the battlefield could hear it. It was the cry of a man whose heart was shattering into a thousand pieces.

Old Lady Jegra turned to Raven and said, "It's time."

Raven stretched out her hand from across the battlefield, as if to try and clasp onto her luv one last time. Raven smiled at her Jegra and mouthed the words, "I love you."

Old Lady Jegra smiled in return and nodded, as if to say, *I know*. She then pried the dagger from her back with a grunt and, ignoring the fact that she'd soon bleed out, turned to one of the Grendoks.

"I need you to grow large and toss me up there," she said, pointing her blade at the giant squid monstrosity hanging above them.

The Grendok nodded and quickly grew to a monumental size. Scooping her up in his palm, he boomed, "May Pan be with you, my empress." Then, cocking his arm back like a catapult, he flung Old Lady Jegra high into the air.

She sailed through the sky, and brought the korridium blade down onto the glowing hide of H'aaztre's true form. Piercing it, she clung to him like a silver-haired tick intent on drawing blood.

Drawing out another blade, she cut open her own chest where the suture scar yet remained. She plunged her hand and fingers inside her own chest, screaming out with a sickening, pain-laden cry that turned into a horrid moan.

Finally, she clutched the Dygra crystal in her fist and tore it from her own chest. Then, with all the strength she yet possessed, began to squeeze it in her hand.

"Everybody get behind me," Lycia said. "All of me."

With that, all the Lycias took formation and erected energy bubbles. Their shields grew into one massive protective energy barrier and they continued to combine their powers to deflect the inevitable blast and save as many people as possible.

Old Lady Jegra looked down at Raven one last time and smiled. "I'll miss you," she whispered.

In a brilliant flash of pink light, Old Lady Jegra and her Dygra crystal exploded. The fiery explosion split open the golden rift even further, and H'aaztre's terrible form was slowly sucked into the new spacetime fissure.

The monster howled in protest and his tentacles whipped wildly about as if they were trying to clutch onto something to anchor himself from being swallowed up.

The blast of energy kicked back and washed over the energy barrier erected by the Lycias. When a portion of the energy shield faltered and then collapsed, dozens of soldiers vaporized in the blink of an eye.

H'aaztre's golden tentacles were flailing about as he continued to attempt to clasp onto something when a powerful blast came out of nowhere and knocked him deeper into the rift.

Jegra stood upon the battlefield with a massive battlecruiser cannon from one of the downed ships. It was the size of a smokestack.

"Oh, please," his demonic voice boomed, "you've tried that already."

"This one's bigger," she grunted, hoisting the cannon above her and taking aim. She wasn't mistaken, either; this one was so massive that her feet began to sink into the concrete, large chunks shattering under the duress of the immense weight of the warrior and her weapon.

She fired another super massive canon blast into H'aaztre's side and he roared out in agony. It seemed that Old Lady Jegra's sacrifice had severely weakened him.

Like all wounded animals, H'aaztre was more dangerous now that he had shown he was vulnerable. Overcompensating, he fired a beam of white energy at Jegra.

It happened so fast that she hadn't time to react. She barely had time to flinch...but when she didn't feel her flesh burning off her body, she cracked open an eyelid and looked around.

Unexpectedly, everything around her slowed down to an incremental tick. The energy blast of white light glided to a stop and vibrated mere feet from her face, where it hung, not vaporizing her.

Just hovering there like a javelin of energy, buzzing in protest at whatever invisible force had seized it, she realized she'd forgotten to breathe and suddenly took in a large gulp of fresh air.

When Jegra looked to her left, she saw Brei'Alas standing next to her, palms extended as she used her time-manipulation abilities to save her empress.

"Don't worry, Your Grace. I've got you."

"Brei'Alas!" Jegra cried out, tears instantly flooding into her eyes and pouring over her lids.

"Go on," Brei said, "Get out of here."

"But you'll die!"

"It'll be an honor to die for a woman like you. But, you need to go. These people need you more than they need me."

"Brei," Jegra said, her hand unable to touch the other love of her life. If she lost sweet, innocent Brei, she wouldn't know what to do with herself. "I can't lose you too."

"Jegra," Brei said in a stern voice, speaking to her empress in a curt manner. "I don't know how long I can hold it," she said, her nose starting to bleed as she looked over at Jegra one last time. "Just know that…I love you. I've always loved you."

"Please," Jegra pleaded. "Come with me."

"You know I can't," Brei said, turning all her focus back to the task at hand. Then, in an authoritative voice, she shouted, "I SAID GO!"

Jegra, tears streaming down her cheeks, turned and ran.

A few seconds later, Brei'Alas screamed as she lost control of her time-freeze and the light flared all around her and Jegra. In that last moment, she realized she'd failed. She hadn't been able to hold him back.

Without warning, H'aaztre's energy beam suddenly changed directions and was redirected into the atmosphere.

Brei collapsed to her knees, stunned that she was still alive. She looked over to see the Lord Emperor standing beside to her. His veins pulsed hot pink and his entire heart lit up like a glow light beneath the folds of his robes.

The most massive forcefield she'd ever seen wrapped around the three of them and Jegra, stopping in her tracks, turned to see what had happened.

H'aaztre roared out in fury, his rage shaking the very ground around them, in an earthquake of his making.

His great fury and rage consumed him; he released another energy blast, but again, Dakroth stepped into the line of fire and deflected it with another energy shield.

Both arms pressed together, palms open, he released his largest energy blast yet. It tore across the battlefield, tearing up the ground as it shot out of his hands like a brilliant and mighty shaft of light.

"I grow tired of you," Dakroth roared out over the blast. "Now, die!"

H'aaztre and Dakroth's energy collided and they deflected each other's trajectories, both shooting off at random angles.

But even as he over-exerted himself, he knew it wouldn't be enough to knock the squid entity back into the rift.

Jegra returned to Brei's side and embraced her, sobbing as she took the girl in her arms. The thought of losing Brie was too much for her to bear. Depleted, Dakroth collapsed to his knees, beside them.

That's when a faint voice came over the comm, Jegra's pendant transferring the call. "Please tell my sister I'm sorry and that I love her."

Jegra looked at Brei, who was just as perplexed as she was and then, together, their eyes settled onto Brei's holopad device on her wrist. The message was coming from there as well.

The comm channel was open fleet wide, so that anyone could hear it, including enemy soldiers. Reaching down, Jegra turned up the volume of her pendant.

The final message came through clearly, and Jegra recognized the voice.

"Raven, if you're hearing this, I'm sorry. I'm sorry for everything. I'm sorry about Mom and Dad. All I ask is, someday you find it in your heart to forgive me. I was young and strong-headed. I didn't know what compassion was. But, now, I know that what I did was wrong. I hurt you. And I'm sorry. Just know...I love you, *big sister.*"

A sonic boom shook the entire battlefield and forced those below to cover their ears. As they looked up, they watched the *Shard* streaking across the sky— like a silver teardrop—as she headed on a direct collision course with the monster itself.

Raven screamed out, "Lianica!" But, there was nothing she could do. In another blink of the eye, the *Shard*, Lianica Blackstar, and her valiant crew, collided with H'aaztre—exploding in a massive ball of flame that could be seen from outer space.

Howling in rage and pain, H'aaztre slowly slipped into the rift. His tentacles whipped around limply like streamers ravaged by the wind, unable to take purchase of anything. He sank away into the glowing fissure, and the rift slowly sealed itself up, locking H'aaztre away forever.

As flaming debris rained down around them, Raven collapsed to her knees, completely stunned. Not only had she lost her lover, but she had lost her sister on the same day.

"I never got to tell her how much I missed her," she said, her voice cracking.

"She knew," Ladgara said, placing a hand on Raven's shoulder. "She knew."

A short distance off, Brei'Alas gazed up with forlorn astonishment. "Barrion was on that ship," she whispered.

Jegra gently reached over and touched Brei's face, wiping away a tear from her cheek. Before she could console her further, though, a soft *thud* drew their attention to the emperor who lay on his side a short distance from them.

"Rhadamanthus!" Jegra screamed out. She scurried over to him and, dropping to her knees, clutched his hand in hers. "You saved us," she said. "You saved us all."

"No," he said, looking into her beautiful brown eyes one last time. "I saved *you*."

Tears instantly burst forth and she pressed her forehead to his. His glowing veins pulsed through every centimeter of his body, as though they were counting down to his final breath.

"I will miss you…wife…" he said with a light cough.

"I know," Jegra replied, her bottom lip quivering as she held back the torrent of sobs that threatened to overtake her.

Slowly, the pink energy surging through his veins faded and his blue flesh cooled in the evening breeze of Dagon Prime.

He smiled at her one last time and then, his head fell back and the lustrous red of his eyes faded until they seemed black. He lay in her arms, an almost calm expression on his face, as he peered sightlessly up at the hazy sky.

Jegra clutched him in her arms, and cradling him as she would a babe, she rocked on her knees and sobbed.

In the end, he'd proven himself a noble warrior and a fine emperor. And, bending down, she kissed his lips one last time and did something she never thought she'd have the strength to do—she forgave him.

High in the upper atmosphere, above the clouds of Dagon Prime, over the capital city of Primea, numerous flashes sparkled like gems filling the evening sky.

Three hundred heavily armed Dragonian battleships jumped into the system. They surrounded the enemy fleet and, then, upon every monitor and holovid screen within communications range, there appeared a Dragonian lizard woman dressed in royal battle armor.

She held a silver staff with spiky protrusions and green emeralds inset throughout the length of it. She slammed it on the floor with a resounding *clank* that rang out loud and clear.

The lizard woman cleared her throat, and announced, "This is Queen Li'lek Zira Barocco the IV of the Dragonian Empire. I demand that all enemy ships surrender to the might of the Allied fleet immediately, or face utter destruction. This is your first and final warning. Do not test my resolve."

Cheers erupted as everyone on the ground watched the Nyctan and Nephilim Fusion fleet jump out of the system in a full retreat.

Nyctan soldiers that were left behind by their own fell to their knees in defeat. Even Lance Bishop turned toward Jegra Alakandra and, falling to one knee, bowed his head in humility and shame, but most of all, reverence to the empress. "Thank you," he said. "Thank you for freeing my people."

Jegra looked down at him and smiled bittersweetly. He had been forced to fight her against his will. He'd been tortured when he'd refused. But in the end, he was only one among the tens of thousands who were the victims of H'aaztre.

At this sight, every remaining soldier of the Knights of Caelum dropped to their knees and faced the empress. The prophesy had been fulfilled. The *Daughter of Sol* had vanquished a great evil and saved their people from death and destruction.

Danica and Raphine sauntered over to Jegra's side, and, extending a green hand, Raphine helped Jegra to her feet. As she rose up, Brei'Alas and Grendok hoisted the emperor's body above them.

"We will light the pyres for you, my friend," Grendok said, looking at the emperor's peaceful face.

As they struggled to carry him away, Raven, along with her crew, came over to lend a helping hand. Deunan, Lycia, and Gamagor joined them and—

together—they carried the body of their deceased emperor off the battlefield.

Danica, Raphine, and Jegra embraced one another, and touching their foreheads together, they let out a collective sigh of relief. The war for the galaxy had finally come to an end. And they'd won.

BOOK 5
EPILOGUE

The bard played a song on his lute, an ode commemorating the empress, Jegra Alakandra, and her victory over the ancient evil that came from another galaxy to conquer hers.

He sang, his voice melodic and pure, of her many conquests, of how she began as a slave and rose to champion of the gladiatorial arena. Of how she went from champion to lover and how she'd tamed the wild heart of the emperor himself.

The song told how she'd defied all odds and became empress to an entire galaxy. And how, as empress, she gained the trust and love of her subjects. It was a song for her; it was a song for the galaxy.

The reception hall of Arena Palace on Thessalonica bustled with the sound of waiters and banquet guests. Everyone Jegra had ever known or loved had come to this momentous occasion; everyone had arrived for the wedding of the century.

Grendok sat in the front row, his head buzzing with the amount of mead he'd already consumed, prior to the ceremony.

Raven stood to the right of the altar, along with Raphine, who held the rings. Danica and Brei'Alas stood to her left.

As bridesmaids, Raven and Raphine had the honor of giving the first toast, which Raven was dreading. But she took her duty seriously.

She waited for Brei'Alas to settle back into the row of women getting married today. That's when the bard changed his tune from the ballads of the galaxy to the wedding march.

All heads turned to the end of the aisle to see the empress in her glorious wedding gown, being walked down the aisle by Kregor, whose avocado colored tuxedo was fitted perfectly to his muscular physique. Although Jegra had informed him that this role traditionally went to a father figure, she wanted him to walk her down the aisle, because of all the men she knew, his heart was purest. In a moment of self-deprecation, he'd chalked it up to having a lizard brain—small and undemanding, yet always noble.

Jegra looked at the faces of her two fiancés, Danica and Brei'Alas, both as lovely as the day she'd met them. Each of them meant worlds to her. As she stepped up to the altar, the reverend turned around, revealing that it was Skuld.

"You're also ordained?" Jegra asked. But before he could speak, she smiled and answered her own question, "But, of course you are."

He grinned from behind the fishbowl-styled helmet, which had been decorated for the occasion by a wreath of rare turquoise orchids, and proceeded with the ceremony.

Jegra read her vows first.

"Danica, the road to happiness with you has had its fair share of twists and turns. Unexpected setbacks seemed to plague us from the start. But no matter what happened, we always came back together, stronger than ever. I loved you from the moment we met, for the strong woman you then proved yourself to be; I loved you when you did the impossible and transformed yourself for me, against your people's customs. I know you've made sacrifices, probably more so than anyone here. But through it all, you've always been the keeper of my heart."

Jegra turned to Brei'Alas next.

Brei'Alas fidgeted when Jegra looked at her, so much so that Jegra had to reach out and place her hands on Brei's arms to stop her from vibrating off the dais.

"There aren't enough words in the galaxy to explain what you mean to me, Brei. You are everything I always wanted in a partner and more. You're kind and thoughtful; you question everything, and your heart is always in the right place—no matter what difficulties you face. You held me in my darkest hour and guided me out of that darkness. You are my light and my soul."

Brei was ugly crying by this point, and Jegra cupped her hands around her cheeks and kissed her.

Danica, meanwhile, wiped a tear from her own cheek and sniffled.

"In that case," Skuld said, "please, bring out the rings!"

Raphine handed the rings to Jegra, two simple, matching bands of finely wrought korridium with blue sapphires evenly inset along the outer circumference. But when the audience realized the empress's ring was not among them, the shift in music alerted them that something special was coming down the aisle.

Everyone turned back toward the aisle to find Lycia accompanied by her trusty feline companion, Allie, ushering Jegra's wedding ring to the altar.

Upon a cerulean velvet cushion rested a glorious ring. It was crafted of three intricately carved bands, one of pale blue pluradium, the most precious alloy of Dagon Prime, one made from the light aquamarine gemstone of Arkadia, and finally the lustrous platinum alloy palladium, from Earth. When they arrived beside Jegra, Lycia took the ring from Allie's back and handed it to Danica.

"You may place the ring on her finger," Skuld informed Dani with a regal wave of his hand.

"Right," she laughed, feeling silly for blanking on what she had to do. She promptly placed the ring on Jegra's finger and kissed her.

"With the powers vested in the Commonwealth Alliance, the Dagon Empire, and the Intergalactic Wedding Commission, I now pronounce the three of you—married."

Cheers erupted as everyone in attendance rose to their feet and gave a seemingly endless round of applause. As Jegra and her two partners headed back down the aisle, hand in hand in hand, people threw rose petals into the air.

Lycia sidled up to Raven, and Allie circled about and then curled up at their feet where she began grooming herself.

Grendok shouted out in a voice that calmed the applause: "Long live the empress! Long live Jegra Alakandra!"

The hall erupted with calls to honor the empress and toasts to the union. Amid the cheers, Lycia leaned over and whispered into Raven's ear, "That's gonna be one hell of a honeymoon."

Raven's usual poker face façade melted away and she bellowed with laughter. It was so sudden that Lycia shot her a nervous glance and then, realizing how her quip must have sounded to her, she, too, broke into a fit of laughter.

Lycia, calming her giggles, spotted Deunan and Gamagor in the audience and waved. They waved back, both smiling broadly. "What happens now?" she asked without looking at Raven.

Raven smiled. "Now we eat, drink, and live our lives."

"I'll drink to that," Grendok said, suddenly appearing by their side as he tipped back another frothy mug of mead.

"Where'd you get that from?" Lycia asked, laughing at the satyr's steadfastness to remain in a state of perpetual drunkenness.

"Yes, indeed!" he answered, half-sloshed. He then smacked Lycia firmly on her buttocks; her eyes widened and she perked up.

Raphine leaned in and said, "Don't worry, he's always like this."

"I know," Lycia said, turning to Raphine. Their eyes met and Lycia froze. She'd never beheld a creature of such beauty her entire life. And what's more, they were virtually the same age.

"I'm, uh, I'm…Lycia," she stammered.

"I know," Raphine replied, smiling back at her and tucking a tuft of forest green hair behind her green ear.

Raph laughed then slipped her arm around Lycia's waist and turned to watch the three queens of Dagon leave. Lycia merely looked down at Raphine's slender green fingers resting on her hips and smiled to herself. It was love at first sight. Right then and there, she knew this was the woman she'd marry. *Someday.*

Grendok raised his mug high and smiled, knowing they'd soon be at the banquet hall, and with the knowledge of a hearty feast to come, he smiled and took another long swill of mead, wiped the foam from his muzzle, and let out a long, satisfied belch.

BOOK FIVE
FINIS

BOOK 6

THE CHRONICLES OF

JEGRA

A SONG FOR THE GALAXY

1

The *UCC Titania* hung languorously against the black backdrop of a star speckled expanse like a bloated caterpillar. It wasn't a pretty ship, but most large fighter carriers were simply overstuffed cargo vessels housing state of the art warships.

Inside her main hangar bay, there was a row of Warhawk stealth fighters parked along the back wall. They were painted in non-reflective matte-black, which allowed them to disappear into the darkness of space.

At the end of the row sat a new prototype ship, but unlike the others, it was twice as long and had a cherry red paint job with yellow warning stickers that gave it a hot-rod appeal. On the side was painted "Warhawk WX-9."

The WX-9 was an FTL capable fighter. The first of its kind in the United Cosmic Commonwealth fleet. Although the Nyctans had Faster-than-Light capable fighters, a technology they'd acquired through their allegiance with the Nephilim, they were now a defeated people and what little remained of their armada was stationed to protect their homeworld and surrounding moons.

Captain Simon Calvec leaned back in his ready room chair and sipped a cup of steaming Belizean honey tea as he studied a 3D holographic display of the ship deployments for the sector. Right now, he was shuttling supplies between Nyctan and the Seyferrian Republic. The two satyr worlds, Qu'Mar and Veridion, also had provided additional medicine and aid to help with Nyctan's gradual recovery and eventual reformation.

Although the Dagon Empress, Jegra Alakandra, had called it "vital aid work necessary to rebuild the Nyctan's homeworld," beneath all the pretense it was just another occupation. Albeit, a very subtle and polite occupation.

Still, Calvec felt it was the best course of action. If they sat back and did nothing, the Nyctan interim government would destabilize and fall apart. Millions of people would die from famine and starvation. And, as with any great culture ravished by war, the entire civilization would take two steps back while the rest of the star systems marched on without them.

Without an official ruler to take the throne, the Nyctan Dynasty was no more. All they could hope to become is a pale imitation of their once illustrious selves. But with the United Cosmic Commonwealth Alliance's help, Nyctan could rebuild, regain economic independence, and maybe one day join the United Cosmic Commonwealth Alliance, UCCA.

And while the UCCA managed public and diplomatic affairs, the military branch of the alliance, known simply as the UCC, handled the more demanding chore of policing the newly formed cosmic alliance. A cosmic alliance that integrated all the peoples of all eight major star systems and three empires into one united allegiance. It was, without a doubt, more fragile than an Oszarkian egg.

Holding his mug in both hands, he took one more sip and then set it down on his desk. He reached up to touch the hologram, and, using small pinches and rotations of his fingers, he rotated the image and then zoomed in on the Outer Rim territories. Much of the fleet had been sent to protect the trade routes from marauder attacks.

In the aftermath of the war, several new factions of space pirates had sprung up, and there were raids on cargo ships daily. Something he hoped to remedy once the prototype ship of his was cleared for mass production. In another month, he'd have an entire fleet of new Warhawks to take the fight to the space pirates.

Just then his door chimed and, taking a deep breath, he swiped the holovid projection away and looked up from his desk. "Enter."

The doors parted with a pneumatic hiss and his chief of security, a beautiful Seyfferian officer by the name of Daz Ryley Ta'miel, entered.

She was stout, but as solid as a brick, and sported platinum blonde hair that complimented her dark copper skin rather nicely. Her chest was overly large for her petite size and seemed to fill her uniform—if not pushing it to its bursting point.

Regardless of her looks, it was her training and modifications that made her a real contender. With her nanite and genetic enhancements, she could pick up a Spartan tank and toss it across an entire battlefield, if she wanted to.

"Lieutenant Commander Daz, how may I help you?" he asked, the steam from his mug rising in front of his gaze as he stared at her with his amber, Dagoni gaze.

She blinked at him with her sky-blue eyes, which she could change at will, thanks to her enhancements. "Captain, as chief of security, it's my duty to inform you that a mutiny is currently underway aboard this ship. For your safety, I have to ask you to come with me."

Calvec laughed. "A mutiny? And I'm just hearing about this now?" He gave her a disbelieving look.

"Sir, this is no joking matter. I'm afraid that some of our crew have locked themselves in the hangar bay and are making demands. Worse," she added, her posture stiffening as she locked her hands behind her back in a formal manner, "they've made threats against the safety of the ship and her crew."

This caught Calvec's attention and any doubt he'd had about the nature of the news quickly turned serious. "What kind of demands?" he asked, rising from his chair.

Daz glanced down at his blue hands, which now formed two balled-up fists. "They demand you turn over control of the ship to them, or they're going to detonate the neutron bomb that's on one of the heavy raiders."

Calvec huffed in anger then folded his arms across his chest as his strategic mind began to run through all the possible scenarios that could play out.

It didn't seem right to him that they only wanted control of the ship. They wouldn't even be able to man the controls, let alone fly it. At least, not without a much bigger number of mutineers. No, he was certain they were interested in something else. This was just a backdoor approach to getting what they wanted.

"It doesn't seem likely that they're after control of the ship. I'll bet credits to creylons they want access to the departure codes so they can take a ship of their own. Without clearance to disembark, the Titania's automated turrets would make short work of them before they could get away."

"Do you think they're after the prototype, sir?"

"It's possible. Do you know who's calling the shots down there?"

"Lieutenant Afriel, sir. I think he's the highest-ranking personnel on the hangar deck."

"Afriel?" repeated Calvec, stroking his chin.

"What is it, sir?" asked Daz, seeing that the captain had fallen into deep contemplation.

"It's probably nothing. But if I remember correctly, Afriel was one of the orphans that grew up in the massive complex for those who'd lost parents in the war and had nobody to care for them. It was called 'the Compound.'"

"I remember that place," Daz said. "It's where they inculcated strict discipline, duty and honor into the kids at an extremely young age. An ultra-nationalist program to ensure the children wouldn't grow up to be recidivist delinquents once they left the Compound."

"Yes. And a lot of those orphans ended up joining the military right out of school," the captain continued. "Others opted to join fringe groups, which promised to fill the hole left by a life chock full of abandonment issues. Of those fringe groups though, one in particular springs to mind. The one that drew in the largest numbers of children...the Harbingers of Purity and Light."

"The Harbingers?" Daz asked, speaking out loud. "Isn't that the radical extremist Demeris Ferrison's organization?"

Calvec shook his head in a displeased fashion and grunted in the affirmative. "It sure is," he replied. Although, by his tone, Daz could tell he wasn't too thrilled about it.

Walking around his desk, he motioned for Daz to join him as he headed toward the exit.

The doors swished open in front of them and they promptly stepped out onto the bridge. As they entered, he snapped his fingers several times, drawing the attention of the surrounding officers.

"Sub Commander T'Vok, you have the bridge," Calvec informed his XO. "Keep things locked down here and keep communications open." Turning to the two security officers stationed at the door, he addressed them with a nod and said, "You two, you're with me."

Calvec, Daz, and the added company of the security detail all piled into the lift and the doors hissed shut behind them.

A minute and a half later the lift doors parted and all four stepped onto deck fourteen, the same deck as the main hangar bay. They strolled down a long corridor which gradually curved to the left, until they came upon the main hangar doors

Another four security officers met them at the hangar bay doors. When they saw the captain and the chief of security, they all stepped into line and saluted.

"At ease," Calvec said. Then, turning toward the door, which was rigged with explosives, he said, "Update."

"At least five personnel have locked themselves inside the hangar bay," the security team leader relayed. "Lieutenant Afriel seems to be calling the shots in there. If you want, I can patch you through to him now." He handed the captain a two-way receiver that was plugged into the wall panel and then, tapping on his holovid display, activated the comlink. With a nod, he signaled the captain that he was live.

"This is Simon Calvec, your captain, speaking. I would ask you all to surrender and come out peacefully, but I have a feeling you want to make a statement with this little mutiny of yours. So, let's skip the formalities and get to brass tacks, shall we? What are your demands?"

Afriel's voice came back over the comlink in that unique manner of talking that all those from the Compound had. It was almost like a southern dialect, except more punctuated with ominous pauses strewn about. It reminded him of how someone might speak to you as a friend but with hidden resentment.

"Ah, yes, Captain my Captain. I just want you to know we don't wish to bring harm to anyone. We're still loyal Dagon citizens, after all, even if we do get court-martialed for our divergent political beliefs. Please, believe me when I say, Captain, all we want is to be granted safe passage off of this ship."

"Is that all?" Calvec asked in a somewhat sarcastic tone. "No other demands?" There were always more demands. No criminal worth his weight in korridium ever asked for only one thing.

"Ah, Captain, I can hear the frustration in your voice as you fish for clues. But you won't find any here. As I said, we don't want to harm anyone. But we will if you push us to it."

"Let's hope it doesn't come to that. I assume you're after the Warhawk prototype?"

"It appears you can read minds, Captain," Afriel laughed. "Very good. But this is just one of the items we'll be taking. It's my birthday today, and I think I'll just help myself to whatever tickles my fancy."

"Out of curiosity, Lieutenant, what makes you think you will get away with this? I'm two seconds from blowing these doors and storming the hangar with a fully armed security detail."

"You want leverage, do you, Captain? How very by-the-book of you. Alright, if you promise not to blow those doors, then I promise not to detonate this neutron bomb aboard your ship."

Calvec laughed loud enough for everyone to hear.

"You'd need the activation codes before you could do that," he said. He looked over at Daz and shook his head confidently. There was no way Afriel had the codes. After pausing for dramatic effect, he spoke into the receiver, calmly and coolly. "I think it's time to face the music, Lieutenant. Surrender yourselves and you might get lucky and avoid the gallows."

"A life in prison, then? As kind of an offer as that is, I think I'll pass, Captain. Also, I think there's something you need to hear. *Echo, Echo, Tango, Infinity, Alpha, Omega, Echo,*" Afriel said, reciting the neutron bomb activation codes verbatim.

"How in the bloody galaxy did he get those?" Daz asked in complete bewilderment.

Only she and the captain had clearance to access those codes, and neither of them had granted any such authorization. She shot the captain a startled look when he turned to her to confirm it was what they both feared. Those were, in fact, the authentic activation codes.

Without warning, the ship's automated voice interrupted the intense silence and spoke in its mellifluous manner, <<Neutron bomb signature detected. Automated red-alert activated.>>

"Graddak!" Calvec cursed under his breath. Then, bringing the receiver to his mouth, he growled, "Fine. We'll permit you to disembark."

"There now, I knew you'd come around to seeing it our way. And, Captain, just to be safe, we'll be taking the neutron bomb with us. That way, if those automated turrets do decide to take us out prematurely, you'll be coming along for the ride."

"Before I grant you the access codes, Afriel, tell me one last thing. Why throw away your entire military career? What could entice you to risk a court-martial and death by hanging?"

"You, a proud Dagoni yourself, should know the answer to that. We have a mongrel ruling our great empire. Sullying it with her impure blood and her lack of cultural understanding. Dakroth married a common bitch and then died, leaving the large-chested cow in charge of the empire. Needless to say, there are those not happy with this turn of events. The articles of the empire are quite clear: a non-Dagoni can never inherit the throne. She is an unlawful ruler, and we want her ousted."

"You must be aware that the articles of the empire also make exceptions for times of war and in case the emperor is unceremoniously lost in the line of duty. In this case, the empress meets both prerequisites."

"Semantics, Captain, a technicality. In the end, the articles mean whatever you want them to mean as long as you have the power to bend the public's perception to your will. With this neutron bomb, we now have that power."

"To what end, Afriel? What's the end game here?"

"We were once feared throughout all the Commonwealth. From one end of the galaxy to the next, they spoke of the mighty Dagon Empire. Now we're nothing but a laughingstock. Instead of conquering worlds and entire star systems, we're relegated to policing the intergalactic trade lanes and sniping at petty thieves and pirates. Meanwhile, that fat-assed Vek'miel sits on Dakroth's throne, wearing his crown, and tarnishing it with her menstruating, impure, alien filth."

"Those are bold words coming from someone of your station, crewman. The empress you dishonor with your slanderous tongue saved our world and countless others like it. She may not be pure in blood, but she's sure as Helios pure in spirit. And if you utter one more libelous slander about our beloved empress, I'll personally hunt you down to the ends of the galaxy and cut your tongue out myself."

Afriel balked and paused for the rest of his men to stop their snickering. "If only I could take your threat seriously, Captain. But I'm afraid, like the rest of our military, you've let the Terran whore defang you and brainwash you with her feminine wiles. But that changes nothing. The Harbingers of Purity and Light have laid claim to the neutron weapon. And you will heed our message or face the consequences."

Calvec cut the comlink and turned to Daz. "Get these assholes off my ship. That's an order."

"Yes, Captain," Daz answered. "With pleasure." Taking the receiver from him, she put it to her lips and cleared her throat. "Lieutenant Afriel, this is

Lieutenant Commander Daz, chief of security. You've been granted clearance for departure from hangar bay A-7."

A flood of hoots and cheers came back over the comm before Daz cut off the link to the hangar. She looked over her shoulder at the captain, who just raised his hands and addressed the security detail with silent gestures.

The moment the ships were away, the security team breached the hangar bay doors. A loud explosion erupted in the hangar and the captain and his security team emerged from the smoke onto the main hangar deck, plasma rifles drawn.

They were too late, however, as they arrived just in time to see two Falcon heavy dropships and the prototype Warhawk passing through the blue negative-energy shields and into outer space.

Daz growled under her breath and let off several blasts of her plasma rifle. The blasts merely hit the energy barrier and dissipated. And she would have wasted a whole coolant cartridge, too, if it wasn't for the captain gesturing with his hand for her to lower her weapon.

"Stand down, Lieutenant Commander. They're already gone."

"A bunch of back-stabbing, traitorous, vek'miels…the whole lot of them!" she snarled, releasing a flurry of obscenities.

"Alright. Let's find our calm and regroup. Lieutenant Commander, I need you to return to the bridge and get me a secure channel with UCC command. I need to warn them that the Demeris Ferrison has just acquired a neutron bomb."

"Yes, sir. Right away, sir," Daz said, giving a salute. Then, swiveling on her heels, she slung her rifle across her back and urgently strode across the hangar deck toward the gaping hole in the corridor.

Looking back up at the parting ships, Calvec scowled. In all his years of service, he'd never once experienced anything as embarrassing or shameful as losing face to a bunch of traitorous turncoats. And although he knew there'd be hell to pay for his failure, he wasn't going to stop hunting those deserters down until he'd rounded up every single last one and strung them up himself.

2

A happy melody played in the distance, rising from the streets of Arena City like a sweet spring breeze. It filled the dusty nooks and crannies of the market place and wafted in and out of the open windows along with the sounds of the nightlife stirring as the desert sun gradually sank beyond the horizon and gave way to the purple majesty of the evening.

The song, to all within earshot, was played on an ancient lute, commiserating the trials and tribulations, losses and victories of the patron of Thessalonica, that famed warrior and gladiatrix, Jegra Alakandra.

The bard's song told of how she had begun her harrowing journey as a slave and through great trials and tribulations became a champion of the arena. It spoke of how she went from famed champion to lover of the great Emperor Dakroth, may his soul forever rest in peace. It sang of their great love affair, and how Jegra had tamed the wild heart of the promiscuous emperor himself.

"Do you ever tire of hearing that tune?" asked Dani as she sidled up next to Jegra on the palace balcony that overlooked the warm glow of the city lights in the valley below.

She was dressed in her royal gown of white with gold embroidery, signifying she was Jegra's queen. And Jegra, queen of queens, had on a tangerine-colored gossamer dress of numerous translucent layers that flowed on the breeze and gave the appearance of a chimera consisting of a grand lion's mane and a jellyfish with countless flowing arms.

"Never," Jegra replied. "On most days I can't get it out of my head. The melody is pretty catchy."

Danica smiled and held out a glass of Nova Centauri Red for Jegra. She took it and sipped lightly, raising an eyebrow as she took in the particularly fine vintage.

"Is this…?"

"Yes," Danica said, "It's from Dakroth's reserve."

Jegra nodded and looked at the cup as she cradled it in both hands.

"Your Excellency," a demur voice called out and Jegra turned to find Raphine standing in the entrance of her chambers. When Jegra made eye contact with her, she said in a soft and solemn voice, "It's time."

Jegra let out a long sigh and reached out and took Dani's hand. "Will you stay by my side, wife?"

Danica smiled. "Always."

Together they followed Raphine out into the large hallway and down several flights of stairs before coming to the grand hall. There, friends and loved ones greeted them, including Raven and her crew, but Jegra didn't have the luxury of time to chat. She merely nodded at all the faces and walked past them as they sent her sad glances.

As promised, Danica accompanied Jegra out onto the main courtyard and the long rectangular pool that stretched out to the end of the green grass of her palace lawn.

Their hands still clasped, they looked up at the evening sky and beheld Dagon Prime hanging there like a giant green and blue swirling marble. It was aglow with the setting sun, which was incrementally receding behind it.

A flurry of golden light came down on top of them and whisked them away, their light particles swirling into the sky as they beamed toward the capitol city of Primea—already lighting up the southern hemisphere.

When they rematerialized, they found themselves standing at the beginning of a very lengthy dock. It was decorated with thousands of ornate flowers, brought in from every region of the empire.

At the end of the dock was a boat, and lying on the boat was the body of Rhadamanthus Dakroth, dressed in his finest burgundy and gold embroidered robes.

Standing there waiting were Brei'Alas and Grendok and the newly elected high chancellor, Marchela Vanesquia.

Vanesquia bowed as Jegra approached and kept her eyes down until Jegra uttered the words, "Rise."

As wife to the empress, Brei'Alas also held the title of queen, and so merely bowed her head most subtly.

Brei'Alas and Danica leaned into one another and gave a peck on each other's lips. Then all four women turned to Grendok.

Grendok Baphomet, ruler of the tenth satyr dynasty, dressed in his royal attire, looked the part of a king.

"I appreciate you doing this," Jegra said, smiling down at the five-foot-tall satyr. "You honor us."

He smiled briefly and then picked up a torch, dipped it in oil, and then, striking a flint, lit it up. He used it to light several other torches. The end of the pier glowed as he handed the first torch over to Jegra in ceremonious fashion.

"The honor is all mine," he said.

Thousands of Dagon and non-Dagon citizens alike lined the banks of the bay. Aliens from all parts of the system had come to pay their respects and light paper lanterns in memory of the emperor.

Dakroth may not have been the best ruler Dagon Prime has ever had, but he was the emperor they needed to get them through their darkest hour.

Jegra looked down at her late husband's handsome blue face one last time and, at that moment, she was taken back to when he'd first visited her in her chambers beneath the arena.

She'd just finished a match and was covered in blood, dirt, and sweat. And yet he came to her and made love to her there. And she remembered thinking to herself, if he loved me as a dirty slave, he'd loved me all the same as his wife.

She never thought in a million years this handsome, elfin lover of hers would propose. But then he did, and the rest is, as they say, history. A colorful, trouble-filled, and not always perfect history—but it was her history.

Smiling, a sparkling tear balancing on the edge of her eyelid like a morning dewdrop, she playfully whispered, "*Bastard*," and then tossed the torch onto the funeral boat.

The oil-soaked wood and body of the emperor went up in a blaze, and, using long poles, Jegra, Danica, and Brei'Alas pushed the boat out to sea.

At the same time, the funeral attendees—the sons and daughters of Dagon, those who felt the loss of the larger than life personality of Rhadamanthus Dakroth—including anyone who'd ever crossed paths with the enigmatic and quite eccentric ruler and came out of it unfettered by his ill-tempered bullheadedness—lined the shores by the thousands to honor his memory.

Men and women and aliens of all gender and species walked barefoot upon the white sands of the *Primean* shoreline, their white funeral robes fluttering in the evening breeze. Together, they lit the candles of their paper lanterns, each lantern a personal message giving their condolences and well-wishes written in beautiful golden ink, and sent them into the sky.

The dreamy orange glow of paper lanterns gradually filled the air and wafted about in the evening sky like fireflies helping to guide the emperor's soul to the afterlife.

Jegra and her two wives, Danica and Brei'Alas, lit their lanterns and together, they let them float off the open palms of their hands to join the great migration in the sky.

The tear balancing on Jegra's eyelid finally rolled down her cheek and she brushed it away with a gentle touch of her thumb.

By her decree, the funeral ceremony was not being televised. All televid drones and recording devices were banned, all except for the official historical biographer and his photographer, who captured the moments in full, high definition virtual imaging.

Jegra watched until the flames had consumed both her husband and the boat. She watched the flaming debris sink into the ocean where it was swallowed up. Only a small smattering of flaming oil remained, but the minuscule amounts quickly burned up, dissipating on the watery grave.

The people, in their mourning, slowly turned back to the mainland and made the sad march back to the palace gardens where they would place flowers at the steps of the great staircase and say their prayers.

Jegra wanted to be the first to place her flowers at the steps and so teleported there with Danica and Brei'Alas.

"It's sad," Brei said.

"What is?" Jegra asked, giving her a peculiar look.

"That I didn't get to know him better."

"Believe me, wife," Danica said, "you would not have enjoyed that. He was not...a pleasant man."

"Still," Brei, replied, "he was a big part of both your lives. I just feel like I'm missing out on knowing you both as well as I could have, you know, if I'd known him better."

"Oh, sweetie," Jegra said, giving Brei a side hug, "we will have a lifetime to get to know one another. This is but the close of one chapter. The next begins from this moment onward."

"I suppose," Brei said, resting her head against Jegra's bosom. Danica sidled up to Brei's other side and sandwiched her in the middle. They all linked arms in a loving embrace and then gently set their flowers down onto the steps.

"Now what?" Brei asked.

"That's it," Danica said. "Now we go about our lives."

Jegra tapped her pendant, and three golden beams of light came down and fetched the trio. Their particles danced about in a swirl of energy and were whisked away, back to Thessalonica.

All three materialized in the hallway leading into the grand hall where Jegra was hosting a reception for her closest friends. An informal dinner celebration to end the evening on a high note, rather than the glum, emotionally drained evening that so often follows a funereal ritual.

"You girls go on ahead," Jegra said to Dani and Brei. "I'm going to freshen up."

They nodded and turned to enter the large doors. Brei looked back and smiled and waved at her. Jegra smiled and waved in return.

And the very moment they passed through the threshold of the doors, Jegra clutched her stomach and raced to the nearest restroom.

She burst through the doors and immediately shuffled over to the first stall. When she pushed the door open it hit someone, and an angry voice called back, "It's occupied!"

"Raven?" Jegra asked, recognizing her voice.

The door slowly swung open and Raven was standing there, clutching her stomach, too.

Unable to hold it back any longer, Jegra turned toward the sink and, barely making it in time, vomited into the sink pan. In turn, her gagging and spewing triggered Raven, who spun back around and vomited into the toilet.

After they'd thoroughly emptied all the contents of their stomachs and then some, Raven and Jegra turned to face one another.

"Are you sick?" Jegra asked.

"Not exactly," Raven replied. "I mean, it's just a bit of nausea, that's all."

"You?"

"Just a bit of teleportation nausea. It'll pass."

Raven gulped, choked down her gag reflex, then scurried back into the stall. Another blast of vomit exploded out of her and Jegra, reaching out a hand in the desire to help her, asked once more, "You sure you're not sick?"

After a long pause, Raven sighed, sat back on her knees, and then spilled the secret she'd been keeping for about a week now. "I'm pregnant."

"You're what?!" Jegra gasped.

"It's a long story." Raven pushed up and went over to the sink. She cupped her hands beneath the faucet and let the water flood over her hands then immediately took a drink. She sloshed the water around and then spat into the sink next to Jegra.

"You have to...*urk*..." Jegra spun back around to vomit again, gripping the edge of the porcelain sink so fiercely it cracked under her relentless grip. But when nothing came, she took a deep breath to calm herself and then slowly exhaled.

"False alarm," she informed Raven. Jegra straightened back up and turned around. "But maybe I was wrong about the teleportation sickness. Usually, it wears off by now. Maybe I am coming down with something."

They looked at one another again and Raven squinted at Jegra's face. Her skin was practically glowing it was so radiant, and she looked extremely youthful and full of vigor for a woman who'd just been through hell and back, lost a husband, and had the entire burden of ruling a Galactic Empire resting on her shoulders.

Raven's left eye flashed hot pink and she rubbed her chin contemplatively as she studied Jegra's vitals.

"Did you just scan me?"

"Yes," Raven replied. "The good news is that you don't have a fever. But your standard heart rate is slightly increased. So, you may want to get that checked out at your next physical."

"It's probably nothing. I probably just caught something going around."

"Unlikely. Your immune system is the most advanced I've ever encountered. Apart from an active nano-virus tailor-designed to kill you, there's nothing I know of that could make you sick. Unless..." Raven flipped her wrist over and opened her holovid scanner. Speaking aloud, she said, "Ultrasound scan," and waved the glowing panel in front of Jegra's abdomen.

Inside Jegra's uterus, the faint pitter-patter of a small heartbeat could be heard.

Jegra looked down in utter shock.

"By the looks of things, you're pregnant too."

Jegra looked back up, touching her lower abdomen, her eyes closed in concentration.

Utterly and completely astonished, Jegra's jaw fell open. Shaking her head with disbelief and a healthy side of denial, she said in a surprisingly uncertain voice for someone in her situation, "But I haven't...I mean...I haven't...you know."

"Had sex with anybody?"

"Not recently. I mean, just..." she looked over at Raven her eyes slowly growing larger. Jegra meant herself—that is to say, Old Lady Jegra from a future timeline, whom she'd incidentally bumped into—and, well, the rest was history. She nodded with understanding.

"Okay. Anyone else other than *her?*"

"I don't *know...*" Jegra's voice trailed off as she thought about it for a moment. Then, whispering, "*Impossible,*" she looked to Raven with sad eyes, simultaneously flooding with tears and reality-altering recollection.

"What is it?"

"I mean, it was just the one time. It was strictly a spur of the moment thing. And, she wasn't even supposed to be virile."

"Who's *she?*" Raven pressed, eyeing Jegra suspiciously.

"Callestra," Jegra confessed. She couldn't help but blush, feeling slightly embarrassed. This was the first time she'd told anyone of her dalliance.

She took a deep breath, pausing long enough for Raven to shoot her an inquisitive glance which conveyed her keen interest in hearing the rest of this story. She obliged.

"She came to me to ask for permission to marry Dakroth. Of course, I said yes. I'm not one to stand in the way of true love. And, well, I may have jokingly brought up invoking the right of prima nocta and, then, one thing led to another and..."

"You got yourself knocked up."

"Completely unintentional," Jegra said, waving her hands defensively. "I assure you."

"I'm not judging," Raven said. She paused and then, a slow grin spreading across her lips, she stared long and hard at Jegra.

Unable to shake the unnerving feeling of Raven's prying eyes, Jegra brushed a long tuft of brown hair behind her ear and asked, "What?"

She knew *that* look. It was the same look Raven gave after she'd accidentally kissed her before her surgery and found out there were no hard feelings. The look of complete and total relief mixed with pure happiness.

"I'm just so relieved to not have to go through this alone," Raven said in a long breathy voice which she slowly exhaled as though she were letting it all out.

She immediately teared up, sniffled, and, wiping her nose, marched right up to Jegra and threw her arms around her. Burying her face into Jegra's shoulder, she let the torrent of sobs take her away.

Although unexpected, especially coming from someone as grounded as Raven, Jegra quickly wrapped her arms around her, hugging her tightly in her arms.

Right then and there, she knew that as tough as Raven was on the outside, and as brave as she was on the inside, there was still something that deeply terrified her—because it terrified Jegra too. *Motherhood.*

"It'll be okay," Jegra said. "I've got you."

Raven drew back and then took Jegra's face in her hands, and sniffling, she gave Jegra a short, very light, platonic peck on the lips, a deep, heartfelt gratitude wrapped up in a simple gesture of sisterhood.

Jegra placed her palms on Raven's face and, both faces enshrined by one another's gentle touch, Jegra said, "Let's skip all this pomp and circumstance and go get refreshed. Then we'll have a long talk, just woman to woman."

"I think I'd like that," Raven answered, smiling at Jegra.

"It's settled then," Jegra said, taking Raven's hand in hers and towing her behind her.

As they exited the restrooms they nearly collided with Danica. "Pardon my intrusion," she said, stopping in her tracks before glancing down at their clasped hands. "I was just coming to check on you."

"Raven and I have urgent business to discuss. I don't want any interruptions this evening, and so we will be using the guest quarters; if that's all right with you, my luv."

Danica knew it wasn't a question but more of a statement wrapped in courtesy. She nodded and then bowed slightly, "As my empress wishes."

"Don't do that," Jegra said.

"Don't do what? Danica shot her a wounded look.

"Don't get all jealous. It's nothing like that."

"I don't get jealous," Danica snapped. Then, softening her tone, she added, "I'm just worried what Brei'Alas might think, it being so soon after the marriage ceremony and all."

"I apologize," Raven said, withdrawing her hand from Jegra's. "I've caused a problem."

She turned to leave when Jegra's hand shot out and clasped onto hers again. "No, there's no problem," Jegra insisted. She turned her hardened gaze back at Danica and gave her a look that urged Danica to tread carefully or there really would be a row.

After a long, intense eye-lock, Danica finally answered, "You shall have your privacy. I'll see to it, my luv. In the meantime, I must go save Brei'Alas from the drunken advances of a certain satyr we all know."

"Ah," Jegra said with a light chuckle, "yes, please do that. Rescue your poor wife."

Danica bowed her head and then spun around on her heels and marched back down the hall toward the celebration.

When Jegra turned back toward Raven, she found her staring curiously.

"Why didn't you tell her I was with child, too?"

"Because that's not for me to tell."

Raven smiled and then looked down at their hands, still clutched in their embrace.

"I miss her," Raven said, her eyes still fixed on their linked hands.

"I know," Jegra replied in her most soothing voice.

Raven looked back up at Jegra's deep brown eyes and smiled.

"You still have me."

"I have a version of you, yes. It's just not..." Raven shook her head and then decided to leave it alone. "Never mind."

Jegra placed her hands around Raven's face again and, leaning in, kissed her Prussian blue lips. This time the kiss was tender and lasted a fair bit longer than their first peck on the lips, seeing as neither of them wanted to break away.

"What was that for?" Raven finally asked.

Jegra smiled but did not answer. If whatever Old Lady Jegra had with Raven was a fraction of what she and Raven had together, then that would be enough to fuel the imaginations of a thousand and one romantic poets.

And in one look, Jegra relayed the deepest felt *I love you,* she could without actually committing to the words themselves.

In the distance, floating on the evening breeze and rising from the party that continued somewhere within the confines of the palace came the sweet melody of Jegra's song, which was being played on a harp. This added to the serene atmosphere and Raven's sparkling amethyst eyes locked onto Jegra's earthy brown ones, and the two felt at ease in each other's company.

3

The carnival rides were lit up with a thousand and one blinking lights. The sounds of bells and buzzers echoed up from the game booths and the aroma of deep-fried torgack and roasted zi'zap on a spit filled the night air.

Adults laughed and lovestruck couples held hands as they strolled aimlessly through the park, steeling sweet glances of one another through lust-filled eyes. Children buzzed here and there in an excited giddiness that wouldn't abate.

Three weeks had passed since Dakroth's funeral and Lycia and Raphine could scarcely believe these were the same people who were so deeply in mourning just weeks prior. Everyone seemed lighter somehow. Especially now that the Dagon festival of the harvest, their culture's most cherished holiday, was in full swing.

The festival of the harvest came with a weeklong celebration which ranged from costume parties to lavish dinner banquets and dancing. Unique to Dagon culture, perhaps, was that it all accumulated in a massive open-invite orgy under the harvest moon.

But for the younger folks, the street fairs, pumpkin carving, and the numerous carnivals were where all the excitement was at. And since neither Lycia nor Raphine had ever been to any of the events, they decided to begin with the carnival and maybe work their way up to the more adult-themed events.

Already on their sixth date, Lycia couldn't remember ever being so happy. Somehow, Raphine managed to make her feel whole again and not simply the product of a mad-science experiment gone horribly wrong.

Pausing for a moment, they both studied their surroundings. They scanned the booths and the carnival rides, trying not to let the flashing lights of the fairgrounds distract them. Children buzzed by them, some racing off to play games while others headed straight to their favorite rides.

"Did you give my proposition any further thought?" asked Lycia, batting her purple painted eyelids at Raph and sticking out her bottom lip and pouting playfully just for good measure.

"We'll see," Raphine replied with an amused laugh. "I will say this much, you sure seem determined to get into my pants."

"I mean," Lycia brushed her hair out of her eyes and looked at Raphine, "I like sex. It's just a part of who I am. But if you're not comfortable with it…then I'll totally understand. I don't want to rush you into anything, you know? Besides, I'm so head over heels for you that I'll wait for you as long as it takes."

"I'm a Bre'lal woman," Raphine informed her girlfriend, slowing to a stop and taking Lycia's hands in hers. "We're taught to be courtesans from six years of age. I was just holding off to see if whatever this is between us is real. Because, the truth is, I like you, too."

"Is that a yes, then?" Lycia asked, brushing a tuft of purple-turquoise ombre hair behind her ear and seductively biting her bottom lip as she waited for Raphine's reply.

As she batted her eyes at her girlfriend some more, she released a flood of pheromones so strong that those passing by couldn't help but turn their heads to look at the two nubile women standing in the middle of the fairgrounds.

Raphine breathed in deeply. "I love it when you do that," she said.

"Do what?" Lycia asked, feigning ignorance.

Raphine took in another deep breath and held it. "Your scent, how you make it smell like cherry blossoms in the spring. I could breathe that scent all day long, forever."

"I don't know…but forever is, well, such a long time and who knows that the future holds."

"You don't know? What do you mean, El?" Raphine used her pet name for Lycia, her initial, though her voice sounded worried.

"I mean, it's almost too good to be true. Don't you think?"

Not following Lycia, Raphine shook her head and shrugged slightly.

"All I mean is, most days I can't help but pinch myself and ask, can all this be real? Or am I just dreaming?"

"Seriously, you can't tell?" Raphine asked in a mildly wounded tone.

Lycia stared at her with a blank expression before, very gradually, a subtle smile cracked upon her lips.

"Oh, you little vek'miel!" Raphine growled, and then playfully punched Lycia in her arm.

"Vek'miel?" Lycia asked, rubbing her arm and pretending to be ignorant of the Bre'lal term for cunt.

"It means..." Just then she cut herself short as Lycia began giggling at her antics.

"Oh, shut up," Raphine said. Then, grabbing Lycia by the back of the neck, reeled her in. After a long, sultry kiss, she drew back and looked deep into Lycia's eyes.

"Do you kiss all the vek'miel you encounter with that much tongue?" Lycia teased.

"As a matter of fact, yes," Raphine replied, squinting at her with an impish grin. Then pulling her in again, she whispered, "I shall silence these lips of yours with another kiss."

After another long snog, Raphine drew back and sighed, both of them beaming as they stared at one another, their cheeks flushed rosy pink as their pulses raced.

"You're the smartest, most beautiful woman I've ever met," Lycia said, tracing her fingers along the soft lines of Raphine's cheek and then brushing a strand of forest-green hair out of her eyes for her. "Your dedication to my mother is unparalleled. You're honorable and you seem to get me like nobody ever has. I want to be with you." Then, drawing Raphine's hand to her breast, Lycia added, "This, right here, is one-hundred percent real, my luv. And no matter what happens, you'll always have a place here, in my heart."

"Oh, El, you're such a romantic." Raphine smiled and let her eyes settle onto her hand which rested upon Lycia's left breast. As she felt Lycia's heart gently thumping underneath her clothes, she said, "But, you know, Jegra is basically my surrogate mother. She found me when I was on the run from the Syndicate and took me in. She gave me a home, gave me a purpose, and has always treated me like her own daughter."

Lycia just looked at her with a blank stare.

Raphine slowly looked back up, an impish and slightly crooked grin forming on her pursed lips. "So, when you stop to think about it, we're kind of like adopted sisters."

Lycia laughed out loud at the unexpectedness of Raphine's disclosure and then grabbed Raphine's waist and drew her close. "Stop it, you're making me wet, big sis."

Raphine laughed and then kissed her again, gently biting Lycia's lower lip, and giving it a tantalizing tug.

"I think we need to find a more discrete place to, you know," Lycia said, scanning the faces of the crowd that were stopping to stare at their unrestrained public display of affection, "continue with our little dalliance."

"How about up there?" Raphine said, pointing a slender finger up at the giant Ferris wheel looming in the distance. "Maybe we could fool around a bit more on that."

Lycia turned and looked up at the enormous Ferris wheel and smiled. Then, leaning close to her girlfriends' ear, whispered, "You read my mind."

"You better believe it," Raphine said, turning her mouth to whisper into Lycia's ear, "which is why I didn't wear any panties tonight."

With that, Raphine sashayed toward the Ferris wheel ticket line, her hips swaying seductively as she went. The tan miniskirt was complimented by her shirt with rounded neckline and faux ripped sleeves, while her long, firm legs trailed down into black tactical boots.

"You're killin' me," Lycia said out loud. "You know that, right?"

She jammed her thumbs into the waist of her white jean shorts into which she'd tucked a vintage, charcoal gray V-neck t-shirt. Unlike Raphine's tight-laced boots, however, she opted for more casual, loosely tied, sneakers.

Raphine glanced over her shoulder at Lycia, who seemed lost deep in thought, and asked, "El, are you coming or not?"

Lycia didn't need to think twice about it and quickly raced after her. No sooner had she joined her girlfriend than their fingers effortlessly wove together before locking tight in a firm coupling of one green and one blue hand.

Although bi-racial relationships weren't uncommon among Dagon and Bre'lal, the two nubile young women drew more attention than most.

"Mommy, mommy!" a small boy said, tugging on his mother's shawl to try and get her attention. "That lady looks like the empress, but blue."

Lycia winked at him and then turned and clamored into the gondola-styled ride with Raphine.

They quickly settled into their seats and waited for the operator to shut the door. With a lurch, the gondola began to move and the giant Ferris wheel was off, albeit at a leisurely pace.

"You know, luv," Lycia said, "the revolution takes thirty-five minutes. There's a lot one could do with thirty-five minutes, if they felt so inclined."

"Is that so?" Raphine laughed and slid onto the bench styled seat next to Lycia, the gondola rocking gently to and fro as all the weight inside shifted to one side. "And what, pray tell, did you have in mind, El?"

She tossed her forest green hair over her shoulder with a shake of her head and nestled into her girlfriend's side.

At the same time, Lycia ran her hand up Raphine's smooth, green thigh, her fingers coming dangerously close to slipping up Raphine's already rather short skirt. Grabbing hold of her thigh, Lycia slid it onto herself so that they were locked scissor fashion, their pelvises touching.

Raphine let out a short gasp as they came together and, then, looking deep into Lycia's hungry eyes, she nibbled on her bottom lip with lubricious anticipation.

"I can think of a few things," she answered, throwing her athletic blue leg over Raphine's and then reaching up Raphine's shirt, her fingers fiddled a bit before undoing her bra. While her bra slipped off, Raphine's slender green fingers fiddled with the brass button on Lycia's white denim shorts.

A steamy white fog coated the gondola windows as the heat inside intensified. Their lips crashed together hungrily and their slender hands slid up and down one another's bodies as they passionately made out. Soon enough, Raphine slipped her fingers down into the front of Lycia's pants and Lycia let out a sultry moan.

"I'm not the only one who didn't wear any panties, it seems," she said, smiling at Lycia.

Lycia shrugged. "I'll let you in on a little secret. I never wear them."

"Never?" Raphine asked, a genuine question lingering in her tone. "Not even during that time of the month?"

"Nope. Genetically enhanced to repress my hormone levels so I don't menstruate."

Raphine raised an eyebrow. "You have no idea how much I envy you right now."

"If you think that's impressive, wait until you see this." Lycia leaned back and, closing her eyes, took in a deep breath. There was a long pause and when nothing seemed to be happening Raphine was about to say something. But a thin blue shimmer caught her eye and she leaned back and watched as Lycia coated herself with the thin film of a Dagon forcefield.

Lycia brushed her hand across her chest and shoulder, as though she were shooing away an Angorian weaving spider, and threw out her hand. The forcefield mold of her image floated off her skin like a ghost before its ethereal visage settled into the seat opposite them.

Slowly opening her eyes, she looked over at Raphine's astounded face.

"How are you doing that, El?" Raphine asked, reaching out to touch it.

When her fingers brushed the forcefield representation of Lycia, it dissipated, vanishing in a flicker, similar to a soap bubble that had been pricked.

"I still haven't mastered it yet, but I want to be able to create a forcefield version of myself to use in combat."

"That's amazing," Raphine said. "The fact that it looked exactly like you shows you've come extremely close to achieving something no Dagon has ever achieved before. Not even the grandmasters of the Dygra Divinitus are capable of harnessing their energy with such precision detail."

"It's still a work in progress," Lycia said. "I just wanted to show you what I've been working on while you're away."

"Thank you," Raphine said, taking Lycia's hands in hers. "I appreciate you sharing yourself with me."

"Is there anything you want to share with me?"

Raphine smiled and took Raphine's hand and slowly guided it in-between her thighs and up her skirt. Lycia looked down, her eyes widening as she watched in wonder and a burning anticipation. When she raised her eyes again, they stopped at Raphine's gorgeous smile.

"You mean other than a thousand orgasms?"

Raphine laughed. "Hopefully more, luv."

"If you feel we're moving too fast, we can stop if you want."

Rolling her neck, she kicked her head back and moaned. *"Mmmm...don't stop, El. Your touch feels amazing,"* Raphine said, her voice cracking as she had to hold back a small orgasm that had snuck up on her.

The two leaned in to share another kiss when, all of a sudden, a deafening boom and a level five tremor shook the entire Ferris wheel.

Screams rang out and Raphine and Lycia looked outside to see what all the commotion was when a giant fireball plumed upward from an explosion somewhere down below.

Both women fell back as the flames lapped at the windows of their gondola. Sitting up, they quickly pulled their clothes back into place and buttoned up. Peering out the window, her face pressed against the glass, Raphine said, "We have to get down there and help those people."

Without warning, a hot wind briskly danced over her skin, and she turned to find Lycia peering out of the open gondola door.

Another explosion, this time a further distance away, sent up another fireball and Lycia, still peering down at the chaos, informed Raph that, "Some complete lunatic is firing off a plasma canon down there."

The melody, Jegra's song, was playing on an automated music box which, having been damaged in the subsequent blast, began to wind down, and its melody changed to one with ominous undertones.

Lycia got on the comm. "This is her majesty's personal security. We have a terrorist situation at the fairgrounds. The assailant is armed and dangerous. I'm requesting immediate backup."

"Meet you down there?" Raphine asked, as golden light came down to fetch her.

Lycia glanced back over her shoulder and smiled and blew Raph a kiss. Then, gradually turning back to the open entrance, she leapt out of the gondola without so much as a second thought.

4

Back in her chambers, Jegra dimmed the lights and offered Raven a fruit-juice cocktail. Raven accepted it and they sipped their drinks in silence for a few moments before settling onto the edge of Jegra's bed.

Sitting there like a couple of nervous teenagers, they both broke the lingering silence at the same time.

"Sorry. You go," Raven said.

"No, you go first," Jegra insisted.

Raven nodded, took a deep breath, and then announced, "I feel the same way about you, you know." It was hard for her to express the way she felt in words, since gushing about her feelings was about as foreign to her as a strange alien species from beyond the Outer Rim.

Even so, she knew that she had to get it off her chest sooner or later. And, if she was being completely honest, a better time probably wouldn't present itself again. At least, not anytime soon.

Before sharing her feelings, she took a deep breath and tried to calm her fluttering heart. "I just haven't been brave enough to admit it until now."

"Nonsense," Jegra replied, playfully nudging Raven in the ribs with her elbow. "You're the bravest woman I know." Then, tugging at Raven's hand, she said, "We have so much more to discuss and the evening is already wearing on."

"Alright," Raven said, allowing herself to be drawn into Jegra's charisma. "But, just so you know, I have to get an early start tomorrow. We're headed to Correllia City on Corel to give the *Skywend* a complete overhaul."

Jegra smiled and, without realizing it, found her hand resting on Raven's thigh. Almost as soon as she was aware of it, Raven's hand pressed firmly down on hers and their eyes settled onto their braided fingers before rising back up to get lost, once more, in each other's permeating gazes.

Six hours later, Raven sat up in bed, the pearl-colored satin sheets slipping down her blue, naked body. She took in a deep breath, noting that she smelled of sweat and the lingering musk of sex, and then it all came flooding back to her. She looked over at Jegra sleeping peacefully beside her and thought to herself, *what have you done, Raven?*

Sliding out of bed, careful so as not to wake the sleeping empress, she gathered her clothes and dressed quietly.

Once she'd dressed, she gently set a gift for Jegra on the side table next to the bed and then quietly tiptoed across the ornate floral patterns of a large, hand-woven rug then a cool marble floor until she came to the door. She gently twisted the doorknob and slipped into the warmly lit hall. As she stepped outside, careful not to make a sound as she latched the door behind her, she turned around only to run smack dab into Danica who stood, arms folded across her chest, looking rather miffed.

Shit, Raven thought to herself, *I don't need this right now.*

Danica uncrossed her arms and took a small step forward. "I just wanted to welcome you to our sisterhood," she said, to Raven's bewilderment. "If Jegra ever chooses a third wife for her harem, it will be you. And, well, I just wanted to let you know, you have my blessing."

"What?" Raven asked, taken aback by the unexpected nature of Danica's words. By the look on her face, she had been certain that she was going to get lectured. Instead, she was invited by the head wife to marry Jegra. "Are you sure?"

"Our empress is poly through and through, luv. I have learned to accept that. It's who she is. And if I didn't love that about her, I couldn't love her in the way she needs to be loved. The question is, can you accept sharing her with a former enemy?" Danica gestured to herself, her eyes welling up with tears.

"Oh, my dear Danica," Raven said, reaching out and taking the woman in her arms. As she embraced her, she whispered into her ear, "I forgave you a long time ago. Now, it seems to me, you need to learn how to start forgiving yourself."

Danica began sobbing into Raven's shoulder, and still unaccustomed to public displays of personal affection and heightened emotions, she just stood there stiffly, allowing time for the awkward moment to pass.

"Are we good?" Raven asked, resting her hands-on Danica's shoulders and craning her neck to look into her eyes.

Danica wiped the tears from her cheeks and laughed at her silly emotional outburst. "I apologize. Here I am being all emotional like this." Sniffling, she wiped her nose with the back of her hand and let slip an embarrassed laughed at her own outpouring of feelings. Then, taking a breath to better compose herself, she answered, "Yes. We're good."

Raven turned and glanced back at Jegra's door. "You take care of her, now. You hear?"

Danica looked toward Jegra's chambers too and nodded silently. "I always do."

Raven smiled and then turned up the hall to take her leave when Danica's hand caught hers, halting her in her tracks.

Raven looked down at their hands and then back up at Danica. They stared into each other's eyes, a strange mix of new love, old resentment, and mutual respect swirling about. And although Danica didn't say it with so many words, Raven knew she was screaming out from the depths of her soul about how sorry she was for all the trouble she'd caused her.

Raven gave Danica's hand a gentle squeeze then slowly drew away. As Dani relinquished her grip, Raven nodded, as if to say, *until next time*, and at the same moment, they turned in opposite directions and parted ways.

Raven exited the main palace doors, descended the large stone staircase and then marched across the palace lawn at a brisk pace. Chief of palace security, Raphine Agnar, was making her early morning rounds when she saw Raven and waved to her from across the garden. Raven nodded in acknowledgment but didn't stop. She'd had enough "girl talk" to last her a lifetime.

A few meters later she came to the loading ramp of the *Skywend's* open cargo bay and paused briefly, looking back over her shoulder one last time at the palace.

A million different thoughts danced through her mind and, for once, she felt almost overwhelmed. Luckily, she had a week to focus on her ship and maybe work some stuff out. In the end, the only thing she was certain of was that she loved Jegra with every part of her being.

She touched her abdomen and looked down at her stomach. Somewhere inside her womb, there was a life growing and she knew that she wouldn't make a suitable mother. Life in the coldness of space was no place for a little one. Which is why she was going to ask Jegra to take the baby when the time came.

The first rays of dawn were peeking through the curtains, but it was the sound of the *Skywend's* engines that roused Jegra from her deep slumber.

She sat up in bed, stretched her arms over her head, yawned, and then brushed her messy hair out of her eyes. That's when the sparkle of something caught her attention from the corner of her eye.

She looked down at the object sitting on her bedside table. It was an open ring case with a beautifully carved palladium ring set with three large purple sapphires, the color of Raven's eyes. A note was tucked underneath, and she reached down and picked it up.

Reading the short message aloud to herself, she whispered, "Something to think about. Yours always, Raven."

"Marry her," a voice said from beyond the shaft of light that lit up a section of the floor in Jegra's room.

Startled, Jegra grabbed the sheets and covered herself. Looking toward her chamber doors, she found Danica leaning in the entrance with a tender smile pressed upon her lips.

"What?" Jegra laughed, fumbling to try and hide the ring even though she knew it was too late.

"You two have had this slow-burn romantic thing going on and off for years. But, eventually, both of you will realize you're perfect for one another. And, as your wife, I'm telling you, you need to marry that woman."

Jegra laughed and then turned her attention back to the ring. Plucking it out of the container, she held it in her fingers, examining it more closely, and asked, "Are you sure?"

Danica strode into the room, passing out of the shadows into the beam of light where she settled onto the end of the bed, next to her wife. Reaching out, she took Jegra's hand in hers and said, "For the last time, marry the woman. You have my permission and my blessing."

Jegra laughed at Danica's stubborn-headed persistence in the matter and said, "Well, if you insist."

"What's going on?" a voice called out to them. They both turned in time to see Brei'Alas enter the room with a catering cart full of breakfast delights: cheese danishes, apple and custard strudels, and butter-soaked croissants with strawberry jam.

"Raven proposed to Jegra," Danica informed Brei.

"That's wonderful!"

"It is?" Jegra asked, practically beside herself as both her wives strongly urged her to consider marrying any other woman, much less the rogue Captain Raven Nightguard.

"Yes. She's, like, your soulmate."

"I thought you two were my soulmates," said Jegra, scanning their faces for some kind of revelation that would elucidate everything. Instead, she just received wide-eyed grins that merely confused her even more.

"We're like your high-school sweetheart and your first crush," Brei'Alas informed her. "But she's like…everything you need in a partner." Brei turned to Danica and said, "Right?"

"I've been telling her just that," Danica said with a shrug. "But she's not listening."

"Wait," Jegra said, throwing up her hands. "Just hold your horses. So, let me get this straight, you're both telling me I should say yes to Raven's proposal and marry the woman?"

Danica let out an annoyed sigh, took Raven's ring out of Jegra's hand, grabbed her left hand and then slipped the ring on.

"There," she said, "It's final."

Brei, getting excited, clapped her hands together giddily and sang out, "Oh, joyous day! Now I get to plan the perfect dream wedding! All you need to do is pick the wedding date."

Jegra looked at her with a peculiar look. "You just had a wedding. Our wedding."

"I know! But this is different. This is like…like your *real* wedding."

Jegra threw her arms up and sighed out loud. "I give up." Falling back onto the bed, she held her hand up in front of her face and studied the ring. "I can't believe I'm going to get married to my third wife."

Danica walked over to the breakfast tray and, standing next to Brei, picked up a croissant and took a bite.

"I'll get your clothes picked out for today and then we're going to get you made up. After you're looking like a proper empress again, you're gonna call Raven and say, *yes*."

With that Brei scurried off excitedly and disappeared into Jegra's closet.

"A bundle of joy, that one," Danica said, chewing on another mouthful of bread.

Jegra laughed and then sat up in bed. It dawned on her that she had forgotten to share with Danica a very vital piece of information. Slowly, she turned toward Danica, and with a sheepish grin, she said, "Babe, I almost forgot to tell you. I'm pregnant."

Danica almost choked on her bread and coughed it up. Dropping the soggy morsel back onto the tray, she dusted the crumbs off her hands.

"You sure? Does Raven know?"

"It's not hers," Jegra said, rubbing the back of her neck self-consciously. "It's actually Callestra's. I was meaning to tell you, but with everything that's happened things just kept getting pushed back and pushed back."

"How far along are you?"

"Around three months."

"You're going to keep it?"

"Is that alright with you?" Jegra asked, scooting to the edge of the bed and nervously fiddling with one of her braids of hair.

"Is it alright? It's more than alright. It's wonderful news. After everything that happened, I wasn't sure you'd ever…what I mean to say is, I can't give you a baby anymore. When I was made into an Avatar, it sterilized me. I couldn't bring myself to say anything until now."

"Oh, Dani," Jegra said, opening her arms for her. "I had no idea."

Danica rushed over and took Jegra's hands in hers, seating herself next to her on the bed. "I want you to know, that whatever you decide, I will always support you, come rain or shine, through thick and thin. You've always been there for me and you've always fought for me, even when I didn't deserve it. Now, it's my turn to fight for you and your happiness. As your wife, that's my solemn promise."

Jegra ran her fingers through the back of Dani's hair and gently squeezed her neck and then reeled her in. Their lips crashed together and the giddy, lightheaded momentum carrying them, they fell back into bed.

"I'm the luckiest woman in the galaxy," Jegra said between hot, steamy kisses.

"You know it," Danica teased. Leaning over Jegra's open mouth, her forked tongue slowly slid down until their mouths were once again locked in a deep, French kiss.

Just then Brei came out of the closet with a bundle of clothes in her arms and tossed them onto the end of the bed. Throwing her hand onto her hips, she looked down at the two lovebirds and let out a loud sigh.

"Come on you two, that's enough. Now isn't the time for sex. Now is the time for planning a wedding!"

"Raincheck?" Jegra asked.

Danica smiled, "You read my mind."

With that, Jegra got up and strolled over to the sonic shower while Dani and Brei argued over which outfit to dress her up in.

As they bickered like a couple of sisters, Jegra couldn't help but smile to herself and think that she might enjoy the domestic life more than she realized. At the end of the day, it was just nice to have people she loved and who loved her back. And, for now, that was enough for her.

5

With a loud thud, Lycia touched down on the ground just as Raphine manifested beside her in a swirling eddy of golden light.

"Over there." Lycia pointed in the direction people were fleeing from. That's when she saw the little boy from earlier. In all the commotion, he'd been knocked to the ground and separated from his mother.

The boy sat directly in the path of a panicked mob stampeding toward him and without hesitating Lycia threw up an energy bubble around the kid. Several people rebounded off of it, not realizing what had hit them as they scrambled back to their feet.

Lycia was soon standing over the boy and reaching down, she said, "Let's find your mother, shall we?"

He smiled at her and took her hand. She scooped him up in her arms and began scanning the frightened faces for any trace of the child's mother. A few seconds later she saw a woman in the distance cupping her mouth and shouting for her son.

Lycia moved toward the woman, using her shield powers to divert the flow of oncoming bodies. A minute later she handed the boy off to his mother. The boy, who clung to his mom's neck like a Semelian koala, buried his face in her neck and wept. The mother thanked Lycia profusely and almost seemed reluctant to leave, until another explosion erupted nearby.

Lycia expanded her shield, deflecting the debris, and then pointed at the exit gate and shouted at the mother and her child, "Go!"

Raphine drew her blaster from her back holster and began cautiously making her way toward all the flames and chaos.

Together the two of them surveyed the damaged area but didn't find much more than singe marks from heavy blaster fire. Luckily, there were no signs of any dead bodies.

"Over there," Raphine said, motioning with a stiff hand in the direction of some of the red and white striped tents.

Lycia nodded and then, with a superhuman leap, flew into the air and over the tents. There was a loud boom followed by the immediate flash of blaster fire.

"Shit!" Raphine growled as she sprinted off after Lycia.

The plasma cannon was unusually powerful, but Lycia's energy shield had held up well enough. Still, she knew that another heavy ordinance plasma blast like that one might knock out her shields.

Looking up, she saw a man with glowing yellow veins standing before her, his chest heaving as he breathed laboriously. Apart from the mysterious radiant energy surging through him, he looked like death walking.

"Xarthon?" Lycia asked, baffled. "What in the bloody universe happened to you?"

"Your wretch of a sister did this to me. And, sure enough, I was naïve enough to think she'd have a cure for me. But, no! All I am to her is just some guinea pig with mere hours left to live. But before I die, I'm gonna finish what I started and take you with me."

"I politely rescind the offer," Lycia snarled.

Xarthon laughed, but his laugh was interrupted by a fit of coughing. Black ooze dripped from his mouth and dribbled down his chin. It was his blood.

He wiped the blood away with the back of his hand and then hoisted the heavy plasma cannon, aiming it at Lycia.

The chime on his plasma canon's recharge indicator bleated out a few tones to let him know he was primed and loaded. With wild eyes and a macabre grin that stretched across blood mottled teeth, he raised the cannon onto his shoulder and fired another blast.

Lycia threw up her blue energy shield, but the blast was much more powerful at close range and it obliterated her energy field. The blue blanket of energy broke apart like shattered glass, and she went flying through the air.

Crashing through one of the booths, a rack of stuffed animals tumbled down and buried her under an avalanche of annoyingly cute plush toys.

As she emerged from the pile of soft cuddly animals, her clothes were singed to ash and scarcely clung to her. Grabbing what little there was left of her shirt, she tore it off and tossed it. She did the same with her jeans and then, reaching up, she tapped the bracelet on her wrist.

A dark gray liquid quickly began to spread across her body like an oil slick coating the surface of everything it touched. It wasn't liquid, though, it was smart-nano-fiber technology so fine that it flowed as a liquid-like substance.

Once every inch of her blue nudity was fully coated, the liquid hardened into a skin-tight material with futuristic hexagonal patterns.

Bright yellow lines ran down the sides of the gray track-styled suit. As the final elements of the suit locked into place, a blue flash of energy surged through the suit as Lycia's energy shield became operational.

Lycia casually walked through the burning debris around her, the smart-suit protecting her from the flames. A plush, Skallekian dolphin sitting on the tabletop was set on fire and gazed at her as though it was desperately pleading with its impossibly large round eyes for her to put it out of its misery.

Cracking her neck, she turned to Xarthon, a less than amused look on her face. "Look, Xarthon, you need to take a breath and get it through your head…the war is over."

"Your war, perhaps," he snarled. "Not mine."

"I don't know if you heard," she continued, "but project *Shooting Star* was declassified and the Seyfferian Republic granted all of us full Seyfferian citizenship. They integrated the non-activated Lycias into the healthcare industry, giving them jobs as nurses and senior caretakers. While those who'd been activated as class-9 elite warriors opted to go their way, many taking on paramilitary gigs or signing up as IGS bounty hunters. Everything worked out in the end."

"Worked out?" he barked, sickly-looking sputum gathering in the corners of his mouth like that of a rabid dog. His veins pulsed with light and, looking at her from sunken eyelids, he grinned a crooked grin. "Don't you get it? I'm an abomination! A monster!"

The plasma cannon chimed again, reminding him it carried a full charge, and he slowly raised it and took aim. That's when the muzzle of a blaster pressed itself against the back of his head.

"I wouldn't do that, if I were you, space cowboy."

Xarthon's eyes slid to the far corner of his eyelids as he tried to see who'd gotten the jump on him.

"I should have known Jegra's palace security would take an interest in this bitch of a clone."

Raphine pressed the muzzle harder against the base of his skull, provoking a grunt from him. "Watch your mouth, asshole. That's my girlfriend you're talking about."

Xarthon laughed hysterically and both women's eyes met, their thoughts perfectly in tune. *This guy has lost it*, they thought.

In their moment of distraction, Xarthon threw back his head, nudging the gun out of the way, and with a firm thrust of the elbow, he nailed Raphine right in her diaphragm.

Winded, Raphine collapsed to her knees and Xarthon spun around and pointed the plasma cannon at Lycia. Its orange glowing muzzle grew brighter and she realized that without the protection of an energy barrier, she'd be completely vaporized.

"No!" Lycia shouted. And with that, she let off a powerful Dygra crystal blast from both palms.

The energy ran off Xarthon's back like rainwater and he laughed. "Stupid wench, your powers don't work on me."

"I wasn't aiming for you," Lycia snarled.

Xarthon then looked at his plasma canon to find the coolant cartridges had been melted and his weapon was quickly overheating. Effectively rendered a ticking time bomb, he spat angrily at the ground and tossed the weapon to the wayside. It was no use to him anymore. "*Gah!*"

Xarthon shoved Raphine to the ground as he raced past her, not looking back as he fled the scene. Lycia ignored him for now and ran to Raphine and helped her up. "This thing's gonna blow. We have to go. Now!"

Back on their feet, they ran together, dashing away from the pulsing plasma canon. The high-pitched whine of the weapon overheating urged them to seek cover fast, and they leaped over the counter of one of the food trucks and tumbled inside.

As they fell to the floor, Lycia kicked the support bar that held open the window awning and the metal sheet slammed closed, securing them inside just as the plasma cannon self-destructed.

A massive explosion erupted from the gun as a plasma ball of fiery death rose, expanding like rising dough, engulfing everything around it. The scorching hot flames slapped against the side of the food truck like waves of fire and the truck rocked violently. Hotdog buns and sausages fell out of the cupboards and rained down onto the two women.

Once the Worcestershire and other random condiments had settled, Lycia and Raphine looked at each other. After a brief pause, they both began to laugh and hugged one another. Then, holding up a big, plump sausage, Lycia grinned and wiggled her eyebrows at Raphine as she dangled it in front of her face. Raphine rolled her eyes, let out a vexed sigh, and then bit the tip of the sausage clean off.

With a mouth full of meat, she teased, "That's what'll happen if you ever cheat on me." With that said, she turned her head and spat out the awful processed meat stick and grabbed a napkin from a pile and wiped her tongue clean.

Lycia raised an eyebrow and Raphine plucked up the remaining bit of sausage and then gently tucked it into Lycia's cleavage. With a gentle double tap, she pressed it down between her breasts, leaving the ugly tip of the wiener sticking out. Raphine then stuck her tongue out at Lycia and slowly rose to her feet.

Lycia plucked the sausage out from betwixt her boobs, chortled lightly then tossed it aside into the pile of other spilled foods which resembled a veritable smorgasbord.

Raphine reached down and grabbed Lycia's hand and helped her up to her feet. A minute later, the two of them emerged from the singed and still smoking truck and looked out at the singed and still smoldering fairgrounds.

"My gods..." Raphine gasped at the sight of destruction. Everything had been scorched by the plasma blast and half the park was either completely obliterated or on fire.

"Come on," Lycia said, smacking Raphine in the side of her arm as she prepared to take chase, "he's getting away."

Before she could race off, however, a royal security team greeted them. "Ma'am, Her Majesty's Royal Guard at your service. What's the situation?"

Raphine waved her hand at the destruction and informed her team, "I need you to put out these fires and then check to see if anyone's been wounded."

"Yes, ma'am," the six-man security team promptly marched off to carry out their orders.

"Let's go," Lycia said, heading off in the direction they'd seen Xarthon go a few minutes earlier.

Raphine jogged alongside Lycia until they caught up to Xarthon who was limping across one of the hydronic fields where the humans were growing Earth fruits and vegetables. His leg had been licked by a stray bit of plasma and he wasn't doing too well.

"Xarthon!" Lycia shouted. "Stop right there!"

He stopped, then slowly turned around.

"It's too late," he snarled. "I've only hours left before this infernal disease kills me. You might as well finish me off and put me out of my misery."

"I think not," Lycia said. "Instead, how about we get you cured and then you go to jail for a very long time."

He scoffed at the notion and then replied, "I don't think so."

Drawing out a smart-patch, he slapped it on his neck. Almost as soon as it made contact with his bronze skin, it began to glow hot orange. His head slowly turned and he looked right at Lycia with his sickly gaze and smiled one last time. "See you in Helios, kid."

"No!" Raphine shouted, throwing out her hand. But she was too late. Xarthon's head exploded and his body, going limp, crumpled to the ground.

The yellow light pulsing through his veins gradually faded until all that was left was a pile of pallid flesh lying in a wide-open field.

"What the Helios was that all about?" Raphine asked.

"Old grudges," Lycia said.

More security forces teleported onto the scene and Raphine motioned toward the dead body. They nodded and went over to take care of it.

She then went up to Lycia, who was staring off in the distance and, sidling up beside her, took her hand in hers.

"I believe you still owe me a good time."

Lycia laughed. "What? You're not having a good time?"

Raphine laughed too. "Well, it's been exciting, I'll say that much." She paused and then turned and met Lycia's gaze. "But I was thinking more along the lines of…maybe you buy me a few drinks and then we see where the evening goes."

"Are you sure?" Lycia asked, her amethyst eyes sparkling deviously.

"Yes," Raphine answered, chewing on her lower lip in anticipation of the inevitable kiss they were about to share.

"In that case," Lycia replied, I know just the place.

Thirty minutes later their bodies materialized in front of Scarback's Bar in the dusty town of Mardok.

A small town of three-thousand, it was more famous as being a safe harbor for smugglers, black-market dealings, and the numerous gambling establishments and sex-parlors that line the strip than anything else.

"Seriously?" Raphine asked, giving a sour face. "Your idea of a sexy date is Scarback's?"

"I know the new owner and I'm certain I can get us a few drinks on the house."

Curious as to where this would go, Raphine shrugged and followed Lycia inside. When they entered, all eyes turned to them and then, realizing Raphine as Her Queen's Royal Guard, slowly turned away and kept to themselves for the remainder of the evening.

It was then that Raphine noticed that the bartender was none other than Grendok, or—at the very least…a Grendok, one of the satyrs many salty clones— that she smiled.

"Ladies! Ladies! Welcome to my humble establishment," Grendok said, slinging a towel over his arm. Then, skipping around to the other side of the bar table to join them, he gestured for them to follow him. "Right this way, if you please. I have a special booth picked out for the two of you."

He led them over to a corner booth, wiped the table, and then slapped down a couple of menus onto it.

"Thanks, old friend," Lycia said.

"Anytime," Grendok replied. He looked over at Raphine once more, smiled at her with his infamous yellow-toothed-grin and, then, with a nod toward the bar, said, "I'll have my android server bring over the first round, on the house. Feel free to take your time, ladies. I'll be right over here if you need me."

After he skipped away, Raphine turned to Lycia and gazed longingly into her eyes.

This caused Lycia to grow self-conscious and, brushing her ombre hair behind her pointy-tipped ear, asked in a conscientious tone of voice, "What?"

"I know we've only known each other for a few weeks, but it feels like I've known you for…"

"Like forever?" Lycia asked, finishing Raphine's sentence for her.

"Yeah. What is that?"

"It's called having a connection."

Raphine took Lycia's hands from across the table.

"In that case, get in here."

They both leaned over to share another kiss when a robotic voice said, "Here are your drinks, ladies."

They turned to see a buxom bar wench wearing an all too revealing maid's outfit lean forward, and slap two mugs of Dragonian ale onto the table.

The bright orange drinks sloshed haphazardly, some splashing onto the bar wench's over-sized breasts. As orange ale drizzled down into the valley of her cleavage, she stood up and returned to the bar where she then struck a sexy pose and maintained it until she was needed again.

Grendok, who'd gone back to drying glasses with his towel, simply chortled as the young lovers did what young lovers do. Made out in front of the regular patrons as though they were the only two in the entire bleedin' universe.

6

Skuld and Gyllek busied themselves with the *Skywend's* overhaul, fixing all the parts of the ship that had been damaged in the course of the last dozen battles or so and which, therefore, needed a complete replacement.

As they buried their heads in the tangle of red, green, blue, and yellow coated wiring that made up the guts of the wall paneling of the ship's cargo bay, Kregor lumbered up the loading ramp with a literal ton of supplies slung over his shoulders

"Will that be all, sir?" she asked, her hands clasped behind her back in a semi-formal stance.

"No need to call me, sir, kid. I'm just the ship's first officer."

The bright-eyed Seyfferian girl, wearing the official navy blue and gray uniform and black beret of Seyfferian security, stood at the base of the loading ramp, her attention rapt on the large reptilian officer.

Kregor set down the supplies with a resounding thump and then turned back to see the girl, who couldn't be more than nineteen cycles old and seemed fresh out of bootcamp, staring up at him.

"At the behest of the Empress Alakandra and the Seyfferian High Council, I've been instructed to aid you and the crew of the *Skywend* in any way possible."

"You can start by telling me your name," Kregor said, crossing his thick, green arms across his meaty chest. He gazed past his intimidating brow at the girl with his deep-set yellow-green, serpentine eyes and blinked with his double eyelids.

The girl's posture stiffened and she replied, "I'm Corporal First-Class, Sendaya Eschelle Vortesh, of the Seyfferian Republic Security Force, sir."

"The SRSF? Impressive. And how old are you, Corporal First-Class?" Kregor asked.

"Yeah," Gyllek chimed in, looking up from a spray of sparks that framed her dark yet undeniably curious gaze in a halo of fluttering embers.

She raised her welding goggles and looked down the ramp at the girl from behind a jumble of wiring and loose panels. "How old are you?"

"Uh...I'm twenty-one cycles to the week. Why? Is there a problem with my age?"

Gyllek eyeballed Sendaya suspiciously, her feline eyes blinking slowly as she mulled over the information, then mumbling something indiscernible under her breath, pulled her visor down and went back to welding and soldering.

"It's not important," Kregor said with a chuckle. "You just look awfully green...err, no offense."

"None taken, sir."

Just then the cargo hold doors slid open with a pneumatic swoosh of compressed air and Raven Nightguard emerged onto the cargo bay deck dressed in her trademark leather fatigues.

"Captain on deck!" Kregor shouted. This time it was his posture that stiffened as he swiveled on his heels and saluted. Gyllek and Skuld both stood up and saluted in return. Raven glanced at her crew and, without saluting, said, "At ease, everyone. We're not a formal service and so any official title is just honorary."

"Captain, Ms. Nightguard," Sendaya said, looking up the loading ramp, "It's a pleasure to meet you. And, I just want to be the first to say—"

"Why are you standing down there?" asked Raven, interrupting the girl mid-sentence. She peered down at the girl with a probing gaze from atop of the loading ramp.

"I wasn't invited onboard yet, Captain. No offense to your fine crew. I'm sure the proper protocols merely slipped their minds, seeing as how awfully busy they all are."

"Indeed." Raven turned and smacked Kregor in the arm and said, rather tersely, "Well, invite her aboard, Commander."

"Yes, Captain. Sorry, Captain." Turning toward Sendaya, he gestured for her to join them in the cargo hold. "Corporal Sendaya First-Class, please accept my deepest apologies, and welcome aboard the *Skywend*."

Sendaya smiled and then clambered up the ramp. As she reached the top, she stuck out her hand and said, "Captain Raven Nightguard, it's a pleasure to finally meet you face to face."

Raven eyed the girl up and down then turned to leave without so much as another word. As she went, Sendaya continued her best to make a good lasting first impression.

"Honestly, I've heard so much…about you…I…uh…"

If it hadn't been for her smart bracelet pulsing with blue light, Raven would have stayed behind to properly greet the girl. But a code blue was the highest bounty warrant. If a code blue was coming in over the needle cast, then she wanted to be the first to jump at it.

She glanced at the girl abruptly, her face calm and collected, and then turned without so much as shaking Sendaya's extended hand, leaving Sendaya slightly perplexed.

Slowly lowering her hand again, Sendaya looked over at Kregor. "Did I say something wrong? I've been told I sometimes come on too strong."

"The captain doesn't much care for fame. Although her reputation precedes her wherever she goes, she prefers to keep a low profile. Don't take it personally. I wouldn't."

"I see."

"At any rate, Corporal, there are a few things I need to run past you," Kregor said, as he started into the corridor. He looked back to make sure she was still with him. She was and he continued briefing her. "Seeing as we don't go by rank on this ship, I'll call you by your first name."

"Copy that," she replied, cheerfully, her hands clasped behind her back as she strode beside him and listened to his every word with attentive ears.

"Additionally, while you're here, I expect you to pull your weight. It's not our choice to have been audited by the Commonwealth Alliance Liaison for quality checks and controls, but our class of vessel sort of requires a formal check to make sure we're not all engaged in illegal activity."

"I assure you, Commander, I'm the consummate professional."

"Good to hear that. As for work around here, the ship just had a complete system overall. So, we're still ironing out some of the kinks. Right now, I think I could use your assistance running through the ship's boot-up sequence. After that, I want you to run a scan on the newly installed autopilot and make sure there's no lag. Once that's completed, I want you to test the fusion quadcore steady-stream stability. Got all that?"

"Got it!" she said spritely.

Kregor started down another corridor when a gorgeous Bre'lal woman with emerald-green skin and forest green tresses of hair breezed past him. Sendaya's eyes widened as she looked at the most gorgeous woman she'd ever seen.

"Hi," she said in a barely audible voice, "my name's Sen. I mean, Sendaya. But you can call me Sen."

Angellyk smiled and nodded at her. "Nice to meet you Sen," she said, reaching out and taking her hand in hers. "Oh, you poor thing," Angellyk said, "your hand is frigid. Come here and let me warm you up." Reeling the girl in by her slender arm, Angellyk mashed Sendaya's face into her ample bosom and gave her a warm embrace. Rubbing her shoulders and arms to help warm her up, Sendaya practically melted into this goddess.

"Better?" Angellyk asked, holding the girl by her shoulders and looking into her gun-metal gray eyes with her teal ones.

Sendaya, left speechless, could only nod.

Angellyk turned her gaze to Kregor and said, "I'm headed to the cargo hold to assist Gyllek and Skuld. Do you need me for anything?"

Kregor shook his head. "Not right now. But, I'll call you later when my shift ends."

She smiled, swiveled her stunning eyes back to Sendaya, then took her leave.

Awestruck, Sendaya slowly turned her head back to Kregor, and asked, "Who in the world is that?"

"Angellyk Adronis of Arkadia. A veritable goddess if there ever was one. But don't get any ideas, kid, she's my girlfriend," Kregor replied, smiling proudly as he crossed his large arms over his beefy chest.

"You're dating *her*?" asked Sendaya, scarcely able to believe it. "You?"

"What?" he asked, somewhat defensively. "You don't believe a guy like me and a girl like her could ever...?"

She shot him a skeptical look as she eyed him up and down. "Hey, I'll have you know that I have a certain charm," he said.

Sendaya glanced back at Angellyk before carrying on. "I meant no offense, sir. It's just that, I never took Dragonians for the romantic type. And, well, she's a veritable goddess."

"On that, we can both agree," he replied, joining her in watching Angellyk's backside as she strolled down the hall.

Angellyk turned and looked back only to find them both looking at her. Kregor and Sendaya both waved at her in the same, awkward, slow fashion and she raised an eyebrow, smiled at them, and blew a kiss.

After a brief pause, Kregor cleared his throat and said, "You know that kiss was for me, right?"

Sendaya looked at him and smiled. "Naturally."

He laughed and then, slapping her on the shoulder, said, "I think I might like you, Sendaya. Now, come along, I hope you don't mind rolling up your sleeves and getting your hands dirty because we've got work to do."

She nodded and trailed after him, treading closely on his heels.

Raven arrived in her personal quarters and undid the flap on her leather Qipao styled vest. Letting out a sigh, she sank into her chair at her console and tapped the pulsing light on the touch-panel display.

The monitor lit up and a familiar face greeted her. She smiled and, stretching her arms over her head, locked elbows behind her head and leaned back in her chair.

"Admiral Grendok, it's been too long."

"My dear Raven, it's always a pleasure to see those stunning amethyst eyes and beautiful face of yours."

Raven smiled, accepting the Galliforn manner of greeting with flattery, and then crossed her legs. "So, what do I owe the pleasure of this call?"

"I'm afraid it's a bit of business. I just got word from the United Commonwealth Alliance supercarrier, *Titania,* that a top-secret prototype fighter has just been stolen.

"The *Titania?* That's Simon Calvec's ship? He wouldn't be one to let something like that slip away from underneath his nose. At least, not without one hell of a fight."

"It's more serious than that, I'm afraid. All signs indicate that the ship was taken by those within the ranks of the military loyal to Demeris Ferrison. Bloody turncoats, the lot of them, if you'll pardon my coarse language."

"So, the snake rears his ugly head."

"If Demeris Ferrison is active again, and if he has the prototype fighter, you can bet your bottom credit that he wants it for the neutron bomb on board."

"Wait," Raven said, sitting up and leaning forward, both hands clasping onto her knees as the tension built in her neck. "Are you telling me that the most wanted terrorist in the Commonwealth has managed to get his hands on a neutron bomb?"

"It's my belief that Ferrison will try to sell the fighter to the highest bidder but keep the bomb for his nefarious purposes. Whatever the case may be, I need you to do what you do best, my dear, and find that fighter and retrieve the bomb."

"And Ferrison?"

"Dead or alive, my dear."

She smiled puckishly. "As long as the gig pays, Admiral, I'm happy to oblige." Although Raven wasn't in the habit of killing, she was quite certain that for a man as evil as Demeris Ferrison she'd be quite willing to make an exception.

"The credits have already been needle-cast to you and your crew's bank accounts. Also, in honor of the new Cosmic Alliance Treaty between the Seyfferian government and the Dagon and Galliforn Empires, I'm asking you to take on an additional crewmember."

"Let me guess, Corporal Sendaya Eschelle Vortesh?"

Grendok smiled his trademark yellow-toothed grin and then, swiping up, added, "I see you've already met. I apologize for the inconvenience, and, yes, the corporal is a bit high-strung. But she'll mellow out with time. Just show her the ropes and see to it that she doesn't get killed."

"Copy that," Raven said.

"I'm sending you're the coordinates of the *Titania*, now," informed the admiral. Grendok's hands, although out of sight, typed busily. A few nanoseconds later, a holo-vid map popped up in front of Raven's face. "You're to rendezvous with Captain Simon Calvec in the Barrion system. Once debriefed, use whatever means necessary to find that ship and retrieve the bomb."

"Yes, sir. You can count on me."

"I have every confidence you will deliver. Also, please keep in mind the sensitive nature of this mission. Everything I've discussed with you should be kept on a need-to-know basis."

"Yes, sir," Raven replied. Grendok nodded and then his feed cut out and the monitor went black.

Raven sat back in her chair and took in a deep breath and then slowly let it out. Then, slapping the touch-panel, she opened the ship-wide comms.

"This is your captain speaking. I need this bucket of bolts ready for dust off in T-minus six hours. So, get to work people."

Back in the cargo bay, Gyllek and Angellyk looked at one another. "Oh, goody! A mission!" Gyllek chirped with bubbly excitement.

"Drats," Angellyk lamented. "I was hoping to have a few more days of R&R. There was a day spa on Correllia I wanted to try."

"I can program a spa setting into the holovid suite for you, if you'd like," Skuld said, looking up from his work and locking eyes with Angellyk. She tossed her forest green hair over her shoulder and smiled at him.

"You'd do that for me?"

"I'd do anything for you," Skuld said nervously. As their eyes lingered, he cleared his throat and then went back to fixing the wiring.

"You're wonderful," Angellyk said, and she leaned in and kissed the visor of his EV suit, leaving blue lipstick imprints.

Angellyk stood and turned to leave when Gyllek called out to her, "Let me know when it's ready so I can join you."

Angellyk looked back over her shoulder at Gyllek and replied, "Sure thing, kid. We'll get our nails done."

Gyllek began to clap excitedly and turned to Skuld. "I love painting my nails. There are so many colors."

"Indeed, a nearly endless spectrum to explore."

"A spectrum!" Gyllek said, fanning her hand in front of her face as though she were envisioning a rainbow with a million colors. "I know the perfect color to celebrate your love of Angellyk, too," she said, still eyeing her fingers.

"Um…what's that now?" asked Skuld.

"I saw how you were looking at her. You love her!"

"*Shhhh!*" Skuld hushed the girl with a finger to his visor. "Not so loud.

Besides, that's preposterous. She's dating Kregor and, if you've already forgotten, she's the captain's ex, too. I don't have a chance with such a magnificent specimen of a woman."

"Don't say that," Gyllek said, resting her hand on his arm. "You're a great catch."

"If you want, I can put in a good word for you."

Skuld chuckled, a bubble floating up to the top of his fish-bowl style helmet. "That won't be necessary. But I appreciate the thought."

"Alright, but I still think you should tell her how you feel," Gyllek said. Then, looking down at the tangle of wires sitting in front of her, she let out a vexed sigh. "Well, you heard the captain. Back to it."

Six hours later, the *Skywend* lifted off from Correllia, its thrusters kicking up eddies of air that swirled away like miniature twisters.

Rising higher, the sleek frigate left the neon lights and the towering skyscrapers of Correllia, the capital city of the Seyfferian Republic, behind.

All things considered, the Seyfferians came out of the war the least battered. The alien entity H'aaztre wasn't able to hack their defense grid-like he had hoped and was waiting until he'd amassed a big enough army to crush their world.

The imposed galactic siege had been mainly to try and cripple their resources, but due to their extremely advanced matter reconstitution technology, they were able to turn waste into water and garbage into common household necessities with a touch of the button.

Given the replication technology of the Seyfferians, the siege would have lasted indefinitely. At least, until H'aaztre became strong enough to destroy them, that is.

Luckily, Jegra intervened when she did and sealed the ancient being away in an extradimensional pocket universe. The rest, as they say, is history.

As the city shrank away in the distance of the ship's main view portal, Raven looked back over her shoulder at everyone seated on the bridge with her. "Alright, ladies and gentlemen, hold onto your seats, because we're going to make the jump into FTL."

Raven glanced over at Sendaya, pausing briefly before turning the rest of the way around. The girl was breathing rhythmically, trying to calm herself in preparation for her first faster than light space flight.

"First time?" Kregor asked, looking over at the young girl who was practically hyperventilating. He noted her fingers clasping onto the ends of her chair arms with such white-knuckle vigor that they looked like tiny skeleton hands.

She nodded, nervous perspiration glistening upon her brow. She seemed to want to reply but all she could muster was a groan from the back of her throat as she fought off her instinct to be sick. This was followed up with a nervous gulp.

"Just take deep breaths. It's a little disorienting at first, but nothing too bad. You'll feel a bit of motion sickness. A time-lag. And then everything will snap back to normal."

She nodded again, still breathing as if she were practicing for a Lamaze class.

"Here," Angellyk said, holding out her hand. "Take these."

Sendaya graciously accepted the two yellow tablets and looked down at them. "What are they?" she inquired, studying the pills.

"They'll help with the motion sickness."

"Thank you so much," Sendaya said, very much relieved to be getting something that would help, and popped the pills into her mouth. With an uncomfortable gulp, she downed them without the aid of drink. Almost instantly she began to calm down. "I can feel it *worbekking alrebby...*" she said, her words growing sloppy and languid as she began to nod off.

A few seconds later she was out like a light.

"What?" Angellyk said, glancing at all the faces staring back at her in shock. "Her incessant heavy breathing was grating on my nerves." Throwing her arms across her chest she puffed in annoyance at being judged by everyone and mumbled, "I can't be the only one."

Kregor chuckled and spun back around in his chair to co-pilot the ship just as Raven throttled up the FTL. "Don't sweat it hot stuff," he said. "No harm, no foul."

Skuld leaned over and gently spoke into her ear, "You did what you had to do."

She turned her beautiful teal eyes to him and batted her purple eyelids. "I did do what I had to do. Thanks, Skuld, for understanding." Reaching across the aisle, she touched his leg and gave it a gentle squeeze. "You're always so considerate."

"I'm considerate," Kregor said under his breath, a twinge of jealousy behind his grumbling.

Raven cleared her throat, putting an end to the lighthearted banter and then said, "Buckle up, folks, because here…we…go."

The throbbing hum of the engines died down as the plasma-ion thrusters cut out and then, with a high-pitched whine followed by a deep thrumming sound, the FTL kicked in. In a flash the *Skywend* jumped out of the system, a loud sonic boom echoing in its wake high over the glow of Correllia City.

7

The *Titania* hung against the backdrop of a green and yellow crab nebulae like a fat larva speckled with a thousand glowing lights. She was waiting to rendezvous with the *Skywend*. Her rotund hull had many bulbous portals and several large vents above her bow that made her looks unappealingly insectoid.

Captain Simon Calvec paced his ready room, anxious to begin the manhunt which would bring down the radical extremist, Demeris Ferrison.

Although many agreed with Ferrison's racist preaching and he had drawn a loyal following of ultra-conservative Dagons dissatisfied with the direction of the current monarchy, he still amounted to little more than a terrorist.

Not only was he wanted for blowing up women and children in the culture center attack on Arena City three years ago, now he'd stolen a neutron bomb and the military's prototype fighter right out from under Calvec's nose. Something he was still sore about.

As he paused to glance out his window again, his comm chimed and he tapped the holovid device mounted on his forearm. Raven's face lit up in a holographic projection and she greeted him with a familiar nod.

"We've arrived, as per the request of the UCC command. Requesting permission to come aboard, Captain."

"Permission granted, Captain." He tapped the yellow alert box on his screen and swiped it away. Once the holographic display cooled to green, a yellow beam of light touched down in his ready room in front of his desk and Raven and a massive Dragonian dressed in tactical gear appeared before him.

"This is my first officer, Commander Kregor Zekkidion," Raven informed Captain Calvec, gesturing to her immediate left with a wave of her upturned palm.

Captain Calvec rose to his feet and gestured for them to take a seat. "Please, make yourselves comfortable."

Raven smiled and slouched down into the seat and crossed her long slender legs. Kregor, meanwhile, merely crossed his arms and chose to stand. Looming over Raven's shoulder, he resembled an ever-vigilant gargoyle statue looking out for its congregation.

"I hear you have a pest control problem," Raven said. Although she was half-teasing Calvec, since the two of them went back to their academy days, but at the same time, she was also being quite serious.

Demeris Ferrison was the nastiest kind of vermin there was, this side of the Badlands, and he didn't hesitate to kill men, women, and children if it helped his cause. A cause relegated to the past, when Dagons believed in a purity myth so prevalent that it lingered to this day.

Jegra's becoming empress had upset a conservative element of the Dagon culture, and Demeris Ferrison found this small agitation the perfect itch to scratch at and the perfect opportunity to spread his brand of racist and xenophobic ideologies.

As within most societies, the ultra-conservative element was the most self-entitled and self-serving and, so too, the loudest when it came to expressing their gripes. Instead of taking the time to understand other cultures, they merely harped on how other cultures degraded Dagon purity. As if a race or a culture's purity was an intrinsic part of nature and not a part of the natural progress and evolution of a species.

The narrow mindedness of the ultra-conservatives usually made them a laughing stock and the butt of jokes on liberal talk media televid outlets throughout the Commonwealth. But with Demeris Ferrison's militant and violent tendencies, they sought to legitimize his dangerous worldview. And, the sad truth was, it probably touched a vein that went deeper than the surface of day-to-day affairs, proving that age-old racism and xenophobia still festered at the heart of Dagon culture.

Now, to make matters even worse, the man who wanted to watch the world burn had managed to get his hands on a neutron bomb. A bomb so powerful that it could extinguish all life on whatever planet it was unleashed upon.

A bomb so controversial, that even the military had limited their stockpiles for fear of getting into a cold war styled arms race with the other galactic bodies in the Commonwealth.

And even when H'aaztre was sowing chaos and tearing the galaxy apart with his armies, the military still withheld using neutron bombs—saving them as only a last resort.

But Raven knew just as well as Calvec did, Demeris Ferrison didn't fear what normal men feared. He nurtured a far too single-minded vision to worry about the consequences of his actions. Which made him an extremely dangerous man.

"The last time anyone had heard or seen Demeris Ferrison was shortly after the bombing of the cultural center on Arena City," Captain Calvec informed his guests. "After the empress made a public statement calling for his immediate capture and arrest, he went underground for a while. And his timing couldn't have been better, since the whole war with the Nyctans began just as he'd hidden away."

"I mean no disrespect, Captain," Raven said, leaning forward and clasping her hands together as she rested her forearms on her knees, "but, I have to ask. How did he get the neutron bomb off your ship in the first place?"

"He had inside help, I'm afraid. Sympathizers to his cause. Good men and women who, until they revealed themselves to be conspirators, served as hard-working soldiers and crew aboard my ship." Swiping his hand up, a holovid carrousel with images of the crew popped up.

With a flick of his wrist, he brushed his hand across the series of images and the files glided through the air toward Raven, who held up her wrist for her holovid bracelet to intercept the files.

The file transfer happened instantaneously, and Raven, having collected the data, immediately began swiping through the dossiers one by one. Studying the crewmember's personal information, their medical histories, and their psyche evaluations, she began to identify possible weaknesses and methods of tracking them.

"Nobody of note," Raven said, relieved that she was dealing with your standard radicalized criminal and not somebody higher up the organized crime food chain. "As far as I can tell, all of them are low ranking officers."

"They're probably just dissatisfied with their low station and the amount of grunt work heaped on them," Kregor said in his usual gruff fashion. Raven nodded.

"It makes sense. It's much easier for a master-manipulator like Ferrison to convince them to come over to his side and join his pet cause. Likely all he had to promise them was a little more personal power."

"I expect better of my people. I know the war has taken its toll. But I run a tight ship and this form of betrayal is unacceptable. Once these traitors are behind bars and awaiting their court-martial date, I'll resign my commission. Until then, however, I won't rest until they're caught."

Raven nodded with understanding. As captain, he had to set a good example by doing the honorable thing.

In the Dagon military, a mutiny aboard the ship usually involved the captain setting off the self-destruction sequence, blowing up the ship, and killing everyone aboard. Which is why mutinies never happened aboard Dagon battleships.

But now that the UCC fleet was mixed, integrating other aliens from the allied worlds within the new United Cosmic Commonwealth Alliance, the rules had changed. It wasn't acceptable to blow everyone up in the name of valor and glory.

Of course, this didn't mean the Dagon military was any less strict than it once was. Quite on the contrary. For his failure, Calvec would face his court-martial and maybe even some prison time.

"I'm here to help in any way I can, Captain," Raven informed Calvec.

Turning toward the viewing windows of his ready room, Calvec looked out at the green and yellow gas swirls of the nebula.

"I'm glad to hear that. Admiral Grendok informed me you'd be comfortable coloring outside the lines if necessary." He paused dramatically and then took a breath before continuing. "I need you and your crew to track these men down and apprehend them. Then, you need to make them tell you where Demeris Ferrison is. I don't care how you do it. Just so long as you get them to talk. Once you've located Demeris Ferrison's whereabouts, I want you to contact me immediately over an encrypted communique and I'll meet you at the decided upon coordinates where we will neutralize and extract the threat."

"A good ole fashioned bag and nab," Kregor said, popping his knuckles as a wide grin spread across his lizard lips. "Nice."

"As much as I wish I could join you, the UCC has given me different orders. I'm afraid the war took the largest toll on the Nyctans. Countless innocents died, their cities rendered little more than ash, and unless they receive help in rebuilding what they've lost, the Nyctans are all but doomed to extinction."

"Maybe it serves them right for aiding and abetting an evil tyrant in the first place," Kregor said, callously. Raven shot him a sharp glower and he shrugged.

After all, facts were facts and history is incontestable. If they didn't want to be viewed as historical tyrants and mass murders, then they shouldn't have engaged in mass murder, as far as Kregor was concerned. And those who'd turned a blind eye to it were, in his estimation, cowards of the highest order and deserved everything they got.

"Many feel that way," the captain continued. "But the empress does not. She has this…shall we say…sense of empathy? And although this emotion is unfamiliar to hardened warriors like you and me, it is this very same compassion, this deep feeling for the plight of others, that has allowed her to champion a greater good." The captain paused and turned to look Kregor in the eye. "You know, Commander, there was a time when I would have agreed wholeheartedly with Demeris Ferrison and his message. That was before the empress taught me how futile that path was, and how ignorant. The path of fear and hate only leads to more fear and hatred. It's like the serpent devouring its tail until there's nothing left." He paused and turned back to the large vista outside his windows.

"Apologies, Captain," Kregor said, feeling he'd upset the captain's sensibilities. "I spoke out of turn."

"No, no. It's quite alright. As a free citizen, your opinion is welcome aboard this ship. Just remember, it is that very freedom of expression that my officers proudly serve to uphold and protect."

"I think," Raven interjected, "the captain has pinpointed that aspect of the empress which makes her such a natural-born leader." She waited for both men's eyes to settle on her before continuing. "Jegra has shown us that instead of tearing each other down, we can build each other up. And that instead of constantly warring with one another we could be thriving. And that this ability to look past our differences and embrace one another's unique traits with compassionate understanding and love is the hallmark of a great society…a society that has evolved beyond petty squabbles regarding the primitive notion of blood purity or non-issues like the exact gradient of our skin to fully embracing itself for what it is—a mixture of peoples, beliefs, and idiosyncrasies."

Both men nodded. "I couldn't have put it better myself," the captain said. Kregor, meanwhile, folded his arms across his chest and grunted as he nodded in agreement. After all, Raven was right. Jegra had come at a time when the galaxy was at a tipping point. The affairs of the galaxy could have very easily gone in a completely different direction, sliding back hundreds of years of progress. Instead, Jegra showed them a better way. A way to get beyond their hang-ups and short-sighted prejudices perchance to grow as a united people.

"Alright then," Raven said, rising to her feet. "We thank you for your time, Captain, and I'll be sure to let you know when we've located the mark. Until then, godspeed, sir."

"And you," Calvec replied. The two captains reached across the table and shook hands. After the formalities were finished, Raven drew back and tapped her bracelet, opening a comlink to her ship. "Skuld, we're finished here. Two to teleport back."

A beam of golden light came down and Raven and Kregor's bodies began to break apart into little hexagonal photon packets. As the light packets whisked away, carried on the beam, Captain Calvec turned back toward the nebula outside his window and watched as the *Skywend* shot across his field of view and then jumped out of sight in a glorious flash of light.

As soon as he was sure they were gone, Calvec turned to the televid display hanging on the wall of his ready room and opened an encrypted channel. A few seconds later, a blue Dagon with slicked back white hair and a sycophantic expression turned and looked at him with wide, bulging eyes that seemed as insane as they were intense.

The man ran his fingers through his hair and, upon recognizing his caller, smiled. "Ah, Captain Simon Calvec, what do I owe the honor of this impromptu call?"

"You very well know why I'm calling you. I did as you asked. I had the bomb planted on Raven Nightguard's ship while she was aboard my vessel chatting up a storm about the empress."

Demeris Ferrison leaned back and grinned even wider, his eyes maintaining their large, hypnotic hold. "Excellent," he said, steepling his fingers under his chin and ruminating on things for a solid moment. "Good work, Captain. You're proving yourself to be a loyal cog on the machine of liberating the Dagon spirit from the shackles of impurity and disease that has taken root in our once great society."

"Spare me the lecture, Ferrison. I upheld my end of the deal, now you uphold yours. Is my family safe?"

"Tsk, tsk, Captain. What do you take me for? A common barbarian? I assure you that your family is being well taken care of here. Esteemed guests of my private estate, if you will."

"I want to speak to my wife and daughter," Calvec said.

Demeris Ferrison nodded then raised his hand and snapped his fingers at somebody offscreen. A few nanoseconds later Calvec's wife and child were staring back at him through the televid screen.

"My luv," he said, reaching out to try and feel his lovely wife's face. Although her eyes were full of tears, she kept it together so as not to appear weak in front of a well-known galactic terrorist. "Are they treating you well?"

"Yes, my luv," she answered. "We are both fine. But I don't have long to talk, and there's someone here wants to say hi to you."

"Daddy?" a smallish voice asked.

Calvec looked down at the bright-eyed face of his eight-year-old daughter staring back at him and he smiled warmly.

"I miss you, daddy," she said.

"I miss you too, sweetheart," he replied. "I miss you too the third moon and back."

"When can I see you again, daddy?"

"Soon, sweetie. Very soon. I promise."

She smiled once more and then, cutting off their conversation prematurely, the camera swiveled back around and focused on Demeris Ferrison again.

"No!" Calvec growled.

Ignoring the captain's protest, Ferrison said, "As you can see, they're perfectly fine. And as long as you continue to play nice and do as I say, they'll remain that way. But if you so much as think of double-crossing me," Ferrison paused and sneered, then continued, his voice rougher and more callous than before, "I'd hate to think what would happen to your lovely family."

"I swear…if you lay a single finger on either of them, I'll…"

The televid cut out with Demeris Ferrison looking unamused, then went dark.

As soon as the screen went back to a scrolling series of beautifully painted scenes of Dagon Prime, Captain Calvec buried his face into his palms and broke down.

8

Neon green and red flashes scorched the hull of Jegra's imperial space yacht. The only distinguishing markings being the rune that came from the Dagoni letter "J" of her alien given name. The sleek white vessel rocked intermittently as more blaster fire pelted it from the three encroaching ships.

The much larger pirate ships consisted of an old, but heavily modified frigate, a cargo ship with grappling guns, and a smaller, more maneuverable, vessel roughly the same size as her yacht.

Streaking past her main window, the small skiff peppered her ship with a series of intense, green plasma blasts. Jegra could tell by the color that they were bypassing ship's auxiliary power straight into the weapons. A dangerous bypass that frequently caused smaller ships like that to overload. But space pirates were never ones to play it on the side of caution.

<<Shields down to 32%>> the female voice of her computer intoned. Suddenly a loud blast rattled the ship as the bright red plasm from the frigate's massive plasma canons made a direct hit. <<Shields down to 12%>> the computer corrected.

"Shit," Jegra said, rising from the pilot's chair. She tossed the loosely woven plait of her long hair, which was held together by a weave of smaller braids, over her shoulder and made her way to the back wall of the ship's cabin.

She paused in front of the smooth wall and tapped the small tab on the mandarin collar of her smart-suit. A seam on the front of the suit from her collar down to her crotch opened up and she quickly peeled it off.

Shedding the nanofiber suit and letting it fall to the floor, Jegra stood up against the wall and leaned back, taking in a deep breath as the cool metal met the skin of her back.

Strangely enough, the surface didn't appear fully solid and began to gradually sink into the wall as if it had the consistency of a thick mortar.

Another few seconds and she sank beneath the metallic surface. The liquid engulfed her, flowing over her face as though someone had doused her in a bucket of silver pudding. After having enveloped her fully, the wall rippled momentarily and then went back to its normal smooth consistency.

In the adjoining room, Jegra appeared on the other side of the wall, her body completely coated in the metallic substance. It slid down from her head and across her body like wet glistening mud after a mud-bath, and gradually coated her in a uniform shine.

The metallic suit stopped at her neckline, and she tossed her long tresses of hair over her shoulder. Then, the liquid metal traveled back up her neck and engulfed most of her face, leaving an opening large enough for a visor.

She blinked her brown eyes and the opening rapidly filled with blue energy as the negative barrier energy shield formed a faceplate visor.

Naturally, this new, high-suit was beyond anything the Commonwealth currently had. Jegra had found the blueprints for it in Old Lady Jegra's things and had replicated all the necessary parts and built it herself, according to all the specifications.

The suit let her long tresses of brown hair dangle out the back while the rest of it began to harden into actual shapes and metal plating. Where there were lines for her joints and points of articulation, the suit turned into a mesh weave of intricate hexagonal links similar to chainmail.

Another loud blast from outside shook the ship and the shields went down. Jegra tapped the side of her helmet and said, "Gladiator mode," and the suit reformed itself to resemble high-tech gladiator armor.

Before it could harden again, a piece of the suit extended from her right thigh, forming three tendrils that wove themselves into a long spear. She plucked it off and the spear slowly morphed into a battle-axe in her hands.

Right on time! Red beams of light lit up her ship as half a dozen space pirates brandishing high powered plasma pistols illegally boarded her vessel.

They all turned to see the silver gladiatrix standing before them, pausing briefly out of shock at the unexpected sight.

"Oy! It's a Knight of Caelum," one of the pirates said in a coward's voice.

Another one shoved him aside and blurted, "That ain't no Knight." He raised his blaster, which had a knife welded to the end of it and added, "It's some kind of woman robot or sumptin'."

"Do you know who I am?" she asked.

"Yeah," one of the pirates said, stepping forward and raising his blaster. "You're a dead woman."

He fired off a blast from ten feet away and everyone watched as the energy dissipated against the armor, washed over it, kind of like hot grease sliding off of a non-stick frying pan.

"You were saying?" Jegra asked with a crooked smile.

"Oh, *shiii*—" the man barely had time to react she moved so fast. Lunging back, he raised his blaster to let off another blast only to point the sparking end of a severed blaster at her. "Gah!" he groused. "The guns are no good against her. Use your blades, men."

Each of the pirates drew out their knives, swords, and daggers and slowly surrounded Jegra. She noted that the leader's dagger had a skull pommel and two red rubies for eyes.

"You best give up, lady, cuz we got you surrounded."

"Surrounded?" Jegra balked, putting her hand dramatically to her chest and looking around. "The only thing I'm surrounded by is a circle of dead cowards."

This seemed to piss the pirates off royally, and they roared out in unison and charged her from all sides, the sharp ends of the daggers glinting angrily as they bore down on her.

Jegra easily dodged the swipe of the first blade, and, throwing her elbow back, nailed the man in the face. His nose broke with a crunch and he screamed out as blue blood gushed from the flattened cartilage.

Dropping her shoulder, Jegra got under the man, who leaped into the air to bring down his blade, but he overshot her and toppled to the floor.

This allowed Jegra an opening to rush the leader, and she tackled him hard. Both of them crashed to the ground as two other pirates leapt onto her back.

Jegra rose with the grace of a panther then tossed the two clinging to her back to either side of her. As she looked back down, the leader kicked his metal-toed boot right into her crotch with a resounding "clank."

She looked down as his foot and then back at him. "Really?"

Annoyed, she reached down and clasped him by his unprotected crotch.

He yelped out in pain as she hoisted him off the ground by it and, then, spinning around, tossed him into his men. They all went down like bowling pins.

While they were getting up, Jegra's axe dissolved in her hand and, melting away like rice paper doused with water, it slid through her fingers and dribbled onto the floor.

"That can't be good," she said to herself.

Just as the pirates were regrouping, the rest of her suit began to melt from her body and drizzled to the floor too, just like her axe had. Every piece of it liquified and gathered into a metallic puddle at her feet.

Standing in front of the pirates with nothing but her birthday suit on, she timidly covered herself up and muttered under her breath, "God damn it."

"Seize her!" the pirate leader shouted, pointing a finger at her from his robotic arm. His other hand clutched his groin and gently massaged his battered and bruised manhood.

It took all five pirates to restrain Jegra, and although she was accustomed to fighting with little to nothing on, she decided to restrain herself long enough to see what this was about.

"What do you want?" she growled.

"What do you think we want? Your ship." Slowly drawing close to her, the leader stroked his beard and smiled a gold-toothed grin. "But first, a bit of payback." Incrementally, he unzipped his pants and Jegra looked down as his hand slid inside his pants.

"Wrong answer," she said, and, with the snap of her neck, she headbutted him so hard he collapsed onto the ground in a heap—his hand still in his pants.

A few seconds later, he regained consciousness and quickly scrambled to his feet, his nose gushing blue blood. "You'll pay for that!" he snarled and drew his skull dagger.

Inching up to her, this time taking extra precaution, he nodded at his men to hold her tight. They did as asked and she struggled in protest but no sooner had they latched on to her than the skull dagger cut a line across her chest just above her breasts. The knife clanked when it hit her Dygra crystal, and the pirate raised an eyebrow. "What's this, now?"

"It's none of your concern," Jegra said, her voice low and menacing.

"A crystal, is it? I bet it's worth a pretty penny on the black market." With that, he began to dig the blade into Jegra's flesh in an attempt to cut out the crystal.

Jegra screamed as the korridium blade, the only metal that could pierce her superhuman skin, sliced into her. For the first time in a long time, she felt the lacerating twinge of real pain cut into her and, unexpectedly, an overwhelming excitement came over her as the gladiator inside her stirred to life.

Before the pirate could get very far with extracting the crystal, another beam of red light filled the room and three more pirates manifested. This time it was a woman flanked by two large Dragonian lizard warriors in full battle armor.

"What's taking you *va'pa mashtaq* so long?" the woman asked, turning around and making eye-contact with Jegra with her one good eye. "Oh, shit," she said, recognizing the empress immediately.

"Ladgara?" Jegra asked in a shocked voice. Although she was surprised, it wasn't entirely unexpected to see that the self-proclaimed Pirate Queen herself was behind this little hijacking.

"You idiots!" Ladgara growled. "Do you know who this is?"

She marched up to her man holding the bloody knife, grabbed him by his collar, and hoisted him off his feet in a show of great strength. A series of electronic styled veins lit up under her skin, showing that, like Raven, she was heavily modified.

"You bleedin' moron," she continued, berating him even further. "You told me it was just an ordinary yacht. Some rich bitch. You didn't tell me it was the mother-fucking-empress of the Dagon Empire, you fucking dimwit!"

"Apologies, my queen," he said. "But, in all fairness, you told us to jam her transponder codes to prevent her from sending out a distress call. Besides, the yacht is unmarked. How were we supposed to know?"

But his words were short-lived because Ladgara, her temper flaring, headbutted him into a plane of unconsciousness. The unlucky man promptly collapsed back to the ground a second time.

"Let her go," she said, pointing at the other pirates who were practically piled onto Jegra in an attempt to pin her down, although, it didn't seem to be working out as they'd hoped seeing as she managed to still stand upright even with all of them hanging onto her like a bunch of spider monkeys.

Doing as commanded, they all let go of her and then quickly stepped back, giving the empress room to stand up on her own. Once free of her captors, she cracked her neck and rotated her broad shoulders, letting out some of the tension.

Jegra raised her wrist and tapped the bracelet on her arm. A smart suit unfurled, and a milky white liquid coated her skin then congealed into a pleather-like catsuit. She tapped it once more and the suit grew two turquoise stripes that ran down either side of her.

"Your Majesty," Ladgara said, pressing her hands together apologetically and groveling. "Please accept my deepest felt apologies for my men's behavior. Believe me when I say, they're complete imbeciles. The whole lot of them." To demonstrate she meant it, she kicked her man, still lying at her feet, in his gut just as he was attempting to get up a second time.

"Oomph!" he groaned, flopped onto his other side, and clutched his bruised ribs.

"Your involvement in the war helped us prevail over our enemies," Jegra said, her eyes fixed on Ladgara's single good eye. "For that, I am eternally grateful and am willing to overlook this little incident—just this once."

"Oh, thank you. Thank you so much, Your Grace," Ladgara said humbly, bowing deeply in a show of her appreciation.

When she rose back up, Jegra was standing directly in front of her, her face mere inches away. Ladgara tensed up, as she hadn't seen her move nor heard her, and drew back a step.

Ladgara's bodyguards grunted and took a step forward to try and get in-between Ladgara and Jegra, but Ladgara simply raised her hand and motioned for them to stay back.

Jegra leaned in so that her lips brushed Ladgara's blue elfin ear, and whispered, "I know you're the one who got her pregnant," she said in a cool and commanding tone.

Alarmed that Jegra knew what had gone on between her and Raven, Ladgara's pupil dilated and snapped to the corners of her eyelid and beheld Jegra's face from the edge of her peripheral vision.

"About that, I can explain."

"I'd rather you not," Jegra said. The two women stared long and hard at one another before Ladgara finally broke her gaze and turned her face away in shame.

"W-what are you going to do?" Ladgara asked, her voice trembling slightly as she felt a genuine twinge of trepidation.

"Right now, nothing. But if you so much as show your face to me again, I'll have you shackled and made into my personal servant for as long as I see fit."

Ladgara prided herself on being the type of girl who never felt fear. The truth was, she was used to a world of lawlessness, back-stabbing, and every man and woman for themselves. Heck, even when she was with Emperor Dakroth, she'd been rather careless, treating him as just another one of her many inconsequential flings. He seemed to quite enjoy that about her.

But Jegra was different. When she threatened you, it wasn't about posturing or puffing up her chest for show. It was a promise. And one you needed to take seriously.

If she was being completely honest, a life of scrubbing toilets and changing linens wasn't the worst fate she could think of. Although it came pretty damn close. She'd probably slowly go out of her mind and then hang herself from the empress's balcony using the empress's bedsheets.

"Understood," Ladgara said, raising her hands as if to say she surrendered while taking a cautious step back.

To Ladgara's shock, however, Jegra promptly reached out and clutched her wrists. Ladgara's widened as Jegra drew her in, her chest smashing into Jegra's. As they drew close a second time, she noted the empress's eyes were lingering on her full, dark painted lips.

Before she knew it, the empress had pulled her in tight, and their mouths came crashing together in a sultry kiss.

Jegra's pink tongue slipped into Ladgara's black painted lips and, feeling herself getting turned on, Ladgara took Jegra's powerful body in her arms and kissed her back.

The remaining pirates all glanced at one another with raised eyebrows and equal parts confusion and arousal as the two women made out with one another.

Thirty seconds later, Jegra shoved Ladgara back so hard she slammed into the rear wall with such force that it dented the metal plating.

Ladgara coughed up a spattering of blood and, wiping her chin with the back of her hand, chuckled and wheezed, "I suppose I deserved that."

"Now, take your men and get the hell off my ship." Jegra raised her arm and extended a finger, pointing at the airlock opposite them.

Ladgara grunted as she pushed herself out of the indentation on the wall and then tapped the pendant on her long, black leather trench coat with red lining and trim. "Bring us back," she said. "We're finished here."

Red beams of light came down and fetched everyone. As Ladgara began to port away, she looked through the energy distortion at Jegra and smiled.

"Give Raven my best," she said before dissipating in a beam of light.

Jegra puffed at a tuft of hair that had come undone and fell across her face, then brushed it behind her ear. She let out a long sigh and then returned to the cockpit of her ship.

When she arrived on the bridge, she found her entire computer system gutted. The pirates she'd been playing slap and tickle with were just a distraction. In typical pirate fashion, Ladgara had double-crossed her.

"That blue-twat-waffle-licking pirate hag," Jegra groused to herself. "She fucking jacked me."

Jegra ran to the window in time to see the remaining pirate ships slowly turnabout and move away from her as they prepared to make the jump to FTL.

9

Jegra slammed her first onto the console, opening the commlink to the lead pirate ship. "You fork-tongued Vek'miel!" Jegra shouted, slamming her fist onto the glass. "Get back here this instant so I can wring that pretty little neck of yours."

"As much as I like it rough," Ladgara's voice came back over the comm, "I'm afraid I'm going to need to take a raincheck, Your *Worshipfulness*. Until next time."

Just then, all three pirate ships jumped away in a trio of blinding flashes of light.

Peeved, Jegra slammed her fist against the glass one last time for good measure and then fell back into her plush Alcantara leather seat and slouched down.

As she lamented her loss, her mind kept winding it way back to the sultry kiss she'd shared with Ladgara. It was the best kiss she'd had in months. And, still feeling a bit steamy, she let out a hot and bothered sigh.

Interrupting her thoughts, Jegra's smart bracelet began pulsing blue to green and back to blue while chiming frenetically, as though it had something seemingly urgent to tell her. She quickly sat up and tapped her bracelet and a female's voice intoned <<After running a ship-wide diagnostic, it's been found that the ship's auxiliary life support is currently at 43%>>

"Just great," griped Jegra in a sarcastic tone, nervous perspiration already beading up on her forehead. Feeling hot, she unzipped the top part of her suit and threw open the flap. Falling back into her seat again, she fanned her cleavage and tried to cool herself and gather her thoughts.

It was slowly becoming clear to her that the pirates hadn't only gutted her computer systems, but they'd taken her fusion quad-core Hyperborean drive, and most of her battery packs too. She could tell by the rising temperature that they'd only left one battery pack for the auxiliary life support. And it was already being taxed to its limit by powering the ship's backup systems.

It would continue to gradually overheat and roast her until, after another hour or two, all of its power would be completely spent. Then, the heat would die down, and she'd stop burning to death and would begin to rapidly freeze to death instead.

Luckily, she had her Knights of Caelum battle armor combination EV suit safely stored in the storage locker along with several oxygen tanks that would allow her to survive for at least three more days. If she put the suit into stasis mode, she may get a month out of it.

It wasn't ideal, but it would buy her enough time to maybe get picked up by a passing freighter.

Although she was certain the pirates couldn't have gotten through the korridium locker, seeing as it would have taken them a week to cut through it with an industrial-strength plasma cutter, they had still taken nearly everything else of value of hers. They'd even stripped the long-range sub-space transceiver. All she had now was short-range comms. So, broadcasting an SOS via needle-cast was out of the question.

All she could do now was wait for a passing ship that came within range of her primitive radio. Her smart bracelet might be able to boost the broadcast a little further, but not by much.

Jegra let out a drawn-out sigh and, kicking her feet up onto the console, stared out at the stars.

Stuck adrift in the dead of space, she did the only thing she could do. She reached under her seat and pulled out a bottle of Nova Centauri Red. Biting down onto the cork with her bare teeth, the plucked it out and spat the cork onto the floor. Kicking back her head, she guzzled the smooth red liquor from the bottle with such gluttonous haste that some of it dribbled down the sides of her mouth and chin.

The red trails of wine continued from her chin and ran down her neck in several branching streams until, finally, it came back together in a delta and disappeared into the valley of her cleavage.

She wiped her chin with her hand, ignoring the rest of the glistening mess as she sat back and continued to gaze out at the stars. If she'd come to the end of the line, well, even she had to admit this wasn't the worst way to go. There were far worse ways to die.

Just then a blinding flash of light caused her to raise her hand and shield her eyes. As she peered out the window, blinking as her eyes adjusted, she let out a huge sigh of relief. A familiar ship came into focus.

Nearly as soon as the *Skywend* had appeared just beyond her bow, a beam of golden light had appeared on her bridge, and she swiveled around in her chair to see Raven standing in the center of the cabin, staring at her with big worried eyes.

Seeing the red streaks running down Jegra's face and neck, Raven rushed to her side and fell to her knees. "You're hurt!" she exclaimed, touching Jegra's face and neck as she assessed how bad the damage was.

"No," Jegra laughed, shaking her head side to side as she took Raven's hands in hers, "I'm just a little bit drunk, is all." An involuntary hiccup escaped her lips and she covered her mouth and blushed with embarrassment. "Excuse me."

Raven let out a huge sigh of relief and, still sitting on her knees, placed her forehead on Jegra's shoulder. "Oh, thank the gods."

As she rested her head there, she happened to glance down and see Jegra was wearing the engagement ring on her finger.

Raven took Jegra's hand in hers and raised it.

"You're wearing my ring," she chirped, excitedly.

"I am," Jegra said, smiling down at her.

"So…is that a yes?"

Jegra held up the ring, her lips stretching across her face in the biggest smile she'd managed all week. "It's a hell yes!"

Raven practically screamed and covered her mouth. She wasn't one prone to acting all girly like this, but the news of Jegra accepting her proposal was overwhelming.

Raven climbed onto the chair with her brand-new fiancé, her legs straddling Jegra's thick thighs. Settling onto her lap, Raven looked down as Jegra wrapped her arms around her waist. At the same time, Raven brushed a tuft of brown hair out of Jegra's face so that they could better gaze into one another's eyes.

They slowly moved in for a kiss but just before their lips came together Raven pulled away again. Raven began sniffing the air. Shooting Jegra a peculiar look, asked, "Is that Ladgara's perfume I smell on you?"

Jegra let out a vexed sigh and immediately responded with an embarrassed look. "It's a long story."

"Don't tell me you and that vek'miel…you know…?" Raven paused, letting Jegra fill in the blanks of what she meant.

"Oh, God no!" gasped Jegra, a horrified look settling across her face. "I do have standards, you know."

Raven let out another sigh of relief and began laughing. Jegra raised an eyebrow and asked, "What?"

"I just realized that I'm totally jealous of that vek'miel."

"Jealous of that cunt-guzzling bandersnatch? Don't be."

Raven's smile twisted peculiarly and she shrugged. "I guess I've never loved someone enough to feel jealous over them before. It's a weird feeling; I don't like it."

Jegra laughed. "Don't worry, babe. With time, you'll learn to navigate your feelings alongside the best of them."

"I sure hope so," she said, laughing at her own naiveté.

Although she was Dagon, she never viewed herself as detached from her emotions like much of her people. Her culture frowned on being overly emotional, but she'd never realized how deeply that mindset had impacted her. Now, here she was confused about feeling jealously for the first time.

Drawing Raven into her arms again, Jegra looked up at her heliotropic eyes and smiled. "I hope smelling like that overly ripe space-twat doesn't put you off from kissing your one true love?"

Raven laughed again and bent down and kissed Jegra on her thick rosy lips. After breaking away, she took a deep breath and whispered, "Never."

A static hiss, crackle, and pop interrupted their little snog-fest and Kregor's voice came over the comm. "Captain, is everything alright over there?"

Raven sat straight up, slid off of Jegra's lap and tapped the side of her ear. Electric veins of circuitry pulsed under her skin and she cleared her throat and replied. "Everything's fine over here, Commander. But space pirates gutted the ship and left nothing but its metal carcass. I'm afraid you'll need to latch onto us with the magnetic grapplers so the *Skywend* can tow the empress's ship to the nearest space-dock."

"Copy that," Kregor replied. "I'll get right on it."

With that, the comm cut out. Raven, who stood beside Jegra, who gazed up at her with dreamy eyes, looked back down at her luv. Seeing her wearing that ring brought a smile to her face once more.

"I still can't believe we're going to be married," Raven said.

"Not only that, but I can't believe we're both having babies."

Raven's eyes grew wide and she looked properly mortified. "I nearly forgot I was pregnant," she laughed, cupping her hands around the five-week bulge of her abdomen and inspecting it.

Jegra gently reached out and placed her soft, fleshy hands over Raven's blue ones. "Don't worry, it'll be fine. I'll be right beside you every step of the way."

"You'd better," Raven said, eyeing Jegra sternly.

Jegra laughed. "Thank you for saving me, by the way."

"No problem, babe. You'd do the same for me"

A yellow beam of light drew their attention to the center of the cabin again and Sendaya appeared with two suitcase-sized containers of equipment.

When she saw the captain and the empress in an intimate embrace, hands-on stomachs and what not, she diverted her gaze. "Apologies, ma'am, I didn't mean to intrude."

"It's fine," Raven said, taking a step back and letting Jegra's hands slide off her stomach. She then tugged on the edge of her leather outfit and forced the creases out.

Jegra rose from her seat and looked over at the young face of the Seyfferian girl. "And who might you be?"

Raven cleared her throat and then said, "Your Grace, may I introduce to you Sendaya Eschelle Vortesh, Corporal First-Class, of the Seyfferian Republic Special Security forces. She's working with us under the order of the UCC on her first field mission."

Jegra extended her hand, "Glad to make your acquaintance, Sendaya. My name is Jegra Alakandra, Empress of the Dagon Empire."

Sendaya took the empress's hand and immediately noticed the ring. Then she looked at Raven and back at the empress. "It's a pleasure to finally meet you,

Your Majesty. I've heard so much about your exploits. You're a living legend. And, I wanted to inform you that, although I wasn't yet out of the academy when the war started, I accelerated all of my courses so I could join you in your cause as soon as possible. I apologize for not trying harder."

"It's quite all right," Jegra laughed. "It wasn't the kind of war one looked forward to fighting in. We lost a lot of lives, and it took a toll on more than just the empire." Jegra looked out the windows as her countenance grew serious. There was a lingering silence, and then she turned back to Sendaya and smiled again. "Don't let us keep you, Corporal. I'm sure you have plenty of work to keep you busy."

"I do. And, congratulations, Your Grace." She nodded at Raven and Jegra shot her a perplexed looked before realizing she meant the engagement.

Holding up her ring again so she could admire it, she said, "Ah, yes. I'm the luckiest woman in the galaxy. Not only do I have two beautiful wives at home whom I adore more than anything, I also get to marry my soulmate."

Raven blushed as she found Sendaya's eyes drilling into her with piqued interest. She then cleared her throat again and said, "Well, Corporal, we'll leave you to it."

Sendaya stepped aside and bowed slightly as both women passed by her on their way to the sliding doors. The moment they stepped off the bridge and the doors hissed shut behind them, she set to work setting up her gear.

"Where are we going?" Jegra asked as she trailed after Raven.

"Once the grapplers are attached, the *Skywend* will feed power directly into your ship. Sendaya will plug in a portable A.I. to help regulate ship functions in place of the mainframe the pirates gutted. Everything should come back online as per usual."

They stopped outside Jegra's quarters and Raven turned to her, her back pressed against the door. Jegra brushed a strand of purple hair out of her eyes and she smiled.

"You didn't answer my question," Jegra said, smiling at Raven with a frisky twist of her lips.

"I don't know what it is, but this pregnancy is making me unbearably—"

"Randy?" Jegra interjected, finishing her sentence for her.

"Yeah," Raven laughed.

"Me too," Jegra said, brushing Raven's face. "What do you think we should do about it?"

"Oh, you know," Raven said with a modest shrug.

Both women laughed and then, Raven slammed the palm of her hand down onto the wall panel and the door swished open. Both women tumbled backward into the bedroom together, their hands fast at work undressing one another with urgent haste as they fumbled their way to Jegra's bed.

Falling into bed, they had just landed in each other's arms when, all of a sudden, there was a loud clunk and the artificial gravity shut off.

Crackle...skkkkt... "Sorry about that," Sendaya's voice came over the comm, "I'll have the artificial gravity back on in about ten minutes."

Jegra and Raven floated over her bed looking into one another's eyes. The claret satin sheets rippled in the air like an ocean wave and the two of them slowly reached out and clasped onto one another.

As their bodies came together, Jegra looked into Raven's amethyst eyes and smiled. Sliding her hand down between Raven's lavender thighs, she said, "That's plenty of time for me to make you gush like Ennead waterfalls of Theta Prime."

Raven bit her lower lip and moaned as Jegra's sensual touch sent a surge of ecstasy through her entire body.

"All nine of them?" Raven asked, letting out a small gasp of hot breath as Jegra's fingers worked their magic.

"Is there any doubt?" Jegra asked, her pink lips hovering over Raven's plum ones.

Raven let slip a lustful moan as she clutched Jegra's forearm and pulled it tightly into her body. Her fingernails bit into Jegra's skin, drawing the slightest trickle of blood that floated away in small globules in the zero-G environment.

Her entire body shuddered as she orgasmed and she let out another breathy sigh. Sweat peeled away from her skin and glinted in the air like morning dewdrops. Holding Jegra in her arms, Raven placed her forehead on Jegra's cheek and whispered, "Only eight more waterfalls to go."

Amused at the fact that she was able to bring such pleasure to the woman she loved, Jegra snickered softly to herself and then peered into Raven's sparkling purple eyes for an indiscernible amount of time before sharing another sensuous kiss.

Light as a feather, their bodies gently spun in the zero-G space with the gentle rotational speed of a rotisserie, their arms and legs linked together to keep them from drifting apart in the weightless atmosphere.

10

On the surface of Nyctan's moon of Endiva, aquamarine swirls mingled with browns and deeper blues like the paints on an artisan's pallet. As the only inhabitable moon of the Nyctan homeworld, it was the perfect place for a secret base of operations. Which explained why Raven, Jegra, and the crew of the *Skywend* had traced the transponder signal of the prototype fighter to Endiva.

"You've gotta' hand it to them," Kregor said in his deep baritone. "They have some pretty massive balls to come back here and try to hock stolen military tech to the Nyctans."

Jegra kicked her long legs up on the side-console and leaned back in her chair. "Especially given the fact that the Knights of Caelum now patrol this sector and are hunting down all the rogue Nephilim who went AWOL after the war," she informed, fiddling with a plait of her long brown hair.

"That's always the problem with fanatics," Raven added, "they only see things in terms of their warped worldview. They may have a vision, but they lack foresight and the means to execute that vision. It's why they always, inevitably, resort to violence. Unable to imagine other possible means to achieving their goals, they try to seize power with brute force. And those who don't respect their vision can be pummeled into submission with the threat of further violence and fear."

Jegra uncrossed her legs and sat up. Only now had it dawned on her that Raven wasn't talking about the tyranny of the Nyctans, but the tyranny of Dakroth.

"I'm sorry," she said, gently reaching across the space between them and touching Raven's arm. "I didn't know he'd hurt you so badly."

Raven shook her head. "It's in the past now."

"That may be, but the trauma lingers. It will take time to heal. And feelings like that don't just go away. It's something you have to live with. Just know, that you have people here who care about you; we're your family."

Raven's eyes flooded with tears as she looked at all the smiling faces looking back at her.

"We love you, boss lady," Gyllek said from the back.

"You're like our surrogate mother," Skuld added. "You took us in when nobody else would."

"You saved my life," Kregor said. "A debt I'll always work to repay."

"You've given me the happiest years of my life," Angellyk said, smiling fondly at Raven.

Sniffling, Raven wiped a stray tear from her cheek and turned her face away.

After mustering up the courage to share with everyone what was so hard to get off her chest, Raven took a deep breath and bit the proverbial bullet. "The bastard raped me," she finally admitted, sharing the dark secret she'd carried inside her for so many years.

The cabin of the ship grew so silent you could hear a pin drop, and everyone shared astonished looks at the shocking revelation. It was hard to imagine a woman as strong as Raven being a victim.

"After my sister betrayed my family," Raven began, "and turned my parents over to the secret police, Dakroth accompanied the raiding party that broke into our home. I was only a young woman finishing her last year of the academy, and he found me hiding in the kitchen pantry. Prying me from my hiding place, he belittled me for my cowardice and not having the fortitude to bring my parent's crimes to light as my sister had. At that moment, I saw in his eyes his disdain for anyone who betrayed him, and he tore my clothes off and defiled me as they trucked my parents off to the other room. I caught the heartbroken glimpse of my father as he caught the horror of what was happening to his daughter from the corners of his eyes. I knew he blamed himself. I wanted to call out to him, but by the time I gathered the courage to scream out the blaster shots rang out. They'd been executed in the next room."

"I'm so sorry," Jegra said, trying her best to sound consoling even though she knew it was likely a futile endeavor given the horrendous nature of Raven's harrowing tale.

"After he was finished with me, he left me cold and naked on the floor. I remember him spitting on me and then telling the guards to leave me. I laid there weeping, staring through the doorway at the corpses of the only two people I ever loved." Raven paused to take a breather and then continued, "From that day forward, I swore to do everything in my power to make him pay for what he did to me. But then this fucking war happened and…" Raven slammed her fist down on the main console and it blurted out some angry tones in protest of the abuse.

Jegra rose from her seat and went over to Raven, reaching out to embrace her and hold her in her arms. When Raven tried to turn away out of shame, Jegra gently reached down and took her chin in her fingers and guided her tear-soaked face back to her.

Then, sinking to her knees, Jegra wrapped her arms around Raven's neck and held her, squeezing her long and hard in her loving embrace. Raven broke down crying as she let it all out.

In the blink of an eye, years of trauma and pain seemed to melt away. A weight she hadn't even realized she'd been carrying lifted from her and everyone watched the strongest woman they knew pick herself up and put herself back together.

"Sorry," she said, wiping a tear from her cheek and sniffling. "I think this pregnancy is making me overly emotional."

"What?! You're pregnant?!" Kregor practically shouted the question as he turned to face Raven, his jaw agape with utter astonishment.

"Oh," she said, brushing her hair behind her ear and looking up at all the stunned faces in the room. "Did I not mention that?"

"It's the first I'm hearing about it," Angellyk said. "But, how should I know, I'm the last to hear anything around here." She folded her arms to try and pout, but it was no use. She was simply too happy for Raven. "Ah, who am I kidding. That's wonderful news!" she smiled at Raven when Gyllek's small mouse-like voice chimed in.

"Also, the boss lady is getting married to Empress Jegra!" Pointing at Raven's ring upon Jegra's finger, she added a revelatory, "See!"

"What in the Seven Rings of Thorgath is going on?" Kregor cried out, his eyes finding the sparkling purple sapphires and crystal-clear diamonds of Jegra's engagement ring. "Did I slip into some kind of parallel dimension?" he asked, his hands on his head as he looked around the room in complete and utter bewilderment.

Skuld, who sat at the far back, cleared his throat and pointed at Raven's finger. "Allow me to be the first to congratulate the both of you and wish you a long, prosperous marriage."

"We appreciate that," Jegra said, looking over at Skuld.

"Can I name the baby?" Gyllek asked.

"Sure," Jegra teased, not being sincere, although by the excited look on Gyllek's face it wasn't clear she understood the nuance of Jegra's fib.

"Oh, shut up," Raven said, giving Jegra a playful shove. Then, turning to Gyllek, she said, "If you make a list of names, I'll take them under advisement," Raven clarified, doing her best to find a way to assuage the girl's expectations without crushing her. "But that's all I can promise."

Jegra laughed and then, swaying back into Raven's arms, they kissed in front of everyone.

"Oh, good! I have so many ideas," Gyllek said, clapping her hands giddily.

Kregor stood up unexpectedly and everyone turned toward him. "I'll be in engineering checking the air-filters if you need me," he informed them. And, with that, he stormed off the bridge.

"I'd better go talk with him," Angellyk said, rising from her chair. "The poor man's lizard brain is probably having trouble processing all the exciting news."

A copper hand pressed down on her forearm and she turned her emerald eyes toward Sendaya.

"I'll do it," she said. There was an anxiousness in her voice, as though she were dying to get away and do something productive.

Angellyk nodded and sat back down.

"I'll go with you," Gyllek said and joined Sendaya as she exited the bridge and stepped out into the corridor.

Skuld and Angellyk made eye contact and then both slowly got up and slipped out with what, strangely enough, seemed an anxious sort of excitement.

Jegra did a double-take as she put two and two together and then turned to Raven with wide-eyed revelation.

Jutting a thumb over her shoulder, she turned back to ask, "Does Kregor know about those two?"

Raven reached down and drew up Jegra's hand, flashing her ring. "I mean, what do you think?"

"Ooh…poor guy," Jegra said, feeling sorry for him. Kregor was a kind soul, but like many of his kind, he wasn't accustomed to processing lots of complex emotions. Receding into his masculine shell and hiding behind all that Dragonian bravado was one way of avoiding having to grapple with his feelings.

At the same time, though, this put a strain on his relationship with Angellyk, and it seemed she was maybe shopping around other options at the moment.

Raven shrugged and said, "Maybe he won't figure it out. As long as he stays oblivious, he's happy as an Octagonian clam."

"Yum!" Jegra said, her stomach growling something terrible. "Speaking of clams, I could eat a whole bucket of Octagonian clams right about now." Drawing an octagon in the air, she added, "I love their little octagon shapes. So scrumptious!"

Raven laughed. "Later, babe. I'm afraid you and I have a mission to prep for."

Jegra sighed and then looked back at Raven. "Right," she said, then, motioning with her hand for Raven to lead the way, she said, "After you, future Mrs. Alakandra."

Raven shot her an uncomfortable look and said, "I don't think I'll ever get used to that," and then turned toward the moon lingering outside the main view portal.

"You don't need to take my name," Jegra said. "It's an ancient Earth custom and is quite outdated anyway."

"Raven Alakandra," she said, trying out the name. "Raven Alakandra," she said more assertively. Then, shrugging, she turned to Jegra and said, "I think it's starting to grow on me."

Jegra laughed and the two of them exited the bridge.

The shuttle set down several clicks outside of the camp and Jegra and Raven stepped out. They had on black tactical gear and wore black camo face-paint.

Checking her holovid band, which was set to night vision, Raven held up two fingers and pointed in the direction of the basecamp. "Six clicks that way."

"Right," Jegra whispered. Then, gesturing for Raven to go on ahead of her, she said, "After you, babe."

Raven nodded and then started off at a brisk trot. Jegra ran after her, her eyes trailing down to Raven's perfectly sculpted ass.

"Babe, are you staring at my ass?"

Without taking her eyes off of Raven's backside, Jegra replied in a defensive tone, "No."

Raven glanced back to catch her lying and then narrowed her eyes at Jegra. Jegra responded in kind by sticking her tongue out at her.

Raven reached up and touched her ear, a surge of pink energy coursing through the circuitry like veins just beneath her lavender skin.

<<Adrenaline boost activated>> a faint computer voice intoned.

Jegra looked over at Raven who merely smiled at her and shot her a strangely competitive look. "Try to keep up, if you can."

In the blink of an eye, Raven shot off like a racehorse sprinting out of the starting gate, except she was running about twice as fast as even the fastest of stallions of the Zornth highlands.

"Holy shit," Jegra muttered to herself under her breath as she was taken by surprise. Without hesitating, she tore after Raven, dirt flying up as the ground beneath her feet exploded with the force of her powerful footsteps.

Soon she caught up to Raven as they sprinted at inhuman speeds across the rocky terrain of the moon. Their momentum was so fast that each footfall shattered the rocks beneath them, leaving a debris field of only pebbles and dust.

A couple of clicks outside the base camp, Raven dug in her heels in and skidded to a halt. Jegra hit the brakes too, and when she came to a complete stop beside Raven, she noticed the circuit like veins beneath Raven's skin glowing hot pink across her entire body.

Raven panted, her hands on her knees, as she caught her breath.

Jegra shot her a curious look. "I didn't know you could do that," she said between a couple of deep breaths. In the distance, the dust trails they'd kicked up in the wake of their high-speed dash slowly dissipated on a gust of wind.

"An adrenaline kick with nanite enhanced muscle enhancement and regeneration. I can push my body to extremes for several minutes. But much more than this and I risk overloading my biological system."

"Still, quite impressive."

Raven smiled and then turned to the faint glow in the distance. She checked her wrist again and then exhaled quietly.

"Good, they still haven't noticed us."

"From here on in we go silent, I take it," Jegra said.

"Yep," Raven answered, tapping her bracelet. "Stealth mode," she said, and with that, a cloak went up around her and she vanished into her surroundings.

Jegra hit her bracelet too and said, "Invisibility mode," and her black tactical smart-suit disappeared, but she remained visible, along with the gun straps and utility belt, and these scarcely managed to cover her private bits.

Raven cleared her throat. "Um, babe…you might want to try that again."

Jegra looked down at her naked body and then grumbled, "Shit" under her breath. She fidgeted with the bracelet some more until, finally, it chimed and the cloak activated and she disappeared discreetly into her surroundings.

"Alright, let's go," Raven said in a hushed tone. "Once we're inside the camp, just stick to reconnaissance. We'll meet back here in fifteen minutes."

"What if something goes wrong?"

"Don't let anything go wrong," Raven responded.

"Copy that," Jegra answered.

The air rippled around two shimmers, and the ghostlike outlines faded into the night.

11

Down on the surface of the azure and viridescent moon, Hela emerged from a spacious canvas tent at the center of a large camp. The camp site was situated atop a rocky bluff that overlooked a sprawling wetland that stretched as far as the eye could see.

Hela brushed her short-cropped black hair with a wave of her hand and cut across the encampment. She had on safari-style clothes and sported khaki shorts and a white button-up top, a tan leather vest, and military-issue black patent boots.

The light colors looked good on her as her dark blue skin stood out. Behind her, two additional Lycias followed her out of the tent and marched behind her to the opposite side of the camp which bustled with scientists and other Lycia clones hard at work setting up lights and making dinner preparations for the coming evening.

The faint yellow sun had already begun to sink into the distant horizon, taking on a lime-colored hue, when Hela finally arrived at the far end of the camp. A group of UCC soldiers met her there and stood next to a Warhawk fighter painted in bright red.

"Did you get the neutron bomb as requested?" she asked, as she approached the group.

"It's right here," Lieutenant Afriel said, patting the side of the fighter as though it were a pet.

When he turned back toward Hela, he was instantly taken with her. She was the most beautiful woman he'd ever seen. A scar running down the left side of her face made her stand out from the rest of the Lycia clones, and he couldn't help but feel his heart skip a beat.

As a Dagon, he picked up on her pheromones right away. She was flooding the entire area with a veritable pheromone storm so as to better influence those around her with her persuasive powers. Feeling the sudden urge to pounce on her and tear her clothes off, he shook the primal thought out of his mind and composed himself.

Hela shot him a sideways glance as she inspected the fighter and then ducked under the nose of the plane and ran her hand along its underbelly.

Her hand stopped on what she was looking for. She tapped on the release panel, and the bomb bay doors opened revealing the shiny new warhead for her to play with.

"By the Progenitors, it's gorgeous."

Unexpectedly, a fight broke out just over her shoulder and Hela turned to see what all the hubbub was about.

"I get her," one of Afriel's men shouted.

"No, she's mine!" the other growled.

The two men tussled about on the ground like a couple of swine rolling around in the mud. Hela sneered in disgust at the primitive attempt to win her favor and then turned to Afriel and shot him a look that blamed him for the ruckus and questioned his competence as a leader.

Embarrassed, Afriel drew his blaster and, raising it above his head, let off a shot.

The squeal of the blaster ringing out caused the two soldiers mucking about in the dirt to stop what they were doing and lookup.

"You two idiots get up," Afriel growled, kicking their boots as they scrambled to their feet. He holstered his weapon and continued berating them. "Get ahold of yourselves. She's testing you to see how you'll react when distracted. But you two let your lizard brains take over and are no better than a couple of damn leathernecks."

The two men rose and fell into line. "Sorry, sir. It won't happen again, sir."

"It had bet n—"

Two shots rang out, drowning out Afriel's next words, and both soldiers dropped to the ground, glowing holes in their chests.

Looking to his left, he saw Hela with his blaster in her right hand. Its muzzle still glowed with residual heat and white smoke gradually wound its way into the sky. He looked down at his holster and then back up at her. She took three steps and nonchalantly handed the blaster back to him. He accepted it and holstered it a second time.

"Demeris Ferrison has no use for weak minded fools in his little operation. He's looking for real soldiers loyal to his cause. The question is, Afriel," her sparkling purple eyes fixing themselves on him caused him to feel a shiver shoot down his spine, "are you strong of will? Or are you one of these impotent specs of dirt?" She pointed her slender blue finger at the two, still smoking dead bodies.

Zora, the sole woman in Afriel's group, looked at him with disgust and then turned her back and slowly fell in line with Hela.

Afriel frowned, realizing that Hela had been calling the shots all along, and he was just a pawn. He looked down at the smoldering remains of his two men and, then, turned back to Hela and replied, "I'm loyal." There was a subtle desperation to his voice. "Use me however you see fit."

Afriel gave her the Dagon salute and she smirked, unimpressed by him. Nodding her head and beckoning for the other woman to follow her, she made her way back to her tent. Hela's two bodyguards and her new acolyte, Zora, trailed after her. Zora glanced back over her shoulder and shot Afriel a disgusted look before continuing one.

"Vek'miel," he cursed under his breath.

All of a sudden, a strange feeling settled over him. A feeling as though he was being watched. When he looked over his right shoulder, a third Lycia, one he hadn't noticed before, stood watching him from a short distance. She wore standard-issue body armor and held a stun rod. She leaned against a stack of cargo crates and tapped the baton in the open palm of her hands and smiled at him with a thin, almost scornful grin.

"Great," he muttered to himself. "Now I have a ghost."

Still smiling that unnatural saccharin grin, she clicked her tongue at him and shot him a wink. Not the friendly kind of wink either, but the intimidating "I got you right where I want you" predatory kind of wink. He turned away, realizing it would be best to pretend she wasn't even there.

Nothing to do, Afriel had turned to the ship and taken a step toward it when the guard's stun-baton crackled with angry blue electricity. He looked to her and she shook her head, informing him it was a bad idea.

Afriel cautiously raised his hands in capitulation, turned around and headed into camp to see if there was anything to eat. As he walked toward the base camp, he checked over his shoulder and, sure enough, his shadow was right there with him, twirling that baton nonchalantly in her left hand and smiling at him with that nerve-racking grin every time he looked back at her.

After dealing with that peon-size moron, Afriel, Hela felt gross. Just being in his presence made her skin crawl. Besides this, she was covered in sweat and grime from the day's work and was in dire need of a bath.

Hela entered her tent, plucked a handkerchief from her back pocket and dabbed at the sweat and humidity clinging to her damp skin. The sour smell of her sweat-soaked body caused her to turn her head and take a breath.

Craning her neck to the side, she wiped the grime from her skin and gently dabbed at the opening in her shirt which teased a bit of blue cleavage. She cracked her neck in the other direction and then turned to the Bre'lal servant girl, dressed in rags, who'd appeared from behind a partition.

"Apologies, mistress. I didn't hear you come in. Do you require anything of me?"

"Draw me a bath, Selestria."

"As you wish," she replied, taking a deep curtsy without ever raising her eyes any higher than Hela's knees. In fact, as a servant girl, Selestria never made deliberate eye contact with her mistress. It would be too bold of her. She was merely here to serve.

Having received her orders, Selestria quickly scurried off. Sitting down on the end of a wooden stool, Lycia groaned as she bent over and began to untie her boots. Although most modern work boots had magnetic ties, she preferred old fashion rope-string because she could make it as tight as she liked. And she liked it tight.

After she got her boots off, she peeled off her socks one dank foot at a time, making a sour face as the ammonia scent of her sweat stung the insides of her nose a second time.

She sat up, shaking off the sick feeling that briefly came over her and began to undo her shirt. After unbuttoning her shirt, she slid it and the safari vest she wore off her shoulders.

She let everything fall onto the floor without a care and then unfastened her belt. Halfway across the room, she wriggled out of her pants and then undid her sports bra and panties.

She found the Bre'lal servant finishing up the bath on the other side of the partition, she nodded at the girl, letting her know she could leave. She humbly bowed and swiftly gathered her things before disappearing out of the tent with the quietness of a mouse.

Hela dipped a foot into the steaming hot bath and instantly sucked air in through her teeth—then let out a string of "oohs" and "ah-ah-ahs" in response to how hot it was. As she slipped into the water, she let out a refreshing moan and then lay back and closed her eyes.

She took in a deep breath and, letting out a yawn, proceeded to speak to the presence she felt in the room with her.

"You do realize that I can smell your musk, right?" she asked calmly. "So, whoever you are, you have two seconds before I scream and alert an entire camp of genetic super-soldiers, loyal to me, that you're attacking me."

A shimmer moved in front of Lycia's bathtub, just beyond her feet. A few seconds later, Jegra decloaked and stared down at the naked woman sitting before her.

When Hela saw that it was the empress standing in front of her she raised an eyebrow. "I wasn't expecting you. A second-rate assassin, perhaps. But not the empress herself."

"I guess I'm full of surprises."

"I wouldn't expect any less from the Empress of the Dagon Empire. How's that going by the way?"

"It's going..." Jegra replied. She scanned the room to see if there was anyone or anything she needed to worry about, but it seemed secure enough. She then turned to Hela and folded her arms under her large chest. "Let me cut to the quick, here. I'm not here for you. All I want is Demeris Ferrison."

Hela smiled in that sinister grin of hers and then dipped her fingers in the water and stirred them about as she mulled it over.

"As much as I'd like to help you, Your Eminence, I'm afraid I must decline your more than fair offer. You see, I swear no allegiance to anyone but myself. It just so happens that Demeris Ferrison's goals align with my own at the moment."

"And what goals might those be?" asked Jegra.

"Your downfall, of course."

"Me? Why me?"

"Because," Hela said, rising out of the water, her dark purple nipples hardening in the cool air. "I despise everything about you." She stepped out of the tub, ignoring the fact that her body was dripping wet, and sauntered over to Jegra. "I hate you down to your very genetic code, and if I could reach inside myself, I'd tear it out." She clutched her chest, her nails digging into her blue skin as she clawed bloody lines into her flesh.

"I'm sorry you feel that way," Jegra said.

Hela smiled falsely and let go of herself. Almost instantly the scratches healed on their own. Then, grabbing Jegra by the chest straps of her tactical suit, Hela hoisted her up and, leaning into it, threw Jegra over her shoulder and out of the tent.

Jegra tumbled to the ground, crashed through someone's campfire, sending up a spray of hot orange embers, and rolled five more times before skidding to a stop.

A dozen Lycias stood up, reaching for their weapons as they readied themselves for whatever it was that had crashed their dinner party. When they saw it was Jegra, they stopped and turned back toward Hela's tent. Hela emerged in a gold satin robe which she quickly cinched up before pointing a finger at the intruder.

"Well, what are you waiting for? Seize her!"

Lycia after Lycia bull-rushed Jegra, charging headfirst without so much as a care in the world about what happened to them.

Being a veteran warrior, however, Jegra easily deflected their attacks using defensive Judo, Aikido, and Bai'Jamin. As more Lycias joined the assault, Jegra continued her dips, leaps and pirouettes. Spinning and twirling, lunging backward, leaning out of the way, and swaying side-to-side, she looked like a professional ballerina. What's more, the Lycias couldn't land a single blow to her and, one-by-one, they toppled to the ground or flew through the air with the greatest of ease.

"Somebody take that bitch down!" Hela screamed, stamping her foot on the ground out of frustration.

"We're trying," one of the Lycias shouted over the din of other Lycias grunting and hollering as they continued to press on.

"She's only using defensive moves," another one said.

"You're genetically superior in every way," Hela barked. "Don't tell me this outdated model is giving you so much trouble you can't land a single strike! Use your powers for crying out loud."

"Outdated model?" Jegra said, echoing Hela's insult. "I resent that remark. I'll have you know, I'm more of a classic."

A dozen Lycias surrounded Jegra, their eyes flaring pink as Dygra crystal energy began to seep from them.

Soon they raised their hands and blasted Jegra with a dozen energy beams. Under the crushing pressure of so much energy, Jegra dropped to her knees. As the pink laser blasts heated up, they gradually ate away her clothes, her entire suit burning up and being rendered little more than ash which fluttered away on the breeze.

With a grunt, Jegra began to stand up, showing that her stamina was unrivaled.

Scarcely able to believe her eyes, Hela shouted "More! More power!"

Sweat began to trickle down each of their strained faces, as the clones grunted and gave even more of an effort to their high-powered energy beams.

The pink blasts intensified as Dygra energy poured out of their hands and came crashing down upon Jegra's back, forcing her to collapse onto her hands and knees.

"Finally," Hela muttered to herself, giving a subtle and celebratory fist-pump. She then watched as the rocky ground beneath Jegra's flattened body began to fracture, stress lines growing out from under her. Soon enough, her body sank into the ground several inches, the energy beam pressing her into the terrain itself.

Satisfied that nothing could withstand such forces, Hela raised her fist high above her head and shouted, "That's enough."

Abruptly, the Lycias ceased their energy beams and took a step back. Smoke and steam rose off Jegra's bare back and there was a long silence that permeated the evening air as they all watched with keen interest to see whether she'd survived the uncompromising volley.

"Good," Jegra said, pushing herself back up to her hands and knees. Her hair hung down in front of her face, but she peered out between the openings of her bangs and growled in a gruff tone that indicated she was done horsing around. "Now it's my turn."

Rising to her feet, Jegra's eyes glowed hot pink and the Dygra crystal in her chest shone brightly, wisps of energy leapt off of her body in arcs like miniature solar flares. At the same time, her long hair fanned out around her like a thousand tentacles and slowly undulated on the energy currents.

Throwing out her arms, she unleashed a massive amount of energy that rolled away from her in a series of intense capillary waves that resembled ripples on the water after a rock has been dropped in.

Unable to brace themselves, the energy wave impacted with devastating force and all the Lycias flew into the air, most being carried twenty feet or more before crashing down again.

As Lycias were flung out of the way like pebbles from a grenade blast, Hela gritted her teeth and braced herself. Crossing her forearms in front of her, she leaned into the wave as it crashed into her too.

She grunted through her clenched jaw and resisted with all her strength. But the energy wave only seemed to increase in strength and pushed her back in the dirt with such force, her feet began to leave drag marks.

As the energy wave washed over her, the sash to her golden robes unraveled and the body-length fabric unfurled behind her and, like a cape, flapped wildly about in the air currents.

Once it passed, she stood up, pulling her robe closed and covering up her breasts. She then glanced down at the tracks her feet had left in the ground, stunned to find she'd slid back about thirty meters. Raising her eyes, she peered across the distance at Jegra, who hovered about three feet above the ground, pink Dygra energy rolling off her skin like steam rolling off the Esperia hot-springs on the ice-moon Riverion.

"W-what in the seven moons of Vespa are you?"

Jegra's hot pink eyes glowed so fiercely that they almost appeared white. When she turned her gaze toward Hela, her blazing eyes cooled, returning to their natural color, and she slowly lowered back to the ground, touching down on both feet.

"I am the Empress of the Dagon Empire. Who are you—that dares to defy me?"

Hela squinted at Jegra for some time and then, her eyes flooding with tears, she dropped to her knees to plead for mercy.

"Forgive me, my empress. I didn't know. But the stories are true. I see it now. You truly are the Mother of Dagon."

One by one the other Lycias looked at one another and, following Hela's lead, they all took a knee and bowed their heads in the presence of their one true empress.

Raven decloaked next to Jegra, her blaster rifle shouldered as she scanned all the bowed heads, checking for signs of further malcontent. When she looked up again, like a wave moving through a crowd, the Lycias kneeled one by one as far back as she could see, until the entire encampment had submitted to the empress's authority.

Hela slowly rose back to her feet and turned her cold gaze toward Jegra. "I underestimated you, Empress of Dagon. But, it seems you have underestimated me too."

"I'm sorry?" Jegra asked, unprepared for Hela's reveal.

"It's a trap!" Raven hollered just before the EMP grenade Hela was holding in her palm detonated.

Jegra and Raven collapsed to the ground and, both threats neutralized, Hela motioned with a wave of her fingers for a couple of the Lycias to go check on them. Unlike the Lycias, Jegra and Raven weren't genetically modified to withstand high electrical disruptions to their nervous system.

The two Lycias bent down and checked both women's pulses and then looked back up. "They're alive."

"Excellent. Now, tie them up and continue making the necessary preparations. There will be no one to stop us this time."

Both Lycias nodded and rushed off to continue with their work. As they scurried off to carry out their duties, Hela linked her arms and looked down upon the fallen empress. *Mother of Dagon?* perhaps. *Living legend?* sure. But, in the end, she was still only mortal.

Raven groaned as she came to and said, "My head feels like scrambled eggs." Looking over her shoulder, she found Jegra sitting with her back to hers, both of them tied up.

"What the hell hit us?" Jegra asked, her lips numb as though she'd just come from the dental clinic. She strained against the restraints, but the rope was some kind of Kevlar weave that was nearly impossible to break out of...even for her.

"An EMP bomb," Raven answered. "It knocks out every electrical device within range. If strong enough, it can knock out a biological organism's electro-chemical system too."

"Shouldn't we be dead then?" Jegra asked.

"My nanites are insulated, so, although they might shut down, they reboot within thirty seconds and begin to repair any lingering damage. As for you, well, whatever makes you impervious to everything else must have allowed you to survive the blast."

"Why are you naked?" Jegra asked, realizing Raven's bare back was sticking to hers due to the humidity and sweat.

"I suppose they didn't want me to use the laser cutter I keep in my tactical vest. Or the korridium blade in my boot. Or the plasma torch I had in my belt. Or the shaving file I—"

"I get it," Jegra said, cutting Raven off. Raven nodded and then looked around for something to use that might help free them.

"Do you hear that?" Jegra asked.

Raven stopped what she was doing and listened. "Actually, yeah. What is that?"

"It sounds like a droning tic. Some kind of a mechanical device."

They both turned their heads to discover a giant neutron bomb sitting beside them, rigged with a digital clock that was counting down in incremental tics. The bright glowing letters read T-45 minutes before detonation.

"Um..." Jegra said aloud, pondering the truth of what she already knew to be the case, "is that what I think it is?"

"If you're thinking it's a goddamn big bomb, then, yeah."

They both went back to struggling against their restraints, desperate to escape the moon before it went up in a blaze of neutron radiation.

"We have to get out of these restraints," Jegra said. "Three million people live on this moon."

"Not only that," Raven said in a dire tone. "If it goes up, the debris will rain down on Nyctan like a meteor shower and wipe out entire continents."

"Hey, wait," Jegra said, craning her neck to see over her shoulder. "Don't you have a mental link to your ship?"

"Yes, but I need to squeeze my earlobe to activate it."

"Lean back, maybe I can bite your ear for you."

Raven shrugged and leaned back. It was worth a shot.

Jegra twisted her head as far as her neck would allow and tried to bite Raven's ear, but instead she just clacked her teeth in the air.

Raven began to giggle. "That's not...please, don't do that."

"Sorry," Jegra said, twisting back around and trying to flex to break free.

"Ugh," Raven said, as Jegra squished her into their restraints which seemed to wind tighter any time they applied additional force to them.

"Sorry." Jegra relaxed and tried to think of another way to escape this nightmare boobytrap.

"Maybe don't do that either," Raven said. "Wait, what about that energy wave thing. You could use that to dissolve these ropes and—"

"I'm afraid not," Jegra said, interrupting her before she got her hopes up. "At least not for another day or two. I used up a lot of Dygra energy and the poor little thing needs to recharge before I can bring myself to that level again."

After it seemed as though they'd exhausted every possible option, they both sighed and sat in silence, contemplating every wrong step they'd taken which had led to this moment.

"What to do, what to do," Jegra murmured, tapping her fingers on the ground.

Raven looked up at the sky and tracked a wandering star. She knew it was probably the *Skywend* whizzing by overhead, but even though they were so close, it was still so far, far away.

12

The automated countdown continued to tic down incrementally. Jegra and Raven shivered as the evening grew cold. "Any colder," Jegra complained, "and my nipples will be as hard as diamonds."

"In that case," Raven said between chattering teeth, "maybe you can use them to cut these ropes."

Jegra giggled and then squirmed some more, but it was hopeless. The restraints wouldn't budge.

Jegra turned her head and checked the clock face. "Only five minutes remaining."

Raven blew at a tuft of her hair that dangled in front of her eyes and then let out a hopelessly vexed sigh. "I guess this is..." she trailed off as a thought dawned on her.

"Goodbye?" Jegra inquired, looking over her shoulder to try and see if she could make out Raven's mannerisms.

"Ring!" Raven shouted.

"Ring?" asked Jegra, rather confused at the unexpected turn the conversation had taken.

"Yes," Raven said, gleefully, "your ring. The engagement ring. It's korridium and diamonds. It should be strong enough to break us free."

"Right!" Jegra said with equal exuberance. She twisted the ring into the side of the restraints until it had bored all the way in. Then she started to slowly inchworm her way through it. "It's working!" she shouted excitedly. "It's really..." this time it was her voice that trailed off.

"Don't leave me in suspense," Raven said. "It's what?"

"Stuck," Jegra replied.

Raven rolled her eyes and sighed again.

They both hunched their heads, unable to think of anything else that would aid in their escape.

The loud sound of a plasma sword igniting startled them and they whipped their heads around to find the glossy battleship-gray armor with his flaming sword standing before them. The intricate design of the armor revealed it was the rank of Commander and the Knight stepped forward, his plasma sword crackling in the cool air as he approached.

He raised the sword high, the light of the molten hot blade lighting up both women's startled faces. The soft reverberation of the sword hummed in the evening air like a giant insect fanning its wings in slow motion.

"No, wait!" Jegra said, "We're allies."

The sword came down with a flash and both women flinched. When, after a brief pause, they realized they were both still intact, they opened their eyes to find their restraints severed in twine and laying on the ground beside them.

Jegra rose to her feet and said, "Thank you, Sir Knight. Now tell me your name so that I may honor you."

The Knight reached up and tapped the side of his helmet. It retracted, revealing the familiar face of Lance Bishop.

"Lance?" Jegra said excitedly when she saw his face. Giddy with excitement, she leaped up and pounced onto him, her naked body pressing firmly into his armor.

He blushed and said, "Lucky for you we were passing through this sector when we detected three Dagon battlecruisers de-cloak. They fired on your ship and then jumped out of the system before we could engage them. Your crew said the two of you came down here on a secret mission." He looked to Raven, who was being hoisted up by Jegra.

Raven turned to the bomb and said, "Thanks for all your help, Sir Bishop. But we have bigger concerns right now."

Bishop drew a wafer-like device the size of a hockey puck out from under his cape and marched over to the bomb. Slapping the device onto the shell with a magnetic clack, he pressed a button, and the top of the device lit up bright green.

In another instant, a high-powered green teleport beam came down and whisked the bomb away in the blink of an eye.

Jegra had heard of high-powered teleports too powerful for biological organisms but able to transport large, inanimate objects like parts for starships and heavy machinery in the blink of an eye, but she'd never seen it in person till now.

"Brace yourselves," Lance Bishop said drawing out two metallic balls and throwing them at the ground. The moment they hit the dirt, an igloo sized energy bubble went up around the three of them.

Jegra looked up in the sky and saw a brilliant flash. She turned away, shielding her eyes from the blinding hot light. A second later she looked back up in time to see a shock wave rippling toward them from the neutron explosion.

It crashed down on them like fiery rain, burning up the grass and vegetation all around them.

The swamps began to blister and boil and even the minerals in the dirt were charred, turning into dark charcoal.

Once the wave dissipated, the Knight's energy shield automatically turned off.

Jegra and Raven stood on the only green patch in several square kilometers and watched the gray wisps of putrid smoke rising from the scorched earth.

"All those people," Jegra whispered.

"My team alerted the cities; we believe their defense grids were strong enough to survive the blast. But I'm afraid the vegetation and animal life on this half of the moon has all been but expunged."

Jegra balled up her fist and looked up at the sky. At the same time, Raven reached up and gently squeezed her earlobe.

"Raven to the *Skywend*, three to teleport up."

"Roger that, Captain," Kregor's voice came back over the comm in her ear. In another nanosecond, a golden beam of light came down and fetched them back to the ship.

"Can't this thing go any faster?" Lycia asked in an impatient voice. She looked over at Raphine, who manned the flight controls.

"Actually, yeah. This Star-Racer has a top FTL speed of two and a half times the speed of light. Nothing much else but the *Shard* was as fast as this little Stallion."

"Then kick it into gear. You heard the distress call, Jegra needs us."

"Alright, but don't say I didn't warn you. Buckle up and hang on to your seat."

Raphine pushed up on the lever, increasing their speed and the two of them leaned back and watched as the time distortion grew disorientating.

Raven and Jegra came out of opposite dressing rooms at the same time and nearly crashed into one another.

"After you," Jegra said.

"No, after you, I insist," Raven replied.

Jegra looked Raven up and down and smiled. She had on black jeans with rips across her blue thighs and a charcoal gray t-shirt of Jegra's with a Felix the Cat image on it that hung a little too large on her but allowed the V-neck line to accentuate her cleavage. The top, stretched thin from use, had lost its elasticity and slid off Raven's left shoulder, adding a bit of sex appeal to the outfit.

"You look nice," Jegra said.

"You do too," Raven rejoined.

Jegra looked down at her metallic-coated, spice-brown catsuit. Once again, her chest was too big to zip it up all the way, but it held her girls well enough and she felt comfortable. The military issue utility belt she wore around her waist contained everything she might need and also gave a bit of flair to the otherwise mundane outfit.

"I'm glad you think so. It's just something I threw on."

A voice clearing in the distance caused them both to glance up and see Lance Bishop looking at them.

"Sorry to interrupt, but we have more pressing concerns, I'm afraid."

"Tell me," Raven said, walking up to him.

"Hela's fleet knocked out your hyper-drive before they jumped. Your team is making the necessary repairs, but there's no way we can catch up to them before they hit their next target."

"And where would that be?" Jegra asked.

"My sources informed me that their on a direct course to the Dagon homeworld."

"It makes sense," Raven said. "They're going to blame the attack on Endiva on the Dagon military. Hela's likely masked her ship's hyperdrive signatures as a Nyctan warship to try and provoke a military response. Once Dagon forces engage with her, all she has to do is retaliate by detonating a neutron bomb on Dagon Prime."

"But what will that achieve? The Nyctans surrendered themselves after the war and, even if this tactic does inflame tensions between our two governments, they don't have a large enough fleet to mount a full-on attack, let alone adequately defend their planet."

"I think that's the point. In retaliation of any attack, the politicians of your world will veto any peaceful declarations you might attempt to make and send warships to a defenseless Nyctan."

"It seems the terrorist Demeris Ferrison wants the complete annihilation of the Nyctan people," Lance Bishop said in a grim tone.

"We can't waste any more time," Jegra said, turning to the knight. "I beseech you, Sir Knight. Allow us to take passage on your vessel and we'll do everything we can to stop the annihilation of your people."

"I would," Bishop said, shooting her an apologetic look, "but the entire reason we returned to our world was that our hyperdrive is on the fritz. It's in worse shape than this one." He gestured with a wave of his hand at the bulkheads around them.

Raven and Jegra turned toward each other, worry lines pressed into the disconcerted looks on their faces.

Just then a flash from outside alerted them to the presence of a ship. All three walked to the port side observation windows and peered out at the Star-Racer flying in formation with the *Skywend.*

"Did somebody call for a ride?" Lycia's voice came over the comm.

"Lycia!" Jegra chirped. "You have no idea how glad I am to see you."

"Raven to Kregor," she said, touching her ear, pink circuitry lighting up beneath her skin. "Beam us onto that Racer and then finish making repairs here. The moment you all get this ship's FTL back in working order, bring a team of knights and make haste to Dagon Prime."

"You got it, boss," Kregor replied.

Another flash of golden light whisked them over to the Star-Racer and the next thing Jegra, Raven, and Lance Bishop saw were the smiling faces of Lycia and Raphine.

"Welcome aboard," Raphine said, giving Jegra the Dagon salute. Jegra saluted her in return and then quickly found her seat.

"As much as I'd love to catch up with the two of you, we need to put the pedal to the metal."

"Pedal to the metal?" Raphine asked, unfamiliar with the Earth idiom.

"Yeah," Jegra replied, pointing her finger out the windows at the direction they needed to go, "we need to floor it."

"Floor it?"

"Burn rubber."

"What? Why? That's not even eco-friendly."

"You need to step on it."

"Step on what?"

"Hightail it outa here," Jegra continued. By now she was just messing with the girl to see how flustered she could make her. But, as she said, they were on a tight schedule so decided to let it be for now.

"Step on the high tail? Huh? I'm so confused right now," Raphine said, turning to Lycia for clarification.

"It means we need to go real, real fast," Lycia informed Raphine.

"That I can do," she said. "Alright everyone, prepare for the high tails to be stepped on."

Lycia raised a finger, prepared to correct her, but Jegra just shook her head and gestured for her to let it slide. Lycia agreed and let Raphine have her moment.

Everyone took their seats and, as Raphine throttled up the FTL, Lycia said with a sly grin, "Hold onto your tits, folks. We're about to jump to ludicrous speed."

"Ha!" Jegra laughed, getting the reference. She looked around at all the blank faces that turned to her for clarity but realizing explaining it would take more time than they had, she shrugged and said, "Never mind."

The Star-Racer pulled away from the *Skywend* and turned around, its hyperdrive spooling up as it prepared to dash back to Dagon Prime. In fact, at the speed they were attempting, they'd either burn out their FTL drive and have to jettison the core or they'd set a new record.

Raphine raised her hand, three slender green fingers pointed upward. Then, one by one she retracted her fingers, counting down to zero as her other hand throttled up the FTL to full.

Meanwhile, outside the ship the stars began to stretch all around the sleek racing vessel and, in the blink of an eye and a flash of light, the Star-Racer jumped away.

Hela's fleet of warships dropped into geosynchronous orbit of Dagon Prime.

The small armada consisted of three large battlecruisers, two small frigates, and half a dozen smaller, corvette type vessels which all hung high above the Dagon atmosphere, weapons armed and targets locked.

"The defense grid has not been activated," one of her bridge officers informed her.

"Good," Hela said, a crooked grin forming on one side of her mouth. "They didn't know we were coming. Jam the communications of those orbital platforms before they activate and prepare the second neutron bomb for deployment."

"Yes, ma'am," he replied and swiveled back around in his chair, dutifully carrying out his orders.

The dark Lycia with plum eyeliner and thick mascara that had been following Afriel around sidled up next to Hela and smiled. "My love, why the glum face? We are on the eve of a great victory. Your victory!" She paused and then turned to Hela. "Don't tell me you feel as though you're betraying your people? After all, did they not betray you first? Did they not order your termination as a failed prototype and force you to find refuge in a world filled with copper-skins?"

"It's not that, Artemis," Hela replied. "It's the empress. I can't shake that sneaking suspicion that she's more than human. She's something we've never encountered before."

"Like what?"

"A demigod."

"A demigod?" balked Artemis.

"Yes, Artemis. She may very well be the first mortal goddess we've ever encountered. And, if so, I don't think betraying her is in our best interests."

"What are you saying? That we should throw Demeris Ferrison to the sharks?"

Not answering right away, Hela merely grinned at Artemis. Then, with a simple shrug of her shoulders, she replied, "All I'm saying is that we should leave that as an option. Until I decide on what our best course of action is, we shall continue to follow the original plan."

Artemis smiled, bowed, and touched Hela's arm for a short moment before taking her leave.

Hela watched her go and then turned back to the viewscreen. Soon, Dagon Prime would burn with the fire of a thousand suns.

13

SMACK! **Brei's arm** slapped Danica across her face and roused her from an otherwise peaceful slumber. She squinted with one eye past the dainty arm draped across half her face and, letting out a puff of agitated air, peeled Brei's arm off her and, with a soft grunt, shoved the lackadaisical limb away.

Brei's arm flopped back onto her own face, hitting with a slap which aroused her briefly, causing her to mumble something about bunny slippers and carrot juice. But her drowsiness soon won out again and she quickly slipped back into a deep sleep.

Before Danica could slide out of bed and start her day, however, Brei rolled over onto her stomach. Her other arm, fully extended, swung right back around, like a fleshy blue pendulum, and slapped Danica right smack dab in her right tit.

"Ow!" she yelped, and then, with a wave of her hand, she manifested an energy bubble and used it to shove Brei out of bed. Brei toppled to the floor with a harsh sounding thump and startled awake.

Standing, she rubbed her sleepy eyes and asked in a dreary sounding voice, "Whu-what happened?" Her question was immediately followed by a yawn and she stretched her blue arms over her head, the bubble gum pink t-shirt with the baby blue unicorn-bunny printed on it slid up her thighs revealing her light yellow cotton panties and blue midriff.

"Oh, sweetie," Danica said with feigned concern, "You were chasing bunnycorns again in your sleep and rolled out of bed."

"I was?" she asked.

"Indeed. You were talking in your sleep and mumbled something about trying to lure them in with carrot juice."

Brei shrugged, as that sounded about right. She often dreamed of luring bunnycorns into the palace garden with her so she could frolic about the grounds with them.

Danica nodded anxiously, praying to the Cosmic Progenitors that Brei bought the fib, sat up in bed, and looked over at Brei with big, rueful eyes.

Reflections danced across Danica's silver satin kimono robe which stood out in stark contrast to Brei's gentle pastel colors. Involuntarily triggered by Brei's yawn, Danica stretched her arms over her head and yawned too.

As Brei swayed on her feet, half asleep and half awake, Danica climbed out of bed and sauntered over to the glass, cylindrical shower stall that stood about ten feet from the bathtub off to the far corner of the massive suite.

Both tub and shower stood on sandstone tiles and butted up against Jegra's indoor pool. The pool itself ran along the entire length of the back wall, and although it was only three lanes wide, it was regulation length.

The pool and the palace wall were both made out of transparent aluminum smart-glass which could change opaqueness and tint. It could turn obsidian black, if one wanted it to. The bedroom wall ran parallel with the surface of the water which passed under it, and continued beyond, allowing the pool to jut out of the empress's sixth story suite and hang in mid-air.

Six stories up, the all-glass suspension pool looked out over the palace gardens which provided beauty and privacy for the empress whenever she wanted to take an early morning swim.

Of course, the pool could be retracted back inside the main palace when need be, and the bedroom flooring would then slide over the top of it, concealing it entirely beneath the floor paneling.

Still groggy, Danica was happy to take a nice, relaxing shower. She slipped out of her satin robe, letting it slide off her shoulders and onto the floor. The silver garment pooled at her feet like liquid mercury and, stifling another yawn, she climbed into the sonic shower.

She ran a sonic scrub cycle over her skin, causing it to ripple with a series of small capillary waves. The series of waves undulated to the tones of the sound waves. Once the cycle had finished breaking up any grime or dead cells that had built upon the surface of her skin, she switched the shower into water mode and stood under the rain-style shower heads and closed her eyes.

Piping hot water rained down on Danica as she raised her face into the soothing drizzle. As streaks of glistening water cleansed her cerulean skin, she ran her hands through her long, silvery hair and squeezed the water out. She took in a deep breath and, eyes closed, reached for the shampoo.

Unable to find it, her hand began to probe the edge of the shower stall, when all of a sudden, she grabbed onto something soft and round. She squeezed it once, then another time, feeling around with her fingers. "What in the world?" she murmured aloud. She opened her eyes and found Brei had stepped in with her.

Brei stood in the shower entrance, toothbrush hanging from her mouth like a lady's cigarette, as she looked down at Danica's palm clasping her right breast. When she slowly lifted her eyes and met Danica's gaze, Danica quickly retracted her hand.

As a private woman, Danica didn't want to share a shower with anyone. It was her alone time. And although Brei was technically her wife, she was too bubbly and exuberant for Danica's taste, especially before she'd had her morning coffee.

Danica cleared her throat, loudly, and shot Brei an easy-going look. "What are you doing, luv?"

"Showering with you," Brei answered, her words distorted by the toothbrush in her mouth.

"Do you mind?" Danica asked, throwing her hands onto her hips and glaring at Brei from behind a furrowed brow.

"Oh," Brei said, realizing she was hogging the shampoo, "here." She handed the bottle to Danica and then lathered herself up.

As soapy bubbles ran down Brei's petite body, Danica, mouth agape, merely stared at her with a healthy exasperation.

"And why, pray tell, must you shower with me, again?"

"Don't be silly, silly. We need to conserve water," Brei said. "It is a desert world, after all. Which is why I like to brush my teeth and wash my hair all at the same time."

After Brei washed the shampoo out of her hair and eyes, she looked down at the suds swirling about on the shower floor. Danica, wondering what it is she was staring at so intently, looked down too, only to find a golden stream gushing out of Brei and arching gently across the distance between them.

Some of it splashed Danica's calf and, reeling back as though she'd seen a terrifying mouse, she yelped and drew back so vigorously her back slammed into the glass of the cylindrical shower wall.

"For crying out loud, Brei!" Danica shouted, "Your piss just touched my leg."

"Sorry," Brei said, quickly adding, "but, I'll have you know, peeing in the shower is one of the best ways to conserve water. And, besides," she added pulling her toothbrush out of her mouth, "it all goes down the same drain pipes anyway. It all ends up at the recycler where its filtered, cleaned, and then put right back into your morning cup of coffee."

"You disgust me," Danica said, staring at Brei with heavy eyelids weighted down by her every pet peeve in the galaxy staring back at her.

Brei merely smiled a pasty grin and spit the toothpaste out and then gargled water, noisily, just to annoy Danica even more.

"Oh, for fuck's sake," Danica said.

Brei snickered to herself again when, all of a sudden, Danica shoved her into the shower stall glass—hard.

"Oomph," Brei gasped, the wind getting knocked out of her. When Danica's hands slid up her sternum and settled on her throat, she grew slightly worried and said, "Hey…Dani…wait a minute now. I was just messing—"

Before she could finish her sentence, however, Danica leaned in and silenced her Prussian blue lips with a kiss.

A couple of intense moments passed and then the two women drew apart. They stared at each other in shock, both of them grappling with how aroused they felt.

In the next instant, their lips crashed together again as their hands desperately groped about each other's bodies trying to find that passionate embrace that felt the most natural.

Drawing back, water pouring down their faces, they stared into one another's eyes. "You're so nasty," Danica said in a sultry tone.

"And you love it," Brei teased. Then she ran the head of her electric toothbrush down Danica's chest, abdomen, and finally down between her legs. They both looked down and Brei bit her lower lip as devious thoughts on whether or not she should do it passed through her mind.

When Danica looked back up at Brei, she narrowed her eyes and said, "Don't even think about—" but before she could finish, her eyes grew wide with the shock of it while Brei just smiled up at her with that charmingly crooked impish grin of hers.

Danica opened her mouth to protest when Brei turned on the vibrate mode of her toothbrush. The toothbrush was, of course, pressed up against her clitoris and the high buzz or a million vibrations surged through her most sensitive area and caused her to cover her mouth and smother a gasp.

Caught off guard by how the vibrating toothbrush felt indistinguishable from her own favorite vibrator, Danica fell back into the glass and let out a loud, sensual gasp.

Leaning back, Danica bit her lower lip and moaned loudly as she soaked in each tingly, orgasmic sensation that surged through her entire body.

"You were going to say something?" Brei asked.

Her neck flexing from another surge of pleasure, Danica shook her head "no" and simply let the water and vibrations wash over her. Moaning again, she reached out and grabbed Brei by the back of her neck and drew her into her, locking on leg around hers so that their bodies became meshed together in a tangle of limbs.

Brei's body slid into Dani's and the two women started kissing again. As they fell into one another, Danica's body shook periodically with aftershocks of tiny orgasms that continued to pulse throughout her entire body. That's when the televid chime rang, signaling they had an incoming call.

"Graddak," Danica groaned as she pulled away.

"Ah, do you have to take it?" Brei asked. "Maybe we can ignore it?"

"It's coming through on the private line, so..."

Brei nodded halfheartedly, her head slumping with disappointment as she pulled away from Danica.

Dissatisfied and testy because she had to stop a rather hot session with her second wife, Danica opened the shower stall, stepped out, fetched a towel from the nearby rack and dried off.

After she'd wrapped herself up in the towel, she looked back over her shoulder to see Brei standing in the shower watching her. As Brei's eyes stared longingly at her from across the distance, the young woman smiled and absentmindedly raised her toothbrush and put it back into her mouth, and then continued showering as she brushed her teeth.

Danica shot her a sour look, scarcely able to believe what Brei had done, but quickly shrugged off her dismay when it became clear to her that Brei was none the wiser as to what she had done.

Danica shook her head in disbelief and thought to herself, *that was such a Brei thing to do.* The girl's head was always in the clouds. So much so that half the time she was completely unaware of what was going on around her. This level of aloofness, however, only added to her appeal. Because even though the woman didn't know where she was half of the time, or what she was doing there, she was always the sweetest and most innocent one in the room. And Danica loved that about her.

As Brei began to hum a merry tune to herself, Danica, wrapped herself tightly in the white towel, turned back and made her way over to a poolside bench. She effortlessly settled onto it with a lady-like, knees closed, side-saddle pose and composed herself. She straightened her back and shoulders, tossed her wet hair behind her, cupped her hands over her lap so as to prevent anyone from peeking up her towel, and then said, "Admit call."

A hologram of Raphine's face lit up in front of her. "Danica, I'm glad I got a hold of you. We have the empress and are returning to Dagon Prime in the Star-Racer. But I'm afraid Hela and a team of renegade Artemis clones have a six-hour head start on us. If they're not already in orbit, they will be soon. You need to activate the defense grid and mobilize the fleet. Defend Dagon Prime until we get there."

"Copy that, chief," Danica said. She was about to stand up and report to duty when Raphine stopped her.

"Wait. There's someone here who'd like to say hi."

Danica smiled and sat back down. The blue hologram of Raphine's likeness flickered and then morphed into Jegra's smiling face.

"Hey, babe," Jegra said, "how is everything?"

"Everything's great," Danica said. "I was just taking a shower."

In the background, Brei stepped out of the shower and plucked her toothbrush out from her mouth and asked, "Is that Jegra? I want to say hi."

Dani, flushing with embarrassment at getting caught taking a shower with Brei, merely smiled and nodded. "Mmmm-hmmm."

"Tell her that I miss her."

"Brei misses you," Danica said, still blushing.

"Also, tell her that we shagged like a couple of bunnycorns during mating season."

Danica gulped and gave Jegra an apprehensive look. "She's such a kidder that one. Heh-heh." The nervous laughter tacked onto the end didn't seem to do much to dissuade Jegra of the truth of it, though.

Jegra merely laughed and said, "I'm glad you two are finally getting along. Just hang tight and I'll be with you again in about six hours. Until then, the safety of Dagon Prime rests in your capable hands, my loves."

"See you soon!" Brei chirped, her cheerful and beaming face appearing next to Danica's in the holovid display. Danica merely nodded in her usual stoic silence and then cut the televid feed.

Danica turned her face to find Brei's face right up in her face. "Do you mind?" Danica said in her usual disgruntled fashion.

"Oh, you know you love me," Brei said. And with that, she licked Danica lips and nose like a cat and then spun around and skipped off to busy herself with Brei'Alas things.

Danica let out a pent-up sigh and then smiled. It was true. She never, in a million years, imagined she'd be attracted to a woman like Brei, accident-prone, astonishingly optimistic about everything, and aloof as they came. It was infuriating.

Yet, for whatever reason, the same nagging disgust for her unrefined, unsophisticated, free-spirited nature, had...over the course of the past few weeks...turned into a strange romantic infatuation with the woman.

As a Dagon, Danica felt both anatomies pulling on her emotions, tugging her heartstrings in totally different directions. Her female side was attracted to Jegra which made sense. Jegra was powerful and strong, while Brei was the opposite of those things. She was fragile, sensitive, and dainty. Which is why Danica's male side was attracted to Brei.

She felt a deep-seated need to protect her, care for her, and be something she'd never felt she needed to be for another person before—empathetic.

And, somehow, in this confusing swirl of biology and physiology and having multiple wives, along with learning to become a better person, she found a balance and, perhaps more importantly, a solace in both women's companionship.

Right now, though, Danica had more pressing concerns to attend to than her wanton gratification. So, without any further delay, she strode across the room to the massive walk-in closet that all three of them shared and put on her admiral's uniform.

A few minutes later, Danica beamed up to her ship, the *UCC Eos.* Materializing in her ready room aboard the new flagship Dagon vessel, she tugged at her cuffs and stepped through the automated sliding doors and onto the bridge.

"Admiral on deck!" one of the officers shouted and Danica nodded at all of the faces which turned to her. Men and women alike gave her the Dagon salute and she merely linked her arms behind her back in a casual manner and turned toward the main wall-sized viewscreen at the front of the bridge.

"At ease," she said and found her command chair waiting for her. She fell back into her seat and crossed her long, cerulean legs. As she read through the ship's updates via her holovid, she shifted in her seat and re-crossed her legs again. Her white mini skirt rode up but she ignored it.

"Ma'am, a fleet of ships just jumped into the system and their weapons are armed."

Danica leaned forward in her seat. It was Hela's fleet. And just as Raphine had warned her, they were coming in hot.

"They're scrambling the defense grid before the orbital platforms can fully activate," the navcom officer informed her.

"Bring plasma canons online. Shields to maximum. Let's welcome our new guests with a little Dagon hospitality."

"Yes, ma'am!" the female security officer, Menita, said cheerfully as she brought the weapons online. Then, under her breath, she added, "It's about time I get to blow something up."

Danica slowly stood up and, brushing out the wrinkles in her skirt, said, "Target the lead ship and disable its engines."

"Aye-aye," Menita replied and with a manic grin, she pushed a series of buttons and purple streaks of hot plasma erupted from the primary batteries of the *Eos* and streaked across the black expanse.

14

A dozen golden pillars of light touched down onto the lush ground, and in the blink of an eye Jegra, along with Raven, Raphine, Lycia, Security Chief Menita Dev'bok and Captain Simon Calvec, accompanied by a troop of six elite Grendok soldiers, solidified in the clearing next to some damaged cryostasis pods.

Jegra had on fitted leather armor consisting of a bodice with rope ties to cinch tight, shoulder guards, and a skirt replete with leather pteruges to cover her powerful thighs. Although she showed some leg, her leather, knee-high boots were fastened with back-straps and had armor-plated kneepads and toe guards.

Captain Calvec wore the standard black-ops tactical gear which included a glossy black breastplate and glossy black bracers with matching shin guards. He pulled out an all-black machete—even the blade was forged from obsidian black steel—and cut away some vines that hung over the crash site.

Jegra waved her hand and the squad of Grendoks, decked out in green and brown military camo with brushed metal breastplates and shoulder armor, all fanned out and took up strategic points as they kept an eye on the perimeter.

Unlike the standard satyr forces, the Ram's Spear team had long, forest-green cloaks draped over their shoulders, a sort of signifier that they were an elite unit apart from all the rest.

Embroidered on their cloaks and their badges was the insignia of a gladiator helmet with ram's horns set against a shield with arrows protruding from it. Laurel leaves framed the emblem nicely, giving it a vintage appeal that harkened back to ancient times. The times when the gladiatorial games were first founded, over three centuries ago.

Menita Dev'bok wore her tan military uniform with matching cap, the UCC insignia of an artistic representation of the empress.

The image depicted Jegra dressed like the goddess Athena, battle axe in hand, charging into battle with a baby celestial squid trailing over her shoulder, its tentacles getting lost in the flowing locks of her hair. The seven constellations of the united commonwealth framed her and acted as the border to the image, which was printed on all military uniforms in the UCC fleet.

Menita Dev'bok squatted down and pushed aside some tall grass and studied the indentations in the mud beneath. She popped open the top buttons of her shirt and fanned at her blue skin, which glistened in the unremitting humidity of the jungle.

A moment later, she plucked out a cloth from her back pocket and dabbed herself dry, first her chest and then her face, as she wiped away the excess of sweat. Finally, raising her fingers, she pointed in an easterly direction.

"An entire series of footprints head off in that direction," she informed everyone.

Raven's eyes flickered and then glowed hot pink as she used her infrared optics to look at the residual heat-signature in the footprints.

"It seems all the footprints have cooled. I'm guessing it's been more than four or five hours since the pursuit took place."

"Alright, people. Listen up," Jegra said, clapping her hands a couple of times to get everyone's attention. "I want everyone to spread out and comb the terrain for any signs of the vice admiral. If anyone finds anything, get on the comms. Captain Calvec, you take the Ram's Spear team and fan out in that direction. Lycia and Raphine, I need you up in those trees. And Chief Dev'bok, you're with Raven and me."

"Well, you heard the lady," Raphine shouted, as people loitered about, "get to it!"

Everyone quickly spread out and began to canvas the jungle as ordered. Raphine and Lycia looked at one another and then, smiling, Raphine said, "I'll race you."

"Try and keep up," Lycia said, a small semblance of a smile curling onto her lips before she darted off, getting a head start on Raphine.

They raced up some giant trees, their footfalls as light and silent as those of elves. Leaping onto the high branches like a couple of acrobats, they darted from one tree to the next, swinging and somersaulting through the air with expert precision. They continued leaping from branch to branch, heading deeper into the jungle until they disappeared entirely.

Jegra looked toward Raven and Menita and, then, breaking into a brisk jog, headed into the thick of the lush jungle. The remaining two women turned to one another, and silently nodded as if to say *let's do this*, and quickly took off after the empress.

As they raced through the jungle, vines and leaves whipping by their faces, Lycia and Raphine gained a five-kilometer lead on the rest of the group. That's when they heard a strange noise.

The sound of a twig snapping signaled them that they'd inadvertently triggered a boobytrap. The trip-rope flew up and clotheslined them both, sending them freewheeling down through the branches.

They crashed to the ground with a thud, the wind rushing from their lungs. Both Lycia and Raphine groaned and then painfully rolled over and tried their best to push themselves up to their feet. But it was no use. Raphine collapsed back down into the dirt, followed by Lycia.

Once they'd caught their breath, they managed to push themselves back up to their knees and sat back on their heels. A shadow crept over their faces and they both looked up with startled eyes.

"Don' run wit'cha fleeting feet, ye vek'miel," a voice ordered in a thick accent. They both looked up and then raised their hands in surrender.

In the distance, disruptor fire erupted and Jegra raised a fist, halting Raven and Menita a safe breadth behind her. They paused in silence when, with a crackle, Captain Calvec's voice came over the comm.

"We've encountered a squad of Artemis clones. The Ram's Spear is holding them off, but something doesn't feel right. I believe this may just be a diversion."

"Do what you can, Captain. I have complete faith in your unit." Jegra lowered her glowing holovid bracelet and looked over at the others. "It seems they were expecting us."

Raven finished a scan of their surroundings, turned to Jegra and gave a shrug. "I'm not getting anything. If they do have a base out here, it's likely too far underground for my sensors to detect."

"It could just be one giant goose chase," Menita said.

"How do you mean?" Jegra asked.

"Think about it. The Lycias abducted the vice admiral down here, leaving ample evidence for you to find. Then, stationing a couple of squads down here to toy with you, she beamed the vice admiral back aboard her flagship. As you're preoccupied with a game of hide and go seek in the jungle, they've taken Danica up there." Menita pointed up at the sky and at the day moon that lingered over them.

Raven turned to Jegra. "It would explain why I'm not getting any readings. There's simply nothing out here to detect."

"And what if your assessment is wrong, chief?" Jegra asked, throwing her hands on her hips and giving Menita a stern look.

"Then you have an elite ground force led by Raphine and Lycia. Surely, they'll be able to handle anything that comes their way."

"Alright," Jegra said, shifting her hips and letting her arms fall to her sides. "Assuming what you say is the case, my next question is, how in the bloody galaxy are we going to get aboard that ship undetected?"

"Leave that up to me," Raven said. Reaching up, she touched her ear, a flare of circuitry flashing just under her purple skin. "Did you get all that?"

"Sure did, boss. You want us to collect you now?"

"Ready when you are, Commander."

Just then, the *Skywend* decloaked in the sky above them.

Raven turned to Jegra and smiled.

"That's my girl," Jegra said.

A few moments later, all three women were greeted aboard the *Skywend* by Angellyk.

"Ladies," she said, then, turning to Raven, she added, "Welcome back aboard, Captain, the ship is yours again."

"Where's Kregor?" Raven asked Angellyk.

"Oh, you know him. He had a parting gift he wanted to give the terrorists."

They *Skywend* buzzed the treetops, flying over Captain Calvec and the Ram's Spear and fired off several massive disruptor blasts. The volley of plasma fire tore through the jungle, vaporizing the automated plasma turrets that had pinned down Calvec and his men.

Once the turrets were destroyed, the *Skywend* slowly pulled away and

Captain Calvec stood up and saluted them, sharing his gratitude for the assist.

The Ram's Spear team all shouted "Oorah!" and then boldly turned back toward the clearing in time to see a dozen Artemis clones rushing their position.

Calvec turned to his men, threw up his fist and shouted, "Advance!"

With a deafening bleat, the Grendoks leaped up and bounded across the clearing, blasters firing as they went.

Raphine and Lycia were shoved up against the cement wall of what appeared to be a bunker set in the middle of the jungle.

"Hey, watch it!" Lycia said, pushing herself off the wall and making a couple of fists as she postured menacingly, trying to scare off the natives of the Mewiki tribe.

Raphine reached out a green hand and held her back as she leaned in and snapped, "Touch me again and I'll break both of your arms! Yeah, I'm looking at you…tough guy!" She motioned with her fingers that she was watching the largest of the tribal warriors and he just returned her gaze with an unamused chuff.

"Look, we don't mean you any trouble," Raphine began, addressing the old shaman, "we're just looking for a man named Demeris Ferrison."

"Ferrison trog naut?" a tribal shaman with large saggy breasts the size of watermelons and a subtle shadow of stubble said to them in a disgusted tone.

Then, seeming to get irate, they shook their coconut maracas that were tied to the end of a long staff at them, waving it about over their heads. Then they grumbled something under their breath, and then spat at the ground.

"What did she say?" Raphine asked, turning to Lycia. Apparently, the universal translator couldn't translate this form of Dagoni dialect.

"You don't want to know," Lycia said, making a sour face.

The shaman, who embraced their Dagon intersexuality fully, maintaining both sexes equally as many shamans of the Mewiki tribe tended to do, mumbled another choice phrase and Lycia raised an eyebrow.

"Bek'vek, beth'likek, amigrak?" asked Lycia.

The old shaman motioned with their staff and growled in their atypically course voice, "Var'tek, avek, amigrak."

"Ven'beshal, vek'miel," Lycia said, letting out a rather lengthy sigh.

"What did she say?" asked Raphine, keeping an eye on the old shaman from the corner of her peripheral vision.

"They said we need to strip off all our clothes."

Raphine laughed and then turned to the old shaman, "I don't think we'll be doing that, thank you. If you're worried about us, why not just run a scan and…" she started to hold up her smart-bracelet when the shaman slapped her hand away and adamantly shook their head.

"No, no, no. You strip. Inspection."

Lycia and Raphine looked to one another and Lycia shrugged. Both of them did as asked and took off all their clothes in front of the shaman and small group of warriors.

While the old shaman walked around them, looking them both up and down, they then clicked their tongue and two tribesmen rushed forward and held Lycia against the wall.

"Hey, now," she said, eyeing them both. "You best tread carefully."

The old one hobbled up to her and said something that made Lycia laugh out loud. "Alright, old bat, but you better buy me dinner afterwards."

Raphine watched as the shaman placed one hand on Lycia's lower abdomen, the other hand pressed firmly at the small of her back, and then began to rub their hand in small circles on Lycia's blue skin.

Their hands gradually moved down further, feeling for something internal, and pressed hard enough it made Lycia laugh.

"Ah, haha, that's my bladder. If you press any harder there, I might accidentally pee on you." She then looked up at Raphine and whispered, "I just realized I have to pee."

Raphine smiled and nodded.

"Ib'vek," the old one replied apologetically.

"Oklivat, mek'veelek?" Lycia inquired, asking what it was the shaman was hoping to find with her examination.

"Some-bom-bom," the old one answered. "Artemis eb'vek om-bom-bom zek'va'jek."

"She's looking for a bomb," Lycia told Raphine, who watched in nervous discomfort. "She says that one of the Artemis clones hid a plasma grenade inside her fanny pack. And by fanny pack I mean love-tunnel. Which is to say vag—"

"Yeah, got it," Raphine said rolling her eyes.

"Some-bom-bom tarshall em'veelek!" the shaman said.

"She says it took out half of her best warriors."

"Why? For what purpose?" Raphine asked in a shocked tone. Murdering primitive people with advanced technology was against the peace accords, and now Hela's army of rogue Artemis clones had broken a galactic law.

"Because they're a bunch of genetically modified vek'miel programmed to kill," Lycia replied.

Raphine shrugged. "Fair enough," she replied.

Lycia turned to the old shaman who removed their wrinkled hands and stood looking up at the young, powerful Dagon female. If it wasn't for her blue skin and pointy ears, Lycia was the spitting image of Jegra. "Arvel, meli'kek? Artem bek fe'kek?" Lycia asked, peering back into the shaman's amber-colored eyes.

"What did you just ask her?"

"If she saw any other faces like mine," Lycia said, realizing if the Artemis clones had brought a prisoner along with them that perhaps the Mewiki would have recognized her.

"Arvel, melikeke, Jegra's avek fe'kek."

"The great Jegra's wife," Lycia replied.

"Danica," Raphine acknowledged, looking to the old one's eyes as she drew near, the wooden phallus in hand. The old shaman then gave a rotten toothed grin and held up the phallus.

"Dis wan divek weevek, naut bavek embu fe'kek," the old one said in the gruff manner of an elderly person who'd smoked far too many cigarettes in xyr day.

"You're in luck," Lycia told Raphine. "She says you're not one of the blue ones, so you're free to go."

"No exam?" Raphine asked, a nervous smile forming on her forest green lips.

Once the old one waved their staff in the air and said, "No exam'vek." they was satisfied that the two women were safe.

After turning back to their warriors, they made a series of clicking noises and waved the staff around. Their tribal warriors quickly brought them their clothes and kneeling down, handed them back respectfully.

As soon as Raphine and Lycia finished getting dressed, the old shaman stamped the pommel of their staff with coconut maracas on the ground and said, "Artemis invek belovek."

Raphine turned to Lycia, who was zipping up her vest and shot her a curious look.

"She said the Artemis clones took her below ground."

"Tuk, tuk," the old one said, motioning for the others to follow after them. "Weevek, tuk tuk."

"Let me guess, she wants us to follow her."

Lycia smiled and then slapped Raphine on the back. "You're a quick study, babe."

Of the six Grendoks in team Ram's Spear, only two remained standing. The others littered the clearing along with the dead bodies of nine Artemis clones. The tenth they held hostage.

Calvec held his left arm, the burn mark visible beneath his singed uniform. "Tell me where the vice admiral is," he ordered.

Artemis just scoffed and said, "Why don't you recognize your inevitable defeat and scurry back to your beloved empress and suckle her giant tits as she strokes your hair and sings you soothing lullabies."

"Insolence!" Calvec roared, and then with a firm strike, he backhanded her across her jaw. The smack rang out and both Grendoks increased their hold on her arms as she tried to take a step forward and test the captain's resolve.

Drawing out his obsidian blade, he pointed it at her and in a deep and threatening tone, said, "You will watch that tongue of yours or I'll cut it out of your mouth."

"I'd like to see you try," Artemis said, daring him to do it.

Instead, he merely thrust his blade into her gut, cutting her abdomen wide open. Then, with his free hand, he reached inside her. She moaned out in agony as he shoved the full length of his forearm inside her lower abdomen and rummaged through her bowels.

Just as it seemed she was about to pass out from the pain, Calvec pulled out a small device. Without even wiping off the entrails and blood that clung to it, he quickly lobbed it high into the air. It exploded over them with an intense, fiery blast.

Everyone standing directly under the blast crouched down as hot wisps of plasma spread out in the sky like tentacles grasping for something to cling to. Luckily, the fiery hot tendrils didn't touch anything, slowly cooling and dissipating in the chilly atmosphere.

"H-how did you know?" Artemis asked with her dying breath.

Calvec grabbed her chin with his fingers and drew her fluttering gaze to his. "Someone had to program and embed all of your protocols into those little clone heads of yours. Why else do you think the empress keeps me around? For my winning personality?"

Artemis laughed, coughing up blood, but soon enough her gaze went blank and her head drooped.

"That's for my wife and child," Calvec said. He then turned to his men and thrust his chin at the pile of bodies. "Toss her over there with the others. Then burn the evidence."

The remaining two Grendoks nodded and, dragging the eviscerated Artemis over to the pile of dead bodies that looked identical to her, they tossed her onto the heap then sprayed it down with an accelerant which they retrieved from their utility bags fastened to their belts.

While the first Grendok finished dousing the pile of bodies, the other one drew out a cigar and a cigarette lighter. Lighting up the stogie, he took a couple of puffs before passing it on to his mate. As he did so, he said the words, "For Pan."

The second Grendok took the cigar, had his puff, then, repeating the same words, "For Pan," flicked the barely spent cigar from his fingers and flung it onto the pile of blue bodies which instantly went up in a blaze of fire and smoke.

In unison, they repeated their mantra, "For Pan."

15

Electrical sparks rained down around the bridge crew as the bulkheads groaned and shook violently, alerting everyone to the fact that they were under attack.

One of the electrical grids in her chair's arm-mounted touch panel overloaded and a spray of white-hot sparks singed Hela's arm. Yelping, she gripped her arm and winced from the pain.

"Where did that bloody ship come from?" she growled, staring at the large Dagon vessel that looked like a massive boomerang hanging in space.

She'd never seen anything like it. It was practically as large as a space-station and guessed that it held around three thousand people.

"It's the *UCC Eos*," Artemis said, returning to the bridge. She had on a special power suit. "It's the first jointly produced battlecruiser of the United Cosmic Commonwealth alliance. It's the planet's main defense, in case the orbital platforms are down."

"Why didn't anybody tell me they had a super-dreadnought?" Hela groused.

"Permission to teleport over to that ship and create a diversion so that you'll have time to deliver the neutron bomb," asked Artemis, turning to Hela with a devious grin.

"Permission granted, luv," Hela said, and reaching out, she reeled Artemis in by her waist and kissed her on the lips.

Artemis smiled and then, turning back around, she marched over to the teleportation pad tucked away in the corner nook at the rear of the command deck.

She stepped onto the pad, tapped a few buttons on the wall panel, and a beam of red light came down and whisked her away.

Roughly ten seconds later, she manifested on the hydroponics bay of the *Eos*, where all the vegetable crops of the ship's food stores were grown.

With a ratcheting click of her armor, she raised her right arm and shot off a twenty-foot flame. The flame-thrower arm attachment worked perfectly, and she turned to the crops as workers screamed out in terror and fled their posts.

A large tongue of flame lapped at the foodstuffs, scorching them and burning everything to a darkened crisp.

The fire alarm, along with the intruder alarm, went off simultaneously and in five seconds, a security team beamed into the hydroponics bay with fire-extinguishers and plasma rifles, cocked and loaded.

"Surrender and come peacefully," Menita said, her blaster drawn but not raised, as she glared at Artemis.

Artemis just scoffed and, without a concern in the world, trained the flame thrower onto Menita and her security team.

The flame shot out as it did when it incinerated the crops, but this time something stopped it. The fire splashed against a forcefield and went in every direction but forward.

Once the flames stopped, Artemis lowered her weapon and smiled at Menita, who was doing her best to generate a low-level energy barrier.

"A Dygra user," Artemis smiled. "I was so hoping to meet a real challenger. I'm glad it's with another *Oldstrong*, like you."

Artemis abruptly lunged forward and struck Menita with a powerful backhand. The suit's motors and servos whined as they responded to her movements.

Menita, taking the brunt of the blow, flew twenty feet into the air, spiraling like a rag doll tossed from a moving vehicle. She crashed down in the middle of the crops with bone-shattering impact.

Her security team advanced on Artemis's position, but she easily deflected their energy shots with her own forcefield and tossed the men about like mere playthings.

Obviously, she'd been wrong. They were no match for her. "Is there not even one among you worthy enough to challenge me?" she asked as she nonchalantly tossed the last security officer into the wall.

He hit the wall with a back-breaking crunch and cried out from pain before rebounding off and crumpling to the ground, paralyzed from the waist, he tried to drag himself up but collapsed again.

The sound of a throat clearing gave Artemis pause and she slowly turned around to find the vice admiral herself, Danica Valencia, grinning back at her.

CLANK! CLUNK! *CLANG!*

Danica's metal fists banged away at Artemis's power suit. As Artemis defensively parried, Danica pushed forward and growled, "Maybe try me if you think you're such hot stuff."

"Finally," Artemis said, grinning. "An opponent who won't disappoint me."

Artemis returned a powerful blow and Danica braced herself. The powerful strike sent Danica sliding back ten feet, but she absorbed the hit with her synthetic arm.

"Now, let me show you how a real warrior does it," Artemis snarled, staring down her aquiline nose at Danica.

"Tsk, tsk," Danica said, raising a finger. "You've forgotten one vitally important thing."

"And what might that be?"

"A good offense is always a good defense."

That's when Artemis heard the beeping and looked down at the small, medallion sized device stuck on her forearm armor. She tried to pry it off but it was magnetically sealed.

"No!" she screamed just as the wispy, spider-silk spread out from the device and then ignited with hot plasma, revealing a dozen glowing tendrils. The tendrils whipped about her entire body like the angry tentacles of a Kraken.

In the next moment, her eyes went wide as a hundred burgundy lines opened up on her cobalt flesh. The super-hot tendrils had sliced through Artemis's limbs, torso, and neck like a sculptor's wire cutting through clay. Chopped into a dozen pieces, her body fell to the ground in bloody clumps.

Menita, cradling a broken arm, sidled up next to Danica. "What happened to the no-kill order?"

"Apologies, Lieutenant Commander," Danica said. "But this woman came on a suicide mission to cause as much havoc as she could before somebody took her down."

"A diversionary tactic?"

"That would be my guess."

"For what, though?"

"Launching an attack," Danica surmised, turning her amber eyes back toward Menita. "I need to get back to the bridge. But you need to attend to that arm and make sure these men get to the medical bay, ASAP. That's an order."

"Yes, Admiral," Menita said, but unable to salute due to her arm being shattered, she merely bowed reverently.

Back aboard Hela's ship, *The Vortex*, she walked up to the cold storage containment unit in cargo bay three and watched anxiously as a green indicator filled up a bar on the viewscreen. When it reached 100% a chime sounded and the storage container decompressed with a hiss of air.

The large steel cylinder let out a flood of rolling steam that rolled onto the floor of the cryonics lab and Hela stepped back and watched as the clamshell lid automatically opened. Inside, a naked Lycia slowly sat up and yawned.

Once her eyes cracked open, she began frantically clawing at her tubes, tore out her IVs, and ripped off her EKG monitoring wires. Coughing up slime, she gasped for breath, and then snarled in a bitter tone, "That bitch killed me."

"It's okay," Hela said, stroking Artemis's slicked-back hair and stroking her back with a gentle, feathery touch. "You're back, safe and sound now...with me."

Artemis turned to see her face staring back at her and she smiled and let out a small chortle. "I can't believe it. The memory transfer actually worked."

"As I promised you it would."

"Your genius never ceases to amaze me, luv."

"You know I'd never let anything happen to you, right?" Hela asked, her hand resting on her doppelganger's shoulder.

Artemis wrapped her arms around Hela's waist and hugged her tight. "I know," she replied.

"Don't grow reckless," Hela warned her girlfriend, tenderly stroking her hair. "There's only about three downloads before the memory transference starts to degrade."

"Then I'd better make the best of my new body then," she teased. Then looking up into Hela's sparkling amethyst eyes, she craned her neck as Hela bent down, their lips meeting halfway, and they fell into what became a rather passionate kiss.

Danica arrived on the bridge just in time to see the enemy flagship fire a projectile down toward the surface of Dagon Prime.

"Shoot whatever that is down," Danica ordered.

"Sir, there are life signs on board."

"Hold," Danica said, raising a fist. "Delay that order. Scan for species."

"It seems to be a cluster of drop pods. Eight in all. Their bio-signature is…Dagoni." The ensign looked up at her with worried eyes. They couldn't fire on their kind.

"Clones then," Danica grumbled.

"Affirmative."

"Vek'barvek betch'leimek," Danica cursed. In Dagoni, it roughly translated to "That flat-assed slut-mule."

"What should we do Admiral?"

All eyes turned toward her. If she fired on the pods, she'd kill eight innocent lives. And, although until recently clones were illegal throughout the Empire, their use during the war against H'aaztre to help liberate the galaxy meant that new laws had been erected safeguarding their personhood.

If she fired on eight innocent sleeping clones, she'd better have a very good reason for doing so. And since there currently wasn't any *official* reason that she could think of to prevent a shipment of clones, she knew she had no leg to stand on.

"Monitor that shipment of clones and update me with their landing coordinates as soon as you can get a geotag."

Danica turned and walked over to the teleportation pad in the middle of the bridge, and stepped onto it. Her bracelet chimed, and she held it up just as the ensign sent her the data.

"Coordinates have been sent to your holovid bracelet, as requested."

Danica nodded and then turned toward the lift doors which opened just in time for Menita to arrive, her arm in a 3D printed, carbon fiber mesh-cast.

"If the admiral wishes, I can assign a security detail to accompany you down there."

"That won't be necessary, Lieutenant Commander. I'm sure it's nothing I can't handle."

"Aye, aye, Admiral."

"You have the bridge, Lieutenant Commander Dev'bok. Keep a close eye on those ships. If they so much as try anything suspicious, you have my permission to blow them out of the sky."

"Yes, Admiral," Menita replied, bowing slightly.

Menita promptly jumped up and marched over to Danica's command chair and sank into it just as golden light flooded the room. In a flash, Danica was whisked away.

Birds sang out from the jungle trees and Danica looked around. She spotted the cluster of pods sitting in a nearby clearing and walked over to them. All eight of them were open and all signs of their contents were missing.

She drew her blaster, realizing there were probably eight genetically enhanced, super-soldiers lurking somewhere in the vicinity. Not only that, but she was almost certain that, in all likelihood, she had walked straight into a trap.

Danica held up her bracelet and, speaking aloud, said, "Admiral Valencia to the *Eos*. It looks like that I am going to need backup sent down after all."

Her words came back to her as an echo replete with static interference. She tapped her holovid bracelet but it was no use. They were jamming her com-signal.

That can't be good, she thought to herself. She scanned the tree line for any signs of movement, but there wasn't any. Not a chirp or the distant buzz of a cricket's wings. Just a deathly quiet that had settled across the entire region like an ominous sign.

The lingering silence only confirmed her worst suspicions. She wasn't alone. The dangerous blue assassins hiding in the trees had frightened off all the wildlife. And just like Aldebaran, a sickening silence that warned of an ever-present danger was the only thing she sensed from her surroundings.

Without warning, a hot-pink laser blast struck one of the pods near her head, sending up a spray of sparks. Already on edge, Danica immediately hit the ground, diving into the dirt and keeping herself as flat against the ground as possible.

She peered out from behind the leaves of a large fern as the pod hissed again, and shot out another spray of sparks from its fresh wound. Glowing embers gently fluttered down around her like forest fireflies and she stayed calm even when one of them brushed her arm, burning her slightly.

"Come out, come out, wherever you are, Vice Admiral. It's only a matter of time before we find you," a woman's voice called out to her.

Project Warrior, as Dakroth had referred to it, was always meant to be a secret. Lycia was never even supposed to see the light of day. Especially not after one of the prototype clones malfunctioned. It couldn't process the Dygra crystal energy and Dakroth had ordered it terminated. This clone was, of course, Hela.

Hela, while waiting in a chamber to be gassed and then burned like common refuse, somehow managed to escape from incarceration and break out of the facility.

Danica had always wondered who had helped Hela escape her impending termination, but now, with it brought to light that she was one of Demeris Ferrison's top generals, it all made perfect sense.

He had every reason to save her from Dakroth so that she'd swear an oath of allegiance to him and his cause. At the same time, he could use her to enact his perfectly orchestrated revenge.

"Hela?" Danica said, speaking loud enough for her to hear her through the thick jungle foliage. "Let's talk about this."

"I'm afraid you've mistaken me for someone else. My name is Artemis. I'm the model after the Hela series was terminated. All, that is, but for one very special one who survived against impossible odds."

"Artemis?" Danica repeated, hoping to distract her.

"Your beloved emperor had a problem with us too, though. You see, our sexual drives didn't work to his liking. Once he got bored having his way with us, he had us put on ice and shelved. It was only the hyper-sexual Lycia series that he was proud to keep."

"Do I hint a twinge of jealousy?" Danica asked in a mocking tone.

Another Artemis, from a different location, spoke up.

"Of course we're jealous. He doted on her as though she was his daughter. And he loved her enough to erase her memories after every conjugal visit."

"The emperor had many fetishes," Danica admitted. "But what you're saying doesn't make sense. If he was fooling around with one of his prototype clones, I would have known about it."

"Are you so sure?" a third Artemis inquired from the shade of a hundred thousand leaves. "He was dating that red-skin too, and you knew nothing about that."

Danica frowned. It seemed the emperor had kept more secrets from her than she realized.

"Fine. Assuming everything you say is true, why team up with a terrorist like Ferrison? What do you get out of it?"

"We get to live," a fourth Artemis answered.

The first Artemis joined in again. "And until we pay back our debt of gratitude for the life he gave us, we will help him achieve his every dream."

"Even if those dreams amount to other people's suffering?"

"A small price to pay, you might say. After all, the cost of freedom is never cheap."

A branch snapping above her alerted Danica to the fact that she was being hunted while she spoke. She rolled onto her back in time to catch the wrists of an Artemis, stopping her blade from penetrating her eyeball.

Danica grunted and threw the Artemis off of her. Then, springing to her feet, she wasted no time and dashed into the woods.

As she raced as fast as she could over uneven terrain, a knife whisked past her ear, slicing a few strands of her hair as it barely missed her, and then lodged itself into a tree right in front of her. She paused, looked at the knife, and then carried on running for her life.

"Run all you want, Vice Admiral; we'll find you."

Seven Artemis clones slowly emerged from the jungle, fully armed with tactical gear and painted in jungle green and brown camouflage. They sidled up next to the team leader, Artemis II, and waited for further orders.

She raised her fist in the air, and then slowly extending the same arm, she pointed in the direction Danica had run off. With that, all the Artemis clones sprinted into the forest, their footfalls as silent as a panther's.

Some of them leaped up onto tree branches and bounced around the jungle canopy like elves right out of a fairytale book, while others stayed close to the ground and tracked Danica's footprints.

Artemis II smiled and then, plucking her dagger out of the tree in front of her, she turned and followed after her team at a leisurely pace.

16

The black bag was promptly removed from Danica's head and she was shoved into a holding cell. When she spun around, the two guards were already headed out the door so she couldn't get a good look at them.

"Danica? Is that you?"

Danica slowly turned around, stunned by the voice she recognized. When she saw Brei's battered face, she cried out, "Brei!" and they rushed together, running straight into each other's open arms.

Danica stroked Brei's hair and asked, "What did they do to you?"

"I was shopping in the market like I always do, and two men in the crowd abducted me. I knew they must be Ferrison's men because they did it in broad daylight. But I did what you said to do. I resisted. Until they knocked me out."

"You're my brave girl," Danica said, a tear rolling down her cheek as she examined the black and blue marks on Brei's face. "I just have to know what they did to you."

"It's okay. It looks worse than it feels, I'm sure." Brei reached up and brushed the stray tear away from Danica's cheek with her thumb.

They looked away from one another, diverting their gazes when it became clear they wanted to kiss. But now wasn't the time.

"Do you know where we are?" Danica asked, looking around the cement holding cell.

"No, when I came to, I found that they'd black-bagged me like they did you. Also, I think they might be using energy dampeners because I can't use my powers in here."

Danica held up her hands and tried to summon an energy bubble, but Brei was right. Something was preventing her from using her Dygra crystal powers.

No sooner had they begun to search the holding cell for structural weaknesses than the door creaked open and Hela stepped into the room.

"You!" Danica hissed, her tone as cold at the dead of winter on the ice-moon of Osallas III.

Hela didn't respond but merely stepped to the side when the notorious man himself entered the room.

"Demeris Ferrison," Danica snarled, her eyes drilling into him with utter disdain.

Brei'Alas did a double-take, looking from Danica to Demeris and back again. "Wait, but this doesn't make any sense. He looks exactly like..."

"Long time no see, little sister."

"Sister?!" Brei gasped. "Demeris Ferrison is your—?"

"Big brother," Danica admitted, not taking her eyes off of the traitorous snake for an instant. "And a traitor to the empire."

"It was smart of the empress to send you in her stead. She must have suspected the family resemblance and surmised I wouldn't kill my blood."

"On the contrary, big brother," Danica said, her voice like icicles, "I volunteered for the mission myself."

Demeris kicked his head back and laughed. "Same old Dani. Always so full of righteous indignation for anyone who dared sully the reputation of her great Dagon Empire."

After a brief pause, Demeris relaxed and Danica took a step back, forcing herself to remain calm. "What do you want, D?"

"What I've always wanted. I want that impure, illegitimate pink-skinned wife of yours to abdicate the throne and step down as ruler of the empire."

"But," Brei interjected, "the people actually like Jegra. Recent polls have shown that—"

"Screw the polls!" Demeris growled without so much as looking at her. Instead, he kept his gaze fixed on Danica. "The people have been brainwashed into accepting an illegitimate, illegal alien as their ruler when, by royal decree, it should be a pure-blood Dagoni!"

"Let me guess," Danica said, rolling her eyes. "You're going to be the one to fill her shoes, is that it?"

"On the contrary, little sister. I'm not exactly what you'd call a people person." This caused Hela to snicker and Demeris glanced over at her with a wry smile that hinted at something more than a platonic relationship. "I plan to hold elections. A democratized monarchy."

"Let me guess, you've rigged the system and already have a man on the inside. A candidate who you'll promote using whatever twisted narrative you've devised to sway the people to your side?"

"Am I so transparent?" Demeris raised his palms and gave an indifferent shrug. "Well, I guess you'll just have to wait and see. I'll be keeping you here until things blow over."

"Like Helios you will!" Danica shouted and she ran up to the glass barrier and slammed her fists against it. The glass merely absorbed the energy of the blow and transferred it into a kind of high-pitched warble, its tones rippling across the glass from the impact.

Demeris Ferrison smiled and then, still not acknowledging Brei's existence, turned and exited the room.

Hela turned to follow after him when Danica called out to her. "Hela, wait...there's something you should know about him."

Hela raised her hand and silenced Danica with a gesture. "I don't want to hear your lies. Demeris has told me plenty about how you sold him out to Dakroth and forced him to go underground."

"I did no such thing!" Danica growled.

"More lies," Hela said, shaking her head. "A pity. Of all his enemies, you were the one he spoke of with the most reverence." And with that, she exited the room and slammed the heavy metal door shut behind her.

"What were you going to say?" Brei asked.

"He killed Ophelia."

"Ophelia? Emperor Dakroth's first wife? I don't follow."

"It's a long story. But, in a Torvian nutshell, Ophelia Rhadamanthus was the love of Dakroth's life. It was as though they were cut from the same cloth. But then she met that enigmatic brother of mine."

"A love affair?" asked Brei.

Danica nodded. "After months of them seeing each other in secret, one thing led to another, and they eloped together. Needless to say, Dakroth was devastated and swore he'd kill them both. He hunted Demeris down and, after five long years, finally cornered him in Sector B-13."

"The coordinates of the rogue black hole," Brei said, nodding along with Danica's story.

"Let's just say there wasn't always a blackhole there—not before Ophelia's disappearance. Dakroth had detonated a prototype anti-matter bomb, hoping to take out Demeris Ferrison's ship. But things didn't go as planned and it ended up taking only half the ship into the event horizon."

"Let me guess, the part of the ship that Ophelia was on."

"She wouldn't have been dead if it weren't for Demeris's dogged pursuit of her affections. And Dakroth blamed him for her death; that's why my brother went underground."

"A tragic love story, for sure."

"It changed the emperor," Danica said, looking down at the floor. "Being betrayed like that by the woman he loved most in the world."

"What happened next?" Brei asked, invested in the story.

"A time of reckless abandon and promiscuity. He tried to soothe the pain by chasing all manner of ecstasy. Sex, drugs, you name it. But it still wasn't enough. Eventually, Dakroth ordered that Nividium be created, a drug so powerful it would make him forget. The same drug that almost ruined my life."

"It's okay," Brei said, reaching out and touching Danica's arm. "That's all in the past now."

Danica folded her arms under her chest and turned away slightly as if losing herself in thought. She took a deep breath before continuing with her story.

"Eventually, Dakroth was able to forget Ophelia. At about the same time, the trade war with the Nyctans began, distracting him even further. But, old habits die hard, I suppose. And before I knew it, he had snuck off to continue with his dalliances. In due course, he'd built up a new harem. But even the doting affection of more than a dozen wives couldn't mend the wounds of his broken heart. Eventually, he became obsessed with a certain gladiatrix. And that obsession turned into a misguided passion—because this woman reminded him of Ophelia—a woman he'd tried so hard to forget."

"You mean Jegra?"

"Yes," Danica replied, turning back toward Brei and looking into her eyes. "It was this weird concoction of love and hatred that drove him to manipulate and torment Jegra in the way that he did. In fact, having her kill his entire harem, in his scheming mind, was simply a means to an end. It marked a fresh start for him. There was no doubt in the emperor's mind that Jegra would come out victorious, and as a test of her fealty, she passed with flying colors thereby endearing herself to him all the more. It wasn't until she bested him in a battle of wits that he finally accepted the fact that she wasn't Ophelia. She wasn't a simple-minded girl who'd merely run off with the next pretty smile that doted on her. That she was, perhaps, something more."

"Love, truly, is a fickle thing," Brei said, placing her hands on her hips. Slowly looking around their prison cell, her mind shifting back to the task at hand, she asked, "So, what do we do now?"

Danica smiled. "Now, we get out of this shit-hole and stop my brother."

Jegra stood on the command deck of *The Vortex*, Hela's ship. Her team of Dagon and Galliforn soldiers had the bridge locked down as they'd successfully taken the ship.

"That was too easy," Menita said, holstering her blaster.

"It does seem like they gave up fairly quickly," Raven added, looking around the room at all the officers on their knees, the muzzles of plasma rifles pressed against the backs of their skulls.

Kregor, dressed in full Dragonian battle armor, marched up to Raven and Jegra. "The ship is secure," he began, addressing Raven first and then turning his gaze to Jegra. "It's all yours now, Your Majesty."

Jegra nodded and then turned her back to them as she gazed out of the view portal. "A distraction on top of a distraction."

"What was that, Your Grace?" Menita asked.

Jegra looked down and shook her head silently to herself before responding with an answer. "It's just something Danica once told me."

She looked up at the stars for a while and turned back toward the others.

"She was always running through strategy with me. But something that made her stand out above all the rest was she knew how to create diversions. One thing she mentioned was creating a diversion to divert you to another diversion."

"As I said, it's a wild goose chase," Menita reiterated, letting out a disappointed sigh.

"Yes, but now I know where Demeris Ferrison is keeping Danica."

"Where?" asked Menita. Raven looked at Jegra with a probing gaze as well.

"Thessalonica," she said. "He's keeping her in the old ruins outside of Mardok."

"How can you be so sure?" asked Raven.

"Because," Jegra said, "hiding them from me right under my nose while sending me on a wild goose chase is exactly what Danica would have done."

"Do you think she's in league with Demeris Ferrison?" Menita asked.

Jegra laughed out loud and shook her head. "No," she replied, "I'm afraid it's much more nuanced than that. You see, Demeris is Danica's brother."

"He's her what?!" Menita stopped herself short of cursing and began to pace.

"It would seem Ferrison is toying with you," Raven said.

Jegra nodded. "Probably trying to get under my skin."

"We'd best not give him the satisfaction," Menita said, swiveling back around with a determined look on her face.

"Oh, honey, it's too late for that," Jegra informed her. "He got under my skin a long time ago.

She held up her holovid smart-bracelet and tapped on it. A blue hologram lit up showing several unsavory characters. It appeared to be old security footage.

Zallek, the drug dealer that had gotten Danica addicted to Nividium, appeared. He was talking to someone off-camera. Jegra tapped her bracelet and brought the volume up.

"I want you to handle this personally. She can't be with that pink-skinned Terran. Dakroth is smitten with the Earth-bitch, but there's no way in Helios I'm going to allow my blood to be tainted by that greasy swine."

The camera shifted showing Demeris Ferrison handing three vials of Nividium to Zallek. He accepted them and then said, "And my part of the bargain?"

"I'll get you in touch with Onelle Te'Legra Agnar. I hear she's looking to expand her black-market trade and Nividium is the perfect commodity. She's looking forward to your call."

Demeris Ferrison handed Zallek a holo-chip and Zallek quickly tucked it into his pocket then held out his hand. They shook.

As they clasped hands, Zallek added, "Consider it done. Your sister will be so doped up and out of it that her relationship with the gladiatrix will all but be over."

"You best make sure of that. You need to ruin Danica in a way that makes her unredeemable in Jegra's eyes. I can't have them be together."

With that Demeris Ferrison's blue holographic visage turned and vanished off camera. Zallek held up the vials in his hand and let out a deep and sinister chortle.

The holovid feed cut out and Jegra looked up, her eyes brimming with tears.

"Her brother forced her to become addicted to Nividium just to break you two up?" Raven asked, unable to believe the extent of the cruelty on display.

"It was worse than that. While she was under Zallek's control, dependent upon him for her next fix, he took advantage of her nightly. Of course, that wasn't good enough for him. Zallek wanted to dominate her completely and to let me know it. So, he sent me this video."

Jegra held up her holovid bracelet again and this time a short smut film played. All three women watched with revulsion at what unfolded before them.

The short clip showed Zallek choking Danica out. He then continued having his way with her without ever removing his hands from her throat. Once he finished, he just got up and walked off, as if nothing ever happened. A few minutes later, Danica's lifeless body spasmed, then, gasping for air, she sat up.

Still doped up on Nividium, however, she quickly fell back down onto the bed, her arms and legs sprawled about her, with only a shallow breathing filling the silence. Then, the video cut out.

"By the Progenitors…" Menita said. "That's devastating."

"I was planning on killing Zallek myself," Jegra said, looking down at her feet, her fist tightening into a ball, "but Onelle Te'Legra Agnar beat me to it. Still, I can't seem to bring myself to erase this footage…because it reminds me of how I failed her. A failure I must never allow myself to repeat."

"You won't," Raven said, placing a hand on Jegra's shoulder. "That's a promise."

"I'm afraid it's a promise I'm failing to live up to," Jegra said, turning back toward the view portal. Just as she looked out at the horizon of Dagon Prime, the cusp of Thessalonica's atmosphere began to rise into view.

17

The shaman raised, her wooden staff and pointed at the bunker entrance and murmured, "Bi'vek." Almost as soon as she'd pointed at the entrance, the large, red-painted metal door swung open with a resounding clank and Demeris Ferrison and Hela emerged.

"It's him!" Lycia whispered. She took a step forward, wanting nothing more than to engage them when Raphine grabbed her by her wrist and shook her head.

"As I recall, you brought backup for just such an occasion."

"That's right," Lycia whispered, almost having forgotten about her most loyal companion in the entire galaxy.

She put her fingers to her mouth and then let out a shrill whistle that cut through the jungle trees like a laser beam.

In the distance, there was a thunderous roar and both Demeris Ferrison and Hela startled at the sound and drew out their blasters.

They put the bunker to their back and scanned the trees.

"We're not alone," Hela informed him.

He nodded in agreement and took a cautious step forward.

In the shade of the trees, Lycia hopped up and down like a boxer about to enter the ring and slapped her arms repeatedly. "Here goes nothing."

With a blur, she disappeared from sight and then, an instant later, reappeared about three hundred meters away. Now just meters from Demeris Ferrison and Hela.

Hela and Lycia's gazes met, their eyes locking like an electrical storm over Gamidon, and they scowled at one another. "You again," Hela snarled.

"Miss me?" Lycia quipped, raising her fists and bouncing up and down like a prizefighter. She then brushed her nose and with a quick slide moved in to strike Hela when, out of the blue, two Artemis clones wearing stealth invisibility suits appeared out of thin air and tackled Lycia to the ground.

They pinned her down and held her there as Hela stood over her. Looking down at Lycia with a sour expression on her face that did little to hide her disdain, Hela raised her blaster and pointed it at the center of Lycia's chest, right above her Dygra crystal.

"I'll give you five seconds to surrender yourselves," she said loud enough for the team of warriors hiding in the woods to hear. "Or I put a bolt right through her chest."

"I'll give you five seconds to say your prayers," Lycia spat back angrily. Clone or not, sister or not, Hela was as soulless as they came and Lycia wasn't going to give her the satisfaction of killing her. Not without one hell of a fight.

Lycia rolled her tongue up and sounded a shrill, high-pitched whistle. As soon as she'd made the call, a deafening roar sounded from the trees and all three of Lycia's attackers looked up in time to see Hela be whisked away by a purple blur.

Everyone turned around to see what it was, only to find Allie, the Lafor'allenthal panther, dragging Hela to the ground. Hela screamed out and tore her arm away from the panther's maw just in time for one of the other Artemis soldiers to engage the large cat.

But Allie, having caught the scent of the woman who had shot her back on Correl, was in no mood to play games. She pounced on the Artemis clone and bit down on her jugular.

With a sonorous growl that sent shivers down everyone's spine, there was a wet sounding crunch, like maize being plucked from the stalk, as Allie tore out Artemis's throat.

As Allie prowled about, circling her kill and licking her chops, she turned her lime green eyes to Hela who, cradling her wounded arm, scrambled back toward the bunker, dragging herself through the leaves and dirt until she had her back firmly pressed up against the cool concrete wall.

"Stay away from me, you beast!" The alarm in her voice was very real and Allie merely growled menacingly and narrowed her green, cat eyes at her.

Petrified, Hela shouted, trying to make her bark sound bigger than her bite, if only to hold the cat at bay. "What? You want an apology, you stupid cat?" She screamed and kicked both legs, slinging rocks and dirt in Allie's direction. "Fine! I'm sorry!"

Allie replied with a deep rumbling growl and paced back and forth, her tail twitching in an agitated fashion.

Demeris Ferrison sidled up to Hela and trained the gun on Allie, holding the cat at bay. "Whoa, there, big kitty. He said. "Nice kitty. Stay."

Off to their right, as they were preoccupied with the large cat, Lycia swept the legs of the second Artemis, knocking her off her feet and onto her back.

Then, springing to her feet, Lycia kicked the Artemis clone squarely in her jaw, knocking her out cold. The woman collapsed face first in the dirt and Lycia turned to face Demeris Ferrison and Hela. As she approached, she patted Allie's head and said, "Good girl."

Demeris circled Lycia, who began to circle him in turn. They eyed each other up and down. Meanwhile, off to their side, Allie held Hela trapped up against the bunker wall, her bloody maw dripping with the leftovers of the Artemis she'd just mauled.

Growling in a deep and vicious tone, Allie let Hela know that she hadn't forgotten her or the fact that Hela had shot her.

Demeris sneered as he looked at Lycia. "I was curious as to what to expect from the famous mongrel clone of the emperor and his pet pink-belly. I have to say though, I'm not as impressed as I thought I'd be."

"Ditto, micro-dick," Lycia replied.

"Very mature," Demeris Ferrison retorted.

"I'm nineteen, I can afford to be uncouth. But you, old man, what's your excuse?"

"Excuse for what?"

"For being such a douche."

"Right," he said in an even less amused tone than before. "Anyway, as much fun as it has been, I'm afraid you're just a distraction I don't need right now."

He slowly raised his hands and clapped twice. A nanosecond later about two dozen Artemis clones appeared all around them.

Lycia and Allie looked all around them only to find themselves flanked and outnumbered.

"As you can see, we have you surrounded."

"Surrounded?" Lycia laughed. "All I'm surrounded by is fear and dead women. You just haven't realized it yet."

Hela scoffed and then said, "See, Demeris, I told you she was cocky."

"Lady, I'm the daughter of the Mother of Dagon, so you best watch your tone."

The Artemises cocked their plasma rifles and trained them on Lycia and Allie.

Lycia smiled and, keeping her eyes locked with Hela's, gently waved her hand as though she were casting an evil curse on her.

"What are you doing?" Hela asked.

"Shhh," Lycia replied, putting a finger to her lips and hushing her. This annoyed Hela and she smacked her teeth and then drew up her blaster and pointed it at Lycia's head.

All of a sudden Lycia ghosted herself, making a dozen energy copies of herself, or echoes as she preferred to call them.

"Interesting," Demeris Ferrison said, raising an eyebrow.

Lycia then pointed at the Artemis clones and her echoes promptly bounded off and engaged the enemy clones in hand to hand combat. As they did so, she grabbed Demeris by his throat and hoisted him off his feet.

Hela turned to fire when Allie leapt up and bit her forearm. Hela screamed out, firing off a shot that slammed into a nearby tree.

Charging forward, Lycia slammed Demeris into the concrete wall of the bunker with bone-shattering force. Demeris Ferrison cried out in agony as a couple of his ribs fractured and coughed up a spattering of blood.

He stared at Lycia with an intense gaze full of abhorrence and wiped the blood driveling down his chin with the back of his hand. "Do it, girl. Kill me. But fair warning to you. If you go through with it then you'll never know where the bomb is hidden and all those lost lives will be on you!"

Lycia squeezed his neck harder, choking him so he couldn't breathe. Just as his eyes began to roll back in his head so only the whites showed, a voice cut through the din of the battle and called out to her.

"Lycia! Don't do it. We need him alive."

Lycia glanced over her shoulder to see Raphine emerge from the trees. She nodded in acknowledgment when, interrupting the afternoon's skirmish, a golden beam of light touched down in the middle of all the chaos.

Soon thereafter Jegra appeared in the clearing and quickly glanced around, scanning her surroundings. Even as a battle raged on all around her, her nerves were tempered by the steel of the arena and not a combatant on the ground had the strength to stand up to her, with, perhaps, the exception of Lycia. Although raw and lacking in training, Lycia would make a formidable warrior one day.

Surprisingly calm, Jegra marched resolutely toward the bunker when a rogue Artemis landed right in front of her, squatting down as her powerful thighs compressed underneath her. She sprang up and lunged at Jegra, wailing like a banshee, and tried to assault the empress. But even though she was fast, she was no match for the champion gladiatrix.

An unconcerned look on her face, Jegra merely backhanded the girl and sent her flying up into the trees to the astonishment of all the onlookers. The sheer strength it took to hit someone hard enough to get them to rise off the ground was impressive enough. But to send them soaring a hundred meters through the air was downright remarkable.

Thanks to Jegra, the Lycia echo that had been grappling with the incapacitated Artemis soon found herself without an opponent, so she looked over to her right and found a sister echo who was currently engaged in the heat of battle. Racing over to her, she ran straight into her likeness and the two visages of Lycia melded into one.

Their combined energy made the new echo slightly stronger and she shoved the Artemis off her and regained her footing. Each time an Artemis fell, the Lycia echoes would recombine, thereby creating stronger echoes to continually fight the gradually tiring Artemis clones.

As Jegra approached Demeris Ferrison's position, he smiled coldly—the kind of smile sociopaths give when they try to emulate real emotions but can't seem to make them feel genuine. "I see you've decided to grace us with your presence," he said to Jegra as she approached the entrance of the bunker. But she merely ignored him.

Instead, she kicked her powerful leg forward and broke down the heavy steel door to the bunker. Then she looked at both Hela and Demeris Ferrison, first one and then the other, then ducked inside without saying so much as a single word to either of them.

Lycia shrugged then shoved Demeris so hard he knocked himself out against the unforgiving wall of the concrete bunker and collapsed to the ground.

Raphine, along with several tribal warriors, arrived in time to apprehend him. At the same time, Lycia reached out her hand and clutched Hela by her arm.

"Ow!" Hela groused.

"Come along, sister," Lycia said, shoving Hela inside the bunker. "You have some explaining to do."

As they began to pass beneath the mantle of the door, Lycia's echoes all returned to her like iron filings being drawn to a lodestone. As she re-absorbed all their energy, all the Artemises they'd been fighting collapsed to the ground, exhausted and defeated by her ghosts.

Danica clenched her metal fist then punched the security glass of her prison cell. It reverberated with a low sounding resonance that seemed to evenly distribute the energy of her blows.

She moved to a different spot and punched it again. And then again, and again.

"I don't think that's doing anything," Brei said, covering her ears with the palms of her hands.

"What?" Danica asked, not hearing Brei over the din of vibrating glass. "I couldn't hear you over the noise."

"I said, I don't think it's doing anything."

Danica nodded, and then with a powerful strike, hit the glass again. As the sound died down, she answered, "I'm searching it for weaknesses."

"How much longer do you think it will take? My ears are killing me," Brei said.

A look of determination settled over Danica's face and she stuck her tongue out of the corner of her mouth as she focused all her attention on one small pinpoint on the entire surface of the glass. Then, she pulled her arm as far back as it would go, winding up for a big one, and used all her strength.

Her fist struck with immense force but instead of a loud vibrating twang, there was a crackling sound as the glass shattered all at once and crumbled to the ground in a million pieces the size of small pebbles.

Walking across the glass, her boots crunched on the white fragments as if she were stepping on freshly packed snow. She paused to look back over her shoulder at Brei and smiled.

"You coming or not?"

Brei returned her smile with one of her own and, whispering under her breath to herself, said, "You're awesome."

"What was that?" Danica asked, her ears still ringing slightly from the terrible racket.

"Nothing," Brei replied, quickly scurrying after her.

They arrived at the exit door together and Danica was about to throw it open and march on through when Brei raised her hand and stopped her. "I've got this," she informed her.

Brei then casually opened the door and stepped through onto the other side and out into the corridor.

"Hey, you there! Halt!" a guard shouted. Brei looked over as two guards closed in on her. Growing frightened, she crouched down and covered her head defensively.

As if by reflex, a time distortion rippled throughout the entire room and continued throughout the rest of the facility. A brief moment later, both women, once again, found themselves standing in front of the very same door.

Danica stepped forward and was about to march on through when Brei reached out her hand and stopped her.

"No, wait, there are two armed guards out there."

"You used your powers, didn't you?"

Brei blushed and brushed a tuft of hair behind her ear. "Yeah. I guess once you knocked out that glass our powers came back."

"Good to know," Danica said, cracking her knuckles. "Oh, and by the way, I think you're pretty awesome too," she said, smiling.

Then, gently nudging Brei aside, who merely stared back at her with a lovestruck gaze, Danica flung open the door and boldly stepped outside as her energy shield formed around her body like a thin, glowing veil.

"Hey, you there! Halt!"

The sound of bones crunching and faces getting mashed in echoed back into the holding cell with Brei and she cringed. Every crack, thwack, and crunch made her twinge with sympathy pain as the guards screamed out.

One thing that Danica had learned to be in the arena was efficient, exacting, but most of all, discriminating. While overly powerful gladiators like Jegra could afford to dance around, pandering to the crowd, Danica was a regular person. It was kill or be killed.

She knew that in hand-to-hand combat, if you hesitated for even a split second, your enemy would get the upper hand. Which is why she never wasted a single move. It also happened to make her style of fighting quite brutal, because she'd strike like a viper and go for incapacitation before her opponents even knew what had hit them.

This made her quite vicious in the arena, but doubly so in real life, when her own life was on the line. It made her more than just a little discriminating—it made her absolutely, one-hundred percent lethal.

Roughly sixty seconds later Danica walked back into the room dusting off her hands. "That felt good to get out of my system."

"Felt good, did it?" asked Brei.

Shaking out her hands and laughing at herself, Danica looked up and said, "Yeah. And, stranger still, I feel oddly aroused right now."

Brei bit her bottom lip, contemplating something scandalous as she stared at Danica.

"What is it?" Danica asked, growing a little self-conscious.

"Nothing," Brei said, still beaming like a schoolgirl with the biggest crush in the world. Wisps of energy gradually began to rise off from her skin like steam rising from one's skin after a hot shower. As she charged her time-powers, even her hair began to rise up into the air, undulating on the small currents of energy that emanated from her.

Another time distortion rippled through the room and, time resetting, the sounds of bones crunching and faces getting mashed in replayed itself all over again.

This time, however, when Danica walked back into the room dusting off her hands, Brei raced up to her, leaped up into her arms, and kissed her long and hard.

Their tongues danced about playfully inside each other's mouths until, finally, Danica drew back and asked, "What in the world was that for?"

"For saving me, you damn sexy goddess."

Danica laughed and set Brei back down on her two feet. "Alright, we'll have plenty of time for that later. But right now, we need to focus."

"Right," Brei said. Just then a pretty moth flew into the room and she became distracted all over again. "Hey, a butterfly!"

Danica rolled her eyes and grabbed Brei by her wrist. "Just stay close and follow me."

The screeching sounds of wrenching metal came echoing up from the depths of the bunker, and a few minutes later, Hela flew out of the entrance, crashed down into the dirt, and rolled several times before skidding to a stop.

The Mewiki stepped aside and Raphine watched her struggle to get up. She spat out a twig and some leaves, ignoring the numerous scrapes and cuts she'd just been dealt.

As soon as she managed to get back up onto her feet, Jegra marched out of the bunker with wild eyes. "Where is it?"

"Where's what?" Hela asked jeeringly. She reached up and wiped the blood from her lower lip and then spat at the ground near Jegra's feet.

"Don't play stupid with me, you little blue snot. You damn well know what. The neutron bomb. Where is it?"

"I don't have any clue as to what you're talking about. I'm a scientist. I have an aversion to violence. And, as you just saw, the only thing down there is lab equipment."

"Lab equipment for making bombs," Lycia said, emerging from the bunker a few moments after them.

Hela ignored her and said, "Equipment for sensitive science experiments."

"What kind of experiments?" Raphine asked.

Hela turned her head and narrowed her eyes at her.

"If you must know, I was studying the medicinal property of several types of fungus and mushrooms."

Jegra marched up to Hela, hoisted her to her feet and then gripped onto her shoulder.

"A likely story, but what would Demeris Ferrison want with medicine?"

This caused Hela to laugh. "Ha! Demeris doesn't care about medicine. He wants me to figure out how to make hallucinogenic drugs for him."

"Why?" Jegra asked.

Hela shrugged. "Beats me. As long as he deposits the credits, I just do what

I'm told."

Seeing as Hela's story was a dead end, Jegra squeezed her arm again, forcing her to whimper. As she let up, she drew Hela close and asked, "Why don't you stop beating around the bush and tell me what I want to know. And, just to be clear, I'm only going to ask you this one last time. Where. Is. The. Bomb?"

Hela just laughed in Jegra's face as if she were nothing but a joke to her. Of course, this made Jegra all the more furious.

Fed up with Hela's obstinate and continuous antagonism, Jegra squeezed down on her shoulder so hard that she shattered her rotator cuff. Hela screamed out in agony. "Even if I told you...*ngh*...it wouldn't do you any good...*ngh*. Demeris is the only one who can disarm it."

"I didn't ask you if you could disarm it," Jegra said. "I asked you if you knew where it was."

"Yes!" Hela finally admitted. "I know where the fucking bomb is. But why would I tell a bitch like you? You shattered my arm. And to think, you almost had me convinced you were worthier than him." She nodded at the unconscious body of Demeris Ferrison. "But now, I see that he was right about you. You're just a primitive simian that's been given the keys to a castle, but cannot even begin to fathom the kingdom that lies beyond."

Lycia's hand flew out of nowhere and smacked Hela's jaw dealing her a sting so fierce that it stunned her.

"That's the empress, you're talking to. You will show the proper respect."

"It's all right," Jegra said, raising her hand, gesturing for Lycia to restrain herself. "She's not going to talk."

"Then why not just kill her?" Lycia asked.

"Because," Jegra said, "killing her won't do us any good. It would only make her a martyr. One that Demeris could use to rally others to his cause against us."

"Listen to your empress," Hela said. "After all, Emperor Dakroth taught her well."

"That's enough," Jegra growled. "You don't get to speak his name. Not ever."

"Oh, did I touch a nerve? What's the matter, Jegra? Do you miss spreading your legs for him? Bending over so he can have his way with you? You liked that, didn't you? You liked giving up that power and putting your fate in the hands of a dangerous, powerful man like Dakroth. I can see it in your eyes."

"I warned you."

Fearing the look in Jegra's eyes, Raphine took a step forward but just as she moved in to attempt to take Hela away peacefully, Jegra reached up and backhanded the blue bitch with a powerful slap that knocked her out cold.

Hela collapsed to the ground and Raphine and Lycia quickly collected her while Jegra stood by, taking in a couple of deep breaths to try and collect herself. She then cracked her neck, rolled her head back and forth across her shoulders, and stretched.

After finding her calm, Jegra threw out an arm and pointed at where Demeris Ferrison lay unconscious. "Get him to his feet."

Raphine took Hela while Lycia went over and hoisted Demeris up by his arms and tried jostling him awake. When that didn't work, she reached down and grabbed his nut sack in her hand and squeezed hard enough to pop his balls like grapes.

"Arrrgh!" he cried out loud, abruptly snapping back to consciousness.

"Wakey wakey, eggs and bakey," Lycia said, slapping his face to rouse him further. Once he was awake enough to know what was going on, she propped him up against the bunker wall and stood aside as Jegra drew up close.

Nose to nose with Demeris Ferrison, Jegra asked in a low and deceptively calm voice, "Where is the bomb?"

"I'll tell you what, oh great empress. If you get down on your knees right now and suck my big blue cock, I'll tell you right where the bomb is." His lips stretched into a wide, smug grin and he stared at her with a look so sincere she knew he meant every word.

Instead of stooping to his level of depravity, however, Jegra merely held his gaze and said in a hushed tone, "Wrong answer."

Bringing up her first, Demeris flinched, fearing she might strike him—or worse, snap his neck. Instead, she just tapped her holovid bracelet, and said, "Two to teleport."

A massive cylindrical beam of golden light came down from the sky and then split into two, slightly smaller, cylinders of light that promptly engulfed them. Standing inside the radiant energy, Jegra's and Demeris Ferrison's forms began to break down into hexagonal packets of light and then were whisked into the sky.

Raphine and Lycia looked up at the blue sky overhead, following the glittering trail of light back to Thessalonica.

18

Blinded by the shining Thessalonica sun, Danica quickly shielded her eyes. The sounds of servos of electric motors coming to life warned her that they weren't alone.

"Get down!" Brei hollered and tackled Danica to the ground. They rolled in the dirt together just as a barrage of fire rained down on their position. They quickly scurried to one of the old Doric columns of the ancient ruins.

Covered in dust and sand, Danica leaned to the side and peeked out at the five Centurion war robots that littered the grounds. They were stationed all along the perimeter with one standing directly over the mouth of the temple entrance.

A flurry of hot laser blasts sent her back up against the pillar and she looked over at Brei, who was spitting out sand from her mouth.

"Centurions. Lots of them."

"Maybe I can use my time powers and…"

Danica reached over and grabbed Brei's face and pulled it to hers. They looked into each other's eyes and then kissed. "It wouldn't do us any good," Danica relayed. "We'd just be trapped inside again. At least now we're out here, still alive."

"I have an idea," Brei said. "There's a new technique I've been wanting to try. But I'm going to have to ask you to trust me."

Danica nodded and then watched as Brei cautiously stood up. She looked down at Danica and began to jitter. It seemed she was moving extremely fast and her image became blurry for a moment. Then she snapped back into focus.

"What was that?" Danica asked.

"I've been skipping through time at super-fast intervals. Mere nanoseconds. Basically, I oscillate between the past and present, always moving forward two and back one to progress, or back two and forward one to regress. As long as I maintain a steady state of fuzziness, nothing in the present will be able to hurt me."

"Are you sure about this?" Danica asked. "What you're proposing is dangerous."

"I know," Brei said. "But there's only so many times you and Jegra can save me. I need to do this."

Danica nodded and then watched as Brei's body blurred out again. Like a fuzzy, partly translucent ghost, she stepped out from their shelter and called out to the war machines.

"Hey, bolts for brains! You looking for me?"

The Centurions opened fire on her position but to Danica's amazement, the laser blasts simply passed right through her.

Brei proceeded to the nearest Centurion; it kept focusing and refocusing on her, but it couldn't get a lock. She materialized briefly and opened its access panel and then pulled down the off switch. The machine turned off, and, with a fading hum, it sank to the ground.

Confident in her ability, she blurred out of sight again, walked around the sleeping robot, and began to inch toward the next one. Like the first one, it too couldn't get a lock on her fuzzy visage, but it fired off several shots just to test her. And as before, the energy beams simply passed through her.

She managed to disable the second Centurion as she'd done with the first one. As she turned to march across the open square to the Centurion opposite her, the one standing above the entrance shot off a grenade. It hit the ground and Brei looked up and turned to Danica with what she intuitively knew was a startled look.

The grenade exploded and Brei flew up into the air. She crashed back down onto the ground and her body solidified again. Just then, the remaining three Centurions opened fire on her.

"Oh, no you don't!" Danica shouted and stepped into the fray. She held up both palms, generating an energy shell around Brei and a shield for herself.

Laser blasts ricocheted off her shield and pinged off in random directions. Trying its luck a second time, the Centurion on the high ground launched another grenade, but Danica was ready for it.

She created an energy bubble over the Centurion and deflected the grenade back down to it. With a loud boom, the machine blew itself up.

The other machines seemed to take note of this, as their primitive A.I. was excellent at calculating the dire outcome, should they resort to any further use of their grenades. As such, their second set of arms unfurled and their giant sawblades turned on with an angry-sounding buzz.

Only two Centurions remained, and Danica wasn't in a good position. Luckily, Brei was waking up and had already blurred herself again. She nodded at Danica, signaling her that it was okay to drop the shield.

Danica did so and Brei took off at a brisk pace, making a beeline for Centurion number four.

As Brei distracted it, Danica turned to the other one and, increasing her shield output, pushed it back out into the wide open, orange sands of the Thessalonican desert.

It began firing everything it had at her. Lasers, grenades, helios missiles. Danica was able to knock it all away with energy discs. Once the barrage had ceased, she used the discs like Frisbees and, with a wave of her hand, threw them back at the machine.

The discs embedded themselves into the Centurion, sending out a spray of sparks and small electrical discharges. Even though it was damaged, it didn't appear that any of its vital systems had been hit. As such, it tried a new tactic and scuttled toward Danica.

Set on a direct collision course, the Centurion nearly bowled Danica over before she got up an energy bubble. Throwing up her blue energy shield just in time, the machine got high-centered on the top of her bubble. Its crab-like legs wriggled about, trying to find something to cling onto, but it was no use. It was surely stuck.

"Just great," Danica muttered. She had to hold the energy shield up for as long as she could, otherwise the massive robot would topple onto her, crushing her beneath its mass.

If she expanded her bubble, then it would eventually teeter off, but then she'd be in close quarters with it and would have to dig in, using a purely defensive barrier. Either way, she was stuck.

Out of nowhere, a laser blast hit Danica's Centurion dead between its eyes, exploding its head and torso.

The dead husk of the bot fell to the side of Danica's bubble, and, as black smoke began to rise from its remains, she stood up fully and dropped her shield. Then turning in the direction of the blast, she saw Brei'Alas holding the severed arm of her Centurion, using it as a blaster.

It would have been an otherwise epic scene, except for the fact that Brei was stark naked.

Danica smiled and, raising an eyebrow, asked, "Where in the seven moons did all your clothes go?"

"A side effect of distorting time all around me. Synthetic materials always seem to have a hard time making the journey; they break apart after a few seconds."

Brei tossed the gun onto the sand beside her and then threw her hands up onto her hips. "Told you I didn't need saving."

"That you did," Danica laughed.

After a moment in the sun, Brei shielded her eyes and fanned herself with her free hand. "It's blazing hot out here, babe. You got that extra smart suit on you that you always carry for emergencies?"

"Maybe," Danica teased. "But, then again, maybe I like you better like this."

Brei's smile grew wide as did her eyes as her mouth fell open. "Oh, you do, do you?"

Just then, a sandworm slithered by Brei's foot and she began hopping around.

"Eek!" she screamed. "Sandworm!"

"It's just a small one," Danica said, strolling over to where Brei was dancing in frantic circles.

"I hate sandworms!"

Danica reached out her hand and said, "Actually, I do too. Come along, luv. We best be getting back home."

Brei took Danica's hand in hers and the moment they locked firm, Danica slapped the smart bracelet onto Brei's wrist, and a liquid-like substance secreted from it, coating her entire body in a milky film.

Once the milky substance had covered every nanometer of her, it hardened into a plastic-like pleather. Brei tapped the bracelet and the suit changed colors, turning light gray with teal sports lines.

"Thanks," she said. "I'd hate to get a sunburn you know where."

Danica simply nodded and then turned in the direction of Arena City. "If we get a move on, we might make it to the outskirts of the city by dark."

"That's twelve hours away," Brei said after letting out a bothered sigh. "And we don't have any water."

"Don't worry," Danica said, as she reached up and squeezed both of her breasts. "I have enough breast milk to sustain us."

"You what?" Brei asked, her eyes trailing down to Danica's chest. She wasn't wrong, her breasts were much more plump than usual.

"I started taking hormones so I could be a good surrogate for breastfeeding when Jegra's new baby comes."

"And you want me to just…what…suckle you like a newborn?" asked Brei, an uncertain smirk on her face.

"Do you see any breast-pumps or bottles around here?" asked Danica as she fanned her hands across the barren desert landscape.

Brei contemplated it a bit longer, stroking her chin and then, with a lighthearted shrug, replied, "All right, then. I'll do it. But let's not mention this to Jegra. She'll never let us hear the end of it."

"Agreed," Danica said, opening her vest and unzipping her smart suit underneath.

Brei waited for the mammary to emerge in all its glory. It looked like a giant, engorged blueberry and, slowly, she bent down gently latched her lips onto Danica's maroon colored nipple and began suckling.

Once she'd had her fill, Brei wiped some excess drizzle from her chin and sighed out a refreshing sigh. "That's better."

With that, Brei bent over and moved in for another helping of breast milk. Danica merely grabbed her face and held her at bay, even as her tongue slid out from her mouth and extended itself in an attempt to get to Dani's nipple.

Danica simply rolled her eyes again. "Save some for later, hot stuff. We have a full day of marching through the blistering heat of the desert and we'll need to save every ounce we can for later."

Brei stood back up and nodded. "Right. All right then, we best get a move on."

Brei looked around and then walked over to the Centurion, its grenade launcher canopy open. She reached into the canopy's opening and pried out a metal rod. Snapping it off, she turned to Danica and slammed the staff length piece of metal into the sand.

"What's that for?" asked Danica, tucking her girls and zipping her special ops suit back up.

"Walking stick," Brei replied. "Also, if we run into any of those nasty sandworms, we can defend ourselves." She thrust the metal rod forward like a lance and pretended to skewer a giant sandworm.

Danica nodded in agreement and then went over to the nearest Centurion's corpse. She plucked out a couple of grenades and fastened them onto her tactical belt. Then she tore off a piece of its metal plating and used some of the loose wiring as rope to tie it to her arm as a makeshift shield.

After testing it out, she grabbed some more wire and yanked it out. Drawing it up against the machine's sawblade arm, she severed the wires and then tied the ends together. She tossed the wire-rope over her shoulder and turned back to Brei.

"Now, I'm ready."

"Who are you even?" Brei asked. "You're like some kind of survival wizard."

Danica shrugged. "I am a trained officer in Her Majesty's Imperial Navy, after all."

As they set out into the desert, Brei finally said, "I still can't believe you made me drink your breast milk." After a moment's thought, she added, "I can't believe you drank your own breast milk."

"It's not that bad. We grow up on the stuff. I honestly don't think we ever get tired of drinking it. We've been conditioned by years of evolution to like it. Besides, we could make a fortune selling the stuff, considering Dagon's are lactose intolerant to everything but their mother's milk."

"You're weird," Brei stated conclusively. "But," she admitted, "it's not a completely terrible idea."

"I have some extra hormones I can share with you once we get back. We'll start a business together."

Brei laughed out loud and then grew silent as she fell deep into thought.

This caught Danica's attention and she slowed to a stop and turned to look at Brei. She stared at her for a few seconds and then asked, "You want more don't you?"

"By the seven moons of Vespa, yes! More than anything!" Brei stated without hesitation. Licking her lips thirstily, she let out a long and overly loud sigh.

Danica laughed and threw her arm around Brei's neck and drew her close. With Brei's face mashed into her chest, Danica kissed her on her forehead, and said, "I love you too, you little weirdo. Now, let's go home."

That's when the glint of something off in the sand caught their eyes. "What's that?" asked Brei, extending her finger in the direction of the flickering flash.

"I don't know," Danica said, sliding off her metal shield. She handed it off to Brei and then said. "Wait here while I go check it out."

Danica began to skip down the sand dune toward the metallic object.

"Like Helios," Brei shouted out to her. "I'm not just standing around doing nothing."

They slid to a stop next to the metal cylinder and then looked at each other with alarm.

"Are you shitting on me?" Brei asked.

Danica shook her head. "No. It's: 'are you shitting me.'"

"What?" Brei asked, somewhat confused. She'd heard Jegra use the term a million times.

"Never mind," Danica said. It wasn't important. Not now that they'd found the neutron bomb.

"But why would he just leave it out in the desert unattended like this?" Brei inquired. She put her hand to her forehead to block out the brilliant sunlight and looked all around for signs of more Centurion robots or some more guards.

"I think I might know why," Danica said.

Brei's eyes met hers and the pit of her stomach dropped out.

"He's going to kill everyone on Thessalonica just to prove his point?"

"It will look like retaliation from the Nyctans. Quite clever, if you think about it."

"But that will destroy the peace Jegra worked so hard to bring to our worlds. It will devastate the fragile alliance we've struggled to achieve."

"That's what terrorists do, sweetie. They destabilize entire governments simply to sew fear and distrust."

"We have to stop it," Brei said, slamming her fist into the palm of her hand.

Before Danica could reply, however, Brei blurred out of focus. Realizing what she was about to do, she reached out her hand and shouted, "No, wait!"

But it was too late. Brei had already plunged her phased hands deep into the guts of the bomb.

19

Jegra and Demeris Ferrison's bodies materialized at the center of the arena on the moon Thessalonica. As they solidified, the crowd erupted into cheers.

"Ladies and gentlemen! Making her exciting return to the arena, the undefeated and still reigning champion, the famed slave who became a queen, the Mother of Dagon, your empress, JEGRA ALAKANDRA!"

The stadium erupted with twenty-thousand voices roaring in excitement. The din sounded like a rushing waterfall and drown out everything else, including the announcer's pleas for the crowd to simmer down.

Jegra shoved Demeris Ferrison aside and raised her arms. Another wave of screams and applause tore through the crowd.

Televid drones flooded the stadium, entire swarms of them coming out of the ventilation ducts from all over the arena. At the same time, the monitor counting the number of active televid viewers quickly racked up some of the highest numbers anyone had ever seen.

Represented as a graph, the bright purple bar that represented Jegra quickly surpassed all of Dakroth's honor bouts, then it surpassed all the most popular humiliation bouts, including Danica's. At last, Jegra surpassed her own most popular bout, and the numbers kept growing. This match wasn't only going to be a ratings smash—it was going into the record books as the most viewed event in cosmic history.

The announcer cleared his throat and finally got the spectators' attention back. "Facing off against the esteemed Gladiatrix of the Galaxy is the Scourge of Seven Systems, the indomitable, cold as ice, evil as sin, butcher of women and children, Demeris Ferrison!"

"Boo! Boo! Boooo!"

The audience cheers quickly turned into jeers and leers. People spat and made lewd gestures. One Bre'lal woman, so worked up over it, jammed her fingers down her throat and gagged herself. A blast of vomit shot from her mouth, and, after the spray died down, she wiped her mouth with the back of her hand and spat her fowl, sour sputum at the arena floor.

Another man pulled down his pants and began to piss into the arena. Luckily, none of these things could reach Jegra—or her opponent—who stood safely at the center.

Jegra turned back to Demeris and stared him right in the eyes.

"You think because they chant your name that you mean something to them? You're nothing. You're just a rating's grab. That's all you've ever been."

"Where's the bomb, ass wipe?"

Demeris sneered and replied, "You know the deal. Blow me, and I'll tell you." He laughed and then, at the sounding of a trumpet, the reserve gladiators brought out the racks of weapons.

Jegra gestured for Demeris to take his pick. He grabbed a couple of scimitars and turned toward her.

"Aren't you going to arm yourself?" he asked.

"No need," Jegra said, motioning with the wave of her hand for him to come at her.

He shrugged. "Suit yourself."

Demeris charged Jegra and swiped his blades frantically. She dodged every slash and thrust of his untrained attack.

Still wounded, Demeris grabbed his ribcage and groaned in pain. He was overexerting himself and, so, slowing down, he turned and decided to make a more discerning attack.

"I'll ask you one last time," Jegra said, slowly backing up as Demeris walked toward her, blades in each hand. "Where is the bomb?"

"That's the beauty of it," he said, his eyes bulging with twisted excitement, his grin manic. "I don't have any fucking clue. I had Hela dump it somewhere in the desert. And since it's too small to scan from space, you'll need every man and woman you can get to comb the entire fucking desert. But, by then, it will already be too late."

Demeris Ferrison began to laugh maniacally, tickled by his evil genius.

Jegra just stood up straight and placed her hands on her hips. "Are you quite finished?" she asked, obviously unamused by his self-aggrandizing.

"Oh, Your Worshipfulness," he said condescendingly, "I haven't even gotten started."

Lunging forward, he thrust his blade straight into her gut. Jegra stood firm and looked down at the bent sword.

Demeris tossed the useless piece of metal aside and, gripping the handle of the second blade with both hands, he swung it as hard as he could—aiming for her neck.

The sword struck Jegra's neck and shattered into several pieces. Startled by her invulnerability, he raced back to the weapons rack and searched for something made out of korridium. But all he could find was korridium tipped arrows.

"This will have to do," he mumbled. Then, an arrow in each hand, he charged Jegra again.

He stabbed and jabbed, swiped left then right, spun around and thrust the spear into Jegra's right thigh. She grunted and then simply plucked the arrow out of her leg and tossed it onto the dirt in front of his feet.

He crouched down, keeping a rueful eye on her, and picked it up. Once he had his arrow back, he sprang up and lunged at her again. And, again, she evaded his moves.

After toying with him for a while, Jegra gave Demeris a little slap and sent him tumbling across the arena. His body rolled across the sands like a tumbleweed. He collided into the weapons rack with a violent crash, and the crowd erupted with cheers.

Battered but not defeated, Demeris Ferrison pushed himself up to his feet and spat a thick glob of blood onto the ground. He grabbed a spiked shield and put it on. In his other hand, he took up a half-sized battle-axe.

Clanking the axe on the shield, he stood up and looked at all the viewers. Televid drones buzzed over him and he shouted out, "I am the destroyer of worlds. Boo me all you want. Vilify me. Spit on me. But know this. I fight for Dagon. I fight for not only the memory of the greatest empire that ever was, but I fight to bring honor and glory back to the Dagon namesake!"

The crowd died down as what Demeris Ferrison was saying caught their attention.

"You may fight for those things," Jegra interjected, "but how you try to achieve them leads to needless suffering."

Jegra and Demeris came nose to nose on the battlefield. Although she stood about half a head above him, he looked up into her eyes with as much disdain as she returned to him.

Then, unexpectedly, he smiled. This tipped Jegra off to the fact that something wasn't right.

Demeris raised his open palm and Jegra caught a glimpse of dried beige dust with red specs.

He blew on his palm and the dust flew into Jegra's face.

Immediately she sensed a strange sensation and coughed and hacked to get it out of her nose, but it was too late. She'd already inhaled the dust.

"What was that?" Jegra asked, taking a couple of steps back away from the lingering cloud.

Demeris Ferrison started to laugh again, his tone quickly turning menacing. Then, golden tentacles began to tear out from his back.

"No," Jegra whispered, backing up, "it can't be."

"Your fear betrays you, Daughter of Sol. The Gilded Master was never defeated; you were only meant to think you had won. But you see, I've been here all along. Watching you. Studying you. Analyzing your weaknesses."

"No," Jegra screamed out. "We defeated you."

Demeris Ferrison's feet rose off the ground and he levitated into the air. "No, you only delayed the inevitable."

As the return of H'aaztre loomed over her, Jegra took a deep breath and then unleashed her most powerful Dygra blast; the same one she'd used in Hela's camp.

The energy wave blew everyone and everything back. Even the people in the stands were smashed into their seats and pressed up against the walls. The concrete of the stadium fractured with large cracks and the energy wave was followed by a massive boom.

When Jegra looked up again, the hybrid H'aaztre and Demeris Ferrison still loomed over her. "Your Dygra energy has no power over me," he laughed. "Now, submit to my will and I might just spare your life."

Trembling, Jegra knelt on one knee and bowed her head before the Gilded One. Her eyes downcast, she didn't know what to do. She knew that she couldn't fight him on her own. H'aaztre was just too powerful.

The last time she fought him, she'd had several armies and the entire galaxy united behind her. But now, it was just her. A humble gladiator standing upon the sands of the arena. But she knew that if she was going to die, at least she would die a gladiator.

H'aaztre settled back down onto the ground and slowly walked up to her. Reaching out his hand, he touched the top of her head and said in his demonic sounding voice, "There, now. Was that so hard?"

A shockwave rippled across the desert sands and knocked Danica and Brei'Alas onto their asses. Danica looked over at Brei, who had, in the ensuing wake of the wave, solidified again. Only now, she was holding the detonator trigger in her hands. They both looked at the bomb and then at each other.

"I don't believe it, you fucking did it!" Danica screamed out in utter disbelief laced with utmost joy. "You fucking disarmed the bomb."

"I did?" Brei asked. "I mean, I did!"

"I could just kiss you," Danica said, grabbing Brei by her face and drawing her in. She kissed Brei's lips and then her cheek and all other parts of her face.

"Okay, okay," Brei giggled. "I love you too."

A small tremor shook beneath them and they struggled to their feet.

"What was that?" asked Brei.

"Whatever it was, it came from the city."

Brei handed the detonator to Danica and then scurried up the side of a small dune. Just as she reached the top, a Falcon Heavy dropship flew over their heads.

"Hey!" Brei shouted up at the passing jet. "Down here!"

It flew on, not noticing them.

"It's no use," Danica lamented, tossing the failed detonator aside. "They can't hear you."

"Well," Brei fired back, "whip out them milk-titties and flash them or something. Get their attention!"

"My tits? Why don't you flash them your tits?!" Danica shot back defensively.

"Because!" Brei shouted, her hands clutching her chest, "Mine aren't as big as yours. They won't even see my titties from way up there." Brei pointed up at the sky, adding in an urgent tone of desperation, "But they might see your huge, milk engorged, melon-sized ones."

Danica rolled her eyes yet again but laughed at Brei's proposition. Her breasts weren't spotlights. But Brei's mind was so wonderfully unique and her spirit so pure and full of fun that Danica was, for the first time in her life, truly enjoying herself.

Before they could argue the point any further, the dropship circled around and returned to their position. Setting down thirty meters from them, the large plasma thrusters kicked up a small sandstorm, and they both shielded their eyes with their elbows and forearms.

Once it died down, they looked up to see the back ramp lower, and a familiar face appeared and sauntered down the ramp, stepping onto the sands.

"Lycia?" Brei asked. "Boy, are we glad to see you!"

Lycia smiled and then called out over her shoulder. "Found them!" As she turned her gaze toward the bomb, her eyes grew large with alarm. "Is that...?"

"Don't worry, this one here disarmed it."

Lycia raised her eyebrows and bobbed her head. "Good job," she said, turning to Brei, who merely grinned proudly.

"Come along, you two. We've got to get back to Arena City. I have a feeling something is going down in the arena."

Danica and Brei climbed aboard the dropship and greeted Raphine, who piloted it.

Lycia went and collected the bomb, hoisting it onto her shoulder as though it were a sack of potatoes. She then marched it back onto the ship where she safely stowed it in the netting.

"Don't want this to fall into the wrong hands again, now, do we?" she asked herself rhetorically, patting the bomb ever so gently.

When Lycia turned back around, Danica and Brei'Alas had begun strapping into the bench seats that ran along the interior wall.

"Um..." Lycia mumbled, only for Danica to look up at her. Lycia pointed at her breasts and then at Danica's. Danica looked down to see two dark rings soaking through her black shirt. "I think you might be leaking."

"It's just milk," Danica replied matter of factly and then finished buckling herself in.

"Delicious milk," Brei whispered to herself, licking her lips.

"What?" Lycia asked.

"What?" Brei asked, embarrassed that Lycia had heard her. Instead of admitting what she'd said, though, she feigned ignorance and pretended not to know what Lycia was talking about.

A small red and orange firebug, that matched the color of the desert at sunset, flew down from the dusty overhead rack and Brei, getting distracted as was her habit, pointed at it and said, "Ah, a pretty firebug!"

"Never mind," Lycia replied with a laugh. "I'll go see if we have an extra shirt in the storage locker that you can change into."

Lycia moved to the front of the cabin at the same time the dropship's plasma-ion turbines spooled up.

The ship climbed upward like a majestic whale, and once it reached the proper altitude, Raphine pointed the nose in the direction of Arena City.

"Hang on to your butts, ladies, cuz we're about to punch it in three, two, one..."

Raphine smashed the throttle forward and opened up the afterburners. The Falcon Heavy's engines roared as it tore through the wispy clouds high above the rolling dunes of Thessalonica.

20

Dazed and confused, the crowd slowly gathered themselves and turned their attention back to the fight, which had, seemingly, paused. Murmurs ran through the tiers of spectators as what they watched didn't make any sense. Jegra knelt submissively before her opponent, the Butcher of Endiva, Demeris Ferrison.

Demeris brushed back Jegra's long brown hair in a loving fashion, exposing her neck. Then, raising the korridium plated axe in his right hand, the only metal that could penetrate Jegra's nearly impervious skin, he prepared to sever her head from her shoulders.

"Is this your great champion?" Demeris Ferrison shouted up at the stunned audience. "Is this cowering woman who trembles before me pissing all over herself worthy of your adoration?"

A dead silence settled over the entire stadium and not a single person uttered a word. Was this the end of their empress?

Demeris Ferrison scanned all the faces looking back at him and he snickered. "That's what I thought," he said, taking the crowds silence as confirmation that he'd already won.

Slowly turning back to his task at hand, he prepared his final strike, "What is it you gladiators say, again? Victory or death? Well, at least you can die just as you began…as a worthless and unimportant slave."

Just then, a lone voice cut through the silence and cried out, "WE LOVE YOU JEGRA!"

Jegra's heavy-lidded eyes slowly raised toward the crowd. She searched the stadium stands to try and see where the voice had come from. She scanned all the faces until she settled upon a group of familiar ladies. Lycia, Raphine,

Danica, and Brei'Alas all stood together up in the stadium stands watching her.

She knew it was Brei who'd shouted out her love and affection. Her eyes, now brimming with tears, then settled on Danica, or, to be exact, whatever it was she was wearing.

Impossible though it seemed, Dani had on a baby blue t-shirt with a pretty pink bunnycorn on it. It was about two sizes too small and showed off her chest in a manner so risqué that it was downright absurd. Danica would never wear such a thing. Not even if it was the last article of clothing in the galaxy.

No, this wasn't right. This wasn't real. This was all just…

Jegra looked back over at Demeris Ferrison and the mass of golden tentacles undulating over him. She squinted hard and remembered what Hela had told her about making hallucinogens for him.

Had he dosed her? If so, with what? Some kind of fear serum? That must have been it. Her worst fear manifested itself the moment he had dosed her, and it had rendered her petrified. But this wasn't real. The baby blue and pink bunnycorn shirt proved it.

"None of this is real," she murmured under her breath.

"What was that?" he asked, pausing his lethal blow simply out of curiosity as to what the great Jegra's last words might be.

Jegra looked him squarely in the eyes and repeated her words—this time in a more commanding tone.

"None of this is real."

"Oh, I assure you, it is very real. As will be your death."

"No!" Jegra screamed, struggling to her feet.

Demeris panicked and brought the axe down, but Jegra caught his wrist, stopping him. She didn't make eye contact but merely kept her eyes cast upon the sands. In her mind, she replayed a thousand and one glorious battles. Then, she scoffed and said for all to hear, "Victory or death. You don't even know the meaning of the words."

With a chilling snap, she broke his arm and he squealed out in pain like a Tharterran hog being taken to the slaughterhouse. His axe landed on the dirt with a thud and, clutching his forearm just above the break while the rest of it dangled loosely, and almost tripping over his own feet, he scrambled back.

Disarmed and no longer a threat to her, Jegra let go of him and watched as the visage of H'aaztre retreated away from her, putting as much distance as he could between the two of them.

Jegra took a step forward, her downcast gaze blotting out her eyes with a dark shade and giving her an ominous look. Again, he scuttled away like a frightened crab. But unlike a crab, he had no shell to retreat into. No place to run to and no place to hide. He was exposed to the blazing hot Thessalonica sun, which beat down upon them with its sweltering intensity.

"You're not him, and this isn't real."

"See! She's gone insane!" Demeris Ferrison shouted up at the crowd, trying to convince them that their great leader was acting mentally unstable.

Jegra looked back up at the crowd and peered into their eyes. She spun in a circle, making sure to scan the myriad of faces from all over the Commonwealth and beyond. She held up her fist and shouted in a voice filled with rage and determination, "Victory or death!!!"

The entire stadium erupted with cheers and then quickly settled into a familiar chant. From their lips, they chanted her name with praise and adoration.

JEGRA! JEGRA! JEGRA!

She glanced back at where Danica, Brei, Lycia, and Raphine stood and smiled up at them. Then, Lycia held something up. It was the lifeless shell of a disarmed and dismantled bomb. Demeris Ferrison's bomb.

A wide grin spread across Jegra's lips as it dawned on her the only leverage he'd had over her was now gone. Slowly, deliberately, she turned back to face Demeris.

"Wait…why are you looking at me like that?" He backed up further, raising his good hand defensively while he let the other drop down to his side. "Let's talk about this."

"You killed innocent Nyctans. You killed and maimed innocent Thessalonicans. You even murdered your own beloved Dagoni people. But, perhaps the most grotesque crime of all, you sold your sister, the woman I love, into bondage and sexual slavery. All for what? So, you could die here, upon the sands, pissing yourself like the coward you are."

"Die?" Demeris scoffed. "So be it. But it will be a martyr's death. In time, the people will come to understand my sacrifice here this day. Everything I did…it was all for the greater good. It was to regain that glory that was taken from us."

"I hate to disappoint you, but there never was any such time. Those glory days you're so fond of never really existed. Things have always been messy and complicated. That's just the way the world is. All you can do is face each day with an open mind and an open heart. After all, you only get out of the world what you put into it. The question is, do you only want to sling mud and hate, or do you want to spread love and kindness? I know which one I choose."

"Which is why you'll never defeat me, pink-skin. Your constitution is as weak as your belly is soft. You choose to do right over doing what you must, but let me tell you, hate can be a powerful motivator. Hate can—"

Demeris Ferrison's head suddenly evaporated into a cloudy pink mist of brain matter and blood laced with particulates of bone finer than the grains of sand they landed upon.

In the mere blink of an eye, Jegra's fist had moved so fast that even the televid drones couldn't catch her movements on video. Even the slow-motion replay up on the large viewscreens on either end of the stadium merely showed a blur passing through Demeris Ferrison's body and then his head instantaneously rupturing and turning into a cloud of gore.

She stood ten feet beyond Demeris Ferrison's back, holding her clenched fist out in a warrior's pose. Slowly, she craned her neck back around and looked over her shoulder at his headless body, which teetered for a bit, gently swaying back and forth.

In the next instant, his decapitated torso toppled over and fell into a heap on the ground with a hollow-sounding thud, just as little droplets of mist condensed on the arena sands coating the surrounding area in an unbroken crimson veil.

"You forgot one important thing, Demeris," she said, addressing his corpse as though he could still hear her. "I'm the Mother of Dagon. And a mother protects all her children, at any cost. The world be dammed. And you, dickhole, picked the wrong mother to mess with."

As a mother herself, Jegra knew that a mother's love was so great she'd burn down the world to avenge her children. It was this same passionate emotion that surged through her now, empowering her to overcome the hallucinogenic-spawned illusion of H'aaztre and defeat her opponent once and for all.

Jegra casually got up and shook the drops of blood from her knuckles. She had more to say, but the day was getting on and she was tired, thirsty, and wanted nothing more than to be with her lovely wives.

"Ladies and gentlemen," the announcer's booming voice sounded with a crackle of the speakers, "the continued reigning and still undefeated champion, Jegra Alakandra!"

The audience erupted with cheers and applause that flooded every inch of the arena. Streamers of confetti and fireworks went off and Danica, Brei'Alas, Lycia, and Raphine all embraced one another in one massive group hug and jumped up and down excitedly.

Jegra, unable to keep a straight face, began to laugh at their exuberance and, from somewhere in the distance, cutting through the white noise of celebration, came the gentle melody and the soft voice of a bard singing a familiar song. A song for the galaxy—her song.

Three-thirty rolled around, and the celebrations in the streets of Arena City hadn't died down yet.

Tonight, the fans of the Intergalactic Gladiatorial Games had seen something they hadn't seen in ages—the champion defending her title and her honor in the arena.

Jegra hadn't had an official match since she intervened in Danica's humiliation bout, but now, after several years of her absence and declining ratings, she made a comeback in a big way. It was also the first time a member of royalty fought for a title belt in the arena and not just for show.

But more than simply another victory notch on her belt, Jegra had defeated the terrorist Demeris Ferrison and foiled his plot to destabilize the peace she had struggled for the past several years to instill in the hearts and minds of the people. Perchance to forge a new galactic trust among the various planetary systems.

Now, at long last, she could rest. And as she stowed away in her palace overlooking Arena City, the people celebrated her great victory. Not only was the war still fresh in their minds, but today's spectacle was one for the ages, and it gave them a great hope that the peace Jegra had brought to their world and countless others would be a lasting one.

"How long do you think they'll keep on like that?" Brei asked from the balcony window of Arena Palace.

"At least well into the morning," Jegra replied. "Now, come back to bed, my love. We grow cold without your warmth."

Brei turned around. Her pink, babydoll chemise teddy's lace V-neck looking fetching on her soft blue skin, she smiled at the bed full of practically naked women.

Like Brei, most of Jegra's harem wore comfortable teddies or lingerie. Raven had on a bright yellow camisole, minus any bottoms, while Danica wore dark purple floral lingerie with garter straps, and Jegra had on floral lace lingerie in tangerine.

All the wives lay tangled up on the bed, all relaxed and lounging as they chatted about everything and nothing.

It was the first time they'd all been together during a time of peace and tranquility without anything to interrupt them and prevent them from catching up with one another—that is, until the fireworks going off over the city had distracted Brei and drawn her to the window like a moth to the flame.

Danica sat up and opened her arms, inviting Brei into them. As Brei made her way back to the bed, she swung by the bowl of fruit sitting on a table at the foot of the bed and plucked some grapes from it. She popped one into her mouth and fed the other one to Danica.

At the same time, Jegra and Raven's hands were clasped, their fingers threading together like a couple of lovestruck teenagers. They brushed their noses together with Eskimo kisses, basking in one another's company.

"So, have you two lovebirds decided on a wedding date?" Brei inquired, looking across the bed at Raven and Jegra with inquisitive eyes.

"Not exactly," Raven said, looking to Jegra to see if it would be all right to share the news. Jegra nodded. "You see, we sort of already tied the knot."

"You did?" Danica asked.

"When?" Brei chimed in.

"We had Grendok do it in secret aboard the *Skywend* right before all this bomb nonsense began. Naturally, as the king of Galliforn people, he has the authority to—"

"Wait? Grendok is a king?" Brei gasped out in disbelief.

Jegra looked over at Danica and Brei's blank faces. "I thought you knew…"

"Apparently," Danica complained, "I'm the last one to learn anything these days."

"I'm sorry about that," Jegra responded. "I'll try harder to keep you in the loop from now on."

"It's okay," Danica said, waving her hand nonchalantly. "This one keeps me busy." She wrapped her arms around Brei, who settled in and reclined against her soft, warm body. Burying her face in Brei's hair, she kissed the back of Brei's neck and let the lilac scent of her purple and pink ombre hair fill her nose.

"What about the babies?" Brei asked, eyeing the slight baby bump on Jegra's stomach. It was barely noticeable, but it had been three months since her pregnancy began. "How are they doing?"

"We're only three months into our pregnancies, but so far so good."

"Do you know if you're having a boy or a girl?"

"Boy," Jegra answered.

"Girl," Raven said at the same time.

They laughed at their simultaneous gaffe and then repeated their answers but spoke over each other again which, in turn, prompted more laughter.

"That's wonderful! Maybe someday they'll become the rulers of the empire."

Jegra laughed. "It's a nice thought. But they have no royal blood in them, and so have no traditional claim to the throne. My baby is from Callestra Van Morgan, and Raven's is from Ladgara Vassex."

"Ah, bak've'mesh," Danica grumbled, cursing the name of her sworn enemy and waving her hand about in the air as though she were swatting at Borellian mosquitos. When she looked up, everyone was staring at her. "That woman is a pain in my neck."

"But even though these kids of ours are mixed blood, we will love them all the same."

"Purity is overrated anyway," Danica added.

Raven laughed out loud and Danica shot her a wounded look. "What?"

"You didn't use to think so," Raven reminded her, a touch of the judgmental hidden in her voice.

"She's right, you know," Jegra said, defusing the building intensity between them before they started going at it like a couple of alley cats. "There was a time when the thought of being with me made your skin crawl."

"I was a narrow-minded fool back then. Like my brother before me, I bought into the lie we told ourselves, that Dagoni people were superior to all other races and therefore destined to inherit the world. We believed that we were the last bloodline descended from the Progenitors themselves, and that we one day would ascend to godhood and rule over the cosmos as they once did."

"You do realize how absurd that sounds, right?" Raven asked.

"I do now," Danica replied. "It took being tortured, humiliated, sold into slavery, battered and broken, and wishing I could just roll over and die to finally understand what Jegra had been through. And through it all, she still chose to find the good in others. It was then that I realized, nothing I had believed served a greater purpose. At the end of the day, no matter our race or what planet we come from—we're all the same. We're all just trying to survive the best we can in a vast and indifferent universe. And, like Jegra has always said, if we don't have love, then we don't have anything."

They shared a smile, and all their past squabbles and gripes with one another melted away in one act of mutual acceptance.

They didn't love each other in the romantic sense, but they loved the same woman with the same fiery passion, and that bonded them in the rarest of sisterhoods. A sisterhood more loyal than even that of the Carcosan virgins.

They were the wives of the one true empress of Dagon. And they had made a solemn promise to forever remain faithful to Jegra, as long as their hearts beat and they continued to draw breath from their breasts.

"Wait just one nanosecond," Brei said, thinking out loud as if a startling revelation had dawned on her. "If Lycia is half Dakroth, then what about all of the other clones? Couldn't they claim the right to the crown too?"

"Not as long as I'm alive," Jegra informed her. "Which will probably be for a very long time, given what we know about Old Lady Jegra's timeline."

"You see," Danica informed Brei, "Jegra claimed only one legitimate daughter and heir to the throne, and that's Lycia. As far as Dagon customs go, only the legitimate child of both the empress and the emperor can be crowned the new ruler of the Dagon Empire."

"Phew!" Brei said, wiping away the perspiration on her forehead. "That's a huge relief."

"Okay, ladies," Jegra said, letting a yawn slip out. "It's already four AM and the Northeastern sun is rising. We best get some shut-eye before tomorrow, because we have Lycia's coronation to attend."

"I still can't believe you're abdicating the throne," Danica said. All the other women nodded along with her consideration.

"I'm with Danica on this one," Raven chimed in. "I think you should hold off. At least for another year. So much has happened, it just seems…"

"Premature?" Jegra asked.

Raven, Brei, and Danica all nodded.

Jegra shook her head and looked away, her eyes cast down at the ornate carpet on the floor, a melancholy look settling across her face.

"You might be right about that. But, this war, everything we've been through together. It's taken its toll. I've done all I can hope to do. The rest will be up to the next generation to handle."

"Regardless, we still love you," Brei stated emphatically. She then crawled across the bed to Jegra and looked down into her upside-down eyes as Jegra rolled onto her back to gaze up at Brei's beautiful amber eyes. Inverted on the center of the bed, Brei bent down and kissed Jegra on her lips.

Danica smiled and looked over at Raven, who'd already nodded off to sleep.

Then, like a tiny blue Torpsian koala, Brei curled up in Jegra's arms, and they, too, drifted away, letting the Sandman take them to that blissful realm of serene and uninterrupted slumber.

Danica's eyelids grew heavy and she dozed off, coming in and out of sleep just as the sun peeked above the distant horizon.

Blowing in on the early morning breeze came a familiar tune. It was that familiar song again—Jegra's song.

Its notes and soothing melodies swirled about their sleepy heads, filling the room with a kind of reverie that slowly put everyone and everything at ease.

Stifling a yawn with her fist, Danica, barely able to keep awake, reached over and detached her prosthetic arm. She set it on the bedside table and then, rolling over, took one last gander at the coterie of beautiful women in bed with her. She clutched a pillow in her good arm and drifted off to sleep.

21

Golden rays beamed in through the windows and basked Jegra's body in their warmth. An early morning groan of protest escaped her lips and she rolled over and covered her face with a pillow.

A few moments later, the bustle of noise and voices chatting drew her back out of her lazy slumbering and she awoke to find herself lying in bed alone while a busy swarm of wives raced about her room preparing themselves.

"What's going on?" she asked in a long, drawn-out manner as she stretched her arms over her head and let out a long yawn.

"We slept in!" Brei squealed with nervous excitement. "That's what."

"What?!" Jegra asked, sitting up in bed.

"Don't worry about it," Danica consoled, "we only overslept by forty-five minutes. We still have plenty of time to get ready for the coronation."

"The royal hairstylists and dressers will be here soon to start working on you," Raven said, reaching out her hands and offering Jegra to take them. Jegra did so and Raven hoisted her out of bed. "And you, babe, need a bath."

"Ugh," Jegra grumbled, rolling her eyes. "Do I have to?"

"YES!" all three wives shouted at the same time from various locations around the room.

This startled Jegra and she scanned all their faces with a shocked look. "Do I smell that bad?" she asked, sniffing her armpit just to be sure.

"It's not that," Raven said. "It's just that the dressing of the Empress takes three hours and you're already behind schedule as it is."

"Alright, alright," Jegra said as Raven nudged her toward the bath. "I'm going."

Jegra peeled and sunk into the large pool-styled bath built right into her floor. Raven stripped and came in with her, which caused her to raise an eyebrow. "What are you doing?"

Raven wasted no time and grabbed a charcoal loofah and a bar of organically made soap with small orange flecks of dehydrated Correllian mango mixed in.

"Somebody needs to scrub your back."

Jegra dipped down in the water as Raven attacked her with the loofah. "Ow," Jegra yelped, "Not so rough."

"Sorry," Raven said, using a gentler touch and softer circular motions, applying the soap with one hand and the loofah with the other.

The mango soap and charcoal blended to create a gray, creamy lather. Once it was thick enough, Raven held out her hand and Danica raced by in time to hand off a large men's straight-edge shaving blade. The same kind that traditional barbers used to use.

"What's that?" Jegra asked, her eyes widening.

"I'm going to shave every nanometer of your body from the neck down," Raven said.

"Everything?" Jegra gulped. She looked down at herself when Raven quickly reached around from behind her and pressed the blade to her throat.

"Don't move a muscle," she whispered into Jegra's ear and then slowly grazed the surface of Jegra's throat with the impossibly sharp blade.

The scraping noise it made against her hardened skin was oddly satisfying and she closed her eyes and let Raven do her job. As she breathed in the scent of mango, she couldn't help but feel like she was being overly pampered. Not that that was a bad thing. It just wasn't something she was used to.

After Raven had finished, Brei helped Jegra out of the bath and began to dab her body off with super soft towels. The towels were made from Tuluvian cotton, much like Egyptian cotton, and were of a super fine weave and extra soft.

Almost as soon as Brei had finished, a full team of dressers and stylists burst into the room like a small army. They descended on Jegra and brought her over to a hairdressing and makeup station which had manifested in a golden beam of light.

"See you later," Brei said, giving Jegra a peck on the lips.

Jegra was about to speak when Raven added, "We'll see you at the coronation."

"I, ah…" Jegra began as she turned around only to run smack dab into Danica's lips, which silenced her.

"Mmmm," Jegra said as Danica let the sweet juices of the peach she'd been eating flood into Jegra's mouth. They kissed a little more deeply, still smacking on one another's lips as a team of Bre'lal and Salamandarian women pried them apart.

Jegra smiled at Danica and then let the women do their jobs. Danica clapped her hands and motioned for the other wives to accompany her.

"Come along," she said, "There's much to do and too little time to do it in."

Lycia looked at herself in the mirror. She was covered head to toe in the most ornate and elaborate dress she'd ever seen. It was silver with silver floral embroidery running up the full length of the dress.

Its mock corset doubled as light body armor and had the same floral pattern, laser-etched korridium design that continued up to the chest. Armored breastplates covered the strapless dress, and linking the two plates together was a replica of Jegra's tyrannosaur tooth which she had strapped to her metal gladiatrix bikini. A small design flourish that made Lycia recognizable as Jegra's daughter.

She felt like a Sultan's daughter, and in addition to the extravagant dress, her very skin had been garishly encrusted with over a thousand diamonds.

Appearing by her side was Raphine, who was dressed in a fancy evening gown but looked like a peasant wearing common rags compared to Lycia.

"I look ridiculous."

"Perhaps. But you must look how your people expect their future empress to look."

"I'm all sparkly," she said, turning slowly and examining the fine details of the ornate and garishly extravagant dress she had on.

"You look stunning," Raphine said, her smile widening as she watched Lycia roll her eyes.

In the background, Allie whined and Raphine threw her hands on her hips and turned to the giant indigo panther.

"I know, but try telling her that!"

"I'll always be envious of how you two can do that."

Raphine smiled and then translated the thoughts that Allie had sent her. "Allie says you look like a thousand glittering fireflies, by the way. Her way of saying you look stunning."

Lycia smiled and turned to Allie. "Thanks, puss. You're pretty darn gorgeous yourself."

Allie chuffed lightly and began grooming herself with her large pink tongue.

Lycia turned back toward the mirror and studied herself a little while longer before letting out a prolonged sigh.

"You ready for this?"

"As ready as I'll ever be, I suppose."

Raphine held out her hand and Lycia took it. As they headed toward the balcony, Allie got up and followed them.

Lycia stepped out onto the main balcony of the Imperial Palace on Dagon Prime. Thousands had already filled the square and cheered as she appeared to them. She raised her left hand and waved and smiled, but it all felt so artificial.

"Just keep smiling," Raphine whispered from the corner of her mouth.

"But my face is already tired," Lycia whispered back through her artificial grin, a hint of distress in her words.

"That doesn't matter," Raphine said. "You need to set a good first impression. Until just a few weeks ago, nobody even knew you existed."

"All this whispering is making my face even more tired," she said. This of course was met with a rather sharp pinch from Raphine, who pinched Lycia's ass so hard she was forced to muffle a yelp with a bird-like chirp.

Just then Jegra's yacht, a large shuttlecraft with four decks, a pearlescent hull, and a sleek and elegant design flew over the crowd, drowning out their cheers with its plasma ion turbines.

The massive shuttle circled about, rose up and then set down in the palace garden, disappearing behind the gleaming spires of the palace.

"Princess Alakandra," a familiar voice said from behind them.

Lycia and Raphine turned to see Admiral Grendok in his dress uniform extending his elbow for Lycia to take.

"It's time."

She nodded and then, squeezing Raphine's hand tightly in hers, she said, "Don't leave me."

"I won't. I'll be by your side the whole time."

With her free elbow, she accepted Grendok's offer and all three turned to the crowd one last time before retreating inside the palace to go to the throne room where Lycia's coronation would be completed.

Somewhere close by, Hela opened the cryosleep pod labeled Artemis CLXVIII. The air of the cylinder decompressed with a hiss and a steady stream of steam bellowed out as the supercooled liquid hydrogen leaked onto the floor, flooding the room with a uniform mist.

The sleeping Artemis clone inside slowly cracked her eyes open and took a moment to process the fact that she'd been awakened. "Where am I?" she asked in a coarse voice unaccustomed to speech. That's how Hela knew that she was brand new.

Hela let out a huge sigh of relief and, taking her hand in hers, said, "You're alive. I saved you."

Artemis sat up and immediately felt a terrible headache. Groaning, she pulled her hand away reached up and began to massage her temples to help alleviate some of the needling pain.

"I wasn't sure the backup would work this time. The nature of your demise was, well, shall we say, rather grisly? But, lucky for you, I was running an active scan on you down in the arena to monitor your vitals and I managed to salvage an eighty-nine percent accurate neural map."

"Back up? Neural map? What are you talking about?"

Hela looked at the Artemis sitting in front of her and held up a mirror. "There's something you need to know."

She took the mirror and looked at herself. After a moment of silence, she burst into laughter.

"It was the only way," Hela informed.

Artemis climbed out of her capsule like a vampire rising from a coffin. Her legs a bit wobbly underneath her, like that of a newborn foal, she finally got her footing and straightened up. "You thought making me into one of your abominations would make me happy?"

Hela backed up slowly and tried her best to explain. "The circumstances were rather bleak. You need to understand, I hadn't tried a backup of anyone conscious, let alone under as much duress as you were. That fact that the neurological engram took is rather quite miraculous."

Artemis clutched Hela by the throat and slammed her up against the wall of the lab. "So, you resurrected me inside this unholy vessel?"

"Demeris," Hela gasped, "You're choking me. I can't...*ack*...breathe...*ack*."

Artemis's eyes only grew larger with rage and her hand squeezed down even tighter. "Tell me why I shouldn't let the life drain out of you right here and now?"

"Lycia," Hela gasped before her words were choked off completely.

"What about that half-breed?" Demeris Artemis asked.

Hela tapped Artemis's hand and she finally let go.

Collapsing onto her hands and knees, Hela's lungs rattled as she took in a deep breath. She took in too much air too quickly, and started coughing. Once she could speak, she looked up.

"As we speak, the empress is handing the crown over to Lycia, who will be inaugurated as the new Empress Regnant of the Dagon Empire and the United Commonwealth Cosmic Alliance."

"What does that have to do with me?"

"Have you looked in the mirror lately?" Hela said, a sinister grin curling onto her lips.

She slowly stood up, her lab coat flapping like a villain's cape on another gust of air kicked out by the stasis pod.

Demeris Artemis turned toward the wall mirror in the lab and examined her blue naked body. A smile slowly cracked her lips as it dawned on her what Hela was hinting at.

"We will replace the empress, and you will sit on the throne in her stead," Hela shared.

"Argh," Demeris groaned, her hands reaching up to her temple. "These headaches..."

"A small side effect of the process, I'm afraid. I wasn't able to get a clean imprint of your neural map since Jegra pulverized your head. But," she said, reaching into her pocket and drawing out some pills. Extending the three white pills in her hand, she added, "These should help alleviate the pain."

Demeris Artemis hastily snatched the pills out of Hela's hand and quickly popped them into her mouth. She swallowed them with a hard, dry swallow and then, closing her eyes, took a deep breath and let the pain recede away.

"Feel better?" Hela asked.

"Much." Demeris Artemis opened her eyes and turned back toward the mirror. Studying her new body some more, she smiled a truly wicked smile.

Hela reached up and tenderly touched Demeris's face. She'd fallen for him, even though she knew he was stubborn and had a single-minded vision that he obsessed over. But she also loved Artemis, and combining them had been her life's greatest achievement.

She drew his gaze to hers and looked upon her creation with great admiration. They looked into one another's eyes for a few seconds before Hela rose to her tiptoes and kissed Demeris Artemis's mouth.

She didn't kiss her back, but, rather, clutched her tightly by both wrists and shoved her against the lab table. The table rattled and a couple of glass beakers fell to the concrete floor and shattered.

Demeris clutched Hela by her throat with one arm and began tearing off her clothes as fast she could with her other. As she did this, her male organ unfurled and gradually began to stiffen with a startling erection.

"Whatever happens, just remember...you made me into this," Demeris Artemis growled. "This freak of nature."

"Wait," Hela said. "I didn't mean for..." before she could finish her sentence, however, Demeris tore her pants down and penetrated her. "*Ngh*...I just wanted to...*ngh*."

A sense of euphoric delight came over her as she was ravished. She liked it violent. She liked it dangerous. She didn't even consider this rape. To her, it was just foreplay. And, truth be told, she could totally understand needing to blow off a bit of steam after waking up in a different body.

"*Ngh*...I'm not...*ngh*..." Hela's eyes rolled back as the pleasure and pain combined to form an orgasm inside her center that slowly trickled out along her extremities as Demeris Artemis continued to ravish her. Soon, her groans of pain gave way to moans of pleasure and she leaned back and let him have his way with her.

Demeris Artemis's hands ran up Hela's chest and then came to rest on her throat. Slowly, she began to squeeze down, choking her again. When she asked,

"Do you want me to stop?" she merely shook her head.

"No," she whispered.

A cruel smile spread across Demeris Artemis's lips and she squeezed down harder, chocking Hela while continuing using her male organ in standard fashion.

A couple of minutes later, Demeris Artemis groaned out loud and then finished inside Hela. Satisfied, Demeris shoved her aside and she collapsed to her knees and then slid to the side, her head slumped as she looked dejected sitting on the floor.

Although sore, she ignored the minor wound inflicted upon her and just sat there in quiet obedience while Demeris looked down at her in disgust and then, with a smack of her teeth, abruptly turned away.

Before heading out the door, however, she snatched up Hela's lab coat for herself and wrapped up her nudity. Making her way over to the exit, she paused in the entrance and fixed her pink gaze upon Hela's face one last time.

"Get yourself cleaned up," she said in a judgmental tone. "We will continue with the next phase of your plan."

Hela smiled when Demeris acknowledged it was her plan. She had made him proud of her, and this filled her with overwhelming joy.

"I told you he never loved you," said a woman's voice a moment after Demeris had left the room.

Hela looked up to see her Artemis step out from the shadows and sidle up next to her. Had she been cloaked this whole time, watching the assault unfold?

"If you were watching, why didn't you stop it?"

"Because," Artemis III replied, "you never would have believed me. But now, you know. And, besides, it's not like you tried to resist. You wanted this to happen."

"So, you're blaming me for this?"

"Oh, that's so typical of you. Twisting everything I say around. Maybe try harder next time to pretend you don't like it so much."

Artemis extended a helping hand and helped Hela up. Hela had made her bed, now she had to sleep in it—bloody and cum-laced though it may be—it was her own bad choices which had gotten her into this mess. Artemis wasn't about to clean it up for her.

"Knowing you, my luv, you're already plotting your revenge. I can see it in your eyes and sense it by the slow, calm and collected beating of your heart that signifies a silent rage burning you up on the inside"

Hela looked at her and rubbed the bruises on her neck and smiled. "You know me too well, my luv," she said, her eyes narrowing and a cold, vicious smile forming on her lips.

In the next instant, Artemis drew back, a startled look taking hold of her as her throat grew impossibly tight and her insides began to boil. Choking, foam began to bubble up from her lips. Artemis crashed to the ground and began convulsing as though she were having a grand mal seizure.

Holding up a small translucent tab the size of a small seed, Hela said, "You don't think I couldn't have stopped it if I'd wanted to? I made you. And I can end you whenever I want."

Artemis III reached up with her hand to try and clasp onto Hela's sleeve but fell back down, spasmed once more, eyes rolling back in her head. Then, as one last breath escaped her Prussian blue lips, she rolled onto her back and was dead.

"The test was to see if you loved me or not. But there's a defect in the Artemis series that prevents any of you from experiencing anything in the way of genuine compassion. All you can do is emulate the emotions. But Demeris is the first consciousness I've implanted into a clone that seems to have genuine emotion. It may not be a perfect pairing, but at least I know where I stand with him. You, my dear, were just another failed attempt."

Hela tore off her ripped shirt and stripped off her tattered underwear. She then undressed the dead Artemis laying before her and put on her clothes.

Once she'd finished getting dressed, she stood back up and looked down at the dead body that resembled her own down to the genetic code one last time. "What I won't do for this goddamn empire," she said. Then, with a hop in her step, she briskly turned and exited the lab, leaving Artemis's corpse lying cold and naked on the floor.

At long last, the final moment had arrived and Jegra took off her crown and set it atop Lycia's head. Then, she whispered, "I'm proud of you," and took a step back and knelt.

Lycia drew up the ceremonial scepter and tapped both of Jegra's shoulders.

"Your service to this glorious Empire is done, and in this hallowed passing, I now accept the mantle of Mother of Dagon and the title of Empress Regnant. You served Dakroth well and I hope, you will heed my call, shall I ever need to summon you back to my side."

"I live only to serve the one true empress of Dagon," Jegra said, looking up at Lycia.

Lycia extended her hand and Jegra took it and kissed it.

"Rise, mother. Someone of your stature needn't kneel before me. I still have so much to learn from you."

"In time, my daughter. In time." Jegra rose and the two embraced. The crowd cheered and Jegra and Lycia turned together and descended the stairs.

The esteemed members of the council and high-ranking officers of the imperial navy applauded as they strode passed. Jegra looked over and spotted Captain Simon Calvec who stood off to one side of the red carpet with his recently reunited wife and daughter by his side. He bowed reverently and Jegra nodded in return.

They made their way along the red carpet and the doors were drawn open for them. They walked through the large hall and then out to the main entrance where Raphine, dressed in her ivory colored battle armor, and her royal guard with their royal blue capes and shimmering spears awaited them.

As they exited the palace a flurry of flashes from buzzing televid drones temporarily blinded them.

"This way, Your Grace," Raphine said, touching the small of Lycia's back and ushering her toward the hover coach drawn by mechanical stallions.

Jegra and Lycia climbed on board the ivory-colored carriage with red quilted leather seats. They would make their way through the main streets of the city, waving to the crowd and making a show of this momentous occasion as it would be written in the history books.

Jegra looked into the crowd and saw some human faces. There were Lycia clones, and Artemis clones, too. There was even a woman wearing a white lab coat that stared at her with an unnerving smile. But when Jegra made eye contact with her she feigned a cough and looked away.

Jegra's gaze lingered a minute longer, but the woman started chatting with one of the humans and Jegra brushed it aside as just her mind playing tricks on her.

As Jegra turned to step up into the coach, two Grendoks appeared by her side and helped hoist her up. She took her seat next to Lycia and the automated carriage started up the street, the clap of the robotic horse's hooves on the ornate brick path, designed with a fading chevron pattern, made a rhythmic beat that seemed to relax them both.

"I still can't believe I'm now the ruler of an entire galactic alliance of over eight-star systems," Lycia said.

"I couldn't think of anyone better suited for the job," Jegra said. "You have the charisma of your father and you have my sense of justice. You're kind to others, although you certainly can be a little mouthy at times."

"I prefer to think of it as sassy," Lycia retorted and they both laughed.

Lycia placed her hand on Jegra's lap and said, "I know I don't say this enough, but I never thanked you for everything that you've done for me. You even let me run when I needed to run. And you let me come back when I needed a home to come back to."

"Oh, sweetie," Jegra said placing her hand on Lycia's cheek. "This will always be your home." They both leaned in and hugged as the horses trotted along.

"I love you, mom," Lycia said, her cheek resting on Jegra's shoulder.

"I love you, Lycia, my daughter," Jegra replied, as she softly stroked her cheek. "Never forget that."

Lycia sank back into the plush leather seats, ran her fingers across the gold stitching, and took a deep breath.

"Don't worry," Jegra consoled. "We're almost done with this dreadfully long day. Once we finish here, I'll attend the banquet and you can go home, if you wish."

"No," Lycia said, taking Jegra's hand in hers. "I think I'd like to spend a little bit more time with you."

As she held Jegra's hand she turned her arm over and noticed the tattoo running up the inside of Jegra's forearm. "What's...*car-pe di-em* mean?" asked Lycia, sounding out the words and hoping she pronounced them right.

Jegra smiled. "It means never let a single moment pass you by. Take every chance, both good and bad, and come what may, you've at least learned something from the experience."

"I like that," Lycia said. Reaching back into the handbag she had, she pulled out her makeup wand, which was no bigger than a pen and was capable of burning makeup directly into the epidermis, and lasted for days. Of course, it could also be modified, scorching deeper into the layers, for making permanent tattoos.

Holding it up to Jegra's arm, she scanned the romantic styled letters of the tattoo. Then, holding it up to her arm, she burned the exact font into her forearm, giving herself a matching tattoo.

"From now on," Lycia said, admiring her new tattoo, "this will be a tradition that passes from empress to empress."

"I love that idea," Jegra replied. "A kind of unspoken initiation. A secret ceremony only among those of us who have had the pleasure of serving as the Mother of Dagon."

"You know I'll be getting more tattoos, right?" Lycia said. Then, gesturing with her hand, making circular motions over her chest, she added, "Like...all over my body."

Jegra just laughed and playfully nudged her with her shoulder so she popped up, but she quickly latched on to Jegra's arm and placed her head back down, resting it upon her shoulder again.

"I wish this moment could last forever," Lycia said with a satisfied and pleasant sigh.

This brought a tear to Jegra's eye and she threw her arm around Lycia's shoulder and drew her close. Lycia rested her head on Jegra's breast and smiled as the horses carried them toward the throng of adoring fans that awaited them on the outskirts of the city.

22

Evening rolled around and Thessalonica's horizon had cooled to a deep purple hue. Sitting on a bluff that overlooked Arena City, was Jegra's palace. The palace lights came on and lit up the evening sky like a beacon of hope that shone across the violet tinted dunes.

Inside the great hall came the sounds of merriment as the banquet ran overly long and the dignitaries and guests from other worlds got properly drunk. Their loud chatter carried out into every wing of the palace and Lycia, properly exhausted, decided to slink away.

After making an appearance and schmoozing with the dignitaries from the other planets as well as the governors of Dagon's twelve city-states, Lycia was beat. So, she used the secret passage behind the curtains that framed the tapestry and entered a side passage that led out to the main corridor.

A couple of her royal guards spotted her and quickly ushered her to the other end, fending off several drunken attempts by the attendees to get a word in edgewise with her. Once they'd helped her to the far end, she exited the main hall and took the adjoining hall back toward the residential wing of the place.

Navigating the various corridors and passages of the palace, she realized, was like navigating a veritable labyrinth. Leaning against the wall in the center of the corridor, she slipped off her heels and sighed with a great big breath of relief that sounded as though she were thankful just to be alive.

"This way, Your Majesty," the guardsman said, gesturing for her to make her way to the end of the long passage. When she arrived, he opened the door for her and then took his post. Another guard was on the other side of the door and he gestured for her to continue up the passage.

She walked along, feeling exhausted and sleepy. She yawned and as she tilted her head back, then, in the reflection of the glass upon the large windows that lined the hallway, she caught a glimpse of the guard behind her with a syringe in his hands as he was about to strike her from behind.

She quickly spun around but, regrettably, was too late. The syringe entered her neck and she mumbled a curt turn of phrase before passing out into the arms of the soldier.

Three Artemis clones decloaked and one of them began undressing. "Help me get her out of these clothes," Demeris Artemis said, slipping out of their tactical outfit. "We have to be quick about it so as not to draw any suspicion."

Afriel did as asked and began stripping Lycia's dress off of her. One of the other Artemises helped while the third stood at the end of the corridor as their lookout.

Once they'd managed to get Lycia out of her dress, Demeris Artemis quickly shed her clothes and started pulling on Lycia's dress. At the same time, Afriel and the second Artemis placed teleportation enhancers onto Lycia. In a swirl of red light, all three beamed away.

"Quick," the Artemis on watch, said, "someone is coming."

She raced up to Demeris Artemis and helped her strap up the back of the dress, then, drawing up a makeup wand, she did Demeris's makeup to match Lycia's.

"What about the jewels?" Artemis asked.

"Don't worry about it, I'll come up with some kind of excuse." Artemis hastily finished with the straps and then quickly stepped up against the wall and tapped her holovid bracelet and vanished in a shroud of invisibility.

"There you are," a voice came from behind.

Demeris Artemis spun around in time to find a green Bre'lal woman saunter up to her and, leaning in, kiss her on the lips.

"I've been looking all over for you."

"Well, here I am," Demeris said, trying her best to sound youthful and cheery, just as Lycia always seems to sound.

"I see you've already begun to try to get out of your gown," Raphine said, looking at some of the loose straps on her back.

"I just want this night to be over with," Demeris said in an overly whiny sounding voice.

Raphine laughed. "No need to play it up with me. I know how much you hate social functions." She reached down and took Lycia's hand—or what she thought was Lycia's hand—and then nodded up the corridor. "Come along, El, I have some nice bath salts and some birtchkum oil waiting for you. I'll give you a nice long, relaxing massage. It's guaranteed to take your mind off everything and put you at ease."

"Sounds glorious!" Demeris exclaimed, switching from whiny to overly enthusiastic.

Raphine towed Demeris by her hand and guided her up the corridor. She then raised her wrist to the wall and a secret passage opened. The two of them ducked inside and Demeris looked back as the door quickly sealed shut behind them, not giving her shadow time to follow them in.

It didn't matter though, she could take on a measly Bre'lal woman if she needed to. But right now, she just had to play along long enough to convince Lycia's pet girlfriend that she was the genuine deal.

After her long back massage, Demeris rolled over and pulled Raphine close. Raphine only had on a towel which she'd wrapped up in after their bath together.

Holding her hand, Demeris smiled and said, "You're too good to me. I don't deserve you."

"Maybe, but, then again, perhaps you can make it up to me," Raphine said as she unfurled the towel and let it drop to the floor.

Climbing onto the massage table, she slid her green body along Demeris's greased up one, the birtchkum oil allowing her to glide effortlessly across the blue skin as though it were the wide blue ocean itself.

Raphine gazed into Demeris's eyes for the longest time, causing her to grow self-conscious. "What is it?" For a split second, Demeris thought that she might know something. But when Raphine smiled, all her worries melted away.

"Nothing, I just love you. That's all." All of a sudden, Raphine felt something and looked down between their legs and then back up at those beautiful pink eyes. "Oh, yeah?"

Demeris Artemis looked back up and smiled coyly. "I hope it's alright."

"It's fine by me, my empress," Raphine said, taking the shaft of the vestigial organ in her hand and gently stroking it. "Anything for the Mother of all Dagon."

"Isn't it weird," Demeris said, "that none of the females in Jegra's species have penises?"

"Their males don't have ovaries either," Raphine pointed out. She then stopped mid-stroke. "Is this your weird idea of foreplay?" she teased.

"Sorry," Demeris Artemis apologized, trying not to sound overly suspicious. "I've just been distracted as of late."

Raphine slid it between her legs and slowly sat down. As she did, Demeris Artemis let out an audible moan filled with unimaginable pleasure. Were these Lycia bodies more sensitive than normal bodies? No wonder they were so horny all of the time. If sex felt like this every time, she wouldn't want to ever stop having it.

"And my species has seven biological sexes and is entirely pansexual. Something we have never taken for granted," Raphine informed her. "Allow me to demonstrate."

She tossed her forest green hair over her shoulders and arched her back, pushing her hips back as far as she could as she rode her girlfriend's erection.

Raphine knew that in Dagon culture, having a penis was no stranger than having arms or legs. Both sexes had them. It was normal. The same went for ovaries.

Although the vestigial penis worked well enough in most of the genetically female half of the species, it didn't always produce sperm. And while most of the genetic male half of the species had ovaries, their uteruses were often underdeveloped. But in both cases, there were enough instances of men having babies and women impregnating their partners as for it not to be unusual to anyone.

People in the Dagon species were primarily intersex and therefore intersexual. That's just how it was.

As for gender, she understood that it depended more upon the individual and their particular mood for the day. If you felt more like a woman in one instant, or a man in the next, or something in between, there was a wide range of variations to choose from and everything was perfectly acceptable.

Nobody looked twice at a short, bearded predominantly male looking person with saggy breasts in a floral summer dress or a woman in slacks with an overly large bulge in her crotch area. These sights weren't oddities on Dagon Prime. They were the norm.

Nowadays, instead of standing in the way of people's gender identity, they supported one another. The fashion and makeup industries boomed too because instead of catering to only half the population, they had a vaster market to appeal to.

Demeris reached up and grabbed Raphine's avocado-colored hips as she rose up and down on her.

"Do you feel good?" Raphine asked.

She continued riding with slow, deliberate motions, never going as fast as Demeris would have liked. But this little tease prolonged the session and drove her wild with a state of pure orgasmic reverie.

"Don't ever stop," Demeris replied, her eyes closed as she soaked up every little sensation.

A few minutes later, Demeris climaxed, gasping out for breath, and then fell back onto the narrow massage bed. Panting, she tried to catch her breath as Raphine simply laid down atop of her, their glistening flesh coming together.

It wasn't the best sex they'd ever had, but it wasn't the worst either. Raphine chalked up Lycia's decreased stamina to being exhausted by the day's events. She wrapped her arms around her and stirring in and out of wakefulness, she whispered, "We can do it again if you want."

Demeris sat up rather abruptly, forcing Raphine off her. "I think I'll just turn in for the night."

As strange and sudden as that was, she then climbed off the table and went over to the bed without so much as waiting for Raphine. Fetching the nightie that was waiting on the edge of the bed for her, she slipped it on and then climbed under the covers and pretended to go to sleep.

Raphine, finding it peculiar that Lycia was treating her like a common servant girl, grew angry and stamped her foot. "You're not getting rid of me that easily." She then marched over to the bed, climbed in with her blue-skinned lover, and, cozying up to her, wrapped her arms around her and spooned her.

Demeris looked out of the corner of her eyes, trying to seem incognizant. She didn't know how Lycia normally acted, but when Raphine's hand reached around and began to gently massage her female parts, she bit her bottom lip and moaned. Her entire body was still sensitive from their last session.

After a minute, Demeris reached down and clutched Raphine's hand in hers. "As much as I'd love to go another round with you, my luv, I'm spent. Do you think we could do this again some other time?"

Raphine looked down at her lover and smiled. "Sure. Anything my empress wants."

"I don't mean to brush you off…it's just that…"

"No, I get it," Raphine replied. "You're exhausted. Get some rest."

She bent down and gently kissed Lycia on her lips and, with that, Raphine rolled over and stared at the wall with a look of intense frustration. This wasn't like Lycia. She never turned down sex. Never.

And for whatever reason, it didn't feel as though she was kissing her back. She was just receiving the kisses. There wasn't any passion or desire behind the touch of her lips. It was as though she were merely carrying out a formality.

Is that what our relationship has become? she wondered. Had they shot past the honeymoon phase already?

When Lycia came to, she snapped awake, took in a deep breath, and shook her head as she forced herself to be clear-headed. Eyes wide open, she tugged on her arm only to find she was strapped down to some kind of surgical table.

Another jerk of her wrists and her feet confirmed that she was bound and shackled. "Where am I?"

"You're in my private lab aboard the *Avarice.*"

"The pirate ship?"

"I had to get off Dagon Prime and make myself scarce, now didn't I? Well, the nice thing about pirates is that you can always strike a deal with them because they all have a price."

Hela stepped up to the side of the bed and pulled the light over her so that it shone down on Lycia's torso. Drawing up a scalpel, she licked her lips and looked down at Lycia's chest.

"What are you going to do?"

"You have a Dygra crystal I want."

"No," Lycia protested. "You can't."

"Oh, but I can," Hela said, pulling on her surgical mask. "I was denied my rightful place by Dakroth's side. Now I have to settle for second fiddle…no thanks to you."

"Me? But I didn't do anything."

"You stole my legacy," Hela said bitterly. With that, she pressed the knife into Lycia's blue flesh and created an incision.

Lycia screamed out, her breathing shallow and rapid. "Don't do this," she said. "I can give you whatever you want."

"Thanks, but you already are," Hela answered, cutting even deeper into Lycia's flesh and drawing out more screams from her lips.

Hela cut deep, and Lycia's eyes rolled back as the pain became unbearable and passed out.

Hela ignored Lycia's vitals and simply cut around the bonds to the crystal. After another few minutes, Hela set down her scalpel and reached into Lycia's chest and drew out the crystal. Holding it up in the air with bloody fingers, she smiled as she examined its pink, pulsing beauty.

"At last," she whispered. "I have my own Dygra."

Lycia started to come to at just that exact moment and opened her eyes. She saw Hela holding up the pulsing crystal and then looked down at her chest only to find a gruesome and gaping hole where her energy source once was.

Lycia screamed with everything she had left and promptly passed out again. Hela merely removed her mask and then waved over a doctor she had on standby. Handing the crystal over to the other medic, she climbed onto an operating table next to Lycia's.

"I want this inside of me."

The doctor merely nodded and setting the gore smattered crystal in a metal tray beside him, he then picked up a new scalpel and drew close to Hela.

"Will you be needing any anesthetic, doctor?" he asked.

"No," she said. "Just do what you're here to do."

He nodded and then pressed the blade into Hela's chest. As he sliced her open, she bit her bottom lip and moaned sensually. Pain for her was the purest form of pleasure. And she could feel the orgasm already building inside of her.

Reaching up, she clutched the doctor's hand in hers and growled, "No need to be so clean, doctor."

Then, holding onto his hand she dragged the blade down her chest, all the way to her abdomen to the complete dismay of the ship's regular physician. She cried out with lust laden moans as she helped him to mutilate her flesh.

Of course, being a Lycia clone, the nanites healed her mere seconds later, repairing her flesh in real-time. It was only when the doctor drew over the neutralizer lamp that its blue light seemed to put the nanites to sleep, and he was able to operate without interference.

Ignoring the strange, sadistic enjoyment she got out of each lacerating kiss of the scalpel, he continued with his job as commanded. Three hours later, the crystal was surgically transplanted into Hela, and he closed her back up. He tied off the last stitch and then cut the thread.

While he tidied up his tray of medical tools, Hela looked over at the unconscious Lycia lying beside her. With the blue lamp lighting up her chest wound, she looked like a gutted fish.

"You may not realize it, dear sister. But you've given me a new lease on life. For that, I'll forever be thankful to you."

It's too bad, then, Hela thought to herself, that Lycia had to die. But she'd served her purpose adequately, and now it was time to move on to phase two of her plan.

With her newly acquired powers, she would commandeer the *Avarice*, and use it to pummel the other bands of pirates into submission. Once she'd amassed herself a small army, she and her army of Artemis clones would descend on the United Commonwealth like a plague of locusts and begin a reign of terrorism that would make Dakroth's bloody campaigns pale in comparison.

Using terror to destabilize the system from the outside, Demeris Artemis, pretending to be Lycia, would work to destabilize it from the inside. Finally, an inside mole would leave the defense grid down, and Hela would attack the empire directly, striking like the viper she was.

After the safety of the empire was called into question, the senate would give Lycia full military authority to expel the foreign invaders. All the while playing up the propaganda to stoke the flames of suspicion and fear, Demeris Artemis would reign supreme.

It had been Hela's plan all along. And now that Demeris Artemis was in the position to become the new ruler of the empire, she'd do anything to see her one true love sit upon the throne.

23

The Dagon senate convened at the capitol building, its grand, white stone walls towering over the other buildings of the central district. It was a building designed to strike a sense of awe in all those who beheld it, with its ancient columns and ornate architecture. It had stood as the beacon of the Dagon Empire for more than three hundred years, ever since the old one was destroyed in the Dragonian and Dagon wars three centuries ago.

As her first official duty as the newly crowned Empress of the Dagon Empire, Lycia was to inscribe a new bill. As Empress, her bill would set the precedent for her rulership.

Lycia pushed through the massive doors to the main senatorial floor which creaked as they swung open, and she gallantly strode in.

Her long lavender dress flowed behind her like streamers of a kite on the wind as the special, ultra-light fabric danced on the slightest undulations of the air currents in the room.

The dress was designed in such a way as to make her look like a mermaid on land, if such a thing was possible. It was certainly aesthetically pleasing, she felt.

The chairman ushered her to the main podium and slammed the gavel with his mallet. "Hear! Hear! All rise for her eminence, the esteemed Empress Lycia Alakandra, newly crowned Mother of Dagon."

Lycia stepped up to the podium as the chairman bowed and backed away. With a small flourish of his hand, he gestured for her to proceed.

"Thank you, Chairman," she said, giving him a subtle nod. Then she turned toward the entire committee and looked up at the five televid drones hovering in front of her—all their telephoto lenses trained on her face.

"Ladies and gentlemen, members of the Dagon Imperial Council, and representatives of the Outer Colonies," she began, reaching into her dress and pulling out a small rolled-up scroll with a red ribbon on it from betwixt her cleavage.

"In these times, where aliens from distant stars can come from beyond the void and invade our space, and our homes, it is my understanding that we need stricter laws preventing future incursions by these so-called illegal aliens."

Subtle gasps sounded like the more liberal members of the senate were taken aback by this sudden change in policy. The conservative senators rose to their feet and began to clap. It was clear that Lycia had divided the room and so too, the people's confidence.

Instead of letting the moment get away from her, she smiled and leaned into the microphone so it could catch her every word. "The Dagon Empire is a symbol of prosperity and hope for many worlds within the empire, and by letting visitors from beyond our borders into our utopia, we have time and again seen our great oasis of peace and prosperity threatened by the corrosiveness of primitive cultures with barbaric practices and a disregard for the sanctity of life."

She paused as another wave of murmurs coursed through the senatorial chambers. She smiled more widely and continued. "We have fended off vengeful and envious races, we have stopped world conquerors in their tracks, but it is the steady erosion caused by a never-ending infusion of impure blood that threatens our great world, and, so too, the very empire itself. I will not let my legacy be 'the ruler who allowed Dagon Prime to grow weak.' I will not let this decay by outside forces to continue. Instead, I will cleanse our beloved empire of this impurity and bring back the pristine and sacrosanct vision that my father, Rhadamanthus Dakroth the Third, had for his cherished empire."

She paused and slid the ribbon off of the scroll and unrolled the document. Clearing her throat, she held it up in front of her face and began to read. "My first writ of legislation, by Imperial Decree, I present my revised immigration policy."

There was a long pause and a murmur of hushed whispers as people asked one another if they knew anything of Lycia's new bill.

"Henceforth, all permanent visas of non-nationals to the Dagon Empire shall be revoked. Only temporary travel visas will be granted. Anyone with an expired visa shall be granted two weeks to file for a new visa or will be fined and deported for overstaying their visa. Anyone deported from Dagon Prime or her occupied territories will automatically receive a five-year ban before they can reapply for a new travel visa."

Lycia slowly rolled up the paper and slipped the ribbon back on. Then, tucking it back into her blue cleavage, she looked up into the televid cameras of the drones and smiled a saccharin grin that was a substitute for the very real pleasure that Demeris Artemis, pretending to be Lycia, took from having dealt a crippling blow to the aliens that threatened the purity and prosperity of *her* empire.

"It is by my decree, as sovereign ruler of Dagon Prime and all her territories, that I invoke my authority as the sole arbiter of the law. This new policy shall be enacted immediately."

Lycia gathered her tresses and stepped down from the podium. Flashes went off as she strode up the aisle, leaving the chairman and other senators with stunned looks.

The laws that Lycia had just passed would set the empire back considerably in terms of trade, international business, and intergalactic cultural exchange. It was a highly conservative writ of law, even by traditional standards, and Jegra, who watched from her holovid screen at home on Thessalonica, couldn't help but feel something wasn't right.

Lycia wasn't the conservative type. She was liberal in almost every aspect of her life. In fact, it was programmed into her as a survival mechanism. She had to be able to adapt to alien cultures, if not to understand the enemy, then to blend in.

Whatever this little stunt was, Jegra had a feeling that it was more than just a plea for attention. No. She was positive something more was going on here.

Jegra sat up in her lounge chair and, stretching her arm over the back of it, turned to face Raphine, who stood behind the sofa watching with equal parts alarm and dismay. Arms folded, she frowned at the sudden developments plastering the televid news monitor. Why would Lycia do this? Didn't she know it would affect her, a green-skin, as well?

"Raphine, go collect your girlfriend and bring her here for breakfast. I wish to have a word with her."

Raphine nodded, and replied, "Yes, Your Grace." She bowed deeply and then quickly left Jegra to her thoughts.

Rising out of the lounge chair with all manner of fancy pillows, Jegra tightened the sash of her satin gown and turned toward the balcony. She didn't step out, but she watched the shuttle flights coming and going.

The sky traffic over Thessalonica was exceptionally busy today, and Lycia's new law would all but kill this level of trade. It was economic suicide, by her evaluation.

And even though Jegra had the protection of the crown, being royalty herself, if she hadn't been the former empress, this law would have surely affected her too.

This turn of events didn't bode well for anyone. Not for the empire and certainly not for those closest to Lycia. Something wasn't right.

This wasn't like her daughter. It was so out of character that Jegra was convinced there must be another explanation for this strange twist in events. And even though she didn't know who or what was behind this, she suspected it couldn't be good.

Something else was bothering her too. In all the commotion down in the jungle of Dagon Prime, Hela had managed to escape capture. If she was out there plotting to ruin Lycia, then Jegra had more worries than just a bit of bad policy.

Hela had proved to be quite formidable, and there was no telling how many clone soldiers she had at her disposal. Whatever she and Demeris Ferrison had been planning, Jegra had the sinking feeling that they were just beginning to find out the true reach of Ferrison's reign of terror.

Although it was closer to brunch, Jegra had the servants set the long, breakfast table and invited Raphine to dine with her and Lycia. If anyone could read Lycia, it was Raphine, and Jegra needed her help now more than ever if she hoped to get to the bottom of this unusual shift in personality.

Fruit platters were practically overflowing with the most delectable varieties of fruits from all over the empire, including the rare star-fruit of Abberdinia. A subtle reminder of the wealth you have as a commonwealth where you combine your economic and cultural surpluses and thereby lend to a lasting prosperity. The very opposite of what Lycia's policies seemed to be working toward.

"Interesting speech today," Jegra said dryly from the far end of the table.

Lycia merely nodded but didn't take the bait. It was obvious that she wasn't interested in talking intergalactic policy at the breakfast table.

Even so, Lycia had it wrong. Jegra cleared her throat and decided a more direct approach was in order. "The thing about diversity of culture is that it always makes yours richer and more prosperous as a people by adding to the wealth of the community." Jegra paused and waited for Lycia to respond, but when it was clear she had no interest in adding to the conversation, Jegra lightly cleared her throat and continued.

"New cultures bring new ideas, new ways of doing things, and ultimately new ways of thinking into the fold. It's this ability to expand one's scope of mind, to gain new knowledge, and to learn new ways of viewing the world around you, I think you'll find, that ultimately proves so beneficial in the realm of multiculturalism. Everyone prospers."

Lycia looked up and shrugged as if such a revelation was no big deal. And, still not caring enough to share her personal views, she went back to eating.

This wasn't like her, though. As long as Jegra had known her, Lycia had never been at a loss for words. She shared her mind regarding virtually everything, especially if it went against her mother's opinions.

Jegra looked over at Raphine, who sat next to her, and raised an eyebrow. Raphine, unable to provide any insights as to this irregular behavior of Lycia's just shook her head and shrugged in disbelief. Jegra and Raph turned their gazes back toward Lycia, who was dishing herself up some more fruit, and stared a while in reflective silence.

Every multicultural society Jegra knew of flourished while those that retreated into fear, hate, and discrimination corroded themselves with xenophobic and insular closedmindedness to the point their foundations gave way and they collapsed under the weight of their bigotry and ignorance.

What these blinkered xenophobes didn't seem to understand was that nobody ever lost their culture by adding to it. They only lost it when they subtracted everything away, including any sense of moral accountability, wisdom, and history, until nothing was left, not even a defensible identity.

Because, and this was the kicker, hate wasn't an identity. It was an attitude. And one that only begot fear and ignorance and then, in a cyclical fashion, fed on the same.

"Ideologies of hate never prosper," Jegra went on to add. "At least, not in the long run. Earth's history, I can honestly say, is full of examples of hateful ideologies that eventually had to surrender to better sense and more evolved moral principles. Principles based on tolerance and compassion."

Lycia put down her spoon and knife and looked across the table at Jegra. She then asked, "Are you saying that your Terran world was more advanced than ours? Than Dagon Prime?"

Jegra grew flustered, her face turning beet red. Raphine placed a green hand on Jegra's and did her best to diffuse the situation.

"I don't think that's what Jegra meant. I think she meant that things like fascism, racism, genetic discrimination, and other hateful ideologies that are propped up by fear and ignorance, have historically always destabilized cultures. It happened on my world, it's happened on yours, and it's still happening on other worlds."

"That's why we need stricter laws and regulations," Lycia informed them. "By suppressing such things before they take root and start to corrode our great society."

Jegra cleared her throat and began again. "Stricter laws only work so well," she informed. "And these laws won't fix things if they don't address the underlying problem."

"And what problem would that be, exactly?" Lycia asked, raising her eyebrow and looking Jegra straight in her eyes. As Demeris Artemis, she was genuinely interested in what the "root cause" would be, according to this outsider.

"Worldviews predicated on hate are divisive," Jegra shared. "They eventually lead to disagreement between groups, usually between the disenfranchised minority and the majority who hold all the power, and this can quickly turn into civil unrest. Protests. Rioting. And finally the call for reform. Sometimes the civil unrest gives rise to revolution wherein the very zeitgeist of a culture is called into question. And, sometimes, this gives way to rebellion and the desire to rebuild a better society. In the end, better societies can only be erected when the people set down their arms and their disagreements and begin to work together toward a lasting peace."

Indeed, it was this precise reason why Jegra had rallied so hard to end slavery and discrimination on Dagon Prime. She knew from her own planet's experiences that this way only spelled eventual disaster for the great empire.

The myth of Dagon purity, the prejudice against clones and mods, and the elitism of believing they hailed from supreme beings simply weren't rational.

Assuming that what you are now was and always has been entirely perfect didn't leave any room for growth or improvement. And, sadly enough, stunted individuals often gave way to stunted worldviews.

Like the belief that your limitedness was somehow superior when, in fact, all it was symbolic of was your inability to adapt or evolve.

And whether Lycia wanted to admit it or not, Jegra knew the sobering truth was that history had time and again born an incontestable certainty: any culture that could not grow or improve was destined to be relegated to the annals of history and become little more than a fleeting memory.

"Maybe so," Lycia rejoined. "But a lawless society will fall apart quicker than one with a few minor lingering injustices. Shouldn't we at least try to make a stable and safe society by first addressing the issues lawfully and diplomatically?"

"Definitely," Jegra agreed. "Your point is well taken." She smiled concisely and was met by Lycia's display of succinct politeness.

Seeing as she wasn't making any headway, however, Jegra decided to change the topic of conversation. "Enough talk of politics," she said waving her hand through the air as though she were brushing the subject aside, at least for now. "How is your fruit?"

"It's delicious," Lycia replied, stuffing several grapes into her mouth. She then held up her glass and a servant raced over to fill it with freshly squeezed Mel'kovian orange juice.

As Lycia enjoyed her breakfast, Jegra leaned in close to Raphine and whispered into her ear. "Does something seem off to you about Lycia? I mean besides her complete shift in political beliefs?"

"I was about to ask you the same thing," Raphine replied in a hushed tone.

They both looked across the breakfast table at Lycia who sat opposite them and was dishing herself up a pile of scrambled Oszarkian eggs onto her already full plate of Quilloxian ham.

"Not just that, but she's eating eggs," Raphine said, raising an eyebrow in dismay as Lycia gorged herself. "She hates eggs. She gets queasy just smelling them."

They both looked up at Lycia as she continued to shovel eggs into her mouth one fork load at a time.

Raphine pointed her finger across the table at Lycia and whispered, "Does that look like a girl who gets sick to her stomach just looking at eggs to you?"

She put her finger down and they both watched in stunned silence as Lycia continued shoveling eggs into her face hole in a rather gluttonous fashion.

"Well, at least she eats the same way as her usual self," Jegra observed, but her voice trailed off as she glanced down at Lycia's arm and something caught her eye. The mother and daughter matching-tattoo that she'd given herself yesterday was now missing.

"You were saying?" Raphine asked. She noticed the puzzled expression settle onto Jegra's face and grew worried. "What is it?" she whispered.

"That's not Lycia," Jegra whispered through the corner of her mouth, staying as discrete as she could about it.

"What?" Raphine replied with a chuckle. It was all a little bit hard to believe. But, at the same time, in her heart, she knew Jegra was right. The Lycia sitting before them wasn't *their* Lycia. This was an imposter. Suddenly feeling ill at the mere thought of it, her face grew deathly serious and she turned her teal eyes toward Jegra. "Please, tell me you're kidding. Because if that's not Lycia, then what we did last night together is going to make me sick."

"I'm sorry," Jegra said, looking at Raphine and placing her hand on her forearm. Then, in the next instant, Jegra shoved Raphine away from the table with a gentle kick to her chair.

Raphine slid across the room till the back of her chair slammed into the wall and she rocked back into place, a startled expression plastered across her face.

Jegra stood up just as Lycia was looking up from her meal to see what all the commotion was about when the table slammed into Lycia's ribcage. The entire table, having been kicked by Jegra, pinned Lycia up against the opposite wall of the dining hall.

She felt the back of her head slam against the stucco so hard that the very plaster fractured all around her. She looked up with a cruel smile and stared across the room at Jegra with half-sunken eyes that were not those of Lycia.

"Who are you?" Jegra growled, marching over to the imposter, who was already trying to push the table back.

Jegra threw up her leg and stopped the table with her foot. Shoving it back again, her superior strength threw the imposter back against the wall again. The small cracks from before expanded, growing out from the epicenter of the duress like the feathery veins spreading throughout thin ice.

"Well, that didn't take you long," Demeris Artemis said with a low chuckle. "What gave me away?"

"You forgot about her tattoo, the one she gave herself yesterday. Our matching mother and daughter tattoos." Jegra held up her arm and showed the doppelgänger the tattoo that Lycia was supposed to have on her arm but didn't.

"Oh, well," Demeris Artemis said with a lamentable sigh and a halfhearted shrug. "You win some and you lose some."

"Who are you and what did you do with my girlfriend?" Raphine asked, looking at this imposter with her harshest glower.

"Isn't it clear by now, ladies?"

They both stared at the wicked deceiver sitting across from them with incredulous gazes.

"I'm Demeris Ferrison." Then, gesturing at her own body, she added, "Or, Demeris Artemis, if we're being technical."

Jegra's face grew more inflamed while Raphine's jaw fell wide open.

"But you and I…we…" Raphine's voice trailed off as tears flooded her eyes.

"And it was glorious," Demeris Artemis said. "I appreciate how well you take care of your woman. Just like a Bre'lal prostitute is supposed to."

Raphine buried her face in her palms and began to weep. This only seemed to bring Demeris Artemis all the more pleasure and a sickening grin spread across her thin lips. That's when Jegra gave a thrust of her mighty leg and smashed Demeris back into the wall again. More plaster debris fell to the floor, sending up a white dust cloud.

"What you claim is impossible. I killed that son of a bitch in the arena," spat Jegra.

"Well, what can I say? That son of a bitch is sitting right here before you in this shiny new body."

"*Ahhh!*" Jegra screamed out fiercely as she kicked the table with all her might. The force was so great that the solid oak table burst through the wall, Demeris along with it, and slammed into the opposite wall in the adjoining room.

Raphine peeked through the gaping hole and waited for the dust to settle before finding Demeris Artemis, or whoever she was, had been rendered unconscious.

"When that Tarbanien shit-stain wakes up, you come and notify me. That's an order."

Raphine nodded in silence and then went over to collect Demeris Artemis. By then a security detail had teleported into the dining room and raced over to assist Raphine with apprehending the imposter.

Jegra marched out onto the balcony, her fists clenched tight, and looked up at the sky and, then, let out a frustrated scream that echoed across the sand dunes of Thessalonica.

Every vein in her neck bulged with the thickness of piano wire and nearly just as tight; her muscles rippled in waves of frustration, and her blood boiled with an uncontrollable rage that turned her sunbaked skin into a dark copper tone.

24

Arms crossed sternly below her chest, Jegra stood on the bridge of the *Skywend* watching the streaks of multi-colored light that rushed by the main view portal. She imagined that the sleek hull of the ship was like that of a large space whale swimming through a colorful sea of shifting light.

Interrupting her thoughts came the pneumatic hiss of the doors to the bridge. Her arms still folded, she turned her head and glanced over her shoulder to witness Raven step across the threshold and onto the bridge.

Raven's amethyst eyes locked with Jegra's brown ones and she let out a pent-up sigh. "Well, I don't think I need to tell you, but that was hands-down the most humiliating televid call I've ever had to make."

Jegra smiled as she got lost in those purple eyes that sparkled like distant galaxies. "Did she agree to help us?"

"Only if we meet her demands."

"Which are?"

"She wants visitation rights," Raven informed Jegra, touching her baby bump and looking down at what was Ladgara's child growing inside her womb.

"Completely out of the question," Jegra said.

"That's what I told her," Raven answered, throwing out her hands as if she didn't know what else to say.

"And?"

"And, I negotiated some more until she agreed to help us."

Jegra squinted at Raven with a discerning gaze and threw her hands onto her hips. "Just like that? No further demands?"

"I didn't say that."

"Alright. Then spill. What aren't you telling me?"

"You're not going to like it. She wants her daughter to be named after her."

Jegra rolled her eyes. "Of course, she does."

"It's just a name," Raven interjected, taking the rational route. "If it helps us rescue Lycia, then why not?"

Jegra huffed in frustration, blowing a tuft of hair out of her eyes. She then grabbed her long tresses of hair and began braiding them out of nervous habit as she mulled it over for a bit.

"Ladgara Alakandra?" Jegra murmured to herself, trying on the name to see if she could stomach it let alone live with it.

"Ladgara Vassex Alakandra," Raven corrected.

Jegra looked up at her and she shrugged, which, in turn, prompted Jegra to let out a frustrated sigh. She stroked her chin a moment and, giving it some further thought, finally amended it to, "Ladgara Vassex Danica Valencia Alakandra."

Raven raised her eyebrows and nodded her head in cordial agreement. It actually wasn't half bad.

A throat cleared and they both turned toward Gyllek who, having caught their attention, sat up on her knees in her chair, itching with the chance to chime in.

Raven nodded at her to go ahead and she promptly exclaimed, "I, for one, love the name Ladgara Vassex Danica Valencia Alakandra! It rolls right off the tongue. Also, Ladgara Alakandra could be abbreviated to Lala. And I love the nickname Lala. I've always wanted to meet a Lala, but so few people are called that anymore."

Jegra's eyes grew wide and she gave Raven a wry grin as if to ask who are these people named Lala they didn't know about, and Raven merely smiled and nodded her head toward Gyllek, who was already spinning about in her chair in a carefree manner.

"It's a good name," Kregor stated. "A strong name." Although he couldn't admit it in front of the others, he'd grown quite fond of Danica over the past few months, even if their little tryst played a large part in his change of heart.

"I can find no objections," Skuld said.

"Nor I," Angellyk agreed. She was sitting on Skuld's lap and had her arms draped around his neck as they continuously rubbed their faces together and gave one another butterfly kisses.

This new ability to touch noses came courtesy of Skuld's new breathing apparatus that allowed his head to be out of the fishbowl styled tank for prolonged periods. Instead of a large bowl atop his head, he sported two metal patches that covered his gills and fed them a constant supply of constantly re-filtered seawater.

Angellyk touched noses with him and they giggled to themselves while Kregor let out a small serpentine hiss of annoyance and rolled his eyes.

By now it was no secret. He felt like a cuckold for having been dumped for a fish. But, at the same time, he needed to be realistic. He and Angellyk weren't going to work out. After all, he'd cheated on her with Danica.

Instead of breaking up with him, however, she just started doting on Skuld, showing Kregor that if she couldn't be happy with him then she'd find someone else to fill that cold and empty void of hers. And by cold and empty void, he meant her heart.

Realizing Jegra was standing just over his shoulder he gulped hard and abruptly looked up.

"How you doin' Big Guy?" she asked, squeezing his shoulder affectionately.

He glimpsed Raven eyeing him from a few feet away and he gulped again, growing nervous as Jegra chatted with him.

"Sorry," he said. "I can't talk right now. I have to concentrate on flying the ship."

He then looked up and stared out the window like a zombie frozen in time. After all, they were traveling through hyperspace. There wasn't anything one could do other than just monitor the console and watch the stars.

"Right," Jegra said, acknowledging the fact that she was getting the cold shoulder as she slowly turned toward Raven with wide eyes and a stupefied grin. "Keep on, my good man. Somebody's gotta keep an eye on all those stars out there." She then playfully slapped his back with enough strength to cause him to wince, and then turned and sauntered over to Raven.

"Be nice, now," Jegra said, wagging a finger at the captain.

Raven folded her arms and looked away with a disgruntled look. "Who said I wasn't being nice?"

"You about made a hardened Dragonian warrior cry with a single look, babe. I think you can ease up a little bit. What happened between me and Kregor is all in the past. And that's right where it shall stay."

Jegra wrapped her arms around Raven's waist and sensually swayed with her until she cracked a smile and shoved Jegra off.

"Not in front of my crew," Raven insisted in an offended yet exaggerated tone. "It's not professional."

"Oh, so touchy," Jegra said, swatting Raven on her perfectly tight ass. Raven just took it and ignored her wife's mischievousness.

"I know that nobody probably cares what I think," Sendaya said, raising her hand as if to signal she had something to say but was too timid to do so without proper authorization first, "but I also think it's a fine name."

"There, you have it. The crew has spoken," Jegra said throwing her hands onto her hips. She turned back to the viewscreen and, hands remaining on her hips, said, "Put a call through to the *Avarice*. It's time I had a word with the Pirate Queen."

The *Avarice* dropped out of hyperspace and Hela looked up at the stars from the bedside window. "Why are we stopping?" she asked, sitting up in bed.

The doctor set down his holopad on the foot of her bed and then looked at her with an almost apologetic look. Without so much as uttering a reply, however, he quickly scurried out of the room and locked the doors behind him.

Hela turned to find Lycia, bandaged and recuperating next to her. She smacked her teeth in disgust at the realization that they'd saved her life instead of just jettisoning her out of an airlock like the damaged goods she was and then she struggled to her feet.

The surgical gown of non-woven polymer she had on only covered her front side. Small elastic bands wrapped around her neck, waist, and thighs ensuring that the gown—which looked like a surgical mask with its pleated folds—would stay on her body.

She glanced around the room for some real clothes, but apart from the bedsheets, there wasn't anything available. She tugged at them, hoping to throw them over her like a toga, but when they didn't budge and the exertion proved too much for her weakened state, she shrugged the idea off and took an unsteady step forward.

Using her IV bag stand as a makeshift walker, she hobbled over to the medlab entrance. When she waved her hand over the sensor and tried to open it, it bleated at her, letting her know she wasn't going anywhere any time soon. She smacked her teeth in frustration and slammed her forehead onto the door.

The pirate wench Ladgara had struck a deal to turn her over. And since there were only two people that would be gunning for her, Jegra or Demeris Artemis, she decided it best not to stick around.

Hela raised her finger and focused hard. Nothing happened at first, but she tried again. Finally, a pink glow emanated from her fingertip and she gasped out with a half-laugh, half gasp of astonishment. The surgery had worked! The Dygra crystal had fused with her and she was summoning power from the dark energy that permeated all of space.

Beyond the Dygra's unique ability to siphon dark energy as if from the ether itself and refocus it, not much was known about them. All attempts to study their unique properties failed. Any time you chiseled away at one, it inevitably stopped working.

Compounding the confusion surrounding the mysterious Dygra, the scans always showed the same energy patterns. An energy pattern which made little sense because it was an infinite loop of magnetically charged positrons collapsing in on themselves in a figure-eight pattern.

All this meant was that the anti-matter positrons traveled backwards in time. How this drew energy from the fabric of reality was anyone's guess. Even the best physicists hadn't been able to crack the mysteries surrounding the Dygra, and so most just accepted the crystals as a kind of metaphysical entity that was beyond understanding.

As a failed clone, Hela's Dygra had not bonded with her as it did in the others. But since she was one of the first stable batches, Dakroth had ordered her not to be terminated. Instead, she was given a new purpose. She was ordered to help improve the Lycia line of clones and prevent any further defectives from happening.

Once she'd succeeded, she decided to stay on the project to try and maybe figure out how to make herself whole again. After years of research, she had finally figured out that a transplant could work, but it would mean the original host's unfortunate death.

Of course, removing the Dygra crystal from a fully-grown adult prematurely always ended up sending the body into shock, oftentimes ending with a full systems failure. Hardly anyone had ever survived her experiments, and those that did were disabled for life. But, seeing as they were all clones, their sacrifice paved the way for Hela's vision of perfection. In other words, they were all expendable. Even her. And, yes, even Lycia.

As an imperfect specimen, however, she used what she'd learned in her experimentation and devised a radical, gene-splicing technique and had, over the past six months, repaired her genetic makeup. This improvement, in turn, allowed her to accept and bond with the Dygra crystal.

And now that the transplant had proven to be a complete success, she felt whole again. She could feel its power coursing through her veins and her energy levels were off the charts.

She pointed her finger at the electronic touch panel on the wall and then blasted it. She laughed gleefully as the circuits exploded, hissed, and popped. The sliding doors to the med-lab fell ajar, and wedging her hands inside the sliver of an opening, she began to pry them apart with both hands.

Even in her weakened condition, she managed to get them all the way open and, proud of herself, she stepped through and dusted off her hands.

"I'll teach you to stab me in the back," Hela grumbled as she stepped into the corridor, her finger pulsing with the glow of hot pink energy. She then severed her ties to the IV drip, plucking the tubes out of her arm, and turned and made her way up the hall.

Before she could reach the junction at the end of the corridor, however, two brawny pirates unexpectedly rounded the corner, causing her to freeze in her tracks.

They stopped too when they saw her; they shared looks, not knowing whether to report her, drag her back to the infirmary, or have a little fun with her first.

"Oy," the big one said. "You ain't supposed ta be 'bout here, yeah?"

"Maybe she wants a bit of fun," the other one said, grabbing his junk and making a lewd gesture. "I got your medicine stick right here, pretty lady. Guaranteed to make you feel better."

They both laughed at the lewd remark while Hela merely smiled at them in a cordial fashion that seemed as though she might be okay with their suggestion.

Then, raising her bright pink finger, she blasted them both without a nanosecond's hesitation.

Wide-eyed with the shock of the sudden attack, they collapsed in a heap on the floor—dead before they ever hit the ground.

A few steps later she realized she was still too weak from the surgery and had no choice but to use the wall for support. After a short pause to catch her breath, she began to make her way up the corridor again and toward the main hangar bay.

It took an aggravatingly long time, but she finally managed to make her way to the *Avarice's* huge hangar. The doors parted as she came to them and, leaning in, she peered inside.

Amazed by how massive it was, she estimated that it likely held two hundred raiders, which lined the ceiling like sleeping bats, and at least a dozen Falcon Heavy dropships, six bombers, two railgun ships, and eight transport shuttles.

And although a ship this size would usually be bustling with Dagoni personnel, it belonged to Ladgara and her pirate horde, and by the looks of things, she barely had enough personnel to keep the thing afloat.

As such, the hangar deck was primarily empty. All but for a single mechanic working on repairing a power coupling. Hela steadied her hand and let off a bright bolt of energy which pelted him in the back.

He yelped out like a dog that had gotten its tail pinched in the sliding door and then, his head slumping forward, he fell across the unit he'd been working on and slid to the ground.

Hela continued on her mission and slowly, painfully, stepped over his corpse before making her way to one of the open shuttles. Not wasting another nanosecond, she clambered up the ramp and into the ship.

Once safely inside, she reached up and tore off her medical gown and tossed it to the floor. Then, pulling open a cubby on the back wall which resembled an overhead storage bin, she drew out a fresh set of gray boxer shorts and a black t-shirt. The t-shirt had Ladgara's pirate symbol—the skull of the Oorn, a hideous hybrid of tentacled Nautilidae and hominid. But, in this case, the skull had boar-like tusks that gave it an unholy appearance.

She then found the drab gray engineering overalls hanging in the back of the locker and slipped them on over her underwear. She grunted from the excruciating pain of every little movement and decided to tie her sleeves off at her waist, instead of stretching to get into them and accidentally popping open her stitches.

Having finished dressing, she settled into the pilot's seat and began spooling up the ship's systems and engines.

As the plasma ion turbines roared to life, she looked out the window to find Jegra standing in the middle of the hangar deck. At first, it seemed she was gazing down at the ground, but her eyes slowly rose and locked onto Hela and held her in their trance. A few golden sparkles of the teleportation beam fluttered about her as she finished materializing and then, like embers cooling into nothingness, they faded away again.

"Going somewhere?" Jegra asked, cracking her knuckles.

Hela's heart began to race and she pleaded with the ship to hurry up its launch sequence, "Come on, come on, come on."

Before she could ignite the thrusters and take off, however, Jegra leaped into the air and came crashing down in front of the shuttle. With a powerful strike, her first impacted the nose of the craft and sent it skidding back across the landing pad.

25

Sparks flew everywhere as the shuttle tilted sideways, its half-wing catching on the metal floor of the hangar bay and etching three-centimeter grooves into it. With the squeal of metal, it skidded backward until it smashed into the rear wall, knocking cargo containers down all around the damaged ship.

With a clank, the shuttle rocked violently and then rolled onto its side, getting wedged up against the hangar wall and leaning at an unnatural forty-five-degree angle.

The sudden impact caused the automated collision system to alert of danger. "Collision detected. Safety protocols engaged."

The intense heat from the friction and sparks had jarred some paneling loose inside the cockpit of the ship and caused a control panel to short and burst into flame. Hela struggled to unbuckle herself as smoke began to fill the cabin. Falling from her seat down to the side paneling of the shuttle's cabin interior, she covered her face and coughed then groaned as the coughing sent a surge of pain through her chest.

She touched the Dygra crystal glowing in her skin then crawled to the emergency hatch, twisted the red lever, and slipped out the opening. Along with a trail of smoke, she slithered out onto the mangled half-wing of the shuttle.

A surge of adrenaline helped mask her pain, allowing her to clamber to her feet. Climbing up, she stood on its hull, still tilted at an awkward angle and wedged between the wall and some heavy equipment. She glanced back to see Jegra marching toward her position, cracking her knuckles menacingly as she came.

Another pop and hiss erupted from inside the shuttle and flames leaped out of the hatch. Hela screamed and shielded her face with her arms so as not to get licked by the flames, which quickly settled down when the ship's automated fire-suppression system released a flood of white fire-retardant foam and dowsed the fire.

Drudging up the courage to force herself to leap off the side of the shuttle to the floor, she inched up to the edge and peered over. As she leaned in to get a better look, however, the shuttled jolted and shifted beneath her feet.

Another scream escaped her lips and, losing her footing, and her balance, Hela tumbled to the floor. Hitting the deck like a lead weight, she smacked her head on the metal plating hard enough to cause her to see spots.

"Oomph," she gasped, as the air rushed out of her. Struggling to keep conscious, she slowly pushed herself up to her hands and knees where she saw two metal boots standing before her. Craning her neck upward, she found Jegra standing over her, arms crossed as she stared down at her with an unforgiving gaze.

"Parley?" Hela asked, half-serious. She was, after all, aboard a pirate ship and interstellar trade law dictated any request of parley be legally observed in all instances where there wasn't an immediate threat to the ship or its crews. This, she figured, had to count.

Jegra merely frowned and reached down and roughly grasped Hela by her hair. Jerking her to her feet, Jegra's eyes widened when she saw that Hela now had a Dygra crystal.

"What did you do?" Jegra growled in her most menacing voice as she held back the avalanche of rage threatening to burst out of her.

Hela merely snickered before another surge of pain flooded through her body and forced her to groan just before she blacked out.

Ladgara raced onto the scene with a team of six armed guards and looked around in dismay at her banged-up hangar deck. Holstering her weapon, she cried out, "What in the Seven Rings of Thorgath did you do to my ship?!"

"You can put it on my tab," Jegra said, her tone unfeeling. Ladgara looked up but merely nodded. She could tell that the infamous Gladiatrix of the Galaxy was in no mood for any backtalk, scheming, or duplicity.

Ladgara raised her hands and gestured for her men to leave. The band of pirates all promptly holstered their weapons and turned about, returning the same way they'd come.

Jegra dragged Hela's body by her hair over to Ladgara who reflexively caught the unconscious woman under her arms. "Here," Jegra said, handing her off as though she were discarding a piece of trash.

"What do you want me to do with her?"

"I don't give a fig. Feel free to shove her out of an airlock for all I care," she boldly said. "Just don't let me set eyes on her ever again. Because the next time I see this conniving, duplicitous, laboratory reject, I'll be twisting her head off with my bare hands."

Ladgara gulped and nodded in reply. She was taken aback by Jegra's tougher warrior persona; she'd never seen this side of her before—the warrior empress side of her–for which she was renowned. She watched in awe as Jegra marched off the hangar deck to go and fetch Lycia from the infirmary.

Back aboard the *Skywend,* Jegra arrived on the teleportation pad with an unconscious Lycia in her arms. Everyone gasped when they saw that Lycia had been surgically mutilated like some kind of mad scientist's guinea pig.

"Quick," Jegra said, her eyes flitting to Skuld and his new breathing apparatus. Under normal circumstances, she'd have complimented his new look, but right now she didn't have the luxury of time. "Prep the surgical bay, ASAP."

He nodded and quickly raced out into the corridor on his way to prep the medlab, as asked. Sendaya quickly followed after him and called out as she jogged to catch up to him, "I'll come too…I have medical training and am a certified nurse."

"Excellent," Skuld said, looking back as she finally caught up to him. "I'm glad to have you with me." She smiled up at him and he smiled back and, not wasting another nanosecond, they walked briskly up the corridor, side by side.

Jegra had slowly begun to carry Lycia to the infirmary when Raven sidled up alongside her and matched her pace.

"I know you well enough to know what you're planning, babe. And you need to know it's risky."

Jegra gave her a sideways glance but then kept her eyes on the task at hand. "Look, I understand your concern. But the fact remains, I have a Dygra crystal I don't need, and Lycia will die without one. I think the answer here is obvious."

"Just," Raven began as she reached out and touched Jegra's arm, "hold up a minute." This prompted Jegra to stop, and she glanced down at Raven's hand as though she wanted to break it off. Raven promptly withdrew her hand and said, "Hear me out. A Dygra has never bonded with anyone of your species before. We don't know what removing it will do to you. If it's anything like my species, you could end up frying your nervous system permanently."

"It will save my daughter's life," Jegra said in a manner that relayed she'd already made up her mind. "That's all that matters. Or are you saying my daughter isn't worth saving?"

Raven scowled and shook her head. "You know very well that's not what I'm saying."

"Good," Jegra said tersely. "Then this conversation is over."

Upset, Raven did the only thing she could do and stepped back, allowing Jegra to continue on her way unimpeded.

She folded her arms and grumbled for a bit before deciding it'd be best to give Jegra a few minutes to cool down and then she'd go be with her.

"Women," a voice said in a disenchanted manner which was followed up with a languorous sigh. "You can't live with em' and you can't live without em'. Am I right?"

Raven looked over to find Gyllek leaning against the side bulkhead along the corridor wall, one boot up against the wall while she balanced on one leg, her arms folded across her chest. She gazed at the captain in a sapient fashion—as though she knew from experience how troublesome women could be—even though she'd probably only heard it from Kregor.

Raven opened her mouth to say something in return when, without warning, Gyllek pushed off the wall, shot Raven a classic homeboy nod, and then strolled off mumbling something about how bitches be cray-cray.

"What a peculiar kitten, that one," another voice chimed in, sharing Raven's thoughts precisely. Even so, the unexpected voice startled her and Raven spun back around to see who it was.

A scowl settled over her and she crossed her arms sternly when her eyes locked onto Ladgara, who stood opposite her.

"Who let you on board?" Raven asked, clearly annoyed.

"Don't get your panties in a bunch, sweetheart. I'm not actually aboard your ship," Ladgara replied defensively.

Raven waved her hand in front of her and watched as it passed through the hologram of Ladgara, confirming she wasn't actually there. It was just a holographic projection.

"I hacked into your ship's holovid emitters so I could call you. Don't worry; this channel is encrypted so nobody will be listening in."

"And what, might I ask, do you want, Ladgara?"

"I just wanted to say I love the name you picked out."

This caught Raven by surprise and she raised an eyebrow. Shifting her hips, she uncrossed her arms and relaxed a bit. In a softer voice, she asked, "You do?"

Ladgara turned toward Raven and her visage reached up to touch Raven's cheek. "I'm not as callous as everyone thinks. I do feel things, you know. Sometimes even passionately. Like I do with you and our ba—"

"Don't," Raven interrupted. She turned her back to Ladgara and folded her arms again. This wasn't a relationship. This was just a consequence of two people having a one-night stand.

Ladgara withdrew her hand as a hurt look settled across her face. "I may not get a chance to say what I want to say again, so please, let me have this one moment."

Raven incrementally turned back around and nodded, allowing Ladgara to proceed with whatever it was she needed to get off her chest.

"You may not believe me, but, in my own way, I do care for you."

"You don't even know me," Raven said, letting out a slight scoff. "We had a one-night stand. That was it."

"Still, after all these weeks, I can't get you out of my mind. It may not have meant anything to you. But, for me, it was unexpected. I fell for you that night. And, sure, maybe we can't ever be together in the proper sense, but I just want you to know that should our child ever need anything, and I mean anything at all, I will blaze across these haunted stars to come back to you both. That is my solemn promise to you."

"I appreciate that," Raven said. They stood, sharing a lingering look. Soon enough, the long pause grew awkward, and Raven cleared her throat. "I need to be going now."

Ladgara nodded and watched as Raven walked right through her image. The image flickered and Ladgara turned around as Raven headed up the corridor without looking back.

Ladgara raised her hand as though she wanted to call out to Raven one last time but then shook her head, deciding against it. Lowering her hand again, her eyes downcast, she stood all alone in the corridor with only her thoughts. A moment later, her hologram flickered and then her image disappeared.

The *Avarice* and the *Skywend* pulled away from one another and the two vessels turned in different directions. Then, nearly at the same moment, they both jumped away in a flash of brilliant light.

Ladgara, feeling dejected, returned to her quarters to have a drink. If she couldn't be with Raven, then she'd do her best to forget her in a wash of liquor.

Upon entering her chambers, she found Hela lounging on her bed, her feet stretched out as they rested on the back of a nearby chair.

She still had on the gray overalls and, gritting her teeth as she fought off the spike of pain, slowly sat up in bed. She watched as Ladgara unfastened her holster and set her blaster on the countertop with a clunk.

"It seems like you had a rough day. Want to talk about it?"

Ladgara, ignoring Hela's attempt at small talk, tore open the flap on her leather jacket to let her skin breathe. She placed both hands on the counter and let out a hefty sigh.

"Look," Hela said, breaking the silence. "I just wanted to swing by and thank you. When I heal, I will repay you ten-thousand-fold. That's a promise."

When Ladgara didn't respond, Hela grew worried and slowly stood up. By the bed, she gestured with her hands, exposing her wrists as though she expected Ladgara to shackle her. A gesture of servitude.

"You saved my life, Ladgara. I will be your indentured servant for as long as it takes me to repay you in kind. Use me, abuse me, I don't care. I'm yours to do with as you please."

Still, Ladgara didn't look up. Instead, she closed her eyes and let out another damning sigh.

"I'll use my cloning technology to make you immortal. We can rule the stars together. What do you say?"

Still, Ladgara didn't break her stoic silence.

"What's the matter?" asked Hela, slowly drawing back now that she sensed something wasn't quite right. Her finger began to glow, although she hid it behind her back so as not to alarm Ladgara, but she was prepared for a fight.

Finally, Ladgara spoke up. "You see, hon. The thing is, I love all my children. And by extension, for some strange reason, I care for their families and friends. This includes Raven and her kin. And, the thing is, you have a dangerous obsession with Lycia, the daughter to Jegra, wife to my beloved Raven."

"What in the Seven Moons of Vespa are you talking about? You're the Pirate Queen. You have hundreds of illegitimate children. But, this one…this is one you choose to love above all the rest?" Hela laughed mockingly.

Ladgara raised her gaze and looked right at Hela with the eyes of a stone-cold killer. "A very unhealthy obsession," she continued, ignoring Hela's ribbing. "One I know you can't simply let go of any time soon." Ladgara drew close and, pressing her index finger into Hela's forehead, she added, "You're sick. In your twisted mind, you think you can make people do whatever you want. And when they don't kowtow to your every desire, you discard them like failed lab experiments."

"You think you have me figured out, do you?" Hela slapped Ladgara's hand away which prompted Ladgara to laugh. "But, you don't. I guarantee you don't have a clue what I'm about or what my plans are."

"Maybe not. But I've known enough people like you in my day to know you'd stab anyone in the back to get what you wanted."

Hela whipped out her hand and pointed it at Ladgara. Realizing they didn't share a trust, she had to weigh her options. "Don't make me do this. We can still rule the galaxy, you and I. With your command of the Outer Rim and my genius, we can still dominate this crippled empire. I will make you into a legend! Don't throw that away for a child you never even wanted in the first place."

Ladgara didn't hesitate. She reached for her blaster off to the side. Simultaneously, Hela, released a laser blast before the pirate queen could draw her weapon, and a hot pink bolt of Dygra energy drilled into Ladgara's head.

Sparks sprayed out as her head flew back. Ladgara's body hit the shelf, knocking some drinking glasses to the floor and then collapsed. Lying in a pile of broken glass, Ladgara's head rippled, distorted for a brief moment, then flickered before disappearing entirely.

Instead of Ladgara, however, lying in her spot was a pleasure-bot which was using a Ladgara simulation as its skin. Now, its dark metallic gynoid body lay sprawled out on the floor, the glowing hole where its left eye used to be slowly cooled as its right eye flickered a couple more times before going dark.

Hela gasped out in shock at the realization it was just a hologram then turned just in time to see the real Ladgara emerge from the dark corner of the room, blaster drawn, its muzzle glowing as the charge heated up.

Ladgara fired off two shots right into Hela's chest before she could even react. The girl staggered back, a stunned look settling across her face before she slowly dropped to her knees.

There was a sizzling sound as she clutched the Dygra crystal in her chest. The crystal's pink glow slowly faded, pulsing a couple of times before growing dark. What was once a hot pink gem of radiant energy cooled to a dark burgundy chunk of lifeless stone.

Still clutching her chest, Hela looked up with betrayal in her eyes and snarled, "I'm just going to resurrect again, you know? And when I do, I'm coming for you. So, you'd better sleep with one eye open, because when I find you, I'm going to tear your heart out with my bare hands and end you, you back-stabbing scag."

Ladgara just scoffed and fired off a final shot point-blank into Hela's chest. Her body jolted from the hit, and she slowly fell backward onto the bedroom floor. As she lay there, blood trickling out of the corner of her mouth, she gazed up at the ceiling until her eyes went cold and a nonplussed expression came over her face.

"Get in line, sister," Ladgara said, addressing the corpse on her floor as she holstered her gun.

Unshaken by the whole thing, she stepped over Hela's lifeless body and, subsequently, the cold husk of the robot body and went over to her liquor cabinet. She pulled out a bottle of Nova Centauri Red and promptly plucked out the cork, discarded it, and put the bottle to her lips. Kicking her head back, she drank right from the bottle, guzzling the fine liquor with large gulps until it was thoroughly depleted.

Once she'd downed the whole bottle, she tossed it over her shoulder without a care in the world, and wiped her face. As the first bottle shattered on the floor, she reached for another. Uncorking the new bottle, she kicked back her head and proceeded to down it just as quickly as the first.

977

26

Lycia awoke with a startled jolt and sat up in bed clutching her chest. Looking down at the area between her breasts, she watched in befuddlement as her Dygra crystal pulsed softly beneath her blue skin as though it had never been gone.

"What?" she whispered aloud, rubbing her finger across her sternum and tracing the outline of the pink glow. It didn't make any sense. She was certain Hela had captured her and ripped it out of her, taking the crystal for herself. Had it all just been one terrible nightmare?

"Good morning, sleepyhead," a voice said and she looked over to find Deunan sitting up on the sofa. She put the holopad down of the e-book she was reading, the latest pulp episode of Savage Jegra, by the looks of it, and then stretched and came over to Lycia's bedside.

"Deunan?" Lycia rubbed the sleep out of her eyes with two balled up fists and did a double-take to ensure she wasn't dreaming. "What in the Seven Rings of Thorgath are you doing here? What's going on?"

"You underwent a serious trauma. The shock to your system was too much for your body to bear and the doctors worried it might cause a full nervous system failure. So, they did the only thing they could do and induced a coma."

"A coma? For how long."

Deunan took Lycia's hand in her copper-toned ones, which had a muted metallic sheen, and looked her in the eyes. "It's almost been three months now."

"Three months?" Lycia gasped, blinking her eyes rapidly as she tried to process the appalling news.

"Nobody has ever had a Dygra crystal removed without immediate system shock and nervous system failure. Of those that survive, most opt for assisted death rather than enduring life as a near-vegetable." Deunan squeezed her hand and smiled. "The good news is that your body took to the new crystal and your recovery is exceeding all expectations."

"New crystal?" Lycia asked, brushing her fingers across her chest again. She tugged at the medical gown to get a better view of the surgical scars, but her rapid healing factor had nearly erased any trace of the trauma.

"Whose...?" Her voice trailed off when she realized that there was only one person alive who could have willingly risked death to donate their own Dygra crystal to her. "Jegra?" she inquired.

Deunan nodded. "I came the moment I heard you were severely wounded. I couldn't sit by and not be here for you. You're like the little sister I never had."

"So, you decided to join the living, I see," a voice said. They both turned their gazes toward the main entrance to the recovery room only to find Gamagor standing in the archway.

"Gam?" Lycia asked, perplexed as to why they'd both be here at the same time. Had it been that serious? Did they fear she might not survive the whole ordeal?

Gam held up her hand and showed off a ring. "We got engaged!"

Lycia let out a sigh of relief. That explained things. She turned and looked back at Deunan, who smiled bashfully and gave a subtle shrug.

"Wow!" Lycia exclaimed in her weak voice. "Congratulations you guys. I mean that."

Gam was halfway into the room when the doors slid open again and a host of nurses hurried in, darting here and there like a mischief of field mice scattering.

After they'd filled the room and got to work checking Lycia's vitals and making reports, a medical Grendok skipped into the room and scanned all the faces that had turned to greet him.

"Excellent. Most excellent, indeed. You are conscious, my empress," he said with a bow of his head. He then hopped over to her, shined his light in her eyes, took her wrist and checked her pulse. Then he set a stethoscope on her chest and checked her heartbeat and her Dygra's thrum.

"Everything sounds good. Also, your blood work came back clean, which means the antibiotic drip I prescribed has taken care of any infections. As such, I'm issuing a full bill of health. You'll be free to check out later this afternoon."

Lycia nodded as the nurses and the doctor collected what they needed and quickly exited the way they'd come in.

Nearly as soon as they'd left, the doors of the recovery room slid open again and Jegra and Danica briskly entered the room. Both women were so tall and elegant that they drew the admiration of all who looked upon them.

"Your Graces," Deunan said, and she and Gam kneeled down in humble veneration.

"You both may rise," Jegra said, gesturing with her hand for them to get back up. They abided her wishes.

Lycia raised an eyebrow as Jegra's six-month bulge was now rather prominent.

"Somebody is looking a bit knocked up," Lycia said with a half-grin on her face.

"And the prego-sex is amazing," Jegra retorted.

Lycia made a sour face and said, "TMI, Mom."

Jegra strolled up to Gam, and they locked in a powerful handshake as gladiators always did before a match. She then turned to Deunan and gave her a big hug. Deunan stiffened, not knowing what to do, and just accepted the strange Terran greeting.

She never quite understood the appeal of mashing one's warm body into someone else's, equally warm body. The Dagon salute or the Seyfferian method of bumping forearms or elbows was preferable in her estimation to a full-body embrace. Hugs felt weird, almost stifling, as you had to wrap yourself around another person while they wrapped themselves around you.

Lycia looked over at Danica and noticed two blue arms.

"Hey, you don't have a metal arm anymore," she said.

Danica flexed her artificial limb and showed it off. Apart from a small seam that ran down the length of the interior, it was indistinguishable from a real arm.

"It still has all the strength of the smart-metal but is made with lighter synthetic materials. The finest in Dagon engineering." She then held her arm up and added, "Oh, and it can do this."

Entire sections of her arm popped open, like hidden panels, and then rearranged themselves around a central plasma cannon that grew from the center. She then winked at Lycia and then with a slight twist of her forearm it all folded back up and her normal, biological arm re-formed.

Lycia then turned her gaze back toward Jegra. She stared at her for the longest time before she remembered that Jegra was without her Dygra crystal.

When Jegra noticed Lycia examining her, she pulled down the V-neck of her t-shirt and showed that she no longer had the Dygra. Just two large breasts and perfectly sunbaked skin. Then, extending her finger, she pointed at Lycia's chest.

"It has a better home now," she said.

Tears flooded Lycia's eyes and she sniffled. "I thought as much."

Jegra settled down onto the edge of Lycia's bed and clutched her hands in hers. "I would do anything for you, kid. I'd even die for you."

"Don't say that, Mom." Lycia sniffled again, wiping another tear and Jegra leaned across her and embraced her. They held each other for the longest time and then finally, Jegra kissed Lycia's forehead and stood up.

"I'm so glad you're doing well," Jegra said. She then turned to Deunan and Gam and nodded appreciatively. They nodded back and she turned and glided out of the room.

Danica stayed behind and looked back over at Lycia once more. "You've been given a second chance at life. I hope you follow her example and make the most of it."

"I will," Lycia said. She held up her arm and looked at the tattoo—the matching one she'd given herself to bond with her mother—the one that read *carpe diem.*

Danica smiled demurely and then left Lycia to be with her friends.

"Naturally, we'll stay as long as you need us to," Deunan said, breaking the lingering silence that had settled across the room.

Lycia turned to face her and smiled. "That's the thing, though," Lycia replied, "I'll always need you guys. You're my moral compass and my strength. My confidants and my friends."

"Whatever you ask of us, we will heed the calling," Gam said. "Whenever you call us, we shall come to your aid."

"I couldn't have put it better myself," Deunan said, turning her smile toward Gam. They reached out and clasped hands.

"In that case, how would you both like a job?"

Deunan turned her gaze back to Lycia, a puzzled look pressed upon her face. "A job?"

"I want you both to be ambassadors to your respective homeworlds. Deunan, please do me this small favor and become my ambassador to Correllia and the Seyferrian Republic." Lycia then turned her pink, glittering eyes to Gam's lime green ones. "Gam, please be my ambassador to Dragonia and the people of Skallek. As a former champion of the arena and a great warrior, they respect you. They'd sooner deal with you than a Blue skin, like me."

Making a fist, Gam crossed her chest and bowed her head in the Dagon salute. "It would be my honor to serve you, Your Majesty."

"As would it be mine," Deunan answered, doing the same.

Lycia smiled once more and reached out with both of her hands and took each of theirs. "Thank you," she said. "You have no idea how happy this makes me."

The Falcon Heavy dropship arrived at the west-facing side entrance of the royal palace on Thessalonica, its plasma ion thrusters screaming as it set down. Even before the engines had fully shut down, the loading ramp began to open and Raphine raced down the ramp and hopped off, leaving the ship's autopilot to complete the landing on its own.

The various security guards and ground personnel all saluted her as she raced by them and into the royal palace.

Maidservants scurried out of her way as she ran into the main hall and turned up the long passage that led to the west wing of the palace where the infirmary was. Her boots skidded on the floor as she shot around a corner and came barreling down the next passage.

Almost knocking over a fancy vase (along with the pedestal it was on), she reflexively caught the stand and danced around it as the vase wobbled about. Gently placing her hands on the floral enameled vase, she carefully set it back into place and then quickly turned about and continued on her way.

In record time, Raphine had made it to the medical ward and burst through the doors. Sliding to a halt in the center of the room, she looked over in confusion at an empty bed sitting beneath the sunny windows.

She scanned the room but there was no sign of Lycia.

"If you're looking for her, she's out in the garden," a voice informed her.

Raphine spun around to find Brei'Alas pausing in the doorway, looking at her with a smile on her face.

"Thanks!" Raphine said as she raced back out, this time through a different set of doors. These doors led into an adjoining room with lots of medical equipment. She quickly found the doors that led out onto the balcony and went through them. Then, without wasting another nanosecond, she raced over to the railing and, with the prowess of a cat, leapt off the balcony.

Sailing four stories to the ground, she landed with a lightly padded thump then continued dashing toward the garden maze.

She ran through every twist and turn as fast as she possibly could and finally came to the central region of the maze, where Lycia was standing in a strapless pearl gown with a lace v-cut opening that showed off her nice blue cleavage.

Beside her sat Allie, who was getting a pleasant head rub from Lycia. "You're a good girl, yes you are."

As soon as Raphine burst onto the scene, Allie's ears perked up and she turned her big, green cat-eyes toward her. Then, sauntering over, Allie rubbed up against Raph, her svelte, purple cat body nudging Raphine back and causing her to laugh. "I missed you too, girl."

Raphine rustled Allie's ears and gave her a big hug before standing back up and turning toward Lycia.

Still panting softly, Raphine and Lycia slowly moved toward one another, as if they were each being drawn to one another by some invisible force.

A heartbeat later, they met at the center of the garden, both of them staring into the other's dreamy eyes. Raph cupped her hands on either side of Lycia's face and, pressing her forehead to her girlfriend's, whispered, "I was so worried about you."

"I'm here," Lycia said. Before she could utter another word, Raphine kissed her long and hard. The kiss, which started roughly, gradually melted into a sweet kiss of passion. Then it grew into a lingering kiss which, in turn, became a deep, sultry kiss.

Soon they settled onto one of the marble benches that lined the interior of the hedges, and Lycia laid back as Raphine got on top. Straddling her girlfriend's hips, Lycia leaned in and kissed her once more.

A swirling pirouette of their tongues tantalized them and they each felt as though their beating hearts had become one. Lycia had never felt so fully at peace with herself as when she was with Raphine, and she knew that Raphine felt the same way.

Allie seemed to be disinterested in what they were doing and wandered off into the maze, stalking thornbirds as she went.

"I love you more than all the stars in the verse," Raphine said, smiling and batting her blue-painted eyelids at Lycia.

"I love you more than the endless dimensions of this cosmic dream," Lycia replied. And, once more, they fell into one another's embrace and made the sweetest love either of them had ever experienced.

After sharing a beautiful moment, they lay in the garden holding each other's hands and stared up at the vast blue sky overhead.

After a moment of basking in each other's warmth, they heard some voices in the distance and quickly scrambled to get to their feet and make themselves presentable again.

"You have a twig in your hair," Lycia said, plucking the small stick from Raphine's hair.

"Thanks," Raphine replied, brushing Lycia's shirt down and covering her exposed midriff.

They turned when it seemed that whoever it was drawing near would walk into their little secret alcove, but then the voice faded and they looked at each other in puzzlement. Lycia shrugged and Raphine turned and hopped up onto the bench and peered over the hedges.

"What do you see?" asked Lycia, gazing up at Raphine with curious eyes.

"I see Jegra. She's headed out onto the dunes, barefoot. I think she was probably talking to Allie because there's nobody with her now."

"I think I'll go and join her," Lycia said.

"Good," Raphine replied. "I think you two should have some mother-daughter time. Catch up a bit. Because, I think you should know, she sat by your bedside and read to you every single night. On more than one occasion, she dozed off in the chair and slept beside you, always waiting for the moment you'd wake up. I know you sometimes don't feel like a true daughter to her, but believe me when I say that she has the full love of a mother for you."

Lycia smiled at her with tears in her eyes and then blew her a kiss. Raphine pretended to catch it and Lycia waved and then, crouching down, she leaped into the air like a Bastolian cricket.

Lycia landed with a thud in the sand several yards to the left of Jegra. A small dust cloud expanded from her impact zone and she slowly stood up as Jegra turned to see who it was.

Jegra smiled when she found that it was Lycia, and she extended her hand, her wrist bracelets rattling and her arm bracelets glinting in the sunlight.

"I like your dress," Lycia said, eyeing the tangerine, gossamer gown that Jegra had on. It didn't leave much to the imagination, but it was absolutely stunning on a woman like her.

Lycia kicked off her shoes and then brushed down her pearl-colored dress. She smiled and took Jegra's hand in hers and, together, they walked out onto hot sands of the Thessalonican desert as the sun began to set and the deepening pink hues washed across the landscape.

They hiked, hand in hand, to the top of the tallest sand dune that they could find whereupon, arriving at the top, they looked out across the basin wherein the great Arena City sat.

Built up around the lake of Amon-Gorloth, named after the god of the great oasis that gave rise to all life in the universe, it was Jegra's little oasis. Her home away from home.

Beyond her quaint oasis city, however, was an otherwise never-ending sea of sand that stretched as far as the eye could see.

Lycia looked up at the sky and saw the green and blue orb that was Dagon Prime looming large over them. A lush world a thousand times bigger and more beautiful than its dusty ole moon. The real gem in all the empire. But even so, it didn't feel like home.

There was one thing that Lycia would never forget, and which always made her feel at ease. Jegra had once told her, "Home is where the heart is," and Lycia, who had no real home, and Jegra, who was a refugee in a foreign land, could at least call this ball of dirt their home. A place where their loved ones resided. A place where they could always come back to and still find that sense of solace and belonging that every heart yearns for.

Jegra turned her brown eyes toward her daughter and smiled. "My beautiful daughter, tomorrow, you will take the throne and rule this empire as its one true empress. From tomorrow, you will put on the crown and be the fearless leader of all of Dagon that everyone expects you to be. But, right now, you are just my daughter and I wanted you to know how truly proud I am of you and how much I love you."

Lycia playfully shoved Jegra and then wiped a tear from her cheek. "Ah, Mom. You're making me cry."

Jegra grabbed Lycia firmly by both arms and reeled her in and they embraced one another. Lycia took a deep breath and, her cheek perched on Jegra's broad shoulder, said, "It's all so sudden."

"Yes. But I'll be by your side, every step of the way."

Lycia stood up and faced her mom and smiled. She then cozied up to her and nestled into Jegra's side, each of them wrapping an arm around the other's waist. And there they stood, side by side, looking out at the sunset.

Gradually, the warm glow of sunlight cooled to a deep purple and settled across the landscape, like a blanket that wrapped itself around the sleepy moon. At the same time, the horizon turned to a navy blue, which faded into a darker evening sky dappled with pinpricks of stellar light.

The occasional shuttle taking off or landing blended into the starry backdrop and, high in the sky, glints of giant cruisers traveling to and from their destinations could be glimpsed from down on the surface.

As a pleasant and dreary calm came over the valley, a familiar melody wafted on the breeze, its notes inspiring and moving. Its lyrics sang of the great battles and the epic adventures of a woman. A woman who began as a slave in the arena, and who then gained her freedom, only to become empress of the galaxy.

It was a song for an empire. A song for the galaxy. It was her song—Jegra's song.

27

TWELVE YEARS AFTER THE DEFEAT OF H'AZZTRE AND THE ESTABLISHMENT OF THE UNITED COSMIC COMMONTHWEALTH. . .

UCC battle cruisers chased down a modified freighter with pirate markings. Of the three matte-black cruisers, only the lead one fired its plasma canons, sending warning shots streaking across the bow of the enemy vessel.

Lycia stood on the command deck of her ship, the *Avalon,* and watched with narrow eyes, her arms clasped behind her back. She had on a white kimono-styled mini dress with a red oriental dragon embroidered on her back. At the same time, she wore glossy red leather boots that came up to her knees, and her hair was dyed a deep black with an under-layer of bright red, which perfectly matched her outfit.

Adorning her cobalt skin, she had a series of tattoos which she'd accumulated over the past ten years, give or take. She had a Vorteshian knot on her left shoulder that was etched in metallic gold and shone in the dim lighting of the bridge. In addition to this, she sported a flaming skull on her forearm, its flames wrapping all the way up to her mid-bicep, and a single wisp climbing up and outlining the Vorteshian knot.

Upon her other arm, she had a strikingly realistic image of Raphine's naked body which was being serviced by two geishas. It was done in the artistic style of ancient Japan of Earth. This art, in turn, blended and morphed into a tiger fighting an oriental dragon that became a full sleeve which wrapped around her right shoulder and upper chest. The dragon's long scaly tail curled around her right breast, a glimpse of which could be seen gracing her cleavage.

She cleared her throat and then, in a commanding voice, growled, "Target their engines and fire a low yield volley on my command. Remember, I want them alive. That's an order."

"Aye, aye, Your Majesty," the crew replied in unison.

Another volley of plasma blasts and the pirate vessel's engines flickered and then died. A coolant leak sprayed out into space as the ship lost power and went adrift.

"Your Majesty," Sub Commander Naya Ri'Vera said, "will you need a boarding party to accompany your rescue?"

Lycia smiled and shook her head, giving a subtle no. "I *am* the boarding party."

Sub Commander Ri'Vera nodded and watched as Lycia tapped her holovid bracelet and disappeared in a swirl of golden light. She then stepped up to where the Empress had been standing and took command of the ship.

"Alright ladies and gentlemen, lock on magnetic grapplers and set the graviton-anchors. I want that ship locked down."

"Yes, ma'am," the crew stated simultaneously, everyone getting to work on securing the enemy vessel and giving the empress the time she needed to deal with the pirates on her own.

Lycia stepped over two dead bodies, her balled fist glowing hot pink, a trail of vaporous pink smoke trailing her like the smoke of a torchbearer at the gladiatorial games.

Just then, a massive, twelve-foot tall Bakktu stepped around the junction and flared its mandibles when it saw Lycia standing in the open corridor, dead bodies littering the length of the passage behind her.

The Bakktu bleated its strange half-roar half-warble, sounding like a prehistoric beast from eons ago, and then thumped its chest. It seemed a dare for her to shoot it, but she merely shook her hand loose, the pink energy fading, and lunged for it at the same time it lunged for her.

Clashing halfway down the corridor, both their fists collided. There was a loud crack, and their powerful hits seemed to stop the others'. Frozen in their tracks, they made eye contact, when all of a sudden, the Bakktu's eyes widened with a terrible revelation and then it reeled back, clutching his wrist. Howling in pain, he realized every bone in his massive hand was pulverized.

Lycia merely grinned, opened her fist, fanned her fingers and then tightened them up into a ball again. As she squeezed her fist tight, her knuckles popped and she quickly dashed forward.

With a volley of brutal gut punches, she drove the Bakktu back into the bulkheads. Once she'd pinned it up against the wall, it roared out and headbutted her with its massive, thick armor-plated cranium.

An unrelenting crack sent Lycia's head flying back. Her eyes widened as she wasn't quite prepared for the level of power of the Bakktu's headbutt. Any normal person would have been crumpled to the ground by such a blow. But she caught her footing and slowly brought her head back up onto her shoulders and, blood trickling down from the gash on her forehead, she said, "Big mistake."

With lightning-quick speed, she jutted a knee into his inner leg, knocking out a kneecap and dropping the behemoth to one knee. Now, at her level, she headbutted the Bakktu in return, with equally devastating force.

The brunt of the force caused her gash to open up, and her blood spilled down her face, but instead of giving up, she merely craned her head back and unleashed another headbutt. Then another. And another.

She continued to headbutt the Bakktu until the back of its head had left a deep indentation in the metal plating of the corridor wall.

Once it was clear the Bakktu's skull was thoroughly crushed in, blood oozing from its ears and eye sockets, she headbutted it one last time for good measure, and then staggered back, a bit dizzy from her overzealous attack.

She swayed on her feet and waited a few seconds for her body to rapidly heal then used the corner end of her half-cape to wipe the blood from her face.

Her business finished here, she turned up the corridor and made her way toward the bridge. Behind her, the Bakktu finally slipped out of the indentation on the wall and hit the floor with a delayed thud.

Lycia noticed the camera in the upper right corner of the corridor zooming in on her, and she turned and addressed it. "You'll have to do a lot better than that if you think you're going to stop me. You have something of mine. And I want it back."

A few minutes later she arrived at the entrance to the bridge. The blast doors had been sealed shut and, although she knew that she could probably melt through them given some time, it wouldn't be as intimidating as literally knocking down the doors.

She clasped her fingers together, stretching them out, and then rolled her head across her shoulders and cracked her neck. Then, creating forcefield gauntlets with her special energy powers, she grinned and began striking the blast doors, one unrelenting blow after unrelenting blow.

THOOOM! THOOM! THOOM!

After about five minutes of bashing on the doors, she got them to bend and buckle. Then, reaching in with her fingers, she used her super-strength, which she'd inherited from her mother, to pry the blast doors apart.

With only the regular doors keeping her out, she eased back and then lunged forward with a powerful kick. The doors reacted like a high-velocity projectile shooting through aluminum. The metal wobbled and tore away from the epicenter of her kick, revealing a large opening as if an orbital strike had launched a tungsten rod, causing an atomic level wave of destruction in its wake.

She crouched down and squeezed through the opening of the door. Emerging through to the other side, she saw three wranglers with animal control poles, holding Allie in the corner. Meanwhile, two pirate thugs held guns to the back of the heads of two fair blue-skinned children which couldn't have been more than ten or eleven years old each.

The pirate captain, a tentacle-faced Groth'Nok, from the ocean world of Nautileptu, raised a giant musket-styled blaster with oversized coolant cartridges. By the size of the barrel of his gun, Lycia knew it packed a wallop, and the small cannon might be enough to vaporize her in one shot.

"It was only a matter of time, I suppose," the captain said in a gruff pirate voice, "before you came for your kin."

Lycia ignored him and turned her head to the two children. "Rhadamanthus, Lala, are you guys alright?"

"We're fine, sis," Rhadamanthus replied. The guard nudged the back of his skull with the muzzle of the gun to remind him who held the power and urged him to keep silent.

"Kick their asses, big sis," Ladgara replied, the corner of her mouth twisting into a grin.

Lycia turned her gaze to Allie, who strained against her captors. "Hang on girl, I'll have you free in a nanosecond."

"A bit optimistic, aren't we?" the captain said in a condescending tone. When Lycia's eyes met his toad-like ones, he scoffed. "I expected more than a common tatted up scag. Your legend spans every corner of the empire, and yet you look like common space trash." He gestured with a shake of his muzzle at her strange, punk rock geisha-like appearance.

Lycia shrugged. "I didn't come here for fashion sense from a tentacle-faced space frog," she retorted. "I came here to get my family back."

Just then Lycia's body began to glow. The other pirates on the bridge stiffened with nervous tension as she multiplied herself with exact energy replicants; soon there were five Echoes, and the blue glowing Lycias engaged the pirates.

The first Lycia charged the cat wranglers and snapped their poles. They scurried back as Allie was set free and pounced at them, letting out a ferocious roar as she tore into the first pirate.

The other two Lycia Echoes made sure the two guards didn't harm the little ones and crashed into them like an Angorian bull rhino.

They flew back into the walls and the two Echoes reached down and helped the children up. Once Rhadamanthus and Ladgara Alakandra were up on their feet, they absorbed the Lycias, their own Dygra crystals flashing with a surge of energy. Recharged, they turned on the three men pushing themselves up off the floor. As the two kids approached, their eyes glowing menacingly, the pirates scurried back, pleading for mercy.

Lycia's fingers gripped the Groth'Nok by his throat and hoisted him off his feet. His tentacles wrapped around her forearm, trying desperately to clasp onto something that would allow him to pry her off of him.

"A low-level scumbag like you doesn't have the balls to kidnap the royal family. So, I'm going to ask you this once. Who hired you to nab my little brother and sister?"

She pressed the glowing tip of her finger to his head, showing that he had just one chance to answer correctly.

"Scarborne of Par'Vek," he wheezed through his strained larynx. "The commissioner of the IGS."

"IGS?" Lycia asked. She mulled it over for a nanosecond and then, seeing as he had no reason to lie, nodded in acknowledgment. Just as he let out a sigh of relief, she snapped his neck with a twitch of her powerful wrist and dropped his lifeless body to the floor. Turning around, she caught the tail end of the aftermath of the events. Her remaining Echoes re-entered her body like ghosts possessing a person, and she looked across the room at her two siblings, who stood over the pile of smoldering ashes from the two pirates they'd vaporized.

Allie, meanwhile, gnawed on the thigh bone of the leg she'd torn off one of the pirates. An afternoon snack to whet her appetite.

Lycia and her half-brother and sister raced to one another and met at the center of the room. Lycia, falling to her knees, embraced them. "I was so worried about you guys."

"Don't worry, sis," Ladgara said. "We had Allie to protect us."

"Yeah, those meatheads never stood a chance."

Lycia squeezed them tight and kissed their foreheads. "What do you say we go home."

"Yeah," Ladgara replied. "I'm sure Mom is freaking out about us."

"Hey, why didn't Mom come and get us?" Rhadamanthus asked.

Lycia took him by his shoulders and held him out at length. "I'm afraid your mother is off on one of her many adventures."

"Saving the galaxy one world at a time," Ladgara chimed.

"Yup, that's our mother."

Lycia smiled and drew them in again for another hug. Allie, already purring, drew up beside them and began rubbing her giant purple body on them. They all laughed and Lycia reached out and ruffled Allie's ears and rubbed her neck.

"I didn't forget about you, ole girl."

Back aboard the *Avalon*, with her siblings tucked into bed and fast asleep and Allie sleeping at the foot of the bed as an ever-present guardian, Lycia returned to the bridge.

Upon stepping onto the command deck, Sub Commander Naya Ri'Vera rose from the command chair and shouted, "Empress Lycia Alakandra on deck!"

All hands stood up and saluted her with the Dagon Salute. She gestured for them to return to their jobs and they complied.

"I know that look," Naya said. "Something weighs on your mind."

"It's the IGS. They're growing bolder in their abductions. And the new commissioner, Scarborne of Par'Vek, doesn't seem to care a fig about intergalactic law."

"He's trying to chase the heyday when your mother reigned supreme. But nothing will ever match Jegra's success in the arena."

"Nor out of it," Lycia said.

"That remains to be seen," Naya replied, shooting Lycia a warm smile.

"Still, he can't simply abduct the royal children without consequences. Ready the railgun."

Naya raised an eyebrow. "Yes, Your Majesty." Turning to the security station, she hollered, "All hands to battle stations. Prepare a tungsten rod and the 'Kiss from Heaven.'"

"Target, ma'am?" asked the security chief, glancing over at both women.

Naya turned to Lycia, deferring to her judgment.

"IGS headquarters," Lycia said in a stern voice.

The two women turned to face the view portal and watched as the chief of security counted down.

"Commencing a 'Kiss from Heaven' in 3, 2, 1…and firing."

A flash left the ship and disappeared into the depths of space. A few minutes later, the security chief relayed, "Direct hit. Target neutralized."

Somewhere in the depths of space, the asteroid belt where IGS had its main station went up in a daisy chain of explosions. The Intergalactic Gladiatorial Syndicate had chosen the wrong person to pick a fight with.

"What now?" asked Naya, turning toward Lycia with big, beautiful purple eyes.

"If IGS wants to go to war with the royal family, then we go to war. Besides, this alien abduction business needs to come to an end. I've tolerated the trafficking of alien species for sex and sport for long enough. No more. It ends now."

"I'm glad to hear you say that," Naya said.

Lycia turned to her with a curious look and raised an inquisitive eyebrow.

"My father was abducted when I was a child. He died fighting some steroid-enhanced Bakktu. I watched on live televid as the Bakktu crushed my father's skull in with its bare hands. I was only five years old."

"I'm sorry," Lycia said, placing a hand on Ri'Vera's shoulder.

They shared a look that hinted at an unspoken attraction and then Lycia turned back to the viewscreen.

As much as she'd love to take Naya in her arms, peel her out of that uniform, and make sweet love to her, she had made a promise to a beautiful Bre'lal woman waiting for her at home.

And, even though she knew Raphine didn't expect her to remain forever in the confines of a monogamous marriage, she'd promise to remain faithful until after they'd raised a family together.

As long as she had Raph, she didn't need anyone else. That's how deeply her love went for that woman.

"Prepare to make the jump to hyperspace back to Dagon Prime," Lycia said.

"Aye, Your Majesty," Naya said, gently touching her arm just above her elbow and smiling affectionately. "As you wish."

She then raised a finger and pointed at the navigations officer who logged the coordinates and hit the ignition.

A deep thrumming rose from the bowels of the ship as the FTL came to life. A few seconds later the stars stretched into spaghetti thin lines of psychedelic light and the *Avalon* snapped out of its position with a flash.

The stars and galaxies stretched into blue and red lines while the light of black holes and supernova turned white. Additional bands of purple and green, pink and orange, oscillated like a shifting kaleidoscope as the ship flew through the passage of hyperspace.

Set adrift, the crippled pirate ship lingered in space until, after several hours, another flash of light signaled the arrival of a much bigger ship.

Roughly three hundred yards wide and a hundred yards long, the oblong shape had tapered edges which gave it the appearance of a double-headed axe. It was the IGS flagship, a massive dreadnought cruiser fittingly named the *Labrys*.

"Sir, she took the bait. The IGS prison colony has been destroyed," relayed the navcom officer.

"Good," Scarborne said in a deep baritone voice. He clasped his arms behind his back, his long black leather duster jacket making him look like something between a space pirate and a bounty hunter.

The tall red-skinned man, with black tribal tattoos, and long dark dreadlocks that trailed down to his mid-back, was of the mysterious race of assassins known as the Par'Vek.

It was his daughter, Ishtar Bantu of Par'Vek that Jegra had killed. And so, he would return the favor by taking the life of her daughter, Lycia Alakandra.

Unlike his daughter, however, who liked to strike with the speed of a viper, he preferred to stalk his prey like the jungle leopard. Which meant he wasn't in any hurry, but he was steadfast and relentless.

"Sir, what are your orders?"

"Nothing, for now."

"Sir?"

Commissioner Scarborne of Par'Vek turned to his officer and replied, "When you hunt predators, the best ruse is weakness."

"Uh, yes, sir," the officer said, turning back to his station.

"Lycia Alakandra, you will pay for your mother's sins if it takes me a thousand years," grunted Scarborne to himself as he turned back to the viewscreen and gazed out at the stars. "And to my last living breath, I shall grapple with thee."

As long as Lycia felt she had dealt IGS a crippling blow, then she wouldn't see the invasion coming. Victory would all but be his.

28

A spiraling fragment of space rock struck Jegra's shuttle as she returned from her trip to the Outer Rim colonies. A loud metallic *thunk* followed by the crunch of internals and the hiss of a ruptured gas line warranted her immediate attention.

"Now what?" she mumbled to herself as the collision alarm blared throughout the cabin of her royal space yacht, the largest of the shuttle fleet.

<<Main oxygen line ruptured. Recommend immediate bypass.>> the computer voice chimed.

"What do you think I'm doing?" asked Jegra, flustered by the reminder of what she already knew was wrong. She quickly reached over to the control panel and flipped a switch that cut off the gas line to prevent any further loss of oxygen. She then rerouted it through a secondary system.

All space vessels required numerous redundancies for just such an occasion. You couldn't fly in luxurious comfort aboard a four-deck space yacht if it wasn't prepared for long hauls.

Jegra rose from her chair, her gray space suit halfway unzipped, her black lace underwear and the cleavage it cradled was on display. She didn't bother to confine her bosom into a fully zipped suit as she went over to the port side window and looked at the damage.

"It doesn't look that bad," she said to herself. "Computer, analyze where rogue meteorite came from."

<<Calculating trajectory, one moment, please,>> the soft feminine voice of the computer responded. A few seconds later the computer chimed on again. <<Meteorite strike came from IGS Central station situated in sector five of the Badlands Territory.>>

"Someone destroyed IGS?" Jegra asked aloud. The computer responded to her question as though it were meant for it.

<<According to the blast signature, it came from an Imperial cruiser registered as the *Avalon*.>>

"That's Lycia's ship." Jegra returned to the pilot's seat and settled in. She was about to make a call to Lycia to see what was going on when all of a sudden, the port side thruster exploded and sent the ship into a spin.

The emergency alarm started again and Jegra growled, "Shit, shit, shit," as she tried to compensate for the sudden uncontrolled roll.

<<Lost main thruster. Do you require assistance in regaining control of the ship?>>

"Thanks, but I got it," Jegra answered. She gripped the joystick tight and guided the ship back to its original trajectory and then cut the thrusters. Sitting back in her seat, she exhaled a deep breath and then said, "Damage report."

<<Repairs are needed for deep space travel to recommence. Would you like me to scan for nearby settlements that may have the required parts necessary to repair the main thrusters?"

"Yes, by all means, do that," Jegra said gesturing with her hand for the computer to proceed.

<<All advanced civilizations are out of reach.>>

"Of course, they are," Jegra mumbled under her breath. "Options," she said, giving the command for the computer to crunch her other possible choices on how to best get out of this mess.

<<Option one: launch an S.O.S buoy and wait for whomever comes. Possible dangers include pirates picking up the signal before help. Option two: call the royal fleet to pick you up. As empress, you still have sway with the military. Option three: there is a small world orbiting a binary red dwarf system. The planet, known as PL16, has signs of liquid water and vegetation. You could set down and synthesize the parts to repair the ship. High-density part printing will take several weeks.>>

Jegra sat back in her seat and steepled her fingers. Sending out an S.O.S this close to the Badlands was a bad idea. Pirates and marauders would take her for everything she had. And she doubted that they'd be as sympathetic as Ladgara.

At the same time, calling in the Imperial Fleet just for a rescue op was an unnecessary interruption in day-to-day fleet operations. Not only would it cause a terrible inconvenience for all those involved, but it would be rather expensive. And she wasn't going to give the politicians and talking heads on the news media more ammo to assassinate her character. Ever since the people began idolizing her as this great heroine, it would look rather ridiculous if, in the end, she was defeated by a small rock wafting through space.

And, sure, her pride was at stake too. "Great," she said sarcastically, "PL16 it is."

<<Setting course for PL16.>>

"ETA?" asked Jegra.

<<With a single operational thruster with ion assist, it will take three and a half hours before we reach our destination.>>

"Excellent," Jegra said, rising out of her chair. This gave her enough time to catch some shut-eye. "Wake me when we get within range of the planet."

Jegra returned to her quarters and threw herself onto her luxurious queen-sized bed. She propped herself up on a pillow and looked out the massive windows that revealed a starry expanse to her. After all these years, space had finally started to seem normal to her. But, at heart, she was still a Terran. She needed to feel the ground beneath her feet, to feel rooted in something. Space was hollow, empty. And she hated being alone out here.

Soon enough, her myriad thoughts gave way to dreams, and she fell into a deep sleep.

A sudden jolt of the ship and Jegra snapped awake. The collision alarm was blaring again and she stumbled out of bed, rubbing her eyes.

"Now what?"

<<A meteorite strike has decommissioned our secondary thruster.>>

Jegra shambled to the bridge, almost getting knocked off her feet as the ship began to fall into the atmosphere of the planet.

Strapping herself in, she said, "Auto landing sequence engage."

<<Auto landing system is currently offline.>>

"Shit," Jegra shouted, grabbing the joystick. "Hand all controls over to me, now!"

As the ship entered the atmosphere, flames streaked passed the windshield.

<<Manual flight engaged. The ship is now yours.>>

Using her immense strength, Jegra pulled back on the joystick and managed to bring the nose of the ship up. Then, flipping switches left and right she fired all reverse thrusters.

The large, pearlescent space yacht shot through the clouds like a lead weight as it continued to plummet. With white wisps of cloud vapor whipping past her windshield, she mumbled, "Come on girl, you've got this."

On the main view screen, the HUD showed a lush jungle illuminated by the twin suns overhead. The red dwarfs, each slightly smaller than Earth's sun, provided about the same amount of light.

"Over there," Jegra said, pointing at a clearing in the jungle. "If I can get to that clearing, I'll be able to set her down all in one piece."

The computer calculated a course for her to follow with orange dots on the HUD to signal when she needed to fire the thrusters. Following the course laid out by the computer, Jegra managed to set the massive yacht down in the clearing with minimal effort.

Jegra forced herself to let go of the joystick and then let out a huge sigh of relief.

<<Breathable atmosphere detected.>>

"Right," Jegra said, standing up. She felt weak in her knees and fell back into her chair again. Trying a second time, she managed to stabilize herself then brushed down her gray space suit and took a deep breath.

Then, she went to the central lift, opened the glass doors, and climbed in. She mashed the button in the lift and the bottom hatch opened, revealing lush foliage beneath the underbelly of the ship. The glass tube extended down to the ground, lowering her to the surface.

When the elevator doors parted, she began coughing and hacking. "I thought you said this atmosphere was breathable," she groused, covering her face with her arm.

<<Nitrogen content is slightly elevated, but the oxygen content is richer, thereby compensating. Your lungs should get used to the slight atmospheric changes in a few minutes.>>

Jegra nodded and then stepped out onto the fertile land. She walked through knee-high grass and then looked up at the ship to inspect the damage. Both engines dispensed a cloud of black smoke as the plasma had burned away the wiring, along with the paint and anything else before the auto-shutoff took effect.

"Dammit," she said, realizing it would take at least a month to fix everything. *One long month stranded on a strange alien world...just great,* she mused, throwing her hands on her hips and frowning.

Undeniably shipwrecked, she let slip a frustrated sigh and then turned around to take in the view. Her hands still upon her hips, she gazed out across the grassy glade that was framed by jungle trees and foliage and took in a deep breath of fresh air. *At least the view isn't half bad,* she admitted.

Over the next three days, Jegra began her repairs. And due to the extreme humidity of this world, she'd stripped down to her black bikini and nothing else. Seeing as she was alone, except for some indigenous wildlife, she mainly stayed near the ship.

Perched on the half-wing, she reached into the open panel with a wrench and tightened the new gas line. Once it was securely fastened, she sat up and wiped the sweat from her brow.

Her sunbaked skin glistened with a uniform sheen, and she stretched her arms over her head. That's when the subtle sound of a twig snapping caught her ear.

She decided to feign ignorance and pretend to ignore it. She began whistling to herself, though her warrior instincts went into overdrive. From the corner of her eye, she spotted five soldiers wearing ghillie suits that allowed them to blend into the jungle foliage.

She twisted and lobbed her wrench as though it was her battle axe. It flew twenty meters and pelted one of the intruders right in the head. The moment he hit the ground, the others took a defensive position and trained their fully automatic weapons on her.

"Howdy, boys," she said, smiling at the soldiers who closed in on her. *If there are people here with this level of technology,* she thought to herself, then they might have enough material and parts to help her speed up her repairs and get off this planet sooner rather than later.

The lead soldier lowered his gun and removed his headgear revealing that he was human.

Jegra gasped. "You're human?"

"So are you," he said, "…I think…"

Jegra leaped off the wing of her yacht with a stupendous jump and landed before them all. Slowly standing back up, she looked at them with a large grin.

"I didn't know humans had colonized any of the Outer Rim worlds," she said.

The soldier gave her a blank look. "I'm afraid I don't know what you mean by that," the man said. "Our ship crashed here more than a hundred and eighty-nine years ago."

Jegra raised an eyebrow. "But that would mean you're…" she trailed off for a moment.

"That I'm over a hundred years old. Yeah. Aging slows down on this planet. Something to do with the regenerative nature of the atmosphere. It's a lot to take in, I know. But for now, I need you to come with us."

"I have questions," Jegra said.

"I'm sure you do," the soldier said. "And all will be explained in due time. But, if you'll follow us, we'll take you back to camp. There are people there who will be able to answer your questions better than I can."

Jegra nodded and followed the soldier into the jungle. As she passed the soldier she'd struck with the wrench, currently being helped up by his comrade, she said, "Sorry about that."

"No problem," he said, rubbing his head. "If it means I get to follow you back into town, it will have been worth it."

She glanced back to find his eyes staring at her ass, his mouth practically salivating. She laughed lightly and figured she deserved that, then continued on her way, letting the men stare all they wanted.

When they arrived back at the small settlement, which resembled an old Western town, made of tin and aluminum, there was a bit of commotion.

A well-dressed man in a white suit, who sported a neatly trimmed white beard and mustache in the classic style of a Southern gentleman, approached them.

"Commander Leroy Gibbs, Mrs. Gibbs, the Preemar have kidnapped my daughter."

"They have Mercy?"

"Preemar?" Jegra asked, looking to both men.

"The Preemar," Commander Leroy Gibbs informed her, "are the natives of this world. A deep burgundy skinned race of savages."

"Savages?" Jegra said, laughing lightly. Colonizers of new worlds always deemed the natives "savages" when, in actuality, they were usually quite peaceful.

"A group of cannibals," Gibbs added. "Who now have the mayor's daughter."

Commander Gibbs waved for his men to regroup. Just then, an ATV drove up and they all climbed aboard.

"Let me come with you," Jegra said. "I can help."

"In that?" Gibbs asked, eyeing her bikini.

Commander Gibbs slapped the side of the AVT and pointed his finger, signaling to the driver to get going. The ATV tore away, leaving Jegra standing by the distraught looking mayor.

"I'm sure she'll be all right," Jegra said.

The mayor looked over at her and in a slight Southern twang asked, "And just who are you supposed to be, my dear?"

"That's a long story. But my name is Jegra. Jegra Alakandra."

He gazed at her with a blank look on his face; clearly, he'd never heard of the famous Gladiatrix of the Galaxy.

"If you'll join me for an evening meal, I'd be interested in learning how you came to find us. But first, let's get you some proper clothes."

Jegra looked down at herself and then up at all the women, who world long dresses and bonnets from a bygone era. That's when she realized she'd encountered a colony that was a stitch out of time.

"I'd appreciate that," she replied, pausing when she didn't know what title to address him by.

"Oh, apologies. With all the hubbub, I have unintentionally forgotten to introduce myself. I am the mayor of this here settlement. You may call me Mr. Darcy. Mr. Darcy Smith."

He reached out and shook her hand. She noted he wore white gloves and hat, peeking out from the gloves on his wrists, were signs of plasma burns.

"The pleasure is all mine," Jegra reassured him.

As they made their way to the large building at the center of the town, eyes turned to watch this swimsuit model. One woman went as far as to cover her husband's eyes when he didn't stop staring.

Jegra merely smiled and followed the mayor up the dusty street to his mansion.

1005

29

Like shadows slipping through the night, Lycia's three matte-black battle cruisers dropped out of hyperspace and slowed to cruising speed as they fell into geosynchronous orbit with the dwarf planet Praxid.

Lycia tucked in her nephew and niece, who were fast asleep the moment their little blue heads hit the pillow of her queen-sized bed. As she felt the ship drop out of hyperspace, she looked out the window at the small red and yellow planetary body lingering outside.

She recognized it from the star charts but, for the life of her, couldn't figure out why they'd come to Praxid. It wasn't particularly valuable, didn't have any atmosphere or mining colonies, contained way too much sulfur, and it wasn't rich in water. It was a dead rock floating on the edge of their system's inner asteroid belt.

She hadn't even had time to get out of her kimono when her door chimed. She said, "Enter," and the doors swooshed apart with a pneumatic gust of air and Ri'Vera stood in the entrance.

"Your Grace, we picked up a Dagon distress call."

Lycia brushed the covers down and rose to her feet, looking at the serine faces of her beloved little brother and sister and then turned to Ri'Vera.

"You couldn't just have called me on the comm?"

"Apologies, Your Magnificence, but I was off duty and returning to my quarters when the distress signal came through. I was close enough that I thought..."

Lycia waved her hand and dismissed the issue. "Nah, it's alright. I'm just tired. I didn't mean to snap."

"What are your orders, Your Magnificence."

"My first order would be for you to stop calling me Your Magnificence. Just call me Lycia. Secondly, yes, I am attracted to you and I would like to explore these feelings. But I have a good woman waiting for me at home and I need to confer with her first if taking on a new girlfriend is something, she's okay with."

"I uh, I wasn't, um…" Blushing, Ri'Vera turned her face away and began biting her teal painted nails.

Lycia strode over and grabbed Ri'Vera's hand in hers and drew it away from her mouth. Their eyes slowly met again and there was a hot tension. Ri'Vera started to lean in and just as it seemed her lips would brush Lycia's, the empress stepped past her and headed toward the bridge.

"Let's go, Ri'Vera," she called out.

Ri'Vera, feeling embarrassed, straightened herself and then brushed down her uniform. "Yes, Your Magni—I mean, Lycia." She shook her head and mumbled, "Stupid, stupid, girl," to herself and then turned and followed up the corridor after the empress.

They arrived on the bridge at the same time and the Lt. Commander in charge shouted, "Empress on the bridge!"

"At ease," Lycia said.

"Sub Commander?" the young man, whose name was T'Vok, asked.

"I'm still off duty, Lieutenant Commander T'Vok. But I will stay with the empress until she dismisses me."

"Yes, ma'am," he said and then turned and offered Lycia the command chair. She sat in it and asked, "What do we have?"

He pointed up at the vidscreen and the digital grid overlay that mapped the terrain of Praxid. "Our long-range scanners picked up a Dagon distress beacon down on the surface of Praxid in quadrant D-13. But we're not detecting any life signs. Just the transponder, which is set to repeat the SOS every thirty-seven minutes."

"It could be a trap. Pirates often use fake transponder codes to lure in unsuspecting ships before boarding them," Ri'Vera added.

"That's what I initially thought, too, ma'am. But we pinged them back for a Dagon security code and we got a class three transponder."

Lycia raised an eyebrow. "I'm sorry, I'm still new to all this military jargon. What's a class three transponder?"

"It merely means they gave a higher-level security clearance code than expected in a situation like this. Type 1 is a distress call for normal operations. Type 2 is a distress call for diplomatic operations. Type three is reserved for more sensitive operations, usually involving somebody of higher rank, regarding sensitive information to the security of the Dagon Empire."

Ri'Vera nodded and then, clearing her throat, chimed in, "It usually means there's a security risk involved, and it shouldn't be ignored."

"So, then, we have to respond," Lycia said.

"It could still be a trap, though," Lt. Commander T'Vok cautioned.

"A risk we're going to have to take. If there's any chance that it's one of ours, then we need to act." She turned to Ri'Vera and with a smile said, "Ri'Vera, you're with me. Lieutenant Commander T'Vok, you have the bridge."

"Yes, Your Grace," T'Vok said, giving the Dagon salute as Lycia and the sub commander strolled off the bridge.

Once they left, he sat down in the command chair and then said, "I want all eyes to monitor their actions down on the surface. If anything looks suspect, out of place, or even if you just have a bad gut feeling—I want to be the first to know. That's an order."

"Yes, sir," the bridge crew replied in unison.

After suiting up, Lycia and Ri'Vera stepped up onto the teleportation pad. Lycia turned to the operations chief at the standing console off to the side, and said, "Begin transfer."

The security chief, a portly Dagon officer with a crown of white hair and a bald top, merely nodded and ran his fingers across the buttons.

A beam of golden light enveloped both women and in two blinks of an eye, they were both standing on the craggy surface of Praxid.

As golden particles of light faded away like embers of a fire dying as they floated away from their heat source, Lycia scanned the jagged and uneven terrain.

"This place looks like something out of my nightmares," she said.

"Praxid used to be highly volcanic, hence all the sulfur oxide and igneous rock."

Lycia drew up her forearm-mounted holovid display and flicked on the

3D representation of the terrain. Then, pointing a finger between two jagged spires of volcanic rock, she informed Ri'Vera that, "The distress signal is coming from over there."

"Alright then," Ri'Vera said, sauntering on ahead. "We'd best get a move on. We only have two hours of oxygen in each of these canisters, and with this terrain, it's going to take roughly forty minutes just to hike there."

Lycia let out a sigh and then followed after her. As they wound their way down the side of the rocky terrain, they came to the edge of the bluff that looked out over the valley. A blinking red light far in the distance tipped them off that there was indeed a transponder antenna set up about three klicks away.

They hiked the rugged terrain for thirty-seven minutes before finally reaching the transponder and the antenna array. A quick inspection proved that it was, indeed, Dagon. Ri'Vera knelt down to check the time code on the briefcase-like transponder and noted the digital clock face read 36 hours and counting.

"Um…Ri'Vera," Lycia said, reaching back and attempting to tap her on her shoulder but missing.

"Odd, this transponder has been on for three days. You'd think somebody else would have heard it by now, unless…"

"Ri'Vera," Lycia said out of the corner of her mouth.

Ri'Vera finally looked up and saw what had frightened Lycia. Off to the side, in a small alcove, there was a campfire with a large man, about seven feet tall, wearing dreadlocks and a long black trench coat, but no suit.

"Are you seeing what I'm seeing?"

"I'm seeing a dude without a suit on just sitting out here warming himself by a campfire."

"Good, because I thought for a nanosecond there, I might be going crazy."

Slowly, Ri'Vera reached down to her holster and drew up her blaster. She aimed it at the man and said, "State your name, rank, and affiliation, or I'll have no choice but to consider you a hostile threat and defend my empress."

She slowly stepped in front of Lycia, her gun's sights not wavering from her target for an instant.

"My people evolved," he said in a baritone voice, "with four lungs. Two of which are used for breathing. The other two for storing oxygen. And although this planet doesn't have much of an atmosphere, there's enough methane in the air for you to be able to hear me."

"And just…who are you?" Lycia chimed in.

He looked up and smiled, then, cautiously rose to his feet.

Ri'Vera widened her stance and steadied her blaster. "Careful, friend. You're already treading on thin ice as it is. One wrong move and I fill you with holes."

He raised his hands in surrender and smiled. "I have no quarrel with you, blue skin. It's the empress I need to have a word with."

Lycia stepped forward, but Ri'Vera threw out her arm and blocked her. She then tapped Ri'Vera's shoulder and said over the comm, "It's alright. I'll handle this."

Reluctantly, Ri'Vera allowed Lycia to move forward and Lycia walked up to the large man.

"You'd better speak fast because my friend is itching to use that shiny new blaster of hers."

"All this posturing," the man said in a monotone voice. "Is it necessary?"

"I don't know. You tell me. You're the one that went out of your way to get my attention. Well, now you have it. So, spill. What is it you want?"

"My name is Scarborne of the house of Par'Vek. My daughter was Ishtar Bantu of the house of Par'Vek. Your mother murdered her in the arena. And, where I'm from, we pay blood for blood."

"So, you're here to kill me, then?"

"I won't allow that!" Ri'Vera shouted, and she began charging forward, her boots crunching on the uneven surface of the regolith. The muzzle of her blaster glowed as she dashed forward, her plasma bolt charged and hot.

Before she could advance even two steps, however, Scarborne quickly drew a blaster from the inside of his jacket and let off a powerful plasma blast from five meters off.

A bright splash of red plasma lit up their faces as it hit Ri'Vera squarely in her chest, just above her pectoral, and sent her flying backward. She crashed onto her back with a thud, a burning plasma hole in her suit and a raw wound of freshly singed skin.

She screamed out as the pain flooded her body. The burning was bad; even though her heat resistant suit had saved her from a fatal wound, there was no escaping the pain. At the same time, air leaked from the fresh gash in her suit and she started coughing and hacking as the fowl atmosphere seeped into her helmet.

"You bastard!" shouted Lycia. She swatted the gun from Scarborne's hand but he didn't seem to care. When she gripped him tightly by his lapel, he merely reached up and clutched her wrists. Drawing in close, they came nose to nose.

"If she dies, I swear on the ashes of my father, I shall…"

"My dear girl," Scarborne said in a disarming manner, "don't you see? You're a dead woman walking."

"Like Helios I am!" With great strength, Lycia threw out her arms, ripping the leather jacket, and consequently, Scarborne's arms from his body. She screamed out with rage before realizing the fizzle and pop of sparking joint hinges. She looked down to find two prosthetic arms dangling from her hands.

"What is—"

The sound of two consecutively fired blasts ringing out, one immediately after the other, stopped her words. She looked down to find both of Scarborne's real arms, each one holding a plasma shotgun. The first shot had burned away her heat resistant suit. The second had drilled a Siezarrian cantaloupe-sized hole in her abdomen. The shot went straight through her and penetrated the back of her suit, leaving nothing but a hollow tunnel of singed flesh and muscle sinews.

Lycia gasped and staggered back. "No, this can't…"

Her words were again interrupted, this time by Scarborne casually putting her in a headlock. With a firm twist, as though he were trying to snap her neck, he ripped off her helmet and then kicked it away from her.

She gasped for breath but her lungs immediately began to burn from the methane in the air. Collapsing to the ground, she reached out for Ri'Vera who was already blurring in and out of consciousness.

Lycia managed to mouth the words, "Ri'Vera," with her dying breath. Then her eyes fluttered back in her head and she stiffened, a look of agony frozen on her face.

As the LED interior lighting of her faceplate illuminated her suffocating face, Ri'Vera reached out in desperation to try and clasp Lycia's hand, but it was in vain. Lycia was too far away and she was too badly wounded to make it to her in time to save her.

Scarborne chuckled in his deep, resonant voice and tapped his comms badge. "Get me off this rock," he said. A split-second later a red beam of light engulfed him and he was whisked up to his ship, the *Labrys*.

Decloaking next to Lycia's three-ship fleet, the *Labrys* slowly turned, its right wing clipping one of Lycia's cruisers. The cruiser exploded as the IGS flagship tore through it as though it were made of flimsy foil

In the next instant, the *Labrys* jumped away, leaving the Dagon Imperial fleet crippled and the empress lying lifeless on the surface of the hellish planet.

30

Shown to the guest room, Jegra stood next to a mirror, looking at the blue and white gingham dress that was waiting on a hanger for her to wear. It looked like the dress of an 1800's woman, not that of modern society.

This was all the more perplexing to her, since, if these people were from the ancient past, how did they get here? How have they survived this long on their own?

Dissatisfied with the attire, Jegra went over to the closet and opened it. Men's suits lined the entire wardrobe and she smiled. At least one of them, she thought, should be in her size. And, sure enough, she found a fancy gray gentlemen's suit with a vest and a black collared shirt to go underneath. She put on the shirt, suit, and vest, leaving the collar of her shirt open so that it displayed just the top of her cleavage.

Once she'd changed out of her swimwear and into the suit, there was a knock at the door and she said, "Enter."

A woman came in and looked at her and then gasped. Jegra turned to her and raised an eyebrow.

"Oh, my," the woman said, doing her best to suppress a giggle. "You look..."

"Handsome?" Jegra said with a chortle.

"The women here aren't exactly in the habit of wearing men's fashion."

Jegra nodded. "I can change back into something less controversial if you think it will cause too much of an uproar?"

"Nonsense, you're our guest," the woman said. "We want you to be comfortable here. Wear what you like."

Jegra nodded and smiled. The woman stepped closer and curtseyed.

"Allow me to introduce myself. I'm Darcy's wife, Patricia. Patricia Smith."

"It's a pleasure to meet you, Mrs. Smith. I'm sorry about your daughter."

Mrs. Smith diverted her eyes for a moment and then wiped away a tear with her gloved hand. That's when Jegra saw that she, too, had two concealed plasma burns.

"If you don't mind my boldness, I noticed you and Mr. Darcy both have plasma burns."

She looked down at her gloved hands, and feeling self-conscious, hid them behind her back. "Ah, yes. Mr. Darcy rescued me from a plasma fire aboard our ship when it crash-landed on this planet nearly forty years ago. It was the most heroic and selfless thing I'd ever seen anyone do. So, of course, I accepted his proposal a year later. Our daughter, Mercy, was born shortly after that. She turns twenty-seven this fall."

Soon enough a black housekeeper appeared in the entrance and with a slight curtsey, informed them, "Table is all set, ma'am. Will you and your guest be joining Mr. Darcy for supper?"

"Well, Zanda, that's up to our guest. What do you say? Shall we sup together?"

"I'm famished," Jegra said.

Mrs. Smith gestured for Jegra to follow her out into the hallway and they made their way downstairs. When they entered the dining room, Mr. Darcy was already at the head of the table awaiting their arrival.

"Doesn't she look fashionable?" Mrs. Smith said when she noticed Mr. Darcy's eyebrow raise when he saw Jegra wearing a man's suit.

"Indeed, she does." Smiling, he stood up and gestured for them to be seated. Once they'd seated themselves, he sat back down. "Zanda will bring out the meal in a moment. But I just want to get better acquainted with you."

"By all means," Jegra said gesturing for him to proceed. "Let the interrogation begin."

Mr. Darcy laughed and brushed aside the notion that he was interrogating her. "I just want to ask a few questions. That's all."

"Shoot," Jegra said, smiling at him.

"Just to get it out there, are you or were you in the past ever associated with the Icarus Project?"

Jegra shook her head. "I'm not familiar with that. Does it have something to do with NASA?"

"NASA?" Mrs. Darcy laughed. "Heaven's no. NASA was disbanded in 1969 when the Cosmonauts beat us to the moon landing."

"I'm pretty sure we beat them to the moon," Jegra said. "We even have a Mars colony and..."

"A Mars colony?" Mr. Darcy repeated boldly. "That's quite impossible. Mars was destroyed in 1975 due to over mining."

"I'm sorry," Jegra said, "I seem to be confused. You are from Earth, yes?"

Mrs. Darcy laughed. "Of course, we are, dear. Both of us born and raised in Georgia."

Although she was confused by the incongruent timeline, that's all it was— an alternate timeline. And with her older self traveling from the future after H'aaztre's dabbling in the past, using Aldebaran to try and exist in all dimensions of time and space simultaneously, a plot which she proudly thwarted—there's no telling what had become of her current timeline. It was all a lot to take in, but she pinned any pressing concerns for later.

Instead of getting fixated on it, however, seeing as it was entirely out of her control, she decided to keep the small talk moving along.

"I'm originally from Nebraska. My parents were farmers," Jegra shared.

Mrs. Darcy leaned in, "That's wholesome enough. Tell us, my dear. How did you find yourself in the deep, still waters of space? How did you come to find yourself here on New Haven?"

Jegra surmised that New Haven is what they called this world. She then reached for the glass of water sitting before her on the nicely made table and took a sip before replying. "It may sound far-fetched, but I was abducted by aliens and sold as a slave into an intergalactic gladiatorial ring where I was forced to kill other aliens from other worlds for sport."

"Oh, my," Mrs. Darcy said, shocked at the terrible nature of Jegra's experience.

"You know, I never believed in aliens until we crash-landed here and met the Preemar. By the by, my dear, I need to ask...of these aliens you were forced to fight to the death, none of them were ever a fellow human, were they?"

"No," Jegra said promptly. "Never."

"It's a relief to hear you say that. Because the Lord doesn't tolerate murder.

But, killing savages like the Preemar, well, that's another matter."

Both he and his wife had a good laugh at that and then Zanda brought out their food. It was a juicy steak with shallots and a baked potato with chives and sour cream. Steamed carrots and yams on the side along with a side plate of Caesar salad.

"It smells delicious," Jegra said, taking it all in.

"We grow all our food. And this year, Dr. Burns insists that the six hundred head of cattle will be fatter than ever before and that the bounty of vegetables will be the biggest we've ever seen."

Jegra nodded politely and then waited for Mr. Darcy to take the first bite before digging in. She then proceeded to devour her food like a half-starved wildebeest, to the dismay and amusement of her hosts. They kept stealing glances at one another and smiling at the strange little things Jegra did as she ate.

"I apologize for my crude manners, but I haven't eaten human food in, well, far longer than I care to admit."

"You poor thing," Mrs. Smith said. Then turning, she clapped her hands and Zanda appeared. "Zanda, be a dear and bring another course for our guest."

"Yes, ma'am," Zanda said, quickly disappearing back into the kitchen. A few moments later she reappeared with another fresh plate for Jegra.

"You sure?" asked Jegra. Mrs. Smith nodded and gestured at her to help herself.

"I hate to talk business at the table, but I'm curious as to what your plans are?"

"I intend to return to my ship and finish making repairs. I'll be out of your hair soon enough."

"Yes, about that..." Mr. Darcy said, "I'm afraid I can't allow it."

"I beg your pardon?" Jegra said, sitting upright, her posture stiffening.

"You see. We don't mind outsiders joining our little commune, here on New Haven. But we have a strict policy against using alien technology. Your ship will be dismantled and recycled to provide us with the necessary metals we need to keep this colony running."

"But you can't do that. It's my property."

Not being accustomed to such defiance, Mr. Darcy shot Jegra a stern look and then said in a strained voice filled with suppressed anger, "I'm afraid that's just how it is, my dear. Of course, you could appeal my decision to the community board, but they'll merely side with me. After all, you're a stranger here."

Just then a car honked and lights flooded into the room. They rose from the table just as the doors burst in and three soldiers brought Commander Gibbs in on a medical stretcher. He was badly wounded—as though he'd been mauled by a bear.

"Quick, to my study," Mr. Darcy said. As they followed him, he began to roll up his sleeves and asked, "What happened?"

"We were ambushed just outside of the Preemar camp. Tribal warriors flanked us. We dug in and our superior firepower prevailed but not before one of those bastards broke through our defensive line and attacked the commander."

Jegra followed them into the study and watched as they hoisted Mr. Gibbs onto the large leather sofa set against the back wall.

Jegra was about to step further into the room when a hand caught her by her wrist and gently drew her back into the hall.

"Let's leave this to the men to handle," Mrs. Darcy Smith said, drawing the doors shut behind them.

"But I can help," Jegra said.

"I'm sure you're a smart and capable girl," Mrs. Darcy said in a polite fashion that was beginning to grate on Jegra's nerves, seeing as everything she said was anything but. "But we must leave this up to the superior judgment of the men."

What kind of backwards society was this? Steamed, Jegra stepped outside. She found the guard she'd hit in the head with a wrench standing on the porch, smoking a cigarette.

She paced back and forth, her fists balled up at her sides, and huffed in annoyance.

"What's got your goat?" the soldier asked.

"Where I come from, men don't talk down to women. And certainly, women don't snipe at their fellow women."

The soldier laughed. "Things can be pretty old-fashioned around here."

"If by 'old-fashioned' you mean backwards," Jegra grumbled, "then, yeah."

He laughed again and offered her a hit of his cigarette. She obliged and then handed it back.

She exhaled long and slow, releasing a puff of smoke and then immediately began coughing.

"Not a smoker?"

"That obvious?" she asked.

They both laughed.

After sharing a lingering glance, she raised her finger and pointed at the bandage on his head. "Again, sorry for walloping you back there. But, in my defense, you guys did sneak up on me."

"I'm just glad you didn't wallop me again for those remarks I made about your ass."

Jegra smiled and then turned slightly to show off her butt in her nice suit pants. "Why, do you think I have a cute ass?"

He laughed again and then gestured for her to keep her voice down. "Careful. If the Smith's catch you talking like that, they'll send you to reconditioning."

"Reconditioning?"

"It's where they hook you up to this device that's supposed to cleanse you of the evil spirits that infest this world. Or, so they say. In my forty years here, I ain't never seen a spirit. Just those bloodthirsty Preemar."

Jegra nodded. "Thanks for the warning."

"No problem."

"So, tell me about Mercy. What's the deal with her? Why did the Preemar take her?"

The soldier laughed. "Mercy can be a handful. Unlike her parents, she believes in missionary work. She thought reaching out to them and teaching about the goodness of Jesus Christ would be the best way to go. It seemed the Preemar were accepting of her attempts, and they used her as a go-between. She even managed to broker a peace treaty. And our two groups left the other alone, for the most part. However, that all changed last month when some of our children accidentally trampled a sacred burial ground of the Preemar."

"What happened?" Jegra gasped, almost dreading the answer.

"They let all but one of the children go. That unlikely child was roasted and eaten. They sent back his bones. When that happened, Mr. Darcy wanted to go to war. But Mercy talked him down and convinced him that at least one attempt at diplomacy was in order. I agreed, but they kidnapped her. Then, you arrived."

"Me and my expert timing," Jegra mumbled to herself. The soldier merely smiled and put out his cigarette on the porch railing.

"Look, I know nobody trusts you yet, but there's no way we're getting Mercy out of there alive without slaughtering the entire Preemar village. And, although Mr. Darcy will be able to justify such carnage in the name of saving his one and only daughter, there are people here who might find that a bit extreme."

"What are you trying to ask?" Jegra said, smiling at him. She knew that he knew something and wasn't telling her.

Lowering his voice to a whisper, he leaned in and said, "I know who you are."

"You do, do you?" she asked, narrowing her eyes at him and smiling playfully.

"The Empress of the Galaxy, right?"

She looked at him with curious eyes and asked, "And how would you know that?"

"A few years back, my patrol found a downed shuttle with an active power source and decided not to report it. We knew Mr. Darcy would merely have us scrap it for parts. But Commander Gibbs felt we could use it as a backup generator in case of emergencies."

"That doesn't answer my question," Jegra said.

"It has a working televid onboard. Occasionally, some of the men will steal away to tune into the gladiator fights. I've seen all your matches."

"So, you know about the war?"

"Only from the bits and pieces, we could piece together from the newsbites that interrupt the feed. We just always assumed it was too far away to have any direct effect on us. And Commander Gibbs ordered us to keep quiet; he didn't want to alarm the rest of the colonists."

"Smart move," Jegra said. "Mr. Gibbs sounds like a true leader."

Just then the screen door opened and Mr. Darcy stepped out, blood coating his hands. He looked over at the soldier and then, with a downcast face, shook his head apologetically.

"My condolences. Mr. Gibbs didn't make it."

Jegra looked at them both then sauntered down the steps and started walking up the street.

"And where, might I inquire, young lady, are you going at this godforsaken hour?" Mr. Darcy asked, calling out after her.

"I'm going to get your daughter back," Jegra said.

Mr. Darcy was about to protest the absurdity of such a notion and reprimand her for attempting to do a man's job, but the soldier merely held out his hand and gestured for Mr. Darcy to let her go.

"You're okay with this?" he asked, shocked by the entire idea of letting a woman do their dirty work for them.

"You don't understand, Mr. Mayor. She wasn't lying about who she was."

"I don't believe I know what you're getting at. All we were able to pry from her tight lips was that she's some kind of gladiator who was forced to kill for sport."

"She's not just any gladiator, sir. She's the reigning, undefeated champion of the galaxy. She's Jegra Alakandra."

"And how might you know all this?"

"It's a long story, sir. And one I'll share in due time. But right now, I'm asking you to trust me when I tell you, if there's anyone who can get your sweet Mercy back, it's her."

Mr. Darcy looked back up the street at Jegra, who was already fading into the darkness of the evening.

"If you say so, young man. But, just in case she doesn't make it back, you'd better mobilize the boys."

The soldier nodded and then pulled out a pack, tapped the box, and let a fresh cigarette rise to the surface. Then, kissing it out with a touch of his lips, he cupped his hands over it and lit it up using his old stainless-steel lighter.

31

A sickly vaporous haze settled around Naya Ri'Vera as she crawled toward Lycia's unresponsive body. Barely hanging on to consciousness, Ri'Vera managed to fend off the red-rim of encroaching unconsciousness long enough to drag herself across the abrasive surface and bring herself within arm's reach of the empress.

Each rattling breath scorched the insides of her lungs like acid, but she couldn't give up. Not with Lycia so close. Not with the empress's life hanging in the balance. If she could only reach her in time, there was still hope that her life could be saved.

Her bloodshot eyes throbbed in her skull and her every vein was swollen with a sickly, decaying purple as her blood became polluted by the toxic gas seeping into her torn suit.

Ri'Vera somehow managed to get on top of Lycia. Throwing herself across the empress, she wrapped her arms around Lycia's torso and slapped her comm badge on her left breast. Touching herself so close to the raw wound caused a throbbing pain to surge through her.

"*Ungh…*" she groaned. Then, taking in another searing breath, she gasped, "Get…us…out…*ngh,*" she inhaled the deadly mixture of toxic fumes, which mingled with her oxygen supply and finished the sentence, "of here."

The exact moment she'd called up to the ship golden light came down around them both, her lips curled into a subtle grin as she hit the limit of what her body could take and passed out, falling limp across Lycia's body.

Sterile white walls greeted Ri'Vera when she awoke in the medical bay of the *Avalon*. Groggy, she slowly sat up in her bed and rubbed the sleep out of her eyes. It was the first time in months she could remember feeling this refreshed.

In the background, the high-tech medical equipment bleeped and chirped with little updates and she scanned the room wondering how long she'd been under.

A sharp pain coursed through her chest and she cringed. Panicking, she quickly patted her chest and tugged at the collar of her medical gown to see what the damage was.

She glanced down at her right breast and was relieved to find that it was fully intact. The plasma had burned away her heat suit and only singed her skin. The burn marks were already being treated with healing gel.

Letting out a huge sigh of relief, she fell back onto her bed and stared up at the lighting for a while.

After mashing the call button next to her bed about a dozen times to call a nurse but not getting any response, Ri'Vera decided to get up and find someone herself. Sliding out of the bed, her bare feet slapped the cool floor and she headed for the side door to the nurse's station. But as she passed the end of the bed frame, her flimsy medical gown got caught on one of the metal corners and practically tore off from her body.

Her quick reflexes managed to pull it back on, but it was too badly torn to stay on her body so she glanced around the room for another set of clothes. Unfortunately, none could be found.

Still determined to find something to wear, she wandered into the doctor's office and opened one of the lockers. The first locker was empty, so she tried another. The second one had a rank smelling gym uniform and she slammed the door shut, turning her face away to avoid the backdraft of the terrible stench.

She cautiously opened the third locker; it contained women's sexy lace brazier and matching underwear in pastel green and nothing else. She raised an eyebrow, wondering what nurse wore this kind of underwear to work before taking them from the hanger and sniffing them to see if they were clean.

They weren't dirty or smelly, which was reassuring. Probably an extra change of underwear for after work when one of the nurses had a hot date, she surmised. Checking the size, she realized they were a size too small for her. Even so, they'd do in a pinch.

After removing the padding to give herself extra space, she fastened her bra, her cleavage rising from the added tightness of it. She then started to hop up and down on one leg as she threaded the other one through the leg opening as she wriggled into the underpants. Although the bra was a little tight, the underpants fit perfectly. All of a sudden, a loud *ba-thoom* echoed throughout the ship and the entire thing jolted, as though it had been struck by plasma cannons at point-blank range.

Ri'Vera screamed out as she lost her footing and fell onto her ass. Swiftly leaping back to her feet, she rubbed her sore butt and mumbled, "What in the Seven Virgins of Vortesh is going on now?"

She ran over to the wall panel at the opposite side of the room and tapped into the comm. Mashing the button to call up to the bridge, she began to say something but was drown out by a strange monotone garble of fragmented voices followed by a screaming buzz.

She hung up the call, as the interference grated on her every nerve. *Still, if we are being jammed...*she thought, then that meant the enemy ship was upon them.

Sickbay, meanwhile, was a deserted ghost town and it did her no good to stick around waiting for somebody when the ship was under attack. She knew that she needed to get to the bridge.

Exiting sickbay, the sliding doors parted and a dead body fell to the floor, causing her to reach up and smother a scream. She nearly tripped on the body of the guard that lay across the threshold, but carefully stepped over him and out into the corridor.

The guard had a plasma blast in his side and the poor unlucky soul had bled out right next to the medical bay with technology that could have saved him.

Ri'Vera bent down and unfastened his gun holster and belt, her underwear riding up her butt as she stood back up. Running a thumb along the inside of the elastic, she titled her hips and fixed her underwear. Once that was out of the way, she quickly strapped the white leather holster across her hips, along with the belt—which held three additional coolant cartridges—standard for security detail aboard Dagon ships.

She wanted a jacket to cover up her mostly naked body, but the guard's jacket was half charred from the plasma and the other half was soaking in his blood. As such, she decided against it. Clothes would have to wait. Right now, she needed to get up to the bridge.

Another blast rattled the ship, and she fell into the wall panel, the computer lighting flickering as it tried to guess what her hands were searching for as she pushed herself back up. A few more meters ahead, at the second junction, she came across another dead guard who'd fallen back onto the railing of the upper deck.

This poor sap had a plasma blast through his skull and had fallen back onto the balcony railing that overlooked the main engineering department below. She peeled him off the railing and let his body hit the ground at her feet with a thud.

"Sorry, crewman," she whispered, realizing it was a bit rougher than she'd intended.

Not wasting any time, she stripped off his belt too, slung it across her shoulder and grabbed his jacket off him. Just her luck, of all the Dagon engineers aboard, she had to find the shortest one with the smallest jacket.

As she slipped the white jacket on, it covered her shoulders but was barely long enough to conceal her abdomen. Zipping it up, it looked like a belly shirt on her tall slender figure, and although her belly button still showed, at least she didn't feel as naked anymore.

Drawing out both blasters, just in case she ran into trouble, she glanced over the railing at the deck below and saw more bodies strewn about. Then, turning up the corridor, she made her way to the lift. Once inside, she jammed her thumb into the button to take her to the command deck and the lift's lights went haywire and flickered randomly. Then everything went dark.

"Graddak," she growled in frustration, smashing the butt of one of her blasters against the panel and cracking the glass.

Ri'Vera raised both blasters above her head and blew open the hatch to the top of the lift. Sparks flared up and then died down as she holstered her guns. Crouching down, she leaped up and grabbed onto the lip of the opening, dangling in the center of the lift for a moment as she took in a deep breath. Then, with a loud grunt, she hoisted herself through and pulled herself onto the roof of the lift.

Emergency lights came on inside the turboshaft, and she scanned the oval walls for the turboshaft's access ladder. Leaping onto the ladder, she started climbing, one hand and foothold at a time, gradually ascending the inside of the shaft.

It would take about half an hour to climb to the bridge on the eleventh deck. But seeing as the lifts were out of commission, she highly doubted that the teleporters would be working. Also, whoever had taken out those guards might still be roaming the ship. At least this way, she stayed out of sight.

Red alert sounded and crimson LEDs flashed along the wall panels, washing across the room in waves that basked Lycia's blue skin and cast her in a purple tint.

She stood on the bridge, her red kimono mini dress torn and tattered. The bridge had been retaken, and she glowered at the face in the televid monitor.

Bandages covered the area where she'd been shot over ten hours ago. But her healing powers were fast and, currently, she felt as right as rain. The same couldn't be said for the dead pirates that littered the command deck, however.

When she'd come to, the ship was already being boarded by a band of marauders. Her security team did their best to fend them off, but the cost was high.

Of the casualties, Lt. Commander T'Vok was one of them. But before he died fighting by her side, he had killed five pirates single-handedly.

Of the fifty or so that had boarded her ship, and she guessed another fifty or so odd ravagers had boarded the *Veritas* just the same, she'd taken down thirty-five with only minor scrapes.

Naturally, she suspected Scarborne was behind it, since pirates typically knew to stay clear of the Dagon Imperial Navy. But what he could have promised them that would embolden them to attack her ships, she couldn't say.

She turned to the image peering back at her from up on the monitor. "How'd you know that I wasn't dead?"

"Because," Scarborne said with a sinister grin, "if I'd have wanted to kill you, I would have taken your head off down on Praxid. I left you there to suffer, not to die."

"So, what? You're just toying with me?"

The red face on the monitor stared at her with a scathing grin and then he gave a subtle shrug. "All is fair in love and war, my dear empress," he said, his words dripping with disdain as he spoke. "And, believe you me. This *is* war."

"Why don't we settle this, *mono a mono*, in the arena?"

Scarborne just eyed her with an unamused look. She was a genetically enhanced clone, and although he was a skilled warrior, he knew that if it came down to a blow by blow battle, she'd win. No, he wasn't foolish enough to take the bait.

The screen cut out and, a fraction of a second later, another blast from Scarborne's ship took out the *Avalon's* engines. Lycia looked out to see the *Labrys* turn all its cannons onto the *Veritas* and open fire. The ship went up in a bubbly plume of green fiery gas which quickly imploded on itself.

"You son of a bitch!" Lycia shouted as if it would do any good.

Indifferent to her curses, the *Labrys* gradually turned and sailed off into the dark expanse. Its course plotted for the pale turquoise dot which sat on the distant horizon—he was headed straight for Dagon Prime.

Another explosion, this time from one of the shield generators which had overloaded, rocked the ship and a scream rang out from the turbo lift.

Lycia raced over and, gripping the wedge in-between the lift doors, pried the doors apart with her bare hands. As they scraped open, she peered inside to find Ri'Vera dangling from one of the rungs of the maintenance ladder a meter below her.

Lying on the floor, Lycia stretched out on her belly and reached down, extending her open hand for Ri'Vera to take. "Here! Take my hand."

Ri'Vera looked up, and, with a grunt, pulled herself up as she, at the same time, extended her free arm. With a clap, their hands clasped together and Lycia, holding firm, hoisted Ri'Vera up and onto the bridge.

Both women collapsed to their knees for a moment catching their breath. Lycia turned to Ri'Vera to welcome her onto the bridge only to forget everything she was going to say when she beheld Ri'Vera's blue skin wrapped up in lots of white leather straps, a jacket too tiny for her frame, and underwear a size too small and which, subsequently, caused her to bulge in all the right places, accentuating her womanly curves.

"What in the galaxy are you wearing?"

"It's all I could find on short notice."

Lycia got up and extended her hand. "Come on, we have to get this bucket of bolts up and running if we hope to stop Scarborne before it's too late."

Ri'Vera clasped Lycia's hand and let her pull her onto her feet. With a mighty tug that nearly had her toes rise off the ground, she landed firmly on her heels and continued holding Lycia's hand for a bit longer than she probably should have before sliding her fingers out of Lycia's grasp.

They both blushed and then turned their attention to the monitor.

"I don't get it," Ri'Vera began, "why would he be headed to Dagon Prime if he wants to kill you? Why doesn't he just finish the job and…oh, no." She covered her mouth as the realization set in.

"Scarborne is IGS…and has declared martial law. Knowing I won't accept his authority, he's taking every trained gladiator in the system and is going to use them as his invasion force. And my mother is the only one who could convince any of them not to do this. But she's since dropped off the star charts."

"My haunted stars," Ri'Vera gasped, "Thousands will die if we don't stop him."

"Then we have no choice. We must stop him."

Just then a red blip showed up on the radar screen and Ri'Vera turned to Lycia with a worried look.

"More space pirates?" asked Ri'Vera.

"Probably scavengers and a salvage crew swooping in to clean up Scarborne's mess."

"What do we do?"

Lycia slammed her fist into her open palm and cracked her knuckles. "We hide. Then, while they're aboard our ship stripping her for parts, I suggest we take their ship and use it to ram that son-of-a-bitch right out of the sky."

32

A campfire crackled in the distance as Jegra crept through the various bamboo huts of the Preemar village. Avoiding detection, she finally located the hut being watched by a couple of guards. "Bingo," she whispered.

Jegra then stood up straight and walked right up to the two guards who, confused by her presence, held their spears out and mumbled something at her in an alien tongue.

"Sorry," she replied, "I don't understand your language." She then grabbed their spears, and, one in each hand, she slammed the sticks together, consequently knocking the two guards together with enough force to render them unconscious.

She then slipped into the hut, dragging both men in with her. Once inside, she looked over to find the big, beautiful green eyes of a brunette tied to the central support beam.

"Who are you and why in the world are you dressed that way?"

"I'm here to rescue you," Jegra whispered. "Your father sent me."

"You know my father?" Mercy laughed, eyeing Jegra up and down skeptically.

"I met your parents, Mr. and Mrs. Darcy, earlier tonight. We dined together. And, now, I'm here."

"You're mistaken," Mercy said.

"I beg your pardon?"

"Patricia isn't my biological mother. My mother died in the crash. My father, the hypocrite, married the woman he was cheating on my mother with."

"Ah, gotcha. An evil stepmother."

Mercy laughed and then, as Jegra came over and snapped her rope restraints like they were straw, looked up and asked, "Who are you, again?"

"Jegra," she replied, helping Mercy up.

"Just...Jegra?"

"Jegra Alakandra, The Mother of all Dagon, Protector of the Empire, and Savior to the Galaxy."

"All that, huh?" Mercy said sarcastically.

"Yeah, nobody ever believes me. But, I'm here to rescue you, so you can either come with me or stay behind and take your chances with the Preemar."

Mercy followed Jegra to the entrance. "Nah, I trust that whoever you are, my odds of not getting filleted are better with you than if I stay here."

Jegra poked her head out of the hut and then slowly drew back inside. "Yeah, about that..."

Mercy placed her hand on the small of Jegra's back and asked, "What?"

Jegra looked back at her and, in a squeaky voice, said, "Sorry?"

Half an hour later, both women were strung up to a cross over a wood pit of a bonfire. Having been stripped of their clothes, only the deep brown barbeque sauce the Preemar had basted them with, conveniently concealed their nudity.

"Is this how all your great escapes go?" asked Mercy.

"Oh, shut up," Jegra replied. "I'm a little bit rusty."

"You're going to be a little bit dead soon, you do realize that, right?"

Jegra huffed out a puff of air in annoyance, shooing away her bangs. Then as two torchbearers approached, she asked Mercy, "Do you trust me?"

"What?"

"Do you trust me?"

"What kind of question is that? I just met you!" Mercy tugged at her restraints and gave Jegra a vexed look. "And it's going great so far!"

"Ha-ha, very funny."

Mercy rolled her eyes and then looked back at the torchbearers as they stood at the foot of the pyres ready to set the women ablaze and roast them for their evening meal.

A train of Preemar women came out and dumped entire trays of vegetables at the feet of both Mercy and Jegra.

"Look, lady, I don't care if you think you're God. Right now, if you get me out of this, I'll give you anything you want."

"That's all I needed to hear," Jegra said. Then, just as they began to set the pyres aflame, Jegra snapped her bonds, freed Mercy, and, taking the young woman in her arms, leaped up into the air and over the village.

With a padded thud, they landed outside of the village and Jegra set the dumbfounded Mercy on her feet.

"Wait, what just…how did you…who are you, again?"

"I told you, my name is Jegra. And my ship is three klicks this way, so try and keep up." With that, Jegra jogged into the forest and Mercy raced close behind, keeping at her heels.

When they arrived at the ship, Jegra pulled the girl into the glass elevator with her and ascended into her ship.

Two X5 battle androids greeted them inside the main cargo hold, arm-mounted cannons locked onto them. Recognizing the empress, both trained their weapons onto Mercy, and she slowly ducked behind Jegra, using her as a shield. Rolling her eyes at the robots, Jegra ordered them to "Stand down," and they complied.

"Seriously, who are you?" asked Mercy, stepping back out from behind Jegra now that the coast was clear.

Jegra went over to a control panel on the wall, tapped a few buttons and a golden light engulfed them. A few seconds later they appeared in Jegra's quarters.

"Whoa, what just happened?" Mercy said, looking down at her hands and arms with alarm. The sparkles faded but she still felt disoriented.

"I teleported you to my chambers. I'll draw you a bath and fetch you a change of clothes."

Mercy slowly followed Jegra into the other room and gasped when she saw what was a large clamshell shaped bathtub made of stone fed by a waterfall styled fountain.

"You have *this* aboard a spaceship?"

Jegra shrugged as though it was no big deal. "It's one of the perks of being the ex-empress."

"Ex-empress?" Mercy asked. "Alright, say I'm starting to believe you. Who's the empress now?"

"My daughter, Lycia."

Mercy nodded; that made sense.

"Feel free to take your time. I'll take a shower in the adjoining room. If you need anything, just call out to me."

"You have a shower in there too?" She leaned to the side to try and get a better view of the luxurious bathroom aboard this spaceship. She'd never seen anything like it.

Jegra nodded, and then slid open a side panel revealing another large room with a toilet, full sink, and a shower. "I'll just be in here washing if you need me."

Mercy nodded and then went over to the small basin beside the bath and rinsed the burgundy sauce off her body. As the freshwater cleansed her red skin, turning it snow white again, Jegra looked away. As she did, however, she caught Mercy's reflection stealing a glance of her in the mirror. She smiled warmly and then shook her head.

No, she told herself, it was a bad idea. She was too young, and Jegra was married to three of the loveliest women she'd ever known. And although they were all Dagoni and gave her permission to have as many side dalliances as she needed, she wasn't exactly craving anything from anyone at the moment. She was, for the lack of a better word, content.

She stepped through the door and entered the shower stall, slowly sliding it shut, but leaving it a crack open just in case Mercy cried out for her.

The shower stall was lined with granite and Jegra climbed into the shower and turned it on, standing to the side so the initial blast of cold water didn't shock her as it gradually heated up.

Once it was piping hot, she closed her eyes and stepped into the hot shower, and washed off the grime and the smell of three-day-old barbeque.

Once they were both cleansed and wrapped in pristine white towels softer than a Flurien alpaca, Jegra found Mercy standing in front of the tall glass windows that overlooked the jungle canopy. In the far distance, she could make out the dim orange glow of the Preemar village.

"I'm sorry it didn't work out for you."

Mercy looked over her shoulder, catching a glimpse of Jegra as she sidled up beside her. They both looked back out the window together and Mercy sighed.

"It's fine. It'll be a while before the Preemar trust us again, and we'll have to fend off raids for the next few years, but I'm confident they'll eventually see reason. After all, they're not savages like my father says. They're quite intelligent. They just need someone to show them the way."

"Once I repair my ship, I may be able to stick around and help you deal with the Preemar, if you'd like."

"No, you needn't bother with that. It's not your concern. Besides, as ex-empress of the galaxy, I'm sure you have other, much more important things to be doing." Mercy turned to Jegra and, still gazing out the window, she shrugged.

"You'd be surprised."

"Well, at least we can have this evening all to ourselves," Mercy said. With that, she let her towel fall to the ground and then, making sure Jegra's eyes were on her, she sauntered over to the bed, swiveling her hips the whole way.

Climbing onto the bed like a cat, she rolled onto her back and patted the covers, begging Jegra to join her.

"I think I may have given you the wrong idea," Jegra said.

"Nonsense. I saw you looking at me earlier. There's an attraction here. Besides, do you know what my father would do to me if he found out I was a lesbian? He'd probably hand me over to the Preemar himself!"

"Not everyone is open-minded enough to realize love knows no bounds. Others are just intolerant to accept love in all of its forms."

Mercy sat up on the bed and covered her breasts with her arm. "You're not attracted to me, then?"

"It's not that," Jegra said. "I'm married."

"Ah," Mercy said, turning away with a dejected look.

"But they're understanding, and we don't place any demands on one another."

"They?" Mercy asked, her curiosity piqued as her eyes quickly flitted back to Jegra.

"I have three wives, at the moment."

"That's…" Jegra waited for Mercy to finish her thought. "Fucking amazing!"

Jegra laughed. "I suppose it is."

"Seriously, that's my dream. Being surrounded by beautiful women." Mercy fell back onto the bed and stared dreamily up at the ceiling. "Not having to worry about being judged or meeting any expectations."

Jegra came over and settled on the edge of the bed.

Mercy rolled over and, propping her head onto her palms, and gently kicking her legs behind her. "Do you realize that he wants me to marry Mr. Gibbs? He's all but picked out the wedding date."

Jegra opened her mouth to mention something about Mr. Gibbs's fate but then decided against it.

"I could never marry a brute like that. I mean, I caught him picking his nose the other day. Sure, he didn't eat it, but men are so gross!"

"Some are," Jegra replied. "Some can be wonderful."

Mercy raised an eyebrow. "Don't tell me you're into men too?"

Jegra blushed and gave a subtle shrug.

"Oh, wow!" Mercy sat up on her knees, her hands resting between her thighs. "Both?"

"See, I told you that you had the wrong idea about me."

"I'm fine with it. Honestly. I am. Being stuck on New Haven doesn't exactly give me many opportunities to date. Especially the kind of people I'd like to date."

Jegra turned to Mercy and said, "If we do this, you have to know it's a onetime thing. I can't be your girlfriend."

Mercy shook her head. "I wouldn't dream of asking you to be. And, a one-night stand is fine by me. I can't even remember the last time I had sex."

Slowly, they drew together and, their lips hovering dangerously close, Jegra waited for Mercy to initiate the kiss.

Once she was confident Mercy wanted to do this, she crawled onto the bed, Mercy laying back and stretching out as Jegra dappled her stomach with kisses. When she got to her neck, Mercy moaned out loudly.

"Are we really doing this?" Mercy asked.

"Yes," Jegra answered, kissing her mouth with a sultry kiss.

Mercy moaned again as they kissed, and settled into one another's arms.

Exactly fifty-seven minutes later, Mercy flopped onto her back, her entire body gleaming with sweat, and panted heavily. "That was the best sex of my life."

Jegra lay next to her, panting too. "That was the first time I've ever had sex with a human. Not counting the time I had sex with myself."

"Wait, what?" Mercy asked, looking over at Jegra with a perplexed look on her face.

"It's a long story. The gist being, I ran into my future self and, well, one thing led to another."

"That's absolutely mental," Mercy said with a laugh. "And, kind of hot, in a kinky sort of way."

Jegra laughed. "Yes, I suppose it is. But it was also the best sex of my life. Nobody knows your body better than you do."

Mercy smiled and then draped a white thigh over Jegra's golden one. Then, reaching over, she ran her fingers up the inside of Jegra's thigh until they came to hallowed ground.

"Ready for round two?" Mercy asked, her eyes locked onto Jegra's.

"You read my mind," she replied. And the two women came together again, their tender kisses melting into more passionate, wetter, and sultrier tongue play.

Shafts of morning light roused both women awake and when they sat up in bed together Mercy screamed and covered herself.

A troupe of soldiers dressed in green camo surrounded Jegra's bed. She recognized the soldier from the porch and glowered at him.

"What are you doing in my private chambers? And how'd you get past my defense system?"

"You mean those bucket-heads? A small EMP grenade took them out of commission. As for you two, get dressed. Mr. Darcy would like a word."

"You're not going to tell him about this," asked Mercy, afraid of her father's wrath should he find that she slept with another woman.

"What you do in your free time, Ms. Smith, is none of my concern." With that, he stole one more glance at Jegra and then motioned with a single finger for his men to leave the women to themselves so they might get dressed.

"Shit, shit, shit," Mercy mumbled. Jegra placed a hand on her shoulder and she looked at Jegra with larger frightened eyes that seemed on the brink of bursting into tears. "There's no keeping it a secret now. He'll disown me."

"Not if I have any say in it."

"But you don't understand my father. He's a deeply religious man. And I've betrayed his trust and spat on his faith."

"Then, how about you come with me? Leave this place."

Mercy's face grew blank. She could hardly believe her ears. Life in the stars with a woman like Jegra? It was a dream come true. "Do you mean that?"

"Yes. If it's not safe for you here, then at least allow me to offer you protection. It's the least I can do for the good time you showed me last night."

"But I thought you said we couldn't be more?"

"Circumstances have changed. I've endangered your well-being, and, if you want to come with me, then you're with me. If you want to stay here and face the wrath of your father, that's your choice. It's up to you."

"In that case," Mercy said, staring into Jegra's warm brown eyes with her cool green ones. "Take me with you!"

"Yeah?"

"God, yes!" she answered. "This place has nothing more to offer me. And I dream of freedom, up there, in the stars." She looked up at the sky, then, spinning on her heels and practically hopping up and down with excitement, she threw herself into Jegra's arms.

After getting ready, the soldiers marched them back to New Haven where they were greeted at the edge of town by the mayor.

"Dad," Mercy began, but he shot her a stern gaze that shut her up.

"I'll have words with you later, young lady. Right now, you best get on home to your mother," he ordered, pointing a finger up the street. "She's worried out of her mind about you." Then, turning toward Jegra, he narrowed his eyes and stroked his hoary chin. "And what are these whispers I hear about you defiling my daughter like the Whore of Babylon?"

Jegra just shared a glance with Mercy which infuriated him all the more. "Don't look at her, look at me. I'm the one addressing you."

Jegra slowly turned her gaze back to him and noticed the fire dancing in his eyes. She grinned brusquely, but it was to mask the swelling rage she felt inside for having been so rudely insulted. Implying any sexual woman was a mere whore was, in her estimation, worthy of having your tongue cut out. If you couldn't respect a woman's sexual prowess, then you weren't man enough for her anyway.

"Call me a whore again," she said in a steady tone, "and I'll run my thumbs through your eye sockets and crush your skull with my bare hands."

This gave the old man pause, and he narrowed his eyes at her and smacked his teeth in anger. But, this time, he gave it some thought before he spoke. "Back in the day, there are those who would have burnt you at the stake for the crimes of witchcraft. Bewitching young innocent virgins with your seductive magic."

Jegra raised an eyebrow. If Mercy had been a virgin, that was news to her. But somehow, she doubted it. Rather, it seemed that Mr. Darcy simply was in denial and he didn't want to accept that his little girl had blossomed into a mature woman.

"Lucky for you, we've progressed as a society. We are a civil people and believe in a fair trial. The only question is, until your trial date, what should we do with you?" The question was rhetorical as he couldn't stop pacing back and forth.

"Like I told your men, lend me the parts I need to fix my ship and I'll be out of your hair. It's as easy as that."

"You'd assume so, but you've broken several of our laws. And I'm afraid until your trial date, my hands are tied."

"At least state the charges," she said, a skeptical tone threading her words.

He waved his hand in the air as he searched for the words. "For unwholesome and depraved conduct. For sinful behavior that could harm the very sanctity of this peaceful society, we've erected here. For disobeying curfew. For antagonizing the Preemar and potentially sparking a blood feud that will end in bloodshed on both sides. Shall I go on?"

"I'm sure you'll do whatever you think is best," Jegra replied. "Regardless of however primitive your beliefs may be."

"Primitive?" Mr. Darcy balked. "Now, you listen here, missy, you're the one running around like a savage." Furious, he turned to one of his men, and growled, "Throw her in the brig."

"Sir?" the soldier asked, unsure if that was such a wise idea.

"It's alright," Jegra said, reassuring the soldier she was fine with it. "It won't be the first time I've been treated like a commoner among commoners."

"Of course, it's fine! Why wouldn't it be fine? It's the law. And what does that even mean, a commoner among commoners? I've had quite enough of your self-entitled attitude, young lady. Perhaps a night in jail will serve you well."

The soldier grabbed Jegra by her arm and, giving her an apologetic nod, guided her toward the jailhouse.

"Sorry about all this," he whispered.

"It's no problem," she replied. "Happens all the time to me."

"It does?" he asked, shooting her a surprised glance.

She shrugged nonchalantly as they continued up the road.

Once they made it to the jail, the soldier opened the barred gate and allowed Jegra to enter on her own volition.

He shut the gate behind her and secured it. Then, looking at her one last time, his eyes relaying how truly sorry he was for all this, he locked the gate with the key. After tucking the key into his vest, he nodded at her, as if to assure her he'd be there for her if she needed, and then exited the cell.

Jegra sighed out in frustration and sat down on her cot, staring across the empty room at the door. *What have you gotten yourself into now*, she wondered. But, she hadn't any answers.

All she knew was that she needed to find a way out of this mess, fix her ship, and get off this rock before she sparked the next Salem witch trials with her crazy lesbian magic and sapphic influences.

33

Unfolding the double-page spread of the naked Bre'lal woman spreading her legs and groping her naked body in a lewd fashion, the lone pirate manning the bridge of the freighter leaned back in his chair and licked his lips, a lascivious grin forming on his crooked mouth.

"Those are nice," a voice whispered in his right ear. Startled, his head snapped to the right to find a mostly naked Dagon woman crouching down beside him. She smiled and then nodded her head and said, "But my friend's are bigger."

She nodded to his left, and confused as to what friend she was referring to, he snapped his eyes back the other way only to find the Empress of the Dagon Empire smiling at him with an unsettling grin.

She winked and then threw a punch. Before he could even yelp, the strike rendered him unconscious and he slumped forward in his chair.

Ri'Vera gently nudged him the rest of the way out and his body slid from his seat and tumbled to the floor. She then took his spot, slipping into the command chair, and brought up the manual controls.

Lycia stood next to her as she commandeered the ship. Throwing her hands on her hips, Lycia cleared her throat. "I want a collision course set for the *Labrys*. Maximum burn."

"As you wish, Empress," Ri'Vera replied, and then punching the ignition, she opened up the thrusters to full and steered the ship onto its perilous collision course.

The ship rattled as it pulled away from the *Avalon*, which hung dead in space, all her engines shot. As the scavenger's freighter gained some distance from the military frigate, Lycia looked out the cockpit window and could see the stunned faces of the other scavengers peering out the view portals of her ship looking at their ship slowly pulling away.

She laughed and waved goodbye to them. By the stunned looks on their faces, they hadn't expected they'd be the ones getting hijacked while trying to hijack someone else's ship.

Ri'Vera turned to Lycia with a worried look on her face. "What about the prince and princess? And your cat, Allie?"

"Don't worry," Lycia said with a reassuring smile, "I'm sure they'll be just fine."

"Isn't it dangerous though?"

"For the pirates, maybe," Lycia said with a light chortle.

Back aboard the *Avalon*, six pirate crewmen skidded around the corner junction of a long corridor, nearly tripping over themselves as they ran.

"Run for your lives!" one of them shouted.

"It's right on our heels," another screamed.

One man, tripping over his own feet, stumbled to the ground while the others pushed passed without offering any help.

"You ungrateful cowards," the man said, pushing himself up to his hands and knees. Shaking his fist, he added, "Don't think I won't forget this!"

When he rose to his feet, he dusted himself off and grumbled some choice words under his breath. That's when he heard the deep menacing growl coming from just over his shoulder. Shivering with fear, he slowly turned around to confront the beast.

Startled by what he beheld, he threw his hands out in a defensive posture and let out a terror-filled shriek as the shadow of the giant panther on the wall leaped into the air to pounce on him.

The others didn't dare look back as their friend's screams echoed up the corridor behind them. Instead, they raced to the opposite end of the passage, not paying any attention to the broken light fixtures along the way.

As the corridor grew darker and darker, they slowed to a trot and then, eventually, a vigilant and cautious gait. "Over there," one of the frightened men shouted out in alarm. He threw out an arm and pointed at the opposite end of the passage.

In the dark, standing in front of the turbo lift doors, were the silhouettes of a couple of adolescent children. One boy and one girl, holding hands, their eyes glowing red in the dimness as they slowly marched down the hall chanting, *"Redrum. Redrum. Redrum."*

One of the pirates clasped his hands together and dropped to his knees, praying to his chosen god. Two others turned to go back the other way and take their chances with the beast when, to their dismay, blood splatter shot onto the wall as the beast disemboweled their comrade.

As the ghastly children grew close, yet another pirate drew out his blaster and put it to his temple. A shot rang out and he dropped to the floor next to the praying man who looked down at the dead man staring back up at him and, overwhelmed, began to weep uncontrollably.

"Yeah, I'm sure they're fine," Ri'Vera said, giving it a second thought. After all, they trained with Danica Valencia every single morning and knew more ways to kill a person than any couple of ten-year-olds should.

"Yeah, they're fine," Lycia repeated, waving her hand as though there was nothing to worry about. But deep down inside, she still cared an awful lot for those little stinkers.

Naturally, the moment she knew it was safe back on Dagon Prime, she'd send ships to retrieve the *Avalon*. Also, they were smack dab in the middle of a major shipping route. Someone was bound to find them sooner or later and offer assistance. That's what haulers did. They'd simply need to fend for themselves a little while longer.

Ri'Vera rose from the chair and turned toward the rear of the cabin.

"Where you going?" asked Lycia.

"I need to check on their teleportation device. Because if we're going to crash this boat into the *Labrys*, we're going to need an escape plan."

"This model doesn't have teleporters," Lycia said. "It's a heavy freighter and much too old. Unless they spent a god-awful lot of credits on retrofitting the thing, there's only escape pods."

"Not even those," Ri'Vera said, slapping the wall panel and opening a secret hatch. She moved it aside to show a steel door with a little rectangular window looking out into the emptiness of space. No escape pod.

"There's gotta be one," Lycia said, moving to the other escape pod's location. She opened the panel and, sure enough, it was also missing. "Well, shit."

"Any other bright ideas Your Worshipfulness?"

Lycia turned to Ri'Vera with a stunned but pleasant look on her face at the emboldened bit of lighthearted ribbing. Unable to help herself, she smiled. "Are you making fun of me?"

"No, no, no," Ri'Vera retorted in a sarcastic tone. "I'd never do that, my empress."

"Oh, put a sock in it," Lycia said with a laugh.

"So, what's your plan now?"

Lycia stroked her chin as she thought about it. Then, looking Ri'Vera dead in the eyes, she said, you're not going to like it."

"I've got a bad feeling about this," she replied.

Sixty-eight minutes later both women were fully suited up in space suits and stood on the outer hull of the ship as it bore down on the *Labrys*.

"You're right!" Ri'Vera said, screaming into the comm. Her shrieking made Lycia wince. "I don't like this! Not one little bit!!"

"Just jump on my signal. We'll board the *Labrys* and make our way to the shuttle bay."

Reaching back, Lycia took Ri'Vera's hand in hers and then shouted, "Now!"

Together they leaped from the freighter out into the vacuum of space. Butterflies churned in their stomachs as they fell through the weightless medium.

The momentum of the ship hurled them toward the massive hull of the *Labrys* as though they'd been launched out of a slingshot. As they barreled forward, the freighter's autopilot engaged full thruster burn.

Incrementally, the scavenger's freighter pulled away from them. About thirty-five seconds later it crashed into the hull of the *Labrys*, sending up a big fireball. Ri'Vera screamed as the fireball rose dangerously close, but it quickly dissipated again.

Another eighty-seven seconds passed and their boots smacked down onto the surface of the *Labrys*. They rebounded off, floating back up and, thinking fast, Lycia slapped her forearm touch panel and engaged her magnetic boots.

Her feet slapped down onto the surface with a metallic *clank*. Ri'Vera, still screaming for dear life, reached out to clasp Lycia's hand but was moving away too quickly.

"Hang on," Lycia said, calmly. She then disengaged her mag-boots and sprang off the hull plating and floated gracefully upward. A split second later she caught Ri'Vera in her arms and then quickly reactivated her boots. This time they touched down together and ran out the momentum of the fall with heavy footsteps and clanked and clunked loud enough that they could probably be heard inside.

"You all right?" Lycia asked, checking on Ri'Vera.

"I may have peed a little."

Lycia nodded as if to say that was to be expected. "It's okay," she said reassuringly, gripping onto her friend's shoulder and giving it an encouraging squeeze. "Besides, the suit will just recycle it into drinking water anyway."

"It will?" Ri'Vera asked. She eyeballed the drinking straw in her helmet with a newfound disgust but then, realizing she was parched, blew a tuft of hair out of her eyes and surrendered to her thirst.

"Over here," Lycia said, finding the access hatch. She went over and, crouching down, took ahold of the handles and manually pried it open.

The LED indicator on the door seal turned orange, for caution, and she threw open the hatch. A small blast of air came out as the room decompressed and Lycia helped Ri'Vera down into the opening before slipping in herself.

Once inside the small maintenance airlock, Lycia pulled the hatch down and then repressurized the room.

Ri'Vera pushed open the large, circular airlock door and stepped into the main hold of the ship. Lycia followed after her and they both promptly unfastened their space helmets and tossed them back inside the airlock.

"This way," Ri'Vera said, pointing up the corridor.

Before they could get more than a few steps, a crewman stepped out into the corridor and eyed them suspiciously. He blinked twice and then said, "Hey, there. You're not supposed to be on this deck. Who authorized you two to be down here?"

"You're not going to believe this, uh, Lieutenant. But it's raining starships out there."

"Yes," Ri'Vera said in a posh accent, turning to Lycia, "it's quite terrible weather we're having this time of year."

Lycia, smiling, as if to inquire—*are we really doing this*—turned to her and, going along with the bit, replied in an equally uppity tone, "Naturally, I wouldn't be caught dead in such bad weather."

"Dead, you say?" Ri'Vera continued, taking the bit even further. "Oh, heaven forbid we catch something going around—"

Fed up with their shenanigans, the lieutenant cleared his throat. "Listen here, you two. I don't know who you think you are, but I'm reporting you both. I'm calling security."

The officer tapped his comm badge to call security and Lycia stepped aside as Ri'Vera drew her dual blasters. She fired a couple of rapid plasma bolts into the officer's gut, drilling gaping holes in his uniform and, subsequently, his body.

A shocked look on his face, he dropped to his knees and opened his mouth to speak but only smoke came out. Then, tottering, he fell forward, landing on his face. Gray wisps of smoke continued to rise from the wide-open wounds on his torso.

Lycia turned to Ri'Vera and, still in her silly accent, said, "Is it tea time yet? I fancy a cup of tea. Do you fancy a cup of tea, my dear?"

A serious look on her face, Ri'Vera holstered her weapons and replied, "There's no time." With that, she turned and began making her way up the corridor.

"Right," Lycia said, clearing her throat to try and get her normal voice back. "I knew that."

Jogging up the corridor, she quickly caught up to Ri'Vera. Pointing at the end of the junction, she said, "Take a hard left up there and head to the end. The doors to the main hangar bay should be just ahead."

"I still think using the teleport would be better," Ri'Vera said.

"That's what they'll be expecting," Lycia replied. Tapping her temple, she said, "At least, this way we will stay one step ahead of them."

They arrived at the hangar bay and waited for the large sliding doors to part. Once they were fully open, they rushed onto the hangar deck only to find about eight hundred gladiators geared up in full armor standing in formation as they prepared to board the Falcon Heavy dropships lining both walls of the ship.

"You were saying?" Ri'Vera asked in a stunned tone as they froze in their tracks.

"Wait, what's that?!" shouted Lycia, her voice full of alarm as she frantically pointed at the upper right corner of the hangar.

All the gladiators looked over at whatever it was she was pointing at, and while they were distracted, Lycia turned and ran out of the hangar.

Astonished that it had worked, Ri'Vera threw her hands on her hips and stared at the gathering of soldiers in complete dismay. Eventually, realizing it had been a false alarm and nothing was there, the gladiators slowly turned their gazes back to her.

"Really?" she asked, mockingly. "That actually worked on all you knuckleheads?"

Lycia came jogging back into the room and grabbed Ri'Vera by her arm and murmured in an embarrassed tone, "Gotta go, honey. Pish posh. Too-da-loo. Cheerio and all that."

Still holding Ri'Vera's hand in hers, she curtseyed and then yanked the sub commander off the hangar deck, dragging her behind her as she hightailed it back down the corridor.

Confused, the gladiators looked to one another to see if anybody had any clue as to what that was about, but nobody did. The two women who'd abruptly manifested on the deck had disappeared just as quickly, vanishing around the bend as the hangar bay doors slowly groaned shut again.

Lycia and Ri'Vera laughed the whole way up the corridor.

"What were you thinking?" Lycia asked, shocked that Ri'Vera would just stand around judging the intelligence of the gladiators.

"What were you thinking?" Ri'Vera fired back. "Steal a shuttle from under the nose of an invasion force?"

"I thought that crashing the ship into them would keep them distracted!"

"Yeah, but that plan backfired. It barely left a dent."

"All the more reason we need to get down onto the surface," replied Lycia. "The invasion is still happening."

They finally found a teleportation pad and Lycia typed in the in coordinates and set the twenty-second countdown. Hopping onto the pad beside Ri'Vera, they shared a quick flirtatious glance.

"What?" Lycia asked, her cheeks flushing.

"Nothing," Ri'Vera answered, biting her lower lip and batting her eyelids at Lycia as she thought about how badly she wanted to kiss her.

Interrupting their little moment, however, a wave of crimson energy washed over them and, in a swirling eddy of sparkling light, quickly disassembled them and whisked them away.

Reforming on the surface of Dagon Prime, they both looked up into the sky as the *Labrys* steadily sank into the upper atmosphere. A flock of birds flew beneath it as it began its descent through the clouds.

Virtually the size of a small city, the shadow of the dreadnought ship stretched out across the landscape like an ominous shroud and eventually darkened the entire valley.

"What now?" Ri'Vera asked.

"Now, we make ready for war."

34

A cool breeze rolled through the cement cell where Jegra was being held captive, rousing her from a light sleep. She sat up and rubbed the sleep from her eyes. That's when she heard the jingle jangle of keys.

When she looked over at the entrance, she found Mercy unlocking the cell with keys that she, in all probability, had swiped from her father. Throwing open the gate, the young woman waved for Jegra to follow her out and whispered, "Let's go. I'm getting you out of here."

Reluctant to follow, Jegra cautioned, "But if your father catches you helping me…there's no telling what he'll do."

"We'll be long gone before my father ever finds out. Besides, Eli has decided to help us."

"Eli?" asked Jegra. The name didn't ring any bells.

"Elijah Remington, you know, the soldier who's sweet on you. I think he has a bit of a crush."

"Eli, huh?" Jegra said to herself, rubbing the back of her neck and blushing. He was the first good man she'd met in a long time and was a little bit taken aback by the revelation that he might have feelings for her.

"Anyway, he's gathered the parts like you asked."

"He has?" Jegra rose to her feet and stretched a kink out of her neck.

"Yeah. And I packed my bags too," she added, nodding at the two black duffle bags on the floor just behind her, "because I'm coming with you."

"In that case," Jegra said, "we'd best get a move on."

They snatched up one bag each, slinging them over their shoulders, and raced out the back and out into the dark alley. Keeping to the shadows, they came to the end of the alleyway and, careful not to be seen, stole a quick glance up and down the street.

A single street light lit up the area and, across the street, standing at the mouth of the adjacent alley, Eli, dressed in civilian clothes, waited for them.

He checked the area again just to make sure the coast was clear before waving his hand and motioning for them that it was safe to come out. Receiving his signal, they darted across the street and just as quickly vanished back into the shadows.

Meeting Eli there, Jegra affectionately placed her hand on his forearm and said, "Thanks for all your help. I know you didn't have to, but I appreciate it."

"Don't mention it," he said, stealing a quick glance at her hand that lingered on his arm a bit longer than usual. Then, nodding his head at the ATV parked in the alleyway, he said, "This way."

A large crate was tied to the roof of the ATV and Jegra knew it held all the parts she'd requested. Mercy and Jegra climbed into the back seats while Eli drove.

The electric motor of the ATV whined and the vehicle pulled out into the dirt street, its oversized tires kicking up a spray of dirt as they sped around the corner.

In a matter of minutes, they'd reached the outer edge of New Haven. As they approached the eight -foot tall, electrified chain-link fence with barbed wire threaded across the top for added security, massive floodlights suddenly turned on and blinded them.

Eli slammed on the brakes and the ATV skidded to a halt, gravel scattering in front of it.

"Dammit all to hell," he cursed, slapping the steering wheel with the palms of both hands out of frustration. "I told them to leave it open. Instead, those sons of bitches gave me up."

The other soldiers formed a line, and two additional ATVs pulled up and blocked the opening of the gate to ensure they couldn't leave New Haven.

Slowly emerging from the line of soldiers was none other than the mayor himself, Mr. Darcy Smith. He puffed on a freshly lit cigar, the orange glowing tip casting a warm light across his pale skin.

Blowing a couple of smoke rings, showing he was no stranger to the habit, he looked up at the three trouble makers and stared at them with narrowed eyes as he contemplated how best to handle the precariousness of the situation.

"Now, now, Mercy," he said, his southern drawl lingering on every syllable, "I expected this rebellious attitude from a naïve young thing such as yourself, but you, Eli? I must say, I'm sorely disappointed."

"Sir, I can explain. If you'll just hear me out and—"

"You've already said quite enough, son," the mayor interrupted. "Now, I'm not a violent man, so I'd like to deal with this peacefully, if possible. Whichever way this goes depends on ya'll. Surrender and come in willingly, and there'll be no trouble. Or, if you persist in this act of defiance, I'll have no choice but to order these fine young men to arrest the lot of you." He cleared his throat and brushed down his fancy white suit. Taking another puff on the cigar, he blew out the smoke and added, "Now, if you'd be so kind, please step aside so that we can apprehend the fugitive."

"No," Mercy said, stepping out of the vehicle and throwing out her arms. "I won't let you take her. I'm in love with her!"

"In love?" Mr. Darcy scoffed. "You hardly even know this woman."

"I know her well enough to see she doesn't have an ounce of hate in her entire being. I know her well enough to realize she is everything I've been looking for in a life partner. I know she's compassionate, strong, and caring. And that's more than you'll ever be, father!"

By the look on Mr. Darcy's face, it was apparent that Mercy's words had cut him to his core. His face growing beat red, he took another puff on the cigar and exhaled the smoke through his nostrils like a fuming dragon.

"Now, you listen here, lil' missy. I've had it up to here with your backtalk and constant disobedience. I am the leader of this here town. I've kept things going through thick and thin and the least you could show is a modicum of gratitude. And, heaven knows, I don't expect you to respect me. But the people of this town do. And all I'd ask is you do right by them. And this woman," he said, shifting his sunken gaze toward Jegra, "whoever she says she is, it's clear to anyone with eyes in their heads that she's a she-devil in disguise. A temptress. She's trying to steal you away from me. Don't you see, Mercy? She's not good for you."

"She's not stealing me from anybody. I'm my own woman, father, and I'm going with her of my own free will. Whether you like it or not, I'm twenty-seven years old, for Christ's sake. You have to let me live my own life!"

Irate, Mr. Darcy tossed the still smoldering cigar stub to the ground and stamped it out. He then reached over and snatched the handgun off an officer and aimed it at his daughter.

"Now, Mercy, I beg of you, please, step away from the prisoner. Let me handle this."

"You mean like you handled the Preemar? Like you handled things after the crash by instating yourself as de facto ruler of New Haven? No, I won't," Mercy said defiantly. She continued to hold out her arms to shield Jegra from any potential gunfire.

"Mercy," he said, drawing out her name before scolding her further. "I'm warning you. If you don't step away from the prisoner this instant, so help me God, I'll...I'll..."

"You'll do what? Shoot your own flesh and blood?"

Jegra slowly got out of the car and, drawing up to Mercy, placed a hand on her shoulder. "It's all right, Mercy. I've caused enough trouble as it is. I'll just take my things and be on my way."

Mercy spun around and grabbed Jegra by her arms. Tears welling up in her eyes, she sobbed, "No! You can't just leave me here. You promised to take me with you."

Jegra just lowered her eyes and took a step back.

"See?" Mr. Darcy said triumphantly. "Her love was a sham. She used you to get her way. Now, don't you see, baby girl, I'm the only one who has ever cared for you. I'm the only one who's had your best interests at heart. So, please, Mercy, step on over to me and we can put this little kerfuffle behind us."

"I'd rather be roasted alive by the Preemar than live another day under your thumb, father. And whether Jegra wants me or not, doesn't matter. Regardless, I'm not coming home with you."

"Fine, have it your way," Mr. Darcy hollered, his face redder than a beat. "Arrest them both!"

"What?" Mercy asked, taking a step back as two soldiers moved toward them.

Before they could reach them, however, a spear flew out of the nearby trees and pierced Mr. Darcy's chest. He fell back, accidentally firing off a shot that struck Mercy in her gut.

"No!" Jegra shouted as the soldiers drew their weapons and turned to the trees. Opening fire, they unloaded their fully automatic rifles at the tree line, cutting everything down.

As their muzzle flashes lit up the dark, Jegra rushed over and caught Mercy under her arms as she fell backward. Together, they slowly sank to the ground. Resting Mercy's head on her lap, Jegra reached around and applied pressure on Mercy's gunshot wound, the dark red of which was already seeping into her shirt.

Mercy reached up with her hand and touched Jegra's face, "I really did love you, you know?"

"I know," Jegra said, her eyes welling up with tears.

Jegra bent down and kissed Mercy on her lips. When she rose back up Mercy's hand slid from her cheek, leaving a red smear of blood.

Cradling her in her arms, Jegra rocked back and forth on her heels. "No, no, no," she whispered, her voice strained with sadness and rage all brewing to form the perfect storm.

"Mercy!" Mr. Darcy shouted, reaching a hand out to try and touch his dead daughter, but she was too far away.

Eli looked up and made eye contact with Jegra. Tilting his head in the direction of her ship, he said, "Go."

"This is all my fault," Jegra muttered to herself, a tear trickling down her cheek. She contemplated taking the girl's body back with her and placing it in the regeneration chamber. But her ship was fifteen minutes away and even if she'd managed to save the body the brain damage would be irreversible. Jegra then checked her teleporter to see if it was working, but with the ship's main engines out of commission, teleportation wasn't an option.

Eli grabbed Jegra by her shirt collar, yanking hard enough to tear it open and reveal her cleavage. She looked down, surprised at how he handled her, and then snapping out of her shock, looked him in the eyes.

"You have to go," he said, relinquishing his grip, setting her free. "It's now or never."

She nodded and gently set Mercy down on the ground, closing her eyes with a gentle brush of her fingers. Then, getting up, she shot Eli one last glance and then climbed into the ATV. She hit the ignition button, the car came to life with a shudder, and then she slammed her foot down and floored it.

The tires peeled out, kicking up dirt behind the vehicle before, finally, taking purchase. With a lurch, the ATV took off and she swerved around the two ATVs blocking her path. This forced her off course and she smashed through the fence, tearing part of it down and shooting up a spray of sparks in her wake.

Gunfire erupted, as the soldiers fired at the darkened tree line, hoping to hit the Preemar warriors that had ambushed them. At the same time, the ATV sped off down the dirt road, its red taillights fading into the night.

"Stop her!" Mr. Darcy shouted. "Stop that woman!"

"Belay that order," Eli shouted above the din of gunfire.

Mr. Darcy shot Eli a look of betrayal. "You wretched dolt! She killed my daughter."

"No," Eli replied, picking up a rifle, checking the magazine, and then slapping it back in. "You did." Then, with a sharp strike to the mayor's temple, Eli struck him with the butt of the gun and knocked him out cold. "That's for Mercy, you prick."

Eli then turned and joined the fray, lighting up the night with gunfire. He waved for the soldiers to advance, and they stepped over the fallen fence and tracked the Preemar through the jungle and back to their village.

Roughly forty-five minutes later they arrived and proceeded to go through the village, hut by hut, searching for any Preemar. Occasionally, a suicide warrior, called the Pardu, painted in white ash to resemble ghosts, would jump out at them in an attempt to cut down the soldiers. But each one was shot on sight and dispensed with.

Luckily, however, it wasn't a complete slaughter since most of the Preemar had already fled the village and headed deeper into the jungle. Meanwhile, the soldiers lit torches and set the village ablaze, effectively ending the Preemar threat to New Haven.

As the Preemar stood on a distant bluff, watching their village go up in flames, in the distance the sound of plasma ion engines of Jegra's ship igniting could be heard. Back in the camp, Eli heard it too and looked up at the sky in time to see a ship rise into the deep blue. It slowly climbed higher and higher into the atmosphere before darting away in a flash of brilliant light.

"God speed, Empress," Eli said, looking up at the flash of light. Then, turning his attention back to the task as hand, he motioned for his men to wrap things up and head back to New Haven.

They'd sent their message and it would be a long while before the Preemar ever bothered them again.

35

Roughly six hundred meters over the tallest spire of the Imperial palace, the *Labrys* opened all twelve of its hangar doors and began to discharge two dozen Falcon Heavy dropships. Each ship, capable of carrying fourteen fully armed soldiers, fired their reverse thrusters and began setting down all across the outskirts of Primea, the capital city.

Unlike the warriors that lined the flight deck, each wearing full chest plates of korridium armor, bracers, and shin guards in the classical vein of traditional gladiatorial warfare, Scarborne forwent the heavy body armor. Instead, he wore a traditional white gi and navy blue hakama. The kind the grandmasters of Bai'Jamin typically wore.

If this wasn't warrior-monk enough, however, he went barefoot too. A sign of his commitment to martial arts and the belief that forsaking all technology was the only way to become the best warrior possible.

According to the Bai'Jamin teachings, only the weapon and the man mattered, and when they fought, they fought as kindred spirits bonded in the fires of battle and became as one.

Walking over to the open hangar door, he looked out at the dropships fluttering to the ground like scarab beetles. Leaning up against the wall, next to the opening, was a giant double-bladed sword. Taking the sword in hand, Scarborne stood on the cusp of the hangar and looked down, out of the open bay doors.

As the remaining ship slowly rose off the hangar deck behind him, he took a flying leap out of the hangar bay and entered a freefall.

After a short plummet, he landed on the top of one of the dropships, falling to one knee to help absorb the brunt of his fall. Slowly rising back up, his feet able to cling onto the hull of the vessel with surprising adhesiveness, he stood, riding the outside of the dropship, like the warlords of old who stood upon the decks of their mighty sailing ships as they sailed into battle.

"Blood shall rain like the purple waterfalls of Cresia!" he said, as the first wave of dropships touched down. "And no matter how hard the Mother of Dagon tries to protect her children from the prowling wolves of the *Nightglade*, she shall not prevail. For the wolves are hungry and they thirst for blood."

Gladiatorial warriors dressed in full body armor marched out of the dropships and took up formation along the ridge line of the bluff they stood on.

It wasn't long before the first four-hundred ground troops were setting up their base camp while the dropships returned to the *Labrys* to fetch the next wave of soldiers.

Several minutes later, an all blacked-out dropship set down a few meters away from Scarborne's position and, noting its arrival, he leaped off the ship and threw his giant sword into the ground.

The sword wobbled slightly behind him as he strode over to the vessel. Drawing near, the side door slid open and a naked, blue-skinned woman climbed out. She looked the spitting image of Lycia except she had been slightly modified—sporting four arms instead of two and standing about seven feet tall instead of a meager six-three.

This new, improved Artemis clone represented the new wave of designer warriors that Scarborne hoped to procure.

Completely naked, the blue woman met Scarborne halfway, her breasts gently bouncing as she walked. She paused in front of him and raised all four palms to the sky. She spun around slowly, showing him off the goods.

"Do you like what you see?"

"I see you have made a few additional modifications."

"There are many more modifications beneath the skin, I can assure you. An improved healing factor, stronger and lighter bone structure, greater muscle density, but above all else, this..." She turned back around and, aiming all four fists at the black dropship, she fired a massive Dygra crystal blast.

The vehicle, along with its pilot, went up in a ball of flame and smoke. As the husk of the vehicle continued to burn, spewing out dark smoke from the shattered windows, she turned back and threw two hands on her hips while she folded the other set of arms under her opulent breasts.

She smiled at him, her eyes half-sunken with the ecstasy she got from causing pain and destruction, her purple nipples standing erect on her blue skin as the adrenaline surged through her veins.

Scarborne drew close, and took her chin in his fingers and turned her head left, then right, as though he were inspecting livestock. He then looked down at her chest, and, reaching up, he squeezed her mammoth left breast in his right hand and asked, "Is this body capable of breeding?" he asked.

She smiled wantonly and then ran two of her hands up and down his broad shoulders while the other set started to unfasten his belt to try and get into his pants.

"There's only one way to find out," she said, biting her lower lip seductively.

Uninterested, he shoved her aside and said, "I'll take as many as you currently have available."

"I'm afraid that I'm the only one at the moment, luv," she said.

"Then suit up…" He turned to her and, pausing for a moment as he puzzled over something, he finally asked, "What do I call you? Hela? Artemis?"

"Those names are dead to me. They died along with the weak bodies they were attached to. You may call me Persephone, for I will lead your army into battle as your general. As your queen of the damned."

"Very well, then," Scarborne said, and he turned and marched toward the encampment which was already taking shape. "Warrior Queen."

Persephone smiled at his acknowledgment of her, then noticed an uncommon amount of attention coming her way from the other men in the camp. She smiled and, raising all four arms into the air, twirled around to better show off her goods. "Take it all in boys, because this is the last chance you get to see me like this."

The gladiators looked away when Scarborne shouted for them to get back to work.

Persephone pinched her earlobe and said in an audible voice, "Send down the package."

A flash from the underside of the *Labrys* signified it had launched a probe. It came down fast and then fired landing thrusters. The coffin-sized object wasn't a probe though, it was a mobile armory.

It cut its thrusters about three meters above the ground and plummeted the rest of the way, impacting with a solid thud and embedding its nose about two feet into the soil.

The mobile armory decompressed with a hiss and a gust of steam shot out as its paneling unfurled revealing body armor specifically designed for Persephone's unique anatomy, along with an entire array of weapons to choose from.

Everything from blades to fully automatic plasma rifles lined the inside of the armory, and Persephone rubbed her hands together excitedly and said, "Happy birthday to me."

Lycia and Ri'Vera had jogged seven kilometers back to the royal palace, arriving on the grounds thirty-eight minutes after they'd set off. Although Ri'Vera was completely winded, Lycia hadn't even broken a sweat yet.

"We're here," Lycia said, arriving at the front gate of the palace. As they waited for the guard to come open the gate, Ri'Vera placed her hands on her knees and panted heavily as she tried to catch her breath.

The man scanned both women and then, checking his scanner, nodded and opened the gate. Lycia waved at him as she started up the drive and called out to Ri'Vera, "Come on."

"You suck," Ri'Vera mumbled to herself and then forced herself to tag along.

"What was that?" Lycia asked.

"Nothing, Your Worshipfulness," Ri'Vera replied, shooting Lycia a fake grin.

"Nonsense, because when you call me that I know something is wrong."

"No, nothing's wrong. That's the thing. Your perfect stamina. Your perfect ass. And perfect lungs." Ri'Vera poked her finger into Lycia's right tit causing Lycia to laugh. "You're just too damn perfect. It drives me nuts."

"Alright, alright," Lycia laughed, throwing up her hands in surrender. "I'm sorry for being so goddamn perfect."

They continued along for a while and then Lycia asked, "You like my ass?"

Ri'Vera rolled her eyes and replied, "I couldn't help but get a good look trailing behind you the whole way."

"Ah," Lycia said. "Sorry about that. When I get going, I sometimes forget other people aren't…"

"So perfect?"

Lycia laughed again. "That's not what I was going to say."

Ri'Vera laughed and then nudged Lycia with her elbow. "I know, I'm just giving you a hard time."

Another laugh escaped Lycia's lips and she replied, "Well, that's a huge relief."

Before long, they'd arrived at Lycia's quarters, and burst into her chamber through the double doors. Inside her room was the royal grounds housekeeper finishing up dressing the bed. Looking around for Raphine, Lycia turned to the housekeeper as she was on her way out and asked, "Where's Raphine?"

"You haven't heard, Your Majesty? She went into labor this morning."

"That's wonderful!" Lycia said. The housekeeper nodded and went on her merry way.

"Congratulations," Ri'Vera said.

Lycia nodded. She wanted desperately to watch her child be born but, now, she had to deal with a stupid invasion fleet.

"Take off your clothes," Lycia ordered, shooting Ri'Vera a stern look.

Ri'Vera cocked her head. "I don't think we have time for…"

"No," Lycia said, realizing she'd sent the wrong message. She should have realized that with all the flirting Ri'Vera was into her. But she didn't want to sleep with the woman. She wanted to get ready for the upcoming battle.

Slapping a panel next to her bed, an entire section of the wall receded about twelve inches and then slid away, revealing two power suits. One was army green and the other a deep plum with matte paint.

"You're about Raph's size, so you'll take her suit."

"Right," Ri'Vera said, blushing. She'd made a stupid mistake but quickly began to strip out of her numerous belts and underwear.

At the same time, Lycia quickly slid out of her kimono and grabbed two smart suit bracelets and some talcum powder. Turning back around she tossed one of the bracelets to Ri'Vera who reflexively caught it.

Pausing for a moment, Lycia looked Ri'Vera up and down.

"I didn't expect the first time we'd see each other naked would be…like this." She gestured at her own body.

"I'm not complaining," Lycia said, handing her the talcum powder. "You have a great body."

Ri'Vera blushed and took the powder and began applying it to her front while Lycia helped with her back. After she was thoroughly coated, she helped Lycia with the same. After Ri'Vera had finished Lycia's back, she reached back with an open palm and swatted Lycia's ass, hard. A cloud of white powder expanded from the point of contact.

Lycia laughed, hopping forward as she shot a look of admonishment over her shoulder at Ri'Vera. "Hey, now. Behave."

Ri'Vera merely shrugged, as if to say it couldn't be helped, and slipped on her bracelet. With a tap of a button, the liquid polymer, a milky white substance, oozed out of the bracelets and coated her body in a uniform liquid which hardened into a rubber catsuit.

Once their smart suits had completed drying, they tapped their bracelets, turning them a two-tone gray, and went over to the power suits.

Lycia tapped the golden royal emblem emblazoned on the left breastplate of each suit, and with a mechanical murmur, the suits opened up. They both looked to one another and then climbed in.

Electric servos whined as the power suits clamped down onto the women's bodies. Taking clunky steps, their metal boots clanking along, they both moved into the main room and Lycia handed Ri'Vera a plasma sword she'd taken off the weapons rack next to the suits.

Ri'Vera examined the sword, noting it was the same kind the Knights of Caelum used.

"How did you get this?" she asked. "The Knights never part with their swords."

"It's Jegra's," Lycia replied. "But I want you to have it."

Then, drawing out her own weapon, Lycia revealed a double-headed battle axe. Not only this, but it was also a plasma axe. The first of its kind, as far as she knew.

"I see you're keeping Jegra's aesthetic."

"It's iconic," Lycia said. "People now associate this weapon with the Mother of Dagon. If I am to fill my mother's shoes, I only felt it was fitting to use her weapon of choice."

Ri'Vera nodded, understanding Lycia's sentiment. "You honor your mother," she said.

She lowered her eyes and gripped the long handle with both hands. "And now I must prove myself on the battlefield, not as a loyal soldier. But as the Empress of the Dagon Empire."

"It will be my honor to fight by your side," Ri'Vera stated. "And die, if needed, to protect that perfect ass of yours."

"Oh, hush, you," said Lycia with a laugh.

Their gazes met and they stood staring into each other's eyes for what seemed the longest time. Finally, Ri'Vera held out her fist and said, "Victory or death!"

Lycia smiled and, giving Ri'Vera a fist-bump, replied in kind: "Victory or death."

Persephone's dark silver armor with golden trim glinted in the mid-day sun. The gladiator army was now fully suited up and armed. Taking up position along the ridge, they looked out across the valley at the Dagon Imperial forces amassing on the other side.

Her archers stood on the cusp of the hill with plasma tipped arrows ready to go while the main infantry remained behind. In the far distance, across the dell, royal military dropships were bringing reinforcements to Primea. She could see Lycia standing about eight hundred meters away in the open meadow, looking up the hill at them.

Scarborne stepped up beside her and she glanced over at him. All he was wearing was a Bai'Jamin styled hakama, in white and navy blue.

Unfastening his gi, he slowly peeled himself out of it and tied the arms of his gi around his waist, tying them as he would his fighting belt.

His red pectoral muscles bulged as he cinched the knot. All across his muscular body, his skin had numerous tribal tattoos etched in black ink. Each of them a symbol of great trial, achievement, or sorrow in his life.

Across his upper left pec was the name of his daughter—Ishtar Bantu of the house Par'Vek—forever etched onto his flesh. A stalwart reminder of what was taken from him and whose honor he fought to avenge.

"One question," Persephone asked, "when you defeat her, are you going to grant her clemency or will you rape her like you intend to rape this entire world?"

"Honorable deaths are reserved for true warriors, not child murderers or their daughters."

"Then I'll stay out of your way," she said, turning her gaze back toward the battlefield.

"That would be wise," he added, a subtle edge to his voice that spoke volumes of what would happen should anyone get in his way.

"As long as I can watch her suffer, I'll be satisfied."

"Out of curiosity," Scarborne asked, "what is it that you hate about her so much?"

"She is everything I could have been. Nobody knows this, but we were the first two borne of Dakroth's cloning program. But I was activated prematurely, before my incubation period was up, to see if premature clones could be battle-ready. Unfortunately, I proved that it wasn't possible to rush the process. And my life was ruined, while she was allowed to mature normally and finish her incubation cycle."

"Sibling rivalry," Scarborne said, "I know it well."

"You have kin?"

"Seven brothers," he answered. "I am the last."

"What happened?"

He turned to her with his yellow eyes blazing and replied, "I killed them all so that I could be king."

"If you're a warrior king, why join IGS?"

"Because, before H'aaztre came for your world, he came for mine. My people fought valiantly against the monster and his golden army, but eventually, his power proved too great for us and we had no choice but to scatter into the stars."

"And then your daughter, Ishtar, fell in love with Dakroth."

"It was foolish of her to do. Dakroth was young, impetuous and didn't care for anyone or anything but himself. I warned her he'd be a disappointment. But she swore to me she could tame him. In the end, his tolerance of that Terran, that pink-skin, led to her demise."

"So, you found yourself a new army?" She scanned the countless gladiators lining the hilltop.

"It took seven years. While the great Jegra Alakandra was rising to prominence in the arena, I was biding my time. Finding the most bloodthirsty killers on all the worlds to throw at her. My original plan was to use these crazed savages to wear her down and kill her in the arena. But then, Dakroth had to intervene and marry the woman, ruining my hard-wrought plans."

"Hence your hatred for Dagon."

"As a warrior, I admire what your people have accomplished. But every empire crumbles…either beneath the weight of its own decadence or under the iron forged blade of a mighty conqueror."

"And yet, my people survived H'aaztre."

Scarborne turned his gaze to her and replied, "Perhaps," then returning to his position, he took a step forward and raised his fist. "Or perhaps he left you so crippled that you will fall to a mightier conqueror."

"A conqueror like you?" she asked.

Scarborne looked over at her one last time, then, tossing his black dreadlocks across his shoulders, he raised his fist and shouted, "Bring up the plasma cannons!"

"Bring up the cannons!" a field general shouted.

With a heave and ho, sixteen trains of muscular gladiators towing massive ropes drew up eight giant plasma cannons, two lines of rope per each cannon.

Like giant worker ants, the men brought the large cannons, which rested on giant wheels the size of a two-story building, creaked along behind them. The barrels of the cannons were roughly the length of a commuter train three cars-long.

Once the cannons were in position, a series of giant hooks fell from the upper platform of each cannon and drilled into the fertile soil, anchoring them into place.

Even with all of Lycia's powers, she'd be helpless against the full power of these cannons. And, even if she did manage to neutralize one of them, the others would make short work of the palace and all of Primea.

Scarborne walked out onto the battlefield, motioning for everyone to hold. After walking fifty meters, he stopped and peered out across the glade at Lycia who stared back at him.

What are you waiting for? Lycia wondered. She knew that those cannons weren't simply for decoration. So, why was he just sitting there?

A soldier from the backline came running up to her with a folded piece of paper.

"Your Grace, an urgent message." He handed her the paper and then hurried back into formation.

Lycia then glanced out across the glade one more time. A gentle breeze blew the knee-high grass, shimmering waves chasing one another across the landscape while thornbirds streaked the sky. The serenity of that moment, oblivious to the bloodshed that was about to come.

She turned back to the line of warriors and marched up to them. Holding up the piece of paper she shouted, "My daughter is born, on this day. We fight not only for her but for all of Dagon! Let us show these invaders that we have not forgotten where we come from. Let us remind them of our warrior heritage and what we have fought so hard for—to establish a jewel in the darkness that brings light to the galaxy. Let us remind them what the word Dagon really means!"

The soldiers all cheered, their roars rippling throughout the entirety of the front line, traveling from one end to another.

Lycia turned back around, tucked the memo into the only unprotected area of her armor, just above her armpit, and then drew out her plasma axe.

Igniting the plasma axe, the edge heating up to a molten orange glow, she raised it high above her head and shouted, "Victory or death!"

It was her mother's battle cry. The battle cry of a gladiator.

From across the dell, they could hear the IGS soldiers respond in kind: "Victory or death."

Screaming out her fiercest battle cry, Lycia took off, her long legs blurring as she charged forward, six hundred strong Dagon warriors at her back.

36

Wedged beneath the fourth and fifth power coupling, Jegra pulled down on the wrench to try and get the new power converter to seal. Without a steady power flow, the engines had been gurgling and burping all day. She couldn't travel at FTL for more than a short burst before the engines reset and the power couplings needed to cool.

This aggravating stop and go had gotten to the point where she was tired of getting jerked around and decided to try and fix the malfunction herself.

She wore light gray boiler suit styled overalls and unzipped the front to let cool air lap at her chest while she worked under the blistering heat of the power couplings.

As she fiddled with the unit, she presumed the malfunction had something to do with the replacement parts that she'd gotten from New Haven. They were the right parts, but they weren't the right fit. And, now, she was banging on them with the wrench to try and make them the right fit.

While she let out her frustration on the metal connector which didn't quite fit into the socket, she inadvertently nicked a coolant line and blue gel spurted out onto her chest and then began to ooze down her cleavage and into her overalls.

"Cold, cold, cold!" she cried out scurrying out from under the large power couplings and grabbing a rag to wipe off the coolant gel.

After she'd cleaned herself off, she turned to inspect her handy work and smiled at the crooked, battered, and scraped up connector. At least, now it fit.

To ensure that it wouldn't start to leak, she grabbed some aluminum speed tape and wrapped every centimeter of the adjoining pieces. She also wrapped up the hose she'd nicked, fixing the coolant line in the process.

Jegra was finishing the final wrap when her ship's proximity alarm went off. Biting the tape with her teeth, she tore it off then brushed it flat with the palm of her hand.

"If it's not one thing, it's a hundred others," she lamented, setting the tape down. She jogged to the lift, jumped on, and let it take her up to the main deck. On a luxury yacht like this, the bridge was full-sized, the same as any starship. But unlike most starships, this one was completely automated. She didn't require a crew and could manage even complicated maneuvers from her command chair.

Even so, she had an X-5 battle robot helping her navigate because, truth be told, it sometimes got lonely out in the deep reaches of uncharted space. It was nice to have someone to talk to. Even if the someone was just an android.

"What's up, Johnny Five?" she asked. She'd trained it to respond to its nickname.

"An unidentified ship has dropped out of hyperspace and is scanning us."

Marauders?" asked Jegra.

"It doesn't appear so, ma'am. They seem to be scavengers," Johnny Five replied. He brought the ship onto the main viewscreen and zoomed in.

"Junkers," Jegra corrected. "They probably detected I was having engine problems and decided to swoop in and pick apart my ship like the vultures they are. If they board us, Johnny Boy, you know what to do."

"Yes, ma'am," Johnny Five answered in his usual, straight forward robot tone.

She appreciated the updated A.I. software that the X-5 series of robots had over their predecessors. They were much more intuitive; it almost felt like conversing with a real person.

A couple of loud clangors on the outside hull of the ship alerted her to the fact that they'd been nabbed.

"They've deployed grapplers," Johnny Five informed Jegra.

"I know, I know," she said, peering out the cabin window to try to get a fix on where they'd latched on.

Blue energy coursed down the thick wire of the magnetic grappling hooks and electrified Jegra's ship. While the electromagnetic shield was able to deflect most energy charges, the magnetic grapplers bit into the hull directly and scrambled entire systems.

As the lights in the cabin and consoles began to flicker on and off, she realized she was losing her ship. And with the engines still cooling down, she couldn't jump out of the system or even try to outrun them. She was, for all intents and purposes, a sitting duck.

"Just my luck," she groused. "Alright, Johnny Boy, get ready."

Johnny Five turned around, raise his arm, and his hand folded up, then disappeared into his forearm whereby a barrel emerged. A couple spurts of flame signaled he'd activated his flame thrower.

"I am ready to kick ass," he stated almost cheerfully.

Jegra raised a hand. "Wait for my signal."

Another resounding clunk alerted them to the fact that the scavenger ship had coupled with her ship. Jegra ran to the airlock and watched as two figures shrouded in darkness on the other side of the plate glass window hacked the airlock door.

All space scavengers and Junkers used rudimentary hacking equipment to bypass a ship's lockdown protocols. It was crude, but it worked. And if it didn't, well, they'd just use plasma torches to cut their way in.

They finally cracked the code and the airlock depressurized. The light flicked from orange to light blue, and the circular door popped open with a hiss of air.

A couple of astronauts in silver suits and helmets with golden faceplates boarded her ship. One was tall and slender and the other one was taller still and quite bulky. They looked around and, discovering they weren't alone, raised their hands to show they meant no harm and then slowly unfastened their helmets and pulled them off.

The boarding party consisted of two Dragonian men. Both lizard men drew back when they saw an X-5 battle android standing beside her.

"Hey there," the thin smarmy one said, continually glancing at the robot, "it seems you're in some need of assistance."

"I am doing fine on my own," Jegra answered.

The lizard grinned. Then looked around the ship. "I suppose that may be true. But, seeing as we're already here, what do you say we make a trade?"

"I have everything I need. But, humor me, what did you have in mind?"

"Well, looks like we're in need of an FTL, and yours is all busted, so why don't you let us have it?"

"And what do I get in return?" she asked, skeptically.

"You get to walk away with your life intact."

"Ah, I see," she said, folding her arms under her chest and frowning. Then, with a nod of her head, she said, "Johnny, please show these gentlemen out."

The X-5 robot stepped forward and as soon as he raised his flamethrower arm, the large Dragonian threw a magnetic disk the size of a hockey puck. It clamped onto Johnny Five then let out several hundred thousand volts of electricity, frying his circuitry. As the blue tendrils of energy wrapped around him, he started to spasm until, finally, Johnny Five staggered backward and came to a standstill.

With all of his circuits fried, his eyes went dark and his torso hunched over halfway, causing him to resemble a marionette hanging limply by its strings.

The large Dragonian walked up to the robot, just to be sure it wasn't a threat, and nudged it, sending it to the ground. Both lizard men laughed when it was clear that they'd won that round.

When the slender Dragonian turned back to Jegra, he saw that she was clenching her fists as though she were going to have to fight. "I'm warning you, don't come any closer or I'll…"

"Or you'll what?"

"Slap the stupid right off that face of yours."

"Oh, Arzek, it seems we have a feisty one here," he laughed.

"What do you recommend we do about it, Ooran?" the big one asked, deferring to his comrade who, by the looks of it, always pulled rank.

"Anything we have to do to secure this bounty. This ship is a veritable goldmine." Ooran crouched down and then lunged forward. Jegra, having superior reflexes, caught him by his wrists.

"I warned you," she began, but the sneaky devil had some kind of knockout gas up his sleeve and a green puff of gas shot out of his cuffs and into her face.

Dizzy, Jegra relinquished her grip and stumbled backward. Unable to keep her balance, she slowly sank to her hands and knees.

"W-what was that?" she mumbled, her words slightly slurred. In the next moment, she collapsed to the ground and rolled onto her back. Looking up at both Arzek and Ooran, who stood over her, her vision blurred in and out.

Jegra didn't remember blacking out, but her eyes snapped open and she found herself seated on the floor, magnetic shackles binding her wrists and ankles, her back against the aft bulkhead.

While she was out cold, Arzek and Ooran had stripped all her ship's paneling and were taking all valuable items from her luxury yacht and stowing them on their ship. Luckily, they had only been at it for roughly an hour, so the damage was minimal.

Jegra looked down, realizing they'd confiscated her clothes too. Everything but for her mauve lace underwear and matching bra.

Letting out a disgruntled sigh, she growled, "Hey, dickheads, where are my clothes?"

"Seeing how you and Arzek are roughly the same size, and seeing as my friend needed a new pair of overalls, I gave your clothes to him."

She looked over at where Ooran had jutted his chin and, sure enough, Arzek was wearing her overalls and he continued to strip the paneling from her ship.

"So, what are you going to do with me?" she asked, already having a fairly good idea.

"We're gonna sell you to the spice miners on Rieghella."

"Rieghella?" Jegra inquired, not recognizing the name.

"It's a planet beyond the Outer Rim. They have a monopoly on the spice trade there and always pay quite handsomely for sex slaves." He then turned to her and, eyeing her up and down, added, "A female of your…proportions…should prove quite lucrative indeed."

Jegra rolled her eyes. Sex. Power. Greed. That was the currency beyond the confines of the empire. And it was clear that poor Arzek and Ooran had no clue who they were dealing with.

"You honestly don't know who I am, do you?"

"You're a nubile young woman. And that's all we need to know to know your value."

"My value?" Jegra balked, her brow settling into a glower. "I'm no one's property," she stated.

"Wrong," Ooran chuckled, "Right now, you're my property. The sooner you come to terms with that the better off you'll be." He drew out a stun rod and jammed it into her shoulder. The shock caused her to yelp and she fell back into the bulkhead, banging her head against it.

This was the last straw. Finally growing fed up with these two egg-heads, Jegra snapped her binders, stood up, and, taking a bold step toward a cowering Ooran, clutched the sparking stun rod in her hand and glared at him with her broiling dark gaze.

As tendrils of electricity ran up her arm, Ooran looked down at her hand, clutching onto the rod, and then back up at her, shocked that it was having little to no effect.

"What are you?" he asked.

"Mad," she replied.

Jegra jammed the rod forward into Ooran's throat, causing him to electrocute himself. After spazzing out for a bit from the high-power current, he blacked out and she tossed him aside.

The loud thump of his body hitting the ground drew Arzek's attention and, seeing his friend lying on the floor, he tossed his tools aside and marched toward Jegra to subdue her.

She turned and marched toward him, matching his stride. They collided halfway, and Arzek gripped her in his arms and began to squeeze. Trapped in his bear-hug, Jegra slowly leaned back and then snapped her head forward, headbutting him.

Arzek let go of her as he staggered back. When he finally caught his footing, he looked back at her with shock, realizing she hit twice as hard as he did.

Without his friend's guidance, all Arzek could do was keep on fighting. So, he lunged forward and took a wild swing. Jegra easily evaded it. Then, leaping up, she brought her elbow down onto Arzek's cranium with a resounding *kra-crack!* He instantly crumpled to the ground, unconscious before his head ever hit the floor.

Jegra dusted off her hands and then asked herself, "Now, what to do with the two of you?"

Just then, her proximity alarm blared again and she raced over to look out the window of her ship only to find the *Avalon* floating, dead in space.

"That *Avalon?*" Jegra whispered in a puzzled tone. Then, seeing a flash of light from the windows of the ship, Jegra realized there were still people aboard, trying to signal her.

She leaped over Arzek's unconscious body and threw herself into the pilot's seat. She did a quick systems check and was relieved to find that she still had her maneuvering thrusters.

Unable to decouple from the Junker's ship made maneuvering tricky, but she finally lined up the port side of her yacht with the *Avalon's* starboard docking ring.

Approximately ten minutes later, she stepped foot aboard the *Avalon's* empty decks. "Where did everybody go?" she wondered aloud to herself as she roamed the vacant corridor.

She turned right at the junction and headed up the next corridor, looking for signs of survivors when she heard a beastly breathing baring down her neck.

Jegra spun around in time to see a dark object leap into the air. She threw out her hands to grapple with whatever beast was attacking her. Its weight threw her back and she toppled to the floor. When she looked up, a big happy cat face and a wet tongue began licking her face.

"Hey, girl," Jegra said, ruffling up Allie's ears and giving her a good rub down. "What are you doing all by your lonesome?"

"Mom?" a voice called out.

Recognizing her child's voice, Jegra shoved Allie aside and abruptly sat up. Rhadamanthus and Ladgara stood at the other end of the corridor. Scarcely able to believe her own two eyes, she asked, "Kids?"

"Mother!" they cried out in unison and raced over to her. She sat up on her knees and threw out her arms. Both children slammed into her, about bowling her over, but she managed to stay upright, wrapping them up tight in her protective arms.

Kissing their little heads, she asked, "What in the world are you doing here?"

"It's a long story, mother," Ladgara said.

"We got abducted by space pirates!" Rhadamanthus exclaimed.

"But Lycia and Allie saved us," Ladgara added.

"Then the mean man came and Lycia had to go after him."

"Mean man?" Jegra asked.

"Yeah. The devil man," Ladgara replied. "With the red skin and black tattoos."

Red skin and black tattoos? It sounded awfully familiar and that's when Jegra grew worried. Ishtar Bantu had been one of her fiercest opponents. If she was back, that would be bad news indeed.

Rising to her feet, she looked down at both her lovely powder blue children and said, "Come along kids, we have a lot of work to do if we want to get back and help your sister."

"Is Lycia in trouble, mother?" Ladgara asked.

"I'm sure she has it all under control. But just in case, we best get my ship fixed up and get back to her, asap."

"Yes, mother," Rhadamanthus said. And, taking his mom's hand in his, he smiled up at her. Ladgara did the same, and all three walked hand-in-hand, back toward Jegra's ship.

Allie, the Lafor'allenthal panther, trod on their heels, her large padded paws plodding along as her tail twitched happily behind her.

37

Echoes of Lycia spread out like blue specters across the battlefield and protected her blind spots. Each glowing blue ghost ensured she wouldn't be flanked by enemy combatants. With the additional performance of the power suit, she was able to concentrate on her Echoes more efficiently.

Lycia moved so quickly that she was but a blur on the battlefield. A veritable phantom. With every lacerating strike, enemy combatants' blood spatter lingered in the air briefly as time seemingly slowed to an incremental tic.

By the time the droplets were about to drench her in a crimson rain, however, in another split-second, she vanished from sight. While the blood splashed across the landscape by the bucket load, she was already onto slicing into the next enemy combatant.

Her battle axe afforded a wide range of motion. She spun like a Borelian ballerina, moving with the momentum of each strike, severing limbs left and right.

She sliced three brawny men in half in one twirl, then planted her foot, pivoted, and reversed direction. Her plasma axe crackled on the air as it swung back the other way, taking out two more brawny soldiers rearing up behind her. Their faces were full of shock as they watched their limbs part from their bodies, blood spraying from their stumps like tapped fire hydrants as their hearts raced with fear-induced adrenaline.

As she danced her ballet of death, her blue Echoes deflected arrows, spears, and other lethal projectiles. This cleared space for her to unleash the most amount of devastation possible.

Before long, she'd moved so deeply through the sea of warriors unimpeded that if she went much further, she'd be risking isolating herself behind enemy lines.

Not wanting to get trapped on the wrong side of the battle, she decided to hunker down. She widened her stance and scanned the faces of all the warriors, circling her like a pack of hungry L'Thorrellian wolves.

When it became clear that they weren't going to attack, she tried to goad them into it. "What are you waiting for? Don't tell me ya'll are afraid of a little girl like me?"

"They're waiting for their orders. Unlike you, they have discipline. Honor. Restraint."

Lycia turned in time to see Scarborne emerge from the circle of warriors, who'd now formed a wall around her. As he entered the circle, the two of them began to move around one another.

"I have restraint," she retorted, raising her middle finger and giving him the bird. "See? Instead of killing you outright, I'm doing this."

Continuing their little tango, he didn't look too awfully amused by her sally. Instead, he just grunted, as if to say it wasn't funny.

In response to that, she tucked her battle axe under her arm and raised her other middle finger and gave him the double bird salute. She raised her eyebrows as if to draw attention to the act itself and say, *see there...see it?*

Scarborne didn't have any special weapons or armor. Just a traditional gi and hakama. She recognized the style as that of the grandmasters of Bai'Jamin and wondered if he'd been trained by them.

"You're a student of Bai'Jamin, I see."

"While you weren't even a theoretical notion in your father's mind, I was accepting my tenth dan belt at the temple of Cresia, which overlooks the eighteen purple waterfalls of the Cresian palisade. It was there, upon the clifftop, that I joined the order of the Dark Brotherhood."

"Then we are sworn enemies, you and I, for I belong to the House of Light."

"But can you say you're truly a student of the Light when you have not trained with the monks? Your training is rote, a mere program embedded in your mind. You have no experience. You have not spilled your sweat and blood nor forged your warrior spirit through pain and suffering."

She narrowed her eyes at him, then in what might prove to be her dumbest mistake, she tapped the royal seal and unlocked her body armor. Stepping out of it, she left it, holding her axe.

Stretching her arms over her head, she leaned to the left, then right, and limbered up her body in preparation of the fight.

After rolling her head across her shoulders, she began to hop up and down and slap her shoulders. "Let's see if all your talk amounts to anything."

A smirk formed on Scarborne's mouth. "And let's find out whether your programming is that of a grandmaster or merely the inferior imitation of one."

They both screamed out and lunged at one another at the same time. Her hands formed the tiger strike while his tightened into the python strike.

As they engaged one another in a furious bout of Dagoni kung fu, the gladiators formed a tight circle and began to cheer.

Lycia knew this wasn't a fight for sport, though. It was a fight to the death. And whoever emerged from this circle alive, was the true victor. *Victory or death, after all.*

Being quadruped allowed Persephone to slice and dice enemies like a sawmill tearing through timber.

Once she grew weary of slicing and dicing, she changed to a relentless series of jabs and throat slices, stinging each opponent like an agitated wasp, and they clutched their wounds and slowly sank to their knees, realizing all too late that they were dead before ever hitting the ground.

She passed by warriors like a dreadful wraith leaving swaths of men in her wake. Each of her blades left lacerating marks upon their flesh.

One by one her foes fell to her relentless attack. Once she'd felled the surrounding warriors like a woodsman fells a grove, she paused to catch her breath. Her chest heaving, she wiped the blood spatter from her cheek with the back of her hand and inspected it. Then, licking it off, she smirked and turned toward the woman eyeballing her from across the distance.

Ri'Vera threw out her arms and the power suit's robotic arms unfolded from the back of the suit and gave her an additional two limbs.

"How about you try that with someone your own number of arms," she asked. But it was more of a challenge than a question.

Persephone smiled and then looked over her shoulder at Lycia, engaged in hand to hand combat with Scarborne. And by the looks of it, she was getting the snot kicked out of her.

"You care for that one, no?"

"What makes you say that?" Ri'Vera asked.

"Her stench is all over you."

"We're close, but we haven't…that's none of your business," she snapped, growing defensive. "Speaking of close," she added, eyeing Persephone up and down and noting her striking similarities to Lycia, "what are you? Her sister?"

"I'm her, technically speaking."

"A clone, then."

"An improvement."

"Look, lady, I know you're new here and all, but Lycia has never pretended to be perfect. That's what makes her so…"

"Aggravating?" asked Persephone in a snide tone.

"Endearing," Ri'Vera corrected.

Persephone balked. Then, drawing all her blades at once, she narrowed her eyes at Ri'Vera. "I could kill you in an instant," she bragged.

"If you say so, lady. But just know this, I don't come from Dagon pure blood. My family ran drugs for the triads. I grew up in Sagor, outside of Kempor. If there was a harder life, I don't know what it would have been."

"Spare me your sob story. Toughness isn't about where you grew up. It's about how hard you can get hit and still get back up."

There was a long silence and then Ri'Vera screamed and charged forward. Persephone anticipated her offensive attack and decided to counter with an offensive maneuver of her own.

While her upper arms came down with a lacerating strike, forcing Ri'Vera's robotic arms to catch her wrists and prevent her from cutting her down, Persephone thrust two blades into Ri'Vera's gut.

Locked in a stalemate, Persephone smiled and leaned forward and sneered, "You left yourself open.

"So…did…you." Ri'Vera reached up with both arms to thrust her blades into Persephone's neck. Persephone let go of the blades lodged in Ri'Vera's gut and clutched her wrists, stopping her from running her through.

The tip of the blades stopping mere centimeters from her neck, Persephone wrenched Ri'Vera's wrists so hard that she snapped them.

Ri'Vera yelped from the sharp pain and relinquished her blades. Both daggers hit the ground and rattled to silence.

"Nice try," Persephone said jeeringly, still holding onto Ri'Vera's mangled wrists. "But you'll have to do better if you hope to defeat a superior enemy. Or didn't they teach you that on the streets of Sagor outside Kempor?"

"You know," she said with a subtle smile, "they taught me something better."

Ri'Vera raised her wrists and two hidden blades popped out of her bracers and penetrated Persephone's neck. A shocked look frozen on her face, Persephone tried to say something but only managed to gurgle up blood.

"It's called the assassin's kiss," Ri'Vera whispered into Persephone's ear before drawing her arms back and sliding out the blades.

Persephone's neck gushed blood, but before she could react to her throat being slit, Ri'Vera instantly swiped up and severed both of her upper limbs, which were still caught the vice-like grip of the suit's robotic grasp.

As Persephone's healing factor kicked in and her throat began to mend itself, she sputtered, "You bitch! I'll kill you for this!"

Ri'Vera's metal arms discarded Persephone's blue ones and then reached down and took ahold of her lower set. As Persephone struggled to try and break free, Ri'Vera crossed her blades, forming a scissor styled wedge, and then pulled Persephone into her.

Persephone's neck slid into the wedge and then with a wet sounding *shuck*, like ears of corn being stripped down to their kernels, her head slowly rolled off her shoulders and toppled to the ground.

Ri'Vera tossed Persephone's body aside and then reached down and drew out the daggers lodged in her gut. This caused her to groan in pain and she tossed the daggers onto the ground.

She tried to take a step forward, but her abdomen surged with pain, and she faltered, falling to one knee.

Coughing up a spatter of blood, she wiped her chin and then looked over at Persephone's severed head and replied, "Get back up from that, bitch."

A resounding *crack* sounded and Lycia's head flew back with a jarring snap. Before she even recovered from the pummeling, however, Scarborne had miraculously appeared at her right and dealt her a powerful left-hook.

She staggered in the direction of the hit, attempting to be like water and move with the flow. But when she caught her footing, she barely had time to look up before realizing he was standing directly in front of her, just in time to gift her with another thrashing.

All Lycia could do was try to deflect the brunt of each blow. But even with her rapid healing, she wouldn't be able to take much more of this relentless beating.

Their hands and arms moved so fast they blurred out of sight. The other gladiators, unable to tell who was winning and losing fell silent and just watched in awe at the impossible hand to hand combat taking place before them.

Scarborne's fists glistened with Lycia's blood and, pausing momentarily, he raised one hand and licked the sticky crimson substance off.

"It seems," he said, studying his bruised knuckles, "that all you have are defensive moves. So, either you're not much of a warrior, after all, or you're trying to wear me down. Either way, you still won't be able to defeat me. Do you know why?"

"No. But I'm sure you're going to enlighten me," she said between gasps for air.

"Because you have no resolution. Nothing to fight for. You stand for nothing. And so, you will die for nothing."

"I could end you with a touch of my fingers," she said, her Dygra crystal pulsing in her chest to let him know that she still held power over him.

"True. But unless you want my cannons to lay waste to your beloved city, you will resist using your powers."

"I don't need my powers to beat you," she said, cockily, wiping the blood from her lip with the back of her hand.

"Prove it," Scarborne said, a gleeful glint in his eyes. He flexed, his every red muscle bulging with raw strength. Then, with ungodly speed, he launched a volley of punches so fast that his very fists melded into a dozen other fists.

Lycia recognized the "Thousand hand slap" and staggered back as though she were taking a chest full of rapid-fire plasma bolts as if from a mini-gun. Every blow struck her body with such force the impacts sounded like a lightning storm striking everything in sight.

Eventually, he paused to catch his breath. Lycia wobbled on her legs but managed to right herself. Her cracked ribs and bruised abdomen quickly healing again.

"I find your resilience admirable," Scarborne said, "but a warrior you are not. If you kneel before me and kiss the ring—hand your empire over to me, I shall spare the lives of your people and all those you care about."

"And if I refuse?"

"I shall kill you where you stand, have my soldiers rape and pillage your cities, and then when I've broken all of Dagon, I shall set it on fire, out of spite, and watch it burn to ash."

"All that to avenge that little red psycho slut you called a daughter?"

"How dare you!" Scarborne roared, his face contorting with rage. "Don't you dare speak of my beloved child like that!"

He came at Lycia with a fury and she merely sidestepped the blow and batted away his fist with an open palm.

She ducked, predicting his backswing which went over her head. When she stood, she leaned back, avoiding his reverse elbow jab. A nice follow up to his missed backhand, but still nearly not as fast as it needed to be.

"How are you doing this?" he asked, throwing several more punches only for her to casually evade every single one.

"I told you, I'm a student of the House of Light. Or did you think I spent the last twelve years twiddling my thumbs and doing nothing?"

"Impossible!" he growled in frustration. "It takes decades to learn the techniques of the masters."

"If you're already an expert warrior, it takes far less time, I can assure you. Besides, did you honestly think I was losing to a simple brawler like you? While you were doing your best to try and end me with your crude punches, I was memorizing your every move. And now, there's nothing left for me to learn here."

Outraged by her insolence, he lunged at her with the flying knee, but she skipped back and then danced around him. As she circled about, he swung his leg in a precision roundhouse, but it collided with her forearms as she planted herself firmly. A sweep of her foot and she knocked him onto his ass.

Scarborne scrambled to his feet as Lycia danced around him some more. She swatted him on the ass when his back was turned to her and the gladiators watching the fight let out a boisterous chuckle that only seemed to anger

Scarborne more.

Fed up with being mocked and taunted, Scarborne extended his arm and opened his hand. A second later, his double-bladed sword came to him—a special modification using magnetic geo-tracking—landing directly in his palm. Using this tech, he could recall his weapon from anywhere within a two-kilometer radius.

Now armed with his favorite blade, he began a flurry of attacks, which Lycia had no trouble evading. As she leaped back, she grabbed her battle axe off her suit of power armor and ignited the blade. The edges of the axe grew molten hot and she planted her feet as Scarborne came at her, his eyes wild with unbridled rage.

Scarborne brought his blade down with a brutal strike, but his face went pale as he watched his sword melt against Lycia's upward strike, her plasma axe cutting right through his blade.

As they drew back again, Lycia stumbled slightly and coughed. A twinge of pain shot through her and she clutched her side.

Scarborne grinned, realizing that he was finally beginning to wear her down. "It appears you're not invulnerable after all."

"Neither are you," she replied. Then, with a speed that defied the laws of physics, she tossed her plasma axe into the air and raced forward.

As the axe twirled high in the air, she jammed two of her fingers into his pectoral muscle, then tapped his neck and thighs, hitting all the vital pressure points in his neck and legs. Once that was done, she hopped back.

Laughing, he asked, "And what was that supposed to do? Cripple me? I should have you know, I'm immune to pressure strikes."

Lycia smiled. "No, not cripple you. Just temporarily paralyze you."

"What?" he asked. Then, trying to move, Scarborne found he couldn't. His body was frozen where he stood.

His face went blank as he remembered the axe, and using every ounce of strength he could muster, he slowly looked up.

Her axe came spiraling down and cut through Scarborne like a hot knife through Kemporian butter.

Scarborne's body split in half and both sections fell away from the axe that had finally lodged itself into the ground beneath him.

His blood splashed onto the nearby warriors, causing them to reel back in fear. When they turned back toward Lycia, she slowly scanned their faces.

"If a gentle tap from me could do this to your battle-hardened leader…think of what I could do to you if I set my mind to it."

The group of warriors slowly backed away. And then, one of them raised a hand, signaling to a man on the hill. The man on the hill put a large horn to his lips and blew, sounding the call to retreat.

"That's what I thought," Lycia said as the gladiators set down their arms and turned away.

As the IGS army stopped fighting and withdrew from the battle, the Dagon forces let out a cry of victory.

Without the commissioner of IGS, the gladiators had nobody to lead them. So, they did the only thing that they knew to do; they returned to base camp.

After watching them retreat, Ri'Vera staggered up beside Lycia, still gripping her gut.

"You're hurt," Lycia said, concerned.

"It's just a flesh wound," she said through clenched teeth.

"Nonsense, it looks deep."

"I'll live. But what becomes of them?" Ri'Vera nodded at the gladiators which looked confused now that there was no chain of command. They weren't soldiers, after all. They were simple warriors. Slaves who could only follow orders.

And the blue woman who might have replaced Scarborne was dead too. They were without a leader. Without a master to guide them as they'd always been guided.

Lycia looked at Ri'Vera then at the camp of gladiators. Raising a hand, she said, "Hang back."

"What are you going to do?" asked Ri'Vera in a worried tone as Lycia marched boldly toward the camp.

"The only thing I can do."

When Lycia entered the camp, the gladiators parted, making way for her. She was, after all, the Empress of Dagon.

She strode into the middle of the camp and then climbed up onto a large rock that jutted out of the ground.

"Hear me out, my fellow warriors. For three hundred years the gladiatorial games helped define this empire. My father, Rhadamanthus Dakroth, used the games to finance his military campaigns. And while he made grandiose promises of glory and freedom, very few, if any of you, ever saw it. That is why, from this day forward, I am disbanding the Intergalactic Gladiatorial Syndicate once and for all. You are finally free to make new destinies for yourselves. Find wives, have children, or should you choose to stay, volunteer to enter the games as sportsmen, not warriors. Instead of battling your opponent to the death, battle them for the championship title and be crowned grand champion of the arena. The choice is yours, but if you choose to fight, let it be of your own volition. Not because any master holds you on a short leash and demands you fight for him, but because you choose it. Let it be for the glory you might reap as a champion of the arena. Not as a killer, but as a celebrated athlete."

After her rousing speech there was a long, contemplative silence and then, one by one, the gladiators began to cheer. Amid the cheers, a lone voice shouted above the din, "Long live the empress! Long live Lycia Alakandra!"

The cheers grew into chanting, and soon, the entire band of gladiators was chanting in unison, "Long live the empress! Long live the empress!"

Lycia let out a sigh of relief and looked toward the crowd, scanning the area from which the lone voice had invoked her name.

Standing in the midst of the crowd, shoulder to shoulder with her fellow gladiators, was none other than her great mother, Jegra Alakandra. The former empress, and still reigning champion of the arena. She smiled upon Lycia with genuine heartfelt admiration, and mouthed the words, "I'm proud of you."

Lycia smiled back and, holding her mother's gaze, she raised her forearm and showed Jegra her matching tattoo. Jegra responded by doing the same. Mother and daughter, warriors both.

Then and there, Lycia felt deep within herself, an undeniable truth. For the first time since she'd opened her eyes that fateful day and entered into a world of violence and chaos, she knew that everything was going to be okay.

BOOK 6
EPILOGUE

 bard played an old familiar song on his lute, a song commemorating the empress, Jegra Alakandra, and her many adventures beyond the Outer Rim and her eventual return to Dagon Prime.

As the music wafted through the halls of the palace, Jegra raced alongside Ri'Vera to the nursery. They slowed to a walk before taking a deep breath and entering the room.

Lycia, stood beside Raphine, whose arms were full of a gurgling, cooing infant with the cutest little turquoise face which peered up at her mother.

"Welcome home, mother. Meet your granddaughter."

"Oh, wow," Ri'Vera gasped, "she's beautiful."

Lycia smiled and put her hand on Ri'Vera's shoulder. At the same time, Jegra drew closer to the baby. Leaning in, she tried to get a better look at the little bundle of joy that was wrapped up in a fleece blanket as white as snow.

"Do you want to hold her?" Raphine asked, extending the bundle and placing her into Jegra's arms even before she'd had a chance to properly answer.

Jegra nodded, accepting the baby and cradling it in her arms. Unable to see the babe's entire face, however, due to the number of layers surrounding it, she'd finally brushed enough of the blanket aside to better see her granddaughter's tiny face when, unexpectedly, a tiny hand reached up and clasped onto her finger.

"She's strong," Jegra stated, smiling at her granddaughter.

"What's her name?" Ri'Vera asked, leaning in to get a closer look.

"Jessica Avery Alakandra," Raphine replied.

An instant flood of tears filled Jegra's eyelids to the brim as she did her best to hold it together. "My father's name was Avery," she informed everyone, still smiling even as tears began to trickle down her cheeks.

"Who is Jessica?" Ri'Vera asked, in the dark as to Jegra's birth name.

"That's Jegra's Earth name," Raphine replied with a gentle smile. She was a mother now, and although she was exhausted from giving birth, she basked in the warmth of this moment.

Ri'Vera nodded and then edged closer still to Jegra to try and get a better look.

Jegra, rocking the cooing babe in her arms, whispered, "You'll be safe here, little one. And you will be loved unconditionally by lots of mothers and lots and lots of grandmothers and one particularly ornery old goat who just so happens to be your official godfather."

Lycia and Raphine laughed and Ri'Vera, uncertain as to what was so funny, smiled respectfully.

"I'll never let anything in this cold, cruel galaxy harm you, little one. Of that, I promise."

Little Jessica Avery, growing a tad fussy, and squirming about in Jegra's arms, convinced her to, reluctantly, give her back to her mother.

"She's everything I could have dreamed for and more," Jegra said, her gaze shifting to Lycia.

Lycia, on the verge of tears, ran to Jegra and threw her arms around her. As they hugged, Ri'Vera and Raphine smiled at one another.

All four women huddled around the newborn and continued to ogle little Jessica Avery Alakandra. They were making cutesy faces and goo-goo sounds when, all of a sudden, the doors to the nursery burst wide open.

Startled, baby Jessica began to wail as Danica, Brei'Alas, and Raven strode in like the elegant queens they were. Close on their heels came little Rhadamanthus and his sister Lala.

"Is that her?" Rhadamanthus asked, excitedly hopping up and down to try and get a better look at the baby.

"I wanna see the baby, too," chirped Lala.

"You will have plenty of time to play with your niece later," Raven said sternly.

"But I want to play with her now!" Rhadamanthus stated, stamping his foot.

"Why can't we play with her now?" asked Lala.

Jegra smiled and crouched down and placed her hand on one of each of their shoulders. "Right now, little baby Jessica is a little bit sleepy and needs to take a nap."

"Why is she sleepy?" Rhadamanthus inquired, looking up at his mother with the innocent curiosity of a child.

"Because she had a very long journey to get here. But now, she's finally home and she'll need you to help watch over her and protect her."

"And love her?" asked Lala.

"Yes, and love her. With all your hearts." Jegra bopped Lala on her nose and then wrapped her arms around them and hugged them both.

After they scurried along, she slowly rose to her feet and turned to her wives and smiled warmly. She then turned to Lycia and Raphine. She smiled at Ri'Vera.

And as the group of women gathered around the baby, Jegra slowly snuck out the back of the nursery undetected and stepped out onto the balcony.

She found Allie lying off to the side, sleeping in the shade, and went over to the balcony railing. Jegra rested her palms on the railing and craned her neck and peered up at Thessalonica which hung in the sky like a giant pearl.

That was her home, she reflected. As for Earth, it had become but a distant memory. With each passing day, the memory of her homeworld became less and less permanent and gradually began to fade away. She could scarcely recall its features anymore.

But she didn't lament the loss, nor did she try to hold onto it by constantly seeking to refresh her memory. Because the truth was, she'd always felt like an outcast in that world.

In truth, the very memory of Earth felt more alien to her now than anything she'd experienced after she'd been abducted and whisked into the stars.

As a daughter of Sol, she belonged to the stars. And it was in the breadth of stars that she'd found a new world, a new family, and a new place to call home.

In the distance, the bard's song could be heard, its notes echoing up and down the great halls of the palace. Although it spoke of her numerous triumphs and defeats, there was a new verse that sang about the next chapter in her life.

Woven seamlessly into the melody was an additional stanza and a verse about how her children and children's children had children of their own. About how she had forged bonds through love that were more durable than tempered steel. And how, in her great desolation, she'd forged herself a new kind of happiness.

Perhaps the sweetest thing, however, was that through it all, a thread ran that sang of how these children would inherit a kingdom of peace—a kingdom of peace that was all possible because of this stranger, this daughter of Sol—Jegra—the Gladiatrix of the Galaxy.

THE END

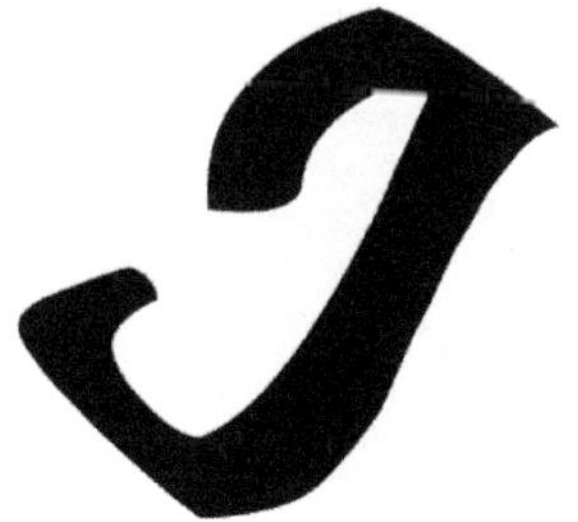

Tristan Vick is a multi-genre author who specializes in sci-fi, fantasy, and horror and has dabbled in mystery and suspense as well. He graduated from Montana State University with degrees in English Literature and Asian Cultural Studies and speaks fluent Japanese. He lives with his wife and three children in Japan. When he's not commuting on the train or teaching English, he spends his time reading, writing, blogging, binge-watching his favorite television shows, and eating sara-udon. In addition to being traditionally published, Tristan Vick continues to self-publish under his own imprint, Regolith Publications. You can learn more about him and his works on his official author webpage at:

Visit Tristan Vick's official author website at:

www.tristanvick.com